Learning Resources

KINGSTON COLLEGE

00133237

Modern Arabic Fiction

Modern Arabic Fiction

AN ANTHOLOGY

EDITED BY

SALMA KHADRA JAYYUSI

COLUMBIA UNIVERSITY PRESS · NEW YORK

Columbia University Press wishes to express its appreciation for assistance given by the Ministry of Information
of Qatar and by the Pushkin Fund in the preparation of
the translation and in the publication of this book.

Columbia University Press
Publishers Since 1893
New York   Chichester, West Sussex
Copyright © 2005 Columbia University Press
All rights reserved

Library of Congress Cataloging-in-Publication Data

Modern Arabic fiction : an anthology / edited by Salma
Khadra Jayyusi.
p.   cm.
ISBN 0-231-13254-9 (alk. paper)
1. Arabic fiction—20th century.   I. Jayyusi, Salma Khadra.

PJ7694.E8M59 2004
892.7'308006—dc22

2004058251

Columbia University Press books are printed
on permanent and durable acid-free paper.

Printed in the United States of America
c 10 9 8 7 6 5 4 3 2 1
p 10 9 8 7 6 5 4 3 2 1

In memory of my grandmother, Su'da al-Khadra, and of my grandfather, Dr. Yusuf Sleem.

My father used to tell us, "Your grandmother would not end her journey to any town in Palestine without having discovered the life history of the other passengers. She would then sit and tell us."

And my mother used to say, "During the long winter nights of Lebanon, your grandfather would sit, surrounded by friends and family, and recount stories he had read in English by European novelists. If he had to go to visit a sick person, no one would move until he returned and finished."

وهاجرتُ فاسطصحبتُ صوتيهما معي
وجُبنا أقاصي الكون نملؤها سـردا
فيوسف يروي مبدعـا ألـف قصـة
وتُنطِقهـم، طوعا، بأسرارهم سُعـدى

When I went to live abroad
Those same loved voices still I heard.
It seemed they came along with me
In what country I might be.
Yusuf would weave a web, made bright
with tales of wonder and delight;
But Su'da's gift was greater yet—
from each stranger that she met
She could draw forth, such was her art,
The inmost secrets of the heart.

—Translated by John Heath-Stubbs

CONTENTS

3   SELECTIONS FROM NOVELS

Note: In some cases the transliterated forms of authors' names reflect an author's own personal preference. This may lead to apparent inconsistencies in the system of transliteration used.

ACKNOWLEDGMENTS

To acknowledge the full debt I owe to so many—to scholars, creative writers, translators, family members, friends, and all those others who have collaborated on various aspects of this work—seems a nearly impossible task. This anthology has been many years in the making. On numerous occasions I was forced to leave this aspect or that in order to devote my time to some other book or project, which, though never more important, was for a variety of compelling reasons more pressing at the time; and that is to say nothing of other, personal constraints. I am all the more delighted, now, to have completed work on this anthology and to hand it over to my most patient publishers.

Like its companion volume *Modern Arabic Poetry: An Anthology* (Columbia University Press, 1987), which supplied the impetus for other such anthologies from Arabic literature, this work owes its initial inspiration to the imaginative mind and enthusiastic spirit of a former director of Columbia University Press, Mr. John Moore. A scholar, editor, or writer possessing the confidence and positive support of a major press, in the person of its director and principal executives, is all the more likely to produce and create with ever increasing vigor. Mr. Moore came to see me in 1979, when I was a guest of Barnard College at Columbia University, and invited me to edit a volume on modern Arabic literature. This was the prelude to a long march into the field of cultural dissemination, which inspired me to found first PROTA (Project of Translation from Arabic), then East-West Nexus for scholarly studies and intellectual discourse, both of which have striven to place the Arabic book in English on the shelves of the world library. If any of the works completed under these two projects have met with success, such success is due in the first instance to John Moore's original interest, while director of the Press, in offering Arabic literature to the English-speaking world, and to his constant support of me and of the literature of my language.

This support of the good literature that Arabic can offer in translation to the world was also strongly upheld by Jennifer Crewe, the Editorial Director at Columbia University Press. Being a literary specialist herself with a deep instinct for good literature, she has faithfully supported my work, and her patience, tact, and good humor have been most helpful. She has augmented my belief in the benefit of the mission I have undertaken during the last twenty years or so to bring good classical and modern Arabic literature to the attention of interested lovers of literature in the English-speaking world.

It was through the offices of Mr. Jassim Jamal, when he was Qatar's representative at the United Nations, that I was able to obtain the initial grant for this present work from the Ministry of Information in Qatar, and I should like to thank him most sincerely for the immediate support he gave my projects and for his great appreciation, as befits an ambassador, of the importance of intercultural dialogue.

The interruption of this work (referred to above), in favor of other pressing projects, did in fact have one positive aspect: it provided a crucial opportunity to discover, on resumption, the many new writers of fiction who had arisen in the meantime throughout the Arab world, including a fair number of new writers from the Gulf region. The development of modern Arabic fiction in recent times presents a major spectacle of achievement and endeavor, exhilarating in its speed, creativity, innovation, and ambition. Twice, indeed, this anthology has needed to be updated. To this end we enjoyed, first, the benevolent support of His Highness Shaikh Dr. Sultan Ben Muhammad al-Qasimi, the ruler of Sharjah in the United Arab Emirates. His Highness's reputation as a lover and promoter of Arabic culture, history, and literature has become celebrated throughout the Arab world and beyond. I thank him in the name of all those who know the importance of entering the world of global culture equipped with the rich cultural and literary repertoire, classical and modern, of which the Arabs can be so justly proud.

I should also like to thank, with all my heart, His Highness Shaikh Abdallah Ben Zayed, then Minister of Information and Culture in Abu Dhabi, for aiding us in the final stages of this work. His Highness's help was instigated through the good offices of Shaikh Ahmad al-Suweidi, a prominent Arab national in the Gulf region and a distinguished personage, whose services to Arabic culture are well acknowledged. He it was who founded the Cultural Foundation of Abu Dhabi, which has now become a major center for literary, artistic, and cultural exchange within the Arab world. I thank him heartily for his most timely intercession on behalf of this work.

Many colleagues have collaborated on this book, and all deserve praise for their ever ready help and advice, which facilitated work on a project encompassing the whole vast Arab world. Special thanks go to Dr. Ferial Ghazoul, professor of English at the American University of Cairo, who supported this work from the very outset and has never tired in providing further support whenever the need arose. Another colleague, deserving equal acknowledgement here, is Dr. Roger Allen, professor of Arabic at the University of Pennsylvania and PROTA's spokesman, who has never failed to lend a helping hand and to answer my many queries on modern Arabic fiction, an area of Arabic literature in which he himself is proficient.

My profound thanks go to those who have uncovered for me treasures of creativity in remote areas of the Arab world and helped me reach the writers of fiction there. Special thanks, in this respect, go to Dr. Issa al-Tamimi, the present, highly energetic Under-Secretary for Information in Qatar, for his efficient help in locating the Qatari writers who have mushroomed in this emirate in recent years. Nouri Jarrah has likewise assisted me in locating writers from Oman, supplying me with their texts, curricula vitae, and addresses, and I should like to thank him most warmly for his enthusiastic help, a help that forms only part of the ongoing services to Arabic culture that he so assiduously carries out.

My most heartfelt thanks go to Christopher Tingley, one of the greatest friends any literary project could ever have. He has acted as second translator for a large part of this work, often as a labor of love, and has shared with me the joys, tribulations, and above all, the pleasure that good literature imparts. His help in the final organization of this work has been beyond price, and I thank him with all my heart.

The first and second translators as a whole, who are the backbone of the work, deserve my deep acknowledgement for their patience and meticulous work. Profound thanks go, too, to the fiction writers themselves, who readily gave me their consent to represent them in this anthology and who answered my many queries. Special thanks go to Muntasir al-Qaffash, himself a short-story writer, for helping me with the difficult process of updating details of Egyptian writers.

To members of my family—brother, daughters, son, and the grandchildren now of university age who have grown up with ever increasing awareness of the necessity of bringing Arabic culture once more to its rightful place in the world—I owe a debt of gratitude for their patience, their care, their constant readiness to shoulder some of the weight that the work on many projects imposes, and, above all, for sharing the vision and often its difficulties and concerns.

It is on a sad note, finally, that I acknowledge the contribution of my late friend Erna Hoffmann. It is, for me, a matter of the most heartfelt regret that she will be unable to see the work for which she provided such sincere and perfectionist assistance during its early stages.

Salma Khadra Jayyusi

Modern Arabic Fiction

INTRODUCTION

Modern criticism of fiction is becoming more and more sophisticated and complex. As critics try to interpret artistic experience in a greater variety of ways, criticism is becoming an interdisciplinary art par excellence. Along with the emergence and development of the novel as a literary form, its artistic and semantic attributes now engage several disciplines of the humanities. The novel has proved to have many more ramifications than the more ancient art form of poetry.

There is a universal common denominator that makes the stuff of fiction, whether novel, romance, short story, or any of the other creative narrative forms that have emerged through the centuries, appealing to listeners and readers everywhere. People have always liked to tell a story and to listen to one. Identification, consolation, comparison, wonder; the normal curiosity that people have about knowing about each other and concerning self and the other; the need to understand one's human condition and explore the significance of human life, to make sense of one's experience, to answer the intrinsic desire to learn about a variety of human experiences and to see examples of how problems of life are solved, to respond to the need to flee sometimes from reality and dwell a little in an imaginary sphere, shifting one's senses to a make-believe world[1]—all these lie behind the importance and popularity of fiction.[2] However, the need for entertainment and pleasure seems to rank high in the hierarchy of reasons behind the love of reading or listening to stories or watching films. The issue of pleasure, which Kant deplored,[3] remains a major and legitimate element here; it is the principal explanation for children's attachment to various fictional forms. Few adults can forget the great pleasure they experienced as children at stories being told to them by their mothers or other elders. There is, of course, even among very young children, an element of empathy and identification. The death of Bambi's mother, slain by a hunter, has brought tears to innumerable children all over the world listening to or watching the tragic scene, but usually children seek to listen to stories or watch films because they are driven by the pleasure and excitement they experience.

The novel's first appearance in the West, in its modern form, has been described over and again by Western critics as a "Western" phenomenon. There are several factors to consider in this respect. The first is that the West, with the gradual success of the battle against illiteracy and the proliferation of learning that secured a large enough reading public, and with the early access to the printing press that fostered written literature and facilitated the journalistic industry as a broad vehicle for the dissemination of the new form, was able to give great impetus and encouragement to novel writing. Quite a few novels by nineteenth-century writers such as Dickens and Thackeray, which later became classics, first appeared in serialized form in various journals.[4]

The second is that the emergence of the novel in the industrialized and, later, technologized West represents a major shift in the social structure and in social and artistic concepts. It gave rise to the common man and emphasized the autonomy of the individual, thus marking the ascendancy of the middle and lower classes, now emerging as "the shaping force of history." It also marked a final shift from the stylized and romanticized representation of kings, queens, dignitaries, and the aristocracy toward the realistically apprehended experience of the ordinary person, previously portrayed in literature as crude, comic, or unworthy of serious treatment. Life, in all its diversity, was now open to the novelist, and men and women from all walks of life filled his/her pages. Many new notions of human interaction were now accessible to the writer, and limitless accounts centering on all of human experience now emerged. The individual apprehension of reality is emphasized and the vista is greatly widened. Several critics, Irving Howe and Lionel Trilling among them, agree that the bourgeoisie and its desire for material possessions constitute the mainspring of the novel. However, more profound than the novel's link to material phenomena was the discovery of the independence of the self and its autonomy, the abandonment of religious collectivity and of the old surrender to the blind force of tradition. The capacity of humanity to direct its destiny and dominate the environment, to wield control over a universe believed hitherto to be utterly controlled by a blind power, had now become feasible, and the whole outlook on life and experience began to change, bringing in measureless riches to the thematic variety of the novel and revolutionizing its points of emphasis. The West, having embraced modernity first, discovered through the forces unleashed by modernity the more profound promptings and independent destiny of the self, its hitherto little explored interiority.

The novel has an elastic, open form that seeks, in most experiments, a finalized ending. Its reliance on print and the written word gives the novel its definitive shape and its quality of constancy. Once committed to print, unless openly changed by the author, it stays fixed, a characteristic that differentiates it from the folk romance that is subject to change in the mouths of various narrators in different cultures and different periods of history. The novel also has the capacity to incorporate many levels of prose according to the particular subject addressed or, in dialogue, according to the personalities of the people speaking them; it can also accommodate long passages of description. Moreover, it can employ several literary modes, turning from discourse to dialogue, from the objective to the subjective. It is the most flexible of all the major literary genres and can develop in unpredictable directions. It can also assimilate other literary styles—the poetic, the dramatic, the discursive, the epistolary, and so on—and can choose its themes from the whole vista of life and periods of history. All these attributes give the novel its particular characteristics.

However, when Western writers speak of the novel, they mean not simply narratives written in the form I have described above but also a more intricate merger of form and content, for there is nothing extraordinary about the form of the novel in its simpler beginnings, and any eloquent narrator relating an actual or fictional account would naturally follow the same strategy as early novels: a beginning, a middle, and an end or climax. But form alone does not make of a narrative a "modern novel." What distinguishes the "modern" novel from a premodern one is its content and intention. Take Jurji Zaydan's (1861–1914) long, historical novels (discussed later), which describe the immense vista of Islamic civilization on which whole generations of Arab youths in the first half of the twentieth century were nurtured. Despite their charm and immense popularity at the time, such novels were decidedly premodern. They reflected a blanket culture, its collective personality, the predictable, well-attuned reactions and interactions of protagonists, the repetitive expectation of their behavior, the anticipated turn of their mind, the absolute purity of character delineation (where the protagonists come out clear and unmitigated in their goodness or evil), their momentous acts of chivalry; or their demeaning actions of cowardice, intrigue, greed, or treachery. Everything was in place; everything was in harmony with well-known qualifications.

However, observing the rise of the novel in Latin America and in the Arab world, to name but two locations, one sees that whenever circumstances that supported the rise of the novel in the West became manifest in these other cultures, the novel made its appearance. In fact, the almost sudden resurgence of the novel after the mid-twentieth century in these two areas of the world, and its quick development over only a few decades from a hesitant form attempted by a few experimentalists to a genre adopted by many very serious novelists sure of themselves and capable of vast ramifications and great ingenuity and inventiveness, perhaps show that the novel is spontaneously suited to the climate of the twentieth century everywhere.

The Arab Fictional Background

In many early-twentieth-century books on Arab literary history, there is a strong voice of complaint that the Arab people had no genuine fictional history.[5] Up to the 1960s the notion of literary dearth and paucity in Arab fictional modes permeated the thinking of some leading Arab critics about origins, literary merit, and creativity. Fiction was one of the major genres said to have had feeble roots in classical Arabic literature. Half a century later these ideas were acknowledged to have been based on lack of research and rigorous thinking. However, at the time the reputation of many aspects of classical Arabic literature, one of the richest and most varied in world literary history, had, through many denigrators who mushroomed all over the Arab heartland, been seriously tarnished. It only attests to the fact that art has its own autonomous growth, its independence and artistic integrity, that despite this disheartening situation for the creative writer, all genres of Arabic literature were preparing to burst robustly into bloom in the second half of the twentieth century. At the end of the forties, poetry was about to have the greatest technical revolution in its history, and some exceptional poetic talents would blossom and create a verse that would stand on a par with some of the best poetry being written in the contemporary world; drama, which had already had a robust beginning in Egypt, was to establish itself strongly in many Arab countries during the second half of the century. As was true of the sixties, fiction was to rise quickly to great experimental heights and scores of novelists and short story writers would join hands to bring the art of fiction in modern Arabic to a place of importance that would compete with poetry and, by the end of the twentieth century, threaten to surpass it in volume and status.

However, research into the literature of the past immediately finds that Arab literary history has never been poor in fictional creations, which were circulating perhaps several centuries before the advent of Islam in 622 A.D. By then, various fictional genres had been nurtured. A comparative examination shows that the remote background of fiction in Arabic corresponds in several aspects to the remote background of other literatures, proving the unity of human creativity everywhere. It is witness to the nonethnic basis of artistic creation that humanity has shown only the smallest differences in the principal literary genres adopted by various cultures and in the way the verbal arts have usually developed over the centuries. Lying behind any differences are external causative factors, usually the environment and ecology of a particular culture, as well as major events in the history of a people and the cultural outcome of this history. The nature of the language can have a conspicuous influence on literature, particularly poetry. However, it is correct to presume that all cultures have produced fictional narratives to fit the particular phase of history they were in and provide an answer to its needs and emphases. The Arabs' greater predilection for poetry, an art that matured and experienced a golden age even before the advent of Islam in the early seventh century A.D., was perhaps due to both: the richness and natural eloquence of the Arabic language and the nomadic nature of the desert Arabs, who were the creators of the finest poetry in pre-Islamic Arabia. Poetry was the art form that could best be carried wherever the tribe moved; it was the register of tribal history and of the valor, wisdom, and emotional attachments of the race.

However, throughout the classical period and a major part of the postclassical period, Arabs created varied genres of fiction, some of which, mainly those of pre-Islamic times, they have shared in fashion and mode with other ancient cultures; still others, created after Islam, were more predominantly of Arab creation.

One major source of pre-Islamic fictive tales and legends is the collected narratives of Wahb ibn al-Munabbih preserved in *The Book of Crowns on the Kings of Himyar* (kitab al-tijan fi muluk Himyar). This book contains many myths and fabulous tales in which the jinn and supernatural creatures, uncanny beings, and events figure greatly. It is testimony to the tarnished status in modern times of classical Arabic fiction that this major early book of narratives, which is a foundational part of the formative stages of fictional creations in Arabic, has been largely overlooked and, as far as I know, has not been assigned as part of a comprehensive educational curriculum.

In the wealth of tales *The Book of Crowns* presents, there seems to have been some negotiation among modes: the mythic mixes with the heroic, the superman often becomes superhuman, and examples depict the romance and passion of ordinary people. Ensconced within the tales of heroism, on the one hand, and within stories of fantastic happenings, supernatural phenomena, and mythic encounters, on the other, are simple accounts of wisdom, clever predictions, quick-witted solutions, and most important, anguished love that ends in tragedy.

Northrop Frye[6] saw these modes in literature as developing one from the other, with the mythic (which he seems to keep outside the realm of genuine fiction) giving way to the legendary and heroic, which he terms "the romance," then down the ladder to the "high mimetic mode," where the hero "is a leader . . . [who has] authority, passion, and powers of expression far greater than ours, but what he does is subject both to social criticism and to the order of nature."[7] The next stage of development is when ordinary men in ordinary surroundings are represented, which Frye calls the "low mimetic mode." Further down the ladder we encounter the hero of inferior powers, of lesser intelligence, in narratives set, according to Frye, in the "ironic mode." Frye notes that during the past fifteen centuries European fiction "has steadily moved its center of gravity down" this list.

One should note, however, that these modes are not so clearly separated in Western literature as Frye proposes. The clear-cut progression is not exact, nor is what he describes as a domination of the "ironic mode" in the twentieth century completely applicable. This strategy, however, does indeed serve as a general map for the gradation of modes, the way one fictional mode gives way to the next as human society changes its systems and relationships and develops toward modernity, but one should bear in mind the possible overlapping of modes and how one mode grows in the teeth of the other. In Arab fictional history the situation is even less discrete, but the gradation described by Frye is loosely present. For example, there is a strong tendency throughout the periods prior to the twentieth century to depict, in both formal and folk literature, experiences relating to the aristocracy and upper echelons of society (what Frye terms the high mimetic mode); but, at the same time, there is a constant infiltration of narratives of the low mimetic mode, even very early in Arab fictional history. There are sudden turns as well. In the first place the progression of modes described earlier was arrested after the advent of Islam. A clean break from the mythic and fantastic tale of pre-Islamic times was immediately effected,[8] and a seemingly rigorous adherence to factuality and away from pure fictional improvisations becomes evident. This took place side by side with the all-too-human romantic stories of unrequited lovers during the Umayyad period, revolving sometimes around the experiences of actual men and women. However, this divorce from the mythic and the legendary romance did not persist throughout the long Islamic period. A vigorous return to the superhuman and legendary narratives, to the heroic superman and the fantastic event, occurs early in the later middle ages (the tales of wonder and marvels and the depiction of the fantastic in medieval travel books; *The Arabian Nights*; the prose folk romances). Another phenomenon occurring as early as the third/ninth century is an adoption of the ironic mode in Arabic fiction, which reflects a quick growth of urbanized attitudes in a maturing civilization.

Arabic Fictional Genres in Classical Times: A Concise Account

Mythical Tales

In the Beginning there is the Myth —*Jorge Luis Borges*

As we have seen, the Arabs began their fiction as all other peoples do, with the mythic apprehension of experience, which is the early human gaze at the universe and a result of the human encounter with its mysteries.

Legends of Heroism

The desert Arabs, who had to fight for survival in an arid region of great scarcity, experienced many memorable encounters of tribe with tribe in fights to secure proprietorship, hegemony, or status. On these encounters intricate war legends celebrating heroism, loyalty, and tribal vendettas were built. Those battle legends were termed "Days of the Arabs" (ayyam al-'Arab).

These heroic stories form part of the living literary repertoire of Arabic literature. They have also found their way not only to the long folk romances of the later middle ages but also to the legendary and exciting narrations, often sung or narrated in rhythmic, rhymed prose, by roaming narrators working with what used to be called in my childhood in Palestine "sundouk al-'ajab" (a chest of wonders).[9]

The Old Arabian Love Story

Varied forms of love stories, both chaste and profane, have been narrated since pre-Islamic times. The early chaste love story of the tragic experience is exemplified, among others, by the pre-Islamic poetry of al-Muraqqash al-Akbar,[10] which set the pattern for the famous stories of the romantic[11] and anguished love poets of the Umayyad period (40/666–132–750)[12] who suffered and often died of unrequited love. This type of love story did not abate with the improvement in fortune, lifestyle, and possibilities that took place after the full establishment of the Islamic empire. These enduring and charming accounts, often tragic or semitragic, formed a genre by themselves and were the purest expression of the ancient Arab soul, full of nostalgia, loyalty, chivalry, and a catching tenderness toward the woman. A number of these stylized and idealized stories survived the centuries because their protagonists were well-known poets.[13]

The contrasting vogue in the love story was also set forth as a pattern of profane love in pre-Islamic times by another poet, al-Muraqqash al-Asghar, venturing out to achieve union and fulfillment in love. The same was true of the Umayyad period, marked for its wealth also in stories of profane love where lovers had no patience for constancy and sorrow. Both kinds of erotic experience form a rich repertoire of the Arabic love story for that age and for all ages.

The Short Narrative or Factual Anecdotes (*Al-Khabar*)

As we begin the Abbasid period in 132/750, several arts of narrative appear. The Islamic insistence on veracity was a deterrent to the creation of fiction during the early Islamic period and perhaps helps to explain the reason behind the pervasive diffusion of an important type of narrative, the factual (or seemingly factual) anecdote (*khabar*, pl. *akhbar*), which became rampant during the Umayyad period and later. This was usually based on what seemed to be an actual episode supported by a list (sometimes a long list) of references to the names of earlier narrators (*isnad*), giving it an authentic or the semblance of an authentic genealogy. Accounts that may have been imaginary assumed the appearance of truth through this procedure.[14]

The issue of "veracity" seems to explain why writers refrained from any long-winded descriptions of fictional events and characters and tried instead to narrate actual happenings or what might seem like actual happenings, mixing history with fiction and thereby recording a vast part of the social and political life of the Abbasids. This method would also camouflage the intention of "indulging" in writing fiction. This genre was a purely Arab genre. It was going to establish itself for many centuries to come as a major method of narration, factual and fictive, and would form the numerous entries to the many large compendiums and dictionaries in which the Arab heritage is very rich.[15] It would exist, side by side, with new fictive genres created by the Arabs themselves or imported from the conquered worlds of India and Persia.

However, Arab creative writers in the classical and postclassical (1250–1850) periods would find several other methods of diversifying their fictional techniques, and some would be original in the extreme.

The Fable

One of the earliest such works was *Kalila wa Dimna,* a collection of fables famed for having been translated by the Arabized Persian and a new convert to Islam, Ibn al-Muqaffa' (102/720–139/756), from the Persian translation of an Indian collection. Ibn al-Muqaffa' used his lucid, succinct style and command of language to produce an immortal text that has enjoyed a considerable number of critical studies and a few translations without losing its charm even in modern times.

These fables were followed by other attempts in somewhat the same fashion later on in the Abbasid period. We find them in *The Arabian Nights*, often relayed in a convoluted fashion. They were also adopted by the famous group of philosophers known as the Ikhwan al-Safa, thus demonstrating the continuation and elevation of this genre in classical Arabic.[16]

The Assemblies (Al-Maqamat)

A purely Arab invention, this genre was begun by Badi' al-Zaman al-Hamadhani (356/968–398/1008), who was followed by many others. Many of the assemblies were picaresque tales about rogues and their wanderings, revolving around the personality of a trickster. They were fully imbued with humor and a comical representation of experience, containing under their humorous surface incisive social criticism and reflecting a widely urbanized lifestyle. They posited a formal acknowledgment of the strong presence of the lower and middle classes in Arab urban life. The varied personalities who populated the *maqamat* were often chosen from the social backyard of Abbasid society: outcasts, tricksters, vagrants, gullible dupes, the nouveaux riches, often antiheroes of some sort or another. In structure, each episode has two main protagonists, one who undergoes the various adventures and describes them in an elevated, eloquent language that is transmitted to his narrator, and it is the latter who relates them to the reading or listening audience.[17]

The Epistle of Forgiveness

The intricate and highly rhetorical *Epistle of Forgiveness* (risalat al-ghufran) by the famous blind poet Abu 'l-'Ala' al-Ma'arri (363/973–449/1057) is a narrative about an imaginary journey to the afterworld, a journey on which al-Ma'arri sends a writer he knows to visit both paradise and hell, meeting and holding conversations with poets, men of letters, linguists, and narrators. It is a major work and a great experiment in intellectual and linguistic virtuosity, and a major literary venture in that it succeeded in transforming the epistle genre into a new literary form with distinct fictional characteristics. It is composed of various fictive episodes in each segment of the journey, each episode preserving its integrity, unlike the convoluted strategy of *Kalila wa Dimna* and *The Arabian Nights*, where the story often branches out into a new ramification before it ends. Despite the difficulty of the language used in these episodes, they preserve their own charm and sustain the interest of the reader even after so many centuries. Other such imaginary journeys followed in medieval times.[18]

A Philosophical Novel

The philosophical novel *Hayy ibn Yaqzan*, by the Andalusi philosopher Ibn Tufail (502/1110–571/1185), is one of the treasures of classical Arabic literature. A mixture of philosophical reflection and storytelling, it has preserved its literary and intellectual excellence throughout the centuries. It is the tale of a man who was born by spontaneous generation from mud on the shore and was brought up by a gazelle on an uninhabited island to attain "the highest degree of insight, both philosophical and religious, by dint of his inborn capacities, by his experience, perceptions and reflections."[19]

On Influences

Whether the Arab experiments described above influenced, as I believe they did, some other European experiments or not, the similarities between them can only stand to confirm my thesis about the nonethnic nature of art, the unity of human creativity, and the way the latter progresses through time. There are several instances to consider here: first, the picaresque tale in the West exemplified by Cervantes (hailed as the father of the Western novel) in *Don Quixote*, which also employed, as we find in the Arab *Assemblies*, two voices,[20] one of which was an Arab voice; the excursion to hell and heaven as we see in Dante's *The Divine Comedy*, highly reminiscent of the earlier Arab versions of, first, the story of al-Mi'raj, the Prophet's nocturnal journey to heaven, and then, the most famous work, the eleventh-century *Epistle of Forgiveness* by al-Ma'arri, mentioned above, which was emulated by the Andalusi Ibn Shuhaid (992–1035) in his epistle, *Al-Tawabi' wa '-Zawabi'*; or the story of a man alone on an island who survives his aloneness and fends for himself, as we see in Robinson Crusoe, a novel reminiscent of the philosophical tale *Hayy ibn Yaqzan*, by the much earlier Andalusi philosopher Ibn Tufail (1100–1185). If these and other forms of storytelling, of which the Arabs were proficient precursors, were written as completely original improvisations by Europeans or were influenced, as I think they were, by the then superior Arab culture in and around Europe engaging scores of European translators, the sum total remains the same: the human creative mind works in similar ways. Often it will either invent, on its own initiative, a mode or form new to its language and culture but that has already been in existence in another language, or consciously assimilate and possess as its own some mode or form created by another culture.

The Arabian Nights

Until recent times *The Arabian Nights* remained, in Arabs' eyes, a secondary example of fictional narratives. The compendium had earlier been seen as embodying a somewhat vulgar lower-class form of expression: its subject matter was characterized by obscenity and unbridled imagination leading into undignified realms of experience; its style—mostly vernacular and laden with grammatical errors—exhibited none of the fine features and high language of the best of belles lettres in Arabic. The "fictional" value of *Nights* was not acknowledged until it was discovered by Europeans early in the eighteenth century, when Antonio Galland published his edited French translations between 1704 and 1717. Galland's translation, with the more extreme pornographic elements expunged, was a best-seller. In 1708 an anonymous English translation appeared, and was followed by several different versions, including one in serialized form. However, it was only after *Nights*—with its extraordinary appeal to both readers and writers of fiction—had created a vogue in Europe and America that the first printed Arab edition appeared, in 1835, from the famous Boulaq printing press near Cairo. Though this edition was followed by many cheap or partial editions, it had no appeal for Arab lovers of literature until well into the twentieth century. It was only then that the Arab world began to appreciate the fictional contents of *Nights*—their originality, their entertainment value, and their broad reflection of the society of their time—and to produce significant studies of this work in Arabic. Still later, and still more important, *Nights* began to influence a number of contemporary Arab writers of fiction, who adopted some of the work's features into their own writings.

The chief structural phenomenon of *Nights* is its open-endedness, its ongoing trail of narration, whereby one story stems from another so as never to arrive at an absolute finale, at the terminal silence that would seal the fate of the narrator, Shehrezad. The new bride of King Shahrayar, she was determined to ward off the death sentence at the end of the nuptial night that had been the fate of all those virgins before her, whom the king had married then killed the next morning. Of course those stories, which were based on historical fact, had to end at a certain point; yet a fine line of narration was somehow always left to lead on to a new beginning. This very complex narrative method, seen earlier to some extent in *Kalila wa Dimna*, arrives at a fullness of sophisticated improvisation and complexity in *Nights*.

Aside from this method of narration, original, nonlinear, and intertwined, it is the social and cultural scene that is of crucial importance in *Nights*—the portrayal of a rich, multicolored social life, intertwined around events and personages, carrying the full breadth of Abbasid city life, mirroring people's interactions in Baghdad's streets, taverns, palaces, courts, river banks, and gardens, as well as its more exclusive, more sheltered boudoirs and canopies. It is a space crowded with human movement, where historical persons such as caliphs, a princess, judges, police chiefs, and vagabonds mingle with improvised characters borrowed from the world of jinn, imps, and demons, or with others formed to embody enduring prototypes and archetypes that would become an integral part of Arabic culture and its concept of the world—characters such as Aladdin and Sinbad who have transcended their original world for foreign horizons. In *Nights,* factuality, or what seems like factuality, is mixed with the wondrous and supernatural; mundanity is entwined with myth, human frailty with superhuman prowess. And above all, there is adventure, whether set within the possible or thrust into the domains of the humanly unattainable. There is no respite for the imagination; rather, a tireless soaring into spaces of an imagined and often unreachable world or into the realm of the senses with their incessant sensuality and passionate urges.

Nights is, indeed, one of the most influential fictional texts one can find anywhere in the world.

The Folk Romances

Then there were the folk romances, of which Arabs created quite a few.[21] These were accounts of battles, of feats of courage and valor, of love and competition, of jealousy and revenge, but also of noble acts of holiness or chivalry. Many of these folk romances were written after the Arab empire began to suffer the attacks of other nations. They were the epics of the Arabs. Although pre-Islamic poetry had a great deal of epic and heroic content and carried in certain poems the epic spirit in all its fullness, it did not produce a single massive epic—probably because the Arab people in pre-Islamic times were not yet one nation facing a single enemy. They mostly feuded with each other within the tribal system or, when faced by a hoard of foreign enemies such as the Persians, only a limited number of tribes faced the outside enemy. When Islam unified Arabs under one banner and the Islamic campaigns started in the seventh century, registering success after success, there seemed to be no need for the reassuring influence of an epic that recounted past deeds of glory. When this became needed after the defeats suffered at the hands of the invading Mongols, Arabic poetry had already been entrenched in the lyrical mode, which is the highest of all modes, and would not happily accommodate the epic. It was left to prose to fill this gap.

Modern Arabic Fiction

The development of the two fictional genres in modern Arabic, the novel and the short story, differs a little from the development of these genres in the West. Like Western fiction, the novel appeared first, as early as the last decades of the nineteenth century, with desultory attempts here and there in the Arab world. These were preceded by quite a few attempts at translations from Western fiction, most of which were from novels, although a few, such as those translated (from the French) by Mustafa Lutfi al-Manfaluti (1876–1924) (discussed below) with the help of intermediaries, were short stories. However, as an independent genre, the short story only became recognized in the 1920s with the rise of several short-story writers in Egypt, among whom Mahmoud Taymur was the most prominent. By the mid-twentieth century it had developed robustly enough to become an established venture and the leading fictional genre, with many short-story writers mushrooming in various parts of the Arab world. This continued beyond the 1950s and well into the 1970s, when the short story kept its higher status and produced great riches within the genre. By the time the novel took firm roots in the Arab world in this same decade, this world was seething with many short-story writers. However, the short story's primacy was, after the seventies, gradually overtaken by the novel, as will be discussed below.

It was a slightly different scene in the West. It was the novel that thrived first in Europe and continued developing toward greater maturity before the short story began to take root in the nineteenth century, becoming an important genre in the 1890s. In America, during the frontier wars and the great movement of a pioneering immigrant spirit, the short story seemed to be a more suitable form, and by the middle of the nineteenth century it had achieved a respectable status. It is interesting to see, at the turn of the twentieth century, a major American journal, *Collier's Weekly*, initiate a vigorous prizewinning competition for the short story, announcing in 1904 its intention of giving prizes to the best three short stories submitted to the journal, offering then what must have seemed a fabulous financial incentive for short-story writers, too large for a single story, even for our own day.[22]

It should be remembered here that these two art forms, in their modern concept, seemed novel to modern Arabs, although written (as opposed to oral) short fiction and brief, self-contained anecdotes that read like stories had been around for at least twelve centuries. But the example of past exploits in short narrative genres was absent from direct memory, for reasons explained above, although it must have seeped into the subconsciousness of writers and become an instinctive artistic approach, providing modern Arabs with a natural affinity for short narratives. This situation will seem clearer if we look at the slow and uneasy development of the short story in England. T. O. Beachcroft speaks of various streams that had been drawing together during centuries to produce the modern art of the short story in England,[23] asserting that even as late as the middle of the nineteenth century "there is still no famous English author whom we think of as a specialist in short stories"[24] and designating Robert Louis Stevenson, who published his first collection in 1882, as the first major writer in the British Isles to become a specialist in the short story.[25] And although the modern short story developed more rapidly in Western countries other than England, its development in the Arab world seems to have been far more rapid still.

However, as it happened, the two major fictional genres seemed, in their *modern* forms, new to Arabs, and writers of fiction were working at the beginning without the guiding spirit of an acknowledged tradition that was only waiting to discover its modern methods and points of emphases. Moreover, because of the attack the heritage sustained at the hands of well-known writers, as explained above, there was a tendency at the time to overlook (or neglect) many inherited prose genres, and it would be some decades before gifted writers would realize the riches of their narrative heritage and begin taking conscious inspiration from it.

Being without direct traditions to build on also meant that writers of fiction were free from established conventions, which was not at all the case with poetry. However, having no direct conventional trappings to tear off, and being outside the inherited cultural institution, fiction writers were not only free, they were also loose, with no anchor in their own language to hold onto, a difficult freedom indeed, in which they had to grope for some kind of foundation on which to base their new standards and their slowly acquired modern artistic concepts and techniques. It is true that they had a model in the Western contribution, but here lay a greater danger: hybridity. If they found in the form of the novel and the short story an already established model on which they could build, they immediately realized that to avoid creating hybrid examples, the other elements in the work of fiction (or drama) had to be genuinely the outcome of their own culture. If the plot, the various beginnings, and the different closures—in short, the general technique of the novel or short story—could be mirrored on Western models, the other elements—characters, events, descriptions, outlook, psychological reactions, emotional responses, and above all tone and *Weltanschauung*—had to spring from the writer's indigenous culture. The new writers had to formulate their own interpretation of the reality around them, and all these had to find their coefficient in a new modern literary language capable of expressing fluently the preoccupations, concerns, and aspirations of modern men and women in the Arab world.

Still in their formative and highly experimental phase, the creative writers of fiction (and drama) gallantly tried to anchor themselves in a new tradition, while being hampered from too quick a development by their inherent weakness in the new art forms and by the natural alienation still felt toward them by critics and audiences alike.[26] The greater concentration on the short story was due, in one aspect, to the fact that the writers of fiction were hesitant to attempt the more demanding art of the novel; publishers were also skeptical about the novel's financial success, while short-story writers could find many literary magazines ready to publish their work. The new freedom that seemed available as writers attempted to build in an empty ground was illusory, for there can be no unrestricted freedom in art. Art has its own built-in rules that can never be successfully flouted. These are essentially silent, unwritten laws that the inspired and highly endowed writer instinctively apprehends; he or she knows where to stop and where to venture, what to adopt and what to leave out. However, in the case of the acquisition of a completely new art form, artistic instinct alone cannot completely secure the best results. The creative writer needs in this case both time for the fermentation of a new experiment and a dedication to his or her work so that the new art form is no longer alien and becomes malleable and accessible to others.

As noted above, the history of literary genres demonstrates a limited number of genres available to the creative writer in any language. Moreover, it also shows considerable similarities of beginnings and development among various cultures, and it is surely expected that the form of the novel in Arabic was to impose itself in modern times as a result of the same phenomena behind the birth of the novel form in the West. It is possible that the early writers of Arabic fiction were conscious imitators of Western models. However, the continuation of experimentation in the genre, the way writers and readers eventually took to it, proves its appropriateness to the historic moment, its utter timeliness.[27]

The Rise of the Novel in Arabic

A study of the rise of the novel in Arabic should focus on the fact that this art form was adopted by aspiring Arab authors not simply as a result of their encounter with Western fictional achievements but also because it was timely for the novel to appear in the Arab world. It represented an answer to a need as well as a readiness in both the literature and the audience of the time for its particular qualifications.

However, it was not enough that there was a "readiness" in the state of art for the introduction and perpetuation of new forms and genres (whether fiction or drama); the process needed a conscious effort to develop their technique, to absorb their particular artistic "flavor," and to familiarize them as reading (and in the case of drama as viewing) material, before they could be established as major genres. High literature was still monopolized by poetry, a situation that prompted the Arab American critic Mikha'il Nu'aima (1889–1988), writing in the second decade of the twentieth century, to express great vexation, calling attention, very early in the twentieth century, to the advantage of relinquishing the obsession with poetry for the advantage of fictional experimentation.[28]

The process of the establishment of modern Arabic fiction (and drama) was begun by introducing the new fiction to the Arab audience through translations from Western fiction.[29] As in poetry, the earliest novels to be translated were from the romantic repertoire, with Hugo's *Les Misérables* translated (through intermediaries) at the turn of the century by no other than the famous Egyptian poet Hafiz Ibrahim, and Goethe's *The Sorrows of Young Werther* translated from the French by the equally famous essayist Ahmad Hasan al-Zayyat in 1920.

The translations that gained immediate popularity in the second decade of the twentieth century were those of al-Manfaluti from French literature, also through intermediaries. His loose, highly personalized translations of four famous works from French literature—Edmond Rostand's play *Cyrano de Bergerac*, Farançois Coppée's play *Pour la Couronne,* Alphonse Karr's novel *Sous les Tilleuls,* and Bernardin de Saint-Pierre's novel, *Paul et Virginie*—quickly won acclaim in the Arab world, and whole generations grew up enjoying them. This was not due simply to his fluent, lucid, vivid, and pure Arabic style, nor simply to the romantic temper of the works, which greatly suited the romantic temper that was gaining sway in the Arab world at that time; it was also due to the generous and humane spirit with which they were imbued, which could be felt in al-Manfaluti's choice of words, his emphases, his preferences, his empathy with those who suffered and endured. Al-Manfaluti also tried to write his own creative work, though with less success, in the form of long short stories, which involved events that could be the basis of a whole novel, centering mainly on the adversities and drawbacks of Arab society at the turn of the twentieth century. This kind of fiction involving social criticism had been started by Gibran Kahlil Gibran (1883–1931) in America, who published two collections of these short/long stories in the first decade of the century: *Brides of the Prairies* ('ara' is al-muruj, 1906) and *Rebellious Spirits* (al-arwah al-mutamarrida, 1908), attacking the internal stupor, the fetters, the inertia, the fanaticism, the ignorance, and the stagnation rampant in the Arab world. For his part, Mustafa Lutfi al-Manfaluti in Egypt was completely involved in the description of the tragic aspects of the lives of the poor and the way poverty and immorality led to adversity. In his *Tears* (al-'abarat, 1916), a collection of ten stories, six were translated and four were written directly by him.[30] Both the translated and the original stories deal with such topics as the consequences of corruption, the weakness of the flesh, the treachery of others, the detrimental influence of drink and gambling, and the cruelty and tyranny of those in power. They illustrate a grim aspect of life, touch on love's many-sided aspects, preach the value of loyalty, chastity, generosity, and self-sacrifice.

The first half of the twentieth century demonstrates greater laboriousness, less audacity, a slower internalization of the tools of good fiction. It is clear that these new forms could not have been established as major art forms in modern Arabic without the diligent and dedicated efforts of a few aspiring authors who worked throughout the early decades of the twentieth century to attain this goal. Experiments in fiction, however, became more pervasive, involving greater awareness of the artistic prerequisites of these art forms, from the mid-century on.[31]

Egypt produced some of the foremost novelists and short-story writers in the modern Arab world and eventually came to be the citadel of modern Arabic fiction. However, early experiments in Arabic fiction also took place in other parts of the world. At the turn of the twentieth century the North American émigré authors known as the Mahjar writers, most of whom were Syrian (these included Lebanese at the time), attempted the writing of fiction of various lengths. Their adoption of modern fictional forms seems natural enough in view of the fact that they were in close touch with Western fiction, knew European languages, and acquired greater affinity with Western taste in both literature and life.

In the Arab world, while the audience seems to have received translations of fiction from European authors well, many critics felt that this phenomenon posed a kind of danger to morals and language.[32] At the same time, other writers expressed their rejection of the old fictional genres, particularly the tales of jinn, ogres, spells, and incantations in, for example, *The Arabian Nights*, and asserted that people had now discarded these stories because they had come to "seek reality."[33] This is extremely important. The idea that modern fiction should be concerned with representing reality—a far leap from the fiction of myths and supernatural phenomena—was not in circulation at the turn of the century, and writers had not yet gained enough modern critical insight to be able to formulate this idea in sophisticated terms. They did not realize at the time that the adherence to reality was the result of the emergence of the middle and, to an extent, of the lower classes who made up the greatest "reality" of the time. But the unknown writer mentioned in note 33 speaks with assurance and a deep insight into the true shift in sensibility, social change, and the literary reaction to the decisive mutations that lay at the basis of the technical and thematic changes in literature and literary sensibility.[34] The real resistance to the adoption of the new genres came from members of the old literary guard who fought the tremendous changes that were taking place throughout modern times in all aspects of literature, only to capitulate in the end.

The Early Precursors in the Novel Form

Writers on the early novel in Arabic tend to speak of Muhammad Husain Haykal's novel *Zaynab* (1914) as the first experiment in the modern form of the novel in Arabic. However, one of the earliest modernized experiments in the novel was the publication in 1912 of Gibran's *Broken Wings* (al-ajniha 'l-muta-kassira), which prompted an immediate positive reaction from another émigré poet, critic, and writer of fiction, Mikha'il Nu'aima, thus launching his career as critic. Although a factual story, and probably largely a true one built on the real experience of Gibran himself, *Broken Wings* is steeped in romantic sorrows and despair. Arab critics writing on romanticism usually overlook the fact that Arab romanticism began, in fact, more in prose than in poetry, with both Gibran's and al-Manfaluti's experiments leading the way. It is also most interesting to note that when Arab romanticism finally took hold of poetry with the rise in the 1920s of the true romantic poets all over the Arab world, Arabic fiction had already moved away from this purely romantic apprehension of experience, even though it was deeply imbued with social and moral concerns and was able to accommodate realistic features as well as comic delineations. The works of Ibrahim al-Mazini (1890–1949) and others, despite their underlying social criticism, were highly entertaining.

Jurji Zaydan

A major contribution, and one that has been overlooked in the literary history of the novel in Arabic, is the massive work of Jurji Zaydan (1861–1914). Zaydan's oeuvre is monumental and has had a great influence on the vision and moral attitudes of several generations of readers growing up in the Arab world.

Jurji Zaydan was born in Beirut to a Christian Lebanese working-class family. Despite difficult financial circumstances, he succeeded in studying an array of disciplines, including Arabic literature, folk, and formal; history; English; Semitic languages; science; and medicine. However, by the time he graduated from medical school in Cairo, he had already discovered his major aptitude as a researcher and writer on history, the Arabic language, and Islamic civilization. In addition to his historical writings, he wrote twenty-three novels, all of substantial length. His first novel, *The Fugitive Memluk* (al-mamluk al-sharid), was published in 1890.

Zaydan's novels differed from the "modern" novel in that they were not as much involved with the common man as with personages of the Arab empire. When men from the common strata of society were introduced, they were often either heroes or villains, sometimes supervillains. His novels also reflected a blanket culture with predictable behavior patterns and logical reactions to good and evil. However, they were free of any relations to supernatural phenomena or transcendental solutions to problems, which was a great leap from the earlier narratives rampant in the Arab world. They stressed either the positive qualities of the person and reflected his or her internal strife and apprehensions when facing problems, or the negative aspects of individuals involved in conspiracies, treason, or infractions. Zaydan's major protagonist was in fact the Arab Islamic civilization in its long march through the centuries, and his novels pointed out its greatest achievements, illustrating, as has never been done before or after, its lifestyle, customs, and the basic *Weltanschauung* that prompted its movement in history. He usually included some romance, which made his novels more attractive to their readers. Some of the novels were tragedies that mirrored the various actual tragic events that punctuated Arab/Islamic history during the days of the empire and after.

Zaydan dealt, in breadth and depth, with a subject matter so vast that it cannot but arouse the greatest admiration. The novelistic narration flowed spontaneously from his pen, crowded with events, descriptions, and recitations. His huge subject matter seemed to be well within his reach; he did not need to invent the wider framework, only the minor human interactions. He described a varied, mobile civilization with its battles, its massive migrations of men and ideas, its mammoth acquisitions, its glorious victories, its tragic vicissitudes. His work, as is the case with all historical novels, was constricted by the facts of history, which left him with no alternative that could alter the outcome of events. However, far removed from the actual mobile spectacle, Zaydan was able to make it more dramatic by an artistic contraction of events and epochs, and the inclusion of universal human associations and modes of behavior.

A man of great vision and sensibility, he appreciated the greatness of a civilization that has been neglected and maligned by others, at a time when Arab and Islamic vigilance regarding this rich heritage had not yet been alerted. He was one of the first modern guardians of Arabic culture and its heritage and was the most zealous of historians, commemorating his vast subject in both fiction and discourse.

These charming accounts, on which the generations of readers in the first four decades of the twentieth century were reared, had more history than art and were inspired more by the Lebanese Christian author's obsession with his subject. Certainly, the novel form was the only adequate creative medium for such a vast enterprise. What shorter fictional form could embody these enormous feats of human accomplishments, cultural achievements, glorious summits, and tragic pitfalls that appeared in his novels in *epic* dimensions? *Zaydan's work is one of the most poignant examples of subject matter that dictates its own medium and celebrates it; the content imposes the form.*

It is unfortunate indeed that a man of this caliber should be almost systematically overlooked or slightingly brushed aside when critics record the beginnings of novel writing in modern Arabic. It is true that his experiment, on the technical level, was decidedly premodern in some aspects, but it was a loyal and mainly realistic description of major moments of history and was an impressive beginning to the fictional venture in modern Arabic. Whatever the reasons that lie behind this neglect, whether due to regional fanaticism or any other kind of prejudice, the fact remains that to speak about the Arabic novel without honoring this great writer is a serious faux pas, an unacceptable injustice both to the writer and to the great spirit that lay behind his writings. Like many early (but acknowledged) experimenters, Zaydan might not have achieved artistic excellence in his creative work, and he might have written in a sprawling style and tried to put too much into the single scene. But his novels—even now with the art of the novel in Arabic—established on sound artistic grounds, are still not only highly informative but also genuinely enjoyable to read. To overlook his matchless oeuvre is a most negative testimonial against the loss of genuine values of judgment in some areas of modern Arab cultural life.

Muhammad Husain Haykal

The same year that Zaydan died, Muhammad Husain Haykal published his much celebrated novel *Zaynab* (1914), a tragic love story based on experiences from the writer's contemporary scene. This, most critics in Egypt insist, is the beginning of the modern novel in Arabic, a proposition that has aroused much countercriticism. Speaking sarcastically, one of the critics of this proposition says, "[it is] as if all that preceded it does not represent more than an introduction to this *event* [emphasis mine] which came as an immense revolution in the world of literature." [35] However, some of this countercriticism contains some partial truth in that the novel presents an Egyptianization of scenery and characters, depicts events taking place on the contemporary scene, and speaks of the individual and his or her predicament; but it certainly falls short of the halo afforded it by many literary critics and historians.

Haykal's *Zaynab* has had more critical accounts written about it, mainly by Egyptian critics, than any other work of fiction before the rise of Mahfouz. It is a story about life in the Egyptian countryside with its customs and norms, about the division of rural classes and the hard life of the poorer peasants. It is also a story of cross-class attachments, depicting the lack of volition allowed women at the time and ending with the death of Zaynab, the main female character, of tuberculosis. It is an early expression of sympathy with the plight of the Arab peasant, a theme that became especially popular in poetry during the 1920s and 1930s, sometimes arriving at a call for revolution.[36] In an artistically positive step forward, away from other fictional experiments such as those by Gibran and al-Manfaluti, especially the latter, Haykal in *Zaynab* breaks free of the sentimentality and spleen with which earlier stories were impregnated. This achievement came at a time when the whole atmosphere was prone to the sentimental expression of a people facing bewildering change in many aspects of life.

Zaynab does not seem to have had much currency in the rest of the Arab world, particularly because Haykal did not continue his fictional career, returning only in the 1950s to write the novel *Such Was She Born* (hakadha khuliqat, 1955), a rather unexciting work for this late period.

Egypt's Early Literary Centrality

In the first few decades of the twentieth century Egypt's literary relationship with the Arab world was through great writers of literary discourse and its quest for poetic leadership. Indeed, poetry criticism was paramount in Egypt, unequaled anywhere in the Arab world except by the great figure of Marun Abboud (1886–1962), Lebanon's and the Arab world's honest, insightful, brilliant, and nonpartisan critic. In the poetic field, the gigantic figure of Ahmad Shawqi (1869–1932), looming above everyone else, was able to sustain the claim of poetic leadership for Egypt. Honored in 1927 at a great celebration in Egypt by the whole Arab world, he was hailed as "the Prince of Poets." Indeed, Arabic letters had their potent stronghold in Egypt in the first decades of the twentieth century, with the triad of the Diwan Group expostulating their ideas on poetry and innovation; with Taha Husain rising staunchly as critic and literary historian, audaciously addressing the hallowed Arab literary past and throwing doubts on diehard concepts of literary history; and with the Apollo group, pathfinders and experimentalists, using their platform, the *Apollo* magazine (1932–1934), to present new guidelines on poetry. Egypt was indeed, at that time, the shaker and mover of literary events for the whole Arab world, and Egyptian writers, like other Arab writers, consecrated their efforts to the service of Arabs' favorite art form: poetry.[37]

By the 1950s Egypt would lose its central place in Arabic poetry, and Baghdad and Beirut, especially Beirut, would become the centers of the poetic movement, with the greatest revolution in the history of Arabic poetry coming out of Baghdad and becoming fully established in Beirut. The citadel of culture in the 1950s and 1960s, Beirut was the meeting place of Arab writers and intellectuals, a place where they could breathe the air of freedom denied to them elsewhere in the rest of a fiercely repressive Arab world; the new poetic movement was bolstered by avant-garde literary reviews and a bustling activity of publishing and journalism that continued to the mid-seventies, when the Lebanese civil war erupted. Egypt's leading role in the prose genres, particularly in fiction, however, would continue to flourish to the present day. This was enhanced greatly by the rise to eminence, in the 1950s, of Naguib Mahfouz (b. 1911).

But before Mahfouz proved his leadership in the field of the novel, the genre had already been attempted by several eminent writers, particularly in Egypt. Tawfiq al-Hakim, an eminent playwright whose great dexterity in the style, mode, and language of drama and versatility in dramatic themes advanced the Egyptian and Arab theater many steps forward, was also a novelist and short-story writer. His first novel, *The Spirit's Resurrection* ('awdat al-ruh) published in 1933, won him success and recognition despite the fact that he used colloquial Egyptian in the dialogue. The problem of diaglossia would plague Arab critics and literary historians for several decades in the twentieth century: Arabs feared losing their hold on their eloquent *fus-ha* (high Arabic), which was the language of their great poetry and prose heritage and, above all, the language of the holy Quran and of the traditions of the Prophet and the great Shi'a leaders. It is interesting to see that this problem has been essentially resolved. Writers of fiction and dramatists often use colloquial language in the dialogue, a device now quite acceptable to the reading public.

Several self-imaging novels were published in the 1930s. Just as al-Hakim utilized his own personal experience to depict life in his novels, so did other writers, and we have in this genre such well-known novels as *The Stream of Days* (al-ayyam), by Taha Husain (the first volume in fact appeared in 1929, the second in 1940); *Ibrahim the Writer* (Ibrahim al-katib, 1931), by al-Mazini; and *Sara* (1938), by al-'Aqqad. These were a mixture of fiction and biography, retaining some of the characteristics of the historic novel in that the author knows what has already happened in reality. Pure fiction in the novel form, with only a few exceptions, would mature later on.

Al-Hakim's depiction of official corruption and low-level bureaucracy as he personally witnessed them when he was a prosecutor in the countryside and then delineated them in his *Diary of a Prosecutor in the Provinces* (yawmi-yyat na'ib fi 'l-aryaf, 1937) is poignant. The same personal experience was utilized in his famous novel, *A Bird from the East* ('usfur min al-sharq, 1938), about the encounter of East and West. This would be a recurrent and popular theme throughout the twentieth century, with a change of emphasis after the 1960s, when the constant migration of thousands of Arabs to the West, by bringing in familiarity, removed part of the curiosity and challenge that earlier twentieth-century Arabs felt toward the West. This is, in fact, a more intricate subject than this introduction can accommodate, but the curiosity that the Arabs had toward the West was part of a romance with the West that fascinated Arab readers everywhere.[38] By the time Al-Tayyib Salih published his seminal novel in the sixties, *Mawsim al-Hijra ila 'l-Shamal*, expertly translated into English by Denys Johnson-Davies as *Season of Migration to the North*, the early fascination with the West had abated and continued to abate later on in works depicting the meeting of East and West, several of which were by women.[39]

The Rise of Naguib Mahfouz

The novel would finally be established as a genre par excellence with the rise of Naguib Mahfouz (b. 1911).[40] The award of the Nobel Prize to Mahfouz in 1988 was not simply a recognition of a single author's achievement but also an acknowledgement of the fact that the Arabic novel had reached distinction on a global scale. It had been said before and after that it was poetry, the first art of the Arabs, that should have been first awarded the global prize, since it was the art in which Arabs had the greatest dexterity and the finest achievements. However, it was more crucial, more telling, more gratifying to see a new art form, less than a few decades old, rise so quickly in the eyes of the world. It was felt, at the same time, that another writer of fiction might have perhaps had the same chance of winning the prize, in this case for the short story: Yusuf Idris, a brilliant writer of unrivaled talent.

Despite their very hesitant beginnings, it did not take much more than half a century for the arts of fiction to grow to a relevant maturity. A great burgeoning of the two genres was seen in the first three decades of the second half of the twentieth century, with the novel gaining ascendancy again by the end of the century. There had been a quick rise of many novelists writing and experimenting with varied skill, from North Africa to the Arab heartland, from the Sudan and the Gulf countries to Yemen. This significant activity in a new and major genre owes its confidence to the work of a few experimentalists, mainly in Egypt, and to the genius of Mahfouz, who was its prime exponent.

Mahfouz's work was a firm bridge over which the Arab novelist crossed to new horizons of modernity and fictional dexterity and courage. Long before critics began to think of the novel as the more vital and accurate expression of modern man, Mahfouz had realized its importance as the literary form most suited to our times.

Of course, there are still many modern experiences in the Arab world that are singularly suited to poetry: great political upheavals, the constant distortion of the rhythm of life, the immutable, unrelenting repression and oppression to which the Arab people have been constantly exposed, whole cities destroyed, feuds among national regions of the Arab world erupting even on a global scale, freedom repressed, people uprooted, heroism and revolution thwarted, all in an atmosphere of constant fear and constant strife. This is the stuff of poetry. However, it would be the task of the novel—more than poetry, which carried a communal voice most of the time—to charter the experiences of modern Arabs and to express more the spirit of the individual in all his or her concerns, the communal but also the private, the externalized but also the internalized in the recesses of the conscience, which only art can reveal best to the world.

By 1951 Mahfouz had already published eight novels, gradually establishing the form in Arabic. However, the publication of his famous *Trilogy*, a three-hundred-thousand-word family saga in three volumes—*Palace Walk* (bayn al-qasrayn), *Palace of Desire* (qasr al-shawq), and *Sugar Street* (al-sukkariyya), published in 1956 and 1957)—was the turning point in contemporary Arabic fiction. The *Trilogy* took a dedication on the part of its author, hitherto unknown among Arab writers of fiction, to complete. It is the saga of a middle-class family in Cairo over three generations, spanning the time from nearly the end of the First World War in 1917 through 1944. The achievement of the *Trilogy* not only compressed the time needed for the Arabic novel's inception as an established art form but also represented the most striking example of artistic courage yet known at the time. Mahfouz had spent six years writing it, working during his free time, for he kept a regular job all his life. The *Trilogy* was an immediate success. It was hailed as a great literary event, and Mahfouz earned acclaim as the greatest novelist in Egypt and the Arab world at the time. This three-volume novel posed the most serious challenge to the great imbalance in Arabic literature,[41] where poetry had for many centuries occupied the pinnacle of creative endeavor.

After the *Trilogy* many Arab writers would take to novel writing, creating new forms and venturing into areas denied to poetry. It would take less than two decades for the art of the novel to burgeon all over the Arab world and establish for itself a place of permanent importance. The old prohibitive fear of writers and publishers about undertaking the venture of writing and publishing long works of fiction was greatly diminished. The sense of estrangement from written fiction of a people whose literary history favored the poetic expression, whose interchange was almost never free of the eloquence and wisdom of dearly memorized single verses or clusters of verses, now disappeared. It is true that Arabs still memorize what they can of their rich and profound poetry, and it is equally true that they still flock, in the hundreds and thousands, to the large public halls to listen to their poets declaim their verses from a platform, mostly addressing the state of affairs in the Arab world. However, the novel has become an ever more desirable form, and people from the Atlantic to the Gulf now read the novels of Arab writers with the feeling and the faith that they are the literature of one people, of one general culture, of one basic *Weltanschauung*. Literary prizes are given not to the writers of one Arab country or another but to Arabic novels and novelists everywhere. The difficulties of each other's colloquial language, when the vernacular is sometimes employed, will continue to pose some problems, although the Egyptian vernacular has won for itself, through the wide dissemination of Egyptian drama, films, and video programs, a pervasive familiarity, and all Arabs seem to have become attuned to it. On the other hand, through the profuse writings in fiction and newspapers, the Arabic language itself is slowly creating for itself a middle language whose affinities are moving slowly away from the standard *fus-ha*, the eloquent high language of poets, without the possible vulgarity of colloquialisms. This has not, however, prevented some writers of fiction, such as Jabra Ibrahim Jabra and Haydar Haydar, from often giving way to the most eloquent and rhetorical of styles in their work or parts of, where an elaborate condensation of meaning and emotion is needed. Everything has become possible in the language of fiction now, and it is an exhilarating experience.

Mahfouz provided a model of dedication, audacity, and perseverance to other would-be novelists, of determination to embrace a vision and see it through. In a lecture I gave at the University of Amherst in 1989, I said about Mahfouz: "Very rarely in the history of literature does a single writer herald the advent of a whole literary era, while introducing at the same time a hitherto alienated medium as the literary genre of the future par excellence."[42]

A great change in literary sensibility was taking place in the Arab world after the mid-fifties. The pervasive motifs of poetry emphasized a high address, a nostalgic approach, an emotional outlook, vehement avowals, grand self-assertions, an insistence on memory, a loud rebuttal of evil. The novel introduced a new calm, a more realistic approach, a more accurate picture of contemporary Arab life, objectifying emotion all the time, stilling undue passion, and painting life in slow motion.

Mahfouz began as a romantic Egyptian, looking back on Egypt's ancient history. His first historical novel, *The Vicissitudes of Fate* ('abath al-aqdar, 1939), was followed in 1943 by *Radubis* and in 1944 by *The Struggle of Tiba* (kifah Tiba). However, by the mid-forties, he turned to the contemporary scene, writing realistically on modern Cairo. *The Khalili Inn* (khan al-Khalili) appeared in 1945, and *Midaqq Alley* (zuqaq al-midaqq) followed in 1947. In the same year he published *The New Cairo* (al-Qahira 'l-jadida). By now he had embarked on his realistic stage, which would culminate in the *Trilogy* in the mid-fifties.

It was with the appearance of his lovely novel *The Thief and the Dogs* (al-liss wa 'l-kilab) in 1961, however, that his new modernist phase was achieved. The emphasis in this novel and in those that followed lay on a modern technique in dealing with characterization, sequence of events, and symbolization.

His later novels are built on the symbolization of one or another aspect of contemporary life. In most of them his emphasis is on social aspects, but sometimes on the ennui and spiritual fatigue of intellectuals. He often chose his characters as archetypes of certain ills that assailed city life: bureaucracy, symbolized by shady government officials; coercion, symbolized by policemen; corruption, symbolized by murderers and thieves; exploited and downtrodden individuals, symbolized by prostitutes and servants. He has also a number of characters from among the affluent classes, with their snobbery, their self-indulgence, their greed, and their spiritual void. In many of his later novels Mahfouz anticipated the great decline in ethical standards that was to befall the Arab world at the end of the twentieth century, the many character blemishes that would become the plague of contemporary life, exhibiting the lamentable results of a century's failed struggle and immense, gratuitous sacrifices.

Mahfouz's characters seem to be the victims of their times and society. Thwarted, betrayed, disinherited, robbed of their rights and of the precious gifts of freedom and human worth, many individuals turned the evil that surrounded their lives onto each other and onto themselves, unable to avert the moral disorders that colonial intrigues, Arab complicity, and the hegemony of a repressive oligarchy that had no real relationship with the twentieth century had imposed on them. They fell victim to petty quests, many capitulating to the blind authority of autocrats and to the allure of possessions and wealth.

If many heroes lack a constructive attitude toward the social world, they are not always portrayed by Mahfouz as complete perverts. They may be simply antiheroes with a mixture of positive and negative qualities, but when caught in the web of a corrupt social order and in the convoluted mesh of their own mistakes, they react violently, sometimes veering toward crime and revenge.[43] With a profound sympathy and understanding of human nature in all its intricacies and contradictions, Mahfouz delineates the complexities and many-sidedness of the individual. Underneath the violent and corrupt mesh of events there may lie a profound forbearance, and in the very grip of corruption and violence there may be love and a yearning for purity of spirit. Although Mahran, the main protagonist in *The Thief and the Dogs* (1961), is now obsessed with the desire to avenge himself against those who had betrayed him, he is still able to seek an old holy man whom he knew as a boy and to rest awhile in the enveloping calm of a religious sanctuary; and in his attempt to escape the police, he seeks a prostitute who loves him and gives him shelter, thus revolving in vain around the pivots of love and faith while he tries to flee a world of treachery that proves that even a thief and a murderer can also be a victim. The drama ends when the prostitute who gives him love and the holy man who gives him pity and forbearance become unattainable, and he is left alone to the police dogs to tear him apart.

In *Chattering on the Nile* (1966) the influence of Franz Kafka and probably Jean Genet and Samuel Becket on Mahfouz can be seen in the superb treatment of the deadlock afflicting the alienated lifestyle of bourgeois men and women who spend their free time on a houseboat on the Nile. A novel of the absurd, it delineates the thinking and behavior of a number of pseudo-intellectuals who seek oblivion from the existing system, in which they can find no redeeming hope, by turning to the sedation and solace of smoking hash, practicing sex, and chattering, with a certain amount of detachment, on the various aspects of contemporary Egyptian life. They meet nightly on this houseboat, looked after by an ageless servant who procures for them both hash and women. Sex is an easy commodity, given and taken freely, a passionless sex, devoid of love and tenderness, exchanged almost with ennui. The ennui is a basic attitude in the novel, and the whole work is a magnification of human impotence. What is stunning, what causes deep anxiety in the reader, is the absence of all longing in this novel, a situation that one would think is still alien to Arab life—or so I thought until I read a recent Palestinian novel by Ahmad Rafiq 'Awad titled *Kingdoms of Lovers and Merchants* (mamlakat al-'ushshaq wa 'l-tujjar, 1997), which describes the same attitudes in Palestinians returning home from exile after the beginning of self-rule in the West Bank. These works, depicting the wildest negative side of

Arab life and its extreme fragility, usher in the signal for the breakdown of values and ideals. What is more alarming is the fact that the breakdown in these novels engages the protagonists not simply as individuals but as members of a group, of a larger entity, proving the social nature of the malaise, revealing its total control over destiny. Mahfouz draws here a view of a section of an elitist society that has arrived, in its despair of social salvation, at stalemate. The young Palestinian writer Ahmad Rafiq does the same. Ideology in these novels, the ideology on which the whole Arab people relied and through which they hoped to breathe one day the air of freedom, the ideology that had kept them alive and hoping, working, and sacrificing for the moment of salvation, was all but false, an illusion. In the Palestinian novel there is one act of will, the quest of salvation through violence, through the most extreme form of self-sacrifice. The suicide bomber happily faces his individual death for the sake of the group, suddenly tearing away the chords of harmony with the natural flow of life through a loud and screaming action, the only willed action in the whole novel, pitiful, agonizing, and blind, keeping the whole dilemma in a state of deadlock.

Chattering cannot help but disturb, even disfigure, the image one sustains of a people still struggling for freedom and liberation, driven forward with the flush of energy and determination and with the glimmer of hope and faith still flowing in their hearts. Mahfouz, as early as 1966, anticipated in *Chattering* the tragic deadlock that was to crown, after a hundred years of agony, struggle, and immense sacrifice, the end of the Arab twentieth century.

It is impossible to go into the whole of Mahfouz's extraordinary oeuvre in this introduction. His many-sidedness has also involved politics and religion. *Al-Karnak* (1974) is a political novel depicting the rude intrusion of politics into personal life as well as the powerful police machine that hems the life of left-wing civilians and curtails, on mere suspicion, their very movements. However, one of Mahfouz's greatest works is the landmark *Children of Gabalawi* (awlad haritna), an allegorical novel written and published in serialized form in Al-Ahram in 1959, banned by an Azhar decree, and republished in 1967 in Beirut. It is a highly symbolized novel, showing the never-tiring human endeavor to achieve the earthly paradise believed to be the rightful heritage of the wretched on this earth. Its seemingly realistic art of description cannot camouflage the undercurrents of the author's philosophy, which the Nobel citation describes as "a spiritual history of mankind." Ending as it does with 'Arafa, the symbol for science, killing Gabalawi, the father who symbolizes the creator, the work caused a big stir in Egypt and, given the atmosphere of ever-increasing religious fanaticism, was probably behind the 1994 attempt to assassinate Mahfouz.

In its subject matter, which deals with what Mahfouz feels is the dubious essence of religious dogma, *Gabalawi* is a unique experiment, an anticipatory expression of the predilection of an intelligent and highly civilized thinker, and as such it is "an anomaly in his novelistic output."[44] When Mahfouz wrote it in the late fifties, he was taking advantage of a more liberal atmosphere in the Arab world, one in which intellectuals spoke freely against religious hegemony, rejected theocratic rule, and called for secularism and freedom of thought. *Gabalawi* was a warning against what was going to come: the dominance of outmoded religious dicta that would pull people (here, the Muslims) away from scientific reasoning and objective interpretation of universal phenomena. Yet despite the prevalence of a more liberal atmosphere, *Gabalawi* was banned. By the seventies, what Mahfouz had warned against began to prevail, and fundamentalism began to sweep in varying degrees of intensity all over the Arab world. This was due to several factors: the success of the Iranian Islamic revolution, which did away with the much hated Iranian regime of the Shah, whose hard-fisted rule was seen as a client kingship subservient to the West; the rise after the 1960s of a massive class of educated young men who had come originally from villages to study at the free universities opened in the mid-twentieth century, after independence was achieved; and the conservative upbringing of these young educated Arabs who now filled thousands of government and other posts, carrying their conservative outlook with them. Other important factors were the political dilemma in the fragmented Arab world; the loss of a large part of Palestine to the Jews through Western intrigue and support; the many repressive regimes that suffocated liberty and individual initiative; and the destructive policy of the West that hampered any robust continuity of such progressive initiatives as the union between Egypt and Syria (1958–1961), coupled with the failure by the 1970s of secular ideologies, whether leftist or nationalist, leaving only a religious ideology to be embraced. A very conservative fundamentalist Islam began to spread slowly but with greater vigor over the whole Arab world.

Gabalawi remains a great allegory with unique qualities and a courageous venture into the realms of forbidden ideas, advocating the rationale of scientific thinking and rejecting the dubious fantasies of blind belief.

However, in other novels, Mahfouz again changes gear, as in *The Beggar* (al-shahhadh, 1965) and *Autumn Quail* (al-summan wa 'l-kharif, 1962), where the personal dilemma of the individual dominates. The two main protagonists, Omar in *The Beggar* and 'Issa in *Quail*, are looking for solutions to existential problems; we witness here not the reaction to a societal malaise but, in Raymond Williams's words, the "dramatic conflicts of an individual mind."

As with many other novels by Mahfouz, there is always a quest, but it is almost never realized. The hero in *The Beggar* tries all kinds of experiences and eventually rejects society, flouting bourgeois standards and expectations. His hostility toward society is not specific but is, rather, a rejection of the very idea of society and its suffocating norms. As such, it produces no action, and only withdrawal can be expected. In such novels one witnesses individual behavior in particular circumstances (alienation, loss, betrayal, failure). Mahfouz has certainly left very few aspects of problematic experiences in Egyptian life untouched and unexplored.

Mahfouz fanatically avoids an emotional participation in his novels and never betrays any sympathy with his characters. A total lack of sentimentality, redundancies, intrusive scenes, or irrelevant descriptions completes a well-knit, compact, and balanced structure. An underlying passion for human justice and harmony is sought, although the harmony is often destroyed by the shattering impossibilities of contemporary life. A great asset is the writer's capacity to achieve poise and control over a new art form, while mirroring through his characters an age of constant fear and fury as well as a sense of pervasive anxiety. However, his novels usually convey an atmosphere of gloom and concentrate on the negative aspects of experience, with very little scope for any alleviating sense of joy or any mitigating innocence. Whatever Mahfouz wanted to say to the world, he said it unassumingly, through his characters. He never played any games with his ideas, and he never pontificated or attempted to address the world from on high.

The word "pioneer" describes the role Mahfouz played in the history of Arabic literature. Through hard work and unparalleled dedication to his art, he engineered the novel's inception into Arabic and established it as an ever-developing and crucially important medium through which the detailed experience of contemporary Egyptian, particularly Cairene life, is narrated,[45] a task that the art of poetry could not fully accomplish. Without him the history of contemporary Arabic literature would have to be written in a completely different way.

General Observations
Modern Arabic Fiction: Content Versus Technique

Most contemporary Arabic criticism of fiction (and indeed, of poetry) shows a predilection for discussing meaning and subject matter rather than technique. Moreover, most teachers of Arabic literature, whether Arabs or Arabists, also favor content, the subject matter usually holding the greatest attention. In most cases, Arabic centers at universities prefer to offer courses on the fiction that discusses social issues, particularly when the subject matter engages women's experiences, especially Muslim women's experiences. At the same time the greatest number of publishers of translated fiction with whom I have had transactions since I launched the Project of Translation from Arabic (PROTA) in 1980, have usually shown a preference for the social topic stressed in fiction rather than for the excellence in technique and form of a work not possessing the immediacy of a clearly socially oriented topic. It was an avant-garde publishing group, Interlink Books, which decided to publish the breathtaking novel *Prairies of Fever*,[46] one of the best postmodern novels written in Arabic, by the Palestinian poet/novelist Ibrahim Nasrallah. Yet this complex and sophisticated novel, in its English translation, has never been chosen as part of a class curriculum, the preference remaining for novels with immediacy and clear assumptions.

This is not to say that content in the novel is less important than technique. In fact, meaning is the backbone of fictional narratives, an integral part not only of the experience of protagonists but, in a novel of quality, of its very artistic makeup. A differentiation exists between the way meaning is handled in discourse and the way it is handled in high literature. This is, of course, seen more poignantly in poetry, where a poetic meaning does not include simply a statement on things but internalizes our own attitude and stance toward things. It should also be so in good fiction. To perceive the world artistically will dress the meaning not just with lofty words, not even necessarily with lofty words, but with the oblique and profound gaze of the artist, with his or her particular sensibility that makes a piece of writing a work of art.[47]

Epic Representation

Three major novelists with epic dimensions in their cumulative works are Naguib Mahfouz, 'Abd al-Rahman Munif, and Ibrahim al-Koni.

Mahfouz's work, discussed above, delineates an epic image of modern Cairo, which is, in fact, the main protagonist of his narratives. Taken all together, it gives an extensive description of both Cairo's upper echelon of intellectuals at a loss how to face contemporary problems and Cairo's underworld, bringing out the varied contemporary malaise that haunts the life of people of all classes but remaining on the grim side of experience, with hardly any depiction of joy and innocence or any reflection of an *optimistic* philosophical interpretation of experience.

'Abd al-Rahman Munif depicts the story of oil in the Arab world, its rise in a vast, forgotten stretch of sands in what is now the Gulf countries, and its consequent arrival at a central place on the Arab map, decked with luminous cities and all the luxury that wealth can buy. His concentration on the depiction of this unusual and colossal experience, which has transformed the various aspects of life in the whole Arab world, has epic dimensions. This has been achieved through his quintet of novels bound together under the general title *Cities of Salt*, a detailed delineation of a grotesque scene that has come to life in the second half of the twentieth century and will remain a decisive historical heritage for coming generations of Arabs.

Ibrahim al-Koni did the same thing with the vast Libyan desert, a neglected and forgotten place on the Arab map that is inhabited by destitute tribes still living in medieval times. However, Koni brought out the rhythm, beauty, and cruelty of place, its history, its fauna and flora, its once artistic endeavor, and above all its wisdom, patience, and nobility, delineating its distinctive characteristics and universal attributes. His work, which constitutes an intense fictional output mostly in novels but also in short stories, is an epic celebration of place and man in place, with clear intonations against the intrusion of a modern life adopted without genuine comprehension of its positive and constructive qualities but stuck at its shallow points of encounter.

Radwa 'Ashur was able to achieve epic dimensions in a single work. Her trilogy *Granada* (1994), on the fall of Granada, the last Muslim bastion in Islamic Spain, relates the painful story of the defeat of the Arabs by the Castilians in 1492, and of the way the Muslim population was either deported or forced to embrace Catholicism. It is a vivid description of treaties dishonored, promises betrayed, human beings forced to suppress their own language and culture and compelled to deny their own faith. It is also the story of a major catastrophe that took place under the eyes of a large Arab and Muslim world that had lost much of its stamina and zeal. 'Ashur's account of the fall of Granada is a most audacious attempt to record history in novel form. It must have perforce needed a minute study by the scholar/artist of the broad qualities and circumstances of fifteenth-century Granada and its level of civilization in Muslim times, then of the dismantling, after the *reconquista* by the Catholic Castilians, of what that civilization had stood for. This novel, written in the 1990s, was perhaps meant to allude to the precarious situation of the Palestinians today, usurped gradually but systematically of their land and identity by the Zionist state, their own country turned into the most massive ghetto in the history of mankind, surrounded by heavily armed enemy garrisons and subject to penury, deportation, and humiliation under the very eyes and ears of the world, including the Muslim and Arab world.

It is a great pity that the situation in Palestine for the last few decades—with its massive disasters, its great human upheavals, its constant movement downward toward deadlock and the pit of desperation, its never-ending tragedies, its love of and nostalgia for lost place, its strangled dreams, its perpetual, never-relenting strife—has not produced any epic depictions by Palestinian writers of fiction. Jabra Ibrahim Jabra (1920–1994), Palestine's most productive novelist, who showed vivid imagination, flowing style, great artistic energy, and ardor for his lost country, would, I think, have liked to write such an epic had he possessed the essential prerequisites for such a grand design. For, in the first place, an endeavor like this would require a stern objectivity in which the personal experience of the author would not be engaged, something that Mahfouz, Munif, and al-Koni have perfected. Jabra's novels revolve around Jabra himself, both in his passionate and other experiences and in his wishful imagination. To give a single example, Waleed, the main character in his fascinating novel *In Search for Waleed Masoud*[48] (al-bahth 'an Waleed Mas'oud), is very much like Jabra himself in his passionate search for friendship and ardent encounters, circumstances that Jabra, the genuine artist, well knew how to elevate into real esthetic heights. However, Waleed is also a very rich man, which Jabra was not.

Mimesis and a Sense of the Apocalypse?

The poet Mahmoud Darwish has offered the broad story of the modern Palestinian experience, albeit in shorter poems whose cumulative power reaches epic dimensions. The cumulative effect of Darwish's oeuvre has now ended in a trend toward an apocalyptic vision of destiny concordant with a deep sense of crisis and blocked horizons. The post-2001 Arab society in Palestine has begun to harbor "a sense of an ending"; that is the sinuous thrust in Palestinian society, that spur to life and the challenge for life, creates the opposing sense of being born again, a revocation of death through death, a noncompliant acceptance of doom but with a vision of resurrection through doom.

One wonders if the state of terror in which Palestinians are living today will soon be read in an apocalyptic narrative of horrific dimensions. The momentous punishment of a whole people is being tragically enacted daily before the eyes of the world. For Arabs, the old ordered image of the world is completely shattered as a tragic situation looms on the horizon through the unfolding story of a devastating global strategy. This horrible sentence, imposed as a result of so much mythmaking by the other, will never need any fabrication of myths to confirm it. It only needs the tools of genuine art. So far, the contemporary silhouette of the ongoing Palestinian tragedy rises far higher than any representation of it in the novel, and it makes a shamble of previous punctuations of the narrative of loss and tragedy, which seem simplistic and shallow in comparison. While discourse has not failed to discuss, analyze, and expose the realities of this terror that hangs like doom on the horizon and honors the great sacrifices offered and endured, neither literature nor art, as far as I know, has been able to match the colossal dimensions of this communal experience. The present-day situation carries the notion of a modern apocalypse that cries to be depicted, not just in historical writings, which are profuse, but above all in art, in fiction, and in other branches of the arts: a Palestinian *Guernica* is now overdue.

How else, if not through literature and works of art of the period, can the present crisis be depicted to an outside world enveloped, for over half a century, in contrived mythological rationalizations? A sense of dark destiny hovers over the world of the Palestinian, a sense of an end that blocks the horizon but is counterbalanced by a sense of a beginning deeply ingrained in humanity's awareness of the impossible. Both are wrought with tremendous human suffering.[49]

The Technological Angle

We have seen above how one of the most crucial questions plaguing the Arab world, that of the relationship of religion to the modern scientific outlook, was expertly explored by Naguib Mahfouz in *Children of Gabalawi*. Two other major modern issues—the effects of Gulf oil on the Arab world and the issue of ecology—have been probed by 'Abd al-Rahman Munif. The problems created by the advent of oil after 1950, as depicted by Munif, have been discussed above, while the issue of ecology is the central theme of part of his novel *Trees and the Murder of Marzouq* (al-ashjar wa ightiyal Marzouq, 1973), discussed below. However, another major issue, that of technology and its influence on human life, has only rarely been touched upon in Arabic fiction.

It is testimony to the nontechnological outlook of the Arab world that writers of fiction have hovered only at the periphery of a world of technology that surrounds them and invades their integrity with its massive weaponry and mechanisms of war and destruction. Although the door is wide open to annihilate them, they have not yet entered this world, a situation that, had they entered it, should have led them to the depiction of a technological dystopia. As far as I know, only one major novelist has done this, the Mauritanian Moussa Wuld Ibno in his outstanding novel *City of Winds*, a potent satire on the assault of technology on a virgin African world and an elegy on the innocence of man soiled by greed and mighty technocratic powers. A symbolic novel engaging the fantastic, it relates the history of human avarice, corruption, injustice, violence, sinister technological hegemony, and, above all, the story of the death of the heart.

However, this aspect of modern life has remained largely absent from fictional writings. There are certainly frequent references to technological aspects of modern life in Arabic novels, but these have not been grasped inwardly by the writer so as to achieve an interiorized sense of the hegemony of the technological world. Perhaps the extreme illustration to the contrary (which only applies to a very early stage in the oil oligarchies and nowhere else in the Arab world) is the hilarious comic description by Munif of a Gulf ruler's first terrorized encounter with the car, an exaggerated but highly symbolic case of representation. However, with the exception of Wuld Ibno's brilliant work, the literary vista does not offer us any images in the opposite direction, in which technology has become a part of everyday life and occupies a firm place in the mind of people.[50]

Although Wuld Ibno's *City of Winds* is not a long novel, it is a major achievement, relating the poignant story of the transfer through the three life cycles that the hero lives: from a world of primitive human transactions that make a slave of man to the world, in the third life cycle, of ultratechnological strategy that changes man into robot, assuring the destruction of those who reject this condition. Wuld Ibno, however, asserts that whether in primitive times or in technological times it is human avarice, injustice, cruelty, and vile aggression that rule the world. In all stages of the triple life of the hero, stretching over several centuries, there is always a Western man trying to squeeze for himself the last drop of goodness at the core of African life.

I doubt whether this genuine apocalyptic feeling prevails all over the Arab world, not just toward the global strategy that puts this whole world in jeopardy but even toward the two clear areas of distress, Palestine and Iraq. For several reasons—deficient insight, a naive outlook on much of the world, an embittered fundamentalism, and a great amount of satiety in several areas of the Arab world—the extent of the genuine apocalyptic situation eludes most Arabs. However, one would expect that the writers and artists who daily face the threat to life and dignity should be able, sooner rather than later, to come out with writings that will honor the great sacrifice and pain suffered. So far, this is still on hold.

Some Observations on the Arabic Short Story
Which Genre for a World in Turmoil?

In its totality, the Pan-Arab output has more or less shown a concordant if not a concurrent history of genres and developments. This has occurred despite the fact that, because of the very special circumstances of both Iraq and Palestine, as well as their people's exposure to unimaginable distress and life-threatening dangers, Palestinian and Iraqi writers may demonstrate certain differences from other writers in the Arab world. Both parties are obsessed with their country and its plight, both are trying to find an answer to the terror that has enveloped them, and both live in expectation of even greater horror to come. A sense of dark destiny hovers over these two areas. It is, moreover, true that although the Palestinian and Iraqi anguish is profound and penetrating, the whole Arab world endures great stress and perplexity. In fact, Arabic literature during the past thirty years or so has fallen into a kind of neoreality that describes a people laboring under a suppressed awareness of a precarious situation, under a forced acquiescence to an unacceptable state of being, to an inner, and still totally impotent, realization of living in an age of ludicrous contradictions.

Mutilation of dreams and aspirations, a taboo on originality and volition, a repressive hand of authority in all wakes of life—these are the emblems of an ailing Arab society at odds with itself and with the outside world. The original trend toward modernity and personal freedom, sought early in the twentieth century,[51] has been blotted out by several factors: authoritarian rulers unable to comprehend the initial meaning of freedom and democracy; the rise of a fundamental tide that is changing the whole personal and social hinges of society; and a submission to the lure of material gain from sources still adhering to a premodern way of thinking and of conceptualizing the universe. Awareness of all this is pervasive among the Arab intelligentsia, but it is either suppressed[52] or provides cause enough for emigration to freer skies. For the majority who remain, the psychological outcome of a life lived under social, political, religious, and moral duress is easily detectable in the literature that has tended to be symbolic, fantastic or allusive, and generally on the murky side. The world around the writer has been muted and bribed out of the modern age, despite the numerous intellectuals and creative talents that populate it. However, the inner awareness of this all-Arab predicament has produced a general nostalgia for *normalcy*, a deep longing for *normal* happiness, for a *normal* capacity to plan one's life, to build one's future with some sort of confidence and forward vision. Except in the Gulf countries, where citizens are assured a kind of secure future sometimes not chosen personally by them, life in the Arab world seems hazy and unpredictable.

The question here is this: Which fictional genre is more capable of describing life and experience in this beleaguered contemporary Arab world? This disjointed world is not, I think, exactly the world of the short story. To yield itself to description, this world needs the detailed, the many-sidedness of experience that only the novel can portray. This neurotic world, which lies now under an anomalous silence, full of muffled protest and suffocated cries, cannot furnish the short story with the calm rhythm it needs and cannot be easily assimilated into its compact, limited structure. This is one of the reasons the novel has gained ascendancy over the short story in the past few years.

The Short Story: Some Characteristics

In studying the general evolution of the modern short story in Arabic, one can easily notice the discrepancy in tone, attitude, and subject matter between the pre-1950s stories and those after. Although the very early examples of Gibran and al-Manfaluti, who both wrote long stories,[53] revolved around sad and often tragic experiences, the story in Arabic after al-Manfaluti and up to the early 1950s reflected a marked tendency to use irony, sarcasm, humor, and wit. There seemed to be a great scope in Arabic short narratives for the comic and the ironic representation of experience. I have tried to show this in the selections I have chosen for the period of the pioneers, of which several stories involve a comic or ironic approach. This is perhaps due to the fact that realistic prose literature in the first half of the twentieth century tended to revolve primarily around social experience and individual human encounters, which gave scope to irony and sarcasm in depicting the multifarious situations of social and personal interactions in an Arab world invaded by modernity but holding onto its die-hard outlook and conventions from premodern times. The political aspect, which carried with it a constant feeling of injustice and anger, remained during the first half of the twentieth century, more the prerogative of poetry. However, after the Palestine disaster of 1948 and the heavy weight of a lost, almost all-Arab war, with the great feelings of misachievement and shock that it engendered, fiction started to engage itself in the political malaise and lost much of its light-hearted approach. The atmosphere of gloom and consternation, or at least of regret, which has overshadowed life in the Arab world since the early fifties, seemed to seep into the fiction of most authors, both novelists and short-story writers, with little involvement in comical representations. Emile Habiby's (1921–1966) creation of a perfect tragicomedy, full of comic depictions, in the novel *The Secret Life of Said, the Luckless Pessoptimist*,[54] is a notable departure from the prevalent gloom in contemporary Arabic fiction.

The short story, like the short play,[55] has the capacity to cover many aspects of life, but unlike the short play, it can accommodate tragedy to a greater extent, although the tragedy it would adopt would be a one-sided episode and would not resemble the classical dramatic tragedies in which the moment of realization of the protagonist's predicament is illuminated. However, by its very structure, the short story can hold its own most effectively, taking time and space to depict the causative factors that lead to the tragic finale, producing shock and pain at the tragic juncture of events. But this is difficult in a short play, which does not have the luxury of being able, by its very technique, to span space and time and offer a full tragedy with all its causative factors. It often begins with the tragic already realized, as is usually the case in the monodrama. And here lies the great difference between the two genres. While in a short story, a tragedy carries its own explanation clearly within its structure, including the causative factors and the consequences ensuing from the progression of events, this cannot happen in a short play because the tragic needs to be realized over *time* and because there is not enough time lapse between the beginning of the play and its end. The tragedy cannot materialize. In contrast, even a very short story can accommodate events that happen over very divergent periods of time.

Short stories in Arabic usually deal with contemporary or at least modern life more than with the historical past, whose minute patterns of everyday behavior would be difficult to comprehend thoroughly and to re-create in fictional narrative. In order to create a worthy contribution, the short-story writer usually needs a rounded perception of society to meet the multifarious capacity of a single collection. In order to fill a cluster of short stories, he or she has to capture the everyday incidents, habits, and social traditions of a period, to know the tastes, fashions of behavior, and ways of thinking and interaction on all levels of experience, including the mundane and quotidian of so many different protagonists. The writer must also comprehend the internalized individual reactions and responses of protagonists, which usually revolve around a single experience of mainly limited consequences, usually one that is culture bound. This stipulates a general, well-honed knowledge of a society, which the writer must be aware of, treating narrower but more numerous social patterns and culling the varied subject matter from all aspects of life. It would certainly be difficult to produce a collection of short stories on Arab life in the classical and post-classical eras targeting the habits and the social interaction in those remote periods, as well as the varied individual behavior patterns of protagonists and their internalized thoughts and experiences. But it is easier to do this in a novel because the gallant venture of the novel gives scope for the delineation of the big issues of past life, designating the communal and universal, often recorded, reactions of people to events and ideas. The novel can accommodate broad and diverse experiences, depicting a past society in its major preoccupations, without having to go into its daily habits and ordinary interactions or capturing its behavior patterns, its moods, and its emotional and spiritual references. The novelist has here the option of creating a narrative about the broad aspects of life, stories of courage, treachery, coercion, quest for freedom, and love (although love is a changeable experience from period to period and from culture to culture), yet the writer would find it difficult to genuinely depict daily transactions of people who lived many centuries ago.[56]

Most Arabic short-story writers are also novelists. However, one should realize that the two genres are not interchangeable but have two separate identities. In modern Arabic literature, there are a number of writers who are particularly endowed with the skill of short-story writing. Yusif Idris, a writer of international status, attempted at some point the writing of novels of good artistic value but was unable to match his short-story skills.[57] Muhammad Khudayyir and Salwa Bakr did the same. Yahya Taher 'Abdallah also attempted some long narratives, but Zakaria Tamir consecrated his great gift to the writing of the short story. All these brilliant authors remain primarily short-story writers by natural endowment, particularly gifted to look at single experiences and depict them with the best tools of the artist. The main factor that determines their identity as primarily short-story writers is the way they gaze at the world. They conceive human experience in a capsule, in the smaller incident, the self-sufficient entity; they re-create their vision in the closed world of the short story, which is usually conceived by them as a totality at the very beginning, as a distinctive form with rules and parameters that is usually written in "full pitch and intensity." These splendid writers have created some of the best short stories in Arabic or in any language, stories that bring to the reader both delight and a deep awareness of life in its universal aspects and its Arab specificity. Their excellence in the genre of the short story is widely recognized, and their work reflects, in Beachcroft's words, the "development in human insight"[58] toward the realization of the stuff of life and experience that is best portrayed in short, crisp narratives; is highly entertaining; and, in the case of the above-mentioned authors, is greatly imbued with the essence of life experienced in small drafts.

This harks back to the way classical writers in Arabic wrote their narratives in the genre of *khabar*, discussed above, anecdotes that were short, compact, and telling. The *khabar* genre took hold of the writer's skills early in Islam and continued to propagate itself in thousands of entries, fictional and otherwise, which filled numerous volumes of literature over the centuries. Modern Arabs were certainly acquainted with many of them, especially the books of al-Jahiz and Isfahani's famous compendium of *al-Aghani*, among many others. Even without a conscious acknowledgement of the effect such a strategy of form in Arabic has exerted on the modern writer, there is no doubt that the short form of narrative must have been entrenched in the subconscious of Arab writers in modern times.

It is possible for a writer to create an extended aspect of the world of the protagonist through a cluster of short stories, forming a broad description of a number of discrete experiences whose cumulative effect would serve the function of a novel, as Ilyas Khouri has done in his collection, *The Small Mountain* (al-jabal al-saghir, 1977). However, the short stories in this collection remain technically independent of each other, each self-sufficient unto itself.

Some stories surpass the length usually expected for the short story, but are not novellas, which are definitely longer and differently conceived than a short story, more like a much shorter novel. But the novellas, despite their limited length, do not belong to the family of short fiction because they can have intricate plots and more than one central theme. The stories I am speaking about are long short stories, of which we have quite a few in Arabic. One of the most poignant is Yusuf Idris's brilliant narrative, "The Abyss of the City," a compact and brilliantly conceived long story depicting heartrending poverty and its chance meeting with opportunity. The story also satirizes the penurious spirit and hard-boiled cruelty of a middle-class man who takes advantage of the poor woman in his service. Despite the impression that a story like this could have been made into a novel, it certainly could not, for the relationship of the protagonists could not permit a greater interchange of dialogue and a more elaborate description of the one-dimensional human situation that exists among the protagonists. Its greater theme, in fact, is its fantastically skillful description of the horrific poverty in the abyss of Cairo.[59]

Offered in this anthology is Mahmoud Shaheen's "Ordeal by Fire," a long story about lust, honor, and the harsh authority of social tradition. A young married peasant woman with irrepressible passion is unable to restrain herself in her husband's absence and covets a young farmer, an honorable man who will not respond to her seductions. She lures to her bed one of the cousins around, but when her husband suddenly arrives and the cousin flees through the window, she names the other as having come to seduce her. The story ends with the elders of the village insisting on trying him in the traditional manner, through the application of live coals to his tongue to decide his innocence or guilt. The story has perfect timing and some extremely well-written passages of high literary quality, especially those that reveal the woman's passion. Although the story depicts an array of events and emotions, it remains concentrated on the central issue of the failed seduction and is not a contracted novel. It contains its own well-spaced and sufficiently portrayed action, running the full cycle of events, which makes it a wonderful candidate for an entertaining film.

SOME SPECIAL EXPERIMENTS

There is an amazing amount of variety and inventiveness in contemporary Arabic fiction; the scene is exhilarating. However, a large critical book would be needed to give a fair and complete assessment of this remarkable endeavor on the part of novelists and short-story writers in Arabic today, a luxury I do not have in this introduction. At the same time, it would be a deficient attempt to speak only generally on the achievements of fiction writers without attempting to highlight at least a few experiments as vibrant examples of the fine heights that modern Arabic fiction has achieved. The following is by no means a comprehensive list. I had wanted to include many more examples, but space and time allow only this limited introduction. The following writers are part of a proud and admirable list of achievers who have brought contemporary Arabic fiction on a par with the Arabs' old and seasoned art of poetry and are on the way toward replacing its primary place in Arab literary history.

'Abd al-Rahman Munif: Oil, Ecology, and Political Repression

As described above, Munif depicts, among other major topics, the story of oil in the Arab world. The discovery of oil led to the creation of an oil oligarchy that seemed in the 1950s at odds not just with the modern world but also with the Arab heartland around it. Munif created the images of several major personages in the area, with their ancient outlook and with their die-hard Bedouin heritage, who found themselves dealing with an all-binding global strategy and, at the same time, with immense wealth—an overwhelming, novel situation that gave them great vulnerability and dictated a need for an army of civil servants, imported mainly from the Arab heartland. Many educated Arabs answered the call to help modernize the once-impoverished area, but among them was a hoard of upstarts and self-interested strategists in the oil oligarchies who spoke with smooth tongues while harboring immense avarice and greed for wealth and power. All these newborn situations were at the core of Munif's enormous fictional strategy. It has been, indeed, a very strange epoch in Arab life, marked by great changes in opposite directions and by exorbitant contradictions. All this has been minutely and creatively depicted by a master novelist, bringing this massive experience into focus and giving it the garb of a twentieth-century epic. No matter what changes will happen to Arab life in the Gulf in the coming few decades, perhaps altering the present scenario completely, this grotesquely bizarre epoch will remain, thanks to Munif, alive in the memory of many Arab generations to come.

Munif is perhaps the most contemporary of Arab novelists. His treatment of current issues of widespread interest in the Arab world and beyond is a great venture into the future. In his quintet *Cities of Salt*,[60] Munif sets the modern history of the oil-producing region within a variety of narrative contexts, using the power of story to paint vivid pictures of life in the desert countries (to which he gives fictive names) and drawing a blanket impression on all of them. He has, moreover, laid down with great skill a scenario that inevitably anticipates what is to come, decrying the corroding consequences of an oil-related contemporary life based on new conventions, a life created with oil money that has introduced an eclectic mixture of traditions and superficial innovative inclusions, pretentiously modern but untenable for progressive modern living.

Munif's audacious venture is one that has not yet been explored fully in other creative prose literature. His great worth as a writer stems, first and foremost, from the unique distinction of being a pioneer who has seen the absurd mode of a new way of living and the impossibility of its enduring, and who has assessed the obstacles thrown by it in the way of the once steadfast march of twentieth-century modernity in the Arab world.

This great modern writer and thinker took up another virgin topic on which he is also a pioneer. In a letter dated January 24, 2002, from Roger Allen, the translator of Munif's ecology-oriented novel *Endings* (al-nihayat),[61] Allen describes how Munif believes the region about which he is writing is "under imminent threat from the policies of its rulers," lamenting how "the desert environment and the numerous ways in which modernity and technology are contributing to its rapid destruction, and to the destruction of the centuries-old nomadic society it has fostered [present a great danger]. . . . His work has been a major eye-opener concerning the predicaments to which his part of the world and the world beyond it have been exposed." Most of the ethical, cultural, political, and social issues associated with oil money have been treated by Munif in ways that mirror the tensions and fears underlying the now placid surface of Arab life in the Gulf region and elsewhere in the Arab world.

Writing about topics yet unexplored in Arabic prose literature, topics that had not yet found their interpretation in effective literary terms, Munif revealed a sensitive and highly perceptive literary instinct, one that clearly did not require the usual period of incubation before it could assimilate and internalize nascent problems and then express them in fine literary terms. In this, his achievement on an artistic level is substantial. There is no doubt that the tools of literature could not yield an easy access at the time and, given the fact that these new realities of Arab life had only existed since the mid-fifties, the Arab audience was not yet attuned to the novelty of his topic or his approach, yet Munif transcended both difficulties with astonishing ease.

Homage is also due to Munif for boldly addressing the issues of oppression and the violation of human rights in the Arab world. Part of *Trees and the Murder of Marzouq* deals poignantly with this issue, but the work that addresses the problem most awesomely is his novel *East of the Mediterranean* (sharqiyy al-mutawassit). This is a harrowing story of the fate of those who stand for human rights and the dignity of the individual and nation. The main protagonist is hounded by the police and exposed to intolerable suffering, entering a dead end from which there is no escape. He is, in fact, the archetype of the most overreaching and horrible experience that lies at the core of the unrelenting malaise in the Arab world.

As in his description of the various drawbacks of the oil oligarchies, Munif does not specify a particular country; instead, he gives a general name that fits most states in the Arab world.[62]

The Adventure of Gamal al-Ghitani: Time and the Novel

Gamal al-Ghitani (b. 1945) is one of the Arab world's most eminent novelists and among its most original. In this short account of his work, I focus on his fascinating book *Kitab al-Tajalliyat* (Revelations), one of the most important modernist works to use the element of mythic time with great success. I will also speak, albeit more briefly, on another important book involved with the elements of time and history, *Al-Zeini Barakat*.

Kitab al-Tajalliyat

Kitab al-Tajalliyat (Revelations) is about anguish that mixes the personal with the communal and the experienced with the imagined, while mourning the loss of both private and historical moments. Without being in the least chauvinistic, this book depicts the life of men, the worth of their manhood and of their life on earth. The author is linked in thought, emotion, and passionate loyalty to three unrelated men, one of whom is his own father.

There is very little relationship to maternity in this book. In this al-Ghitani is unconsciously faithful to the Arabic male cultural tradition of the father–son relationship, which holds high esteem for the father, even to the point of veneration. Here, as elsewhere in contemporary Arabic literature, the esteem of the father reflects an attachment, often tinged with a great amount of tenderness. In al-Ghitani's many-sided strategy, in its conscious and unconscious elements, the writer aims not simply at reviving old literary roots but also at keeping alive the spirit of the culture and its most enduring attributes.[63]

The great concentration on the sadism of historical events, medieval and modern, stands in strong contrast to the love, regret, tenderness, and reverence the author displays as his experience unfolds to exhibit three dimensions of a unified obeisance: his personal love for his father; his deeply ingrained political feelings for Egypt and the Arab world's dead leader, Jamal 'Abd al-Nasser, whose premature death he mourns as the most devastating event to happen to modern Arab people; and last but by no means least, his attachment to al-Husain ibn 'Ali, the grandson of the Prophet and the pretender to the Islamic Caliphate after the assassination of his father, 'Ali ibn Abi Taleb, the fourth Orthodox Caliph, in 40 A.H./661 A.D. Al-Ghitani will have us remember that al-Husain is the greatest martyr in Islam, "the master of all martyrs," and that his slaying at the hands of the Umayyads in the battle at Karbala' has changed the whole history of the Arab nation. Much can be understood through this text about the profound pain experienced through the centuries by the Shi'ites at that perfidious act of villainy, intermittently but most vividly described by Ghitani in his *Revelations*. It is a text that can illuminate what has been ignored in modern times of political Shi'ism and its capacity for redemption through self-sacrifice. Al-Ghitani, through his interplay with time, brings that major historical event into a modern focus, showing its relationship with another present-day act of treachery exemplified in the untimely death of 'Abd al-Nasser, the emblem of national pride and revival, and the sacrificing of his strife, integrity, and steadfastness to the spirit of surrender and compromise. The most important thing here is the true agony—infectious, compelling, beyond the here and now—exhibited by the writer to embrace the Arab nation's and all of humanity's major losses to evil and perfidy.

Al-Ghitani displays the son's feelings of guilt toward the father, not through any maltreatment or stark conflict between them but through the son's neglect to seek proximity and demonstrate overt affection. For example, when the father visits his son, as he intermittently does, his son never insists on him staying the night in his house, a fact that seems to burn the son's heart as he remembers it now, too late for any redemption. Despite the supermodernist technique al-Ghitani so successfully follows, the Western literary disposition against the father is clearly alien to him. The symbolic death of the father in Western culture, the crumbling of the family line in favor of individuals "master[ing] their time outside of linearity"[64] is not tenable. On the contrary, the actual death of the father here is the pivotal point of his resurrection, and the whole novel commemorates the permanent presence of the father in the author's life—a presence tinged with great tenderness but also with deep feelings of guilt. Arabic literature in general, old and modern, does not reflect any great feelings of guilt. It is more a culture of shame rather than of guilt. In my readings in classical Arabic poetry, I realized that feelings of guilt mainly surfaced when the issue had to do with a close blood relation, particularly a father or a brother. However, the Shi'ites have sustained throughout the centuries genuine feelings of guilt about abandoning al-Husain to his fate at Karbala', and al-Ghitani has embodied all those inherited feelings in this triple experience of the father, of the tragic figure of al-Husain incorporated into the deepest religious feelings sustainable, and of the wasted and much lamented leader of modern times, Jamal 'Abd al-Nasser. Part of al-Ghitani's regret about 'Abd al-Nasser arises from the fact that he had not realized, during 'Abd al-Nasser's lifetime, the crucial importance of this leader who stood larger than life, and might have participated in the sotto voce criticism of short-sighted, easily swayed individuals. Like many other Arab intellectuals, however, al-Ghitani had later realized 'Abd al-Nasser's irreplaceable value and regretted, very deeply, the loss to the Arab nation of a man who, had he lived, could have unified the Arab struggle and brought the whole Arab world to a new age of pride and dignity.

The tone of genuine regret that permeates the whole book is tinged with nostalgia, an Arab nostalgia par excellence for things gone and irreplaceable, inherited from many centuries past. In a lecture I delivered on Palestinian nostalgia in Stavenger, Norway, in 1999, I said that "the Arab soul was always annihilated by nostalgia and revived by memory." And al-Ghitani's is precisely the nostalgia that brings back to the Arab reader that very intimate experience of grief and lament, many centuries old.

It is interesting to see how al-Ghitani spans the centuries to make contact with an experience that the urban centuries of the postclassical period (thirteenth to nineteenth century) had abandoned in formal literature. Satiated by the accessibility of the erotic, which was denied in Bedouin times when nostalgia became an integral part of the whole culture, and acquiescing to a political tyranny that nothing seemed to control, the formal literature[65] of the later middle ages lost its touch with the nostalgic aspects of inherited Arabic literature, aspects that found their way to the folk poetry. Nostalgia was revived in modern times in the work of some major poets and has been instrumental in sustaining a glowing yearning for home, country, and comrades—particularly in Palestinian poetry, whose great heights are exemplified in the work of master poet Mahmoud Darwish.

The deep religious revelations are not shy undercurrents in al-Ghitani's novel; they play an overt part and are as personal as they are communal, connecting firmly with the tenacious political passion of the author. Two opposing trends are therefore seen at once: a highly personal attachment to a religious experience laden with the suffering of fourteen centuries, and a relentless political grief, secular and modern, which, because of its failed tragic enterprise and its severe loss of a great political opportunity, immediately forms a link to the older religious grief.

What is immediately realized the moment the venture into the world of al-Ghitani begins is the great fascination with which the novel holds the reader enthralled, how it exemplifies "the pleasure of the text." Mahfouz poses here an immediate contrast. This Nobel Prize winner's initial success in the Arab world at large stems from several reasons that do not, in my opinion, pertain to the pleasurable experience of reading a fictional text. It stems, in the first place, from Mahfouz's authority as a dedicated writer in a genre that, when he started gaining status and popularity, was still not yet firmly established in the Arab world. Through his utmost seriousness as a novelist, his incessant search into social and political questions that have preoccupied the minds of modern Arabs after the fifties, his precision, and his almost fanatical avoidance of redundancy and sentimentality, he set the model for the new novelist in the Arab world. However, his style—though adequate, balanced, and subtly critical of contemporary life in the Arab world, particularly in Egypt—remains lackluster, rather unexciting, and certainly not conducive to literary ecstasy. Having gained early supremacy, his work, however, became an unconscious model for upcoming writers after the mid-twentieth century. Despite the great differences of style that exist now in the Arab world, much of the Arab fictional output has lacked that magical element that Mahfouz could never attain, that exquisite component in fictional narratives that holds the reader fully absorbed. The negative influence of Mahfouz on the general atmosphere of the novel in Arabic has been enhanced by the harsh situation in the Arab world today and has not helped to introduce any real measure of humor to mitigate the grim syndrome that dominates most fictional texts. However, other than al-Ghitani, there are, of course, a few major exceptions: Jabra Ibrahim Jabra, with his luscious fluid style; Emile Habiby, with his expert use of the comic and the fantastic; Haydar Haydar, with his *rhétorique profonde*; al-Taher Wattar, with his delectable gift for telling a story; Ahmad al-Tawfiq and Sun'allah Ibrahim, with their skillful elegance of maneuvering their unusual tales; Hanan al-Shaykh, with her great decorum, exciting surprises, and delicate peripeties that never fall into sentimentality or drab realism; Ghada al-Samman with her bold but refined encounter with reality; Sahar Khalileh, with her exceptional ability to emulate the language and thinking of various social classes; Ben Salim Himmish, with his zestful flights into the unusual, the remote, and the wild, but without losing his hold on the esthetic and the refined; and a few others, who have all had, in addition to their particular gifts, the correct fictional instinct that leads the novelist to the first prerequisite that makes a novel unforgettable: the element of excitement that holds the interest of the reader throughout, leaving a sense of pleasure after the reading is over.

In speaking of the "pleasure of the text," warm mention is due here to a master Arab novelist, the Lebanese Amin Maalouf, who, writing in French, sets the finest example of a narrator of novels. He can address the most serious, complex, tragic, and grim situations, probing into the history of humankind, bringing past to present, merging human experience, positing varied cultures one against the other, and uncovering the roots of present-day predicaments without ever losing the element of pleasure in his highly acclaimed narrations.

A Testimony of a Life

Although one is inclined to believe that *Kitab al-Tajalliyat*, written in the first person, is an autobiographical testimony of a life, that is not exactly so. It is true that the author speaks of his own childhood, and from his fragmentary comments one can form a kind of image of the author, but it is by no means the image of his life. We know little or nothing of full childhood, al-Ghitani's schooling, successes or failures, personal aspirations and dreams, jobs, love life, marriage, or experience of fatherhood. Rather, what are depicted here are the details of his inner life, his psychological reveries, and his political sensibility.

However, the real person whose life is thoroughly depicted is the father. We can reconstitute the whole life of the father from the fragmentary delineations that al-Ghitani offers in an intermittent, nonchronological fashion throughout the novel: the father's early life in the village and the usurpation of his land and property by his own uncle; his decision to emigrate to Cairo to secure a living; his thwarted ambition to gain knowledge through studying in the city; the fact that he worked first as a porter, then as a mail carrier in one of the ministries where he remained throughout his life; his fine character and love of strangers and kin; his hospitality and charm; and, above all, his dedication to the upbringing of his two sons and to securing their education. Here, in the description of the tender care and steadfast devotion the father displays in order to raise his sons to a higher status than his own, is seen clearly the other side of Arab patriarchy, that which reveals a tenacious loving responsibility, often entailing major sacrifices on the part of the father.[66] A thoroughly likable figure is delineated here by the son who, as befitting a fine writer, does this without a trace of exhibitionism or superfluous emotion, beginning the novel with the death of the father, and ending it with the father, as a shy young man, feeling, for the first time, the flicker of the erotic on seeing the bashful young girl, who became the author's mother, passing by.

Al-Zeini Barakat

Al-Zeini Barakat is a story about Memluk Egypt on the verge of the Ottoman invasion in the sixteenth century. The Memluk oligarchy is depicted as corrupt and tyrannical, relying greatly on an intricate system of internal espionage against its own public, with a wide margin for torture and oppression. Memluk Cairo is well described, particularly its mosques, its mansions, and its souks with their great variety of foodstuffs and eating places. One can smell the various dishes prepared in the souks, so vividly are they depicted. Al-Zeini Barakat, the main protagonist, is someone we do not meet in the novel but only read about. His rise to sudden power is meant by the author to draw attention to the frequent rise to power of a certain type of person in the modern Arab world. A master hypocrite, al-Zeini poses as the high official, directly appointed by the palace, who will save the marketplace and the population from corrupt and unlawful deals. Making a cruel example of a few wrongdoers, al-Zeini participates under the cover of justice to benefit greatly from his post. But it is the Ottoman invasion that will be the catalyst of change in this epoch.

Although *Revelations* and *Al-Zeini Barakat* are two novels that treat the element of time in a modernist and nontraditional manner, each has quite a different approach. In *Revelations* the linear unity is completely abandoned as al-Ghitani brings together past and present to show the persistence of the old in the new, the fluidity of a time that never seems to completely close out on past events and will regain life in the hands of the artist. In a testimony he gave several years ago, al-Ghitani said,[67] "I have a strong sensibility toward time, this power that cannot be stopped in its frightening march, in its continuity, in its liquidity that never freezes."[68] He believes that "it is the artist who can save a particular space from annihilation, for he records what the historians do not mention. . . . He penetrates to the essence of reality, to the invisible, the unfelt."[69] Major moments of history have been "mutilated and forged," he asserts, but these can be saved by the artist. "I believe that the artist is a historian of a very special nature, for he preserves particular moments [of history] from dissipating in this horrible universal void called time."[70]

Revelations uses time in a directly mythic sense, emphasizing recurrence and the prevalence of the past in the present. *Al-Zeini Barakat* is situated completely in the past, making links with Arab Egyptian history at one of its very perturbed epochs, an epoch riddled with corruption, espionage, hypocrisy, political intimidation, harsh control over the lives of individuals, internal turmoil and external dangers—a period, the author seems to indicate, resembling our own times. Thus he makes the link with the present by distancing the scene, giving greater scope toward comprehending the terror of the present political malaise by placing the whole in a wide historical perspective and, by this, emphasizing its intolerable continuity. Using the historic mask, he espouses outer form to an inner psychological process that leads to an inner knowledge of the full predicament in which modern Arabs find themselves. The mythic connection in this—and in the story I have selected for al-Ghitani in this anthology, "An Enlightenment to the People of This World"—is one of symbolization and comparison, but the message is the same: history repeating itself with all its cultural emblems and political devices.

It is regrettable that space does not allow any further discussion of al-Ghitani's unique and splendid venture into the possibilities of fiction. One last point to make about the author's experiment involves his conscious search for cultural roots and possibilities. He shuns the entire dependence on other cultures (here Western culture) for models of narrative, asserting that it is enriching to "take inspiration from the Arab heritage in order to create new artistic forms that are unique ... and supply us with artistic tools to depict this passing time and to preserve its essence from extinction."[71]

Ibrahim Nasrallah: A Venture into Postmodernism

After a period as a teacher in a remote corner of southwestern Saudi Arabia, Ibrahim Nasrallah (b. 1954) recorded, in a superior poetic novel, his fantastic and horrifying memories of a lonely and harsh experience. A first novel, it is hardly matched in excellence and originality by any other first novel in Arabic, except al-Tayyib Salih's magnificent work, *Season of Migration to the North* (mawsim al-hijra ila 'l-shamal; 1967). No one could give Nasrallah's *Prairies of Fever* (barari 'l-humma, 1984) a greater tribute than putting it in a league with the work of the earlier masters of the novel in Arabic.

Prairies is a nightmarish experiment in stopped time. Fantasy, despair, lunacy, fragile sentiments, and a constant craving for home, roots, and human affection, for the image of woman, for the least semblance of normalcy all mix and procreate themselves, in this hyperbolized narrative. Exquisitely artistic (and hence not overstated) with extreme situations, with an anguish so amplified that it haunts the reader forever, *Prairies* magnifies the experience of thousands of young Arab expatriates torn out of space and equilibrium as they tried to eke out a living in the remote corners of a region suddenly blessed with oil and fabulous wealth, which awaken it to modern times while it is still in the stupor of a forgotten age in history.

Prairies reflects also the *modern* Arab gaze on the Arabian desert, standing in stark contrast to the early image of the desert in Arabic literature, where the desert was depicted over and over again in verse as the place where existence flourished, forging an intimate link with the vast spaces of sand that harbored memory and the history of the tribe. It was the place where love and war, hospitality and vengeance, and the deeds of valor and honor occurred, the place that, because of its ecological constrictions and deprivations, imposed a way of life built on constant migration in search of survival. Yet it was a place that was also loved and instinctively familiar to the heart. This relationship with place was greatly celebrated by the poets before and after Islam, reaching its utmost symbolic and archetypal depiction in the poetry of the Umayyad Dhu al-Rumma (696–735). In Nasrallah's modern handling of the desert, a widely different and alien image is created of the desert, one with its fauna and flora but with its deadly heart, its fierce resistance to life and joy, its pathetic fixation on dead conventions, all spectacularly depicted in visual, sometimes comic, images that remain in the minds of readers for a long time.

Somewhere near the Red Sea, more than four hundred miles south of Jeddah, lies the town of al-Qunfudhah. Here, too, lives the young teacher, Muhammad Hammad, the narrator and main protagonist.

> This is al-Qunfudhah then
> a city full of water
> a place without a sea
> a city without land
> the desolations of sand
> buries everything.

The novel opens with a strange scene in which five men come to Muhammad Hammad's room and command him to pay for his own funeral. But is it he who is dead? Or is it his roommate, the "other" Muhammad Hammad? A question of identity arises here, of self lost in the other, of another embodying self. The young protagonist's devastating struggle to retain any sense of identity is never resolved in the novel. He continues to straddle the limitless confines of a vast desert prison, where everything negates everything, where the main protagonist is alive and dead, present and absent. The novel is "the Arabic answer to the divided self, the image of the double or shadow of which Jung took account, and which surfaces in the European novel from Dostoyevsky to Herman Hesse's *Steppenwolf,* and from Thomas Mann's *Death in Venice* to Jean Paul Sartre's *Nausea,* and wherever the dialogue in its psychic expression is realized as a discourse between two: I and another, the mirror and its reflections."[72]

By virtue of a negation of chronology and sequence, a cohesive relationship between form and content and a temporal parallelism among events, memories, and dreams, the novel possesses a fresh and original flavor all its own. The central themes are, in fact, the subjugation of human life to the harsh reality of place, the tenacious grip of inherited mores many centuries old, and the blind, automatic nature of the machinery of state. Deprived of everything he covets, the main character suffers total victimization. There is often a complete fusion of actuality and dream, of fact and fantasy, and a strange unity of the animal and the human worlds. And there is, too, an eerie absence of women, who becomes an unachievable dream, a source of torture and fantasy, an undefinable phantom surrounded by taboos and danger. The force of place (here, the desert) is so strong as to confuse time, which runs in every direction, unsystematically spanning the past and the future and then regressing to the past, emphasizing the supreme sovereignty of place. This is a novel of extreme anguish.

Ghassan Kanafani: The Parallelism of Time and Space

For the Palestinians, the premature death of an eminent political writer is a tragic loss, but the assassination of Ghassan Kanafani (1936–1972) by Israeli agents in Beirut was a double tragedy because it cut short a brilliant career in fiction that is difficult to replace. Emile Habiby, after writing his masterpiece *The Secret Life of Saeed, the Ill-Fated Pessoptimist* (1974), never attained in the works that followed the same kind of brilliance. Mahmoud Shaheen's excellent experiment in "Ordeal by Fire" (translated in this volume), also proved difficult to repeat. Ibrahim Nasrallah's first novel, *Prairies of Fever*, remained his greatest literary work even after years of output in both poetry and the novel. Kanafani, however, soared in his creative work year after year, continuing to probe new avenues of life and art. His *All That's Left to You* (1966) is a masterpiece of modernist literature unmatched by any in his time, an experiment in triumph and despair rejecting the chronology of time and the contemporaneousness of place.[73] A previous novel, *Men in the Sun* (1963), had already secured for him fame and recognition with its more realistic but highly charged description of two opposing poles: a desperate need for survival in a brutal world and a frantic fear of asserting one's life in it. The three Palestinian refugees, made penniless by the forced exodus from Palestine and without identity papers that would allow them to travel to where they could find gainful employment, had only one avenue to follow in order to secure their own and their family's survival: to be smuggled into Kuwait in an empty water tank. Giving the middleman/ smuggler (what in Chicano literature would be called the coyote) a large sum of money, which is almost all they had, they coil inside the hot, empty tank on arriving at the frontier, waiting for the middleman to conclude the usual customs processes. When the middleman is delayed by customs officials, the Palestinians suffocate and die in docile surrender inside the now seething hot tank, abstaining, out of fear of exposure to the authorities, from banging for help to secure survival. Their gratuitous death, Kanafani wants to tell us, was the Palestinian's mode of dying in the early years after the catastrophe. This vulnerability is vindicated in *All That's Left to You* when the young Palestinian, crossing the stretches of the desert at night toward Jordan away from scandal in Gaza, encounters an Israeli patrolman and realizes he has to kill him even if he is not sure he will survive. *Return to Haifa*, although written later, in 1969, is of a more facile structure, but it contains an ultimately profound resolution. The young Arab man brought up by a Jewish Israeli couple, who found him abandoned in the immediate aftermath of the chaos of the 1948 exodus and brought him up as their own, is asked to choose between staying as an Israeli with his adopted parents or joining his real parents who had come looking for him. Kanafani flouts all expectations when he, with real artistic courage and sophistication, decides to have the young man choose his Israeli connection. Only an independent and truly artistic talent could, in the late sixties, a period seething with loud slogans on Arab nationalism, anti-Israeli belligerence, and faith in an ultimate Arab victory, dare to make this choice.

As I have said earlier, it is most unfortunate that Kanafani died too early in his career for the artist in him to explore further areas of technical and semantic possibilities. One can sense the struggle in this sternly committed man between the surge of his ever-vigilant creativity and the compelling commitment he has taken upon himself toward his people. With his talent burgeoning and procreating all the time, he had always to remember that there was a large and less sophisticated audience whose spirit he wanted to touch and illuminate. This lies behind the diversity of his output and the sometimes uneven level of his short stories.

Yet Kanafani had the audacity to flout readers' expectations in *Return to Haifa*, giving them a theme that they could not "consume subjectively" or reconcile effectively for themselves, but that they could only "grasp objectively." This has been a perennial problem for the modern writer. There are too many unspoken expectations implicitly contained within the spontaneous author/audience interaction. With only few exceptions, the audience in an age of commitment and heightened politics has almost always formed, to a greater or lesser extent, part of the creative process, lurking as it were in the background of the writer's mind throughout the process of creativity.[74] Exceptions to this are few: Tawfiq Sayigh in the 1950s and 1960s, Walid Khazindar in the 1980s and after, and perhaps Ibrahim Nasrallah in *Prairies of Fever*. Once a writer is caught in the trap of the incessant demands of a voracious audience in constant need of therapy and catharsis, he or she will find very little escape. This is more true of poets than of writers of prose fiction, but we are talking here of committed political writers.

Kanafani's *All That's Left to You*, the most sophisticated of all his writings, has never gained the same wide popularity of *Men in the Sun*, possibly due to the latter's familiar situations, its customary treatment of human relations, and its chronological flow of time. His *Return to Haifa*, on the other hand, also a sophisticated study in the problems of identity and loyalty, still remains within the field of the immediately comprehensible. All three novels achieve a high order of sophistication, but *All That's Left to You* signals a different technical direction.

Kanafani's triumphs were of two kinds. First, for a rigorously committed writer to be able to probe, particularly in his short stories, the mysteries of the human condition in its universal aspects and to succeed with insightfulness and discipline in delineating so many situations that stem from the very essence of human experience everywhere should be seen as a genuine artistic triumph. Second, his great dexterity in handling his artistic tools and his inborn sensitivity to what is appropriate for a work of art is allowed him to elevate many of his committed writings to a high level of artistic sophistication, culminating in his modernist novel *All That's Left to You*. It is interesting to see how many Palestinian writers and poets have shown this unusual capacity, after the debacle of 1948, but particularly in the 1960s and after, to mix art with the demands of a political situation that dominated their lives. However, among the most committed, Kanafani pioneered this trend and proved to be its master.

All That's Left to You unifies time and place, where the desert stretches in time and through time to seal the fate of the protagonists and where time, through place, is an ever-stretching desert, that describes their destiny. The fusion of time and desert is perhaps a symbol of the interminable Palestinian experience of suffering that has been deepened by time and by the way the fertile place (the Palestinian homeland) has been snatched from them. They keep straddling the gaping desert that prepares to swallow them.

The novel revolves around a family in Jaffa, separated in 1948 during the upheaval of the exodus. A brother and sister end up in Gaza with an old aunt, while the mother flees to Amman. The novel introduces Maryam, Hamid's considerably older sister, who has made a relationship with a Palestinian of ill repute, a collaborator with the Israelis by whom she gets pregnant. This is too devastating for Hamid, who feels that, despite the fact that the collaborator agrees to marry her, his family's name has been dishonored. He decides to join his mother in Jordan by crossing the desert at night to evade the heat and the Israeli patrol.

Here a drama is portrayed by Kanafani with great finesse: "Two timepieces monitor the movement of Maryam's preoccupied memories and the movement of Hamid's footsteps across the desert: a clock hung in Maryam's house . . . and Hamid's own watch." Ticking away the time, they reflect the anguished thoughts of brother and sister portrayed in constant flashbacks "as the two protagonists weigh their present situation against the events of both the immediate and the more remote past." The one stable character in the novel is the desert, against whose background events will happen. It is one of the three voices that speak as events heat up, monitoring Hamid's march across it. The finale occurs when Maryam, aroused to frenzy by her new husband's demand that she either undergo an abortion or be divorced, kills him, and when at the same time Hamid encounters the Israeli patrolman and kills him.

Kanafani is also an accomplished short-story writer, roving between the universal and the nationally committed and producing a variety of stories, many of which are unforgettable. It is clear that among writers of fiction he is among those who could produce excellent work in either genre, reflecting a very sensitive perception of human nature and of the finest and most subtle situations and characters.[75]

Edward al-Kharrat: A Modernist Experiment

Edward al-Kharrat was born in Alexandria in 1926 to a Coptic family of limited means. He entered the world of fiction with his first short-story collection, *High Walls* (hitan 'aliya, 1959). A voracious reader and fully proficient in both English and French, he was able, in the late sixties, to rise in the world of Egyptian letters fully armed with ideas on modernism and on the need of literature, both poetry and fiction, for renewal and for forging stronger links with the modernist mode of writing. In 1968, after the shock of the 1967 June War, he gathered around himself a group of disillusioned young writers and started a small review titled *Gallery 1968*, which marked a definite turn to modernism.

Initially, much of al-Kharrat's work had to wait several years before finding a publisher. However, he continued writing, devoting his energy to novels in the modernist mode and winning the confidence of younger poets, critics, and writers of fiction. He concentrates, thematically, on love, sexuality, and politics. His detailed descriptions in his novels of the erotic is highly acceptable to liberals, "who find in his manner of writing an adequate antidote to the more rampant fundamentalist tendencies"[76] in Egypt and the Arab world. His *Rama and the Dragon* (Rama wa 'l-tinnin, 1972), a selection from which is included in this anthology, is the first book in a trilogy, followed by *The Other Time* (al-zaman al-aakhar, 1985) and *The Certitude of Thirst* (yaqin al-'atash, 1997).[77]

Al-Kharrat writes a rarefied prose, often with a touch of poetry in it, reaching at times genuine heights of esthetic refinement, laden here and there with a profound and fresh philosophy on life's existential experiences. I quote from *The Other Time*: "They sail together in a timeless movement"; "The answer that negates every question"; "Joy is more moral than every possible purification."[78] However, this writer can abandon these splendid heights in order to wade in an impossible exercise of phonetics and artificial coinage of numerous words with the same alliteration.[79]

Ferial Ghazoul, in her discussion of three modernist novelists, including al-Kharrat, compares him to the great pre-Islamic poets.[80] She quotes him in a paragraph of nine lines from *The Other Time*, where ninety odd words occur, each containing the letter *gh* (*gh* is phonetically similar to the Parisian *r*, a musical-sounding letter indeed, but too much of a thing can annul its effect). This consonant is so incessantly repeated, often in several consecutive words, as to give one the image of the author bending over his dictionary, exploring it for words and yet more words with the consonant *gh*. This smacks of artificiality. Modernist creations are not a spontaneous mode of writing and will allow a certain chiseling of words, a certain elitism of choice, a certain selectivity, but the above exercise is beyond esthetic endurance.[81]

Ghazoul's discussion of three works by three modernist novelists—the other two are the well-known Tunisian writer Mahmoud al-Mas'adi's novel, *Abu Huraira Spoke, He Said* (haddatha Abu Huraira, qala, 1973), and the Lebanese experimentalist Ilyas Khouri's first novel, *City Gates* (abwab al-madina, 1981)—creatively links their passages of pure estheticism and abundant descriptions to the art of description in classical Arabic poetry, notably to the poetry of the pre-Islamic period. Pre-Islamic poetry, which by the sixth century A.D. had attained an amazing level of artistic excellence, is a great experiment in esthetics that has not received the attention it deserves, although critics and estheticians anywhere would benefit greatly if it were to be explored to its fullness. The art of description, which the old Arab critical cannon in the eighth century and after decided was one of the four major modes required of the great poet,[82] had arrived at a very accomplished state in pre-Islamic poetry. It was often stripped of human experience, as when the poet described his she-camel or his horse, achieving a dehumanized art, a kind of art for art's sake. Ghazoul's linkage of these two remote experiments is a refreshing and positive step toward the unification of the sources of poetic/literary experience in Arabic and, even more important, toward the illumination of specific and enduring traits in the Arab literary heritage. In this she is responding, even more profoundly, to a recent trend in contemporary Arabic letters to bring these disjointed times, these segregated experiences, and this disaffected kinship to their rightful meeting point, where the specific and universal in the creative process take a rectified course, flowing from classical Arab times to join not the hackneyed, the imitative, or the repetitive in the contemporary period, but the modern, the experimental, the fresh, and the new.

Critics agree that this highly experimental novel is not possible to fathom or to telescope in a few words. "The narrative structure is loose, and the semantic aspect is scattered," hiding behind the consciousness of the reader, without, however, disappearing. The parts of the novel follow each other according to the selectivity of memory. The random meeting at a conference of the Christian Mikha'il with his first sweetheart, Rama, a Muslim girl specializing in old civilizations, ends by her inviting him to dine with other conference members at her home. The novel then undergoes many ramifications of themes and modes, where, among other topics, memory, political news, and erotic scandals are discussed in a way that makes the reader lose the thread of events under this huge amount of information and disjointed details. However, "there is a consolidating thread belonging to the two main protagonists that points to the dialectique of their union and their detachment, to their relationship to the world [offered] through minute descriptions and poetic rhythmic projection. Every chapter . . . remains a poignant creation for a love connection, and a model piece for a passionate relation."[83]

When al-Kharrat discusses politics, he is directly comprehensible. He speaks of contemporary political events in Egypt (such as the many incarcerations in Egypt in 1981) and outside Egypt (for example, the massacres of Sabra and Shatila) in order to achieve an extraordinary mix of the public and the strictly private.

Gha'ib Tu'ma Farman and Fu'ad al-Takarli: The Novel of Individual Action

There are quite a number of novels that delineate individual action, often taken against the prevailing mores and social expectations, but the work of the Iraqi writer Gha'ib Tu'ma Farman (1927–1990) is particularly interesting both because it is an early appearance and because the author was a committed socialist who proved by his work that he is a greater artist than ideologue.

The emergence of Arab fictional genres outside Egypt shows similar trajectory in the way young experimentalists in the Arab heartland[84] benefited from both the translations from Western fiction and the fictional experiments in Egypt. However, right at the beginning of the Iraqi venture into the world of the novel and the story we see an awareness of a deeper concept of what fiction should be. The early Iraqi novelist Mahmoud Ahmad al-Sayyid (1903–1937), who spent several years reading Western literature, particularly Russian fiction, is regarded as Iraq's first novelist for his novel *Jalal Khalid* (1928). He came early to the conclusion that writers should write for the people: "I call upon writers to begin writing stories for the people, and to follow the footsteps of the Russian writers, and of the French novelists such as Zola. . . . [Stories] should be written for one purpose only: to delineate the life of people; there is endless material in our society for writers and novelists [to benefit from]."[85]

Al-Sayyid's call to Iraqi writers to talk about people's experiences is, in fact, a call to adopt realism, a term that had not yet gained currency. However, after decades of renewed attempts at story writing, in which the names of Dhannoun Ayyoub (1908–1988) and Shakir Khasbak (b. 1930) begin to appear with strength, we have the rise of two of Iraq's and the Arab world's most accomplished novelists, Gha'ib Tu'ma Farman and Fu'ad al-Takarli (b. 1927). It was Farman in particular who adopted a distinctively realistic mode, publishing his first novel, *The Palm Tree and the Neighbors* (al-nakhla wa 'l-jiran), in 1966. This is the novel regarded as the "true artistic beginning of the novel in Iraq."[86]

Farman's focus is on the city and its people, a far cry from the Egyptian interest in village life and its particular problems seen, for example, in Haykal's *Zainab*. In *Palm Tree* and in his other novels, Farman writes about the poorer quarters of Baghdad, delineating their daily preoccupations, their struggle, and their aspirations. He writes with solicitude and affection, armed with an intimate knowledge of these quarters in which he grew up. His work reflects a well-grounded socialist ideology, which took him to the Soviet Union where he spent most of his adult life.

Social realism prompted Farman to resort to the Iraqi vernacular in his dialogue, a difficult problem for those not familiar with the Iraqi dialect at its most colloquial, the dialect of the poorer community in Baghdad. However, the use of the vernacular gives the novel great credibility when people speak and interact as real people do. *Palm Tree* revolves around two plots set in one of the poorest quarters of Baghdad. The first involves a baker, widowed and struggling for existence, whose fatigued state makes her a target for deceit and exploitation so that she is eventually robbed of her meager savings. The second involves her stepson, whose negative attitude to life undergoes a reversal after he suffers two major shocks and changes from an aimless, disillusioned young man to a resolute man of action—a willed action that he elects to perform after a long internal dialogue that Farman reproduces with great effectiveness and skill.

This novel is very reminiscent of Mahfouz's method of writing. Farman, acknowledging the influence of the master, says that the Iraqi novel was heir to no novelistic tradition in the modern sense and that Iraqi writers, like other writers in the Arab world, had to look to Egypt to learn the tools of the craft. This is true enough, but the Egyptian novel was itself a disinherited form at its beginning and looked to Europe for models. However, Farman asserts that when he wrote *Palm Tree*, he was mindful not of any other literary work but of the period of his own childhood, so "rich and strong and packed with people and events" that he did not need to resort to any other writings for nourishment.[87] This novel's main protagonist is "place"; the poor, decrepit quarter in which most of the protagonists grew up plays a great part in their destiny.[88]

An atmosphere of suppressed gloom reigns over Farman's novel as it does over several of Mahfouz's works. What makes *Palm Tree* an achievement at that comparatively early date in Iraqi fiction is its inner decorum, its planned economy of emotion, the lack of verbiage, the well-ordered parts, the compact structure, and the great control the author has over his material.

This was a mature beginning for the art of the novel in a country with no novelistic traditions of its own—a country, however, that faced the twentieth century with a revolution in art and ideas fermenting in its heart; a country with strong Arabic roots steeped in the classical heritage that were preserved and nurtured particularly in the religious centers of Najaf and Baghdad; a country harboring, right from the beginning of the century, great artistic creativity and a deep eagerness to explore all its creative resources and all the possible avenues of literary and artistic innovations. In only a few decades Iraq would radically change the inherited form of Arabic poetry, at least seventeen centuries old, achieving the greatest revolution ever in the history of age-old Arabic verse, and soon enough it would be home to a good number of original and highly competent artists, both painters and sculptors as well as some masters of the art of Arabic calligraphy.

However, for some reason, the novel's strong beginning in the hands of Farman, al-Takarli, and a few others did not bring forth a large enough number of experimentalists in the novel to make Iraq a center for this creative prose genre in Arabic. Iraq was going to prove its greater dedication to poetry, and new poets appeared in every decade, armed with a rich and infallible heritage of poetry. The interesting thing regarding Iraqi fiction is that its major writers were usually first-class and often very original. After *Palm Tree* Farman would write several other novels that bolstered his name as one of Iraq's and the Arab world's more accomplished novelists. In everything he wrote he continued to be the social observer we first meet in *Palm Tree*, and despite his émigré status he remained deeply involved in his country's life, its social and political changes, and its concern with individual freedom. There is an incidence of "willed action" in Farman's novel *Shadows on the Window* (1979), where he portrays one decisive action that is an act of the will against the apathy and insensitivity of the other protagonists. Farman is trying to tell his readers that willed individual action is essential if people hope to achieve freedom from inherited taboos and repressive social mores, that nothing will really change their lives except a revolutionary act of rejection. What is particularly interesting in the work of this socialist writer is the way he gives value to the individual rather than to the group or community, which is a genuine departure from the masses-oriented ideologues. The individual here acts beyond the limits of what is expected of him or her, of what is supported by the community, even against the blessing of the community. The actions taken by the protagonists are not those of heroes to be revered and emulated but of ordinary individuals who take their destiny into their own hands, who actively reject the communal outlook on the world. This is where Farman's artistic talent outweighed his political beliefs; he was more of an artist than an ideologue.

A major Iraqi writer, Fu'ad al-Takarli is one of the most accomplished novelists of the Arab world. Although his output is not prolific, his works have an artistic sophistication and a penetrating outlook on life, often interspersed with an intellectual analysis that never loses its artistic grip. After publishing the short-story collection *The Other Face* (al-wajh al-aakhar) in 1960, he proved to be more addicted to novel writing, publishing his famous novel *The Far Echo* (al-ra j' al-ba'id, in 1980), *Joys and Sorrows* (al-masarrat wa 'l-awja', 1988), and several others. His novels feature a complex structure of events and personalities. In *The Far Echo* the main character, Munira, is a woman who is both victim and heroine; her relationship with three men proves her superiority of character and her greater strength. The interesting point here is that al-Takarli makes the woman the source of strength and restoration, whereas his male characters demonstrate various types of weaknesses: sexual indulgence and aggression, the incapacity to transcend die-hard attitudes and mores, the incapacity to face life with confidence and rise above adversity. This novel is a great victory for woman, asserting faith in her inner strength and in her capacity to outstrip her experiences and discover a direction for her own life and the lives of others around her. Al-Takarli can sometimes achieve real esthetic heights in his style and, perhaps most important, can touch one's heart with his choice of mood and language. Although *The Far Echo* has a gloomy atmosphere, Munira's courage and profound humanity provide solace, creating a positive attitude in the reader, and, along with the author's bursts of eloquence, alleviating much of the gloom through esthetics.

Two Major Experiments in the Short Story

Yusuf Idris: Master Teller of Short Fiction

In the case of Yusuf Idris (1927–1991), the writer's artistic flair for the short story is indicative of a basic difference in attitude among writers of fiction. It marks out clearly the divergence (often ignored) between the two major arts of fiction—the short story and the novel—demonstrating their basic difference not just in technique but, still more crucial, in the writer's concept of the world and the way he or she handles experience. It is noteworthy that Idris himself stresses his propensity for the short story, making no mention of the novel.

Such a preference stems naturally from the writer's gaze at both the world and experience, which may sometimes impose a line of demarcation between these two arts. Many of Idris's stories comply with the prime requirements of the old short story: that it should be a compact account of a limited event with no desire to extend the bounds of time or, generally, to flow beyond the story's initial purpose, which is to recount an incident or a particular experience on the part of the protagonist or protagonists by providing a brief narration of a single event or aspect of experience and reaching a climax in an unforeseen ending. It is apt here to draw attention to the Arab literary heritage with its thousands of stories in the classical tradition, both fictional and factual, that have filled so many major compendiums and encyclopedias of Arab literary, social, and political history. The clear majority of medieval Arab or Arabized writers wrote in episodic and piecemeal fashion about the broad and infinitely varied panorama of Arabic life in medieval times. The anecdote, typically embodying a short story either factual or fictional, is an Arab literary phenomenon par excellence.

The memory of these thousands of anecdotes, internalized by many a cultivated Arab, must surely have been a major factor underlying the tendency of writers early in the modern Arabic renaissance to turn to the short story rather than the novel as the prime model for fictional narrative. There were indeed further causes, such as the problem of publication in earlier modern times and the reluctance of inexperienced writers with few direct models of longer Arabic narrative to venture on long, multiepisodic fiction that would have seemed more hazardous, more costly in time and consequence, than shorter experiments. Even so, the robust cultural tradition of the anecdote (a factor hitherto ignored, to the best of my knowledge, by literary historians) should be firmly underlined. The modern Arab writer who began his serious adventure in fiction with the short story must surely have inherited his ancestors' gaze on the world, seeing it not as a broad, continuous flow or a totality of life engaging the destiny of protagonists through time, but in terms of a particular experience: specific moments of joy or stress or contemplation; single acts of generosity, hospitality, revenge, loyalty, cruelty, magnanimity, wisdom, open or suppressed sexuality, ardor, sensuality, asceticism, experiences medieval Arabs knew. These experiences stemmed first from pre-Islamic desert life with its limited yet paradoxically universal experience, its dire deprivation of luxuries enjoyed in the adjacent civilizations of Persia and Byzantium, and its ceaseless struggle for survival. Later, these experiences also stemmed from urban Arab life and all the new experiences the city brought to a multi-racial and highly colorful public: licentiousness; an awe of authority; the pomp of luxury, power, and money; periodic adventures beyond the normal limits of space and tradition; a yearning for wealth as an early middle class arose in Baghdad and other metropolitan centers. The classical Arabic anecdote, often an exemplary short story, is most decidedly ingrained in the consciousness of modern Arabs who are in touch with their heritage.

For all this, I am not sure how well versed in classical Arabic literature Yusuf Idris personally was, or whether he ever received the education to furnish this kind of intimate feel for the anecdote. With Idris and a few others, such as Zakaria Tamir and Ghassan Kanafani, there is at least one other major factor: their own personal outlook on the world, whether influenced by their ancestors or not. These writers used the short-story form by instinctive preference, mainly according to the preliminary requirements I have already described.

In fact, the art of the short story is a very special one, not amenable to all fictional talents. A number of modern Arab writers—Haydar Haydar is an example—do in fact write equally well in the two genres, but there are some whose gifts are peculiarly suited to the modes and constriction of short fiction, as opposed to novel writing. Yusuf Idris is a prime example. Idris did attempt the latter genre in *The Illicit* (al-haram), which is good enough. But it does not rise to the skill of his short stories. It is a great pity that Idris died before his superior talent in the short story could gain recognition through the award of an international literary prize. When Naguib Mahfouz won the Nobel Prize for literature, in 1988, Idris felt cheated of what he and many critics regarded as his just deserts. In fact, it was right that Mahfouz should have been awarded the prize. He may indeed have been less attractive as a writer than Idris, but his work, over and above its intrinsic merits, established the novel as an important fictional vehicle in Arabic—a serious achievement in itself. Nonetheless, many continued to feel that Idris had been denied what he above all others merited on the artistic level; as I myself anticipated, the matter was never remedied.

The art of the Arabic short story, where Idris's major achievement lay, was already established in the fifties, when he began writing and publishing. On this foundation he brought the genre to its peak in Arabic and attained, in my view, the highest world standards. His literary worth, the interest and artistic pleasure he arouses in the reader, the variety of his themes, his passion for his subject matter, and his affection and sympathy for his protagonists—all these qualities raise him above any other writer in the Arab world, including the Nobel laureate himself. Mahfouz's grim, often labored depiction of the sordid or futile side of life, usually devoid of any empathy with his protagonists, cannot compare with the endearing way Idris handles even the most squalid aspects of society, evoking not revulsion and alienation but pity, sometimes even heartbreak. This is what happens, for example, in Idris's long story "Abyss of the City" (qa' al-madina). In taking the reader through the deteriorating slums of old Cairo—described superbly, indeed incomparably, by a peerless artist—to the very abyss of the city where decay and deprivation reign, to the world of the servant woman who has stolen the watch of her employer (a judge who has sexually exploited her), Idris uncovers human suffering and degradation in his characteristic way, arousing both pity and horror. What strikes home to the reader is not the petty theft but the utter poverty in which the woman lives, an environment of intolerable human misery. The way in which this abjectly impoverished woman is shown to be exploited on every side can only horrify us and arouse our deepest feelings of pity and even guilt: Idris's best writings positively engage readers' consciences, making them not onlookers but responsible witnesses to human misery.

This Mahfouz never contrives to do. In some of Mahfouz's best works, such as *Children of Gabalawi*, his cerebral qualities may indeed awaken our reflective powers. But in others, such as *Chattering on the Nile*, which reflects the end of all quests for the protagonists, his depiction of decadence and futility ends by alienating us and arousing our revulsion and despair. He narrates the sordid slowly, carefully, at times even heavily, unalleviated by any factor able to evoke pity and tenderness in the reader. (*The Thief and the Dogs* perhaps provides an occasional exception.) Idris, in contrast, writes vehemently, fluently, naturally, speaking from the heart to all our senses, portraying the human condition in the most lively, pathetic, and penetrating way. Mahfouz improvises on this condition.

One senses that Mahfouz the writer is a looker-on, depicting society from a safe corner of middle-class Egyptian life, whereas Idris appears to be a part of the living substance of his stories—as though he has lived all the aspects of deprivation that rural and lower-class Egyptians have known. In his early youth, Idris took active part in a rebellious social and intellectual movement in Cairo. He had grown up in rural Egypt and, by the time he entered medical school at the age of twenty, had witnessed the tyranny and oppression of the Egyptian government of the 1940s. He had suffered considerable hardship, having been brought up in the poverty-stricken home of maternal relatives—the only way he could gain an elementary education (his better-off parents lived in a Delta district still without schools at that time).

In Cairo he was in direct touch with an Egypt preparing for revolution against the prevalent weakness and corruption of the minority governments there. It was in the course of his youth in Cairo and his contact with leftist students that he became a Marxist, something that enlarged his sensitivity toward the ailments beleaguering his country. During his early medical student days, he discovered both a power of oratory and a deep concern for his people. It was then also that his friend Muhammad Yusri Ahmad foresaw Idris's still undiscovered talent and encouraged him to write.

His publications came during an active period of Egyptian experimentation with the short story, already acknowledged as a genre. Many young writers were trying their hands and injecting the short story with considerable vigor—a vigor that found its special outlet and authority in Idris's stories, which were original, rich in form and subject matter, and highly attractive. From the very start he showed a prodigious vitality. In his works, he moves freely across the whole social structure of under-privileged Egypt, showing less interest in any philosophy of life than in how life is actually lived. The 1950s were to be his most fertile period. In 1954, he published his first collection, *The Cheapest Nights* (arkhas layali), in which he was already presenting the voice of the suppressed and suffering plainly and sympathetically; four more collections would appear before he reached the age of thirty.

In the 1960s, he published still more collections. Much of his former viewpoint and breadth of subject and perception remain in these later collections, but there is greater emphasis now on the sheer futility of life and on the deep loneliness that insecurity and public and social chaos can produce. The Egyptian political atmosphere had changed in the 1960s, and intellectuals, Marxist intellectuals especially, had begun to feel alienated from the general political situation.

One of Idris's greatest assets is an understanding of human nature, which lends a distinctly naturalistic aura to his writings. His work—reflecting so much of Egyptian and other Middle Eastern life, with its often crushing poverty, poor government, and, most important, lack of social justice and security—often entails a quest that ends in failure, though not in doom. Many of his protagonists continue to strive for a better life; if he stresses the aberrations and blemishes of Egyptian life and plunges frequently into the tragedy surrounding a world of injustice and constant toil, he can also on occasion bring out the humorous side of experience. The beggar in his small tale "A Very Egyptian Story," for example, is shown not just in his penury but also in his skilled professional capacity to beat difficulties and survive—all this humorously and attractively drawn.

However, the most prominent features of Idris's work are its success as artistic narrative, its attraction to the reader, and its sheer quality as entertainment. This last aspect of narration, so lacking in many writers of modern Arabic fiction, is perhaps the core of Idris's superior success as a storyteller. No matter how well constructed the plot, how vivid the description, or how elaborate the style, no fictional narrative can properly succeed without that quality of inner attraction that holds readers' minds and hearts, leading them on to long for more. Idris's precise and clear style is never sentimental, but neither is it ever dry, obscure, or alienating. His language is uncomplicated and explicit, often reverting to the spoken language in dialogue and so bringing his narrative closer to life. It is a language that abhors redundancies, its economy being a weapon against unnecessary dilution and tedious description, but it does not leave important things unsaid or vital questions unanswered. Above all, he has that magical flair that can transform the most dingy and repellent setting into a place shining with familiarity, even with intimacy, where the reader is not a mere onlooker but part of the scene. Any summary of his plots that is removed from this spellbinding gift of style and language is doomed to failure. His plots are indeed usually strong and well developed, but it is the way he tells his story that clothes his fiction in the mantle of genius.

Idris portrays the whole spectrum of many and different protagonists and, on a universal level, the whole of life within the constricted environment of the Egyptian poor. A wide variety of themes is represented here, reflecting the author's own natural abhorrence of repetitions and of dwelling on a few selected social representations.

Zakaria Tamir: An Exclusive Syrian Experiment

"The novel," according to Zakaria Tamir (b. 1929), "is always far more poorly populated than a collection of short stories, and much more constricted. For the same number of pages, a collection of short stories introduces more characters, more variety and more issues than a novel can ever do." Such was the reasoning of this prolific short-story writer in comparing the art of the two forms. The truth is, however, that Tamir's gaze on the world has always been that of a writer of episodical stories, each one limited in time and space but with the whole oeuvre covering the spectrum of contemporary Arab life; each story has its own artistic worth and encapsulated meaning, but his overall statement, on social and political life in particular, is effected through a string of such stories.

Tamir's ambience is the whole of life around him. He addresses not only social and political problems but psychological and existential issues as well, lingering always on the side of pathos in life, with a touch, every now and then, of Arab traditional wisdom and firm ethical grasp, reflecting a profound apprehension of universal norms and values that defy extinction. For all that, his interpretation of experience is never reactionary; he is abrasively critical of stale values and outdated concepts. An abiding quest for freedom and justice within his society, going beyond the Syrian to the pan-Arab environment, has made him a shrewd critic of the major flaws and deprivations of human happiness in present-day Arab society. For fifty years he has witnessed and endured the constant swerves and strategies of Arab authority everywhere, an authority he sees as directed toward the dehumanizing of a whole people's life and prospects. In this his quest differs somewhat from that of Idris, his prime target being not the poverty and struggle of the individual in society but the voracious appetite of society for stealing, usually through corrupt means, the happiness and well-being of the individual. In his work the individual is either total victim or perfect executioner. For all these reasons, Tamir's approach is difficult to pin down. He employs, as major writers generally do in an environment of censorship and cultural repression, a method sometimes allegorical but mostly symbolic.

The historical disasters that have engulfed and still engulf the Arab world have not led to any retreat of the creative impulse, but they have greatly affected an earlier robust trend toward the comic and the ironic in favor of a stern apprehension of experience, unyielding in its solemn address and its periodic touch of the tragic. Looking at the long list of writers represented in this anthology, one realizes how few of them resort to humor to depict contemporary dilemmas. The pioneers, those who wrote in the first half of the twentieth century, offer us such a contrast to the more contemporary fiction writers that one wonders how the further urbanization deep into the twentieth century did not produce fictive experiments capable of outshining or even matching the early attempts at humor in Arabic fiction. When one delves further into the twentieth century and into the greater urbanization and modernization of life, humor in fiction experiences an unexpected reversal and is greatly arrested in the work of the best writers of fiction, showing clear signs of retreat. This is undoubtedly mainly due to the deep grip and unequivocal infiltration of political malaise in the life of the individual after the middle of the twentieth century. A serious and often somber attitude toward life took hold of writers, who responded to the grim situation with an equally grim depiction of life. One can name exceptions to this among the major writers—Emile Habiby, for example, incomparable in his apprehension of the tragicomic—but the number is very limited. Tamir is another major exception. He writes a kind of bitter humor with an ironic twist that has captured a large number of readers.

In his work Tamir shows no attempt to "contrive" a special "literary" style. To the naked eye, he seems simple and even journalistic in his approach, reflecting the influence of the years he spent as editor of prestigious journals. However, as he remains nearer to the commonplace, his words composing themselves in a basic style, one finds out that all this is a means to express a specific meaning, often highly allegorical and full of allusions. This apparent simplicity hides beneath it a sophisticated design that in many of his stories verges on the satirical, even the comic, and assails the reader unexpectedly with the sudden turns he takes, usually at the end of a story, through the logic of his special kind of narration. What makes this almost neutral language work so well is Tamir's great capacity to manipulate "tone." His work is, in fact, a great experiment in tone, a literary element hardly ever alluded to in modern Arabic criticism, but here representing the very backbone of this writer's achievement. Despite the allusive and far-reaching implications of his intent, however, Tamir's prose enjoys a crisp lucidity and is always clear, almost innocently candid, unemotional, and controlled in his handling of a story, as if he has not just indicted a whole society, satirized a whole epoch, and staunchly condemned an existing way of life. A lover of freedom, he never goes into a crescendo of anger or into a stream of nostalgic lament about the absence of freedom from contemporary Arab life. The depth of his rage never flares up in torrents of telling words but is compressed and let out through poignantly depicted images. And out of all this, his satirical voice emerges not in frenzy but in a low whimper, leaving the reader deflated, frustrated, and conquered by a horrible truth that Tamir so radically reveals without letting forth a single scream. No reader with any genuine sensibility can read him without immediately discovering the despair that is latent in the Arab's daily life, a despair that is camouflaged and glossed over so that life may continue. The reader experiences a kind of national/communal regret and stifled rage. For those who attend the many poetry gatherings that are particularly popular and highly regarded occasions, the opposite reactions are experienced. Poets depicting the state of affairs, mainly political affairs, can arouse in the audience feelings of fervid passion and loud expressions of anger, all terminating in a catharsis at the end that becomes a delusive calm. With Tamir, there is no catharsis. The reader's self-expression is stifled, and he or she discovers all too soon the absolute present-day inadequacy of the individual in a world of turmoil, injustice, and violent strategies. Highly allegorical and rich in allusions, Tamir's style can also resort to representing human frailty and predicaments through animal representations, offering, as we see in one of his stories in this anthology, "Tigers on the Tenth Day," a kind of modern-day fable with great poignancy.

Tamir does not offer his readers any one memorable character—his protagonists seem to symbolize something else. We do not relate to his characters
as actual people who live in the memory with their names engraved in our
consciousness. They are almost all symbols, mainly of an idea or a deficiency
in our lives, primarily the lack of freedom. There is nothing to prevent a short
story from accommodating heroes and heroines that join our life and become
part of our experience, but this is not what we get out of Tamir's stories. His
often nameless protagonists are there in order to stress the antagonism that
exists between the actual ways of the world around the author and those he
dreams of. There is an unmitigated derision in his social and political criticism
against those who hold the reins of power, whether it is the religious, social, or
political authority. When he swerves into scornful sarcasm, his satire is posed
against the deadly and criminal seriousness of a faulted world. The resistance to
the demands of an oppressive order, which is, in fact, extant all over the Arab
world (but experienced in varying degrees of urgency from one Arab entity
to another), has been a persistent phenomenon in modern Arabic literature,
irrepressible but resorting to various forms of expression. Tamir has excelled in
the allegorical and satirical forms. He has indeed made of our hopelessness an
ongoing fable of derisive humor.

There is no doubt that the decades between the early pioneers of modern
Arabic fiction and the fiction of the Arab world today reveal a matchless race
toward the attainment of original and highly meritorious achievements. It is also
clear that fiction, especially the novel, is now displaying signs of competing with
poetry, Arabs' most established and revered art, and may well surpass it in the
near future. This radically changed Arabic fiction must be assessed against its arid
background, only a few decades removed from the contemporary scene. It will
be realized then that this new wealth, this unprecedented activity, this supreme
literary assertion, this extraordinary explosion of the Arab fictional genius, this
unbounded adventure, this flourishing productivity, this liberation, this courage,
and this ambition comprise an unequivocal statement on the vigor and dyna-
mism that mark out the fictional venture in the Arab world today. It is with the
greatest elation that one looks to the future of Arabic fiction and anticipates the
ongoing rise of novelists and writers of other fictional experiments offering a
creativity equal to the best in humanity's boundless heritage.

Notes

1. A make-believe world is a part of a many-sided and fundamental human activity that "includes game-playing, role-playing, daydreaming . . . as well as literature

proper." See J. Hillis Miller, "Narrative," in Frank Lenricchia and Thomas McLaughlin, eds., *Critical Terms for Literary Studies*, 2d ed. (Chicago: University of Chicago Press, 1995), p. 68.

2. Miller suggests that stories influence events in life: "we would not know we were in love if we had not read novels." Ibid., p. 69. However, this is not a pertinent situation. How did people, before the rise of the novel, realize they were in love? In Arab literary history the poets of Hijaz in the Umayyad period (661–750 A.D.) filled the world around them with their tender, romantic, and exhilarating love poems, and many stories were circulated about their often tragic love experiences. This is, of course, a more complicated issue than a few lines can describe. But it should be kept in mind that love, with its many modes and styles—romantic, sensual, heterosexual, homosexual, chivalrous, predatory—has vogues and periods in which a particular mode flourishes or is eclipsed. The whole experience cannot be due to the influence of novels, and although written literature can help set a mood and enhance a mode, it can also be itself influenced by the social, economic, and spiritual climate of a period, which sets the style and temper of the love experience for that period, thus directing its literature.

3. Kant, in his essay on education, seems to find that the main interest in fiction affords merely momentary "entertainment," which he regards as a useless exercise because it weakens the memory, imprisons fancy, and affords no exercise of thought. See Immanuel Kant, *Education* (Ann Arbor: University of Michigan Press, 1999), p. 73.

4. This began, as far as I know, early in the eighteenth century, when the novel became a major genre in English literature, with Scott, Dickens, and Thackeray, especially the latter two, publishing many of their novels in serials in various papers. For a single example, Dickens seems to have begun his publishing career by serializing his *Sketches by Boz* in 1835–36; then had his famous *Pickwick Papers* serialized in 1836–37; then *Oliver Twist* in 1837–38; then *Nicholas Nickleby* in 1838–39. *Dombey and Son* was serialized in 1848 and *David Copperfield* in 1849–50; *Bleak House* in 1852–53; *Little Dorrit* in 1855–57; *Great Expectations* in 1860–61; *Our Mutual Friend* in 1864–65. Several other novels were never serialized, such as his renowned *A Tale of Two Cities* (1859).

5. This negation of history was voiced by many Arab critics and literary historians. It was usually poetry that was treated with greater care, as did Ahmad Amin in his *The Dawn of Islam* (fajr al-Islam), 11th ed. (Cairo, 1975), pp. 55–68. For another important example, see Ahmad Hasan al-Zayyat, *History of Arabic Literature* (tarikh al-adab al-'Arabi), 23d ed. (Cairo, n.d.), p. 393, where he says that the arts of fiction were unimportant to the Arabs. It was Tawfiq al-Hakim who realized the importance of some fictional arts in classical times. He does concede that early classical Arabic literature was deficient for ecological reasons, for among the Arabs "a fresh and beautiful [literary] language developed in a barren environment . . . and it is something for Arabic language to be proud of that it has risen to this level among the sands"; see *The Prime of Life* (zahrat al-'umr) (Cairo, 1955), pp. 182–83. Elsewhere al-Hakim asserts that "It is not the Russians who are masters of the story, nor the English, nor the French, it is we, with the fictional tradition of the Quran, and the [folk romances] of 'Antara and the like, and *The Arabian Nights*, and the *Assemblies* which are basic in the art of the story. It is we who should be regarded as the masters of the fictional art . . . !" (p. 190). See also what 'Abd al-Hamid Ibrahim says about this in greater detail, in his *Prose Love Stories* (qisas al-'ushaq al-nathriyya) (Cairo, 1972), pp. 19–21. By the mid-twentieth

century, the ideas of these writers and many others had already been assimilated into a general outlook enhanced negatively by ideas about deficiencies in several poetic genres (mainly the dramatic, the narrative, and the epic), giving a great sense of lack of achievement to modern Arabs, who were unaware that they were on the threshold of a richly creative period not only in poetry and fiction but also in drama.

6. See Frye's *Anatomy of Criticism* (Princeton: Princeton University Press, 1957); see the first essay, particularly pp. 33–34.

7. Ibid., p. 34.

8. However, this divorce from the mythic and the legendary romance did not persist throughout the Islamic period; a vigorous return to superhuman and legendary narratives, to the heroic superman and the fantastic event, occurs in the later Middle Ages (e.g., *The Arabian Nights*; the "wonders and marvels" of the medieval travel books; the prose folk epics).

9. The wandering narrators carried this chest as well as a bench on which viewers sat. They walked the streets of cities calling for people, mainly children, to come and view the marvels they would reveal. We would each pay a piaster and sit on the small bench with our eyes glued to the glass window, behind which a reel would be passed accompanied by the voice of the narrator chanting: "Welcome and see: This is 'Antar the brave knight, and this is 'Abla his beloved . . . etc." And we'd gasp and choke when we saw other horsemen attack black and sinewy 'Antar, only to feel relief at his capacity to thwart them.

10. The notion generally asserted in modern times—that the dedication and purity of the Umayyad lovers was due to the influence of Islam—is discredited by the fact that such stories, of which the Midad and Mai story and that of al-Muraqqash and Asma' are but two, existed in pre-Islamic times. Arab cultural canons were thus established before Islam.

11. On this, see my study of the Umayyad poetry in "Umayyad Verse," *The Cambridge History of Arabic Literature,* vol. 1 (New York: Cambridge University Press, 1983), p. 19.

12. The most elaborate of these are the story of Midad and Mai in *The Book of Crowns*, and the work of the poet al-Muraqqash al-Akbar in the sixth century A.D.

13. The most famous among these Umayyad poets was the Mandman of Laila (Qais ibn al-Mulawwah), Jamil Ibn Ma'mar or Jamil Buthaina after his beloved; Kutahyyir 'Azza, and Qais Lubna, both also after their beloved women.

14. Jorge Luis Borges, who studied Arabic, was genuinely influenced by the Arab-Islamic heritage. He used the method of *khabar* and *isnad* in his own work, basing it on his knowledge of this type of Arab narrative. See his *The Book of Imaginary Beings* (Penguin, 1969). See also Khaldoun Sham'a, "An Introduction to the Literature of Modernity," in *Method and Terminology* (al-manhaj wa 'l-mustalah, Damascus: 1979), pp. 90–91.

15. Examples include Ibn al-Jawzi's *Stories of the Stupid and Dim-Witted* (akhbar al-hamqa wa 'l-mughaffalin) and al-Muhassin al-Tanukhi's (d. 384/994) collection *Relief After Affliction*, which is full of wise advice, religious exhortations, and descriptions of the repression and violence done to people by rulers and their officials. See also Tanukhi, *The Admirable in the Deeds of Generous Men,* and al-Raqqam al-Basri (d. 321/933), *The Capacity to Forgive*, which deals with the various meanings of forgiveness, reprieve, and apology. It speaks of felons and how they were forgiven, providing a clear picture of the Arab personality at the time and many of its social habits, the way

the ruler treated his subjects, as well as the habits of people in handling their quarrels and differences. Tanukhi depicts some major historic figures, such as the notorious Umayyad ruler of Basra, al-Hajjaj ibn Yusuf, and the poet al-Farazdaq. See also Ibn al-Daya's (d. 330/941?) charming *The Recompense*. With the developments of city life, many books were written about sexual and sometimes illicit topics—for example, those by the encyclopedic writer Shihab al-Din al-Tifashi (580/1184–651/1253): *A Recreation for the Mind by What Is Not to Be Found in Books* (nuzhat al-albab fima la yujad fi kitab), which contains details of sexual practices in his times; *The Return of the Old Man to His Youth* (ruju' al-shaikh ila sibah); and others.

16. See Ferial Ghazoul's illuminating article on the fables used in *The Arabian Nights* and *Epistles of the Brethren of Purity*: "Fables between Our Popular and Philosophical Heritage" (qisas al-hayawan baina mawruthina al-sha'bi wa turathina 'l-falsafi), *Fusul*, special number on the Heritage (fall 1994): 134–52.

17. For a discussion on the emulators of these assemblies in modern times see Sabry Hafez, *The Genesis of Arabic Narrative Discourse* (London: Saqi Books, 1993), pp. 109–110, 129–36; see also Muhammad Rushdi Hasan, *The Influence of the Assembly in the Emergence of the Modern Egyptian Story* (Cairo, 1974).

18. The suggestion has been often made that *The Epistle of Forgiveness* may have been the basis for Dante's *The Divine Comedy* (composed in the early fourteenth century), which is another journey to the afterworld. It is highly astonishing that most European literary historians writing the history of the various nascent literatures that developed in the second millennium around Muslim Spain and the shores of the Mediterranean only rarely attempt to examine the influences that must have affected some of the literary contributions in these languages—for example, the songs of the troubadours and the lyrical poetry in the south of Italy, particularly in Sicily where the Arabs had ruled for two hundred years, almost until the end of the eleventh century A.D. It is beyond the scope of this introduction to go into the details of these influences. But surely it cannot happen that a civilization would flourish for centuries in a certain place, arrive at brilliant heights, and leave no influences behind. Because of its apparent presence in Spanish and other languages, the influence of the Arabic language on other Latin languages has been acknowledged and studied, but other influences have certainly been overlooked by most literary historians. However, during the twentieth century several sonorous voices arose in the West, pointing to those influences on Western fiction and poetry. On this, see Luce López-Baralt, "The Legacy of Islam in Spanish Literature" in Salma Khadra Jayyusi, ed., *The Legacy of Muslim Spain* (Leiden: Brill, 1992), pp. 505–82; Maria Rosa Menocal, "Al-Andalus and 1492: The Ways of Remembering," ibid., pp. 483–504; and Roger Boase, "Arab Influences on European Love Poetry," ibid., pp. 457–82. These chapters are brilliant discussions of influences and similarities.

19. J. C. Burgel, "Ibn Tufayl and His *Hayy ibn Yaqzan*: A Turning Point in Arabic Philosophical Writings," ibid., pp. 830–31.

20. See Fatma Moussa Mahmoud's essay on the probable influences on Iberian writers of the Arab assemblies in Spain, written by such Andalusi Arab writers as al-Saraqusti al-Andalusi (d.1143) and Lisan al-Din ibn al-Khatib (d. 1374). See also her "The Arab Assembly and the Picaresque Novel in Western Literature," *Al-Manhal Review* (Cairo, 1983), pp. 124–32. See also Luce López Baralt, "The Legacy of Islam in Spanish Literature," in Salma Khadra Jayyusi, ed., *The Legacy of Muslim Spain*, pp. 521–22.

21. Some of the most famous include *Banu Hilal*, an epic romance, translated several times into English; *Sayf Ben Dhi Yazan*, an epic romance, rendered in part transalation and part retelling for *PROTA* by Lena Jayyusi, under the title *The Adventues of Sayf Ben Dhi Yazan* (Bloomington: Indiana University Press, 1996); the folk romance of 'Antara, narrated and described by Peter Heath in *The Thirsty Sword: Sirat 'Antara and the Arabic Popular Epic* (Salt Lake City: University of Utah Press, 1996).

22. The magazine offered what must have seemed a tremendous financial boost: one prize for five thousand dollars for the best short story (even taking inflation into account, this amount still seems great and must have seemed like a megaprize for competitors), two thousand dollars for the second best, and one thousand dollars for the third. The journal was bombarded with short stories: more than fifteen thousand were submitted by more than twelve thousand competitors. The experiment having succeeded, *Collier's* continued the competition but phased it out for the year 1905–1906, offering a one-thousand-dollar prize for the best short story every three months. *Collier's* stipulated that the story be no longer than six thousand words, but that it could be as short as the author preferred. It is also interesting to read that the journal offered the minimum fee of five cents a word for publishing short stories, but that there were authors who received an established rate. (See *Quarterly Prizes for Short Stories, as Offered by Collier's* [New York: P. F. Collier, 1905].) It is also interesting to see that among the sixty-eight stories accepted and entered into the first competition, twenty-eight were by women, including the winner of the second prize.

23. T. O. Beachcroft, *The English Short Story* (London: Longmans, 1967), p. 38.

24. Ibid., p. 41.

25. Ibid. It is interesting to see that Stevenson's first collection, which appeared in 1882, was called *The New Arabian Nights*, pointing to influences from Arabic literature that have usually been omitted from any critical discussion by Western writers.

26. Muhsin Jassim al-Musawi mentions that Ibrahim A. al-Mazini—who after being first a dedicated poet and then a critic of poetry found his proper direction as writer of fiction—said that some friend had told him that the novel was not worthy of his status (see *The Arab Novel: Beginnings and Transformation* [al-riwaya 'l-'Arabiyya, al-Nash'a wa 'l-tahawwul] [Cairo, 1988], p. 61). I was also told by the late historian 'Ajaj Nuweihed an interesting story about Mahmoud Taymur, now acknowledged as the father of the short story in Arabic. On a visit to a high government official in Cairo where Mr. Nuweihed was on a short visit, a young man entered with a message from his own father to the high official. When he left, the official turned to Mr. Nuweihed and told him, sarcastically, "Isn't it a pity that this wonderful young man is obsessed with the writing of what they call 'short stories'! What futile business!"

27. For detailed descriptions of the reception and spread of fictional genres and the early attempts at creating indigenous forms, there are several useful books, including Sabry Hafez's detailed and meticulously researched *Genesis of Arabic Narrative Discourse*, and Muhammad Yusuf Najm's classic *The Story in Modern Arabic Literature, 1870–1914* (Beirut, 1952). The first stresses the Egyptian efforts in particular, and the second stresses the efforts of the Syrians (including the Lebanese).

28. His argument, however, revolves around an erroneous hypothesis that "would-be novelists and dramatists, seeing the possibility of becoming able to write verse . . . through learning the laws of prosody, confined their literary activity to poetry and

'here we are today with no novels and no plays.'" On this, see Salma Khadra Jayyusi, *Trends and Movements in Modern Arabic Poetry* (Leiden: Brill, 1977), 1:112. The quotation from Nu'aima is from his *The Sieve* (al-ghirbal), the chapter on license in poetry, "al-zihafat wa'l-'ilal" (Cairo, 1923), p. 119. Nu'aima's assumption that learning the laws of prosody made it easy for a talented person to become a poet is clearly unrealistic.

29. For a list of the early translated short fiction published in peridoicals, see Muhammad Yusuf Najm, *The Story in Modern Arabic Literature,* pp. 15–21, where he lists a good number of periodicals, mainly Lebanese, and mentions on pp. 20 and 21 that the Lebanese were the main translators. See also Sabry Hafez's discussion of the role of translation early in modern times, *Genesis of Arabic Narrative Discourse,* pp. 85–90 and 106–08. See also Najm, *Story,* pp. 21–31, for a list of the novels translated in the nineteenth and early twentieth centuries.

30. The four original stories by Musafa Lutfi al-Manfaluti were "The Orphan," "The Veil," "The Abyss," and "The Punishment," all self-revealing titles.

31. Cf. the rise of the novel in Latin America. For a long time the Latin American novel did not exist as a "definable entity." It burgeoned, however, in the 1960s with the rise of such writers as Miguel A. Asturias, A. Carpentier, Carlos Fuentes, Mario V. Llosa, Gabriel Garcia Márquez, and others. In his *The Emergence of the Latin American Novel* (London, 1977), Gordon Brotherston does not discuss the rise of a middle class and a larger reading public. Rather, he refers to the surge of such fine literature as the birth of a "thread of inner coherence" after World War II, which he attributes to the many movements in Latin America toward greater emancipation. Brotherston compares this Latin American activity to the rise of several major novelists such as Tolstoy, Gogol, and Gorky in nineteenth-century Russia and to novelists in eighteenth-century England. I refer to all this in order to point out how new the novel is in the world and for how many centuries the world existed without it. It also draws an immediate comparison to the burgeoning of the novel in the Arab world around the 1960s.

32. This was not unlike the conservative reaction in the seventeenth century to the appearance of the novel in England. In his *The Social History of Art,* vol. 3, *Rococo, Classicism and Romanticism* (London, Kegan Paul, 1962), Arnold Hauser says, "The novel, which, despite its popularity, represents an inferior and in some respects still backward form in the seventeenth century, becomes the leading literary genre in the eighteenth, to which belong not only the most important literary works, but in which most important and really progressive literary development takes place. The eighteenth century is the age of the novel" (pp. 24–25).

The literary genres dominant in England before the rise of the novel were poetry, drama, travelogues, and discursive prose on various subjects. It is interesting also to see how the novel in English was able slowly to replace drama to a great extent. The profusion of dramatists in, for example, the middle of the sixteenth century, when almost every year one or more plays were published, continued into the century that culminated with the rise of Shakespeare, who wrote *Henry VI* at the beginning of the 1590s. It is also interesting to note that in 1590 at least six other plays by different dramatists were published, including Marlow's *Dido, Queen of Carthage.* In fact, around the time of Shakespeare, there was an explosion of drama and dramatists in England. However, although by the 1640s this great activity remained rather central, it began to abate a little, until drama slowly gave its centrality of place to the novel.

In Arabic, poetry has occupied the central place. In fact, both fiction and drama had to struggle throughout the twentieth century to gain their rightful status.

33. From a 1901 article in *Al-Muqtataf*, a journal that had shown an avant-garde interest as early as the 1880s in the fictional developments that had begun to infiltrate the literary scene. For more on this see al-Musawi, *The Arab Novel*, pp. 48–69; the quotation is on p. 50, with no mention of the writer's name.

34. The experience of my maternal grandfather, Dr. Yusuf Sleem, who shares the dedication of this book, may be helpful in illustrating the timeliness of the modern fictive narrative. My grandfather was a surgeon, but in his private life he was also an erudite man who loved literature and could narrate a long story with eloquence and style. He had read the most famous English novelists as well as those Europeans translated into English, and all his narrations were taken from the rich repertoire of Western literature. His turn-of-the-century audience ranged from family members to neighbors and friends to quite a few local people. This means that some of his audience came from simpler backgrounds, but they all enjoyed the novels of Walter Scott, Charles Dickens, Jane Austen, Victor Hugo, and so on, pointing to a readiness in the audiences of literature in the Arab world to shift their interest from the traditional folk romances, with their flamboyant, transcendental content, to a more modern fiction that speaks of the lives of men and women from all walks of life.

35. See Butrus Hallaq, "The Beginning of the Novel: Between Criticism and Ideology," in Muhammad Barrada, ed., *The Arabic Novel: Its Reality and Horizons* (al-riwaya 'l-'Arabiyya, waqi'un wa afaq) (Cairo, 1981), p. 18. Hallaq adds on p. 19 that this novel is not a real artistic creation and that he totally rejects its evaluation as a pioneering example; see also pp. 26 and 29.

36. On this see my *Trends and Movements*, 1:189–90, 196.

37. On Shauqi, see ibid., pp. 46–51; on the Diwan Group, see ibid., pp. 152–75; on Taha Husain, see ibid., pp. 149–52; and on the Apollo Group, see ibid., 2:369–410.

38. A poignant example of this is the enchantment that Arab readers everywhere felt toward the Egyptian poet 'Ali Muhammad Taha's delightful celebration in the forties of his annual visits to Europe, which he described with ardor and unprecedented joy.

39. See Hanan al-Shaikh's two novels, translated into English by Catharine Cobham: the acclaimed *Women of Sand and Myrrh*, which takes place in a Gulf country but has an American as one of four women who are trying to cope with a different culture and emotional attitudes; and *Only in London W2*, which takes place in London and, among other characters, brings two people, a divorced Arab woman and an Englishman, together in an erotic relationship that uncovers the cultural gaps endured by both lovers. See also Usaima Darwish's *The Tree of Love, the Woods of Sorrow* (shajarat al-hubb, ghabat al-ahzan) (2000), a sensitive and audacious depiction of a very intimate encounter between an Arab woman and an English doctor, here reflecting the attitudes of a truly emancipated Arab woman; Laila al-Atrash's lovely novel, translated into English for PROTA by Noura N. Halwani and Christopher Tingley as *Woman of Five Seasons* (Imra'at al-fusul al-khamsa, 1990 Northampton, Mass.: Interlink Books, 2002), also dealing with a liberated Arab woman choosing to live in London free of her husband's chauvinism and swaggering. While the early novels, such al-Hakim's *A Bird from the East* and Suhail Idriss's *The Latin Quarter* (al-hayy al-latini), reflected an attitude of wonder if not awe toward Western urban culture, Tayeb Salih's famous *Season of Migration to the North* (mausim al-hijra ila 'l-shamal) showed the negative consequences of the cultural shock experienced by the main protagonist. However,

recently, as in the novels of the three women novelists noted above, the cultural differences do not portray shock or rejection on the part of any of the parties, allowing a greater affinity between East and West in the future.

40. See my "The Nobel Laureate," introducing the 1989 edition of Mahfouz's *Midaq Alley,* translated by Trevor LeGassick (Washington, D.C.: Three Continents Press).

41. This imbalance does not seem to exist in, say, English literature. For example, although poetry was well received since Chaucer and even earlier, drama continuously coexisted with it. Out of the three major creative verbal arts (poetry, drama, and fiction), Arabs had very little drama and their right ande original fictive genres were never treated on the same level as poetry or seriously discussed as equal to poetry in most critical works.

42. The same idea was broached at the ceremony of the Nobel Academy on December 10, 1988, where Mahfouz was cited by the academy as having "formed an Arabian narrative art" and bringing it to maturity.

43. This is clearly seen in *The Thief and the Dogs* (al-liss wa 'l-kilab) translated by Trevor LeGassick and M. M. Badawi (Cairo: American University in Cairo, 1984). On his release from prison, Said Mahran faces a double shock: his wife has deserted him and his journalist friend, Rauf 'Alwan, has abandoned his old radical stance vis-à-vis society and the rights of the downtrodden poor.

44. Roger Allen, *The Arabic Novel* (Syracuse, N.Y.: Syracuse University Press, 1982), p. 50.

45. See my "The Nobel Laureate."

46. Translated for PROTA by May Jayyusi and Jeremy Reed and introduced by Fedwa Malti Douglas, with an afterword by Jeremy Reed (New York: Interlink Books, 1993). Quartet Books in London was among the publishing firms that admired the novel but, citing financial concerns about its salability, would not publish it.

47. It is possible to have a poem of sheer description whose esthetic perfectionism is its *raison d'être,* such as the short poems of description that flourished in Arabic poetry during the medieval period. See Salma Khadra Jayyusi, "Nature Poetry and the Rise of Ibn Khafaja," in Salma Khadra Jayyusi, ed., *Legacy of Muslim Spain.*

48. Translated into English by Roger Allen and Adnan Haydar (Syracuse, N.Y.: Syracuse University Press, 2000).

49. Liyana Badr's three-part collection of narratives on the agonizing experience of the Palestinians in Lebanon during the seventies, *A Balcony on the Fakihani* (shurfa 'ala 'l-Fakihani), translated for PROTA by Peter Clark (Northampton, Mass.: Interlink Books, 1997), has perhaps attained the level of the tragedy it is addressing. In this book there is a genuine depiction of the Palestinian apocalyptic experience. All three stories end in deadlock and chaos. The detailed and lively description, incorporated into an enduring narrative of great poignancy, keeps the reader breathless. Based on true but slightly fictionalized experiences, the novel relates the harrowing details of cold-blooded murders and deportations already known to the public, all vested with an esthetic decorum that keeps sound the book's claim to be genuine art.

50. Even the American woman living and loving in the Gulf, in Hanan al-Shaikh's novel *Women of Sand and Myrrh,* forgets all about a modern scientific outlook and resorts to witchcraft to regain her Arab lover.

51. See Salma Khadra Jayyusi, ed., *Human Rights in Arabic Thought: A Study in Texts* (huquq al-insan fi 'l-fikr al-'Arabi. dirasa fi 'l-nusus) (Beirut: Centre for Arab Unity

Studies, 2002), which has many chapters pointing to this problem. This book will appear soon in its English translation.

52. See my introduction to *Human Rights in Arabic Thought,* where this situation is discussed more fully.

53. I am using the word "story" without the word "short" to designate a long short story that is different from a novella. A novella is at least fifty pages long and has different parameters. When a fictional account shorter and different from a novella exceeds the usual length of a short story, I have called it simply a "story."

54. Translated into English for PROTA by Trevor LeGassick and Salma Khadra Jayyusi and published in a new edition (Northampton, Mass.: Interlink Books, 2001).

55. See my introduction to my *Anthology of Short Plays* (Northampton, Mass.: Interlink Books, 2002).

56. However, this is not impossible to achieve in certain experiences if there is enough literature on it. For her historical epic on the fall of Granada, Radwa 'Ashur had pored over numerous books of history and was able to internalize much of the reaction to the desperate experience of the Muslim Granadians, described in a substantial amount of poetry and prose, often by contemporaries of the tragic events.

57. In his brief autobiographical text "Yusuf Idris on Yusuf Idris," he asserts the fact that he is essentially a short-story writer and a dramatist. See Roger Allen, ed., *Critical Perspectives on Yusuf Idris* (Washington, D.C.: Three Continents Press, 1994), p. 13.

58. Beachcroft, *The English Short Story*, p. 40.

59. I had wanted to include the part of this story that delineated the horror of poverty in the slums of Cairo, but the author did not agree to publishing an extract. Unfortunately, the whole story was too long to include in this already large anthology.

60. The novels of this monumental quintet, published as stated under the general title *Cities of Salt* (mudun al-milh), are *The Maze; The Trench; Variations on Night and Day; The Ostracized;* and *Desert of Darkness* (al-tih; al-ukhdud; taqasim al-layl wa-'l-nahar; al-munbatt; and badiyat al-Zalam). The first three have been translated into English by Peter Theroux (New York: Random House, 1987, 1991, 1993).

61. Roger Allen, *Endings* (London: Quartet Books, 1988). See also his *Trees and the Assassination of Marzouk* (al-ashjar wa 'ightiyal Marzouq, 1973), whose earlier part deals with an ecological problem that has afflicted many parts of the Arab world; here it deals with the elimination of trees for the sake of planting cotton, which would yield more profit.

62. For example, the name Taybeh, the town in *Trees,* could be in almost any Arabic country, particularly east of the Mediterranean, where there may be a Taybeh in every country.

63. There are quite a few other examples of this in modern Arabic writings, especially in poetry. On the death of his father, the Iraqi poet 'Abd al-Karim Kassed speaks with grief, love, and tenderness about the poor, unlettered father who aspired to educate his son (just like al-Ghitani's). Returning from the father's funeral, he finds his shadow still in the house:

> I returned to find him in the house
> In front of his small mirror
> Shaving, still shaving
> With his old implements
> His implements he acquired before I was born.

See his cluster of short poems entitled "Tales of My Father," translated by Lena Jayyusi and Anthony Thwaite, in Salma Khadra Jayyusi's *Modern Arabic Poetry: An Anthology* (New York: Columbia University Press, 1987), pp. 291–92.

In one of her poems, Salma Khadra Jayyusi confesses her attachment not just to the dead father but also to the dead mother and the living son:

S . . .
Forever dispersed between father and son,
Hung by her hair to the mother tree.

64. Patricia Drechsel Tobin, *Time and the Novel: The Genealogical Imperative* (Princeton: Princeton University Press, 1978), p. 12.

65. "Formal" as opposed to folk. In folk literature, which never gained the status of formal creative works, the nostalgia persisted. See my "Arabic Poetry in the Post-Classical Period," to be published in Roger Allen and Donald Richard, eds., *The Cambridge History of Arabic Literature*, vol. 6 (in press), on literature in the postclassical period, in which I discuss the issue of nostalgia at greater length.

66. It is interesting that the same self-sacrificing attitude is also transferred to the daughter in modern times. The Egyptian poet Iman Mirsal, writing on the death of her father, remembers his acts of kindness and love:

For the sake of buying a book
of "Translated Poetry"
this man sleeping so deeply
convinced me once that his wedding ring
was pressing hard on his ring finger
He remained smiling as we left the goldsmith
while I was telling him that I did not agree
that our noses were similar.

67. Roger Allen, *The Arabic Novel*, pp. 325–29.
68. Ibid., p. 325.
69. Ibid., p. 326.
70. Ibid., p. 327.
71. Ibid. Al-Ghitani then recounts the sources from which he took his inspiration. These are (1) books by formal historians who have depicted some characteristics of the life of ordinary people, those who usually fall out of history books pertaining more to the microhistory discipline, with particular mention of the historian Ibn Iyas, who witnessed the Ottoman invasion of Egypt; (2) books of geography and city plans; (3) books of magic and alchemy; (4) other world histories, including those that try to imagine the remotest past of humankind, surely unknown to the writers, which lead us to myths and their specificity as well as to folklore; and (5) books of marvels and wonders. He then mentions his interest in the various styles of bygone writers, such as the narratives in al-Aghani; in the simple, unaffected, and direct style of historians; and in the style of Sufisism with its special terminology and ambiguity. It is clear that he had a deliberate interest in studying the rich and varied heritage of the Arabs with the aim of adopting that which he found suitable.

72. Jeremy Reed, from his preface to *Prairies of Fever,* translated by May Jayyusi and Jeremy Reed (Northampton, Mass.: Interlink Books, 1993), p. ix.

73. I have discussed this at length in introduction to my anthology *Modern Palestinian Literature* (New York: Columbia University Press, 1992), pp. 29–32.

74. I have discussed this point about author/audience at length in my chapter "Platform Poetry," *Trends and Movements*, 2:583–94; see particularly pp. 586–87.

75. Kanafani has published four collections of short stories: *The Death of Bed No. 12* (maut sareer raqm 12, 1961), a collection of seventeen stories containing some of his best; *Land of Sad Oranges* (ard al-burtuqal al-hazeen,1963); *A World Not for Us* ('Alam laisa lana, 1965), which contains some of his best stories on the universal human experience; and *On Men and Guns* ('an al-rijal wa 'l-banadiq, 1968), dedicated to the Palestinian experience.

76. From a letter by the late Shukri 'Ayyad, eminent critic and writer, to Salma Khadra Jayyusi, discussing, among other matters, modern trends in literature.

77. After his first short-story collection, al-Kharrat spent some unproductive times, publishing his second creative book, *Hour of Pride* (sa'at al-kibriya'), a collection of short stories, in 1972. His most fecund period came in the 1980s and 1990s, when he began publishing profusely. Among his books were *Saffron Dust* (ghubar al-za'faran, 1986), *Girls of Alexandria* (ya banat Iskandariyya, 1990), and *Stones of Bobello* (hijarat) (Bobello, 1992). In 1996 he won the prestigious 'Uweiss Prize.

78. Pp. 164, 22, and 136, respectively.

79. He repeated the letter *gh*, not a very common letter, obsessively. The *gh* here could be any letter in the word, not just an alliteration.

80. Ferial Ghazoul, "The Modern Poetic Novel: A Model of Genuine Modernism," in *Issues and Testimonies* (qadaya wa shahadat) (Morocco, 1990), pp. 240–41.

81. In certain literary experiments, the repetition of matching consonants for esthetic or even comic effects can appear spontaneously. A great Umayyad poet, Dhu al-Rumma (696–735), said to be simple and illiterate, used a good number of spontaneously selected alliterative words, keeping, however, the esthetic prerequisites of decorum and balance. See my "Umayyad Verse," in *The Cambridge History of Arabic Literature*, vol. 1 (1983), the section on Dhu al-Rumma.

82. See Muhammad ibn 'Imran ibn al-Marzubani (d. 994), *Al-Muwashah,* ed. A.M. Bajjawi (Cairo: Dar Nahdat Misr, 1965), p. 273.

83. Ghazoul, *Fables,* pp. 232–33.

84. Other than Egypt, the Arab heartland comprises Iraq, Syria (including Lebanon), Palestine, and Jordan. It was in these regions that the Arab literary renaissance began in the nineteenth century and then spread to the rest of the Arab world.

85. Quoted in Najm 'Abdallah Kazim's slim volume *The Experiment of the Novel in Iraq in Half a Century* (tajribat al-riwaya fi 'l-'Iraq fi nisf qarn) (Baghdad, 1986), p. 35.

86. N. 'A. Kazim, *The Novel in Iraq, 1965–1980* (al-riwaya fi 'l'Iraq, 1965–1980) (Baghdad, 1987), p. 31.

87. From an interview with Farman by Kazim in Moscow, ibid., p. 230.

88. Farman's other novels are *Five Voices* (khamsat aswat, 1967), *The Wading* (al-makhaad, 1974), and *Offering* (qurban, 1975).

I

THE PIONEERS

Marun 'Abboud (1886–1962)

A Lebanese literary figure of great stature, Marun 'Abboud was predominantly a literary critic, an iconoclast of the finest order, with an honest mind and a personality of great integrity, qualities rare at any time and in any place. His work has been a driving force behind the modernization and development of modern Arabic poetry, as he helped demolish many old concepts relating to poetry and open up new avenues for poets and critics to follow. However, he was more than a critic, he was a litterateur open to many literary disciplines. His short stories are vivid depictions of life around him and demonstrate the full flavor of his life-loving attitude toward the world and to life's essentials. His fiction includes *Faris Aga*, *Accounts of the Village*, and *The Prince with Wheat-Color Skin*. 'Abboud was writing at a time when the atmosphere was still free of the somber and often desperate mood that now dominates the Arab world, and in his fiction, like many of his contemporaries, he was able to achieve a jovial tone and a humorous interpretation of experience.

THE HIGHWAY ROBBER

Bou[1] Khattar returned home dusty and disheveled. He hung up his rifle, put the pistol in the opening in the wall next to it, and emptied the things hidden in his shirt, his pocket, and the folds of his belt onto a stone shelf. Then he sat, cross-legged, in his usual place to the right of the fire.

His wife, Barsitta, came with a jug and bowl, and he started washing his hair and face—which didn't stop him from talking on and on. Every now and then he'd break off to ask her a question, not minding the lather that covered his face. If it stung his eyes when he looked up, he closed them and then opened them again, so as to clear the soap without interrupting his flow of words. He talked on for a long time. When Barsitta poured the water carelessly, he shuddered and swore then quickly realised he'd committed a mortal sin and started to pray for forgiveness, drying his face but still talking. He combed his hair, asking question

---

1. "Bou" is derived from "Abu," meaning "father."

after question but not waiting for an answer or expecting one, till it was time for him to twirl his moustaches and arrange them in the style of one of the folk heroes. This required profound silence.

A few moments later the family gathered about the low round table where they ate their food. Each of them had a large loaf, like a round napkin, on his thigh. They used their hands as forks and the bread as their spoons. Bou Khattar didn't give them permission to speak while eating. If anyone asked a question, he was answered; otherwise everyone was expected to confine his attention to his plate, till their hands met at the plate of figs or molasses that was the family's common dish.

After thanking God for their daily bread, Bou Khattar gave his advice and instruction. He corrected the mistakes of the day, first with his wife then with his children. Finally he turned to his commanders-in-chief, his two sons, Khattar and Shalhoub, to explain the proper way of doing the job, criticising them for any minor faults they might have committed during the day.

"You approached him from the back," he told Khattar. "You should have done it from the front. You told him to hand his stuff over and waited. It would have been better to take him by surprise; you should have hit him, or at least screamed at him, and frightened him to death. And you, Shalhoub," he went on, "if you'd stood at the crossroads as I told you, that swine wouldn't have got away from you—and you can bet that he was the one with the money. Don't worry, it's too late now. There'll be other chances. Make sure you pay attention next time."

"We didn't have much luck today," he remarked to his wife. "You must be furious with us." Imm[2] Khattar gave a subdued smile. Bou Khattar went briefly over some other matters, then heaved a sigh and said, "Kneel down. Let us pray."

He stood up straight, like a pillar, and noticed that the way one of his sons was kneeling wasn't as it should be. He told him off, then the prayers started, with the father and his eldest son leading them: After standard prayers to the Virgin, Bou Khattar repeated several Hail Marys and Our Fathers and begged the Virgin for better luck next day.

He went straight off to bed and lay down on his back. "Barsitta"; he said, tucking himself under the covers, "prepare a packed lunch for us tomorrow. It's Friday lunch, don't forget, so boil some potatoes." A little later he raised his head from the pillow. "My trousers are torn," he said, "do something about it, will you? And my waistcoat's come undone. If I set eyes on him again," he muttered, "I'll really get him."

After he'd been under his cover for some time, his bald, wrinkled head emerged again, and he spoke to his son, "Sharpen the knives and clean the guns; and warm up the gunpowder so we don't have a repeat of what happened today."

Curious, Imm Khattar made a questioning gesture with her hand. Her son signaled to her to wait till his father was asleep. In due course he said, "We came

---

2. "Imm" is a colloquial form of "Um" or "Umm," meaning "mother."

on two men today. We robbed one and the other got away. He was a brave, spirited young man."

He got out a silver ring with "Yazoul" inscribed on it. Barsitta was angry when she saw it. "This is a present for his beloved," she said. "How could you?" Khattar pointed to his father. "Tell him, not me," he said. "If I ever protest or talk about pity, he loses his temper. 'You scoundrel,' he says. 'You're always ready with an excuse! Rob them, and damn their ancestors!'"

Soon the house was quiet except for Bou Khattar's snores as they rose and fell. He was talking in his sleep, threatening this man and ordering that man to surrender, then telling his son, "Search him, Khattar!"

He woke at dawn as usual, crossed himself several times, and prayed to the Virgin while still in bed. Sometimes this would go on for a long time and Bou Khattar would apologize for any shortcomings in his behavior toward her, promising her a quarter of what she enabled him to steal. She was promised such things as a chandelier or a candlestick or incense or candles for her church. And, he promised, if he really did well, then her gift would be a handmade bell.

After about an hour of prayer, they went to their place on the road as usual. The youngest son followed behind them with the packed lunch.

Bou Khattar never forgot to bring his rosary. He prayed continually, and if he suspected he'd left a bead out he went back and repeated it to make up. He wanted his prayer account to be straight, free from mistakes and omissions. How else would the provider grant him good luck?

He was praying and wondering who providence would send his way, when the bell for mass sounded. He crossed himself and asked God's forgiveness for missing the mass, promising to attend it in mind and spirit.

He reached his usual lair at sunrise, as the sacring bell was ringing. He moved his fez slightly back from his forehead, knelt on the ground, and led the Lauds prayer with his sons. Then they lurked, each in his place, waiting for their just and lawful daily earnings. Bou Khattar felt in his heart that the Virgin was pleased with him and would grant him good luck.

He heard someone approaching, singing.

Bou Khattar signaled to his two sons to prepare for action. The person approaching was feeling safe and happy—then he saw a man praying with a rosary in his hand and became alarmed. His fearful reaction surprised him, as the man was only praying, but he put on a brave front and greeted him very respectfully. Bou Khattar scowled and looked at him out of red bulging eyes.

The man avoided his stare and walked on. Bou Khattar made a sign with his rosary, ordering the man to stop, but he ignored it and carried on walking. Bou Khattar shouted at him, "Look, don't make me do something I'd regret! Let me finish my prayers!"

The man realized he'd fallen into the hands of Bou Khattar. "It must be him," he thought.

Bou Khattar went on praying, while the man waited. Finally he came up to him, pointed his finger at him and said, "Hand over everything you've got."

"I haven't got anything with me, Bou Khattar."

"You've got nothing with you? And who told you I was Bou Khattar?"

"I recognized you."

"God strike you blind! All right, hand over everything you've got."

"I've only got ten majides that I borrowed to buy flour for my children."

"May God restore it to you. Hand it over."

"Let me keep it, for the sake of the Virgin Mary!"

Bou Khattar shook his head and gestured to him to hand it over.

After a lot of toing and froing and pleading and weeping, Bou Khattar agreed to share the money with him for the Virgin's sake. The man left mumbling, grateful for only half a disaster.

Bou Khattar crossed himself with the money and slipped it inside his shirt. "What a blessed start to the day!" He said piously.

He gazed at the sky, beseeching his beloved Virgin Mary. "We showed him mercy for your eyes alone," he said. "Give us our recompense."

He heard some people leading mules, talking about prices and good seasons and various other things. "Here comes our luck," whispered Bou Khattar. "There's a whole crowd of them!"

Khattar prepared his rifle and Shalhoub prepared the hatchet, aiming it as if the victim was right in front of him.

There were three men, leading their mules. Bou Khattar gave a great shout, which was echoed and magnified by the river, "O.K., gentlemen, hand it all over, or else!" One of the three, a proud young man, answered roughly and cursed their mother. Bou Khattar fired a shot to scare him and he shot back, but the final, decisive shot came from Bou Khattar's rifle. The young man fell to the ground and his friends surrendered. They were robbed of everything they had, including their clothes and their packed lunch.

Bou Khattar sat down to count what he'd gained on this happy day. There were thirty-five gold pieces and some riyals and a big moneybag full of metal coins, so heavy that it made Bou Khattar groan to lift it.

He looked too at the goods he'd stolen—a carved brass axe, a dagger, a cleaver, and a rifle.

He kissed the ground, thanking his God for what He'd given him. "Kiss the ground, you ungrateful lot!" he told his sons. Then he laughed. "Money and weapons. That's good luck."

He started joking with the Virgin, his eyes fixed on his spoils. "Thank you, mistress, may God give you long life! Today you've given Bou Khattar his chance. I'll give you the best bell that was ever made! Children, open their knapsack, get the food out!"

The three of them sat on a stone in the middle of the river and ate with surprising appetite after their victory. The younger son took a piece of cheese from the knapsack of the men who'd been robbed, and Bou Khattar slapped him.

"Show some respect, you lout!" he said. "How dare you eat fat on a Friday? It was only because of their lack of faith that we beat them!"

—Translated by Salwa Jabsheh and Christopher Tingley

Dhannoun Ayyoub (1908–1988)

Iraqi short-story writer and novelist with a pioneering spirit, Dhannoun Ayyoub was born in Mosul and studied at the Higher College of Teachers' Training in Baghdad. In his lifetime, aside from teaching, he occupied several responsible positions, mainly in cultural services, becoming director of the Institute of Fine Arts in Baghdad. It is clear from his life story how deeply men of honor can suffer from the repressive rule of governments: he was once court-martialed and subsequently emigrated to Vienna in 1954, i.e., during the time when Iraq was ruled by a king. On returning to Baghdad after the 1958 revolution, he was only able to stay there for a short period before having to emigrate again in 1961. Ayyoub spent some period of his life translating from English and Russian literatures. He published his short stories first in the Mosul review that he edited for more than six years, *Al-Majalla*. These and other stories were compiled in eleven collections, including *Stories from Vienna* (1957). Just as in his short stories, his novels *Dr. Ibrahim* (1939) and *The Hand, the Land, and the Water* (1948) mirror social life in Iraq, which he depicts with irony, a critical tone, and an intent at reform. He spent the rest of his life in Vienna, where he died.

THE LITTLE GODS

The wheat field, stretching to the horizon, received the morning breezes with a light rustle. The tender ears swayed on their pliant stems, sending soft waves that rippled over the green sea. The sun shone in a blue sky without trace of cloud, a sky itself like a sea, calm with the silence of the dead. That blue sea above met the green sea below at the horizon, their colors meeting and mixing at the place of sunrise.

A large, dun-colored village stretched along the seashore, its mud huts straggling at random, some as small as a fox's den, others the size of beasts' stalls, like blotches of earth on the shore of that wondrous green sea. The greenness of the wheat shimmered beneath the rays of the warm March sun, which found its way into every pore of the plants, bestowing life on all it touched—except for those living behind the windowless mud walls.

It was a day of sweet calm, following one of rage in which the sky had lowered, the wind howled, the thunder cracked, the rain poured down, yet without any spring cold to nip the wheat. The water had flooded the land, reviving the plants, so that the peasants could rest for two weeks and more; the village lay in unaccustomed sleep, even though the sun was up. No living thing was to be seen, except for the larks sending out long, sweet tones that descended from the sky like angels' whispers, and the swallows chirping then sweeping low to the earth in search of untilled ground to snatch some mud for their new homes.

A mile from the village rose a great, strongly built palace. Three thousand years before, Babylonian peasants had filled this place with buildings of their own. Had one of those peasants been restored to life, he'd have taken the new building for a mighty mansion of the gods, into which grains and foodstuffs poured through every day of the year!

This stately palace was the mansion of the shaikh, the owner of all that broad district and many more like it, possessions larger than the whole of Belgium. The shaikh held sway, too, over the peasants and all the others who worked there; plants, beasts of all kinds, men, the very sun and rain and winds were harnessed to his use. Having all this, he was every bit as mighty, as exalted as Marduk, and Enlil, and Etonabashtem;[1] and they were mere gods of the imagination, whose worshippers saw only their idols, while this was a living god who commanded and withheld, gave life and took it, bestowed happiness or misery—and yet was a man exposed to all the storms that buffet human life.

Shaikh Mughamgham ruled over a very large tribe, which his father, Shaikh Budair, had used to spread terror near and far. In those days there had been less use of irrigation; his father, along with the tribe, had lived on tithes and booty from raids, from the money paid by their terror-stricken neighbors. Not a tenth of the present cultivated land had then been tilled.

Budair never lived to see these new developments. He was succeeded, at last, by his oldest son, Matar, a fierce and awesome ruler whose name had echoed through the times of revolution and the independence that followed. Even in the new state the *diwans*[2] felt his crushing power and influence and fearfully submitted to him, so that he grew ever stronger. He played the despot over his own tribe even, over the members of his very blood family, ruling his brothers with a rod of iron, holding unrelenting sway over his followers, killing and imprisoning with none to reprimand or keep watch on him. His brothers, bitterly though they suffered, found no fault with his actions; for the tribal customs and the traditions of the country had made them used to abject obedience and the endurance of cruelty. Besides, they were all too young to do anything—all except Mughamgham, who shared his brother's qualities and was his trusted counselor. Mughamgham advised him to send their younger brothers, along with Matar's own sons, to receive a modern education in the nearby cities; for this, he was far-sighted enough to see, would confirm their ancient status and fit better with their radiant glory.

Matar died and was succeeded by Mughamgham, who inherited vast possessions and carried on his brother's iron-fisted power and dreadful cruelty. Indeed, he took his tyranny and cruel sway still further, until the peasants made up a song about him. "Mughamgham bowed down to God," they sang. "Then he picked God up, that's the truth, and carries Him on his shoulders!"

---

1. Gods of ancient Babylonian mythology.
2. "Diwan": a hall or large room in which men congregate socially.

As for his brothers and nephews, city life had corrupted some, while others had been exalted by learning. Those delighted with learning were content with little, so that the crumbs from Mughamgham's table more than satisfied them. But the corrupted ones were spurred on to drink wine and gamble and pursue women, so prodigally that all the vast possessions of their ancestors would have been too small to last a single year. Aziz, the oldest of the dead shaikh's children, and bold and cruel and haughty as his father had been, belonged to this second group. But when Mughamgham assumed power, he took Aziz in hand, forcing him to moderate his conduct. Things became strained then, between the uncle who wanted his sway to be as great and cruel as his dead brother's and the nephew who thought himself the legitimate heir, the rightful successor to his father's title and rule. And things were made worse still by Mughamgham's utter failure to produce children, a source of shame in his country, which only served to increase his despotic cruelty.

Now just an hour later, on the day of splendor we described at the beginning of this story, two masked horsemen rode out of the palace gate, wrapped in their cloaks, and galloped at full speed toward the farm, passing fleetingly by the village where the slavish greetings of the peasants were carried to them on the wind. They galloped along the middle of the field, on a track made by the feet of cattle, alongside a ditch large enough to take a boat. The ditch was full to the brim with rain water, but the two horses sped on unheeding, their heads high, showing no interest in the pure water or the succulent plants along the way. No doubt they were stuffed as full as their masters!

Aziz, who was one of the horsemen, turned to his companion. "How high would you put the revenue of this field, Khalaf?" he asked. "You ought to know. You've acted as our agent for enough years now."

"Last year," Khalaf answered, "this village alone yielded twenty thousand dinars, from summer and winter yields combined. On that basis, the revenue from your ten villages should be a full two hundred thousand dinars."

Aziz grunted.

"And do you know," he asked, "how much that cursed man allows me each year? Two thousand dinars, that's all! And if he weren't afraid of my spirit, he'd have given me a mere thousand dinars, the way he does to his cowardly brothers and nephews who are satisfied just to fill their bellies. Two thousand, out of two hundred thousand that belong to me by right. I'd like to break his neck, by God!"

"But he's strong," Khalaf replied with a smile. "He holds vast sway and has many followers."

Aziz laughed, refusing to be impressed.

"All this will be mine," he retorted, "when he's dead and buried. I haven't been wasting my time there in the city. The strongest head cowers in front of me when I show a hundred-dinar note. Curse my stingy uncle!"

He thought long and hard, then said, "Listen, Khalaf. I've finally had enough of this scoundrel. I can't take any more. I've often talked to you about doing away with the man, but you've always put off your decision. My old offer stands. You'll receive the next village as your part in it—you're married, after all, to his cousin Shannouna. When he dies, the whole inheritance will be freed. Shannouna will have her rights, and through her you'll have yours."

"Aziz," the agent answered, "I've been waiting for the proper moment, and now it's come. He's grown suspicious about my relations with you and he's threatening to deprive me of my post. He didn't realize the threat was his own death warrant!"

"It's time to strike, you say? So, what's your plan?"

"Do you remember that quarrel between your uncle and the peasant 'Ammouri? Your uncle beat him with his club, so hard he broke two of his ribs, and the peasant's son threatened in front of the whole village to have his revenge. I warned your uncle to take care, not because I was worried about his safety but to draw attention to the peasant's threat. Your uncle almost spat in my face. He wasn't afraid of buzzing flies, he said. Now, he's invited to the city tonight—the city governor's honoring a visit from the minister of the interior. And since your uncle's driver's sick, he's decided to drive himself. It's only twenty miles, after all. The road passes by that reed thicket, which makes such a wonderful hide for hunting. I've secretly bought two repeat-firing rifles. We'll burn him along with his car, and to hell with him!"

"Wonderful!" Aziz exclaimed. "That's the perfect pretext! Although there's really no reason for all this caution. Who'd dare accuse us anyway, and who'd want to avenge him? Those policemen of his who are virtual house servants, or his wives who can't stand the sight of him, or the peasants who hate him so much? He doesn't have any son, thank God. As for that flock of sheep in the city, his relatives, I'll double their annual income."

"It's just as well to be careful even so," Khalaf answered. "Where's the harm in letting people think 'Ammouri's son killed him? There'll be no one except his father to say he was at home. As for us, we're going to the city now, which will put us beyond suspicion—even if we do find a way to steal out again and hunt this savage tiger down!"

That dark, moonless night, following on from the lovely day, witnessed a brutal and ugly crime—though not the ugliest crime in the Iraqi countryside.

The nephew killed his uncle. How often a brother kills his own brother, or a son his father—and the hand of justice stretches out to the weak and the simple. But as for the strong, they are the little gods who kill as Cain killed Abel, and as the gods killed one another in the old myths.

The gods have had their fill of everything; but they are still thirsty for blood.

—*Translated by May Jayyusi and Christopher Tingley*

Mahmoud Badawi (1910–1985)

Egyptian short-story writer Mahmoud Badawi was one of the early men of letters to seek stimulation and knowledge of technique from his readings (and translations) from Western fiction, particularly in this case from

Russian literature, especially from Chekov. Although not as known in the Arab world as was his contemporary Mahmoud Taymur, Badawi's work on the short story widened the horizons of the genre and paved the way for a more candid delineation of experience. Among his collections are *The First Sin* (1959), *A Room on the Roof* (1960), *The Guardian of the Orchard* (1960), *The Last Carriage* (1961), *A Night on the Road* (1962), *Sad Beauty* (1962), *The Falcon of the Night* (1970), *The Golden Ship* (1971), and *The Other Door* (1977). His oeuvre demonstrates the struggle of early Arabic fiction to find its methods and approach, as his abundant creativity combated the weaker roots of modern Arabic fiction to produce satisfactory results.

THE SNAKE

As I passed Shaikh 'Abd al-'Aleem Bakr, he was sitting under a lotus tree near the farm road, surrounded by peasants and going over the accounts for the water supply for the motor. He invited me to stop for a cup of coffee and help him with the figures.

It was a scorchingly hot day, and I was thirsty and tired as well from riding, so I was happy for the chance to sit in the shade. I had an *Al-Ahram* paper I'd bought from the Bani Husain station, and Shaikh 'Abd al-'Aleem started reading the news, asking me about the opening of the cotton bourse and the plan to bring drinking water to all the villages, about the cooperatives organized to help the peasants and the assembly place they'd already started building east of the village.

The peasants listened in silence. As far as they were concerned, we were enlightened people, way above their mental level. Then Shaikh 'Abd al-'Aleem broke off, and I saw he was watching a man crossing the track where the motor was, followed by the rural watchman, 'Abd al-Basir. As the man came nearer I saw it was Ma'mun 'Abd al-Rahman, a land worker and one of the best peasants on Shaikh 'Abd al-'Aleem's estate.

"Where's the money, Ma'mun?" Shaikh 'Abd al-'Aleem asked.

"Here it is," the man replied.

"Where's the other pound?"

"I've only planted an acre and a third on your motor, 'Abd al-'Aleem Bey."

"You planted one and a half acres. The controller measured it and so did Isma'il Effendi. Every season we have this argument. Go and fetch me another pound."

"This is all I have, 'Abd al-'Aleem Bey."

"Take your money back then, and bring me everything together when you've got it."

"Where from? Do you expect me to sell my children?"

"Go and sell two measures of wheat. Or one or two of those goats that keep eating up other people's property."

"This is all I have. And it's more than you've any right to as well."

"What did you say?"

"I said more than you've any right to, Bey."

"OK. First thing in the morning, we'll be coming to seize your plants and ox."

"You treat us like slaves with your land and your motor. Just how much more do we have to take?"

"What was that you said, you cur?"

Shaikh 'Abd al-'Aleem rose, took his cane and started beating the man hard on the face and chest. We had to pull him off. Then he went furiously back to where he'd been sitting, still threatening to throw the wretched peasant off his estate.

We did our best to calm Shaikh 'Abd al-'Aleem and still his furious anger in some way. The sun was at its highest point now, the July heat so fierce tongues of fire seemed to be coming up from the ground. The land stretched out in front of us—the wheat stubble where the land wasn't planted, and the green maize fields, the young shoots holding out against the drought and intense heat.

The Nile was close by, but it flowed down in a basin, whereas this land was high up and the peasants couldn't benefit directly from the river water to grow their crops. People used it for drinking, though, and sent their cattle to drink and bathe in it, and they'd made a dirt track down to the river for the cattle, and for the women to go and fill their jars.

Shaikh 'Abd al-'Aleem's son, Hasan, had gone down with two other boys from the estate, to play with the mud and build castles on the sands. Shaikh 'Abd al-'Aleem didn't stop him doing it. It was the only game he could play, after all, when he went to the estate with his father.

Shaikh 'Abd al-'Aleem had finished with his accounts now, and the peasants were moving off. He'd just got up to perform the noon prayers when we heard a boy screaming.

"Come quick! It's Hasan, 'Abd al-'Aleem Bey's son!"

We thought the lad must be drowning, and I raced to the riverbank with his father, followed by all the peasants who'd heard the cry. When we got to the top of the slope, we were suddenly rooted to the spot, our eyes open wide in terror, afraid to make a move for fear of unleashing a disaster. There, coiled up, was a huge spotted snake come to the water to get cool, while Hasan was flat against the wall near the hole the snake had come out from, too panic-stricken to scream or even move.

He was frozen to the spot, completely motionless; you could hardly tell whether he was alive or dead. He couldn't go down to the water, or up to the fields. In the water there was just a big she-ox, Ma'mun's, which was paying no attention to anything round about it. But it was right in front of the snake, and we were afraid, if it moved, it would stir the snake up with disastrous results. We stood there riveted, watching helplessly. It was the longest, hugest spotted snake we'd ever seen, like some creature newly up from hell.

We couldn't think of any way of coming on it and killing it—if we startled it, the boy would certainly die. I felt a kind of electricity pass through my body, and I seemed to sense more snakes, crawling along under my feet and coming out from the crevices in the walls. As I stood there I started bringing my foot up and down, shaking it constantly. I looked round in terror, imagining one of the snakes coiling itself round my neck.

Then, in the midst of these terrifying visions, one of the peasants hurled a big stone at the snake, but missed it. If he hadn't acted so rashly, all might have been well; the snake might have gone back into its hole and no one been harmed. Now, though, it reared up in fury and started moving straight toward the boy. There was uproar as we all started shouting together. Shaikh 'Abd al-'Aleem cried out too, and pointed his gun, but his hand was trembling too much for him to fire.

"Shoot, Hassan!" he screamed at one of the peasants. "Shoot!"

"The bullet might hit your son," Hassan said, "or the ox. No one can be sure to hit the snake in the head when it's moving like that."

"Fire, lad. Fire!"

We were all overwhelmed, powerless in our terror and confusion to take our eyes off the boy, there at the snake's mercy. Then a single bullet rang out from behind us, and snake and ox crumpled together. We looked back to see where the bullet had come from, and there was Ma'mun standing a little apart, holding his short rifle. We all knew what a crack shot Ma'mun was. There was absolutely no one else who could have fired that bullet.

Shaikh 'Abd al-'Aleem embraced his son. Then he took out some banknotes and offered them, as the price of the ox, to Ma'mun, who threw them down on the ground with utter contempt and went off on his way, alone, his head bowed, as though he'd done nothing at all.

I never saw Shaikh 'Abd al-'Aleem as despised and humiliated as he was at that moment.

—*Translated by May Jayyusi and Christopher Tingley*

'Ali al-Du'aji (1909–1949)

Tunisian short-story writer 'Ali al-Du'aji was mainly self-taught. He belonged to a group of Tunisian writers in the forties that included the poet Mustafa Khrayyif and the famous folk poet Muhammad Bairam al-Tunisi, all of whom led a kind of Bohemian life. Du'aji's collection of short stories, *My Sleepless Nights*, was published posthumously in 1969, but during his lifetime he published an interesting account of a boat cruise around the

Mediterranean, which appeared in *Al-'Alam al-Adabi* review between September 1935 and February 1936 and was titled *A Cruise Around the Taverns of the Mediterranean*. Du'aji died of tuberculosis.

MY SLEEPLESS NIGHTS

The aunt is so fat that parts of her body move independently as she climbs the stairs. She is breathless, heavily sweating, and calling out jokingly to her niece before she can even see her, "Where are you? Where? This is not a stairway, it is certainly the narrow road to heaven! Where are you, young woman? Damn this fat, it does not even allow me to breathe!"

"Auntie! May you be safe! Please sit down, here is the comfortable chair you like. First let me kiss you."

She kisses her before the aunt sits down and unveils her face. Staring at her niece, she asks, "Zakiyya, what is this? Why are your eyes swollen? Were you crying?"

"I can't hide anything from you, my auntie. That is how it is."

"What made my dear one cry? Tell your loving aunt what happened! Why would you cry in the second year of your marriage? Ah, but you have your mother's character—she, who is now in the world of truth while we dwell in the world of illusion. She used to love crying, may her soul rest in peace. Tell your aunt what happened to you ... "

"I live in hell as you have wanted me to live, ever since you tossed me into the hellfire of this marriage."

"Is it because of your husband?!"

"My husband? Better to call him my executioner. He has the heart of one. Every day he kills something in me. You will find me stiff and dead upon your next visit; unless I melt before that and stream away in tears."

"Take it easy! Tell me step by step what has happened between you two."

"He is a malicious stupid man, an alcoholic who gets drunk every night. He comes home after midnight to pester me and my son. Oh, if only we did not have our son, Hammadi! Auntie, he would always insult me when he first began drinking, and describe me in the ugliest, most malicious way. He would change between names of the ugliest fish or birds. According to him when drunk, I fell in a category between the peacock and the bat. Or the tuna and that nazli fish with the ugly head. Then he would force me to light the fire and prepare mashlush pancakes for him after two in the morning. If I refused, he called me a donkey who knew nothing about cooking!"

"God have mercy on us! God have mercy! He is a devil! And a loathsome devil at that!"

While the aunt spoke, she was eyeing the closed bedroom door. Casting an inquiring look at her niece, she paused, and Zakiyya answered, "He never wakes up before noon—and when he does, it is just to go back to sleep!"

"To sleep?"

"Yes, among the books and newspapers that take all his time. He talks to me only when he is drunk. If he sobers up, it is only to read books and to write. His papers fill the whole house. He raises hell if one of them is lost. How I wish you'd had me marry someone as illiterate as myself! I cannot bear to live with this man anymore!"

"It sounds unbearable!"

"Would you believe that he returned last evening swaying drunkenly, disgustingly, smelling like a monkey, and then he tripped on a book that Hammadi had thrown on the floor, which I had not noticed. He poured out his anger on the child and slapped him so hard he almost killed him. We had a tug-of-war . . . "

"With the child or the book?"

"The child, Auntie! Hammadi! But he slapped me too."

"He slapped you and you did not mention that first? Oh! This matter is more serious than I thought. How dare he raise his hand against his wife, the mother of his son? This is unbearable. So it has come to slapping! Listen to me, my girl. You're young, so open your ears and listen to the advice of your experienced aunt: I've been married to three husbands, and I know men better than anybody else. The man who beats his wife is not a man! Listen to me, ask for a divorce! We will sue him, request a compensation, and send him to prison. The law and all the laws of the five hundred religions do not give a man the right to slap a weak woman. You must ask for a divorce! I am telling you, it is not possible to have a regular life after a man slaps his wife."

"So divorce it will be."

"Could you bear to continue living with this boorish man? You said he was stupid and I said to myself, it does not matter, he is like any other man. You said he called you animal names, I said to myself, it does not matter, he could change his appellations and life with him would improve. You called him a drunkard and I said to myself, never mind, his liver will enlarge and he will have to abandon alcohol. You said he likes to read books and I thought, she is seeing his books as her rival and they are better than a human rival. But now that you mention bad treatment and beating, there is nothing but divorce. I will see that you get it in the easiest manner possible."

"How, Auntie?

Staring at her own plump wrists stuffed inside her silver bracelets, the aunt spoke. "If your blood is like the blood that runs in my veins—if your blood is not composed of water, sugar, and orange juice—and if you are really the daughter of my lioness sister Monjiyya, may her soul rest in peace, you will jump to your feet now, collect your things, and come with me. I will take care of the rest."

Embarrassedly, Zakiyya turns her eyes towards the door of the bedroom, then looks down. "Auntie, speak more softly!"

But her aunt is carried away. Trembling, she shouts angrily, "Why should I speak softly? I shall raise my voice and my hand! Speak softly for whom, pray tell me?"

"So you won't ... disturb him."

"Disturb whom?"

"Him. Let him have some sleep, he stayed up very late last night."

—*Translated by Aida A. Bamia and Naomi Shihab Nye*

Tawfiq al-Hakim (1898–1987)

Famous Egyptian dramatist, novelist, and short-story writer Tawfiq al-Hakim was born in Alexandria and studied both in Alexandria and Cairo. When in Cairo, he discovered his love of theater and attended many performances by the most famous Egyptian actors of his day. He also studied at the Berlitz School in Cairo where he read a great amount of French literature. Later on, after obtaining a degree in law, he went to France for his doctorate. Al-Hakim was one of the strong links between Arabic and Western literature and utilized his experiences in the West not only through his creative writings as in his novel *A Bird from the East* but also in his thorough knowledge and admiration of European literature, which he transmitted in many ways to his Arab readers and admirers. He went back to Egypt in 1928 and was employed as deputy public prosecutor in the Egyptian provinces, an experience that produced his lovely novel, *Diaries of a Public Prosecutor in the Countryside* (1937). He began his novelistic career with *Return of the Spirit* (1933). However, his influence as a playwright has been very great and was essential in laying a firm basis for a mature theater in Arabic. As part of his general literary oeuvre, his fiction mirrors his great versatility and his active interest in all aspects of life and in all moods of living, mixing tragedy with comedy, showing the absurd and the realistic. A man of great gifts and charm, Al-Hakim also became famous as an antifeminist but remains one of the cornerstones of modern Arabic literature in its various aspects of fiction and drama.

THE MAILMAN

It was by the seashore that I came across him: an odd fellow, carrying a bag just like those that mailmen use. His whole air was one of languor and stupidity—even the weary way he looked up at the sky put you in mind of an imbecile. He had the bearing of someone who was totally exhausted, at war with himself and the whole world. His vocabulary, I reckoned, would be exhausted after the single word "Ugh!"

I went over to talk to him.

"If I'm not mistaken," I said, "you're a mailman on his day off."

He didn't even bother to look up.

"Day off!" he retorted contemptuously, obviously trying to swallow his annoyance.

"Why not?" I said. "Don't you get time off each week?"

"I've never had a day off in my life."

"But how can the Post Office do that? Don't they have a system for time off?"

"My dear sir, the Post Office doesn't know what time off is."

"What do you mean?"

"Just consider, my dear sir. I get up every morning at dawn, along with the birds, and grab my bag, which is stuffed to overflowing with as many letters as there are grains of sand. Every living man and woman on earth must have a letter in it, and I'm the one who's supposed to do the rounds and give a letter to every one of them, all delivered to the proper place, till the day comes to an end. The bag has to be empty by then—so it can be filled up all over again next day, with fresh letters, all to be delivered once more, one by one, to the proper place. It just goes on and on, day after day; the people never go away and the bag's never empty. In fact the only thing that ever gets exhausted is my patience. But what can I do? If I didn't keep working, the letters would pile up, over two days, and then I'd really be in trouble."

"But that's incredible!" I said. "Doesn't the Post Office have any other mailmen?"

"No. There's only me. I am the Post Office."

"How has that come about? Is it mismanagement or just plain negligence?"

"Don't ask me. I keep complaining how overworked I am, but I might as well talk to thin air. As you can see, things have got so bad now I just don't care any more."

"But can you really deliver all those letters in one day?"

"I just deliver them at random. A person can only be expected to do so much. No one's ever called me to account for any mistakes I've made—and I must have made a lot, of course. The main thing is, when I come back at the end of the day, there are never any letters left in my bag."

As he spoke, he opened his bag, almost as though he'd just remembered it was still there. Looking inside, I saw he really did have a lot of letters.

"How are you going to get all those delivered?" I asked. "It's already twelve o'clock."

"Don't worry. I'll just do what I do every day."

Close by was a fisherman, who hadn't managed to catch anything since he started early that morning. The mailman thrust out his hand toward the man and shoved several dozen letters in his pocket. A moment later the fisherman, to his astonished delight, was hauling his net from the sea with a huge catch of fish inside, while another group of fishermen, a little way off, was still vainly trying to land a single fish. I pointed toward these other people.

"But what about them?" I asked.

"They're too far away," he said irritably, glancing in their direction. "I told you, I'm tired. Why should I have to go and give every one of them a letter? I've given theirs to this fisherman here."

"Do you always treat people's letters like that?"

"Of course I do. Do you think I'm stupid enough to strain my joints and get all out of breath chasing after every creature God put on this earth? If I don't come across people, I give their letters to the ones I do happen to meet. That way I get a bit of rest, in God's safe keeping!"

At that moment a peevish-looking old hag with a dreadful voice came by and, taking a lottery ticket from her pocket, yelled at the newspaper seller to check for her number in the paper. The way she kept bossing the poor man around made cursing and swearing sound polite. Meanwhile a whole bevy of lovely girls in bathing costumes came running along the sands behind her, waving their glistening arms. They had lottery tickets too and wanted to check their numbers. As the old hag approached the mailman, he took a thousand letters out of his bag and stuffed them in her pocket, and a moment later she found her ticket had won first prize, worth thousands of pounds. Her fearful voice rang out in a cry of triumph and victory and sheer joy!

This was too much for me. "Don't you have any decency?" I exclaimed. "Or if common justice means nothing to you, can't you at least show a bit of sense? Look at that ugly old hag. She's so repulsive she couldn't make a grave laugh. How can you give her all that wealth, when there are all those gorgeous young girls just a few feet away, overflowing with energy and youth and full of the joys of life? Life's one long happiness for them. Doesn't just looking at them make you want to break into a smile?"

"Stop bothering me!" he replied, shoving me to one side. "If I had to tell the difference between spring and autumn, or say who's ugly and who's beautiful, or work out who deserves things and who doesn't, I'd never get my day's work done!"

"But doesn't everyone have a letter with you? And doesn't each man's letter give him the same chance as his brother?"

"I told you," he yelled, "I can only do so much! Show a bit of pity, can't you? Isn't there anyone, in heaven and earth, who'll show me some pity, or at least some understanding? Up in heaven they keep telling me my negligence is making people furious with them. And here you are, down on earth, shouting how this person should get something and that one shouldn't. I'm the one who ought to be complaining. I've been working so hard for so long, generation after generation, I can hardly see any more and my brain's scrambled. Listen, all you dear people. My eyes are still just about capable, God be praised, of making you out, and I still hand out what's in my bag, day after day. And that's all I can do!

If I happen to meet someone, or they bump into me, I thrust my hand down in my bag, bring out whatever I can take hold of in my fingers, and give it to them. It's all a matter of chance, according to what comes up. If I were to try and give every man the same share as his brother, I'd find my legs wouldn't move fast enough. I'd break down. You can go on as long as you like, saying how I'm lazy, or unfair, or negligent, but you won't change the way I do things. If people have complaints, they can yell them to the whole world for all I care—it won't make a jot of difference. There have been more complaints about me than there are grains of sand on this beach."

With that the "mailman" went off from the beach, leaving me to my reflections. Then the joyful shouts of the lucky fisherman and the old hag's peals of laughter brought me back to reality. I ran after the fellow.

"Hey," I yelled, like a madman. "Mailman, wait! I forgot to ask you. Could I have some of your letters? Please? Dig me out a handful from your bag!"

He'd vanished. I went and sat on the beach, burying my hand in the sand in sheer despair and biting my nails in my frustration.

"What a fool I am!" I thought. "There was good fortune right next to me, his bag full to overflowing, ready to give me everything I needed. But no! I had to be all philosophical and forget about my practical interests. And that stopped fortune giving me anything. We wasted our time talking—and time was all I got. If I hadn't kept pestering him with my ideas, he would have stretched his hand out to me, and I'd be another Rothschild, or Rockefeller, or Qarun!"[1]

—Translated by Roger Allen and Christopher Tingley

Yahya Haqqi (1905–1993)

Born to a poor family in Cairo, Egyptian short-story writer and critic Yahya Haqqi won a scholarship to the Cairo School of Law, graduating in 1926. Soon after, he began a long and distinguished career in the diplomatic service, representing his country in several Middle Eastern and European capitals. Other than his own language, he was proficient in English, French, Italian, and Turkish. On the literary level, Haqqi is regarded as a pioneer of the short story in Egypt, which he began writing in 1923, but it was not

---

1. "Qarun": A minister of one of the Pharaohs, notorious for his arrogance and oppression. In the folk history of the Arabs he is proverbial for enormous wealth.

until 1944 that he published his famous work, *The Lamp of Um Hashim*, which reflected his deep interest in Eastern and Western patterns of cultural interaction and was translated into English by M. M. Badawi under the title of *The Saint's Lamp and Other Stories* (1973). In 1955, the year he published *The Postman*, he became director of the Department of Fine Arts in Cairo, then counselor for the National Library. His other fiction includes *Antar and Juliette* (1961); *A Suitcase in the Hand of a Traveler* (1969); *The Empty Bed and Other Stories*; *People in the Shadow* (1971); and *Blood and Mud*, three novellas translated into English by Pierre Cachia (1999). Miriam Cooke translated another collection, *Good Morning and Other Stories* (1987). Throughout his writing career, Haqqi reflected a deep interest in developing a sense of identity, and although not a prolific writer, he is considered a cornerstone in Egyptian fiction. In 1975 Egyptian literary circles celebrated half a century of his career.

THE DIVINING STONES

I don't believe in fortune-telling. I refuse even to consider it. I don't understand how anyone can believe in those people who read the sands—people who, most of the time, simply draw the lines as they want to, as many as they want, and could just as easily make them foretell evil as the good fortune they claim to see.

Then there are the cards. Just who laid down that the ace means a letter, the three a trip and the four a house? Who on earth decided all that? And what's to stop their meaning changing just like that, so that, if the fortune-teller says you're going to get a letter, it means you'll be going on a trip; or, if she congratulates you on some money coming your way, she's actually predicting your bankruptcy? I don't see how the life of a human being can be linked up with the numbers on playing cards.

And worse still is the coffee cup. How can someone's fortune, his very future even, be bound to a particular kind of coffee and how thick it is? A fortune-teller once told this man how she'd seen great turmoil in his cup. "I'm not surprised," he said. "That coffee I've just drunk came from the Congo."

All this was going through my head as I sat on a low straw chair in front of the old Sudanese woman who spreads her stones near the enchanted fountain. I'd been visiting her every Saturday for a year—she didn't spread them on Fridays. I'd learned from experience that the stones were lively and truthful in the early part of the week, not talking evasively or holding anything back. Later, though, and towards the end of the week especially, they'd get monotonous and irritable. You had the impression they were bored with words and tired out by people's trivial concerns: all they'd see in front of them was a greedy man eager to get his hands on something he hadn't earned, or a coward fearful of some imagined danger, or scheming women whose hearts are opened up, and—lo and behold—all their declared friendship to neighbors and acquaintances is actually bitter enmity and lasting hatred.

Here's what the old woman told me this time:

"A man and a woman," she said, "are living happily together. But there's a tall, dark woman coming to destroy their peace. In two somethings' time you'll receive a formal paper from the government. I see you in your home now. You'll be getting some new furniture."

I knew who the tall, dark woman was—Umm Mahmoud, the stupid, coarse-grained peddler woman who, not content with plunging my wife in debt, had developed a hold over her and started dragging her off on trips I knew nothing about. I'd warned my wife never to let the woman set foot in the house again, then pawned my watch and chain to pay back the debts.

What about the paper, though—the one I was supposed to be getting from the government? Would it be a letter appointing me to the job I'd worn my shoes out trying to land? I hoped the two "somethings" would be two days, not two months or two years, God forbid!

As for the new furniture, the stones had certainly unearthed one of my fondest wishes, one I'd been hiding deep down inside me: I'd decided some time back that, within a month of getting a job, I'd buy a new mat and a new bed.

The stones filled me with a sense of security, and I started believing in them more than before. If only, I thought, all those people who believed in coffee cups and cards and sand could give up their stupid beliefs and trust in divining stones! Could there, after all, be a more graphic symbol of bustling, endlessly clashing humanity than the stones you could hear rattling in this woman's hand? There, in front of you, were a man and a woman together; then they were separated by, say, a man who tempted the woman, and a dark woman who tempted the man. Wasn't the whole problem of life summed up in that? As for this emerald green stone, didn't it obviously denote wealth beyond one's wildest dreams? The divining stones didn't lie, and consulting them cost a mere twenty khurdas. If you picked up that sum in the street, you wouldn't (as the fortune-teller pointed out) be ecstatic at what you'd found; but you had to consider what it bought you from the stones themselves.

When I got home, my wife came to help me take off my jacket.

"Didn't I tell you," I said, speaking slowly and calmly, "that Umm Mahmoud wasn't to come in here?"

To my astonishment she went pale with shock. Then she rushed out, opened the door onto the stairs, and started screaming down at our neighbor on the first floor.

"Hey, Sitt Asma," she yelled. "Can't you ever keep your mouth shut? Eh? Do you stand guard outside our door, or what?"

Then she poured out a stream of insults so bitter and venomous even I was surprised. And so the first part of the stones' prophecy had been fulfilled. Now, I thought, let the second part come true, and quickly. Let the government send me the papers I'd been waiting for.

On the Monday a little boy came up.

"There's a man downstairs," he said. "Well-dressed. He wants to see you."

I went down, and there was a stranger with a bundle of papers under his arm and, in his hand, an ebony writing instrument fitter to write hieroglyphics than Arabic. My heart started pounding.

"What can I do for you?" I asked

"I'm delivering a summons," he said. "Will you put your signature or seal on this?"

"What is it?"

"A lawsuit filed by Sitt Asma, against you and your wife, for publicly insulting her. The case comes up next Thursday."

As I climbed the stairs, the full force of the disaster struck me. I went in through my door ready for a blazing row.

"Well," I said, "are you happy now? The two days have passed. The quarrel was the day before yesterday, two days ago exactly! By God, the stones were telling the truth, but it wasn't the truth I'd been looking for!"

Next morning there was another quarrel between my wife and the neighbor. My blood boiled.

"Do you want to bring me a new lawsuit every two days?" I demanded.

"Don't get so worked up, my darling," she snapped back. "You'll soon be seeing the back of me."

She rushed out in a fury, and there I was. I'd wanted to prevent a suit that would have cost me fifty piasters, and instead I'd saddled myself with alimony, confiscation, and imprisonment; for, while I was out, two policemen burst into the house, along with some of my wife's relatives and four porters, and carried off all the furniture.

When I got back, I found totally bare walls—they hadn't even left the pitcher. I stood there dumbstruck.

"Is that what the stones meant by new furniture?" I thought.

—*Translated by May Jayyusi and Christopher Tingley*

Ja'far al-Khalili (1914–1984)

Iraqi scholar, essayist, writer of fiction, journalist, encyclopedist, and biographer Ja'far al-Khalili was one of the few old guard littérateurs who excelled in many fields of creativity and research. Born in Najaf, the center of Shi'ism in

Iraq, he moved to Baghdad where he followed a successful career as a journal-ist, founding his own paper, *Al-Hatif,* which was a central medium not only for political and social commentary but also for literary exchange, guided by its editor's fine taste in both poetry and narrative. Among his major works is his *Encyclopedia of the Holy Muslim Shrines* (1965), which was published in many volumes. He also wrote on Iraqi dates, and on social conditions in Iraqi prisons. Among his works of fiction are *From Over the Hill* (1949), *Lost* (1948), *Al-Khalili's Children* (1955), *Confessions,* and *Those People* (1966).

GRACE

Life grew narrower and narrower in the eyes of Miz'il al-Fahham, the coalman, for his family kept growing, the number of children increasing rapidly, and he felt more and more overwhelmed.

Before becoming a coalman, he had tried his hand at several other profes-sions with little success. Now he was middle-aged, past his mid-forties, and still at square one where he had started as a young man. He had just one suit of clothes for the winter and another for the summer and had been in debt since his marriage. Although some people might consider his debt small, Miz'il found it oppressive and was at a loss as to how to repay it, since his income seemed increasingly slight.

He had worked two years in construction, another two as a farmer in a near-by orchard, then five years or more as a seaman on the *Euphrates* transporting goods from one town to another. Later he became a greengrocer for four years, and for the last twelve years he had been a coalman, collecting tree trunks and roots, then kindling them in special holes that he prepared himself according to agreements with the orchard owners. As his children grew up, they helped him dig the holes in the orchards and collect roots and tree trunks, throwing them into the holes in order to kindle them and make them into charcoal. Then he would carry the charcoal to the village or to one of the nearby towns to sell it to householders or retail coal vendors. This work involved profound effort and fatigue, yet he hardly profited enough to sustain himself and his large family. It was because "grace" was lacking.

Miz'il believed "grace" was behind all success in work, otherwise how could some people work together in full cooperation and still not satisfy their needs, except after tremendous toil and effort? Without grace, how could one person effortlessly support twenty people, while twenty people might fail to sustain themselves? Miz'il certainly believed in grace as other people do, and had, since his youth, sought to obtain it through constant prayer and fasting. He tried to avoid hurting anybody or violating others' rights if he ever had to weigh or measure their purchases. He had employed this ideal as a greengrocer, as a con-struction worker, as a farmer, and, now, with his coal. He could give a thousand proofs that if grace were to be removed from even one grain of wheat, a person might eat and eat and never feel satisfied; if it were drained from one drop of water, one might drink and drink without having enough. He believed grace was like an imperceptible but utterly crucial thread in a piece of cloth; if it were to be plucked out, then whole textile factories would not be sufficient to clothe one's body and protect it from heat or cold. Or if life were able to satisfy any without benefit of grace, it would be able to do so only briefly, after which a person would once again be hungry, thirsty, or cold.

For Miz'il and for most people, there was no way to obtain grace but through supplication to God by unceasing prayers, frequent invocations of His charity, and pilgrimages to the tombs of holy men and saints. Miz'il performed these acts with great energy, hoping God would grant him grace, save him and his children their huge efforts, and bless them with some luxury and happiness.

However, time kept passing and here he was, approaching fifty and the mid-autumn of his life if not its end, and God's grace still had not been bestowed on his work or life. Nevertheless, his heart was full of faith, which gave him patience and calm. Then in 1942 the most biter winter in fifty years came along, which would seemingly have been a favorable opportunity for all coalmen, since the price of coal rose to unprecedented heights. Now those who worked in the coal trade could glean double profits and save money for their unknown futures, in case fate should suddenly frown. But the grace Miz'il stubbornly sought evaded him once again; he fell terribly ill, and his sickness consumed his whole family, eating up their assets and lasting so long they couldn't even borrow any more money. His children couldn't work since they spent so much time helping take care of him. The frigid world that looked bright to other coal vendors was black in this family's eyes. For the first time in his life Miz'il felt despair.

For more than a quarter of a century he had been an industrious, pious laborer, always praying to receive the grace of God, but now he had arrived at the point where he feared his end could be worse than his beginning, leaving his family nothing but misery! What was he to do? He was nearly well again, but where could he seek that grace that he might clutch it with both hands and never let it go? His wife had become extremely tired of their life and was bored with her husband's ardent prayers for grace. She had even come to loathe the very word and had threatened to leave her husband and go to live with her own relatives if he ever said it again. She insisted "grace" was nothing but the cleverness to beat life. Cleverness alone was the way people gained profit and the tranquillity that accompanies material success; it was obvious. People hid behind the notion of "grace" to escape other people's jealousy at their cleverness.

When his wife said all this, she wept. Miz'il's doubts were ignited again; maybe grace was, indeed, an illusion, and the solution—if solution there be—lay in seeking to trick life. He needed his remaining strength to discover the secret of the grace in the one grain, the unseen drop of water, and the woven cloth. But how could he discover this trick? Perhaps he needed to make some radical change in his thinking; if not, he would continue to fail at everything he did. The coal business was never going to secure his family's future.

That evening, after facing his wife's rebellion, he thought very hard, pondering the issue from all aspects until he finally decided what to do. He would not even confide his decision to his wife until it succeeded.

Next morning, Miz'il awakened early and woke his whole family. In a trembling state of terror he said he had seen in his dream a most dignified and awesome-looking man who told him he was al-Khidr, one of God's saints, an *imam* who was buried in their own house, precisely in the front corner past the entry, and that he, Miz'il, should erect a tomb for him there, and give people a chance to see it.

News of Miz'il's dream spread quickly. He was known to be a very pious man whom no one had ever known to lie, so Miz'il's story attracted immediate attention. The village people were happy to discuss this new *imam* and proud their village had acquired the mystique of other holy towns. The next day Miz'il told the people he had seen the *imam* again. He looked as he had the first night and repeated his demand that a holy tomb be erected for him. News spread that day even more widely in the village till everyone had heard. On the third day Miz'il confirmed that it had become an unavoidable duty to build the tomb. The *imam* had angrily threatened to remove all grace from the village if its inhabitants did not hurry to construct a proper memorial. Naturally, the idea of grace being removed was a horrendous prospect to the village people.

Miz'il asked the help of the village people. In a few days a tomb had been built for this new *imam* and a legion of candles placed over it. These candles were donated by a village woman who, upon hearing of this new *imam*, had pledged that if her only son be cured of the fever and illness that had plagued him for two days, she would bring candles. Since her wish was answered the same day she made it, she kept her promise. News of this miracle quickly spread. Since almost everyone had a wish or a desire, many people tried this method of pledging with the *imam*. And since many of the wishes were logical ones, within nature's bounds, they had a good chance of coming true in the near future; with the grace of the new *imam*, many were answered. People invariably made good their pledges, so that in a few months the news of this new *imam* had spread to neighboring towns and villages and he became well-known for answering, in the quickest possible time, the prayers of many people. Stories of him often pointed toward the miraculous, and people hurried toward the shrine in groups, or alone, begging the tomb for what they needed. "Grant our wishes, alleviate our pain, cure this disease!" Pledges mounted, as did presents, and Miz'il and his family had a large share of all of it, with the grace of the new *imam*. In only one year after the *imam*'s appearance, Miz'il, who was now known a Shaikh Miz'il as a reward for his service to the *imam*, had built a large house with an entire wing dedicated to the continually arriving guests.

Many traditions now grew concerning the *imam*'s visitation, to which visitors had to adhere. Shaikh Miz'il asked a clergyman to compose a greeting that each visitor could use at the beginning of his visit. The man wrote for him this line, which was engraved with beautiful calligraphy on a silver plate. It became tradition for the visitor to say it as he entered the room where the tomb was:

"Peace and God's mercy and His grace be on you,
O good servant of God and His Prophet."

And when the visitor spoke the word "grace" Shaikh Miz'il and his wife and children would secretly laugh. He had eventually revealed to them "the secret of grace," which he now believed to be the only effective form of grace possible.

Mahmoud Taher Lashin (1895–1945)

An Egyptian short-story writer, Mahmoud Taher Lashin was born in Cairo in the famous popular quarter of al-Sayyida Zainab. He studied and practiced engineering but demonstrated genuine love for literature, helped to this by his knowledge of both French and English and his readings in these two literatures. His stories, published in various magazines show the direct influence of Western literature on his work. He was also a socially oriented writer, concentrating on a social reality that was beginning to show a growing consciousness toward a better control over life and a slow discovery of the flaws in an inherited social culture that was at odds with evolving modern times. Although he chose eminently serious social topics for his stories—marriage problems, polygamy, drunkenness, and prostitution— he, like many fiction writers of the pre-1950 era, was able to introduce into his stories a touch of humor that was both refreshing and entertaining. Three collections of his short stories have been published: *The Sarcasm of the Flute* (1926), *It Is Related . . .* (1928), and *The Flying Veil* (1940).

"Hello"

The time: morning. The place: a spacious room with four desks to accommodate the same number of functionaries. One of the desks, in the most prominent place, was for a large man of majestic demeanor—the chief you'd guess, and you'd be right. At a desk to the right was the youthful figure of Farid Effendi, who took pride in his father's wealth and the post he himself held; while a third place, opposite the first, had, for countless years now, been assigned to Af-fifi Effendi Mandour, a man with bluish-white hair, disheveled eyebrows and mustache, and a dried-up face, appearance, and speech, but who wasn't, thankfully, a man of any great importance in the office and doesn't figure too much in this story.

A wall clock above the door chimed nine. Farid Effendi threw aside the newspaper he'd been studying and gracefully bent his arm to reveal, below the sleeve of his silk shirt, a gold watch and a bracelet of the same metal, both perfectly and exquisitely made. When he'd checked to see the two timepieces tallied, he said, "What on earth's happened to Yusuf Effendi?"

Neither the wonder nor the question was directed at anyone in particular, but Affifi Effendi took it on himself to answer.

"It's not the first time, is it, Sayyid Farid?" he said, his eyebrows and mustaches dancing about. "What do you expect anyway, from someone like that? Do you think a man who spends his nights playing around, along with people as debauched as he is, is going to be punctual in his job? Or any use at all for that matter?"

The chief and Farid Effendi exchanged disparaging smiles, realizing well enough this old, old man was hitting at them with his word "debauched." Affifi Effendi's loud comments sank to a mutter, then to a mere wordless movement of his jaws.

After a while Farid Effendi got up, went to the chief's desk and bent over it so that the two tarboushes touched and the two cuff links seemed to be playing together. Yusuf, he whispered, had spent the night before moving on from one tavern to the next, getting in a worse and worse state, till he just didn't seem the same person any more. He'd bellowed out songs in the street, or demonstrated the Charleston, and delivered speeches in Arabic and every other language under the sun; and when he finally got home, he'd shouted and hurled abuse. He couldn't, he said, stand the sight of his wife a moment longer, and he'd yelled, at the top of his voice, that—

At this point the talking stopped as the door opened and Yusuf Effendi, tall and broad-shouldered, entered the room with a rather unsuccessful attempt at a smile and greeted everyone.

He threw himself down on his chair with a weary air, and the chief asked him, sarcastically, if he was just pretending to be tired so as not to be called to account for his lateness, while Affifi Effendi sniggered, sniffed, and made every sort of malicious insinuation with his eyes. Farid Effendi moved over to where his friend was sitting, with a host of questions quivering on his lips, but Yusuf Effendi saved him the trouble of asking any of them.

"I've divorced her," he said.

The chief banged his desk.

"What's that, Yusuf Effendi?" he said.

"It's all over," Yusuf answered, briefly but firmly, opening his palms as if to say there was nothing he could do about it any more. Then he rang the bell, told the office boy to get him some coffee, and lit a cigarette. The chief, horrified by Yusuf Effendi's air of indifference, nervously shifted his huge fifteen-horse-power body and favored the desk with another bang (which he enjoyed hugely, since the force and manner of the blow so obviously fitted his role as office head). "Vous êtes fou," he said in French, following this with the Arabic translation, "You're mad." As for Farid, he stared at Yusuf in consternation, his cheeks trembling.

"What about the sixty *feddans*, you fool?" he said.

Yusuf Effendi knew deep down he'd done something crazy. The idea of the sixty *feddans* leapt into his mind, almost cracking his head open. Still, he tried to laugh it off.

"Crazy, sensible, what does it matter?" he said. "It's over and done with now."

Soon, though, the regret gnawing at his heart grew unbearable and, in an effort to assuage it, he put his cup of coffee aside unfinished and started pacing up and down the room, wiping his broad forehead with his handkerchief, then using it to pat his full lips.

The chief asked Affifi Effendi what he thought of the matter, and Affifi Effendi didn't let his chief down.

"The man's depraved," he said promptly. "He's crazy. He doesn't deserve any sympathy."

Farid yelled to try and silence him, while the wretched Yusuf, advancing, would have relieved his depression by attacking him if a shout from the chief hadn't finally held him back. Even so, his feelings found their outlet through a torrent of words, as he talked endlessly of the hell he'd lived in, of all the subtle varieties of torment he'd suffered and described to them day after day. All right, he'd married partly out of greed, and, all right, he'd been avidly looking to get something from his father-in-law, a gift or else something when he died. But five years had gone by now, five years that were just five joined-up fetters of constant quarreling and misery and pain, and he was plunged in debt, all through the extravagance of that woman who was so proud of the sixty *feddans* she'd inherit. He'd started drinking too much, too, to try and find a bit of relief, and, just to put the cap on things, all three babies she'd borne had died, victims of her ignorance and neglect—and there was that decrepit father-in-law of his, with his creaking joints, and weak heart, and bad stomach, and hardened arteries, still existing on this earth where he wasn't properly alive or dead. What? Was this the sort of miserable prison to spend your young years in? Down with wealth, and long live freedom!

With this ringing proclamation Yusuf ended his speech—or his defense rather—and the words, and the passionate manner, and the resounding voice made Farid clap as if he was in a front seat at the opera house. Then he got up and shook Yusuf by the hand. "Bravo," he said in Italian, then, in English, "shake on it." "You're a hero!" he added in Arabic.

Yusuf slumped in his chair and started smoking a second cigarette (the first had burned to ash on the edge of the table). The chief gazed at him, his eyes full of sympathetic understanding. As for Affifi Effendi, he just narrowed his eyes but, thankfully, said nothing.

Farid Effendi made a stab at some jokes, to try and cheer his friend up, but his wit failed him. Then, as Yusuf's air grew grimmer with each puff of his cigarette, the others tried to look busy with the papers on their desks so as to avoid conversation. Finally Yusuf threw his stub into an earthenware bowl with sand in it, shrugged his shoulders to dismiss what had happened (and what was going to happen), unlocked his drawer and took out his work, as if it was just another day.

A few minutes passed; then the telephone rang. The chief lifted the receiver. "Yes, Effendi," he said. "Yes, he's here."

He turned to Yusuf and passed him the receiver.

"Hello," Yusuf said. "Yes, this is Yusuf Effendi speaking. Who's that, please? Hello? Oh, emergency. I think you must have the wrong number. Yes, this is Yusuf Effendi . . . Hello. Who? Could you speak a bit louder, please. He was coming here, you say? Hello. Hello. Keep the line open please, operator, What? A crash in a taxi? He's dead?"

Yusuf flung down the receiver, which, instead of slotting back in its place, started whirling about on its cord just above the floor. Then he said, with a stunned air, "Would you believe it? Her father's just died. Today."

There was a general, grim silence, broken only by Affifi Effendi, who muttered, "No more than you deserve!"

—*Translated by Salwa Jabsheh and Christopher Tingley*

Ibrahim 'Abd al-Qadir al-Mazini (1890–1949)

Egyptian critic, writer of fiction, poet, and essayist Ibrahim 'Abd al-Qadir al-Mazini was a member of the renowned Diwan Group with 'Abbas M. al-'Aqqad and 'Abd al-Rahman Shukri and, like them, wrote in many genres. Starting out as a poet with strong romantic tendencies, he shifted in the 1920s to prose writing, cultivating a style that became famous for its humor and engaging portrayal of human situations. Among his books of fiction was *Ibrahim al-Katib* (1931), an almost autobiographical account that won fame on a pan-Arab scale in the 1930s and was later translated into English by Magdi Wahba as *Ibrahim the Writer* (1976). Other works of fiction were *The Magic Box of the World* (1929), *Cobwebs* (1935), *Thirty Men and a Woman* (1943), and another semi-autobiographical novel, *Ibrahim II* (1943), a sequel to *Ibrahim the Writer*.

HOW I BECAME A DEMON OF THE JINN

When I was a teenager, I tried my hand at everything, taking any opportunity that came my way. I only used to think about the moment in which I was living, hungry for my share of life, anxious to get my fill of it. One marvelous summer's night I was wending my way home in the early morning hours—we lived in the Saliba quarter—after a whole night of drinking and listening to music and songs. When I arrived at my threshold, I realized my ninety-year-old grandmother was the only person home and I didn't have the key with me. I said to myself, "Should I disturb my grandmother? She can only rise with the greatest difficulty, and when she walks anywhere, she moves along the walls so she can prop herself up. I should let her rest and go join up with the rest of my family—my mother and brother—after all, the weather is clear and it will be a refreshing walk."

So I turned my back on the door and left. In those days the road to the Imam Shafii mosque had not yet been paved; there were no trams or lights, and no one path was any better than another. So I chose the shortest route, which passed by the Sayyida Nafisa mosque, cut through the graveyard, and eventually merged with the public road again at the other end. I started stumbling along and kept bumping into things because there were so many graves, scattered haphazardly yet all crowded together. It was hard to find my way in the dark. Yet I didn't really bother or think about this; I just entrusted things to my two legs, which proceeded, moving and stumbling along as they did every day and every night.

I remember I was singing the tunes of that evening, which were still alive in my head and heart. One piece kept on eluding me and I felt that my walking intruded on my finding the correct notes. So I stopped, leaned my back against a tombstone, and tried singing it again. I can still picture myself there in my mind today, even though I thought nothing of it at the time; it did not impress me then as a dramatic situation. Why should a lad intoxicated by music and wine bother to think about graves and what they contained?

In the prime of life, when does a man ever really think about death, even though it is a reality close to him? There is no running away from it and no way to avoid its eventual encounter, yet young people look upon death—when it occasionally occurs to them—as they might consider something hidden behind a mountain, without understanding it. It is simply something unknown and far away. Our attention is busy with the climb to the top of the mountain and all the wondrous things encountered on these fascinating slopes! Later, nearer the summit, conjectures about what lies beyond the peak begin crowding into his head and the meaning and gravity of death occur to him bit by bit. Later these thoughts may dominate a mind entirely; after all, the long climb may have sapped the strength and wrecked the body. So toward the top one may become rather stupid, facing the thought of death with a spirit of helpless despair that eclipses any sense of oblivion or personal alarm.

So, anyway, I stood for a while, singing over the grave, projecting my voice into the darkness without bothering about the cluttered tombs or the remains buried beneath me. Once all these people had, like me, been in the prime of their lives, showing all the ignorance of youth, filled with joy and singing, not thinking about that all-embracing oblivion that is the fate of every living creature. Even now, I am still amazed at how I ignored death when I was right in the middle of its motionless sea! Youth is indeed a mercy. What would life be like if our thoughts were filled with death from the cradle to the grave? In such a case everything would be unbearable; men could cease all their endeavors and efforts, however fascinating, immediately. What would be the good of life, the point of any effort, the consolation for all striving, if thoughts of this abyss continually swallowed up mankind? Death is despair, and God has been merciful enough to let life be more powerful. Man's feeling for it is stronger, so it has more control over him.

Youth is a bursting force. Life in youth possesses a sweet magical novelty. In middle age life becomes something familiar, consisting of habitual experiences; now, man feels less alarm when he thinks of someday giving up this life and all its familiar tastes. Some don't even like the taste by now! Were it not that life is a habit like everything on earth, and people are used to being alive and breathing air, they would not consider it a burden to die and be cut off from the world. Habit and fantasy grow along with life and one's feeling for oneself, which is what makes death so hard, makes people sad at the thought of leaving the world. With children and animals, it is the opposite.

As I stood there singing, I spotted a figure approaching—I had no doubt it was a man, since no woman would dare, except in very rare circumstances—walk around these graves at night. I stopped singing, suddenly nervous. It occurred to me he might be a thief, or if he were not, this desolate quiet spot might entice him to robbery. But then I calmed down, thinking, "What am I worrying about? I have nothing on me worth stealing; I have only a few piastres, which won't make him rich if he gets them and won't make me poor if I lose them. Anyway, I am very light and can run fast, and I know all the entrances and exits; I don't think he could catch up with me if I took off with both feet flying. So there is nothing to fear from this approaching person, whoever he may be."

It didn't seem sensible to panic; it would show clearly in my voice and movements, which would only encourage him if he were a sinister character. Prudence demanded, nevertheless, that I hide behind a secluded grave, so I could see him without his seeing me, determine what kind of person he was, and wait until he would be walking in front of me with me behind him—that would be the stronger position, I thought.

Approaching was an old shaikh with a white beard; in his hand he carried a rosary, and he was reciting the name of God and passages from the Quran or something, although I could not really hear him. It annoyed me that this feeble shaikh had startled me, and I felt my inner self moving to take vengeance on him. I let him walk on a little way then sprang out in front of him suddenly, from behind a grave. The poor fellow was terrified and almost collapsed on the ground. I quickly hid myself again, retracing my steps for a grave or two—a distance of a few meters. He was staring all around at nothing. He held himself closely, spat right and left, and raised his voice in a plea to God, seeking refuge from every accursed devil. Then he began reciting again and walking, with me darting stealthily between the graves behind him. His pace quickened and I realized he was still afraid. I leapt to his side once again, stretching out my hand

and tugging at the hair in his beard. He screamed and I ran away to hide. I cut round behind the graves and got in front of him again, almost bursting with suppressed mirth. I waited till he passed by me, then I put my hand out to his waist and tickled him. I swear, the man leapt off the ground as if I had plunged a sword or white-hot iron into his side. I realized the moment was ripe; the poor man's trauma had reached its peak and he had started mixing up the things he was reciting, like someone who cannot remember his words. He was so terrified that he was shouting, "I seek refuge in the devil from . . . " I came up behind him and began making roaring noises, producing the most repulsive sounds I could muster. The poor wretch broke into a run.

In this way, he got away from me. I myself had grown tired of the game and did not attempt a chase. I walked calmly along, brushing the dust off my clothes, and eventually came out on the public road.

After a quarter of an hour or so, I reached the Imam Shafii mosque just as the muezzin was about to chant the call to prayer in his banal tone. People were arriving, making preparation for their dawn prayer, and I saw my friend the shaikh surrounded by a whole group of people. He was exclaiming, "It was like a black cat leaping on my shoulders, licking my cheeks, passing between my legs, and climbing inside my *qaftan*! I sought refuge in God, then the earth opened up and it disappeared into the hole, but it came back again, appearing sometimes in the form of a bear on hands and legs, other times like a grave shroud emerging from beneath the tombstones; the veil had been ripped from its face, and its eyes shone, glowing like angry sparks. I kept reciting as much of the Quran as I could, then it wrapped its face in a ragged garment and sank into its grave. I'll never forget its teeth as long as I live . . . They were like burning charcoal, gleaming red, they clattered around in its mouth like gleaming stars! God be praised, who saved me from its clutches . . . "

Someone asked him, "Did you think it was going to strangle you?"

"Going to?" the shaikh replied. "What do you mean, going to? I tell you, he stretched out two arms as long as minarets and came forward, intending to wrap them around me! The spikes on his chest were gleaming like bayonets! If God had not given me the inspiration to recite the Kursi Sura,[1] it would have been I who died."

Someone else said, "You mean it died? That's strange!"

"It was burned," replied the shaikh. "The Kursi Sura burned it to death. Then I kept walking till I reached this road . . . "

He turned around to point to the direction from which he had come, and saw me behind him. Astonished, he cried out, pointing, "That . . . Tha . . . that's . . . "

No one except me understood what he was shouting about or pointing at, while I suppressed the laughter welling up inside me. I looked behind me as

---

1. The Kursi verse is in the chapter of Yasin, the twenty-fifth chapter of the Quran. It is regarded as a central Quranic verse, recited as a prayer to avert evil or to summon good.

though to see what he was pointing at, while the trembling man clung desperately to the people around him. Some asked, "Where? Where? We cannot see anything."

The man wiped his face with his hand and calmed down. "Odd," he said, "very odd indeed . . . this gentleman looks just like it."

I couldn't contain my laughter. "Do you think my face is like a demon's?" I sputtered.

Standing nearby was someone whom I knew, someone both clever and cunning. It was clear he was suspicious and was imagining part of the truth, at least.

"Listen," he said to me. "Which way did you come from?"

I realized what he was getting at and replied, "I came from that direction."

This was a lie, at least a half-truth. But I was afraid it would cause a scandal if the truth came out. He asked, "Did you come via Sayyida Nafisa or the Citadel?"

"Via the Citadel, of course," I replied. "Who would dare to walk among all those graves?"

He mumbled something I did not hear then went away. I was saved. I, who had been a demon of the jinn for one night!

—*Translated by Roger Allen and Naomi Shihab Nye*

Muhammad al-Muwailihi (1858?–1930)

Egyptian author of the *Narrative of 'Isa Ibn Hisham*, Muhammad al-Muwailihi is regarded as the bridge between old Arabic fiction and the rise of modern fiction in Arabic. An erudite writer, political agitator, journalist, and social critic, al-Muwailihi was banished for distributing political pamphlets and, after spending time in Italy, France, and England, lived in Istanbul for several years, returning to Cairo in 1887 where he resumed his career as journalist. Between 1898 and 1902 he serialized his *Narrative of 'Isa Ibn Hisham* on the front page of his family's journal, *Misbah al-Sharq*, evoking the name of 'Isa ibn Hisham, the narrator of Badi' al-Zaman al-Hamadhani's famous tenth-century assemblies *(maqamat)*. These assemblies were one of the most admired narrative genres rediscovered from classical Arabic literature during the early period of the modern Arab literary renaissance. Understandably, the episodes, with their smooth flow of language, subtle social critique, touch of humor, and firm link with the classical tradition met with great success, and the whole work was published in book form in 1907. The initial episodes were enlarged by further episodes describing Paris. Many editions of the book were published in the first three decades of the twentieth century. However, it would be quite a number of decades before the evocation of the classical tradition in modern Arabic fiction would be resumed, as Arab writers were more likely to emulate the West's accomplishments in modern fiction until they were themselves self-confident enough to look into the riches of the classical Arabic fictional tradition. This having now become a well-established and successful approach, al-Muwailihi must be regarded as the major founding fathers of this trend.

THE 'UMDA IN THE TAVERN

'Isa ibn Hisham said: "They went on their way to the tavern they had selected, that trough to which people go to imbibe. As we followed behind them, we were all lost in thought. The Pasha turned toward that great hotel, in fact a veritable al-Khawarnak and al-Sadeer,[1] and noticed the electric lights gleaming brightly like rising suns, so much so that darkest night shone in white raiment and its surface seemed like ebony embossed with silver. The lamp standards looked as though they were tree branches glowing with light rather than lamps. The effect was that each pillar became a ray of daybreak piercing the cavity of darkness—and what a piercing it was! It was as if suns were scattered in pitch darkness and stars throughout the dome of the firmament. Beneath these lights the Pasha spotted rows of men mingling freely with women. Apparently favored by continuing good fortune and enveloped in a becoming opulence, they were sitting opposite each other and lounging on sofas.

"Is this a reception for some social occasion?" the Pasha asked me, "or a banquet at a bridegroom's house? What do you think? Could it perhaps be the soirée for a group of demons who have forsaken the earth's interior for its surface; having forgotten the difference between the sexes, they proceed to get on intimate terms with their fellow humans?"

"Yes," I replied, "these people are devils in human forms. They cross land and sea, cut through hard and rugged earth, and fly in the heavens. They can walk on water, penetrate through mountains, and pulverize peaks, turning hills into lowlands, leveling mounds, making deserts into seas, and changing seas into smoke. They force people in the East to listen to sounds made by people in the West, and bring down the remotest stars for you to see, magnify the tiniest spider, freeze the air, melt stones, start gales, weigh light, try to cure the secret ailments of the intestines, and discover unknown facts about the limbs."

"Tell me more," he said, "about these demons of Solomon who live in this era."

"They're tourists from Western countries," I replied. "They're used to civilized living and regard Oriental people with utter contempt. From a perspective of power, their attitude to Orientals is like that of an eagle on the peaks of Radwa and Thabir staring down at desert grasshoppers and pool frogs."[2] With

---

1. "Two famous mountains," in Arabia (as al-Muwailihi's own footnotes tell us).
2. The original text is "'ayns and ya's," they being two letters of the Arabic alphabet, which begin, according to one version of the alphabet, from "'ayn to ya'," while in the standard one now it begins with an alef.

regard to learning, it's like the great sage, Alexander, having to watch a boy spelling out his alphabet.[3] In the sphere of arts and crafts, it's as though Pheidias the sculptor were watching a builder putting up village hovels. Concerning wealth, it would be like a man with a bunch of keys weighing down his waistband looking at a laborer wiping the sweat from his brow beneath a waterskin. Finally, looking at the qualities of mind, it would be like Socrates the philosopher, who drank poison in his devotion to virtue, looking at Herostratus, someone who in his craving for evil set fire to the temple. These are the kinds of claims they make about themselves."

"But wait a minute!" the Pasha said, "Are they really the way they claim to be?"

"Certainly not!" I replied. "They posture and show off and keep bringing in innovations. Their activities are evil and their knowledge is pernicious. They're the people who rob others of their wages. They plunder territories, cross deserts, and destroy common folk. They're the pirates of the high seas who make other people's blood flow. They're the ones who keep duping us with their finery and swamping us with their cheap trash. It's people like them who are referred to in the Quran when it says, 'They have bewitched people's eyes and terrified them; they have brought a mighty enchantment.'

"When they travel to the East, they can be divided into two categories. The first consists of the leisure classes with modern ideas who are besotted by their own wealth and amused by novelties of civilization. As far as they're concerned, there's nothing left to do. So nature takes revenge on them by exempting them from its usual practice and sees to it that they're beset by the twin diseases of listlessness and boredom. They wander around on their own from one area and country to another; that way, they can be cured of their illness by touring countries that are less civilized than their own and retain their characteristics, albeit on a lower plane.

"The second group consists of scholars, politicians, imperialists, and spies, who use their knowledge and ideas to occupy and control countries, argue with people about their sources of income, and crowd folk out of their land and homes. They're the precursors of destruction, even more deadly to people at peace than the vanguards of armies in wartime."

'Isa ibn Hisham said, "The conversation was interrupted by the arrival of our companions at the tavern. They lined themselves up by the kegs, while we sat down near them and waited to see what would happen. The Playboy kept looking to right and left and then spoke to the waiter:

PLAYBOY: (*to the* WAITER) Hasn't His Highness the Prince honored the place with his presence tonight?
WAITER: He'll be back in a moment.

---

3. A pun using the two types of *S* sound in Arabic: one, which uses the strong-sounding *S*, means "to accompany, to go with"; the other, which uses a soft *S*, means "to drag."

'UMDA: (*astounded*) Do princes come here? Is it proper for us to sit drinking somewhere in the same company as them? Why did you choose this place? Why don't we go somewhere else?

PLAYBOY: Don't worry. We're quite safe here. Just wait and see what I'll do to make sure that you don't leave without the Prince shaking your hand and sitting with you.

'UMDA: Don't make fun of me and crack jokes at my expense. What business have we got with princes?

MERCHANT: (*to the* 'UMDA) Don't think it is so outlandish! Some princes are quite decent and down-to-earth people. It's part of their plan to mix with ordinary folks on equal terms in their various meeting places, as well as through the transactions they make with each other.

'UMDA: (*to the* PLAYBOY) Do you know him already?

PLAYBOY: Of course! Otherwise how could I get to sit with him every night? More often than not, I accompany him to his palace at the end of the evening.

'UMDA: You're exaggerating!

PLAYBOY: No. I'm not. Anyway, here's the proof for you!

'Isa ibn Hisham said, "The Prince came back to his seat and signaled his greetings to him. The Playboy stood up and went over to his table, which was piled high with various sorts of wine and candied sweets. Joining the company around the Prince, he started talking to him in a voice loud enough for the 'Umda to hear from where he was sitting."

PLAYBOY: I hope you're in the best of health and spirits, Sir.

PRINCE: Where have you been? I've asked about you several times.

PLAYBOY: I'm at your service, Sir, whenever you wish. The only thing that has prevented me from hurrying to your exalted company was the fact that I've made the acquaintance of two people, one an 'Umda from the provinces, the other a port Merchant. They've clung to me so that I'd stay with them and have insisted that I go everywhere with them.

ONE OF THE COMPANY: (*joking*) You mean "drag them," don't you?[4]

PRINCE: (*poking fun*) Oh, is there a cattle pen around here?

EVERYONE: (*laughing*) What a superb joke, Sir! How subtle and refined!

PRINCE: I've never learned properly how to crack jokes, but once in a while particular words will come to me by chance.

ONE OF THE COMPANY: (*to* ANOTHER) By God, my friend, do you see how subtle and refined the Prince's wit is, and how effectively he manages to incorporate things into whatever he is saying?

---

4. This speech and that of the Merchant that follows it were not part of the original episode published in the journal but were inserted in the first edition.

ANOTHER OF THE COMPANY: You're being very eloquent tonight! Did you get that phrase from the papers?

PRINCE: (*to the* PLAYBOY) What will you have to drink?

PLAYBOY: Excuse me, Sir, but I must go back to my two companions first and get rid of them.

PRINCE: Are they known to be rich?

PLAYBOY: The 'Umda owns a thousand *feddans* of land, ten irrigation pumps, and has a second grade. The Merchant owns the biggest tavern in his town and a cotton mill, and is in line for the third grade.

PRINCE: Then don't deprive them of your company. I see no harm in inviting them to join us.

ONE OF THE COMPANY: (*to* ANOTHER) Get up and we'll make room for them.

ANOTHER OF THE COMPANY: Wait a bit until they bring the round of drinks we've ordered and the bowl of sea dates the prince asked for earlier.

'Isa ibn Hisham said, "The Playboy went back to his companions to bring them over. The 'Umda got up to pay his respects, but, as he did so, dropped his cigarette holder on the marble floor. It broke and sent chips all over the floor. The 'Umda could not control his remorse, but the Playboy pulled him toward himself and said:

PLAYBOY: Come on, we shouldn't be making such a fuss over a cigarette holder at this moment. The Prince is watching and I've brought you an invitation from him to join his company.

'UMDA: I'm not sorry about the holder itself, but it's a momento I received as a present from the district Ma'mur when I presented him with a horse. That's why it's so precious to me. But tell me, how did His Highness come to invite me? How did you describe me to him?

MERCHANT: Yes, do tell us how it happened! Was I mentioned in his presence as well?

PLAYBOY: I said what I said, and I mentioned what I mentioned. As the proverb puts it: "Send a wise man, but don't advise him."

'UMDA: I'd like to hear the details of what was said about me during the conversation, I saw him laughing a lot while you were talking to him.

PLAYBOY: I told him about the clever way you deprived the cotton broker of his fee.

MERCHANT: Talking of brokers, have you heard that His Highness the Prince is selling his cotton this year?

'Isa ibn Hisham said, "The Playboy's response was to grab the 'Umda by the hand. With the merchant behind them, they walked over to the Prince's table. The 'Umda bent low to the Prince's knee and touched it with his hand, then took hold of it and kissed it several times inside and inside and outside. The

Prince smiled at him and gestured to him to sit down, but he declined and remained standing, hands on chest. Eventually, after a great deal of insistence, the Playboy sat him down with the Merchant at his side."

PRINCE: (*to* ONE OF THE COMPANY) Don't forget to remind me tomorrow about the drawing of that horse, Sirin. The duke of Brook has written to my friend the Adviser asking me for a picture of him to show in a racing exhibition in London.

ONE OF THE COMPANY: Couldn't you do that on the day when you've arranged with the Adviser to dine with the irrigation inspector, Sir?

PRINCE: (*to the* 'UMDA) What will you have to drink, my dear Shaikh?

'UMDA: (*treading on the* MERCHANT'S *foot*) If you'll excuse me, Sir, I won't have anything.

MERCHANT: (*restless with pain*) Pardon, Sir, God's forgiveness. Such conduct is not becoming in your company.

PRINCE: Why on earth did you come here if not to drink?

PLAYBOY: They're imbibing as much of the aura of Your Highness's presence as possible. Conformity takes precedence over good manners.

'Isa ibn Hisham said, "The Playboy reached for the cigarette box in front of the Prince and gave one to each of the 'Umda and Merchant. The 'Umda ostensibly avoided lighting it in the Prince's presence; perhaps he wanted to keep it as a momento from the Prince to boast about among his companions. Then a flower-seller came over and whispered something in the Prince's ear, which made him guffaw. He ordered the Waiter to bring a glass for the seller who drank it and then went away. The Playboy then asked the Prince's permission for the 'Umda to order a bottle of champagne, which he graciously gave. The Prince then turned to the 'Umda and asked:

PRINCE: (*to the* 'UMDA) What's the crop in your area? How much cotton have you got per *feddan*?

'UMDA: By Your Highness's breath, I've been getting seven per *feddan*.

MERCHANT: That's an excellent yield, but prices are falling. Have you sold your cotton yet, Sir, or are you keeping it?

PRINCE: (*to* ONE OF THE COMPANY)
I'm not going to pay more than twenty pounds for that dagger we saw today. If it had had the date of manufacture on it, I'd have paid the price the owner is asking for it.

ONE OF THE COMPANY: It wouldn't hurt you to go up to thirty.

PRINCE: What do you have to say about tomorrow's horse race?

ONE OF THE COMPANY: I'm sure the Prince's horse will win.

'Isa ibn Hisham said, "When the bottle they had ordered arrived, the 'Umda searched hurriedly in his pocket and brought out the bananas. He wiped one of them and offered it to the Prince, then distributed the rest among the people present. One of them found some wool sticking to his banana, so he left it on the table."

ONE OF THE COMPANY: (*to the* 'UMDA) Are these bananas from your farmland? Do you ripen them in wool where you come from?

'UMDA: No, my dear Sir, they're from the New bar. They haven''t been in my pocket for long; only the time it took us to walk here. I've got some oranges, dates, and custard apples as well.

ONE OF THE COMPANY: Would I be correct then in assuming that you're in partnership with Hassan Bey 'Id in the fruit trade?[5]

MERCHANT: The gentleman isn't involved in commerce. The profits involved are fraught with risk, so not everyone is willing to take it on.

'UMDA: (*to the* WAITER) Bring us a bottle of English champagne as well.

ONE OF THE COMPANY: (*to* ANOTHER) It looks as though the *feddan* has produced ten!

ANOTHER: In the real-estate bank!

PRINCE: What does "English" mean?[6]

ANOTHER: It means that it comes from the same nation as the pound.

Isa ibn Hisham said, "Meanwhile the flower-seller came back and had a word in the Prince's ear. He got up at once and went out followed by the flower-seller. The members of the company slunk out after him one by one. Eventually, they had all gone, and the 'Umda drank what was left in the Prince's glass, then leaned over to the leftovers on the tray and took some food."

MERCHANT: (*to the* 'UMDA) You should ask the Waiter for some more before His Highness the Prince comes back.

'UMDA: I won't order anything unless His Highness is present.

PLAYBOY: I don't think His Highness will be coming back tonight. When he gets up utterly drunk and goes away with a flower-seller, that's usually the case.[7]

'UMDA: But I didn't see him pay anything toward the bill.

MERCHANT: Perhaps he has a standing account here.

PLAYBOY: Let's ask the waiter.

'UMDA: (*to the* WAITER) Didn't His Highness pay anything?

WAITER: He didn't pay anything before he left.

PLAYBOY: How much is the bill?

WAITER: A hundred and twenty-one francs.

---

5. In the original episode, the speech was given by one of the people present.

6. This speech replaces a short piece of description in the original episode: "The Prince got into the carriage and left."

7. This speech was added to the first edition.

'UMDA: I don't believe that His Highness would leave without paying his share of the bill. In that case we'd better wait for him.

WAITER: Whenever the Prince gets up and leaves like that, he won't be back. If you don't want to pay for the Prince's drinks, I'll add them to his account.

'UMDA: If I were to pay for anything at all, it would be for what His Highness the Prince had to drink and that alone.

While they were talking and arguing in this fashion, a Deputy Governor entered. The 'Umda got up to welcome him and insisted that he join them. He then turned round and addressed the Waiter in a loud voice:

'UMDA: Bring me a detailed bill listing exactly what His Highness the Prince had to drink and eat, how much the drinks cost for the Prince's companions, how much we drank with the Prince, and how much the Prince drank before we arrived. Ask the Deputy Governor what he will have to drink and then come back so that I can pay you the entire amount required.

DEPUTY GOVERNOR: I won't have anything.

'UMDA: How can you refuse our offer of a drink when His Highness the Prince graciously accepted just in order to please us![8]

DEPUTY GOVERNOR: Then I wouldn't mind a glass of cognac.

'UMDA: Good heavens, no! You should only drink champagne just as His Highness the Prince did when he was with us.

PLAYBOY: (*to the* 'UMDA) Why haven't you introduced us to the gentleman?

'UMDA: The Deputy Governor, this gentleman (pointing to the Merchant) is a very influential merchant, and that gentleman (pointing to the Playboy) is one of Egypt's refined wits.

PLAYBOY: (*to the* DEPUTY GOVERNOR) I believe you've come to Cairo as a follow-up on the inquiry into grades currently being submitted to the Ministry of the Interior.

DEPUTY GOVERNOR: That's right, I was in the Ministry of the Interior today. God willing, everything will turn out as we want.

'UMDA: (*to the* WAITER) Another bottle of champagne.

DEPUTY GOVERNOR: That's enough! I want to go inside to join my colleagues, the judges and the public attorneys.

---

8. In the original episode, there is a discussion at this point between 'Isa ibn Hisham and the Pasha about princes. The Pasha expresses his surprise that princes should descend to visiting common pubs, but 'Isa explains that princes are bored with living in palaces and prefer to meet people. And, in any case, it is better for them to behave like this prince and mix with their own people, rather than consorting exclusively with foreigners as some of them do. At this point in the conversation, the 'Umda reappears.

PLAYBOY: There's no need for you to move. I'll invite them to join us. A and B are both in their party and they're great friends of mine.

DEPUTY GOVERNOR: Don't bother yourselves. It would be more proper for me to go in and join them.

'UMDA: (*to the* DEPUTY GOVERNOR) That being so, we'll all come in with you, and the waiter can bring us a bottle of champagne.

DEPUTY GOVERNOR: I've no objection to that, if you wish.

'Isa ibn Hisham said, "They got up and joined the other company. The Waiter brought a bottle of champagne, and the 'Umda asked them to drink some. They declined, he insisted, but they still declined. Then he started to stammer in a drunken stupor, swearing he would divorce his wife if they did not drink with him. He took a glass and stood there leaning on the Playboy so that he could drink with them. He had barely placed the glass to his lips when he began to choke and could not stop himself; the wine spilled all over his clothes and left a stain. The Playboy, assisted by the Waiter, hurriedly pulled him inside to put his sorry state to right.[9] We waited for a while for the 'Umda to reappear. Eventually he emerged, somewhat recovered from his drunken stupor but still staggering as he walked. He made for the exit, with the Playboy whispering to him on his right and the Merchant flattering him hypocritically on his left."

—*Translated by Roger Allen*

Mikha'il Nu'aima (1889–1987)

Born in the mountains of Lebanon, Mikha'il Nu'aima was a Lebanese-American poet, critic, biographer, writer of fiction, and philosopher. He studied at the Russian Teacher Training College in Nazareth, Palestine, then attended the University of Poltava in Russia, before emigrating to the United States in 1911, where he entered the University of Washington to study law. He soon became an active member of the group of Arab writers in America, founding, with al-Raihani and Gibran Khalil Gibran, a vital literary movement that was soon joined by such prominent poets as Ilya Abu Madi. Nu'aima, like most of his contemporaries, wrote in many genres and discovered his abilities as poet, critic, and writer of fiction simultaneously, becoming known as early as 1920 in all these fields and winning immediate recognition for his lovely short story "Sterile," published in the

---

9. In the original episode, there is a discussion at this point between 'Isa ibn Hisham and the Pasha about princes. The Pasha expresses his surprise that princes should descend to visiting common pubs, but 'Isa explains that princes are bored with living in palaces and prefer to meet people. And, in any case, it is better for them to behave like this Prince and mix with his own people, rather than resort exclusively with foreigners as some of them do. At this point in the conversation, the 'Umda reappears.

famous collection of the North American Arab Group, *Majmu'at al-Rabita al-Qalamiyya* (1921). His short-story collections include *Once Upon a Time* (1927), *Meeting* (1946), *Akabir* (1956), and *Abu Batta* (1958).

UM YA'QUB'S CHICKENS

Um Ya'qub was past ninety. In the eyes of villagers she was a widow, but in her own she was still a woman with a husband. Her sheep-merchant husband had left for Mosul seventy years before and never returned. In all those long years not a shred of evidence had suggested he might still be alive. Rumor had it that he had either died by accident or been stabbed to death by a thief after his money. But Um Ya'qub did not care about such speculation; she regarded it as slander motivated by jealousy. She often said the promptings of her heart assured her that her husband was still alive. "After all," she said, "one's heart is one's guide."

Her more malicious neighbors believed that the man had not gone to Mosul in search of sheep at all. He had lied to his wife, they said, abandoning family, home, and property, and moving to a remote country to escape his wife's bitter tongue and extreme stinginess. He himself had a jolly disposition and a pleasant, peaceful nature, and was warmly generous and hospitable. In contrast, Um Ya'qub had a face that stiffened against smiles, a tongue foreign to pleasantries and a hand opposed to giving. Besides all this, she was barren.

As for calling her "Um Ya'qub,"[1] the villagers did it out of courtesy and wishful thinking. It was only fair to admit, however, that she had at least one virtue—honesty. She never tried to disguise the bitterness of her tongue, the scowl on her face, or the tightness of her fist. She would even brag about them, explaining her peculiar philosophy: "Life is a struggle and people are enemies. If you smile or laugh with someone, he deems you weak and oppresses you. No one smiles at an enemy but the idiot. Life is coarse and a soft-spoken person only hardens others' hearts against him. Someone with a quiet voice loses respect, becomes the butt of others' jokes, and fails to find his daily bread. Living means saving, not squandering. If your pocket is full, your belly knows no hunger. Squandering is eating more than you need to stay alive, and wearing more than you need to cover your nakedness. Saving is collecting the drops that spill over the cup of survival."

"Any kind of charity is a crime. If God had willed us equal, we would be so, but God must have seen some wisdom in bestowing His wealth on some and

---

1. "Um" (written also as "Umm") means mother. In many Arab countries, such as Palestine, Lebanon, Syria and Iraq, it is customary to call married men and women by the name of their first-born male. This is a sign of respect. However, sometimes a childless married man or woman may be called by the name of a would be son: "Um so-and-so" for the woman and "Abu so-and-so" for the man.

withholding it from others. If you feel pity for the poor, offering them your own sweat and toil, you are turning against God's wisdom and will. And hospitality is nothing but foolishness! Let people eat and drink according to what their own hands produce. Haven't many eaten your food and made fun of you afterward?"

Um Ya'qub lived her own philosophy daily, a virtue rare among philosophers. She ate only one meal a day, consisting solely of bread. The sharp eye of the most talented tailor could not have discerned the original material or pattern of her clothes, so mended and patched were they.

If you could have seen Um Ya'qub leaning on a stick with a hooked head, her back so bent she seemed to be heading into the earth, you would have thought her grave was only a few steps down the road. You would have thought the slightest breath could blow her over onto the ground. But then when you learned she had not lost a single tooth, that she could still thread a needle, mend her clothes, and wash them with her own hands, that time had erased nothing from her memory, and events had not softened the sharpness of her tongue— you would have changed your mind. You would believe her assertion that she planned to be a hundred years old or more before they buried her. She hated death bitterly and often repeated, "Death? Let it never come! I want to live!"

Why did Um Ya'qub cling so firmly to life when she always went to bed hungry and no one in the village liked her company? First, she preferred mere breathing to death. Long life was a divine gift given only to those with whom God was pleased. Secondly, she had a hen unique among chickens. Rarely do two creatures—particularly of different species—have such a bond! If she died, the chicken would surely die of grief. No doubt her desire to live had much to do with her love for her chicken. And finally, she wanted to live to spite her neighbor who had been wishing her dead for a long time, expecting her death from day to day. Um Ya'qub hated her neighbor more than death.

Her neighbor was even stingier and meaner than she was. She did the basest things in exchange for a loaf of bread or a few pennies; she stole others' property when they turned their backs. Um Ya'qub had accused her more than once of stealing things from her house, and called her "Mother of Warts" since her nose and chin were full of them. This nickname had long replaced her original one, "Um Zaidan"—Zaidan died when he was only two years old. Later she had three daughters, now aged ten to fifteen, and always beat them before providing their scraps of bread. She could not tolerate a mouth that ate at her table unless it was accompanied by two hands that worked and produced more than the mouth ate.

The breach between the two neighbors was chronic and irreparable. They never exchanged a "good morning" or "good evening" but only traded dirty looks, grumbles, mumbles, and endless supplications to heaven to rain down upon the other one fire and ruin.

But God is merciful. If He slaps with one hand, He strokes with the other. God had plagued Um Ya'qub with proximity to the "Mother of Warts," but He had also blessed her with Seniora's friendship. Seniora was her hen, the creature closest to her heart. Um Ya'qub spoke her name emphatically, adding a kind of grandeur to it. And in truth, Seniora was a lady, a noble dame among her species. Her bright, black feathers were crowlike, but her stride reminded one of a quail. Her rosy crest, nattily tilted to the left, obscured her eye, and her slim blue legs ended in slender feet and good strong claws for digging the earth and picking in the garbage. Um Ya'qub's favorite summertime pleasure was to sit on the threshold of her house watching Seniora dig small trenches in the smooth earth. Lying on her side in the ditch, the chicken would scatter dust with her feathers until she swooned with cleanliness and joy. Then she would surrender to her hennish pleasure, sleeping the sleep of innocence.

Nature had not deprived Seniora of any of the fine accoutrements of chickens save for her tail. The missing tail was replaced by an upright feather, hooked on the end, which looked like an insignia of nobility. In addition, nature had given Seniora a unique brain—hence the possibility for mutual understanding between woman and hen. When Um Ya'qub asked Seniora to come, she came; when she told her to go, she went. The chicken could distinguish gestures of approval or disapproval from the subtle human moves of Um Ya'qub, and understood when it was permitted to roam freely about the house, and when it was not. She knew that Um Ya'qub did not mind cleaning up the trail of dirt she left behind after making her rounds, inspecting all the corners of the house. Often the chicken's flirtation with Um Ya'qub led it to jump into her lap and take a peaceful nap there while Um Ya'qub would gently pet its feathers, lifting it to her lips to kiss the rosy crest with admiration and affection.

Seniora also never neglected to get her share when Um Ya'qub broke bread. The chicken would circle around her, repeating in its peculiar language, "Your bread is delicious, Um Ya'qub. Feed me and God will feed you." Um Ya'qub would become generosity personified; she would not eat a bite without passing one to Seniora. The chicken ate, thanked Um Ya'qub, wished her a long life, and laid five eggs a week—except in winter, when it had to rest. Um Ya'qub took the eggs every Saturday and sold them to a rich lady in the village for a high price—they were fresher and bigger than anyone else's.

So infatuated was she with the chicken that she practically gave up going out altogether. When questioned about this, she would reply, "Do you think I have time, my dear? I am a woman of responsibilities. Who will feed my chicken if I don't? Who will give it a drink if I don't? Who will guard it? These days there are more bastards than foxes and jackals."

One day Um Ya'qub checked the coop as usual and did not find the anticipated egg. Terrified, she began wringing her hands and blaming herself loudly, "May God disgrace you for your stupidity! You have fallen into the trap that you always feared! Your chicken has betrayed her home and laid her egg in the coop of the Mother of Warts!" Um Ya'qub had long been suspicious any time she saw her chicken mingling with those of her neighbor; but she tried to have compassion for Seniora's friendship with her neighbor's rooster, looking upon them together with some measure of sympathy and satisfaction.

Several days passed and no new eggs were found in the coop. Um Ya'qub was about to go mad. She seized the chicken, shaking her finger in its face. "Where do you lay your eggs, ungrateful wretch? What about yesterday? The day before yesterday?" Seniora replied with an ambiguous cooing. Her secret remained a mystery.

Um Ya'qub began to check her chicken's rear every morning, and came to the conclusion that her suspicions were justified: Seniora had not stopped laying eggs but had simply stopped laying them in her own coop. Um Ya'qub was certain the eggs were ending up in the coop of the Mother of Warts, and this notion made her wild.

Two weeks later, in extreme anger, Um Ya'qub went to her neighbor's house, calling her names and demanding that she give back her ten eggs. A fierce fight broke out. The neighbors were shocked by the women's filthy curses. But the fight accomplished nothing. The Mother of Warts would not hand over any eggs, and Um Ya'qub would not cease leveling her charges.

Things went from bad to worse when, a day after the fight, Seniora disappeared entirely. Um Ya'qub asserted that the Mother of Warts or one of her daughters had hidden her. She went to other neighbors asking for their support, but they all denied it, insisting that she had no proof. Some tried to console her, saying the criminal must be a fox. Neither her heart nor her mind would be consoled. Her health deteriorated, her eyesight dimmed, and her breath became short. Finally she took to her bed, giving in to depression, weeping, and fasting. Three weeks later she died.

As the small funeral procession was leaving her house, the ten-year-old daughter of Mother of Warts shouted loudly, "Seniora! Seniora! Here is Seniora!" A chicken with a hooked feather on its rear approached the house slowly, paying no attention to the crowd but stepping with great dignity. Behind it came nine baby chickens scrambling to keep up with their mother. Seniora would turn to give them encouraging clucks. Her voice was filled with pride. They entered the house together and examined every corner. Stopping finally at the bed of Um Ya'qub, a shocked Seniora clucked and stared as if to say, "Um Ya'qub! Where are you, Um Ya'qub? Here I am with the babies that God has given me, where are you, Um Ya'qub?"

—*Translated by Admer Gouryeh and Naomi Shihab Nye*

Jamal Sleem Nuweihed (1906–1994)

Jamal Sleem was born in Lebanon, the daughter of a Lebanese doctor famous for his narrative skills in story-telling and a Turkish mother. She lost her parents at a young age and emigrated to Syria with her brothers who were officers in the army of prince Faisal, the first Arab ruler of Syria after the Ottomans. From there she had to emigrate again, this time to East Jordan with her brothers who, after the fall of Syria to the French, moved to East Jordan and were officers in the army of the newly founded East Jordanian state under the then prince 'Abdallah, the great-grandfather of Jordan's present king. Because of this constantly interrupted life, she had very little formal education. However, her self-education during the long hours she spent alone in her brothers' absence was grounded on the firm basis of the major books of history and literature published in Arabic, and she mastered the knowledge of Arabic letters. She married 'Ajaj Noweihed, a prominent writer-historian who himself was highly knowledgeable about Arabic literature, which allowed her to continue her wide literary interests. She went with him to Jerusalem where he founded the review, *Al-'Arab* (1932–1934), and it was then that Jamal began her writing career, with many short stories, which she published in *Al-'Arab* under the name Sawsan. She continued to write fiction and poetry throughout her life but, being the reclusive person she was, she published very little of her work. Three novels, however, among many others, were published: *Procession of Martyrs* (1965), *A Stranger in One's Country* (1989), and *A Wedding in Paradise* (1991). In the 1980s she wrote for *PROTA* a most valuable collection of folk tales, which were translated by *PROTA* and published by Interlink Books in 2002, under the title of *Abu Jmeel's Daughter and Other Stories.* Later on she managed to write, just before she died, an account of her own life and of that of her family, which is a historical treasure mirroring the social and political life east of the Mediterranean throughout most of the twentieth century. This major work of over twenty-five hundred handwritten pages awaits publication and translation for the benefit of those in various disciplines who are now studying the Middle East and its evolution into modern times.

FALSE TEETH

Sana' drew back the curtains to let in the sunlight and the spring breezes, breathing in the fresh air as if wanting to rid herself of the choking gases she felt filling her chest. Her eyes had a wilted look, her eyelids felt heavy, like those of someone who'd lain awake all night, nursing a secret anxiety and a painful sorrow. Suddenly she heard her father's voice, speaking to another person behind the trees in the garden. Stunned, as if hit by an electric current, she drew back. As her arm struck the window, she realized what was happening and lay back on her bed, weeping in her despair. She knew who the man was that her father had been talking to. It was that vain old man, fabulously rich, who put on youthful airs and had promised to give her father a thousand pounds[1] to help him restore his finances and so revitalize his trading business, which had suffered

---

1. The reader should remember that this is a story written in the 1930s, when a thousand pounds meant a great amount of money.

a sudden setback. The money was to be given to him in return for the hand of his daughter, a girl highly praised for her beauty and strength of character. Her father, 'Abd al-Salam Effendi, had accepted this bargain laid down by Yahya Bek, a man who claimed to be no more than forty but was in fact much older. He was able, it was true, to keep up a decent appearance, on account of the leisure and luxury wealth brings. But when he retired to his bed, away from prying eyes, he looked very different—his mouth like a gaping cave with the dentures out, his eyes red and bulging. He'd be racked, too, by fits of coughing. Anyone who knew him, seeing him in this state, would never have believed this was the same elegant Yahya Bek who put on such a show of youth and vigor and met his friends with such laughter and good cheer.

To begin with, Sana' had rebelled furiously against the engagement. Her father, a wise and experienced man, who knew the secrets of people's hearts and the way they behaved, had reacted with forbearance and kindness. In any case, he loved his daughter very much and was concerned for her happiness. It was his financial plight, and his hope of regaining his past status, which had persuaded him to give her in marriage to Yahya Bek, well aware of the comfortable, luxurious life she'd lead. Like many others, he'd been taken in by Yahya Bek's false appearance. The disaster would have been far easier for her to bear, had she not already chosen for herself, without her father's knowledge, another fiancé with whom her happiness and hopes were bound up. For quite some time now she'd cherished this secret in her heart, confiding it to no one but waiting for the day the young man would be in a position to approach her father for her hand. This young man was a writer, whose devotion to his craft had held him back from seeking money through trade. It was as though he was waiting for some miracle to help him find his bearings, so he could ask for his beloved's hand.

Just how had love brought these two young people together? Love is like air, there are no barriers to block its entry to hearts ready to receive it. All we can say is that, no sooner had Sana' and Nabeel met than they felt deeply attracted to one another. When the marriage arrangement with Yahya Bek was made, Sana' found a way of letting Nabeel know; she gave a letter to an old family servant who loved her dearly, and the servant delivered the letter into Nabeel's hand.

The night of the engagement arrived, and a great celebration was in prospect, with all the town's most prominent people in attendance. In the men's sitting room were gathered judges, rich merchants, and high dignitaries; in the women's were assembled all the town's most fashionable women. Everything was ready for the engagement ceremony except the bridegroom, who'd failed to make his appearance. People waited and waited, and so did 'Abd al-Salam Effendi, beginning to feel highly nervous now at the absence of his prospective son-in-law. As time passed, people began to fidget, and some even left the party. 'Abd al-Salam hurried over to Yahya Bek's house to see what was keeping him, and there he found Yahya Bek barricaded in his room, refusing to open to anyone. Finally, though, he did open the door, and 'Abd al-Salam Effendi, going in, was met by an astonishing sight. There, before him, was a quite different-looking Yahya Bek.

Not feeling it right to inquire about this change in the man's face, he simply asked the reason for his delay. Yahya Bek embarked on a litany of moaning and lament.

"My teeth!" he yelled. "Who's taken my teeth?"

Concerned as 'Abd al-Salam Effendi was about the delay in carrying out the ceremony, he couldn't help bursting out laughing at the comical sight there in front of him: the toothless bridegroom, with his odd, lamenting voice, as he cried out, "My teeth! My teeth! Who's taken my teeth?"

Suddenly, a youthful voice was heard, coming from the other side of the house. "What's the matter, Uncle? What's happened to your teeth?" 'Abd al-Salam Effendi looked behind him and saw a most handsome young man, soft-voiced and with an attractive smile, betokening self-confidence and a cultivated manner. He'd never seen the young man before but realized he must be Yahya Bek's nephew.

"My dear Nabeel," Yahya Bek replied, "I've lost my false teeth. I've searched through the whole house, and I can't find them. It's my engagement ceremony, and the guests are waiting. How can I show myself there without my teeth?" He was simply too agitated to go on.

As for Nabeel, standing there in the middle of the room, he had a curious smile on his lips. He gazed at his uncle, then said, "Uncle, listen to me for a moment. Just listen to me, then do exactly as you like. I would, though, ask you to hear what I have to say in front of this wise witness, this good man whose daughter you've chosen to marry without even thinking about false teeth and the disastrous way yours have gone missing. You're a rich man, Uncle, a very rich man, and I'm your nephew, whose sole livelihood is through a pen that never dries and a heart that never despairs. But these days, Uncle, ink and paper don't get converted into bread and butter. Several times now I've asked you to help me, so I can start making my way and build my life on a surer foundation. And each time you've refused, mocking the way I live, running down my profession. One day I told you I was in love with a girl from a good family and wanted to marry her—and you just sneered at me. How, you asked, could an impoverished young man like me ever presume to think of marriage? But Uncle, why shouldn't a young man think of love and marriage, when an old man like yourself does exactly the same, just because he's rich? I couldn't bear to see you snatch away the very same girl I'd fallen in love with, all on account of money. I couldn't bear it. I had to stop the marriage any way I could, and the only way of stopping it was to get hold of your false teeth. I have them now, and I won't give them back unless you agree for me to be the groom and not you. That way, the ceremony won't be wasted."

Nabeel then looked at 'Abd al-Salam Effendi and spoke, pleadingly but firmly. "Sir," he said, "I must seek your agreement even before I seek my own uncle's. If it should please you to exchange the autumn for the spring, then I ask you to exchange my uncle for me. He, I assure you, was poor at my age, and money comes and goes. Men make it through their diligence and hard work."

'Abd al-Salam Effendi smiled, feeling a great affection for this smart, handsome young man.

"Son," he said, "I admire your resources and the clever trick you've played. If your uncle should choose to abandon his quest, I shall be most happy to have you as a son-in-law."

Yahya Bek looked stunned but felt, too, a surge of affection toward his nephew. He'd lost the battle, he decided, and shouldn't allow himself to behave in a shabby way. He gave in, promising to cover the expenses of the party, to pay the dowry he'd been planning to pay on his own behalf, and to provide the newly-weds with a new house, fully furnished.

And so a night of misery was transformed into one of blissful joy.

—*Translated by May Jayyusi and Christopher Tingley*

Fu'ad al-Shayib (1911–1970)

Syrian writer and one of the short-story pioneers in Syria, Fu'ad al-Shayib was born in the town of Ma'lula. He studied law first in Damascus then in France, where he also studied French language and literature. As a young man he worked in journalism and teaching, then occupied many prominent positions in the field of culture and cultural information in his country. He was one of Syria's prominent intellectuals, a connoisseur of literature and, with his ideas on freedom and human justice, able to wield great influence on the rising generations of writers. In 1958, on the occasion of the union between Syria and Egypt, he was decorated with the Medal of Merit. His collection of short stories, *The History of a Wound,* was published in 1944.

HOW MISERY WAS BORN

A Legend

God created misery on the evening He created happiness.

His wisdom in doing so is unassailable. His reasons impossible to refute or controvert.

Misery was a rib he took from the side of happiness, as he created Eve from Adam's rib.

The universe had to be filled with creation. First, there was happiness. . . . When the Creator made happiness and traced the last part of the last line with His brush, He stood back, tired and perplexed. His eyes expressed rapture and a feeling of heaviness, as if He had never been so drained by any of His paintings as He had by the splendid one before him. He paused to admire His work: it was a beautiful maiden, exulting in a resplendent beauty, like that of a morning shining behind the translucence of a rosy horizon.

As He prepared to blow life into the inert picture, He knew that He was offering the world a gift of beauty and ugliness at the same time, a gift of both good and evil. It was not a light that radiates in the morning or a darkness that spreads in the evening, but a mixture of the two taking form in the same spirit in daytime.

But how are we to explain this emanation that preceded its bringing to life? This is a mystery lost in the mist of original creation. Without any long period of prior reflection, the Creator, in his glory, blew on to the new picture. He covered His face with his hand and turned it away from His work. This happened in the morning.

Installed in His tower, the Glorious One was obliged to rest, before He reached the last day of creation. In His awesome isolation He felt that none of His creations was worthwhile.

The Creator was suffering beneath the burden of His cares.

He wished He had not produced a universe and created a soul.

Was happiness not the aim of excellence in original creation?

Why is the Glorious One not at peace with this concept of the ultimate aim?

Why are the tips of His fingers not steady? Why do the lips tremble, murmuring those questioning words, while the heart is brimming with melodies?

What is this floating mist carrying an unknown idea in its womb?

Happiness took Him by surprise; when does happiness ask for permission? This was the first time it had stepped with its rosy feet anywhere in the universe. It crept inside its master's tower like the golden threads of the sun.

It stood before Him, bashful and coquettish, the most superb of all created things.

The Creator, about to frown and reprimand, now rejoiced and spread His radiance. Happiness was shimmering in a haze of the softest dreams and smiling with the freshest blooming hopes. It bent like a branch drunk with the singing of birds. It was like a spring borne on the petals of sweet flowers.

It bowed to God, and He welcomed it smiling. It settled in His lap, light and graceful. But what His arms could embrace, His disturbed and anxious soul rejected.

On the evening of this splendid creation, happiness felt pain on the left side of the body. A certain paleness touched the rosy cheeks, two blue veins jutted out from between the delicate temples, and the eyes were ringed with black circles of sadness.

The mouth was surrounded by arrows, which formed two lines, like two burning swords that appeared above every smile. Whenever a smile formed, it was stained with blood; when it spread, it shattered; when it danced, it died.

The Creator soon realized the secret of the pain. He felt the side of the maiden, where the pain was. His fingertips felt a jutting rib.

It was not the Creator's wish to see happiness suffer, but such paradox lies at the heart of creation. Something in the universe had to be.

The Creator took out the painful rib and for the first time happiness knew great joy, as well as a vast emptiness.

Happiness asked, "What do You intend to do with my rib?"

The Creator replied, "I shall reduce it to ashes and scatter it on wind of the precipice!"

The maiden shouted in anguish, "Do You really intend to do that? Is that Your will? Use it to make something for me."

He asked, "What kind of thing?"

She said, "Something like a stick to lean on or a scepter to hold."

The Creator blew on the rib removed from the suffering side, so reaching the end of His act of creation; thus He closed the final circle.

The result was an ugly head set on a small, skinny body, and two hollow eyes sunk in a high forehead. The mouth was small and the lips thinly pressed together, as if the new creature harbored an eternal pain. After some hesitation, sad and shuddering with horror, the Creator said, "The will of creation is sacred. The mist is dispelled, the veils of the unknown have been withdrawn, and the great emanation has taken place. Let us call him 'intelligence.'"

Happiness said, with a coquettish attitude of a new mother, "Let us rather call him 'misery.'" And so it was.

When misery moved here and there to cast his first glances on the creatures, happiness felt her brightness shining like a full moon.

They went out and roamed the world together. These two opposite creatures had one common bond, no matter where their travels took them: it was their recollection and yearning: his memory of having once been a part of a whole, and his yearning for the side from which he sprang; and her memory that she had once been a perfect creature and her yearning for the rib lost for ever. God often looked at His creatures as they went on their way. He would see misery and happiness walking side by side, each holding the other by the waist, she leaning on him and he resting his head on her side.

—*Translated by Aida A. Bamia and Christopher Tingley*

Mahmoud Taymour (1894–1973)

Egyptian short-story writer and dramatist Mahmoud Taymour is regarded as the foremost pioneer of the modern short story in Arabic, whose work has influenced many aspiring writers throughout the Arab world. He came from a literary family and was well grounded in Arabic literature as well as in Western cultural achievements. Like many of the pioneers of the short story in Arabic, he offered a comic representation of experience that reflected the contradictions and absurd situations of the quickly changing world around him, an orientation that grew weaker over the years as the Arab world plunged, at ever greater speed, into major political dilemmas. He published several fictional and dramatic works, among which are: *Rajab*

Effendi: Egyptian Stories (1928), *Al-Haj Shalabi and Other Stories* (1937), *A Concubine's Heart and Other Stories* (1937), and *The Little Pharaoh* (1939). These early works were followed by a number of collections, such as *A New World; Um Ahmad the Baroness and Other Stories; A Husband by Auction, I Am the Murderer; The Blue Lamps; Sun and Nigh; Today's Girls;* and others. A collection of his stories translated by Nayla Naguib appeared in 1993, titled *Sensuous Lips and other Stories.*

THE ELEMENTS OF THE ABLUTION

When I was a pupil at primary school, I got to know another pupil in my class whose name was Zankaluni—a boy who moved slowly, like a tame elephant. We were all very fond of him, even though his stupidity had become a byword among us. The poor fellow would do his very best to memorize his lessons, spending a good part of the night at his exercise books and textbooks, but when morning came there still wasn't a thing in his head.

Shaikh Barakat, the teacher of religion, used to start each period with the same question, which he'd shoot directly and mercilessly at Zankaluni, "What are the basic elements of the ablution, Zankaluni?" Zankaluni would stand gaping like a stone statue, and the teacher would add, "Zero, Zankaluni! Dry bread for you, Zankaluni! Detention on Thursday afternoon, Zankaluni!"

We'd see this tragicomedy repeated in every one of Shaikh Barakat's periods, and in the end Zankaluni only managed to join us at the lunch table once or twice in the whole week. On the other days we'd see him sent off to sit against the wall of the dining hall, where he'd gaze at us out of his tiny eyes, in a sort of stupor, and chew quietly at his piece of bread, as if it didn't bother him at all to go without. From time to time he'd even favor us with a foolish smile, and sometimes, too, we'd throw some hazelnuts or Ibrimi dates in his direction, and he'd snatch them up and swallow them down greedily.

And so it went on, with the elements of the ablution blocking our friend's path and pouring the cup of deprivation on his head. They didn't, though, manage to make any inroads on his fatness—quite the reverse. His great body simply got bigger and bigger!

One day the teacher asked him the usual question, then adorned the register with a large zero as before and inscribed his venerable name on the "dry bread" slip. Finally he stood in front of him and contemplated him for a long time.

"Tell me, Zankaluni," he said at last, "what *do* you know? What single thing can you do well in this life here below?"

Zankaluni went on scratching his head but gaped and said nothing. Then one of the bad boys of the class stood up. "He can sing, sir," he said boldly. "He's got a lovely voice."

Now the teacher of religion, for all his sternness, was a tolerant man who loved a joke; often, indeed, he'd stop the class for a while to tell us amusing stories about things that had happened to him. "Is this true?" he asked Zankaluni at once. "Can you really sing?"

We all answered for Zankaluni together. "It's true, sir," we chorused. "He *can* sing."

Zankaluni obviously believed what we'd said, because he sat down, took a passage from the Quran and got ready to recite it. A profound silence fell over the whole class and off went Zankaluni, intoning in a singsong voice. It was as if a bomb had exploded and fragments of it were flying in all directions, and we all burst out laughing. The teacher saw the joke and started to smile, then we saw him hide his face behind his handkerchief. As for Zankaluni, he was well into his recitation now, growing more and more passionate. The teacher went up to him. "You're a clever boy, Zankaluni," he said. "I'm giving you ten out of ten."

So Zankaluni was able to join us again at the lunch table and leave his humble place by the wall. Indeed, as he reached for his food he'd point mockingly at the others who were subjected to the dry bread punishment; he'd wink at them maliciously, and hurl Ibrimi dates at them, and cackle with laughter. From that time on Zankaluni was top of the class in religion; he always got the highest mark.

One day, while Shaikh Barakat was examining some of us, the headmaster came into the class and stood there, listening to the pupils and scrutinizing them. Then he leafed through the teacher's register, and his eye was caught by the outstanding marks given to Zankaluni. He was delighted and called him out. "Muhammad Zankaluni!"

The "tame elephant" moved ponderously by his little bookshelf, while Shaikh Barakat's face grew solemn and he began to wipe the sweat that was pouring down his brow. The headmaster addressed Zankaluni. "You're a clever fellow," he said. "Can you tell us the basic elements of the ablution?"

We looked at each other in wonder and alarm, our hearts beating faster. A dead silence lay over the class, and Zankaluni's lips didn't move. The headmaster thought the pupil might not have heard him, so he repeated the question. Then, suddenly, Zankaluni sat down, took his Quranic fragment from the shelf and started intoning in his loud, ugly voice.

The headmaster turned to Shaikh Barakat, who'd grown pale and was vainly trying to conquer the agitation he felt. Then we heard the headmaster say, "That's enough! Zero! Dry bread, Zankaluni!"

A few days later we had another teacher of religion, and Zankaluni went back to his old place by the wall in the dining hall, making do with the dry loaf and any dates and nuts his fellow-pupils were charitable enough to provide him with.

But he never once tried to understand the secret behind this revolution in his affairs.

—Translated by Michael Wickens

2

SHORT STORIES

Amina 'Abdallah

A short-story writer from the United Arab Emirates, Amina Abdallah's early experimenting with fiction, represented here by one of its cogent examples, shows a genuine artistic sensibility and a good control of literary language. Her work has not yet been collected in book form.

FURY

As Amina was in one of her usual moments of contemplation, she discovered with irritation that her only wealth was her slim figure, wide expressive eyes, and pursed lips, nothing else. It was these attributes that her very rich husband, 'Abd al-Rahman al-Musa had liked, and it was for this that he brought her one day from her world in the Fishermen's Quarter in the east of the city, a quarter sharp in smells and full of communal joy, to this quarter of fine, well-lit houses, looking up to the future and imperiously arrogant.

However, 'Abd al-Rahman al-Musa did not seek to marry from the Fishermenís Quarter solely because of Amina's young and fresh beauty, for he had a remote blood relationship with her family that he had avoided speaking openly about. He had already occupied many high positions, which had established his relationship with the market. He had formed several companies in cooperation with foreigners, and his companies had enlarged and merged with other institutions and factories that covered all kinds of activity and whose capacity to enlarge seemed endless.

My husband—the word seemed strange when she repeated it slowly. She wondered how others must view him.

She could see that he was a man of tremendous energy and great clout, showered with various assignments, enjoying a high appreciation in certain quarters. What a difference to her first love! Her husband was well balanced, friendly and cheerful with certain people, quick-witted, a perfect man to run a conversation in the assemblies of men that demanded a very special decorum.

She thought now of his elegant appearance, which, in fact, irritated her; a face well built, a pair of golden rimmed glasses, and a laugh that showed gold teeth at the back of his mouth, but a laugh that ended in barter and coldness. You could see from the way his lips closed that any dialogue with him was impossible. He was clever with others like a fox, but also with her, and would never relinquish this role in their conversation together. His inner self was never transparent to her, and their relationship often suffered long periods of silence in which she refrained from talking to him.

How do I really feel toward him? she asked herself.

This question had always worried and confounded her. After a candid contemplation she realized that she neither loved nor hated him. However, she involuntarily felt proud of his success, proud to be the wife of a flourishing businessman. There was, moreover, something else that had established itself in her depths, causing her dejection and an inclination to self-abuse: she felt gratitude toward him. Was it because she lived now in this large, polygonal house occupying a considerable area of land, with its domes and high slanting roofs, and its garden full of all kinds of flowers and a swimming pool in its center? Was it also because she had now four servants and many possessions and could travel widely?

She did not find an answer to this feeling, which, every now and then, aroused her rebellion.

However, this did not prevent her from mustering everything she had to be soft and desirable and to wait for him after his night out, which he spent with his friends enjoying all kinds of diversions that always included gambling.

When he returned home, the only relationship between them was sexual. Looking for an answer as to why she made up and prepared herself for him, she found that that was expected of women, something basic. The whole relationship could be nothing more that an unannounced exchange of operations.

She raised her head and looked around her quickly, feeling some tension as she found herself sprawled on a proud-looking easy chair and realizing she was nothing more than a static part of static things, all of which seemed antagonistic to her: the antique clocks with their inflated bases and their pendulums forever moving, with a maddening perseverance, right and left, showing time that moved and piled up in the background, chiding her; the oil paintings with their shining surfaces showing women looking stupid and wearing dresses that were wide at the bottom and bare at the shoulders and breasts. Exactly opposite her there was the basin of colored fish.

At the beginning, when she left the Fishermen's quarter, she tried hard to accommodate herself with this world of things, which seemed exciting at first then was transformed into an infernal place. The walls, colored with elegant and fine hues, the carpets celebrating their beautiful colors, and the paintings, and vases and figurines, all of these emphasized her bitter feelings of alienation. She was a desert plant killed by humidity and too much nourishment.

Her feelings afterward changed into indifference, and she accepted the fact that she now owned luxurious clothes and gold and jewels, exchanging her natural instinct, which looked for the sun, human faces and voices, and adventures in narrow streets odorous with the humidity of walls, with the retreat to a cold, lifeless corner in the house of 'Abd al-Rahman Musa.

She wished to be freed of the encroachment of these things around her, which existed because this whole life was based on showiness and hypocrisy. She raised her body and pulled the thread of the velvet curtain, in order to look at the garden. She saw Muhammad al-Milbari intent on trimming the bushes and cutting off the weak branches. The garden looked artificial, and its esthetic appearance seemed devoid of any modesty.

Her distressed spirit trembled, her eyes gazed now at the newly created houses beyond the garden. Among the dwellers of this high-class, nouveau riche neighborhood there was hot if silent competition over beautifying the houses with beds of flowers, possessing the most original models of new cars, the number of dinner parties held every week, and the kind of guests received. Usually high employees of companies and individuals in eminent positions were the most favored guests.

In these houses where dejection and alienation were covered up and where pomp and luxury were the means for human interchange, she had found women like her, and it was impossible for her to stifle the gasp of dismay at the hair-raising stories that happened in this house or that. Each of these women suffered suspicion of her successful husband. All of them had one quality in common: they were all prone to gossip.

Yesterday her neighbor, Hussa bint Bakhit, looked at Amina and asked her to relate the various stories she had come to know about Hussa's husband, and then Hussa, in turn, would tell Amina what Hussa's husband had told her of the secrets of 'Abd al-Rahman Musa. Then Hussa gratuitously began telling her quickly what she knew of 'Abd al-Rahman Musa's secret.

The world turned in Amina's eyes, for she realized then the secret of her husband's intermittent trips and his return laden with luxurious presents for her. The feeling of falsehood wound around her neck like an accursed, dominating snake. She feared the consequences of the urge she felt to commit an act that would wound his feelings, to lure one of those many men who formed the circle around her husband, with their shining faces and their gambling eyes that always stole wicked looks at her, men who loved snatching fleeting relationships. As for love, her heart, she felt, was unable to love.

The wicked clock struck its moaning tune: one, two, three rings. On the fourth she felt her body shake and was overcome with the desire to direct a blow at a world that tormented her, to shake it to awakening. Things began to whistle in her ears, she felt a murderous paralysis, and she sensed the heaviness of those daily rituals and politesses in this world, the absence of good will. Her fingers became tense and she attacked the clock's hands, trying to tear them off and causing them irreparable damage, while the pendulum was breathing its last movements. Her battle with things became more intense, and the vases scattered in small fragments, while the twigs of yellow flowers fell mercilessly on the floor.

By this time the fish had already left the bottom of the pond and begun revolving around the glass wall of the basin. She raised her hand to break the fish basin, but the idea of the fish out of the water and convulsing in front of her eyes stopped her. She hurled her body over the easy chair, which swallowed her indifferently, with all her anxiety and rebellion.

Her old neighborhood appeared to her imagination, the familiar faces passing in a long procession. It was like a moving caricature where they were laughing and shouting and exchanging funny nicknames. Then the ditches of the streets and the stagnant gutters appeared to her eyes, the dogs and emaciated sheep, the shy but mischievous boys as they surrounded the cars of strangers, gazing at them, evaluating them, and rubbing their noses with the sleeves of their greasy robes. She also saw in her mind's eye those men who still remembered the days of the sea and pearl diving but now sat under shades in the evening, stretching their legs as much as they could and filling their isolated world with sarcastic comments full of the wisdom and prophecy of silent spectators. Her husband had fallen many times under the barbs of their sharp tongues, and they often said that he lived by flattery and by expropriating the money of others. She could also glimpse the women with their many children and their proud gestures, who were ever ready to kindle little battles then snuff them out with affection and laughter.

When she visited them the first time, her sensibility was wounded by the confusion and the fishy smells. Then she ceased her connections with them. However, she now felt the urge to throw herself in the lap of that world with its firm relations and its great capacity for love, but she felt she was already too spoiled to endure a life of hardship.

The world was free and on the move, she thought, inviting people to get involved in it, but where were the tools for entering this world?

This is what she told herself.

Her thoughts moved between the eastern and the western quarters.

Her heart beat strongly now, for the time of his arrival was drawing near. When he arrived, she was going to scream in his face for her deliverance.

He was cheerful and the ecstasy of drink appeared at its highest in his eyes. His face now reflected signs of protest and pity as he gazed at the broken objects. He wanted to scream in her face, Are you quite mad? But instead he began to laugh, for the sight of an angry woman excited him. When he felt that a thundering rebellion was about to break, he collected himself and tidied up his thoughts. For he had already come to know these states of mind in his wife, which had become worse and worse with time. At this moment he felt fear from the surly fishermen spirit that had been now kindled in her.

When she looked at his face, which still carried the remnants of laughter, it seemed strong and firm. He was everything, the master who had clout and wealth and the source of her affluence. Her strength began to dissipate.

He pulled her from his arm while he was fighting the numbness of wine in his veins and whispered in her ears, "Tomorrow, I shall take you to the psychiatrist, darling."

—*Translated by May Jayyusi*

Yahya Taher 'Abdallah (1942–1981)

An Egyptian short-story writer who was born in Karnak near Luxor, Yahya Taher 'Abdallah was a largely self-taught man who was able to evoke admiration within Arab and Egyptian literary circles because of his deft and authoritative handling of fictional narrative. He used to recite his own fictional work in Cairene coffee houses. His work is characterized by great originality of theme and approach, a vivid style, and a sharp perception. It is, moreover, deeply rooted in Arabic literature and tradition and in Egyptian folklore. When he died in an automobile accident in 1981, he had already published one novel, *Choker and Bracelet (1975)*, as well as several collections of short stories: *Three Large Trees Producing Oranges* (1970), *The Drum and the Chest* (1974), *The Prince's Tale* (1978), and *Images from Earth, Water, and Sun* (1981). In 1984 a collection of his stories was translated by Denys Johnson-Davies as *The Mountain of Green Tea*, and Mary Tehan translated his novel *Choker and Bracelet* in 1997. His premature death was a genuine loss for the Arabic short story.

WHO'LL HANG THE BELL?

This is the light from a funeral, O my *Emir*. The rich man has died today, and tonight I shall pluck for you from his life the fruit that is bitter and the fruit that is sweet that perchance you may sleep.

The day he learnt God's Book by heart

His mother hung a blue bead in his pierced ear and said, "To ward off the evil of the woman who envies and the man who envies," and she sprinkled the floor of the house with salt. When the men brought the bundle, his mother undid it and said, "It is of the money of the Moslems," and she scattered its contents before the women's eyes: the *jubba,* red and embroidered with gold and silver thread; the tarbush, a red Moroccan one; the yellow slippers made of camel's hide; the green belt; and the white *qaftan* with black stripes.

When Sabir—for that was his name—put on the *shaikh's* clothes and was about to go out with the men, his mother kissed his hand and said, "O our master,' and she wiped away the tears of joy with her black headcloth.

In the mosque of 'Abdullah

Sabir made two complete prostrations of prayer and thanked his Lord. When he had finished, he kissed the hand of his master and teacher, Shaikh Suleiman, and received from his right hand the wooden sword and led—he who was so young—the procession of men round the lanes of the village.

In the house of his mother and father

He pushed aside the plate of *besara* and said to his mother, "Mother, I've eaten enough," and he put his hand to his cheek and thought, "You will never travel by train; your eye will not see Cairo, Mother of the World, along whose ground trams run; you will not enter al-Azhar,[1] Sabir, and live the life of the boarders and keep company with the sons of Syria and Morocco."

Sabir asked his Lord, "Why, O Lord, did You create my father a watchman over the fields and barns of others, scaring away birds from the grain with a catapult?"

Also in the house of his mother and father

He said to his mother, "I'm hungry, Mother," and he took his hand away from his cheek and thought, "There's no point, my boy, in putting on the wings of a bird so long as you possess the robe of sheikhs. You know the Book of God by heart and there is no flaw in your voice. God's words are beautiful when recited and God's words are suited to both funerals and weddings. Be the son of your day and do not be in opposition to your fate. Shut yourself up in your village and recite the Quran at its weddings and funerals. When you have saved sufficient money, buy a riding animal and get onto it and go and recite the Quran at the funerals and weddings of distant hamlets, and he who today is satisfied with an onion will tomorrow eat a morsel dipped in honey, and he who today is satisfied with an egg will one day eat a duck."

Spiteful Mother Nature, with her seasons, is not to be trusted

A cold day came and tore apart two of Shaikh Sabir's vocal cords.

A rainy day came, severed two of Shaikh Sabir's vocal cords, and cracked his windpipe.

Shaikh Sabir picked the remains of meat from between his teeth with matchsticks and said to himself, "When a man's ambition grows weak, black thoughts come and gnaw at his soul so that he takes to the house as old women do."

On a Saturday he went out to the people in the garb of a man of knowledge

He said, "Every disease has a cause and every cause has a reason. O my brothers, there is an illness that can only be alleviated by cauterization, and there is a disease in which nothing avails but potions sold by chemists. Likewise, treatment by herbs is known only by me who am an expert in blending herbs. As for the black ant, it can easily be driven out from houses if I write one of God's verses on a piece of paper the size of my finger and you stick it with paste to the door of your house.

"So, too, am I able to drive away jinn and suck out the poison of scorpions. Also, I take away fear from every fearful soul who is met by an *afreet* on a dark

---

1. The religious (Islamic) university in Cairo.

night. O inhabitants of my village, O my people, have no fear of the bite of the snake or the flea."

When the stars told him of his day of good fortune

He entered the souk and went to the assembly of Shamardali, shaikh of the merchants of the fish market, and made greeting to him. Shamardali returned his greeting with an even warmer one, standing up and shaking the stranger by the hand and seating him alongside him on the pelt that covered the bench; he ordered him coffee and a *narghila* and enquired of him his purpose in coming.

"The very best," said Sabir. "For how much do you sell fish and for how much do you buy it?"

Shamardali said, "I buy the *kantar* for half a silver coin and I sell it for one silver coin."

Sabir said, "I shall sell you two *kantars* for half a silver coin. How many *kantars* will you buy?"

Shamardali replied, "All you've got."

Sabir said, "I have a lot."

Shamardali said, "I shall buy from you half the souk's requirements, say ten *kantars*."

Sabir said, "People say, 'That which is agreed upon from the start, will end well,' and I say to you, Shaikh, let's have half the price right away and I'll carry out my part of the agreement in two days, and I shall pay for it with my head if I don't fulfill it."

The sheikh of the fishmongers said, "I am in agreement and my money is ready."

Sabir said, "May it be with God's blessing—bring the witnesses and the notary."

And this is the text of the agreement, O my Emir

With God's blessing, we give witness, we the witnesses, that every day the stalwart shaikh, Sabir the son of So-and-so from So-and-so, will sell every ten *kantars* of good fish to the sheikh of the fishmongers, Shamardali, son of So-and-so from So-and-so, at the rate of a quarter of a silver coin for a *kantar*, and the contract is valid for the period of a lunar month and is renewable if so desired by the seller and the buyer. In accordance with this contract the buyer shall pay to the seller immediately half the amount in silver, and the contract shall come into effect after two sunrises, and if the seller fails to comply with the contract he shall pay for it with his head.

In the house of his mother and father

The mother said, "My son, you have sold air and have been paid in silver."

Sabir replied, "O mother, I sold fish; he who sells air is not paid in silver."

The mother said, "You sold what you do not own, son.

Sabir said, "The fish are in the water, mother."

The mother said, "But you do not own the fish of the water, son."

Sabir asked her, "And who owns the fish of the water, mother?"

The mother said, "No one, my son, no one."

Sabir said to his mother, "The bags of money are under my belt. I shall enter the lane of the carpenters and a carpenter will make me a boat of mulberry wood. I shall buy it. The fisherman who sticks to his job will catch much fish. Instead of fishing at the shore, he will take the boat and cast his net into the water, collect up the fish from the water, pile them up on the shore and take his daily wage from me. The porter who carries the fish and puts them on the cart, I'll pay him, too, the price of his labor and the sweat of his brow; so too will the driver take his wage from me when he transports the fish from the river bank to the souk. Thus shall I carry out the condition that is laid upon me and remove the sword from off my neck."

The mother said, "May God protect that mind of yours, my son."

The fox's conversation with the watchmen

The month passed, and Sabir said to Shamardali, "Let's renew the contract." And after that month, there passed yet another and another, and Sabir bought the boat, and then a month and another and another and another passed, and Sabir bought two boats and said to Shamardali, "I do not want to renew the contract."

Shamardali asked him, "Why not?"

Sabir said, "The contract has been unfair to me, Shamardali. Let's write a fresh contract and you be content with half of what you are earning today." Whenever there passed a month and another and another, Sabir would buy another fishing boat and would call out to a fisherman who was carrying his net on his shoulder and say to him, "Get on to the boat, that's better for you than walking to fish along the bank on your two feet." After a year and a half, Sabir said to Shamardali, "Be content with a quarter of what you earn, Shamardali."

Shamardali said, "What has come over you, man?"

Sabir said, "Be content, my friend, for you earn without getting up off your bench."

After a year, Sabir revoked the contract between him and Shamardali, and when Shamardali sold fish at the price at which Sabir sold it, they shared the market equally. But Sabir lowered the price of his fish and kept on lowering it, so buyers fled from Shamardali and Shamardali fled from the souk with what money remained to him. He spent the rest of his life in a tavern owned by a Maltese.

Thus did Sabir come to be without a competitor in the souk

He bought a fishing boat for every fisherman going along the bank on his two feet with his net on his shoulders, and he warned the fishermen against taking the small fish, saying to them, "The small fish of today is the whale of tommorow."

And he changed the scales and ordered the town crier to proclaim in the souk: "Selling as from tomorrow will be by the kilo and not by the *okka*." And he brought an expert on the classifying of the different sorts of fish and, giving him a handsome wage, said to him, "Appraise the sorts of fish and choose for each sort a name and fix a price, for just as people are slaves and masters so it is also with fish."

Sabir said to his men, "Put on sale half the souk's requirements of fish and salt away the rest. In this way we shall raise the price of fresh fish and fix the price of the salted fish."

Sabir said to himself, "Here I am, with my superior brain, ruling the souk with the heart of a lion, king of the animals."

Sabir's conversation with Time

Sabir looked out from the balcony of his palace and addressed Time:

"King of fresh fish and of salted fish—and yet I'm old.

"Creator of thriving business in the souks—and yet I'm alone.

"My business sets in motion boats, fishermen, porters, drivers, carts, mules, donkeys, and the painter's brush[2]—and yet I'm static.

"My carriage is drawn by a white horse and by a black horse—and yet my days are drawn by a black night and a white day to the cemetery.

"They stand aside for me in the street, for me the king, the whip-bearer—and yet I am departing; and they are remaining.

"Just as the money lies in my coffers so shall I lie—cold as silver.

"O Time, you are the sole one I have not vanquished—it is as though you were the king.

"With my gold I shall buy the most beautiful of your daughters, O Time, that she may wear mourning after I am gone. If I am incapable of doing it, her belly will swell from any son of a whore and my consolation will be that tongues of fire will remain alight in the souks telling all comers of the news of me."

—Translated by Denys Johnson-Davies

Ibrahim 'Abd al-Majeed (b. 1946)

Egyptian novelist and short-story writer, Ibrahim 'Abd al-Majeed (also written Maguid or Majid) was born in Alexandria and studied philosophy at its university, graduating in 1973. One of the avant-garde younger Egyptian writers of fiction, he has published to date several novels and short-story collections. His first book of fiction was his collection, *Little Scenes Around a Big Wall* (1982), followed by *The Tree and the Birds* (1987). He published his

---

2. In Egyptian villages, fish shops are often decorated with pictures of fish, boats, etc.

first novel, *The Hunter and the Pigeons,* in Baghdad in 1986. Other collections and novels followed: his novels, *Lanterns of the Sea* (1993) and *No one Sleeps in Alexandria* (1996), and his short-story collections, *Closing the Windows* (1993), *Spaces* (1995), and *Old Ships* (2001). This prolific writer has lived in many parts of Egypt and, for some time, in Saudi Arabia. He now works in Cairo as Director of the General Directorate of Culture, which deals with literary affairs throughout Egypt. He also edits the *Al-Thaqafa 'l-Jadida* Quarterly.

THE TREE AND THE BIRDS

[1]

On Salim's first day of work he noticed how the sun dominated the sky, and the earth was tortured by drought. All the ground seemed barren but for thorns. The superintendent had told him not to move from this position, for it would be his job to furnish the trains with water from the Crow.

He did not know why they called the apparatus "the Crow." He does not know to this day. A wide pipe rose vertically for three meters over a tank in the ground. The pipe was bent at the end for one meter and bore a rubber hose dangling downward. The train would halt, and the driver inserted the end of the hose into his tank while Salim opened the valve on top of the pipe. Water would gush forth from the ground tank. The trains did not exceed two or three a day. No train ever seemed to return, nor did any driver. Even the weekly train, which hauled water to the ground tank, was always different, as was its driver.

Salim and Hassan divided the day between them. Under his flimsy roof of three wooden boards, Salim wondered why Hassan never talked to him. Each would work either the day or night shift for a month, then switch. However, Hassan was always frowning and never greeted Salim or answered his own greeting no matter what time of day it was.

Salim realized that the days would pass in a meaningless blur, so he planted a tree which grew bigger and bigger and helped him to feel the passing of years. Everything else around him remained the same. The desert thorns never grew taller, or disappeared. The Crow became rusty but remained rooted. The tracks stretched quietly toward the two horizons. The distant wall separating wilderness from city never crumbled. Even the supervisor disappeared; no one came to check the work. Yet Salim realized the world was wider than his surroundings. Surely the trains traveled to villages and far-off cities. His work was important for it gave the trains water to run on. What really surprised him was that the tree, now billowing with leaves, never invited birds to land on it. Perhaps no birds could reach this vast territory. But what good is a tree without birds?

One autumn morning Salim found the tree chopped off near the bottom of the trunk and lying on the ground, broken. Its branches were twisted, and his heart felt devastated, as if it had fallen onto the tracks and been crushed by a train. Since Hassan was nowhere present, Salim was sure he had done it.

In the barrenness of the area, the leaves of the tree had been a green oasis that had uplifted his eyes when the sun fell upon it or the morning dew made it glisten. It had helped him endure the sight of that savage Crow. Not wanting his grief to continue, Salim planted one of its branches. He fashioned the others together into a simple shack. It was a hard day. Trains passed carrying heavy military equipment. When he asked a nervous driver, "What's going on?" he was answered with one word, "The war." In the evening Hassan arrived, smiling.

"Why did you cut down my tree?"

"I don't like birds."

"But the birds never even came!"

"What do you know? I see you've planted a new tree." Hassan's voice was indifferent.

Salim spoke firmly. "If you cut it off, I shall cut you up. And don't you ever enter this shack."

Hassan, who was stronger than Salim, remained cool. "Even though five years have elapsed since the beginning of our friendship?"

Somehow this annoyed Salim more than anything. How had five years passed so quickly?

[2]

In his small room over the low house where he lived, Salim contemplated the fact that he had never had any relationship with his neighbors. A year ago a horde of bulldozers and workers had demolished the houses around his. Their inhabitants had packed up their belongings and moved to the other side of the town so a new weaving factory could be built in place of them. His own house had, for some reason, been spared. It remained alone in the middle of rubble that was soon purchased by merchants during the day or stolen by thieves at night. While the factory was being built, the din never ceased. Apparently the builders worked all night and all day. One morning Salim awoke to find the factory surrounded by a high wall, and his house was behind it.

He could not see over the wall and no one from the outside could see in. For a long time Salim had thought of quitting his job. He felt it was stealing his life from him. But one day he returned to find his own house locked tight with huge locks, and he realized he would have to move somewhere else. He decided to live next to the tree and the Crow and the birds! Indeed the second tree had grown tall and many birds had come to stand on the Crow! Salim brought some wooden boards and enlarged and fortified his small shack. He noticed that Hassan was erecting his own shack nearby; perhaps, Salim thought, this might now lead to a real friendship. Hassan still never offered more than a greeting when they passed.

Now Salim placed his attention on the birds, drenching the ground with water, letting them drink, hop, turn over in the water, and dance. He didn't understand why they would never roost on the tree, but only on the Crow. He bought seeds for them in the city and scattered them on the ground as they chirped. He tried to tame them. He would signal to them to stand on the Crow, which they would, and to come down again, which they would. They would even alight on his palms, or shoulders, or head. In the evenings before Hassan came out of his shack, they would scatter. Salim never feared for their safety with Hassan; when he, Salim, worked at night, they never came during the day. He would dream of them continuously. They spoke to him a lot. They said that Hassan spent half the night gathering uneaten birdseed off the ground and eating it. The other half of the night he shook the tree so the nests would fall; this made the birds laugh, since there were no nests.

Salim regretted that he could get the birds neither to nest in the tree nor stand on its branches. In his mind the tree grew and grew, becoming enormous, then shrank back to its old dry stick. In his dreams their chatter fondled him till he awoke, laughing. Sometimes Salim worked with the birds roosting on his shoulders or head; the drivers of the trains did not seem to be surprised. He realized the number of trains had decreased substantially. Now a whole week went by and only one or two trains might pass. And when he saw many green trains passing without stopping for water, and without emitting smoke like the old black trains, he thought surely his job was finished.

But one day the superintendent limped toward him again. Salim could see that his face was all wrinkled and his hair white under a black beret.

"At last you return, Sir."

The superintendent glanced around him. "Do you live here now?"

"Yes."

"Don't you ever go to the city?"

"Rarely—only to buy what I need."

"The city has changed a great deal."

Salim did not feel that had anything to do with him in any way. The birds were jumping from one of his shoulders to the other, and from his head to the Crow. The superintendent didn't even look surprised but continued speaking and smiling.

"The cloth factory has been demolished—so has your old house. Large new buildings have been erected in their place. New hotels." ("Quite a few years must have gone by," thought Salim.) "Where's Hassan?"

"Maybe he's sleeping in his hut."

"Does he still chop down trees?"

Salim was amazed at how much this fellow knew! The superintendent continued, "I realize your work here is slight now. The green trains don't use coal and don't need much water. But don't worry, and please don't abandon your post until I return again!"

"When will that be, Sir?

Salim suddenly felt very small. He also felt he was speaking about something so far away that he could not even imagine it.

"Perhaps in ten years. Perhaps tomorrow. But don't be anxious."

The superintendent stretched out his hand and lifted a bird from Salim's right shoulder onto his left. Then he departed, leaving Salim alone again in the huge space. As he left, all the birds had alighted on the Crow; now one hopped down to drink and Salim shouted at it. He opened his palm and it came. He spoke irritably, "For a long time I've been teaching you love. Why did you fly down before I signaled to you? Now, drink!"

But the bird did not drink. It flew off, followed by the other birds. They spread out into the air and Salim felt the universe had two oppressive sides that were crushing him. But at this moment, an old black train, belching out with thick white clouds, chose to stop for water.

The driver was telling him about the war. "You know, when that first phase of the war ended, many young drivers disappeared. I think they'd been called to fight and were blown up in the desert, or lost in the sand. Maybe they were killed by bedouins who took their weapons and water."

On went the black train and its carriages laden with heavy military equipment. Later many green trains would pass laden with equipment, the trains that never stopped. Another war was going on.

[3]

When Salim saw Hassan standing with the ax in his hands and angry sparks flashing in his eyes, he also noticed that his legs trembled. Hassan had grown old. Salim decided to attack him. Most of the previous night he had heard the intermittent sound of blows, which he imagined to be a sharp wind on the train tracks. And as had become his habit since the birds abandoned him, he heard their voices crying that it was impossible for anyone to resist thirst; he imagined he was hearing the bird he had rebuked. It never occurred to him that Hassan was out there cutting at the tree. His own legs were shaky too! He approached the tree and began stripping its thick leaves.

"What are you doing?"

"I want the branches. We can dry them and kindle them at night."

The space around them felt wider than the whole earth and sky. For that matter the earth could have been the sky and vice versa. There was no one else in the universe. Hassan chopped off a branch and offered it to Salim. "Go, plant it, make yourself another tree."

"Why did you cut off my second tree too?"

Hassan smiled. "This is the fifth tree. You forgot!"

The face of the earth seemed darker than on his first day. The thorn shrubs were high and huge. The tracks seemed to be coming out of their places. Even the Crow seemed more crooked than usual, and the faded hose dangled from it like a fighter that had thrown away his weapons. Salim took the branch and planted it. That night he said, "It's a merciless winter."

Hassan was blowing on the fire. He had moved his possessions into Salim's hut; now they were living together. When they were frightened by a loud crash outside, Hassan said, "The Crow has fallen! Its pipe has eroded and come down."

The black trains stopped coming. When Salim would open the valve to drink or wash, he noticed its pipe was filled with holes. Water gushed through like from a fountain. Now the weekly train came once a month to fill the ground tank. Finally it also disappeared. Salim dug a well to drink from. Hassan dug another well for himself. Gradually they drank from one well.

Salim's thoughts strayed back to his first day on the job. It was a miracle they could travel so far; he wondered how old he was now. Hassan surprised him by asking, "Aren't you ever going to return to the city? It has changed so much."

Salim said, "The superintendent asked me the same thing a long time ago."

Hassan said, " They've demolished the new buildings and rebuilt the cloth factory."

Salim placed some old pillows behind his back. He thought, "Maybe they just wanted to get rid of my old house."

Hassan said, "I've heard them speaking of a new war."

Salim did not comment. All he said was, "Are you going to cut the new tree too when it grows?"

He was still dreaming of the birds. Now that the Crow had fallen, perhaps they would return to stand on the tree.

But the wind was blowing outside. Thunder crashed as loudly as if the mountains were toppling onto one another. Lightning filled their hut with awe. Hassan placed the teakettle on the fire, saying, "We have enough wood for another year. We won't die of the cold."

—*Translated by May Jayyusi and Naomi Shihab Nye*

Muhammad 'Abd al-Malik (b. 1944)

Bahraini short-story writer and novelist, Muhammad 'Abd al-Malik is an experimental and sensitive author, deeply concerned with the plight of downtrodden individuals. He describes the various reactions of these people to all kinds of exploitation, including class exploitation, and the ways in which they interact with their deprivation and insecurity. However, he is also prone to humor which he introduces in his descriptions of some social situations, as we see in the following story. He writes in a vivid and effective style, usually free of mawkishness and redundancies but sustaining a sufficient emotional appeal. He published his first collection, *The Death of the Cart Owner*, in 1972 and his second, *We Love the Sun*, in 1975. Other collections are: *The Fence* (1982) and *The River Flows*. He has also experimented with novel writing, publishing *Jizwa* in 1980.

THE ILLUSION

Hamid Faraj, director-general of the Central Woman's Hospital, received a quiet telephone call saying, "Su'ud al-Dhahab's wife is on her way to the hospital."

No sooner had he heard this news than Faraj summoned the head doctor of the present shift into his office and spoke to her, in a voice feigning calm, "A person's worth is proven, for better or worse, when tested." His tone was serious, reflected by his lined forehead and frozen eyes, as well as his smoking, which he did only rarely these days, having announced in the local newspapers that he had joined the Committee Against Smoking. However, his mind at this moment was not lucid enough to be decisive or define his plans.

The doctor was silent, awaiting explanation of what was meant by "being tested." Mr. Faraj, well-trained to mask confusion and worry with apparent composure, said, "You know very well, Dr. Nawal, how historical and important to the hospital these visits are!"

This only increased the moment's ambiguity. Dr. Nawal asked, "What visits, Mr. Hamid?"

"Su'ud al-Dhahab's wife!"

"And what will she be doing here in the hospital?"

"She'll give birth, like other women."

Now everything seemed quite clear to Dr. Nawal and she said, "Of course, we'll do our duty, naturally."

Faraj replied, "That's not enough!"

"We'll prepare a private room."

"That's not enough."

"We'll welcome her at the main gate." Sharply, she added, "Unhabitually."

Gazing at her, he answered, "And what else? That's still not enough."

"What do you suggest then?"

He lifted the telephone receiver and spoke to all departments of the hospital, uttering short, clear orders. He took out another cigarette while the first one was still burning between his fingers. Dr. Nawal recalled that he had headed the Committee Against Smoking for the last three years. He banged the receiver down nervously. Then he walked with sure steps, ordering, "Do not leave the operating room."

An emergency state was declared in the Women's Hospital. The hospital divisions resembled a military barracks during wartime. Rushing nurses with blanket-covered beds, with food and baffled patients, collided with one another in the halls. A cacophony of raised voices swirled in the air. Heels echoed everywhere. More nurses appeared, asking in surprise, "What's happening?"

It was very difficult for them to get a good answer since no one was speaking calmly. Faraj stood at the center of the storm, personally supervising the movements of the staff like a captain issuing orders to the crew of his drowning ship. He panicked when he discovered that the private room overlooking the eastern garden had been occupied for the last two days. His voice rose in frustration, "The lady must leave the room at once!"

The head nurse replied, "But all the other private rooms are occupied!"

"To hell! To hell! The room must be emptied at once!"

"But her surgery is still fresh . . . "

"Take her to one of the wards."

"At once, at once, sir. Is that all?"

Faraj looked relaxed for the first time. "This is only the beginning."

And he flashed like lightning down the long corridor to the operation room, followed by a crowd of nurses and technicians and doctors. Mr. Hamid Faraj had been transformed to a man at the peak of his energy and vitality, recovering the gusto that had left him years ago following three exhausting operations on his intestines. He arrived in the operating room in only a few seconds and was welcomed by a young woman doctor. "Everything is in tip-top shape."

"You will help Dr. Nawal the entire time."

"I've anticipated this."

"And after the delivery you will monitor the lady's health from hour to hour."

"Then I must be relieved of my duties at the Number Four wing."

"I shall see to it that you are. Tell Rose, the head nurse, to bring me reports on the infant step-by-step."

"Alright—anything else?"

"More later."

Faraj went to the main gate preceded by a wheelchair and followed by Dr. Nawal, along with nurses and curious visitors. They all took their places in two facing lines, holding medicines, sheets, and incense, as a blue Mercedes Benz approached the gate. In a few moments Mr. Hamid Faraj was opening the car door himself, with the wheelchair close behind. A middle-aged woman descended from the car, clearly in an advanced state of labor and nearly collapsing. She was carefully placed in the wheelchair, which flew immediately from hand to hand amidst the commotion. Faraj himself looked as if he were in labor for fear that al-Dhahab's wife might fall out and the child be born on the floor. What a disaster that would be! Faraj was too distraught to keep up with the speedy procession and began calling out, "Take care, take great care! Take it easy, but hurry up!"

Rashid 'Askar, the driver of the blue Mercedes, was not in an enviable state himself, since he had been taken completely by surprise, and the quick procession forced him to run and run, holding his slippers between his hands. In his state of stunned confusion, he imagined this crowd of people intended to kidnap his wife for an unknown reason.

The procession stopped at the large delivery room, which could not accommodate so many people. Faraj beckoned to the nurses, who broke into smaller groups. And he faced Rashid 'Askar who decided to hurl his questions out at once, although his mind was at peace now that his wife's procession had stopped at the right place. His mouth opened, but Faraj quickly interrupted, "Everything will be fine, just fine."

'Askar stuttered, "I am quite sure of that."

Faraj added, "I only hope our care will meet with your acceptance."

"We're unable to thank you enough."

A smile broke on the face of Mr. Hamid Faraj. He felt ebullient: his feet were light on the ground. Suddenly the delivery room's door opened and a nurse rushed past pushing a long bed, with a smile of victory and pride on her face. Directing her words to Faraj first, she announced, "It's a boy!"

Faraj turned to where 'Askar was standing and said, "Congratulations, congratulations! It's a boy!"

An older nurse uttered a ululation of joy. All faces wore smiles. Then the procession proceeded to the private room prepared for al-Dhahab's wife and quickly cleaned away all vestiges of all insects and cockroaches, in an expert communal fashion never before witnessed in that hospital. The long procession preceded the middle-aged steps of Rashid 'Askar who followed shortly behind.

His wife was smiling, surrounded by a large retinue of doctors, nurses, section heads and technicians, some carrying sheets, equipment to measure blood pressure, and pages of reports. 'Askar addressed the group. repeating, "I simply can't thank you enough."

Hamid Faraj said, "We apologize for our limitations." After a long pause, he asked, "And when will His Excellency arrive?"

Immediately Rashid 'Askar remembered the surreal quality of their strange welcome. Now these words fell on him like a strange unexpected bird out of the sky. He had almost forgotten his initial surprise till this moment riveted him, and explained it all. His thoughts were interrupted by Hamid Faraj saying, "If His Excellency does not like visitors, we'll take the necessary precautions."

Rashid 'Askar stared in astonishment at Faraj as the latter continued. "And by the way, what will you call His Excellency, the newborn?"

'Askar exchanged looks with his wife. And now just as Faraj was about to open his mouth and ask more questions, he was stopped by a voice from the end of the lobby, the tremulous voice of a panting man, tongue faltering on the words before he announced them, "The wife of Su'ud al-Dhahab has arrived!"

And he ran. Mr. Hamid Faraj was running again. He ran despite the great exhaustion that had afflicted him, and the whole hospital began running again, from all directions, headed everywhere. In the corridors, rooms, lobbies, on the street opposite the main gate, in the delivery rooms, bathrooms, and in the wards. The only person who remained composed and motionless was Rashid 'Askar, chauffeur of the Manager of the Investment Company whose job had given him the opportunity, for the first time in his life, to enjoy the use of a Mercedes Benz for one historic occasion. Intoxicated, he said to his wife, "The Mercedes Benz is a hero!"

And they embraced in the few moments of privacy they had, while the hospital swarmed to the front gate and before orders to empty the room could arrive.

—*Translated by Salwa Jabsheh and Naomi Shihab Nye*

'Abd al-llah 'Abd al-Qadir (b. 1940)

Iraqi short-story writer 'Abd al-llah 'Abd al-Qadir was born in Basra. He took a degree in literature from the University of Baghdad and worked first in teaching, then, until 1980, as secretary-general for the Union of Iraqi Artists and a director of theater and folk arts at the Ministry of Culture. In 1980 he moved to the Emirates where he now works as Executive Direc- tor of the 'Uweiss Prize for Culture. He has written regularly for the press and participated in numerous literary conferences and seminars in the Arab world. His interest in drama prompted him to write his own plays and a study of theater in the Emirates, a virgin subject at the time, titled *History of Drama in the Emirates* (1986) and followed in 1997 by *History of Theater In the Sharja Over Two Decades*.

He is a prolific short-story writer, having published ten collections to date among which are: *The Woes of Hunchback Alwan* (1990), *Elegy on Gilgamish* (1991), *The General* (1994), *Request for Asylum* (1996), and *The Yankee* (1999). In 2002 he published his whole works in two volumes. In 2003 he published his last collection to date, *The Gate of Freedom . . . The Gate of Death*.

THE BIRTHDAY PARTY

'Alwan's house was full today, with more than one beautiful bride. They were like bright, fragrant butterflies, their colorful clothes like a garden radiant with flowers and trees. Their eyes sparkled with joy. But 'Alwan had long since ceased to feel joy, and on this particular day, his youngest daughter's birthday, he was sadder than ever. She'd invited all her friends, and, while they danced with happy faces, he looked on with the deepest sorrow. For him all festive occasions lacked something in exile, just as all sorrows were heavy. His eyes glistened with tears as he watched his little girl leaping and chirping like a bird of paradise, her hair flying as she moved. If only, he thought, she could have celebrated her birthday in their homeland. He prayed to God her wedding day would be in his home- town, where the two of them had been born and he had lived all his life.

The sound of song filled the whole house, the nine candles danced as they burned. The tables were laden with food, and every so often a light flashed as commemorative photos were taken. But such a day failed to lift the spirits of the weary, downcast 'Alwan.

What a long life it had been! How in heaven had it passed?

"Why don't you ever celebrate your birthday?" his little boy asked him.

"I'll celebrate my fiftieth," he answered. "Ha, ha, ha!"

It was a long time since 'Alwan had been able to laugh like that, and the boy was taken aback.

"Mother," he exclaimed. "Father laughed."

The little guests were surprised too, as they heard all their fathers laughing in their turn. The news spread through the house.

"'Alwan laughed, you said?"

"It's a miracle!"

"Where did the sun rise today?"

Still 'Alwan went on laughing till his mouth was wide open and he had tears in his eyes.

"God make it a good omen," people said.[1]

"What's made you laugh, 'Alwan?" his wife asked.

"I was thinking of my father, Fatima," he answered.

"So why has he made you laugh now?"

"Because once, around forty years ago, I asked him to celebrate my birthday."

"Did he agree?"

"No. He shouted at me and pinched my ear so hard I thought he'd pulled it off. Then he called to my mother.

'Come over here, Umm 'Alwan,' he said. 'Your son wants to turn the world upside down.'

'What's happened?' mother said. 'What have you done, 'Alwan?'

'Just imagine,' father said. 'He's actually asked me to throw a birthday party for him!'"

Birthday parties had been something really new in those days—and anything really new, they said, was a delusion, and delusions led to hell. Every year, though, 'Alwan had gone on dreaming of a birthday party, and when he grew to be a young man he'd celebrated his birthday all by himself, too timid and fearful and shy to announce the occasion openly.

His little girl came up to him.

"But father," she said, "didn't you ever visit your friends on their birthdays?"

"People never celebrated their birthdays then," 'Alwan said.

"No one at all?"

"Well, just once it happened. A friend of mine called Wameed invited me to his."

This boy Wameed ('Alwan told them) was the son of the city governor, who went to the same school but never felt at ease with the sons of major functionaries like the police chief, or the army commander, or the governor's assistant.

---

1. There is a common fear in some parts of the Arab world that hearty laughter may lead to misfortune. The invocation of a good omen is to drive away evil.

He disliked them, regarding them as pampered, and so he only mixed with boys from a lower class than his own.

One day he told 'Alwan, "It's my birthday next Thursday."

"You mean you celebrate your birthday?" 'Alwan asked, surprised.

"Yes. Why not?"

"Didn't your father shout at you and pinch your ear?"

"No. Would you like to come, 'Alwan?"

"What, me? To a birthday party?"

"Yes. What's so strange about that?"

'Alwan was so happy he could have flown through the air. He arrived at his own alley panting, with his satchel on his back and holding on to his jacket to stop the pencil and the eraser and the four *fils*, which was great wealth to him, from dropping out. He got home, ready to kick the door open and announce his news. Then he stopped suddenly, remembering his father, and tried to stifle his panting.

"Will Father fly into a rage again?" he wondered. "How am I going to tell him?"

He went into the house finally, put his satchel down under his iron bed, put his books in their place (he didn't have any desk or shelves for them), then looked at the faces in front of him. It was a bitter evening, and his father was warming himself by the newly lit fire, while his mother was tidying the room and the old radio wheezed out a light song. His father, head bent, seemed to be following the tune.

'Alwan sat cross-legged on his bed, stealing looks now at his father, now at his mother, and sometimes at his little brothers and sisters playing in the room. His mother looked back at him, surprised at the way he was sitting there. Had he failed his exams, she wondered? No, it couldn't be that. She knew how intelligent and hardworking he was. So what was wrong with him?

"'Alwan," she called. "Come here. I've a job for you."

'Alwan got up and went over to the east side of the courtyard. He trembled a little as a cold breeze stung him, but he strove to control himself.

"All right, Mother," he said rather fearfully.

"What's the matter with you?" she asked. "You don't look yourself at all. What's happened?"

"Nothing, Mother. Nothing's happened."

"I'm your mother, 'Alwan. I always know what you're thinking."

'Alwan was afraid his mother really would read his thoughts—he'd never managed to hide a secret from her. He loved her as dearly as she loved him. Even when she was angry he could feel her tenderness, which made him less inclined to try and hide things.

Trembling from the cold, and from his news, he said:

"A birth—"

"You're not going to start on again about celebrating your birthday?"

"No, Mother."

"Well, what is it then?"

"Wameed, the city governor's son. It's his birthday next Thursday."

"The governor's son? What does that have to do with us? The governor's a wealthy man, 'Alwan."

"Wameed's my friend."

"Well, then, send him your best wishes."

He was on the verge of tears now.

"Wameed's invited me to his birthday party."

She gazed at him tenderly, her eyes widening in disbelief.

"Are you sure, 'Alwan?"

He told her he was. She passed her hand over his hair, then said, "In that case you're going!"

'Alwan was beside himself with joy. He picked up the broom and started sweeping the courtyard, no longer feeling the cold or the stinging air.

"But what am I going to wear, Mother?" he asked.

With quiet resource, Umm 'Alwan told her husband the news, making sure to catch him in a good mood. He started scowling and drawing himself up, but she begged him, softly and calmly and tenderly, to let 'Alwan go. In the end he had to agree.

Umm 'Alwan was busy the whole week getting 'Alwan's clothes ready. She made a new shirt for him, washed his jacket and his only pair of trousers, and ironed them with her own hands. Then she borrowed one of her husband's neckties, which he wore only on special occasions, and polished his old pair of shoes after having them repaired at the cobbler's.

When the longed-for Thursday came, 'Alwan was a different boy. Everything about him shone: his face, his hair, his eyes, his clothes, his shoes. His mother took care to buy a present for him to take, which cost her some hundred and fifty *fils*—a big sum that she took from the money she kept aside for the family's clothes and the preparations for the feast.

In the afternoon of this bitterly cold winter's day, his mother took him personally to the governor's house, a mansion overlooking the great river, surrounded by spacious gardens. The governor's yacht was moored in front, and there were armed police guards at the lofty gate and quantities of different-colored lamps on all the walls. Umm 'Alwan was highly nervous and turned to her son, who was carrying his present in a state of awestruck excitement. There was a clear doubt in her gaze.

'Alwan stumbled as she looked at him. She took his hand.

"Is it true?" she asked. "Did the governor's son really invite you to his birthday party?"

"Why shouldn't he, Mother?"

"Because he's the Governor's son and your father's just a simple employee."

"He's my friend."

"How can I take you in with all these police guarding the gates? And how will I find you after the party?"

"There's no problem, Mother. Just leave me to go in, and when the party's over I'll come back here."

He hardly finished his sentence before running toward the main gate. She watched him lovingly, following him as he went right up to the gate. There, as he tried to enter, one of the guards shouted at him to stop. Guns were pointed at him, and Umm 'Alwan stifled a scream.

"'Alwan!" she cried helplessly. "Son!"

'Alwan had stopped dead in his tracks. But next moment a voice came out from the garden.

"Welcome, 'Alwan," it said. "Come on in."

It was Wameed, with his father the governor, welcoming the guests. The blood returned to Umm 'Alwan's face and she started breathing more easily, thanking God her son was safe. 'Alwan felt safe now too and entered the broad gate between the two rows of police guards, who'd lined up in readiness for the governor's exit.

Umm 'Alwan sat there on the sidewalk, watching the ships sail down the great river. It was wretchedly cold, but she was too concerned about 'Alwan to go all the way back home and let him return on his own.

Time passed, and still she sat there, feeling as though the hours had stopped, asking passersby every so often what the time was. The sun sank behind the palm groves, and the colored lights of the mansion were switched on. The ships, too, began to turn on their lights. She grew ever more anxious. Her pulse quickened. She started to regret letting him have this adventure and was even more afraid of her husband's reproof if she was late.

As for 'Alwan, he went in stunned at what lay before him. The garden stretched all around the mansion with scores of fruit trees and flowers of every kind. There were driveways for cars, and garages with several cars of various colors inside. Wameed led him to the entrance of the mansion, a large door with glass panels, and from there he climbed a flight of marble stairs and entered the main hall. He gazed around him in speechless amazement, fascinated by the lights and furniture and colorfully dressed guests, the girls dancing in the arms of young boys of the same age. His eyes widened and he found himself tongue-tied.

He was offered a plate heaped with food whose name he didn't even know. He longed for his brothers and sisters to be able to share it with him and wanted to put a piece of chocolate in his pocket to let his mother taste it. She must be thirsty now, he thought suddenly, squatting there on the sidewalk, and he wished he could slip a bottle of the soft drink into his pocket too. He didn't, though, dare do any of this under the eyes of all those strangers. Everyone, he thought, must be watching him in this strange, new atmosphere.

The time passed all too quickly for 'Alwan, but he decided he should be the first to leave and so keep his promise to the mother he loved so dearly. He was worried at the thought of her waiting for him on the sidewalk, opposite the governor's mansion. He began, very politely, to take his leave, but was stopped by Nuha, Wameed's sister. She was a year younger than he was.

"Take this bunch of flowers with you, 'Alwan," she said.

"For me?"

"Yes, for you. Why didn't you dance?"

He laughed.

"Me? Dance? Because it's—it's shameful, Nuha, for a man to dance."

"There's nothing shameful about dancing."

"My father says dancing's just for women."

To his acute embarrassment, a number of the guests overheard the conversation and started laughing. He took the bunch of flowers and left. Nuha and Wameed walked with him to the gate of the garden, but he asked them to go back for fear of embarrassing his mother.

Night had settled on the river. The streets were lit with small lamps, and a mournful song could be heard from the deserted café nearby.

Umm 'Alwan seized the young boy's hand and tugged him briskly off.

"Why did you stay so long, 'Alwan?" she asked.

"I came at the time you said."

She hurried along, while 'Alwan talked on and on about the party, describing the women's clothes, the men's conversation, the soft manners of the boys, the taste of the pastries, the different kinds of fruit, the grandeur of the furniture, the shine of the floors, the bearing of the servants. When they reached home he just went on talking. His brothers and sisters gathered around him, and even his father, while telling his rosary beads, shared his wonderment. Then, finally, his father laughed and sent the children off to bed.

"One day, 'Alwan," he said, "you'll be a grown man. Then you can celebrate your birthday too."

'Alwan went to bed, to float in a long dream about birthdays.

Turning suddenly, 'Alwan saw all his daughter's young guests listening to his story, while his wife, Fatima, gazed at him with compassion and love, wondering at the way he'd kept this memory of childhood suffering through so many years.

"Cheer up, 'Alwan," she said finally. "This year we'll celebrate your fiftieth birthday!"

—*Translated by May Jayyusi and Christopher Tingley*

Muhammad 'Abd al-Wali (1940—1973)

Born in Ethiopia, Yemeni novelist and short-story writer Muhammad 'Abd al-Wali studied in Cairo and did his higher studies at the Gorky Institute in Moscow. After the success of the 1962 revolution in Yemen, he returned to his country and held several important positions, such as the chargé d'affaires for Yemen in Moscow and Berlin. The last position he held was director general of aviation in Yemen. 'Abd al-Wali is one of the best-known writers of fiction in the Arabian Peninsula. His work reflects a preoccupation with the human condition in its more tragic or at least more

pathetic aspects, treating, cogently and with sensitivity, problems of alienation, loneliness, artistic dedication, oppression, and the opposing aspects of
human behavior, speaking of vulnerability and of strength, of failure and
of noble endeavor. His premature death in an aviation accident while still
in his prime put an end to a most promising career. He published three
collections of short stories, *The Land, Salma* (1966), *Something Called Longing* (1972), and *Uncle Salih* (1978), as well as two novels, *They Die Strangers*
and *Sanaa: An Open City*. A complete collection of his work was published
posthumously in Beirut in 1987.

AL-SAYYID MAJID

He sat on the steps facing the gate of Al-Qal'a's prison, watching the new prisoners being led in and the soldiers chaining their feet. His face contorted in
pain. He began counting the prisoners until he got tired of it. Or perhaps the
numbers he could count were restricted to single digits, but the numbers of
prisoners kept rising ... twenty ... thirty ... forty. He scratched his head, deeply
perplexed. His eyes wandered around the scene. No one could have told if they
held any tears. He would fix his gaze on the stone set deep into the ground and
on the hammer that rose and fell with monotonous rhythm over the chains.
When he realized the flood of prisoners had ended, he went rapidly down
the steps and addressed the last man who had entered, trying to speak amiably.
"Please tell me, are any more people left outside?"

He gestured toward the gate.

The prisoner did not grasp his meaning and answered simply, "No, there is
no one left."

Majid nodded his head, as if he had expected that reply.

Now the prison yard was filled with dozens of new inhabitants, each carrying
his mattress and jumbled clothing, which had been pawed and searched through
upon entry. Each man was trying to find a place for himself in the narrow prison
rooms. The older prisoners were quick to offer them spaces in their own cub-
byholes, while al-Sayyid Majid's eyes continued to stare stupidly around him.
He began sauntering among the prisoners wearing his dirty tattered shirt and
bare feet, trying to smile as if in welcome. He did not offer anyone a spot next
to him, for he realized they were a different breed.

Slowly he approached Haj Ahmad al-Haddad, who stood transfixed on the
prison steps, also observing the new arrivals. The new ones traded warm embraces with old comrades. Then would flow the rush of eager words, the spilling
questions with no satisfactory answers.

Majid spoke, "Did you notice? They are all young men."

He did not wait for an answer from al-Haddad. He scratched his head deliberately as if he were counting the number of white hairs that grew there.

Al-Haddad said abruptly, "It is Ghaitha bint al-Dheeb who sent them here—Gaitha bint al-Dheeb."

His voice rose loudly as the prisoners continued to laugh among themselves.

Majid spoke soothingly, trying to calm his friend. "They are all of Sanaa—God knows who is left on the outside."

No one paid any attention to this conversation by the steps of the mosque.

Gradually the prisoners came to know one another, and Majid, being one of the gentlest of the crew, came to be a friend to most of them.

No one ever minded giving Majid what he asked for since a smile of wonder seemed always to be planted on his lips. He'd say, "I want a cigarette and matches." Then he would rush off to a corner where he would fling himself down and smoke with pleasure.

Since Majid was the quietest madman in Al-Qal'a, he wore no chains. It was said he rarely raved and often sang—each time he smoked, he would hum an old tune sadly. He had forgotten most of its words.

When he was tranquil, he would choose someone, sit beside him, and stare into his face, asking, "Why are all you young men in here? What did you do? Who is left outside?" He would ask many other questions as well but never wait for the answers. Suddenly he would bolt away to go sit with someone else . . . and so it went.

The prisoners wondered about Majid's history. As with other things here, complete stories were never available, details remained perennially vague and the truth opaque. Once someone had said, with conviction, "Majid went mad when he fell in love with a girl and married her, only to find she was betraying him. Because of the fervor of his love, he would not leave her, so he had a nervous breakdown and lost his mind."

Others said Majid had been an ambitious youth who had wanted to make his way among the ruling family. Because he was of Hashemite[1] lineage, he began to groom himself to compete with the imam.[2] He made contact with the Freedom Party members,[3] attended their secret meetings, and debated the issues of underdevelopment and terrorism. News of this reached the imam, who had adopted Majid and planned to make him one of his supporting pillars. When he heard of Majid's mutiny, he arrested and tortured him until he went mad. Then he threw him into prison, where he had been for more than twenty years. He remained calm, thoughtful, and kind, except for certain rare moments when he would fly into a rage, rip his clothes, and attack any person near him.

---

1. The Hashemites are the descendents of the Prophet's family through his daughter, Fatima.
2. The imam was the traditional ruler of Yemen.
3. The "Freedom Party" in Yemen (or the "Party of the Liberals") was formed in the 1940s to fight the oppressive rule of the imam. It succeeded eventually in instigating a revolution against the ruler and his royalist forces, succeeding in 1969 in completely overthrowing the Imamite establishment and forming a republic.

Majid was one of the few who had visitors from the outside. He never discussed his visitor, and no one saw who visited him, yet the crier would sometimes call out in his loud voice, "Sayyid Majid! Sayyid Majid, you have a visitor."

Majid would hurry off, humming his sad tune, and disappear outside the door for a while. Then he would return carrying qat, cigarettes, and sweetmeats. Occasionally he carried clothes. One day a prisoner said Majid's visitor was his mother, that his family had some money, which assured him of clothes and food, cigarettes and qat. Majid's real obsession in prison was qat. You could often see him in front of other rooms, gathering the crumbs of qat discarded by prisoners. Then he would retire to his favorite corner near the mosque and settle himself down again, munching at the stems and twigs.

If his desire for qat overwhelmed him, he sometimes provoked the other prisoners, trying to snatch the qat from their hands. They would kick him out of their rooms. But he continued to gather the scattered dregs, sometimes arguing with other mad inmates, who also wanted them.

Once a prisoner said he had known Majid as a child, that his name was ʿAbdallah Majid, that he had worked in Dhamar over twenty years ago, and was famous for his knowledge of religious jurisprudence and tradition. He added that Majid used to be fond of good qat even then, and that his salon was very famous and was visited by many men of knowledge—judges and sheikhs, that Majid used to dress elegantly in brilliant white garments, and that he had many turbans that he changed frequently and that always looked very clean. The reason for his madness, according to this prisoner, was his addiction to qat, for he chewed it daily until midnight.

There was no one to verify the story, even though al-Muzayin, who had been there a long time and become the official prison crier, said that Majid had already been in prison a long time before his own arrival, that he had once regained his sanity and been sent home to his family. Muzayin said that when Majid was released, his mother received him happily, but after only a few days he was returned to the prison. A rumor spread that he had tried to assault her sexually.

Since that day Majid had not left the prison.

Like all the mad inmates, he remained a perplexing puzzle. No one knew anything certain about his past, and they all lived through their days much as he did, in bewilderment and baffling confusion, with no longer any present or future.

Still, Majid remained an affectionate friend to others, despite his proclivity for snatching qat from under their noses.

Things dragged on till one day something new happened. The crier's voice rang out while the prisoners were still in their corners chewing qat or preparing supper: "Everyone to his place! Prisoners, everyone to his place!"

A crowd of soldiers entered with thick clubs in their hands. They were beating the ground and yelling angrily, "Come on! Hurry up! Each to his place quickly!"

The prisoners sprang away, and the clatter of chains echoed in the yard. Each man tried to get to his place before a blow could strike him—some even dropped their untouched qat. A genuine panic ensued, as the prison guards continued shouting. When one of the prisoners sputtered, "As you wish ... but may I get a little water?" the guard bellowed, "No water, no nothing!" and struck him on his back. The man moaned and fell to the ground.

The guard swung to repeat the blow, but other prisoners were already dragging their comrade to his room. His empty water can tumbled into the gutter without anyone noticing.

Majid walked hurriedly to the mad section of the prison, staring anxiously about him. He stopped before he got there, looking around at the prison yard that was abandoned except for the soldiers, who yelled, "Shut your windows and no one look out!"

Some of the soldiers threw stones at open windows.

All this took only a few minutes, but they were long terrifying minutes that passed like centuries. Majid had withdrawn into a quiet corner. The soldiers paid no attention to the mad inmates.

Suddenly the lights were turned off and an intense darkness reigned.

The hearts of the prisoners were filled with terror.

What had happened? What was going on?

Questions were whispered in every room. Some tried to peer out from the cracks in the windows, despite the darkness. But stones would pelt the windows, as if the soldiers instinctively sensed the prisoners' eyes.

The yard was completely dark. Fear stymied everyone's comprehension. One terrified prisoner whispered, "Even the sun has disappeared." Another tried to be funny, though his voice trembled, "I heard the soldiers commanding it to stay in its place." No one laughed.

The prison's inner gate opened and everyone heard the loud clanking of chains. The hammer echoed unpleasantly. They heard rapid blows on flesh and the moans of a human being.

One of the prisoners tried to count the number of hammer blows to determine the number of new prisoners.

One . . . two . . . three . . .

He could not continue after the sharp cries, "Enough, no more! God knows you've got me! No more beating! No more!"

The guard yelled, "Be silent, you rogue!"

Another shouted, "Beat up that bastard!"

The blows continued. They heard the sound of someone being dragged on the ground, his chains scraping.

The victim of the beating cried wildly, "Enough! Enough! Damn you, enough!"

The hammering on the chains continued violently. They heard the sound of the lower dungeons being opened. One of the huddled prisoners wept convulsively, "They are killing us, I tell you they are killing us."

His comrades tried to quiet him, but he was hysterical. A soldier beat the door of the cell with his club. "Are you going to be quiet or should we teach you how to behave?"

His voice made the prisoner weep silently.

Other prisoners threw themselves to the ground, covered their heads with their blankets, and tried to shut their ears.

They could hear the thud of bodies on the dungeon floors. Bodies being dragged. "Enough, I told you!" "Man, you are hurting me, let me walk!" Bodies were flung onto the floors of the dungeons.

More minutes passed, long and mute ones. Then the doors of the dungeons clanged shut. Soldiers were banging on stones with clubs. Some still pelted stones at the windows. Afterwards a wary quietude ensued. A whisper, "They are going to take us out and beat us."

"They might execute some of us."

"God forbid! Maybe they are just bringing in new prisoners."

"But why all this intimidation?"

"Perhaps the newcomers are very important."

"Who do you think they could be?"

Muttered questions. "We know there are many of them."

"No, perhaps only five or six."

"Didn't you hear those chains? Man, they are more than ten!"

No one that night knew much except for Majid, who had crouched in his hidden corner and observed everything.

In the morning the soldiers forbade the prisoners to pass by the dungeons where the newcomers had been placed.

Each cell tried to find out from other cells what had happened.

No one knew but everyone guessed.

Majid went about as usual, skipping peacefully, though his face was shadowed with sorrow. After some hours he passed by the dungeon door, humming his usual tune, and heard the voice of a human being from within. "I want a cigarette . . . I want a cigarette."

Majid kept walking as though he had heard nothing. When he passed some fellow prisoners near the mosque, he said painfully, "Oh, how I'd like a cigarette." One gave him a cigarette. He took it and turned to another, saying, "Could I have another cigarette? Many cigarettes. Many more."

The prisoner rebuked him, for he was discussing the awful night with his companions.

To other prisoners Majid said, "Oh, I'd like a cigarette, many, many cigarettes."

They gave him some, then told him off when he kept asking for more.

He left them and went to others. He continued collecting cigarettes and even smiled in the face of the soldier who sold the cigarettes, saying, "Could you give me one?" The soldier gave him what he asked for.

He proceeded slowly to the dungeon, looking left and right. No one was watching him. The soldiers were watching the other prisoners to make sure they did not pass in front of the dungeons. Majid was not being watched. When he arrived in front of the dungeon, he crouched low and pressed his hands close to a narrow gap beneath the door. He rolled the cigarettes underneath it.

He rose and shook the dust from his body.

A voice reached him from inside, from underground.

"Thank you . . . thank you . . . we also want some matches."

And Majid went off, looking for some matches.

—Translated by Lena Jayyusi and Naomi Shihab Nye

Jamal Abu Hamdan (b. 1938)

Born in Amman, Jordanian dramatist and short-story writer Jamal Abu Hamdan obtained a B.A. in law from the Arab University in Beirut and has worked as deputy head for legal affairs of the Royal Jordanian Airlines. He also worked for many years in the field of journalism, especially in Jordan's two leading papers, *Al-Ra'y* and *Al-Dustur*. Although not prolific, his volume of short stories *Many Sorrows and Three Gazelles* (1970), made an immediate impact in avant-garde literary circles, with its highly symbolic stories deeply involved with the Palestinian and Arab social and political scene. He is also a fine playwright, having written such plays as *A Box of Biscuits for Mary Antoinette* (1968) and *The Night of Burial of Actress Jean*, a monodrama (1992), which was translated by PROTA and published in its *Anthology of Short Plays* (2003). As well as stories written for children, he has also published two more collections of short stories, *A Place Facing the Sea* (1993) and *Searching for Zizya'* (1999); a long story, *Kingdom of Ants* (1998); and two novels, *Beautiful Death* (1998) and *Plucking the Wild Flower* (2002). He lives in Amman, Jordan.

THE CLOUD

"See how beautiful it is," I told him. And before he raised his head, I continued, "I mean, the play of light on it."

He gazed at it for a while as he kept on walking, then said, "I envy you!"

I waited for him to explain.

"Because you saw it before I did," he said.

"No one can possess the clouds," I said.

"That's not true. Beautiful things belong to those who see them first."

He went up close to her and pointed to the cloud, but she did not look up. She gazed at his face and said nothing.

A little later the moon rose. I expected one of them to speak. I remembered that he had once told me how he used to play with other children in the moonlight, until the moon set on the western horizon of the city. One night they had come upon a high wall and played near it for a while. When the moon began to slip down to the west, the wall had blocked their view of it. Because he and the other children needed the moon, they scattered, and he had never seen them again.

He never would have believed that a wall could screen out the moon. At the precise moment when the moon slipped behind the wall, the world looked strange and ambivalent. And so he had gone indoors and stayed there. . . .

The moon was making its transit now, but they did not see it. They stood in silence, his hand on her shoulder.

"She's with me now," he had told me a few days before, as we were coming down a narrow road on the Mount of Olives. "I only come out for her sake." I had smiled. "As for the city," he had continued, "it lives inside me."

We went into a small, empty church and stood inside. When he spoke it was in a whisper, because echoes frightened him, "Look at this unique view of the City from here."

We were standing at a small window of violet glass.

"Why do they always use violet glass in all the churches here?" she asked. No one answered.

After a while I remarked, "I've noticed that your paintings have almost no violet color in them at all."

"I keep the sad colors for myself," he answered. He paused, then added, "I have not yet painted my masterpiece."

We left the church and continued down on our way, passing another church on the slope of the mountain. Some people greeted him from inside. He approached the gate, picked a flower, and gave it to her. A little later he drew near her, held her hand and the flower in it as they walked together. I walked with them.

At the wall he asked me, "Do you know when this wall was built?"

I shook my head.

"Do you know that this city has a special smell?" he asked. She clung to him, nestling. I gazed at them. "Just like the special smell of a mother," he said. "The city and the mother have the same smell."

We walked on.

The next day I departed, alone.

They got here together. We did not exchange greetings as they entered, nor did we exchange much talk. Through all the days that followed I did not ask them a single question. Their world seemed so fragile that it could not bear another question mark. . . .

This morning I remembered that this was the anniversary of the day they had first met each other. They used to celebrate the occasion, but today they did not mention it at all. I brought a carafe and placed it between them, making an excuse that I had some work to do in the next room. I felt pleased. My veins filled with a blood that was not my own, for I felt that their world might still get back some of its softness. I was happy.

I did not hear them say anything. Then there was the sound of shattering glass, followed by silence.

I stood in the doorway. She was sitting sideways in the far corner, angry, but also very sad. He was mesmerized in his place, as though strung tightly between the two poles of the world . . . I was afraid to speak.

The carafe lay in pieces on the floor, exactly half way between them. I looked down at it for a long time. No one had wanted to break it. It had fallen as though through a will of its own. I looked at him. He had no desire to speak. When I was about to turn my gaze toward her, he shook his head and said, "But we are in Amman now! Not Jerusalem!"

I understood, Oh, God! I had feared that time might unfurl a moment as intense and searing as this, for I had known on what burning surface it would fall.

I could say nothing. I went out.

—Translated by Sharif Elmusa and Thomas G. Ezzy

QAIS'S ROAD BEGINS HERE

Once, during one of his many incarnations throughout the course of time, Qais ibn al-Mulawwah discovered that in the desert—his desert—many cities had sprouted up. Before he could get over his shock, he was taken by an urge to write out the name of Laila,[1] a girl he had once loved. He bent to the ground, but when he stuck out his finger to write, it touched a hard, solid surface.

He raised his head and saw an engraved plaque at the gate near which he was kneeling. He went up to it and read, "This is the city of builders. They raised it on the surface, like this, in solemn ritual, while nature watched, indifferent, and while history was changing its course."

Qais ibn al-Mulawwah searched the plaque for a drawing that might help him understand what he had read, but could find nothing. Then he entered through the gate.

At first he was not taken too much by surprise. Of course, just inside the gate the city loomed up suddenly before him, but he had learned, during previous incarnations, not to allow himself to get carried away with astonishment. He looked around him several times, shaking his head. He missed the softness and warmth of the desert sands, and this regret affected him deeply. However, now it was more important for him to look for a place soft enough to write out the name of Laila, as he had always done before. He looked down at his feet and found that he was standing on a black road, whose surface seemed as smooth as the skin of a snake. It slithered along until it lost its head in a square surrounded by buildings.

He went forward, feeling very happy with the alternating patches of light and shade before him. He began to walk in zigzags from one to another. He became so absorbed in the pleasure of this that he took no notice of the hubbub around him.

---

1. Qais ibn al-Mulawwah (d. 688?) was a poet of the Umayyad period famous for his chaste love poetry. His love for Laila, his cousin, drove him to madness when her father married her off to another man from a different tribe, and he came to be known as "the madman of Laila."

The city clock rose up like a giant in the middle of the city. Time flowed from its fingers in a regular, rhythmic fashion. Qais ibn al-Mulawwah paid no attention to it. However, when its chimes began suddenly to ring they drowned out all the city's din, and pushed him out of the shade into a sunny spot. He could not understand where this push had come from. He looked up at the sun to determine what time it was, then continued along his zigzag course, in and out of the shade.

He began to feel an intimacy with the shade and took to walking more slowly, almost forgetting his previous desire to write Laila's name in the sand. Soon, however, the desire returned to him, and he began to search the place for a sandy spot; but always his eyes clashed with huge masses of concrete and glass, which blocked him in all directions.

"This whole place was sand once," he said to himself. "I knew it well. How were they able to do this?" Yet he felt no resentment toward them, even though he could not understand their reasons and desires. He felt that the shade where he stood was receding. He looked around and walked on.

When he felt tired, he began climbing a hill he had been walking toward for some time. Soon there were no more buildings. Qais had discovered the hill only after fatigue had hit him, and so he could feel no strong reaction to his discovery. He continued his climb, watching the movement of his feet.

He was on the verge of collapsing with weariness before he reached the top. However, when he noticed a cypress tree there he quickened his footsteps toward it. The fact of its presence seemed strange and surprising. Once he had regained his composure, he rested his head on the trunk of the tree and looked upward.

At that moment a flock of sparrows was passing in the sky, rapidly and far overhead. As he watched them fly by, Qais ibn al-Mulawwah felt a warm pleasure fill his pores.

"Now the shadow of the flock will surely be reflected in my eyes!" he said and continued to look at the sky, brimming over with joy.

He turned to watch them as they arched over him and flew toward the city. They alighted on thin parallel wires that were strung out from the roofs of buildings and gleamed in the sun. Qais ibn al-Mulawwah felt something break in him. When the faint voices of the birds reached him, he listened carefully, and sorrow filtered into his soul.

"They're different," he said. "There is a clear and distinct difference in the depth of their voices. These wires are making them lose their real voices."

He listened more intently, and after a while he began to forget to contrast them to what they had been before, as these new voices became more familiar to him. As they faded away, he turned his attention to the wires they were perched on. "God!" he thought, "How well they look together!" He tried to compare them to the chaotic order of green, tender twigs, but gave up the attempts and leaned back on the trunk of the cypress tree.

A young girl came and stood near him. Her image was reflected in his eyes, and he stood up, frightened. The girl only laughed at this reaction. When she stopped laughing, Qais ibn al-Mullawah asked her, "Is your name Laila?"

The girl smiled. She had blue eyes and fair hair, and Qais liked her dimples. He waited eagerly for her answer, and when she said "No," he felt disappointed and defeated. He lowered his head and fell silent.

The girl asked him what he was doing there. He looked at the tree.

"Do you like cypress trees?" she asked. Before he answered, she added, "I like its shape. It looks like a spear thrown from heaven."

Qais ibn al-Mullawah was stunned and gazed at the tree for a long while. When he turned his eyes away, he was almost in agreement with her.

"Where did you come from?" she asked.

"From the desert."

The girl's eyes gleamed. "The desert! I've read about it! What is there in the desert?"

Qais ibn al-Mullawah murmured something incoherent.

"Aren't there any cypress trees in the desert?" she asked.

He shook his head.

"There are no cypress trees in the city either," she said. "That is why I come here sometimes."

He looked at the city, which he had left behind only a short while ago.

The girl pointed. "That's my city."

Qais ibn al-Mullawah tried to speak, but the words "desert" and "city" jostled each other chaotically on his lips. The girl gazed at him, wondering what he was thinking, while he said to himself, "I shall ask her about this: What is it that has changed this same old place I used to know into a city?"

However, he did not utter a single word. The girl smiled, and Qais said, "Your name is not Laila."

The girl was surprised at his insistence. But she overlooked this and, with another smile, said, "No. But if you want to call me that, it's all right."

Qais ibn al-Mullawah felt embarrassed. In an effort to extricate himself he began, "But if your name is not Laila, then how . . . " He did not finish his sentence.

The girl chuckled. "You can call me whatever name you like. All it will take is the juggling of a few letters."

Then she turned and walked away. Qais ibn al-Mulawwah followed. When he caught up with her he was silent, and the girl said, "I've got to be in the City by sunset."

"Just like that?" said Qais ibn al-Mullawah.

"You can walk with me on the way, if you want."

Qais ibn al-Mulawwah walked by her side.

The road the girl chose was narrow and very winding. On either side a tall wall rose high. Qais ibn al-Mullawah walked with her, but the place soon lost its interest for him, and he stopped asking questions. The girl began to gaze at the upper edge of the wall on her side.

Suddenly Qais spoke out, "This is the city . . . " He did not finish.

The girl waited, than added, "Narrow and cold as stone . . . Aren't the desert sands warmer? I've heard they are . . . "

Qais ibn al-Mulawwah bowed his head and did not answer. The girl took his hand in hers. He felt in it a warmth that did not feel as though it could belong to a blonde girl. He held it for some time, then loosened his grip, looking at her.

"So, you are not Laila!"

The girl laughed limpidly. "I haven't asked you your name! What does it matter?"

He missed having her hand in his. This feeling fell like lead on his soul. He drew nearer to her and groped for her hand, but at that moment the narrow road opened out suddenly, to reveal the wide expanse from which the city loomed.

He trembled, and dropped his hands to his sides.

"I'm here," said the girl. "Where will you go? Will you return to the desert?"

Qais ibn al-Mulawwah smiled bitterly and said, "The desert is very far away now ... I don't know if I can reach it."

The girl was surprised and after a while said, "Then stay in the city!"

Qais ibn al-Mulawwah looked around him at the place and noticed for the first time that the city had its own order and harmony, as had the wires on which the birds had perched. It was divided into carefully organised, colored areas. However, he could not train his eyes on it in a steady gaze; instead, he stole stealthy glances at it. An embrace of familiarity fell over everything. He looked at the girl.

"Will you stay in the City?" she asked.

"I would have liked to stay," he answered. "But I know it very well now. I might return later. But for now ... "

"I'll go back to the gate with you," the girl said.

They walked together. Qais ibn al-Mulawwah was no longer interested in the things around him, for they had lost their strangeness and their element of surprise. The buildings were casting longer shadows out into the sunlight, but the alternating patches of sun and shade no longer intrigued him. He noticed there were many colored arrows painted along the sides of the road.

"These fix direction for us," the girl explained, "Here is the gate."

Qais ibn al-Mulawwah stood under the arch of the gate and felt something pulling him back to the city. The girl waited for him to speak, but he did not. She waved her hand, turned, and went back.

He remained standing at the gate and soon noticed the plaque again. He approached and read the engraving anew, stopping at the phrase, "history was changing its course." He saw now that there were two more words that had been carved after it, but they had been partially eroded. The second word was "it," but he could not tell whether the one before read "to" or "from."

Qais ibn al-Mulawwah wished that the girl was still with him so he could ask her about them. But he did not think much more about the matter, for he saw another city just out on the horizon and began to run toward it, while the wind that blew between the two cities played in the fringes of his cloak.

—*Translated by Sharif Elmusa and Thomas G. Ezzy*

Abu al-Ma'ati Abu al-Naja (b. 1938)

Egyptian novelist and short-story writer Abu al-Ma'ati Abu al-Naja is a writer with a broad vision of the universal human condition whose work has contributed an added flavor to the experimental works written by the second generation of short-story writers in Egypt. He has had several collections published to date, among which are *An Unusual Mission* (1980) and *The Leader* (1981). He has worked and lived in the Gulf area for several years. His latest collection is *On This Morning* (1999). The General Egyptian Council for Books has published several collections comprising most of his work: the first, *A Girl in the City* (1992), contains three of his collections of short stories: *A Girl in the City* (1960), *An Inscrutable Smile* (1962), and *People and Love* (1966). The second, *Illusion and Reality* (1993), contains three other short-story collections: *Illusion and Reality* (1974), *An Unusual Mission* (1980), and *Everyone Wins the Prize* (1984). The third, *Return to Exile*, contains his two novels, *Return to Exile* (1969) and *Against the Unknown* (1974). Al-Naja has also written criticism on fiction, published in his book *Many Ways to a Single City* (1997).

PEOPLE AND LOVE

If you are one who uses public transportation to go to work every morning, you will no doubt have experienced that strange connection that, for the period of an hour, more or less, binds you to people you do not know and have not had the slightest freedom in choosing. It may seem hard to give these relationships a name or even define their true flavor, for each time they are different, varying according to whoever sits or stands beside you. You may be at ease with this one or find this other one repellent, and occasionally you may even be oblivious of his presence.

But after a number of days or weeks, something may happen. You may find you have begun to feel at home with some of these faces you meet day after day. They may come a little earlier or later, but you will inevitably see them again. You will notice that your eyes have begun to grow used to their appearance, especially their clothing, and that puzzling, short-lived sensations have begun to be associated with their presence and sometimes their absence. Then you will realize that your relationship with them has entered a new phase, where you can't deny its existence entirely but at the same time don't really admit to it.

It's possible for the relationship to become frozen at that stage. Or, as happened to me, it may enter a new, exciting phase. But somehow I can't define, even now, the decisive moment at which my relationship with the No. 9 bus entered that new phase.

To begin with, I had gotten used to some of the faces—would exchange greetings, ask about the time, or complain about the buses with them. As time passed, however, the faces I had become familiar with receded into the background's dense fog, leaving room for two faces, which became the only ones I saw. They were the faces of a young man and woman whose names I did not know and doubt that I shall ever learn.

They were students. They used to board the bus at Station Square and get off at the university stop. She would arrive first, or he would, and the expectant face would be reduced to anxious eyes. Then suddenly—and this would happen every day as if it were happening for the first time—the anxious watchfulness would transform into a radiant glow. They would shake hands, their features would soften and animate, and they would speak in whispers so low you marveled they could hear one another. I wondered at the power of words when I saw the girl's eyes shining so brilliantly that all other signs of life in the wide square, even at a busy time of day, evaporated. Those happy eyes were the only riveting point of focus in the scene.

But sometimes the noisy square would steal the girl's gaze for a few moments and she would turn her head right to left or smooth her hair, although the wind had not touched it. Sometimes she would stand on one foot, lightly tapping the ground with the other. But I could see all the same that her awareness of the young man beside her had not dimmed in the least; with his rough, short hair, his eyes behind their gold-rimmed spectacles, constantly following her, and his firm, round face, he was everything in the square to her, even everything in the world.

When the bus came and the people rushed towards it wildly, as if they had suddenly lost their minds, I would feel uncomfortable somehow—the young man and woman in the midst of that stupid crush lost their mysterious invisible frame that an observer could sense enclosing them where they stood, setting them apart from everyone else. For an instant they seemed commonplace in the midst of dozens of pushing hands and feet. Yet as soon as they had taken their places on two seats or were standing beside one another in the aisle, they would regain that mysterious frame, which, in the bus, seemed almost palpable. I noticed that the passengers, perhaps unintentionally, would leave a circle of space around them, allowing them to move in comfort and somehow be protected from the press of people everywhere. The bus would heave and the passengers be jolted at every bend and traffic light. The circle of space around the boy and girl would get narrower, and their whispering be drowned in the roar of the bus. From time to time I would lose sight of them, but then I would catch a glimpse of a lock of hair, a hand pressed against the roof of the bus, or the side of the golden spectacles as the boy tilted his head, and I continued to be aware of their distinctive presence in the midst of the heavy mass of humanity. Even when they got off and disappeared behind the walls of the university, they lingered on in my mind for a while.

Because of them, my relationship with the No. 9 bus had taken on a special flavor. Now this part of the day radiated a glorious aura of expectation and recollection. The images of the two young people even started infiltrating the rest of my days, casting their gentle shadows over my daily preoccupations before I really noticed it.

For a long time I thought that I was the only fascinated follower of this love story that had chosen the No. 9 bus as stage for some of its scenes. Later, on the morning one seat was left empty on the aisle, I realized other passengers had filled the space around me in the theater and were following the scene with similar attention. Although the boy and girl were no closer to the empty seat than others, a flurry of hands indicated to them that the girl at least should sit down. She hesitated a moment, perhaps preferring to remain at her friend's side, but he motioned to her to take the seat. Till now it could have been accepted as a common courtesy shown to any young lady standing, but next the young man in the seat beside her got up and motioned to her friend to sit down too. He hesitated a second, then took the seat. He may have thought the young man was getting off at the next stop and been surprised when he didn't. At that moment I scanned the nearby faces, young men, older people, all gazing around furtively and glancing at the couple. I felt that the couple's presence had overflowed the seat they were sitting on and we were all attached to them by invisible strings. When they moved, heads turned, someone craned a neck, lips fluttered with conversation, or eyes blinked.

From that morning on I became aware that the passengers' interest in the scene was no less wonderful than the scene itself. Indeed, it had become a part of it, until, as time passed, the observers became the most exciting element. Any passenger who obtained a seat near the couple was not going to give it up, while one who ended up at a distance from them spent his journey trying to catch a glimpse, although at a distance one could make freer comments. And just as the artificial barriers between members of an audience are lifted when the curtain goes up in the theater, and strangers often exchange comments on the play, so the bus passengers frequently found themselves speaking. And the love story with its single scene, which altered little but was never boring, had become the chief topic of conversation. It was the magic thread linking this odd collection of people and creating a strong unity that, on a bus like this, could only be achieved when facing a common disaster.

Oddly enough, the boy and girl seemed oblivious to all of us who were so involved with them in our minds. Maybe the imaginary frame protected them.

It sometimes happened that the young man would put out his hand to lift the window and then forget to remove it from the seat back or his companion's shoulders. Or he might move closer to her to whisper something into her ear, and the whispering would go on and on. When they stood in the aisle and the bus jerked into motion, he would put his arm around the girl's shoulders to prevent her falling and she would move closer to him, as forgetful as he that the motion of the bus was once again smooth.

Perhaps because of all this—or for no reason at all, since these obvious sorts of things had been happening ever since they had been traveling on the bus together—the bus raised its first shout of protest against the love story it had been following with fascination. Strangely enough, the bus, which had never expressed its fascination in more than a whisper, did not hesitate to shout to announce its opposition.

As sometimes happens in the theater, the shout came from the back rows, no one knew from just where, and the words were blurted, "They've gone too far!"

"Where do they think they are?"

"They've no consideration for people's feelings, my friend."

These voices certainly weren't expressing the opinion of the whole bus. Some faces expressed a silent irritation at the shouters. While the protesting voices increased, growing louder and advancing to the front rows, and I imagined them bending the invisible frame, the sympathetic faces did nothing. The best they did was to try to conceal their annoyance with the shouters.

The only thing that the whole bus continued to do was to show its particular interest in the two young people. Our interest began to take on a new form when for one day, then two, then three, they did not appear. After three days we realized it was not simply a schedule alteration: after three days the whole bus missed them both.

For the first time a dialogue started up between the supporters and opponents in various parts of the bus. I said to my neighbor, whom I recognized as one who had protested the slight intimacies, "Have you noticed? They haven't been here for three days."

"I was expecting it. There was nothing serious between them."

"How do you know that?"

"Neither of them was wearing a ring."

"They're still students."

"Perhaps he was making a fool of her."

"I don't think so. He seemed serious, and . . . "

"Now you're thinking the way she did." He laughed. "Have you fallen in love with him too?"

"The whole bus fell in love with both of them."

"If they'd been engaged, no one would have gotten annoyed."

"Isn't it enough that they loved one another?"

"Enough for them. Not for the bus."

"Why does the bus have to butt into their business?"

"They're the ones who butted into the bus."

We both laughed.

More days passed without them returning. A despondent sense of having lost something descended on the whole bus. The expectancy in people's eyes turned to despair. The barrier between supporters and protesters fell away in a shared feeling of guilt. Our conversation kept going, like one voice repeated by many voices: "Do you think they'll come back?"

"I don't know. Maybe."

"They were magnificent."

"Do you know, I can't stand this bus anymore."

"I've thought about taking a different bus."

"Why don't you?"

"They might come back."

"There's nothing more beautiful than the sight of two lovers."

"Why are people so keen on destroying lovely things?"

"It was the bus that . . . "

"Perhaps they haven't parted for good. Maybe they just had a quarrel."

"Everything is possible, but this won't change things for the bus."

More days passed, but they didn't return. The No. 9 was simply any bus now and the people simply passengers. The hidden threads that had connected us were severed, and the old, hesitant expectations disappeared from the eyes, replaced by singular, everyday cares. The bus became simply a place that resonated with oaths and apologies.

I considered changing my route many times, but I never did. I don't know why. I was surprised to find one morning that the girl—whose name I still didn't know—was sitting right beside me. How had I failed to notice her before that moment? Absolutely it was she, and she was alone this time. I almost asked her where he was and why he wasn't there. Perhaps she had been on the bus alone another day and I hadn't noticed. Nothing about her had changed, and yet she was entirely different from the girl who used to be with him. Her eyes were strangely unseeing. Her hand hung by her side and only the wind stirred her hair. I realized I was sitting in his place. I looked at her hair, then looked at the people around us, wondering if the other passengers would notice that I was in his place. I fantasized that some eyes looked at me with irritation and I shifted in my seat. The girl's head was still bowed as more and more eyes discovered her presence. Faces grew closer to one another, commiserating. Why had I chosen this wretched seat? If I left it I imagined no one who recognized her would take it. Why did all these eyes encircle me? Only the girl noticed nothing. She was imprisoned in another frame in time, a frame that allowed her no movement. And she was alone inside it. The bus traveled on, the road continued, and the passengers who knew the story turned their heads before getting off, to take one last look. I couldn't face their eyes, and the window saved me. Even then I could see the bus in the center of the road, the eyes inside it coming closer, merging, becoming one enormous eye in an enormous head that filled the bus and every inch of space in it so the girl could not move.

On subsequent days the girl continued to travel by herself. The enormous eye stopped staring, and the sympathy and grief in its gaze faded to indifference. Now the glances dispersed in all directions, preoccupied with their own lives. Even my eyes often failed to recognize her, and on the occasions I was startled to see her at close range again, she seemed to be slightly frail, indistinguishable from other girls. Why had I not noticed how pale she was, with cheeks slightly protruding and a forehead a little too broad?

And yet, often as I walked on any road where there were people, an inscrutable dream would take shape in my mind. Someday I would meet them again, walking together. Even though many months have passed and the girl has not boarded the bus in ages, I still think of this, especially when I see a boy and girl walking together, wherever they may be.

—*Translated by Hilary Kilpatrick and Naomi Shihab Nye*

'Abd al-Hameed Ahmad (b. 1957)

A short-story writer from the United Arab Emirates, 'Abd al-Hameed Ahmad studied up to secondary level, then acquired a wide literary knowledge through his own reading. He began writing in 1973 and has shown great concern over the immense and irreversible changes that have taken place in the Arabian Gulf area as a result of the oil boom and the sudden wealth it brought to the region. He has a poignant sensibility for the pathos and tragedies that have resulted from this new life and delineates his impressions sometimes directly in the tragic mode but at others with a comic apprehension of experience. He now works in journalism in the Emirates and, having served for several years as head of the Union of the Writers of the United Arab Emirates, serves as deputy head. He has gained a distinguished status in journalism and is now editor-in-chief of the prestigious English-language weekly *Gulf News*. His first collection of short stories, *Swimming in the Eye of a Savage Gulf*, appeared in 1982, and his second, *The Alien Farmer*, in 1987.

THE ALIEN FARMER

[1]

A crowd of men, women, and children was gathered around a shack standing on an elevation south of the quarter where huts had been built for the poor. Men with wraps around their nostrils, frightened children, women crying and breaking into loud wailing.

A voice was heard: "The door is locked."

Another voice: "The smell's so bad, it's unbearable."

A third voice: "It smells like dead mice."

The sun was burning hot. The sand was hot as live embers. Faces were running with perspiration. As more people approached the shack, the noise increased and the clamor intensified. In spite of the stink of hot breath combined with that of human sweat, the smell from the shack had a strange effect, overpowering, sharp and pungent.

A voice was heard saying, "This is Marish's shack, isn't it?"

Another voice: "But Marish has left it and gone away."

A woman's voice: "He himself told me he was going back to Oman."

Another voice: "Who did he leave his shack to, then?"

"Maybe it's the donkey—his donkey."

Someone commented, "It's all very odd."

The first speaker replied, "Marish wouldn't leave his donkey behind. He'd be sure to take it with him."

The men tightened the wrap around their noses. There were murmurings of revulsion and disgust.

"Ugh! What kind of a smell is that?"

In the middle of all this noise and commotion a child asked his mother, "Who is Marish?" But his mother didn't hear him.

[2]

When he climbed the tall palm tree and reached the top, its spathe opened. There was a smell, something like the smell of semen. Desire filled his mind. His longing for women increased—the women he saw around so often but had never touched—in all his life he had never touched a woman.

At noon he carried the seedlings under his arm and returned to his tent. He ate some dates and drank some coffee, then lit his pipe and sat down to enjoy the taste of Omani tobacco. He stretched out on a straw mat and pushed aside the palm branches that made up his shack wall, to allow some air to come in. He tried to sleep, but his mind kept going back to the time he and his brother left al-Batina[1] to head for the United Emirates in search of work.

The donkey had carried the goods and walked in front of them. Marish enlivened it every now and then with a rap from his stick. They crossed mountains and rocky valleys and deserts. How long did the journey take? Marish could not recall—except that it was a long hard journey. His brother had said, "Al-Batina is now a long way off."

"We've got to get to the coast."

"I'm going to miss it, Marish."

"It's vital for us to find work and earn a living."

"When shall we be back?"

"God only knows."

His brother became a confectioner, a good one, and became well known all over Dubai. Marish had settled in Jumaira.[2] As he cast his mind back on all this, the tears came to his eyes. He tried to fall asleep again when he remembered

---

1. A district in the Sultanate of Oman on the Arabian Gulf.

2. A village in Dubai, one of the states of the United Arab Emirates.

that Bou Jassim[3] had asked him to call at his house to slaughter two lambs in celebration of the circumcision of his two sons.

He picked up his knife and went in the direction of Bou Jassim's house.

[3]

Someone said, "It's getting hotter. The smell is suffocating."

A young man wearing glasses said, "We've got to call the police, and the health officers as well."

"Why? Can't *we* deal with this?"

The young man replied, "This smell might start an epidemic."

A man suddenly broke forth from the crowd, saying, "Whoever said that Marish had left for Oman?"

A woman's voice answered, "He told me so himself."

The man replied, "But I myself saw him four days ago sitting in the shadow of a palm tree. He seemed to be despondent."

The various sounds commingled. The swarming bodies heated the air even more; the noise grew louder. Voices rang high in the air. The child again asked his mother, "Who is Marish, Mother?" But his voice was lost in the hubbub.

[4]

Sad and lonely, he had smoked a lot of tobacco. Salem had passed by, he had not seen him for quite some time. Together they smoked and meditated. Astonished, his friend asked, "But why do you want to go back?"

Bent with pain, he answered sadly, "How can I live here? No one takes any notice of me any more." After a pause, his eyelids quivered and he whispered, "I can't stand indifference, being forgotten."

" But ... "

With tears in his eyes he interrupted his friend: "No one cares about palm trees any more, and lambs are now slaughtered in special slaughterhouses in the market."[4]

"But you can work as a guard on one of the municipal plantations, or even as a porter. I've worked as a guard. Or, better still, why don't you work with your brother in his shop?"

"My brother died two years ago."

"May God rest his soul."

---

3. "Bou" is derived from "Abu," meaning "father."
4. This is an allusion to the many profound changes that have taken place in the Gulf countries since the discovery of oil, a subject that deeply preoccupies this author, as well as other authors from the Gulf area.

Rubbing his nose fiercely, he poured his friend a cup of coffee. "To work nowadays, you need an identity, citizenship, a passport. No one will hire me."

He fell silent. Sadness and despair took hold of him. "Decent folks are dead and gone—there are few left. No one remembers me now."

The pair fell silent and exchanged perplexed and worried glances.

"You mean to leave after having lived here for thirty years, as if you'd never set foot in this country, Marish?"

"I'll go back the way I came. I'll build a plantation in al-Batina."

Marish gathered his things together and they both stood up. Before leaving the shack he said, "Do take the donkey, Salem. It might come in handy for you."

Salem took him to the bus that was leaving for Oman. They exchanged a long embrace, their breath mingled, and tears fell from Marish's eyes as he waved goodbye to his friend.

[5]

One day when I was eight I heard that Marish was coming to help my father to graft the palm tree in our palm grove. I was delighted that I was going to meet Marish at last, for I had heard so much about him without ever seeing him.

As we were waiting in the shade of the garden wall I asked my father, "What does Marish do?"

"He is a farmer, my son."

"Has he any children?"

"He lives alone in his shack, no wife, no family."

"Why doesn't he get married?"

"He is Omani and very poor. Who would take him for a husband?"

I heard someone clearing his throat and saw a man approaching, carrying an axe and limping. His beard was long and black. His head was wrapped in a yellowish *ghutra* that had once been white. His eyes were narrow. His right nostril was red and disfigured as if rats had gnawed at it. He wore a loincloth striped with blue and green and a white shirt stained by sweat and dust.

He spoke to me playfully, in a teasing way.

My father smiled and remarked, "You never stop your joking, do you, Marish?"

Marish's laughter was unique in its liveliness. I watched him all the time.

When he and my father had finished the work, my mother offered them coffee and dates, and jokingly said to Marish, "We'll arrange to marry you to Hantouma. What do you think of that?"

I knew Hantouma. She was black and cheerful. She used to bring fresh water to the village on her donkey. Once she said to me, jokingly, "You're always clinging to your mother's skirts."

Marish laughed his characteristic laugh and said, "I don't want her."

I came to like Marish. From then on I saw him everywhere, in the streets, beneath the palm trees, at feasts and other such occasions, and at celebrations of weddings and circumcisions, at the well, and at the seaside. He joked with everyone, and his singular laughter was often heard echoing in the village alleys. Years went by, and I left to study abroad. When I came back, I heard no one mention his name or say anything about him.

[6]

The shack was almost hidden by the crowd surrounding it. The sun was blasting the place with its heat. The noise was increasing, a mixture of questioning, humming, and chatter.

Surprise and fear were growing on the faces of the children. The foul smell mingling with human sweat was dreadful.

"People! Something's got to be done."

Another voice: "What shall we do? Call the police?"

Another suggested, "No—we'll break the door down and find out."

Another voice: "The heat's unbearable, let's break down the door, there's really no choice."

Many voices were saying, "Let's do it then."

Heads were craned high to see. Three men charged at the door. A loud crash was heard as the door broke down. Noise and commotion prevailed. The place was filled with the sound of wailing women and frightened children. The strong foul smell burst forth like a waterfall, clogging the nose before dispersing in the warm air.

"Ugh—what kind of a smell is that?"

Men yelled in fright: "May God give us strength."

[7]

The next day Um 'Abdallah sat chatting with her neighbor, Um Husain. Her eyes full of tears, Um 'Abdallah said, "Alas! He died like a dog."

"They say he was found swollen like a bagpipe. Abu Husain swore that nobody would be able to identify him. His face was all puffed up, you couldn't even see his eyes. He said that he saw worms coming out of his mouth and nostrils."

Um 'Abdallah spat on the ground, buried the spit in sand, then said, "Is that the way for any human being to die? What a life!"

"What times we live in! Times in which a brother forgets his brother!"

Um 'Abdallah continued, "My husband told me that Abu Nasser met Marish about five days ago, and when he asked him why he had not left for Oman yet, Marish explained that he was stopped at the border and prevented from crossing to Oman because he had no passport. He had tried to explain his circumstances, that he was of Omani origin but had moved to the United Emirates thirty years before to look for work. No one believed him. So he had to come back."

Um Husain was touched, and said, "Then in effect they have deprived him of his family and country."

Um Abdallah went on, "But Abu Abdallah says that he was never given a United Emirates passport either."

"May God forgive him and rest his soul."

A heavy silence prevailed, then Um Husain said, "Do you realize that Marish did not die naturally?"

The eyes of the other woman widened.

"What?!"

"Those who broke into the shack said that they saw many wounds on his body and found a deep wound in his neck and black dry blood on the floor beneath him. Close by they found a scythe."

"Did he commit suicide?"

She questioned fearfully, placing her hand on her cheek. Then she let go a sigh and said, "Alas, Marish! It is frustration and grief that have killed you! You died lonely, no family and no wife."

For a whole month the place was preoccupied with the story of what had happened to Marish.

The story was narrated by women and men amidst tears and lamentations and feelings of guilt.

Before the story everyone found so touching had been forgotten, Um 'Abdallah's youngest son came up to her and asked, "Who is Marish, Mother?"

—Translated by Sharif Elmusa and David Wright

TEMPTATION

He didn't know when he'd first started thinking about water. He'd just set off, striding down to the sea, and that's how the others saw him—with amazement striking them dumb, as, all of a sudden, one of his hands dropped off on the road. He didn't take any notice—didn't stop to pick it up or shed so much as a single tear over it. He just left it there and moved swiftly on, indifferent to their stares. It had shocked him before it shocked them, but he was already over that now. It had started with a finger splitting away from his palm, followed by a second, then a third, and a fourth, and a fifth, at each step he took, till finally they'd all dropped off; when he looked at his hand, there were no fingers there at all.

The sea held more temptation, a deeper attraction and charm. And there he was, walking along, stubbornly intent on reaching it. It was as though some devil, some power, a kind of murderous impulse, pushed him ever onward to the water. There it loomed far off, glittering like silver or like shells under the burning sun, and there was its glorious azure adorning the vast distance, awakening days of childhood past. He redoubled his pace, taking ever longer strides, and when the fingers of his other hand started dropping off it didn't surprise him this time. They could go, just like the others; everything was leaving him, but it wasn't important.

Still he gazed and walked on, a trunk on two feet, with a head on the trunk. Before him was the vast blue whose temptation was limitless, dating from some immemorial time, different, utterly, to anything else he knew, beyond all else in its pain and exquisite suffering and its tragic joys. Soon now, with just a few more steps, a few more tremors, there would be the water waiting for him; and he'd enter it anew, curling up in its warm delightful heart, like one more fish amid the weeds and shells and utter whiteness—alone in a calm and quiet space, beyond all the various din.

Suddenly the blue of the water vanished, along with the red of the sun. One of his feet had parted from his trunk, dropped down in front of him, and he'd tripped on it, falling flat on his face, smeared with sand. He raised his head and cursed the decaying body; and he cursed, too, the sarcastic eyes and the pitying whispers and cruel sounds coming from those other mouths. The water wasn't a far-off dream any more. There it was in front of him, and soon now he'd feel it forever, let his limbs go forever. He'd let those other people vanish as well; and as for the bitter fields, let them burn too in the noonday sun, be branded with the fires of their misery and perpetual tragedy, along with the bodies and voices and heads bloodied with suffering.

Water—water. When had he first started dreaming of water, longing for it with such anguish? He rose on his single foot, bore his body up, and stood facing the sea. Then, like a bird with a broken wing, he started hopping toward the water. One hop, then another, then another, and still another; but once more he crashed down on the ground, a mere trunk with a head, and no limbs at all—like a fish or a snake. Had he reached the water, he told himself, he could have swum, with fins grown on his trunk in place of the limbs dropped on the road. Raising his weary head, to the clear blue sky, he saw the blue of the sea. The sea was there! In just a few moments he'd be like a fish and float into the warm, far-off depths, free of everything, of night and day. The sea was there, sounding in his ears like a mythic, primordial song, the waves clamoring without end, wave after wave, surge after surge, dash after dash. He could hear them as he lay there, stuck on the earth.

Just one more thrust now and he'd be back in the water. He started crawling along on his belly, in anguished desperation, panting constantly, like a fish taken from the sea and on point of death. The surf was playing gently onto the white sands, the sea drawing ever nearer. He could smell its damp coolness, along with the smell of weeds and pebbles and moss and small fish. He tried to think: when had he started dreaming of water? But his memory oozed away with the sweat of his body. All he could recall was a longing that ate into his guts like a murderous desire, like a first delightful, agonizing tremor.

It was a thirst like enchantment that had driven him to the sea, pregnant with its hoard of memories and a myth sunk deep in oblivion. As he crawled on, he didn't care now about his split skin, or the limbs that had dropped off one by one, or the voices issuing from the gates of hell, or the drops of blood coloring the earth, leaving a bloody thread behind. A great star of joy shone in his eyes as he saw the water nearer than his own heartbeat, its arms wide open to receive him; there was the lofty blue, calling to him with the longing of a body known so very well.

One last crawl and he'd be in the water, would drown, once and for all, in its everlasting sweetness. One last crawl. But the head rolled right away now, parted from the body that lay lifeless on the wet ground, mute like a stone, while the eyes in the head gazed longingly on the blue and white waves that threw another dying fish onto the shore.

—Translated by May Jayyusi and Christopher Tingley

Daisy al-Amir (1935)

Iraqi short-story writer Daisy al-Amir was born in Alexandria, Egypt. She lived in Iraq and Beirut, and for a short period in the 1950s she lived in Cambridge, England, where she pursued her study of English. She has worked in Beirut as Director of the Iraqi Cultural Center. In her stories, al-Amir has been able to depict images of a woman's loneliness and fear in the face of war or entrenched social traditions. There are several collections of her short stories: *The Faraway Country We Love* (1964), *Then Returns the Wave* (1969), *The Happy Arab Home* (1975), *The Whirlpool of Love and Hate* (1979), and *Promises for Sale* (1980).

THE NEXT STEP

'Alya, the most popular girl in our city and the daughter of a wealthy and prestigious merchant, was elected Beauty Queen. The news passed quickly from mouth to mouth, and the next day it appeared in the papers.

We were not surprised. In our minds, we had all already crowned her Beauty Queen—and Queen of Culture, of Elegance, of Gentility, and of Modesty as well!

What more can I say about 'Alya's other qualities? Well, aside from all this, she was devoted to charitable works, and this naturally endeared her to all our hearts—we, the children of this nosey city . . . Yes, I admit it! We were a meddlesome lot of people, even though inquisitiveness is properly a characteristic only of small towns. But our town had been small once; it had grown rapidly after the founding of its large university, which attracted many professors, intellectuals, and students. It was our town's rapid growth that had preserved its original tendency toward snoopiness.

We used to know the history of every single person who came to our little-big city. I cannot say exactly how the details became known and spread so quickly, but I do know that every bit of news was relayed speedily from one to another, as though its spreading were part of our daily duties. I do not deny that keeping a lookout for news was a great diversion for us natives. Newcomers were preoccupied with the affairs of the university and its intellectual life, while we, the shop owners, the café frequenters, and the backgammon players, had nothing else to do than indulge in gossip. However, we were not malicious, I can swear to that. We simply related the news just as we heard it, without any exaggerations. This was a virtue acknowledged by the newcomers themselves. We would dig up some item and then relay it among ourselves, never blowing it up or adding anything to it. Moreover, we never felt joy at others' misfortunes; on the contrary: we felt elated at happy tidings and sad if the news was painful . . .

And that day we were happy, for 'Alya had a prominent place in our hearts! She had grown up under our eyes. We had loved her as a child, and our love had grown as she had grown, and so had our interest in her and her life . . .

Yes, that day she had been crowned Beauty Queen! Silently, our eyes asked the question: "What next? When will the next step be?" We wanted to celebrate her wedding, to see her settle down. In our minds we selected as candidates the best young men of our city, sons of natives and sons of newcomers alike. However, our conjectures as to her future husband found no echo, except in our most private conversations.

We thought hard about ways to transmit to her our mental strategies for her future and wondered what her reaction would be if she were to hear of our schemes. Would she realize that they were only due to our love and care for her? Or would she think us meddlesome and curious, heedlessly disrespectful of her privacy?

One day someone came to me wearing an anxious face and told me he had heard from a confidential source that 'Alya had been consulting the city's medium.

'Alya consulting a medium!? I felt great anger build up in my head and would have slapped the bearer of that tale, had I not feared that this might cause gossip about 'Alya herself. The talebearer had more to tell me; I could see it in his eyes. But I rejected it with all my heart and shouted in his face, "'Alya has her pride! She would never love anyone who didn't love her! Not even Old Man Fate himself would let her stoop to magic to make someone love her! She is a woman to be worshipped! Any man would dream of her looking at him just once!"

But after a while the truth became plain to us: 'Alya was indeed visiting a medium. Our curiosity almost killed us. At first, however, we could do nothing but remain silent.

Who could this man be, whose heart 'Alya was trying to read, we asked ourselves. We were ready to kill him if he did not love her . . . But, we thought, if 'Alya loved him then we had to love him too, for her sake.

The only thing to do was go to the medium herself and beg her to tell us the truth, to help us help 'Alya and to satisfy our murderous curiosity. But the medium held back and would tell us nothing. The secrets of the craft could not be revealed. However, we could see in her eyes two conflicting tendencies, equally strong: one, to come out with the secret; the other, to keep it.

Finally, the character of our old city gained the upper hand over professional ethics, and she divulged the truth to us.

Afterwards we stared at each other, stupefied:

'Alya had been resorting *to magic in order to be able to feel love! What did it mean?*

—*Translated by Sharif Elmusa and Thomas G. Ezzy*

Yusuf Habashi al-Ashqar (1929–1992)

Lebanese novelist and short-story writer Yusuf Habashi al-Ashqar was born in Bait Shabab, Lebanon. He studied at St. Joseph University and the Lebanese Academy of Fine Arts, where he read philosophy. He worked at the Social Security Fund in Beirut. Ashqar was one of Lebanon's most accomplished writers and was deeply involved, in his writings, with the struggle against bourgeois culture and values. He published four short-story collections: *The Taste of Ashes* (1952), *Winter Night* (1954), *The Old Land* (1962), and *The Parasol, the King, and the Death Obsession* (1981); and two novels, *Four Red Mares* (1964) and *Roots Don't Grow in the Sky* (1971).

The Banquet

Winter. And War. War. Will it ever end?

War is everything. War is knowledge. War is the provider. War is the despoiler. War is power. War is everywhere, within the hearing of everyone and in the heart of all.

It is War that we ask about winter, about flour, about light and warmth.

Winter is cruel, O War. Will it ever end? In our village only firewood remained outside War's will. Praise be to firewood, for War would be God without it.

War *is*. It will never end. It has found rest in our eyes, in our houses, in our malice, and in the beast in us. It is the banquet in our houses, the guest of honor in our halls. With its gaping single eye it looks around and enjoys the wasted world.

Today the winter laughed, with the jingle of golden bracelets on its wrist.

The sun rippled through the clouds, one layer, two layers, three, its fingers moving like those of a guitar player. Its fingerprints stuck like kisses to the bricks of our houses.

Give us your bracelets, O sun. Gold can be stored for time of war.

The gravel on the roads has dried up. All that remains of the mud is a brown dampness in the soil. The dead grass, like an old woman who disguises her age, adorns itself with a few pearls, which fall, drop by drop, against its will.

On the roads we collect the sun's charity.

How generous you are, O Lord! Your sun rises upon us—we who deserve frost, we who blaspheme against the generosity of your mind and the gift of your freedom.

His face is dark, dark. I know who he is. But what is his name? This is the first time I have longed to know his name. His face is dark, the color of dark brown tobacco. His hair is blond; his eyes like the sky in summer. He walks down the long sandy road. His shoes, studded with nails, strike into the damp soil the rhythms of a poem. His sweater is red, his trousers black. On his shoulder hangs a long rifle. How old is he, this young man?

Along the road young women stood looking at him as he flashed past them like a tongue of flame.

"Where are you going, soldier?" I asked him. "Enjoy the sun, for soon winter will take back the bracelets, rub out the fingerprints, and cramp the fingers. The sun will disappear. Wait for it to disappear and then go."

He did not look back. The long sandy road came to an end and, beyond it, the red sweater was swallowed up in the pine forest.

"O War," I said, "winter is back. And who said it had ever been over?"

In winter everything looks like everything else. The clouds obscure differences. Differences descend into the shade. Similarities ascend to the light. The red sweater is light.

"Young man, they'll spot your red sweater and they'll shoot you. Take it off. Take it off, you fool, and enjoy the sun."

The rumble of cannons can still be heard. It's as though it will never fall silent. The village of Kafr Millat listens to it in awe, kneeling as in a huge church. Jiryis is sitting at the edge of the stone bench, hunched over, his elbows on his thighs. His coat covers the bench, and his wool hat covers his head and face. Only his nose and eyes can be seen. The nose and the eyes are not enough for communication. The face is what matters. One must see the face. One cannot communicate with symbols or parts. Only features communicate, and only the face has features.

"Will this war never end?" Jiryis asked. His two sons are at the battlefront.

"You'll get a chill, Jiryis. Come in."

The roof of Jiryis's house is no longer made of mud. A part of the Jiryis has died: the same Jiryis who used to level the roof of his house with a stone-roller.

His sons had covered the roof with a layer of concrete and left the roller on the roof without a handle. The roller has no meaning. It's simply there, just like Jiryis himself when his sons left him and went to the battlefront. Why this war, O War?

"There was hunger during the First World War," Jiryis said. "We fled to the plains, and we survived. This war breeds fear. Where shall we escape this time?"

War is everywhere, everywhere. Where shall we escape?

My eldest daughter swims like a fish. The water in the pool is blue. The sea is navy blue, spotted with white, waves and foam. His wife is lying there on the terrace like a bundle tanning in the sun. Her lips suck on a cigarette.

And I, lying in a chair, am constructing dreams of a woman far away. I'm writing in hieroglyphics so no one can read them, except her. She knows hieroglyphics. She's old, very old. She's a queen called Hatshepsut.[1] The war came and took our dream to the battlefront. Our dream too wears a red sweater.

Jiryis's sons came back. Their mother heated some water. They took a bath, shaved, and went out chasing after the girls. Jiryis slept twenty-four hours, got up, pushed the roller with his foot, and sang, "They are back, they've returned." He jumped on the roller and rolled along with it, his hair flying in the wind. He kept waving his hat as though he were the leader of a dabke dance troupe, waving a scarf.

It's drizzling.

You don't start with a passive verb, smart boy. You don't start with "and," and you don't . . .

"I am dead against grammar," I told her, "and I'm against prisons as well, and against harnessed, bridled, obedient horses. You and I are the rule. Everyone else is the exception."

Yet she kept on reading her grammar book and pointing with her trembling fingers even at the commas.

It's drizzling.

Jiryis dances along with the roller. The Amchit[2] radio station broadcasts the following bulletin: "An exchange of fire is reported between Hut Street and the Sodeco quarter." The Sanayi'[3] radio announces "an exchange of fire between the Sodeco quarter and Hut Street." I turn off the radio.

"But they'll go back to the war, Jiryis," I tell him in my heart, "and you'll go back too, to the stone bench and cover your head and face with your hat."

I'm strolling with my son along the Manara Corniche. I hold his hand. It is getting bigger. He is no longer so small. I look at his face; soon his beard will be sprouting. I press his hand. He will grow up and leave on a ship like that one over there. The ship is lit up like a bride on the altar steps, all in white and swaying proudly. He will leave on a ship like that, dreaming of things in which I will not figure. Our partnership will be broken by him. With me it will remain intact. He will sail like the ship and return only occasionally.

We stopped. I looked at him. His thick lips and blue eyes were laughing. Entranced, he looked at the lightning that ploughed a deep furrow, planted

---

1. Queen Hatshepsut: Egyptian queen of the 18th dynasty; daughter of Thutmose I; married her half brother Thutmose III. She built the magnificent temple in the Valley of the Queens on the west side of the Nile near Thebes, and erected two obelisks at Karnak, 1485 B.C.

2. Amchit: the radio station of the Christian section in Lebanon, in the East.

3. Sanayi': the radio station in West Beirut.

with black trees. The trees ran toward us. Lightning tore through the length and breadth of the forest and set it on fire. It made the hair on my son's arms stand on end. He closed his eyes.

"Are you afraid?" I asked.

"No!" he said.

It's drizzling.

"Lend me your eyes," I said. "We could see together, feel together. How I need to see with that wonder in your eyes!"

Jiryis put his hands on my shoulders. His head was bare, and he was not wearing his coat. His seventy years glowed in his eyes like seventy candles lit in celebration of his sons' return.

"Every time they return I light the seventy candles. Every time I am born again with them and I dance on the roof for the prodigal who is found."

It's drizzling.

As we stood on the barren ground, we listened to the sound of gunfire. The tree in front of our house had no leaves. It was all buds.

"I love this tree's nakedness," I said. "It's more beautiful than the naked vine."

"Like the nakedness of a new lover," he said.

The light of the seventy-first candle glowed in his eyes.

"Come in," he muttered, "you'll get wet."

"What about you?" I asked.

"Joy is my protection," he said. "Joy is an antidote to sickness, hunger, and death. Joy is resurrection."

He went under the tree. I followed him through the open cellar. It was piled high with firewood pushing against the ceiling.

Who would have thought that we would come back to firewood?

"Firewood has saved us, and yet the day will come when we'll forget it."

"Won't I be like firewood to you during the war, and you'll say one day, 'there was the war. There was firewood, and there she was'?"

"Can time destroy things it can't reach?"

"Meaning?"

"I mean that what is between us is outside time if you wish it to be so."

He looked at her eyes. How long? He didn't know. Like a wanderer, a poet, a creator, he lost his life in her eyes.

"I love your gray hair."

"I wish you hadn't fallen in love with any particular part of me."

"Why?"

"The love of any one part only lasts as long as the part itself."

"And yet I love your gray hair."

"Gray hair is just the beginning of the road to death."

"My love will give you life, will ward off death. It will open the road to eternity before you. I love you. I love you."

The sun was orange. It entered the room through the windows, coloring the walls and her face.

"Wheatstalk, Wheatstalk," he called after her.

The firewood was piled up against the ceiling. Jiryis was sitting on the stump of an oak tree, relaxed. Raindrops collected on the branches of a tree above and fell at random.

"I hate grammar. I hate prisons. I love you, a wheatstalk growing in the wasteland."

By the cellar, under the tree. The small brick house boils with noise. Faris is sitting on the stone wall, smoking. Occasionally he moves towards the locked door and listens. His two little girls circle around him. The smaller one is crying. Mucus covers her lips and chin. Faris strokes her hair, wipes away her tears and mucus with his shirtsleeve, and takes her in his arms.

"What's Faris doing, Jiryis?"

"He's waiting for his wife."

"And where's his wife."

"In the house."

"Is she cross with him?"

"No, she's giving birth."

Our neighbour's wife is having a baby. All by herself. Just like a ewe. Her husband's only role is to wait. She's having a baby all by herself. She doesn't scream or yell. I wanted to hear her voice but could not. I imagined her biting her fingers, clutching the bedsheets, writhing like a woman making love. The baby will come out soon. She will wash it, carry it, and put it next to her in bed. The world will receive her baby without a celebration, without gifts. In no time the child will be running fearlessly in the fields. The child will not be scared of the dog, the donkey, or even the tarantula.

"Jiryis, what's the name of the dark young man with blue eyes and blond hair, who wears a red sweater, carries a long rifle, and who went along the sandy road and disappeared at the edge of the forest?"

"Antun, the son of As'ad al-Ifriqi. You know his father, don't you?"

"Yes, when he died, his wife sent an announcement to the patriarch and the patriarch himself sent a message of condolence."

"Al-Ifriqi deserves the patriarch's attention. He left his children ten million pounds although he couldn't count to ten. During the First World War we fled together onto the plains. We were both nine years old then. He had five loaves of bread that he put round his waist like a belt and slept on so no one could steal them. After the war he left for Africa on his own. As'ad deserves the patriarch's attention, even though the patriarch did not know him. His son is like light. He carries his old rifle and goes after the troops begging them to take him with them. As'ad had great luck. He died before he had to wait in the house, on the terrace, on the road, for his son to come back from the battlefront. He was always a lucky fellow."

Love is like a fire. It dies down when it is not fed. "Don't forget me. Rub your glances upon my eyes and bend over my face like a young poplar. If you only knew how much I love poplar leaves. Don't you love their silvery sheen shimmering and their copper-plated faces?"

"It's going to snow," Jiryis said.

"How do you know?"

"The clouds are dust-colored. The birds have closed their wings and hidden in their shelters. Look at that flock: do you see how they're fleeing away?"

"Fleeing away? I don't know. They're just flying."

"You town people are still ignorant even though you've been to many schools. Can't you tell the difference between flying and fleeing away? I've just said it's going to snow."

Through the open cellar the wind blew playfully, carrying with it the musty smell of the soil, the dead grass, the green pine needles, and my pipe's tobacco. And I love you.

"You make love like a volcano and you think about it like a saint."

"Our family marries late. I'll marry you today on my thirtieth birthday. I shall make love to you like a saint and think about it like a mistress. Is that what you want?"

"Why are you always in need of two faces, my Wheatstalk—two feelings, and two kinds of behavior?"

"Why do you call me 'Wheatstalk'?"

"Your skin is the color of wheat. I await your gifts as the wheatstalk waits to turn into a loaf of bread."

I knew that she spoke with others too. I knew how much she needed comforting words, love words, words that intoxicated her, words that she would keep like yeast to foment her dreams on dreary nights. My Wheatstalk is royally hungry, but I've learned for quite some time now that there's no such thing as royalty, kings, kingdoms. To love and not to be disappointed is the epitome of intelligence, pride, enjoyment, a banquet of pleasure. But in order to avoid disappointment, one must give, one must love giving, one must love oneself. Be narcissistic, through others, and you'll be saved. Narcissistic: what's in a name, anyway?

"Jiryis, I shall leave you. I must go."

"Where to? I'll come with you."

"No. No one will come with me."

"All right. Take your coat."

"I won't take anything."

"I told you it's going to snow."

"No, it won't. The sun will return, and the dark young man will come back wearing his red sweater."

Jiryis shook his head while still gazing at the firewood on the cellar's floor. I picked up a stick and walked away.

"Be careful, Jiryis," I said. "Don't throw your cigarette ends on the firewood."

"Shame on you," he said. "Jiryis is not the kind of person who is told not to burn, kill, or destroy. I am life's guardian. Don't you see how I sit here every day waiting for my sons' return?"

"Believe me, believe me," he said, and stood up, pointing a finger at my face. "If I didn't wait for them with every pulse in my heart, they wouldn't come back. But they do come back and they'll always come back, and we shall soon spit at war."

"Let's spit at war," I said.

Jiryis started dancing.

The fog was very low, almost licking the ground. I leaned on my cane in the empty church square. There were a few green trees: a sign of early spring. From far off I heard the sound of a car's engine and a loudspeaker shouting, "Fighters, kill that you may live. Learn the art of death, and then you'll also learn the art of life. Fighters . . . " The sound faded into the fog.

"I cannot imitate the prophet Jeremiah. I am—spontaneously—against death. More reflectively, I am against martyrdom. In principle I am for the homeland as a means and against the homeland as an end. Truly, I am against a homeland that spills the blood of its citizens and neighbors. Glory belongs to mankind, not to the homeland. In any case, glory is a glass of arack, no more. It makes you drunk only while it sits in your stomach."

In spite of all this, she kept singing for glory.

I stretched out along the top of the church wall. I felt as though it was going to collapse. "The earthly wall is collapsing," I said to myself. "God is not in the church."

God sees War above church endowments. He sees the monopoly of endowments. Which monopoly? God is not in the church, even though the women have decorated it with their expensive white, red, green, yellow, and blue scarves: a cascade of interlocking colors. They decorated the church almost a month ago. And yet War comes, and God does not return.

I entered the church. It was cold. The icons were cold, the statues were cold, the pews were cold. I sat down. No one talked to me. The church was empty.

From the inside of the church the noise of gunfire grew. The church is the very opposite of guns, and yet it was absorbing the sound of gunfire and playing with the echo. Playing, did I say? Is there anything more serious than play? Play is the most serious thing we do. Do we give ourselves, heart and soul, to anything else with such fervor? Games presuppose victors, and is there anything more lustful than to be a victor? War is a game too, a red game, a blood banquet, serious to the point of death. In other words, it has all the crass stupidity of everything that leads to emptiness. Nothing is more beautiful than life.

I stretched out in a pew. I could still smell the incense from the Mass that was now long over. I closed my eyes. I felt a hand shaking me roughly. I saw him in his black gown standing over me.

"The church is not a place to sleep in," he said.

"The church is a place to exercise freedom," I said.

"Which freedom?"

"There's only one freedom: the freedom of speech, action, thought."

"That's for unbelievers. Get out of here, or behave with decency!"

"Is sleep a sign of irreverence, Father?"

"Yes. In the presence of God, it is."

"God! But God is everywhere. God is in one's bed too."

"Silence! Spare me your philosophy. Freedom, philosophy—meaningless words!"

I leaned on my cane and left. The church that God has left in the hands of His servants is like a house abandoned by its owners. No one takes better care of his property than the owner himself.

I ran out to meet her. War is everywhere, where the early spring is. Her door was open. I did not knock. She too is everywhere.

"What's wrong with you?"

"I was thrown out of God's house."

"What took you to God's house?"

"I was just passing by."

"You're lying."

"It's true. I was lying in the church. I was sleeping there. That is why the verger threw me out."

"Tell the truth."

"I swear I'm telling the truth. I went to pray."

"For what?"

"For a cure."

"From?"

"My hope and my role in life."

She stared at me.

"My hope," I continued, "for a true, free deliverance and my role as a powerless witness to the wasted world."

"And did you pray?"

"No. But I shall. I shall catch up with the dark young man."

"You're crazy."

"I'll catch up with the dark young man wearing the red sweater. I'll have him take it off and I'll give him my clothes to wear. They'll spot him and they'll kill him."

"Stay with me. Stay here a while."

"No."

"Leave the dark young man alone with his dream. Don't ruin it for him. Death is an issue only for those who do not believe. For the believer it's so easy. Leave him alone. Don't spoil his song."

I sat down and reflected. The room was real, alive: a half-full cup of coffee, records on the sofa, an open book, an ashtray filled with cigarette ends, a pair of slippers, everything in disarray like life itself. Could it be that life is just that, a state of complete disarray? Could it be that the yearning for order is simply the unconscious yearning for death?

She stood up smiling because I had stayed. She put on a record that had one of my favorite pieces. I waited for my piece with anticipation. Suddenly I was listening to it. I wished it could last longer, but it did not. The record wanted to say other things that had no significance at all.

Essentials don't take too long to say. I grabbed my cane.

"Where are you going?" she asked.

"To catch up with the dark young man wearing the red sweater. I'll have him take it off and give him my clothes."

"Stay here with me."

"No."

"Don't you love me?"

"It's unimportant."

"Are you angry?"

" . . . "

"Is it because I speak to other people?"

"I'm beyond being possessive."

"Because you're a failure. You talk about freedom because you're a failure."

"Yes, and more, because I'm a coward. I didn't know how to shrug off the love of life like the dark young man."

"And are you going to try?"

"Yes!"

"A saint!"

"No, a devil who worships God."

"You won't go. You won't go."

"Take me with you to the banquet," my daughter begged. I walked away but she clung to my arms.

"What's the broker's banquet to you?" I asked.

"Take me with you, please."

I took her with me.

Here I am having dinner with the pockmarked broker. He eats with his dark blue eyes, his thick lips, his fat fingers, his red face. He eats with two appetites. He eats with his eyes.

A week ago he tried to sell me to a butcher of a wholesale merchant.

The banquet is for the rich. The dining table is long, like those found in monasteries. To my right is a blonde young woman, to my left a fat brunette. To the right of the blonde woman sits the consul. The landlord sits next to the fat woman. At the head of the table is the guest of honor, the lawyer, carrying in his hand a blue rosary the same color as his socks. To his right, the hostess: to her right, the businessman wearing a black coat and an astrakhan hat. Next to him is the consul's wife, then the retired military attaché wearing khaki. (He cannot forget himself in khaki.) The host sits modestly at the head of the table. The broker is everywhere, just like War itself.

The broker is trying to sell the host, who is a businessman himself, a consignment of stolen Italian tiles. The broker is very careful about legal transactions: he has brought the lawyer along to take care of them. The host will not buy stolen goods. Why? Because. The blonde woman looks at the lawyer. "Money does not have a particular smell," the lawyer says. He inhales deeply. "Money has no country," replies the broker. "Money has no religion," the businessman says.

The host is tense. He knows the truth of what they're saying, but he will not buy stolen goods, because he's afraid to. He say's he's not a member of the "club"; only the members can get away with stealing.

The lawyer whispers to the businessman, leaning over the hostess's empty seat. The hostess is in the kitchen.

"I can guess what you're whispering to him," I said, clapping my hands. "You said the host was a coward."

"I didn't say a coward."

"Yes, you did."

"You shouldn't guess," he said, fondling his rosary.

"I heard it, I heard it. I'm not just guessing," I insisted, clapping my hands again.

The hostess came back, carrying a tray full of fruit. The conversation stopped.

The house is hot. The heat is suffocating. The businessman is sweating, but he takes off neither his coat nor his hat.

There's a chill in the conversation. "The tiles will stay in their crates tonight," I mumbled. "Too bad, they'll stay in the cold warehouse."

The lawyer is looking at the brunette next to me. He's pontificating about justice and injustice, upholding the former. The broker eats up the lawyer's words, assessing what profit he can make out of them. The businessman is talking about fair profit, the military man about nobility on the battlefield. The radio is reporting that sniping incidents have been reported on all fronts. The consul is making predictions about the result of the war, while the lawyer offers conflicting suggestions. The lawyer has a nicer voice. His words are more powerful and more appealing.

"God, the lawyer certainly knows a lot!" the blonde woman whispers to me.

There's a power cut. My daughter and Mark are playing. Mark is a poet. His hair is disheveled. His shirt is open. He's barefoot. He is redecorating the house and changing the position of the lamps and vases.

Candles are flickering in the hallway. The butane lantern sits on the table radiating light. Mark has stuck flowers in the chairs and the windows.

My daughter is a painter. She's borrowed Mark's reading book, opened it on the table, and drawn on it the story of Asterix, her youngest nephew.

The lawyer is talking to the fat woman. The military man is talking to the hostess. The consul, frowning, is analyzing silently. The businessman and the broker are discussing horses. The blonde woman is feeding the lawyer the two apples she has peeled.

"Why two?" I asked.

"It is improper to give him only one."

"Why?"

"One apple suggests Eve's deed."

The conversation is about horses. We're sick and tired of horse talk.

The light of the lantern shines on half of the blonde woman's face. My daughter is pasting her drawing on the wall. Mark is drawing dizzy circles on the floor with a piece of chalk. He has written his name under his circles.

The night of Kafr Millat is red. Bullets are crossing the sky.

The night of Kafr Millat is groaning. A thousand voices from a thousand wailing throats.

The night of Kafr Millat is day. People are in the streets.

The night of Kafr Millat is insane. Lanterns are running around in the streets. Faces cannot be distinguished one from another.

The night of Kafr Millat is the valley of resurrection. Its church bells are ringing until they almost crack.

The dark young man is dead.

"What a waste of a good deal!" the middleman said. "All those tiles."

"Don't worry," the lawyer said. "We'll sell them to the party."

"The party takes," the businessman said. "It does not buy."

"I have connections in the party," the lawyer said.

"My God! He has so many friends," the blonde woman said.

Mark and my daughter messed up the decorations. They tore out the pictures and rubbed out the drawings. They drew on the floor a long rifle and a sweater, and colored them with the red nail polish, which they took from the blonde woman's purse.

I cried out like a madman. "I told you, I'll run after him and have him take off his red sweater. The red sweater gave him away. I told you they'd spot him, you bitch!"

The blonde woman screamed. Her eyes looked like two pools of blood. She left the table. The lawyer's hand followed her.

"Why is the Flower of the Banquet crying?" He stroked her hair with the rosary. His hand touched her face.

"Why is the Temple's Goddess crying?" He asked again.

The lawyer stood up, sternly pointing his accusing finger at the two children. "They have stolen the red nail polish and drawn meaningless lines with it on the floor."

—Translated by Adnan Haydar and Anthony Thwaite

Ibrahim Aslan (b. 1939)

A largely self-educated man, Egyptian novelist and short-story writer Ibrahim Aslan has worked as a civil servant in Cairo. His early collection of short stories, *The Evening Lake* (1971), won him recognition in Egypt and the wider Arab world. He is skilled in delineating the physical and psychological details of a situation, which he usually picks from ordinary everyday life around him. A later collection of short stories, *A Night's Rosary*, appeared in 1992. He has also published two novels, *Birds of the Night* (2000) and *Tales from Fadlallah 'Uthman* (2003).

IN SEARCH OF AN ADDRESS

Shortly after midday a thin man was walking with straight steps, along the sidewalk of the long street that divides the city in two. The sidewalk was crowded with men and women moving in both directions, and the sunlight shone from the roofs of the vehicles creeping along the asphalt street.

The thin man was wearing a pale gray suit and carried a folded newspaper in his hand. There was no hair on the crown of his head. He walked for a while down the long street, then stopped by a metal trash basket that was hanging on one of the tall poles and began to watch a crippled man who was crawling across the sidewalk, blocking his way. Finally the cripple leaned his back against the wall under one of the shop windows and stretched out his hand to the passersby, looking at them with anxious eyes.

The thin man stood and watched him for a moment; then he shifted the newspaper to his left hand and with his right took out a handkerchief. He wiped the sweat from his face and the crown of his head and sighed weakly. He had no sooner put the handkerchief back in his pocket and begun to walk on, than he stopped again and his eyes narrowed.

A few yards away a fat man stood gazing at him, his jaw hanging open and his eyes wide.

The two men stood facing each other for a while, and the thin man constantly shifted his eyes from the fat man to the asphalt of the street and back again. He kept on doing this till the fat man suddenly approached him, with a wide grin of surprise on his face. He came up so close that they almost touched and said:

"*Ahlan wa sahlan!*[1] It's good to see you!"

The thin man retreated a step, coming very close to the trash basket. As they exchanged glances, he murmured, "It's good to see you, sir!"

The fat man said in a loud voice, "Don't you remember me?"

The thin man looked at him. He managed a little smile, as he replied, "No, really, I don't, not exactly—although your face seems familiar."

The fat man, who was wearing only a shirt and trousers, and was hugging a few packages, said, "Come on, you know me. I'm Sayyid al-Biltagi."

His eyelids quivering, the thin man repeated, "Really, I'm sorry, I'm sorry . . . "

"Aren't you . . . aren't you . . . ?" The fat man jerked his head irritably. "Your name's on the tip of my tongue, it's on the tip of my tongue . . . "

The thin man said, "My name's 'Arif, 'Arif al-Saqqa."

The fat man lifted his hand over the packages, grasped the arm of the thin man and shook him, shouting, "'Arif al-Saqqa. Yes, 'Arif al-Saqqa. That's who you are. Exactly. *Ahlan wa sahlan*. Another moment and I'd have remembered.

---

1. This is equivalent to saying "Welcome" in English.

But how come you don't remember me? Don't you remember Sayyid al-Biltagi, who sat behind you in class? Right behind you?"

"You were at school with me, sir?"

"Of course, I was!" And patting him on the shoulder, the fat man whispered, "You must be getting old. Your memory's going"

"I was at Farouk School."

The fat man laughed uproariously. The drops of sweat on his temples rolled down over his short, stout neck and the bare part of his chest. He said, "Farouk School? Didn't I tell you you're getting old, and your memory's going?" Then he continued sharply, "Well, how are you?"

The thin man smiled. "All right."

The fat man craned his neck. He stared at the thin man's face more carefully. "But what's happened to make you look so old?"

"Circumstances."

"Circumstances? How come you're so calm about it, lad?"

The thin man laughed. He said in a confused voice, "Calm? How do you mean, calm?"

"How do I mean? I mean how are *you* so calm about it, you old devil? You, the most mischievous pupil I ever set eyes on?"

"You don't say!"

"Hey! Come on! Come on! You were a real little devil. Well, it's good to see you!"

At this moment he dropped one of the packages he was holding against his chest. As he tried to bend his short body, he almost fell against the thin man's chest. He said, "Listen, do you remember Mabrook?"

"Mabrook? Mabrook who?"

"The dark boy, brother. You know! The one whose lunch you used to grab."

The thin man laughed, "Did I grab his lunch?"

"Of course you did!"

"That's really strange! I don't remember it at all."

"At any rate, you do remember him?"

"What?"

"It was a very odd thing."

Again he looked around, then pointed with his chin to the packages he was carrying: "I thought I'd buy some clothes for the kids. Listen. You're married, of course."

"Who?"

"You."

"God, no. Never."

The fat man shouted, "I don't believe it!" What's this, 'Arif? I don't believe it ... "

"God, I've had other matters to think about."

"Other matters? What other matters, man? What matters were those?" He frowned. "Financial matters?"

"No, not at all." The thin man laughed. "Matters of another kind."

"They really must be, if you're still not married. I can't believe it! I'm absolutely flabbergasted!" Then he shouted, "Tell me, how's your mother?"

"May you live long, she's passed away."

"Indeed, there is no power, God bless her soul, or strength except in God. Listen, where do you work now?"

"Well, as a matter of fact—I don't do any particular work."

"That's just like you! You never could settle down to anything. But don't you remember Mabrook? The dark boy, brother?"

"I believe there was a dark boy. But I want ... "

"That's just like you! You never did settle down to anything. But who would have thought we'd go all this time without meeting? Eh? Who would have thought it?"

The thin man said, "That's quite true."

"And who would have thought we'd meet again like this? Eh? But where do you live now?"

"I live in al-Agouza."[2]

"Well, I live in al-Hilmiyya al-Gadida."[3] He burst out laughing. "When I saw you, I couldn't believe it! That 'Arif, looking so serious? I can't believe it, I thought. I'm really surprised."

The thin man laughed. "Why?"

"Why? You, the biggest joker ever, ask me why? You ask me why, lad? Listen, do you remember when we went to the Aquarium?"

"The Aquarium?"

"When we had the school officer with us, and we went out on a jaunt and had some food?"

"It was a long time ago, you know."

"A long, long time ago, when we played on the hill, and you jumped and hurt yourself. How come you don't remember?"

"I jumped! Me?"

"Yes!"

"Why?"

"I don't know. We were playing on the hill, and you laughed and jumped."

"Did I hurt myself?"

"Of course you did."

"Where was that?"

The fat man looked at a woman who was crossing the street in a leisurely way, her dress revealing a large part of her back. He winked and said, "What do you think of that, eh?"

The thin man smiled and did not answer. The fat man again pointed his chin at the packages held tightly to his chest, and said, "I thought I'd buy some clothes for the kids."

---

2. A quarter in Cairo.
3. A quarter in Cairo.

"Do you have kids?"

"Samira, 'Abdu, and Mursi, and another on the way."

"That's marvelous! Marvelous!"

"Listen, I'll give you my address so you can come and visit me. You must see the kids, brother."

"I will, God willing."

"Seeing you has just reminded me. Do you remember Mursi Effendi, brother, the schoolteacher? Good grief! You really were a little devil! Well, *ahlan wa sahlan.*"

The thin man chuckled. A fine net of wrinkles formed around the corners of his eyes. The fat man shouted, "Laughing and playing and jumping and hitting people! Good grief!" Then he shouted, "You poured ink over the backside of the boy who sat in front of you!"

The two men laughed helplessly, with all their strength, alongside the trash basket. The fat man's laughter was uproarious and varied, while the thin man shook as he laughed, bending forward and biting his lower lip every now and then.

The fat man shouted, "I used to sit right behind you, and I saw you."

The thin man gripped his newspaper tighter, and there were tears of laughter in his eye.

"Did you see me?"

"Yes. I saw you pouring ink over his backside. And I reported you."

He clapped the fat man on the shoulder. "Did I really do that?"

"Yes. I reported you. We were just kids."

"What did the headmaster do?"

"He must have beaten you."

"Did he beat me?"

"I don't remember." He stamped his feet on the ground. "You must have run away."

The passersby watched, keeping clear of them as they walked. The thin man threw his newspaper in the trash basket. "Did I run away from him?"

"Yes. You must have jumped. We were on the top floor."

"No way. We were on the ground floor."

He put his hand on the fat man's shoulder. "What did the kid do?"

"Which kid?"

"The kid whose backside I poured the ink over?"

"He must have cried. Yes. He cried, and his face went blue."

Caught by a fit of violent sneezing, the thin man jerked his head. "Did he cry?"

"He did. And he complained to his mother."

"Where is he now?"

"I don't know. He must be dead."

The thin man said in a weak voice, "I'm exhausted, man." He took out his handkerchief and began to dry his eyes.

While the fat man was adjusting the packages clasped to his chest, he said, "You were a real little devil. Good grief! Laughing and playing and . . . " The sound of a vehicle braking split the air. The fat man shouted, "Look! It's held up at the traffic lights."

He blurted out the last sentence, jumped off the sidewalk, and rushed towards the bus, which was now about to move. The thin man wheeled round. He saw the hands helping the fat man climb aboard the crowded vehicle. Reaching out his hand, he whispered, "The address! You didn't give me the address."

Just as he said this, the vehicle moved. He stopped, his face more wrinkled than before, feeling his chin with his long fingers. Some passersby pushed him slightly, and his eyes met the eyes of the crippled man in a swift, burning glance. Then the thin man shook his head and moved back with a heavy mechanical step. He leaned his back against the trash basket, and for a long time looked into the distance where the bus had disappeared.

—Translated by Sharif Elmusa and Christopher Tingely

Sa'id 'Aulaqi (b. 1940)

One of the finest authors from South Yemen, short-story writer and dramatist Sa'id 'Aulaqi writes on a wide range of subjects, including detailed histories of the two revolutions of North and South Yemen. Whether on political or social themes his writings are based on reality but a reality made thrilling and imposing through fiction. His short-story collection, *Emigrating Twice*, was published in 1980. He has also published a play entitled *The Inheritance* and a literary history of drama in Yemen entitled *Seventy Years of Theater in Yemen* (1980).

THE TRIAL

I entered the coffee bar at a harsh hour of the afternoon. I ordered a cup of tea and dipped my tongue into its bitterness.

"You are a despicable person, Majid . . . but I understand you. I don't blame you at all, you're just like other people, no better, no worse. Good-bye, contemptible man!"

Such was our heated parting—I did not speak that day. I let 'Afaf choose her words freely and pour them over my head like cold water. I let her enjoy her last day with me to its fullest and contented myself with sitting beside her like some wooden statue, as she decreed our parting . . . and we parted in silence.

On that day I did not care. I knew it was the natural end of our relationship; marriage was the furthest thought from my mind.

One year passed, then two years, and three. During that period I lived more and more in bitter struggle with myself. I wondered why people create constraining customs for themselves, then curse them uselessly. All my attempts to contact 'Afaf met with failure. After the third year I still sat alone, spinning my pain, cursing the act of memory, and chewing on my silence.

Behind that silence I was hiding something heavy and suspect. I used to try to liberate myself from it so I might accomplish something real and important, something that would restore me to my previous possibilities.

But a fire seared the back of my head. I decided to break the rule and rebel against tradition. I decided to ask her hand in legal matrimony. The pain I had suffered away from her was absolutely cutting and unbearable; it had smelted me and dissolved me into madness before cleansing me of my vileness and giving me this new intent.

I walked on a straight dirt road, where the houses lined up together harmoniously, like match boxes, all of them one-story mud houses—one-story, one window—but their walls were huge and firm, and their paint was old.

This was an unforgettable place to me, its nooks and corners immortalized, since it was the place I first saw 'Afaf.

Today I noticed a large tent, its sides strung with tassels. From inside came the strain of dance music, accompanied by drumbeats. My ears followed the music that grew louder as I approached—suddenly a long drawn-out ululation hit my ear, after which the drums went berserk.

I was confused . . . then utterly overwhelmed when I realized they were celebrating 'Afaf's wedding . . . her wedding! Could anyone have believed that 'Afaf would be getting married on the very day I went to ask for her hand? Is that possible, Your Honor?

The judge rapped with his gavel. I was a tragic figure in a comic play.

I awoke to the café owner's voice asking me to pay for the tea. I paid and left the coffee bar, more certain than ever that were I to sleep with a thousand women, 'Afaf would never leave my mind.

"From 'Aziza, Fathia, Um al-Khair, and 'Alawiyya Radwan to 'Afaf Mohammed 'Issa on the occasion of her blessed wedding, with all best wishes."[1]

You are a despicable person, Majid, so be despicable . . . why not?

My chest heaves as the heart madly pumps blood into the veins; each night I shed new reserves of patience and become more certain that the impossible is truly impossible.

I returned to my house like a deposed emperor being led into exile. After what had happened, it seemed to me I could not become wise even if I lived for a thousand years. The present and future dimmed to a faded tableau, shadowed bleakly by the past . . . there was no escaping the fever of memory.

Now it is three years since 'Afaf's marriage, Your Honor. And I still burn with grief. When will your verdict be passed?

The accused man standing before you is the greatest embodiment of moral disintegration and indifference, a man without a heart, the devil himself. 'Afaf,

---

1. This is an open declaration of gifts, often of money, offered to the bride (or groom or both) and announced loudly at weddings by a special announcer.

his victim, was in his grasp, she had given herself to him, confident of his gallantry. And what did he do but rob her of a woman's most precious possession, then turn his back on her love by refusing to marry her? What more can he want, Your Honor? What more?

For three years I experienced no rest. 'Afaf's memory beseiged me and dug a grave for me in every city where I traveled. 'Afaf, 'Afaf, 'Afaf . . . a nymph, a fairy, an enchantress. The legend of earth and sky, moon and stars. Fountain of inspiration, overflowing spring of tenderness.

If only I could now shut my eyes and be something else, something unknown to me, something of complete indifference to others, something that does not think or dress or see. Something chained up in the exile of memories.

Your Honor, honorable members of the jury . . . I have emphasized repeatedly to you that the negative stance of my client toward the events that led to these consequences is the greatest evidence of the psychological state that he has been in and remains in, which led him to his state of delirium. He stood at a loss between two choices, the first driving him forward toward realizing his dreams, desires, and ambitions, the second constraining him within the prison of tradition and society. He was torn apart. Isn't what this miserable wretch has suffered enough? Doesn't he deserve compassion and care instead of being left a prisoner of his own conscience to the point of collapse?

I would not exaggerate, gentlemen, if I were to say that some might see him as a saint, a prophet in an age that has no prophets.

So I am a prophet, and the age of prophets is past and gone. Does this satisfy you, 'Afaf? The session is adjourned for deliberation.

'Afaf, dark brown hair, willowy form, the color of coffee with milk . . . magical evenings under moonlight by the sea . . . Um Kulthoum's[2] songs, the sweet nights of longing and love, the fire in my heart and the belly of the sands and folds of the sea . . . the past, present and future . . . undefined symbols on her lashes.

A TRIAL

Since this court is given over completely to this case, it permits the defendant another opportunity to recount his story from the beginning.

The sun was setting and the chill reclaiming the sky. Nothing moved but the wind, which carried small particles of dust. The air seemed dense with illusory fog. I walked on a straight road where houses were lined up close together like matchboxes, one-story mud houses, their walls huge and steadfast, their paint old.

She appeared in the doorway . . . I saw her face and green filmy dress, covered with tiny white flowers, like glittering stars . . . my eyes fell to her small rubber shoes. She stood lightly on the earth, almost weightlessly. She called to a small

---

2. Um Kulthoum was the Arab world's greatest twentieth-century female singer.

child, who was playing with a pile of soil, and smiled. I heard her voice, sensed her smile like the pricking beak of a dove in my heart. My fingers stopped playing with the key chain in my pocket. I saw my face reflected in the darkness of her eyes and wished that I could live there. My throat went dry as I murmured my prayer.

The peak of wishes! The pinnacle of dreams!

She seemed so beautiful, I suddenly felt limitless—everything surrounding me blurred. Time lost its boundaries; 'Afaf was everything I had dreamed of—she seemed to possess something I had dreamed of—she seemed to possess something I had not known existed—something new, wonderful, and amazing that moved within my heart, touching where no one had touched before.

The child approached her. She lifted him up, smiling, and nuzzled against him, kissing him on the back of his neck. Her voice filled me as she spoke . . . I learned he was her little brother, and I felt that I too was a child full of health and joy. Her words and kisses were the glittering ocean in which I swam. She disappeared behind the door, closing it gently, and suddenly I stood alone on a dusty noisy street. I clenched my fist and opened it, looking inside, but discovered only my throbbing heart.

Dust swirled in the light beams. The world, the sunset, and my soul were unhinged. I searched for my happiness but could not find it.

Everything in my life lost meaning until I met her for the second time, in the center of the city. She was alone, walking calmly, a confident smile sparkling on her lips.

I told myself that I should not act like a fool. But I swallowed and decided to act quickly, making a move toward our acquaintance, whatever the price. Everything happened suddenly. I approached her with some mysterious notion of the words that would pass between us. I smiled. I spoke, feeling as though I were wading in a sea of dough. I said strange words I cannot remember, then lowered my head with embarrassment. I must have looked silly, shifting between one sentence and another with all the streets of the city around me watching. But she was gentle and full of self-confidence; instead of running away, she entered my heart and quietly sat there.

She said, "When a person speaks extensively in the classical form, I know that he is undergoing some crisis!"

We went off together, feeling already close.

"And why did you refuse to marry her, since you loved her so much and she returned your love?"

"I never knew that I loved her this much, your Honor. The best days of our lives are always the days that have passed, because we do not feel happiness until after we lose it. We do not know what is right until we have committed what is wrong. I was happy in the past, only I did not feel the happiness in the literal sense of the word! When I would think of marrying 'Afaf, I would think of other people . . . my mother, my father, my family, my friends . . . I would think of society and what it would say of a man who married a woman that had been intimate with him out of wedlock. I would think of honor within the narrow limits set by society. Do you know what it means for a person to flout the inherited code of honor, Your Honor? It means that he walks lightweight in the street, wind tossing him around, and any old broom is capable of sweeping him away."

After our first date I could not sleep a wink. I sat musing on how I would talk with her, what we would do . . . where we would sit, what she would say. Then our meetings became more frequent, and we grew extremely close.

"Let me see your breasts naked . . . Solomon's treasure is found only in legends!"

"You are, mad, mad! But I love your madness . . . you are tender and marvelous."

I was mad and marvelous.

With dreamy sea breezes filling my nostrils, I kissed her, and it was our first union. In the confusion of our first union a thick fog settled over the seven seas, the sailors mutinied . . . the captain was killed . . . the ship captured . . . the pirates ravaged her . . . the pirates triumphed . . . the ship was lost and all her cargo sank!

'Afaf cried a lot, so I buried my head in the sand and the embryo died before it was ever born.

'Afaf, where are you? I want to dissolve tenderly with you again, I want to weep all the tears there are!

Our relationship continued, studded with mundane details—a delicate film covering an open wound. Each night I fancied I would do something noble, but each time I remembered the illicit nature of our relationship, I would fall silent.

'Afaf spoke from her heart, "I love you, I love you very much, Majid, I adore you."

I did not answer. I lifted my hand and touched the sky. The moon slept. 'Afaf breathed deeply, and a moment of exquisite lucidity overwhelmed her. She said, "Love is everything in life! It is life itself—our life and the lives of those who live with us, who were born before us, and who will be born after we die. Without love life is not worth even a handful of dust."

I watched her face, caressed by the breeze. Locks of her hair were fluttering in the air. Then I looked back at the sea, at the place where it joins with the sky . . . I did not say anything.

"Why are you suddenly silent? What's the matter?"

No, please, do not get impatient with me, my love, do not say harsh things. Let me dream . . . I know I must be dreaming. Be gentle and calm—it is enough that you are by my side.

"Why do you haunt me with your silence?"

I had to say something. I found myself saying, " Love is mercurial, it does not suffice as a good foundation for our marriage."

She placed her fingers on my lips to silence me. Her lips quivered as she spoke through her tears, "Enough! Don't go on. Don't kill the memory of our past times together. You are acting despicably, Majid, but I understand you."

Her words hurt me. She said, "Don't be under the mistaken impression that I built my relationship with you with the hope of marrying you. I did what I did voluntarily, because I wanted to. Be sure that I would do the same thing without remorse if the days turned back and the opportunity arose again."

I envy her, Your Honor, believe me. I envy her courage and daring and intense self-confidence, her sincere faith in her beliefs and actions. I lack such faith. I am weak next to her; I did not deserve her to begin with! She is stronger and greater and more honorable than I!

No use. The trial will never be finished. The verdict will never be passed and I will never forget 'Afaf. Only sleep delivers me from the exile of memories.

But I am also afraid of the sad night that awaits me, its long empty hours divided into minutes and seconds . . . afraid of 'Afaf and her phantom that disturbs my sleep. How miserable can a person be when he lies awake alone, thinking of his beloved in the arms of another man?

This is the whole story, Your Honor . . . what is your verdict? The verdict will come after the deliberation.

Who can accuse or pass judgment? Who can set himself up as judge? Who can see the truth and find the way?

I am the accused, the guilty one. I stand alone, an outcast in an insignificant corner of the world. I know nobody, no one knows me. My friendship cannot be bought or sold. I am the criminal and the judge and the executioner, and I shall pass sentence on myself.

Now everything in this city seems impossible, everything! The city is suffocating me. I hate everything now. The city spins a web of confusion that suffocates me. No, it's not the city—it's the people—society is the cause! but 'Afaf is the one who must pay the price.

Tonight I shall pass my own sentence and let 'Afaf fall forever from my memory.

I went down into the street after midnight that night. My feet led me across the alleyways and streets on the path they had been ordained to follow for years . . . the rhythm of my feet competed with my breathing until I almost panted trying to match the two movements. The dagger hidden under my jacket was strong enough to kill ten oxen! I stood in front of the intended house. I broke the window so I could open it from the inside. Soon I had found my way through the darkness to the bedroom where 'Afaf slept in the arms of her husband . . . I tiptoed toward the bed.

"From 'Aziza and Fathia and Um al-Khair Radwan to 'Afaf Mohammed 'Issa on the occasion of her blessed wedding with best wishes . . . "

I thought I could express my burning emotions and find peace.

Like lightning I saw my hand rise and fall with the unsheathed dagger in it down onto the bed, repeated blows accompanied by hysterical cries . . . I did not know I could make such sounds. My heart was weeping its burden of love, hate, despair, recklessness.

In a few minutes the neighboring houses lit up. Windows opened. Then the house was filled with people. The police recorded in their log that an assault had been made against an empty bed—the intended victims were not in the house when the incident occurred. The experts recorded twenty-five stab marks on the empty bed.

Red and white spots blurred my eyesight. I felt numb. I was in a mobile cage, wearing strange white clothes, guarded by two armed policemen.

The motor cage took us to an isolated building in a city suburb, surrounded by a thick stone wall. An old guard opened the gate and the car entered. I saw a sign that read "Mental Hospital."

"You are despicable, Majid . . . you are gentle and marvelous."

I am mad and marvelous.

Your voice, 'Afaf, stands behind me, rules the world, transports me to the countryside of sun and open spaces. Each time the moon sleeps, I remember the days when I used to write your name on the sky.

—*Translated by Lena Jayyusi and Naomi Shihab Nye*

Tawfiq Yusuf 'Awwad (1911–1989)

Lebanese novelist and short-story writer Tawfiq Yusuf 'Awwad was born in Bharsaf in the mountains of the Matn region. After studying at St. Joseph College, he read law at the University of Damascus. He worked in journalism, first as one of the editors of the well-known Lebanese review *Al-Makshuf,* then founded his own magazine, *Al-Jadid,* in 1941, which he made a platform for writers. In 1964 he joined the diplomatic corps, representing Lebanon as ambassador in many countries of the world. He became known as a novelist with his early publication of *Loaf of Bread* (1939), but his most famous work is his novel *Windmills of Beirut,* which he wrote while ambassador in Tokyo. Published in 1972, this novel won immediate fame as a sensitive reflection of Arab society in general and Lebanese society in particular during the post-1967 Arab-Israeli war. In 1976 Leslie McLoughlin published his translation of this novel, which he titled *Death in Beirut.* 'Awwad has several collections of short stories: *The Woollen Shirt (1937), The Lame Boy (1937),* and *Frozen Rain and Other Stories.* In 1988 'Awwad won the Saddam Hussein Prize for literature.

THE WIDOW

In Ras Beirut the splendid white house with the beautiful garden round it was in the middle of a frightening storm, which howled like the sound of metal scraping on metal. It was raining heavily, but the rain would stop suddenly when it had covered the glass of the western window with water, which would then glide down the window pane and begin to trickle, leaving small, scattered drops that soon dissolved and allowed the light to enter the room. But as soon as the rain started falling again, the window would again cover over and the room would grow dark. It was a rough January night such as the Beirutis hadn't known for years, and this prompted Helena to light the fire to try and keep warm. While attending to this, she'd peer out through the window from time to time and think about her dead husband. Whenever the memory of him passed through her mind, she blocked it, staring at the glittering, smoldering embers in the hearth and spending long minutes without moving.

Helena had become a widow five days before.

Her sister came from Saida for the death of her brother-in-law and stayed with her for four days, repeating the formulas people always use to people in mourning, hugging her, tidying the house for her, and crying with her. She left on the afternoon of the fourth day, after advising her to forget and reminding her that we're all food for death and that tears don't bring the dead back from their graves.

For all her efforts Helena couldn't forget; rather, she found herself trying to remember Kameel by recalling his features and his movements and the things he'd said. Although she'd spent five years of her life with him, not counting the year of their engagement, she remembered him only in a very vague way, as if he'd died five years not five days before!

As the dark, stormy night raged on, with her soul as desolate as the weather, it occurred to the widow to go to the cupboard and look for the letters Kameel had written to her during their engagement. She went next door to their bedroom and, as she saw the empty bed, an overmastering terror combined with the cold of the room to make her shudder violently. It seemed to her that Kameel was standing behind her, preparing to take off his clothes and throw himself on the bed. Then she imagined him lying there, a lifeless body, pale, with drooping moustaches. She stretched her hand toward the cupboard and fumbled to open it with fingers that shook badly. She took a small box from the drawer and returned hurriedly to her seat near the fireplace, not daring to look behind her.

There was a pile of letters written in his beautiful handwriting, on smooth sheets of paper, all alike, decorated with a rose in the corner. It was a special romantic paper that Kameel particularly liked, together with the luxurious blue envelopes, also romantic, in which he used to enclose the letters.

Here was a letter describing their life after their marriage, and there was one in which he asked for her love and kissed her hand. A third one described a nightmare in which he'd seen himself die; but, he added, he didn't want to die because he wanted to be happy and make her happy. Yet another passionate letter was sent to her from Aleppo, where he went on business. And here was his first letter, where he confessed his love, his tears, and his beating heart. As Helena read it, she remembered his first kiss. He'd asked, "Can I kiss your neck?"

Then he'd kissed her neck and blushed. She remembered their engagement too, and the wedding. She saw all her past life between the lines, scene by scene, passing in front of her across the fireplace then rushing headlong into the gulf of eternity.

Suddenly her eyes lit up, as she saw a paper different from the others, a flimsy, yellowish paper, with fingermarks still visible on it. She took it from the box, ignoring the other letters, and as soon as she opened it she recognized it. It was the letter that had never been delivered.

There was a story connected with the letter, and Helena recalled it as she read and reread the words in front of her.

It happened before her engagement. She was twenty-one then, and Said Hattam was in love with her. He married two years after she did but soon tired of his wife, Henriette, and they were now separated. In fact Said loved Helena and she loved him. They were neighbors, but she couldn't remember how they met; She might have seen him every day and paid no attention to him. But one evening he met her at a party and talked to her privately. He was very aggressive, and spoke to her in words no young man had ever used to her before! He had, she recalled, said, quite literally, "Listen Helena, you're beautiful all right, but I don't love you. Do something to make me love you."

Helena held a clear memory of his strange words, as well as the way he looked when he talked. He'd been insolent to the point of offensiveness, saying these words as casually as if he'd been remarking that the weather was bad and he wished it would clear up so he could take a walk. Then he'd given a confident smile, sure that the matter was one for him alone: if he decided to fall in love with her he would, and she'd have no choice but to respond to his love; and if he chose not to, nothing would happen between them. Helena had felt a certain revulsion for him and a need to maintain a distance between them. There was something else too, call it fear, which weighed on her. She hadn't dared to answer him, and as people around them were engaged in a general discussion, they'd felt obliged to take part in the conversation and abandon their private talk.

Said had finally got what he wanted. His fiery looks were too much for Helena, and one day she fell in his arms and he kissed her on the mouth without her permission. She wanted to resist but melted helplessly in his embrace.

One day she prepared a meal of tabbouleh, for which she was famous in the neighborhood. She invited her neighbor Said among others, and her friends came with their brothers and their brothers' friends. There were more than twenty people gathered there, boys and girls, under the lemon trees in the garden. Brothers and sisters went their different ways, each looking for a companion to snatch a mouthful of tabbouleh from, except Said, who didn't favor any girl in particular but moved from one to the other, very elegantly grabbing a bite here and a bite there. His face was almost entirely covered with olive oil, parsley, and *burghul*.

When the party was over, one of Helena's friends, Mary, approached her and indicated him out of the corner of her eye.

"Who is he?" she asked.

When the guests left, Said lingered behind and, as he was leaving, indicated Mary out of the corner of his eye—she was walking in front of him, tall and slender—and asked Helena, "Who is she?"

Helena's heart beat violently, but she couldn't refuse to tell him.

"She's . . ." she replied, "an old school friend of mine."

Then Said explained that he wanted to know her because he liked her.

Said and Mary had their wish. In spite of her jealousy, Helena agreed to what Said wanted and arranged for them to meet at her house two days later. Helena decided not to tell Mary that she already loved Said and that he loved her, so the three of them sat together, with Said's attention and endless flow of words being totally devoted to Mary.

It was amazing the way he could talk when he was sitting with a young woman! He could talk about anything he wanted; he could laugh, cry, get angry, stand, or sit. He'd totally captivate his listener, to the point where she'd forget herself and everything around her. It was as if the ear and the heart together opened to every word he uttered, and to every movement he made, and to the sad or joyful expressions on his face.

Remembering that meeting as she sat there in front of the fireplace, Helena sighed, and her face took on a strange smile that she wasn't even aware of and that was visible only to the periodic flashes of lightning that traversed the window.

Next day Said gave Helena a letter, which he asked her to give to Mary!

Helena knew she'd lost her chance with Said because he was falling in love with Mary, and it was with a grief-stricken face that she took the letter. He didn't seem to understand, or rather he pretended not to understand—perhaps he understood and simply didn't care, didn't feel the least concern about Helena's jealousy. He'd loved her and now he loved Mary; he could love them both at the same time! He didn't say this in so many words, but just said boldly to Helena, "I'll always love you. But take this letter to your friend!"

Then he bent his head and kissed her, with the kiss of a father trying to console his child for a toy he'd broken. But the toy was Helena's heart, a heart that was shattered within her, bleeding and awaiting death and burial. She didn't utter a word, but simply burst into tears, and Said, seeing her weeping, kissed her a second time on the forehead and laughed. Then he left, requesting her once more to take his letter over to Mary and wait for a reply.

Still sitting in front of the fireplace, Helena took hold of the shabby, yellowing letter and read it for the tenth time: "Mary, you're beautiful. I'm surprised I haven't met you before. I'd like to kiss the mouth I snatched the tabbouleh from yesterday. Said."

The handwriting was big and uneven, and the few words had filled the whole page of a paper torn from a copybook. The letter had no elegance whatsoever. How different from the paper Kameel used for his letters!

Helena didn't deliver the letter to Mary. As soon as Said left, she opened it, read it over and over again, and cried. Then she crumpled it in her fingers and was about to tear it up and throw it away, but finally held back. "No," she thought to herself, "I'll keep it." She kept it in the box where she later placed her fiancé's letters, and from this time on her feelings for Mary changed to hatred—which was unfair, because Mary knew nothing of Helena and Said's relationship. Yet she didn't hate Said, who deserved hatred. She no longer knew what she felt for him.

Mary came to visit her that evening.

"Helena, do you know that Said loves me?" she confided, blushing.

"Has he told you?"

"No. But he doesn't need to tell me how he feels about me. I saw it myself. Can't you see his love for me almost bursting out of his eyes and the way he acts? You know as well as I do that we girls have a sixth sense about these things. My heart tells me: Said loves you, he loves you, he loves you."

"Do you love him?"

"All I know is I'm happy, happy, happy!"

Helena would have liked to jump up and shout in Mary's face. "You're a thief." she wanted to shout, "and you say you're happy? It's my happiness you're stealing!"

She would have liked to give this thief a resounding slap in that face that shone with such joy! She would have liked to take her by the hair, then drag her out of the house, push her down the steps, and never see her again. She would have loved to do all those things, but she didn't. Instead, she smiled and said, "That's fine! Said's a wonderful young man. He's a friend of my brother's. You can meet him here, at my house."

Had Helena acted like this out of curiosity, to find out how the romance between Mary and Said would end, or was she slavishly carrying out Said's orders to her?

Whatever her motive was, she arranged a meeting for Said and Mary for the following morning. Mary arrived first, then Said. The house was empty, as Helena's mother and sister had gone out for a visit and her brother had gone to work.

Said came in, with his usual smile, ready to make conversation, and greeted Helena in a pleasant manner that implied that she was a mere go-between for him. Before he even asked about Mary, she told him, "She's here, I invited her for your sake."

Then she went to the kitchen and pretended to be busy. As she went in she noticed a shining meat knife. She picked it up, gazed at it and burst out crying; then grimaced and checked her tears. "How good it would be to die!" she reflected, still looking at the knife. "Wouldn't it be better to kill myself than live this kind of life?

She'd loved two other young men before, but her love for Said was different. He showed no delicacy or good manners, yet he'd stolen her heart, from the first moment, and she would have liked to remain his till her last breath. And here he was, betraying her with her own help, in her own house, and on the same couch where he'd kissed her for the first time. He was betraying her with all the cruelty of an animal, before her own eyes. A stab to her heart with this knife would put a sad end to the romance. How would Said react, she wondered, if he saw her dead body?

While she was lost in her sad thoughts, she heard Said's loud laughter in the sitting room. It was a long peal of laughter, daring and insolent, like everything he did. She held her breath in fury, then ran out of the kitchen into the living-room. She didn't want to die any more, she wanted to be revenged against Said and Mary. They'd see!

What she saw startled her. Said and Mary were embracing; his head was between her breasts and she was kissing his hair. Sensing Helena's presence, they looked at her, Mary smiling stupidly. Helena fell to the floor, in a faint.

When she recovered consciousness, she was lying in bed with a bandage around her forehead, over a painful wound. Said was sitting near the bed. He smiled, and said, "You lied to me. You didn't give Mary my letter. Did you tell her I loved you? Is that why she refused to stay, too embarrassed to look you in the eye?"

Helena simply replied that her parents were about to return and he'd have to leave.

All this had happened six years before and was brought back by the letter lying in her lap. She touched her forehead, searching for the wound and the bandage, and was relieved to find nothing there. She took the tongs to stir the fire, then, realizing the flames were almost extinguished, she bent down to blow at it. She kept blowing and blowing, while the ashes flew round the room and onto her hair and blackened her face. When she raised her head again, she felt a certain dizziness and unpleasant ideas came into her mind, like wounded snakes twisting themselves through her head. She imagined she was married to Said Hattam and that he struck her in the face with a jug, as he did with his wife. She saw herself kneeling at his feet and kissing them, covering them with her tears. Then he'd come back to her and she'd see the love shining in his big, black eyes. She'd feel his strong muscular arms holding her at the waist and pulling her toward him. He'd bring her close to his mouth with its drooping lower lip and would kiss her passionately, then push her away and desert her for other women. But he'd come back, she knew. Oh, she was so happy!

She didn't think about her dead husband any more; she didn't want to remember him. She hated the way he'd given in to her slightest whim. She'd spent five years with him, as well as the engagement year, without ever seeing him take his eyes from her face, or raise his voice, or go against her wishes; he spent his life serving her, not acting like a master. She used to boss him around, take him on visits, pay for their cinema tickets because he'd given her control of the household expenses. "We must do this," she'd tell him, and he'd agree. If she said no, he'd fall in with her wishes. "Just as you like, darling," he'd say. "Do whatever you like, I want you to be happy."

"Poor man," she thought, "he wanted me to be happy! He did everything I wanted, never refused me anything I asked! He was such a good-hearted man, so attentive and caring! Always there to do anything I wanted, hurrying into action if I so much as whispered, or blinked my eyes, or made any move."

Helena went back to her husband's letters and tried to read them with tenderness; but soon she carefully gathered them up and locked them in the box. Then she went to the bedroom, opened the cupboard and put the box away, in a tomb like her husband's tomb. She closed the cupboard carefully, with the yellowing, faded letter still outside, then sat down by the fire. The storm outside was still raging round the house and pounding at the doors and windows. The widow stretched her right hand toward the fire and spread out her fingers to warm them up, listening to the long laments of the storm. It was as if nature was sharing in her grief—not for her husband still covered with fresh mud but for her lost love. The only thing left her from this love was the shabby piece of paper she was nervously squeezing in her left hand.

—*Translated by Aida A. Bamia and Christopher Tingley*

Shukry 'Ayyad (1921–1999)

Born in Manoufiya, Egyptian short-story writer, scholar, and critic Shukry 'Ayyad studied in Egypt, obtaining his Ph.D. in literary criticism in 1953. He received a Rockefeller fellowship and spent the year 1955–56 in America. Dr. 'Ayyad was Professor of Arabic Literature at Cairo University until his early retirement, after which he worked as visiting professor at King Saud University until 1986. A fine writer and distinguished critic and scholar, his many books have been highly praised in literary and academic circles and continue to be used as works of reference. Before his death he was preparing to found a new avant-garde literary and intellectual review, a plan that, through his death, lost the creative impulse of its founder. His several collections of short stories include *The Locksmith* (1958) and *My Gentle, Beautiful Wife* (1976). He also published a novel, *Bird of Paradise*. In 1997 he published his *Short Stories: Six Collections in One Volume*.

THE LOCKSMITH

I went to visit my newlywed sister to find that she and her husband had an unusual problem. Her brother-in-law was living with them. He had his own key to the apartment and used to leave very early in the morning, locking the door with his key. This particular morning, when my sister wanted to get some bread from the vendor, she looked for the second key, which usually stays in the house, but couldn't find it. She tried to remember where she'd put it, but all she could remember was that some of her husband's relatives had been staying with them as guests. They had probably taken the key with them by mistake.

Her brother-in-law had left for Sharbin with the first key, while her husband's relatives had taken the second key to Upper Egypt. So my sister and her husband were left inside the apartment with the door locked. This is the way my sister described their peculiar situation, as she looked pleadingly at me through the small window in the door, like some prisoner who does not know why he has been imprisoned. Her husband, on the other hand, was looking over her shoulder, giving an encouraging smile befitting a man.

It was only with the greatest difficulty and after asking many questions that I managed to grasp this matter of the key. As you can see, it is a complicated story. I don't believe my sister, or for that matter, any woman—when she is telling stories about things that have been lost. The one thing I have learned from painful experience is that no housewife is ever really a housewife until she gets used to leaving things in a different place each time, so that she has to turn the house upside down looking for just one thing. This well-known habit is a harbinger of glad tidings—that she'll give birth to a large number of children and will eventually become a revered grandmother. But my sister was still a new bride, and it was not right for me to scold her in front of her husband. Scolding wouldn't work in any case. The important thing was to get them both out of this predicament. It was possible for her to lower a basket from the window down to the street, and I would put in it bread and anything else she needed. In fact when I made this suggestion, my sister looked glum, and for the first time I discovered that she was a genuine human being. For the first time I really loved her—not the kind of compulsory love people call brotherly affection. I suddenly discovered that my sister hated the idea of being locked in, my sister who had stayed at home ever since leaving primary school and who had never left the apartment more than once a week.

I kissed her in my imagination (I am not used to kissing my sisters) and told her that the door would eventually be opened. Before she could ask me how, I was on my way down the broad staircase.

I walked down the street that had been turned into a series of hills and valleys because builders were working on a neighboring house. I felt happy—I had the subtle sense of being a hero. I was dealing with the matter quickly and decisively, feeling pleased with myself at every step I took. My first stop was the building supply store at the beginning of the street. I searched among the oil brushes, faucets, pails, sinks, locks, and a whole host of other things, some of which were hanging along the walls, some of which were on the floor, while others were displayed on counters or suspended from the ceiling. Eventually I discovered the owner sitting among his wares like a grandfather in the midst of his children and grandchildren. He himself resembled an old brush: a man of brown complexion, gaunt, with a huge mustache and a mud-colored *gallabiyya*. I am always getting into stupid messes by making shopkeepers think I am there to buy something, whereas all I actually want to do is ask for directions. To avoid that, I asked the man curtly whether he had anybody to repair locks. He looked at me for a moment—he was obviously deeply involved in some complex calculations, for his lips kept muttering some figures—then he pointed his index finger upwards.

"The cinema next door," he said. "You'll find somebody working there called Mahfouz. Ask for him."

"You mean, over there?" I asked, repeating the question just to make sure.

"Yes," he said.

I went to the cinema, the entrance resembling a public toilet. It was just before sunset, and work had not yet begun. I asked the doorman for Mahfouz.

"Hey, Mahfouz!" he yelled several times.

Then he turned to a young man wearing a European suit, who was standing outside the theater.

"Is Mahfouz inside?" When he found out that he was not inside, he turned back toward me. "Okay, fine," he said shaking his black bearded chin at me, "Ask for him at the hashish den. Whenever he is not here at the cinema, that's where he's got to be, one place or the other. See that tree standing there by itself? That's where the den is. Ask for Mahfouz, and you'll find him right there."

I thanked the man for his detailed explanation and made my way to the hashish den. It was a mere bench placed under the tree. In front of it there was a tea crate with a number of water pipes laid out in it, and a pottery brazier, alongside which squatted a slender young man with a few strands of black hair sprouting from his chin. On the bench sat a man whom I recognized at first glance; I often used to see him on the bus in the morning. He always used to wear the same suit, which was much too small for him. I don't know why I thought of him as being a primary school supervisor. Next to him on the bench sat a fat man wearing a Kashmir *gallabiyya* and a fez. As I made my way slowly toward the group, I saw that the fat man was inhaling with relish from the water pipe.

No sooner had I asked for Mahfouz than a man who was sitting on the ground at the far end of the bench leaped to his feet. I hadn't noticed him at first.

"What can I do for you?" he asked in a coarse, tremulous voice like the sound of an ancient organ.

"Are you Mahfouz?" I asked, scrutinizing his thin bent frame. I noticed that his hair, his beard, and even the hairs on his chest were white.

"At your service."

"Okay, Mahfouz . . . "

I explained the whole thing to him, by which I mean, I only explained what he needed to know. I didn't go into details about the brother who had gone to Sharbin or about the relatives who had gone to Upper Egypt. He listened to me with considerable patience.

"Wait here a minute," he said in his humming and wheezing voice, "I'll be back in a minute."

He came back a while later with a small box strapped to his shoulders.

We headed toward the house. He was walking in slow, measured steps as though he knew the way. I kept thinking about this man's strange life, spent between the café, the cinema, and repairing locks. Something strange happens to me every time I look at people; I get the feeling I am a child looking at the moon. I crave to reach them, to get inside their souls and to discover what lies there. I feel the same intense pain as that of a child who cannot reach the moon. In fact, it is even worse than that, even though I do not cry and scream like children. Thus, as we walked side by side, I felt he was far away from me, very far. Eventually we reached the apartment.

By then lights had come on. My sister and my brother-in-law were peering through the small window in the door, like two faces on the screen of the old cinema where Mahfouz worked. The man put his box down and took out a bunch of keys.

"In the name of God, the beneficent, the merciful," he muttered.

I noticed when he was trying the keys that his hand was trembling.

"This is a foreign lock; it must be opened from the inside," he said in his quiet voice after he had tried the last key.

A thought occurred to me.

"Could you unscrew the lock from the inside if he were to give you a screwdriver?" I asked my brother-in-law.

"I have a screwdriver," he said smiling, "but I already tried it. It's useless. You may be able to unscrew the lock from the outside, but the tongue is stuck inside."

"It's okay," Mahfouz said, humming and wheezing. "Be patient."

I saw him looking at the window at the top of the stairs; then he walked to it and looked from there at the skylight over the apartment door. He was measuring the distance between the two with his eyes.

"In the name of God, the beneficent, the merciful," he said after some reflection. Then he put one foot on the ledge of the window.

"What are you going to do, Mahfouz?" I called out.

"Be patient," he said looking at my brother-in-law. "Would you mind opening the skylight."

I looked at the distance between the two windows. It was in fact the equivalent of a full pace, but anyone who wished to undertake such a move had to stand on one of the windows with one foot, lean on the wall with one arm, then stretch his other arm and leg to bridge the gap and thus achieve the posture of someone who had been crucified. He would have to stay for a moment dangling over the high staircase. Who of us would do such a thing? Mahfouz whose hands were shaking as he tried the various keys in the lock? Not very likely.

Before I was able to assess the gravity of the situation, Mahfouz was in fact dangling over the staircase. We all held our breath for a few agonizing moments. Then Mahfouz managed to put his foot and arm on the other ledge. Now things were easier. All he had to do now was to move the foot that was on the staircase window. If he lost his balance now, he would be highly likely to fall inside the apartment and be badly bruised. But there was no question of his killing himself and ending as a mutilated corpse on the floor.

"Praise be to God!"

I didn't see how Mahfouz took the lock out, but a few minutes later I entered the apartment to find the lock in pieces on the floor. Mahfouz was crouching there and fiddling with it. There remained the basic task of finding the right key for the lock, but that wasn't easy. Mahfouz's hands were shaking badly, and my brother-in-law was trying to help him. It was obvious that they didn't see eye to eye. Mahfouz may have wanted to calm his nerves a bit, and so he stopped fiddling with the lock's mechanism.

"The pins," he said by way of explanation. "This one has four. Every lock has pins; some have three, some four, and some five. In one lock you'll find them arranged one way and in another, another way. You have to take the lock apart in order to make a key for it. This is how all foreign locks are."

"Okay," I said, "never mind all that, we're just glad that everything worked out all right. But you shouldn't have gone to all that trouble."

"What do you mean, so much trouble! After all you came to me with a problem and I was supposed to solve it, right? There's no question of trouble. Our lives are in God's hands."

Mahfouz finished making the key and put the lock back in the door. My sister made him a cup of tea, which he drank with gratitude. He left after getting paid.

For a while we sat in the living room and talked about many things. Mahfouz was almost forgotten. Suddenly my sister spoke as though she had remembered something: "Would anybody have believed that the man could climb over the skylight? Is that so easy to do!? Good grief, what if the man was a robber!"

She started looking back and forth between the dish cabinet and the gleaming, new dining room chairs; almost as though she was afraid that he might come back late at night to steal a chair.

In my imagination I did not kiss her this time.

—*Translated by Adnan Haydar and Samuel Hazo*

Muhammad 'Aziza (b. 1940)

Tunisian poet, short story writer, and critic Muhammad 'Aziza was born in Tunis and obtained his doctor's degree from the University of Paris VII in 1974, where he specialized in the sociology of culture. He occupied several important positions, first as director of the international branch of Tunisian television, then as director of information at the Organization of African Unity in Addis Ababa. After joining UNESCO in 1975, he became chief of the Arab Section of the Cultural Sector of UNESCO in 1978. In 1989 he was appointed rector of the Euro-Arab University in Rome. He has written many books of criticism under his own name, notable among which are his *Theater in Islam* (1969) and his *Thoughts on Contemporary Arab Theater* (1972). He has, however, published his creative work under the pseudonym Shams Nadir. These works include his two collections of poetry, *Silence of* the *Semaphores* (1979) and *Books of Celebration* (1983), while his collection of fiction, *The Astrolabe of the Sea*, appeared in 1980.

VENGEANCE

Go away fly, I am with child by my lord. —*Proverb from the Atlas region*

As the sun faded on the rim of the horizon, the lost horseman pressed harder against the sides of his mount, recklessly pushing it to the limits of its endurance.

The young man had shown often enough that he was no contemptible coward, but now he was shivering with fear. Ever since the mysterious disappearances had begun in the region, playing such havoc among the males of the Banu Rabi'a tribe to which he belonged, he had known only too well how dangerous it was for a man to lose his way in the empty immensity of Al-Rub' al-Khali, the Empty Quarter in the southern desert of the Arabian Peninsula. The frantic imagination of his brethren had populated the area with giant bats and voracious beasts and terrifying ogres.

He had never really believed these tales himself. Yet the regular disappearance of members of his tribe was a plain reality, and he could think of no really clear arguments against the stories. These strange disappearances had begun a year after the end of an affair that had caused great unrest. It had happened when he was still just an unruly lad, but he remembered all the details nonetheless.

It had begun as a mere tale of jealousy. The beautiful Aicha Kandicha from the Kalb tribe, which was allied to their own, had many suitors, but the final choice lay between the chief of the Banu Rabi'a tribe and his own cousin. She chose his cousin, and their marriage sealed a long and beautiful love story, but the rejected aspirant nursed a relentless hatred. Seven days after the wedding celebrations, the two former suitors came together with some of their companions to drink to the marriage. Soon the treacherous effect of the alcohol made itself felt, and quarreling led on to an indiscriminate brawl. The adversaries were separated, but one of them, the husband of the beautiful Aicha Kandicha, fell to the ground, never to rise again; he had been killed on the spot by a vicious blow to the temple. Mad with grief, Aicha Kandicha did not weep, hardly sobbed even, but demanded that the ancient tribal law be applied.

The two chiefs met and discussed the matter at great length. Given the strategic issues involved, it was not advisable that their alliance—so necessary as a counter to the machinations of other, hostile tribes spurred on by Banu Chaddad—should be severed.

They therefore decided to apply customary law, which, in certain cases, permitted the ancient laws concerning the shedding of blood to be set aside. It was agreed that the Banu Rabi'a tribe should deliver a thousand white she-camels and a herd of white goats to the parents of the unfortunate victim, in reparation for the harm done. This arrangement was accepted by all concerned except for the widow, who for three days persistently demanded that the ancient laws be carried out. All efforts to shake her determination failed, and finally, at a loss for further arguments, the chief of the Kalb tribe advised the parents to let her be, convinced that time would have its healing effect on her wounds.

It was on the fourth day after the agreement made between the two chiefs that they realised Aicha Kandicha had disappeared. In her tent they found all the belongings she had not felt it necessary to take with her and, attached to the central prop of the tent, a cloth drenched in blood and inscribed with the single word "THA'R"—"vengeance." It was thought that Aicha Kandicha had been overcome by grief and had slit open her wrists, inscribing this word with her own blood before leaving the encampment. The chief of the tribe gave orders that the demented woman should be found before all her blood was shed, for suicide was totally forbidden and could only bring shame and damnation. They followed the traces of blood till they could find no more, and they looked for her for seven days.

They made a thorough search of all parts of the encampment, looking into every nook and cranny, every possible hiding place that might serve as a tomb. They even searched to the very borders of the pasture lands. But all was in vain, and they had to face the fact that Aicha Kandicha had mysteriously vanished into thin air. They abandoned the search, and thereafter it was totally forbidden to mention her name, so as not to invoke the anger of the gods, al-Lat, Manat, and al-'Uzza, and bring down their wrath for the unforgivable act. As time went by, the members of the tribe began to forget the regrettable affair that had almost destroyed their alliance and to lose their deep sense of unease at the widow's disappearance.

But exactly a year later a strange happening revived their old fears. The chief's son, who had strayed without an escort on the other side of al-Rub' al-Khali, failed to return, and again the search was in vain. Since then no man from the tribe of Banu Rabi'a who had imprudently strayed ever returned alive, and no trace of him was ever found.

The lost horseman was seized by a fear that he made no effort to hide. Then, desperately scanning the horizon, he noticed the faint glimmer of a campfire. He guided his horse towards it. "At last," he thought, "I've found someone. I'll spend the night here, then I'll go on tomorrow at dawn."

As he approached the fire, he made out the form of his future companion, shrouded in a splendid *burnus* and standing with his back to him. As he stopped his horse and approached the fire, the *burnus*-clad figure turned, and he saw an extraordinarily handsome young man with a marvelous glimmer in his large eyes. The sight mesmerized him, and he answered the customary greetings mechanically. The young man invited him to spend the night in a cavern, and the horseman, feeling a strange languor stealing over his limbs, followed him without any resistance and seemed to accept everything that followed with remarkable detachment. He found himself standing at the entrance to an immense cavern, extremely well lit with reflections from the multitude of mirrors covering its walls. Along the sides of the cavern were two rows of statues—of totally naked men it seemed—with icy white hair and hollow eyes.

The horseman silently followed the young man, and the images in the mirrors seemed to multiply. At last they reached the end of the cavern.

There, exquisite music met his ears and the smell of food awakened his hunger. Pulling aside white embroidered curtains, they entered a splendidly decorated hall, where the horseman gazed in admiration at a central fountain made of beautiful blue and green tiles. The music, he noted, came from a series of instruments played by no human hand—there was a lute of mother-of-pearl, a *qanun*, and a *rabab*. A low table attracted his eye, filled with ready-cooked meats and other food and wine. The young man invited him to bathe, then, without another word, disappeared behind a curtain, where the horseman glimpsed a low bed.

He undressed mechanically, then stepped onto the sculpted steps of the marble basin set deep in the ground. The water caressed him, embracing his anguished body; and it was at this moment, when he was beginning to feel rested, that she appeared from behind the curtains where the young man had disappeared. Never in his life had he seen a lovelier, more bewitching creature. She joined him, completely naked, in the voluptuous waters, and as they bathed the horseman felt his desire overcoming him. She slipped coyly from his embrace, urging him first to calm his pangs of hunger. To the sound of the tunes played by the invisible orchestra, they ate and drank profusely. Then she led him to the foot of the bed behind the curtains, where the metamorphosis, which no longer astonished him, had taken place. Overwhelmed by the heat of his desire for her, he wanted to make love to her immediately, but she pushed him aside, then opened her thighs wide to expose her naked body, out of which the horseman saw a mass of gaily colored butterflies rise up. So great was his excitement now that he no longer felt the torpor into which their magical flight had plunged him. He pulled the beautiful damsel toward him and covered her body with his own, the flutter of the colored wings growing slowly calm above the intertwined bodies.

That night the horseman knew ecstasies he would never have dared to dream of, used as he was to the harsh embraces of the desert women. Everything seemed new to him and so exciting he lost count of the acts of love. He lay there totally drained, mesmerized, inert, embracing the beautiful body in his loving arms, and fell into an irresistible slumber.

He was woken by a cold breeze whipping his skin. He felt a deadly weakness through his whole body and a sharp pain in his neck. The stars were fading above, and the Twins were apart. He had the sensation of seeing his body emptied of its blood, lying in its place on the same bed where he had known such voluptuous joys. He could see on the neck, very clearly, the marks of the teeth that had torn into the flesh and sucked out all the blood.

The body, about to depart, had barely energy enough to open its eyes and see that it was lovingly embracing a skeleton swarming with fetid worms.

It was then, before he sank into final unconsciousness, that he realised that Aicha Kandicha was about to add another statue, another petrified trunk of man to the collection lining her gallery of ice. It was then he knew that the implacable curse on his tribe would never end till the bloodsucker's vengeance could find no more victims.

—*Translated by Mona N. Mikhail and Christopher Tingley*

Samira 'Azzam (1925–1967)

Palestinian short-story writer Samira 'Azzam was born in Acre, Palestine, and became a refugee in Lebanon in 1948. She worked most of her life in radio broadcasting, either as an employee or as a freelancer, as well as working as a journalist, writing on literature and life. Her short stories, many of which revolve around the Palestine experience in the diaspora, are characterized by precision and control and stem from a realistic modern experience in the Arab world portrayed with skill and compassion and spun around a single point of action or a single idea. She published four collections in her lifetime: *Little Things and Other Stories* (1954), *The Long Shadow* (1956), *And Other Stories* (1960), and *The Clock and Man* (1963). Her fifth collection, *The Feast from the Western Window* (1971), was published posthumously.

TEARS FOR SALE

I never knew how Khazna could manage to be, at the same time, both a professional mourner for the dead and a professional beautician for brides. I had heard a lot about Khazna from my mother and her friends, but actually saw her for the first time when a neighbor of ours died. He was a man wasted by illness long before the age of fifty. So we were not surprised one day when a neighbor called out to my mother and announced without sadness, "Ah, Um Hassan! Around us and not upon us . . . so-and-so has passed away . . ."

The wake for this man was a chance for me to sneak off unobserved with the boys and girls of the neighborhood. I felt I was going to spend an exciting day. I was not against that at all. We would all be able to stare at the waxen face of the dead man, to watch how his wife and daughters wept for him, and to see how the hired mourners clapped rhythmically while they chanted their well-worn phrases of lamentations and mourning.

Hand in hand, my girlfriend and I were able to squeeze between the legs of the people crowding in front of the dead man's house, to a place not far from the door. Here were numerous children who had come, like us, to taste the excitement that accompanies death. We did not move from our places until a big fist, Khazna's fist, pushed us all aside as she stood, filling the door with her great, broad frame. In a matter of seconds she had assumed an emotional face, unraveled her two braids of hair, extracted from her pocket a black headband that she tied around her forehead, and let out a cry so terrible that I could feel my heart contract. Khazna pushed her way through the women crowded into the room to a corner where a jug of liquid indigo stood. She daubed her hands and face with the indigo till her face was so streaked with blue it looked like one of the masks salesmen hung up in their shops during feast days. Then she took her place at the dead man's head, let out another piercing cry, and began to beat her breast violently. From her tongue rolled out rhythmic phrases that the women repeated after her, and tears began to flow from their eyes. It seemed as though Khazna was not just lamenting that one dead man, our neighbor, but, rather, was weeping for all of the town's dead, arousing in one woman anguish over a lost husband and in another sorrow over a dead son or departed brother.

Soon one could no longer tell which of the women was the dead man's wife or sister. If the keening women paused a moment in fatigue, Khazna would revive their sorrow with a special mournful chant, following it with another terrible cry. The tears would gush forth once more, the sobbing would become more intense, the sounds of anguish greater. And in this room of grief, Khazna was the center, with a tongue that did not tire and a voice like an owl, a large woman with an uncanny ability to affect sorrow. If one could say that reward is given in exchange for the amount of effort expended, then only a sum so large as to move in Khazna this seemingly inexhaustible store of anguish could compensate her for this tremendous performance of sorrow.

I still remember Khazna when the men came to carry the dead body to its wooden coffin. She stood beside the deceased, begging the pallbearers to be gentle with the dear one, to have mercy on him and not be too quick to cut his ties with this world. One of the men, fed up with Khazna's chatter, finally pushed her away so that he and his companions could lift the body. Black scarves were waved in farewell, and the women's exhortations poured forth, this one charging the dead man to greet her husband in the other world, that one asking him to speak to her mother there. Khazna proceeded to fill the neighborhood with shrieks so loud they could be heard above all the other cries.

Once the men had left the house, the procession of mourners made its way slowly down our street, bearing the coffin upon which the fez of the departed one bounced up and down. Then it was time for the women to rest a little from the grief they had imposed on themselves, and they were invited to eat at a table set in one of the inside rooms. Khazna was the first to wash her face, roll up her sleeves, and stuff her big mouth with as much food as her hand could reach. But I also noticed that she was careful to secrete some extra food in her bosom. If she felt that someone noticed her doing this, she would smile wearily and say, "It's just a bit for my daughter, Masʿouda . . . I got the news of death before I had time to fix her something to eat. And, of course, eating the food of the wake is an act pleasing to God."

That day I realized that Khazna was not a woman like other women and that she was almost more necessary for the ritual of death than the deceased. I never forgot her big mouth, her dreadful grip, her wild flowing hair. Whenever I heard of a death, I would head for the house of the deceased with my girlfriend, propelled by my curiosity, my desire for sensation, my search for something I could tell my mother about if she herself were not there. The sight of Khazna herself would divert me from the face of the deceased. I would find my eyes riveted on her person, watching her hands as they moved from her breast to her face to her head. Those blows, together with the dirges and chants, seemed to have a special rhythm, a rhythm designed to intensify the pain of the family's loss and instill anguish in the visitors at the wake.

Some time passed before I had the opportunity to see the other face of Khazna—as she appeared in her role as *mashta*, or beautician for the brides. There at the wedding she was—the same black hair but now combed back and adorned with flowers, the same ugly face but made up so it scarcely resembled that mourning face streaked with indigo. Outlined with kohl, her eyes seemed much larger. Her wrists wore heavy bracelets (who said the trade of death was not profitable?), and her mouth would open in loud laughter and only half close again, while she chewed a huge piece of gum between her yellow teeth.

That day I began to understand that Khazna had as special a place with brides as she had with the dead. Her task began the morning of the wedding day when she would appear in order to remove the bride's unwanted hair with a thick sugar syrup. She would pencil the bride's eyebrows while conveying in whispers (or what she thought were whispers) the sexual obligations to come. If the girl's face reddened in embarrassment, Khazna would first laugh mockingly and then reassure her that two or three nights would be enough to make an expert of any bride. She, Khazna, would guarantee this, she insisted, provided the bride used a perfumed soap and a cream hair lotion (which she could, of course, buy from Khazna herself).

In the evening the women would come dressed up and perfumed, wearing flowers in their hair or on their shoulders, to hover round the bride on her dais. Then Khazna's ululations would rip the sky over our town.

Khazna performed memorably on the dance floor, circling constantly while she joked with the women, using words so rude they provoked laughter. And when, amidst the winks of the guests, the bridegroom would come to take his bride, Khazna would conduct the couple ceremoniously to the door of the bridal chamber, for she had the right to watch over them. At that time I did not really understand why Khazna took such care to stand at the door of the bridal chamber, waiting for something, in curiosity and nervousness. But as soon as a sign was given, a knock at the door and the showing of a bloodied handkerchief,[1] she

---

1. The bloodied handkerchief is the sign of the bride's virginity. It used to be a general custom in the Arab world to await the consummation of the marriage and the assertion of the bride's good moral conduct by the showing off of the virginity handkerchief. Except in very traditional and rural society, this habit has now been abandoned in the Arab world.

would let out a memorable ululation for which the bridegroom's family had apparently been waiting.

When the men heard that ululation of Khazna's, they would twirl their moustaches. The women would rise together. In a single movement and from every direction or corner would emerge a ululation of pride and exultation. Khazna would then depart, content, her pocket full, followed by expressions of good wishes on all sides that she would see a happy wedding day for her daughter.

Mas'ouda's happy wedding day was something to which Khazna looked forward and for which she put away bracelets and other treasures. For she had no one else to inherit all she had collected from the town's wakes and weddings.

But heaven decreed that Khazna should not have her happiness. That summer the germs of typhoid fever took it upon themselves to create a season of death for Khazna unlike any other season in memory. I will not forget that summer. The sun would not rise without another death in the town. It was said that in one day alone Khazna lamented three clients.

The typhoid fever did not miss Mas'ouda, and death had no pity; it chose her despite Khazna's pleas.

One morning the town woke up to the news of the death of Khazna's little one, and people's curiosity was aroused almost at the same moment the wretched child's life ended.

How would Khazna grieve for her daughter ... would it be in a manner unknown to ordinary mourning occasions? What chants and dirges would she recite in her own bereavement? Would it be a wake that would turn the whole neighborhood upside down?

I could not overcome my own curiosity and my pity for Khazna's loss, so I went to her, I sought her, as did crowds of other women who went to repay some of their own debt to her over the years.

Her single room was small. About twenty people sat, and the rest hovered near the door. I did not hear Khazna's voice and searched for her, looking across the tops of peoples' heads. To my surprise, she was not crying. She sat on the floor in a corner of the room, grim and silent. She had not bound her head with a black scarf nor smeared her face with indigo. She did not beat her breast nor tear her dress. She sat there not moving, not making a sound.

For the first time I found myself seeing a Khazna who was not affecting emotion. I was looking at the face of a women in such pain she seemed about to die from that pain. Her sorrow was mute, her suffering that of those who feel deep loss, who experience total bereavement.

A few of the women tried to weep, to cry out, but she looked at them in such a stunned way, as though rejecting their demonstrations of grief, that they gradually fell silent, astonished and indignant.

When the men came to take away the only creature who had ever given her the opportunity to express her emotions honestly, Khazna did not cry out or tear her dress. She simply looked at the pallbearers with dazed eyes and, like one lost, followed them down the street toward the mosque. At the cemetery she laid her head down on the fresh earth that housed the little body of Mas'ouda, and she rested on the grave for many hours. Only God knows exactly how long she stayed there.

People returned from the wake saying many things about Khazna. Some said she had become so mad she appeared to be rational; some said she had no tears left after a lifetime of wakes; and of course someone said that Khazna did not cry because she was not given any money.

A few, a very few chose to say nothing, letting Khazna in her silence say everything.

—*Translated by Lena Jayyusi and Elizabeth Fernea*

Layla Ba'albaki (b. 1935)

Lebanese novelist and short-story writer, Layla Ba'albaki is a Shi'ite Muslim who rose to immediate fame with the publication of her first novel *I Live* (1958), which announced, in a lively and expressive style, the rejection of traditional values that have circumscribed women's lives in the Arab world. The novel was translated into French and other languages and was followed in 1960 by her novel *Deformed Gods*. Her collection of short stories, *A Ship of Tenderness to the Moon* (1964), was a cause of controversy and spurred a lawsuit by the public prosecutor on moral grounds, which the author won, thus scoring another victory in the battle for women's liberation. Ba'albaki is decisively the major feminist among women writers of fiction in the mid-twentieth century Arab world and the founder of the trend of open confrontation with male chauvinism and patriarchy. She lives in London.

FROM MARE TO MOUSE

My skin was still warm. I stroked my neck with my fingers, felt the pulse in my green, dilated veins. I pulled my dress over my breasts and closed my eyes.

Again I felt the weight of its fabric on my knees. I bent my head to rub my chin against where it draped my shoulder. It was clinging to my back. Suddenly, I smelt a particular smell, and I became oblivious to the real world around me. I became a white mare, cantering slowly up to the bank of the river. She arches her neck into the air around her. Her head touches the clear sky. She contemplates the river as it winds among the tree trunks, the grasses, the faraway mountains, the houses, and the valleys. With a toss of her head she is lifted by a white cloud, which sets her down on the surface of the water. She listens to the singing of the frogs in far and nearby ponds, and watches the multicolored butterflies as they dance. The mare says in her heart, "If I had not been born a mare, I would have chosen to be a butterfly: these wide open spaces, the sun's rays, and the face of the moon would then belong to me . . ."

One day the mare was drinking from a fountain. She had just returned from a journey to snowy regions. She had seen a new world, clean and bright, where trees had turned into white candles on the mountaintops and the houses looked like children wearing white fur coats and red hats . . .

These images still hovered on her eyelids as she drank. She was thinking that the water was delicious. Then she heard cautious footsteps approaching and, out of the corner of her eye, she saw a man. She cannot understand why she did not kick the man. Instead, she sniffed at him, and his smell seeped into her body and lodged itself in her heart. The mare let the man draw nearer. She let him put his hand on her body, fondle her, wrap his arm around her long, proud neck. She let him take her with him to the city . . .

When I opened my eyes, my face was tilted toward the ceiling. The image of the mare was no longer there. I rubbed my temples with my ten fingers and felt the warmth of my body accumulate in my ears. The ceiling looked snowy white and dazzled my eyes. My eyes wandered to the upper corners, where a slight darkness gathered, then traveled down and focused on the edges of the windows. There were six windows on the three walls. I breathed. A slow chill of fright seeped into my joints as I noticed how narrow the windows were. They had no glass; they were long, very long, and were barricaded with many iron rods. Each was bracketed from the outside by two wooden shutters, which were fastened with rusty screws and painted with a pale green paint that was chipped and peeling. On the light brown, uncarpeted tiles inside stood a large round table, which appeared, from where I sat, to be without legs. A long chair seemed to be crawling along the floor, and on it I discovered the man—the same man who had been with the mare—there with me in the room.

From the ceiling downward the room seemed like a dark corridor, subterranean and cold. But when I found the man in it, it became a bottomless hole in the ground, inhabited by rats. I myself was a mouse, and the man was the owner of the house.

Again I became totally lost to reality.

I became a little mouse, slightly larger than a cockroach, clammy and emaciated. There was no down on the fur of its flaccid body. Its nose was red and its eyes a pale frozen yellow. The mouse lived inside the man's chair—an old chair, which had been bequeathed to him by his father and to his father by his grandfather. When the man put out his lamp, the mouse would leave its hole and make its way, fear gripping its heart, to the table. There it would eat the remnants of the man's food and sip the dregs of his coffee. Then it would nestle into the pit of his arm and go to sleep. Whenever the man moved in his sleep he would squeeze, nearly smothering it.

During the day the man would prepare a trap. He would set up a box with pin and hook and bait it with a piece of bread and butter. He moved it around a lot—from behind the door to under the table or the chair to inside the cupboard—all over the house.

He should know, thought the mouse, that to get rid of me he is actually going to have to sever his own arm from his armpit . . .

I laughed as I imagined myself a mouse with a transparent body, leaping into the air, onto the furniture, onto the man's nose; and the man chasing, hunting it out to kill.

I laughed, and my husband poked his nose out from behind his magazine, startled. He frowned, then said, mockingly: "Now this Christine Keeler—she's a real woman!"

He said this several times, then buried his nose again in the pages of his magazine.

I stopped laughing. I looked at him. He was stretched out on his back in the chair, his feet propped up on the edge of the table among ashtrays, empty glasses, a half-full bottle of water, and a silent transistor radio. He had wrapped himself in a green-and-white-striped bathrobe, which was open to the waist. His skin was dark at the chest, pale over the abdomen, then dark again below. His head seemed alien to the rest of his body, as though it had once belonged to another person, a man he had met on an evening—full of drink and women with dyed blonde hair—and then on leaving, at the rack in the entrance hall, each had taken the other's head by mistake, neither knowing the other's name or address . . .

At this idea I laughed again. My husband moved his borrowed head, and I took in the lines of his face in a glance.

No sound came from that face. I did not resume my smiling as my husband lost himself anew in the pages of his magazine. I remembered I had seen that face by chance before. But when? Where? What had changed in it?

I found it difficult to go back, to go back in time. I closed my eyes. As toward the end of a long, dark hallway, I reached back over seven years . . .

It was the beginning of summer then, just as it is now. I met him at the house of a friend. The minute I saw him, I whispered in her ear, "That's him!"

He came up to me and asked what country I was from. I told him I was from here, from this country. Then he asked why he had never met me before. I answered that I had been in Europe, moving from one capital to another, studying ballet; that I had come home to spend the summer with my mother but would be going back soon. His voice was troubled as he asked why I had chosen an art that was so alien to our sun, our land, and our dark complexions.

I told him a long story, about a little five-year-old girl. One afternoon, when the sun was pale, her mother took her by the hand down cold streets, along which the windows of houses were all closed. They stopped in front of an old brick house, and her mother rang the bell. An old man with a very white and wrinkled face opened the door. He stretched out his long, thin fingers to shake hands with her mother, then plunged them into the little girl's hair, ushering them in. He sat the little girl at a piano and began to give her her first lesson, while her mother sat in a corner, shedding warm tears . . .

I told him how exciting these piano lessons had been for me at first. I found them fun—a kind of game that I could boast about to all my young friends. I also told him that my mother was a foreigner, who had lived thirty years with my father, dreaming of her distant homeland and yearning for it. When my father died, her dreams died also, and she planted them in me. Another time my mother took me to a small house belonging to a woman who spoke my mother's language, and thus began my first ballet lesson.

I told him how my mother had sold all her rings and bracelets in order to send me to Europe; how later she sold the furniture of our house to keep me there; and how afterwards she mortgaged the piece of land in my father's village in order to visit me in Paris and take me to Rome. Then, how she did all this cheerfully, while her hair grew white and mine grew long and black. And how I excelled in the dance, and that I might be participating in a program at the Paris Opera that coming autumn.

He did not say a word. He held my hand as he helped me down the stairs of my friend's house. He roamed with me in the empty streets of Beirut. He walked me to a house with a garden, but he did not ring the bell. The door of the house remained closed. He sat me down alongside the trunk of a tree and never opened his mouth.

Then I told him how there, in Europe, I was like my mother here: yearning for my country, for the sun that burns and makes people sweat, for our sad songs, for the stars that glow in the pitch-black nights, for belly-dancing, silver bracelets, and people who go barefoot. How even so, I would not be able to live, I would suffocate, if I could not make the dance my profession. I would always be a stranger in both places, I concluded.

Still he did not speak, not even one word. He pressed my waist and drew me nearer to him. He poured his breath into my ears, and I felt a fountain was gushing from out of the tree trunk and flowing over my face. I took refuge against his breast and saw stars dangling from the branches. He clung and clung to me, wrapped his arms around me and asked if I was happy. I answered that I was walking on bare, open ground, that a misty rain was falling over me, and that everywhere were wooden rods that burned quietly, giving off a reddish blue light. He told me I was a stalk of sugarcane, ripe for harvest: a lost stalk that was looking for red earth in a hot country to plant itself in. If I gave him a taste of my sweetness, he said, he would be ready to slit his own veins and give me his blood. If I married him, he would let me dance forever, between heaven and earth, until the world extinguished itself . . .

I married him, and my mother died of grief.

I became pregnant with my daughter and forgot how I had caused my mother's death. I believed that she was no longer desperate, or sad, or disappointed in me; and that she would return to me in another body. I believed that I was now carrying her inside me, just as she had once carried me, and that I was going to suffer the pains of delivery so that she would forgive my mistakes. And, as a matter of fact, my daughter did turn out to look remarkably like my mother . . .

But my dancing. Since he had promised I could go on with it after the birth of my child, I had to lose a little weight. One day I was lying on my bed, while a masseuse worked on my body. I will never forget that day. My husband barged in and told the masseuse to leave the house immediately. The he screamed in my face that he would not tolerate seeing his own woman opening and stretching her legs as she danced in front of other men. I would learn to be a mother before I opened a school to teach others how to juggle their bodies, he said; I should be a wife, take care of household duties, before bothering to entertain others . . .

And now we are in this room in the mountains. He sits in front of me, slowly leafing through the pages of his magazine. I pull down my silken dress and feel its softness on my warm skin. I feel incapable of thinking clearly about that morning. I know that I said nothing. I lay, frozen, on that bed for hours, until the sun disappeared and darkness came. I neither screamed, nor wept, nor moved . . .

He had killed something in me, stifled it so that no blood came through the wound. I folded inward on myself and over my little girl. I gave her my milk, washed her diapers with my own hands, embroidered her dresses, and taught her how to walk and talk.

For five years I dragged along, crawling those years on my face.

And now, at this very moment, after five years, I meet the man again. My husband. A few moments ago I was sprawled on that chair he sits in now, while he lay stretched out over me. I watched his movements on my body.

For five years he has entered my home and left it, has slept with me and eaten, while I was in a long, dry, heavy coma. But I am waking up now. I am waking up . . .

I opened my eyes so wide they almost split and discovered a few white hairs on his temples. On the floor between his feet I saw a glass of water and a red rose, like the ones they sell at nightclub entrances. I also saw a package of menthol cigarettes.

I opened my nostrils wide and smelt the smell of a woman, a woman who came to him secretly in the dark. I let out a laugh that was hilarious and sardonic.

My husband frowned and asked angrily, "Why are you being hysterical? Have you gone crazy?"

I ordered him to drop his magazine and look at me. Surprise and embarrassment forced him to obey, and the magazine fell from his hand. Stunned, he watched as I tore my dress off my body and hunched naked in the chair.

"Don't take your eyes off me." I said. "Soon I will be moving again. Once I was a mare, and you turned me into a mouse. But charms weaken with time, and sooner or later the charmer loses his magic staff. Look at me! I am moving my hand! I am moving my foot! I am getting out of my chair! I am walking! I am becoming a mare again . . . "

And before his eyes I began to dance. To dance. Galvanized, I watched myself and asked myself in my heart, "Where has this courage come from? How has my courage returned to me?"

Sweat poured from every cell in my body, while he repeated that I had gone mad. My little girl circled me, happily laughing and cooing, while he kept repeating that I was crazy, crazy . . .

I slowed down a little, then took my little girl in my arms, carried her into my room, and stood with her in front of the mirror. For five years, I had not seen myself.

From Mare to Mouse.

I put on my clothes as my husband continued to read his magazine. I picked up my child and went away—very, very far away.

—Translated by May Jayyusi and Thomas G. Ezzy

Liana Badr (b. 1950)

Palestinian novelist and short-story writer Liana Badr was born in Jerusalem to an educated nationalist family. Her father, a doctor, was incarcerated for many years during her childhood because of his political views. When out of prison, he did a great amount of patriotic and philanthropic work, opening his practice to the Palestinian refugees in Jericho's three refugee camps. Her mother joined in her father's struggle, and the family's constant exposure to the scrutiny of the secret police has led them from exile to exile. Despite this very unsettled life, Liana Badr was able to finish her education and obtained a B.A. in philosophy and psychology from Beirut Arab University. However, she was never able to finish her studies for an M.A. because of the Lebanese civil war. She was an editor on the cultural section of *Al-Hurriyya* review and undertook collective work in the Union of Palestinian Women in Jordan and in the Sabra and Shatila camps in Beirut. These experiences are reflected in her 1979 novel, *The Sundial*, which was published in English by the Women's Press, London, in 1989. She has published two collections of short stories, *Stories of Love and Pursuit* (1983) and *I Want the Day* (1985). Her collection of three short novellas, *A Balcony Over the Fakihani* (1983), contains some of the most moving and poignant accounts of Palestinians in Lebanon. It describes the notorious 1976 Tel al-Zaatar massacre by the Phalangists where Palestinians and poor Lebanese, the inhabitants of the camp, were besieged, bombarded, and starved out, and the conditions in which at least fifteen thousand people were killed in the Israeli invasion of 1982. This book has been translated into English for PROTA by Peter Clark and Christopher Tingley. Liana Badr now lives and works in Ramalla, Palestine.

COLORS

The child was fascinated by the colors flowing from the paintbrush in her mother's fingers. Each dawn of each day the doctor's wife in the small farming town woke and shook the sleep from eyes swollen with palm and orange pollen, irked by the allergies such fine grains could produce. She would rise while the sky was still veiled in darkness, then, with no morning coffee, with not so much as a glance at her sleeping family, would head straight for the easel propped in a corner of the room where the patients waited. There by the window, with its prospect of craggy, rose-colored mountains, she would take her place and begin weaving the details of the scene onto the taut canvas, with a patience understood only by those who knew of the disease so soon to end her life.

The child marveled at her mother's colors, marveled how they spread over the canvas, taking shape little by little, till at last a town nestled there in the lap of the mountain, with its houses of mud and adobe, the roofs tiled and the floors of wood, a town surrounded by gardens and orchards, the green land plowed by the wind and cut through by water channels, heavy with the smell of vegetation and wild mint. She wondered too, as she dressed for school and reluctantly drank her morning milk, how her mother could bring the town to life in her painting in spite of the bars that crossed the window and blocked the view.

As the sun rose, heralding the arrival of the clinic's first patients, the slow movement of the mother's hand began to falter, till at last she would withdraw, taking with her the easel and the tubes of paint and the turpentine-soaked brushes, leaving behind, on the canvas, the rubber tree that bent under its own huge weight out there in the yard, and the rustling palm trees that needed two ladders to climb, and the birds still twittering in the ablutions basin in the court-yard of the mosque nearby.

The child picked up her satchel and set off for school, and all the way she mar-veled at her mother. In class, when the teacher asked her to draw an eggplant, her fingers dragged and stuck, because she resented the plump form with its purple-black coat and its green hat that became a dark charcoal circle on the paper. Still her fascination with her mother's painting grew, the painting where one shade of purple flowed into another, tint by tint, just as they did on the craggy face of the Mount of Temptation outside. Forty days the devil had spent in those caves, put-ting the youthful Jesus to the test, and when he had failed, he tumbled down onto the plains below, to be turned into a grain of salt. Perhaps the mother completed her picture of Jericho in forty days, or in more, or in less. I really don't know.

It was 1967, and my mother, the doctor's wife in that small farming town, was gone now. She hadn't lived to cram herself into the tiny car bearing its load of passengers across the bridge to the east bank of the river. As for the doctor, he had rushed to the hospital, eager to offer his services in the crisis, only to return dejected from a scene of empty beds and deserted corridors; even the driver of the ambulance had piled his family into the vehicle and gone. And when he went on to the police station to ask for a weapon, he found the cells deserted and the chains heaped up by the door. He tried to flag a line of tanks moving full speed away from the battlefront and was nearly mown down. So, at last, he admitted the truth of the disaster his friend had prophesied, bundled his children and some neighbors into the small gray car, and set out himself for the bridge and the east bank.

Small bridges. Napalm, with its burning smell like the smell of molten as-phalt. Dark metallic planes pounding the hundreds and thousands of refugees fleeing from the camps around Jericho. Fallen bodies by the roadsides, trampled by the desperate feet of those running for safety. A crazed hysteria built up as rumors grew of what the invaders would do to anyone they caught. Napalm. You can't imagine the smell of napalm.

Boiling asphalt, bubbling on human faces and human limbs, the skin blackened. There. Here. Here. Or there. There was no here or there any longer.

No return. Simple. That's what the invaders said.

A year. Two years. Ten.

In the years that followed the girl was to wander till she was dizzy, seeing, in all those distant countries, no tree, no sky like those of her own country. After many days she came at last to a bewildering city, a city of towering buildings and burnished glass and spacious boulevards. It was called Beirut.

In Beirut she grew to know a sea the color of liquid turquoise, and she strove faithfully to print it on her memory, to learn all its different states. But that was hard enough to do at the best of times, let alone when the nights were lit by flashing explosions and the days echoed to shells pounding off walls and down alleyways. Even on New Year's Eve the flaming shells still rained down, the sky spattered with mortars the militias fired to bring in the new year.

Her only escape was to breathe in the smell of the sea that hung in clouds of mist over the shore; or to take in the smell of the stone on the railroad tracks where the trains had once run to Jaffa and Haifa. There were stones shaped like roc's eggs, or artillery shells, or dinosaur's eyes, or like ultramodern sculptures, all fashioned by nature millions of years before.

One day her cousin arrived on a visit from the Occupied Territories, just as she was returning home from her job in the magazine archives near the Green Line, worn out from the constant darting into entrances to dodge the shelling. He went into the kitchen and prepared a dish of fresh green fava beans. "Do you remember these?" he asked. She looked at the steaming beans. "I'd forgotten them all this time," she answered. She realized now how she'd forgotten the taste of home-cooked food, in this busy city where people made do with a quick snack or sandwich in passing.

"What gift would you like me to bring you?" he asked. That was a gesture no one had made since she'd arrived in Beirut. This custom, to offer a gift of one's own choosing, belonged to her relatives in her own country. She thought long and hard, then said, "I want a bird. A golden yellow canary."

She'd grown used, as she lay anxious and wakeful after a night of shelling, to the twittering of the birds at dawn; it was only when she heard their morning chorus that she was finally able to sleep. At such times the city felt to her like the mighty oak tree near their home in Jericho, which had been thronged with birds you never knew were there till everything else was silent. The only time Beirut was silent like that was at the very first light of dawn.

Her cousin left, promising to send her mother's painting of Jericho. But every morning the canary's song filled the house in the earliest dawn, weaving itself into the first rays of silvery light, till the sunlight was transformed into tapestries blazoned with lilies of gold.

Soon the canary began to need a family of its own. An orange-feathered female was brought in and immediately began to sit on a clutch of five eggs.

Four. Then five. Then—all over again!

And the eggs never hatched!

When she asked about it, people told her hundreds of canaries had failed to breed in Beirut that year, in the spring of 1981, because of the constant fierce shelling. That amazed her. The sounds of war had become mere background noise by now, a part of the place. Unless it fell in the street where they happened to be, no one asked any more about the type of shell, or how big it was, or what color it was. It was as though the bombs had lives of their own, better than the lives of men and women living to a pattern of coincidence, with chance meetings in the streets regarded as happy events, taking the place of calling on people. Things like parties and visits no longer existed that year when booby-trapped cars sprang up like mushrooms after rain.

Nothing was left but never-ending nightmares, office buildings and apartments and houses crashing down on people's heads. And when the children in her building couldn't go out in the street any more, to ride their bicycles down the pavement or walk to the corner shop for sweets, she thought of the canary family. Perhaps hatching the eggs would be a source of entertainment.

She discussed the matter with the neighbors when they gathered in the stairwell during bouts of indiscriminate shelling from the East Side, and following this the female canary was sent to the home of a man in a nearby building, who bred pigeons. This man was an expert on birds and paired her off with better results.

Before the canary family returned, with a new clutch of eggs that were beginning to hatch, a relative came from Palestine, bringing the painting she hadn't seen for fifteen years. Birds soared in Jericho's sky, grapevines clambered along the roadsides, armies of ants marched under trees and among cornstalks that waved like lazy straw fans, swaying branches mingled with the taste of wind and the scent of underground water pouring out into the gardens.

Every morning, first thing, she'd gaze at it before going about her daily affairs, plucking herself from the nightmares bred by the endless blackout. She'd listen to the distant echo of the shelling, gearing her ears to the hum of fighter planes staging mock raids over various parts of the city. The singsong cries of the street vendors peddling their fresh vegetables would float up to her balcony, mingling with the smell of gun oil and the stench of garbage that piled up ceaselessly as the city workers continued their strike. Then her body would dwindle to tiny points of light, so sharp was her desire to become absorbed in the painting, a very part of it. Closing her eyes, she'd touch the brambles they'd warned her against as a child, breathe in the fragrance of the honeysuckle that spilled in such profusion over the fences of the town—then find herself back where she was.

The day the canary family was due to return, there weren't any canaries after all, hatchlings or any other, or even any people come to that. That July a formation of Israeli fighter jets swooped down over a particular row of buildings; and amid the hell of wailing and condolence that followed, the widowed women, the children crippled or paralyzed, the distracted people wandering in search of a missing father or brother or friend, the worry that gnawed at her was what to tell the children about the new canary family they'd awaited so eagerly. How did you explain, to children, that canaries can be killed in an air raid too?

There was less sky now. What there was was cramped between the sandbags stacked on the pavement and the mounds of earth set up to give protection from the shells. Terror drifted, like black smoke, through alleyways and into the entrances of buildings. The city shrank toward the sea, till nothing was left but the Corniche, thronged with people seeking a breath of air in summer or a touch of warmth in winter. Makeshift souks were set up in tents across from Le Rocher, with tape decks blaring out the voices of the latest singers—meaningless words set to meaningless music. Along with a Lebanese friend she went into a tent selling all kinds of goods and tried on some eye shadow. "Which looks better," she asked her friend, "the brown or the silver?" "The brown gives your eyes more depth," her friend answered, "but the silver makes them brighter. The silver makes you look happy." She didn't get the chance to choose between the two. A fire engine roared by, announcing an unexploded bomb found in a nearby street, and they fled before the place was wrapped in black smoke.

When the Israelis invaded in 1982, and she found herself, exhausted, amid the dust of another Arab city, she knew she'd left Lebanon for good. Faced with the loss of everything she'd known before, finding how she missed it all—the people, the neighbors' voices, the turns of particular streets, cracks in the pavements she knew by heart, the different taste of the air, the smells things had, the colors of noon—she wrote to her Lebanese friend to ask her to send a few things she'd left behind, including the painting that was still there on the wall of a room whose floor had been almost totally destroyed by the bomb. And six months later the friend managed to gather together a few photographs and send them off, together with an old shawl embroidered with birds of paradise, and the mother's painting.

Patiently the girl waited for her things to come, and to her amazement everything arrived—except the painting. And when she inquired further, she learned the driver had stopped off for a few minutes to make a delivery at the offices of one of the factions in the Becca Valley. Could it be he'd presented it to an official he wanted to placate, or had one of them simply been taken with it, like the gunman who'd forcibly confiscated a painting of some golden swans from a friend of hers when she moved from one neighborhood to another? Did it perhaps have to do with the more stringent border controls they'd set in place just recently to combat smuggling? She'd heard the border officials were less strict with people who gave them presents. Perhaps the driver had won over some border guard with her mother's painting!

After trying in vain to seek out either driver or painting, she thought of placing an advertisement in a newspaper, explaining that the picture had a special sentimental value, as the only souvenir of her late mother, and requesting that it be returned, but soon thought better of it. What was to say the person who'd taken it would read the particular paper she picked out? And in any case, who dared, these days, to talk of things they'd lost?

She'd never known, till she left Lebanon that second time, on the ship headed for that new country on the coast of North Africa, how blue could turn to a dull, leaden gray. As the ship slid over the thick, oily waters, entering a region of dusky night, everything within her was glinting and glimmering like flashes glancing from the blade of a knife, the knife severing the cord that bound her to Asia—her beloved Asia, tight and cozy as a nest whatever the distances within it. Still her ears rang with the lapping of the water against the ship's hull, and still the violent sickness surged within her from the movement of the sea. It was as though she had left an oasis to venture on a land of endless, shifting dunes. What was she to do, on the other side of this sea of sand?

In the new country her longing became ever deeper and sharper. She couldn't breathe easily any more, couldn't savor the air as once she had. Shadows fluttered like giant butterflies beneath the glare of a sun beating straight down. She had no idea how to pass her time. She didn't know how to embroider, like the grandmothers who'd spent years decorating their gowns with scenes of harvest and clusters of grapes. For her such a thing was out of the question. When she was a child, the teacher had tweaked her ear, scolding her for the crooked eggplant she'd drawn or the banana that, under her clumsy fingers, had come to look like a nail clipping on a grubby floor. Her hands hung stiffly, uselessly, at her sides. The street before her eyes was quite empty, apart from the few employees who walked down it at the peak business hours. There were no neighbors to shelter with in the stairwell during air raids, no housewives to share bread with when things ran short, or split meager rations of sugar and tea. All was silent here. What was she to do when her work was finished and that deadly emptiness came to haunt her? Birds! Once again she brought in birds for the children; and yet they could never be the same as the birds lost in the smoke of that explosion. What was she to do?

She rummaged through the house, for colored pencils and a school sketchbook from which she tore a page. Then she stood at the window, with its screen of bars set out in an Andalusian pattern. Should she, she wondered, draw the scene in front of her with the bars or without? The house opposite had balconies with wooden lattices, and its walls were whitewashed, with blue trim round the windows. The woman marveled at what her trembling fingers were doing on the face of that white sheet, whose gaping mouth seemed ready to devour her. What was it her hand was drawing, plunged there among those vibrant colors? Still she drew, on and on, eager to end what she had begun, to know what her hand was capable of doing.

She couldn't believe it, this child who'd left her country that day across the wooden bridge splintered by constant bombardment, this girl, or woman rather, who'd swayed on the back of a ship speeding over the waters from one continent to another. She couldn't believe what was revealed by the unfolding colors, what was springing from the fever that gripped her still till the drawing was complete.

A small farming town was taking shape among the trees, a town with houses of mud and adobe, with tiled roofs and floors of wood. It was surrounded by orchards and gardens, its red soil plowed by the winds, heavy with the smell of vegetation, like no other place.

—Translated by Sima Atallah and Christopher Tingley

Shawqi Baghdadi (1928)

Syrian poet and short-story writer Shawqi Baghdadi worn in Banyas, Syria, took his degree in literature from the University of Damascus, and has been active in the literary life of Syria, helping to found the Union of Syrian Writers in 1951. A deep believer in the necessity of Arabization in North African countries, particularly Algeria, who were dominated by the French language, he went as a university teacher of Arabic literature to Algeria where he stayed for five years. At home in Syria he has fought for national renewal and spent several years in prison for his outspoken struggle against regression and autocracy. Baghdadi is predominantly a poet but has also published books of fiction, the best known being *Her Home at the Foot of the Mountain* (1978) and *A Night Without Lovers* (1979).

TANYUS ON EARTH AND TANYUS IN HEAVEN

At 6:30 in the morning Tanyus 'Atallah came out of the small café in the Upper Quarter of Tartous and walked toward al-Manshiyya in the town center. He was still savoring the taste of the coffee, neither strong nor weak, that he'd been drinking.

Suddenly he was racked by a bout of coughing. He was walking through a patch of ground that was empty except for some big stones that had been dumped there for building work, then forgotten. They had moss growing on them now, making the pile look like an old dung heap. Tanyus threw himself down on one of the stones, put his arms on his knees, and let the bout work itself out. His body shook convulsively with every cough, and every so often he'd raise his head as if to call for help, then look up at the sky, as if seeking some cool breeze to come before he choked.

Suddenly he found he was bringing up blood in his spittle, which was staining the moss growing on the stone. A distant passerby saw him collapse onto the ground and ran up to find him unconscious. Then, the moment he saw the blood, he drew back in fear, because Tanyus 'Atallah had long been known as consumptive. In a few minutes people had gathered around, but no one dared approach the man sprawled out there on the ground. His movements became slower and weaker, then stopped completely, and they couldn't tell whether he was dead or simply unconscious. The truth was, though, that Tanyus had died almost instantly, and it was a corpse the doctor found when he came.

The body lay there on the ground, and still no one ventured to come near. The doctor had gone off on other business, and the others were wondering which of his relatives would come and take him away. Or would somebody from the health department maybe come and do it? People continued to gather round, men and women, pupils and other children. The bell was rung, first at the girls' school then at the boys', but many of the pupils just stayed there in the ever-growing throng.

Someone had brought a white sheet to throw over the body, but it couldn't cover the spatters of blood on the moss, and no one dared go and fetch the fez, which had rolled some distance off, and place it under the sheet.

"We're late," a pupil said to one of his schoolmates. "What's the first class?"

"History."

"Let's skip it, shall we? What do you say?"

The other boy nodded his agreement, his eyes riveted to the white sheet and the shape of the body underneath.

An old woman shouted at a servant girl who was carrying a basket full of meat and vegetables.

"Get off home," she yelled. "Go on!"

But the girl, fascinated by the scene, hardly budged. She just raised her basket a fraction and put it down a couple of steps to the right. Meanwhile, a smartly dressed man, who thought a lot of himself and felt he knew more of life than the rest, spoke up.

"I think you'll find," he said in a cocksure tone, "that germs die when the carrier does."

"You're wrong there, sir," said an old veiled woman. "The germs don't die."

The sun was rising higher in the sky, and it was getting hotter all the time. But still the spectators hung around, as if waiting for some miracle, or for something extra to be added to the scene of death before them.

A woman crossed herself.

"Did you hear the church bells?" she whispered to her neighbor. The other woman said she hadn't.

"That's odd," the first woman went on. "Why haven't they tolled the bells? The poor fellow's been dead for over two hours. Why hasn't the priest come? Is he out of town maybe?"

"Suppose they don't toll the bells?" said a young man with jet black hair and eyes, as if to himself. "What will happen to the dead man's soul? Where will it go?"

The old woman eyed him with astonishment and alarm. Then, not daring to answer, she simply crossed herself and retreated a few steps. Some of the people had left now, but still more kept coming, making the crowd ever bigger.

"It really is strange," the smartly dressed young man said, amazed. "Doesn't he have anyone to fetch him? Where are his relatives?"

People looked at one another, but no one spoke. He did have relatives, as most of them knew, but they certainly wouldn't be coming. He'd quarreled with them bitterly some years back, and, on top of that, he'd sold the only piece of land he owned ten years before and was now penniless and destitute, while his relatives owned a whole village and some houses in town. In any case, they had just as much to fear from infection as anyone else. And yet, people kept saying, Tanyus's body could hardly be left there forever, could it? There was a government, wasn't there? And at least a priest to say a prayer over the man's body, so that his soul could make its way up to heaven?

Three men among the crowd volunteered to go to the town hall and talk to the municipal and health authorities, while two more went off to the church to ask why the priest hadn't come and why the church bells hadn't tolled.

"Maybe the priest hasn't heard about it yet," the alarmed old woman said to her neighbor.

Once more the young man with the black hair and eyes spoke as if to himself.

"If Tanyus had had any money," he said, "the bells would have been tolling out two hours ago."

The old woman turned to him, utterly scandalized.

"Don't talk such blasphemy, lad," she protested. "It's the morning. Maybe no one's even told him."

"Well, anything's possible," the young man answered, with a sly smile. "But where do you think this poor man's soul's gone, with the bells not tolling?"

At the other end of the crowd, a man was telling his friend a long story about Tanyus 'Atallah. But the friend, who was apparently better informed, was just nodding from time to time, or else correcting him on some point.

"No, Abu Qadri," he said. "Everyone knows he was sick but couldn't go to the sanatorium. Where would he have found the money for it?"

"But how did he live, I wonder? Some kind-hearted person must have been helping him out. It must be that. The whole 'Atallah family had disowned him, you know, and his adopted son got married a long time ago. He went to live with his wife's family in Banyas."

Suddenly a little boy went up to the body and tried to take off the white cover. Everyone shouted at once.

"Hey! Come away from there!"

The curious boy, who'd wanted to see what a dead man's face looked like, almost dropped down with fright. A second later he'd slipped through the crowd and disappeared from sight. The two schoolchildren, though, were disappointed, wishing the boy had managed to pull the cover off, so *they* could see a real dead man's face for the first time.

At last, around half past ten, the lines of spectators opened to make way for a newcomer, raising their hands to him in greeting.

"The Father's come," one of the old women exclaimed, with deep satisfaction. "Thank God!"

The priest was a tall, hugely built man, whose long black robes made him look even taller, and his beard was so black it looked as if he'd dyed it. But for all his vast bulk, he had a smooth, soft voice, so soft the listener would start looking right and left to see where the sound was coming from. Surely it couldn't be coming from this colossus! Many devout believers heartily regretted this inconsistency, wishing he had a voice as mighty and strong as his body—then he would have been a model priest, without peer in the whole district. Many people loved him, regarding him as a perfect example of a man of God, while others were sickened by him and, by their own admission, had stopped going to church because they couldn't stand his effeminate voice when he said the prayers. Tanyus 'Atallah, people remembered, hadn't exactly been pious in spite of his illness. They'd often heard the priest impressing on him that he of all people, with one foot in the grave already, should be devoting himself to worship.

The priest came forward, hurrying at first. Then he slowed his pace and finally stopped a few paces from the body. He raised his hat, his eyes fixed on the bundle on the ground, lying there all covered in white. Then he shot a sidelong glance at the onlookers, to make sure they were all watching him.

At 6:45 in the morning the soul of Tanyus 'Atallah left his body, rose a little to hover above the crowd, then soared up toward heaven. It was filled with joy, the way children feel on the way to the festival square, for Tanyus 'Atallah had had no place among people below. He'd lived among them, it was true, but he'd had no real place. For them he was already dead, long since blotted from their concerns, and because of that his soul had always felt itself imprisoned and estranged, regarding life as a chain tying it to a place it disliked and where it was disliked in turn. Now, this morning, it felt true elation for the first time, like the joy of a bird escaping its cage to join a wide and limitless sky.

There, on the borders of space, the soul of Tanyus 'Atallah stopped before the wide gates of heaven with their polished white wood and waited for these gates to open so it could enter the promised place. Yet, oddly, the white gates remained fast shut, leaving the hovering soul exposed to the fearful heat of the sun. It cried out, in a high voice, that it was there, waiting, and, when no one answered, let out a higher cry still. At that a voice was heard, asking the soul what it wanted. The question astonished it. It approached the bolted gates, saying, in a pleading tone, that the heat of the sun was so strong there, that it wanted to come in as soon as it could.

"But these gates," the voice answered, "are only open to the souls of people who've died."

"I'm the soul of a poor consumptive man," Tanyus 'Atallah's soul answered. "I've just now died."

"How can that be," came the voice again, "when the bells haven't tolled? If the bells haven't tolled, it means no one's dead."

"But Sir," the soul exclaimed, "I swear I'm a man who's died. I'm as dead as I can be. I don't know anything at all about the bells not tolling."

"You'll just have to wait till your owner's death has been officially announced. Sorry, that's the rule."

Deep sorrow filled the soul of Tanyus 'Atallah. It leaned against the lofty gates, which soared up to limitless heights, then crouched there listening for the echo of the tolling bells, announcing someone had died.

For a full hour and more the soul of Tanyus 'Atallah remained there without uttering a word. Then it rose and once more approached the barred gates.

"Have the bells tolled, Sir?" he whispered softly.

"I haven't heard anything yet," the voice whispered back.

"Suppose they forgot to toll the bells down there? What would I do then? Where would I go?"

"You'd have to go straight back to earth," the voice answered.

"But there'd be no place for me on earth. They'd expel me for sure."

There was no answer from the voice, and Tanyus 'Atallah's soul decided to return to earth, so that it could at least find out what had happened.

At first the town seemed a mere black lump without proper form. Then the soul saw people walking gaily about, with everything going on just as before. There was, it saw with astonishment, a huge crowd gathered around the body now. It tried in vain to find out what was so attractive, why they were prepared to stand there for hours.

An old woman seemed the most affected by the spectacle. The soul approached her and spoke tenderly and affectionately.

"Tell me, dear lady," he said, "why haven't the bells tolled?"

The old woman, though, gave no reaction, seeming to hear nothing. The soul turned, next, to the smartly dressed gentleman, but he seemed not to hear either. Suddenly the soul, consumed with rage, yelled at the crowd at the top of its voice.

"Answer me, won't you? Why haven't the bells tolled?"

Realizing no one could hear, it felt a sudden urge to weep, to dissolve into floods of tears, but found it had no power to do it. It withdrew a little, then hovered over the motionless body, as if wishing to embrace it and fall asleep by its side, or else enter it anew. At last it decided to return and once more made its ascent toward heaven.

There was, Tanyus's soul felt, some kind of conspiracy against it, condemning it to roam through space, with no place to settle either in earth or in heaven. As it approached the great gate of heaven, which was still closed, a sense of deadly weakness overwhelmed it.

"Have they tolled the bells yet, Sir?" it asked feebly.

There was no answer. The soul withdrew a little, then turned to roam solitary in space.

Meanwhile the priest, rather impatiently, finished his prayers. Indeed, it seemed to the people gathered around him that he hadn't even opened his mouth. Still, with him, they made the sign of the cross with deep reverence, then joined him on his short trip back to the church.

After the priest had left, the people mostly scattered. The women all returned home, keeping their ears open for the tolling of the church bell. At last, after half an hour, the townsfolk heard the dismal peal, and people living further off asked who the bell was tolling for. The news soon spread, and when the tolling was done, no one was left near the corpse except for a few stray children and dogs.

When the soul of Tanyus 'Atallah was still far from the gates of heaven, it heard the faint echo of the church bells. It gasped in disbelief, then listened more keenly to be sure it had heard right. Then, when it was sure the bells had truly tolled, it sped off to the white gates of heaven, which were still barred.

"Don't you hear the bells, Sir?" the soul shouted. "They're tolling. They really are! Tanyus 'Atallah's dead, he is! A real, final, proper death!"

Still the great gates stayed immovably locked. But down at the bottom end of them the soul of Tanyus 'Atallah saw a small, narrow door turn and open half way, and it quickly slipped through. The moment it was inside, the door snapped shut again.

—Translated by May Jayyusi and Christopher Tingley

Salwa Bakr (b. 1949)

Egyptian short-story writer and novelist Salwa Bakr was born in Cairo and started writing her short stories in the 1970s. She was immediately recognized as a potentially major fiction writer when she published her acclaimed novel and short stories under the title of *Atiyya's Shrine* (1986). A collection of short stories, *Zinat in the President's Funeral,* appeared in 1986 and was followed by at least six collections and four novels. Her collection *The Wiles of Men* (1992) was translated by Denys Johnson-Davies (1995), and other short-story collections include *The Dough of the Peasants* (1992), *Rabbits* (1994), and *Opposing Rhythms* (1996). Her novel, *The Golden Chariot Does Not Rise to the Sky* (1991) was the basis of a film and has been translated into German, Dutch, and English, the latter by Dinah Manisty in 1995. *Description of a Swallow* was translated by Hoda el-Sadda and titled *Such A Beautiful Voice* (1992).

Salwa Bakr is a most gifted and original writer. The universal aspects of her fiction are based mainly on Egyptian experience that transcends, through her skillful and insightful handling and her deep understanding of human nature anywhere, the realm of the national to the wide spaces of universal human experience. Her approach and style are complex and can harmoniously accommodate composite elements of sometimes contradictory nature, often mixing the comic with the deadly serious and always aiming at an illumination of one or more important aspects of contemporary life that need revolutionizing.

DOVES ON THE WING

They carried out their plan very efficiently. The first one, the one with the deep scar on his short neck, boarded the bus at the main terminal. Then, after the bus had made its way through the central shopping area, creeping along like a tortoise because of the masses of cars and people and the merchandise spilling out all over the pavements and onto the streets, the second one leapt on the bus the moment it slowed down at the first stop in the old district—where buildings now vied with one another to soar up into the sky, stifling the lovely gardens that had slumbered peacefully there such a short time before. The third, sharp-eyed, with a lean, straight body translating itself easily into sudden lithe movements, clung to the bar fixed to the door at the rear as the bus set off from the stop at the public garden that separates the old district from the other districts. Every district had its distinct identity, reflected in the street lighting (sometimes faint, most often nonexistent), the broken pavements, and the regular potholes in the street, to which the bodies of the passengers responded by going up and down, or left and right, whenever the bus landed in one of them or the driver tried to go round them. The moment the third man had boarded the bus and made sure his two partners were there too—the first one standing at the front, behind the driver, the second sitting in the last seat at the back—he raised his hand as a signal to go ahead and pushed his way through the standing passengers to the front, upon which the other two produced gazelle horn knives and pointed them at the backs of the driver and conductor. Then the third man whipped out his gun and aimed at the passengers. "Put your hands up," he said, "and just don't move."

Stunned, the passengers hesitated for a few seconds, then raised their hands. So did the conductor, in spite of the Belmont cigarette burning between his thumb and forefinger, the one his friend the street vendor had given him before calling out to sell his wares, then jumping off the bus. The only one whose hands didn't go up was the driver; he clutched onto the steering wheel and followed the instructions of the leader with the gun, slowing the bus right down. This hold-up, he thought sadly, could only put back the moment when he got home and dropped on his bed like a stone, sinking into a sound sleep and so getting a little relief from the pain and toil of a long day. No doubt, too, the passengers would insist he change course when the thieves had run off, heading for the nearest police station to file a complaint. He gave an angry grunt. Here was one more reason, he reflected, just one more to add to all the other reasons, for cursing the ill-starred day he was appointed a driver in the Public Transport Department. Meanwhile there were thirty-five of its clients on the bus, six of whom had fallen into a deep sleep after the first stop or two, probably because they lived in the district at the other end of the route; these, for a few minutes at least, were still unconscious of what was going on and so were saved the trouble of putting up their hands. Then the man with the gun yelled out at them, frightening them so much that they sat up and raised their hands like all the other passengers. Even the little boy who'd been sitting on his mother's lap and who'd been smiling and gaily putting up his hands because he supposed everyone was playing "Doves on the Wing"—even he got upset and started crying when his hands stayed up too long, and his mother didn't, the way she usually did when they played this game, say "put down the dove" and lower her hands into her lap. But the man with the gun glared at him, and the boy buried his face in his mother's bosom. She was tense as well and had started worrying, not about the one pound five piastres wrapped up in a piece of cloth and hidden away between her breasts—she didn't suppose the thieves would be so mean and low as to search the secret places in her bosom—but because they might seize the goose in the basket under her seat, which now kept stretching out its neck and moving it inquiringly from side to side. For the moment, though, the thieves didn't share her concern about the goose or about all the trouble she'd taken to feed it and fatten it so she could take it to her daughter, a bride of less than a week, whose home she was now going to on this bus, to spend the night there and slaughter the goose next morning. All the thieves were worried about for the moment was collecting the passengers' money just as quickly as they could. The one in the rear started ordering the passengers to get all their money out and to take their watches off if they had them, and he also told them all, men and women alike, to give up any items of gold jewelry such as rings and earrings. The one farmer on the bus, who was not only carrying nineteen pounds thirty piastres in his pocket but had a gold crown in his mouth as well, decided—a true child of our times—to keep his mouth tight shut and quietly hand over everything he had in his pocket, not letting the smallest grumble escape his lips. In contrast, the young conscript soldier sitting next to him had his mouth wide open, unable to believe this was actually happening on a bus that was supposed to be taking him to the nearest place to his military unit (from which he would still have to walk at least three kilometers across the desert to reach his destination): the whole thing was like a scene from some American gangster film. It was true he had no more than twenty-five piastres in his pocket, and the thieves, damn them, were more than welcome to it, but he was bitter and worked-up because he'd saved the provisions his mother had given him rather than eating them all straight off: three boiled eggs, a loaf of home-made bread, onions, and a large fig. The thieves, though, passed him by; the one collecting the money didn't, for some reason, bother to ask the soldier for his money—probably he'd learned from the wise saying, "What can the wind gain from bare tiles?" Not wanting to waste his precious thief's time, he didn't even glance at the soldier who (whatever the words of the popular song might say) obviously wasn't the Pride of the Egyptian Nation but told the old man in the next seat to produce his wallet and empty the contents. The old man pleaded with him. "For the Prophet's sake," he begged, "let me keep just five pounds. My daughter Loza needs a pair of shoes to wear to the children's festival at school tomorrow." But the thief told him to keep his mouth shut. The thin black man sitting in the back made a similar request (with three pounds difference in the sum involved); then, when the thief took no notice, he moaned and grumbled and cursed his own stupidity and lack of foresight, because if he'd stayed in the café and played backgammon and smoked the *nargila*, the one pound fifty would have been well spent instead of being stolen by thieves. But no, he'd decided to be sensible and wise; rather than spend money on pointless games, he'd told himself, make your children happy by buying them some fruit. As for the young man with the thick glasses who was carrying books, the man with the gun told him to stop scratching the floor with his feet, because it was setting his teeth on edge; he'd cut those feet off, he threatened, if it happened again. When four pounds sixty piastres had been extracted from the young man, the money collector announced that the operation was complete.

"What about the conductor?" asked the man with the gun.

"We've done him," said the money collector. "He didn't have much on him anyway."

This annoyed the man with the gun. He grunted irritably.

"We'll take it anyway," he said, "just to get back at the government."

He hurled some insults at the passengers and started telling them again what he'd do if anyone tried to move, but the money collector interrupted him.

"That woman with the child's got a goose," he said. "Shall I go and grab it?"

The man with the gun considered this for a while but, fearing the goose might expose them with its honking, he didn't answer his partner, instead ordering the driver to open the bus doors, which had stayed shut since he got on. Then he made a sign to his partners to join him. "Come on," he ordered. "Jump off, quick!"

The bus sped away in a twinkling, and the thieves ran like the wind to a piece of wasteland behind the old mosque, in a distant street parallel to the one where they'd got off. There they sat down to catch their breath, count the money, and examine the articles they'd stolen—the latter consisting of three wedding rings (one of silver and two that broke between the teeth of the man with the scar on his neck, showing that they were mere polished brass) and five watches (two of them not working and another two at least thirty years old and not worth a thing). The combined money from the passengers and the conductor amounted to the grand sum of sixty-eight pounds ninety-three piastres.

"Bastards!" yelled the man with the gun bitterly.

He was backed up by the man with the scar, whose only wish at that moment was to smash anything he could lay his hands on. Finding nothing suitable on the wasteland, he took his shoe off and banged it on the ground.

"Scum!" he said. "God damn a country with passengers like these!"

The third man, who'd pointed his knife into the driver's back, was struck by the force of his friends' words. The whole situation was so ridiculous his laughter rang through the empty wasteland.

"We'll have to forget about eating kebabs or getting drunk tonight," he said. "We've ended up with nothing." The second man fingered his scar, as he always did when he was worked up.

"A great, fat bus full of people," he went on, "and we come out with a lousy sixty-eight pounds! Just our luck! God, this lot had already been robbed before we came along!"

The thin, nervous-looking man joined in his partner's bitter and cynical laughter.

"The ones who robbed them must have been big thieves," he answered. "Really big thieves! It's a big-time game they're playing. Ha, ha, ha!"

—*Translated by Hoda El Sadda and Christopher Tingley*

LITTLE THINGS DO MATTER

Next day, after I'd read in the daily paper about the thieves who'd robbed a whole bus, the doorbell rang, and I opened to see Um Muhammad, the maid, puffing and panting from climbing the six floors to my apartment.

"Come in and sit straight down, Um Muhammad," I said at once. "You're out of breath."

"You wouldn't believe it," she gasped, sinking down onto the floor near the door. "I waited for that cursed bus from the crack of dawn till nearly nine, and the moment I went to get on it, it suddenly raced off and disappeared. So I sat down on the pavement again and waited for the next one, and even then I had to push and shove and only just managed to get on. Good God, it was just one solid mass of people."

"Public transport's become the most horrible crush," I said consolingly. "People are just selfish now, they only look out for themselves. They rush about, knocking up against one another, totally wrapped up in their own affairs, without caring about anyone or anything. Imagine, Um Muhammad, just two days ago there was a report in the *Akhbar* of how a gang of thieves seized the right moment and took the money off all the passengers on the bus. And all they got, after all that, was a miserable sixty-eight pounds!"

Um Muhammad was taking off her veil and the black *gallabiyya* she had on over the worn-out dress in which she usually cleaned the house. She paused for a second.

"The world's full of swine," she said. "Empty stomachs have turned people against one another. That's why I always prefer to be paid in small change, which I can carry in different places, on account of pickpockets and so on. I spread it, if you'll excuse my saying so, all over my body. Some I hide in my breasts, and some, just to be on the safe side, I stash away in my hair, with a scarf tied over it and the veil on top of that.

I tried to tempt her into discussing the exciting things that had happened on the bus.

"Can you believe that, Um Muhammad? All the money the passengers had was sixty-eight pounds!"

She asked whether she should start cleaning in the bedroom or the living room. Then, showing no surprise at all, she said, "Maybe it was the beginning of the month. People had just collected their salaries, and that's why their pockets were full of money."

"For Heaven's sake, woman!" I replied impatiently. "I say all they had was sixty-eight pounds, and you think it must have been the beginning of the month?"

Um Muhammad didn't answer, hurrying, instead, to answer the telephone, which had started ringing. She picked it up, spoke for a moment, then said, "It's somebody called Safinaz."

Safinaz was an old school friend of mine, an unknown painter who suffered from the usual chronic depression, the sort most people in our country are afflict- ed with. It was because of that that she paid no attention to her appearance and hardly ever smiled—or, if she did smile, immediately said, "Lord, have mercy on us!"[1] She'd be continually muttering too, always adding "Dear God" as a footnote. Safinaz came from the sixth generation of an old aristocratic family, but all she'd inherited was her Circassian race, a fair skin, and a quarter of the old house where she'd lived with her mother since her divorce from her cousin. Following the events of the past few years, this dear friend of mine had first become a member of the crumbling middle class, then finally joined the ranks of the impoverished lower class. She was employed in a run-down museum no one ever visited, and her salary was barely enough for herself and her son to live on.

Safi (as I always call her) greeted me and reproached me for not calling her more often. Then she went on to pay me a full morning visit by telephone: she told me about herself, and about her son, and how things were going in her world. Then—surprising me with one of her odd, thought-provoking ideas that always seemed to me to have a tinge of charming madness about them—she added:

"What do you think? Only last week I was in the subway, and my mind started wandering, and I thought: one day young people will have forgotten altogether what a bus conductor or train conductor looks like. The very word 'conductor' may go out of use, just be a memory from the past."

"Of course," I said, laughing. "And the same goes for a lot of other things too. Look at the gas stove, for instance, or the earthenware pitcher. My neighbor's

---

1. An expression often used by Egyptians and other Arabs following laughter, due to a supersti- tious belief that too much laughter and happiness will inevitably be followed by misery and tears.

little girl went to visit her mother's aunt in the village, and do you know what she said when she saw the pitcher? She said she wanted a drink from the vase. Ha, ha, ha! Do you know, twenty years ago my mother sold all her brass pots and pans by the kilo, but now people cook with aluminum pots, and you never see the brass polisher any more."

"I remember when I was at school," Safi said, mispronouncing the *r* in her delightful way. "I remember our house in the country with palm trees all round and Hassan the train conductor with his white hair and his dark blue uniform with big brass buttons on it. He always carried himself with such dignity. I can still see him now, along with the canal and the palm trees and the lovely old houses. How everything's changed!"

This was my chance to talk about the thieves on the bus.

"Let me tell you a really funny story," I cut in. "These three armed thieves robbed the passengers on a bus, and when the police caught them, they found all the stolen money came to a mere sixty-eight pounds."

"I'm hardly surprised," Safi said calmly. "The whole country's out of control. Just imagine, two days ago a man on a motorcycle snatched a gold chain and pendant off the neck of my colleague at work as she was going home in the afternoon, and managed to make off with it. Things are completely out of control. Dear God!"

I tried to make myself clearer.

"I told you," I said, "they were caught by the police. And anyway, you've got the wrong end of the stick. It's the detail of the sixty-eight pounds that's so comical. What a miserable sum! The whole thing's completely ridiculous."

But Safi didn't react, telling me, instead, about a savings club she'd formed with a group of colleagues, whereby she was paying ten pounds a month to collect two hundred pounds after three months. She was planning to use the two hundred pounds to pay the English teacher who gave her son private lessons, because the boy was so weak he couldn't tell one letter from another. Then I told her how I had to go to my husband's cousin's wedding that night, just one more social obligation that was really a wearisome chore. I didn't like my husband's aunt, or her children, because they were snobs who judged people by how much money they had. That, said Safi, was how all the nouveaux riches acted in this country. She wished me luck.

In fact I was lucky at the wedding that evening, as my husband and I sat at a table where the guests included a police officer and, between the munching and the laughing and the talk of drugs and thieves and furnished apartments and investment companies,[2] I found a chance to talk to him.

"Did you hear about the bus," I said, "and the armed thieves and the sixty-eight pounds?"

---

2. "Investment companies" flourished in Egypt in the 1980s, amassing enormous sums of money due to the high rates of interest they offered their clients. In 1988 they were dissolved by government intervention following charges of fraud, after many Egyptians had lost all the savings that were often their only source of livelihood.

He was a pleasant, intelligent young man.

"It happened on the Aboul Seoud line, didn't it?" he said, smiling.

I was delighted he was actually willing to talk about the incident and even seemed to know something about it.

"As a matter of fact," I said eagerly, "the story on the crime page was mainly about the arrest of the thieves. It didn't say anything about the number of the bus, or the route. Just imagine, all the passengers had was sixty-eight pounds!"

For some reason this made the officer laugh.

"Of course," he said. "Passengers on the Aboul Seoud line are bound to be very poor. They'd have hardly any money on them."

Then he asked my husband, who's employed at the airport, whether the duty free shop there sold men's perfumes at reasonable prices and whether perfumes there were cheaper than the ones sold downtown.

As it was getting late, and I was feeling sleepy, my husband and I left the wedding. On the way home I thought about my conversations with the police officer and Safinaz and Um Muhammad. I hadn't discussed the incident with my husband yet, but I told him the story now.

"Imagine!" I said. "A great, fat bus, with fifty passengers at least, at the end of the day, and all the people had in their pockets was sixty-eight pounds. My God, just thinking about it almost drives you crazy!"

My husband sighed, but said nothing. In fact he seemed indifferent, as usual, to what I'd said; he always, I knew, thought I overreacted to things. Yet all of a sudden, as we crossed the street, he said: "Life's become just unbearable. If I got the chance to leave, to go anywhere, even to the other side of the earth, I'd go."

Suddenly I was overwhelmed by pain and sadness and a deep sense of loss.

—*Translated by Hoda El Sadda and Christopher Tingley*

Muhammad Barrada (b. 1938)

Born to a poor, traditional family in the old city of Fez, Moroccan short-story writer and critic Muhammad Barrada pursued his Arabic studies at home and in Cairo, despite the restrictions imposed by the French occupation. He awoke early to the plight of this occupation and became involved in the issues of national liberation. In 1975 he received a doctorate in Arabic literature and for many years lectured at the University of King Muhammad V in Rabat before he took an early retirement and went to live in Paris. In 1976 he was elected head of the Union of Moroccan Writers and remained in this position for many years, editing its review, *Afaq,* and participating in many pan-Arab conferences. His first short-story collection, *Skin Flaying,* was published in 1979. After this collection, he began writing novels. *The Game of Forgetfulness* (1993) is a charming, half-autobiographical account, set in Fez and Rabat, of love, anguish, and loyalty. Other novels are *The Fleeting Light* (1993), *Roses and Ashes* (2000), and *Woman of Forgetfulness* (2001).

THE TALE OF THE SEVERED HEAD

My blood flowed on the pavement. My head was separated from my body as though a sword had cut it off with a single blow. It pained me that my lifeless corpse should lie there, discarded on the asphalt, to be run over by a bus or truck. I tried to order my hands to raise the corpse but realized they were no longer obedient to my command. My arteries and veins jetted a wild fountain on the ground, and the stain spread as if eager to finish up some government project for a crimson lake.

The passersby went on their way, their eyes glancing off my spilled blood. They merely avoided the red spray and did not even turn. I heard an old man muttering, "Oh God Almighty!" (he had stepped in the red puddle and stained his shoes).

I did not even see my murderer before joy flooded through me: *my severed head was still capable of movement and speech.* My eyes darted back and forth. What to do? What *could* I do with my chopped-off head before busybodies noticed this strange phenomenon and put my head back with its dead body in some silent pit?

Shutting my eyes, I focused, like a yoga master on a single point, all that remained of my being. I murmured: "God, grant me wings to carry me far, far away, that I may live, if only for a single day."

Before I had finished the last word, my head began to rise smoothly into the air ... no need for wings! Quickly I set my course and headed south.

From above, Rabat appeared to me a snake's hole, a lair, a mangy jackal, a rusty sword, a sea serpent spit up by the ocean, a beehive without bees, a bleak, bald pate of a rock ...

Twice I sighed. Intoxicated by the sun's heat stinging my cheeks, I went on. I flew through a flock of birds and they fled from me, crowding toward their own haunts, alarmed by the sight of a lopped-off human.

The sea disappeared from sight as I cut through the air with astonishing speed. Below me I saw the world spread out before me without distortions, without secrets. But inside my brain the question still throbbed: "Severed head, what will you do when you come down to earth from your wanderings?" I controlled my flight as much as I could, my nose a vent gulping in air that then passed out through the veins of my neck, doubling my speed. I began to understand the secret of 'Abbas Ibn Firnas's[1] attraction to flying: we need to be detached from earth to increase our appreciation of the commonplace. Everyday life recovers its poetry whenever we live with absolute confidence in our powers. I did not regret the loss of my body so long as I could fly and see and speak. Believe me,

---

1. A Muslim Andalusian scholar, poet, and inventor (d. 887 A.D.) credited with developing the manufacture of crystal and with making experiments with flight, wearing a feather suit and wings and gliding from a precipice.

my mind was clear, my intellect doubly lucid . . . my consciousness broadened to the point of madness. I thought, these powers need testing . . . I would land at the first gathering I saw: let it be the grounds of the Jami' Al-Fana'[2] so that I could argue with the dervishes and storytellers and con artists.

I hovered over the heads of the people in the square, making a buzzing noise to attract their attention. Faces turned upward in amazement. Fingers and voices were raised: "There's a man's head flying up there!" cried someone.

A motley group of people gathered round me. And I wasted no time—my desire to address them was overwhelming.

"You wretched men," I said. "Here you are still waiting expectantly, still turning from reality to superstition. The truth would dazzle you, so you anesthetize yourselves with tales of 'Antar,[3] of Zayd,[4] of the Land of Waq Waq.[5] You're dreaming. You dream of beautiful houris, whose ample breasts incite burning passion, who promise to satisfy your lust—but your lust masks hunger, defeat, repression.

"My miserable people, I have come to knock at your rusted doors and shake your shabby hearts so you will break your silence, call a spade a spade, face reality and your own capabilities, which then will grow, develop, and finally rise up, a giant with a thousand arms . . . "

The words burst from my mouth with thunderclap speed and electric tension. I wanted to say everything I had stored up, everything I had never before been permitted to say openly. The people listened dumbfounded. Some didn't understand what I was saying, some were whispering about this disfigured freak addressing them. The dervishes themselves came over, now that I had outclassed their performance.

They said, "It must be a flying saucer whose covering has fallen off."

"Or a mechanical head they've filled with this recorded speech."

"Whatever it is, we don't have to put up with anyone taunting and insulting us!"

Before the dervishes could wrest control from me, I turned back to the crowd, "How many of you are out of work? Have you ever asked yourselves who is responsible? Why you grow old in your prime? Why you dine on superstitions and

---

2. The main mosque overlooking the square named after it in Marrakesh, Morocco.

3. This is a reference to a historical figure, the poet 'Antara ibn Shaddad, who lived in Yemen in pre-Islamic times and was known for his chivalry, courage, and love of his cousin, 'Abla. He was a black man, the son of an Abyssinian slave woman, and was discrimated against until his courage and valor imposed his worth on his tribe, 'Abs. Later on, in medieval times, a heroic folk legend grew around his name and exaggerated the original historical story to fantastic proportions.

4. This is a reference to Abu Zayd al-Hilali of the Banu Hilal tribe who emigrated to North Africa. Here, too, a great legend, one of the most potent and famous in Arab folklore, grew up around his name and deeds.

5. Legendary islands mentioned many times in the *Thousand and One Nights*. They are described as out of reach of humans, except through the help of great feats of magic and courage.

old tales? Why you subsist in this sunbaked wasteland on crumbs and snake brains and the contaminated flesh of starved cats?

"I know you demonstrated for jobs . . . but what happened? They promised to employ you to pave a great highway . . . but what about the gulf that separates you from the owners of those winged automobiles that will cruise down that great highway? Here we are in a giant grave that embraces the living dead. Are you content to keep on playing the role of "good citizens," in whose name God is glorified and thanked for His bounty and blessings and praised in public and in private; to Whose will you submit. Are you satisfied to live miserably in a bountiful land?

" . . .You wretched people are like al-Tirmidhi's[6] saying about Abu al-Dardaa:[7] 'The best of my people are at the beginning and at the end of our history; the lot of those between is sorrow.' You are those whose lot is sorrow!"

The crowd began to murmur.

"This severed head has gone too far."

"We're happy in our misery; why does he have to reawaken our sorrows and reopen our wounds? Where are the Governor's spies? Why don't they report this troublemaker?

Other voices interrupted confidently, "They are giving him time so that he'll discharge all his ammunition. Then they will be able to tell whether he is a lone agent or whether some foreign hand has trained and sent him."

Another voice: "But he isn't afraid—look, even though his throat's been cut, he is still saying things that are true—at least he's not lying."

I was rolling gradually to the center of the circle, examining the faces and smiling with satisfaction, for I had at last roused this apathetic group to argument, made them listen to some new tunes.

Suddenly the crowd drew back to make way for some firemen. Surrounded by police, they were carrying a gigantic net attached to a long iron pole. I laughed aloud as I watched the net fall on me from above; I didn't resist. I laughed and everyone was astonished. Galvanized by the increasingly bizarre situation, their voices rose, and their confusion grew as they argued about what to do. I heard the head of the operation yell out, "Don't touch him! He may have toxic or explosive materials on him! Put him in the cage so we can carry him to court!"

I felt light-headed as I looked out of an iron cage, which the firemen had hoisted to their shoulders on a plank. The crowd began to walk in procession behind me, but the police drove them off. I cried out in my loudest voice, "Farewell! Demand your rights! Demand mutton, and chicken, wine, and good sex! Question—and question yourselves!"

The voices clamored in reply, "Let him speak . . . There shouldn't be any punishment just for speaking out . . . He's given a good speech . . . Since when has the government feared words?"

---

6. This is a reference to Abu 'Isa al-Tirmidhi, a famous ninth-century A.D. collector of the Prophet's traditions.

7. An ascetic who lived in eighth-century Iraq.

Before disappearing into the van, I cried out, "Demand an open trial for me!"

In the governor's office it became clear that my case was a complicated one. The experts and consultants and judges were all perplexed: neither texts nor tricks nor force could aid them here.

The governor entered, wearing white silk gloves. He assumed an air of dignity and diplomacy as he asked me, "Wouldn't you call this inciting to riot, Severed Head? You came from outside to stir up the people; you told them your daydreams and your communist delusions . . . don't you know the law?"

As I didn't want to prolong the discussion I merely replied, "I came in search of my body, which I'd been told was in the South."

"And since you're so clever, as reports of your maneuvers in Jami' al-Fana' inform me, how did you come to be taken in by this ruse?"

"Crowds enchant me: I always feel they are like oyster shells hiding wonderful secrets—why is it that *you* are so careful to keep them slumbering in their idleness? Nothing was left to me but my tongue, so I said to myself, 'Let's see what this little flapping bit of flesh can do.'"

"You are playing with fire."

"You know that death itself has penetrated but did not overcome me."

An elegant youth entered hurriedly to whisper in the governor's ear. The governor turned and asked me, "Do you have any specific requests?"

"A forum from which to address the people."

"Request denied. We shall now begin your trial."

"I'm supposed to be dead."

He quickly smiled, as though he'd found the appropriate solution.

"In this case, we will call on one of our dead judges to try you."

I remained alone in the cage, waiting. From time to time echoes of cheers reached me: "Long live the Severed Head!"

I don't know how long I dozed. I opened my eyes and was startled to find beams of light flooding over me, from searchlights trained on the cage. Footsteps sounded continously, and the hall filled with a great throng of people, gleaming in their robes and decorations. The same cold and nervous smile overspread the face of the governor. I continued to regard everyone with tranquility. After a short while a loud voice announced, "His Excellency Bil-Baghdadi Pasha, summoned from his tomb to render judgment in the case of the Severed Head."

The notion tickled me. I laughed aloud in delight. At least they knew how to compensate for their own impotence. The wisdom of their ancestors would be greater than their own poor wit. Not bad at all. We would see what the government judge would say.

I don't know what he was told of my crime, nor do I think it farfetched that they added to the list that I was the one who had had his quisling son dragged to death the day of independence. My senses and awareness were heightened to such a pitch that I was not able to resume conversational games or assume sarcasm. A yearning to fly returned to me, and I regretted I hadn't slipped away when first I sensed danger.

Bil-Baghdadi Pasha stroked his beard, running his fingers through its white hairs. He appeared proud of the service he was offering to a post-independence government. At last he confidently pronounced his judgment:

"You have already taken care of the body—therefore return this head to its body and cut out its tongue."

Note: Here ends the Tale of the Severed Head. Properly speaking, the Tale of the Severed Tongue should follow: however, this latter experience is a common one, which we have all undergone and continue to undergo, and there is nothing to distinguish this particular *instance* or set *it apart from the common run.* Therefore, with apologies, our story ends.

—*Translated by Anne Royal and Elizabeth Fernea*

Muhammad al-Busati (b. 1936)

Egyptian novelist and short-story writer Muhammad al-Busati is a government employee. He lived in Riyadh where he was seconded to the Saudi Arabian government. He is a prolific writer who has published novels, novellas, and collections of short stories. His work shows originality and variety and often an involvement with peculiar situations and odd characters. Among his early works, his best-known collection of short stories is *Conversation from the Third Floor* (1970). He has demonstrated great creativity over the years, and a rich crop of fictional works has appeared since the 1990s, including the short-story collections *The Bend of the River* (1992), *A Faint Light that Reveals Nothing* (1993), *A Sunset Hour* (1996), and *Prisoners* (2002). Al-Busati has also published several novels: *Houses Behind the Trees* (1993), *The Tumult of the Lake* (1994), *Voices of the Night* (1998), *Other Nights* (2000), and *Firdaus* (2002).

A GAME OF PURSUIT

Bassyuni had just circled the garden and climbed an inclining mulberry tree onto the fence, when it suddenly occurred to him to look down before jumping, once more, to the ground on the other side. He saw Al-Hajj, crouching between the trees by the stream, as if he had been waiting for him.

"So it is you after all!" Al-Hajj exclaimed. "You're the one who's been breaking my guava trees!"

Bassyuni grabbed on to the fence and stared in silence. Al-Hajj swung his cudgel up at him. It barely missed his face, chipping the fresh clay beside him and sending up a spray of fine dust. As long as he remained high on the fence, Bassyuni thought to himself, he would be safe.

Al-Hajj was a short, fat man. After his third leap he seemed about to explode with anger: he puffed and panted and strode around in circles, muttering, "So it is you, after all!"

Bassyuni craned his neck over the edge of the fence and saw Al-Hajj crouching over a pile of stones on the side of the road. He quickly made for the stream. Al-Hajj looked up, afraid Bassyuni would fall on him. Bassyuni struck him twice with his staff, then jumped into the water and crossed to the opposite bank.

He looked back and saw Al-Hajj's fat, round face, floating on the surface of the water. Bassyuni was quite astonished that he had not heard any noise when Al-Hajj fell into the stream. He stood, watching him struggle to get back onto the other bank, and burst out laughing. Then he went into a crouch; he took big bites of the guava fruit he had stolen and threw a few of them out into the water, watching them bob and swirl around Al-Hajj's head.

Once Al-Hajj reached the bank, he anxiously looked around. Reassured that no one else was watching, he relaxed and wrung out the hem of his *gallabiyya*, searching all the while for his shoes in the grass. He avoided looking at the other bank but could hear Bassyuni's constant taunts and gurgles of laughter. When he tried to stand up, the damp *gallabiyya* clung to his rear and he decided not to move until Bassyuni had left.

Bassyuni watched him closely, laughing and periodically kicking guavas into the water. Then abruptly he stood and disappeared into the cornfields. Before he got near the village, he took off his *gallabiyya*, washed it out in a small canal, then spread it out to dry on the branch of a tree, under which he went to sleep.

When he awoke, the shadow of the tree had spread far beyond him; his *gallabiyya* had dried and was fluttering lightly in the breeze. He was gazing at the sun's disc as it sank behind the village minaret, when his ear, which he had kept pressed to the ground, picked up some sounds. Cautiously he lifted his head and crawled closer to the tree trunk. There he buried his three remaining guavas in the mud and sat peering around him. Soon he saw al-Hajj and another man, both apparently searching for him.

"He can't have left this area," he overheard Al-Hajj explain. "Had he slipped down to the village, I would have noticed him."

"Don't worry, Hajj, we'll catch him yet. . . . Where could he possibly have gone to?"

They seemed to have done searching the cornfields and were standing by the roadside. Bassyuni pulled his *gallabiyya* over his head, but that movement seemed to attract their attention, so he cautiously folded his *gallabiyya* and bent his legs to leap into the water. Just then a violent blow to the face knocked him over onto his side. His assailant dashed up and brought his huge foot down hard on him, and another man cried out, "Don't let him go!"

Bassyuni realised that others had to be around and that they had found his hiding place and would continue to beat him until Al-Hajj arrived. He clutched his stomach where he had been kicked and began to groan and writhe with pain. Then he suddenly leapt away and raced along the canal toward the village, thinking how easily he had fooled them this time.

But when he reached the village, there they all were, standing under a tree. One of them cried out, "Where do you think you can go?"

Bassyuni just stood there looking at them and ran his fingers over his swollen lips; then he quietly put on his *gallabiyya*.

In the village he was known as "Rubber Wheel," or "Palm Tree." No one knew much about his origins; perhaps no one really cared to know. Whenever his name came up, some elders would assert that they had seen him around ever since he was a little boy, when he had always been in the company of an old woman who carried a wicker basket and sat at the foot of the bridge on market days. Others believed he was one of those migrant laborers who had come from afar to dredge the canal and had simply stayed on. He used to carry a wooden cudgel, taller than he was.

As far as Bassyuni himself was concerned, he had no interest whatever in discussing the matter. He rarely ever spoke to anyone. He would stroll down the village's main street, his *gallabiyya* split in the front, strutting proudly on his large feet and holding his shoulders high. Whenever he looked around, he would do so suddenly, wheeling his whole body. He had a special way of bending forward that villagers liked to watch: he would hold his legs tightly together, as though they were glued, and then bend forward from the waist to form almost a right angle; then he would stretch his arms up in the air and stare at his fingers. When he was done with this, he would bend further, until his face touched his feet. All the while he would be very quiet, stealing glimpses from the corner of his eye until he was sure they had all seen him in this position. Then abruptly, without warning, he would straighten up and look around, extremely proud of himself. Some of the bigger boys would try to imitate him, but none were as clever as he.

He had never done anything shameful that might warrant expulsion from the village. He had never, for example, exposed his intimate parts to either men or women, although many somehow expected that some day he would.

However, whenever he saw the villagers sitting in front of their homes, he would suddenly stare at them. They would fall silent and wait expectantly for him to say something, but he would only stand and stare, sighing from time to time. They could have used this as an excuse to chase him away, but they would only move to do so when their women, who usually sat behind them, would whisper in amazement, "Look how he moves his belly!" And sure enough, his upper abdomen would be blown out to such proportion that it showed through the split in his garment. He would stay that way for a moment, as though this were the normal state of his body; then he would exhale and deflate.

He had generally not been considered a disruptive influence until the day he had discovered that spot in the marketplace. It was just a high wall, rather dilapidated: they saw him sitting on it one afternoon when the souk was bustling with people, and from that time on he roamed the streets much less frequently than he used to. When he did, he drew behind him a train of noisy young boys, who obeyed him and took it upon themselves to defend him from the bullies who liked to lie in wait for him on rooftops and in the bends of the village alleys. They even defended him against adults when they tried to chase him off the streets. Bassyuni would silently watch his defenders throw stones at his assailant until he was forced to retreat, while he waited for them at the end of the road.

One day these boys had hoisted a flag atop the ruined wall where he liked to sit. It was a large square piece of white cloth, which they had attached to a tree branch they had meticulously peeled. After joyfully brandishing it in a procession through the village alleys they had dug a hole in the adobe and stuck it there, propping it up with small pebbles to withstand the winds . . .

Now, when the men crossed the market place toward him, they found him dangling his feet from the wall as the flag flapped above his head in the wind.

The marketplace was empty; the lights of the coffee houses were visible, but still only faintly. The young boys, who had been sitting together at the base of the wall, fled at the approach of the men to the bank of the stream.

The men were accompanied by the two guards who had once beaten Bassyuni in the market place and followed by several older lads who had gathered from all over the village.

"Come down!" they shouted.

Bassyuni peered at them, then suddenly leapt down from the wall and raced off toward the canal. They followed in hot pursuit.

Once outside the village he stopped to catch his breath, listening for their shouts. The roads leading to farms were all deserted, and it was almost dark. Close by stretched dense field of sugar cane. From it, Bassyuni saw a mongoose stick out its head and look cautiously around. A hush fell over the croaking frogs, and the wind that had been swaying the canes subsided. Silently in the dim light the mongoose emerged, rolled over onto its back, then straightened up and burrowed its muzzle into the grass.

Bassyuni was so taken by this sudden silence that he got down on his knees and began to creep stealthily, hoping, perhaps, to take it by surprise from behind. But, just as he came within inches away, the animal darted off and swiftly disappeared among the canes.

Bassyuni had just begun to feel a little relaxed, when he heard the voices of the villagers coming toward him from all directions. It occurred to him briefly that he might as well give himself up; then he decided to crawl quietly into the cane field . . .

"He must have gone into the cane field!" someone cried out.

Bassyuni looked back through the stalks and saw them converge on the very spot where he had entered the field. Their number seemed to have grown, and he noticed faces he had not seen before. They were all standing in silence, listening for the slightest motion that might give him away. Then suddenly one of them snapped his head around in another direction, and they all followed suit. Darkness seemed to embrace everything.

Had they stopped their search? Bassyuni became uneasy because he couldn't make out what they were looking at. He crawled back to the edge of the field and stuck his head out.

Now was the time to make a break for the village. He noticed that the men were gazing intently at the far end of the field. From it came a constant rustling movement in the cane. The two guards were entering the field on either side of the noise, while a few others stood poised on the road. Were they chasing the mongoose?

Bassyuni heard a dignified-looking, elderly man—one of those he had never seen before—whisper loudly to the others, "They will never be able to catch him before morning. What we need is a few men to go in after him."

The rustling noise had subsided now, and the two guards came out of the field and stood with the others. It began to look to Bassyuni as though they were actually chasing someone else. He even walked by them several times and looked them in the eyes, but no one noticed him.

They might be playing a game with him, he thought.

One of the guards shouted into the sugar canes, "Come on out! We won't hurt you!"

"What we need is a few men to go in after him," repeated the distinguished-looking old man, this time in a loud voice.

A couple of the men dashed into the field. The old man leaned on his cane, watching them. He was wearing a pair of shiny new shoes and a turban.

Bassyuni was very surprised that he had never seen him before in the village. He went to the bank of the canal and sat there, stretching his legs. Perhaps they didn't realise he had caught on to their game, he thought to himself. What if he let out a loud scream? He imagined them jolting upright amidst the cane and decided to wait where he was until the others had entered the field as well ...

"Why don't you go in with them?" The old man, who was the last one left on the road, had turned and was talking to him.

Bassyuni was still buoyant with the feeling that he could take them by surprise if he so wished. He got up and approached the old man, thinking that were he to leave now, he would not see the end of the game. Since they were alone, he wanted to reveal his identity. He came closer, but the man pushed him away. He came closer still and whispered, as though confiding in him, "It is I!"

He burst out laughing when he saw the old man shrink back and look anxiously around. He proudly threw his arms into the air and headed toward the sugar cane field. He stood watching the men as they bent groping for him through the cane. Then it occurred to him that what the old man had suggested made sense: Why indeed shouldn't he join them?

He entered the cane with his head high, pushing away at the stalks, very happy with all this rustling and rattling. Someone crawling on all fours tugged on Bassyuni's *gallabiyya* and whispered: "Shhh! Quiet, he'll hear you! Keep your head down!"

Bassyuni kept silent, thinking that no doubt they wanted him to join in the game. Cautiously he bent his head and followed the man, who seemed a dark mass moving swiftly among the canes. The man complained that his hands were thoroughly scratched, and from time to time he scraped off the rough, dry mud that clung in patches to them. Bassyuni would have advised him to stand erect, as he was standing, but others were crawling all around so he decided to say nothing.

"Get lower," whispered the man, "lest he take you by surprise."

Bassyuni watched him wriggle on ahead of him. He tried to discern the place where they were but the canes were thick. He got down on his knees and crawled slowly. The silence was thick, and he could hear men breathing heavily close by . . .

Eventually the man said that they were probably lost among the reeds, perhaps left behind by the others, and he cursed the man who had suggested that they enter the cane field.

Bassyuni listened in silence, while the wide leaves of the sugarcane slashed at his face from every direction and their sharp edges cut him. The smell of the roots, mixed with the stench of the damp earth, filled his nostrils.

The voices of the men were now far away. It occurred to him that this would be an opportune time to reveal his identity, so he nudged him in the back and waited; but the man paid no attention and continued crawling. He nudged him again.

"Hey! What are you up to?" the man shouted breathlessly.

Bassyuni came closer. The man muttered something, pulled free, and crawled away. Bassyuni tried to catch up with him. The man grumbled angrily, stood up, and ran through the cane.

Bassyuni listened for a moment, and the only voices he heard were far away. He crawled in various directions but could find no one. Then, through the cane stalks, he could see a dim light, and he sensed he had come to the other side of the field.

Despite the darkness he could make out the contours of vast stretches of newly tilled land and a small hut, built under a huge sycamore tree at the head of the field. Its door, he guessed, would be facing the open space.

Bassyuni could hear voices coming from the opposite direction. He looked toward the bridge and saw some of the men standing at the edge of the field. He thought of approaching them, but then he heard a voice closer, from the direction of the hut, whispers that were soft yet clear as rustling straw. He moved toward the hut, thinking he would find one of the men inside.

But as his feet sank into the soft straw at the entrance, he suddenly felt a violent blow to the chest, as if someone was trying to throw him to the ground; and when it seemed unavoidable that he would fall, he tried hard to fall inside the hut. He heard a man's voice murmuring, as well as the soft weeping of a woman. He quickly retreated to the edge of the hut, but the man came after him, threw him down, and sat on him.

The woman wailed: "Oh no! What terrible luck! I am disgraced, 'Abd Al-Samad!"

"Be quiet, woman!" whispered the man, loosening his hold on Bassyuni's neck. "It's only Bassyuni."

"Bassyuni? Oh, what a relief!"

But she burst out crying anew when Bassyuni propped himself up on his elbow, looking at the two of them as if he had just grasped the truth. He laughed.

The man gripped his neck once more and said: "What are you laughing at, you son of a bitch?"

The men's loud voices were coming closer. The woman said fearfully, "It's him they're coming after!"

The man furiously slapped Bassyuni and stood up. In the soft light he slipped long drawers and a vest over his naked skin. Then he leaned to find his *gallabiyya*, which he threw over his shoulder.

As he reached the door he turned and said, "If you dare utter a sound you know what will happen to you." Then to the woman, who was still crying, he said, irritably, "Stop crying!"

"You want me to stop crying? Where are you going?"

"Let me tend to this night, which doesn't seem to want to end peacefully!"

He stood outside the door, blocking it with his back, which suddenly seemed huge.

Bassyuni glanced sidelong and noted her bare shoulders in the light that fell on her as she looked for her dress in the straw. He hoisted himself up on his elbow and stood.

"Watch out, 'Abd Al-Samad! He's about to get away!"

'Abd Al-Samad looked inside and said, "Be patient, Na'ima!"

"I'll keep quiet . . . but please don't go off and leave me behind."

The hut was made of bamboo covered with dried-out corn reeds, through which Bassyuni tried to peek out. He saw men come over the bridge, then suddenly veer off onto the tilled land and pass out of his field of vision. It appeared from their voices that they were heading toward the entrance of the hut.

"Who's there?" challenged one of them.

"It is I, 'Abd Al-Samad."

"Who? 'Abd Al-Samad, the guard?"

"Yes."

"Have you been there long?"

"For a while."

Another voice, which Bassyuni made out to be that of the first guard, asked, "'Abd Al-Samad, have you seen that fellow Bassyuni go by here?"

"No . . . what's up?"

"Where the hell did he go? . . . That idiot's been causing a lot of trouble in the village!"

Bassyuni thought he might be able to see them if he looked from between 'Abd Al-Samad's legs. He slowly began to crawl, but the woman gave him a kick in the side.

"That idiot, 'Abd Al-Samad, has made fun of al-Hajj Shaker."

"The sheikh of the village?"

"Yes. He pushed him into the canal."

Bassyuni was furious and was about to dash outside, but she grabbed his shoulder, covered his mouth with her hand, and dragged him further inside.

'Abd Al-Samad felt the movement behind him and turned around, as though looking for something.

"Is there someone with you, 'Abd Al-Samad?"

"It's just my son, sleeping inside."

Now he could justify looking inside. He peered without seeing anything, coughed twice, and turned back to the men.

"That oddball has been making fools of the villagers, 'Abd Al-Samad."

"God only knows, Hamdan!"

"We have been chasing him since early afternoon."

"Why don't you wait till morning?"

"Morning! What morning? You know quite well what will happen to us if we return empty-handed!"

"What can happen?"

"The sheikh hasn't slept a wink. He insists we catch him tonight."

Bassyuni's nostrils filled with the smell of her sweat. Her warm, soft arm was around his chest. He pinched her armpit. Frightened, she moved against the wall and covered herself. He reached out for her. She brusquely pushed his hand away. He tried again and felt her teeth sink into his palm. He took a deep breath and gleefully flexed his foot, which was in the circle of light. When she slackened her jaws, he wished she would bite him again. He crawled toward her, took her in his arms, and drew her to him passionately . . .

'Abd Al-Samad felt that if he kept his voice loud he could stop them from coming any closer to the hut.

"At any rate, do you plan to spend the night searching?"

"You should have heard the way al-Hajj was screaming at us!"

"Come on, man, go home and sleep, and stop this fuss!"

He tried to make this sound like his final word and turned to enter his hut. But by the way they stirred, he knew that if he did enter, they would come right up to the door.

One of the guards cried out, "Do you want him to keep us searching till morning?"

"'Abd Al-Samad, he pushed him into the water!"

"I wish he had drowned him after pushing him in! Maybe then he would have saved us all this trouble."

"Don't speak like this, Hamdan!"

"I am fed up! Who can accept to be beaten in front of his wife and children?"

"Be quiet, men! Bless the Prophet and hold your peace!"

"I'm holding my peace alright, 'Abd Al-Samad. Don't you see me keeping to my own business?"

'Abd Al-Samad had glued his back to the entrance of the hut, his ears at-tuned to every movement that took place behind him. He could hear her angry groans, as well as Bassyuni's breathless heavings. The men were still standing, and his legs suddenly felt like they were giving way.

"Watch out for him, 'Abd Al-Samad."

He stared in their direction, his *gallabiyya* hanging from his shoulder, submitting to the gusts of the wind.

When all had become quiet inside, he lifted his head and heard a noise like that of straw being crushed under huge feet; and he remembered that there was straw only on the floor of the hut.

He saw the men turn around and move off toward the bridge. He felt the *gallabiyya* slip off his shoulder. He picked it up, folded it, and entered the hut.

Gaping at him was a wide hole in the wall. He could hear her heaving breath in the corner and felt irritated at her soft weeping. He was sure that she was lying with her face in the straw, but he avoided looking at her. Instead, he slipped out through the opening and went away. The field of sugarcane stretched quietly before him.

—*Translated by Mona N. Mikhail and Thomas G. Ezzy*

Zayd Mutee' Dammaj (1943–1998)

Yemeni novelist and short-story writer Zayd Mutee' Dammaj was born in Abb and pursued his secondary and university studies in Cairo. On his return to his own country, he was appointed a member of the Shura Council and occupied various prominent positions in the government. He comes from a revolutionary family that lost many members in the war against the *imams*, and his writings are full of descriptions, artistically presented, of the corruption and injustice of the rule of the *imams* and their high officials, and of the struggle against them. His lovely novel, *The Hostage* (1984), is a fine exposition of the cruel practices that were carried on in prerevolutionary days and has been translated into English for PROTA by May Jayyusi and Christopher Tingley. He has at least three other collections of short stories: *Tahish al-Hauban* (1973), *The Scorpion* (1982), and *The Bridge* (1986). Dammaj was a fine creative writer with a special sensibility for various important aspects of human experience: love, beauty, the way the humorous intertwines with the tragic, and how nobility and pride face and challenge intrigue and moral frailty.

A Woman

Each day I'd look for her eagerly at the nearby *zalabia*[1] shop, vying with the simple people in their jokes and odd, silly stories. I'd take the hot *madrat*

---

1. A pastry fried in oil.

al-bur'i[2] with powdered thyme and cumin and hot *busbas*[3] and stand sipping it in front of the shop, watching its handsome young owner, Rizq, exercise all his skill in making the *zalabia*; he'd repeat the same endless process in his light-handed style, and the hot oil in the great brass pot seemed to make him more handsome still. He'd learned the art from his father, and from his older brother Shu'i, who'd grown lazy now, being content to sell tea at the entrance to the shop, along with a pot of beans that would be quickly sold out in the first hours of the morning.

Again and again I'd hear his father and younger brother scold him, sometimes curse him even, because he never cooked enough beans; to which he'd answer it wasn't his job to cook beans, that he cooked the little he did for his own breakfast and sold any that was left over. His real job, he insisted, was making *zalabia*, which his father had handed over to Rizq, his younger brother. This unfair distribution of work would, he went on, would have been a source of constant strife between him and his father and brother, had it not been for the interference of that woman, who always settled the dispute in young Rizq's favor.

I've never tasted *zalabia* in my life, but I still got a lot of enjoyment and pleasure from sipping the piping hot *madrat al-bur'i* and watching the graceful movement of young Rizq's hands as he made the *zalabia*, while customers waited eagerly inside the shop, or outside, or at the narrow entrance to the alley.

Every so often I'd gaze at the woman I'd finally come to look out for, watching how she'd elbow the men and fight with them for her place. She was a woman of siren-like allure. I would have put her at thirty-five, but I knew she was actually older than that, because lazy young Shu'i had told me quite specifically she was forty and maybe more.

She'd take her place early in the morning, on a long wooden chair, almost like a table, which stood against the dirty wall of the shop. In front of the customers was an actual long table, which was dirty too, soiled with the remains of *zalabia* and oil and tea, and all the other mess customers leave.

While waiting for the hot *zalabia* pastry, she'd take a cup of tea from Shu'i, with some *madrat al-bur'i*, following this up with the delicious *ruwani*[4] dessert; after which you would have thought her eyes were riveted on the pan of seething oil that was frying the *zalabia* pastries young Rizq made with such skill.

Young Rizq, so handsome and good-looking, with his curly hair and rosy cheeks, his well-shaped nose and smiling lips and straight neck, like a bust of Alexander of Macedon. He sensed her eyes were locked on him. When, though, she realized someone was looking at her, she'd turn her eyes quickly away, then dart looks here and there, trying to make out faces a little further away—after she'd had her fill of gazing at young Rizq.

---

2. "Madra" means bowl; "bur'i" is a soup made with dried peas.
3. Hot red peppers.
4. A kind of cake drenched in syrup.

The smile, calm, serene, enticing, never left her lips. She was like the Mona Lisa. What excited me most, though, was her firm bosom whose treasures were revealed for all her attempts to conceal it, standing out clearly from her embroidered cloak, the two breasts seeming almost to pierce through the red silk gown. "Those breasts of hers," I heard a man sitting nearby say, "are enough to get the angels excited." Sinking into this ample bosom was a chain bearing something like a Quran, or the eagle of the revolution or republic.

She didn't mind her natural charms appearing, or care about people gazing where these charms showed most. All she cared about was the *zalabia* and the tea she drank as her eyes devoured the youthful Rizq with the appetite of someone eating a piece of *ruwani*. And because she was the focus of interest for the men who were always there, I imagined I was the focus of her interest!

I never said anything, deliberately hiding any feelings I had toward her, and she acted the same way. I felt, too, that we shared mutual concerns that brought us together, for, as soon as she'd finished her daily meal of *zalabia* and was done with the visit, with its constant stealthy gaze toward the young man, she'd leave the shop and approach me, passing close by me on the pretext of struggling through the crowd and rubbing her breasts against my body. How I'd thrill when this happened! And the number of sleepless nights I'd endure as a result! I kept picturing her . . .

Her mouth, seen from a distance, seemed to be adorned with two gold teeth where the canines should be, and she appeared to wear gold bracelets over her bare wrists; and I'd see henna heightening the beauty of her soft, tender fingers, and black dye of lovely patterning. There was a greenish mole, too, on her left cheek, which made her more alluring still, over all her other beauty and loveliness. I thought at first the mole was artificial; then I realized it was natural, increasing her radiance and beauty, as though she were the star of Yemen. There was no trace of make-up on her lovely face, for she believed in beauty natural and unspoiled.

I got used to the jostling and the crowds at the entrance to the *zalabia* shop. I'd become a besotted lover of the place, just so that I could see her.

Sometimes young Rizq wouldn't be there, and his old father, with his attempted youthful airs, would take over, filling the place with his piquant jokes and gleaming gold teeth, and the bristling of his proud mustaches, and the shining tip of the valuable old dagger bound to his slim waist, and the densely embroidered turban, which swayed proudly this way and that.

Once in a while both father and son would be absent, and their place would be taken by Shu'i, Shu'i the tea and bean seller, whose beans sold out so quickly, for all his laziness and unattractiveness and unfriendly air.

Young Rizq, like his father and maybe his brother Shu'i too, would wonder why I always stood in front of their shop and their pot of oil constantly seething with *zalabia*. What got on their nerves more than anything was that I was always just a spectator! Not that I was the only one like that: there were plenty who liked to stand sipping hot *bur'i* in front of their shop.

Maybe, I told myself, it was because I gazed at that woman. It's true the others gazed at her too, but did I, I wondered, gaze at her more? Perhaps I did. But why should they be so struck and amazed, so resentful at seeing me standing there in front of their shop like others among God's creatures? I always stood on the sidewalk, after all, and that was a public space belonging to the government!

~

She'd sit in her usual place in the *zalabia* shop, with a glass of Shu'i's tea in her hand, her eyes on the pot of seething oil frying *zalabia*, waiting for her hot piece.

There were times when she seemed distrait, but that would soon pass off and a smile would return to her lips. Then she'd start looking once more at the faces of her fellow-customers eating their morning meal there.

~

She wasn't the only woman who liked her *zalabia* for breakfast, or some *bur'i* here, but she was the only one who'd jostle among that strange mixture of people crowding into the place, people of varying age and bearing and clothing, this man in a smart suit, that one in peasant garb, another wearing school clothes, a fourth in military uniform, and so on.

It was these she chose to sit among, while the other women sat at the entrance to the narrow alley nearby, hidden behind their colored cloaks.

~

The gleaming of her two gold teeth fascinated me totally, like sparking ecstasy or uncontrollable desire. For the hundred and tenth time I gazed at her avidly, or for the thousandth time, or for centuries and whole ages and time without end.

She it was always, of no more than medium height, yet of such womanly beauty and allure that whole crowds of customers for *zalabia*, and *bur'i*, and *ruwani*, and *kabab* would be dying for her. Every one of them was captivated by her and desired her; every one of them gazed, as I did, at her charms.

I felt myself consumed with jealousy, especially when I saw how she allowed her breasts to rub up against them just as she did with me. So many times I'd come close to fleeing from her, to any other place at all.

For all her fiery eyes each morning, I was convinced she hadn't slept a wink beforehand. She didn't sleep during the night! I reckoned she spent the whole night enjoying herself instead! For all her glorious beauty, there were clear signs of exhaustion in her face and on all of her body—even on her clothes. That dreadful vision, still clinging to my mind, of how she must have spent her wakeful night only made my ardor more intense.

I wished I could spend an hour with her late in the night, stay together with her till the time came to sip *bur'i*, and eat *zalabia*, and *ruwani*, and *kabab*. Or rather, through all eternity!

I became filled with mingled, violent feelings. I feared temptation, and I was afraid of committing some scandalous error, like embracing her in front of people and within their hearing, or letting my hand stretch out, unthinking, toward her entrancing body. I felt I'd known her since childhood, that she'd fed me all kinds of succulent things whose sweetness was still on my lips.

Finally I decided to leave the place, so as to get right away from her. I was fond of *bur'i*, it's true, but there were plenty more places in town for that. Next day I went off to Bab al-Yaman;[5] and no sooner had I sat down in the place selling *zalabia* and *bur'i* than, to my surprise, I found her there. Yes, there she was, gazing toward me, gazing at everyone there, as if the place hadn't changed at all.

I fled once more, to Suq al-Milh,[6] for my usual breakfast, but once more I found her at the *zalabia* seller's next to the *bur'i* seller's place where I was. It was she and none other, with all her disarming charm, her calm, serene, enticing smile. Here too everyone adored her and gazed at her charms. And I felt, as well, how she rubbed her ample breasts against them, just as she did against me.

Once more I fled, to yet another place—Bab Shu'ub[7] this time; but there she was once more. It was as though she and I were still at Bab al-Sibah, in front of young Rizq, the *zalabia* seller. Everyone, I felt, loved her and desired her and took pleasure in gazing at her charms.

I fled from her further still, to Bab al-Qa'.[8] There the *bur'i* seller and his wife, who made *zalabia*, weren't in separate shops but on the same corner, working

---

5. The Gate of Yemen, or of Freedom. It is the southern gate of old Sanaa.
6. The Salt Market, one of the markets of old Sanaa.
7. One of the northern gates of Sanaa.
8. The gate leading to the Jewish Quarter of Sanaa.

and selling together in the same narrow alley. And no sooner had I begun sipping my *bur'i* than I found her in front of me, eating her *zalabia* pastry as usual.

So back I went to Bab al-Sibah, meaning to tell her frankly of my feelings toward her. But I couldn't pluck up the courage. She'd leave the eating place while I stood sipping my hot *bur'i*, drinking in her whole body, imagining the things she must have experienced the night before.

And I thought how she'd constantly jostle God's creatures as she left the eating place, till she reached the place where I was standing, then how she'd push me away with a motion that wasn't, I felt, meant to entice me.

This repeated itself a hundred times, a thousand times, for a lifetime, and over ages and all eternity. It's still repeating itself.

—Translated by May Jayyusi and Christopher Tingley

Zaki Darwish (1944)

Palestinian short-story writer and novelist Zaki Darwish was born in Berweh in the Galilee, which was razed to the ground by the Israelis after the 1948 debacle. He now lives in Judaidah where he has been the headmaster of the Shi'b secondary school. He obtained a B.A. in Arabic literature and education from the University of Haifa and has been active in the literary life of Palestinian Arabs in Israel, heading the cultural section of the Union of Palestinian Writers in Israel. He has also edited the *Aswar* review and been editor-in-chief of *Nida' al-Aswar*. He began writing his short stories early in life and had at least four collections published before the end of the 1970s: *Winter of Estrangement* (1970), *The Bridge and the Deluge* (1972), *The Man Who Killed the World* (1977), and *The Dogs* (1978). In 1983 he published his first novel, *Exodus from the Ibn 'Amer Plain*. Zaki Darwish's style is robust, vivid, and gripping. His characters have depth and intelligence and his plots are often original, even haunting at times. Some of his work has been translated into Hebrew.

THE WINDOWS

It wasn't the sea breeze that drew me to the west-facing balcony or the chants of the evening fishermen as the sea whispered and reflected delicate twilight tints. Nor was it the blood of the sun painting my curtains. These were things I'd noted in the past, at times when my mind was quite clear. Yet the face of truth changes constantly.

Our quarter always hugs secrets, but does it the way a fool grips a prize so tight it slips from his hands. Why do people so love to have secrets in their keeping? If they didn't have a secret to tell, they'd simply invent one.

I, though, kept to myself, in a room that faced the sea to the south and west and, on the west side, looked out over the variously shaped roofs of the city. Here I created a narrow world that broadened according to circumstance. It had a modest library quite unlike the modern literary idea of one (above all the poetic idea of one), and alongside the bookshelves was a collection of records whose music sounded strange in the modern city streets, soft, drowsy melodies far removed from the piercing cries of body and throat, infusing you with a kind of sweet depression or melancholy. In the corner I had an old-fashioned bed with kitchen gear stowed away beneath it. Forgive me if I'm more specific here. They were things for making tea or coffee, because I'm not the energetic type: I like to have just one meal a day, in the least crowded places, then try and ease the stomach's pangs with cigarettes and cups of tea and coffee. I don't like tiring myself out; in fact I'm so sad I'm practically paralyzed. Have you ever known sadness like that? Perhaps it's not the right way of putting it, but when I fall into this haze of misery, I do seem to lose all ability to move. A kind of smoke comes down over the world, blue smoke especially, as the deepening roar of the sea becomes unbearable.

Is there a particular time of day for my sadness? No, I don't think so. Sometimes the smoke gathers at the peak of joy, the sea roars when the weather's clearest, and it's in the light of the loveliest summer nights that I lose the power of motion.

So that's how I am: a tired, sad man. Can you kind people keep a secret? There've been times, more than one, when my sadness has filled me with terror. They say men don't weep, but that's a lie. I've held back the tears more than anyone, not one tear flowed from my eye when I've lost so many people, old and young, to death; and yet I've wept for myself. Please keep the secret locked in your hearts. My countrymen have called me a deaf rock, but here I am quite exposed. You have to weep for yourself, at least once. In spite of everything, a person's life is something precious and dear.

I took to standing, constantly, at the west window that looked out on a small balcony a mere two meters long and a meter wide. The sea flooded once. That time its rage was real, the kind of rage everyone could see. It was during the October winds, God help us, winds that whipped up the sea, strange winds such as I'd only read of in the geography books. The papers flew from my desk, and some of the books tumbled from their places on my old shelves. The window was flung half open and slammed against the wall, shattering the glass. Only then did I realize that the wind was real, that the sea's rage was real.

I went out on the balcony to close the wooden window against the fierce strength of the wind and, turning to one side, looked across at the balcony next to mine. Then I left the window to slam against the wall. That, God be praised, was the first time I saw her there, as she stood in the storm, hearing nothing of the noise the window had made. She was looking west, out to sea, and I looked out in the same direction. There was a boat being tossed about by the surging waves, turning this way and that as the winds blew on. As she leaned against the decrepit wall, I gazed at the picture of the sea and its reflection on the girl's face.

She seemed utterly downcast. Then the boat won through to the shore at last, and Mahmoud, a young man from the quarter, leapt out and looked up toward the balconies. The girl, turning back, closed the door, and I'd found a secret to occupy myself with. Then I added to the secret, to create a beautiful love story, starting with that west balcony and the windows facing out toward the sea.

I tried to see her again but without success. The young man, though, I saw several times, and the first time I smiled at him—my first smile, perhaps, since coming to live in the quarter. I regretted it at once, because it seemed to my swirling imagination that he'd realized the motive behind that smile. Still, he grinned back, revealing fine white teeth. "Hallo, Ustadh," he said.

He was the first man who'd called me that—the usual way of addressing mysterious-looking men. Can I say it was then that my friendship with Mahmoud began? No, I don't think so. He went away for a time, then suddenly reappeared. As for that delightful girl, I didn't see her again, but I found out she lived in the room next to mine. Between her balcony and mine, though, was a window tight shut and curtains that were always drawn. Many times I heard, through the window, an alluring female voice that I was able to connect with the girl's face as I saw it that first time. Then matters developed quicker than I'd expected, spurred on, perhaps, by the repetition of events. The blue boat, appearing on the blue water, became the signal for the next-door balcony or window to be opened. Did it make me feel jealous? No, I swear to God. It was a pleasure to me to watch the clever moves they made as they tried to outwit other people.

He'd stand there every evening, on summer nights when the horizon was so beautiful and on winter nights when it grew black. Then the smoke encircling my world would turn translucent, the noise grow less fierce, the spinning of the universe become gentle. The days passed with a strange swiftness.

Time passed quickly.

One evening Mahmoud stood facing east, like a man long in prayer, but the curtain on the west window didn't stir. There was no alluring voice, no movement from the balcony door. Sadness gripped me all at once; night fell quickly and the sea grew dark. A cigarette floated on the water, working its way south. I closed the door and played a sad record, because I'm a very sad kind of person and very tired.

Next morning, as I dragged myself along a narrow alley, I found Mahmoud there in front of me, looking pale and exhausted. "From love!" I cried to myself, from the depths of my heart. He greeted me sadly, then walked on.

Another day the same thing happened and, trailing my misery and weariness along with me, I entered my room through clouds of smoke. Then the smoke grew, so that I could no longer sit there in the room, and I raced down the narrow stairs and out into the street. There I saw him once more. The night had fashioned a new kind of sadness for my soul. I caught a glimpse of his face, pale under a street light, and cried out to myself once more, "From love!"

I wanted to go up to him, but his sadness filled me with a sense of shame. The secret had to remain as it was. He saw me and smiled, a faint smile I felt too wretched to return. I made to drag myself off to the shore, then felt his great hand on my shoulder.

"Good evening, Ustadh."

"Mahmoud . . . "

He said little, only that he was sad and tired and wanted to go away.

"Don't go away," I said.

He stared at me.

"And why not?"

"Just don't go away, that's all."

"I feel sad."

"That's why you shouldn't go away."

"And how about the sad way I feel?"

"The sadness will turn to slow death in some strange land."

"And how about the tiredness I feel?"

"The tiredness will turn to endless torture in some strange land."

My evenings became tormenting, beyond endurance. All at once I'd lost the thread that bound me to the horizon and the sea and the sky. Can you believe that? I even lost my old pleasure in misery, and I lost the soothing numbness that came with tiredness. There was no meaning any more to the rest I found in torpor. I thought of a fresh banishment, and the notion filled me with horror. The roaring grew louder and smoke filled the room ever more densely.

Every so often I'd hear that alluring voice and remember Mahmoud. Then, one afternoon, walking the half-empty streets as the winter wind blew away the last leaves on the one fig tree in our quarter, I found myself, on a corner, face to face with the girl, and all the months of waiting and longing and wretchedness came out in a rush.

"Where have you been?" I cried.

She froze where she stood.

"It's not fair!" I cried bitterly. "It's not fair!"

Her eyes widened in fear. In my weakness I was pouring out my heart to her, but it was of myself I was speaking. As for Mahmoud he was vanishing utterly behind clouds of smoke, on a far horizon. So very far away.

—*Translated by Raya Barazanji and Christopher Tingley*

Harib al-Dhahiri (b. 1964)

Poet and short-story writer Harib Al-Dhahiri was born al-'Ain in the United Arab Emirates and studied computer science and business administration in Portland, the United States, then specialized in the administration of airplane fuel. He is one of the founding members of the Short Story Club in the Emirates and the director of its branch in the capital, Abu Dhabi, and in 2003 became the director of the Union of Emirate Writers. He regularly contributes articles to various publications in the Emirates and has published one collection of short stories, *Mandalin* (1997), and two collections of poetry: *A Kiss on the Cheek of the Moon* (1999) and *The Sun of Your Lips* (2002). As can be seen from the following story, al-Dhahiri has spontaneously absorbed a more modernist trend and writes with a completely different style and approach from most other writers. This is a very interesting point for the literary historian who follows the development of Arabic literature in the past few decades.

THE DEATH OF THE CANE

Search for your grandfather! There's no trace of him in the crannies of the quarter, in the alleyways heavy with the sticky mud that clings to the soles of your feet. Come on! Spread out and search for your grandfather!

"Your world," the old woman said, squeezing the udders of a scrawny cow, "isn't the way it used to be." The old women fell silent, but the quarter didn't. People could talk of nothing but the grandfather's disappearance and of the merriment pouring out on all sides. It was borne to them on the north winds, redolent of incense and perfumes from the far country. Merriment took its grip on the men and women and children, but the old woman's milk stayed cold till the winter sun licked what remained of it.

Then, when the rounded face of the sun glowed, they saw the grandfather approaching, with the swift steps of a man racked with hunger. In his haste the shoe was plucked from his left foot, and he swiftly grabbed it up from the midst of the thick dust. Your great-grandfather's face is like the barren land, which gave birth to him one day, before he reached this sour end of his life!

"What did you expect after all?" the young lads said. They were moving in a circle in the midst of the festival courtyard, wearing their special hats with the holes cut out in various shapes, their flowing hearts mirrored in glittering eyes. "So where's the problem?" they said. "Of course our grandfather's coming. He had three legs, but the third one's gone from the hand with the silver ring. His arrival's frightening, awesome, just as his sudden disappearance was. But let's forget how he went away. He's here, that's the worrying thing. What does he want, do you think? He must be coming to tear us away from here. Our grandfather hates festivals, and he hates us having them. When he arrives, he'll tell us just what folly made us leave our homes, and join in this pointless festival all together. Still, maybe that's not what he's come for. Let's hear him out. Let's find out why he's come back." The eldest of the group added, "Our grandfather hasn't brought his cane with him—the one he never lets out of his hand. He never used to be without it."

All of them, old and young, drew one stop closer, then moved back and let him come in among them, striving to read the meaning of his stubborn silence.

"Perhaps," they said, "his face will speak before his tongue does. He's frowning, though. His eyes are red, searching the features of this throng of the Freij people, as if he's seeing them for the first time!"

It was as if some blow had struck him, as if a lingering smoke had come to obscure their festival headwear. His eyes shot suddenly upward to take in the crowd. The cheerful girls quickly stopped their swaying dance, and the dance of thought began in the minds of the revelers. What does your great-grandfather want? They were used to his old, knowing air, but this was something new to them.

"Perhaps," they said, "he's come to tell us why he went off so suddenly. And yet, by the look on his face, it's something different he has to say."

The grandfather's rasping breathing grew easier, and his body began to relax after the fatigue of his trip. There were black smudges on his clothes. The women, who were officially in charge of the festival, made their careful observations on this.

"Perhaps," the old woman said, "he's come back from some fierce, fiery battle, and that's where he lost his cane. Or perhaps he dug a hole and buried it, so he could go back and fetch it when things calmed down."

"Come on," another woman broke in. "Let's get on with the wedding. You've seen he's back. He always hated festivals anyway!"

Before she could go on, he held up his right hand and pointed to a rope, half of it consumed by fire, the other half blackened.

"This," he said, "is all that remains of your quarter!"

Everyone's face turned red and sullen, in the very midst of the heady joy. Fear surfaced in the eyes of the reveling people, and every mouth fell silent—except for that of one woman whose screams pierced the walls and the dumb alleyways, as she wailed over her suckling infant left alone in the burning heart of the blaze.

"Why are you screaming like that?" the old woman asked.

"It's joy," the grandfather said. "It brings madness to young and old alike."

He beckoned to them, and they trooped behind him like prisoners. They crowded around the battered old coach and its driver, who'd been huddled inside for so long his brows were flecked with white, his hair hanging long. His hands were there on the steering wheel. He drove off at a fearful speed, and inside were faces tinged with sadness and sorrow. The old woman locked hands with a trembling young woman who carried a piece of wedding cake, her clothes redolent of incense, a rusted key to an old door tied on the end of her scarf. The door perhaps had burned to ashes now. The key would stay with her till the day she died.

The coach climbed a sandy slope, then juddered erratically downhill and came to a stop on its shaky wheels.

Cries of "God is great" rose in the air, and fear crept from the burning eyes. The grandfather said nothing. The women were crying out, every one. Smoke filled their nostrils, mingled with their panting breath; and now they surrounded the fire with water and earth, trying to put out what was left of it. The grandfather seemed to have lost the weight of his sixty years. The crackling flames were put out at last, but still the smoke rose, along with the secrets it bore, its blackness swirling to waken new terror deep in people's hearts. Empty bubbles seethed up, bearing the smell of weariness and angry thoughts. Questions arose, from murderous voices. "Who did this terrible thing?"

Perhaps your grandfather knows. But perhaps he'd rather say nothing. Maybe he'll announce who did it when the fire's finally out. Just look at your grandfather! He's grappling with the fire, with matchless strength. He's stronger even than the youthful students.

"You want to know who did this?" the old woman asked. She cackled aloud. "You've forgotten," she went on, pressing hard on the bundle in her hands, "the biggest scoundrel in al-Freij! He wants his revenge against our grandfather, because our grandfather thrust his dirty beard down on the sand, and trod his neck, so he'd never again dare steal the wedding gear. But why is he pouring out his venom on the whole quarter? The licking fire has found his own grubby house, his own windows, brought its smoldering, fetid smell there too. Look at the quarter, pale with fear, everything twisted out of shape. Our grandfather loved its mud walls, loved its grains of sand. He'd stand in the shade, waiting for the young ones to come back from school. The place would echo as he endlessly cleared his throat. He'd lean on his cane, the cane that made the round of the wayward sons of al-Freij, while their mothers cried out so bitterly. 'Go on,' they'd say, 'give them a good thrashing! You're the only one they're afraid of!' And our grandfather would answer: 'Too much merry-making's bad for the soul.'"

"Where's the cane?" the sons of al-Freij cried. "The cane! Where's the cane? They've carried it off on the fiery coffin!"

—*Translated by May Jayyusi and Christopher Tingley*

Lutfiyya al-Dulaimi (1942)

Iraqi writer of fiction Lutfiyya al-Dulaimi lives in Baghdad, where she has been working at the Ministry of Culture. Her main preoccupation in her writing is the situation of women in the Arab world. She depicts with sensitivity and precision the plight of liberated Arab women and the way they are consigned to loneliness when they abandon the traditional role of women in Arab society and, at the same time, are not fully assimilated into the general society where men dominate. Her novel, *Who Inherits Paradise?*, was published in 1987, and she has published several collections of short stories: *A Path to the Sorrow of Men* (1969), *The Statue* (1977), *If You Were in Love* (1980), *The World of Lonely Women* (1986), and *Seeds of Fire* (1988). Her work is original and precise and reflects a preoccupation with the inner life of women and their tribulations, while at the same time preserving the element of pleasure for the reader.

LIGHTER THAN ANGELS

Some time before midnight I was swept by a strange wave of merriment, felt light with an overwhelming joy that opened in the depths of my soul. My heart told me I could soar now, could move, in the thick darkness of night, with all imaginable freedom, released from the old clogs of day and its rules. I couldn't tell just what had woken in my heart the flaming desire to cut free from the earth; but before going further—as the unlooked-for joy drove me on to a deeper bond with life—I should, I decided, count up the promises of life to-morrow would bring; the reverse of what I'd done before, when I used sleep as a refuge to forget the misery of my fate. And so I opened my handbag to count what money I had left, from what I'd earned selling the books of philosophy and history in the Sarai market and from selling a painting by a recently dead artist at the Baghdadi auction. I had, I found, sacrificed philosophy, and history, and art, to spend two thousand dinars on a pair of badly made leather sandals, plus a further three thousand dinars on a kilogram of coffee. I realized then just how foolish I'd been: after all, I reflected, with deep regret, I wouldn't be able to travel, move from place to place, however many pairs of shoes I bought, while the coffee would keep me awake more than ever, to count the miserable tribula-tions of my life instead of forgetting them. The money gained from philosophy and history and art would mean constant alertness, with the pleasure of sleep postponed. I took a sip of the coffee, and found the taste heavy, sealed, it seemed to me, with the nectar of the minds I'd sold at the market and the auction. To get over my sense of remorse, I sat down in front of the television to watch a performance of Beethoven's Fourth Piano Concerto. The Japanese pianist began to shine, to glow, seeming ever lighter as her fingers touched the piano, as if she were melting into a great and holy ecstasy, the whiteness of her body standing out against the blackness of the piano keys, and the blackness of her dress against the white keys, so that two rivers of black and white pearls could be seen flow-ing from the instrument. The pianist seemed to vanish, while the keys moved on, as if they themselves were playing the music, unaided by a woman's fingers. The hot, humid south-east winds seeped in through the window overlooking the garden, and I felt a stickiness, like the stickiness of dates, forming on my body, dampening my face and neck and blouse with a kind of drizzle from some place unknown. I thought of writing him a letter but found no ink in my pen; and so I called out to him, hoping he'd hear my call, through some special bond, in that faraway country. I felt my body swimming in its solitude and in the sticky south-east winds pouring into my blood; my hand, though, moved in a total void, so that I couldn't feel my skin with the tips of my fingers. I feared my fingers had lost their sense of touch. Had he tried to touch me, I thought, would his fingers have found the same void? I wished he'd appear at that very moment of my helpless longing, hurry across the expanse of the oceans to prove to me that my body existed; but he couldn't hear me as I communed with him, calling to him from a world floating amid oblivion and tragedy. And so I began, all over again, the search for my absent body, lost to me in the southern winds and the piano concerto, telling myself once more that he wouldn't hear me. All language had become a silent conspiracy now, filled with a poison blocking out the promptings of the heart, so that he, the one I wanted, wouldn't hear me, and my voice, like my body, would be wiped out.

Still I didn't stop searching. I tried to feel my arm, my face, my breast, my leg, but met only a still more awesome void. The long night, and the poisonous storm, had emptied me of weight, of blood, of existence itself; the very body in which I existed had turned to void. He should come, I told myself, stop me vanishing like this. How would he recognize me, otherwise, in my annihilated state? For a moment I imagined him laughing at my sheer stupefaction, at my illusion that my body had been voided amid this sense of tragedy. But, since it wasn't an illusion at all, how would he ever recognize me? Would he sense my presence by catching my voice? And how, and why, and where? I started searching for myself once more but found nothing of my body, and I rose, trembling with fright, feeling robbed of my time. I went to my room and switched on all the lights and stood in front of the mirror on the huge cupboard; but I couldn't see myself in its bright glass. There was nothing but the wall and the painting copied from Goya's naked Duchess of Alba that I'd bought from a penniless art student (he'd taken pleasure in signing it with his name in red ink, just to stress it was a fake). I gazed at the painting, but still the Duchess of Alba lay back in her royal, naked luxury, reflecting, in her mindless ecstasy, the history of a woman whose body, in turn, summed up the history of an era. It seemed, finally, that this indifferent, naked duchess was mocking me because I couldn't find myself, while she could see me with her legendary eyes. Filled with sadness, I reached out for my hand, my hair, my lips but found nothing; just the void and my annihilated body. I looked at myself but found nothing as I tried to trace the contours, my fingers failing to touch anything rounded, to follow the rising and falling forms of a human body. Terror took hold of me, just as poison seeps into the blood, and I began to realize the horror of my state: I was turning into nothingness. Wanting to test my other senses, I turned on the radio. I was immediately engulfed, straight off, by sounds crossing one another in all directions. There were wars of voice and language, their weapons released in tunes and sighs and screams and missiles of scandal. The Fourth Concerto, I saw, had ended. The screen was filled with stiffened corpses now, corpses quartered and mutilated, belonging to people who'd been tortured, their limbs cut off like fruit, their blood set flowing in the colors of all languages. There was violet blood, and green blood, black blood and red and blue and yellow blood; the lovely, tender grasses were sucking it up greedily, while the eyes of the camera snatched close-ups of human faces in the agony of death, and gleaming blue flies circled round about, waiting to pierce the bodies, and birds of prey flew low beneath a wondrous sun, and those on the point of death breathed their last dreams. Now the lens caught the eyes of a small dead boy, filling the screen with them. I thanked God then that

I didn't have a body open to such horrors. I praised God, and redoubled my thanks that He'd spared me this, turning me into a bloodless void. I switched off the television and ran out into the garden, to pass between some rough, tearing branches; but I couldn't feel the pricks that had given such pain and smarting and irritation before. Out in the street were just cars hurrying by. I went back into the house, firmly locked the big wooden door, then locked all the other doors and rushed to fling myself on the bed that had so often refreshed me with its coolness; but I felt no coolness now, nor any softness from the cover with its rose flower decoration. Nor, though, did I feel any pain in my neck; the pillows seemed to me like silken bubbles, and my hand passed over spaces that had once formed my body. Then sleep overcame me. I must have slept for a long time, for I woke to find myself engulfed by the glow of a strong sun, streaming through the vines and lemon trees, reflected from the glass of the window. I'd forgotten what had happened the night before, was surprised by my total absence, as I saw the bed still tidy and cool, as though untouched by my body and its warmth. I burst into tears and—when I found neither tears nor a face—felt as though I was spilling my very soul. I went out into the garden, then on to the street, to be assailed by the din of cars and voices, but I could see no people. Then I came running back and dialed the number of my friend, jerking her out of her sleep. I couldn't find myself, I shouted. Could she find her body? I heard her laugh, half asleep as she was, at what she supposed was some crazy behavior of mine. I shouted to her to touch her body and tell me what she found. She laughed again and asked what was the matter with me, thinking, no doubt, I'd been taken over by some figment from a new story. I should let her sleep, she pleaded, for another half hour. I, though, pleaded with her in my turn, begging her not to leave me to face the terror of my transformation alone. I couldn't convince her of what had happened to me; in fact I don't think she'd even properly woken up. Yet again I begged her to look for her body. Then I heard her terror-stricken scream, as she cried, "I can't find myself either." Then, seized by panic, she cried out, "Let me see the other people here." I didn't, I told her, feel hunger and thirst any more, and this had freed me from the consequences of material existence. I'd never know violence or hunger again, and I was going to use my nonexistence to do every kind of beautiful thing, to let the songs pent up in my heart burst out. "You'll be able to do that?" she said. When material nonexistence takes us over, I told her, it's the resurrection of meaning. She wondered, she said, about our inborn greed, and how it would prompt us to react to all this, but I assured her our voices would remain, and the word, after all, had its desires and pleasures; then, before she could protest, or be consumed by despair, I put down the receiver and hurried back into the street. But I found nothing there, except the cars and buses streaming down the road, with no one driving them. Then, as I gazed at the roads and sidewalks, I saw scores of shadows, with no need of bodies to cast them, reflected from the asphalt. Voices were crossing one another, clashing, laughing, and joking together. Suddenly I felt my soul soar upward, and I was seized by the tremor of a piercing joy, assured of my escape, of my deliverance from all the many dangers and the demands of a body with blood and heartbeat. I was truly rid of the ever exigent body, as well as all the shackles and desires and taboos with which its existence was shot through. I was free of hunger and the need for clothes, free of pain, and disease, and murderous weapons, and all the frightening, stupid problems besetting us through our human history, which concern all those thousands and thousands possessing bodies. I was utterly liberated, could mix with the crowds of hurrying shades, could move around in the void, in an everlasting nonexistence. Something I took to be my heart told me the whole goal of being was to attain disappearance, to vanish and transcend the myth; all had turned, now, to a nation of wondrous angels, without body or fear, or fate leading on to annihilation, their shadows enfolding only precious secrets. This, my heart said, was something none had ever dared dream of and none had ever known before. They'd passed over now, from the tremors of the blood and desires of the body, to the joy of air and void, merging perfectly with the great space.

—Translated by May Jayyusi and Christopher Tingley

Ahmad Ibrahim al-Faqih (b. 1942)

Libyan short-story writer and dramatist Ahmad Ibrahim al-Faqih was educated in Libya and in Britain where he studied drama at the New Era Academy of Drama and Music in London and obtained a Ph.D. in modern Libyan literature from the University of Edinburgh. He first worked in Libya as a journalist, supervising the production of the literary journal *Al-Ruwwad* (The Pioneers), and helped found the weekly paper, *Al-Usbu' al-Thaqafi* (Cultural Weekly), which he edited until 1976. He then moved to London and for ten years was editor-in-chief of *Al-Ufuq* (Horizon) review, published in English and dedicated to the dissemination of Arabic literature and culture abroad. He later held responsible cultural positions in Libya and other Arab countries while writing and producing his experimental and often highly original fiction and drama. His gift as a story-teller was recognized early when he won the 1966 first prize at the Higher Council for Literature and Art in Libya for his short-story collection *No Water in the Sea*. His writings are concerned with the human condition in general but often also with the problems of modernizing and freeing the minds of people from the inhibiting hold of outmoded social and cultural traditions. He has published several collections of short stories, among which are: *Fasten Your Seat Belts* (1968), *The Stars Disappeared* (1976), *A Woman of Light* (1985), and *Mirrors of Venice* (1997). He has also published several novels: *Valley of Ashes* (1985); his lovely trilogy, *I Shall Offer you Another City, These Are the Borders of my Kingdom*, and *A Tunnel Lit by One Woman* (1991), which has been translated into English and published by Quartet in London; and *Homeless Rats* (2000). He has also written some accomplished plays, one of which,

The Singing of the Stars, has been translated into English by PROTA and published in PROTA's *Anthology of Short Plays* (2003). His work has been the focus of a number of critical essays and of some graduate studies. Much of his creative work has been translated into English and other languages, including Chinese.

LOVE ME TONIGHT

That particular smell struck him at once.

He had paid for his ticket, gone down a long corridor, passed through a red-curtained doorway to the warmth of the room itself. For a moment he stood in the entrance, taking his coat off and brushing the rain out of his hair. He waited for his eyes to adjust to the subdued lighting, and it was then that the smell came flooding out to him: a mixture of perfume, sweat, smoke, and wine; a blend that had, no doubt, accumulated over the year, matured and become an ingrained part of the place by now ...

Suddenly he wanted to rush out to the street again, where there was rain, lights, sky, and air. He wanted to go back to the hotel, where his colleagues in the delegation were all sound asleep now, after the tiring journey from Tripoli to this city. If they were to know that he had come here, they would be shocked. He had only slipped away to have those couple of drinks he'd been hankering after for so long. He should get out now, while the going was good!

But from somewhere in the room, a drum was summoning him. Its beat seemed to come like a wind from some far, far place, calling him by his name: "'Abdallah!" Its rhythms spoke a language arcane with insoluble riddles and unfathomable secret to which something deep inside him recognized and leapt up in response. Out of all the instruments of the orchestra he was aware only of the sound of the clay drum, which was being played by an old black man. It was as though an African tribe were communicating with one of its sons who had got lost in the thickets of some mighty forest. Soon he would fall prey to ravenous tigers; the drums were trying to warn him, to tell him which path to follow ...

This was not the usual kind of nightclub. Everything here gleamed and glistened in soft light; carpets, curtains, marble pillars, the tables at which the customers sat, even the very customers themselves, all reflected an incandescent glow, as though phosphorescent dust had been sprinkled on their faces, heads, and clothing. The waiter who took his coat and led him to a table used the kind of language you hear only in the most exclusive salons. The audience all sat listening to the music in silent and rapt attention, as though what they were watching was not a floorshow but a religious ceremony.

'Abdallah's anxiety sharpened. Something strange and drastic was about to happen: perhaps a man in Samurai dress would leap into the stage and ritually disembowel himself; there would be a public scandal! Or even worse, perhaps this club was a front for a gang of thieves who used this plush setting to lure its victims. He became filled with a sense of his own imminent death. Next day's headlines would read: "Unidentified Murder Victim Found in Sin Quarter." And he, "Shaikh" 'Abdallah, as they had called him in his village because his conduct had always been beyond reproach, what memories would he be leaving for his little daughter, for his only son, ten years old and about to become a man? He cursed the weakness that had led him to this place!

However, there was no resisting the magic spell cast by the drum. He had never heard anything like the pulsating rhythm that continued to throb out the essence of all the stories, poems, and myths that had ever sprung to life within the vast girth of Africa. His fears receded. He ordered and avidly sipped, one after another, three glasses of wine, giving himself up to the wild and ancient visions the rhythm aroused in his mind . . .

After a while the stage cleared and the floor was opened to general dancing. The old Negro had been playing without a let-up, and the sound of the playing reverberated from the ceiling itself, calling 'Abdallah to join in. A surge of joy filled him: it would be a dance like no other; he would not stop dancing till he was completely free of all those burdens that were weighing down his soul, until he fell exhausted to the ground.

He was on the point of getting up to do this, when he realized at the very last moment that it would be impossible. In the fever of his impulse he had forgotten that among the dancers—in fact, in the whole club—every man was coupled with a woman and every woman with a man. In his country, men and women did not dance together, and so he had never learned how.

He felt foolish. Shame and frustration turned his legs into rubber and the blood in his veins to water. He looked around to find another customer who, like himself, was not dancing. But it was to no avail. He was the only one in the whole place who was not dancing.

The waiter who had seated him stood close by, facing his direction, a slight smile on his face—which, 'Abdallah was certain, was a smile of contempt and derision. 'Abdallah sensed that the situation was getting more embarrassing by the minute. The feeling of weakness in his legs went from bad to worse. He sank back in his seat and addressed the waiter in his mind: "Tell me, Waiter, what is it that makes you laugh? Why is it so strange for a customer not to join in the dancing? Is it that you can tell I come from Tripoli? Well, my regal gentleman concealing your horns under a veneer of phosphorous, what's the matter with that? Who are you to talk, when your own morals have been polluted by a corrupt and decrepit civilization? Do you sneer at the women in my country? Before you can even mention them, you should go and wash your mouth out with rosewater. There they have a sense of decency. Do you really want them to be like women in your country, whose femininity and humanity no longer have any meaning? Who go to cafés and clubs to drink wine and consort pub-licly with men? Is that what you call freedom? Or perhaps you'd call it virtue!

I know you look down on the way people get married in my country: a man marries a woman he sees and gets to know her for the first time only on their wedding night. That is exactly the way that I did it, and I was delighted to accept this human being whom Fate had sent me. How can you possibly call this way of doing things 'coercion,' you pimp, when at the end of every night you bring men into your own wife's boudoir? What's that? Did I hear you say the word 'love'? The slaughter of virtue like a sacrificial lamb? Or is there some kind of love other than the one you sell in your emporia of lust? No, no, you man of phosphorous, you can keep this kind for yourself and trade in it as you wish! But rest assured that, however many pornographic magazines you send us, you will never get us to relinquish one iota of that sense of honor that marks our actions! In my country a man will still be ready to kill his daughter on the spot if he finds out that she has believed the filth in your magazines and fallen in love with a boy behind her father's back . . . Why are you giving me that strange look? I haven't lost my mind yet!"

"Come here!"

'Abdallah said this out loud, so harshly that he startled the waiter into coming right over.

"Bring me another glass. This time make it double."

The dancing came to an end and the drumming stopped. Couples returned to their tables, while the club's announcer introduced the resident magician, who came rushing up on the stage, unfolding a handkerchief and pulling a large number of doves out of his pocket.

But 'Abdallah's attention became focused on something entirely different.

A young man and a girl were sitting at a table just opposite his own. They might have been there all along, but it was only now that he became aware not only that they were there, they were, precisely, mere children. What else could you call a boy of seventeen or eighteen and a girl slightly younger?

'Abdallah was intrigued. What kind of parents would allow, at this time of night . . .? He adjusted his chair slightly so that he could concentrate all his attention on them. She was wearing a simple sky-blue dress that reached to just above her knees, while he had on a full black evening suit. She had that kind of simple and serene beauty that reminded him of the most beautiful poetry he had ever read, of vistas at sunrise and sunset . . . There was an angelic quality to her face. The name "Cinderella" came immediately to mind: she seemed to have walked right out of that famous fable.

The boy's features were those of a child, but his trim stature was that of a man and reminded 'Abdallah of nothing so much as a knight on a flying steed, traversing the heavens in order to pluck a maiden from a high moonlit balcony, just as it happens in the dreams of young girls . . .

'Abdallah tried to eavesdrop, but they were saying very little: a whispered word, a gesture from him, and her face was wreathed in a smile of complete understanding. They sat there totally absorbed in each other, their faces registering surprise now and then, when applause for the magician's act broke through and reminded them they were not the only two people left on earth.

After the magician, the band returned to the stage, along with five women, naked except for long colorful feathers that concealed parts of their bodies. As they started to perform, the young lovers looked up briefly, broke into giggles, and soon had eyes only for each other again. They were so utterly delighted with each other that 'Abdallah felt that before meeting they must surely have gone through some terrible suffering. In fact, as 'Abdallah came again under the spell of the old Negro and his drum, he felt that his rhythms were transmitting stories about them: in some previous existence they had been two old folk, worn out by time, who had been transformed at the moment of their meeting into a boy and girl at their peak of youth and beauty; if they should ever, even for a single moment, separate, then they would be turned into two old crones again. They would have to journey to the ends of the earth to find each other; otherwise they would fall to the ground dead, dissipate like steam into the air, or, they would find that God had turned them into mice, tortoises, or ants . . .

'Abdallah realised that there was such a thing as genuine love and that he was now witnessing it in all its wonder and power. Whoever came to know love like this could never be touched by disease or poverty or hunger—not even by death. These children, when they left the nightclub, would not be drenched by the rain pouring down outside: the rain would know that they were in love. Neither cold winters nor hot summers would ever upset them because they were in love . . . No one would ever charge them for food, for bus tickets, for rent, because they were in love . . .

It was only now that he began to realize what a tragedy it is to live without love, to spend one's life as a prisoner of a society that regards love as lechery. He was the one who had been turned into a mouse, a tortoise, an ant! Not for a single day had he ever been able to experience his humanity! Every illness, every problem that had ever beset him had been caused by his lack of love. And when death itself finally came, it would be only because it realized that he had spent his entire life without finding love . . . His entire youth had slipped through his fingers like water. There had been no joy, for even a single day, in all his forty years—not even the excitement of a love letter sent by a woman, no matter how frivolous and false. If that had happened just once, then his whole life, in fact the very face of the whole world, would have been altered . . .

Guiltily he looked about him. The drum was telling him and everyone else who was in the club that it was all his fault. He had surrendered himself willingly to societal traditions, had assumed a mask that he had talked himself and all those around him into believing was a real face. And now that he knew the importance of reassuming his true face, he discovered that he no longer had any face of his own at all . . . The drumbeat was continuously, impulsively speeding up and slowing down again, rising to fever pitch and then subsiding. It had stripped 'Abdallah naked for all the world to see and now was playing with him, tossing him up at the ceiling, dropping him down in a heap on the floor. He blocked his ears in order not to hear it, but the beat penetrated his entire being, arousing unending surges of pain and agony inside him. He closed his eyes as his anguish turned to sheer rage in his blood . . .

When he opened them, the boy and girl were standing. The floor show was over, and it was time for general dancing again. The boy took her by the hand and led her up to the dance floor. He slid his arm around her supple waist as though he were afraid it might break. For a while they danced slowly, heads resting on each other's shoulders. Then at one point she raised her head to look into his eyes. He bent down to her. As lips and bodies came together, they both became a single entity . . .

'Abdallah was so possessed that he forgot himself. He became, so to speak, a third element, joining and intermingling with them. The breathlessness of the moment wiped away all aggravation. That kiss, which had brought the two of them together body and soul, was a prayer that would bring them the blessings of God and would delight the angels in heaven . . .

No! exclaimed the strident voice inside his brain. What they are doing is a crime against morality, against their families. In our society what counts is not love but virtue. In our society they would both be severely punished!

But who is to say that this love is not a virtue? 'Abdullah himself argued. In fact, God's anger may well be aroused by abstinence from such experience! The greatest crime of all would be for God to give mankind the spirit of youth and for man to reject such God-given bounty.

But the force of his own logic recalled to him the fact that he had sacrificed his own life on the altar of those same ancient traditions he had once thought so noble and as a result had turned himself into an old man at the age of fifteen. He felt utterly miserable, and the feeling gnawed away at his heart, until he wished he had a dagger, a revolver, or poison to put a quick end to his misery.

When the two young lovers returned to their seats they were holding hands and nuzzling each other happily. 'Abdallah could not stand it any longer.

"They're killing me!" he cried out loud. He did not care if people thought him mad.

"Are you talking to me?" asked a woman's voice at his elbow. His face was seared by her drunken breath. It was one of the showgirls. Her performance over, she had put on her clothes and come into the hall. The only empty seat was the one by him.

"No!" he replied. "I was talking to myself! What business is it of yours, anyway? I enjoyed your dancing . . . " He paused, then continued, his speech rapid and confused: "You don't realize it but they're out to get me—of course that's no concern of yours—but why are you sitting there? Oh no! No! I didn't come here looking for a woman! I am a man of principles—oh, please forgive me!"

She looked at him in amazement. It was obvious that the drink had brought him to a sorry pass.

"Shall I tell you a secret?" he went on. "Do you realize I've never once received a love letter in my whole life? That's why they're out to kill me tonight. They may have done it already. Look at my eyes. Am I dead?"

"Are you all right?"

"Yes, I'm fine, but that's none of your business, and that damned drum, too, it has nothing to do with the story of my life, which it's been telling people openly all night. I knew right away that something was being set up for me in this—"

At that moment the young man and the girl got up and left, hand in hand. 'Abdallah reached for his glass, but the dancer stopped him.

"You've had quite enough," she said. "What's the matter? You're shaking." She stretched out her hand to feel his forehead. He did not resist. She saw at once that he had a fever and gestured to the waiter to bring him his bill and help him up. "You need some rest. I live close by. You can come with me."

Almost unconscious, he paid, put on his coat, and leaned on her shoulder.

When they got outside the street was deserted, and rain was still pounding down. 'Abdallah turned toward the dancer, as though he were just now noticing that the person next to him was a woman.

"Someone has to love me tonight," he pleaded, "or I will collapse dead in the rain! I will die like an insect, a miserable ant! I beg you to love me! Love me just once! Love me tonight, that's all; just tonight!"

Tears were pouring unrestrained from 'Abdallah's eyes. The drum whose rhythms had been with him the whole evening was still echoing inside his head as he stood there in the street. But this time it was not transmitting an old folktale or a message from an African tribe to its son who had gone astray in the forests. Now the tribe realized that its son had fallen into the hands of wild tigers. There was no way of rescuing him. He was gone forever; he would never be the same man again. Palms kept pounding away on the drum, and this time the message was one of bitter weeping that the wind and rain carried to the furthest corners of the world.

—*Translated by Roger Allen and Thomas G. Ezzy*

Mustafa al-Farisi (b. 1931)

Tunisian novelist, short-story writer, and poet Mustafa al-Farisi was born in Sfax and studied history, obtaining a doctorate in 1955 with his thesis on the Qarmatians. After independence he was employed in the Tunisian Ministry of Information, and from 1959–62 was head of the Foreign Section of Tunisian Broadcasting. He then moved to be the head of SAPEC, the Tunisian film organization, and later became secretary general of the Tunisian Society of Authors. He has had great success as a writer of radio plays and has also been a successful writer of short stories, including his collection, *I Stole the Moon*. In 1966 al-Farisi won a literary prize for his novel published that year, *The Curve*. As well as fiction, he has written and published plays and poetry in French.

WHO KNOWS? MAYBE . . .

Her room overlooked the street and the sun came in through the big window, spreading its fresh, gleaming rays over her flowering plants. She'd potted them herself two weeks before and given them the vigorous encouragement of cheerful youth and innocent maidenhood. But today, every now and then, her glance wandered from the flowers toward an open window on the second story of the block of flats opposite. A young man about the same age as herself kept looking in her direction; he'd disappear from view and come back to the window; then vanish only to reappear once more.

Hind smiled, waiting for what would come next. She busied herself for a moment with her flowers, then suddenly looked up—and there was the young man, looking at her intently, his dreamy eyes fixed on her window. The young man realized he'd given himself away and was embarrassed for a moment. Then he returned to watering his potted plants and removing the dead leaves from them with every appearance of unconcern—but stealing periodic glances at Hind. The pot he was watering filled and overflowed, and the water ran out, falling in generous quantities on the head of a passerby who was sunk in daydreams of his own. The man opened his umbrella and held it over his head. "God!" he muttered resentfully, "the amount of rain we're getting this summer!"

Summer! That year it was still raining at the end of the summer, though on this particular day the sun was at its most resplendent. But that has very little importance for our story, since as soon as Hind caught sight of her neighbor, and as soon as the neighbor caught sight of her, neither sun nor rain came into the picture. Watering the flowers became a daily duty, if not an hourly one, and stealthy glances and shy smiles were the natural result.

Hind had taken out a lease on her apartment the same day the neighbor moved into his apartment in the block of flats opposite. From that day, from the moment the two windows looking on to the street were opened, Hind and her young neighbor were moving constantly to and fro—a brief meeting and a briefer parting; silent, dreamy glances and shy, hesitant smiles. From the first day—that first Sunday when the sun had come out so brilliantly, as if to take its revenge on the earlier Sundays of the rainy summer—Hind and her neighbor glanced or smiled at one another, across the wide street, once a day at least. The long hours of the weekend would bring them together.

Every encounter must have a pretext of some sort—theirs was that their flowers, like their dreams, needed frequent watering, but done hesitantly, like the glances sent from one window to the window opposite. She'd bought potted flowers and he'd bought a type of plant that he hoped would flower but that produced no blooms. But the young man wasn't bothered by this barrenness; the important thing was the pretext. He had his pretext, even if it didn't flower.

If the good-looking young man and his pretty neighbor kept casting interested glances at each other, if they were constantly exchanging stealthy looks, why, some readers may ask, didn't they speak to one another, without having to resort to their pretext? But Hind and her neighbor were shy, and it isn't easy for two shy people to start a conversation. Then again, no one had introduced them; they'd made each other's acquaintance purely by chance, at their windows. They hadn't met anywhere else even once, not at the baker's or the milkman's or the butcher's. So what could they do?

The search for a scheme that would let them meet at the baker's or the butcher's taxed them to the utmost, but their efforts went unrecorded and no meeting took place.

They engaged in long conversations with the shopkeepers. They dawdled in the street. They walked around the white block of flats or the yellow block of flats ... perhaps ... maybe ... perhaps. But these schemes were a failure. It was as though some accursed jinn had resolved to keep them in suspense and, by making it impossible for them to meet, was preventing the miracle they so desired.

Just think of it! Hind would often go into her room and open the window—to water her plants, of course—and just at that moment the good-looking neighbor would be going down the stairs to have a word with the grocer, asking him how he was and how his family was, and lingering over a cup of coffee or tea. And if Hind did happen to catch sight of him, it was only to see a bicycle vanishing down the street or turning round a corner, bearing all her dreams with it. Her hopes were centered on meeting this stranger who was her neighbor. How unfeeling bicycles were! Hind began to hate them because they prevented young men from walking. What had God given people legs for?

Then, of course, there was the postman. He knew Hind, and he knew the good-looking young man; he was the person who brought them their daily ration of joy or depression. He knew that the good-looking young man was called Tawfiq and that he worked at the Central Bank. And he knew that Hind's real name was Fatimah—but what girl these days keeps to the name her father chose for her? Fatimah indeed! Maybe this name suited the tastes of girls in the first century, or even the fifth. But in our day and age?

The postman, then, knew both Tawfiq and Hind, and he could, if he'd wanted to, have brought them together. But is it a postman's job to bring together sweethearts who've kept their feelings to themselves? It wasn't his business to do it, even if he'd known about the fine thread of emotion that bound the window in the white block of flats to the window in the yellow block. How could he be expected to bring them together when he had no inkling of their love, any more than anyone else did who came along the street or lived in the blocks of flats? No one knew about this thread that made the fragrance of Hind's flowers pass from her window to the window opposite or about the thoughts of that good-looking young man who spent evenings standing behind the curtain of his window, looking toward the window across the way. Nothing would tear him away from it till the light went out. Again and again he'd remain standing there as the light shone in Hind's room, his head full of obscure and distracted and perplexed thoughts.

In his long daydreams he saw the girl he loved sitting at her small, elegant desk with so many books and papers in front of her and a pen between her tender lips, pondering the answers to the questions in front of her. "The poor girl's tiring herself out," he'd say to himself; or, "She'll pass. I know she'll pass. A girl like that never fails an exam. She couldn't fail." At other times he saw her in his dreams, lying on a comfortable bed, her wide eyes eagerly devouring poetry—now calmly, now passionately. And he'd say to himself, "Her poetry's from me and it's to me." Then, still in his dream, he'd come upon some scattered pages on the floor of the room and pick one of them up. Beautiful handwriting. Green ink on blue paper. And what tenderly poetic expression! He'd read it and reread it, again and again. "She's enchanting ... didn't I tell you she was enchanting?" Then he'd close his eyes and go into a long reverie. After a while, though, he'd open his eyes in alarm. Could it be that other things were going on behind those curtains drawn across the window of his pretty neighbor? How could anyone know? But then he'd pull himself together, reproaching himself for his suspicions.

One Sunday evening, when he was looking out of his window on to the street, he noticed a red car stop in front of his neighbor's block of flats, and a young man he'd never seen before got out. The young man stood on the pavement for a moment, then, nonchalantly putting his fingers to his mouth, let out an impudent whistle, which Tawfiq didn't like at all. And what happened next he liked even less, because the cheeky young fellow, having whistled for some moments without receiving any response, vanished into the hall of the building with the same nonchalant air. Tawfiq checked that he wasn't still in the street: no, he certainly wasn't there now. The white block of flats contained ten apartments at least, each of these being occupied by a family and sometimes by two or more families; the strange young man might be making for any one of them. But Tawfiq gave no thought whatever to these possibilities, certain that the young man was making for the flat of his pretty neighbor. A cheeky young fellow whistling like that in the sight and hearing of everyone passing by in the street! There must be some kind of familiar relationship between him and Tawfiq's neighbor. And the red car! And the way he disappeared into the building! All these were clear signs of a close connection between the pretty girl and the cheeky young stranger.

For the first time Tawfiq felt a pain gnawing inside him. He was depressed because he didn't have a red car like the one standing in front of his neighbor's block of flats. No doubt the girl of his dreams was a materialist, like all modern girls; she wouldn't appreciate his feelings or have any respect for what was troubling his soul! But he quickly rebuked himself for this nonsense. How could he think such things?

He stood for a while, poised between reproachful doubts and feelings of remorse. Then, suddenly, he caught sight of his pretty neighbor leaving her block of flats with a large basket in her hand. He could see what was in it: empty bottles that she was obviously going to take back to the milkman. The girl passed the red car, playfully tapped its roof, and walked on.

Tawfiq felt a limpness spread through his whole body, weighing down his arms and head and legs ... she'd deliberately patted the roof of the car, just as though she was flirting with the owner of the car, indirectly, through that heap of red metal and glass. "That's it!" Tawfiq said to himself. "I'm going to put a stop to these goings on. I love her. I don't suppose she knows about my love, but that doesn't matter. It's enough that I'm a man and I love her. She's at the grocer's now or the milkman's. She'll be making breakfast for that cheeky stranger and sitting down at the same table with him and eating the same food from the same set of plates ... it's too much! I must find a way of talking to her. I'll put the whole thing to her and tell her I love her."

Tawfiq pondered what he was going to do. Then it occurred to him to go down to the street and offer to carry the heavy basket she had in her hand. He'd carry her basket, and he'd suppress the resentment he felt toward that young idiot! If there had to be a sacrifice in the cause of getting to know the girl of his dreams, then he'd sacrifice his pride and carry the basket up to the entrance of the flats.

"The pleasant man never loses a bargain." That was what his boss at the Central Bank always said, and he was quite right. Tawfiq made up his mind accordingly and skipped down the stairs like a child. He reached the entrance and was on the point of leaving when he was stopped by a friend of his coming in. "Where are you off to?" he said. "What are you running like a madman for?" "Oh, no reason," said Tawfiq. "I just want to get a drop of milk from across there ... the shop's just close ... wait till I get back."

"You know I hate milk. You've probably got some beer or tea. Let's go up."

"You go up and let yourself in. You can start getting the tea ready and I'll be with you in a few moments."

But his friend clutched the bottom of his jacket and stood in his way. "I'm in a hurry as well," he said. "Listen for a moment and then I'm off. I've brought you the telescope. Here, take it ... are you going out hunting?"

"Something like that," Tawfiq shouted, snatching the telescope from his friend's hands. He shot off down the street like an arrow, while his friend remained rooted to the spot, at a loss to account for all the hurry.

Tawfiq reached the grocer's shop and looked round at the faces of the customers. But he didn't find the bride of his dreams among them, so he turned back toward the white block of flats. Then, at the very moment his glance fell on the entrance to the flats, he saw her disappearing into the hall with the heavy basket in her hand. He boiled with anger and stood cursing the stupid friend who'd blocked his way and spoiled his plan.

He continued on his way home, quite oblivious to everything around him. When he reached the entrance to his block of flats, he stopped for a moment to direct a last glance from the road toward the window on the second floor and found his attention caught by something that he hadn't noticed before—a site, in the street dividing his window from the window of the white block of flats, which was wide enough for a third building. He'd also paid no attention to the piles of bricks and steel mesh that had begun to fill the site about a week before. He watched now as the machines were set up alongside the bricks and steel and timber, with the workmen around them busily engaged in their noisy work.

He didn't linger in front of this scene but went into the block of flats and started climbing the stairs. "It's going to be pretty noisy here for the next few months," he thought. He reached his flat on the second floor and went in, locking the door behind him. Then he hurried to the window, opened it wide, took the telescope, and raised it to his eye. He aimed it toward the window opposite but couldn't see any life or movement in the apartment of his pretty neighbor because of the curtains. A cold sweat broke out on his brow, and a violent trembling ran right through him, forcing him to sit down. How he would have liked to see what was happening behind those curtains, which hid from him the mystery that had perplexed him all day.

But for those curtains, he would have realised that the owner of the red car hadn't come to visit Hind. He'd actually come to take out his fiancée, Thurayya, who was an old friend of Hind's and had come to lend her a tea service.

Hind was going to give a small party in honor of a good friend who'd just had a beautiful baby girl, to be named "Hind" at the request of our Hind, the owner of the window opposite. But Tawfiq didn't know about all this. The malicious jinn was lying in wait for him—so who could hope to set him in the right direction?

Hind's friend had just drawn back one of the curtains and asked: "Who's that person looking this way through a telescope—over there—from the window opposite?"

Hind completely ignored the query. "There he is again," her friend went on. "He's putting his telescope down. He looks a nice young man. Do you know him?" Hind didn't answer this question either, but went to the window and threw a hurried glance at the window opposite. Her friend quickly started to smooth her hair and straighten her dress. "Why does she have to play the spy like this in front of her fiancé?" Hind wondered.

She felt a sense of annoyance rising up inside her. If you'd told her she was annoyed because she was jealous, she wouldn't have believed you. But it was jealousy, of course, brought her back to the window and made her draw the curtain with unwonted force. "I see what's going on now," her friend observed, more slyly than anxiously. "That young man's pestering you. But he won't annoy you for long. When that new building's up to five stories, you'll be able to open the casement as wide as you like. It'll be finished soon."

Hind smarted at her friend's words, and the smart increased as the building rose higher. As each row of bricks was added, the rising wall got nearer to the second floor. These workmen were playing a strange game. All they had to do was raise the wall a few feet a day. Why were they going so fast? It was as though they knew about the two windows and were intent on cutting the fine thread of emotion that had bound the two young people together for so long. They meant to cut it just as quickly as they could, and that was why you saw them scurrying about to put up the ill-starred block of flats. Often the two sweethearts stood there, each at their own window; often they lingered to exchange stealthy glances; and often the water spilled down the wall and sprinkled the heads of people passing by on the pavement.

Hind prayed hard for a downpour of rain, hoping that the workmen would stop work on the building or at least have to slow down, so that the hour of parting could be postponed. As for Tawfiq, watching the rising building from his own window, he was wondering about a possible stoppage of work, perhaps because of a strike by the workers protesting against . . . well, against something or other that didn't suit them. But the summer, which had sent such a heavy load of rain earlier, now decided, during its final days, to win the public's approval and do its duty as a summer. It allowed the sun to come out and shine with extreme brilliance and liberality. The workmen didn't go on strike either. All their demands were met, and a good number of their difficulties were settled amicably, without any disturbance or dispute; so you could see them intent on their work, with satisfaction on their faces, all singing the same song, to the effect that "work well done ennobles the worker, and the man who does good work is a creator in his trade"—or something of the sort.

So the building went up with surprising speed, till the heads of the workmen were level with Hind's window. The inevitable day arrived: the workmen were level with Hind's feet, then with her chest. That was one Monday morning. It was as though the same idea had come to the sweethearts at once, for they both stayed at home, standing at the window and watching the building opposite as the workmen raised the level of the wall brick by brick. Then a second idea struck them together, both of them deciding not to lose their last opportunity, for at the same moment they raised their arm and waved to one another. And just as the wall was finally cutting off all communication between them, Tawfiq and Hind were rushing headlong down the stairs. In a few seconds they'd met at the entrance to the new building.

For the first moment neither of them spoke, because they were completely out of breath from running; but soon they were chatting away and the cloud had lifted. They spent that evening together at the cinema, and one Sunday, two weeks later, Tawfiq was carrying two heavy baskets to his home. That evening he gave a party, and one of the people he invited was the Thuraya's fiancé, the owner of the red car. Oddly enough Tawfiq no longer saw him as the cheeky young whistler who'd once given him such sleepless nights.

When his red car drew up in front of the door of the yellow block of flats, he was whistling as usual, but it didn't sound cheeky or offensive any longer. On the contrary Tawfiq enjoyed it and found it had a pleasant ring to it. Hind, too, was there again to receive the guests—it was she who'd prepared the party and chosen the food and drink.

When the workmen finished the new building, it was the most elegant in the whole district, being painted in a number of different colors, in the modern fashion. Over the entrance was a mosaic, done with great skill and in the best taste.

If you ever chance to pass the new building and curiosity prompts you to slip into the hall, you'll find some wooden pigeonholes in one corner, each one well known to the postman and to its owners. Over one of these there's a white label, neatly inscribed "Hind and Tawfiq—Second Floor." Then you'll understand why Tawfiq gave the telescope back to the friend he'd borrowed it from to go hunting ... or something like that.

—*Translated by Michael Young and Christopher Tingley*

Ilyas Farkouh (b. 1948)

Jordanian short-story writer and novelist Ilyas Farkouh was born in Amman, studied philosophy and psychology at the Arab University in Beirut, and now works as a journalist and in publishing. He has published four collections of short stories, *The Slap* (1980), *Amman's Birds Fly Low* (1981), *Twenty-One Gun Salutes for the Prophet* (1984), and *Who Will Plow the Sea?* (1986). He has also published one novel, *The Height of Sea Froth*. Farkouh has also done some interesting translations from Western literature, including stories by the brothers Grimm, and is a permanent member of the Jordanian Union of Writers, participating, as guest reader in its cultural meetings. He has also participated in many international and Arab conferences on literature.

SHOULDERS

On the Palestinian Exodus from Beirut, 1982

As the place grew crowded, the noise began to rise and there wasn't enough air to breathe any more; it had grown thinner, as people were cramped ever closer together. What I feared had come: a sense of choking suffocation, seeping into my very blood. My heartbeat quickened, and the sweat trickled more and more, all over my body. All my senses woke; I was ready to meet whatever sudden crisis might arise. I was, I found, still living in a state of constant alert.

All this had begun so very long ago.

The endless need to be on the watch. The flickering and nervous starts of the eyes. The glances shot in every direction: there's danger from this side; there's an explosion here, just lying in wait. That way seems calm, but it's evil, cunningly dressed up. The evil all around dries the spittle and makes people's limbs convulse, stretching out and shrinking back, always on the move. There was never any peace. The calm and quietness made the hair bristle up on our heads. A sense of suffocation pressed down on our souls, and our breathing quickened.

I heard my friend's voice, echoing my own feelings.

"This is the final suffocation, my friend."

I asked him what he meant, and he reproached me.

"Don't you understand?"

"No," I said, "I don't understand." But he didn't offer any explanation. In front of us the sea stretched to the edge of the misty horizon, while the Suicide Rock jutted up, solid but featureless, from the mossy forest of the water. Down to our left, on the desolate sands of the beach, a man and a woman were walking, close to the waves with their eager tongues.

"Yes," my friend said. "This is the suffocation." It was a long time ago, when the sea itself was less broad than our dreams, the sky itself too narrow to harbor all the birds of our coming joy.

I spoke to him of these things, realizing, now, that he was thinking of all those newspaper headlines, with their endless clamor and warnings of approaching disaster.

He just patted my shoulder, saying nothing. I quivered beneath the touch of his fingers and turned angrily to face him.

"You only read about the bad things in the world," I said.

He gave a brief, unenthusiastic laugh. Then, looking not at me but at the Suicide Rock, whose features were getting gradually clearer, he retorted, "What about you?"

"I don't read the things you read," I said quickly.

He shook his head repeatedly.

"That's true," he said, speaking each word clearly and distinctly, as though he were bringing it out from some cherished hoard of treasure. "All you ever read is poetry."

His lopsided way of looking at things, as though nothing existed in the world but politics, annoyed me. I knew, deep down, that his fears weren't groundless, but still I was loath to give up those parts of life I so loved.

"Are you criticizing me," I said, "for the way I see life in poetry?"

"No," he said. "But it's more practical to see the world through the world itself."

I dropped my gaze, turning my eyes to follow the tongues of the waves as they licked at the feet of the couple on the shore.

We'd run away from the waves, laughing. Once her shoe fell from her hand, and she bent down to grab it, but the wave was quicker, carrying it away as it retreated, then bringing it back upside down. She, my lovely woman, stood still there, on bare feet that had sunk down into the soft wet sand, and laid her free fingers

on the waist of her wide blue dress. At that moment she looked like a young
woman mourning something close to her heart. She stood there sulkily, awaiting
consolation from a kindly word or a gentle hand laid on her shoulder.

⚯

"You're not with me," I heard him say.
"I'm with you," I said, "and with them."
"Those two over there?"
"Yes, those two. Look at them. Just look!"
There they were, alone on the sands of the desolate beach. The man was
staying close to the woman, who was pressing her head against his shoulder and
trying to hide from him—perhaps from all of us—what the winds were reveal-
ing above her knees.
My friend started muttering.
"That's what you're interested in," he retorted. "That's what you're interested
in, admit it!"
The woman was trying to gather the edges of her dress, which was flying
upwards now as the wind blew it out.
"Yes," I grunted. "I am. I am interested in it."
The woman, realizing there was no point in trying to fight the wind, let it do
as it pleased. I saw her place her hand on the shoulder of the man, who gathered
her into an intimate embrace; then I saw them merge into a single moving figure and vanish—vanish behind the smell of the salt, and the sweet taste of fish,
and the sea breezes that, for the moment, had nothing hurtful in them.

⚯

The ship swayed with the movement of the sea; and we swayed too, clashing against
one another with our shoulders. We saw the houses of the city, the city that had
bid us farewell with bullets, fade slowly from sight; and I remembered the words
of my friend as we watched the women swirling all along the harbor, waving not
handkerchiefs but guns: "Do you understand, now, that bullets can be tears?"
I hadn't answered, trying to evade her eyes as they searched for me among
the crowds of people. She would come too, she'd told me; and when I'd refused,
her grief had shown itself in tears of bitter suffering.
"I can't stand goodbyes," I'd said.
Still the tears had flowed. She didn't realize I was a wall unable to support
even itself.

⚯

I saw everything the others saw, and more than those saw who were so far
away from us—those who knew of us through the voice of the radio, or who

watched us, excited by it all, alongside a goal scored by Italy or Brazil, following our progress, onto the decks of the ships, as we flickered out from their television screens.

I saw, there, all life had allowed me to see of a city that had given me so much but had now faltered at last, powerless to let me keep hold of my lovely woman, powerless to let her keep hold of her firm-hearted man, to know a single day's joy together—or further joy beyond that.

"You're the one I lean on." She'd said that repeatedly, till at last the sun tore aside the curtain of the night and I slipped away from the warmth of her side. The city harbor was a place woken to doomsday; the sky beyond a blue mantle filled to overflowing with farewell shots and the cries of those remaining behind:

"Don't leave us! Where—?"

We saw, over our shoulders, how the sea swayed with us as we climbed the steps, one by one, toward the deck. I saw, over my shoulder, how her face floated, distraught, above the other faces, a face speaking no words; how her hands were thrust out toward me through the tears and the bullets.

"Don't leave us!" Still the noise swelled, as the place filled with jostling shoulders. I tried to slip through, but constantly the spaces closed up; people's breathing quickened, till it rose, in its agitation, above the very roar of the engines; shoulders were jammed tight, so close they seemed joined as one—coming together as my face had come together with her soft shoulder, where it sloped gently down toward her swelling breast, receiving my tears and welcoming them, as it would welcome a fighter who had been defeated without knowing why.

"Why?" she asked, as I gently touched the head laid on my breast.

I violently stubbed out my cigarette, fury swelling up inside me.

"Ask them," I said.

The next day would bring the meeting the world had been waiting for—and that we, in the depths of our hearts, had so striven against, so tried to forestall.

We were silent for a few moments, unable to speak from the longings twined together in our hearts. A cool breeze, blowing softly toward us from the open window, brought me no relief.

"Please don't leave me," she begged again.

I held her more tightly to my breast. She slipped her arm beneath my shirt and held me close to her.

"You're the one I lean on," she said.

I kissed her shoulder, so smooth and firm, so close to me.

All this happened so very long ago.

From that day on there was never enough air to breathe; it grew thinner, and people were cramped ever closer together. What I feared had come: a sense of choking suffocation, seeping into my very blood. The sweat trickled more and more, all over my body. All my senses woke; I was ready to meet whatever sudden crisis might arise.

The ships' sirens sounded, and a great hubbub rose, along with a hail of bullets.

I find, now, that I'm still living in that state of endless alert.

And still I'm haunted by a world that—given over though we are to constant sailing and constant departures—refuses to lose its old taste, and by memories of the shoulder of that lovely woman.

—Translated by Salwa Jabsheh and Christopher Tingley

Gha'ib Tu'ma Farman (1927–1990)

Iraqi novelist and short-story writer Gha'ib Tu'ma Farman was born in Baghdad. He studied Arabic literature at Cairo University then completed his degree at the University of Baghdad, graduating in 1954. He worked as a journalist, moving between Syria, Lebanon, Egypt, and China, then left for Moscow in 1960 to occupy the position of translator at the Foreign Languages Publishing House in the Russian capital, where he remained up to his death. Farman is regarded as one of Iraq's foremost novelists. Despite his long sojourn abroad, he has retained in his work the details and flavor of daily life in Iraq, as well as the emotional and psychological attitudes of Iraqis toward social and existential problems, with a thread of universality running through all his works. His first, early collection of short stories, *Millstone Harvest* (1954), was followed by his collection *Another Newborn* (1960). His first novel, *The Palm Tree and the Neighbors* (1965), immediately placed him among the best social-realists of the novel, a status that was confirmed by his later works such as *Five Voices* (1967), *Labor Pains* (1974), *The Crows* (1975), *Shadows on the Window* (1979), and *The World of Sayyid Ma'rouf* (1982). He early depicted the Baghdadi bourgeoisie, reflecting an optimism that began to disappear gradually in his later work with the entrenchment of social injustice and the continuous deprivation and loss in Iraq and the Arab world.

UNCLE, PLEASE HELP ME GET ACROSS

"Uncle, please help me get across . . . Help me get across . . ."

Stretching out her hand in front of her, cocking her head to one side, and trying to gauge the pressure of the cold air on her face, she took a few short, cautious steps. She could hear noises around her: people's voices, which meshed together in her ears; the sounds of cars speeding by, and the blasts of air they sent whipping against the side of her face and penetrating her whole body.

Her fingertips touched a hard object and held on to it. She ran her palm over its cylindrical surface. She clasped it with her arm and pressed her body against it. Then she put her foot a little forward until it touched the edge of the pavement, then put out her leg and raised her arm until she felt the drops of rain falling on it.

It's still raining, she thought. Eh, how miserable this is! . . .

She clung tighter to the post and could hear the sounds of cars as they cleaved their way through the water from the rain.

"Uncle, please help me get across! . . ."

She said it in a louder voice, turning her head toward the passersby, waiting desperately and anxiously for a hand that would reach out to her.

The noises were getting louder around her, and the passing cars splashed spray on the side of her face as they sped by.

"Uncle, please help me get across!" she shouted again in the din of muddled noises—people's voices, machine sounds, and the sounds of nature. Then she heard the engine of a car stopping near her, the sound of a door opening and slamming shut, and a soft, feminine voice, saying, "Close up your jacket well . . . You'll catch a cold."

Instinctively, she brought her hand to her chest and touched the upper part of her dress. She could feel a new chill going through it, piercing the bones of her chest. Some strands of hair had fallen over her brow down to her eyes and were bothering her. Her feet were two numb pieces of ice. With one foot she rubbed the surface of the street and felt the oozing mud. It annoyed her, the way the mud stuck so persistently to her feet, penetrating the fissures in her toes and soles.

"Uncle, God give you health," she pleaded, "won't you please help me get across?"

Two men were talking together nearby. She heard all they said.

"May God give you a long life, Uncle! . . . Help me get across!"

"Where do you want to go?" she heard a voice ask next to her. "It's raining hard . . ."

"Uncle, my good-for-nothing brother has gone away and left me, and I want to get to the other side . . ."

She waited as a warm hand touched her arm, then crept downward until it touched her hand. Meanwhile, the owner of the hand was still speaking to his friend:

"I'm not drinking today . . . Why should I? Do I own a money factory? . . . Let's sit in a café instead and take it easy."

Her palm grew warm. Feeling a sense of security and tenderness, she had the courage to give the stranger's hand a light squeeze.

"I swear, I have no money—only forty fils, God is my witness . . ."

For some odd reason, which she could not fathom, she wished their conversation would go on longer. He was coming closer to her now. Giddily, she waited for him to speak to her in his gentle tone. She visualized this frantically and ingenuously, a sensation of numbness seeping into her body. She did not budge her hand as it lay in his, for fear of disturbing him. With a feeling of dreamlike ecstasy, she waited for him to take leave of his friend. These moments of waiting created for her a different world—a world of mistiness and of transparency.

He lifted up his hand and put his other hand on her shoulder. She imagined that he was young and tall . . . God! How wonderful to be so protected! . . . How sweet to surrender with a mind that was blank, just as her eyes were blank, to a gentle hand . . .

"You must be cold," he said to her, for he saw her in a tattered dress, with her feet bare and her hair disheveled. "Don't you have an old coat?"

"No," she answered, in a low voice.

She felt ashamed, as though she were appearing before him quite naked. She imagined that he was gazing intently at her eyes.

For a few moments the two of them stood silently, side by side, as if she'd known him for a long time. When his body softly and inadvertently nudged hers, she shivered with cold—or with something else . . .

Then he led her across the street to the other sidewalk. Cars were going by rapidly, and mud splattered her bare legs, but all fear and anxiety had left her, as though she were walking in an empty, open place. She wished that the street would widen endlessly and that she could go on walking like this, completely relaxed, yielding without difficulty, like a cat being stroked by a gentle hand . . . The street noises around her became quiet in a peculiar way . . .

When she got to the other side, she felt a cold piece of metal being pressed into her hand. She was afraid to close her palm on it, afraid that the hard metal would absorb the warmth she had been feeling there.

"Here, take this, this is for you."

"Uncle, God bless you, I don't want money," she answered spontaneously. There was something else she wanted to express, that was emerging elusively in her mind, but she felt him pat her shoulder and go away . . .

She fingered the piece of metal until she realised it was a ten-fils coin. At this, her heart throbbed with a great, spontaneous joy.

She sat at the entrance of a shop, bringing her legs together, laying her hands in her lap, and tucking her head between her shoulders like a turtle. She listened to the hubbub around her and to the sound of a drainpipe, whose waters were splashing onto the cobbles of the street with a loud, monotonous noise. Every now and then she could hear a roar of thunder—sometimes very far away and sometimes getting closer, almost at the nearby roofs, crashing above her head. The chill seeped through her cold and shivering body.

This went on until she heard the voice of her brother approaching, imitating the sound of a car horn. Then she heard the squealing of brakes coming out of his throat and laughed, raising her head.

"Where have you been, Dirty-Face?"

His face really was dirty—stained with burnt black oil—and his clothes were black and stiff as leather.

"I went to see our sister, but they wouldn't let me in."

"Why?"

"Whenever it rains, they won't let me in the house. They say I'll dirty the floor tiles."[1]

She went into a reverie and did not answer. Her thoughts were in a different world; her extinguished eyes gazed in the void; the moment of illumination shone in her like the whiff of a fragrance that had touched her lowly world . . . She was alone with him, crossing the tumultuous street, her hand in his, his tall figure shading her. This one time, her miserable life went to sleep and allowed her soul to be colored with a joyful green dream . . .

Sitting beside her, her brother eyed her affectionately. He was talking to her as though he were simply talking to himself: "You haven't seen the new house where our sister is working now . . . You'd think it was a palace, in a garden you'd think was Sa'dun Park!"

He gazed at her face. When he saw she was pensive, he nudged her with his elbow.

"Hey, Khairiyya, why are you so distracted? Don't you want to hear what I have to say?"

"What, Kazim? What were you saying?"

"I'm telling you about our sister's new house, in Karrada."[2]

"Yes?"

"New—first-class—"

"Did you go inside it?"

"Only once . . . My sister let me in. They had all gone to the cinema, and she was alone in the house. She let me into the kitchen—What a kitchen they have!—You'd think it was painted with milk! . . . I sat on a tiled floor that had a colorful design on it, and Badriyya brought me a plate full of rice and stew. I ate it all up! . . . "

He looked at her. She wasn't paying attention.

"Khairiyya, are you hungry?"

It was as if she hadn't heard him.

"Khairiyya . . . I'm talking to you. Have you eaten today?"

She roused herself and turned her head to him.

"Yes," she said, "I ate at Um Khamees's."

Kazim sighed. The shining kitchen, the brilliant plates, and the silvery pots and pans all loomed large in his imagination. These were sacred memories for him, brightly colored memories that were as fantastic as a dream, on which he nourished himself often, as would a little ram who'd been mistakenly put into a field rich with grass for just once in his life. A desire, harsh as hunger, rose up inside him

---

1. Tiled floors are a sign of a family's affluence. Floors in the homes of poor people are usually covered with mud.

2. An upper-class quarter of Baghdad.

now: the desire to feast once more on memory. In the deep lake of his soul a joy quivered, and he felt the sweetness of memory and licked his lips.

"Then she left and went away . . . Do you want to know the truth? I had not eaten my fill—not completely . . . I got up and went looking for more food. At a distance I saw a table with a large bowl full of apples, pomegranates, and oranges . . . It shone like the eye of the sun! I said to myself, 'This is your chance, Abu Jawad.[3] Why don't you snatch an apple or a pomegranate or something?'" I walked slowly, slowly, until I reached the bowl. At that moment I saw Badriyya, sitting at a dressingtable and putting on makeup—painting her eyebrows and lips . . . That damned girl, she copies their lifestyle! . . . I pretended to be looking at the small coffee tables, but suddenly Badriyya shouted at me, 'Why are you coming here? You'll dirty the carpets, and they'll scold me . . . '"

He fell silent for a moment, then took on a sly expression. "But she knew what I wanted, and said, 'I'm afraid you want an apple . . . All right, take one and get out. Don't let me see your face . . .'"

He closed his eyes and went limp. Then he said, in a dreamy voice, "What an apple! You'd think it was a melon, big enough to feed five people . . . "

He fell silent again, laying his cheek on his shoulder, gazing at the surface of the street. Then he said, in a tone of surprise, "But that damned Badriyya! . . . How beautiful she's become!"

And, as though aware he'd said something stupid, he continued, "But of course! . . . If she doesn't become beautiful, who will? Me? With my ugly face and my failed life? . . . "

He turned his face toward his sister and was surprised to see her cheeks wet with tears.

"Hey, Khairiyya! . . . You're crying! . . . By al-'Abbas,[4] tell me, what's bothering you today? Have those orchards your damned father left all been flooded?"[5] he asked sarcastically.

She remained silent. The drainpipe also had gone silent, and the spattering sound of the rain had subsided. She stretched out her hand to him, and it touched his chest.

What could she tell him? She herself did not know what had happened to her. She was fourteen years old and had never felt as devastated as she was feeling

---

3. In several Arab countries it is customary to call people by the name of their firstborn. Hence, a man whose eldest son is 'Amr will be called "Abu 'Amr," i.e., "Father of 'Amr." However, in the case of a bachelor, it is not unusual to call him "Abu the-name-of-his-choice," in order to achieve a greater respectability in addressing someone. Here Kazim calls himself "Abu Jawad."

4. Al-'Abbas was the son of 'Ali ibn Abu Talib, the Fourth Caliph and the originator of the Shi'a sect. 'Ali had married the Prophet's daughter, Fatima, and had several children by her, among whom were al-Hasan and al-Husain. 'Ali also married other women, and al-'Abbas was his son by one of these. Al-'Abbas is regarded as a saint and is believed to render a quick reward or a quick punishment. Hence, for Shi'ites, to swear by him is a serious matter.

5. Here, of course, Kazim is being ironic.

that day. It was as though two pincers had opened the closed shell of her heart. A bright light had crept into the dark corners of her soul . . .

She had been born blind. Her father had died before she had ever touched him or heard his voice, and her mother had followed a few years later. While her mother was alive, she had felt some sort of happiness, as if she'd had one eye; then that eye had been extinguished and total darkness had covered her life. Afterward her older sister had left her to work in the houses of the rich, and her brother had grown up and was working in an automobile service station. She remained alone, the world rising up in front of her like a thick wall that can't be broken through. She felt she was swimming in a murky darkness . . .

Every morning she sat next to Um Khamees, the baqilla vendor. There she would eat some food—bread soaked in simmering bean sauce. With the time passing very slowly, she would wait for her brother till noon; then she would wait for him again till evening, when he would sit with her a while before they both went to sleep in the same bed, in a little place walled by sheets of metal, which they shared with a group of peasants who had left the countryside and come to the city looking for work . . .

The next day she got up early, ate at Um Khamees's, and sat waiting for her brother.

It rained all morning, which made her fretful since the roads were becoming muddy and slippery, and the oozing mud would work its way into the fissures of her soles. She would become at one with this world, which frowned and disseminated meaningless anger . . .

When she sat down to eat, the rain was falling about a yard away from her.

"The poor! . . . " Um Khamees was saying plaintively, "Even God is angry with them! It may be that You have a purpose in this. God of the Blue Tent! . . . How often do I have to kindle this fire? It keeps dying out! . . . Ai! It's only the poor that He defeats! . . . "

Khairiyya listened to her as the rain came closer to the only dry spot left, until the whole area had become muddy.

She got up and felt her spirit ripping. The smell of extinguished embers from Um Khamees's stone fireplace rose to her nostrils . . . God! What kind of life was hers? Mud, rain, and blindness! . . . She was an orphan, always hungry and lost in this world . . .

"I must go to Kazim! I feel that my soul is about to leave my body!"

Her feet slipping on the soft, muddy pavement; she felt her way with her two hands.

"It's true, He must have a purpose in all this! . . . For I am blind, and the world is so slippery! . . ."

Walking through the rain-drenched alleys, she went to her brother. He was in the process of leaving the service station. On seeing her, he exclaimed, laughing:

"Hello there! . . . Hello there! . . . What a sight you are today—just like a gutter-worm!"

The rain had drenched her clothing, and her hair, which was dripping water onto her neck and exposed chest. Her teeth were chattering. She flung her hands around his shoulders and hugged him hard. She felt a warmth in the deepest part of her, and he felt intoxicated by a feeling of manliness, pride gleaming in his eyes.

Rushing out into the street, which was crowded with the carts of food vendors, he told her: "Ask for whatever you want! Your wish is my command!"

When she said nothing, he hurried over to a *kabab* vendor, and in two minutes came back with a couple of loaves and some pieces of *kabab*. They began to eat. As he ate automatically, he would frequently stop chewing to sing, in an acidic voice, some popular songs, just to make her happy.

Suddenly his voice died down.

He threw down his remaining piece of bread and went off. She stayed there waiting for him, the rain paralyzing her into patience. Desolation returned to her, and once again her spirit clouded over. She remained alone with the rain and the mud . . .

Using the wall for support, she made her way to the pavement of the large street. Then she shouted, "Uncle, please help me get across!"

Stretching out her hand in front of her, cocking her head to one side, and trying to gauge the pressure of the cold air on her face, she took a few short, cautious steps.

She remembered the warm hand that had reached out to her, and the moment of illumination, and the sweet, childish dream that had made the thick wall transparent, that had turned it into a gray mist that embraced her soul and opened in the deepest part of her female hunger, which stirred in her greedily and blindly. Then she relaxed into a kind of weary surrender, as though she'd found a green bench where she could take shelter, as though her sorrows had magically melted away or turned into an elusive, inscrutable joy.

After she finished recalling the images of that day, a luminous joy enfolded her soul. She turned to her brother and asked, "Kazim, I am pretty, aren't I?"

But she received no answer.

She reached out her hand, but it swam in a void.

"Hey, Kazim, have you left me again? What's going on with you today?"

She got to her feet, exclaiming, "Hey, Kazim! . . . Where have you gone?"

With her fingers she touched the hard, cylindrical pole. She drew nearer to it and put her arms around it.

"Uncle," she pleaded, "may God bless your dead! . . . Please help me to get across . . ."

And she awaited the hand that would reach out to her. As she waited, hope shone in her; she imagined that she would feel the touch of that warm hand again—one more time.

—*Translated by Lena Jayyusi and Thomas G. Ezzy*

Jamal Fayiz (b. 1964)

Born in Doha, Qatar, Jamal Fayiz obtained a B.A. in geography from the University of Qatar. He is the head of the Department of Cultural Activity at the General Department of Youth in Qatar and writes weekly for newspapers. He is the secretary of the Qatari *Al-Hayat* review and a member of the Literary Salon in the Jisra Club. A short-story writer, he is also a playwright and has had several plays acted on stage in Qatar, thus contributing to a nascent and active drama movement in his own country. He won the second Rashid Ibn Hameed Prize as a short-story writer in 1994 from Ajman, the United Aab Emirates, and has so far published two short-story collections: *Sara and the Locusts* (1991) and *Dancing on the Edge of the Wound* (1997).

THE REWARD

[1]

It was the second year running he'd won the prize for Best Employee. But it was the first time the new director of his department had attended the award ceremony. As the award was presented, by the director-general of the company, the director stood there clapping, then delivered a speech on behalf of the department, expressing his great joy that the award had been won by one of its employees. He would, he announced, be asking for a raise for the employee in due course, and he promised before everyone that he'd promote him if he should win the prize again the following year.

[2]

Next morning the employee went to the meeting room with the others, and the director indicated he should sit alongside him. He thanked him but said he'd prefer to sit with his colleagues. When the director repeated the invitation though, he went to sit next to him, awestruck as he looked down the table at the head of his section and the others attending.

The director cleared his throat, and everyone looked at him. He began once more to compliment the best employee, expressing his wish that all the other employees should strive to be like him. He ended his opening remarks with a joke that made people laugh till the tears streamed down their faces, and they fell off their chairs like so many autumn leaves or else shook as though a sudden earthquake had struck. All, that is, except for the best employee, who sat there looking serious and somber.

[3]

Three days later the employee went to the director's office, armed with a proposal for a new project.

"Computers," he said with a smile, after the usual greetings, "have the power of magic. If my project's implemented, the administration will be better organized. Its output will rise—"

"Leave the file with me," the director broke in. "I'll study it."

[4]

Over the following days he kept asking the director about his proposed new project, but all to no avail. Eventually the director started referring him to his secretary.

[5]

After three months he could only get to see the director by special permission— the director ordered him to submit anything he wanted through his secretary. He was surprised at this. He asked the secretary if he could see the director, and his request was rejected, first orally then in writing. Still he insisted; he must see him, he said. The days passed, but still his resolve never wavered. Finally he received a bombshell exploding in his face—and a piece of paper that said, "Thank you for your services"

—*Translated by Salwa Jabsheh and Christopher Tingley*

Sulaiman Fayyad (b. 1929)

Egyptian short-story writer and novelist Sulaiman Fayyad was educated at Al-Azhar University and taught at the Teachers' Training College in Al-Giza, Cairo. He fought as a volunteer in the 1948 Palestine War in Gaza. He is a member of the Cinema Guild of Film Makers and has made contributions to radio and television. A socialist, he believes in realist and socially critical fiction, beliefs that are reflected with sensitivity in his work. He has published six collections of short stories and one novel to date and is currently preparing a comprehensive dictionary of the Arabic verb in all its facets—semantic, phonetic, and grammatical—as a basis for the development of modern Arabic. His short-story collections include *June's Sorrows* (1969), *The Eyes* (1972), *Time of Fog and Silence* (1974), *The Picture and the Shadow* (1976), *A Woman with Honey-Colored Eyes* (1992), and *The Cocoon* (1997). His novel, *Voices*, has been translated into English by Husam Abu al-'Ula.

THE GRAY-COLORED VEHICLE

Suddenly he spots them, just a short distance away, lurking. The white *gallabiyya*s they wear give them away in the dim light of night. They are standing at the mouth of the side alley off the old road, exactly between the two street corners. They are whispering softly and they glance up often toward him. They seem to be in on something, lying in wait for someone, some passer-by ... Lying in wait for *him!* For him alone! ... They are positioned right between him and Zaitun Station,[1] and the train to Al-Khanikah,[2] to Khadija ... All of a sudden they seem to grow larger. They loom as shadows do, across the sands, or on walls in the light of a setting sun, or in the light of a dim lantern that swings back and forth: like terror, like fear; like nightmare; like the moment of pain in a severe illness or the anguish of total poverty and the hunger it brings in its wake, with no hope of deliverance, with only shame for oneself and anxiety over wife and children ...

What do they want, these two? The two pounds in his pocket? He stops in his tracks. This has been a cursed night from the beginning, he thinks to himself, certain that if he advances even one step further he will never get to Khadija. He will never reach the station, or the train, or Al-Khanikah. The two pounds will be lost and he with them—fallen in the street, slain or wounded, to remain there till morning ...

He affects an air of nonchalance and begins to move carefully, so that they do not notice he is backing away and run out to take hold of him. In his mind an idea is flashing: to appear to be slowly advancing, but in reality to sidle backward until he is far enough away to break into a run and disappear into the winding alleyways before they can reach him; then, to find another, safer, way of getting to the station ...

Now he feels he is far enough away. He can no longer see them and, consequently, they can no longer see him. Perhaps they will never see him again; perhaps they will think they missed him in the dark ... But perhaps even now they have started after him! Stealing along toward him under cover of the walls, the old archways, the huge square pillars ...

---

1. A station in Cairo
2. A popular quarter in Cairo

He turns suddenly, assailed by terror, the specter of all the possible dangers on a dark, inscrutable night, in a dreamlike reality. He starts to run, taking as much care as he can that his military boots make no sound against the street's asphalt, the trolley tracks, or the pavement tiles. He runs in his favorite, well-practiced style, in a semicrouch, to give his steps extra speed and steadiness. He runs in an irregular pattern—on the pavement, between the tracks, under the archways, and in the open space of the street. The street seems wide and shaded, like a dome, like a desert in a dream, like the sea at sunset; like mute space through which the dream carries him, stretched out on his back or sitting, flying wing-less over buildings, trolley tracks, eagles' nests, treetops, the crescent-shaped iron arcs atop the minarets, the crosses outstretched on church towers . . . He is aware as he runs that he is in reality and in a dream as well: in a reality like a dream, in a dream like reality. The nightmarish confusion of this awareness makes him feel he is on the verge of suffocating, of screaming, of resisting, of surrendering to death and the rhythm of terror. He is afraid to enter the alleyways for fear of finding himself closed in by it on all sides and thus more vulnerable to its onslaught. The old street, narrow by day but spacious and long at night, gives him greater freedom to escape. Yet amidst this freedom he will be exposed to *them*. They will be able to see him wherever he goes. He wants to collapse in the street or call out for help to whomever there may be behind the doors and windows, to the desk clerks in the entrance halls of the hotels . . .

Then all at once he sees help, in the form of a van parked nearby to his left, where the road runs into the square. In the light of the cigarette shop there he catches a glimpse of some of his confreres, whom he normally hates. One of them stands smoking near the front of the vehicle, learning on it. This must be the driver; the others must be sitting inside the van. They are now his only succor in the sleeping street, his only means to Al-Zaitun, Al-Khanikah, and Khadija.

The color of the van is indistinct in the weak light that filters into the square from dusty lanterns and the windows of the shop. None of the light falls directly on the men, and he sees them as dream figures. He recognizes them by their woolen coats, the red bands around their arms, the berets worn tight over their heads and held fast like iron rings.

These are night guards. Everyone regards them with misgivings, as people regard regular Army soldiers with fearful apprehension and the civil police with wariness. He himself, whenever he sees them, always feels an instinctive guilt, a sense that he has done something wrong. Yet now he is completely drawn to them. They alone are his means to safety, to Al-Khanikah and Khadija.

They are sitting in the luminous darkness of his night dream, on two wooden benches that extend the length of the back of the van. A large rectangle of color-less canvas, held in place by separate iron rings, covers them like a tunnel. Their backs are bent, their elbows rest on their knees, their hands are clasped, and their eyes are trained on the square as they survey it and keep their watch through the back opening of the vehicle's carriage. He realizes that they have seen him and he knows he needs them. At the same time, he might have a button missing, his beret on crooked, his collar open, his clothes rumpled. In a panic he fumbles with his uniform, driven by fear of scrutiny, his fear of the night guards . . .

He is in front of them now, near the opening in the back of the van. He sees there are four of them. None of them speak. They fix their eyes on him. With difficulty he makes an effort to control his panting, his agitation.

"Good evening, Patrol."

He is answered by a nod from one of the guards—a studied, controlled gesture.

"There are two thieves," he says. "They are lying in wait for me. They want my money."

They gaze at him with indifference.

"There," he adds, "in that street. By the Bab al-Hadid Square."[3]

They remain unmoved.

"I am on a short leave," he cries, begging for help. "My wife has left me, in anger, and gone to Al-Khanikah. My children are very small. They are lost without her."

One of the heads ducks back. A finger taps on the glass of the small window of the cab, where the driver is. A hand with its fingers closed tight signals him to wait a little. Then the hand makes a gesture that tells him that the driver will be following them shortly.

One by one they leap from the vehicle, as if answering the call of a siren that cannot be heard. They fall in around him; then with him they start forward, in step, at double-quick time. He gets an urge to laugh: four grown-up men, bounding about like children, playing a little game . . .

At the head of the street they split up into two groups. Each jumps under the archways on both sides. Mahjoub finds himself alone in the middle of the street. They egg him on in hissing whispers that make him want to run back to his children, to wait until morning and see then to the matter of his wife, with greater clarity. But he is afraid to turn back.

The two men are still there, talking in whispers. Glancing up at him as they did before, one after the other. Always glancing, conspiring, waiting for him . . .

Before he gets there, before they make a move, two of the night guards are on them, and the other two rush at them from across the road. There is no argument: no one speaks, no one utters a word. Simply, the guards surround them and begin to hit him. The two men retaliate. Hands, feet, and the sounds of heavy breathing are intermingled. Watching all this, Mahjoub feels a sudden immobility, a paralysis, like a heart attack, like the impact of a thunderbolt, the sudden rush of a car from a side street at a person running and unable to stop. He finds himself without a role. It occurs to him to continue on his way to the Al-Zaitun train or to turn his back on a quarrel that seems, at that moment, not to concern him at all.

---

3. This is the main Cairo station. It has a statue of Ramses II set up in the square facing it, with a fountain playing at its feet.

Suddenly his attention is drawn to the cry of one of the guards: "The son of a bitch has run away!"

"Should we chase him?" a voice calls back.

"No need. This one is enough for now. We can find out who the other is from him."

Mahjoub is about to thank the night guards and hurry along to the station, but at that moment the van roars up on them from out of the darkness, its horn blaring, the ground trembling beneath its weight. It screeches to a halt, leaving deep ruts in the ground, scattering broken pebbles.

The man in the white *gallabiyya* shouts: "I haven't done anything!"

One of the night guards, fiercer than the others, pushes him toward the vehicle carriage. "Get in!"

"Where are you taking me?"

"Don't ask. It's none of your business."

"Whose business is it, then?"

The fierce one slaps him. "Shut up! Get in!"

The man in the white *gallabiyya* gets in. Mahjoub thinks of taking his leave: let the guards take the man to hell itself . . . Two of the guards climb in after the man, and then two more. Mahjoub remains standing. He does not understand what is happening. He is about to thank them when a voice comes from inside the vehicle: "Get in."

Stunned, he looks at them, asking himself, "Why should *I* get in?"

"And the train?" he reminds them. "I will miss the train . . . "

The same voice answers: "That is not our business. Get in."

He has no choice. "Alright."

The guard says, "We will give you a ride afterward . . . to Al-Khanikah . . . "

Al-Khanikah?! How do they know he is on his way there? Mahjoub is struck to the heart with terror: perhaps this is a dream after all! His skin prickles with fear, all the way to his scalp. He remembers what his grandfather told him once: "If your arm were a policeman, you should cut it off . . . Cut off even your right hand before you ever resort to the court . . ." And now he finds himself riding with them, like a man drugged and controlled by others. Opposite him sits the man in the white *gallabiyya*.

The vehicle plunges them across the street, past Station Square and onto that very long avenue, flooded with light, which leads to the open desert. The man in the white *gallabiyya* shouts at them, "Are you taking me to the police precinct?"

No one answers. Mahjoub thinks that no doubt they are taking him to the precinct, for this is police business. He thinks of the charge he will be asked to make against this man, but can find nothing specific. He assures himself that there must be some sort of charge, or the night guards would not have taken the man into custody.

"But what is the charge against me?" resumes the man in the white *gallabiyya*. When no one answers, he tries to make light of the whole matter.

"Is it because I am still up at this hour? *Everyone* stays up . . . Look at all those private cars running around with people in them . . . " He laughs, then adds, "Here's one being driven by a woman. Why don't you ask her where she's been and where she's going?"

No one answers him. And no one laughs with him.

"Is it because I am still up *without* a private car?"

No one answers, so he repeats his question: "Put my mind at rest—what is the charge against me?"

No one answers, so he shouts: "Tell me the charge against me! Then I'll stop bothering you and be quiet . . . I'll even accept a death sentence from you! All I want to know is, *why?*"

His outburst sinks into the depths of the dark, silent night. It is lost in the rumble of tires, under the treading of feet returning home just before daybreak, with its diffused rays of radiant light . . .

Once his cry has faded, the fierce guard growls, without turning to look at him, "Shut up!"

But the man in the white *gallabiyya* does not shut up. He continues shouting, "What is the charge against me? I didn't do anything! I didn't plan to do anything! I didn't steal, I didn't kill . . . "

Deep inside Mahjoub something surges and leaves him thoroughly shaken. He must, immediately, emerge from this dream game. He makes a great effort to doze off but cannot. Everything is a nightmare: the guards, the vehicle, the night, the man in the white *gallabiyya,* and the blurred objects—trees, blocks of building, street lamps—that flash into sight and recede into darkness in quick succession.

The man in the white *gallabiyya* is not a dream, Mahjoub thinks; even now, he is deceiving him and the night guards by feigning innocence. But the pounding of Mahjoub's heart increases to the point where it aches with pain and terror, and he realizes what this means: the man in the white *gallabiyya* has had no evil intent toward him. But then, why did he put up a struggle? And why did his friend run away? And why is he shouting now, so vehemently? Mahjoub thinks: the innocent one shouts and the accuser shouts; the defense shouts and the prosecution shouts. Only the public keeps silent, as do the night guards, as do the judges who sit stony-faced until the rapping of the gavel is needed to protect the prosecution from the voice of the man in the white *gallabiyya* and from his defense . . .

At the end of the protracted protest, one of the night guards shouts at the man in the white *gallabiyya,* "Shut up!" He reaches out his hand and slaps him, as though he were silencing the other secret reverie that wells up in the man's heart. The man gasps at the force of the blow and moans. Mahjoub senses the man's blood streaming down his chin. He does not see it, but he feels it when he sees the man's hand wiping his mouth. Mahjoub feels he has to speak, and not appear soft in what he says to him.

"Don't you and your friend waylay people who pass by on the road?" he asks, accusingly.

Despite the slap, and the blood, the man laughs and cries out mockingly: "I? We are the ones who waylay people on the road? And what are *you* doing now?"

The guard who slapped him is furious. He brings his hand up tight against his chest, then lashes out at the man's face with the back of it. The weight of the blow falls on the nose. The man stands, clutching his nose in pain, but two of the others pin him down. The vehicle shakes with the struggle. The man in the white *gallabiyya* cries out for help from passersby, from sleepers, but the vehicle hurtles along. No one wakes out of his slumber. No passerby pays any attention. Perhaps because the whole thing is happening in a gray-colored vehicle . . .

At last the man says, "Let us go to the police."

He pleads, again, "Take me to the police."

The fierce guard replies, "We are not at your service, or at the service of the police. We will take you where we like."

The man in the white *gallabiyya* realizes, and Mahjoub realizes with him, that a bizarre and terrifying drama is about to take place. The man explodes, cursing, and swearing. The guards hold down his hands and give him several quick blows across the face. He stops cursing and swearing.

Mahjoub, afraid that his turn will also come, asks him, "Well then, why were you standing there with your friend?"

One of the guards frowns at him in disapproval of his question, his weakness. But the fierce guard says, "Answer! Speak up! Why were you standing there with your friend? Why did you accost one of us in the street after midnight?"

The man, still overcome with weeping, turns his face to Mahjoub, as though telling him that he is the cause of his misfortune.

"I?" he says. "Did I subject you to any harm, Sergeant?"

Mahjoub is silent for a moment. Then he asks, "Why were you there, talking and pointing at me?"

The man cries out in amazement. "What is happening tonight? Have I fallen among madmen?"

Madmen! The word jolts Mahjoub, stirs up his shame. He realizes he was just being foolish, and still is. Two people talking together, he thinks to himself, what is the crime in that? And if one of them should happen to point to the other or at anyone else . . . But it was happening at night, damn it! Couldn't they have found another place for their conversation?

"You were pointing at me!" he shouts, thrusting aside his shame and embarrassment in front of the night guards. "You were about to attack me!"

The eyes of the man in the white *gallabiyya* open wide. Sobbing and laughter blend in his throat, pleading and swearing.

"Me? I've never seen you, except in this vehicle!"

"Stick to the subject!" a guard shouts at him.

Without turning his head he says, "I have not deviated from the subject." Then he says to Mahjoub, harshly, assertively, as though he has just realised it, "You are the cause, then!"

Then he asks him, "Don't you have a wife?"

At this point a guard slaps him. Mahjoub puts out his hand to shield him, and the guard yells scornfully, "Have you weakened? He is talking about your wife!"

Mahjoub is at a loss. What is he to do? He takes refuge in silence. The man in the white *gallabiyya* rescues him from his embarrassment.

"You have a wife, and you have children, is that not so?" He does not wait for an answer, but adds, "I, too, have a wife and children, and I was . . . "

"Sure, of course you were!" shouts the fierce guard. "Come off it! Since you have a wife and kids, why aren't you home taking care of them, watching over them like a hen?"

The guards laugh. Mahjoub does not laugh. No anger shows in the man in the white *gallabiyya*. Mahjoub realises what has happened. He can almost phrase the man's next words before the man says them: "And where is she now? I wanted her to return to me for the sake of the kids . . . "

"Ah!" Mahjoub sighs, his voice rising in pitch. "And the other man who was with you?"

"He is my wife's brother. I was trying to work out with him how to get my angry wife to return home, but he was being obstinate."

Mahjoub is speechless. The guards remain silent. They do not look at the man in the white *gallabiyya*. They look only at Mahjoub. He feels their mocking eyes. Their gaze is fixed upon his face, taunting, humiliating. Yet they neither chide, nor blame, nor turn against him.

"Another trick you're playing on us!" shouts one of the guards. "You can be sure that we're not taken in by lies—especially by obvious lies, like this lie of yours!"

The man in the white *gallabiyya* swears that his story is true. Mahjoub believes him: he, too, had been on his way to bring back his wife from her family's home . . .

"If a man wants to make up with his wife," says the guard, "is it likely he'll spend his time standing with her so-called brother in the street?"

All four burst out, in rapid succession, muzzling him:

"Why didn't you go to her house, then?"

"Why didn't you meet her brother at his house, instead of out in the street after midnight?"

"Listen—you're a liar!"

"And a thief!"

"Listen—why did your friend run away then?"

"Why did you fight us when we arrested you?"

"You were resisting the government!"

When the barrage of questions is lifted, the man in the white *gallabiyya* is silent for a long time. Then he starts laughing vexedly, in a voice choked with weeping. He beats one hand with the other.

Mahjoub realizes that no one would be able to answer those questions. He knows many of these games, plays them on the soldiers under his command, as do officers on him whenever they are angry at him. He, too, had been on the way to bring back his wife: it would have been possible for any guard or police-man to stop him in the same fashion and accuse him of a crime that had taken place in the next neighborhood; or, to stop him as he was returning with his wife and say to him, "Prove that she is your wife . . . "

He screams in his heart of hearts: A curse on everything!

He hears the man in the white *gallabiyya* muttering through his teeth, "Dogs! Bastards!" then resuming his sobs. Mahjoub would like to rescue him from this predicament, from the night and the vehicle and these guards.

He says to the night guards, "Let's let him go . . . I—I forgive him."

The night guards laugh, and the man goes on weeping.

"Be quiet," one of them warns Mahjoub.

"You put us through a lot of trouble for your sake," a second adds, "and then you go and weaken, like a woman!"

The fierce one adds, "He cursed us. He has to be punished for what he did to you, and to us."

Mahjoub feels that their glee and excitement have reached fever pitch. They have found something to do this night. He resumes his silence.

"Dogs! Dogs!" exclaims the man in the white *gallabiyya* again.

Mahjoub cries out to him in pity: "Don't say that! Don't say that!"

He feels that because of his insults they are going to wreak a terrible ven-geance on him. They laugh together in the man's and in Mahjoub's face. Out of terror and vexation, Mahjoub is about to laugh with them as well. He occupies himself with looking out of the vehicle. The smell of the desert, the night dew, and the coolness of air fill his nostrils. The lights of the street lamps have disap-peared. All hope is extinguished. The desert is still dark, and the night, like the sea on a summer evening, is heavy, still, and damp . . .

The man looks around, cries out in fear as he sees the desert through the back opening of the vehicle.

"Where are you taking me?"

The night guards laugh. "We are going to hold a military tribunal for you!"

"For me? What an honor!" he blurts, in a flash of hysterical panic. Then he protests, "But I am not a soldier!"

"You had resolved to attack a soldier. And you resisted us."

"I never resolved any such thing!" insists the man, pleading. "And I didn't resist you. I didn't see who you were in the dark. Relieve me!" In the silence that follows he bursts out, "Then why? Why then? Why?" And the words slip out: "Did I commit your crime?"

These words, involuntarily spoken, rob him of his speech. They prompt the guard to ask him, with a sly and provocative hatred, "And what is our crime?"

The man in the white *gallabiyya* answers dully, as though in a trance:

"Kidnapping someone from the street."

With teeth clenched, the guard asks him in the same tone, "And what else?"

"Listen, why are you against me?" returns the man in the white *gallabiyya*. "I am not your enemy." Then he mutters, audibly, "If I *were* an enemy, an armed enemy, you never would have dreamed of kidnapping me ... "

Mahjoub fervently hopes that no one has heard him. The fierce guard slaps him, shouting, "Shut up, you dog!"

Immediately, as though on a cue the driver has been listening for, the vehicle jerks to a convulsive halt, shuddering in fright.

Two of the guards promptly jump out. The fierce one pushes the man in the white *gallabiyya* toward the opening and bellows, "Get down!"

The man in the white *gallabiyya* lifts the hem of his garment as he steps out onto the vehicle's footrests. All at once he jumps, clearing them, and runs away into the night and the desert. Two guards chase him. He swerves toward the dunes, which are now outlined in the light of the false dawn. His feet sink into the soft sand. His steps grow heavy. His pace slows. The guards seize him. They bring him back, beating him all the while as he submits to their blows.

"What are you going to do with me?" he cries out fearfully, once they are back at the vehicle. He turns to Mahjoub and pleads, "Tell them, Sergeant, I didn't do anything ... "

"Shut up, you dog!" roars the fierce one

"I?" The man's retort is surely suicidal. "I? *You* are the dogs! ... Dogs! ... Bastards!"

They walk him a distance through the desert to the slope of the mountain. Mahjoub is afraid of lagging behind and being reprimanded, of staying apart from the man in the white *gallabiyya,* whom they may well be about to liquidate. He follows them. They stop.

"Leave him," the fierce one says.

"But he will run away."

The guard laughs with relish. The others understand and smile. They leave the man in the white *gallabiyya* free to go.

"But where should I go?" he pleads, "Don't leave me in the desert. My children are at home."

The guard in front of him gives him a push. "Go to them," he says, friendly, persuasive. "And hurry. This is your chance."

The man in the white *gallabiyya* looks around him warily. He stares into their faces, one by one, and stops at Mahjoub. The light of the false dawn is not enough for either of them to see the other's face clearly.

"Should I go?"

Mahjoub turns to the guard for reassurance.

The guard's face is smiling. "Yes," he says, innocently, "Let him go. We have pardoned him."

The man in the white *gallabiyya* turns to Mahjoub. "*You* say. Should I go?"

Mahjoub thinks for a moment, hesitant because of the guard's innocent smile. Whether he stays or goes, he will not escape. He says to the man in the white *gallabiyya,* "Yes. Go."

Mahjoub turns his face away from him.

The man in the white *gallabiyya* realises that he will not be saved, he will not escape. He does not run . . . he starts off slowly, like one who has lost hope and surrendered. Mahjoub watches him trudge away, his feet heavy in the soft sand. He wishes he would make a break for it, on the chance he might get away. He wants to shout at him to run, to drop to the ground, to crawl . . .

Suddenly he sees the guard unholster his revolver and quickly take aim. Mahjoub's impulse is to throw himself against the guard's hand, to cry out a warning of imminent death. But in his mind's eye he sees his house and children and Khadijah; he sees the sunshine and the light of the moon. He turns his face away, withdrawing into himself. Out of the corner of his eye he sees the guard's hand grip the gun, firm and unwavering. His finger pulls the trigger. The discharge shatters the night air and the calm of the desert. The mountain reechoes its reverberations. Mahjoub hears an enormous cry, its echo embraces the echo of death. He turns toward the man in the white *gallabiyya:* his arms are up and flailing, he falls on his face like a stone, as though the bullet has struck him in the head or heart. He writhes for a second, then is still. No dust stirs, nor does the morning star fall tumbling into emptiness, nor does the mountain sink in shock . . .

The fierce one blows coolly on the barrel of his gun, stone-faced, as is done in movies. Silence reigns over the mountain and the desert, over the night guards and the false dawn, which is now dissipating. The guards move silently, away from the man in the white *gallabiyya,* and return to the gray-colored vehicle. Mahjoub sees that now they are five. It takes him a minute to realize that the driver is with them.

The driver looks at him suspiciously. The fierce one looks at him suspiciously. They all look at him suspiciously. Mahjoub's heart sinks between his ribs. He feels like a mouse in the eyes of a cat.

"Did you see anything?" asks the fierce one.

Mahjoub swallows. He grabs on to the thread that has been thrown out to him and immediately answers, "No. I saw nothing."

"Did you hear anything?"

"No. I heard nothing."

"Did I say anything?"

"No. You did not say anything."

Another guard asks, "And I?"

Mahjoub says instantly, "You did not say anything."

A wave of sincerity engulfs Mahjoub. He cries, pleading, asserting to ward off all evil, "We did not say anything! We did not see anything! We did not hear anything! Nothing happened! Nothing, nothing at all! Nothing, nothing . . . "

The fierce guard smiles and puts his hand on Mahjoub's shoulder.

"You are one of us," he says.

Back at the steps of the van, everyone climbs in. The vehicle's motor is running. The face of the fierce one looks out and says to him, "Get in."

He does not get in. He tries to get in. He does not get in.

"Don't you want to get in?"

Mahjoub shakes his head. "No thank you," he says politely.

"Alright, laugh!" the fierce one commands him.

Mahjoub laughs until tears come.

"Alright, wipe your tears," the fierce one says.

Mahjoub wipes his cheeks.

The fierce one laughs. "We will take you to Al-Khanikah. We told you that before."

"I know," Mahjoub answers. "You will take me to. Al-Khanikah. I know. You said that."

"Alright," the fierce one says, "you are free."

The vehicle jerks to a start and moves away. Mahjoub stays rooted to his spot. He feels the ground move backward with him on it. Toward the man in the white *gallabiyya*. Then suddenly the ground is moving him forward, toward the gray-colored vehicle. There is impact. He falls, crushed.

He remembers that at home he wears a white *gallabiyya*.

—*Translated by Lena Jayyusi and Thomas G. Ezzy*

Khalil al-Fuzayyi' (b. 1944)

Saudi short-story writer Khalil al-Fuzayyi' has worked as a journalist in the Eastern province and, like so many other writers from the area, writes much about the past but also about universal human experience, at times mixing realism with nostalgic notions and at others offering a comic description of human behavior. He has published several collections of short stories, among which are *The Clock and the Palm Tree* (1977) and *Women and Love* (1978).

The Autumn of Life

Nothing pleased the people of our village more than a wedding celebration. Consequently, as soon as even the idea of marriage crossed someone's mind, the whole village rushed to nominate this girl or that as the prospective bride. Sometimes this was carried out in people's minds without being made the subject of general conversation; at other times it would become the major topic of conversation in the village. There were times, moreover, when some went so far as to consider a marriage between two people as settled, when in fact both the girl and the man involved were in complete ignorance of the matter. This tendency had become a common tradition with us, and was as much a part of our daily lives as the sequence of night and day. It may have given rise to curiosity, interest, or even bewilderment among newcomers to the village, but they soon became accustomed to it—the way they became accustomed to the many other peculiarities of our beloved village.

One of these village peculiarities was Um 'Ulaiwi. She was an imposing woman—much more imposing than a woman ought to be—and she had a sharp and vicious tongue. Nevertheless, she could be the soul of kindness—that kindness that was typical of our village folk—and despite her hard and relentless appearance, she had a soft heart that was full of love. Although she had never born any sons, she had inevitably been called by the name "Um 'Ulaiwi".[1] Her marriage had lasted only ten years and had resulted, to her disadvantage, in only three daughters, who were expected, like all other village girls of their age, to stay at home drying palm leaves and turning them into artifacts, baskets, hand fans, etc., in their free time. Um 'Ulaiwi's marriage had ended traumatically, for she had lost her husband when he drowned during a spell of the heaviest rainfall the village had ever seen. This rain had frozen and had fallen in hailstones as big as watermelons. The village butcher always claimed that this was a lie he could never believe. He had come to live in the village years after that particular winter, and when they told him the story, he refused to believe a word of it and claimed that it had to be greatly exaggerated. This was not the butcher's major flaw, however. His major flaw was simply the fact that he was a butcher, for his profession was not held in high esteem by our village. Other artisans with skills like his, such as bakers, blacksmiths, and carpenters, were nonexistent in our village because in our eyes these professions were regarded as degrading and not fit for any proud and worthy person.[2] Needless to say, those persons who were most convinced of this scale of social status were the same people who would not hesitate at any time to commit theft or assault others, without any feelings of guilt.

Um 'Ulaiwi's life followed a humdrum routine. Her daughters stayed at home while she worked in the field that she had inherited from her husband. Her elderly uncle, who was old enough to prefer the prospect of death to that of facing Um 'Ulaiwi's bad temper, helped her manage her affairs.

The village had been going through a bit of a slump, and people were eager for exciting news. So, when a rumor of Nasser the butcher's intention to marry arose, it spread like a fire among dry stalks. A thousand questions popped into people's minds as to who would be the poor unfortunate girl who was fated to marry a butcher. Pointed fingers fixed on spinsters, divorcees, or widows—which included, of course, Um 'Ulaiwi.

"Why shouldn't Um 'Ulaiwi be the bride?" one of them asked.

---

1. This means "the mother of 'Ulaiwi." In other Arab countries, she might have been called by the name of her firstborn girl, but here she is called by the name of a son she has never born, perhaps as a good omen, so that she will have one some day.

2. Manual work has traditionally been looked down on by Arabs since pre-Islamic times, and classical Arabic poetry is full of allusions to this.

As the majority of the villagers would never have consented in any case to the marriage of their daughters or sisters to a butcher, no one would be better suited to this match than Um 'Ulaiwi. For fear of her sharp tongue, no one had yet considered marrying her. But when rumors of the butcher's marriage intentions reached Um 'Ulaiwi's ears, she began yearning for one concrete sign that Nasser was actually considering her. For, in spite of all other considerations, she still longed for the warmth and contentment that married life offers, as well as for a husband to protect her and look after her affairs. She had often wondered what would become of her once her daughters had married and as she grew older. A good husband was what would protect her from the treachery of time. She was no longer young—this was something that she had never denied—but neither was she all that old, for she was hoping that her life's journey would be a long one. She was not yet forty, and Nasser could not be less than fifty. Age in this case was not an issue; they were close in this respect, and many women her age had married and spent the rest of their lives in peaceful happiness. Had she not been rumored to be so sharp-tongued, she would have found a husband to accept her long ago. And besides, the butcher, as she knew from her frequent trips to buy meat from him, had many fine qualities that other village men, who claimed to be above him, lacked.

As soon as she heard that the butcher was thinking of getting married, she wished with all her heart that he would propose to her. After making sure that her daughters were not around, she asked one of her friends, "Haven't you heard what everyone's saying about Nasser the butcher? He's thinking of getting married . . . "

"How silly of you to ask!" answered her friend. "Of course I've heard! Hasn't everyone?"

Um 'Ulaiwi probed further, asking, "What else have you heard?"

She asked this in a cunning manner, which did not pass unnoticed by her friend, who answered, "I've heard that he intends to ask you to marry him."

Um 'Ulaiwi feigned anger, but she made no answer and kept herself busy clearing the coffee things and preparing to offer another cup to her friend, who had already consumed an enormous quantity of dates.

"Honestly, be frank . . . " pressed her friend. "Are you willing to have him for a husband or not?"

"All I want is a good ending to my life," answered Um 'Ulaiwi.

And then she managed to change the subject quickly, worried that her friend might find out her true feelings on the whole matter.

As she was seeing her friend off, her uncle came rushing in, his face beaming and his cloak about to slip off his shoulders.

"Good news, my niece! Good news!"

"May it be the best of news," she said, with an anxiety she made no attempt to hide.

But he went on, without paying any attention to what she had said: "Nasser the butcher wants to pay us a visit tonight, after dinner!"

So, the rumors had been correct after all . . . Here he was, taking the crucial, decisive step . . . She felt lucky he was thinking of her. Immediately her mind flooded with all kinds of thoughts: of the wedding, of her daughters, of the happiness she would find; of the autumn of her life into which she was about to put as much spring as it was in her power to; of her poor dead husband . . . People would certainly condemn her for having a butcher for a husband . . . of a man presiding over her household.

But her uncle, who was leaning on his stick, did not give her much of a chance to go on with her contemplation. He wanted to know how she felt about the visit.

Surprised that he needed to ask, she answered, "Of course he's welcome."

Her happiness was beyond description. She wanted to tell everyone around of Nasser's intentions. She considered telling her daughters—or at least her eldest daughter, who was already seventeen—but she decided to wait until things were finalized. Then she would break the news to all her daughters, for she was sure that their happiness would match hers . . .

After evening prayers her uncle called in a few of the neighbors, and Nasser arrived. As was the custom, Um 'Ulaiwi remained inside, waiting impatiently for the moment her uncle would come to tell her of Nasser's proposal.

Time passed slowly as the men discussed issues pertaining to the marriage. As for her daughters, they were unaware of what was happening, for they were used to having their uncle come and spend the evening with neighbors after prayers.

Um 'Ulaiwi who had been dreaming of her impending marriage to Nasser, had defended him strongly whenever any of the other women had criticized him. She often explained these attacks to herself as due to jealousy and envy, and God help anyone who stood against her opinion, for to her he was an honest, flawless, and good man, regardless of what everyone else might think.

She was tempted to sneak through the corridor to eavesdrop on some of the men's conversation, for that gathering happened to be the most important event in her life. She mustered up patience and decided against it; but time was passing so slowly, and the whole matter needed no time at all . . .

Finally came her release from suffering: even before she saw him, she could sense her uncle's approach. He was about to break out dancing with joy. However, his line of thinking at that moment was very far from hers, definitely not aware of the calamity that was about to fall.

"Nasser the butcher is asking for your eldest daughter's hand in marriage," he said.

It wasn't really the uncle's fault. He had been thinking of her eldest daughter all along, for in the village it was not unheard of for mature men to marry younger girls; Um 'Ulaiwi had encouraged the visit when he mentioned it to her, and it had never crossed his mind that she had been thinking of her own marriage. But now, as soon as she heard his words, she jumped at him like a rampaging hurricane. In an endless stream of slanderous words she cursed the butcher, the butcher's father and grandfather, and as many of his ancestors as she found possible to think of.

—Translated by Sharif Elmusa and Thomas G. Ezzy

Fat-hi Ghanim (1924–1998)

Fat-hi Ghanim was a major Egyptian writer of fiction, though, like many of his generation, he has tended to live in the shadow of Naguib Mahfouz and other more prominent figures. Following graduation from the School of Law at Cairo University, he initially worked as a civil servant, and it was while working in his administrative capacity that he was inspired to write his first fictional works: *A Gilden Irona*, a collection of short stories, and *Al-Jabal* (The Mountain) (1965), a novel that deals with the intrigues surrounding the smuggling of ancient Egyptian antiquities in Upper Egypt and the plans to move people to a "modernized" village. From the outset Ghanim has experimented with fictional techniques, something reflected both in his short stories—in such collections as *The Experience of Love* (1958) and *The Spiked Iron Fence* (1964)—and in his celebrated multinarrator, four-part novel *The Man Who Lost His Shadow* (1966), which was translated into English by Desmond Stewart in 1966. He continued in this experimental vein, with varying degrees of success, in a stream of novels, including *Those Days* (1966), with its fracturing of narrative time; *The Idiot* (1966), where the narrative is viewed through the lens of a mentally handicapped person; and *Hot and Cold* (1970), which incorporates an almost Joycean stream of consciousness technique. More recent contributions include *A Little Love and a Lot of Violence* (1985), *A Girl from Shubra* (1986), *Ahmad and Daud* (1989), and *Woman of Beauty* (1991). Wider recognition of Ghanim's contributions to Arabic fiction has recently come in the form of the Saddam Hussein Prize for Literature (1989) and the Egyptian State Prize for Literature (1995).

THE ENGAGEMENT PRESENT

Ibrahim 'Abd al-'Aal al-Halawani was no ordinary man. A stickler for morality, he'd never told a lie in his life, either a harmless white one or the really harmful black sort. He hated malice and double-dealing and couldn't bear to see the accepted way of doing things flouted. All this made him a shade neurotic. Whenever he encountered something wrong, or found out an immoral act, his eyes would glisten, the veins on his neck would bulge, and his voice would turn shrill.

His upbringing could well have had something to do with it. His father, Haj 'Abd al-'Aal al-Halawani, had been a big landowner in Sharqiyya province and a good and virtuous man, who'd died when Ibrahim was ten years old, leaving in Ibrahim's heart a splendid memory recharged whenever he met one of his father's friends or acquaintances. These would all speak of him with deference, enumerating his many virtues, and, as Ibrahim listened, his father's image would glow in his mind, shining and radiant, the image of a hero or one of God's pious saints.

Perhaps Haj 'Abd al-'Aal's widow, Ibrahim's mother, played a part in her son's moral upbringing too. She lived like a nun after her husband's death, acting as a servant to Ibrahim and her other children, giving them all the love and tenderness it was in her power to bestow.

Ibrahim came to feel he'd somehow adopted his father's personality, even after he'd left the village and gone on to university, before eventually becoming an official in the Ministry of Agriculture. His colleagues there nicknamed him "Sheikh Ibrahim" because of his strict adherence to the moral code.

When he was twenty-five, his mother started nagging him to get married. He himself felt no inclination that way—it was almost as if he'd convinced himself his mother should be the only woman in his life. But finally he succumbed to her insistence, perhaps because he was reluctant to have endless arguments with her or (as she herself believed) because he wanted to make her happy.

It was his mother who chose the bride-to-be, a Cairene girl who lived in the apartment next to his aunt's in Shubra. His mother had seen her several times when visiting this aunt and been dazzled by her beauty. She admired, too, the goodness of the girl's mother, who would, she felt, be a good mother-in-law for her son Ibrahim.

All the agreements were made, and one morning Ibrahim went to the goldsmiths' bazaar, with his fiancée and her mother, to buy the engagement present.[1]

They went into the large shop of a well-known goldsmith, who realized why they'd come the moment he set eyes on them. He produced, for their inspection, rings and earrings and a variety of brooches, till their eyes were dazzled by all the gold and the diamonds and rubies and emeralds.

The prospective bride seemed nervous, and her hands kept trembling as if the jewelry stung her; but she managed to hide her anxiety behind a thick veil of shyness. She wouldn't give the smallest hint of what she liked. She'd be completely happy, she insisted, with whatever Ibrahim chose.

As for the bride's mother, she showed her true colors, constantly asking about prices, announcing demurely that she didn't want to involve her prospective son-in-law in the purchase of an expensive engagement present. Ibrahim was touched by her solicitude. He became ever more enthusiastic, telling her, in fervent tones, that price was immaterial, that nothing could be too good for her dear, beloved daughter.

---

1. It is customary to buy the bride-to-be not only a ring but a further piece of jewelry, usually a bracelet. This engagement present is called *al-shabaka* in Arabic (meaning "that which fastens" or "that which joins").

While these heartfelt exchanges were at their peak, something strange happened. The goldsmith told them one of the gold bracelets he'd been showing them had disappeared. Everyone fell silent.

Ibrahim didn't follow the goldsmith's drift at first.

"Maybe you dropped it," he said guilelessly. "Have a look."

"Sir," the goldsmith answered, "I made a thorough search while you were all talking. It's only now I'm telling you."

"So what exactly are you saying?" Ibrahim asked, beginning to realize what was up.

"I mean there were twenty bracelets before, and now there are nineteen."

"I don't understand," Ibrahim said.

"If you don't mind," the goldsmith said firmly, "I'd ask you to look for the bracelet. It might have fallen into the turnup on your trousers. Or maybe one of the ladies put it in her handbag by mistake."

Ibrahim's eyes glistened with anger, and the veins on his neck swelled up.

"What are you implying?" he bawled.

"Sir—"

"You're accusing us, aren't you? You are! We've more honor than you, and your father, and all your ancestors before him!"

Ibrahim was sure his resolute tone would put an end to the problem. These empty accusations were monstrous. He was, after all, an honorable man, the son of the pious Haj 'Abd al-'Aal al-Halawani, whose memory everyone at home revered, and these ladies were his fiancée and her mother. How could anyone have the smallest doubt about them? It was inconceivable!

And yet this stupid, insistent goldsmith stuck to his guns. In fact a grim frown came over his face.

"There are only the four of us here," he scowled. "One of us must have the bracelet."

"Then it must be you, you scheming swine!" yelled Ibrahim.

The goldsmith's voice became colder than ice.

"I don't want any scandal," he said. "But if I don't search you, the police will."

"The police!" Ibrahim shouted. "Don't you know who I am?"

"The best, most honorable man in the world, I'm sure. But there's no alternative. Either we search you or the police will."

The prospective bride had started weeping, while the mother was trembling all over.

"I'm the one who's calling the police," Ibrahim bawled. "Against you!"

The bride's mother intervened.

"Let them search us here," she said, terrified. "Then the whole thing will be over."

"That's out of the question, mother."

"Don't worry, son," she said. "Just forget all the fuss and let's get on with it."

"We have a young lady here," the goldsmith hastened to explain. "She can search the ladies upstairs."

"Just hurry up and search us," the prospective bride said tearfully. "Let's get it over with quickly."

All eyes were on Ibrahim—the one person who'd refused to be searched. He started feeling a trifle apprehensive, in case his fiancée and her mother should think the worst of him.

"All right," he whispered angrily. "Go ahead and search me. My trust is in God."

The prospective bride went upstairs with her mother to be searched by the female employee, while the goldsmith searched Ibrahim. The bracelet wasn't found on any of them. Suddenly the female employee bent down on the floor next to the goldsmith and picked up the bracelet. At first the goldsmith beamed. Then he turned pale and started apologizing to Ibrahim, the bride, and her mother.

But apologies were of no avail with Ibrahim. What had happened was a disaster and a scandal too. He wasn't going to leave the shop till he'd avenged his honor along with the honor of his prospective family. The police would have to be called!

"I'm going to talk to the emergency police," he said. "And I'm using your telephone to do it."

"Sir," the goldsmith said, "the whole thing's over now. I'm truly sorry."

"It's not enough to apologize, not after what you've done. You should be put in chains."

"I beg you to forgive me, sir. We all make mistakes."

"But not with ladies."

Ibrahim rushed to the telephone. The goldsmith clutched at his hand, but Ibrahim shoved him away.

"Just forget it, son," the mother cried. "Please, I beg you—"

"Be quiet," Ibrahim bellowed. "I know what I'm doing. You can go if you want to, but I'm staying here—"

The mother came and embraced him, but he pushed her away furiously and started dialing the number of the emergency police.

"You're only going to harm yourself, sir," the goldsmith said. His voice had a strange, stern tone now.

The mother clung grimly on to Ibrahim's hand.

"We're the ones who'll suffer most," she said beseechingly.

"Why?" Ibrahim yelled viciously.

"Tell him, madam," the goldsmith said. "Tell him before I do. I'll have to do it, madam."

"I had the bracelet, son," the mother whispered. She started weeping, became convulsed, and finally fainted away.

The goldsmith told Ibrahim what had happened, sprinkling the mother's face with water all the while. The female employee had found the bracelet on her; or rather, the mother had produced the bracelet from her clothing, handing it to the employee and begging her not to expose her in front of her daughter's fiancé.

"I realized what had happened quickly enough," the goldsmith went on. "These things go on a lot, and we're used to them. A trifling incident, my dear sir—let's forget all about it. Jewelry's a temptation to women. I'm not upset, believe me. It's happened with ladies from the best families. Sometimes they go even further than this, but we always manage to iron things out, and work goes on. It has to, in the interest of human relations and, to be quite frank, of good business too. If I'd started sending customers to prison, I'd have had to close this shop twenty years ago."

Ibrahim listened to the goldsmith in amazement, shocked to the core. It was as if he was seeing a new world, or simply dreaming.

He gazed at the mother, as she lay there across a number of chairs arranged like a bed, being hugged by her daughter. Suddenly the thief had become a victim, and the daughter was eyeing him as if he were some savage beast, whose very sight scared her to death. He looked at the female employee and saw her lip curled in contempt. It was clear he was the one she despised.

"What have I done wrong?" Ibrahim whispered.

"Don't worry about it, sir," the goldsmith said, for all the world as if Ibrahim was the one in the wrong—a criminal indeed.

Ibrahim's head was spinning. This was all quite beyond him. Theft was a sin, a heinous fault, a crime, but here everything seemed reversed. He needed to understand; and, above all else, he wanted to make his moral position clear to them. But how should he behave? What should he say? He wasn't going to consider marriage now, but he'd try and be gallant, like the goldsmith. He went up to the prospective bride.

"I'll go and find a taxi," he said.

"Get lost!" she yelled.

Ibrahim looked at the goldsmith, as if for support, but the man returned an icy blank stare. Then he looked at the female employee, who stared back at him with steely, insolent eyes.

"What did I do?" he whispered.

As his eyes fell on the mother's prostrate body, he felt guilty, with a guilt he'd never imagined existed. He went over once more to his prospective bride.

"Please forgive me," he said, as endearingly as he could.

"I'm not marrying you," she said woundingly. "I wouldn't dream of marrying you. You're cruel!"

He'd decided to put off any thought of marriage. And now here was his fiancée proclaiming *her* firm rejection of the whole idea!

He felt dizzy. Everything was swirling around him, below him, above him. Everything was swirling inside him as well.

"All right," he said, in a sorrowful voice. "But please, let me just understand . . ."

—*Translated by Roger Allen and Christopher Tingley*

Nadia Ghazzi (b. 1935)

This Syrian writer of fiction was born in Damascus into a family that has provided scholars and lawyers since the fifteenth century. Nadia Ghazzi trained as a lawyer and combined her practice of law with the profession of writing. She has authored several books of fiction, including *Very Special Issues* (1991). She has also authored a book on the flowers of Syria, *From the Orchards of Syria* (1990).

THE MAN WHO SAW HIS OWN FUNERAL

Shall I buy a car? Or should I buy some land? I could have five *dunum*s at 100,000 a *dunum*. Or should I maybe get a house and start a new life? I could have one deep in the country. There'd be no windows as fine as mine, no sunflowers more glorious than the ones I'd plant by the patio. I'd furnish the house with woolen carpets. The price for sheep and lambs has gone up, and there are some luxuries I really love.

Shall I buy a car? Or should I buy a drill for wells? I could drill a well, and water would come gushing out of it, drawn up from the belly of the earth by all that elaborate olive-colored machinery. I could lay down metal piping, hundreds of meters of it, to irrigate the land, with outlets all over the place.

Shall I buy a car? Or should I buy twenty gold bracelets? One could be fashioned to have a couple of diamond snakes' heads. Another one could be inlaid with sapphire and emerald. Ten could have sovereigns and half-sovereigns hanging from them. Real treasures those. They just get more valuable as time goes by.

Shall I buy a car? Or should I buy some racehorses? I could build spacious stables for them, and every day, as dawn came to the village, I could wash them down, their muscles quivering. I could comb their blazes with a special comb and set lucky charms of porcelain over their eyes. As each day broke, I'd caress them, the way city women caress the shoulders of their loved ones.

Shall I buy a car? Or should I take another wife? I could get a bride from a long way off, a slip of a girl the age of one of my own daughters, who still hasn't learned how to fleece a sheep and doesn't know how to grind wheat in a hand mill. I'd buy her a color television, and she could twiddle the knobs with her lily-white hands, and I'd load those arms with jangling bracelets. I'd adorn her neck with pearls.

Take a wife? God forbid! That's just a troublesome dream, a wild flight of fancy. And yet it could be done. Of all the many ideas I've pondered since my hair turned white, that's the vain fancy that keeps coming back to my mind!

After weighing it all up, Abu Ka'dun decided to go ahead and buy a car.

At nightfall he came home and counted up his money. He counted it twice and found it came to 550,000 Syrian pounds. It had taken a lot of effort to get that—year after year he'd scrimped and saved. He'd gained a profit from wheat, and the mortgage on the olive trees had brought a good return. The summers had been kind and the prices for his produce grew. His green cucumbers had danced amid the flat leaves resting on the soil, danced a dance of prosperity and joy.

Now he'd made his final decision, he summoned his wife.

"Listen to me," he said. "Thirty years you've been my wife and made the bread for the household, tossing the dough from one rough hand to the other, slapping the flat loaves onto our ancient oven. I'm as old as you, who are the mother of my sons and as loyal as the grains of wheat in my fields, which produce, each one of them, forty grains more.

"I'm going to the city now, far off to the north. For you, and for your children, I'm going to buy a car, one big enough to carry us all. It will help us move around. When it comes I'll pay for it to have its own tarmac road. We'll have our own private tarmac road, and a white car we'll hose down every day with water from the cistern.

"Yes, mother of my sons, raiser of my grandsons and granddaughters, I'm going there. My mind's made up. I'll put on a new *qaftan* and wrap the *kufiyya* round my head with its black *igal*, and make my way to the city of Aleppo. They sell cars with wonderful bodies there, so I've been told, and with sturdy wheels, specially designed for country folk like us.

"Prepare me some food for the journey. Wrap it carefully, and I'll set off tomorrow, at dawn. I won't be away long, for I'm part of you, flesh of your flesh, and I never feel easy unless I'm by your side. Away with any pointless fancies I've had up to now!"

That evening his wife stoked the oven, then rolled up her sleeves to prepare the fine dough in the great copper kneading trough. Every so often she'd sprinkle in some water and squeeze the dough with her strong tight hands—an example to all those city women who'd end up with aching necks and shoulders if they tried to do anything similar.

With the joy of anticipation she patted out the loaf over the round cushion, then tossed it onto the side of the hot oven, where it stuck the way an infant clings to its mother. Some of it swelled out into bubbles, while the rest stayed flat. Then it was ready to be prized from the belly of the oven.

Um Ka'dun spread out the loaves to let them breathe a little. Then she took some of them, folded them, and packed them up tight with the rest of the food, ready for the journey. She took the packet to her revered husband, who set off at first light, grasping the black bag in which he'd put his money. He reached the main road designed by the engineers and geologists and waited for a car to take him north to Damascus.

A shared taxi came along, and he took a corner seat, clinging on to his bag and food. The car ate up the miles, passing fields of wheat and black volcanic rocks, leaving behind the tough, colorful thorn bushes. At last it brought Abu Ka'dun to the capital, with all its rush and bustle.

From there he'd move on to the north. First, though, he had to buy some presents for his friends in Aleppo—some Damascene sweets, made with pistachio nuts and Turkish delight, along with other concoctions like the *kinafa* and *baraziq* and *ghuraiba* that melt in your mouth.

Around midday he made his way to the place where the public vehicles waited and got on one bound for Aleppo. He didn't opt for one of the fast ones, preferring to travel on a small bus, what they called a microbus, which stopped in the main towns or anywhere else the passengers wanted—it was cheap, a lot cheaper than the regular buses that sped by like lightning, with no thought for the likes of him. Off he went, with his black bag and his packet of food, enough to keep him going over his return journey to Aleppo.

He didn't talk to any of the passengers, didn't ask anyone where he came from or where he was going. He was on his guard and absorbed too in his own private thoughts. He preferred to be a nameless unit on this nameless journey.

The bus started off, on its leisurely way, along a road that was tarred like silk. There were more and more bends, and the vehicle shook and sighed, going round them at its own slow pace. Then it pushed on more freely over the open plains.

When they reached Homs, where some passengers got off and others got on, Abu Ka'dun remembered being totally alert; and at Hama, too, where there was another shuffling of the passengers, he was careful to keep on top of his weariness. The vehicle refueled at Hama, then set off again, though not before the driver had had a *falafil* sandwich bursting with pickles. Abu Ka'dun could have done with a *falafil* sandwich too, even if he was from the south of the country, but he curbed his appetite in the interests of economy, taking some bread from Um Ka'dun's packet, along with a couple of boiled eggs, eggs laid by his own chickens. As he cut these and spread them on the bread, a rather uncomfortable aroma pervaded the bus, but he ignored it, making a sandwich of his bread and eating it.

People were replete now, and Abu Ka'dun, filled with his eggs and bread, succumbed to tiredness. As the bus rocked endlessly on, weariness weighed down on the eyelids of the careful passenger. For all his efforts, he couldn't stop himself dozing off from time to time. He'd drop off, then wake up, then fall asleep again. The vehicle stopped at some desolate spot, and people got down. Then the journey resumed, only for the bus to stop once more in the middle of nowhere, at a place where passengers could go on to their villages or to some ruins behind a hill.

Every time the bus stopped, he'd open his eyes and look round, without taking things in. Then he'd sink back into sleep, and the dreams floating around his mind would start up again, dreams about cars and roads and fields.

Sleep had overcome Abu Ka'dun completely!

Then, at last, night came. And still he slept on, like a babe in arms, or a bridegroom on the morning after his wedding night. The bus's shaking took him back to a world of infancy. He was like a newborn baby now, sleeping in a cloth-lined cradle that was like an old blanket, folded and made secure with a black cord, hung between two trees, where the gentle breeze played with the leaves and the baby could hear the chirping of birds along with the rustling leaves. Still he slept. He heard the noise of the wheels and the drone of the engine. And still he slept on.

Chance decreed that a wicked man should come and sit behind Abu Ka'dun. It decreed that this stranger should see how the smart, reserved villager, every ten minutes or so, checked his black bag, touching it gently as he might one of his own children. And it decreed that this wicked man with the unkempt hair should realize the bag contained a valuable treasure. Why else should the owner show such concern?

Luckily for him, and unluckily for Abu Ka'dun (or was it the other way round?), this man with the money had fallen asleep, was in a deep slumber now, as the night wore on and the bus still moved on north.

When the stranger had made sure the bag's owner was fast asleep, and when he could see the people around were asleep too or else sunk in their thoughts, he got up quite calmly, took the bag from under Abu Ka'dun's feet, then went to the front of the bus and asked the driver to stop.

It's normal enough, with these small buses, for drivers to stop at places on the way. And so the driver stopped as he'd been asked and the wicked man got briskly off, wishing him good night and showing no sign of anxiety. Then the bus moved off into the darkness once more. Soon the engine was droning and moaning again, as the bus carried on with its passengers, toward Aleppo. Abu Ka'dun opened his eyes, then returned, fast asleep, to his cradle.

The thief, nervous now, hid behind some thornbushes till he was sure the bus had really moved on. There was no moon to light up the desolate spot he'd chosen, so he lit a match and opened the black bag. A feeble light fell on the vast sum of money, such a sum as he'd never seen in his life.

He snapped the bag shut, then, having made sure it was secure, got up and crossed the road to wait for another vehicle, which he could flag down, on this pitch-dark night, to take him back in the direction he'd come from. He was burning with impatience.

He had no ally on this night, no companion but the beating of his heart, which reverberated in his ears and in his head and arms and chest. As he stood there panting in the darkness, it was as though he'd been transformed into a pump.

Still he stood, clutching his bag, his hair all over the place, hoping for the headlights of an approaching vehicle, which would take him from this spot among the thornbushes and the silent tarmac, to his township, to his family. There he'd be able to calm down, climb into the obscurity of his striped cotton blanket, hide the cash round his waist, and go to sleep.

Next morning he'd be able to eat some nice warm *kishk* garnished with mint. He'd think about buying some land, and a car. He'd hide the money among the rubble and the trees, in a place not even the lizards knew about. Then he'd divorce his wife and send her back to her family, along with the children, so he could marry a girl appropriate to his new status. With money you can have beauty, whereas a louse just breeds nits.

A louse was all he'd been before. He'd married a she-louse and they'd produced nits swarming out among the ruins, lunching off dried bread dipped in black tomato paste. And now he'd be a wondrous bird of paradise. He'd seek out some flighty *naghnuna*, who'd toy with him the way he was toying with the money in his hands, here on this dark night.

He held the bag in his hand. His hair was disheveled and his throat dry. He didn't feel the cold of the night, and he wasn't hungry, though he'd had little enough to eat, and he wasn't thirsty either. His mind was focused on one thing above all others—to get home. He wanted to snuff out the flame of fear flickering in his heart.

Headlights blazed. Oh, let them come nearer! Beasts of prey were everywhere in the night. There were hyenas that prowl around, and can smell their victims' blood, black snakes that slither by, bite, and pass on. Perhaps *abu 'l-fasa'* might come stinking along—that small wild creature, about a quarter the size of a cat, with its long body, as slender as a small pipe. It sends out a poisonous scent onto its victim, which drives away other creatures, leaving it free to devour the body.

When headlights glimmer, they open up an island of light in the still night, in the lonely places where there's not even a twinkling of stars. Still the shifty thief stood there, a dim point on a dim background, awaiting liberation; filled with fear, of the night and of a chilly prison cell.

All of a sudden, away in the distance, a glimmer of headlights appeared. Quaking to the very core, the man took a firm grip on the black bag and stood right out on the road, waving his hand pleadingly, beseechingly. What time it was he had no idea.

As it happened, the driver didn't see the stranger in his headlights. He was nodding off at that moment, or confused, or thinking about something else, or he was somewhere else, or blind. The car, careering along, struck the cursed wretch, tossing him right up in the air. For a moment he felt as though he were in some spaceship hurtling toward earth. He did his best to hold onto the bag, so it wouldn't fly out of his hands. Then he felt a violent blow, shattering his head and his limbs and heart and brain.

The bag was the only witness of his death there, so late in the night.

The body lay on the ground, in this utterly desolate place. Snakes slithered by, and those wild creatures, the hyenas and mosquitoes, wouldn't go near him. The night advanced, then, little by little, began to pass, as the gray colors of morning glimmered. Then came the dawn. A radiance spread through the world, revealing a well-built tarmac road, making everything plain, calling on anyone passing to discover the man who'd been killed, crushed in a hit-and-run accident; killed because the driver was otherwise occupied, or asleep, or drowsy, or blind, or didn't really exist.

In the morning the body was found, all twisted up and smashed. The only clue to identity was the black bag, which was opened by the police. They swiftly inspected the scene of the accident, chalking an outline of the body on the tarmac, then the body itself was taken to the hospital in the nearest town, so the pathologist could establish the cause of death and record it on the certificate. They had a look, too, at the tarmac, to assess the speed of the vehicle from the skid marks. Then they recorded the incident as death by misadventure, caused by a person unknown.

Opening the bag, they found 550,000 Syrian pounds, along with the identity card of one Sulaiman ben Asim al-Ma'sum, known as Abu Ka'dun, from one of the villages of the Hauran in Syria. In his fifties, poor man. No doubt he'd come from his village to trade.

There were legal procedures, and official reports, and the family of the "deceased" was informed of the accident. Distress swept through the village. The men straightway left their irrigation work, dropped their hoes, and ran. The women ran out of their houses without their veils, grieving and listing the merits of the man who'd enjoy his wealth no longer.

When the white ambulance arrived, bearing the shattered corpse, the keening of the women and girls rose higher still, while the small children stood there agape, their faces yellow with horror. Um Ka'dun struck her cheeks and tore at her face with her nails. She plucked at her hair, tossing pieces from it as she went from the house to the ambulance.

When the body had been delivered, the police expressed the usual condolences, then showed the official reports, including the details of the black bag, which was to be duly handed over, along with the money inside, to the legitimate heirs.

And what, meanwhile, of Abu Ka'dun?

As the bus reached the heights above Aleppo, it slowed down and the passengers started gathering their bags, ready to get out. Abu Ka'dun, woken by the general stir in the vehicle, yawned, then, with an automatic movement, stretched out to feel his bag. It wasn't there!

"Driver!" he yelled. "Police! Help! My bag's been stolen. I put it under the seat, and now I can't find it. Driver, where can I get hold of the police? Help! Driver, I beg you, don't let any of the passengers off. Please, in the name of God, keep the doors locked. Put the lights on, so we can see the other passengers' bags."

The driver did as he was asked, and the passengers all submitted to a thorough search, but to no avail. Weeping and striking his face, Abu Ka'dun reported the theft of his bag to the police, along with details of the precise sum of money, his identity card, and further personal documents. The other passengers were questioned; then, when it was clear none of them had the bag, they were allowed to leave.

And so this man who'd been robbed was right out on a limb, physically and mentally too. You can't lose half a million Syrian pounds and fail to be shaken to the core. He sat down on the kerb and wept. There was no point at all, he knew, in trying to find the bag. The thief must have been one of the numerous passengers who'd left the bus while he was fast asleep.

He still had his packet of food, but he couldn't eat the things his wife had prepared. He didn't even have any appetite for a *falafil* sandwich now. He could only sit back, for the rest of the day, on a seat in the park, feeling like a stray cat. Then, going through his pockets, he found he had enough cash to get to Damascus and took the next available transport, gazing out of the window all the way, looking at the ground, looking for hiding places, looking for his black bag. Perhaps it had been thrown out behind the thorn bushes.

So he continued till he reached Damascus, and there a friend lent him the money to get home. Then he set off for the Hauran.

What, he wondered, would his wife say to him? What would the young men say? How would his in-laws greet him, his daughters, his grandchildren. Never mind, Sulaiman Abu Ka'dun, he told himself. You won't die of grief. Disaster's struck, and you'll just have to bear it in patience. You didn't have to fall asleep on that cursed journey. You should have fought against it. You should have held out, keeping hold of your bag as you would an injured child.

You've been struck by disaster, man, he told himself. You'll just have to put up with it. Perhaps the years to come will make you prosperous again. Perhaps, if you save, you'll still be able to get the money for a car. Before old age finally creeps up on you.

Abu Ka'dun was still in this anxious state when he reached the road leading off to his village. Then, in the deepest distress, he left the vehicle, wondering how on earth he was going to explain the theft of the bag to his household.

He walked, dragging his feet along. Or rather his feet dragged him, till at last he reached the hill overlooking the village and saw the crowd gathered there. There were women wailing and children sobbing. A funeral in the village!

Who was it that had died? One of the elders of the village maybe? Or the headman? Or was it someone in the prime of life? Or some young bride? Abu Ka'dun headed for his house, to find people gathered there. He heard the voice of his own wife, keening and wailing. There were people coming and going, and a fresh grave was being dug.

Woe to you, Sulaiman, he thought. Who's died in your house? No sooner does one disaster strike than another comes, straight off like this, to hit you. A worse disaster, more wretched still. Woe to you, Sulaiman! Not for the money you've lost, or the car you haven't bought, or the weary weight of the years. None of this could be equal to a fingernail of one of your sons or daughters.

His knees buckled, and he couldn't speak now. He was drawn along, as if by a magnet, to his front door.

Then, suddenly, the people stopped wailing. They actually stopped wailing! The roses of the garden all bloomed at once, their petals bursting open in amazement.

The gravedigger raised his spade, then dropped it as he stared aghast at Abu Ka'dun. As for the returning traveler, he looked at his sons one by one, seeing their eyes swollen from so much weeping. Why, he wondered, were they staring into his face so intently, so oddly, their eyes almost popping out of their heads?

He went into his house, where the women were still wailing, seated round a wooden coffin. Someone, clearly, was waiting to go on the next stage of his journey. He counted his daughters. There they all were, safe and sound. Then he saw his wife, up against a wall, staring at him—she seemed as pale as a page in an exercise book. You'd have said she was hanging from the wall.

She cast her eyes towards the wooden box, then towards Abu Ka'dun. She looked back at the dead man, then once more at Abu Ka'dun. Then she fainted.

People were rushing up to him, congratulating him, kissing him, believing and yet not believing. The children gathered round their father, kissing his feet and hands and mustache. The women gathered round Um Ka'dun, rejoicing, sprinkling water over her face and rubbing leaves of basil round her nose. And amid all the talk bursting out, the returning traveler unraveled the story of the body that had turned up, and the story of the stolen bag returned to its owner.

God is great, let everyone proclaim it!

Allahu akbar! The traveler has returned to us, safe and sound.

It was clear now what had happened. How the bag had been stolen; how the thief had been knocked down at dead of night by a speeding car, after he'd filched the bag and fled into the thorn bushes, then stood there on the other side of the road, on the trunk road, where the cars go so fast; how he'd been waiting there for someone to stop and take him home.

Allahu akbar. Allahu akbar, cry it out! Right has prevailed and wrong been crushed. A car passing in the night struck the wretch down, visiting him with a wretched death. Blessings have returned to those who merit them. Abu Ka'dun has got back his bag and his money.

And it was the bag that betrayed the thief.

—*Translated by Peter Clark and Christopher Tingley*

Gamal al-Ghitani (b. 1945)

Egyptian novelist and short-story writer Gamal al-Ghitani was born of a poor family and reared in the old Gamaliya quarter of Cairo. He first studied at the College of Arts and Crafts and for six years worked as a designer of Oriental carpets, traveling all over Egypt in the course of his work. The 1967 June war had a major impact upon him, and through the years 1968 to 1976 he worked as a war correspondent, largely based on the Suez Canal front. A leftist, his writing is very concerned with the social and political issues of the day and particularly with Egyptian history in the 1970s. He has been imprisoned and lost his job more than once. A writer of great stature and originality hardly paralleled in modern Arabic, his style is rooted in the Arabic literary tradition, and he has successfully attempted to reintroduce the old Arabic "tale" form, in contradiction to other writers who model their fiction on Western styles. Among his collections of short stories are *Remembering What Has Happened: The Diary of a Young Man Who Died a Thousand Years Ago* (1969), *Surface to Surface* (1972), *Siege from Three Directions* (1975), *Al-Zuwail* (1975), *Fruits of Time* (1990), *Singer of Sunset* (1997), and *Approaching Eternity* (2000). His collection *A Distress Call* was translated into English by Suad Naguib (1997). He has also written a number of novels, among which are his famous *Incidents in the Za'farani Alley* (1975), translated into English by Peter O. Daniel (1986), and *Al-Zaini Barakat* (1981), translated into English by Farouk Abdel Wahhab and published by Penguin. A more recent novel, *The Book of Revelations,* is a superb attempt at merging the past with the present and the personal with the national and universal and, together with *Al-Zaini Barakat*, has been discussed at greater length in the introduction to this book.

AN ENLIGHTENMENT TO THE
PEOPLE OF THIS WORLD

I read this manuscript several months ago in the library of one of the old mosques in Gamaliyya.[1] It aroused my astonishment with its strange theme, as it did not have anything to do with problems relating to the religious law. These pages contain, rather, the diary of the warden of the prison known in Mamluk[2] times as al-Maqshara. Many pages of the manuscript are lost, but I preferred to publish what I found because of its rarity and peculiarity. I did not interpolate anything, except on a very few occasions. I also noticed that the author did not determine which sultan was reigning when he controlled the affairs of al-Maqshara, although I feel it was most probably Sultan al-Ashraf Qaitbay,[3]or al-Ashraf Qansuh al-Ghuri,[4] the last of the Mamluks. The reader or researcher may find in these pages some useful material and some important accounts of what went on in Egypt during those distant times.

---

1. An old Cairean street and district. This story takes place in the old Fatimid city of al-Qahira, Cairo, during the Mamluk period. The city was laid out in the form of a rectangular palace city by General Gawhar for the Caliph al-Mu'izz. A street ran from Bab al-Zuwayli (also known as al-Mutawalli Gate), the southern gate, to Bab al-Futuh, the northern gate. Gamaliyya Street runs approximately parallel to the east of this street, from the famous al-Husain Mosque to Bab al-Nasr, another gate a little to the east of Bab al-Futuh.
2. A warrior caste, originally slaves of non-Arab extraction who were dominant in Egypt and the Middle East from 1250, when they usurped supreme power, to the nineteenth century when they were decimated in the notorious massacre of the Tower. c. 1840.
3. The eighteenth Burgi Mamluk Sultan of Egypt (1468–1495). He was originally a Circassian slave brought to Egypt by Qalawun as a member of Qalawun's bodyguard, which was housed in the Citadel built by Salah al-Din.
4. The twenty-second Mamluk Sultan (ruled 1500–1516) and also the second last of the Burgi rulers. He had been a former slave of Qaitbay.

May God forgive our past and present sins.

God help and aid us . . .

Forgive our sins, O Sultan of Sultans! Overlook our faults, You, the most Merciful! It is You we worship, and it is from You that we ask help. God, give Your blessings to the greatest of your messengers, who was a prophet when Adam was still between water and mud . . . and on all his family and companions.

Since I was assigned one of the strangest jobs of my epoch by which I could serve my master, the sultan—and in the light of the strange events that happened to me in that job (which might seem painful to some and amusing to others), and since I used to spend most of my time in al-Maqshara, I said to myself, "Let me write down part of what I see and hear, and—who knows?—it may happen that my master, the most noble of our day, might read what I have written and know to what extent I have exerted myself in his service, and suffered pain, and almost met death. His heart might feel compassion toward me then, and he might grace me with a gift of a thousand dinars from his bounty."

The prison I command is situated near the Futuh Gate,[3] between this gate and the mosque of al-Hakim bi Amrillah.[6] It is called al-Maqshara[7] because it was built on the site of a former threshing ground. Common people, rabble, *shaikhs*, and all the people of Egypt say that it is one of the ugliest and most horrible prisons, where prisoners suffer indescribable misery and grief. However, those who say this have never even seen it from the inside. What would they say, one wonders, if they had been inside it themselves? If men or women pass by it either secretly or openly, they are prone to say—either secretly or openly—as they draw away from the building in awe, "God! Save us from its evil and misery!" I hear them say this and I mockingly say in my heart, "None of you should think that it is too far-fetched for you to enter al-Maqshara. Maybe today you're among your family, near your wife—and the next morning in the lowest dungeons of al-Maqshara!"

On the evenings I spend here, I sometimes feel tired of this kind of existence. During the second half of the night, the calm becomes thick as death, and the darkness becomes frightening even to those accustomed to it. I often hear voices coming from the neighborhood around the prison, so mixed that you cannot discern the voice of a man from that of a woman or distinguish even one single word. I then go out and walk around the wall enclosing the flat rooftop of the building. When I come near the center, I hear some hissing noises, squeaky protracted sounds that send a shiver down my spine. It is from here that the spiral stairway begins and then plunges to a great depth. There are narrow hollows in the walls on each side of the stairway where a man can neither fully lie down

---

5. See n.1 on Gamaliyya.

6. The Fatimid ruler al-Hakim ruled (996–1021) built his mosque beside Bab al-Futuh Gate. It fell into ruins but was restored by the Ismaili sect around 1980.

7. Threshing grounds. The prison was built, as the story goes, in a place used previously for threshing.

nor stand up to his full height. These are the places where the prisoners are chained. I sometimes go down, preceded by the jailers lighting up the subterranean vaults for me. Often, I ask myself, "What can an old man who has spent seventy years here be thinking about now? Or, for that matter, a young man who has been here only one or two years?" I contemplate their faces. I joke with them mockingly, and I might even hit them suddenly and shout that there can be no hope for them at all. For the faces seem ugly and repulsive. If you want to make one of the new prisoners cry like a woman and even admit he is no better than a woman, then tell him that two of his children have died and that his wife has filed suit for divorce and is remarrying. When the night descends, moreover, the bats come out and you can hear the noises their wings make as they crash against the walls, or you can see them eating the lotus fruits snatched from a nearby tree. Sometimes the prisoners scream up from below, and often an obnoxious, appalling odor flares up suddenly. The jailers seem then about to flee the place. No one knows the reason for the odor.

A head jailer came and told me that Emir Tabaqtabay had sent a group of prisoners to be placed in our custody. I asked him how many they were. He said forty. In an hour's time, when the night had completely descended, we heard a loud din downstairs. I stood at the edge of the wall of the roof, eager to see the new prisoners. This is my habit. Whenever there are some newcomers, I feel a great urge to see them immediately, and I start guessing who they might be. But please note this: I never know who comes to al-Maqshara except after I receive him. And who knows—? It might sometimes be a prince, may be the *dawadar*[8] prince himself, or the supreme commander of the armed forces. No one in the whole of Egypt, or among the Arabs or Persians, is too elevated to enter al-Maqshara. If one were [obliterated words in the original] . . . Whatever goes on in his heart, and why, and how he finds things now. He had been a prince that very morning, a great prince, drums beating at his door, and the retinue preceding his carriage in the streets. Before I bind him with iron chains, I beat him once and twice and thrice and let him suffer indescribable insults and agony. No, no one is too elevated for al-Maqshara. You are a prince? You are a prince in your own home and over your own women only. I tell him, "They may be destroying your home, raping your women, stealing your property and possessions." The higher in status a man is, the more pain we inflict on him. This is what our master orders. Praise be to the everlasting master!

I went out to walk around the walls. The road beneath us was wide and free of pedestrians. It seemed completely still. This was because a few days earlier our Sultan had banned walking in the streets after dinner and ordered that the Mamluks were not to leave their lodging quarters and go down masked into the

---

8. An elevated rank during Mamluk times. The position's official title was "Bearer and Keeper of the Royal Inkwell," but it involved a great amount of power.

city. I struck the stones in my hands and called one of the head jailers and asked him, "When will the newcomers arrive?" He said, "In an hour or so." I asked, "Do you yet know who they are?" He answered, "Peasants." I shook my head in indifference. This thing arouses nausea. He asked where he should put them, and I said to put them in the small hall. He asked, "All forty?" I replied, "Yes."

God help and aid us . . .

Each of them was like a reed or a bamboo shoot. Their clothes were tattered, their hands tied to each other, their eyes protruding as if they had been hurled together at doomsday! No noise from them, not a murmur. As for the night, it was completely calm with nothing to disturb its calm. Since I was not going to sleep for some time, I thought I would try to find out something about them. One of the head jailers said that I would not find anything to please me there. All of them were repulsive. I asked one of them, "What have you done, son of a whore?" His voice came out thick and rattling: "By God, I committed no crime and do not owe a single dirham to the Sultan's treasury." I lashed another. He received the lashing calmly as if to say, "Hit me more, if you want, but return me to my wife and children." Then he said that they had been sowing in the fields when they were raided by the cavalry, who surrounded them, rounded up forty of them, and put them in chains. Then the man was silent and an old peasant shouted, "They took us claiming we were bedouins, sir. They had been unable to arrest a single bedouin from amongst the mountain dwellers and arrested us instead so they could tell the sultan . . . 'Here, we have arrested forty outlaws'—but we have not disobeyed and have not . . . " I went round them and noticed four very young boys, which any of the prisoners would love to be with. A head jailer shouted ordering them not to scream during the night. He added that the sultan intended to put them on display shortly. Their wails rose like women. I yelled at them and they fell silent. I saw that their necks were thin and their bones jutted out. I noticed a young man with wide eyes. I asked him, "Are you married? Is your wife young?" He did not answer. He had broad shoulders. I said to him with deliberate calm, "You will never see your family again. Think of this and contemplate it thoroughly." He remained silent. I told him, "You are the first whose head is going to fall—or may be you will hang at the Zuweila Gate. Aren't you afraid?" He said, "I am sad and trembling all over." I said, "This should not be a barrier." I signaled meaningfully with my hand and winked. He asked me suddenly, "How long will I stay in prison?" I was silent for a moment, deep in thought, and then said, "Do you really want to know?" He did not answer. I said, "If you escape decapitation and hanging, you might spend ninety years in here—that is, if you are fated to live that long—or one year, or twenty; but you will never leave this place without a decree from the sultan. And who will take your case to our master the sultan? Do you know the Viceroy of Cairo or another great prince who can intercede on your behalf?" I saw fear overshadow his eyes. I said to myself, "Here is someone who does not know what is awaiting him, so let me tell him and observe what emotions show on his face, and try to guess what goes on in his heart." The rest of the rabble was listening with the greatest attention. I continued, "This will happen to you, if you do not die of the plague, or if the bats do not suck your blood. You must know that the bats in al-Maqshara are as big as men, and the scorpions huge as mules. Moreover, if I feel bored one evening, I might bring you up to me and strip you naked, and then cut off your [obscene words, which I preferred to delete]. You must also know that whatever we do with you—imagine, anything at all—no one will even question us. Not a single man will ever raise his finger in protest. Not one woman will weep for you, and no wife will ever mourn you." I said to myself that I knew very well what was going on in his mind and soul, so let me rouse in him things that might make him drop dead. "Our very sultan," I said, "hasn't got the power to do what I can do. Can he say what I can say to any of the prisoners in the sultanate?" The old peasant whispered, "By God, our prince, we haven't done anything." But a head jailer hit him in the face and silence hovered over them all.

The moon, stretched on the wall of the sky, looked suffocated and ravaged. I approached the broad-shouldered young man. "Of course, you do not know all the kinds of torture we have here. Woe to you if any of your friends here point at you and declare that you possess a sum of money, even if it is only ten dinars . . . You will then be handcuffed and will be placed on a stake, your limbs and head will be wrung, your teeth extracted and pounded into your scalp . . . or we might tear out your breasts and grill them and feed them to you." I noticed that the steadfastness of his look faltered now and his lips trembled . . . I put my face so near his that my nose almost touched his and suddenly let out a huge scream, and he retreated, stumbling. I began to box his chest softly and gently, all the time knowing what this was doing to him. I shouted, warning him and the rest of them that he would never see his mother again, never, never, and would never hear his wife calling to him as he returned from the fields. In the dungeons downstairs, he would even forget the names of his children and how they look. I addressed them all as I straightened myself: "Even a bloodhound will never find any trace of any of you."

I called a head jailer, and he raised his truncheon. They rushed down the narrow spiral stairway, weeping like women. The lower they went, the more faint their screams grew. In the lowest vaults some of the men who had spent sixty or seventy years in prison would try to find out who these newcomers from the outside world were—the world that they no longer knew. One evening when I went down myself to put the tall Emir Aqbay in prison, I heard a man screaming from a dark place we had passed, asking if there truly existed a real world outside. I heard another asking how people outside were and from what quarter the new prisoners came. Voices followed each other until tall Aqbay almost died of terror; but he did not die.

I leaned my arm now on the stone wall and saw the city dead silent. It was a night somewhere between autumn and winter. Very soon the rains would come, the marketplaces would turn muddy, and al-Maqshara would become a terrifying and horrendous place. I remembered at that moment that I had not performed my evening prayers. I asked forgiveness from my Lord and went to my room. One of the head jailers followed me and said that the sultan was to order that these prisoners be put on display in perhaps two or three weeks. I did not answer him but asked him to bring me the prayer mat.

God help and aid us . . .

A few evenings ago, Sheikh Mas'ud stopped me in the alley just after I had left my house and told me, "Don't you fear God on Doomsday?" I said, "I take refuge in Him and to Him I turn always. Why? Have you seen me debauching? Or lax in performing my religious duties? Have you heard from the rabble that I blasphemed against the Lord? No, by God, Sheikh Mas'ud!" He answered, "Neither this nor that; but I hear that you inflict on the prisoners all sorts of torture, that you crowd many in a place too narrow to contain them, where they are unable to perform their ablutions or to pray, and can even see each other's forbidden parts." I told him, "Every job has its good and bad sides, Sir, but know that all that has reached you is a pure lie, from beginning to end." He said, "There is no power and no strength save in God." I asked him to pray to God to forgive me. He said, "O God, keep us from grief and evil." I left him, feeling resentful against him. Did he take me to be the commander of the Shama'il treasury or of the Qal'a or Daylam or Irqana prisons? Is it any fault of mine? Was it I who created prisons? Was it not the second caliph of Islam[9] who initiated the prison system, who bought a house in Mecca where those who deserved to be incarcerated were thrown? "By God," I said to myself, "it would not be strange if you too came to the Maqshara, Sheikh Mas'ud!" At the end of the day and beginning of evening, when people in the marketplace are pushing each other to the Lemon Market, vendors shouting, young boys returning home, the movement increasing in the market, and the selling and buying intensifying, then I appear. Calm and quiet descend upon the place, as if the world has suddenly come to a stop. At that moment a thought rises up in my mind: that all these people will one day come to the Maqshara and fall under my command—not all of them at once but each in turn. Each has a preordained period that he will spend there, or die in the process.

I went up to my room feeling extremely depressed . . . I ordered Prince Mughulbay to be brought in. He was the one who had conspired against the sultan, occupied the Sultan Hasan Mosque,[10] and tried to usurp the sultan's throne . . . He was an old fox. Neither a Mamluk, nor anyone from the upper or lower classes, dared stand in his way. I said to myself, "I'm going to screw him and make him . . . [*here the paper was destroyed and the description of what happened stopped, but*

---

9. Caliph Omar ibn al-Khattab, an early convert to Islam and one of the Prophet's greatest companions. He was the second of the four Orthodox caliphs and ruled from 735–744 A.D.
10. Built by Sultan Hasan (ruled 1347–1351, 1354–1361) as a madrasa-mosque (college-mosque), it is considered to be the finest example of existing Egyptian Arab architecture. The walls of this huge edifice are 113 foot high and are built of cut stone brought from the pyramids. It stands opposite the citadel and, following the custom of the day, is cruciform in shape.

what follows does not really separate events too much from their natural flow.] . . . and I don't know what for. I was about to draw my sword and cut off the head of anyone I saw, but the catastrophe was too great, and my spirit calmed down. The problem would have to be solved calmly. If it should become public it would be a scandal and my head would fall . . . What black days await me? Everyone will instigate the sultan against me. The prince of the army himself will mount me on a mule, front to back, and expose me in the streets of Cairo: "Stone him," "Beat him." "He has tortured my son," "He has killed my husband," "He has cut off my arm," "He put me on a stake and pierced my . . . with his heated dagger," "He coveted my wife and imprisoned me thirty years in order to have free access to her," "The lecher," "The adulterer." Oh God, have mercy and help me! The rabble will slap me, and the town crier walking in front of the procession will shout, "This is the punishment of those who do not keep proper custody of the Sultanate's prisoners." And what prisoners! Merely forty peasants. If any had been killed in the street, not a single finger would be raised, no lips would move! I assembled the jailers and began beating and kicking them. I saw their bodies tremble with terror. I shouted at them, "Do you know what horrors are awaiting you? You know al-Maqshara best. It will become a place where no one can reach you." But I called them again some time later and said, "If this should spread and become public, I shall kill you all." I folded my hands on my breast and prayed to God that the sultan would not order the outlaw bedouins to be put on display. Then I went out roaming the streets aimlessly, feeling a live coal burning my heart. Some men carrying red banners and beating drums came toward me, preceded by a man who was whirling swiftly without falling or even getting dizzy. He had around his waist a red cloth. which flapped and swirled swiftly as he turned. The men were shouting enthusiastically . . . *Allah* . . . *Allah*[11] . . . I walked slowly until they passed. Evening was drawing near, and very soon the night would suddenly fall. The air blew so cold, it pierced my bones. I stood perplexed; the movement in the street was increasing briskly. I remembered my children and my wife at home. I wished I could ride a horse that would speed me swiftly away. But, I thought, they will catch up with me anyway. I did not know what to do and told myself, "Stand firm, stand firm." I went down the three steps that led to an old low mosque. The air inside was stuffy. I stood piously and remembered their number: forty peasants . . . It is in God's hands.

Praise be to God, I have repented and I am the first of believers . . . God forgive us and give us reprieve! Lord, do not let my enemies rejoice, and do not let me be among the heretics. I beg You for mercy according to Your saying, "God loveth the repentant, those who purify themselves." Our sins are many, and our obedience is ready. All of us are prone to make mistakes and have shortcomings. O God, were it not for the sins of sinners, then the generous trait of forgiveness would not be. Were it not for the shortcomings of people, then the clemency

---

11. These are the chants of dervishes belonging to a Sufi (mystic) sect.

and patience of the forgiver would not be shown. God, I take refuge with Your beloved Prophet of whom You sent down the verse, "We sent him as a bringer of mercy to the world."

God help and aid us ...

I asked a head jailer, "Have any of the people seen you? Have the Mamluks shouted at you?" He answered that no one saw us at all. The Mamluks do not come down from the Qal'a tower after sunset, and the *Wali's* guards do not roam the streets except in the dead of night. And yet who are we? Aren't we the soldiers of the sultan? Everyone in town knows the name of each one of us. Moreover, heavy clouds had gathered above us, almost reaching the houses ... The first among them screamed when he saw me, "What have I done, Prince?" I struck him with the whip on his face and watched the long swelling appear suddenly after the blow. Another man shouted like a woman, "Woe to me and to my family!" Others said that they had not committed any crime and that none of them had ever cheated anyone or disturbed a human soul ... Some of them said that they were the most obedient of all the people of Egypt, obeying everything that had been decreed and everything that would be decreed. "So what have we done that you should fall on us while we were selling lemons in the market place, and take away our camels and loads, and put us in chains?" They said that they were poor people and that their families would die of sorrow for them, having gone to Cairo and never returned. "I have ten children, sir!" "As for me, I have staked all my life on a basket of lemons that I carried slung over my neck to sell in the market." I listened to what they were saying, feeling contentment and peace in my heart. I said nothing. The peasants that the *dawadar* had brought were not like these, they did not shout and scream like them. But this was natural. The others had come straight from their villages, while this lot were in an extraordinary situation. A man leaves his home and never returns! His wife and children will never know what has happened to him. In a few days, the sultan will ask for the outlaw bedouins who had wreaked havoc in the land and who had been rounded up by the *dawadar* prince to be put on display. Some of them will be decapitated, while others will be hanged, their skinny bodies dangling at the Zuweila or the Shi'riyya Gates. Some corpses will become decomposed and their flesh putrified but find no one to bury them until a pious man eventually will. No one would argue about his death, each one of them would pass away, giving up his place in life, leaving no news of himself behind. I told them while they listened attentively, as if the trumpet had been blown on the day of judgment, and the whole world had been destroyed. "You are the anarchist bedouins, and no matter how much you scream and say differently, you are the highway robbers, attacking the caravans of pilgrims. You will say, 'We are lemon vendors; we plant them and sell them'; but no one will listen to you." I circled around them, deliberately watching their protruding eyes and terrified features, seeing hope mingled with despair on their faces. Strange! Are these heads that will be stuffed with straw in a little while? I felt a chill come over my skin. A notion came to my mind but I pushed it away, and took refuge from the accursed devil in God. The heavy clouds were pregnant with rain, and in a little while it would pour down like a torrent, and their screams would rise to the heavens—but even if the whole world heard them, who was going to ask any explanation from the commander of *al-Maqshara?* I retreated a few steps and shouted at the head jailer to throw them in the middle level and to chain each one of them with three iron chains. Before he went down to them, I asked him, "How many are they?" He said, "Forty-two." I asked, "And how many were the prisoners of the prince?" He said, "Forty." I bowed my head in contemplation for a moment, then told him to send me two. I took out my dagger from its sheath, and its blade glittered in the air.

Thus end the papers of the manuscript, suddenly, but I know that there must be missing parts. All that I hope is that these were not destroyed completely. I kindly ask, therefore, all those fond of studying old manuscripts, if they should come across the parts that would complete these strange accounts, to be so kind as to send them to me . . . so that I can publish them and have people benefit from them.

—Translated by May Jayyusi and Anthony Thwaite

Huzama Habayib (b. 1965)

Huzama Habayib is a Palestinian short-story writer. Born in Kuwait, she lived and studied there, obtaining her B.A. in English literature from the University of Kuwait in 1987. She then worked for three years in Kuwait, first as a research assistant at the University's English department, teaching Arabic to non-Arabic speakers, then as an editor and translator at the *Al-Watan* newspaper. Forced to leave the country in 1990 as a result of the Gulf War, she returned to Jordan, where she first took a post as editor and translator for the *Basma* review and now works at the Ministry of Education in Amman. She has translated several books and articles on various non-literary subjects. She has so far published four collections of short stories: *The Man Constantly Duplicated* (1992), *Remote Apples* (1994), *A Shape for Absence* (1997), and *A Sweeter Night* (2002). She has been awarded two literary prizes: the Youth Short Story Prize (1993) and the Mahmoud Sayf al-Din al-Irani Short Story Prize (1994). She is a promising writer with a leaning toward the realistic description of experience.

HEART FAILURE

"Heart failure. She's in a serious state."

"Is it very serious?"

"You should have brought her to the hospital before. It's a matter of hours. The chances are very slim. Where's her mother?"

"Has she asked for her mother?"

"Straight away."

"Her mother's in Damascus, Doctor."

"You'd better send her a telegram, quickly. She might just get here while she's still alive."

"Can I see her?"

"No, please. She mustn't be excited in any way. It's better that way for the present. You follow me?"

"Zahia, do try and stop the baby crying!"

"What should I say in the telegram to her mother?"

"Zahia, I told you to stop the baby crying!"

"What can her mother do for her anyway?"

"Zahia, the baby's crying!"

"We could telegram her uncle to book her mother a seat."

"Zahia, stop the baby crying!"

"Didn't you hear what the doctor said?"

"Of course I did. But the baby's hungry."

"Give him some milk then."

"How can I?"

"How about contacting her uncle? To save time?"

"I can't. There isn't any milk."

"Good idea."

"Take him home, then, and put him with his brothers."

"His brothers aren't there."

"How is she now, doctor?"

"Where are they then?"

"No change. The pulse is weak."

"I left them at the neighbor's."

"Is there any hope at all?"

"The neighbor's?"

"Very little."

"I couldn't leave them at home."

"Will you people stop that baby crying!"

"Zahia, stop the baby crying."

"I've told you! He's hungry!"

"What's the time now?"

"It's passing so slowly."

"Nurse him with some milk."

"I can't. There isn't any milk."

"I'm so worried."

"Don't keep on worrying."

"I'm worried about the two boys."

"The neighbor will take good care of them."

"I can't be sure of that."

"I told you. Don't worry."

"It'll be all right."

"There's some hope, the doctor says."

"Hardly any."

"Still, there's some hope."

She sat on a long bench, watching a scene in which the characters never stopped moving backward and forward, right and left. She crossed her legs, and her skirt rose to reveal part of her upper leg. She quickly jammed the leg against the other one till the two seemed to fuse. She pushed her shining pink shoe right under the seat, then spread her arms over her lap to try and control the confusion written all over her face. She gazed at the shining white tiles. They were very big and spotlessly clean, with the sharp smell of dettol very evident. She raised her head and fixed her gaze on the cream-colored walls. A black skeleton, almost wholly decayed, stared back at her. It had several cigarette stubs in the middle of its lung, and a cloud of gray smoke had collected in the chest. "Smoking is a principal cause of cancer, and of diseases of the chest and heart." The skeleton was fully life-size, as large as hers; and yet hers was agitated now, the size Zahia's would have been if she hadn't been holding the baby; the same size as Dawud's, but Dawud's body was agitated too, looking as anxious as Dawud himself; the size of the doctor, who was slight, just like the hope he gave them every so often—the size of Hala's body stretched out there on the bed, in a gloomy closed room, waiting for a few hours to pass, just a few bare hours! The size of the body of Abu Samih, Hala's uncle. He was coming and going. They were all walking to and fro, except Hala's body and hers, the lungs of all their bodies holding worries and gray clouds that never cleared. The poster was the size of the skeleton itself, with a violet background and deep red lines that found a reflection in the lung of each of them. The baby was crying its eyes out now. She took him from Zahia and put him in her lap. Her skirt creased up and her legs opened, to reveal parts of her upper legs.

Dawud gazed at her anxiously. Be patient, her eyes told him. God will be with you, they said, and with Hala, and with me too. God will be with me too, Dawud. But Dawud's eyes didn't see her, only Zahia, and the baby crying again, and Abu Samih, and the huge, clean, white tiles, over and over again. Dawud's eyes saw the baby, but didn't focus on her lap, or on the creased skirt pushed back to reveal her legs, parted a little where the full thighs were provocatively exposed; and there was another thing, dark, showing between the two thighs, something far away, not clearly visible perhaps, but its presence felt for all that, because it was something eyes, ears, nose, tongue, teeth, and hands wanted to seek out. She felt abashed. "Shame on you!" she told herself. She brought the baby up onto her breast, closed her legs, and pulled down her skirt. The worn-out black skeleton and the thick cloud of smoke glared at her angrily. Feeling more ashamed than ever, she jammed her legs together still closer, feeling as though a hot iron rod were burning between them.

The doctor was saying Hala had just a few more hours to live, repeating that hopes were slim—that there was really no hope at all. "Hala's dead." Hala was dying, and when she was dead the baby would stop crying. Dawud would slump down alongside her on the seat, his perfume seeping into her. "Be patient," she'd tell him—but he'd put his head in his hands and weep. Zahia was screaming. The doctor and nurses heard her and told her to stop it. "Shh! Shh!" There were other sick people there, some would die and some live on. Zahia stopped screaming, then started up again, more quietly now. Abu Samih was resting his head against the great poster of the black skeleton and weeping softly. The poster was very tall, stretching from the middle of the wall right up to the top, so that Abu Samih's head only just reached between the skeleton's two legs, and the ashes from the cigarette stubs were dropping over his head. She was weeping too, of course. Taking the baby to her breast and jamming her legs together, she gathered up her conflicting feelings and wept.

Dawud was leaving the hospital, alone. She followed him. The baby cried with Zahia, she said, but not with her. She told him how she loved the child, how she'd like to keep him with her, just for a little while at least. She told him how she loved all his children: Ahmad, Ashraf, and Amjad. Amjad was still very small, it was best he stay there with her, while Ahmad and Ashraf stayed on with the neighbor. And yet, why not take those two as well? It was better they stayed together with their nursing brother. They wouldn't be any trouble to her at all—she loved them, and they'd be a consolation to her. Zahia, of course, had five children of her own, and his children, so very young and full of sorrow, would be a burden. But she was on her own, with no children—no anything. His children would be hers, just for the time being of course. Dawud agreed, and so she took the children; and when Amjad was asleep, she went out with Ahmad and Ashraf to the shops. She bought a toy ambulance with a revolving blue light on its roof, and Ashraf took a fancy to a clown that climbed a barrel, then suddenly fell off it, only to start climbing all over again; and so it went on. She bought that as well. Then she took them to a restaurant and bought them some big hamburgers. Children always loved big hamburgers. She ate some too, so as to get closer to them. They knew, they told her, that their mother, Hala, was dead, and they cried a lot, but they loved her because she was like their mother. She hugged them, and in the evening she told them the story of the charmed prince and didn't force them to drink milk in the morning, and she bought them so many toys and let them stay up an extra hour in the evening, which their father, Dawud, never did. They loved her so much, just as they loved their mother, Hala; they told her how they wished she could stay with them forever. Amjad loved her too, they said, and didn't cry with her the way he did with their aunt Zahia. And they told her their father, Dawud, would love her just as much as they did. Then she said she loved them very much, so very much, and she'd like to stay with them, but she—here she fell silent. (She had to fall silent here.)

At night she helped them on with their pajamas and gave Amjad some milk, and she made dinner for Ahmad and Ashraf and sat with them. They talked and laughed; then they heard a knock at the door. It was Dawud. She was in her wide pink nightgown, cut low at the neck to show part of her full, ivory breasts. No, it had better be her sky-blue nightgown with the thin shoulder straps that flowed gently down her body. The slit on its side reached just above her knee, revealing something of her full, white thigh. No! She'd better not show herself in that particular nightgown. What would he say about her? A single woman, living alone—what did it mean, that she had such an alluring, revealing nylon nightgown? He'd be right too. It had better be her violet cotton nightgown. It was sleeveless, true, and fitted tightly and provocatively over the curves of her ripe, well-rounded body; but it was the right one, because the caller was Dawud. When she saw him at the door she pretended to be surprised and ran to her bedroom like lightning, in her bare feet, to put on the robe. He stayed at the door, and she came shyly back, getting over her surprise. He apologized for coming so late. "Not at all!" she insisted. "Make yourself at home." He asked how the children were. "They're all fine," she said. "Amjad's asleep, and Ahmad and Ashraf are having dinner." Then he asked how she was herself. "I'm fine, thanks," she said. She gazed into his face. It was sad and gaunt-looking, with the stubble of his beard showing irregularly here and there. Ahmad and Ashraf went up to him and hugged and kissed him, and he kissed them, in turn, on the cheek, the forehead, the neck, and the ears. She felt a warmth seeping into her. She asked him to come in, and he did, sitting on the sofa with Ahmad leaning up against him, while Ashraf climbed onto his lap. He thanked her for the way she was looking after his children. It was the least she could do, she replied; then, after a brief silence, she added that she loved children. A further brief, planned silence, then she said, "all children." Another silence. She felt, she said, as though his children were really hers. But no, that wasn't right, that was surely moving things on too quickly. He told her how he missed the children, how the house felt totally empty and dead. He'd call by next morning, he said, and collect them. She couldn't protest or ask to keep them with her any longer—they were his children, after all, not hers—but her pain and sorrow were clearly visible. He could feel her pain but didn't say a word (not now, because he was going to speak later on). He ate dinner with them, and Ahmad and Ashraf were happy. She was like Mummy, they told him, she bought them big hamburgers, and played with them, and told them the story of the magic frog. She shyly gathered her robe around her body, so as not to reveal her white breast, and he felt embarrassed too. He listened to them, smiling but saying nothing.

Next morning, when he came to take the children, Ahmad and Ashraf stayed close to her, leaning their heads against her legs and crying. They asked her to come with them, insisting they loved her the way they loved Mummy. They asked her to come and live with them—always (they should insist on this, in front of Dawud). She felt embarrassed, but a vibrant joy swept through every inch of her body. She wanted to say, "I wish I could," but that wasn't possible. He thanked her again, then said goodbye, took his children and left. She watched them till they disappeared from sight, then turned pale, feeling as though melted wax had frozen over her stiffened legs.

A few days later he rang her up. Dawud rang her up, his voice coming tenderly over the phone. He asked how she was and told her the children missed her, and she said she missed them too. He missed her as well, he added, and she replied that she missed him as well. He didn't know what to do, he went on. The children were crying night and day, and he didn't know what to do. Aunt Zahia looked in every so often, but couldn't do anything; the children didn't like her very much anyway. Abu Samih came too, but didn't know how to handle the children, any more than he did. Ahmad kept asking for her, night and day, while Ashraf wanted beans with tomatoes. As for him, he'd burned his shirt ironing it and been late for work. She laughed and so did he, then he told her the children wanted to see her and he did too. She promised to look in and see him, or rather see them (it was important to say "him" first, then correct it to "them"). She did look in on them, and Ahmad and Ashraf rushed to greet her. She changed Amjad's diapers, prepared his meal, and put him to sleep. She cooked dried beans with tomatoes, cleaned the bathroom, washed the dishes, tidied the rooms, washed the boys' pajamas, and washed Dawud's shirts; then, in the evening, Dawud came home, greeted her warmly and had dinner with her and the children. She left then, but returned next day, and the next, and the next, and every day the children greeted her still more warmly, and he greeted her still more warmly. Once Ahmad asked for stuffed zucchini, and once Ashraf asked for *mujaddara*.[1] Once, too, Dawud asked for an okra dish. She loved all this, loved it and longed for it too. No sooner had one day ended than she started waiting for the next. She became, by common consent, part of the family and felt she loved them so much. She loved Ahmad and Ashraf and Amjad, and she loved—Dawud. Poor Dawud, he was a man on his own. He couldn't change Amjad's diapers, didn't wash the dishes properly, left the rooms unswept, didn't know how to cook dried beans with tomatoes. He didn't know the story of the magic frog, and he couldn't take Ahmad and Ashraf out to eat big hamburgers when they wanted to. She didn't blame him. How could she? He was a man, and men didn't understand these things. Sometimes she'd see him standing there in an apron with his sleeves rolled up and wearing women's slippers, and she'd stifle her laughter and feel sorry for him at the same time. She'd see too, though, how his trousers were rolled up to the knees almost, and she was shocked at the thick hair on his legs. She hadn't had the chance to see this hair before. She drew her own legs together as she sensed the wetness between them.

The neighbors started talking about them (you shouldn't ignore that). So she stopped visiting them for a few days. He phoned her, asking, anxiously, why she'd

---

1. A national dish in Palestine, Jordan, Syria, and Lebanon, made of lentils and rice or lentils and crushed wheat.

stopped coming, with concern and longing in his voice. The children, he said, missed her and asked for her all the time. She started crying, and he got worried again, asking her what was the matter. But she just went on crying (this was something he must work out for himself); she said, simply, that she couldn't visit them any more and hung up. (Surely he'd understand now.) The days passed, and she didn't visit them, and they didn't visit her. She was burning with love for him, and he was burning with love for her. She lifted the receiver, dialed one number, then the next, then hung up. He lifted the receiver, rang one number, and a second, and a third, then hung up. Then, at last, he phoned to say Ahmad was sick, and she hurried over to him and Ahmad. He opened the door, pressed her hand with great warmth, and she surrendered to the warmth. She felt wet in every pore of her body, felt as though she hadn't seen him for years. She rushed to see Ahmad, who was running a temperature, and asked Dawud if he'd called the doctor. Yes, he said, he had, and the doctor had said it was a minor fever that would pass. Ahmad looked at her, his face drawn and pale, and called out to her, and she went and sat by him, wiping his forehead. He had a fever, just as she had! She brought cold water, along with a towel that she dipped in the water and laid on his forehead. "Don't leave us," Ahmad said insistently. "I love you. We all love you." But she knew it wasn't possible. How could she let that happen, betray her dear friend Hala? Marry Dawud? Hala would never forgive her, and she'd never forgive herself. But Dawud loved her; he told her so. And she loved him; she told him so. But she couldn't! She'd go on loving him and loving him, and she'd love the children, and cry a lot. Maybe she'd never get married at all, devote her whole life to them. Only she couldn't marry him. (Yes, that was a much better way.)

"The danger's passed, thank God. Everything's back to normal."

She woke to hear the doctor's voice, sounding relaxed now. Everyone relaxed in fact. Zahia stopped walking round and round. Abu Samih, for the first time in hours, sat down and stretched his legs out in front of him, calm and quiet. Even the baby, now, was calm in her lap. Dawud rushed up to the doctor: "Is Hala all right then, Doctor? Can I see her, please?" The doctor gave a pleasant smile. Hala would be just fine, he told him; there was nothing to worry about at all. Dawud loved Hala, and Hala loved him. She loved Dawud too, but Dawud didn't love her. He seized the child from her lap, not even noticing the raised skirt that revealed her legs. He carried him and fondled him, while her lap remained empty and her skirt raised. Abu Samih and Zahia said goodbye to him and left. They'd shared the anxiety and fear, done their part of walking to and fro over the shining, clean floor, and now their role was over. Dawud embraced his little child and followed the doctor, wanting to see Hala. He thanked her, of course, for sharing his anxiety, saying what a faithful friend she was; and then she was alone. The tiles were white and clean, bearing no trace of the footsteps of Abu Samih and Zahia, and tomorrow fresh people would walk on them, anxious and sad, leaving no trace either. Every year millions of anxious, sad people would walk on them and leave no trace. They were white tiles, clean and flat, like water. If you cut through water, it becomes whole again, by itself, in a few seconds, leaving not the remotest trace. She looked at the poster gazing across at her, and that seemed silly and unconvincing too, especially as it was wearing a colored sports cap and funny sunglasses. Even the cloud of smoke looked meager now against the violet background with the red lines. And she'd never seen a skeleton wearing sports shoes before. It was utterly ridiculous.

And so she left alone, as she'd come, waiting for the next heart failure.

—Translated by Salwa Jabsheh and Christopher Tingley

Emile Habiby (1921–1996)

Palestinian novelist, short-story writer, and journalist Emile Habiby was one of the most distinguished literary figures in occupied Palestine, as well as one of the most original writers of fiction in the Arab world. After completing his secondary education in Acre and Haifa, he worked as a laborer in the port of Haifa, then as a broadcaster for the Palestine Broadcasting Corporation. In 1940 he joined the Communist Party and became editor-in-chief of its weekly organ, *Al-Ittihad*. After 1948 he joined Rakah, the Israeli Communist Party, which he represented for nineteen years in the Israeli Knesset. In 1969 he published his first short-story collection, *Six Stories of the Six-Day War*, after the June War of 1967, followed by his famous novel, *The Secret Life of Saeed, the Pessoptimist*. Translated by PROTA in 1982 (with a second printing in 1984 and a third in 1999), this novel deals deftly with the conditions of the Palestinians in Israel, using a style that mixes the comic with the tragic in order to bring out the painful contradictions of life under siege. His novel *Pieta* appeared in 1985, and his last work, *The Squadrons of the Ogre's Daughter*, was published in 1992.

THE MANDELBAUM GATE

"Why don't you admit she wants to get out of here?" the Israeli soldier shouted. He was standing, hands folded together, at the Mandelbaum gate, when I told him that we'd come with our mother, who intended, with formal permission, to get through to the other side. I pointed to the Jordanian side of the gate.

It was the end of winter, and the sunlight anticipated the spring. Wherever the rubble had left a patch of land free the earth had overtaken it with green. Children with long hair covering their temples played amongst these waste patches. They were a subject of curiosity to the children who'd accompanied us to say goodbye to their grandmother. "Boys with braided hair?"[1] they questioned, "how can that

---

1. A reference to Orthodox Jewish children, who grow their hair and wear it in braids or locks.

be?" In the middle of this area was a wide paved square, sheeted with dust, in the quarter that we knew as al-Musrara. The square was equipped with two strategic gates, made of whitewashed iron sheets and buttressed inside with stones. The width of each gate allowed for a car to enter or exit.

The soldier uttered the word "exit" from between his teeth with a rancor intended to impress. Getting out, by which he meant leaving paradise, carries with it a profound significance that outweighs the importance of getting there. And this customs policeman wanted to make things clear, so he made a point of telling us as we were exchanging farewell kisses with our mother: "People who leave here never come back."

I suppose that similar thoughts preoccupied my mother during her last days among us. For, when our relatives and friends gathered in her house the evening prior to her departure for Jerusalem, she said: "I've lived long enough to witness my own mourners." In the morning, when we came down the sloping alley to the car, she looked behind and waved to the olive trees, and to the old dry apricot tree, and to the threshold of the house, and asked herself how many times in twenty years she'd climbed this alley and descended its slope.

And when the car passed by the cemetery at the outskirts of the city, she exclaimed, calling the dead among her relatives and peers and saying farewell to their graves: "How is it that I'm not to be buried here? And who's going to put flowers on my granddaughter's grave now?" When she undertook the pilgrimage to Jerusalem in 1940, a fortune-teller had told that she'd die in the Holy City. Was his prophecy going to come true, after all?

At seventy-five she had not yet experienced that heartrending realisation, that feeling accompanied by a spiritual void and depression in the chest, not unlike the pangs of conscience, which comprises the deep yearning for the motherland! Were she to be asked for a definition of the motherland, she would be confused as to how to reply. To her mind it might mean the home, the washing bowl and the *kubbeh* basin and mortar that she'd inherited from her mother. How they'd laughed at her when she'd wanted to carry this washing bowl on her travel, although she was prone to forget the *kubbeh* mortar and basin. And wasn't the motherland also the morning calls of the *laban* vendor, the kerosene seller's clanging bell, the coughing of a sick husband, the nights of her children's weddings, the children who'd left this threshold one after another, secure in the promise of their marital homes but leaving her alone?

As she looked back a last time, she felt that threshold could speak out and give witness to the times she'd stood on it, suffocating her tears as she relinquished her respective brides and grooms.

I brought you into the world, an unfeathered fledgling, and taught you how to chirp, to fly, and to make your nest, and when you grew up and developed wings, you flew away, and all my toil was gratuitous.

If she had been told that all this comprised the motherland, she would have been none the wiser. But now, as she looked out at the forbidden land and awaited the signal to advance, she turned to her daughter and said, "I wish I could sit for a last time on my threshold!"

Her middle-aged brother, who'd come from the village to say goodbye, shook his head with alternate signs of pain and surprise in his face. This mysterious "thing" that his sister had to leave behind because she couldn't carry it with her was also precious to him. Our neighbour told him, "Like it or not, in the end you'll have to sign the sales agreement. The law's on their side."

The old villager then turned to me and said, "Listen, nephew, my father, my younger brother, and I were once guarding the land that was planted with cucumbers when a flock of partridges flew down on to the plantation. My younger brother was quick to raise his rifle, as was expected of a man, while my father just laughed. Do you remember how your grandfather used to laugh? He'd say, 'Boy, hunting partridges is men's work!' But my brother was obstinate. He came back to us after an hour's activity, carrying, to our general surprise, a live partridge. And the little devil prided himself on his exaggerated achievement.

"'But we never heard a shot!' my father exclaimed

"'I charmed the rifle,' the young hunter answered.

"He then made me solemnly promise not to divulge the secret to our father, if he took me into his confidence. The truth was that he'd seen the bird being carried in the jaws of a ferocious cat, and had pursued the animal from one thorn shrub to another until he succeeded in saving the bird from the cat's jaws . . .

"But, nephew!" he continued. "Do they really expect me to sign the sales slip for all these memories? How little the power of their laws is!"

I advise you never to visit Mandelbaum Gate accompanied by children. This is not because the demolished shells of houses invite their curiosity to look inside for the "magic lamp" and the "Aladdin's cave," and not because the little boys' curls and braids reaching their shoulders would tempt the children to ask embarrassing questions, but because the street that leads to Mandelbaum Gate is never empty, even for a moment, of cars that traverse it, with real European speed, either coming from "there" or leaving "here." And always elegant American cars, their occupants smartly dressed, with starched collars and shirts of every color, or wearing military uniforms that were intended to be stained with whiskey and not blood.

These cars belonged to the forces of the Mixed Armistice Commission, the United Nations Truce Supervision Organization, the United Nations forces, as well as to the ambassadors of Western states, their consuls and wives and household cooks, their bars and pretty women. The cars would stop for a short time at our gate, while the drivers exchanged greetings with the soldiers as a token of courtesy. Then they would cross the area designated as no-man's-land and repeat the procedure with the other party's soldiers, cordially exchanging cigarette packets and jokes. What transpired from this was a Jordanian-Israeli competition enacted at both gates.

The law of death, whereby those who enter do not return, seemed powerless to affect these passengers. For His Excellency the Chief Supervisor can have lunch at the Philadelphia Hotel in Amman and dinner at the Aden Hotel in the Israeli part of Jerusalem, while his polite smile never leaves his lips in either place.

When my sister began entreating the soldier standing at our gate to allow her to walk with her mother to the Jordanian gate, he told her, "It's strictly forbidden, madam."

"But I see foreigners coming in and out as if they were in their own country!" my sister replied.

"Anyone on earth has the right to come and go by those two gates, except the people who live there," the soldier said.

Then he added, "Please stay away from the road. It's a public thoroughfare and very crowded." He interrupted his speech to engage in conversation with the passengers of a car. Both parties laughed. As for us, we lacked all comprehension of the joke.

The customs officer said, "Everything has an end, even the hour of parting."

And from our gate to theirs an old lady hobbled out, supported by a stick, and began slowly to cross the endangered territory, looking behind her every now and then, as she waved her hand and went forward. And why at this precise moment did she remember her son who'd died thirty years ago when he fell into her arms from the attic? And why was she also, now, struck by the remorse of conscience?

A tall soldier appeared from behind a rubble pile on the other side, wearing a *kufiyya* and *igal* on his head. He received the old woman and stood talking to her, and both were looking in our direction.

We stood there, with our children, waving. A second, equally tall soldier, only bareheaded, engaged us in conversation. We kept looking to the other side, while he warned us against taking a single step forward.

He said to us, "It's as if she'd crossed the valley of death from which nothing returns. This is the reality of war and restrictive frontiers and the Mandelbaum Gate. But please, make way for the United Nations' cars to pass."

Suddenly a little body pulsing with life cut free from our group like a ball skilfully placed toward the rival team's goal. This small thing ran forward across the "forbidden land," and to our surprise we saw my young daughter running toward her grandmother, calling, "Tata, Tata," as she crossed the danger zone and reached her grandmother, who took her in her arms.

From a distance, we watched the soldier with the *kufiyya* and *igal* lower his head. My own eyesight is so very sharp that I saw him scratch the earth with his foot, while simultaneously the hatless soldier near us unconsciously repeated that action. The soldier standing with his arms crossed at his office door went inside, and the customs policeman was suddenly busy rummaging through his pockets for something he'd just discovered was missing.

And miraculously occurring, before our eyes, was the feat of a little girl crossing the "Valley of Death from which there is no return" and returning from it, having contradicted the reality of war and frontiers and the Mandelbaum Gate.

And this was done by a little ignorant girl unable to differentiate between the soldier who wears a *kufiyya* and *igal* and one who is hatless. And what an innocent naive child who didn't feel that she'd been transported across oceans to a different country but accepted it as a literal journey between two gates.

With her father standing on one side and her grandmother on the other, why shouldn't she be free to come and go between them as she did every day at home? And the cars coming and going across this median territory resembled those she saw every day near her house. Here they speak Hebrew and there they speak Arabic, and she speaks the two languages with Nina and Susu!

It appears that the customs officer despaired of finding whatever it was he was looking for. He stopped his search abruptly, just as he'd started it (everything has an end, even a predicament!) and in a consolatory voice, said to the soldier, "An ignorant little girl!"

"Gentlemen, please back away from the street, the cars here travel fast, and we don't want a child to risk falling between the wheels."

Do you understand now why I advised you not to come to Mandelbaum Gate accompanied with children? Their logic is simple and uncomplicated. How sane it is!

—*Translated by Sharif Elmusa and Jeremy Reed*

Ghalib Halasa (1937–1986)

Jordanian novelist, short-story writer, and critic Ghalib Halasa studied at Cairo University and worked as a journalist in Cairo, Beirut, and Damascus. His collection of short stories *Bedouins, Blacks, and Peasants* (1976) reflects many of his experiences in some of these countries and also shows his intimate knowledge, usually ignored or overlooked by modern Arab writers ('Abd al-Rahman Munif being the prime exception), of bedouin mentality and attitudes. In these stories Halasa employs his knowledge symbolically to reflect the present-day situation where oil and what it brought about in terms of money and power prompted a revival of old bedouin culture and mentality, sometimes at odds with modern life. Another short story collection is *Wadi', Saint Milada and Others* (1971). His most famous work is a novella entitled *Ordeal by Fire* (1964), which also reflects his deep knowledge of peasant traditions. He wrote several novels, including *Laughter* (1971), *Sirocco* (1975), *The Question* (1979), *Weeping on the Traces of Ruins* (1980), *Three Faces for Baghdad* (1984), and *Sultana* (1987). His critical works reflect a wide knowledge of the contemporary Arab novel.

A MIDNIGHT VISIT

Zaidan wanted to put out the lantern, but his wife said that the dark fright-ened her.

He asked how she could be afraid with him sleeping beside her. She an-swered that when the light went out, she felt she was sleeping outdoors.

"When we've picked enough grain, we'll sell it and buy a house near your father's," he said.

"Being near my father's is not important," she replied. "Wherever you go, I'll go with you."

He realized she was apologizing for her fretfulness about living in a tent, and he was pleased that she was being thoughtful. He decided that he would never take her away from home again. When he married her, he had known that she came from a line of wise and tender women; he had always felt she was of an especially refined nature. Once he had saved up enough money to buy a house and a few *dunums* of land, he would become worthy of her. This was the reason he and his brother had emigrated.

He told her that he was sorry for having separated her from her mother and friends. His voice had a ring of genuine sadness to it, and he was afraid she might look down on him for this. But she surprised him: with a surge of her large body she wrapped her arms around him and clung to him.

At the same moment he heard the man's voice from outside.

"Zaidan! Hey, Zaidan!"

And before he could respond, or even feel astonished at a visitor who came at such a late hour, the bedouin burst in on him, saying angrily, "Why didn't you answer, you *peasant?*"

Zaidan rose to greet him.

"Why didn't you answer?" the bedouin insisted.

In confusion, Zaidan said, "Welcome . . ."

He sat when the bedouin sat, and started to pull the quilt up over his wife's reclining body. With his cane the bedouin rapped on the quilt above his wife's leg and said, "Get up! Don't you show respect to your guests?"

The bedouin's face was dry and bony. Long, dirty braids, pitch-black, hung from beneath his *kufiyya*. His eyes glinted fiercely and his face was shaped like a rectangular pyramid, with his nose forming the pointed tip. On his chest two belts crisscrossed, holding in their leather loops bullets for his rifle.

Suddenly the bedouin stood up. Thinking he was going to leave, Zaidan reached out his hand in farewell. But the bedouin ignored the extended hand, spun around to behind the reclining woman, and nudged her in the back.

"Get up, girl!" he said. "Heat some water for me! I want to have a bath!"

The woman fixed her eyes on her husband's, but Zaidan lowered his gaze, looking down at his two big, rough hands. She flung the quilt off of the top part of her body, took hold of her black gown, and put her head through the collar.

Then, kicking the quilt away, she stood up. The gown hitched a few seconds around her hips before dropping down. Her legs showed, bare and round, their whiteness tinged with a red flush. Disgust came over Zaidan at the sight. It was as though he had seen his mother naked.

"Get on with it!" the bedouin said to her and sat down again, turning his back to Zaidan. He sat quietly, but with a distinct air of menace.

Zaidan sat hunched over, ashamed of his strong, muscular body. He felt it excessively large; he wished he could be slight and lithe, like the bedouin. He began to hate his own broad palms and his shoulders, which, he imagined, were swelling out across the width of the tent. He saw himself through Sahloul's eyes, peering through his aristocratic pride at these peasants with their huge bodies, at their slow, heavy movements, at their funny accent with its monotonous ring and its slow, stumbling enunciation . . . His hatred for himself increased.

The woman began to gather small pieces of wood. She fixed them into the ground with their tips together, forming open triangles that the air could pass through. With her forefinger she dug in the ash for an ember, then wiped her thumb with her gown. She rubbed her nose, leaving a bit of ash on its tip. Then she turned—sitting all the while—and took up a leather bag, into which she looked for matches. She turned the other way and got the kerosene can. With supple fingers she poured a few drops onto the sticks and lit the fire. Her face was flushed, absorbed.

The bedouin stirred, and Zaidan realized that she had aroused him. Through his internalization of the bedouin's desire, Zaidan began to desire her too. He felt this desire as something new and strange, as though it were incestuous.

The bedouin's back was almost completely turned away from him—only his braid and protruding cheekbones were visible. His 'abaya had slipped from over his stooping back. Underneath the 'abaya he was wearing a white qunbaz. His shoulder blades jutted out, and between them there was a deep hollow. Zaidan's eyes were glued to that hollow: he felt a great urge to touch it, to feel his hand gliding between the two shoulder blades; he could feel the touch of the white silk on his fingers, and the bedouin's protruding bones . . .

Suddenly he felt that he had to do something to resolve the matter quickly. He began to tremble as he heard his heart pounding like a drum in his ears.

Smoke filled the tent and collected around the lantern. Through the smoke and the tears it brought to his eyes, he saw his wife's face—fierce, proud, intently watching the flames.

"More wood, girl! Put on more wood!" the bedouin said.

These words hit Zaidan like a blow. They made him aware of the boundaries of his body and the distance that separated him from the bedouin. He had the feeling that each of them was a discrete unit with its own place on the floor of the tent. With a flash of unsettling intuition, the truth of the situation revealed itself to him now: the purpose of the visit and his own impotence to do anything about it.

He avoided looking at his wife's face. He was afraid of their eyes meeting, of the insistence in hers that would demand him to dare, to act. He asked himself,

"What is the bedouin going to say once the water is heated? Will he take off his clothes in front of her? Will he take her to bed on the mattress with his body wet? And she—how will she act?"

It occurred to him that she would deal well with the situation. She seemed collected, which meant that she had a plan laid out. He was reassured and comforted by this idea.

The bedouin started coughing. With each cough his shoulders rose and fell.

"Girls tell their mothers everything that happens to them away from home," he said to himself. In a flash he saw her mother's face; he saw the village market, its shops, the patrons of the single coffee bar, the olive trees, the mosque's minaret, and the early morning light that enveloped them all . . . *He plunged his dagger into the hollow between the bedouin's shoulder blades. The bedouin's back was as hard as oak wood, and he did not strike with sufficient strength. Through the rip in Sahloul's* qumbaz *he could see the small red scratch, from which flowed not one drop of blood . . . Laughing, the bedouin turned to him. Still laughing, he reached for his rifle and fired at him . . . Here, here in the forehead the bullet pierced; and it was not only the point of impact that hurt but his whole head that became full of thunder and pain . . .*

Squatting with his head bent down was giving him cramps, but Zaidan dared not shift his position. He was afraid. The violence that had just been filling his head made him want to keep his eyes on the bedouin.

From outside came the neighing of a horse. For some reason he could not quite grasp, he considered this a good omen. The story-teller in the sheikh's house finished one of his songs with a *rababa*. Consequently, Zaidan told himself, everything would end well . . .

The bedouin was speaking to his wife now. Zaidan remained silent. His wife did not answer, and she directed a quick, black, flashing, conspiratorial look his way. He did not understand its meaning, but it cut through him like a sharp blade. His heart heaved, and dizziness overcame him.

"*We married our daughter off to a man, Zaidan,*" her mother's angry, haughty face *was saying to him. "This is how you dishonor her in a foreign country!*"

"*Try to understand me! Try to understand me . . .*"

"*You have dishonored her in a foreign country . . .*"

"*Yes, I am a man! Look! . . .*" He drew his dagger stealthily and came down with it on the bedouin's back: once, twice, three times, four, five, six . . . And the bedouin toppled over, jerking his legs like a little goat that has just been slaughtered . . . And there was Zaidan on a horse, his wife mounted behind him, galloping across the mountains and the night . . .

Suddenly he discovered that the bedouin was looking straight at him.

"I see you're being silent," he said. "Be careful, now, that you don't get angry!"

"No," said Zaidan.

The bedouin laughed out loud. Zaidan felt embarrassed. He did not know what to do. He began to laugh accommodatingly. The bedouin turned his face away. *Will he take her to bed with his body wet?* He craned his neck toward the woman and pointed his thumb at Zaidan.

"He's not angry!" And again he laughed out loud.

Should he laugh too, Zaidan thought, with the insult lying like a heavy weight on his chest? Then he remembered his wife's flashing, conspiratorial look, and its message now seemed clear to him: "Leave everything to me! I will kill the bedouin while his body is all covered with soap!"

That made sense. After all, she was the one he was going to be taking to bed, not he . . .

Only something else had happened, and he did not know what . . . His wife was casting a frank, direct glance at him, as though she disapproved of something or as though she had asked a question and was waiting for a reply . . . The bedouin was smiling . . .

"Thinking ruffles the temper," he said to the woman. Then, he addressed Zaidan, "Why are you so quiet?"

He turned to the woman and laughed, as she looked at her husband in disbelief.

So, there had been a private exchange between her and the bedouin in which he, Zaidan, had not shared. And at the same time he felt the weight of her surprised look, which insisted that he do something.

"What do these two want of me?" he asked himself. A violent anger took possession of him. In it he tried to escape from the black light that shone in her eyes. "What does this woman want of me? Am I supposed to die so that she can remain pure and chaste, untouched like a king's daughter? What does it matter if he sleeps with her?"

Sahloul was his master, and hers too. As long as they chose to work for him, they had to bear the consequences.

He began addressing his words to her mother: *How was I to know that he intended to sleep with her? I thought that he was simply going to have a bath and then go back home . . . That's their custom in this region . . . We are their servants—we have to do it . . . Why did she let him sleep with her? Was it my fault she preferred him to me and seduced him . . .*

He hung on to this thought like a lifebuoy: she preferred the bedouin to him; she preferred the bedouin . . . But all the while he sensed that there was some flaw in this line of reasoning that he found so convincing. It would come out: after the night visitor had left and Zaidan was face-to-face with her, or the next day when he faced the other peasants in the field, or back at the village coffee bar as he sat with friends, that flaw would make him realize that there was something he had been expected to do that he hadn't done . . .

The bedouin was talking to his wife, and she was looking at her husband with that same gleaming look of disbelief. The rhythm of the bedouin's word stuck in his head like a song whose lyrics he had forgotten. He was afraid to remember them. Deep down he knew that the bedouin was asking her how a woman as beautiful as she was could have married a boor like him, who was unable to feed or protect her. Her response was still the same strange, surprised look.

Zaidan convinced himself that he had heard nothing. His eyes were glued to the bedouin's back, to the hollow between the shoulder blades. In his imagination he touched it as he would touch a familiar thing, as he would put his hand on the shoulder of a friend. He longed for the bedouin to look at him with sympathy.

"Is the water hot?" asked the bedouin.

The woman nodded automatically.

Suddenly it seemed to Zaidan that what was happening was completely natural. It was not the end of the world. His wife, who was more intelligent than he, had realized that there was no need for all this fear and torment. The bedouin had come to them as a friend . . . He began to laugh.

The bedouin took off his *kufiyya* and threw it onto the mattress. His long hair made him look like an emaciated girl. Standing, feet apart, he pulled his hands out through the sleeves of his *'abaya,* which he threw violently behind him. Then he turned around. He saw Zaidan and his eyes narrowed.

"Are you still here?"

Zaidan stammered.

"Do you want me to undress in front of you? Have you no shame? Get out!"

Zaidan did not stand but crawled out of the tent on all fours. Outside, he felt an urge to leave this place far behind and never return. He heard the bedouin's voice calling him from inside:

"Hey, Zaidan, don't go far! I want you to make us some tea!"

Without thinking, he answered that he would not go far.

The open space was vast and dark. Some tents were lit by dim lanterns, occasionally eclipsed by moving shadows. In one of these tents, he knew, friends of Sahloul's were sitting, watching him in his nocturnal adventures and laughing: they had seen the fire kindled; they had seen Zaidan come out of the tent, leaving his wife to Sahloul . . .

He felt the slap of humiliation and impotence.

He turned toward the tent and saw that the front screen had been lowered. He walked to it and stood behind, listening. He heard the sound of water splashing.

A cold breeze blew from the west. "They must have seen me as I left the tent," he thought, but that didn't mean much. With his finger he looked for a slit in the side of the tent and found it. He widened it and peered in.

The bedouin was squatting naked on the floor. His hair was covered with soap. He was as slight as a child, and over him stood Zaidan's wife's large body.

"This is perfectly normal. The man wants a bath." He saw her first rub him with a *loufa,* then pour the water . . . And Zaidan decided that as soon as his wife had finished bathing Sahloul, he would go right in and put the teakettle on the fire.

His wife was standing behind the naked man. She reached her hand out and rubbed his chest with the *loufa.*

Zaidan felt sick. He left his place and walked some distance away. Immediately, he sensed that he was being followed. He looked around him, then stopped and listened, but he heard nothing.

"Who's there?" he shouted. His voice faded into the emptiness. It was just an illusion, he told himself.

He walked anxiously along the slippery ground of the downward slope. On the other side of the valley a hill rose, black. All the while he felt that they were watching him, that they would take him by surprise and he would have to answer their questions: *"What are you doing here? Why did you leave your wife with the bedouin? How come you let Sahloul in—aren't we big enough for you?"*

He considered returning, but when he remembered his wife's hand reaching down over the bedouin's shoulder, he felt revulsion, and changed his mind.

He paused and started listening. Definitely, someone was following him: the sound of footsteps was distinct. "Run away, Zaidan!" he said to himself. "From now on he will come every night . . ."

Then, he glimpsed his pursuer's frame reflected in the clear water. He was quickly getting closer, so Zaidan hurried away to avoid him. He could make out a large boulder and hid at its base. The man's footsteps got louder, but Zaidan was sure he had lost him.

He stayed a short while before continuing his way toward the hill. No doubt his pursuer had given up and gone back. The image of his wife flashed into his mind: reaching down with the *loufa* over Sahloul's shoulder, rubbing his chest . . .

Then from nearby came the voice, boldly breaking the silence, "Who's there?"

A mad urge to escape came over Zaidan, but the man's voice was insistent and would certainly be followed by a shot if he did not answer.

"It is I," he said.

"Who are you?"

"Zaidan." He rose to his feet.

The man approached without speaking. His body was large; this meant he was not a bedouin. Zaidan started to tremble.

"I came out to pass water," he said.

The man did not answer.

"Who are you? Khalil? Good evening . . ."

The man faced him silently.

"There's a cold breeze. It feels like it might rain . . ."

The husky man continued to look at him without saying one word in response.

"How's the wife? Are you on your way home? The night is still young . . . Welcome, as the Arabs say, ha! ha! . . . Come over and have some tea, really . . ."

Then suddenly he fell silent. Khalil knew everything! He turned to go.

"Good night," he said.

Khalil grasped his shoulder and kept him from walking on.

"Zaidan, who have you got at home?"

"Khalil! Khalil, you . . ."

"Take it!" Khalil said to him.

The metal felt cold in his hand.

—Translated by Lena Jayyusi and Thomas G. Ezzy

'Abd al-'Al al-Hamamsi (b. 1932)

Egyptian short-story writer 'Abd al-'Al Hamamsi was born in Akhmim in Upper Egypt. He worked on his father's land before moving on to Cairo, where he worked in the cinema and other cultural avenues and became deputy president of the Egyptian Writers' Union. A very sensitive writer and a strong observer of human behavior and psychology, he has published four collections of short stories, *The Chicks Have Wings* (1967), *The Voice— and Others* (1979), *The Ethiopians' Well* (1990), and *The Joy of Bells* (2003). His *Complete Works* was published by the General Egyptian Book Organization (1995–2003). He has also written critical articles and interviews.

CAIN SUFFOCATES THE MOON

Yesterday in the sky over our town the moon appeared suffocated. From the rooftops, and in the narrow roads and dark alleys the processions of children went, beating on old tin cans and brass objects, entreating the houris to free the moon. But it remained constricted despite the importunacy of the children. The reverberation of tin cans sounded like the ritual of primitive prayers offered to a dead god.

It was then I remembered you. I recalled your sarcasm at the expense of grandmother and the Reverend Danial, the deacon of the church of our Lady Dumyana that's situated close to our house. I thought of you also with a geography book in your hand, explaining to us the phenomenon of the moon's eclipse, while grandmother scolded you and cursed the nature of a school that had taught you such blasphemies and shown you how to write from left to right. She believed it was the houris who strangled the moon, because their love for it remained unrequited. As for Reverend Danial, he assured us that the damage was done by Cain, who strangled the moon out of revenge, because in illuminating the desert one night it revealed Abel's corpse to the crows, who raucously shredded it and so awakened the angels who reported his misdemeanor to Adam.

I remembered you and slept. In my sleep I was visited by a dream—I saw your hand encircling and pressing the neck of the moon! I didn't see your face: it was hidden behind dark clouds. But I know your hand intimately, its fingers, its veins, and the tattoo on its palm.

Your grandmother died a few days ago. People said that her corpse flew off with the coffin from the shoulders of the pallbearers. Not being at the funeral, I couldn't validate this anomaly. I had remained behind in order to go through her possessions. I got hold of her rosary for myself, that rosary fragrant with the scent of camphor and the dust of graveyards. I came out with the rosary in my hands and knocked at Reverend Danial's door, and of his hospitality drank freely of a vintage wine that an American missionary friend had brought him from the orchards of Jaffa and Galilee.

An hour ago I returned from Danial's house. The headiness of the wine I'd consumed still lit my veins, and I was fired by the impulse to confide in you, as I used to when we were intimate as a close-knit family. Do you remember how we sang during the harvest season; my father, my mother, my grandmother and Sara, and the guests with whom our large house would resound, our big house with its stories and corridors that no one frequents now?

Some years ago, your father ceased to be the *'umda* here; he lost his post subsequent to his bankruptcy. The commissioner of police and his assistant arrived, together with the various dignitaries, and transferred the telephone to the new *'umda*'s house in a scene not far short of a scandal.

Before the catastrophe occurred, the processions of chiefs and religious leaders used to come to our house and sit in the large yard under the mulberry tree, whose roots were so deeply earthed that it defied the flood water that obstinately beat at its trunk. I loved the river to which you used to drag me naked and teach me how to swim. One summer I almost drowned when I was with you. After the old fisherman had felicitously rescued me and pumped the water from my body, you told me that if I'd drowned, people would have spread the rumor of the story of Cain and Abel. At the time I didn't understand what you meant. I knew the story of course. I'd read it, but failed to see its connection with the incident of my drowning.

I might have forgotten the entire experience, were it not for the old fisherman reminding me of it. I saw him a year ago, begging in the middle of the road. He'd lost his eyesight but knew me when he felt my hand. He told me that you could have rescued me before I went under, but that you'd let me go down without doing anything, and only his timely intervention saved my life. I returned home that day trying to retrieve the details of the occurrence, and I dreamt what I now relate. I saw you sitting next to me reading the story of Cain and Abel in an old gilded copy of the Bible. You'd grown a thick beard and were wearing a *qaftan* over your trousers. When you'd finished, you asked me not to believe the story, saying that the whole thing was nothing more than a legend and that Cain and Abel were inventions, as Adam died childless. He was sterile, and it was the Greek historian Herodotus who'd invented the story from his imagination.

I woke up immediately after these words. It *was* a dream. You were in Cairo at the time, and I in the Upper Egypt countryside. I remember the day I came to see you in Cairo. I'd been unable to close my heart to Sara's entreaties, and the day remains indelible in my memory. You welcomed me tepidly, shunning the embrace I offered you. Even before your servant had offered me a cup of tea, your wife wanted to know in which hotel I was staying. My world clouded over. I swallowed hard and replied that I intended to sleep in the courtyard of the Hussein Mosque, for the old women in my town had asked me to read the *fatiha* at the Hussein shrine.

I observed you to see the effect of her question on you but couldn't discern any trace of surprise in your face. I got up and left without talking to you, and I walked the streets in a daze, feeling totally lost and alone. In my confusion I asked a man the way to the railway station and watched as he scrutinized my face minutely. He was accompanied by a girl whose white face and eyes revealed her inner suffering. The man took hold of my hand, while retaining his grip on the girl's wrist, conducted me through winding alleys, and, in a pitch-black impasse, drew a knife to my face and robbed me of everything my pockets contained. When the girl pleaded with him to leave me the fare for my ticket home, he slapped her in the face. She knelt at his feet and offered to relinquish her share of the night's proceedings if he'd leave me with enough money to buy a ticket. In the end he gave me the fare and went off with the girl.

I was terrified and ran off like a madman. When I encountered a policeman I threw myself at him and told him my story. Much to my surprise he guffawed and asked me if I was from Upper Egypt. When I answered in the affirmative, his laughter grew even more boisterous and, before disappearing amongst the crowds in the square, he said: "One of you once bought the tram" (referring to an incident in which a Cairene confidence trickster once persuaded a man from Upper Egypt to "buy" one of the city's trams.)

As I finally walked toward the station, helped by the directions of a little girl who sold bread, I kept asking myself about your nature, Ibrahim. For, despite the fact that I hated you ferociously, I wasn't comfortable with the decision of my conscience to indict you. It's always been my belief that we should extend tolerance to the nature of all individuals and that commitment to others is insignificant in comparison to one's own inner conviction. Everyone must navigate his ship in accordance with his own compass. Those people who insist on carrying the misery of humanity over their shoulders are invariably the eccentric and odd, who are unable to disburden themselves of some crookedness in the course of history.

I went back to marry Sara who'd lost all hope of your return. The midwife aborted her child despite the fact that she wished to keep it, as it had been engendered by you. I tried to make her hate you, but I failed in this respect. You still live in her blood. On my part, I couldn't force myself to dislike her; her warm nature wouldn't permit it. Her heart's a seemingly inexhaustible fountain of tenderness, a generative warmth that would be sufficient to appease the majority of mankind. But your presence divided us, it kept me from penetrating her spirit. While I'm permitted to explore the depths of her femininity, she expels me to the surface should I try to possess her spirit.

A few days ago she told me that she didn't share my belief in your evil. I was talking to her about you, enquiring into your nature, and asking why someone who had no cause to be embittered should behave in this way. She answered that one shouldn't discuss a person in their absence, for their rationale isn't easily analyzed. Then she turned her back to me and went to sleep.

In the morning she asked me why I'd refused to expose you when I clearly hated you so much. I couldn't find the answer. I'm a man of little self-perception. I often grieve for the suffering of mankind and would be prepared to embrace death rather than have anyone shed a single tear. When I was a little boy and you used to read me stories about heroes condemned to suffer, I used to undergo agonies on their behalf and swear in my heart to become a new Christ who would redeem their miseries. I still feel similarly, although at times contradictory thoughts pass through my mind. Often, when I face the harshness of people, I find myself ready to hate everything, and I wish that the opportunity would arrive for me to blow the entire world to smithereens and ash. When I informed Sara of this, she greeted me with total silence.

A few months ago your father committed suicide. He'd lost all his wealth, and we'd experienced the misery of those who are deprived of their worldly status. People abandoned us completely. Our drawing room, which had formerly gathered people from all social classes, was empty. The only strangers to call were the police investigators.

The bankrupt cotton merchant died without ever knowing the secret of his ruin. I know it, and so do you. And I know of your connivance with the brokers in return for a huge commission. In the face of the horror of the incident and its consequences, I thought of exposing you, denuding you, or even stoning you. But I couldn't. I rejected the idea, knowing, as a prisoner might, that the cause of my suffering was a false one.

My silence told on my nerves, and I could find no reprieve except in knocking at Reverend Danial's door and drinking his wine. When the wine had loosened his tongue, the Reverend would start talking about Christ and Judas, he'd chant hymns, and relate those hallucinatory stories about the fig tree that put forth leaves, and about the scent bottle with which a harlot anointed the feet of a man who was supposed to have beatified the poor with his teachings, before being dragged by the merchants in a rancorous procession to the cross. He also spoke of the patriarch who'd appointed Simon the carpenter a minister of the Virgin's Church in return for three sheep and ten cocks. And he spoke of the way he was being ignored, he, the orthodox servant of the church. He'd then undergo convulsive fits of tears and, with his nerves overstrung, he'd throw me out of the house and I'd find Sara waiting for me. Sara is my own torture. She herself is tormented by something in her psychological make-up. She gives of herself with a tenderness that permeates my body, and perhaps that of all humanity, but she remains above all a stranger to me. Her spirit is in constant flight from me.

Sometimes she tells me that she hates you to the point of death; but I realize then that she's lying. She'd have her body dismembered in return for seeing you one minute, for the satisfaction of feeling your arms crush her body, your lips drawing fire from her, for your heat to consume her. Her own suffering tears me to pieces.

When your father died, your mother told me, "Everything dies, but life proceeds from death. Nothing ever dies." I understood by this that she hoped Sara and I would have children. I told her that Cain had killed not simply Abel but the whole family. He'd killed the family's future progeny. I was thinking how Sara's womb seemed infertile to my seed. Rice plants don't grow on the equator. Your mother understood. . . . She said nothing!

It isn't Danial's wine that's responsible for this outpouring. A long time ago, when Reverend Danial was telling me his scriptural tales, I found you. And when you used to take me to the cinema in the next town to see Tarzan films, strange things used to happen inside me. I'd dream of a world without people. I was its sole inhabitor. I used to come out of the theology classes at school and hurry to the graveyards at the east of the town and let my thoughts take flight. I'd ruminate on humanity, the world, and the story of our earthly existence. I used to grow confused by the naive dialogues I established with spirits. Then I'd try to convince myself and the company of skulls staring at me from broken graves that existence, school, our home, the cotton ginneries, the minarets of mosques, the domes of churches, the graveyards, all of these things lacked an external reality and existed only as a projection of my inner self. Nothing and no one existed apart from me, and when I died, everything would vanish with me. And yet I might not die. I might be the world, and who knows, I might be God himself!

I expounded this to Sara yesterday. At first she said nothing, then, when I repeated my ideas, she put out her hand and felt my brow. She told me I was sick and that my heart was suffocating. "Come with me to the roof and breathe in the air," she said.

Above the roof the night-sky was pitch-black. We looked for the moon but couldn't find it. Sara's eyes scanned the clouds before she said to me, "A whole day's passed without the moon appearing. It's a day like a lifetime. The houris are still strangling it." "Perhaps," I answered. Then I remembered Danial, and thought of you, and corrected myself. "Perhaps it's is not the houris," I said, "but Cain who's responsible for this."

Then I asked her to light a candle until the moon returned.

—Translated by May Jayyusi and Jeremy Reed

Akram Haniyyah (b. 1953)

Palestinian short-story writer and journalist Akram Haniyyah was born in Ramallah on the West Bank. He studied English literature at the University of Cairo, then worked as a journalist, becoming, in 1978, editor-in-chief of the *Al-Sha'b* newspaper, which is published in Jerusalem. His writings and his work as a journalist under occupation have worried the Israeli military rulers of Jerusalem and the West Bank, and Haniyyah was hounded, prohibited from traveling, and then in 1986 imprisoned and later deported. He has lived in exile until the Palestinan Authority was able to place its headquarters in what remained of Palestine. He now lives with his wife, 'Adila, and their daughter, Shams, in Ramallah, where he is editor-in-chief of the daily *Al-Ayyam*. He has published five collections of short stories, the first of which, *The Last Ship . . . the Last Harbor* (1979), won him immediate recognition. This was followed by *The Defeat of Clever Hassan* (1980), *The Account on the Second Taghreeba of Hilali* (1981), and *When the Jerusalem Night Is Lit* (1988). These four collections have been published in one volume under the title *Rituals for Another Day* (Cyprus, 1986). His latest collection is *The Secrets of the Sparrow* (2001).

That Village on That Morning

Aware of the intrusion of noise, Abu Mahmoud al-Qasimi partly opened his eyes in response and listened, then closed them again, expecting the silence to return. When the sound increased in volume, he muttered to himself, "Even the dead can't sleep in peace."

Determined to find out the cause of the noise, Abu Mahmoud loosened his graveclothes, and, using his freed hands, worked his way towards the surface. As he thrust his way through the ground above him, so the uproar grew louder.

The biting morning cold stung his face as soon as he periscoped from the grave. Al-Qasimi found himself shielding his eyes from the rays of the warm sun, which he had not seen for twenty years.

After a few moments he felt sufficiently at ease to look around him. Glancing toward the east, he could make out the village houses crouched at the foot of the mountain. Memories flooded back to him, and he found himself recollecting, "That's the home of the mayor, 'Adnan, and that's the house of Sheikh Abu Sufyan facing the mosque; but where's my house?"

His questions were interrupted by the increasing hubbub, and he turned to face the other direction, only to see a huge bulldozer closing its steel jaws on the cemetery soil and uprooting the modest tombstones and the bones of the dead.

Unable to believe what he saw, Abu Mahmoud opened his mouth in order to cry out, but his voice, which had remained dormant these twenty years, was too faint to be heard by anyone. "What's happening?" he questioned. "How can the sanctity of a graveyard be violated?"

Scrutinizing the driver's face, he observed that it was round and fair-skinned, crowned by blond hair, and belonged to a man in his thirties, dressed in shorts and a shirt unbuttoned at the neck. The man was proceeding calmly with his task, his lips closed on a cigarette, which was no sooner extinguished than it was followed by another.

Abu Mahmoud's body was now entirely outside the grave, but astonishment continued to numb his senses. Questions were buzzing loudly in his head, which he had thought consigned to permanent repose. "What's happened? This fellow certainly isn't from our village and his features are Jewish. What's happened and where's my house?"

He looked again at the village, its haphazardly scattered houses invested with a funereal quiet. "The men must be on their way to the fields now," he thought, "and the children heading to school. What's brought this intruder here? What's he doing driving a bulldozer in our village cemetery? How can he violate the sanctity of the dead?"

Abu Mahmoud felt deeply distressed but was determined to do something. Winding the white fabric of the shroud around his body and hitching it up under his arms, he started to walk toward the driver of the bulldozer to enquire into his intentions. As he progressed slowly toward the man, who continued to operate within a few meters of him without being conscious of his approach, Abu Mahmoud found it difficult to flex his feet when they'd been laid out in the grave for twenty years.

No sooner had Abu Mahmoud advanced than a dust storm swirled off the road alongside the village and in its approach to the cemetery revealed a procession of military and civilian vehicles lined up in a row near the bulldozer. Seeing this, Abu Mahmoud came to a standstill and concealed himself behind a gravestone to see what would happen.

The company dismounted from their cars. Their features were alien to him. "They don't belong to our village," he whispered.

They grouped around the bulldozer. Although he couldn't recognize a single face, they were all identifiable as men of the military government, the border police, the Keren Keyemet[1] officials, the Gush Emunim[2] representatives, journalists, and others.

The situation was too knotty for Abu Mahmoud to unravel and too oppressive for him to tolerate. "It is, after all, my village, my grave, the graves of my family and forbears. I must know what's going on," he said, emerging from behind a gravestone and, with visible anger, striding toward the crowd.

The first person to notice his exhumation was a soldier, who cried out at the sight of someone reeking of the grave, dressed in graveclothes, and with the pallor of death on his face. The initial reaction to the advancing man was one of stunned amazement, but once some of them had recovered their self-possession, one of the border police pointed his machine gun at the newly returned man and shouted, "Stop!"

Though Abu Mahmoud knew that the language in which the command had been issued was foreign, he stood still. The soldiers approached him cautiously, their eyes scrutinizing his every detail, while they formed a ring around him. A soldier of superior rank approached and bellowed at Abu Mahmoud, "Who are you?"

---

1. An arm of the Jewish Agency that existed before the establishment of Israel for the transfer of Arab land to Jewish ownership.
2. A fanatic religious group that believes it has a religious right to the whole of the land of Palestine. This group lived mostly on land confiscated from its Arab owners in the West Bank.

"And who are *you?*" replied Abu Mahmoud calmly.

"I'm the person in authority here, so answer my question."

"I'm 'Abdallah Khalil al-Qasimi."

"Where from?"

"From this village."

"Where's your identity card?"

"My identity card? What do you mean?"

"What are you doing here?"

"I was lying dead in my grave when the noise of a bulldozer woke me."

A murmur arose at this, and the crowd that had gathered looked suddenly frightened, until the soldier resumed his questioning of Abu Mahmoud.

"You're crazy! I asked you who you are and what you're doing here."

"I'm not crazy. Who are *you* and what are *you* doing here?"

"I would have you know that we're the representatives of the State of Israel."

Al-Qasimi was thunderstruck by the answer, but after a momentary pause he regained control of himself and cried, "Why are you bulldozing the cemetery? That's a sin."

"It's our land."

"Your land? All of my ancestors are buried here."

"It's our land and we're going to build a settlement on it."

"But . . . "

The conversation was abruptly terminated by the sound of a military jeep approaching the cemetery. Everyone treated it as the focal point of attention. The jeep came to a stop, and a man in his fifties wearing a military uniform got out. It turned out that he was the commandant of the district.

The newcomer, apprehending that something was wrong, searched for the answer in their eyes. He was alarmed to see a man wrapped in a shroud, standing in the midst of the gathering, with anger showing in his eyes. The commandant briefly referred to the man who'd been questioning Abu Mahmoud and received a full summary of what had taken place. With the hint of a smile on his lips, and evident concern in his face, he strode towards Abu Mahmoud and asked him, "Were you born in this village?"

"Yes."

"When did you die?"

Abu Mahmoud needed to reflect before replying, "Five or six years after the emigration."

The commandant resumed his questioning: "Where were you during the year of the emigration?"

"I was here in my village."

"Did you never leave it during that time?"

Abu Mahmoud hesitated for a while, then hurriedly said, "No."

The commandant paused before going on with measured deliberation.

"Didn't you go to the defence of your village and countrymen?"

Roused by the question, Abu Mahmoud, tumbled into the trap.

"Of course I did," he replied hotly, the words issuing from his mouth like bullets.

"I fought both the English and the Jews. I had a rifle that I had inherited from my father, and I fought at Ya'bad and Bab al-Wad. I was renowned for my courage."

Things now grew clearer to Abu Mahmoud as a flood of old memories mixed with feelings of nostalgia and bitterness resumed possession of his mind. This train of thought came to a halt when the commandant, sensing that he had made an important find, shouted, "So you're a seasoned saboteur!"

"Saboteur . . . ?"

"Shut up! Where's the rifle . . . where did you bury it?"

"It's an old one . . . My father got it from the Turks when he fought in Yemen."

"Where did you hide it?"

"It's buried beside the olive tree in front of my house."

"And where is your house?"

"My house . . . it used to stand by the mosque, but it's disappeared. What have you done with it?"

Advancing from the rear of the crowd where he had positioned himself, a man whispered something in the commandant's ear, then made his way towards Abu Mahmoud. "What's your full name?" he asked.

"I've already told you—'Abdallah Khalil al-Qasimi."

"And do you have a son by the name of Kamal?"

Abu Mahmoud's heart throbbed with alarm.

"Yes," he cried in a frightened voice, "He's my youngest son, and the child I love best of my family. What's happened to him?"

"We've dynamited the house," the man said stridently. "Kamal's a saboteur."

"My house! What's happened to Kamal?"

"He's in prison."

Stunned by these words, Abu Mahmoud screamed aloud. He advanced on the commandant waving his fists, for anger and frustration had revived in him the strength he had when living. The soldiers grabbed him and returned him to his former place.

Silence invaded the cemetery, a quiet broken only by Abu Mahmoud's moans. The commandant was thinking, "There'll be a problem if we jail him—how can we jail someone who's risen from the grave? The bulldozer will erase the cemetery, so we're denied the possibility of reburying him. What shall we do with him?"

One of the commandant's assistants, sensing his perplexity, stepped forward and whispered in his ear, "We can send him to Jordan."

Four men quickly led Abu Mahmoud off and threw him, in spite of his protesting cries, into the rear of a jeep, which took off at high speed towards the east.

$\rightharpoonup$

The vehicle came to a halt on the banks of the Tajriba River.[3] Four soldiers marched Abu Mahmoud to a shallow ford within the sight of the opposite bank.

"Cross over to the other side," shouted the soldiers.

The shout startled Abu Mahmoud from the stupor that had enveloped him. Thousands of images flooded into his mind. Kamal . . . his home . . . his wife . . . the olive trees . . . the rifle . . . Ya'bad . . . the woods . . . Bab al-Wad. As he looked about him, an idea suddenly flashed into his mind. Advancing toward the river bank, he looked around him for the last time and saw the soldiers motioning him to cross to the other bank. He saw, too, the hills and the trees lit by the morning sun. He moved forward with passionate eagerness, murmuring something to himself, and as he did so, his resolution increased and a hot tear leapt from his eyes. Then he threw himself into the river.

Moments later the waters of the sacred river were bearing the body of Abu Mahmoud al-Qasimi as they rushed on with insurgent force to empty themselves into the Dead Sea.

—Translated by Lorne Kenny and Jeremy Reed.

Jameel Hatmal (1956–1994)

Syrian short-story writer Jameel Hatmal studied Arabic literature at the University of Damascus. The high artistic quality of his work was first acknowledged when, at the age of twenty, he was awarded a major prize as a short-story writer by the Syrian universities. From then on his reputation grew on a pan-Arabic scale, and he is now regarded as one of the best fiction writers among the many short-story writers in the Arab world. His approach is original, reflecting, in some stories, a subtle underlying irony springing from his long experience of urban culture in the big Syrian cities. At other times it reflects a streak of Syrian cynicism almost unique in the Arab world. From 1981 on Hatmal participated, as an independent writer, in the conferences held every two years by the Union of Arab Writers. He also took part in the Conference on the Arab/Dutch Novel and Short Story held in Amsterdam in 1993. At the end of his short life he went to live in Paris, where he founded a Committee for the Right to Freedom of Arab Creativity and Creative Writers. Four collections of short stories have been published: *The Little Girl with the White Hat* (1981), *Emotions and Reactions*

---

3. The River of Temptation, i.e., the Jordan River.

(1985), *When There's No Country* (1993), and a collection tellingly entitled *Stories of Illness . . . Stories of Madness* (1994), which reflects his experiences as a heart patient in Damascus and Beirut.

HOW MY GRANDMOTHER WAS MURDERED

This isn't a detective story, even though the "police" played an indirect part in it and even though it's long been my ambition to write a story of that sort. And it isn't a comic story either, even if one of its main characters, its main character in fact, is my old grandmother, with her blue eyes and her goodness of heart verging on naïveté.

My grandmother was born in the second decade of the twentieth century, and although that made her, strictly speaking, quite old, she was in good health even so, for one simple and very obvious reason: she didn't think much. She'd been used to living that way since she was young, because my grandfather—or the man who eventually became my grandfather—had saved her the trouble.

She'd been one of the most beautiful girls in the village. In fact, that had been her only quality. My grandfather had returned in fetters, being chained, according to custom, at the entrance to the village, until his father should slaughter a goat and entertain the people to show his joy that his son had come back as an "educated" young man, one who'd managed to pass his first "certificate" and so become one of the few people in the village to hold it.

Having acquired this certificate, my grandfather began work as a teacher and had of course to get married, which made it imperative that a bride be chosen. Her name was Dalla, which, as you all know, means the kettle from which Arabic coffee is poured—or perhaps it's derived from *dalal*, meaning "coquetry." But my grandfather, not liking the name, called her Adele, and so she came to be called.

Adele, as I mentioned, didn't think very much. In fact she didn't think at all. She was extremely good-hearted, and anything would make her happy. She knew well enough how to bear children, and how to wash dishes and pots, which was another hobby of hers. She'd still indulge this hobby, it's said, even when my grandfather had become better off and provided her with a maid—who may, for all I know, have been an old mistress of his that he introduced to my grandmother in this new capacity.

The important thing is that my grandfather, who was a very irritable man, died young, leaving my grandmother alone except for a number of children who were rapidly growing up and leaving her. There's a whole collection of stories about her good-heartedness, or her naïveté—it comes to the same thing. Once, for example, during one of my grandfather's trips, she agreed to lend a man all her furniture, so that, as he told her, he could get married. He then sold the furniture and ran off with the money. Another story tells how she once exchanged ten coins for a few lengths of cloth—and the coins were ten gold liras! All this made my grandfather's temper worse and worse, and she never understood why.

Finally, when my grandmother was alone, all her children being married and having children of their own, she went to live in a small room, just like the rooms of all the old grandmothers we hear of in stories. It had an old iron bed in it, as well as various strange things, including a huge number of buttons—collecting these had become a hobby with her, though all her children and grandchildren found it very odd. In fact, one very small grandchild used to overturn the bags of buttons on the floor, searching among the buttons for the smallest and largest ones, and sometimes some of them would get lost.

My grandmother, in her turn, used to find her grandchildren's behavior very strange. One of them had fled his father's house to live on his own, and one granddaughter married a man from another religion. The incident that surprised her most, though, was when one of the grandchildren was put in prison. My grandmother couldn't understand how such a thing could happen when he hadn't stolen anything, and hadn't killed anyone, and hadn't ... And yet he'd been put in prison. When she asked why, they told her it was because of "politics," a crime whose meaning she never fathomed.

How could her grandson be imprisoned for politics? She couldn't understand. And when she started missing him a lot and told his father—her son—that she wanted to see him, her son told her sadly, "We can't. It's not allowed."

My grandmother didn't understand this prohibition. She wanted to see her grandson, and that was that. That was something she did understand, and she supposed his father was just making fun of her and didn't want to take her with him—especially as he wasn't visiting her and bringing her fruit as much as before. And so my grandmother started neglecting her hobbies. In her sadness she no longer washed dishes so much and no longer troubled to add new buttons to her collection. She'd take the small straw seat and sit in a sunny corner, with her head on her palm, and start shaking her body to and fro, to a tune that came out like a groan. And if someone asked her, "What's the matter, grandmother?" she wouldn't answer.

One day, in confidence, she told her daughter the reason for her sorrow: her son, she said, didn't want to take her to see her grandson. Her daughter assured her he wasn't able to, that he couldn't even get to see him himself. That made him very sad, which was why he didn't visit her much any more.

My grandmother didn't say anything to that. In fact, she no longer left her room to go and sit in some sunny corner. She just became sadder, and more and more silent, perhaps thinner and thinner. Should I finish the story and talk about the part the police played, or is the whole case clear to you? Do you know how my grandmother was murdered?

—*Translated by May Jayyusi and Christopher Tingley*

MORNING IN THE CITY

I'll give him a name that's neutral, say "George"—he could be Portuguese, or Egyptian, or Italian, or Syrian, or Senegalese. George, or the man we'll suppose to be called George, wakes up at seven o'clock. He turns on the light in the room, because morning's late coming here. Then, when he's washed his face, he leans the little mirror by the window, where some light can seep through the curtains, and starts shaving. His appearance must, after all, be in accordance with the wishes of the superintendent where he works.

At half past seven, George goes down the stairs toward the bread seller. What a blessing it is, he thinks, that she's so close by; that makes him feel very happy on all those mornings when it's so cold. The little bread seller, who's almost an old woman, murmurs a few words of welcome, then hands George a loaf of bread as usual. George nods his head and thanks her inaudibly, then starts climbing the stairs toward his apartment, or, rather, toward his moderately large room, counting the stairs as he goes, knowing the number by heart. He only counts them, it should be said, when he's going up, because it somehow comforts him to find the number getting smaller and smaller. He arrives there, out of breath, and finds, as usual, that his wife's awake and so is his child. In fact, let's suppose he has two children.

As George hurries along to the metro station, his only thought is that the metro should come quickly. It doesn't usually hang around, and he sometimes finds he can catch it just as he reaches the station. Most days George finds a seat, because he lives near the beginning of the line. Then, at the sixth stop after his own, he sees that the thin woman who usually comes into his coach seems exhausted as usual and, though he sometimes thinks of offering her his seat, he finally doesn't; it was done in his old town, but people don't, he notices, always act that way here. At the seventeenth stop George begins the process of counting the stairs at the metro station, reflecting, as usual, that this station must have been built before electric escalators were invented.

The moment he arrives at his workplace, he goes to the superintendent, who hands him his instructions for delivering pieces of furniture to buyers—this is his job—in the truck waiting for him there. This truck he returns to its exact place around five in the afternoon.

At five George walks down the stairs of the metro station, but he doesn't count them. On the metro he starts counting the stops in reverse, and when he's arrived, he returns to his habit of counting the stairs up to his home, whose number he knows exactly. It should be said that this habit of counting worries him sometimes, but he only feels that way when he's in the middle of counting.

When he arrives, he mechanically kisses his wife, who's getting dinner ready. He doesn't say much, watches television, sometimes maybe plays with his child (or his two children); then, around ten o'clock, the lights in the room go out.

At seven o'clock next morning, George—or the man we'll suppose is called George—wakes up. He turns on the light in the room, because morning's late coming here. Then, when he's washed his face, he leans the little mirror by the window, where . . .

At half past seven, George goes down to the bread seller. But when George walks to the metro station, he doesn't feel able to hurry the way he usually does. At the sixth stop he doesn't notice the thin woman, because he's leaned his head against the window and closed his eyes. When the metro reaches the seventeenth stop, George doesn't get up to go out—he doesn't even open his eyes. Then, or a little later, the superintendent will notice George hasn't arrived, and he'll record this.

At the last metro stop, George doesn't get out. He's still leaning his head against the window, more limply than ever, even though the driver's sounding his whistle and announcing, in monotonous tones, that this is the last station. The passengers getting off see there's a clean-shaven man in one of the coaches, whose body's leaning so limply it's ready to fall.

After five in the afternoon, the woman who waits to hear George's slow footsteps on the stairs, who's getting dinner ready, is going to wait a long time, a very long time . . .

At seven o'clock on the morning of the next days, the light won't be turned on in the apartment—or large room, rather—and you won't find a man leaning a mirror against the window and start shaving, or the bread seller murmuring the regular morning greeting to George. He isn't coming down to her any more.

And at seven o'clock on another day, Yusuf—or whatever his name is—who might be Portuguese, or Lebanese, or Maltese, or Algerian, turns on the light, and, when he's washed his face, leans the small mirror and starts shaving, in this city where morning's late coming. And there's another bread seller, and another set of stairs in an old building, and in the metro stations. Yusuf gets ready for all this. He wakes at seven o'clock, turns on the light, leans the mirror . . .

—*Translated by May Jayyusi and Christopher Tingley*

Haydar Haydar (b. 1936)

Syrian novelist and short-story writer Haydar Haydar gained recognition with the publication of his collection *Tales of the Migrating Seagull* (1968) and is now regarded as one of Syria's foremost writers of fiction. His is a new and uncommon world, where the writer interprets human experience in the light of both the universal and the national. He employs a vivid and dramatic style that stirs up at times an atmosphere of mystery and even suspense. Haydar has published several collections of short stories, among which are *A Flare of Light* (1970), *The Deluge* (1976), *The Mountain Goats* (1978), and *The Twighlight of the Gods*; and some remarkable novels, among which are *The Time of Desolation* (1973), *Mirrors of Fire* (1992), and

The Leopard (1977). His novel *A Banquet for Sea Weeds* (1983) is an incisive and powerful indictment of stalled revolutions, a direct critique of events in both Algeria and Iraq.

THE DANCE OF THE SAVAGE PRAIRIES

THE BODY

Summer. Overflowing pavements. A white illuminated world. The morning bustle, quick, invigorating. A period of one's childhood, suffused with warmth, sears the heart.

A memory flowing and bustling, carried by the wind from the green hills. The wind saturated with the smell of grass, forest leaves, and the expanse of sea.

The Square. Nubile schoolgirls pass by with their short colored dresses. Rosy faces, throbbing with health and liveliness. The wind that springs up lifts the short dresses a little, then higher. Suddenly the morning glitters. Summer glows, reflected from the marble of white and brown flesh. The smell of grass and sea disappears.

The atmosphere is agitated now by the smell of something hot, delicious, and painful.

Inside a glass café, at the edge of the opposite pavement, a face alien to the world. A neutral face, monotonously chewing gum. When the wind lifts the dress of a passing girl, he presses the gum between his teeth causing a small explosion.

His face, except for the retinas of his fiery eyes, appears to be undefined, neutral as a rock, while observing the summer and other things.

Except that something else can be observed, behind his neutrality—a kind of annoyance mixed with a harsh disgust. His gestures, inside the café, in the midst of the mechanical din of people, are slightly neurotic, while anyone observing him closely would doubt that he is thinking of anything in particular.

The truth is, he is simply there. Sitting on a chair, an empty table in front of him. His left ankle resting on the opposite leg. A hand, loosely hanging, seems to have been forgotten there, while the other is on the top of the table, its fingers moving to a monotonous and meaningless beat.

Between this man, sitting behind the glass front, and the outside world there is a white curtain and then there is the glass. His eyes, sharp as a hawk's, pierce through the screen, the glass, the streets, and the bodies of the passers-by. They pierce faces, the half-exposed breasts, the thighs that dazzle the eyes and inflame the blood.

Although the face perched behind the glass appears to be immersed in its own sense of anatomy and personal solitude, something else might move behind this cold reserve. Something that, on breaking out, sweeps away the neutrality to give the face an expression full of pain and desire.

The man sitting on a chair in the café is constantly changing: his depths singing with secret desires, residing in his fiery sphere, the sphere of the five senses, center of energy and action.

From a time impossible to recall, objects had taken on their hard fiery form there. Transformed from the objective world, drawn by a power overwhelming to the force of reason, to the sphere of fire and sensation where the absolute, the private, and the brutal desire for possession are to be found. Place, time, and people were involved in this transformation. All formulae seemed to have been molded in his depths, in the image of his desires.

His name was Muhammed. However, after a series of special procedures and painful, physical, sensual experiences, he came to be known as Alazrak—"The Blue."

His gait as he swaggers with his Spartan body, the wind playing with the blue scarf around his neck and his hair falling in waves to his shoulders, is reminiscent of the gait of actors playing the role of a roughneck.

At such times, as he cuts across pavements and people, he would imagine that all eyes were fixed on him. Frightened eyes, awed by his athletic walk. There walks Alazrak!

Perhaps he hears it echoing in his depths. The throb of an inner intoxication would rise in his blood. He would stretch his body high, strutting like a peacock, surveying with his sharp eyes the passing human flies.

Alazrak is the beautiful beast of the city. Bewitcher of girls and possessor of the sharp dagger that he draws only to plant in the heart of a man who deserves death.

He sees in the fleeting faces, the glass fronts and the lighted sky, his own solid dark face. A woman once said, "In your barbaric face, there is a cruelty that women desire and at which men tremble."

In the streets of the city bounded from the west by the sea and from the east by the African forests, Alazrak had asserted his existence among the gangs of looters and the vagrants; the alcholics and the gamblers; the prisoners and the police.

This had begun at the end of a wintry day in a remote village of the Oras[1] mountains. On that day his father had rebuked him for abandoning school and starting on the road of robbery and vagrancy. That evening their discussion became heated and the father had attempted to teach him good conduct by beating him up. But the cruel blows on his head had pained Alazrak and he rebelled and foamed, "Enough. Enough. You are killing me, you madman."

When the brutality of the blows increased, Alazrak sprang up like an enraged tiger. He twisted his father's arm and slapped him, then threw him to the ground smashing his face and teeth in. Then he fled the house, never to return.

---

1. The Oras mountains, or Aures as they are known in English, are in North Eastern Algeria, part of the massive Saharan Atlas. They were a center of the Algerian revolution that ended in 1962 in victory against the French colonization of the country.

Now as he reclines on the café's chair, he remembers bits of his argument with his father: "You swine, you dog. You hit your father?! How will you face your Lord on the day of judgment, you enemy of God?"

Just as he recalls his father's face bloodied and humbled, he recalls how he cursed him, spitting in the air, "Leave me alone you and your God! From now on Alazrak will be his own lord and master."

THE REVENGE

He descended on the city that had fought the invaders after years of occupation filled with bitterness, terror, and brutality. He had arrived in the last week before their departure. The week that was named the week of terror and blood. In those terrifying days Alazrak witnessed the foreigners demolishing the city with explosives and hunting and sniping at the children. He saw the massacres of old men and the rape of young girls in streets and squares.

The invaders were celebrating, in that tragic manner, the rituals of their hatred and defeat, as if they were setting up games in a riotous carnival colored by blood, fire, vengeance, and blind chaos.

In the week of blood and explosions, Alazrak entered upon his dangerous course.

The killing of innocent women, children, and old people in that gratuitous fashion had aroused in him something like nausea, which was later to explode in sudden spasms of hatred.

There he is, avoiding main thoroughfares, quickly crossing dark corners. Suddenly a bullet rings out, hitting a wall.

Alazrak freezes for a moment, observing the flash of bullets from one of the windows. He finds the window and pinpoints the fenced house. Cautiously, he advances, his back to the wall. With the agility of a panther, he climbs the wall surrounding the house. Broken glass, embedded at the top, cuts his hands. He jumps into the courtyard, disappearing among the trees. As soon as the shooting stops, he climbs a tree close to the window and crouches there. Just before dawn Alazrak smashes the window and enters the room. At the noise, the light is switched on in the drawing room where Alazrak surprises his opponent. He flings the fair-skinned colonist on to the brilliant white marble floor. The colonist's green eyes protrude, pleading for mercy. Coldly he sits on top of his chest, stifling his voice. He pulls out his knife and slaughters him like an animal, then flees.

As he runs away, what he had witnessed in the week of terror passes in front of him, with fragments of stories told to him in his childhood about the brutality of the invaders, the torture camps, the acts of extermination, of burning and rape.

With the sun and solitude, these fragments have fused together in his depths, spreading thick shadows of depression, dark moods, and an untamable drive toward death.

THE SHAME

After drinking coffee and smoking countless cigarettes during the day and greedily drinking beer in a frenzy at night, Alazrak's other world begins, alone or with members of a gang from the wolves of the city.

There is always a store to be burgled or the bedroom of a woman to be raided, followed by bloody clashes with the outcasts and drunkards of late nights. After that the wild roaring of the hot blood in the nerves calms down.

"The police, the bastards!" Alazrak says to himself as he sees their blue cars invading the streets with their shrill sirens.

"If only I had a machine gun to gun them down like dogs."

Those who had occupied the city after the departure of the invaders had stiffened his inner resolve. As he observes them in every quarter, at every corner, in the squares, schools, factories, park, and beaches, his soul becomes a permanently boiling volcano.

"Those pigs!"

He clenches his teeth and spits in the direction of the blue sky.

In prison, the police officer sarcastically asks, "Hey! How do you find yourself now? Si[2] Alazrak? How strong is your determination?"

As he stares into the policeman's face, he glimpses the desire for murder in his eyes.

"You've had it? O Alazrak!" he says to himself.

Once they had been given freedom in the city, they had turned into hunters. Orders had emphasized the need to consolidate the authority of the state, and licensed the liquidation of all lawbreakers.

This wild beast, this outlaw Alazrak disturbs the peace of the jungle.

"Alazrak! you son of a whore, you and your band have fallen. You think the state is like your father, you trampled on his face and walked away? Ha. We'll show you how you'll return to your folk a woman who has lost her virginity, you swine, you fornicator."

The baton now appeared from one of the desk drawers to fall on his head. The second blow hit the central spot at the back of his head, and a red flame erupted, lighting up the world. Alazrak screamed like an animal being slaughtered, "Ayie, ayie, you have killed me, you pig. You dog of the state."

Fire raced through the veins and nerves, bursting out. The area of the blow started to sting and glow. Crimson shapes began to emerge in the sky of a cruel world.

Alazrak met the third blow with his raised, manacled hands and, like an enraged bull rushing into the arena, he rammed his head and hands into the face and stomach of the police inspector. He tore into his face and broke some of

---

2. "Mr." in parts of North Africa (e.g., Algeria and Morocco).

his ribs, then he mercilessly crushed his head as he had once crushed his own father's.

As a result of this, Alazrak spent three months in the prison hospital, receiving medical treatment and nursing the shame and dishonor of having been raped.

THE NIGHTMARE

He felt exhilarated as he watched the city burn. He saw himself soaring in a sky of fire and blood. The fire was consuming the police stations, the jails, the mosques, the shops, and the army barracks. All the symbols and old idols that had crushed and distorted his spirit were burning to ashes in the raging fire. He saw himself dancing naked over green hills. As he dances, pustules, boils, and hateful-smelling germs emerge from his body. When the dancing halts, he slings incendiary missiles to fan the flaming fire. As the flames erupt in waves, so do his desires erupt from their prison, breaking down the barriers that had repressed his spirit, dormant under layers of fire.

Now he is purged and returns to his original nature. And here is the fire, laying bare the desire, awakening it from the bondage of its sleep, and reconciling it with its origins. Here is Alazrak shouting out primitive cries, some meaningful and some not, in this colorful ritual celebration.

The bird of the spirit had taken off from its cage, toward the forest and the sea.

"To hell with you, you oppressive heritage!" The city of nightmare, the city of fear, arrests, hunger and murder, had become a burning hell.

With pagan joy, Alazrak takes wing, passing over the city of ruins in the direction of the forest. And with the tranquility of a child whose eyes are the color of the sea and the sky, he lies down on the green grass and, naked, sleeps in his mother's arms.

SEA

Beyond the city stretches the sea. A blue heavenly child, frightening and sublime. The sea and the virgin African forests encircle the city. The city, which Alazrak perceives as a cage or cemetery. He moves in the subterranean alleys, as if he were a beast thrown up by the forest into the city's compound. In the streets, the cafés, the bars, the interrogation rooms, and the prison cells, he can hear only the sounds of taming, of familiarity, concord, and obedience, and he recoils.

Suddenly he feels nauseated, and he spits. Sometimes in the middle of the street he takes out his penis, tracing with his urine strange obscene words attacking the state, the police, the city, gods and fathers, commands and prohibitions and conventions.

Then he rushes with animal-like screams across the city toward the jungles.

This time, however, the prison wound went deep. Although he feels, as he reclines on a chair in the café, the need to break out of his human condition toward his natural absolute, he now realizes that his swift movements toward freedom have become constrained.

He had to do something to erase the stigma. Although he spent many sleepless nights dreaming of raping his rapists, killing all the city's policemen, and blowing up the jail, these substitute nightmares, while soothing to the nerves, seemed like a temporary sedative unable to heal the wound.

On this tranquil morning Alazrak feels less disturbed. The rays of the equatorial suns as they pierce the sands, the heads, and the tops of trees seem bearable near the sea.

Lying on a blanket of hot sand under a primitive sun is like a truce. Reposing under this white glare after two years of solitary confinement makes things look brighter and breeds joy. His child's heart opens up now like a flower at dawn, free and intoxicated among the half-naked bodies of girls and women lying on the sand. Two girls stretch out two meters away from him. One presses her breasts into the hot sand, while the other's breasts and thighs receive the sun's kisses.

The two girls whisper to each other in an audible voice while he observes them from the corner of his right eye and listens.

The conversation must now be about him.

"Isn't that Alazrak?"

"Look at his muscles and his huge chest."

"Ooh. Yet do you think that he makes love in the way he kills?"

"Will you take a bet on the length of his organ?"

"Listen. Do you think that they really raped him in prison, as it's rumored?"

The other laughs, mimicking the incident. "In that case his organ must have atrophied and become a cunt."

"Ha ha ha. In that case he will compete with us in catching men."

They disappear, laughing together in wanton fashion. They must be imagining him during the act, a man's rod going in and out of his backside under the eyes of that laughing pig whose ribs he had crushed.

Alazrak's mood clouds because of these imaginings. The sun, the sea and the two girls become vibrating red patches. The bell in his head has started its loud ringing.

With the spring of a wild cat he finds himself beside them. He opens his legs, cornering them. They are now between his legs. Their eyes face a huge upright figure whose face overflows with bitterness, terror, and hatred.

"Take it, you two. That's it! It's yours."

He had unsheathed his organ and was shaking it with both his hands, long, erect, and tanned by the sun,

"Is he big enough for you, you whores?"

Despite his gratification following the incident by the sea after his release from prison, Si Alazrak did not rest until he had lured into the forest two members of the gang that had raped him. There he extinguished the fire in himself after he had tied them up, then he cut off their penises and left them bleeding among the trees.

SCENE OF THE KILL

Once again, the café. Pavements glitter under the summer sun. The white screen hanging behind the white glass emits white heat. The day is like a shroud. From the half-naked bodies of schoolgirls, whores, and passing women a hot flame radiates, exciting desire. Si Alazrak fidgets on his chair. The hot center of energy expands, and he feels ablaze. The brutal ringing in his head and nerves has started again.

He springs up. A taut body, bursting with energy and desire. A single violent need to kill or rape engulfs the body like a tornado. That's him following with unsteady steps a girl walking along the pavement. She turns and he follows. Her back is half bare. Every now and then the wind lifts her dress and her red panties glow in the sunshine. Alazrak's temperature rises and his pulse quickens. He sweats. To regain his balance, he lets out his breath, then whistles. His whistling is well known. He concentrates on observing the rhythmic movement of her backside squeezed in by her underpants, whose outline is seen under the flimsy dress.

She was now within earshot and within reach of his hands.

"O for that smooth marble dome. Are you a woman or a virgin, my beautiful ewe?"

He says this as he presses his palm on her soft swinging bottom. The girl is frightened.

She turns around and they face each other in an empty alley.

"Oh it's you?"

"The girl from the beach! What a happy coincidence! This is a real wedding, then."

"Oh have mercy, Si Alazrak."

His big hand is on her mouth, covering half her face. He gives a voluptuous laugh. He drags her to the dark entrance of a building like a wolf dragging a sheep to his lair.

"If you scream, I will kill you."

Now the knife was at her neck, the gleam of death flashing from it.

"O Si Alazrak! I appeal to your honor!"

"Did you say my honor? You are my honor now."

"O Alazrak! I am a young virgin."

"Not bad. We'll conduct a little experiment, my ewe, to see which of us is the man and which the woman."

He was pressing her against the wall while his hand was pulling up her dress and tearing at her panties.

"Take it, my ewe! It's yours now."

He took her hand and pressed it into her palm: "I heard that your brother is a policeman and that you complained to him after the incident by the sea. Tell the truth."

"But he's never harmed anybody in his life!" said the girl, trembling.

"Did you tell him about the incident or not? Anyone harming Alazrak will never get away with it. Now it's your turn, next time it will be the turn of your dirty policeman, my ewe."

He pressed her against the wall. The girl moaned. He plunged his face into hers, then into her bosom, exposing her breasts. She groaned with pain. He was pushing at her, she resisting, compressing her legs together. He arched his back a little, then plunged, forcing her legs open, crushing her supple body between his body and the wall.

"Ooh, my magnificent Alazrak. Be reasonable, I am a virgin. Ah!"

She had loosened up under his thrusts giving him the opportunity to be free in his movements.

His excitement overflowed and he started lowing like a bull bearing down on a cow.

Their bodies fused together. With a slow, impassioned movement he penetrated her, as a knife penetrates a wound, and a supressed scream, intermingled with pain and desire, escaped from her.

Alazrak had triumphed. His pulse became normal and the summer seemed to him to stretch like a joyful band of marble white light over the city.

THE EMERGENCE OF THE SPIRIT

There is Alazrak, a wanted and pursued man. The law wants him while he wanders alone fleeing through the prairies. An obsessed and deviant thief had subverted the dignity of the law and had breached morality. Thus they branded him as they sought him. During his flight across the valleys and forests that encircled the city, he raids farms and isolated houses for food. Some nights he is forced to sleep hungry in the open or in lairs and mountain caves. In the open air among the trees and rocks Alazrak returns to his pure nature. He builds his private kingdom among the rocks. The limitless sky, the wind and the rain, penetrate the veins in his body, unclogging the pores blocked by the contaminated cities, by the stench of the pigs, patriarchal prayers, and the coffinlike cafés, bars, and shops. His spirit is gratified, and he recovers his lost childhood, the childhood that had been violated.

The birds and animals of the wild combine with the spacious silence of land and open air to give him a feeling of joy and peace.

"Who had been more cruel?" He asked himself.

"You chose wrongly Si Alazrak."

A mysterious voice reached him from behind. He turned in a panic: "God of the devils, who is there? Man or demon?"

He sprang up, knife in hand.

She was standing on an overhanging rock. He rubbed his eyes to brush off the dream: "Who are you?"

She towered over him like an apparition. Gigantic. Transluscent in an enchanting dawn. Her face the color of the prairie flowers. She seemed to him to glow in the halo of light.

"What are you doing here?"

He moved as slowly as a spacewalker. Sat on a rock. Ran his fingers through his floating hair. Opened and shut his eyes with difficulty.

When he looked up, the wind was whistling around the high barren rocks.

She reappeared. Still standing on top of the rocks, the wind blowing through her wheat-colored hair. A pebble she flung to him fell near. She smiled: "Are you deaf or are you mad? Say what you have come to do here?"

He stood up and started walking. He trod the damp grass while dawn was spreading. He could not climb the rock. An invisible force prevented him. The light of the blazing sun exploded in his eyes. He felt something pulling him backward, so he lay down between the blades of grass.

It was a joyful morning. A bird was singing sweetly on a tree. In a short while beautiful colorful birds arrived and began a festival of song and joy. Alazrak was enchanted. A strange overwhelming joy swept through him and he burst out singing and dancing and laughing.

THE SECRET

The girl of the prairies reappeared. The same distance remained between her and Alazrak. Alazrak was unable to comprehend. He tried to ward off the nightmare in an attempt to distinguish truth from illusion, but he remained lost.

"Alazrak! You've made a mistake! The road does not pass through here—your road."

"From where then?"

She seemed different from city girls. There was a magic halo surrounding her sweet, innocent face. The faces of city girls throb with lust and depravity.

Alazrak had not forgotten her first appearance. It was as if the grass had unfolded to reveal her or that she had fallen from a distant star.

She knew that Alazrak had fled the inferno of the city that demanded his head. When she began talking, her words were strange and surprising. She talked of the history of the murderous city and the misery of people and their hunger, of the violations of the oppressors and the bestiality of their instincts, then went on to talk of the murdered and the martyrs, the prisoners and the exiles.

She related to him the incident of her father's death under torture and of his burial here in these prairies, and she said that she came here in search of her father's wandering spirit that demanded revenge.

He heard her repeating words that rang in his depths like a bell: "Love and murder cannot coexist. It is either love or murder."

She was talking in a subdued tone, while the sunset flowed tenderly on her face, so full of sorrow and beauty.

Alazrak wanted to say something about himself, about his inner torment and his black history, but felt powerless.

Her face inspired confidence and trust. From that transluscent, sad face a warm light stretched, engulfing his depths in joy and peace.

Alazrak was transformed as he listened. At one point he felt he had become a different person while she talked to him of the conditions of beggars, hobos, of naked, hungry people plunging like dogs into garbage bins in search of a crust of bread; while she talked of the insane whose nerves had been destroyed by the war, of the unemployed, of the retired fighters, of the thieves, and of the peasants inhabiting tin shacks while the oppressors, heirs of the invaders, occupied the palaces, the farms, the beaches, and the parks, all the while sucking the blood of the homeland forcibly and violently.

Nowhere was there someone as sad as he was now. His heart almost broke as he listened. He felt impotent and alone, that he had chosen a wrong path. He wondered about the reasons for his loss of direction, where the trauma had originated, and why he had met this apparition at such a late stage.

Within seconds the nightmare was back. He saw the city swept by an earthquake that hurled it to the center of the earth.

At the back of his head, at the center of organic damage, sharp pains arose.

He raised his head, shaking off his anger, and heard her distant and dwindling voice calling on him to return to the city where they would meet. When the phantom had disappeared, he felt as if his heart were bursting through his ribs. He felt that he'd lost something precious that could not be recovered.

Something had dissolved in him during the nights of misery, pursuit, and exile. Alazrak wondered about his situation. Was his existence superfluous, his birth a mistake? Why did he flounder, not knowing how to adjust and harmonize with the world?

He did not find an answer to his questions, either from inside himself or from the outside world. Impatience roused a scream in him that pierced the peace of the prairies: "Mother, oh Mother! Where are you? Take my hand in this darkness. Return me to the womb."

The echo spread. It spread until it flooded the plains and valleys. Alazrak was now crying like a child who, in losing his mother, had lost all sources of compassion.

PEACE

Alazrak did not see the prairie girl after that date, neither did he enter the city again.

At the gates of the city he fell, brought down by a bullet that tore through the back of his head and came out from his forehead. Alazrak fell alone and bloodied, without uttering a cry. He lay sprawled at the gates of the city, then curled up like a child in its mother's womb and peacefully subsided.

The hunting of the brutalized, the thieves, the deviants, the beggars, the homeless, and the unemployed had begun.

Orders had been issued to purify the city of these pests in the interest of law and order. The killing of Alazrak came as the crowning achievement of the period of purification and as a consolidation of the calm and peace that reigned over the city.

—Translated by May Jayyusi and Anthony Thwaite

Gamil 'Atiyya Ibrahim (b. 1937)

Gamil 'Atiyya Ibrahim was born in Giza and subsequently lived in two places that left a deep imprint on his writings: old Egypt, near the 'Amr ibn al-'As mosque and the churches and seminaries of this region rich in Coptic and Islamic monuments; and the Giza region, near the famous pyramids. Since 1980, however, he has lived in Switzerland, although he visits Egypt twice a year to collect material for his novels and short stories. He initially studied business administration at 'Ain Shams University, then joined the Academy of Fine Arts, obtaining a diploma in art appreciation and criticism, as well as an M.A. in prehistoric African art. A member of the sixties generation, he played a part in founding the review *Gallery 68*. He writes both novels and short stories, marked by their candor and their preoccupation with seeking original material in the world of everyday life. Shunning the sentimental or the sensational, he is a master of understatement, probably unmatched for the matter-of-fact way he addresses even the most crucial issues. His first novel, *Asila,* was published in 1980 and republished in 1994. It was followed by *The Sea Is Not Full* (1985), *Down to the Sea* (1986), and his trilogy *1952* (1990), *Papers of 1954* (1993), and *1981* (1995). He has also produced two collections of short stories: *Mourning Befits Friends* (1976) and *Side Conversations* (1994). A number of his stories have been translated into English and German, and his novel *Down to the Sea* was translated into English by Frances Liordet and published by Quartet Books, London, in 1991.

AN OIL PAINTING

When Munir asked if he could make an oil painting of me, I agreed, telling myself I'd really like to see such a picture. I felt Munir always painted the truth in his portraits and, when I looked into his eyes, I had the sense he was piercing to my very depths. He took his pen and drew a number of lines, watching me closely all the while.

I saw my face and eyes appear from many angles, and thought, "Is that really how I am?"

As he dabbed his brush on the papers with swift strokes, Munir would start talking to me about his past. Then he'd stand back from the painting and look at it from different distances, talking all the time but without finishing his sentences, while I'd keep grunting to show I was following him.

I'd taunt him too, saying his political views were wrong and his analysis of things was faulty, and he'd pitch into me in return and start defending himself. I'd tell him the forties generation was responsible for all the disasters that had overtaken the country, and he'd laugh at me.

As I posed for him, keeping totally still, I'd let my thoughts stray, then come back to him to say something else and contemplate the way he was scrutinizing the portrait.

Whenever I entered his studio, I was gripped by a sense of awe, as if I was in some holy place at the time of prayer. There were books piled and scattered in corners and, over the tables, scores of canvases, paintings, inkwells, and colors.

He was an artist.

As he plied his brush, he'd talk about student demonstrations and the life of prisons and whores, and I'd get totally confused, not knowing if he was talking about the demonstrations of 1946, or 1968, or 1972. He jumbled up different events, leaping from one to the other without pausing for breath.

I'd tell him, bluntly, that he was one of those who'd betrayed the revolution of 1946. And then he'd start up with his remarks, some of them true, some not, about all the Egyptian politicians and intellectuals, throwing out unfinished sentences as he painted on, saying how the real problem of the country lay in the absence of democracy, that the new generation knew nothing of its country's history.

The trouble with Egypt, he'd tell me, was that its leaders didn't read French, didn't visit art galleries, didn't listen to music. Then we'd both start listening to Sibelius; and the moment Sibelius's melodies began to seep and echo through the studio, I'd feel a profound tension, for his melodies are full of the preoccupations of Finland, where the universe bears down, cruelly and harshly, on people's souls, because winter's so long there; the icy lakes and gloomy forests instill fear, and life, under their dominion, is lonely and filled with ghosts. We were at one in our love for Sibelius.

Few people, Munir told me, had the capacity to listen to Sibelius; Egyptian big shots had no interest in anything beyond Um Kulthoum and Muhammad 'Abd al-Wahhab,[1] though 'Abd al-Nassir had once expressed his admiration for *Scheherazade*.

I could see he hated the police and people in authority, mocking leaders and their speeches and attacking their pretensions, not in the way politicians do but

---

1. These Egyptian singers are the two most celebrated singers of the twentieth-century Arab world.

in his own unique manner. That man's broad shoulders, he'd maintain, must stop him sleeping properly—and in that case how could he lead a whole nation? As for that other man, he was too ignorant even to distinguish between *ts* and *ds* when he talked, so how could he be trusted in any political capacity?

I learned, too, to pay close attention to the way speakers walked. He maintained that the leaders in most Arab states suffered from piles, and, when I smiled, proceeded to demonstrate it through pictures of them. I'd inspect the pictures of Arab leaders on the point of getting up or sitting down, or as they walked, and I became convinced they suffered from inflamed prostates as well. He gazed at me closely, to see if I was being serious or just sarcastic, then said, "It could well be." He claimed, too, that the inflammation from piles affected people's mental powers.

Sometimes he'd offer me something to eat or drink; at others he'd have a very serious air and we'd go off to the studio the moment I arrived. He'd tell me he had a number of appointments, and I'd sit for him in silence. He wouldn't speak himself for some time, just dab at the portrait with his brush. Then his features would relax, and he'd smile and start talking.

I learned how to arouse his interest. At the start of the sitting I'd tell him something about my travels, or about Ibrahim or Salma—for instance that Salma suffered from a psychological condition, or that Ibrahim had had a quarrel in the Atelier the day before, or that al-Hadi had delivered a Nazi speech in the café, attacking everyone, or how, on one occasion, I'd missed my plane. Then he'd start talking about himself.

I brought him a printed sheet once and told him how the university students were distributing pamphlets attacking him. In fact, it was a friend of mine who'd prepared and printed the paper, at a press he owned. He took the paper, read it through with indifference, then said, "Poor people!"

A little later he returned to it, read a few lines, then threw it to one side and said something about art in French. "Quite," I answered—though I hadn't actually understood what he said. Then he took the sheet again, angrily, and said, "These people don't have any honor."

"They certainly don't," I said.

"No one," he went on, "has any interest in soiling my reputation except the tools of the authorities or failed artists."

"Quite right," I said.

His last exhibition before the 1967 June war had consisted of oil paintings of garbage cans, several of them filled with garbage and set up on dilapidated tables. The bins reflected a light that came and went as though by some inner illumination.

I coveted Salma and would show my admiration for her in the presence of Ibrahim and Munir. I was besotted by her legs. Once I even crawled up in front of her and asked if I could kiss her feet, but she refused. I knew Munir had had a relationship with Salma before I met her. Ibrahim, too, asked me not to try and see her, and I knew he was hovering around her as well.

The portrait was pretty well finished now, parts of it already complete. Everyone made comments, some sarcastic, some admiring.

Munir told me about the pamphlets attacking him, accusing him of betraying the 1946 revolution; he'd come across several of them, he claimed. They became the main topic of his conversation, and he talked about them with animation, though I think he realized they weren't genuine.

As I sat in his studio at noon, I'd visualize the streets I grew up in, then come back to him, to find he was still plying his brush with soft strokes. As the portrait neared completion, I realized my eyes were narrow and long. I'd always thought they were wide.

One day Ibrahim turned up full of excitement and told me Salma was having a relationship with an Englishman called Henderson, who was studying Arabic.

"I know him," I said.

"Salma's finished," he said. "Henderson's done for her."

Ibrahim was sorry about it, while I, for my part, was swept by a surge of jealousy I had difficulty hiding. Eagerly I asked him to tell me what had happened to Salma, sparing no detail. Henderson and Salma, he said, had gone in a car, with another couple, to one of the suburbs near al-Ma'adi.[2] There they'd taken a sailing boat and, when night fell, they'd all plunged into the Nile in the moonlight, seeking, by this means, to cleanse themselves from disease. Henderson, it seems, had had a lifebuoy, a rope, a censer, incense, and some Indian books to draw the good spirits to the riverbank. As they bathed, they'd listened to a special kind of music.

I was eager to know more about Salma. How, I asked, had they gone into the river?

"They went in naked," he answered bluntly. "One after the other."

"Naked?" I said.

"Yes."

I felt a choking sensation, and my hatred of the British grew stronger. To possess Salma was like stealing the pyramids. I'd always thought of her as something more than a mere woman.

I repeated to myself, "Naked!"

Aisha, Ibrahim said, had given a full account of all this to some of her friends, claiming she'd been cured of a number of diseases after going into the water. The silver light of the moon, she went on, had engulfed her as she swam, and she'd felt a profound ecstasy, which cured her of the madness that had driven her to periodic attempts at suicide.

I told Munir everything I'd heard, but he wasn't interested this time, saying merely that the new generation was inclined to a licentious lifestyle. He'd known Salma, he said, since she was a student at the College of Art, and from the start she'd never shown any shame at standing naked in front of her female

---

2. A suburb of Cairo.

fellow-students. Nakedness, he went on, was a weapon used by weak people. A strong woman never stripped naked unless she wanted to, but Salma was mentally sick.

He started adding some dark colors to the portrait, to define the eyes. He'd look at me as he painted, still plying his brush. Our problem as human beings, I told myself, as I looked at the painting, is that we always have to be either a man or a woman, or else something in between. Salma's problem was that she was a woman and we were all men around her.

As the portrait neared completion, I discovered something strange about myself. To begin with my features had been clear; then they'd begun to assume a hint of boorishness. A hard, piercing look had appeared in my eyes, and there was a small, fading smile on my lips, lost amid the shadow that stretched from my chin to the side of the room.

"The portrait's changing," I said. "It's taking on a different look."

He only painted what he saw, he answered. He simply looked for the essence.

I knew he was going to finish the portrait and add it to his gallery—that for him, as my image faded, dissolved into the painting's space, I'd be just an experiment in color.

When he was on the point of completion, I told him, furiously, that it was the picture of a murderer set amid nightmare.

"That's what I see," he said.

I felt dejected then.

—*Translated by Salwa Jabsheh and Christopher Tingley*

Ilfat Idilbi (b. 1912)

Born in Damascus to an upper-class Damascene family, Syrian novelist and short-story writer Ilfat Idilbi is a largely self-educated woman who has become prominent in Damascus literary circles and an active participant in her country's various cultural and literary organizations. Her stories, mainly documenting the images and structure of old Damascene life and their transformation under the impact of twentieth-century modernization, are unique in their kind and strike a nostalgic note. She has published several collections of short stories from which many stories have been translated into German, Russian, and other languages: *Damascene Stories* (1960), *And Laughs the Devil* (1970), *Goodbye Damascus* (1963), *Stingy in Tears* (1972), and *Behind Beautiful Things and Other Stories* (1996). Her novel, *Damascus, Smile of Sorrow* (1980), was translated into English by Peter Clark, appearing under the name of *Sabriya: Damascus Bitter Sweet* (1995), and is currently being made into a film by the Syrian Cinema Institute.

THE CHARM

Her neighbor said, trying to be comforting, "What's the matter with you, Um Safi? Why make such a thing of it? You think this is the first time a man has taken a second wife?"

"How can he do this to me?" cried Um Safi, wiping her tears. "If I'd heard this from anyone but you, Khadooj, I wouldn't have believed it. I would have said no, it's gossip—vicious . . . " She stopped. "Oh," she cried again, "how can he do this to me—Abu Safi—after twenty-five years of marriage!"

Khadooj sniffed sarcastically. "How indeed? Sometimes I wonder about you, Um Safi. You should know by this time that trusting a man is as stupid as trying to carry water in a sieve." Then her manner changed. "But look, my dear, there's no time to waste. I'll take you to Um Zeki. She'll give you a charm to stop everything before it's too late."

"But how?" Um Safi frowned. "You just said his wedding was set for tonight."

"Yes, yes, but Um Zeki can do wonders."

"In such a short time? In a few hours?"

"That woman can do anything, believe me. She's known for stopping weddings at the last minute, for bringing husbands and wives back together after they've fought for years. She's even managed to separate the closest and most loving of couples."

"But how?"

"Does it matter how? She just does it. But there's no point in ever going to see her unless you have a gold lira. No work unless she's paid in advance. And it's a fixed price: one lira per job."

Um Safi hesitated.

"I have a gold lira," she said.

"All right, let's go."

Um Safi rushed to dress, then she opened her own private chest and took out the gold lira. For a moment she held it tightly in her hand. Years ago she had promised herself never to part with it, this gold lira that was heavy with memories and had become a symbol of her own blessings and good fortune.

She had had many difficulties in her life, bad days, hard days, but she had never considered spending the gold lira. No, it was not a simple matter to use it.

Whenever she rearranged her chest, she would take the gold lira from its box, deep in the folds of the garments; just looking at the piece filled her with happiness, and often she would let her imagination bear her away, into the past.

Twenty-five years ago. The day she had come to this house as a bride. Many times during those years she had sat, the gold lira in her hand, looking first at the winking gold and then at the courtyard where she had worked and lived and raised her children. And she would see the courtyard as it had been on her wedding day, filled with festively dressed guests, the lemon and bitter orange trees decorated with lighted lanterns. When she crossed the threshold for the first time, she had been lucky: the traditional bit of dough on a green fig leaf, handed to her by a cousin, had stuck successfully to the wall of the courtyard. Her family had smiled and congratulated each other on this good omen, an omen that their daughter would settle peacefully in her new home and that her life would be filled with joy. They had sung:

> The sacred words of Yaseen will protect you.
> Oh flower of the grove
> You are the bloom, of rose, or iris,
> That crown the head of the sultan.

The women of the bridegroom's family had welcomed her into the courtyard with joyous cries of ululations. They sang:

> No, you're not too tall, to be ugly,
> Nor short enough to be squat.
> You're as good as the best *halawa*
> Fresh and sweet, sweet.

The groom's mother had taken her hand and led her to the place of honor, a platform decked with flowers, made comfortable with carpets and satin cushions. And all the time she had remembered to keep her eyes lowered modestly, so as not to be, as they said, "one of those impertinent brides who gazes into the faces of the guests."

But still she had managed to steal a glance at the courtyard, realized she would live there for the rest of her life, and had loved it then as she loved it now: a spacious courtyard with luxuriant shade trees and high arched doors with a fountain whose jet of sparkling water rose into the air and fell back, splashing, into a silvery pool. The lilac tree had bloomed for the wedding day; its branches were heavy with clusters of pale mauve flowers. When one of the girls' pretty heads touched the branches, blossoms floated gently down to decorate the courtyard floor with lavender petals. The windows and doors were festooned with jasmine, its scent stronger and sweeter than all the perfumes worn by the wedding guests. The twenty young girls had carried decorated candles, and had circled the fountain, the flames of the candles leaping as they sang the traditional bridal song:

> Blessings on the bride!
> God's blessings on the bride!
> Oh beauty,
> Oh beauty,
> Oh rose blossoming in the garden!

Um Safi sighed. She remembered herself then, how proud she had been of her beauty, circling with the girls, proud of her fine blonde hair woven by the beautician with glinting golden threads, which fell free over her shoulders, almost reaching her knees. The long transparent veil of white net had been fastened on her head with a wreath of lemon blossom, the symbol of purity and virginity, of innocence.

The shouts and chants of many people outside had signaled the arrival of the groom.

An old lady had said to her, "They're singing that marriage is a harness for men, a chain, but that real men can handle it. They're singing to your husband because he's leaving the company of bachelors. But they say that if he cares well for his future wife and his home, they'll shout congratulations."

The women's joyous cries of ululation rose higher.

From under her eyelashes she had looked toward the door and seen her future husband for the first time, coming toward her, surrounded by members of his family. She had cast her eyes down. A young relative of hers had whispered, "Don't forget. Don't talk to him till he gives you something for your hair."

He was before her. The beautician put her hands in his. She felt her chest rising and falling alarmingly, her heart pounding. To this day, twenty-five years later, she could not explain that strange disturbance in her body. Had it been fear, awe, joy? Or all of these?

They had entered the bridal chamber. The door closed behind them. They were alone. She sat beside her husband. She felt again that strange disturbance in her chest. He was nervous too, she thought, for he was fingering his worry beads. A moment of thick embarrassed silence passed. Then he came close, took one of her hands and uttered, in a soft, gentle voice, the traditional first sentence of a husband to his new wife: "You and I—against the world." He paused. "Or is it you and the world against me?"

She almost looked at him but remembered the words of her young relative and turned her face away coquettishly.

He smiled. "Oh yes," he said. "Now I remember." He lifted a lock of her light hair and kissed it. "Your fair hair is like silk, my love. I shall cherish it with my life. It has no price but gold." He reached into his pocket, took out a gold lira, and put it into her hand.

At that moment she had vowed to herself that she would save the gold piece, as a token of blessing, of good fortune, in memory of this wedding day. She had raised her head, meeting his eyes for the first time and answered him speaking clearly and directly from the depths of her heart. "You and I—against the world."

She had honored that vow. For twenty-five years she had stood with him against the world, a good wife, faithful, loving, caring. She had borne him nine children, four young men now as straight and tall as palm trees, five young girls, each, she thought, as beautiful as the moon. And how could he do this terrible thing to her now? Take another wife? How could he? How could he forget those years?

Maybe Khadooj was right. Men were faithless, deceitful. She had never believed that, but she realized now that her husband had changed over the years.
After his uncle Bakri had died and left him the mill and the orchard, he had
never been the same. He had become more cross, more irritable, so short-tem-
pered that the smallest matter seemed to annoy him. He had withdrawn more
and more from family life, and he was always creating excuses to be away from
her. How stupid she had been! How foolish not to have noticed that something
was going on! She had always had complete faith in him, had never suspected
he might be thinking of someone else.

The gold lira. Yes, she would spend it. She had no doubts now. She went to
Khadooj and said she was ready to see Um Zeki.

Um Zeki took the gold piece.

"After the evening prayer," she said, "go alone to the roof of your house.
Circle the roof seven times, repeating this charm each time."

Um Safi nodded. But she felt oddly numb. She had done something she
had sworn never to do. She had given up her gold piece, the piece heavy with
memory, all for a charm to stop the marriage of her husband.

"Mother, what's wrong," her children said. "Mother, your face is so pale and
sad."

She didn't answer. She was waiting for the call to evening prayer to end. As
the *muezzin's* cry died away, she stole away from the children, up onto the roof,
as Um Zeki had instructed her.

Rain poured down. The night was full of darkness and foreboding. Fear
filled her, suddenly; she had not expected to be afraid. She was trembling, but
she straightened up in the rain and began the first round, chanting as she had
been told to chant:

I send you Hani and Mani
And the fiercest jinn of all, Khohramani the ruthless,
In his rose tarbush and his leather slippers
To bring you back, now, now!
In any way, in any way,
From wherever you are,
Quickly, quickly, quickly!

As she finished the verse, a bolt of thunder crashed above her head. Lightning
cracked the black sky, the rain fell in torrents. Um Safi froze in terror; she could
not move; she felt she was nailed in place on the dark, wet roof. It seemed as
though she saw before her the ghosts of those evil jinn, Hani, Mani, Khohramani, in horrid glimmers of horns and tails. She thought she could hear, in the
distance, the howling of rabid dogs and the crying of the owl.

Her heart was pounding so hard she felt it might drop down in her body or
stop beating forever. "Oh, what have I done?" she moaned to herself. "These
jinn are dreadful creatures!" She cried out. "Oh Abu Safi, beloved husband, what

have I done to you?" He was the father of nine children, after all, and still the most handsome man in the street, despite his age of forty-five. How could she have taken it into her head to condemn him to this horror? He would come to some terrible harm and she would lose him forever.

"No, no," she cried. "May God forgive me for the evil I've committed! Please, God, let Abu Safi live safe and sound, even if he does marry another. May God forgive me." Then she added, "And please compensate me for the loss of my gold lira."

Um Safi tried to move from the place where she stood, crying, in the rain. She pushed along slowly, feeling her way with hesitant steps through the darkness, along the edge of the wet roof. Then she stumbled, her foot slipped, and she catapulted down, down into the courtyard below.

But she did not die. Her fall was broken by the full branches of the old lilac tree, the tree she had watered and cared for during the twenty-five years of her marriage.

She had cried out as she fell, and her children rushed to help. Safi, the oldest son, lifted her gently down and carried her to her own bed.

"What in God's name is the matter with you, Mother?" he asked. "What were you wandering around on the roof for, on a night like this?"

Um Safi turned away from him and from the other children who had gathered round her bed. She was ashamed to tell them about the charm, but she could not help saying abruptly, "It's because of your father. He's taking another wife. His wedding is tonight."

A shocked silence. Silence like the dead moment before a storm. Then the storm broke. The children all began to talk at the same time, and the babble of agitated voices grew loud, louder. Safi stood up, screaming and cursing and shouting so his words were incomprehensible. He was running out of the bedroom when his sister called, "Safi! Where are you going? How can you run off with Mother in such a state?"

"I'm going to him," he shouted, "to bring him here."

Um Safi gathered herself together. "Bring your father here? Why? What for? Where is he?"

"I don't know, Mother, but I'll find him, wherever he is, and I'll bring him back here. Wherever he is," he added, shouting wildly.

Um Safi opened her mouth and shut it again. "So that's the way it is," she said to herself. "That's the spirit, this Khohramani, the fiercest of the jinn." He had always been there, her oldest son, her strongest son. He would have helped her, but she had never asked him. She had not even thought about him. And she had wasted her gold lira and destroyed her memories.

"No, my son," she said finally. "God bless you for thinking of it, but don't confront your father now. You know how stubborn he is. I've asked for God's help. Please don't make a scene, Safi. Don't give the neighbors something to chew on . . ."

"Don't be silly, Mother," Safi interrupted. "People are already gossiping about us. So what difference does that make? Do you want me to let my father get married again so you can commit suicide and all of us can stand by and watch?"

He slammed the door behind him.

The room grew quiet. Safi had voiced everyone's worst fears, including those of his mother. Um Safi closed her eyes. A strange peace was creeping over her, as she realized that her son had grown strong and independent; he was now a man perfectly capable of defending her if she needed him.

In a short time Safi returned with his father.

Um Safi closed her eyes and pretended to be unconscious. Abu Safi stood at his wife's bed. He could not meet the nine pairs of accusing eyes, so he bowed his head in humiliation, and murmured:

There is no strength but the strength of God.

There is no power but from God.

Fate, destiny; what is written on the forehead the eye must see.

We pray to God, we turn always to God, in His mercy.

But even the holy words, spoken eloquently, could not make those accusing eyes disappear. Abu Safi's sense of humiliation and shame was almost too much to bear.

"I must get the doctor for Um Safi," he said, and ran out of the house. When he came back, the children would have calmed down, he told himself. The doctor's presence would help smooth over the embarrassment of this day.

By morning news of the events in Um Safi's and Abu Safi's house had spread through the neighborhood. The women came to inquire after Um Safi. She felt poorly from the effects of her fall, but cheered up a bit when Khadooj came and whispered in her ear, "You see, Abu Safi's marriage has been stopped. The stream returns to its bed." She smiled triumphantly. "Didn't I tell you? Um Zeki is a wonder. Her charm never fails."

—*Translated by Basima Bezirgan and Elizabeth Fernea*

THE WOMEN'S PUBLIC BATH

Our household once suffered from a unique problem. My grandmother—who was over seventy years old—liked nothing more than to go to the public bath at the beginning of each month. The souq bath, as she liked to call it, seemed to have a special flavor for her, which we, who had never experienced it, could not understand.

We used to fear that our grandmother might slip on the slick floors of the bath, a thing that often happened to the bathers, and break her bones, now grown brittle and frail, or else that she might catch a severe cold as she came out from the warm atmosphere of the bath into a chilly street and thus contract an illness from which she might never recover. But how were we to convince our grandmother with these arguments? It was impossible that she would give up a habit she had practiced since childhood without ever being afflicted with what we were now cautioning her against. She was determined to go to the baths for as long as she could walk. The more my mother tried to convince her not to go, the more my grandmother tenaciously held on to her custom.

My mother never tired of criticizing her mother-in-law and arguing with her, trying to show the fallacy of her ideas, even though she did this subtly. Whenever the subject of the public baths came up, my mother started counting their drawbacks from a sanitary and social and even financial point of view.

What most annoyed my mother, however, was that my grandmother, on her public bath day, would completely monopolize our only servant. Starting early in the morning, she would call the servant to her room to help her sweep it, then change the sheets, and then wrap the bundles of clothes to take to the bath. Then she would take the servant with her to the bath and bring her back only at sunset, completely exhausted and unable to do any more work.

I watched this strong, undercurrent conflict take place in our home between my grandmother, who tried to hold on to her old status in the house and was most reluctant to relinquish it, and my mother who tried her best to ease her mother-in-law out of her former place of authority and occupy it herself.

And despite the fact that daughters usually side with their mothers, I used to feel a strong sympathy with my grandmother. She had suddenly grown old when my grandfather died a short time before, and her shadow receded from the household little by little, while my mother's spread in its place. This may be life's normal procedure of taking, then relinquishing, I learned, but people surrender to it neither willingly nor with conviction.

I used to feel the pain tearing at my soul when I saw my grandmother retreat to the seclusion of her room and stay there for many hours after she was defeated in an argument with my mother. I often heard her muttering bitterly to herself or saw her shake her head continuously and monotonously as she sat in silence as though reading the whole book of her long life, conjuring up the memories of her bygone days when she was the undisputed mistress of this house and the one who had the first say in it. Often I watched her release her anger through the beads of her thousand-bead rosary, fingering them nervously as she repeated, "Oh, Benevolent God! Dispose of our affliction!"

But who could be her affliction if not my mother?

Eventually, her anger would calm down, little by little, and she would forget the cause that led to it. What better way to cleanse the soul and aid it in bearing the tribulation of fate than the repetition of God's name in devotion?

It occurred to me one day, as I watched my grandmother prepare for her day at the bath, that I might also accompany her to it. I had never before been to a souk bath and was eager to discover the secret attraction it held for my grandmother. When I expressed my wish to her, she became very happy. My mother, however, considered my suggestion too impulsive and told me, loud enough for my grandmother to hear, "Did this obsession with the souk bath also seep into you? Who knows? You might contract a contagious disease like scabies and pass it on to your brothers and sisters!"

But my father intervened and said decisively, "What is that to you? Let her go with her grandmother. All of us went in our childhood to the public baths and no harm ever befell us."

My mother let me off, reluctantly, while my grandmother smiled, proud of this victory, for my father rarely sided with her against my mother.

Grandmother then got up and took me by the hand to where her huge chest stood. She produced a key from her pocket and opened the chest. This was a great honor indeed, because this ancient chest had never been opened in front of anyone else. A strange though familiar aroma emerged from the chest, a smell that can come only from the chests of old women, the smell of age, of the past, of the years folded and put away. My grandmother brought out, from the bottom of the chest, a *buqja* of red velvet embroidered at the corners with beads and sequins. She unfolded it and took out a wine-colored *meyzar* strewn with golden stars, a *meyzar* the like of which I had never seen. Then she passed to me white bath towels embroidered at the edges with silver thread and said, "These are all new and have never been used. I have kept them since my wedding day. And now, since you are to accompany me to the baths, I give them all to you as a present. Woe to me, I who have never been accompanied to the public baths except by servants."

She then heaved a long sigh and called for the servant to carry the bundles of clothes and towels and the big bag containing a bowl, soap, comb, washcloths, *lufa*, Aleppo powder, and the henna that was to transform my grandmother's white hair to jet black. Then my grandmother put on her cloak and we went to the Afif baths not far from our house. Often, in my goings and comings, I had read what was inscribed on the plaque situated on its low gate: "Whoever seeks good health from the Benevolent Lord, Should seek God first, then the Afif Baths."

We entered the baths. The first thing that drew my attention was the manager, who was a huge woman sitting cross-legged on a bench to the right of the entrance, with a casket in front of her in which she collected the revenue. To her side was a *nargila*, decorated with flowers, with a long hose whose mouthpiece the manager caressed with her lips as she looked haughtily at those around her. When she saw us enter, she welcomed us without moving from her place. Then she called Um 'Abdo, the overseer. She, a middle-aged woman, hurried to bid us enter. She had well-trimmed eyebrows, kohl-blacked eyes, and clean, clean clothes. She had adorned her hair with two roses and a sprig of jasmine. She was, moreover, eloquent in speech, quick of movement like a spinning top, never resting for a moment. Her wooden thongs made a rhythmic tapping on the bath floors. She was more a hostess of the baths. Taking my grandmother by the hand, she led her to a special stone bench that looked like a bed. Our servant then hurried over and spread a prayer mat over the bench and my grandmother sat there to take off her clothes.

In the meanwhile, I was fascinated by my surroundings. I liked the vast outer hall. It had a pool brimming with flowing water. Narrow benches against the walls were covered with colored rugs on which were thrown the clothes of the bathing women. The walls themselves were adorned with old yellow and pocked mirrors and with plaques engraved with wise sayings, several of which made it clear that "Cleanliness is part of faith."

My grandmother encouraged me to take off my clothes. I did and then tried to wrap myself with the wine-colored *meyzar*. Since I did not know how, Um 'Abdo helped me and wrapped it firmly around my body, throwing one of its edges over my left shoulder, like a sari. Then Um 'Abdo helped my grandmother down from the bench and to a small door leading to a dark corridor. There she called at the top of her voice, "Marwa! Come and take the *Bey*'s mother!"

Suddenly, out of the dark, a shriveled, gray-haired, middle-aged woman hurried toward us. She had a face on which misery had dug deep furrows and was naked except for a discolored cloth that dangled from her waist down to her knees. She welcomed us with a twangy voice, chattering words I did not understand, because of the din of splashing and voices, the hot steam that veiled my vision, and the nauseating smell of sweat and steam, all of which made me dizzy. For a moment I thought I was going to throw up and leaned on the servant. It took a few seconds for my head to clear as I got used to it all. I was also better able to peer through the darkness by now. We soon arrived in a small hall with a large circular pool in the middle, around which several women sat, chattering and bathing themselves.

"Why don't we join them?" I asked my grandmother.

"This is the Middle Hall," she said. "I have reserved a chamber in the Inner Hall. I am not used to bathing with the rabble."

I followed her, and we entered through a small door to the Inner Hall. I stared around in wonder. In each corner of the square hall there was a large white marble basin where women sat, completely involved in massaging, sponging, and washing themselves, in constant movement, as though in a race. From glass-covered round openings in a high dome, the sun's rays flooded in to light up the entire hall.

The din here reached its climax, the tingling of bowls, the splashing of water, the screams of children, and the voices of the women that were getting louder so as to make themselves heard. My grandmother stopped to greet a friend of hers, while I watched a violent quarrel between two young women. Both were married to the same man and had just met for the first time. The quarrel became heated and led to their throwing their bowls at each other. Gallantry took hold of some of the other bathers, and they separated the two wives before they could hurt each other.

We advanced into the hall a little. The screams of a child now dominated over the din of the bath. His mother had put him in her lap and had wrapped one leg around him and was now scrubbing his hair with soap and pouring hot water over him until his skin became red, as if flayed. I looked away, afraid he might die in front of me.

Inside the chamber I felt a little depressed. The initial enchantment was gone. It was, after all, a small room with a basin. Its only attribute was that it was private, shielded from the other women.

A huge woman with a pocked face and a thick husky voice met us in the chamber. She was Um Mahmoud, the supervisor. She took over from Marwa, who was being constantly called by the other bathers: "Cold water, Marwa! Cold water, Marwa!" The poor woman hurried each time and filled two big pails from the pond of the Outer Hall and carried them with such difficulty as to arouse pity.

I went back to my grandmother and found her sitting on the tiled floor in front of the basin. She had yielded her head to Um Mahmoud, who sat behind her on a low wooden stool. The washing of the hair was an exacting ritual. It had to be done exactly seven times, neither more nor less.

I stood at the door of the chamber, amusing myself by watching the others. Young women went in and out of the Outer Hall for recreation. Proud of their youth and of their colorful *meyzars* embroidered with gold thread, they swayed as they walked, like Indian women in an incense-filled temple. Little circles of light fell from the ceiling and danced on their lithe bodies, accentuating their luster. But it saddened me to see the old women sitting next to the walls, chatting with each other, while the henna paste on their heads melted and ran in black trickles down the furrows on their foreheads and cheeks. They waited, patiently, for some attendant to come and wash it away.

Suddenly, there were ululations, and I looked up and saw several women around a pretty young girl for whom they were singing.

Um Mahmoud, the supervisor, said, "Our baths are well-attended today. We have a bride, and a young woman who is honoring us with her first public bath since giving birth to a baby, and of course my lady, the *Bey*'s mother, may God preserve her for us."

My grandmother was proud to be associated with a bride and a new mother. And it pleased me to stand in front of our chamber, watching the bride and her party. A plump, white-skinned middle-aged woman wearing a royal blue *meyzar* sang the ululations, joy emanating from her. From the words of her song, I understood that she was the mother of the bride. She sang:

> Seven bundles I prepared for you
> And the eighth is in the chest
> We thank you O God,
> That You did not make her need anyone.

Another woman, the bride's relative or friend, answered:

> You have entered the gate of the Middle Hall
> Wearing the gold-threaded Saysabani sash.[1]
> Whoever is not happy about your wedding,
> May he die an infidel.

---

1. A kind of *meyzar* or wrap used by bathing women who would wrap them around their bodies like an Indian sari. The best kind was enmeshed with red and blue golden threads.

The bride's mother sang again:

> The bird chirped and flew away
> among the vine leaves.
> How lovely is the bride in the Baths,
> her brow studded with dew drops.
> The city's gate is high,
> but I surrounded it with my little finger.
> And for seven long years now
> I have been pining for this day.

But the nicest song was that of the bridegroom's mother:

> Daughter-in-law I chose you
> Against the evil eye.
> Damascus girls are numerous,
> but my heart loved and wanted none but you.
> Nuts, hazel-nuts and dates
> The heart of the enemy is wounded.
> Today we are joyful
> And the enemy sees no joy.

The songs and the ululations ended when the bride and her party sat around a large bowl filled with Damascus meat pancakes and another filled with fruit. The bride's mother became active, distributing the pancakes all around. I also got one of them.

There was one secluded corner, however, where a woman with her four children sat around a plate full of rice and lentils and turnip pickles. They were so involved with themselves that they were oblivious to everything else taking place in the hall. When the plate was emptied of its food, the mother produced from her basket a large head of cabbage, which she raised high and brought down with full strength on the floor of the bath. She did this over and over again until the cabbage split open into several pieces. These her children snatched and munched with great joy at their sweet taste.

Not far, on the bench nearest the wall of the furnace, another secluded group attracted my attention. In the midst was a young woman about sixteen, looking bored and discontented, as if enervated by the heat emanating from the place near where she sat. She was surrounded by three women, one in particular fussing over her, most likely her mother. She soon began rubbing the young woman's body with *shaddad*, a yellow paste smelling of ginger, which my grandmother told me strengthened the veins of a woman after childbirth and made them stronger than before.

Um 'Abdo, the overseer, came and asked after us, bringing glasses of licorice juice, a present from the manager. Then she lit a cigarette for my grandmother and I realized how important my grandmother was.

My turn had arrived now to take my bath, and my grandmother gave me her place. I surrendered my head to Um Mahmoud to scrub as she wanted and as the rules of the profession dictated. After having my hair washed seven times, I watched Marwa washing one of the women. The attendant wore a rough cloth mitten to scrub the woman. She began slowly, then quickened her rubbing, and some gray residue came off the woman's skin.

After we had finished sponging and scrubbing, Um Mahmoud asked me to go back to wash my hair again, this time for another five times. I surrendered to her completely because I had promised myself to fulfill all the rituals of the public bath, no matter how trying they were. When Um Mahmoud finished the washing, she poured on my head a bowl of Aleppo powder mixed with water, which gave a special fragrance to the hair and would linger for several days to come.

Um Mahmoud then stood at the door of the chamber and shouted in her husky voice, "Marwa! Towels for the *Bey*'s mother!"

The attendant in turn moved with alacrity to the door of the Middle Hall and called out in a voice as shrill as a cock's, "Um 'Abdo! Towels for the *Bey*'s mother!"

Her voice mingled with that of another supervisor standing in front of the opposite chamber, also asking for towels for her customer.

Um 'Abdo appeared, her Shibrawi[2] wooden thongs tap-tapping on the floor. She brought us a heap of towels and, distributing them between us, said, "Blessings. Blessings. I wish you good health after the bath." She took my grandmother under the arm and walked her to the Outer Hall and helped her climb the bench, then assisted in drying her and putting on her clothes.

My grandmother had to wait her turn to pay. A loud argument was going on between the manager and a middle-aged woman and her three daughters. The woman was claiming special half fees, insisting that she was a widow and that her daughters were all unmarried. The manager was sceptical, for the oldest girl was a mature young woman and quite beautiful, but she finally accepted the mother's claim after she swore the most sacred oaths that she was telling the truth.

My grandmother then advanced and slipped something into the manager's hand, saying, "This is for everything, including the cold drinks and the service."

The manager glanced at her hand and broke into a big smile, looking very happy. She said to my grandmother, "May God preserve your high status, Khanum. And may you come here often."

My grandmother next turned to the supervisor and the attendant and the overseer, who had come out of the Outer Hall to see her off, and distributed tips to all three.

I must admit that I have never known my grandmother to be so generous as on that day. She looked contented and proud as she accepted the good wishes

---

2. Very high wooden clogs, often studded with mother-of-pearl and made with silver front strings over the toes. Brides used to wear them on their wedding days to look taller.

showered on her by those who had just received her generosity. She then gave me a proud look as if to say, "Have you now seen your grandmother's status? And would you mention this to your mother who values me lightly?"

Then she emerged from the bath, erect and dignified, an extra lilt to her steps, quite different from her stooped and humble walk at home. She had been exercising her prestige in the only place she could.

And I realized her secret of the souq bath.

—Translated by Elizabeth Hodgkin, with the help of the editor, and Ahmed Essa
—Translated by Roger Allen and Christopher Tingley

Suhail Idris (b. 1925)

Lebanese novelist and short-story writer Suhail Idris was born in Beirut. He studied at al-Maqasid al-Islamiyya College and obtained his Ph.D. from the University of Paris in 1953, writing on the Arab novel and foreign influences on it. He also obtained a diploma in journalism from the Higher Journalism Institute in Paris. On his return home he founded, in 1953, the prestigious monthly, *Al-Adab*, which has served the cause of modern Arabic literature most decisively. The review reflected not only its editor's spirit of literary avant-gardism but also a crucial vision of Arab cultural and political unity, proving the great cohesion of contemporary Arabic literature and its natural transcendence of political barriers and artificial frontiers. In this undertaking, Idris's services to modern Arabic literary thought are remarkable. His credentials enabled him to occupy several pioneering positions: he was one of the founders of the Union of Lebanese Writers, its president for eight years, and one of the founders of the Union of Arab Publishers in 1984. The publishing firm he founded in 1960 and attached to his review has also served the cause of Arabic and world literature, by publishing numerous translated works, especially from French literature. Idris's first novel, *The Latin Quarter*, about the life of an Arab student in Paris, appeared in 1953 and won him immediate fame. He has published two other novels, *Al-Khandaq al-Ghamiq* (1958) and *Our Burning Fingers* (1962). His many collections of short stories include *Bitter Tears* (1956) and *Have Mercy, Damascus* (1961).

NADIA'S IMAGE

My mind was numb with exhaustion, and my limbs were stiff from sitting so long. Since two o'clock in the afternoon I'd been sitting here on this chair, at this table in the Sorbonne library, reading this book, without so much as raising my head. The clock in the outer yard was striking eight. Its chimes echoed through the halls, arousing feelings of awe in all who'd entered this great cultural citadel.

I shifted in my chair and raised my eyes from the book. I was about to get up and walk round the library for a few minutes, to relieve my numb brain and the weakness in my limbs, when my eyes focused, mesmerized, on a chair at the next table.

My God! What on earth was Nadia doing here?

A few moments later, of course, I'd been brought back to reality and was laughing at my error. No, it wasn't Nadia, but it was very like her. If I hadn't known Nadia's features so well, I would have thought it really was her but grown just a little thinner.

I put on my glasses and regained my calm. Then I began to gaze at the face, which was so near and yet so remote. No, her eyes were even blacker than Nadia's, though they were less bright and expressive too, and her mouth was different from Nadia's, its two corners more deeply etched—a larger mouth, it now seemed to me, than my Middle Eastern girl's. The hair, pitch-black, flowing freely and apparently carelessly onto the shoulders, was exactly the same as Nadia's. I couldn't compare her figure, as she sat in her chair, with Nadia's, but I imagined her to be taller though not more graceful. It would have been unfair, though, to say that Nadia's neck was prettier than hers. How could my girl's neck compare with the long, graceful, elegant, very white neck I saw in front of me?

I gazed and gazed at the face that had now recreated Nadia's image in my memory, clearing away the dust that had gathered on it over the past three years, bringing her back to me, full of energy and life.

A few years before, I'd left my country for the French capital to carry on with my higher education, and Nadia and I had promised to keep in touch with one another. We'd write often, we said, letters filled with what we would have said to one another if we'd been together, and so continue our relationship.

I did write Nadia many letters, telling her of the feelings of love and longing her distance from me had aroused and giving impressions of my life in Paris. She wrote to me in turn, sending me, as my sister and closest friends did, all the news from my country that she supposed would interest me. She also asked me to give her more news about my life in Paris.

During my first weeks in the French capital I felt my love for Nadia grow sharper. In my mind I relived, over many long hours, our former meetings together, imagining her close to me, feeling that I could never have enough of her beauty, sensing the warmth of her nearness. The most beautiful of these memories was our last meeting in a park, stolen from beneath the watchful eyes of our families. That day I plucked up courage, for the first time, to take her hand and kiss it—a kiss that carried all the love and longing I felt for her. At first Nadia tried to draw her hand back from mine, but I still held it and she let it stay there. When I looked up, I saw that there was a blush on her face and a look of reproof in her eyes.

But after I'd been in Paris for two months, the memory of my love for Nadia began to sink within a sea of oblivion; the dissolute capital was beginning to open my eyes and tempt me with its dazzling lights. I began, naturally enough, to enter its life, to be no longer a stranger watching from the outside but the hero of great events. I began living, to the full, the life every Middle Easterner seeks to live in his own country but is denied as he clashes head-on with conservatism and tradition and ends up a mere symbol of deprivation. Here, in Paris, pleasures abounded in all their colors, so many and various and novel that they filled all my inner emptiness and made my being overflow.

As one might expect, my urge to write to Nadia weakened and my letters to her became fewer and fewer. She wrote to me, in one letter, that she expected Paris to turn me away from her. Yet, she said, she felt no despair at this, for I would soon grow bored with the lights of the French capital and return to her with a deeper love and a clearer mind. I found that I had nothing to say to Nadia now and decided that I would feel more comfortable if I stopped writing to her altogether. It had begun to strike me how very foolish I would be to miss this chance of throwing myself, with all the force of my body and soul, into the life of Paris.

After this Nadia wrote to me many times, begging me not to stop my letters. She knew, she said, that my love for her was weakening, yet it would be a great consolation to her to see my writing and read what I had to say. I turned a deaf ear to this. What did she expect from a man whose conscience had been destroyed by Parisian women, who'd thrown over it a thick curtain of neglect and indifference?

It was exactly a year after I'd left my country that I received the last letter from Nadia. It was full of pain and despair, and the things she unfolded to me should have melted the cruelest heart. But did I have any heart left to be melted now?

It was several months before I realized that Nadia had stopped writing. It was as if she'd despaired of me—or perhaps she supposed her long silence would rekindle my longing for her and the desire to return to her love. If so, she was wrong, for Paris had drained all the longing from my heart and emptied it of old desires. Why should a soul yearn for the image of paradise when paradise itself was within reach every day?

Two more years passed, years so long they could have drowned a whole life in a sea of oblivion. How could Nadia's image stay clear in my memory when so many other images had been piled upon it, images more brilliant and marvelous and dramatic than hers? Each of these images reflected a rich experience in my life. What spirit had been able, now, to chase all these other images into the corners of darkness, leaving only Nadia's image, clear, sweet, and wonderful, in the face of the girl sitting before me in the Sorbonne Library?

I raised my eyes again and was surprised to find her looking at me with interest, as if she too was going back through the memories her presence had awoken in me. Then she realized she'd been gazing at me and lowered her eyes, plunging herself back into her book.

I stopped reading myself and began, naturally enough, to think about Nadia and about what must have happened to her over the past three years. For a long time I tried to silence the voice of conscience, which was now rebuking me and raising feelings of regret. "What real meaning has there been in the life you've led in Paris?" it asked me. "Just what have you gained by sacrificing Nadia and her love?"

While I was reflecting on all the different things that might have happened to Nadia, the Sorbonne clock struck ten, which meant that the library was about to close for the day. Quiet sounds were heard as the students prepared to leave. A few moments later the girl came toward me on her way to the door, giving me the same interested look I'd seen in her eyes a little while before. Emboldened by this, I plucked up courage to follow her and caught up with her at the outer gate. I had no difficulty starting up a conversation with her; I was used to doing this well enough, and I usually managed it successfully.

Within a few days Gilberte and I had become good friends, and we began to sit regularly next to one another in the Sorbonne library; if she arrived first she'd reserve me a place alongside hers, and I'd do the same if I was first. Gilberte very quickly became curious about our language and the way it's written and said that she'd like to learn it. I said I'd be happy to teach it to her, and we agreed that I'd give her an hour's teaching every day, beginning with the alphabet.

A question soon surfaced in my mind, for all my efforts to avoid it: "Have I fallen in love with Gilberte?" I began to realise that this French girl was occupying my thoughts as no other girl in Paris had done. I was well aware of the slight quiver that would pass through me when I looked at her, making my heart beat faster and giving me rather confused feelings. The cause of this, I knew, was that Nadia's face kept looking out at me from Gilberte's, arousing in me the old chaste love that my very different experiences of love in Paris had only served to raise to an exalted loftiness and sanctity. When I was near Gilberte, I felt the same old, contented happiness I'd felt when close to Nadia, and I soon realized that the love that had begun to grow in my heart for Gilberte was beginning to cleanse me of the false, wanton feelings in which I'd been submerged during my three years in Paris, that it was returning me to the kind of clear, pure atmosphere in which Nadia and I had lived for so long.

It was clear that Gilberte had also begun to love me. Her joy when she came to see me was clear, and she'd speak to me with deep affection, as if she'd known me for years. I noticed, too, how utterly rapt she would become whenever I talked to her about the East and its secret enchantments. She told me more than once that one of her greatest wishes in life was to visit the desert and get to know the bedouins in their tents, and she made it clear that her desire to learn Arabic stemmed from the hope that she could one day visit the Arabian desert and talk to its people in their own language. Once she laughed and said, "I might meet a handsome Arabian prince there, who'd take me and marry me!"

I laughed in my turn and told her she wouldn't be able to stand bedouin life for more than a week. She'd soon, I said, be thoroughly disenchanted with the East. But she wasn't convinced.

"As long as I loved the prince," she said, "I wouldn't mind what hardship I had to take."

Then she took my hand.

"Forgive me, dearest," she went on. "I love you too, even though you're not a prince!"

I laughed and pressed her hand, gazing into her eyes.

Then, one evening . . .

Gilberte had suggested that we leave the Sorbonne library at eight and go and watch an American film that revolved around the psychology of love. We were both rather tired from studying, and this seemed like a welcome break from hard work.

We left the library, and a chill, more like the chill of a Parisian winter night, cut through our bodies. When we reached the cinema, Gilberte told me she felt cold, so cold that she was shivering. We quickly entered the cinema, where, I was sure, the warmth would soon restore her. But when I held her hand, the coldness of her body was passed on to mine, and I began to shiver too. I had to rub her hands in mine to get them warm, and, slowly, I felt that the warmth was coming back to them and that the color was returning to her face and the light to her eyes.

Going back to the film, I began to follow the story closely. It was a serious psychological film that needed total attention, but after a few minutes I felt Gilberte place her arm round my shoulders and leave it there. I pretended not to notice, but then she began to squeeze my shoulders and draw me toward her. I turned to her with a quizzical look.

Only then did I see in Gilberte's eyes what I'd seen in the eyes of so many other girls I'd known in Paris, and I saw, on her lips, the apparition of those desires that remain active and alive, even though they've been suppressed and muted. With this there came back to me the memory of so many feelings I'd had during my time in Paris, feelings I felt I must stifle totally, so as to rid myself of the nausea they inspired in me. Gilberte must have felt my revulsion, for she drew back her arm and pretended to be absorbed in the film. We left the cinema, and when we reached her metro station, I realized, to my surprise, that I hadn't once raised my eyes to look at her on the way. I kept them lowered as we shook hands and exchanged a brief goodnight, and perhaps her eyes were lowered too.

I slept worse that night than I've ever slept before. Nadia's image was lost among the images of scores of Parisian girls or, when present, would sometimes lose its innocence and purity and sanctity, would bear expressions full of temptation and have cheeks aflame with desire, lips trembling with passion.

I avoided the Sorbonne library for several days, so as not to see Gilberte; I stayed in my room at the hotel where I lived, leaving it only to go out and eat. During those days Nadia returned to share my life with me, with an insistent presence. She would appear, especially, from the pages of my books, and my longing for her would grow stronger. I realized then that the love I'd felt for

Nadia when I was in my country was a deep and chaste love, flowing from the depths of my soul, the only passion that could ever bring me to the highest pinnacle of unblemished happiness.

Once more I began to wonder what had become of Nadia now. Hope made me believe that she still loved me and was waiting for me to come back home. More than once I thought of writing to her, but I hesitated to do this after three whole years of silence—a silence that I now regretted bitterly. Still, I consoled myself with the thought that I'd be going back in just a few months, and that I was now firmly decided, the moment I arrived there, to ask for her hand and make her my wife.

I began to get used to working in my room at the hotel, to living within myself on the wings of imagination and listening to my conscience as it stood in judgment over me. Then, late one afternoon, when the Parisian spring shone over Paris with color and flowers and smiles, I felt I needed to go out. I went to the Luxembourg Park and sat under a leafy tree, watching the children play round the big fountain and push their boats out onto the calm waters.

A few minutes later two hands closed over my eyes and blocked the light. I sat still for a moment or two, waiting to hear something; then the hands were taken away and I heard a gentle laugh. I looked up and joyfully exclaimed, "Nadia!"

She turned suddenly pale, and the happy smile was dashed from her lips to be replaced by a rather sardonic one. She slowly moved away and said:

"I always thought it was another girl you loved in me, and now you've given yourself away. What a naïve Arab you are!"

Turning quickly, she hurried off and was lost among the crowds of picnickers.

I'd meant to find Gilberte next day, and apologize and assure her that I loved her. Then I received a letter from my sister, telling me, among all the other news, that Nadia was engaged and that the marriage would be taking place shortly.

—*Translated by Salwa Jabsheh and Christopher Tingley*

Yusuf Idris (1927–1991)

The Egyptian short-story writer, novelist, and playwright Yusuf Idris is the foremost short-story writer in the Arab world. From the beginning of his creative career, he demonstrated the caliber of an international writer of high standard. Idris was born in the Egyptian Delta and, after spending an unhappy childhood living with relatives in order to gain an education, he studied medicine in Cairo and worked as a health inspector for a time before practicing medicine. He began writing his short stories when he was still a medical student and, at the same time, became involved in the political and social affairs of his country, an involvement well reflected in his fiction. His early stories drew immediate acclaim, and he continued to write prolifically. His 1965 novel *The Illicit* was made into a movie. He also wrote some interesting plays, including his acclaimed play *Al-Farafir* (1964), which was translated into English. But his greatest strength lay in his short stories, which are unmatchable in technique, subject matter, and the capacity to bring in pathos and involve the reader emotionally. Idris has a capacity for graphic and moving details. His work reflects his great empathy with people's psychological and emotional reactions to life's experiences and places a special emphasis on the plight of people in less fortunate circumstances, such as poverty exploitation, particularly of women. He has published many collections of short stories, including *The Cheapest Nights* (1954), *A Matter of Honor* (1958), *The Language of Aye Aye* (1965), *House of Flesh* (1971), *I Am the Sultan of the Law of Existence* (1980), and *Kill Her* (1982). He received well-deserved great acclaim for his novella *Abyss of the City* (1964?), and his works have been translated widely into several languages. English translations of Idris's works include Roger Allen's *In the Eye of the Beholder (1978),* Wadida Wasfi's *The Cheapest Nights* (1978), and Catherine Cobham's *Rings of Burnished Brass* (1984).

THE BET

It was one of those dog days of summer. The country road stretched away into the distance, and it was so hot not even a fly or a crow could stand it. It was noon, and the heat stifled everything into quiescence; even the few wafts of breeze were soon lost. Al-Sharqawi's hashish den was the sole haven along this road writhing in the intolerable heat.

There were four regulars in the den at the moment. The cotton season had filled their wallets, and their pockets were bulging with coins of different sorts. Their conversation was languid and drawn out. Beyond them, Salih, the seller of prickly figs, was squatting beside his basket, bent over it and drifting off into a gloomy silence as he brushed the flies from his figs and sometimes from his face as well. Al-Sharqawi, the owner, was trying to fight off his sleepiness as he sat there with the unlit gas burner in front of him. He was paying no attention to Farag, the road sweeper, who was squatting by one of the posts that supported the den's roof, begging al-Sharqawi, in the intervals of a long and patient wait, to let him in for a smoke on the water pipe.

Then the stranger arrived.

He was a tall, sturdily built bedouin type, wearing a gown made from old calico and short enough at the bottom to reveal a pair of skinny legs. Around his waist was a broad woolen belt, tied behind, and on his head a brown scarf and a worn-out headband with threads hanging down. He had sharp features that were made more conspicuous still by the sweat streaming down his face, and his eyes looked as though blood might actually gush from them.

The regulars sitting there returned his greeting. From his shoulders he lowered a panting lamb and asked for some water, and al-Sharqawi pointed to the jug buried in the ground. The man drank what was left in the bottom of it, then sat down on the bench. The water had moved rapidly from the inside of his stomach to the outside of his face.

No one could think of dozing off with a stranger in their midst, and it wasn't long before conversation started up. The regulars learned where the new customer was from and where he was going; and when they found he owned absolutely nothing and had neither money nor hashish with him, their manner soon turned to derision.

As they were starting to get bored with all this, Salih came to life again. He stopped brushing the flies off his figs and took an active part in the conversation, describing his figs in glowing terms, saying how incredibly succulent they were. No sooner had you eaten one, he said, than it went straight to your heart and breathed new life into it!

Salih was the only one talking now, as the others found their mouths watering at the thought of his figs. Then one of them started things off by buying five of them. The others said it was too many, but he ignored their comments, claiming he could gobble down the entire basketful.

Everyone laughed. Then, still laughing, they asked the bedouin chief, as they called him, what he thought. They were quite taken aback when he replied, in his soft, courteous voice, that he could eat a hundred.

They all said it was impossible to eat as many as that. Even a bull, they said, couldn't eat so many. But the more they poked fun at him, the more he kept insisting he could, and even put the small lamb down as a wager.

When the bet had been taken up, one of the men produced his wallet and prepared to pay for a hundred figs—if the man managed to eat that many. Salih was beside himself with glee as he peeled them, while the man ate and the rest of them counted. Even Farag, forgetting about his smoke, left the place where he'd been sitting and started helping Salih with the peeling.

The two of them simply couldn't keep up with the man, who sat there downing one fig after another, at an incredible rate. It was so easy he might have been dropping them into a bottomless well. Al-Sharqawi stared at the man in amazement, all thought of sleep driven far away. He started whispering along with his customers, and with Salih, and Farag, all of whom were counting.

At forty the man loosened his belt.

At sixty he asked for some water, and al-Sharqawi rushed off and filled the cup from the canal.

At ninety he asked for some more water, poured it down his throat, then let out a prolonged belch. Slowly and confidently he finished the hundred figs, and then, just for good measure, downed another one in honor of the company present.

Almost the moment he'd finished, he scanned the silent, dumbfounded expressions on the faces of the other men, waited a moment to catch his breath, then picked up the lamb, wished them a quiet farewell, and was gone.

They kept looking at his stomach, till he'd finally vanished. Only then did they find their tongues again.

"He must be one of the western bedouins," al-Sharqawi said, nodding his head up and down. "I reckon he put a spell on the figs and called up a genie before he downed them all." He looked right and left and uttered an oath, spitting in his pocket as he did so.

"Maybe he's got worms in his guts," Salih suggested, "and they gulped the whole lot down, one after the other."

Farag cleared his throat.

"Bedouin are just like camels," he said. "They have two stomachs."

One of the men with the swollen wallets assured them all the bedouin would burst by and by, and fall down dead. They'd stumble across him for sure in a day or two, floating in the canal or crumpled under the bridge.

The far-fetched notions came thick and fast, with any attempt at rational explanation or conjecture abandoned. There was nearly a fight over it.

As for the man, he was proceeding on his way. He could feel a stomachache coming on, but all that concerned him was that he'd eaten. Just for a while the pangs of hunger had been stilled—come what may.

—*Translated by Roger Allen and Christopher Tingley*

An Egyptian Mona Lisa

This isn't my first attempt; it may even be the third or fourth. Every time I think of writing it down, I get the feeling the language I'm using is much too crude, too stilted and hollow to put what I want to say into words. The language we use to speak and write was, I feel, created to depict imposing phenomena and great sensations, things like rocks, for instance; and even if we reduce the scale a little, I still sense it's meant to depict things like sand and pebbles—whereas what I want to portray is something soft, musical, delicate, and subtle, like those tiny particles that seem to cling to the sunlight when it pours into a dark room. No! It's not even like the sound of a violin or the plaintive warbling of a flute, but, rather, a melody you can only hear when the world's cacophony dies down and all creation is silent. Your entire being is purged then of all those anxieties and ephemeral, earthbound feelings that always manage to distract you. You're infused, totally, with the proper sense of the words "mercy," "love," "affection," and "man," all of them timeless concepts in whose fulfillment the abiding hope of humanity lies. There's plenty of strain involved in preparing yourself for this sensation and a lot of contemplation and silence too. But when it's been done at last, you'll find a gentle, soft melody seeping in to your inner self, not just through the ears but through your very being, as an actual part of it. This is done, quite simply, by transforming your very self into the melody, till the two merge in one profound, transparent unity.

How can I find words to describe it, when all our words are fashioned with particular concepts in mind, things that are totally clear, evoking no doubts or stirrings of the spirit? How can I find words to describe a tenth of the excitement, or just one hundredth of that shuddering sensation, or the incredible palpitations, so muted they can hardly be heard at all?

How can I find colors to describe the complexion of Hanuna, the Christian girl? It wasn't white or flaxen, it was neither European nor Oriental, neither Upper Egyptian nor from the northernmost part of Lower Egypt. It had a blue tinge to it; not the kind of blue you associate with lifeless things but, rather, the blue of dawn breaking or of a calm sea when the waves are transformed into gentle cries turning back to their home on the humble, prostrate shore, calling you on to plunge into the sea and follow its blue expanse for ever.

How can I begin the story, when I've no clear-cut beginning in mind? It's just a series of relationships between people—a common birthplace, the days of infancy, then childhood, a faded black blanket, a room with no one in it but us, holy bread, then a New Testament with lots of pages in an Arabic with a special flavor to it.

I was an adolescent then, at that stage of life when you feel there's a world there, something that's real; that there's morning and sun and moon, and people too. Far, far away there are lands on this side of the salt sea and across and beyond it. Then there were the pumps, incredibly large, black, and oily, with their perpetual slow, solemn noise. Vast quantities of water were drawn into the sluices by some secret magic then emerged, roaring angrily, in a headlong torrent. Cows and sparrows there were too and pious saints of God, holy scriptures and verses that had to be memorized, all about a strange, incredibly beautiful heaven and a hellish fire that made your whole body shudder, retribution, torture, this world and the world to come. Then there was Sheikh Mustafa's cane; now that was something very urgent and immediate. His turban used to tilt forward more than it should, and he had long legs, coming to a point at a pair of knees that looked like the heads of matches. He'd cross his legs, letting his faded, gaping shoes dangle, and when he shook his turbaned head at you and said, "Listen to me, boy!" that was something very real, something we couldn't see or feel, something quite apart from things like the Night of Power,[1] or death, or the steady affection I felt toward my father. There was something about the sheikh's will. It kept out of sight, reluctant, apparently, to show itself. Perhaps it was worried at the effect it might have on us; for, if we'd encountered it, we might all have died of sheer fright. It really was something quite unusual, different even from demons, who do finally, after all, have something amusing about them. This, though, never remotely provoked laughter: it was severe, grave, protective, and compassionate, all at the same time.

"I want to be like you," I told Hanuna, even though I didn't really mean it.

---

1. The Night of Power (lailat al-qadr) is the twenty-seventh night of Ramadan, the month of fasting. Muslims spend a long part of this very holy night in prayer and supplication and also ask God to grant their specific wishes.

She must have been a year or two older than I was. She was certainly taller, though not as strong; but in any case, she was always more intelligent and had more common sense. It's at this point, in fact, that I can't put things into words. Her soul had a feeling that radiated like a glow from nowhere, which reached you through some indirect path. It enveloped her words, her walk, the way she'd raise and lower her head and chew the small piece of consecrated bread with her front teeth—a rite of such bizarre innocence and purity and elegance that it made you believe. She didn't seem like an earthly creature at all, more like someone from a further stage of humanity, forging a link between the angels and themselves.

I can't remember what it was she said to me; to tell the truth, I can't even remember if she replied at all, or what it was she had to say about the Gospel, holy bread, and the Kyrie Eleison (which, she told me, means "Lord, have mercy"). Some months earlier I'd heard the priest who came from the city recite it at Africa's wedding. All I can remember is that her replies made me aware there were other people in the world beside Muslims. Up till that time I'd imagined the whole world was Muslim. This other, new religion was filled with things that woke your imagination and stimulated curiosity; and all the more so when I learned from Hanuna that the Christians had a church in the local capital, with a large picture of the Messiah in it, as well as candles and electric chandeliers. Everyone, she said, sang there; in fact, their whole worship involved singing.

I couldn't understand any longer just why I felt such a bond with Hanuna, as my thoughts followed her on her way to sleep. Could it have been because I wanted to learn more about this religion of hers, or was it surrender to that irresistible, unending radiance that drew people and things toward her, transforming everything she did into some sparkling event, delightful and subtle and exiting?

One thing I do know though. I won't say I began to feel a firm bond tying me to her; rather I slowly became aware that I never left her, as though I were her shadow. It was only when I wasn't with her that the feeling came; when I was, I never realized what I was doing. I was enmeshed, totally, in one long, continuous meeting with her. My only concern was to look at her and follow what she said and did, like a person baffled by some unbelievable, constantly recurring miracle, who can't distance himself from his feelings, remaining in a state of baffled intoxication that he can't leave and that won't leave him for a single second.

As far as I can tell, that's just where the problems of this world start. We simply won't tolerate what happens in the world, the spontaneous interplay of events along with those impulses of energy and growth that come into being, then develop, disperse, and flourish. With our foolish wills and the laws drafted by our narrow-minded ancestors, we're forever interfering with everything. We take it for granted someone has evil or, sometimes, good intentions, and so we poke our noses into things, striving all the time to make injunctions, to suppress and disrupt, and so pervert the rules of life itself.

What possible harm could there have been, I wonder, in letting a relationship like ours continue? It was like a small, gentle flower amidst the impenetrable forests of people's temperaments and characters and those complex, intermeshed social relationships of which we knew nothing. What did it matter that I was the pump engineer's son, while Hanuna's father was a local big shot? Or that I was a boy and she was a girl? Or that people gossiped a lot (even though there weren't many living in our settlement)? They all had homes the Irrigation Ministry had put up for them near the enormous pump building. There it was, a settlement with its own little society, together with the pumps, in some faraway place in the northern part of the Delta; a small representative set of people (though it seemed to me then like a quarter of the world), Muslims and Christians together. But for all that, there were a thousand problems, a thousand thousand thorns to prick and hurt relations between these few human beings in this spot at the ends of the earth.

It all started when my mother complained to my father. He'd lost one of his legs; either it had been amputated or else mashed up in the pump propeller, I don't know which—the whole subject was mostly avoided, since it seemed to bring back such painful memories. Ever since it had happened, though, my father had been dominated by my mother. Since he only had one leg, my mother grew three, along with ten hands and a hundred tongues. And so, one day, my dear father stopped me on my way to Sheikh Mustafa's school and told me plainly I had to come straight home afterward.

He didn't want, in his kindness, to hurt my feelings by mentioning Hanuna's name or the things we'd been doing together, preferring to leave me to work the rest out for myself. I had no inclination to argue either. To tell the truth, I'd decided instantly to disobey the injunction and carry on meeting Hanuna without telling him. How could I just stop doing something when my own will had no control over it anyway? It was simply the way I was. It seemed as natural as being hungry or being thirsty and drinking; I just did it, without any recourse to thought, or weighing up the different possibilities, or making decisions. When we're young, we tend to be more honest with ourselves, and what we want is more heartfelt than life itself. Finally we were young children in a world that didn't submit to life or its laws, to a life regulated, legislated, and governed by grown-ups. They always had to interfere, and, when they did, it forced us to stop and deceive them, to tell lies and hate them as much as we hated to be punished.

I've no idea what happened to Hanuna.

Our usual meeting place was by the millrace, the deep center into which all the water pours from the major canals and from where the pump apertures raise it up to a higher level, to that of the Mediterranean. Then it can be pumped out again and fed along the irrigation canals. The Delta water level, in the northern part especially, is below sea level, which is why it has to be pumped higher. But I didn't find her there. I waited for a long time, gazing at the water as it rushed through the millrace, spinning round in huge circles that became gradually smaller and shallower. Then they started spinning even faster, till they made a funnel-shaped hole. A man could be swallowed up in that, people said, and never come out alive.

She didn't come. Finally I went and stood a little way from her house. By this time, I was beginning to realize just how mean-spirited grown-ups could be: they'd done their dirty work, and that one long, sweet day was over for ever.

I spotted her in the window. It was late afternoon, and the sun had changed from the fearful, hot ball of noontime fire to a gentle yellow lamp lighting up the window and the room beyond. And there, in the middle of this vivid yellow floor, stood Hanuna. The sun's rays gave her face a strange-colored glow, which shone out through the gloomy iron bars, a glow that transformed her face into another sun, smothered, faded, and hidden. Still I stood there, waiting for some gesture, a glint in her eye even, to show she'd seen me or wanted me to be there. But she stayed silent and motionless—the very picture, indeed, of the Virgin Mary herself, like that picture hanging in her room, but hanging, now, there in the window. I had to see her. I knew her mother, who, though reputed to be so hotheaded, had always been very good to me, seeming, almost instinctively, sympathetic to my friendship with her daughter. Often I'd sneak an orange or some sweets into my pocket, and she'd regularly ask me to give my mother her regards—which I never did, knowing well enough how the two women felt about one another.

The door was open. Should I knock? I went in.

Hanuna's mother was just that moment coming out of the kitchen, her face, along with her clothes and the strands of her white hair, covered with soot from the stove. She smiled momentarily, as if realizing why I'd come. Then her expression froze. It was as though she'd suddenly remembered the problem and the threat. She stumbled and stuttered, but couldn't get a single word out. Then she turned back towards the kitchen, as if she hadn't seen or heard a thing.

What was I to do now? I took her gesture to mean approval and shot into the room like an arrow, to find Hanuna standing there smiling, waiting, with her head still bowed. Although I couldn't see it for myself, her expression was, I'm sure, one of delightful, innocent cunning, of the kind lovers often have. Then, to my astonishment, she acted in a way I'd never seen her act before: she put out her hand for me to shake. I put my own hand out with all the energy I could muster and shook hers so firmly it seemed to hurt her. We'd met often enough and walked and done things together, but this was the first time we'd shaken hands. Her hand was small, whereas mine, for all the two years' difference in our ages, was larger. But it wasn't just that. Hers was a slender hand with refined, delicate fingers at the end, so that you felt as though you were clutching a collection of pencils. They weren't pencils, though, but fingers on a hand, alive and warm, as though all her particular vibrations were focused within them. It wasn't just a hand but a pounding heart, the same heart I'd heard beating before. When I brushed past her breast with my face, something awestruck, something feverish swept through me.

"You look like the Virgin Mary!" I told her.

She raised her eyebrows in alarm and disapproval. Then she smiled again, as though I'd simply said something clumsy. Yet she asked me, even so, how she looked like the Virgin Mary.

"When I saw you through the window, Hanuna," I replied, "you looked like the Virgin without the Messiah"

How I loved calling her by her name—as though just pronouncing it brought enjoyment and left an enjoyable taste in my mouth. " You're Hanuna," I went on. "I'm the Messiah and you're the Virgin. Let me be your Messiah, and you'll be my Virgin."

She almost struck me. In fact she did slap my hand, but very gently, to scold me for saying such a thing. But by now the idea had seized hold of my mind. It wasn't just a whim of the moment; it must have been growing inside me that day we were alone together, as usual, in their home. I'd gazed at the picture of the Virgin Mary caressing her child, Jesus the Messiah, its colors old and faded. From Mary's head rays shone out in all directions, while Jesus was a beautiful baby, smiling happily like a son who knows he's in his mother's arms, that she'll cherish him and love him. Mary was smiling too. There was just a trace of a smile in her face and on her lips, as though she knew someone was painting her portrait and she wanted it to include the smile of a mother really happy with her son.

As I turned to talk to Hanuna, I suddenly felt I wanted to be a baby once more, so that I could cuddle into her embrace, and she could be as happy over me as the Virgin Mary was with her Messiah. But when I asked her that day to be my Virgin, with me as her Messiah, I wasn't really thinking of becoming a little baby again, embraced by its mother. Behind it, rather, was a desire that had long been burning fiercely inside me. I wanted to hug Hanuna, to take her in my arms and embrace her. I wouldn't do it violently or brusquely, for I was aware how slender, delicate, and fragile she was. No! I'd embrace her gently, with loving affection. I wanted to enclose her completely in my arms and chest, to make her smaller and then put her some way into my own heart. That, it seemed to me, was the only way of stilling my constant wish to be close to her and bound to her forever.

I wanted to get really close to her, so much closer than we'd ever been with girls when we'd played at being married in the old storehouses.

Hanuna gazed at me for a long time. It was the first time I'd seen her gaze at me in such a strange way. I'd often wondered what she thought of me, how she felt toward me. I didn't feel the way she treated me showed any sign of a particular "special" relationship—rather that she saw me as a boy of fourteen, just another boy to those eyes of hers that had seen sixteen springs come to full bloom. There was something there, bound together by companionship, by familiarity and mutual agreement, but nothing more than that.

Suddenly, now, I sensed a certain gleam in her gaze, possessing that quality I'd so often yearned for, the quality of emotion. I felt it was a look being directed at me, Muhammad, and that she was using it to say a lot of things the eye would be ashamed to put into words. The look she was giving me was the only way of expressing it. In fact, the eye was just incapable of putting such things into words—or so it seemed to me—and *her* eyes above all. Faced with such a glance, all I could do was move closer to her. We'd often been close together as we walked and had even linked arms, but this was the first time we'd ever moved this close. For all the dreams and desires swirling inside me, I'd never imagined that what was happening now would ever happen: that Hanuna would suddenly clasp me to her bosom with a rapid, trembling gesture and plant a furtive kiss on my forehead. Naturally I blushed crimson; then I raised my head, bringing us face to face. We were both panting. Then came the second, incredible surprise. I found her leaning toward me—I was a little shorter than she was—then, before I knew what was happening, she'd kissed me on the lips. Like the first kiss, it was soon over, but we were both quivering with excitement. I felt her trembling lips, pursed together, as she imprinted them on mine. The kiss was swift as lightning, but it sent electricity through me, and there was the flavor of mint too. Every pore in my body opened up to it, and my heart sprang to life, like a bird awakening in early springtime. The whole thing left me dazed and excited; I'd never felt anything quite like it before. It was as though the kiss itself made me aware, all of a sudden, that Hanuna was a girl, with that quality distinguishing the female sex. She had the attribute that makes women wear particular colors and that kind of clothing, put on all kinds of perfume and jingle around in bangles, rings, and necklaces. It was the same thing that made her breasts swell out and gave her a skin as soft as silk, made her voice like a tuneful melody. How different that sound was from a man's voice, coarse as his body, prickly as his chin, and dark as his face and the hair on his chest.

So Hanuna was female! The reason this so surprised me was that I'd never conceived such an idea before or even dreamed of it. For me Hanuna was like the Virgin Mary, like a goddess: the great promoter of those happy feelings with which creation abounds. Good God—may He be praised and forgive me my sins—she was female! As I still embraced her in my arms, it flashed into my mind, for the merest fraction of a second, that this was the eternal virginity of creation I held in my hands. That was the feeling I had, and it wouldn't go away; it fell into the chamber of my mind and refused to leave. There it stayed like the profoundest of aspirations, a prisoner of veneration for convention, reason, and tradition, a wish that the smaller self would fuse into the larger, that you could love God to the stage of utter oblivion, that the eternal bond between you and the great cosmic secret would be forged at last.

Even if I'd managed to picture Hanuna as a female human being, to bring her down from heaven to earth as a body with flesh and bones, still I could never have linked such a picture with myself. I couldn't conceive of anything between Hanuna and myself that might lead me to treat her like other girls. Like someone possessed, I strove desperately to return the saint to her place. Again the feeling came that she was the one great thing above all else, that the beauty,

grace and superior quality she bestowed on the world set her above the level
of mankind, raising her to the heavens. I made a mighty effort to recapture that
feeling, hoping it might restrain this young man now quivering in response to
the call of womanhood. Hanuna herself, with equal suddenness, had been born
out of the same call.

But I was trying for the impossible. All the saints in the world can't prise apart
man and woman, those two great forces in life, when they've once come together.
There's always a third factor involved too, the fiendish law that can't be defied.
And so I returned her kiss, shaking all over my body, every bit as excited as she
was. To do it, I had to summon up all my virgin manhood. I didn't care any more
whether she belonged on earth or in heaven, whether she was a saint or just an
ordinary girl. She loved me and I loved her, and she had started it all. What I had
to do now was seize the chance with joy, to bathe naked in that strange, surprising sea that had suddenly opened up between her lips. How her heart pounded as
she lay there on the sofa, with my ear close to her bosom, a pounding that almost
made the heavens and earth shake! It made me tremble. In her face I sometimes
saw the earth in all its beauty, sometimes the heavens in all their sanctity. Now,
for a moment, she looked refined, now earthy, she blushed and then turned pale,
seemed depressed then wore a virgin smile, stirred up like the sea in all its awesome splendor as it urges and seethes. There she was, speaking yet saying nothing,
while her body swayed from side to side, speaking without uttering a word. She
was a virgin, and so was I. Neither of us knew it; or we may have wanted to know,
while knowing all the time. Suddenly the blinkers were taken away, those blinkers
that shield our eyes, preventing us seeing our true selves, as we are in our very
depths. The fever we felt wasn't the kind to make you swoon into unconsciousness; it was an obsessive quest for achievement, for pleasure and discovery—and so
part of the cosmic secret itself. At last it was revealed! It was the same feeling you
have on the Night of Power, as you stand there waiting for that moment when
the gates of heaven open before you and heaven's secrets are revealed. You have
the same feeling when a woman divests herself, before your eyes, of the greatest
secret she has, for you and you alone.

Each time I tried to think of her as a girl, a female, I felt on the threshold of
some enormity that would make earth and heavens shake or as though I were
about to commit some heinous crime, the worst possible crime a human being
could commit. I remember how, each time I felt this way, overwhelmed by a
sense of deprivation, I held her, squeezed her tight, and bit her. There she was,
alive and warm and female. I groveled in her, in my own feeling of deprivation,
in her saintliness, in the greatest crime a human being can commit, in the fact
that she was a human being, and in the time I spent worshipping her. I'd worshipped her before, and now here I was holding her, in a fashion inconceivable
in the wildest fantasies.

What can I say? Should I say the saintliness that wrapped her round, giving
a certain air to her voice and even the movements of her hand, simply sprang
from the female in her, womanly rays, sacred and gleaming, rays of her whole

kind and femininity, focused and magnified in Hanuna's light, all femininity and female? Many years have passed now, and I've known plenty of women. But she was the female that day, and ever since, to this very day, I've never had the same sense of being the man, that man.

It was as if the water in the millrace had slowed to utter calm and the pit it made had been leveled out, with everything becoming quiet and still again; as though the sea bursting out from between her lips, across the whole world, had a surface like glass once more.

She looked shy, yet as though she regretted nothing. I felt shy too. We'd hardly finished trying to put ourselves to rights when something flashed by the door, and I knew at once what it was. It came from the glasses of Mi'wad Efendi, her father! He was a tall, refined man, with eyes that always looked tired and always, whatever the time of day, had in each corner a piece of white-colored mucus or some residue from iritis, I'm not sure which.

I felt shy. But I was like a believer too, who, for the first time in his life of faith, achieves absolute, unquestionable communion with his Creator. The wonder's complete then, and faith becomes a mission for him, a certainty prepared to sacrifice life itself for the cause, in all simplicity. And so, when Hanuna scuttled from the room like a frightened cat, and my heart started pounding as it does when young boys are caught, I stilled the pounding with all the zeal of a visionary filled with faith, who, by so doing, can restore the link with what he'd been doing some moments before. For me that meant Hanuna and everything connected with her. This believer, I told myself, would carry on his relations with her, come what may. The world might be turned upside down; Mi'wad Efendi might strike me or quarrel with my father; Hanuna's mother might give mine a piece of her mind, or maybe my own mother would throttle me; my father might drag his old gun from the cupboard and shoot the whole Mi'wad family or else just me. Well, let it all happen! The worshipper prays to his God, the beams of the sun lead back to the sun itself, the night will always have its stars. My relation with Hanuna was still more inevitable than these. It had endured and always would, till the day I died or we both died together. It might even last beyond death itself.

These amazing feelings were all well and good. But, as Mi'wad Efendi stood there, tall and sedate, my expression somehow changed. It seemed to be borne off. All the blood in my body seeped from my veins, as though pouring out and drenching the floor of the room. I stood there, motionless, my eyes dry. My head was bowed low, and I awaited my punishment. Yet I knew, too, that everything had finished before he arrived, that he could have no idea of what had actually happened. But there I was, still waiting for him to punish me. If only he had! If only he'd struck me or cursed me, or even told my father so he could punish me. But all he did, after a long silence, was say:

"I thought you were a gallant boy, Muhammad."

That's a word to stick in your mind for life, never to be erased. It rings in your ears constantly, rising up, suddenly, from the darkness of the past, forming itself on your lips as you repeat it, while a shuddering shame envelops you just as it did when you heard it for the first time. Whenever you remember it, you recall it completely, with the same tone and manner in which it was said. I don't know if months or years have passed since it happened—the days passed bleak and full of tedium, stretching aimlessly and without end. Again and again I'd go to the house, hoping for a glimpse of her, knowing, though, that fate had struck, that her parents had given her the strictest orders not to see me, that I should perish on her account. Sometimes, very rarely, I'd catch sight of her from a distance and gaze my fill at her with a faraway look, like a man looking up at the stars, with the holy passion prompting me every so often to move nearer, to venture into her sight. I'd call to her, now whispering, now aloud, beckon to her with a trembling hand that sometimes felt cut off from me, at other times as though it could leap in the air along with my whole body, to come between her eyes and the horizon. Not once did she seem to recognize my existence, as she stood fixed in the heart of the square yellow window with its iron bars. Surely, I felt, surely she must know I was there; yet she was not aware of my presence or else refused to recognize it. She must have promised her parents, and Hanuna's promise was sacred like Hanuna herself, never to be betrayed. I'd melt with passion as I remembered her, as I shall remember her always till eternity itself, every move she made, every word she uttered, every look that spoke on her features. I'd melt with longing and passion, ready to die from the memories. Did my love have to seek final fulfillment? Wasn't it enough just to be near her? Wasn't that easier than the void this final break brought with it? I felt like the hero in one of those Arabian Nights stories, who was left in a palace with seven gates and ordered not to open the final one. He lived happily in the palace but couldn't resist the last, alluring temptation of that seventh door. And so he opened it and saw what no eye had seen and no mind conceived—then found himself outside the palace in the very magic spot where he'd entered, along with six men clothed in black who sat there constantly weeping and wailing. Those were the ones who'd followed that same course before—and now I'd become the seventh. Did I really have to open the seventh door, seek out the greatest happiness? Now I was sorry and wept; the world had become bleak, the days never ending like a gray, withered old crone, the nights without midnight or dawn or morning, life itself without time. Then autumn came. Rumors spread that I refused to believe; the day was fixed and the night came. There was celebration all over the colony, but its heart was in the great central square. Lights pierced the darkness with their sparkle; there were countless candles, sending the smell of their wax far and wide. Her cousin had come in from the countryside to marry her, and now they were celebrating the wedding. The clergyman who visited from time to time had arrived from the state church, and everyone was singing and repeating after him, "Kyrie Eleison, Lord have mercy, God have mercy." Hanuna came, in her snow-white clothes and jasmine necklace and veil, her face made up too heavily. Her gaze, though, wasn't painted; it was distracted, terrified, and lost. As the many hands pushed her forward, she moved like one hypnotized and playing a part. The smile on her face was pale and fearful, and by her side was a young man she might never have seen before that evening, a big man in a black coat, with thick black moustaches, his hair gleaming from the brilliantine he'd used. The bridegroom strutted proudly, like someone who'd just clinched a favorable deal, savoring the moment, booming with laughter, for no apparent reason sometimes, from the very depths of his chest. And beside him walked Hanuna, meek as a dove beneath the touching, thrusting hands, her smile pale, her eyes wandering and searching for something among the stars, as though she were the Virgin who'd lost her Christ. The Virgin was submissive, patient, solitary, searching the heavens for some escape. Who knows? Perhaps she was looking for me as I crouched on the roof, watching with suffering and longing, as everyone repeated, "Kyrie Eleison, Kyrie Eleison."

—*Translated by Roger Allen and Christopher Tingley*

A VERY EGYPTIAN STORY

There are odd moments when two strangers meet and both start cursing their fortune in their own way, frankly or obliquely, according to their particular natures.

There was this taxi driver, plump and round and good-natured, the father of three boys who were all at university. He was expert at telling stories and jokes, and here's what he had to say:

I was driving along near the Sheraton, when suddenly, at a crossroads, I saw a legless beggar blocking my way with what was left of his body. I stopped, and, to my astonishment, the fellow thrust himself, with the agility of a monkey or some sort of reptile, round to the door on my right, opened it and swung his body in next to me.

"Drive on, master," he panted.

What was this? "I could give you some money, maybe," I said. "But take you on board? What are you talking about?"

"Master," he said, "I need to go to Shobra al-Khaima, or Shobra al-Mazallat. Take me, please. I'm a proper customer, not just a beggar. Please, hurry!"

I was still hesitating; but, seeing his urgent manner and then the handful of coins he half took from his pocket, I decided to move on. Away I drove, along the Nile Corniche, all the while reflecting on this customer. His clothes were tattered, his body dirty, and, though he was actually still young, he was disheveled in a way that added ten years to his age. My suspicions returned, and I stopped the car.

"What's this all about?" I said. "I'm not going on till you tell me."

"Would you like some Coca Cola?" he asked.

He called the coke seller over, and gave him a full ten piastres for the two bottles. When we'd both drunk, he said, "Look, master, I'm a beggar."

I can see that, I thought.

"And," he went on, "I needed a cab to get away from a policeman."

"You mean," I said, "the vagrancy police were after you?"

"No, a man from the traffic police."

"But what do you have to do with the traffic police? You're a beggar."

"It's a business matter."

What sort of business, I wondered, could he have with the traffic police?

"Yes," he repeated. "It's a business matter."

Then he told me his story.

"After I lost my legs," he said, "in a metro accident, God opened the heavens for me. When people saw me crawling about on the ground, they'd give me money just like that. I started earning fifty, sixty piastres a day. 'This is the grace of God,' I thought. Then, soon, it dawned on me that I had an asset—my lost legs—and one I ought to start capitalizing on. I learned to seek out all the best spots to beg and came to know the habits and moods of people there and of people walking in every quarter of Cairo. Oddly enough, the people who were charitable and gave me something were either the very poor or the very rich—it was the ones in the middle, like you, who seemed to show less pity. I learned too, after a lot of experience, that people who live in Cairo soon get hard-hearted, through seeing so many things. It's the new arrivals whose hearts are still full of mercy, and their pockets full of money.

"And so, finally, I fixed on that corner near the grand hotel, where I got in your car. It's a marvelous place, the perfect spot to take a lot of cash. There are traffic lights and, when the cars stopped at red, I'd quickly pass down the row before the lights went green again and the cars moved on. Even so, the lights didn't, I found, stay red long enough for me to cover all the cars and their drivers. So, one day, I went up to the traffic policeman.

"It only took a few words. He agreed to keep the lights at red till I'd gone right through all the cars. Then I'd nod to him, to show everything was okay, and he'd switch the lights to green."

"You son of a— " I said. Was that why those lights stayed red so long, and others like them too!

"Did you give the traffic policeman anything?" I found myself asking.

"Of course I did. Fifty or sixty piastres a day."

"And how much do you earn in a day yourself?"

"Two or three pounds, or a bit more. Five or six when it's really busy."

"I see. And why are you running away today? What's happened?"

"Today's a feast day. (Many happy returns to you!) I was making a real pile of money. So, I thought, let me get away before the policeman comes along and wants his share."

I thought it over.

"Well," I said, "that's not very clever, is it? The policeman's only going to get you tomorrow instead."

"Oh no," he said, giving me his young, intelligent, very Egyptian smile. "No, there'll be a different policeman tomorrow, and I've got a separate arrangement with him. Today was this policeman's last day there."

We'd reached the destination now.

"Just here, master," the beggar said.

The fare was forty-three piastres, but he gave me fifty—a full seven piastres tip.

"I tell you what," he said. "If you drive up to that traffic light every day, around ten o'clock, and take me on board, I'll give you fifty piastres a time."

—*Translated by Lena Jayyusi and Christopher Tingley*

Walid Ikhlasi (b. 1935)

Syrian novelist, dramatist, short-story writer, columnist, and literary commentator Walid Ikhlasi was educated in Aleppo and took a higher degree as an agricultural engineer at the University of Alexandria. Ikhlasi has led a life as rich in literary productivity as it has been in travel. In 1988 he came to the United States as guest of the Visitors' Program of the State Department. He is one of the founders of the People's Theater in Aleppo and has presided for a period over the Union of Arab Writers at its Aleppo branch. Ikhlasi has distinguished himself both as dramatist and writer of fiction. Many of his plays have been presented both in the theater and on Arab television, and his works have been translated into several languages. His first collection of short stories, *Stories*, was published in 1963. His other collections include *Blood on a Dusty Morning* (1968), *The Mud* (1971), *The Report* (1974), *Black Grass* (1980), and *The Rose Inn* (1983). *The Hoopoo Bird Tales* (1984) confirmed his reputation as one of the Arab world's best writers of the short story. He has published several novels, among which are *Winter of the Dry Sea* (1965), *Sandalwood Flower* (1981), *Ember Gate* (1986), which is one of the most sensitive works of fiction in Arabic, and *Pleasure House* (1991). He has also published at least ten plays, among which his acclaimed play *The Path* (1976) was included in PROTA's *Anthology of Modern Arabic Drama* (1995). Ikhlasi is one of the most distinguished and prolific literary personalities of Syria.

MADMAN

As the bus plowed its way down the long, long road, I sank back in my seat, lost in a dreamy sleep. Then, when I woke, I tried without success to strike up a friendship or even a casual acquaintance with one of the other passengers. Actually, I can't even remember, after what happened to us, just how many passengers there were.

I stole a glance at the book in the lap of the passenger next to me and recalled part of my dream. "Is that an Egyptian edition," I asked him without preamble, "or a Lebanese one?"

"It's a special edition," he answered, so coldly I felt discouraged from further conversation.

"How strange!" I cried joyfully to myself. "I saw Plato's *Republic* in my dream, just a little while ago." I turned back to the man. "A special edition?" I said. "A third edition, do you mean?"

"A university edition."

"It's just like the dream," I reflected, "where I was reading a special illustrated edition of Plato's *Republic*." Then I laughed to myself, because coincidences like that really don't happen.

I asked the man if the edition was illustrated, but he simply glared at me. "Is Plato's *Republic* something you read for fun?" he shouted.

I snatched the book from the man's lap, flipped through the pages, then returned it to him. "You're right," I said. "There isn't a single picture in it."

The man made no comment, so I turned my attention to the driver planted behind his wheel. Some of the passengers were sleeping, and some reading, while others were watching the countryside and the villages flash by. Then I noticed, to my astonishment, that the driver's eyes reflected in his mirror had an odd look and were becoming stranger with every minute that passed. I stopped smoking, and I forgot about my neighbor and Plato's *Republic*. Instead I focused intently on the driver's face where it filled the oblong mirror. He was eyeing the passengers one by one, his eyes glowing with madness and a mocking evil. I nudged my neighbor, who didn't move to start with.

"Look at the driver," I said. "Doesn't he have a peculiar look?"

Indignation showed in his face. "What's odd about him?" he muttered. Then he dozed off again.

I held my breath as the driver's features slowly crumbled into a look of authentic madness and the bus gathered speed. I had the impression of some lunatic leading us on to hell.

"We'll be passing through some dangerous hills soon," said an old man sitting in front of me.

As the driver's gaze met mine, I had the sinking feeling he was mocking me and all the rest of the passengers. I became more frightened with each passing second. There was going to be a disaster, beyond all doubt. I must warn these innocent people!

"Stop the bus!" I yelled. "Stop the bus!"

The bus sped on, while the other passengers turned toward me in astonishment.

"Stop this driver," I screamed again. "He's leading you to your deaths!"

"We've all got to die one day," said a man behind me.

"But this driver's crazy."

"Crazy?" a few of the passengers shouted. Their eyes focused on me. "Crazy?"

"Just look at him," I insisted. "You can see it in his face." I hesitated for a moment, then yelled out, "Save yourselves!"

"My God," shouted a passenger in the rear of the bus, "you're the one who's mad!"

At that moment the bus came to a halt. The driver left his seat and came up to me so calmly I couldn't believe it.

"If you don't like it in here, my friend," he said, "why don't you just get off?"

A number of passengers voiced their agreement. When I didn't move, the driver said, "I'm not taking the bus any further unless this man either gets out or apologizes to me."

"Apologize to him, son," one old man said. "We want to get home."

"Me? Why should I apologize?"

"Why shouldn't you? You call him crazy, then you won't apologize!"

I took another look at the driver's eyes and saw they were brim full of madness and a sly malice. His contempt for me was obvious. The duel was going to begin now, as though we'd already agreed on the rules. "We want to get moving," one passenger yelled.

"If you want me to go on," the driver said, "this man has to leave the bus."

"The man's crazy," I screamed. "He'll lead us all into a ravine. There are some dangerous bends ahead of us!"

The driver addressed me with a calm fit to rouse Job himself to fury.

"Who's crazy?" he asked. "Me or you?"

Protesting voices rose from front and back alike, demanding that I get off. I felt humiliated.

"All right," I said. "I'll get off. Do any of the rest of you want to save yourselves?"

No one answered. As I left the bus, I heard sighs of relief behind me.

The sun had just set, and the land around me stretched out toward a horizon that was terrifying and tinged with red. The bus pulled away quickly, and I continued to watch it with deep anxiety. A few seconds later I saw with my own eyes how it swerved off the road and hurtled down into a valley. Then, a few seconds later, came a mighty, shattering explosion and flames rising higher and higher. The burning colors fused with the grayness, pervading the whole landscape.

—Translated by Admer Gouryeh and Christopher Tingley

THE MERRY NIGHT OF THE DOG

[1]

Intoxicated with anticipation, I saw the vast horizon emerging from the darkness before me. A sense of timelessness prevailed as my longing tumbled across the city toward that suburb where I would meet my dear friends.

My life had entered a new phase. Here I was, carrying my philosophy degree from the University of Damascus, traveling the road to Aleppo, my city, which I had first loved, then hated. Now my love was rekindled for the suburb where our worries had been born and our rancors nurtured; there lived the young woman whose breath I could imagine embracing the cool of those first summer days.

There lay the familiar dirt road on which people had fled the days of vengeance. The asphalted road joined the suburb's Nairab Gate to Aleppo during other days of peace. I had opted for "peace" now, carrying my dreams with me, imagining my first night home with my young companions downing bottles and bottles of our national wine until morning, and singing in unison, leaving no margin for hatred. We were going to meet outside our neighborhood's limits. I represented the Dari[1] family and the three friends waiting for me were from the Wawi[2] family. Fire facing fire. But this night would be all coolness and peace, wine and sheer intoxication of joy; mists would rise above the large quarter that had been drowned in a pool of spite for more than fifty years. Dagger versus dagger, gun versus gun. But tonight! Love was going to balance us—four people would meet secretly to mock a stupid conflict that had plucked away the flowers of two families for too many vengeful years.

The Nairab Gate loomed in front of me. My heart longed for my beloved, whom I would not be able to see yet but whose image remained before me like a luminous twilight stronger than darkness or day. I had decided to bypass my own family also and go straight to the room on the outskirts of the quarter lit by electricity pumped to the orchard. Oh, that abandoned orchard had been a haven for nights of revelry after the well's waters dried up and the planting of cotton exhausted all the subterranean waters! I was full of news and books and longing to share.

The car devoured the road like that longing devouring me. A crescent-shaped cemetery surrounded the area, so death and life seemed to mingle. My senses felt sharp enough to imagine the fragrance of my beloved, as well as the dark odor of family blood that had flowed profusely into this ground. Finally the air coming over me through the open window was too strong and I had to close it. Memories penetrated even the glass. In the past our family had planted vegetables, living like a tame herd on the banks of a shallow river that flowed down from a majestic grassy hill. The waters dispersed into a large plain outside the city. At that time love was still legitimate, shining joyously whenever a male child was born. The mud roofs would be lit with wooden torches, and ululations would resound that frightened the wolves gathering at the outskirts of the village. Later our quarter enlarged, with the First World War, becoming a little town, an adopted child of Greater Aleppo. In those days people loved, got mar-

---

1. Ferocious. As the author points out, the name did not suit their family's original profession as farmers or their later interest in learning.
2. Jackal, a symbol of sly smartness and even tameness.

ried, and experienced happiness. Hatred was unthinkable. They only heard of vengeance in the recounted tales.

Despite all the changes, I loved her. I had decided to transcend the boundaries between us like a proud stallion that pays no attention to trivial reins. Her family had long engaged in smuggling and lived on the far edge of the neighborhood. They shot bullets toward the sky with every personal victory. Their family name derived from the intelligence of their long-ago ancestors called al-Wawi. Our family had acquired the name "Dari" despite their profession as farmers, then later as men of knowledge—two professions that had nothing at all to do with fierceness.

Her first name was Laila; anyone called Laila deserves to live a thousand years. I used to wish I had been named Qais,[3] but heritage had branded me with my grandfather's name, reminding me forever that vengeance can be passed on. Laila and I, Wawi and Dari, sharpened teeth and innocence, blocked walls and hope.

Laila was childhood to me. I had emerged from the world of innocence and abstract notions of vengeance to the study of philosophy. I discovered a very complicated world leading only toward the world of simplicity again after a simple childhood that had often pushed me to a world of complications.

I told my old friend, the ancient cab driver, "Hurry! Hurry!"

A laugh emerged from his silent face. "Don't be afraid, things haven't changed since your last visit. The sun still rises every day."

I felt more pessimistic, suddenly. "And the night comes every day too." He continued, "None of the two families has been killed in your absence."

The last slain man from the Dari family had been my cousin, last summer, and the last slain man from the Wawi family was killed a few days later. Then the mad storm had thankfully subsided.

Despite the car's speed, I felt we were approaching too slowly. Problems of "vengeance" did not matter to me anymore in any way. I made a final decision that this meeting tonight with my friends from the Wawi family would release us from the mad orbit of time; we would celebrate the beginning of a new life, which I had dreamt of all the way from Damascus to Aleppo.

[2]

The heart of the Bab al-Nairab quarter throbbed with a dignified calm. My contemplation was tinged with slight apprehension, but a larger sense of confidence and calm seemed imminent. The main street of the old neighborhood triggered a crowd of memories; this old place had been a seething cauldron once, but now the fires would finally subside. My longing to see my own family

---

3. The Majnun (madman) of Laila. One of the greatest lovers in Arabia's history, he was demented for love of his cousin, Laila. It is customary in modern times to nickname an ardent lover "Qais" or "Majnun Laila."

tried to tempt me away from my decision, but I resisted it, traveling on toward the end of the quarter near the cemetery where the orchard, friends, and renewed innocence awaited me.

The driver begged me not to tell anyone that he had driven me to the orchard. My family would be angry if they knew he had taken me anywhere but home. I promised him, then asked him to say a prayer for us. He asked what he should pray for. I said, "Pray that love remains a child, happily playing, whom no one would molest."

He smiled and drove off.

Embraces, wild salutations, merriment! Suitcases were flung open, wine bottles emerged, embraces gave birth to warm, sweet tears. We spent the night like an unbroken circle—Ahmad, the agricultural engineer, Muhammad, excellent in math, and Kamal, about to complete his degree in civil engineering. Those three were on one side, but I completed the circle. Rancor, which had remained kindled in our families' hearts, subsided. I thought of our mood as a clear glass of affection that no darkness could blemish.

We had decided upon this meeting before finals began, committing to the hour and date. None of our families knew we were together, since we all knew we would be chided for breaching the law of the tribe. In that square room built of mud we met, but the narrow space was enough to welcome us. We filled it with jollity and smoke.

"Let's drink to the salt that we sprinkle on all old wounds!"

"Long live knowledge, which has infinitely broadened the horizons of our minds!"

"I wish I could kill all ill will in the world—but I hate even the word 'kill'!"

"Come on, let's bury the dead!"

We shouted for the past and the future. Outside the darkness was cool. We could see the dilapidated wall of the cemetery. We drank and drank till all the old feuds became amusing myths. Then Muhammad exclaimed suddenly, "I agree to your marriage to my sister, Laila, the cousin of these other friends of yours who love you!"

I was overcome with happiness. "May all the lovers in the world be doomed if I do not worship your sister and cousin, the flower of the neighborhood!"

Glasses flew in the air for joy. We had to bring out the earthenware bowls to drink from, and our ceremony became more primitive. Love, oh primitive, primordial love.

After we had played in the land stretching between the orchard and the cemetery, watching the funerals of family and strangers with astonishment. We had grown up and used to meet behind the gravestones or in the shade of the castle overlooking the quarter. We had played closely, cheek to cheek. Now we vowed eternal love, which we had learned about in books. We discussed children's names, Salaam for Peace, Mahabbah for Love, Wi'am for Harmony . . . but who was that brave one among us who would be first to mention love, harmony, and peace among the rest of our families who had been so penetrated by hatred?

My marriage would be the first announced between the enemies. Now the bullets of joy could erase the echoes of treacherous shots that had punctuated our histories. "Let's drink for unity!" "Let's toast the last person who was killed!" We toasted wildly past midnight. I stared at Muhammad, who was a male replica of Laila, then leaned toward him to kiss his forehead, and he let me. I had never dared to touch Laila yet, though I longed for her—despite the obscenities I had learned during my wild youth, with her I was always shy. Once I swore to her that I would kill anyone who stood in my way to her, and she was angry with me a whole week. "Haven't we had enough of killing?"

Once she told me, "Look, all of Aleppo's old and new quarters have developed and improved and known peace and calm, except ours. We still mix killing with our crushed wheat."

We had pledged to one another that we would not leave our neighborhood after our marriage. So many other young couples fled their little homesteads the minute they found a scrap of success—we would be different.

Suddenly Kamal spoke, his tongue slurred with drinking, "Do you know that we four are absolutely unique in this wide city of Aleppo?"

He tried to stand in the middle of our circle but he swayed. "We do not know hatred. Do you know why? Because we have known love. Not only that, but we have also thought with one language. I'm an engineer, but I've stumbled onto the right language as you have. And what is it? It's enlightenment, culture. Let's drink a toast to enlightenment, to the new culture, to philosophy . . . to all of you, my dears!"

He stumbled toward the earth, but our loving arms caught him. The radio played the music it always plays after the newscast. We had heard nothing of the news. I shouted as loudly as if I were out in the wilds, "Men are fighting everywhere, but we've found the road to peace!"

Her shadow was burning my face.

[3]

A stray dog became our circle's fifth member. Anxiety had begun circling in my head like a crowd of bats; I was imagining my father's attitude toward the declaration of my love. He had lost his own brother in the fifty-year feud. I could see my mother's face shouting at me, "The Wawis have killed my nephew!"

Pessimism was sticking out its tongue. I faced it with a new glass of wine, trying to wipe away the past's image, but the bats were still flying. A mad desire burned in me to go out into the open, knock on Laila's door, and tell her family that I loved her, then be killed, my corpse torn and strewn to every corner of the city.

The hungry dog began to smell my feet. I threw him a chicken's leg. Ahmad held his head amidst our wild toasts to one another's families, "Let's make this dog drink from the wine of our love!"

We applauded the idea like madmen, dancing. The gray dog had slipped through the opening in the door, staring back at us meekly. The news mumbled the smell of a civil war somewhere, while Muhammad and Kamal pried open the dog's mouth. I poured wine into the black pit. It was as if the dog understood our innocent merriment and did not resist. He seemed now grateful to us for the food and drink with which we had filled his stomach. He fell to the ground like a child, asleep.

I would unsheathe my philosophic sword before thousands of men from the Nairab Gate. I would wave it in their faces, but not one drop of blood would be shed. Even if men from the two families shouted in my face, I would respond with silence, striking in all directions. What if not a single thing moved or changed? The stones would still be there and the rifles hidden under the trees. Maybe philosophy would be lost in the labyrinths of the big quarter, like doomsday.

Someone shouted, "Do you think this dog is dead?" We stared till we could see it breathing, slowly, slowly. I felt joyful. "This dog will not die!" Ahmad said, "Why should he, when he has drunk the wine of love?" He said we needed to honor him further. Suddenly the dog was an issue.

I kept wondering, "Does Laila dream about me as I dream about her?" Aloud I said, "Sing to the dog like a mother would do." But no one responded.

I wanted a wedding celebration in which dignitaries and a wide array of guests would celebrate. I wanted the *fatiha* to be read on the graces of marriages and the burials of hatred. I wanted to see Laila dancing for peace between the two families, her hand in mine, swaying to tamborines and flute, then all of our families joining the circle.

Morning was coming and we had decided to go outside. We wrapped the drunk dog in the rug and carried him on our shoulders. We chanted slowly as mourners, "Read the *fatiha*—brother vengeance has passed away."

Our laughs burst forth, our echoes ascended into the skies. We lit up the dawn's silence, which was now crawling out from behind tombstones and houses where people still turned in a deep sleep.

As we danced, the dog's pliable body nearly flew from our hands and we struggled to keep it balanced. "Read the *fatiha*—brother vengeance has passed away!"

Then a light appeared in one of the houses and something strange happened, which our wine-soaked visions could not comprehend. Bullets poured on us like rain, from all directions, sparks mixing with the dawn's early threads of light.

[4]

Later, I could not distinguish the faces encircling my bed. Everything around me seemed like jelly. After a while I realized I was lying in a hospital and my right leg could not move. A stray bullet had entered its bones. Faces, faces, but they all eluded me. Relatives, friends, a few with slings on their arms or white gauze bandages around their heads. I did not want to ask about anything. In my drifting hallucination I remembered only a dog carried on our shoulders and a night of merriment that pledged to bury a moldy old vengeance.

After a few days the faces returned to congratulate me for having escaped death. I asked what had happened but got no answer. I asked about my leg and the heads bowed down. I asked what had happened to the dog and learned that it was alive and thriving. This made me happy until I learned that my leg bones were completely shattered, a terrible revelation, until I learned the even worse news that followed it.

Our merry band had been paving its way between the homesteads of sleeping people when a man from the Wawis and another from the Daris each awoke. Each of them saw a man from his own family shouting the traditional funeral lament, with death being carried on the shoulders. Blood had boiled in each head, thinking a member of his own family had been slain. Both had raised their weapons immediately and sent fires screaming in the skies. One bullet, another, till a river of death poured over the heads. The whole quarter awoke to the massacre, and axes and knives were brought out. Blood poured forth, a few walls were demolished, women were screaming, and the oldest women prodded their men on to vengeance. The sun emerged, only to be swallowed by clouds again. The man who told me all this stated, "Twenty dead, a hundred wounded."

Our hours of merriment had ended with twenty slain and a hundred wounded. I closed my eyes in shame. We had come together to heal the wound and now . . . I was told Muhammad had miraculously escaped but Ahmad had been killed immediately. Kamal had been hit in his arm and side and would live, just like me. I felt permeated by the sorrow around me. My mother had been hit in the brow but was covering her wound with a black band. I asked an old relative, "Until when . . . until when, you people?"

"Until the sorrow is over and the reckoning complete."

But who would do my reckoning? I was thinking of Laila. Would she be able to stand me, leaning on my cane? I asked my relative, "Can't the government interfere and help put an end to these massacres?"

A shadow of contentment hovered over his wrinkles. "I think they'll demolish this quarter with the pretext of beautifying it."

I was glad to hear that but could not express it. I pretended to be thinking deeply. A few days later my chest felt like it was exploding with its secret and I asked my relative, "Would you carry a message from me to Laila al-Wawi?"

He was completely silent. After a few moments he spoke, averting his eyes, "And what have you to do with the daughter of the enemies, son?"

"I love her! I love her, don't you understand?"

"Well anyway, she's one of the victims of that dawn."

The sedative had subsided, and my leg throbbed with waves of pain. Now my whole body froze. I was roving in a desert where Laila's famous Qais was howling, asking after his beloved. My thoughts were strangely calm. "Should I do as Qais did? But his Laila was alive . . ."

All I could do after I left the hospital was go back to the cemetery that had witnessed our childhood and our love. I circled a half-built grave, then sat thinking about the futility of our lives and philosophies, and the ludicrous dreams my friends and I had had about changing the mood of the quarter.

Maybe there was no silence after all. The machinery was briskly in motion, moment by moment, stones falling at its feet and roofs tumbling. The old castle seemed terribly remote, as if it would never change, despite all the other frightening changes taking place.

—Translated by May Jayyusi and Naomi Shihab Nye

Isma'il Fahd Isma'il (b. 1940)

Kuwaiti novelist and short-story writer Isma'il Fahd Isma'il is one of the best-known authors outside the Peninsula. As well as specializing in commerce, psychology, and public administration, he earned a B.A. in literature and drama criticism and has been deeply involved in dramatic and cinematographic activity in his country. He is a prolific writer who has written many collections of short stories and novels, as well as a number of books of criticism and literary history. Among Isma'il's collections of short stories are *The Dark Spot* (1965) and *Cages and the Common Language* (1974); and among his novels are his lovely novella, *Lightspots of Stagnation* (1971); *The Drum* (1972) and *The Other River Banks* (1973); his novel in two volumes, *The Nile Flows Northward* (1981, 1982); and his more recent novels, *It Is Happening Yesterday* (1997), *Far Away to This Place* (1998), and *A Distant Sky* (2000). He has also written a critical account on the Kuwaiti short story, *The Arabic Story in Kuwait* (1980).

THE STRANGE WORLD OF A TOY STORE

The shopping center is jammed with customers. I am overwhelmed: how to deal with all the customers and their questions at once. "What is the price of this toy?" "How much for the train?"

The first day I worked here, the manager told me, "A toy salesman needs two qualities: patience and a keen sense of observation." He added, "Keep your eyes wide open because those little devils quickly grab up anything they can lay their hands on."

Yesterday while I was busy with the father of two kids, I noticed a dark child outside, about six years old and by himself. He seemed very preoccupied with the show window.

I felt I knew his kind. I was watching him constantly while he stared at the toys. I said to myself, "Be careful!"

When the customer left, he entered. His eyes were fixed on my face.

"This car . . . how much?"

I smiled when I saw his little finger pointing at a big car that runs on batteries. I said, "A dinar and a half—would you like to buy it?"

He looked surprised, then mumbled, "It is too much!"

I could not help smiling. "What is your name?"

I could not help stroking his hair. "Where is your father?"

"At work."

"Ask him to buy it for you!"

He looked at me, uneasy. "He won't buy it."

"Why not?"

I wished I could do something. He hesitated a moment before leaving. I felt at ease again, thinking, "The crisis has passed peacefully."

Suddenly he was back. He stood near my feet, looking up at me, and I thought, "Now I must be careful."

"May I see it?"

His voice had a lovable, conciliatory tone. I thought, "Why don't I just make him happy?"

"Alright, but be quick." I brought it to him. He took it carefully and examined it affectionately. "It is pretty!" He put his arms around it.

I remembered the words "Those children grab very easily anything they can lay their hands on."

He spun a full turn around. What was he thinking of? But he did not hold it any longer, he handed it back to me.

"How does it work?"

I thought, "He is a nice boy . . . why don't I give him some happiness?"

"I will show you, but quickly." I sat beside him. "Look, it is moving!" The car took off cruising about the aisles of the shop. I watched him; he was smiling and his face radiated happiness.

"It is *beautiful!*"

A customer entered and I lifted the car from the floor. "That's enough." As the child turned to leave, I thought, "The second crisis is over peacefully," and I turned my attention to the customer. "Yes, sir?"

"May I see that car?"

Another customer entered the shop and another; for a few minutes the shop was very crowded. When finally I had a few moments to myself, the car had disappeared.

I thought, "It was not sold!"

Today, although I was busy, I saw yesterday's child. He was standing behind the glass with a look of amazement on his face.

I thought, "How dare he come back?" and was about to shout my surprise when I noticed my stolen car with him. He was clutching it to his chest.

I was torn between a persistent customer with three busy children, tirelessly touching all the toys, and the boy outside the shop. I was almost rude to the customer to get rid of her. Thinking, "I must get it back!" I raced out so fast that I almost bumped into the boy, who was coming in. He pushed past and preceded me into the shop, and I followed, demanding, "Give it to me!"

He smiled innocently.

"How did you steal it?" And I snatched it away from him. He said nothing. He was looking amazedly toward a large train.

I had to make sure the car still worked, so I clicked it on and it cruised about the shop. He spoke confidently. "I didn't hurt it at all."

He puzzled me. He was speaking like a grown man! I asked him, "Why did you steal it?" and he said, "I didn't steal it—I just took it to play with."

What made me maddest was how he didn't look at me when he talked to me. "So why did you bring it back?"

"I'd had enough of it."

"The devil!" I thought to myself. Those little hands that grab . . . He was still staring at the train. "So what else do you want?"

My question sounded menacing, even to me. I almost added, "Do you want me to call the police?" but it was then he answered simply, "I want this train!"

I grabbed his little arm and pulled him toward the door, muttering, "Enough, you little thief."

He whined, "Stop, you are hurting me!" and I relaxed my grip. His feet were holding firm. "Why don't you go?"

"I want the train."

"You must be crazy!"

"But I returned the car."

"I don't believe it . . . the train for the car. Get out or I'll hand you over to the policeman."

Desperate sadness covered his face. I added, "The good boy does not steal." A customer passed us, entering the shop. I watched the child leaving, dragging his feet, until he disappeared behind the main gate of the shopping center. I thought, "The crisis is over."

Another customer entered, and a third, and fourth, till the shop was crowded. A quarter of an hour later when I had a moment to breathe again, I noticed what had happened. But how was this possible? When did the train disappear?

—*Translated by Aida A. Bamia and Naomi Shibab Nye*

Abdu Jubair (b. 1948)

Egyptian novelist and short-story writer Abdu Jubair was born in Esna in the south of Egypt and read religious studies and Arabic at Al-Azhar Mosque University in Cairo, then studied English and spontaneous translation for two years at Al-Azhar's College of Languages. He now works in Cairo as editor of *Al-Musawwar* and *Al-Hilal* magazines. One of Egypt's most promising avant-garde writers of fiction, he has published four works of fiction to date, some of which, such as his novel *Moving the Heart* (1982), ran into several editions in various Arab countries. His latest work is his collection *Farewell: A Crown of Grass* (1986).

FAREWELL: A CROWN OF GRASS

I was leaving in the morning, about ten o'clock. Perhaps the train would be late, as usual. I felt like leaving even earlier but that was the earliest train.

Voices filtered toward me, cocks crowing, donkeys and sheep. From all directions they penetrated the night. Gradually, the light strengthened inside the window frame, then footsteps approached me.

"Get up, son, take your breakfast."

I didn't know what to say. It might have been five or six a.m. already, but it was imperative to move from beneath the covers; what could I say on a morning like this? A headache was exploding inside my head. All night my dreams had been disturbing, a series of miniature nightmares between the blanks. Now . . . the *hilba*[1] with milk and tea. My mouth tasted terrible. Where were my slippers? I could hear my sister's voice. Would I enjoy the journey? I wanted now to sit next to the window and let my spirit wander the empty land, the fields, those small creatures crawling on the thin belt of green, or the birds landing on the horizon.

Last night my father had asked, "Have you prepared everything for your trip? Are you ready? Why haven't you said farewell to everyone before now? You shouldn't always forget this."

I had been postponing it purposely for three days. Now I was stuck. I would begin with my aunt, then my grandmother, then the house of my uncles, then our neighbors. All would be present to celebrate my departure, and undoubtedly at least one would cry. That would be Salwa. Didn't she realize that all of this was nothing but futile play? She took things with a murderous seriousness.

"Haven't you had your breakfast yet? It's getting cold! Can't you move?"

I got up and turned on the old wooden radio to the chanting of the Quran, in a sweet clear voice. Where were my slippers?

I was tired of looking for them. I felt weighted, even dizzy. Then I found them, as usual.

I opened the window. Cool breezes entered and felt uplifting. But I quickly became cold and moved away. If the light should fall in a certain soft pattern on my high brass bed and its faded coverlets, this place would feel like a dream. But it kept reminding me more of a room filled with shrouds.

---

1. Special seeds known to be good for one's health. They are ground and eaten either with milk or in puddings and cakes.

In the bathroom I dipped my fingers into the bowl and splashed my face with cold water. I returned to bed, covering myself partially with the faded eiderdown, and sipping my *hilba* with milk. I followed it with tea and a cigarette.

Time was crawling around me and the noises increased.

"Boy, are you going to get some *ful*."[2]

"No, I'm going to get milk from Um Muhammad."

"Then I'll get the *ful*. Husni, Husni!"

Two people conversing. Beyond my window life was going on. Their sounds disappeared. My cigarette tasted like salt. Now birds chirping loudly, like they chirped once when my father claimed he was about to go mad from the noise. What could I do on this very difficult morning? Would I go out? Shouldn't I go out?

My father passed by and laid down his orders. "You must go see your grandmother immediately." He gave me money and told me to pass by the shop, and I heard the hoarse tiredness of his voice and felt his deep eyes penetrating me with their arrows.

I began to dress, but my trousers felt shrunken and my socks had holes. My head was throbbing.

Three magazines, I needed to remember. I could read them one after the other on the train; at any rate, I was utterly indecisive at the moment. Maybe on the train I would just want to listen to the monotonous thrum of the engines or gaze into the faces of the other passengers. Would that foolish girl meet me?

"Good morning, Fulla!"

"Are you leaving today?"

"Yes."

"Okay."

"Okay what, Fulla?"

Her face seemed tired, a pool of sorrowful waves. My little beast of a sister was the only person from this whole group I might ever want to talk to in the future. I felt optimistic. Did I know what was happening? Hammer blows large as mountains resounded in the emptiness. I wished I could disappear and tell myself happy restful things in an infinite empty space.

"You'll plunge into life, Abu Zayd, take great care!"

This was good Uncle Sulaiman. He did not speak much. He protected his secrets. I suspected he would die in my absence. I could read it in his eyes. The idea occurred to me, and I executed it at once.

"Let me go," I said, "and walk around the marketplace."

The sun was rolling down from the east. At the end of the street, children were carrying some bowls. And I was slipping away down the alley under windows that had not yet opened. I wanted to go on and keep going on.

---

2. Fava beans seasoned with lemons, garlic, and oil, a staple food in Egypt and throughout the Arab world

"A pretty new teacher came to our class."

"She's stupid! I know geography better than she does!"

"Look out, boy, I'll tell her what you said. You are dirty and impolite."

Bold voices echoing behind me. Now that I was leaving everything and everything was leaving me, how could I voice any idea?

The shops were still closed. "Manyous Batriyous, the Grocer of Faith." "'Abd al-Wahhab, the Grocer of Sincerity," etc. I had memorized those signs from reading them so much. I had grown tired even of myself. I was running, should I slow down?

The bazaar was still closed, covered and dark. The wind that blew in its heart told the tale of selling and buying, as rags dangled from the long roof and wooden doors of the shops. As it is said, it is a tiring tale, which makes some happy and others sad. Just as it happens in life all the time. Then I reached the street by the sea. The karozina[3] trees spoke of the coming buds. How, and why?

This town that I will leave in a few hours makes you tell a strange tale. "Tell me please, how long since the train passed?" I had heard this question so many times, standing on the wooden floor of the station with Kamal, Mamdouh, Salah, and the others. We used to go out every evening, walk along the corniche, cross the bridge, and smoke. Then we would walk through the trees of the village to the station. None of us were going anywhere, but we used to look at the tourist girls arriving and departing on the trains. And we used to dream. That time, which has passed, was the time of dreams.

Now I was going to knock on my grandmother's door.

"Good morning, Nabawiyya. Is my grandmother here?"

She was sitting on her wooden sofa in the long hall. She sat upon her thick furry blanket with the water pipe's mouthpiece in her hand. She did not feel my presence until I touched her shoulder. Then she raised her eyes to me in surprise.

"Who? Abu Zayd?"

"Yes, grandmother. I'm leaving today."

"What?"

"I am going away."

"Oh! I used to tell your father to go away and work for a while, then return, but he never did. You're a good boy."

I sat with her a few minutes as I contemplated the things around us; the drum hanging on the wall, the rosaries, and the keys. The doves jumping about in the scaffolding and the brown dog, then Nawiyya, who crouched near the fire turning the coals and preparing the water pipe. The silence filled the rooms of the house with a hushed voice like soft wind.

Then I broke free and leapt from the room, taking the stairs in jumps, like I did when I used to jump and hop for joy.

---

3. Tall shady trees that bear no fruit and grow on river banks in Cairo and the Delta region.

I grasped my aunt's door handle and knocked on the door with the same lyrical beat I had learned from her teacher-son. She appeared, repeating her usual song, which sounded more like moaning. Now she added a new verse. "You'll depart and leave us. You'll depart."

I said only, "Oh!" But I felt that something was moving, she was not like my grandmother sitting on that fur. No. There was something else I couldn't explain. She kissed me until my whole face was wet and I was permeated with her smell. Now I would go to the house of my uncles.

Beyond the heaps of dried dust, the narrow streets, under the palm trees near the old stream, a lone boy was singing in a wounded voice behind a cow. Every moment or two someone would bring another cow or donkey and let it drink, then leave in silence. And there on the outskirts of everything, the house of my uncles stood.

How many times had I sat on the branch of the tree sleeping next to the door? I held a stone and knocked hard. My uncles would be beyond the long corridor that ended in the courtyard of the women and that took such a long time to cross. Maybe they would be walking the cattle or turning over the produce in the courtyards under the tall palm.

I had tried many times to climb that palm, but my dream remained distant, hovering at its cloudlike top.

"Hello!" My greeting was answered by the broken, weak voice of my Uncle Kamal's wife. She gathered her scarf around her and led me down the corridor, reciting the following tale: "Drums beat for fathers and mothers, holy verses are chanted and houses are built. Then, blood flows over the bed and the girls burst into song. Then come the monotonous beats from morning to evening, night followed by day, and the bellies grow big and labor pain comes. Then the scream that pierces like fire! The blood, the pain, the night lullabies, the rocking of cribs and staying up all those hours ... the clothesline! The baths! Then we depart? There—your uncle is in the courtyard."

The wife of another uncle, 'Abd al-Fattah, met me on the way. She stretched her rough hand out to me and spoke in a voice that was more like repressed howling.

I opened the door. My Uncle Kamal sat in his dirty white trousers sieving hay. He lifted the hay from a heap on his right, then sieved it into a heap on his left.. My uncle 'Ibadi's wife was at the end of the courtyard under the umbrella with the scanty shade, standing next to an ox. Uncle Kamal said, "Welcome." Uncle Muhammad was hauling a large grain sack onto Uncle 'Ibadi's back.

I sat near Uncle Kamal, who said, "Walk the way the sea flows. Winds blow from the north toward the south. Always beware of the hay's chaff when it flies about. It would be a mistake to sit against the winds." I don't know why I wished that the wind would blow the grass and cover my whole head, so I might embark on my trip with a crown of grass. I greeted Uncle Muhammad, and he pressed my hand and smiled,. I felt him warning me against the advice of his brother.

"You're going, and . . . " He worked the wooden machine of his mouth, uttering old words that tasted like red clay. I could contemplate the ropes hanging above, or the feet of the cattle, the nests of the doves or the helpless little sparrows. Uncle Imadi removed grasses from his head as he shook his cap. His chest was as formidable as a shield and always stirred awe in the boys.

"This is a dangerous young man," he said, shaking my hand with a powerful, large hand. I felt pierced by my surroundings, as if I could almost burst. \

Uncle Kamal's wife appeared, muttering, with a brass pot and four glasses on a shining brass tray. I took one of the glasses, sipping my tea, greeting the men one by one, hardly able to focus my eyes. On the way home I pressed the hands of my little cousins, giving each a piastre. I climbed the heights to my own home to find the neighbors gathered and my mother with a shine shimmering on her face.

My knees felt shaky. I was surrounded by women in dust-covered black. All faces were moving, and many hands. Should I stop? Should I stop?

My older cousins had gathered; one held a cigarette. I took it from him, drew a long puff, then returned it.

The horse carriage had arrived outside. My cousins carried my suitcase and trunk. I sat on the comfortable leather seat, and they sat on the two sides. The coachman crackled his whip. We rode to the marketplace and stopped.

My father was sitting on his bench in front of his shop next to Uncle Saleem. Our hug felt artificial. I greeted Uncle Butrus the barber and those loitering around his shop, then my father, then climbed back to the carriage where so many armpits emitted the odor of sweat.

We rode. The corniche, water shining under the sun. Trees sleeping on the shore. The long friendly thoroughfare, the monotonous bat of hooves. The smell of air laden with musk. I lit a cigarette like the young men around me. Then we traveled a while among the orange groves. The scattered yellow, the long green stretches, the sun, and sleepiness.

I woke to find myself on the sidewalk at the station.

The train came—the train took me away.

I placed my things on the upper shelf and sat next to the window. Then the train slipped away. The hands at the window, the planks of the station disappeared . . . and the fields began.

Faces crowded the carriage, but I could breathe. I took out a cigarette and lit it, puffing out the smoke, staring into the face of the young stranger with close shaven hair. He was a soldier in civilian clothes, heading toward the war. The fields stretched far, retreating behind the mountains, and the birds were like drops of water falling horizontally, a scenery broken only by poles and wires. Sheep stood on the bridge, with a man behind them riding a donkey. I could see the grass crown on my uncle's head, the ropes on the walls, the dust, and the bends in the road. The faces of women wrapping their black *gilbabs*, and my sister's small face. The chants, the rasp of a microphone, and the long beat of tambourines, the benches covered with cushions, tables of food, the silence of the plantations, sheep and goats under palm trees, cattle sleeping in the court-yard, the sieve, and the brass bed. I could remember the *hilba* with milk, the little children, the young schoolteacher, the moon, the bride on her platform, the henna, the ululations, the dancing women, the sizzle of bullets, the shouts of men, the hands women held together, the packed trunks. The groom would stretch his hand and raise the veil, and she would turn her face far away from him. He'd undress himself, then her, placing a moneybag in her hand to make her laugh. He'd stretch his hand out, undoing her long braids. She'd lean toward him, and he'd lean toward her, kissing her passionately. She'd close her eyes and fall into something like a trance. He'd then raise his body, the embrace, and the blood. He would also see the henna, the *nuqut* [4] and the *shi'riyya* [5] trays, the mornings, the going and coming, the work. The cattle, the sheep, the pregnancy, the pain, the days and months, then the labor screams, the baby, the work, the fields, telephone poles, plantations, knocks, and yourself, yourself, yourself, your-self, yourself, and the face of the soldier, the telephone poles, the fields, the sheep, the carriage, the station, the neighbors, Salwa rushing toward me and clinging, my mother freezing up and my sister shouting, "What's happening?" The fright-ened women retreat a little, but she clings to me until she disappears.

"Are you a soldier?"

"Yes, I'm a soldier from the Order of the Knights. I've fought twice."

As for me, I'm going off to work for the first time and had never thought of this matter before. But you are a soldier from the Order of the Knights who has fought twice on this horse. How can this be? Certainly your feelings com-ing out of the war must be different. How were your feelings when you were in the war?

He looked at me and must have glimpsed my imaginary conversation. I re-treated to my corner once more and stared out of the window.

My sister Fulla came and sat near me. She looked thinner than ever—and was speaking intermittently. I wanted her to talk so I talked too. We talked together until the train stopped.

—*Translated by Salwa Jabsheh and Naomi Shihab Nye*

Nasir Jubran (1953)

Poet and short-story writer Nasir Jubran was born in 'Ajman, now one of the seven states of the United Arab Emirates. He studied communication and worked for the 'Ajman municipality then in the postal service, taking an early retirement. He was one of the founders of the Union of Emirate Writers and a member of its Administrative Committee, becoming at one

---

4. Gifts of money to the bride and groom.
5. A pastry made with vermicelli or rice, milk, and sugar.

point the Director of the Union. He is a chess enthusiast and a social volunteer and was for some time a member of the committee for the 'Uweiss Prize for Culture. He has published two books of poetry, *What If They Had Let the Horses Go?* (1986) and *The Impossibilities of Calmness* (1993), and two collections of short stories, *Miyadeer* (1993) and *Fountain of Shrapnel* (1993).

THIS HARDSHIP WILL PASS

We came home from a long swim in the water of the bay, our loud talk and peals of laughter, as youthful as our wet bodies, resounding to the furthest house in the quarter. Then we parted, and each of us was swallowed up in the small neighborhoods, with their narrow alleys and winding paths. Hamdoun was walking in front of me carrying a thick wooden board. I felt the tiredness seeping into my left arm and put down the tin canister before moving it to my right hand. By the time I was upright again, Hamdoun had reached the corner and waved goodbye.

I walked on to the end of the alley, then bore left and, after a few meters, stopped for a little under a palm tree that is still one of the main features of our home, looking at the sands that the wind had swept into two little hills by the sides of the door. There was dung on them from the sheep and the traces of 'Abboud al-Marwi's donkey. I walked a few steps toward the door, opened it, and went in. There were sea birds swirling around me. Then I put down the canister and took off the cloth sealing its mouth.

I heard my mother's stifled voice from the tent.

"Who's there? Is that you, Yam'an? What took you so long?"

"Here," I said. "Give me the knife."

As she came toward me with the knife, I pointed to the canister.

"Look at this."

"What's in it?"

"I've no idea. But I'll open it. It'll make something for the birds to drink from."

"Do it after lunch."

"No, it's all right. I'll open it while you're preparing the table."

I put down the knife and went to the well with my undershirt in my hand. I put it down at my feet, stood on a square board and washed in cold water, then wrung out my loincloth, put on a fresh one, and went back.

I opened the canister, bending the knife completely, then raised the lid and flung it away, looking inside. What was it in there? It seemed to be a sticky powder of some sort, rather like hardened molasses, though the color was quite different. Could it be some kind of alcohol? God forbid! I raised the canister and threw the contents on the ground outside. Some of it fell on the courtyard in small patches. Then I filled the canister with water and put it right away in a corner where the birds could come and drink from it.

After eating, we spread our little mat in the shade of the wall of our neighbor, the sea captain Muhammad. It was a plastered stone wall with a lotus tree that threw its shade and caught the refreshing breezes, overhanging our own simple home.

We slept for an hour through the heavy heat of the afternoon, only to be woken by shouts and screams and the frightened birds beating their wings. Men were forcing their way into our home, along with tongues of blazing fire. Terrified, I ran to the well, while my old mother went wailing back and stood at the entrance to the tent, watching the burning courtyard with bloodshot eyes. Men's figures wove in and out as they strove to fight the fire. You could see arms thrusting out fearlessly to rescue household objects all on fire, while others were bailing water from the well and throwing sand on the ashes that burned the naked feet. The very trunk of the palm tree was on fire. At last the fire was extinguished and died down, but only after it had burned two sides of the courtyard, leaving just its western side and the sea captain Muhammad's house on the north side. The tent was ruined, and there was still a little smoke coming from some scattered pieces of it. The palm tree, though, was there in its place, resistant to everything that had happened. Part of its trunk was burned, but the green branches hadn't been touched by the fire.

Still the din didn't subside. There were constant questions, and a few women were offering unlikely explanations. The situation seemed familiar enough, and yet nothing quite like this had happened before. People knew what matches could do, what gunpowder could do, but what was the secret of this ground with its small tongues of flames scattered here and there, this fire that burned without anyone touching it?

We were still considering all this when a jeep stopped at the end of the alley and three British military got out, armed to the teeth, with some local soldiers behind. As the men approached, their faces were flushed and ablaze with fury. They obviously had plenty of questions to ask.

Why had they come, we wondered? Who'd sent them to our neighborhood? Who'd told them? Plenty of homes burn in our small town, but we'd never seen a single soldier put on his helmet and brave the fire.

Our neighbors formed a circle around the soldiers, till we were like a packed wall of human flesh. The Britons talked among themselves in their own language. Then one of the Arab soldiers translated, signaling to us to disperse:

"Move away. Go on!"

The fire was still burning in a few places. The leader of the team trampled it with his thick boot, treading down the heads of flame and loosening the blistered sand. He examined the flames at some length, then launched into some lengthy questioning in his own language, while the interpreter translated.

Who had brought this thing here, and where had he found it? And why—and—and—and who did this place belong to? I remembered my father, buried in the earth. Had he been alive, things would have been very different now.

"To Yam'an al-Lasli," I said.

"Is that you?"

"Yes, I'm the owner."

Question followed question, then the interrogation went on with my various friends: Hamdoun and Salloum and the others in the group who'd swum together in the bay. They even questioned poor 'Abboud al-Marwi, who just carries water to people, making a living from his thin donkey."

The leading British soldier wasn't satisfied with the results of his inquiry. He looked at the tent, then murmured some orders. The soldier signaled to us.

"Move off. We're going to search the tent."

The human wall stiffened and people moved still closer together.

The soldier repeated:

"Move off. We want to search the tent."

"Why? What's so serious about this?" a voice said.

"We won't allow it," said another. "It's a matter of honor. We must protect the old woman from strangers' eyes."

One of the local soldiers, standing apart from the others, gazed at the crowd of people. In his eyes a kind of understanding gleamed, stretching a bridge between the other local people and himself. It was as though the very form of the homeland was etched on his face.

The first soldier became threatening.

"Move off, will you! I'm telling you, for the last time, we want to search this place."

"To look for what?" the sea captain Muhammad interposed.

"For the stuff that burns. He might have hidden some of it." He wheeled round on me. "Where's the canister that went missing? If you don't speak, you'll end up in prison!"

"Why?" I asked.

"Because it's dangerous and prohibited material. Anyone caught with it is regarded as a criminal."

"But I found it half-buried," I said. "It had been washed up on the shore by the waves. I picked it up as one of the gifts of the bay, which the sea sends sometimes when ships are stranded there, in the shallow water."

"All right, that's enough. We don't want a whole story. Tell us, where's the canister?"

I pointed to the side of the courtyard that was still standing.

"There."

"Well, why didn't you say so before?"

"No one asked me about it."

"All right. Come and show us."

I went off, and people followed me to where I'd pointed. There was a dead bird next to it, while the other frightened birds were perched on the tent.

"Here it is!"

I pulled it out of the sand that was all around it. On the outside some letters were marked. Eyes blazed, and there was astonishment on the faces of the British, which had turned very red. The soldiers didn't take the investigation any further. They just picked up the canister and left.

The crowd dispersed. I dug a hole, as the good soldier had advised me to, and buried the dangerous stuff in the depths of the earth. Then I spent the night in the open tent. The palm tree embraced the moon, and the sea shared my pillow, and, at the end of the night, the waves sent their tunes and the dogs started howling outside. For some reason I couldn't fathom, it was delightful being awake on such a night.

I tried my best to understand the words of the good soldier:

"They're ashamed. You convinced them. There was hidden evidence here, of their ugly crimes. Don't worry, son. This hardship will pass. May God compensate you."

His face remained etched on my mind. What did he mean by those words? His image rose above the picture of the commanding soldier. I didn't feel like sleep. Was it the phantom of the prison with which I'd been threatened? Being in prison would mean death for me. It would mean the imprisonment of the sea, its usurpation, its separation from me, not mine from it. It would mean my death.

I got up at the crack of dawn, folded my bed, and left the tent. I embraced the earth, contemplated the palm tree and found it, God be praised, still in its full strength. I saw how the small birds were leaving their nests to swim in their boundless horizon. My mother was rubbing the morning dew from her eyes. There was new furniture left there in front of the tent, and good men had been quick to start rebuilding the courtyard. 'Alya', the daughter of the sea captain Muhammad, came in carrying the breakfast tray, and I smelled the sea in her robe. I drew a deep breath and went up to my mother.

"I shan't be long," I said.

"You're going to the sea, aren't you? Well, just don't bring anything else. All we want is fish, food for us and the birds."

"All right, Mother."

I stood facing the sea, gazing at the caravan of waves, breaking one after the other. Then I saw him coming toward me. Still nearer he came with his long strides, crossing the bridge that seemed to me something small, the size of a horse's hoof. He stood there in front of me. Then he patted me on the shoulder and, before rejoining his troop, said, "Dig a deep hole, Yam'an. Hide that dangerous stuff in the heart of the earth. They're ashamed, and you've won the argument, and here they are, burying their ugly crimes. Don't worry, son. This hardship will pass."

I looked again at the sea. The British fleet was carrying out its usual maneuvers. And I understood what the good soldier meant.

—*Translated by May Jayyusi and Christopher Tingley*

Sa'id al-Kafrawi (b. 1939)

Egyptian short-story writer and novelist Sa'id al-Kafrawi was born in al-Mahalla al-Kubra near Tanta. He studied economics and commerce and worked for some time as an accountant before leaving to dedicate himself to writing. His first short-story collection, *City of Beautiful Death*, appeared in 1985 and immediately became the focus of literary analysis and commentary because of its originality and vigor. His novel, *The Edge of the Bay*, is based on his experience in Saudi Arabia, and he has published several collections of short stories: *People and Stones*, *The Ultimate Desire* (1990), *As Far as the Eyes Can See* (1994), and *A House for Passers-By* (1994).

THE BEAUTICIAN AND THE BRIDE

And now, like amorous birds of prey,

. . . tear our pleasures with rough strife

—*Andrew Marvell, "To His Coy Mistress"*

"I beg you to save my honor, Aunt.[1] May God protect you."

The beautician took hold of the girl's braids, rolled them around her hand, then pulled the abundant, thick hair, so hard that she heard it crack in her hand. A maddening pain surged through the girl's body.

"Pull it, Aunt," the girl said abjectly. "Pull it hard. I deserve whatever happens to me."

The beautician pursed her lips, and a line of anger spread from beneath her nose down to her rounded chin. Her crescent-shaped earrings swung as she shouted at the girl, "Sinner!"

Kneeling in contrition, the girl took hold of the woman's dress.

"I couldn't help it, Aunt," she said imploringly. "My body tempted me."

The beautician turned her head away from the girl, still holding on to her braids.

"Dishonor lasts longer than life, sinner!"

She released the braids and turned her back on the girl. Through the window she saw a kite, its claws out to pounce on a small house sparrow, which it caught successfully. The sparrow flapped its wings in despair, struggling between the claws of the bird and uttering pleas for help.

---

1. "Aunt" is here used as a respectful term of address to an older woman. It does not imply a blood relationship.

"Who is he?"

"Hannoura."

"The village idiot! What a humiliation for you, Madawi daughter of Nawasif!"

The beautician began looking through the window again, at the bubbling spring, the turning water wheel, the trees on the river bank, a row of returning animals, the clouds moving along the sky.

'The air's filling up with the *khamisin*[2] dust,' she thought. 'There'll be a *samum*[3] blowing, and the girls' veins will swell with hot blood.'

The wind increased. 'There are more sins in spring,' the beautician reflected, 'and scandals smell very bad.'

She turned to the girl who had risen and was sitting on the wooden bench, her head bowed, weeping convulsively.

"All pleasures are the work of the devil," she said. "You've disgraced yourself and your noble father. Get up."

Madawi stood up, still weeping.

"When did it happen?" the beautician asked.

"A month and a half ago."

"Does anyone know about it?"

"My cousin knows."

"So you couldn't even keep it secret. You're a sad case, Madawi."

The beautician was silent for a moment, then asked, "When's your wedding, girl?"

"Next Thursday, Aunt."

"God protect us on that blessed day! Now, take your brother and get out. I'm sick of the sight of you. May God protect his female creatures!"

The girl left the house and walked on to the bridge, rejoicing in the smell of the flowers in the nearby fields. She'd stopped crying and sobbing now, and the pain had lessened too. Her brother asked her what she was crying about.

"Nothing," she answered warily.

"Has someone upset you?"

"No, there's nothing."

She was less sorrowful now, and the memory of the sinful event flooded back ...

The sun was quite hot that day, in the middle of the sky, and she was standing at the window, leaning against the sill and looking across the thick trees that shaded their garden. Then, hearing the sound of splashing water from the direction of the well in the middle of the garden, she pushed back her braids and stood up straight, looking towards the source of the sound with her sharp, black-lashed eyes.

"Who's there?" she said.

The only answer was a giggle, a friendly voice, and some unintelligible words.

---

2. A hot southerly wind found in Egypt.
3. A hot wind or sandstorm.

"Who's there?"

The idiot let out a raucous laugh that frightened an owl. It darted out from among the branches of the tree and was blinded by the sudden light.

"Oh, it's you, Hannoura," she said.

She looked under the tree and saw the boy stark naked. A deep quiver went through her, and she burned with longing, enraptured by the sight of the strange, strong body. For a moment she wished she could stretch out her hand and touch his arms and chest and take hold of that thing between his thighs. Then she shuddered at her sinful feelings.

She left the window and walked out on to the dry leaves, listening to the boy's confused, meaningless singing. His words reached her ears:

"The lovely girl, pretty . . . as . . . a . . . pic . . . ture!"

She pushed aside the branches of the orange tree and walked to the edge of the well. Water was dripping from Hannoura's muscular body, and the sun shone on him, highlighting the down that was like sheep's wool and his thick, dark, curly, tangled hair. He gaped vacantly at her, and she saw the strong, shiny teeth in his open mouth. He dived into the basin of the well, stayed there for a while, then came out noisily.

"Won . . . der . . . ful water!"

He laughed like a ram, and Madawi laughed too at the sight of him playing with the water.

"Look, a dumb animal!" she shouted jubilantly.

Then she caressed his forearms and stroked his chest. Startled, he laughed and pointed in the direction of the shady trees.

"A grasshopper!" he shouted.

The thin-legged insect, the same green color as the trees, stood concealed in the branches, waiting, with watchful eyes, for some prey on which to make its ferocious attack.

When the girl pinched his chest, he pushed her hand and let out his ram's laugh. She clapped her hand over his mouth in fear.

"Be quiet, you fool!"

A tomcat and a cat in heat were howling near the wall. Then the cat ran on to the roof of the house, with the tomcat hot on her heels, his ears pricked and his tail and whiskers erect.

"Tell me, Hannoura, aren't you ever going to get married?"

He laughed and pointed toward the tree.

"A grasshopper! A grasshopper!"

Whenever the youth moved, he aroused her desire. She tried to clench her teeth, in an effort to stop the surging of the blood within her.

She let her headscarf fall, deliberately, to reveal her coal-black hair, then stared into his eyes, where she saw thunder and flashes of light. She helped him out of the water and he submitted to her wish, docile as a child. He was totally naked, his sexual member exposed to the spots of sunlight that shone so provocatively through the leaves of the trees.

Water was dripping down and across his body. She pulled him by the arm, took him to her room, and closed the door; then she perfumed him with rose water and combed his hair. Seeing himself in the mirror, he neighed like a horse, and she quickly put her hand to his mouth.

"Be quiet, you fool," she said in a strangled whisper. "Don't make a scandal!"

She touched his body and a spark took fire in both of them, moving from the whirling mind to the heart, then flowing into the blood, setting them both aflame. She took him in her arms.

As the two braids were unfastened, her hair floated over her shoulders like ropes; she began to make pleasurable moaning sounds.

He greedily tore the top of her dress open, to reveal breasts that were like two balls of white dough. He seized them so violently that she was frightened.

"Don't be so rough, you idiot!" She whispered weakly.

He pressed his lips together, and the blood ran through the veins in his face.

Hannoura got on top of the girl and penetrated her; she cried, but was too inflamed with desire to feel the pain deeply. He set himself firmly over her, his heart pounding against his ribs like a tolling bell. His idiocy didn't matter now, because he was guided by animal instinct and a primitive, overwhelming pleasure.

The girl became scared at the sight of the blood on her thighs, but it was too late now; she'd fallen into the pit. She closed her eyes and drank from a river of honey, crying out with pleasure; she was running free in a wide, open land, released from her reins, spurred on by her hot-blooded young body.

When Madawi reached the house, she let go of her brother's hand and a tear sprang from her eye.

"How I regret it now!" She murmured.

It was the day of the 'henna',[4] the day before the wedding. The rooster, that creature of God that stands erect, its head raised up towards the sky and its wings beating, sang out its morning song of praise as the Almighty instructed it: "Blessed be the Holy One!" And the other roosters of the world returned his song.

Madawi woke up, chasing from her mind the fear her dreams had contained. Then sighing, she addressed her prayer to the King of the World, "God, you have protected me up till now, please protect me still. The one you protect is never brought to disgrace."

She felt the covers of the clay pots and took the container of yesterday's milk, which was an essential part of her father's and uncles' breakfast. Then she leaned against the wall of the hallway, with her head in her hand, feeling frightened and weighed down by anxiety, as if she was being stifled by cobwebs. She was dizzy: she hadn't slept the whole night, and the maddening worry never left her by night or day. No one else in the house was awake yet.

---

4. A red (or sometimes black) powder, derived from a plant and mixed with water. It is applied to the hands and feet, often in decorative patterns.

Going up the stairs, she stumbled and dropped the milk container, with a re-sounding noise that wrenched her brother 'Abd al-Mawla out of a blissful sleep. When he came out to see what had happened, he found his sister leaning up against the wall, her head in her hand, while the spilt milk ran in little rivulets along the ground. He looked at the milk for a moment, then shouted:

"Look, Madawi, there are worms in the milk!"

The Egyptian *nabk* tree overhung the bridge of the Kasbar canal, stretching out its arms over the water, the bridge, and the children of the village, while Hannoura the village idiot was beating the branches with a mulberry stick to catch the fallen fruit and filling his hands with it. "The *nabk* fruit!" he was shout-ing. "The *nabk* fruit!" The children had gathered round him, in a circle, shouting: "The idiot! The idiot!" and he was shouting the same words with them and laughing inanely. One of the boys, called Rahim, pulled his robe, and Hannoura beat him with his stick, forcing him to fall back against the wall and rub his backside. He drove away the other boys, then stood there gazing at the noonday sun. He threw his fruit up at it.

"Take them, sun!" he said. "Eat them!"

They fell on the ground to form a necklace of fruits.

The youth took off his robe, revealing his strong body, then brandished his stick and hit the ground with it like a furious bull.

"Cover yourself up, you ignorant lout!" the women shouted to the wayward boy. Then they burst out laughing.

"It's as long as an arm, sister!" one of them cried.

Some ululations began and he waved his stick in the air and danced naked.

"The wedding!" he shouted "Madawi's wedding!"

Madawi's father remained where he was after ending his formal prayers, be-seeching God to spare him any scandal. Then he got to his feet, tidied the collar of his *gilbab*, took his slippers, and went toward the door.

The clock of the mosque sounded three times, reverberating through the large courtyard. A bat flew, its wings outspread, as the blind gathered at the pulpit to recite Quranic verses.

Madawi's father had a deep fear of blindness, handicap, or loss of dignity, and he was a man who pondered on God's wisdom and laws. Looking up at the sky with its scudding clouds, he lost his sense of confidence and felt a sorrow that would not leave him. "The corn doesn't turn green in a harvested field," he said under his breath, "and disgrace outlasts death."

He arrived home to be met by the crowd of the wedding party.

"Change my aunt's shawl," he said. "It's dirty."

He stopped at the old house, where his son asked him, "Is anything wrong, father?"

"No," he said. There's nothing wrong."

His granddaughter ran after him calling, "Grandfather, Grandfather!" but he pushed her roughly aside and walked straight to the store room. There it was, hanging on the wall as long as two arms, dark brown, its metal dull. It had two barrels and a pale yellow band, and it had been hanging on the wall for years, evoking the coldness of death. "Get the gun down," he shouted to his son, "and clean it and oil it. I want it to shine for your sister Madawi's wedding!"

On the wedding day, a light wind filled the air with khamisin dust, the "devil's dart" blew the straw in the streets, and the sun looked white in the sky.

The beautician entered the room and, from her bag, took a piece of granite, which she used as a whetstone. She poured a few drops of oil on it, then began sharpening her knife. "There's a smell of death," she thought to herself, "and a smell of young blood. No one wants to open the gate to Hell fire. But the girl can be forgiven: her body failed her, and so did her boiling blood. That's why I'm here, to hush up scandals and give birth to joy."

She looked in the mirror of the cupboard and rolled her hair in a bun on her head, reflecting nostalgically on her lost beauty. "Life's faded," she thought. "Your braids are gray now, and the face in that dull mirror has grown pale."

The village beautician bent down and pulled out the khaki bag that held her equipment: a jar of milk-white cream, a silver teaser for the eyebrows, a reel of thin thread, rose-colored makeup paper for the cheeks and lips. Then she went up on to the roof with the sharpened knife. She gazed at the *nabk* tree and the cluster of dates hanging over the mud wall and the greedy hens clucking with their eggs inside them, while the fathering rooster was crowing and raising its dark red crest to proclaim its uniqueness among the flock. On the wall hung the pigeon houses with their cooing birds.

The sun disappeared among the clouds and the village was covered with dust. A smell of mud and dust covered the place.

The wily old beautician sat down under the branches of the palm tree and took a short nap. She dreamed that she was walking to some moonlit ruins, and the black-browed girl with the braids was there, naked, her bare breasts sinful fruits. She ran toward the girl, who was shouting: "The pigeons! The pigeons!" The pigeons circled the ruins then flew out of sight. The beautician invoked God's grace to remove any curse. The wind had carried the girl away, but the beautician shouted to her, "Come back, girl!" When the call to prayer woke her, the wind had died down and the weather had become clearer. "What a strange dream," she thought to herself. "May God turn it to good!"

She went up to the pigeon-houses. "No one escapes his fate," she said aloud. "The road's closed and God lays traps for his creatures."

She opened a cupboard and took out a glass cup. Then she captured a pigeon, holding the cooing bird by its fluttering wings, and set it down on its back. The bird shuddered in instinctive fear, and the whites of its eyes appeared to be begging for mercy. But the strong hand cut the weak neck, as the bird's crooked claws struggled to find an escape from the death that had struck so suddenly.

The beautician drained the pigeon's blood into the glass cup and, as she did so, caught sight of Hannoura on the bridge, riding a stick like a horse, cheering for the bride amid the procession of children.

"It's all because of you, an idiot," she muttered bitterly. "But that's what God decreed."

Sambo the butcher was driving a milk calf from behind. The animal resisted stubbornly and refused to move, but the butcher gave it another shove, and it moved forward once more.

'Abdel Al-Mawla covered the calf's eyes with a green scarf decorated with shining pieces of metal and colored beads. Then he took the amber stone he'd been carrying in his pocket, put a thread through it, tied it around the neck of the calf, and pulled. He walked the calf round the place seven times, accompanied by ululations and joyful drumming. Then he handed the calf back to Sambo, who took it by the legs, thrust it to the ground, then threw all his own weight on to it.

The animal shook and snorted, then opened its large eyes and stared at the children. The butcher recited the usual formula, "In the name of God, God is great," then slit the animal's throat. The calf gurgled through its cut throat. The sound scared the noonday birds, while the gushing blood scared the children. A small pool formed from the warm and still living blood.

The mother gave a resounding ululation from the threshold and shouted at the top of her voice, "I slaughter in honor of my daughter. Let the rich and the poor eat, and let everyone passing take his fill!"

The evening saw the procession of the trousseau, accompanied by music. A number of carts, pulled by thin-bellied horses continually chasing away flies, carried the brass, the furniture, and the newly upholstered mattresses. There were also baskets filled with groceries, lemonades, and sugar cones, covered by the dresses of the bride.

At night, the Saqiya alley sparkled from the lanterns hanging in the courtyard, and gaily colored flags attached with threads fluttered among the other decorations. The musicians stopped in the courtyard, with the Al-Zawayda grocery at their back, facing Rashad's coffee house, Alfiyya's house, and the *nabk* tree where the children usually climbed to watch festivities.

The wind instruments, the trombones, and the big drum began playing with a sound that resounded in all the alleys of the village, mingling with the ululations of the consummation ceremony taking place in the house of the bridegroom's family. There the bridegroom sat in a copper basin, surrounded by his friends who were proceeding with his bathing ceremony. They turned up their wet sleeves ready to pour water on his body, which had been covered with perfumed wedding soap. When they had finished, they chanted in unison, "Roses were only thorns that bloomed from the Prophet's sweat. Our bridegroom is, by the Prophet, by the Prophet, by the Prophet, like jasmine, by the Prophet!"

Then the bridegroom stepped out, naked, covering his genitals with his hands, while his friends assailed him with chaff: "Keep going, bridegroom, tonight's your night! It's going to be a fine night for you, in the name of Him who knows the unknown!"

There were half a dozen candles burning in front of him, their flames flickering in the night, while three lanterns lit up the wedding procession. His mother and aunts and their closest friends, others who were intimate and others still who were mere acquaintances, let out ululations and threw grains of salt that streamed down like rain. The night promised fulfillment; the whole world seemed to be possessed by joy.

Madawi, daughter of a noble family, was wearing her white embroidered dress; but her heart was pounding like the fluttering of a bird's wings, and she was praying to God for protection. Her cousin Sharbat was trying to reassure her.

"Don't worry! I promise you, having the hymen pierced is just a fleabite!"

Hannoura got very excited, holding up his stick and pointing it at the approaching light that accompanied the bridegroom across the alley.

"The wedding procession!" he shouted stupidly. "The wedding procession!"

The beautician had come in the afternoon, carrying her case. She adorned the bride in red and green and had her wear a new brassiere as white as cotton. She rubbed her body with rose water, thickened her eyebrows with a coal-black pencil, covered her lips and cheeks with an apple-red color, and combed her hair like a town girl's.

"How is everything, Aunt?" Madawi asked. "My life's in your hands."

"All's well, daughter of honorable people."

She turned away and went out into the courtyard in front of the house.

"Let's have some ululations!" She shouted to the girls. "Don't you have any breath in your bodies?"

The ululations resounded through the house and joy reigned; it seemed like an endless night of celebration.

The beautician returned to the girl and looked her in the eye, forcing her to drop her gaze.

"I want your cry of pain to be heard at the other end of the village," she said. "Pigeon's blood can work miracles."

The arrival of the bridegroom and the wedding procession caused a great deal of excitement in the party. "Welcome, you innocent young bridegroom," people shouted. The naive young man smiled, and his mother wrapped a silk scarf around his neck. "Keep yourself warm," she said.

"How's he going to be cold, Aunt Anima?" said his friend Ahmad al-Jammal. "Do you really expect anyone to feel cold with Madawi in his arms?"

The bridegroom walked to the unveiling room. The ululations increased and the crowd grew, while the singing became louder and more tumultuous. He removed the transparent veil from a face as lovely as the moon, looked at the black-browed eyes, and thought to himself: "She's as beautiful as a moon!"

"Congratulations," he said to Madawi, "to you and to me."

The girl lowered her eyelids and the beautician thumped him in the chest.

"Why are you in such a hurry?" she said. "You'll soon have all you want of her!"

The father made his way through the crowds and shouted to the beautician, "Let's finish things. It's late, and people are hungry."

The beautician sent everyone from the room and closed the windows. Then she took her equipment out of the cloth bag and put it under the couple's wedding chair, placing the glass of pigeon's blood near one of the legs of the chair. Outside the music had stopped playing.

The beautician took hold of the bridegroom's thumb and wrapped it in his white handkerchief. Then she shouted at him with sudden anger, "Do you know how to pierce the hymen?"

The inexperienced young man became nervous.

"Yes, Aunt," he said. "Yes, I know."

"I'm sure you don't!" she answered hotly. "Let me help you. You never know with young men these days . . . "

Growing still more nervous, the bridegroom gave her his wrapped thumb, and she drew it beneath the thighs that Madawi, in her shyness and embarrassment, was trying to cover. The young man looked under her dress, but the beautician scolded him, "Are you going to look at me or at the bride, as beautiful as a full moon? Give me your finger."

The thumb penetrated the forbidden land already plowed, entering easily, while the embarrassed young man sweated profusely. Madawi shouted loudly as they'd agreed, a cry that pierced the thick darkness of the night. The aunt undid the handkerchief beneath the bride's lap and stained it with the pigeon's blood, making marks as big as a silver coin. Madawi struggled to rise, moaning, while the bridegroom held her in his arms and told her, "It's over now."

The beautician opened the door and threw the handkerchief stained with the bride's blood out to the crowd. The courtyard rang with ululations and cheering, and the music went on with its various sounds.

Gunfire exploded in the darkness, from revolvers and guns; the night was full of the sound of bullets coming in sudden flashes from the rooftops. Some of them seemed to be flying right up to the stars!

The bloodstained handkerchief fluttered over the heads of the paternal and maternal uncles, a symbol of the families' untarnished honor. As the song says:

Open date fruit, you honored your brothers!

The beloved mother came from the parlor opposite, carrying the tray of sweets and drinks on her head,[5] and the doors opened to make room for it. Madawi appeared, resting her back against the bed and facing the door. Her husband was busy removing his cashmere robe, and the beautician was collecting her material, with a feeling of relief, her face reflecting the happy ending and her

---

5. This is the so-called tray of agreement, brought in at this point to symbolize harmony and good luck.

soul free now of the worries of the previous days. At that same moment a bullet was fired and pierced Madawi's heart. As she cried and moaned, the young man took her to his breast and shouted for help, while, to the horror of the guests, a thread of blood ran onto the white dress. The girl collapsed and died.

"Madawi!" shrieked the bridegroom.

A voice in the courtyard—or perhaps two voices, or three, no one was sure how many—shouted, "It was a bullet! A stray bullet!"

—*Translated by Aida A. Bamia and Christopher Tingley*

Ghassan Kanafani (1936–1972)

Born in Acre, Palestine, novelist, dramatist, and short-story writer Ghassan Kanafani's most vivid memories of his boyhood sprang from the 1948 war in Palestine, which led to the eviction of the Palestinians to the various Arab countries. Kanafani became a refugee with his family, and it was this experience that formed much of the substance of his fiction. He lived for several years in Damascus, where he joined the Arab Nationalist Party (later, the Popular Front for the Liberation of Palestine). After working as a teacher in Kuwait for a few years, he returned to Beirut in 1959 and became the spokesman for his party, writing prolifically in both literature and journalism. His journalism was the reason for his tragic death in 1972, when his car was booby-trapped in Beirut.

A politically committed and popular writer of originality and style, Kanafani published five novels, two plays, and five collections of short stories. His short-story collections *The Death of Bed No. 12 and Other Stories* (1961), *Land of Sad Oranges* (1963), *A World Not for Us* (1965), *On Men and Guns* (1968), and *Umm Sa'd, Palestinian Stories* (1969) were published in two volumes in 1973. Some of these stories are politically committed, but many of them are stories of the human condition that could translate into any culture. This capacity of a committed political activist to transcend, as artist, the politically oriented and depict life in its universal aspects was Kanafani's great achievement. At the same time, much of his politically committed fiction is of very high caliber, avoiding the sensational and the fanatic and sometimes providing, as in his novella, *Returning to Haifa* (1969), a highly unexpected and unideological resolution to an intricate political and psychological problem. His novella *Men in the Sun* (1962) was made into a film and translated into several languages, including an English translation by Hilary Kilpatrick. The film was banned in many Arab countries for pointing an accusing finger at the treatment of the Palestinian refugees and reflecting their sometimes blind and desperate search for survival in the face of terrible odds. Another brilliant novella, *All That's Left to You* (1966), is one of the earliest and most successful modernist experiments in Arabic fiction; it again revolves around the plight of the Palestinians. This novella, together with a collection of Kanafani's stories, was translated by PROTA and published in 1990. His third famous novella is the above-mentioned *Returning to Haifa* (1969).

IF YOU'D BEEN A HORSE

"If you were a horse, I'd put a bullet through your brain."

Why a horse? Why not a dog, a cat, a rat, or whatever else you cared to name, if some animal had to be sacrificed and shot?

He'd heard his father repeat this sentence from the time he'd first begun to master language. It seemed odd to him—that his father was the one person he'd ever heard wish his son were a mere horse. And it was an indictment reserved, too, for him alone. His father never wished this about anyone else, no matter how angry he became.

At first he'd assumed his father hated horses, disliked them more than anything else in the world—that only when his rage had reached its peak would he say to someone, "If you'd been a horse, I would have shot you." He'd supposed, too, that his father hated no one in the world as much as he hated his son, for the simple reason that he never directed the barb at any other living creature.

With time, though, he came to abandon this childish notion; for he found his father loved horses, that he'd had, at one time, a vast experience in this particular field, a way of life he'd renounced only when he'd left the countryside.

Only once could he remember his father being especially cheerful, and he'd seized the occasion to ask straight out, "Why do you wish I was a horse whenever you want to be rid of me?"

His father had knit his brows on hearing this.

"You don't understand," he'd replied, with the utmost seriousness. "You don't understand these things. There are times when it's necessary to kill a horse. When it's the best thing to do."

"But I'm not a horse," he'd answered.

"Yes, yes, I know. That's why I sometimes wish God had created you one!"

With these words his father had swung his broad shoulders around and walked off; but he'd overtaken him and blocked his path. His father had stopped, then inspected him closely, sizing him up with his sharp eyes, and he'd tried in vain to work out what was going through his father's mind.

"Do you hate me so much?" he'd asked at last.

"I don't hate you," had come the reply.

"What is it then?"

"I'm afraid of you."

In the short silence that followed he'd felt how much he loved his father, as he watched him walk around the ladder, loved this unfortunate old man who'd lived the greater part of his life solitary and alone. His youth had been taken

up with horses; then, on a momentary impulse, he'd abandoned everything. His
wife had died after giving birth to a son, and he'd taken this son with him to
the city, selling his horses—Samra, and Beida, and Barq, and Lion—along with
his meadows. He never knew why his father had acted like that, and if he'd tried
to ask he wouldn't have had an answer.

He knew his father well enough to realize that, for him, the past was a thick
wooden box with a thousand locks, a box whose keys had been flung into the
depths of the ocean. Still, seized by the mystery of his father's behavior, he'd
decided to look into the reasons for it at the first chance he had.

Once, when his father had gone back to the countryside to see his few
remaining friends and relatives, he'd taken the chance to pay a rare visit to his
father's room; and there, for the first time, he'd noticed the many pictures decorating the walls, most of them depicting beautiful horses. Sliding a knife in the
gap above, he'd opened the drawer and drawn out an exercise book with black
leather binding, which he'd then sunk back in a chair to read.

It had been hugely disappointing. There was nothing in the book to en-
lighten him: just a long series of numbers and prices and details of ancestry—the
buying and selling prices of horses, and the ancestries of horses stretching back
hundreds of years. Interspersed with all these flat entries were a few random,
unfinished sentences written haphazardly in the margins, akin to the doodles
of a man whose attention had wandered, like: "20.4.1929—they told me to sell
him, or else kill him."

He went on turning the pages out of interest, imagining he'd picked up some
thread that would prove significant.

"1.12.1929—he's the best I have. I won't let him go. They still say I should
sell him, or else shoot him."

"20.3.1930—these are just old people's scare stories. Barq's the most splendid
horse I've seen in my life, and the gentlest too. I won't kill him."

On the last page, in a trembling hand, came the final entry of this strange diary:

"28.7.1930—He threw her savagely off his back by the river bank, then
cracked her skull with his hooves and went on pushing her into the river with
his forelegs. Abu Muhammad fired a bullet through his head."

"That horse should have been killed at birth," Abu Muhammad told me, "the
day he was dropped on the hay. It's really difficult to kill a horse after that. When
a horse lives with you for a few years, he becomes more than a brother almost.
Does a man kill his brother? But your father, God forgive him, wouldn't have
it. This, he insisted, was the most beautiful horse he'd ever seen. 'This particular
breed,' we told him, 'is famous for its beauty, but don't be taken in by it.' All he
did, in reply, was keep saying how noble the horse was. 'He'll lose you more than
he's worth,' we told him. But your father, God forgive him, is a stubborn man.

He didn't kill him, or sell him, or get rid of him. 'Abu Ibrahim,' we begged, 'at least don't mount him.' But he, God forgive him, wouldn't listen.

"You don't remember your mother. She was a beautiful woman, and everyone loved her. Your father, may God smooth his path, loved her to distraction—we never saw any man, in these parts, so intoxicated with love. She was, God have mercy on her, a woman who was beautiful and hugely intelligent too. They were together around a year, if I remember rightly, and at the end of that she gave birth to you. Then the horse threw her, by the riverbank.

"You ask why we wanted to kill the horse? That's a difficult question, lad. Only someone with special knowledge and special experience can answer it, and only someone like that can really understand the problem involved. I'm an old man. Why don't you go and ask someone else?

"Your father doesn't hate you. On the contrary. He's afraid of you and has been ever since you were a child, too weak to pick up the smallest stone. If I were you, I wouldn't ask him why."

～～

Why should his father be afraid of him? He was, as his colleagues at the hospital knew, a quiet person, inoffensive and reserved, with the sort of gentle nature that wouldn't let him kill a fly. So why was his father the one person to fear him? None of his patients had shown any misgivings, surrendering to his scalpel with total confidence. His features didn't arouse fear, and that made his father's apprehension all the stranger.

One night, when he was asleep, he heard a sharp cry of pain from his father's bedroom; when he flung open the door, he found his father writhing with pain on his bed. It didn't take long to see he was suffering from an acutely inflamed appendix, which might burst at any moment.

As the nurses carried him on his stretcher to the operating table, he asked: "Who's going to do the operation?"

"The best surgeon in the whole city," they told him. "Your own son."

When he heard this, the old man struggled violently on the stretcher, trying to free himself from the restraining hands. Then, when his efforts proved useless, he started screaming at the top of his voice.

"Any other doctor," he shrieked, "but not my son! Any other butcher, but not my son!"

"But," they told him, "he has the best success rate of all the surgeons!"

Still the old man struggled convulsively on his stretcher, pain and terror clawing at his throat. Then he violently resisted the anaesthetic.

"He'll kill me!" he yelled. "He'll kill me!"

"That's just nonsense," they answered.

"Nonsense or not, I don't want my son here in this theater, not even to watch. I don't want him here."

It was useless prolonging the argument. He, after all, knew his father better than anyone. When he heard him talk like that, he spread his arms in a gesture of resignation and made his way back to the waiting room.

"It's the most difficult I've ever done," said the surgeon who performed the operation. "The local anesthetic seemed to affect him. He kept talking right through the operation.

"Your father said things it would take the devil himself to understand. He said Abu Muhammad—whoever he may be—was a cool, unemotional man, and that was why he was capable of killing a horse, which the owner himself could never have brought himself to do.

"I wish you could have heard the fine way your father spoke of his youth. He wept when he talked of your mother's beauty—due, I imagined, to the high concentration of alcohol in the room—and went on to say he was responsible for her death, equally with 'Barq.' Who is this Barq, by the way?

"He talked, too, of a horse he'd had thirty years before. This creature had been born on a stormy night, of mixed parentage: a noble mother and a horse a bedouin had brought in from the heart of the desert. In your father's eyes it was the most beautiful horse in the world, with its flawless silver white coat. At the first sight of him, he said, he'd leapt over the fence—he described all this in minute detail—but, when he got the horse to its feet, he noticed a brownish-red patch running in a zigzag down its right side. He'd hardly recovered from the shock, he said, when Abu Muhammad cried out from the other side of the fence: 'That horse has to be killed straight away.' And when your father angrily asked why, Abu Muhammad answered: 'Don't you see that stain of blood? It's a sign this horse will bring death to someone you love. He's marked, at the very moment of birth, with his victim's blood. He must be killed before he gets any stronger.'

"But your father, by his own account, was determined to disprove the legend. The horse, he said, turned out to be easy to ride, obedient and intelligent. He lived there in his stable for a long time, without doing anyone any harm.

"Your father grew silent at this point and finally lost consciousness. And do you know something? I was happier with his silence than I was with his story. That old tale fascinated me so much I was in danger of losing concentration. When he lapsed into unconsciousness, the operation could go on as normal.

"Have you heard any legends like that yourself? Of a horse born with the blood of its future victim on its neck? Your father talked of it with a Sufi's faith. I wondered if you'd ever had arguments with him about it."

It had been almost dawn when he set off for home, his colleague's remarks still turning around in his head. So that was the story of hatred his father had finally revealed, after keeping it secret for thirty years. That was why his father was so afraid of him, had wished he'd been a horse, so he could put a bullet through his brain. That was it!

He reflected on the story, and on the reddish-brown zigzag patch that, like Barq's, covered a large part of his right side and back, the victim's blood according to the old folk tradition, the patch about which a girl had once said, as she fondled it, "That's the biggest mole I've ever seen. Why is it that reddish color, like a patch of blood?" He understood now why his father feared him. It was because he was stained from birth, the way Barq had been imprinted with his mother's blood all those years before he killed her, cracked her skull and pushed her into the river. He realized now what had tormented his father for thirty years, had made him wish his own son was a horse, so he could dispatch him.

Superstition, he thought, destroyed people's lives. His father had lived with this nonsense for thirty years, and a barrier had come between them as a result. And why? All because Abu Muhammad didn't know the simple medical explanation for this birthmark, this blood-colored disfigurement, and because his father—

He stopped suddenly, there in the middle of the road. "My own father," he thought, "tried to destroy this belief, wanted to challenge the old tales. And what happened? It looks as if Abu Muhammad won. My father lost the battle, at terrible cost.

"A brown patch, tending toward red. We know what causes it, but we don't know why it appears here and not somewhere else. Obviously it's a distinguishing mark of some sort. My mother was a good rider, Abu Muhammad said, used to the ways of horses. So why did Barq kill her? What drove him on to crack her skull then push her into the river for no reason? What drove him on to kill her?

"Abu Muhammad won the wager. My father lost his wife, and with it went his youth. And now he's bent on giving battle to his son, and who's to say which one of us will win?"

He walked on a little further, then stopped once more, as a thought exploded, with enormous force, in his mind.

"I handed over an operation," he thought, "of my own free will, to someone less competent than I was, all because I felt hurt by a sick man's ravings. Could it be this other surgeon's killed him through his negligence, because he was so taken by his story? If he has, then I'm the real killer. I could have carried out the operation perfectly well, in spite of the things the old man was telling. And now, what have I done?"

He stopped abruptly, turned around, and started running back toward the hospital. The sun was rising as his heavy steps pounded over the stones of the wet street, a noise that resounded like the trotting of a horse.

—*Translated by May Jayyusi and Christopher Tingley*

Fu'ad Kan'an (1920–2001)

Lebanese short-story writer Fu'ad Kan'an was born in Rashmayya, where he attended seminary before moving to Beirut to complete his studies, which he did while teaching. After that he worked as a literary journalist and lived in

Beirut until his death. His first short-story collection, *Nausea*, was published in 1947 and his second, *First and Last and In Between*, in 1974. Although by no means prolific, he is an accomplished writer who addresses existential and social problems with skill. He sometimes uses local Lebanese vocabulary and expressions, creating a Lebanese atmosphere and often employing a tone of mild sarcasm not devoid of compassion for human frailty.

THE TRAM OF LIFE

Father Simon al-Rawand had discovered that the hardest part of his new mission, as counselor and confessor at the Reform School for Delinquent Girls in West Beirut, was the crowded tram that he was forced to ride every day at the peak of the rush hour. In fact, he had to travel on the tram twice each day, and it was always jammed with people, pressed so close together he could hardly move.

Father Simon would have much preferred to walk, but it was a very long distance indeed from his monastery, Saint Joseph of Arimathea in East Beirut, to the opposite side of the city, where the Reform School for Delinquent Girls stood in West Beirut. Even if he had been willing to walk the long distance, his superior, the Abbot Antonious, felt such a gesture was ill advised, and taxis were out of the question since the monastery did not generate enough from the daily Mass collections to cover the cost.

Occasionally Father Simon considered drawing to his superiors' attention the difficulty he faced, but he worried that they might doubt the purity of his intentions. He also felt that they might see his reluctance as bordering on refusal or even as outright disobedience of the call, particularly since he had declined the abbot's suggestion that Sister Marie Rose, one of the sisters of the Immaculate Conception, might accompany him on his mission.

"Father Simon," he would say to himself, "haven't you been singled out to fulfill a noble purpose by being selected to serve as counselor for these delinquent girls? Didn't you accede to your superiors' command because you believe that the monk's vow includes not only sacrifice but total obedience and strict self-denial? Isn't it God himself who has summoned you? Jesus has called me, so I will not doubt; Jesus has chosen me, so I will not be afraid."

Father Simon's pleasure in the trust his superiors were showing in him was matched by a tremendous confidence in himself. He had rejected Sister Marie Rose's assistance because he had never allowed himself to consort with any of the daughters of Eve. He believed that woman's presence tarnished the bright gleam of inner purity and brought death to the soul of man. And every dead soul, he told himself, is cut out of the body on the day of judgment and thrown into the everlasting fires of perdition.

And how many of his brother monks, he thought, had allowed themselves to fall into that fire, had left the safe refuge of the monastery for the dark clutches of sin. Three there had been, no four. Their guardian angels, he thought, had been unable to keep those poor creatures' hearts free of lustful thoughts and must have had to abandon them. There was Father Zakaria, oh woe on you, Father Zakaria. Whatever made you sit in the confessional, asking the girls at the Reform School those suggestive questions? Whatever made you ask the girls to stick their fingers through the grille so you could pull out their sins? Oh, Father Zakaria. And Father Ezekial, fie on you, Father Ezekial. You were so puffed up with vanity, grooming your beard and scenting your body, that you lost all discretion. Then you were ripe to fall into the hands of the devil who goaded you into impregnating Sister Lucia, and now the two of you are roasting in hell together. What about you, Father Bernardus and Father Gennadius, woe on both of you. All of you have made the order of Saint Joseph of Arithmathea a laughing stock in the hands of this Fu'ad Kan'an!

When Father Simon first started riding the tram to the Reform School for Delinquent Girls, he would admonish himself, "Father Simon, Father Simon, watch your virtue. Don't betray your vows. Don't fall into the same trap as your predecessors, an abyss so deep only the devil itself knows how far down the bottom is. Your own chastity has raised you up in the eyes of your brothers, your superiors, your Lord, and all the saints around Him. Your chastity is all you need to accomplish your mission at the Reform School for Delinquent Girls, to set them on the right path, to lighten their sinful hearts with the radiance of Jesus! Your prudence made you refuse Sister Marie Rose's assistance! So now, Father Simon, don't slip, don't stain your spotless purity with vile thoughts, with sinful deeds that will lead you down the road to death and eternal damnation!"

Such were the admonitions he addressed to himself in the beginning, and he continued to chide himself in this way every day. Every day when the morning bell sounded and he leaped out of bed to pray and recite the rosary; every day when he washed his face, neatened his beard, and straightened his mustache; every day when he boarded the tram, traveled in the tightly packed crush of people, got off the tram, walked to the Reform School, sat in the confessional. In the end he gave himself up to the care of his guardian angel, asking to be led by the hand on that difficult route between the monastery and the reform school.

Still, despite the protection of his guardian angel, he could not help but take the additional precaution of prayers en route. As the train came clanking and groaning its way along the tram line, he would quickly push in among the crowds and squeeze into the nearest corner. There he would draw himself up, close his eyes, and pray from the very depths of his being: "O most blessed Mary, help us overcome the enemy within our hearts. You who vanquished evil and death with your purity, teach us how to avoid the occasion of sin, sin which rots the human soul and enslaves us to the devil." So Father Simon would go on until his destination was reached.

Only when his feet were safely on the ground again would Father Simon relax a little. He would give his cassock a good shake, check his pockets, grasp his umbrella firmly, and straighten his beard that had become disheveled during the squeezing in and out of the tram. The road to the reform school wound along between rows of houses, and he could smell the scent of flowers and hear birds singing in the trees. "Praise to you, O my God, for all Thy wondrous works of nature," Father Simon would intone. And when he reached the Reform School for Girls, he would go straight to the chapel, bow down in prayer, intone a litany, and then make his way to the confessional. He would slide back the screen of the partition and, enveloped in darkness, receive, one by one, the sinners.

For Father Simon, hearing confession was just as much a source of delight and relief as the tram ride was a source of anguish and misery. Through the tiny aperture, he would listen while the girls who were sick at heart unburdened their souls to him and asked him for help. He would sympathize, pour balm on their spiritual wounds, and wash away their sins with prayers of penance and words of absolution. From this confessional he could repeat, with the Prophet Isaiah, "I am he that blotteth out thy transgressions for thine own sake, and will not remember thy sins. Though your sins be as scarlet, they shall be white as snow; though they be red like blood, they shall become white as wool."

From this confessional, he was in touch with a vile world, it is true. The things he heard through that small aperture shook him up, sometimes amazed him, and often sorrowed him. He learned more than he had ever dreamed existed about the kinds and extent of the delinquent girls' illnesses and diseases. How incredibly ignorant the poor girls were! The extent of their ignorance staggered Father Simon. Often he would weep at the spiritual wounds these girls bore, some of which, it must be admitted, had already become infected and could not be cured. But he would do his best. "Pray, my daughter, pray," he would say. "Pray and repent! Repeat after me, 'My beloved Redeemer, Teacher, Beloved Jesus, I repudiate my sins, all the forbidden thoughts and deeds that have caused your bleeding wounds. Beloved Savior, I will no longer be your enemy. After today, I resolve not to resist your love, I resolve with all my strength to surrender myself to You. Help me cut those evil ties that keep me from submitting to You totally, from accepting the sweet balm of your eternal love."

To all of the delinquent girls who came to him, Father Simon appeared just as he did to his superiors, his brothers, his acquaintances: the very model of a good priest, meek, unpretentious, with no sign of arrogance in his manner, no indication of tension or anxiety in his face. His hair was close-cut, and looked like a crown on the top of his head; his beard spread all over his dark red lips and then billowed down to his chest. He would extend only the fingertips of his hand in greeting and then swiftly withdraw them. He would fend off the gazes of his sick charges with the edge of his cape and stare steadfastly down at the ground or up toward heaven. In his heart Father Simon believed that sins were an abomination, not to be tolerated, and yet he could feel sympathy for human weakness and did not react harshly. But every day he would hear more unusual sins through that confessional aperture, things that almost knocked his ear off sometimes, so startling that occasionally he could not help himself from pulling his cape aside for a moment and staring through the screen at the girl kneeling there. "God," he would cry," "what sin could be stranger than that girl's?"

Then he would have to begin his admonitions to himself once more. "Listen, Father Simon, you may have heard about a lot of sins in your lifetime, but never anything like this! Fie and woe upon us all! Oh teachings of monasticism, where are you now when we need you the most? How can we quench the fires of evil that course unchecked through the hearts of these young girls? They all follow the same path as this little girl here, and that leads straight to hellfire!"

Every day, the girl told him, she went from home to the shirt factory in the morning and home again in the evening. In both directions, she rode the tram at the peak of the rush hour, in other words, at the time when lewd ideas and impure thoughts were at their worst among the passengers. Father Simon looked at her. "But she's just a child, a little doll," he said to himself; he liked the idea of calling her a doll. Even so, he had to admit that there was a wicked gleam in her eye, visible even through the screen. "Oh, Father, I have no choice," she said, "I have to choose a man and stick close to him . . ." He stared at her again. "She's just a little doll," he thought, but the expression on her face is that of a hungry cat. "If I feel any sign of desire in the man I'm squeezed against," she went on, "Well, I just let him do it . . ."

Father Simon started, and moved his face closer to the grill. "You let him do what?" he whispered.

"Whatever he wants, I don't pay any attention, I just relax, and then I jump off the tram, but by that time I have his money in my hand."

Father Simon sat back in the confessional, speechless.

What a sin! The sin of the tram!

"Well, Father Simon," he muttered to himself, "this sin that this little doll from the reform school has committed is a double sin; isn't that so, Father Simon? Lechery and theft, theft and lechery. Isn't that what your theology has to tell you? Sin against the sixth commandment: gratifying the lusts of the flesh with an unknown person, deceiving that person into believing he owns something that is not his to own. Clasping, clutching the body of another, for no other reason except that in the tram you have no other choice; is that it, the sin, or is it simply resignation to what must be? But then the sin is compounded by the sin of theft: stealing from a person with whom one has committed the sin of lust! What a sin!

"Yes, Father Simon, a most extraordinary sin, a new sin. Have you ever heard anything like it, Father Simon? And how about you, Leopoldo Casteltovo, our mentor and guide, in your own time, what would you have done if a delinquent little doll of a girl like this came along and asked for absolution? How would you guide her along the path of righteousness and away from the occasions of sin? Wouldn't you have guided her as I did? Isn't Mary Magdalene the only model to give her? She too was a sinful woman who defiled the sanctity of matrimonial love and threw herself into the maw of lust? Isn't that what you would have told her? That Jesus was touched by Mary Magdalene's penitence, had mercy on her, and restored her to life. She poured ointment over His sacred feet and He in turn poured grace into her heart. She loved to excess, but He forgave her in the same proportion. She had trodden the road to hellfire, but He turned her around and set her on the path to heaven.

"Yes, that was it. That was what had to be done.

"But Father Simon, what about the road to hellfire that you yourself tread twice every day, on that crowded tram? Who can guarantee that one day you won't fall and be roasted like the rest. Many women get on the tram when the seats are full; they stand close to you, and their bodies brush against your cassock, Don't you see lots of women every day who act just like this little doll, rubbing against men in the tram and submitting to the sin of lechery. Just look around you, go on, look! See there, here's a young man letting his hand swing back and forth with the movement of the tram, so he can fondle the backside of that woman standing near him. Shut your eyes, Father Simon, keep them shut! Such sights are enough to consume your whole vision. Soothe yourself with the love of Jesus. He commanded the winds to cease, and they were silent. Let him calm your heart and lift the darkness of your nightmare. Oh, look at that woman on the edge of her seat, with the man beside her, squeezing her arm. Oh chaste Mary, dove flying on wings of gold, deliver me from the sins that flourish on this earth! And there is a girl standing and a middle-aged man staring lustfully at her. O Jesus, my heart is pounding, my strength is ebbing away, even my eyesight is fading . . .

"But the Lord has given me eyes so I can survey His earth and wonder at His presence in his creatures," Father Simon thought to himself. "Am I then," he asked, "to stop gazing at the Lord on His Earth, bearing witness to the presence of his people? Am I to avert my eyes forever from the poor men and women who ride the tram? Are they not His creatures as well? He puts them on earth that I may see them and witness their life, so that I, too, may share the tram of life with them. And what of me? Where is my place in the tram of life, where is my place among His creatures, among humanity? Am I, Father Simon, not made of the same clay as that little doll who confessed to me? The Lord said, 'All of us are human, no one is in any way superior to anyone else . . .'"

But his thoughts were interrupted by a wave of strong perfume. He pulled himself together. A woman, was it! Was she a doll, too, he wondered. He turned his back. "There," he thought, "I have turned my back on sin. I have scored a victory over iniquity." He felt better. Sin is only sin after all when accompanied by acquiescence. "'Not what goeth into the mouth defileth a man,' Jesus said, but that which cometh out of the mouth, that defileth a man . . .' Yes, yes, from inside, from the hearts of men, that is where the evil thoughts lurk . . .

"Still, Father Simon, if you stand there motionless in the tram, a sin may creep over you without your even being aware of it! You may not intend to do it or look for it, and you may not accept it, either. But suppose you decide to resist that sin, what do you propose to resist it with? Will you turn your back on sin like you did just now? If you turn your back on any woman, any girl, any doll, you have in fact committed a sin in doing so. You have committed wrong, yes, against your will, it's true, but wrong nonetheless, by using that weapon of resistance merely because a girl stands behind you brushing the edge of your cassock and smothering you with her scent. How can you resist this sin forever, when it is hovering near you every day on the tram of life" (he liked the idea of calling it that). "What rosary, what litany, what psalm will you use when those impure desires invade your very blood and bite into your flesh? What saint, what Joseph of Arimathea, what Casteltovo, indeed what poor priest Simon al-Rawand can help shuddering when squeezed tight against a woman for a hot half hour in a crowded tram?"

Now the crush was getting worse.

The scent of that doll of a girl on whom he had turned his back seemed to be getting under his skin. Father Simon found to his dismay that his body could not resist; her breath was seeping into every bone of his spine; her body was touching his. Why not take a look out of the corner of his eye? No, no! He did not want to see her; he did not wish to feel any sense of capitulation toward her; any sense of pleasure. He resorted once more to his missal and began to intone the prayers, desperately making of them a rope with which to pull himself up out of the abyss: "O Lord, help me. If you are watching over us, guarding us against our sins, who can resist your gaze?"

Resist, Father Simon! Resist and stand firm! That was all he could do. And pray. He stood exactly where he was without moving, just as the doll of a girl had told him in the confessional that she had done. But even so, the crowds of people in the tram, the rocking movement of the overloaded cars, these were all enough to send sin flooding through his veins and deliver the coup de grace.

"Eli, Eli, lamma sabakhthani?" a voice moaned deep inside him. "My God, my God, why hast Thou forsaken me?" But when he turned round to cry in the face of his Lord. "O Lord, forgive me, for I have abandoned you for the sake of this doll of a girl," all that greeted his gaze was the face of an old woman.

Father Simon hurled himself out of the tram.

That day, when Father Simon al-Rawand reached the Saint Joseph of Arimathea Monastery in East Beirut, he hurried to his cell and bowed down with a profound sense of shame. He prostrated himself before the small statue of Jesus that stood above his bed, then looked up, fixing his eyes on the seven wounds of the Savior and taking from their presence some consolation for his broken heart.

Then he begged Jesus to relieve him of his responsibilities at the Reform School for Delinquent Girls. "One thing have I desired of you, O Lord," he said, using David's words from the Psalms, "to dwell in the house of the Lord all the days of my life . . . for in the time of trouble He shall hide me in His pavilion; in the secret recesses of His tabernacle shall He hide me; He shall set me upon a rock."

Jesus was not long in responding: "Father Simon," he said, "have you forgotten your vows? This is not some secular profession you can drop whenever you feel like it. No, it is God's call to work for the good of His church."

Father Simon bowed his head. "Forgive me, Lord, forgive me. Look with compassion upon my weakness. Oh, give me, I entreat you, only pure thoughts, thoughts unsullied by corruption!"

And soon Jesus did look with mercy upon his servant. Simon al-Rawand, touching him on the shoulder and whispering in his ear, "Father Simon, have you not heard me speak in the words of my prophet. You have not chosen me, but I have chosen you. I have ordained you to go forth and do good works and the fruit of your efforts shall remain ... and so that the fruit of your efforts shall indeed remain, I have called you specifically to fulfill a mission at the Reform School for Delinquent Girls in West Beirut. I call on you once more to fulfill this mission and ordain that one of my sisters, Sister Marie Rose, will help you in your work."

Thus, just as Simon of Cyrene helped Jesus carry the heavy burden of his cross, so did Sister Marie Rose help Father Simon al-Rawand bear his tortuous tram ride across the city of Beirut. Just as Jesus allowed Veronica to wipe his anguished brow with her handkerchief, so did Father Simon al-Rawand let Sister Marie Rose soothe him when the rush-hour tram rocked and lurched and the crowds of people were thrown together in a crush that was almost too much to bear.

And on such occasions, from Sister Marie Rose's heart to that of Father Simon al-Rawand went forth the sigh, "Oh Lord Jesus, we suffer for Your sake."

—Translated by Roger Allen and Elizabeth Fernea

Wadad 'Abd al-Latif al-Kawwari (1964)

Qatari short-story writer. Wadad 'Abd al-Latif al-Kawwari studied philosophy and psychology at Beirut University and has worked at the Ministry of Information in Qatar since 1981. She is married, is a journalist, and does research on theater, television, and radio. She has so far written three collections of short stories, *Sorrow Has Wings* (1985), *Good Morning, Love* (in press), and *This Is Life* (in press), and has published two novellas, *Marriage and Tales* (1990) and *Behind Every Divorce Is a Story* (2002).

LAYLA

"Are you an Arab?"

I raised my head from the book I was reading, trying to recognize the small voice. The question was repeated.

"Are you an Arab?"

I smiled, viewing her lovely face with delight.

"How did you know?" I asked.

"Because your hair's black like mine," she replied. "Look there." She touched my hair. "My name's Layla," she added. "Won't you play with me?"

I gazed at the beautiful face, and the long black hair and slim little body. How old was she, I wondered? About six or seven perhaps. If only God had given me a baby since my marriage, she would have been around that age. If only!

I found myself looking back over those six married years. Before that I'd been a student at high school, free to live my own life, beautiful and loved by everyone. Then, suddenly, I found myself wife to a man I'd never met, his desirable quality that he was sole son and heir to a rich man who happened to have paid my father a splendid dowry—a dowry that made him forget his cherished dream of seeing his oldest daughter become a doctor. For all my objections to this forced marriage, I was happy to seek out the merits of my new husband, and the discovery of these spurred me on to keep hold of him and try to make him as happy as I could.

My happiness might have lasted rather longer but for his parents' constant impatience for a child. When six long years had passed, and still I showed no sign of conceiving, they even suggested he take a second wife. But my loving husband, Ahmad, stood by me, refusing to replace me with another woman, striving to defend me for all my obvious barrenness.

Finally, though, he began to seek a way out of the atmosphere of suspicion and accusation that was beginning to choke me. He suggested to his father that he might take me to London—to manage their office there, as he put it, and, while there, have his wife examined by a medical specialist.

I was overjoyed at the idea. I must, I thought, consult a doctor and seek treatment. I just had to have a child to smooth relations with my husband's family, to prove to everyone I wasn't barren as they supposed. Besides, from my earliest years I'd loved children, dreamed of having a boy or girl to fill my life, to share my life by playing and laughing with a baby.

It was from this dream I'd been awakened by the little girl's voice asking, "Won't you play with me?"

"Of course I will, darling," I said. "I may be an old lady, coming up to twenty-two, but I'll be happy to play with you."

I ran barefoot over the green grass of Hyde Park, through to the middle. I became a child again, going up and down on the swing—which was just like the dreams of youth that take us up to the clouds and hide the reality pulling us back to earth.

"Look!" Layla cried. "Here comes my mother!"

I slowed down the swing, feeling overwhelmed by shyness even before it stopped. "My name's Nadia," I found myself murmuring. "I've just met Layla. I've been playing with her to make her happy."

Layla rushed up to her mother, throwing her arms round her neck.

"Mummy," she cried. "I love Auntie Nadia. I want some chocolate, Mummy. Please tell her to come with us."

I gazed at Layla's mother, who, from the way she was looking back at me, seemed very kind—the sort of person, you felt, who had been created just to give. She took my hand warmly in hers.

"Whoever Layla loves," she said, "I love too. They have a place in my heart."

I thanked her, sensing that she was sincere in what she said. Those few words seemed far from any kind of flattery.

"Come on," she said, turning to Layla. "It's late." Layla tried to squirm out of her mother's hand.

"We'll be here again tomorrow," Layla said. "We can play again. Please don't be late."

I kissed her, promising not to be late. Going back home I couldn't stop thinking about this little girl who'd given me such a happy day and made me laugh as I'd never laughed before. The day was a chilly one, and yet I felt a warmth creeping into my body, such as I hadn't felt since arriving in London three months before. How strange human beings are! Moments of happiness send them flying up into the spheres!

When I reached the small apartment we rented in central London, Ahmad wasn't there. He spent most of his days, and part of his nights too, playing cards with his friends. I didn't blame him—I swear to God I didn't. I'd been thoroughly edgy recently, and extremely provoking, starting up quarrels as a kind of relief for my shattered nerves. What made things even worse was the long wait for medical treatment, which I'd started seeking on arrival. Ahmad, as a perfect, considerate husband, understood why I was so irritable and was striving not to provoke me for the time being. Deep down I appreciated his response.

Next day I went off to see my doctor, who gave me a thorough examination. "Everything seems all right," he declared. I thanked him, feeling suddenly full of optimism. There was no reason not to be hopeful. I was able to have children, the doctor assured me, and so was my husband. I simply needed medication to tone up my physical condition. In fact I'd been taking this medication for some time now and, as I left the clinic, I decided it was time to do some shopping. My sister had asked me to buy some records, and I needed to buy gifts for the whole family.

I spent the day going from one store to the next and arrived home in a state of wretched exhaustion. I fell asleep without even taking my clothes off but woke up next morning refreshed. Since I had nothing to do all day, I thought, why not go to Hyde Park? The thought of Layla sprang to my mind, and that made the idea even more attractive. Why in heaven's name hadn't I thought about her the day before? So off I went and found her darting gracefully among the trees while her mother sat with a beautiful child about a year old on her lap. I greeted her affectionately and tried to sit down alongside her, but just at that moment Layla spotted me and ran toward me shouting, "Auntie Nadia! Auntie Nadia!" She flung herself at me, and, as I hugged her, I knew how close she was to my heart, that I loved her even though I'd only met her forty-eight hours before.

"Why didn't you come yesterday?" she asked reproachfully as I released her. "I waited for you the whole day." Then, changing the subject abruptly the way only children do, she said, "Have you seen my brother?" She pointed to his hair. "He's blond," she said, laughing, "but he's Arab!"

I laughed with her. "What's his name?" I asked.

"He's called Ioui," she answered before her mother had the chance to reply, "and my mother loves him very much."

"But I love you even more," Layla's mother said, speaking for the first time. Her voice was grave and sorrowful, brim full of love and fear. I was astonished at the sad, painful way she spoke. Finding no reply, I accepted Layla's invitation to play with her, and the hours flew by.

Layla's mother turned to me that evening, as I was wishing her good-bye.

"Layla's grown very fond of you," she said. "How would you like to come shopping with us tomorrow? That's if you don't have anything else to do."

I answered straight away that I'd be delighted and, before leaving, agreed to meet her in a particular spot. In the shopping mall next day, Layla insisted I choose her clothes for her, and this embarrassed me, because every mother likes to choose her children's clothes for herself. But the pleasant smile on her mother's face melted away all my embarrassment and reluctance. In the children's department Layla picked up a huge number of summer dresses, even though I reminded her summer was still a long way off; and, faced with her joy and excitement, I relented and insisted on paying for all the dresses myself despite her mother's objections. I felt, I assured her, as though Layla were my own daughter, and I begged her not to deprive me of this happiness.

She reflected for a moment.

"OK," she said. "Just as you like. But we must go back now. Layla's father's calling for me at five. Won't you come with us? No one," she added, by way of persuasion, "can tame Layla the way you can!"

I won't deny her compliment made me feel proud, proud of the place I had in the little girl's heart. I spent the evening with them, without any feeling of being among strangers; in fact I felt as though I were in my own home, and little Layla was quite used to me. She spent most of the time sitting on my lap, getting up only to bring something I asked for, and the mother was very natural, behaving and talking in a quite unaffected way. I was happy to have Layla's mother's love but even happier at Layla's love and affection for me, a special bond confirmed by time. Even my husband, who was eager to see her after all I'd told him, said once, "I don't blame you. Layla goes right to the heart." I finished up spending most of my time with her.

We were playing one evening, while Layla's mother occupied herself with her younger child, when I felt a sudden pain. I excused myself, promising I'd come back next day. Layla's mother, fear and worry written all over her sweet face, suggested we call a doctor, but I refused to impose on her. Layla insisted she wanted to come home with me, but I assured her I'd be back with her next day.

Luckily Ahmad was there when I returned, and he was appalled to see how pale my face was. I tried to tell him I was just a bit tired, that it would soon pass, then fainted. How long I was unconscious I don't know. When I opened my eyes I found myself in bed with Ahmad sitting there gazing into my face.

"My darling," he said, "you don't know how worried I've been."

I looked lovingly back and let my hands rest in his. He was happy.

"Congratulations," he said. "The doctor's just confirmed you're pregnant."

I couldn't speak, couldn't find words to express my feelings. The room had never looked so beautiful; even Ahmad, my husband, seemed dearer to me than before. I was to be a mother at last! At last my marriage would have a meaning! The dream of motherhood captivated me right through to the next day.

The doorbell was ringing. Who would be visiting us so early? I rushed to the door, and there were Layla and her mother. I was happy to see them, but surprised too. They'd been worried about me, Layla's mother explained.

"Come in," I cried, not waiting for her to finish. "I'm happier than you'd ever believe possible!"

I hugged Layla lovingly, perhaps because she was the one behind the visit.

"How I've missed you, my little darling!" I cried.

In the living room I told them how I was pregnant. Layla went off into a corner without replying, but her mother, I swear, was as happy as my own mother would have been. After we'd drunk our tea, I noticed Layla's unusual silence and set her on my lap.

"Aren't you happy," I asked her brightly, "that you're going to have a little sister?"

"You'll love her more than you'll love me," Layla answered quietly.

"No," I said. "No, of course I won't love her more than you."

The light came back into her face and she returned to her boisterous play. And God knows, what I'd told her was true. When Layla's mother said she ought to leave, I begged her to let Layla stay there with me, promising to bring her home afterwards. She agreed as usual, knowing how much I loved the little girl.

That evening Ahmad came out with me for the first time, apart from those visits to the doctor. Why don't we, he said, get out of London for a few days? I welcomed the idea. How could I turn down something that would bring us closer together? I couldn't take Layla with me, though, because her mother firmly refused to let her little girl leave her for a whole week. We spent some wonderful days just outside the capital, with Ahmad all love and care. The one thing that upset me was that I couldn't see my little girl, my Layla. The day I returned to London I found myself at her door, and she herself opened it, then stared at me in disbelief. She was beautiful in her green dress and her white cap and shoes. I bent down and picked her up.

"Aren't you pleased to see your Aunt Nadia?" I said.

She wouldn't stop kissing me. "Don't go away again," she said. "I love you. Tell me you won't go away again."

Layla's mother came to greet me, holding her younger child by the hand, and asked me to come in. I never seemed to see her without her little boy. She seemed, I thought, fonder of him than she was of Layla. If I'd known, though, what fate had in store for Layla, I wouldn't have been so hasty in my judgment. The mother went to make some tea, and I sat down to talk and laugh with Layla.

Suddenly I put my hand on the little cap covering her head and pulled it off, saying: "No rain today!" My hand froze in the air. Layla's whole head was smooth. There was no hair on it at all. I took my hand back, paralyzed by the shock. Then her mother was there at the door with tears in her eyes, before withdrawing abruptly. I've never seen such pain on anyone's face. Layla's small hand stretched out to touch my face.

"My mother says it's the London water that makes my hair fall out," she said.

Suppressing my emotion, I told Layla I'd be back in a moment. I rushed into the kitchen to find her mother and closed the door.

"It must be some skin condition," I said, speaking as naturally as I could. "Tell me it is! I'll take her to the best doctors. They'll make her hair grow back."

I couldn't finish. My tears were streaming down and the words stuck in my throat.

Layla's mother was weeping too.

"It's cancer," she said. "She only has a short time to live. I don't know how long."

She hugged her younger child again as if afraid of losing him too. I clutched at the door handle to stop myself falling.

"That's impossible," I said. "She's so young. There must be a mistake."

"I hoped there was," she said faintly, "but it really is true. I have to accept it and learn to live with it."

I thrust open the door and ran into the living room, my tears still falling, and there was Layla sitting on the floor playing with the train I'd brought back for her. She was laughing innocently, unaware how near death was. Summer would be here soon, and she'd never wear the dresses I'd bought for her. They'd still be there, but Layla wouldn't.

I turned back to close the door, weeping bitterly, and felt a warm hand on my shoulder.

"God gave me Layla," her mother said, "and now God will take her again. We mustn't lose hope in God's mercy."

Our eyes met, and I felt the pain she was suffering. She was Layla's mother, and yet she was comforting me, the stranger! It can only have been faith in God's providence that made her able to bear such disaster. I rubbed the tears from my eyes, then rushed to the little girl so as not to lose a moment of nearness to her, to have a treasure of memory when she died. If I was taking her from her toys, surely I had a better right to that than anyone!

"Thank you for the train," Layla said, burying her face in my hair. "Please bring me a bigger train next time." Oh God! She didn't know there'd be no next time. Oh Layla, I thought, if only I could give my life for yours. If only I could banish the specter of death from you!

I spent more and more time with Layla, cutting down on my hours of sleep. My husband, Ahmad, didn't blame me for this. When I told him the truth, he forgave me and hugged me, with pain and love.

"Stay there with her," he said. "And may God help her poor mother."

Day by day life slipped slowly away from the little body. Weariness began to show on the small face, and there was no trace left of her lovely long hair. "When I get better," she kept saying, "we'll play together again. We'll go and have fun on the swings in the park."

Her words of hope tore at my heart. The last time I picked her up, her body was shrunken and so terribly light. She was in acute pain, and her eyes were begging me to help her. Up to the very last moment, when death stilled her voice forever, her hands were clutching at mine, as if she was seeking, in me, a refuge from her illness. Her death was a dagger piercing my heart. Today, as I hug my own Layla, the daughter I had seven months later, I still weep for her, and I will weep as long as strength pulses in my body.

—Translated by May Jayyusi and Christopher Tingley

Bushra Khalfan (1969)

Born in Musqat, Omani short-story writer Bushra Khalfan obtained a B.Sc. in chemistry and works as an environmental inspector in Musqat. She is one of the fast-growing number of women short-story writers whose work is appearing in the Arabian Peninsula and the Gulf states. A trend toward a feminist perspective can be seen in her work as in the work of quite a few other women writers all over the Arab world. Her first collection of short stories is in press under the title *Rafrafah*. Her fiction, which reflects the challenge and freshness of the modern feminine experience in the Arab world, indicates a promising future for this woman writer.

THE TAKERS

Everything's fading, withdrawing far off to a place beyond the shade, before the light. Over there, where things seem bigger—or smaller—or seem to vanish.

"What time is it?"

"I left my watch at home."

"That shows rebellion all of a sudden. This is because forgetting your watch means you're not worried about time. And that means you're not bothered about when you come, or when you go. You're not worried about the rules of work, or about rules generally, which betrays your seeds of rebellion, rebelling about time, about rules and order, about. . . ."

Here you are, holding on to the braids of my hair, as I mount the stairs, my head tilted back. My braids reach to the floor, sweep the porches of sympathy, with illusion. You exploit my patience, hold on tighter to my braids, which loosen between your hands. You take hold of the second knot where I had braided the silk, the incense, and basil. My head, tilted so strangely, feels far more than the pain; maybe it feels love and perhaps hate. I make no effort to escape. You've reached the roots of my hair, and my head, tilted backward, feels torn up from its place, hung there like an ironic smile.

I'm in your power now. You tread me with your dusty shoes, you strike hard at my eye and my ear, but my tongue surprises you with its curses. You kick my jaw so I won't be able to speak.

You're lying on the floor. The light makes you happy and you laugh; then you get up and dance. You pull the braids of my hair, wrap them around your wrist, and drag me behind you. I feel my flesh stick to the earth, feel worms multiply in its wounds as you run in all directions, eager to catch the falling thread of the sun.

I'm a corpse, and you're sitting there with me by a tree, leaning my body on its trunk and wiping the blood from my lips. You set my eye back in its place, fix my ear in its place. You look for the worms under my skin. You whisper how you love me, how you want me as a pampered, obedient wife—how you'll give me back my lost memory and preserve my name.

"You can say whatever you like within the four walls of your room. Outside, though, beware of the friend still more than the enemy, and beware of yourself above all."

You pour water on my body. You wash me with henna. You scrub my face and my hair, hard. It's obvious you're hurting me, but you don't really care. You fill my ear and my hanging eye with cotton, stuff my mouth with soft cotton wool.

"We were there, daughter, we saw what happened. But we didn't say a word. Their looks were lying in wait to snare us. We promised to stay quiet, all except you. You fled from the room and climbed a tree, staying among its branches till dawn."

At dawn I carried my school bag, and my pens and composition notebook, and I wrote a story for the Arabic-language class.

"Your words are full of violence, that's not right for someone as young as you. Why don't you write about nature, about the palm tree, say? Or how about the summer vacation, or the beach, or an innocent love story?"

I leave the specialist puzzled, as she contemplates the color of the ink spilled on my notebook and on the floor. I go in quest of the palm tree, to bury my face in its sand.

"When you grow, and the gardens of your body shall blossom, you'll stare for hours at the reflection in the sea, and you'll search for a partner, to help you reap the fruits and keep your soul from being lost."

"Will he comb my hair the way you do?"

"Yes."

"Will he pour incense and musk on it?"

"Yes, and he'll put henna on those small feet of yours, those feet as soft as almond leaves."

"Will I grow wings?"

"Wings don't grow on girls." I feel fluffy dawn growing on my shoulders. I water it with almond oil. I nourish it, till it grows and flutters on my arm, turning to feathers, strong and shining white. I stroke them till they're fully grown, then fling myself through the small hole at the top of my house. And I fly.

"Take care, a thousand times, before you put anything into words. Seek the proper moment, take every precaution. Don't give them any evidence against you. Burn your feathers if you have to."

"If you don't stop talking, they'll burn your face with acid water, and cut you in small cubes just right for a barbecue. But they won't do that till you've borne them a good many kids."

You light the fire with a bunch of dry leaves and two pieces of white charcoal. You perfume me with the broken sticks, tighten the cover on my head. You wipe away the blood from around my lips, keep tickling me as you pass your hands under my wings. Laughter, filled with joy, grows, courses through my lungs, but no sound comes. My tranquil eyes ask you the time, but you don't reply. Here, the earth beneath me seems warmer, and I remember that I'm dead.

—Translated by Dina Bosio and Christopher Tingley

Shakir Khasbak (b. 1930)

Iraqi novelist, short-story writer, playwright, scholar, and translator Shakir Khasbak was born in al-Hilla and obtained a Ph.D. in social geography from Reading University in England in 1958. He was a professor at Sanaa University in North Yemen and has published several books in the area of his specialization. His first collection of short stories, *Conflict,* appeared in 1948 when he was very young and was followed by *A New Era*(1951) and *A Hard Life* (1954). He has also published several novels and at least three plays. His novels include: *Identity* (1996), *A Trick* (1996), *A Lost Woman* (1997), and *The Sin* (1998), and his two novellas, *Stories of Love* and *The Bird* were published in one volume in 1998. Khasbak belongs to the first post-pioneer generation of writers of fiction in Iraq but has continued and enriched his contribution over the years. He is noted for his skill in delineating the details of everyday life in the Iraqi urban environment.

SUMMER

The moment the hands of the clock struck two, a stream of civil servants poured out of their offices, carrying along with them Hamdi Aboud, an employee in the Ministry of Justice. At the main entrance some wet plaster got stuck to his shoe; tearing off a piece of his newspaper, he wiped off the plaster, for fear it should get onto his trousers. He passed by Muhammad al-Aswad who was sitting ply-ing his daily trade in his usual spot, where al-Mutanabbi Street joined al-Saray Market. He acknowledged Muhammad's broad smile with a nod of his head, for he could not bear standing under the glare of the sun to select a lottery ticket. Anyway, he no longer believed in his luck.

At the corner of al-Mutanabbi and al-Rasheed streets, Hamdi stood in the shade of a balcony, thinking, uncertain about what to do. Should he continue walking to al-Mu'azzam Gate and thus save the price of a bus ticket, or should he sacrifice the fourteen fils and take the bus from this spot in order to protect himself from the heat? . . . A porter passed by, carrying a huge wardrobe on his back, his wet gown clinging to his body. American cars were speeding past. Con-templating a patch of wet plaster in front of him, he decided to take the bus.

Getting ready to cross to the other side of the street, he caught sight of a woman, with full, rounded breasts, coming his way. Eagerly he waited for her to reach him. She had ivory skin, eyes as blue as the sea, and golden hair that was wound into an attractive bun at the back. Her dress, more like an underslip, revealed her ample bosom and a fascinating back. She headed for al-Mu'azzam Gate and he followed her, as if drawn by some magnetic force. Undoubtedly she was European—perhaps German. He had heard a great deal about the beauty of German women and their fresh, healthy bodies. What a life a person could have, in beautiful Germany, among these fantastic women! For could his own life be considered real living? . . .

Turning into the street of the Zahawi Coffee Shop, the woman stopped be-side a deluxe American car. He stood still, watching her movements, until she took off in the car toward al-Sharqi Gate. His imagination persuaded him that, with a faint smile, she had said good-bye to him. He went on his way with a whole range of emotions, from desire to distress, tugging at his heart.

His whole body was bathed in sweat; his drenched shirt clung to his body. The sweat kept pouring down his cheeks and the back of his neck. He no longer bothered to wipe it off, for as soon as he did so, more took its place. It was truly amazing that human beings could have chosen to live in this spot on the earth: in summer, Baghdad was a fragment of hell!

The stop at al-Muazzam Gate was crowded as usual, and some of the people were standing outside the shelter so that they could make it into the bus before the others. Hamdi, however, preferred standing under the shelter to keep out of the heat of the sun. The bus arrived; the crowd of standing people pounced on it, pushing and rudely trampling each other's feet. A second bus arrived, then a third, and a fourth, and still the crowd got no smaller. Hamdi's shirt was soaking wet, so he took off his jacket and draped it over his arm. He did not like resort-ing to this, for he imagined that without his jacket he looked like a stupid or ignorant boy. But the heat was unbearable . . . Without doubt, people's clothes, especially men's, were styled wrongly. Why didn't men wear loincloths, like the people of India for example?

As soon as the fifth bus came into view, Hamdi left the shelter, preparing to force his way onto the bus. After a hard struggle he managed to find a foothold inside the bus, where the air was so stiflingly hot that it was unendurable. Sweat was pouring down the faces of all the passengers, streaking the make-up on some of the women. Passengers' hands were in constant motion, trying to create some flow of air with handkerchiefs, newspapers, or briefcases. A child was gasping for breath, and an old woman was on the verge of passing out. The conductor got into an argument with a passenger. They heaped insults on each other; the driver joined in the dispute, stopping the bus and refusing to go on unless the passenger got off. This cut off the circulation of air inside the bus, making it like a blazing oven.

By the time Hamdi reached home, rivulets of sweat were running down under his suit, from his head to his feet. His head was about to burst, and his nerves were on the point of snapping. He took off his suit and threw himself onto the mat in his underwear. He turned on the fan, but all it produced was hot, burning air. He recalled the director's office and was swept by a flood of longing for a cool, comfortable place ... Where could he find such a place? In this blazing hot room? Or in his room at the ministry, where he was crammed in with four others, at the mercy of one ceiling fan that cast air hot as hell down on them? When he had gone into the director's office that morning, he felt as though he'd moved from summer into winter ... The law he studied at college had taught him that all citizens were equal in the eyes of the law. If so, what gave the director preference over him? Why this discrimination between them? He knew *how* the director had risen to his position; he certainly works harder than him, his head almost burst as he sat bent over his papers in such heat as this. And, in addition, His Honor the Director had not been pleased with Hamdi; he was trying to use Hamdi to conduct some shady piece of business in such a way as to get in the good books of his superiors while making Hamdi the scapegoat! Let him say what he liked—Hamdi would never bow his head to anyone! ...

His wife brought him his lunch on a tray, placing it in front of him in silence. As he averted his eyes from her, they came to rest on the dish of eggplant and rice ... How he loathed eggplant! He was fed up with this food, which scarcely ever varied from one day to the next. He wanted to fling the whole tray away.

"Do we have to eat eggplant every day?" he asked angrily. "Aren't you able to buy anything else? You know I hate eggplant!"

"There isn't anything better in the market," replied his wife.

Sweat was dripping off her face; her hair was so disheveled that she was frightful to look at, and there was a smudge of soot on the tip of her nose. The vision of the European woman flashed through Hamdi's mind, making him feel that he hated his wife with all his heart, that he hated this food, that he hated his work at the ministry, that he hated everything.

"You always blame the market!" he burst out. "But the truth is, you're a lazy cook!"

"What have I done wrong?" retorted his wife indignantly. "The okra is expensive, and the beans are no good. Our daily budget won't cover any more than this!"

As he looked at her, he felt that he was burning up inside and that her words were adding fuel to the fire. It occurred to him that the European woman's breasts had looked firm, despite the fact that she was older than his wife and had probably borne more children. By contrast, his wife's breasts had begun to sag a long time ago, sooner than he had ever anticipated.

In a rage, he yelled at her, "Can't you find any better excuse than this lame one that you throw in my face every day? I know very well that what's wrong with you is laziness!"

His wife's face grew red, the blue vein on the side of her neck swelled, and her eyes brimmed with tears. She tried in vain to restrain them.

"Do you see me sitting idle from morning til night like the rich ladies do?" she said in a blubbering voice. "From early this morning till now, I've been on my feet! But it's just my bad luck that makes you quarrel with me every day . . ."

Her tears flowed, mixing in with the rivulets of sweat that ran down her cheeks nonstop. The sight of his wife seemed unbearable to him, and the smudge of soot on the tip of her nose made her uglier still.

Closing his eyes he yelled at her mindlessly, "Get out of my sight, for God's sake!"

His wife went out, muttering tearfully, while Hamdi watched her with a look of disgust in his eyes. He could not understand what idiotic desire had made him find Nahida admirable. He had known that she was an ignorant woman, who possessed no distinctive beauty. Nevertheless, he had insisted on marrying her, despite his family's opposition. Was it really the sight of her full firm breasts that had captured his heart? How stupid! . . . It was true that the sight of beautiful breasts hit his weak spot, but was it worth all this frustration?

Whenever he had met her in the street, she had tried to satisfy his thirst to see those breasts, for she had understood where his weak spot lay and that they were the most beautiful thing about her. He had not imagined that those breasts would become flabby so soon after the arrival of the first child. If he had, he never would have taken this naive step . . . He had imagined that marriage would be such a blissful state. At night he would fall asleep beside a woman and in the morning would wake up to the sight of those wonderful breasts, the first thing his eyes fell upon. He had spent many nights dreaming about this desire. Had he not got married, he could possibly have become a famous lawyer, or a well-known merchant—anything but an insignificant employee in the Ministry of Justice. This morning even the janitor had given him a sarcastic look after he had heard the director chewing him out . . . If only she had made an effort to keep her breasts from his sight, the thought of marrying her never would have crossed his mind. Many times he had walked by her house, only to find her standing at the window, frequently wearing her nightdress with her breasts showing beneath it, irresistibly enchanting. And what was the result? This miserable, tormented life . . . He wasn't able to support a family, yet the children had arrived one after the other. This burden had been cast upon his shoulders while he was still in the prime of his youth and at the threshold of his career.

Having finished his lunch, Hamdi threw himself down on the mat in an effort to give himself up to sleep. The room was full of flies, and the small fan continued to circulate only hot, burning air. It appeared that sleep was a dream he would never realize in a room like this, even though he was very tired. But what room in the house *was* suitable for sleeping? They all faced the sun at this time of day and were like a red-hot oven. Often he'd had hopes of moving from this house, but rents were continually on the rise, making it impossible to leave. The day would definitely come when people would be putting up reed shacks in the streets to relieve the housing crisis! . . .

He turned over on the mat, his body bathed in sweat. All of a sudden Mahmoud's screams broke out, getting louder and louder. Mahmoud's howling always reminded him of the howls of a repulsive dog that had used to drag itself to the garden of one of his family's next-door neighbors. Again he turned himself over on the mat, but his efforts to ignore Mahmoud's wailing were futile. His mother must have given birth to him on an unlucky day. Why did he have to put up with all this annoyance? Some people spent the summer in Lebanon or in Europe, others lived in air-conditioned mansions, while he was obliged to spend it in a house like this . . .

"Shut up, you curse your parents!" he burst out suddenly. "Shut up or I'll bash your head in!"

The mother's attempts to quiet the child were useless. Hamdi's nerves were growing tenser by the moment. Jumping to his feet abruptly, he rushed out, to find Mahmoud sprawled on the floor.

"What's the matter with you?" he shouted angrily.

"He was fighting with Kamil," the mother intervened.

"If you don't calm down, I'll beat you within an inch of your life!" he threatened.

However, Mahmoud kept up his howling. After waiting a few moments Hamdi pounced on him, lifted him off the floor, sat him down, and slapped him repeatedly. This only succeeded in making him wail louder and kick the floor as if he were having an epileptic fit.

Hamdi went back to his room and lay down on the mat, exhausted. He closed his eyes, trying to doze off, but Mahmoud's howls fell on his ears like the blows of a heavy hammer. The heat grew more oppressive, giving him a splitting headache. He pressed his forehead in perplexity.

"Where can I escape to?" he whispered. "Where? . . . "

He knew very well that Mahmoud would not give up his crying for many hours. The heat, the crying, and the headache were weighing down on him like a horrible nightmare. In astonishment he asked himself how he had let himself get into this mess. His life was ruined, his youth squandered, and he was being persecuted on all sides—at the office, at his club, and at home.

That same morning his boss's anger had exploded like an erupting volcano, and he had heaped all sorts of accusations on him. Hamdi had retorted in terms that were not in the least polite, so there was no doubt that the boss's persecutions would increase. Nevertheless, he was not going to compromise his honor, even if he wasted dozens of years in government service. The boss was an employee, the same as he was, and they both rendered a certain service to the state and received a certain salary in return. The boss had no right to humiliate him as he had done today. Had Hamdi not been certain that the legal profession was no longer a profitable business, and that there were dozens of lawyers who were unemployed, he would have handed in his resignation on the spot.

Mahmoud's rising and falling shrieks were disturbing his train of thought: the vision of his agitated boss was getting all mixed up with the image of Nahida before their marriage and the specter of Mahmoud kicking the floor.

All of a sudden, he sat up. Feelings of despair were making his heart bleed. "Where can I escape to? Where? . . ." he asked mechanically.

Dressing hastily, he went out into the blazing hot street, roaming about with no destination in mind. The street was like a raging fire, so he took off his jacket and carried it over his arm. He didn't know where to go; then, he thought of taking the bus to one of the air-conditioned cinemas.

The air in the bus was on fire, and there wasn't a cool spot to be found. The conductor came up, fanning his face with a large handkerchief while sweat ran down his cheeks. He wiped off his face with his arm as he handed Hamdi his ticket. Overcome with deep pity for the conductor, Hamdi marveled at how he could endure staying in this vehicle for eight hours. Observing the sympathetic looks, the conductor sat down in the opposite seat and fanned his face with his hand, remarking, "It's an extremely hot day."

"Deathly hot," answered Hamdi. "May God help you—This bus is like an oven! . . ."

"If only it always had as few passengers as it does now! . . . An hour or two ago it was so crowded that there was no room for me to move around in!" Then, sucking in his breath, he continued ruefully, "Our profession is one of the hardest . . . But, what can we do? A man must work to earn his daily bread."

"God help you," repeated Hamdi.

Hamdi's nervous tension lessened, making him feel more composed. He wasn't the only tortured person in this life. Here was a man who was more tormented than he—and Muhammad al-Aswad was worse off than either of them. There were millions of tortured people crowded onto this earth. What was the meaning of these absurd contradictions? Why should some people live in idle luxury, while others lived in misery, worn out from hard labor? And why should a man like Muhammad al-Aswad have to live without arms or legs? What was the meaning of life? . . .

Getting off the bus at the Roxy Cinema, Hamdi entered without even trying to find out what film was being shown. The air inside was refreshingly cool. The spacious hall seemed almost abandoned, for all he could hear was the crunching of dried melon seeds in second class. When the film began, his depression gradually began to lift, until finally it almost vanished. He was able to follow the film with eager pleasure. Memories took him back to the days of his youth, when he was longing for a woman; the days when Nahida, with her firm, round breasts, had embodied his sweetest dreams . . .

The film was a story of the infatuation between a university student and a girl who worked in a small shop. It was presented in such vivid colors that it seemed to be showing life in a shining aura: the sky was clear blue, the gardens were very green, the paths were strewn with yellow sand, the sides of the streets were ornately fitted out, the waves of the sea lapped a lovely beach that was littered with magnificent bodies, and elegant people moved about joyfully and happily. The hero and heroine rivaled each other in their beauty, in their love, and in long, ardent kisses. At the end of the film, when the truth came out that the hero was the son of a millionaire, life appeared even more enticingly radiant.

Hamdi went out into the street with a happy, satisfied smile still on his lips. However, a wave of scorching heat woke him out of his dreams. He came to, and behold, the ornate streets and the paths strewn with yellow sand had been replaced by dull and humble Rasheed Street. Swept by a fierce wave of disgust, and a fleeting thought of his wife and children, he asked himself, helplessly, once again: "Where can I escape to? Where? . . . "

It occurred to him he might search in the brothels for a woman in whose arms he could forget his cares. Gripped by a spirit of recklessness, he recalled the days of his bachelorhood. However, an acute repugnance came over him. He shook his head in aversion and went on his way toward al-Sharqi Gate. On his way he passed a tavern, which he entered without hesitation.

Everything in the tavern gave evidence of its sordidness: the soiled tablecloths were torn; the covers of the old seats were faded; the dirty floor was full of holes. Voices were raised in an unharmonious clamor of boisterous shouting and singing. Under the ceiling of the tavern hung a cloud of smoke, which emanated from innumerable cigarettes and made it difficult to breathe. A fan in the ceiling circulated streams of hot air onto the customers.

Choosing an isolated table, Hamdi sat alone. He had decided to spend a few hours away from afflictions and worries. No sooner had he taken the first sip from his glass than images from the American film he'd just seen came to mind. Struggling with conflicting emotions, he longed inexpressibly to hold the heroine in his arms, and his heart almost burst with an anguish that gripped him and weighed down on him like a nightmare. Confused images ran through his mind: of his wife bursting into tears as she stood before him, with her flabby breasts and the soot on her nose; of Mahmoud kicking the floor like an epileptic; of his arrogant boss heaping accusations on him. He was absolutely convinced that life was unbearable.

He was startled out of his reverie by a quavering voice calling out, "Brothers, will you give me a moment of your time?"

Raising his eyes to the owner of the voice, he saw a poor wretch of a middle-aged man supporting himself with his shaking hands on the table in the opposite corner. The din subsided somewhat, until it grew almost quiet. The eyes of everyone present were turned toward the man, who continued speaking in his trembling voice while tears glistened in his eyes:

"Brothers, my son 'Abdallah is a real jewel. All the young men in the Juaifer Quarter speak well of him. My jewel of a son, 'Abdallah, has been arrested by the government, on no charge other than that he went on strike at the factory . . . I went down on my knees to them! I kissed their hands and their feet so that they'd release him from prison, but no one paid attention to me! What shall I do, brothers? . . . What shall I do?"

A gloomy silence settled over the tavern. Whereupon the man added in a choking voice, "Do you sanction this injustice, brothers? Do you agree with it?"

"Damn this tyrannical government!" exclaimed one of the customers. "Damn whoever brought it into being!"

Confusion reigned in the tavern; from every direction curses were being poured on the government. Recalling his tyrannical boss, Hamdi found himself joining in the outpour, which afforded him deep satisfaction.

All of a sudden he was overwhelmed by a desire to see his wife and children. He rose to his feet, staggering, and left the tavern. As he came into contact with the outside air, he felt somewhat refreshed. Nevertheless, he felt a constant ringing in his ears and a sharp emptiness at the center of himself.

Walking along with quick steps, he felt as if fresh blood were coursing through his veins. The stars were shining like diamonds in the canopy of clear sky; the full moon was flooding the earth with silver light; and soft breezes were blowing gently, causing him to shiver slightly.

—Translated by: Olive Kenny and Thomas G. Ezzy

Burhan al-Khatib (1944)

Iraqi novelist and short-story writer Burhan al-Khatib was born in al-Musayyab in the old district of Babylon. He completed his secondary education in Hilla, then moved with his parents to Baghdad where he studied mechanical engineering and obtained a B.S. in 1967. In the same year his first short-story collection, *Steps to the Far Horizon*, appeared, followed in 1968 by his first novel, *Fog at Noon*. His short story "Honor" was published also in 1968, causing him to be taken to court because of its challenge to inherited social conventions. However, he was later exonerated. In 1968 al-Khatib also completed his novel *An Apartment in Abu Nuwas Street*, a narrative on the plight of the Kurds and their exposure to torture, and offered it to the cinema. By now it had become apparent that this young creative writer was an actual rebel against both social and political conventions, and he was advised to leave Iraq. He went to Moscow where he studied literature and received an M.A. in world literature in 1975, the same year, his novel *An Apartment in Abu Nuwas Street* appeared. He subsequently worked as a translator in Moscow while writing novels, short stories, and essays and publishing a second short-story collection, *The New Street*, in 1980. His love of freedom, however, caused him to clash with the Soviet system of government, and he was deported in 1986. He emigrated to Sweden in 1987 as a political refugee and founded the publishing house Orasia in Stockholm in 1991, where he published several of his novels: *Stars at Noon* (1991), *The Fall of Sparta* (1992), *A Baghdadi Night* (1993), *Fragrant Babylon* (1995), and *That Summer in Alexandria* (1998). His acclaimed novel, *Closed Gardens*, appeared in 2000. In his creative work al-Khatib explores Iraqi life within a universal framework, with some existential overtones. It is very clear that his basic struggle has been to escape the clutch of ideology and its constrictions on the individual, while attacking the cruelty and harshness of totalitarian regimes. He has become a Swedish citizen, but he keeps close contact with Arab literary and journalistic activities.

AUTUMN CLOUDS

She raised her voice, smiling. "What's that you said?" she shouted. "I can't understand a thing!" Another wave came, thrusting her away from him. He swam toward her, shouting and smiling too: "The sun. It'll burn your skin."

Her smile widened as she closed her eyes to avoid the drops of salt water flying from the surging waves. She shouted again, her voice almost lost amid the rough sea, "Talk in English, or French. I can't understand what you're saying." But the tiresome breaking waves balked all attempt at conversation. He came closer to her and put on a comic voice, pausing between each word and stressing each sound. "Come and let me put some cream on your back. You'll get sunburned—" As she listened to him, she looked toward the beach, where her family sat under an umbrella buffeted by the strong wind. The holidaymakers had mostly left the beach now. There were just a few left, laughing and running toward the sea, chasing one another, splashing one another with water, then going back to dry themselves and eat something, before running off to the sea once more.

Her lovely smile faltered a little. She shook her head, the waves caressing her. "Oh, no, no, thank you—" He spat the seawater spouting from his mouth.

"Look what the sun's done to my back," he said. He turned to let her see the black and red spots that covered his shoulders all the way to his neck. She waved her arms this way and that in the surging blue water. "I'm used to the sun," she told him. Her candid smile revealed a set of teeth like glistening pearls. She kept shooting glances back at the beach, trying to watch her family. Then she added, "Go a bit further off, then talk. I'm afraid my father might spot us." He too looked toward the beach, where the gale was blowing empty bags and torn newspapers in all directions. "Curse this wind," he said. "The beach is almost empty." She went on smiling her lovely smile, as the wave pulled her back and forth. "I can't understand what you say. Are you Lebanese?" Her bathing cap was pistachio-colored, and she had thin rosy lips.

"No, I'm Iraqi."

"Do you live here or are you on holiday?"

"I've been sent by the government, to do some training at a plant in Alexandria." Her arms were slim and bronzed, her smile truly beautiful. It washed away heartache, like spring rain falling gently on someone plunged in anxiety.

"What kind of training are you doing?" There was beauty in the way she asked her question. Without her the sea seemed meaningless, the waves to be without purpose.

"Mechanical engineering," he answered. Her laughter, her looks, the way she danced in the water. It was all quite entrancing.

"Really? My father's a mechanical engineer too." The waves became calmer, friendlier, and filled with harmony. Nothing meant anything, apart from those eyes of hers.

"I like these signs of fate," he said. "Why don't you go with me to the beach, and I'll put some cream on your back. This sun really will hurt you." She gazed once more toward the beach. The few people scattered there began coming together as the wind blew colder, and some of them even started putting on their clothes. They were smiling and shivering at once. The torn papers and bags flew about as if racing to reach some unknown goal. Umbrellas came down, people started hurrying away. Gray clouds began crawling from the direction of the sea, breaking up the blue sky. But still, from time to time, the sun shone out from behind the clouds. "It looks as if they might be getting ready to leave," she said.

"Where do you live?" he asked.

"Twenty kilometers from Alexandria. Near the plant." She was still looking at the beach.

"They're going to leave," she said, disappointment in her voice.

"I hope I'll see you again." The question left her confused.

"I don't know."

"Shall I give you my phone number in Alexandria?"

"Write it down."

"Just memorize it." Her hazel eyes squinted as she looked toward the beach. Then she said, in a crushed tone: "They're getting ready to go." "Six, one, six—"

"Write it down," she broke in. "I'm bound to forget it."

"Where am I going to find pen and paper here on this beach?"

"I have to go. They're waving to me." The wind blew ever harder, playing roughly with the waves, which broke on to the beach with a mournful sound.

The coastguards blew their whistles to announce the end of swimming for the day, that it would be dangerous to stay any longer in the water. Black flags were hoisted along the line of the beach. She moved away from him, tender emotion evident in her eyes. There was a heavy silence, for all the crashing sea. The heavy silence between them awaited a word, sad or happy, a goodbye or an arrangement to meet again very soon, but their lips were unable to utter a word. At last he said, in a dry voice, "I'll try and find a piece of paper and a pen—"

Her look shifting between him and the beach, she carefully entered the water, the waves playing on her slim body. "Don't give me the paper in front of my family."

A shaft of sun pierced the clouds, breaking on the water drops blown from the far-off waves, then turned to a lovely rainbow, as though a ladder were joining the sea to the sky. She was standing on the beach now, apart from him, framed against a gray gloomy sky.

"I don't know. Write it down and wait for me over there." She pointed her slim hand toward the boats that had been plying for hire. A wave rushed into her footmarks, as if the sea wanted her back in its raging arms. He gazed at her, for some time. The cold wind began blowing once more, carrying his soul above the people, the sea, and the white sands. Then he rushed, like a happy child, toward his clothes, his feet scattering sand on to his small bag, there alongside the great umbrella hopelessly fighting the wind. He looked in his bag for paper, in the pockets of his clothes for a pen, but found neither. He looked around. Where were all those torn newspapers and bags the wind had been blowing around just a little while before? Had paper, all of a sudden, turned into a rarity? He walked aimlessly, his feet sinking into the soft sand. Then he started running toward the brick wall that ran parallel to the long line of cabins facing the sea. He leaped over and started looking this way and that, as if scanning for a rescue ship on the skyline. But the torn bags and newspapers seemed to be in league against him. They'd simply vanished. He ran back to his place, foraged through his pockets, through the corners of his bag, but his hand just grabbed at emptiness. He got up and gazed at the sea where the waves, far off, looked like a school of poisoned fish, striving to come nearer the shore and lie down dead. Then he walked slowly over the soft sand, searching for a pistachio-colored cap among the heads gathered near the buffeted umbrella. That was her family, over there. They were moving quickly, collecting up their belongings, changing their clothes, leaping briskly around. Now the pistachio-colored cap would be visible, now it would vanish, just as the sun lay concealed behind the gray clouds, which were gathering and multiplying now, as if trying to block all light from streaming on to the sea. His eyes wandered over their heads the way a bird flies over a brook. And, as a splendid beam of light pierced the clouds, as it shone over the crashing waves to light up the far distance with shining joy, their eyes met. He smiled at her for a second. Then a fat woman drifted across and stood between them, blocking his view of her. The clouds returned, gathering up the spilled light, smothering the sea once more. The fat woman kept shouting with laughter. She moved heavily. Cigarette smoke hung over their heads, but the wind gusted it away as the woman, with her dark fingers, took the cigarette from between her lips. He went back to his place, searching for his own pack of cigarettes. He tried to light one, but the wind blew out one match after another. He sat there, gazing at the spent matches in his hand, his fingers using them to draw meaningless lines on the cigarette pack. The clouds gathered over his head. The sky seemed far off, the sun pale and imprisoned in the white frozen distance, beneath which the waves broke one on top of another, hurtling toward the beach as if eager to escape being trapped on the horizon. He lowered his head, staring at the pack of cigarettes, where his fingers with the spent matchstick had finished writing his phone number. Tearing the cover from the pack, he let his gaze take in the upturned boats and, behind them, the rough sea with its promise of mystery, of an unknown fate to all who sailed on it. Then he turned his eyes to the small group of her family, finally making ready to leave. He found her, and he saw the endless sea and the sad autumn clouds in her eyes. He beckoned to her to follow him, to where the boats were lying like small whales by the side of the sea. He went over himself, then watched from a distance, his teeth biting hard into his lower lip.

"Watch out, young man," a voice said. "Watch out—" He looked toward the sound and saw the coastguard tugging a small beached whale and setting it next to the upturned boats. Shocked, he gazed at the creature for a while, then asked the guard, "How did that get here?"

"Who knows?" the guard replied absently. "Maybe the sea didn't have room for it any more." Above, the sun shone dully behind barriers of cloud, as if smothered by its thick veil. It grew pale, as if all its light had bled away. As they left the beach, she looked over at him. Her look turned to a call, silent yet resounding, spreading to the far distance then fading away in the roar of the waves and the whisper of the wind. The sun vanished totally, behind the gray clouds. The sedan came and parked at the end of the sandy path that separated the huts overlooking the sea. He rushed over to her, his eyes speaking of a failed, infantile scheme, his hand firmly gripping the piece torn from the pack of cigarettes. Still, as the others carried their belongings to the car, she gazed at him in silent, senseless confusion. He approached the car, and she tried to come closer to him. Discreetly, he raised his hand toward her, but a masculine voice from the car told her to get in. Heavily, with disappointment, he let his hand drop. She looked out of the car window, and her clouded eyes almost let two tears fall. The engine roared into life, and the car pulled off, like some wounded animal. The wheels left two parallel lines on the sand, lines that went on as far as the asphalt road, with no hope of meeting. He stood for a while, his eyes following the back of the car as it drove further off. Then, slowly and carefully, he tore up the small piece of paper, letting it scatter in the wind like a flock of seagulls setting out on their journey.

—*Translated by Dina Bosio and Christopher Tingley*

Muhammad Khudayyir (b. 1940)

Short-story writer Muhammad Khudayyir is from Southern Iraq. He has worked as a schoolteacher in Basra and is a sophisticated, highly original writer of great descriptive power. His stories reflect a dense atmosphere of suspense and repressed emotions, and occasionally an existentialist gloom. He is also a fine critic of literature, something he undertakes not as a professional commitment but as a fulfillment of an inner need to express his original and often compelling views on literature. His short-story collections include *The Black Kingdom* (1972), *Forty-Five Degrees Centigrade* (1978), and *Vision of Autumn* (1995). His short critical discussion of the art of Arabic story-telling, *Bushra Khalfan: The New Tale* (1995), is a revelation in critical discovery and intuition.

CLOCKS LIKE HORSES

This meeting may take place. I will get my watch repaired and go out to the quays of the harbor; then at the end of the night I will return to the hotel and find him sleeping in my bed, his face turned to the wall, having hung his red turban on the clothes hook.

Till today I still own a collection of old watches. I came by them from an uncle of mine who used to be a sailor on the ships of the Andrew Weir company, old pocket watches with chains and silver-plated cases, all contained in a small wooden box in purses of shiny blue cloth. While my interest in them has of late waned, I had as a schoolboy been fascinated by them. I would take them out of their blue purses and scrutinize their workings in an attempt to discover something about them that would transcend time stuffed like old cotton in a small cushion, as I had recorded one day in my diary.

One day during the spring school holidays I was minded to remove one of these watches from its box and to put it into the pocket of my black suit, attaching its chain to the buttonholes of my waistcoat. For a long time I wandered round the chicken market before seating myself at a café. The waiter came and asked me the time. I calmly took the watch out of its blue purse. My watch was incapable of telling the time, like the other watches in the box, nothing in it worked except the spring of the case, which was no sooner pressed than it flicked open revealing a pure white dial and two hands that stood pointing to two of the Roman numerals on the face. Before I could inform him that the watch was not working, the waiter had bent down and pulled the short chain toward him; having looked attentively at the watch, he closed its case, on which was engraved a sailing ship within a frame of foreign writing. Then, giving it back to me, he stood up straight.

"How did you get hold of it?"

"I inherited it from a relative of mine."

I returned the watch to its place.

"Was your relative a sailor?"

"Yes."

"Only three or four of the famous sailors are still alive."

"My relative was called Mughamis."

"Mughamis? I don't know him."

"He wouldn't settle in one place. He died in Bahrain."

"That's sailors for you! Do you remember another sailor called Marzouk? Since putting ashore for the last time he has been living in Fao. He opened a shop there for repairing watches, having learned the craft from the Portuguese. He alone would be able to repair an old watch like yours."

I drank down the glass of tea and said to the waiter as I paid him, "Did you say he was living in Fao?"

"Yes, near the hotel."

The road to Fao is a muddy one, and I kept on putting off the journey until one sunny morning I took my place among the passengers in a bus that set off loaded with luggage. The passengers who sat opposite one another in the middle of the bus exchanged no words except for general remarks about journeying in winter, about how warm this winter was, and other comments about the holes in the road. At the moment they stopped talking, I took out my watch. Their eyes became fixed on it, but no one asked me about it or asked the time. Then we began to avoid looking at each other and transferred our attentions to the vast open countryside and to the distant screen of date palms in the direction of the east that kept our vehicle company and hid the villages along the Shatt al-'Arab.

We arrived at noon and one of them showed me to the hotel that lies at the intersection of straight roads and looks onto a square in the middle of which is a round fenced garden. The hotel consisted of two low stories, while the balcony that overlooked the square was so low that anyone in the street could have climbed up onto it. I, who cannot bear the smell of hotels, or the heavy, humid shade in their hallways in daytime, hastened to call out to the owners. When I repeated my call, a boy looked down from a door at the side and said, "Do you want to sleep here?"

"Have you a place?" I said.

The boy went into the room and from it there emerged a man whom I asked for a room with a balcony. The boy who was showing me the way informed me that the hotel would be empty by day and packed at night. Just as the stairway was the shortest of stairways and the balcony the lowest of balconies, my room was the smallest and contained a solitary bed, but the sun entered it from the balcony. I threw my bag onto the bed and the boy sat down beside me. "The doors are all without locks," said the boy. "Why should we lock them?—the travelers only stay for one night."

Then he leaned towards me and whispered, "Are you Indian?"

This idea came as a surprise to me. The boy himself was more likely to be Indian with his dark complexion, thick brilliantined hair, and sparkling eyes. I whispered to him, "Did they tell you that Basra used to be called the brothel of India and that the Indian invaders in the British army, who came down to the land of Fao first of all, desired no other women except those of Basra?"

The boy ignored my cryptic reference to the mixing of passions and blending of races and asked, if I wasn't Indian, where did I live?

"I've come from Ashar," I told him, "on a visit to the watchmaker. Would you direct me to him?"

"Perhaps you mean the old man who has many clocks in his house," said the boy.

"Yes, that must be he," I said.

"He's not far from the hotel," he said. "He lives alone with his daughter and never leaves the house."

The boy brought us lunch from a restaurant, and we sat on the bed to eat, and he told me about the man I had seen downstairs: "He's not the owner of the hotel, just a permanent guest."

Then, with his mouth full of food, he whispered, "He's got a pistol."

"You know a lot of things, O Indian," I said, also speaking in a whisper.

He protested that he wasn't Indian but was from Hasa. He had a father who worked on the ships that transported dates from Basra to the coastal towns of the Gulf and India.

The boy took me to the watchmaker, leaving me in front of the door of his house. A gap made by a slab of stone that had been removed from its place in the upper frieze of the door made this entrance unforgettable. One day, in tropical years, there had stopped near where I was a sailor shaky with sickness, or some Sikh soldier shackled with lust, and he looked at the slab of stone on which was engraved some date or phrase, before continuing on his unknown journey. And after those two there perhaps came some foreign archaeologist whose boat had been obstructed by the silt and who had put up in the town till the water rose, and his curiosity for things eastern had been drawn to the curves of the writing on the slab of stone and he had torn it out and carried it off with him to his boat. Now I, likewise, was in front of this gateway to the sea.

On the boy's advice I did not hesitate to push open the door and enter into what looked like a portico that the sun penetrated through apertures near the ceiling and in which I was confronted by hidden and persistent ticking sounds and a garrulous ringing that issued from the pendulums and hammers of large clocks, the type that strike the hours, ranged along the two sides of the portico. As I proceeded, one or more clocks struck at the same time. All the clocks were similar in size, in the great age of the wood of their frames, and in the shape of their round dials, their Roman numerals, and their delicate arrowlike hands—except that these hands were pointed to different times.

I had to follow the slight curve of the portico to come unexpectedly upon the last of the great sailors in his den, sitting behind a large table on which was heaped the wreckage of clocks. He was occupied with taking the movements of a clock to pieces under the light of a shaded lamp hanging down from the ceiling at a height close to his frail, white-haired head. He glanced toward me from one naked eye and from another on which a magnifying glass had been fixed, then went back to disassembling the movements piece by piece. The short glance was sufficient to link this iron face with the nuts, cogwheels, and hands of the movements of the many clocks hanging on the walls and thrown into corners under dust and rust. Clocks that didn't work and others that did, the biggest of them being a clock on the wall above the watchmaker's head, which was, to be precise, the movement of a large grandfather clock made of brass, the dial of which had been removed and that had been divested of its cabinet so that time manifested itself in it naked and shining, sweeping along on its serrated cogwheels in a regular mechanical sequence: from the rotation of the spring to the pendulum that swung harmoniously to and fro and ended in the slow, tremulous, imperceptible movement of the hands. When the cogwheels had taken the hands along a set distance of time's journey, the striking cogwheel would move and raise the hammer. I had not previously seen a naked, throbbing clock, and thus I became mesmerized by the regular throbbing that synchronized with the swinging motion of the pendulum and with the movement of the cogwheels of various diameters. I started at the sound of the hammer falling against the bell; the gallery rang with three strokes whose reverberations took a long time to die away, while the other clocks went on, behind the glass of their cabinets, with their incessant ticking.

The watchmaker raised his head and asked me if the large clock above his head had struck three times.

Then, immersing himself in taking the mechanism to pieces, he said, "Like horses; like horses running on the ocean bed."

A clock in the portico struck six times and he said, "Did one of them strike six times? It's six in America. They're getting up now, while the sun is setting in Burma."

Then the room was filled again with noisy reverberations. "Did it strike seven? It's nighttime in Indonesia. Did you make out the last twelve strokes? They are fast asleep in the furthest west of the world. After some hours the sun will rise in the furthest east. What time is it? Three? That's our time, here near the Gulf."

One clock began striking on its own. After a while the chimes blended with the tolling of other clocks as hammers coincided in falling upon bells, and others landed halfway between the times of striking, and yet others fell between these, so that the chimes hurried in pursuit of one another in a confused scale. Then, one after another, the hammers became still, the chimes growing further apart, till a solitary clock remained, the last clock that had not discharged all its time, letting it trickle out now in a separate, high-pitched reverberation.

He was holding my watch in his grasp. "Several clocks might strike together," he said, "strike as the fancy takes them. I haven't liked to set my clocks to the same time. I have assigned my daughter the task of merely winding them up. They compete with one another like horses. I have clocks that I bought from people who looted them from the houses of Turkish employees who left them as they hurried away after the fall of Basra. I also got hold of clocks that were left behind later on by the Jews who emigrated. Friends of mine, the skippers of ships, who would come to visit me here, would sell me clocks of European manufacture. Do you see the clock over there in the passageway? It was in the house of the Turkish commander of the garrison of Fao's fortress."

I saw the gleam of the quick-swinging pendulum behind glass in the darkness of the cabinets of the clocks in the portico. Then I asked him about my watch. "Your watch? It's a rare one. They're no longer made. I haven't handled such a watch for a long time. I'm not sure about it but I'll take it to pieces. Take a stroll round and come back here at night."

That was what I'd actually intended to do. I would return before night. The clocks bade me farewell with successive chimes. Four chimes in Fao: seven P.M. in the swarming streets of Calcutta. Four chimes: eight A.M. in the jungles of Buenos Aires . . . Outside the den the clamor had ceased, also the smell of engine oil and of old wood.

I returned at sunset. I had spent the time visiting the old barracks that had been the home of the British army of occupation, then I had sat in a café near the fish market.

I didn't find the watchmaker in his former place, but presently I noticed a vast empty cabinet moved alongside a gap between the clocks. The watchmaker was in an open courtyard before an instrument made up of clay vessels, which I guessed to be a type of water clock. When he saw me, he called out, "Come here. Come, I'll show you something."

I approached the vessels hanging on a cross-beam: from them water dripped into a vessel hanging on another, lower cross-beam; the water then flowed onto a metal plate on the ground, in which there was a gauge for measuring the height of the water.

"A water clock?"

"Have you seen one like it?"

"I've read about them. They were the invention of people of old."

"The Persians call them *bingan*."

"I don't believe it tells the right time."

"No, it doesn't, it reckons only twenty hours to the day. According to its reckoning I'm 108 years old instead of 90, and it is 78 years since the British entered Basra instead of 60. I learnt how to make it from a Muscati sailor who had one like it in his house on the coast."

I followed him to the den, turning to two locked doors in the small courtyard on which darkness had descended. He returned the empty clock-cabinet to its place and seated himself in his chair. His many clothes lessened his appearance of senility; he was lost under his garments, one over another and yet another over them, his head inside a vast tarbush.

"I've heard you spent a life time at sea."

"Yes. It's not surprising that our lives are always linked to water. I was on one of the British India ships as a syce with an English trader dealing in horses."

He toyed with the remnants of the watches in front of him, then said, "He used to call himself by an Arabic name. We would call him Surour Saheb. He used to buy Nejdi horses from the rural areas of the south and they would then be shipped to Bombay where they would be collected up and sent to the racecourses in England. Fifteen days on end at sea, except that we would make stops at the Gulf ports. We would stop for some days in Muscat. When there were strong winds against us, we would spend a month at sea. The captains, the cooks, and the pilots were Indians, while the others, seamen and syces, were from Muscat, Hasa, and Bahrain; the rest were from the islands of the Indian Ocean. We would have with us divers from Kuwait. I remember their small dark bodies and plaited hair as they washed down the horses on the shore or led them to the ship. I was the youngest syce. I began my first sea journey at the age of twelve. I joined the ship with my father who was an assistant to the captain and responsible for looking after the stores and equipment. There were three of us, counting my father, who would sleep in the storeroom among the sacks and barrels of tar, the fish oil, ropes, and dried fish, on beds made up of coconut fibers."

"Did you make a lot?"

"Us? We didn't make much. The trader did. Each horse would fetch eight hundred rupees in Bombay, and when we had reached Bengal it would fetch fifteen hundred rupees. On our return to Basra we would receive our wages for having looked after the horses. Some of us would buy goods from India and sell them on our return journey wherever we put in: cloth, spices, rice, sugar, perfumes, and wood, and sometimes peacocks and monkeys."

"Did you employ horses in the war?"

"I myself didn't take part in the war. Of course they used them. When the Turks prevented us from trading with them because they needed them for the army, we moved to the other side of the river. We had a corral and a caravanserai for sleeping in at Khorramshahr. From there we began to smuggle out the horses far from the clutches of the Turkish customs men. On the night when we'd be traveling we'd feed and water the horses well, and at dawn we'd proceed to the corral and each syce would lead out his horse. As for me, I was required to look after the transportation of the provisions and fodder; other boys who were slightly older than me were put in charge of the transportation of the water, the ropes, the chains, and other equipment. The corral was close to the shore, but the horses would make a lot of noise and stir up dust when they were being pulled along by the reins to the ship that would lie at the end of an anchorage stretching out to it from the shore. The ship would rock and tiny bits of straw would become stuck on top of our heads, while the syces would call the horses by their names, telling them to keep quiet, until they finished tying them up in their places. It was no easy matter, for during the journey the waves, or the calm of the invisible sea, would excite one of the horses or would make it ill, so that its syce would have to spend the night with it, watching over it and keeping it company. As we lay in our sleeping quarters we would hear the syce reassuring his horse with some such phrase as, "Calm down. Calm down, my Precious Love. The grass over there is better." However, this horse, whose name was Precious Love, died somewhere near Aden. At dawn the sailors took it up and consigned it to the waves. It was a misty morning and I was carrying a lantern, and I heard the great carcass hitting the water, though without seeing it; I did, though, see its syce's face close to me—he would be returning from his voyage without any earnings.

Two or three clocks happened to chime together. I said to him, "Used you to put in to Muscat?"

"Yes. Did I tell you about our host in Muscat? His wooden house was on the shore of a small bay, opposite an old stone fortress on the other side. We would set out for his house by boat. By birth he was a highlander, coming from the tribes in the mountains facing the bay. He was also a sorcerer. He was a close friend of Surour Saheb, supplying him with a type of ointment the Muscati used to prepare from mountain herbs, which the Englishman would no sooner smear on his face than it turned a dark green and would gleam in the lamplight like a wave among rocks. In exchange for this the Muscati would get tobacco from him. I didn't join them in smoking, but I was fond of chewing a type of *olibanum* that was to be found extensively in the markets of the coast. I would climb up onto a high place in the room, which had been made as a permanent bed, and would watch them puffing out the smoke from the *narghiles* into the air as they lay relaxing round the fire, having removed their dagger belts and placed them in front of them alongside their colored turbans. Their beards would be plunged in the smoke, and the rings would glitter in their ears under the combed locks of hair whenever they turned toward the merchant, lost in thought. The merchant, relaxing on feather cushions, would be wearing brightly colored trousers of Indian cloth and would be wrapped in an 'aba of Kashmir wool; as for his silk turban, he would, like the sailors, have placed it in front of him beside his pistol."

"Did you say that the Muscati was a sorcerer?"

"He had a basket of snakes in which he would lay one of the sailors, then bring him out alive. His sparse body would be swallowed in his lustrous flowing robes, as was his small head in his saffron-colored turban with the tassels. We were appalled at his repulsive greed for food, for he would eat a whole basketful of dates during a night and would drink enough water to provide for ten horses. He was amazing, quite remarkable; he would perform bizarre acts: swallowing a puff from his *narghile*, he would after awhile begin to release the smoke from his mouth and nose for five consecutive minutes. You should have seen his stony face, with the clouds of smoke floating against it like serpents that jumped and danced. He was married to seven women for whom he had dug out, in the foot of the mountain, rooms that overlooked the bay. No shyness prevented him from disclosing their fabulous names: Mountain Flower, Daylight Sun, Sea Pearl, Morning Star. He was a storehouse of spicy stories and tales of strange travels, and we would draw inspiration from him for names for our horses. At the end of the night he would leave us sleeping and would climb up the mountain. At the end of one of our trips we stayed as his guests for seven nights, during which time men from the Muscati's tribe visited us to have a smoke; they would talk very little and would look with distaste at the merchant and would then leave quietly with their antiquated rifles.

"Our supper would consist of spiced rice and grilled meat or fish; they would give us a sweet sherbet to drink in brass cups. As for the almond-filled halvah of Muscat that melts in the mouth, even the bitter coffee could not disperse its scented taste. In the morning he would return and give us some sherbet to drink that would settle our stomachs, suffering from the night's food and drink, and would disperse the tobacco fumes from the sailors' heads."

An outburst of clocks striking prevented him from enlarging further, but he did not wait for the sound to stop. "On the final night of our journey he overdid his tricks in quite a frightening manner. While the syces would seek help from his magic in treating their sick horses, they were afraid nonetheless that the evil effects of his magic would spread and take the lives of these horses. And thus it was that a violent wind drove our ship onto a rock at the entrance to the bay and smashed it. Some of us escaped drowning, but the sorcerer of Muscat was not among them. He was traveling with the ship on his way to get married to a woman from Bombay, but the high waves choked his shrieks and eliminated his magic."

"And the horses?"

"They fought the waves desperately. They were swimming in the direction of the rocky shore, horses battling against the white horses of the waves. All of them were drowned. That was my last journey in the horse ships. After that, in the few years that preceded the war, I worked on the mail ships."

He made a great effort to remember and express himself. "In Bahrain I married a woman who bore me three daughters whom I gave in marriage to sons of the sea. I stayed on there with the boat builders until after the war. Then, in the thirties I returned to Basra and bought the clocks and settled in Fao, marrying a woman from here."

"You are one of the few sailors who are still alive today."

He asked me where I lived, and I told him that I had put up at the hotel. He said, "A friend of mine used to live in it. I don't know if he's still alive—for twenty years I haven't left my house."

Then searching among the fragments of watches, he asked me in surprise, "Did you come to Fao just because of the watch?"

I answered him that there were some towns one had to go to. He handed me my watch. It was working. Before placing it in my hand he scrutinized its cover, on which had been engraved a ship with a triangular sail, which he said was of the type known as *sunbuk*.

I opened the cover. The hands were making their slow way round. The palms of my hand closed down on the watch, and we listened to the sea echoing in the clocks of the den. The slender legs of horses running the streets of the clock faces are abducted in the glass of the large grandfather clocks. The clocks tick and strike: resounding hooves, chimes driven forward like waves. A chime: the friction of chains and ropes against wet wood. Two chimes: the dropping of the anchor into the blue abyss. Three: the call of the rocks. Four: the storm blowing

up. Five: the neighing of the horses. Six . . . seven . . . eight . . . nine . . . ten . . .
eleven . . . twelve . . .

This winding lane is not large enough to allow a lorry to pass, but it lets in
a heavy damp night and sailors leading their horses, and a man dizzy from sea-
sickness, still holding in his grasp a pocket watch and making an effort to avoid
the water and the gentle sloping of the lane and the way the walls curve round.
The bends increase with the thickening darkness and the silence. Light seeps
through from the coming bend, causing me to quicken my step. In its seeping
through and the might of its radiation it seems to be marching against the wall,
carving into the damp brickwork folds of skins and crumpled faces that are the
masks of seamen and traders from different races who have passed by here before
me and are to be distinguished only by their headgear: the bedouin of Nejd and
the rural areas of the south by the *kufiyya* and *igal,* the Iraqi effendis of the towns
by the *sidara;* the Persians by the black tarbushes made of goat skin; the Ottoman officers, soldiers, and government employees by their tasseled tarbushes; the
Indians by their red turbans; the Jews by flat red tarbushes; the monks and missionaries by their black head coverings; the European sea captains by their naval
caps; the explorers in disguise. . . . They rushed out toward the rustling noise
coming from behind the last bend, the eerie rumbling, the bated restlessness of
the waves below the high balustrades. . . . Then, here are Fao's quays, the lamps
leading its wooden bridges along the water for a distance; in the spaces between
them boats are anchored one alongside another, their lights swaying; there also
is a freighter with its lights on, anchored between the two middle berths. It was
possible for me to make out in the middle of the river scattered floating lights. I
didn't go very close to the quay installations but contented myself with standing
in front of the dark, bare extension of the river. To my surprise, a man who was
perhaps working as a watchman or worker on the quays approached me and
asked me for the time. Eleven.

On my return to the hotel I took a different road, passing by the closed shops.
I was extremely alert. The light will be shining brightly in the hotel vestibule.
The oil stove will be in the middle of it, and to one side of the vestibule will
be baggage, suitcases, a water-cooling box, and a cupboard. Seated on the bench
will be a man who is dozing, his cigarette forgotten between his fingers. It will
happen that I shall approach the door of my room, open the door, and find him
sleeping in my bed; he will be turned to the wall, having hung his red turban
on the clothes hook.

—Translated by Denys Johnson-Davies

Ibrahim al-Koni (b. 1948)

Libyan novelist and short-story writer Ibrahim al-Koni was born in the
Libyan oasis of Ghadamis in the Northern Sahara. After studying world
literature at the Gorky Institute in Moscow, he worked first as a correspon-

dent for the Libyan News Agency in Moscow, then as a delegate to the Libyan-Polish Friendship Committee when he became editor of its journal *Friendship*, published in Polish in Warsaw. Since then he has been a cultural counselor at the Libyan embassies in Warsaw, Moscow, and Berne, Switzerland. A prolific writer, his chief subject is the desert, with its flora and fauna, with a special concentration on the life of the Touareg tribes from which he sprang. In his work the representative members of these somewhat neglected peoples (the chief, the soothsayer, the dervish, the religious leader, etc.) are transformed into symbolic figures of profound resonance, while his style, in which mystical feeling merges with a genuine love of freedom, provides fresh insight not only into the essential qualities of desert life (which also form the basis of the nobility of old Arab culture) but also into the innate capacity of the human mind and heart to find timeless wisdom under even the most primitive and impoverished conditions. His fiction includes the short-story collection *The Autumn of the Dervish* (1994), as well as many novels, including *Gold Ore* (1990) and *The Bleeding of the Stone* (1990), the last translated by PROTA, and his major two-volume work *The Magi* (1990). He is working on a multivolume novel entitled *The Wizards*.

THE PACT

If any man offend not in word, the same is a perfect man, and able also to bridle the whole body. Behold, we put bits in the horses' mouths, that they may obey us; and we turn about their whole body. Behold also the ships, which though they be so great, and are driven of fierce winds, yet are they turned about with a very small helm, whithersoever the governor listeth. Even so the tongue is a little member, and boasteth great things. Behold, how great a matter a little fire kindleth! And the tongue is a fire, a world of iniquity: so is the tongue among our members, that it defileth the whole body, and setteth on fire the course of nature; and it is set on fire of hell. For every kind of beasts, and of birds, and of serpents, and of things in the sea, is tamed, and hath been tamed of mankind: but the tongue can no man tame; it is an unruly evil, full of deadly poison.

—*James 3:2–8*

The chief was afflicted with a dreadful disease. Blisters ate away at him, oozing with a fetid smell, and worms crawled everywhere on his body, so that the tribe despaired of his recovery and the wise men hurried off to the foot of the mountain and began collecting stones for his burial. Yet the chief himself had not given way to despair. Still, unflinchingly, he fought the wretched worms, scanning the wide horizon with the smile of one expecting a messenger.

The messenger did not delay. He came to him at night, after the wise men had departed, and said, "Because you did not rail against fate and the worms struck no fear in you, because you smiled into the darkness, and found only joy when others abandoned you, I have come bearing an ample reward from my Master. Rejoice in your recovery, which the everlasting law has made the portion of the brave."

The phantom rose then and, drawing near the chief's bed, leaned over him and uttered his words of prophecy: "From this day on you will never again see the face of darkness, nor will harm ever befall you, so long as you remain faithful to the pact."

Fighting to conquer the weakness of his disease, the chief said, "The pact?"

"I shall set a seal on your head," the messenger answered, "for it is my Master's law that none be granted eternal life without a sign to mark him out from other mortal creatures. Rejoice in the everlasting life that is yours, but preserve the pact in your heart and take care never to reveal its secret."

"And what secret," the chief murmured, "is that?"

The messenger thrust his hand into his sleeve and produced an object of metal with a tapering tip like a knife's. Then, uncovering the chief's face,[1] and murmuring a strange incantation, he inscribed secret symbols on his head and brought the tapering object down on the head's right side, so that the chief winced with the pain. Then he brought the object down on the head's left side, and again the chief winced with the pain. "Take care," the messenger said, "that no one's eye fall on the seal of the pact. Know that the eye was fashioned to see; and that, having once seen, it will dispatch the knowledge to the tongue. Should the knowledge reach the tongue, the secret will be out, and the news broadcast everywhere. Take the utmost care, then, for my Master has no mercy on those who betray the pact." And with that the messenger vanished.

The tribe rejoiced at the chief's recovery, yet rejoicing was not deemed sufficient; for the wise men said that if such a man, once diseased and eaten away by worms, had escaped burial with his forebears at the rounded mountain foot and returned to the wide desert, then the law should accord him privileged rights over maidenhead. They raced their camels accordingly, and sang the *shajan muwwals,* then seized and brought to his chamber the loveliest, most pleasing, and accomplished virgin of the tribe, a maiden surpassingly tall, with full buttocks, thick braids, fair skin, and kohled black eyes, able to speak the ancient language of the forebears and to repeat poems and songs and riddles. The chief took delight in the lovely body and still greater delight in the poems, and the eloquent speech, and the wondrous immemorial *Aanhi.* He knew the truth then of the words spoken by the woman who had placed her hand in his by night and had said, "Her form is a joy to the eye, her tongue a joy to the ear. Take her, for she is yours." He took her by the wrist and, when the others had departed, spoke with her and discovered her qualities. But it was close to dawn before he discovered the sign.

---

1. Tuareg men habitually cover their faces.

It was not he indeed who discovered it first, but the lovely maiden, who, sporting with him, found her hands touching two horns on his head. Putting his own hands to his head, he found something hard grown there in the place of the right seal; and, feeling on the other side, found the same hard growth where the left seal had been set. Then it was that he remembered the pact, and abjured her, by the law handed down from the forebears, not to reveal the secret. At that the maiden smiled scornfully, telling him only a foolish woman would chatter about the sacred matters of the bedchamber and giving many wise instances of marriages destroyed by the tongue. Yet the chief, whose knowledge of women was deep and whose life was now so full of joy, could not rest secure. Accordingly, he hatched a ruse to protect the secret of the sign by stifling it in the mouth of the lovely maiden. As the first rays of dawn appeared, she went out to answer nature's call, and he came after her, telling her he wished to protect her from the assaults of the jinn but saying within himself, "I shall accompany her and so be sure she will not reveal my secret to any phantom she might meet."

When they had descended into a hollow, he stood to one side while the maiden disappeared among the bushes that grew thickly there. She dug a hole among the reeds, then knelt over it and bit her tongue fiercely, till the blood poured out; then she covered her mouth with her hand, so that the blood soiled her elegant fingers. Her eyes bulging out, she fought with a thing that was ready to burst in her throat, a thing seeking desperately to issue into the world as she strove with all her strength to force it back. At last it was victorious and, falling to the ground, she turned her face to the earth and rid herself of her burden, crying, "Aawkalgh Aamghaar Ila Iskawn!"[2]

Relieved at this, she returned to her husband, who went back with her to the tent. Yet still he felt no safety in the assurance she had given him, for he had known women too long. Accordingly he unsheathed his sword. "Because you have learned my secret," he told her, "you must choose one of two things: either I must kill you or I must cut out your tongue." The lovely maiden uttered a long wail, then, raising her head, spoke with the courage worthy of a lovely woman versed in the learning of the forebears. "Far better to kill me," she replied, "than to cut out my tongue. For what good shall I have in life if I cannot compete in the learning of our tribe, cannot match myself with other women in the recital of verse, and sing the *shajan* songs?" But the chief, so long versed in the ways of beautiful maidens, knowing from ancient wisdom that the wishes they expressed were not to be countenanced, had no mind to go against the ancient wisdom that day. And so he cut out his lovely wife's tongue, believing his secret now to be firm against the tongue's evil, little knowing how, when he left his wife to bow her head among the reeds, she had already rid herself of the secret she could not keep for a single hour.

---

2. "Woe is me, the chief has horns!"

The rains came, filling the desert brim full. The hollows flowed with water, and the reed bed too had its portion; and soon the herdsmen heard the song the reeds were sending out on the winds: "Aawkalgh Aamghaar Ila Iskawn!"

The herdsmen repeated the song, and at length it reached the camp, where the women poets sang it; and then the boys received it from their lips, till at last the whole tribe had taken it up.

The messenger came by night to the chief's tent and for a long time he squatted, huddled, by the entrance. The chief said nothing, and both listened to the silence. A little before the first rays of dawn, the phantom rose and drew near the chief. Then, withdrawing a strange object of metal from within his cloak, he uncovered the chief's face and passed the object first over the left side of his head, then over the right side. And with that the messenger vanished into the dawn shadows.

When the sun rose, the wise men found the chief with his head resting on the pillow, scanning the horizon with a gaze none could interpret. He was dead. They cast their eyes over his head, seeking the horns; and great was their wonder when they found none.

—Translated by May Jayyusi and Christopher Tingley

Musa Kraidi (b. 1940)

Born in Najaf, Iraqi short-story writer Musa Kraidi studied at the University of Baghdad and has since been a civil servant, holding a responsible position at the Ministry of Information in Baghdad. His short stories are based mainly on the experience of life in his country and display an awareness of the sociopolitical changes of the second half of the twentieth century. He has published several collections of short stories: *Voices in the City* (1968), *Footsteps of the Traveler Toward Death* (1970), and *Half-Lit Windows* (1979).

ONE SUMMER

He hesitated for a moment, noises pouring in at him from all sides, between the pavement and the square that was wheeling dizzily around before him. As he crossed over, he caught glimpses of the many cars, trucks, and motorcycles that all rushed by him at once, then disappeared into the entrance of one of the nearby streets.

He hurried by the water jugs perched in the square like closed fists. Suddenly his vision blurred. The light of his inner vision was now traveling far, away from the surrounding din; it settled on a bench, or a small garden at noon, or a fountain glittering alone in a corner of the capital. He smiled faintly as he gazed at the vehicles' wheels wafting away like floating straw on the dark surface of the water . . .

It was no surprise to Muhsin al-Shatri that he could hear the faint bells of prayer as his oldest sister recited her supplications, her fingers ceaselessly count-ing the beads of her *sabha*. And, in the background, the murmurs of his aunt, who was praying for his safe return from his journey ... She had asked him not to forget to kiss the cheeks of his sick father, her brother, whom she always remembered; he had grown old before his time and had not seen life in all its vast possibilities.

Of course, she herself had grown prematurely old, even before he had, but she had surrendered to her fate and stayed at home.

Muhsin al-Shatri had hidden from them the telegram he had received the day before. The prospect of his home plunged into deep mourning at that mo-ment had been too much for him to bear. He knew too well that this would have been the source of an additional kind of worry for him.

It occurred to him that his father's departure, and later his own, would in no way change the roundness of the sunflower as it turned toward the light; nor would it make the white lilies stop giving off their fragrance.

He saw now the waters of the Tigris from afar, flowing away, and he remem-bered the words of the telegram: "Come immediately. Your father is critically ill."

He pushed toward the crowd, hearing the echoes of his sick father's voice mingled with those of the babble around him. He was looking for transporta-tion. The heat was less than it had been in the morning, but the breezes were stronger. The sun fixed itself on his head like a flaming serpent. Whenever he tried to look closely at people, he found that the sight of the crowd moving under a hot, aluminum summer sky aroused his anxiety and vigilance, even though this had been a familiar sight to him for the past ten years or more. Suddenly he was seized by a strong desire to return home.

But if he did, what would he tell his sister and aunt?

He remembered now his aged father, eyes like two dark lumps of salt, eye-brows like white arches that sloped slightly downward over the two small stars of his eyes now embedded in their deep, lonely sockets. The face had not yet become completely worn, although some of its muscles had shriveled and hard-ened, looking like scars, discolored ...

He had not been surprised, at how pale and lifeless his father's face had looked the last time he'd seen it. His hand, when it touched the two arms stretched out on the bed, had not been able to stimulate one muscle in that face. The bed, in its half-lit corner, stood under a stone shelf that held a water jug, a cup, and several small bottles. It overlooked a square courtyard the size of the room that had been occupied for years by the sick man. When the window was closed, the sun's rays were refracted inside the room, like multicolored blotches of ink, through four round panes fixed in a faded black frame. The wings of flies glinted like mercury as they buzzed through the dust that lay thickly over the decaying wood.

In the space assigned for waiting passengers, he leaned on a wooden pole, rest-ing his body, now drenched in sweat, after having spent a whole hour looking at the colors of the taxis that arrived at the station and those that disappeared quickly into the crowd. He felt dejected again and closed his eyes for a few moments, silently feeling the pain penetrate. He looked down at the ground and saw some wrinkled rinds and some dull-looking *esparto* fibers. When he raised his eyes, he did not see the low sky, which was screened by the humid summer dust. He stayed motionless, feeling acute pain, the sun piercing the skin of his scalp.

For half an hour or more he continued to suffer, like a Buddhist monk preparing his body to be burned. When a taxi suddenly did turn toward him, he saw four passengers get in even before it had stopped in its reserved place. He rushed up to them and became the fifth passenger.

Hardly conscious that he was sitting in the front seat, he paid scant attention to the beads of sweat he felt crawling like ants through the hairs of his chest. He did no more than open his shirt at the neck, welcoming the slap of hot air and wishing at the same time he could surrender to sleep as a fighter surrenders to death. But sleep was impossible, so long as his eyes were intoxicated with this heat . . .

When he turned his head toward the driver's wheel, he saw a huge lump of flesh perched behind it. Surprise lit his eyes, as if he were seeing such obesity for the first time. Al-Shatri exchanged a look with the driver.

The driver smiled. "You are no stranger to me."

"I knew you before you became fat," said Muhsin al-Shatri.

"I was truly thin . . . Yes!"

"That was ten years ago, or a little more."

"That's right . . . You *do* remember."

The car pulled off the main road and stopped at a gas station. Passengers grumbled, feeling the hot air. Once the tank was filled, the driver got in and drove quickly, crossing the last square of the city.

"You know me, then?" he resumed.

"And your father, the butcher."

"You must be al-Shatri, if my memory is correct."

"You have a good memory."

"We used to be friends . . . We also lived in the same alley, didn't we?"

Muhsin recalled the whole length of that alley: its bends, its dust, wet with rain; the mobile wagons, the horses of al-Husain[1] as they passed slowly by; the votive candles, the small lanterns that hung over the thresholds of the houses, which all resembled hollow caves . . . He remembered all that long stretch of film.

An incident, which had been buried deep in his memory, now sprang to mind. It concerned the Madman, who used to wrap his head in a green turban.

---

1. This is a reference to al-Husain ibn 'Ali, the grandson of the Prophet, who claimed the caliphate after the assassination of his father, 'Ali ibn Abi Talib, the fourth and last of the Orthodox caliphs. Al-Husain was defeated near Karbala' in Iraq by the army of the Umayyads and was killed by the victors. Every year the battle scene is reenacted with horses and knights in armor.

Not many had known him, but he became quite notorious as of the day he killed his sister for honor.

She had been a woman of sixty, famous for her piety and asceticism and good deeds, loved by her neighbors and known by all in the place. The Madman had just turned forty then, a strong man with firm features and a thick, hoarse voice. He stood in front of the door of the "cave"—the alley was long and dark—and called his sister. She heard him and thought that he needed something, so she crossed the threshold and peeked out, her head covered with her black veil to avoid the light outside and the eyes of passers-by, as she was not wearing her cloak. The Madman shot two fatal bullets at her, in rapid succession. A scream rang out, and the next moment a woman who had never spoken to a man in her life fell dead . . .

"You must have gotten married. Isn't that so?"

The driver answered quickly: "Yes, yes . . . Several years ago."

"Any children?"

"As many as the years of our marriage."

"Oh. A large number . . . "

"Are you trying to console me?"

"I?" Muhsin laughed, taking his friend to be joking.

He looked over at him and saw that his body was draped in a wide, grey *dashdasha,* full of stains. Because of the heat it had climbed up his body; clusters of black, goatlike hair covered his thighs and his fat legs. The other passengers seemed to be sleeping. The movement around was monotonous and the sun seemed to be sinking toward the horizon.

"I know that you work the Baghdad-Basra Highway. Isn't that so?"

"I've been working this road for three years. It's a good road."

"What do you mean by 'good'? Do you mean it has fewer accidents?"

"No. I mean it is profitable."

He relived the woman's death. He saw her moving in the alley, stretching her arms toward the sky. She had screamed before she fell down. Her black veil came untied. Her hair was tinted with henna. People gathered. Women shrieked. Blood covered the ground in the alley, forming a deep, crimson pool . . .

The news had spread in minutes, like an epidemic, and became the subject of people's conversations. The Madman gave himself up to the police at the city precinct after firing one shot into the air.

"Can you imagine that this car has carried almost"—the fat man paused to remember the number of corpses he had carried with him from the south over the past three years—"more than four hundred funerals?"

"Is that so?" Muhsin's eyes widened in surprise.

The driver seemed to brighten up. "Maybe more . . . I am not exaggerating!"

"Was this during the day or during the night?"

"We work day *and* night! You know . . . " How would *he* know? He went on, without smiling, " Reward is equal to the effort made in getting it, as they say . . . "

Muhsin was overcome by a feeling of alienation as he contemplated the roof of death over his head. He realized that the man whose flesh sagged loosely over the steering wheel was an undertaker par excellence. He noticed that the color of the sky was fading and that the eastern sky was darker now.

He forgot for a few minutes that he was Muhsin al-Shatri, a chemistry teacher for seven years, and became the driver himself, involved in carrying the dead on top of his car at night, binding the coffins with flaxen ropes connected to an iron net. The two sides of the coffin would protrude on each side of the car like two fixed phantoms and would stay there for hours . . .

For the first time, a violent terror seized Muhsin al-Shatri, and he feared he was about to faint with exhaustion. He felt dizzy and sensed a pressure inside his skull. With his left hand he pressed the front of his forehead, while with the other he fumbled for a pill for his headache. He noticed, from the corner of his eye, that his friend was going well over 120 kilometers an hour, but he said nothing. He feared that if he protested the driver might obstinately double his speed or accuse him of cowardice.

However, the other passengers were murmuring quietly as they sat in the rays of the sun, which shone red on the road ahead. Like an arrow, the car now passed a huge truck. Violently shaken, the passengers shouted out; a stream of indistinct words, which Muhsin understood to be a curse on all other drivers, came from the driver's lips. Al-Shatri thought that a crash with the vehicle would have been inevitable had it not been for his friend's skillful driving, which had saved them from certain death.

As he stopped at one of those rest stations where people sit to sip tea or take cold drinks, Abu Jabbar, the driver, suddenly gave a strong, conspicuous whistle, the way people in cinemas do, which drew the attention both of the passengers and of nearby bystanders. His whistle expressed the great wonder aroused in him by the sight of a girl standing next to a luxurious car. Ruefully, he contemplated her graceful form, and was stunned when he saw her blue eyes. Her silky blouse open at the neck, showed summer in bloom.

The fat man started walking slowly toward the cafe, while the passengers got out to eat and to drink tea.

"This is death, my dear Sir!" Abu Jabbar bleated out, like a trumpet blowing. Everyone laughed.

"And what is your opinion of death?" asked Muhsin al-Shatri.

The driver let out a short sigh, which he followed with a sound of disapproval and a shake of his head. His voice came out soft and effeminate, disproportionate to his huge size and sagging abdomen.

"I am stronger than death!" he said.

"Strange . . . "

"Do not be surprised if I tell you that death itself fears me."

"What an unknown lion you are in this world!"

"I am not brave, but I do not fear death!"

"Your heart must be something special!"

"Not at all . . . You see only my huge size, but I have a soft, tender heart. I have a lover, despite the fact that I am married and love my wife and children. I love women . . . People are always deceived by external appearances . . . There is no opportunity for me to be alone with you and tell you the whole story of my terrible conflict with death, but you may say that I am the conqueror of death."

"You must be Ringo, after all!"

"I am not Ringo, but Abu Jabbar, Father of Fortitude,[2] and this is the truth."

"Well, Abu Jabbar, when do we arrive?"

"Don't be in a hurry. Hurry is the instrument of the devil. We'll be getting there in half an hour."

"You advise me not to be in a hurry, and yet you drive your car at such speed. Isn't that a contradiction?"

"I am used to speed. What can I do?"

Abu Jabbar drank his fill of water and black tea. Then he went back to his car and felt the motor with his fingers. His eyes continued to shine for a few minutes with a mysterious joy. But as soon as the girl disappeared from his sight, his eyelids quivered, his eyes narrowed, and, with the air of one who has been hit with something, he straightened up, flipped around like a shark, and called the passengers back to the car.

"Are you tired?" he asked his friend, al-Shatri.

"Very tired."

"We will be arriving soon."

"I no longer care if we do."

"What do you care about?"

"Nothing . . . "

After Abu Jabbar passed the edges of the small villages scattered on both sides of the road, Muhsin saw a herd of cows in the distance, attended by a few men. He visualized them as typical peasants who wore *kufiyyas* and headbands around faces drawn with fatigue and tanned by the rays of the noon sun. Deep in contemplation, al-Shatri was paying no attention to his friend, who sounded regretful as he mumbled vaguely. He now looked at the small face on its short, fat neck.

"Bitch!" Abu Jabbar was saying.

"Who is this bitch?" asked al-Shatri.

"Didn't you see her?"

He understood now that Abu Jabbar meant the pretty girl they had seen earlier.

"Yes, I saw her."

"Her beauty is bewitching . . . Isn't it?"

"You are a great lover. Have you heard of Casanova?"

---

2. *Jabbar* means "invincible; a man of fortitude."

"No . . . But she is a girl who will stay in the memory."

"Maybe. But what do you get out of that?"

"Nothing but regret."

Again Abu Jabbar swore at all car drivers, coming down on them with harsh invective, recounting, without the slightest pause, their achievements in stupid driving, law violation, and exploitation. Then he returned to the girl, calling her a gem.

Al-Shatri said: "Yes, she is a gem, but you did say . . . "

"What did I say?"

"That you love your wife."

"I do love my wife, truly . . . But—"

"But what?"

"I'm bored, believe me . . . all husbands are; they get bored."

Al-Shatri was calm and ready to ask more questions, but he noticed that his friend's cheeks were flushed. He admired his frankness, just as he had admired his skillful driving.

Abu Jabbar began to clarify his problem.

"Believe me, I lie with her in bed, and nothing happens to me!"

"Always so?"

"Most of the time."

"Then you cannot love her."

"I swear by al-'Abbas[3] that I do love her!"

"But you cannot prove it."

"What do you want me to do?"

They approached the outskirts of the city and were presently weaving through the crowded streets to the square. The fatigued passengers got out, and each went his way. It was evening now.

The traces of headache still cling inside your head, as do the features of faces that have passed you by: smiles, entreaties, complaints; from the summer, from the dust, from people. You are like a tool in other people's hands: you are put where they want you to be, and if you wish to run away you find no place to go . . . All your life you keep postponing your dreams in order to appease other people's emotions, to please kinsfolk and the dead, whom you have to visit before they die and then again after they die. There is no escape—and you do not know why . . . You would happily spend your money if that were enough, but it isn't: you have to expend your nerves, your pain, your artificial tears as well . . . This you find difficult to understand, just as you find it difficult to come out with the right words at the weddings and wakes that take place all the time, one following another, like a geometric equation; that occur unremittingly, like all the years of headache, of barrenness, and of deprivation; that hammer away at your nerves and exhaust you, annihilating the very light in your eyes . . .

---

3. The uncle of the Prophet. He is regarded as a very holy figure by the Shi'ites.

You are expected to visit the dying on a hot summer day. And it was on a hot summer day that you left your town, Samawa, and came to Baghdad without a penny in your pocket. But what has changed? Nothing! . . . And now, what can you do? Can you make blood return to his veins? And if you can't, why did you come? People will say that you are an ungrateful son, that you are dried-out, unnatural . . . But what *won't* people say?

You are here, filling a certain calm in a small room in a tenth-class hotel, trying not to shatter the quiet of the place. You close the door on yourself, and there is no telephone.

Return to Baghdad without seeing anyone, and never again allow anyone to question you . . .

Go back!

Muhsin al-Shatri walked alone in the empty, half-dark streets feeling the calm wind on his hands. He was waiting for daybreak, to return to where he had come from. His father's house was not far, but he had to return that next morning, without feeling any remorse. To be a truly undutiful son, one had to put all dead traditions on the shelf. And in order to spend this night quietly, he had to go to sleep . . .

Next morning Muhsin al-Shatri got up late, washed his face and hands, and combed his hair. He was still dressed, as he had never taken off his clothes. After eating, he walked towards the taxi station, to get a car back to the capital. He preferred to walk stealthily in the back alleys, in order to avoid being seen by anyone he knew. He yearned to shorten both distance and time, feeling that he was running away from very determined pursuers. To keep panic at bay, he walked slowly, hoping not to run into anyone. This hope was strengthened by the fact that movement in the streets seemed to be normal: although it was mid-morning there were only a few pedestrians leisurely strolling, indifferent to passersby, whether strangers or acquaintances.

At the next alley, however, he encountered a large crowd of people walking in line behind a coffin. To avoid embarassment, he hid behind the protruding part of a wall that faced the street he had just come out of. But when he looked more closely at the crowd of mourners, he was shocked to find that many of them were friends of his father. He knew their faces.

"He has died, then . . . He must have died yesterday evening!" he thought to himself. When he entered the city, everything had been finished! He felt a sudden agitation: sharp pain stabbed through his joints, his legs trembled, and he felt his dry throat choking. Traces of tears shone in his eyes and fell slowly, mixing with the salt of the sweat that covered his cheeks.

He approached the crowd, heading for the front row of mourners. Wasn't he the son, after all? He hastened forward, looking meanwhile for his brothers and cousins, but none of them were there. Where were they? He thought that they might be at the rear, but this would be unlikely, since it was not the conventional thing to do on such occasions. Where were they?

Some faces were gazing at him now, as if they wanted to console him for his bereavement without uttering any words.

Where were they?

He made his way toward the head of the procession, which seemed like a regiment being driven to the day of judgment. As he approached, he opened his eyes wide in surprise. His body broke into a sweat. The coffin was huge, distinctly huge, big enough for three men. There were many more pallbearers than the usual four—a whole crowd of men, in fact, all looking burdened with the weight.

He let the procession proceed with dignity, in absolute silence. Only the sound of men's footsteps was heard. Despite the somber atmosphere, he overheard some men whispering:

"He died yesterday . . . He was asleep, and died at midnight."

" . . . after his return to Basra, a few hours later . . . "

"He was not ill."

"Yes, Abu Jabbar was a strong man, firm of heart, skillful in driving . . . But all of us will travel the same road."

" . . . his laughter was as huge as his body . . . was larger than . . . "

They were walking slowly, carrying on their palms yesterday's friend, raised toward the burning sun.

—Translated by May Jayyusi and Thomas G. Ezzy

Hasan al-Lawzi (b. 1952)

Yemeni poet and short-story writer Hasan al-Lawzi was born in Sanaa. He studied at the University of al-Azhar in Cairo and occupied several important government posts, including that of the Minister of Culture in Sanaa. He also became Yemen's ambassador to Jordan. Al-Lawzi is a powerful writer with diversified themes and interests. Among his major themes are his deep and committed involvement in the issues of the Yemeni revolution and his aspiration for its success on both the political and the social levels. He has published several collections of short stories and poetry, among which are his verse collection, *Poems for the Difficult Woman* (1979); and his collections of short stories, *The Woman Who Ran in the Glow of the Sun* (1976) and *Hymns in the Temple of Love and Revolution* (1978).

THIRST

Like a dog in the sun-drenched summer, I pant. Like the sun-baked earth I crack with thirst, like a desert I crumble in the flaming wind. My body disintegrates, burned flesh and mottled blood. Away from you, I feel a saw slowly rending my skull, like a malignant well-trained turtle. My world is brutally hard, as narrow and constrained as the contours of my body. Ah, I suffer a murderous siege from which I cannot escape except through your warm soft body. When we meet, I shall be born again as lightning, or I may drip down as quiet drizzle or stand upright, a tall straight-backed form, drenched with the rainbow colors of joy.

The woman I speak to is my beautiful neighbor whose husband emigrated ten years ago, leaving her with a child in her womb ... and now, no one knows anything about him. Some say he has died and others that he will never return, while others insist he will come back one day to impregnate her with more children and titillate her with more joys and juicy sighs! They insist he will return a rich man to save her from the flames of her *tannur* oven, and the bread that she sells in the marketplace to survive.

As for myself, I am a young man of thirty. I am not cultured although I have finished my university education and read some nonacademic books. I do not like to talk politics; it bores me. When I was abroad, I used to enjoy discussing the homeland, the revolution, the authorities, the changes, and the inevitability of a socialist solution to our problems. My colleagues and I used to soar with our aspirations to a distant and glorious future stacked with loaves that would feed the hungry millions. We dreamt of a world rich with beautiful things. But all this has evaporated in the face of the few responsibilities I now carry. I confess they are trivial and do not deserve mention. My family in the village claims half my salary in order to live and better their circumstances. I live here with the other half, which I distribute among rent, electricity, water, restaurants, cafés, the cinema, and the grocer's. I've been like this for the past two years, since the day my neighbor's son died, and I haven't saved any money that would help me get married. Girls' dowries are very high now ... extremely. Despair of ever saving what amounts to a possible dowry has made me squander what I have on anything at all. The important thing is that I try to defeat time, to resist the siege and the alienation. Even the local liquor has started to wear me down, turning me into a swamplike creature yawning with worms, cockroaches, mosses, and disgusting smells. Oh, where are you, you wonderful beer bottles, goddesses of merry evil spirits? Where are you? Yet I cannot live another day without marriage ... "Oh road of outlaws and rebels, do not close your doors in my face, just as the slave traders sealed the doors of their crowded flesh-filled stores ... Don't do that just because I don't have the required price, defined and fixed in the protocol of traditions and worldly vanity. The instructions of the Prophet are now corpses of letters and words imprisoned in the recesses of yellowed books and rusted in barren minds."

The Prophet once said, Give her at least an iron ring.

But we are now in the age of platinum and diamonds.

The Prophet married some of his Companions[1] with only one verse or one chapter of the Quran. Isn't that true?

---

1. The Companions of the Prophet were a group of early Muslims who formed the inner circle of pious men around the Prophet and learned his teachings. The four Orthodox caliphs were among them.

I will only marry off my daughter as my neighbor married off his—for fifteen thousand riyals.

I can pay you five thousand riyals.

It is unacceptable.

I spoke to one of my friends about the crisis I was suffering, and the sexual thirst from which I toss and reel. I also complained about the resistance of my lovely neighbor in her golden tower, armed with fear, metaphysical spears, and a marriage contract that has rotted in the wardrobe of memory. He pitied my situation, introducing me to a man who, he said, would furnish me with what I needed. We made an agreement, and I waited for the man in the appointed place at the appointed time. A quarter of an hour passed and he did not come. Eventually I despaired and gave up the liaison. But just then he appeared from afar, accompanied by a young boy no older than sixteen. They approached me. A chill passed over my body. I asked him about the promised goods and with a strangely meaningful face, he replied, "Well, what do you think?"

"Think about what? Where is the girl?"

"Doesn't he please you?"

"Damn you! Have you forgotten that we are Yemenites? Get out of here immediately or I shall break both your heads!"

God! Can it be possible that I can sink to this level? Animals could not be more disgusting! I felt dizzy, acutely nauseated. I wished I could vomit, spill out all of the sand and stones inside me. I asked a man standing nearby, "Has the earth stopped revolving?"

"How stupid! How can the earth revolve?"

"Then it must have stopped."

He did not pay any attention to me but went on his way, leaving me wearily repeating the last sentence, "Then it must have stopped." It was our misfortune to have ridden the camels across the great fatiguing desert, exhausted by their burdens at the desert's dark side. A little sun, my good men! The pores of our skin ache for a little sun! Run toward the plains and valleys, climb the highest mountain you can find, and you will see strange and wondrous things. Oh! The earth's virginity is in your hands, exposing itself, lying warm and suffering under your feet. Where can I find a sword to rip the impotent clouds from the sky so they stop their endless masturbation? Where can I find a woman into whose flowing body I can pour my fire, pour that passion ripping me apart—and then relax in the shade of her proud breasts like a child exhausted by play? Oh, it is impossible for a person like me to live without marriage. He'd do better to commit suicide alone between four chilly walls as he tries to make love to his murdered dreams.

I tell myself that one day the old woman who brings water to my house will find me lying here, a naked corpse. Maybe she will think of doing strange things with me before she tells the police what has happened. A person's true capacity to retain any moral and ethical values is determined only when the person is alone with himself. I collected my disheveled pains, wrapping them inside my clothes until I looked acceptable, then decided to roam the streets. I would not return until I tired out the police and guards who whistled and yelled, asking for my name and identity card, and where I had come from, where I was going. As I left my house I saw my lovely neighbor, that muffler of a woman who quietly suffocated my breath as ashes suffocate the breath of live coals beneath them. I felt the exhaustion of that dream, which I had followed from one room to another, one street to another, until it was etched on every wall and ceiling; in the graceful shape of trees with wounded desire and glorious limbs; of grass with the smell of firmly compact breasts ready to burst at any passionate touch. I uttered a low greeting. After a century she responded, bashfully, in a low voice. That night I roamed for a long time, and my mind obsessively thought of her, flashing photographic and cinematographic pictures of what might happen between us if we were alone. My legs were jelly as I tiredly returned home. Crossing the street, I saw her room lit up. With whom was she whiling away the time, I wondered. Should I knock at her door?

I entered my house, remaining mesmerized at the window. I stared at her light as my mind tried its best to slip in through the holes and cracks of her room. On a previous day I had surprised her while she was at the window. Her rounded face was uncovered, and I infiltrated the two deep forests of her eyes, kindled with greenness, night, and piercing meteors. Since then I had risen early, hoping to sneak another gaze at her. I burned and continued to burn. The next afternoon I decided I had to tell her something. Anything, I thought, and let what will be, be! I approached her door. I knocked quietly, and she answered. Her voice released bright butterflies.

"Who's there?"

"It's me!"

"What do you want?"

"I want to talk to you."

She opened the door and stood in front of me like a towering wind, laden with warm clouds, children of the storm. She was all covered up with black cloaks and her eyes, those two forests, were shining brightly now, becoming more mysterious, fleeing to the far-off wilderness where rabbits and elks ran wild.

"Say what you have to say."

"How can you live in this large house all by yourself?"

"What's that to you?"

"By God, this is unfair."

"You rude man!"

She spat at me and violently slammed the door. Her spittle coated most of my face. I had no handkerchief, so had to wipe it off with my coat sleeve. Then I went on my way. It was enough for me that I had spoken to her briefly and gazed into her shining eyes, my fiery looks skirmishing with her budding breasts. On the fourth day after this incident I approached her door again. It was open and she was in the corridor. She saw me and rushed to shut the door. But I caught it with my hand and asked, "Don't you feel any repentance?"

She slapped me so hard on the face that the neighborhood children came running. I snatched away my hand that had flown to the place where her slap stung. One of the children laughed loudly. It seemed he knew what had happened. I felt humiliated. A week passed, after which I again knocked at her door. It was evening. My mind had begun to swing drunkenly on some rosy transparent threads.

"Who is it?"

"It's me!"

"You again?"

"Yes, me again!"

My voice was loud, and she gingerly opened the door. She was the one who opened the door and I was the one who invaded her corridor. It was almost as if she expected my attack. I tried to hold her, to embrace her, but she shoved me away.

"What do you want? Get out!"

"I will not get out!"

"I shall gather all the neighbors here around you!"

"Just try to do that!"

"Are you crazy?"

"Unfortunately, you are the last one to know that, although you are the reason for my madness."

I advanced. I was whinnying, and she leapt aside like a nervous wildcat. I embraced her tightly. She relented a bit and uttered a low laugh. She whispered, "Then please come in."

She led me to one of her rooms and asked me to wait there. I thought she would leave me and close the door, then scream to all the neighbors to save her. I thought she would rip open her clothes and tell them I had broken into her house and tried to rape her.

I expected her voice to rise at any moment. But I heard nothing, and then the door of the room opened again and she entered, walked cautiously toward me. She slid a knife from her pocket and thrust it at my head. I grabbed her hand and tried to pry the knife out of it. She was very strong, and she was furious. She held on to the knife.

We began to fight, rolling from one corner of the room to another. I expected her to shout for help, but she did not. She seemed to have great confidence in herself. We struggled long and intensely, and our struggle took strange shapes. She was a summit about to surrender from her heights, and I was holding the secrets of the winds in my palms. The winds were laden with clouds and the clouds pregnant with rain and then the rain began to fall, heavy and torrential. Wild animals trembled and ran to their hiding places. From their lairs and burrows, breathless gasps were rising, stammers were shuddering, males and females were merging together. The whole earth was taking the shape of a ripe and hungry female and suddenly, surprised at the thirst of starving men, she took off her clothes in front of them, laughing. Her valleys, plains, and plateaus relaxed and bathed in the overflow of passionate joy, dizzy with the ecstasy of satisfaction.

The veins spilled over with boiling blood and the ripe flesh mingled with the hungry flesh. And hungry flesh mingled as deeply as it could. The world became a tavern of pagan songs, dances, and merry rituals. And there was the knife, fallen from her surrendered hand. She began to gyrate in wild directions, sinking her teeth and hunger for sex into my flesh, and I was plunging my ribs and growing fire into her body. She was sighing, wailing, and I was panting, groaning. And little by little the voices began to subside and the movements quieted. The rain diminished and stopped. And we both calmed down together. The earth sighed with childish joy and released a far-reaching moan.

—Translated by Lena Jayyusi and Naomi Shihab Nye

Naguib Mahfouz (b. 1911)

Egyptian novelist and short-story writer Naguib (also written as Najib) Mahfouz is the Arab world's first Nobel laureate (1988). Born into a merchant family in the old Gamaliya quarter of Cairo, he studied philosophy at Cairo University, where he began writing fiction. Subsequently he embarked on a long career in government administration and the civil service. His early works were a series of historical novels, and it was not until 1945 that he published his first novel on contemporary Egyptian life. His work depicts, in particular, middle-class life in Cairo, with its changing moods and fortunes. His fictional output has been a landmark in the development of modern Arabic fiction and has rightly made him the father of the modern Arabic novel. He has a large number of novels and nine collections of short stories in print. In 1970 he received the National Prize for Letters, and in 1972 he was awarded the nation's highest honor, the Collar of the Republic. He has received honorary degrees from Denmark, France, and the Soviet Union, and his work has been translated into many languages. Several have been translated into English, including his famous *Trilogy* (vols. 1 and 3 translated by Olive and Lorne Kenny) and *Midaqq Alley* (translated by Trevor LeGassick); *The Thief and the Dogs* (translated by Trevor LeGassick and M. M. Badawi) and *The Quail and the Autumn* (translated by Roger Allen). Roger Allen and 'Akef Abadir translated a collection of his short stories, entitled *God's World*. After the award of the Nobel Prize, Doubleday brought out a collection of his translated works in English.

RENDEZVOUS

Evening, the best part of the day. The chores are done. Everything has been put away in its place. Even the kitchen is so neat and tidy it looks as though it might almost be up for sale. The servant girl has gone to her room to sleep. Now the family can sit together cosily beside the radio and enjoy the evening, enfolded in familial love. Little Lulu isn't asleep yet, though; she never wants to go to sleep. All she wants to do is play, be a nuisance, get into mischief. But what about the husband, the happy husband? What's the matter with him? And the wife? Well, Lulu never allows *her* any time to think. She throws herself at her mother without the slightest warning. Either mother and daughter end up banging their heads together or Lulu digs into her mother's cheek or neck; and then all the makeup in the world cannot hide the marks of her tiny nails. Lulu's not even three yet, but she's already a holy terror.

The wife. She told herself she could feel happy with her daughter, if it were not for the change in her husband. That spoiled everything. Though she had to be on guard every minute in case Lulu hurled herself at her, she still kept sneaking glances at her husband. There he sat slouching in the armchair, first throwing his head back, to stare at the ceiling, then looking down at the radio. In front of him on the table stood a glass, half full. He was with them, and yet he wasn't. She felt that he was closer to them when he went away on one of his business trips than he was now, right here in the same room. What had changed him? What had happened? She had always been able to sense danger. These days she had been tense, fearful, unable to relax for ... how long had it been?

Good heavens, how time goes by when you try to measure it, when in reality your nerves are being torn to shreds because the tension has gone on so long! What did his cruel new attitude mean? There he sits; he won't talk to her or play with Lulu. All he does is drink! Night after night he drinks and drinks. And he smokes like a chimney; a cloud of smoke is always hanging over his head. The whole scene is disgusting. What makes it worse is that, outside, away from home, he socializes and he's successful, he's actually a role model, owns a store where he sells and repairs electrical appliances. He's a respected electrician.

It never used to bother her when he went down to the Khedive Café every evening to play backgammon for an hour or two. He would always bring home some delicious candy or fruit. Back he would come, back to her and to Lulu. The part of the evening that followed was warm with love and happiness. Up to now her short married life had been happy. Cozy evenings at home, good times with the family, visits to the cinema with discussions of the films afterward. Everything contributed to the joy of their life together. Thus occasional arguments had never been serious; by the next day everything had been forgotten.

Was all this past history? Would she ... There was Lulu being a pest again. She never gives up! She was striking out at her father now, but he was paying no attention. He was so indifferent and defended himself so poorly that his small child soon abandoned her attack. She tried leaning on the table and spilled his drink, but even that did not make him angry.

"Why are you drinking so much, my dear?"

If only he would tell her what was wrong, show some glimmer of emotion in the process, even lose his temper with her!

"It doesn't do any harm."

"Oh yes, it does!"

"Don't believe what people say ... " Before she could reply, he went on. "It's just that I'm fed up with spending my evenings idling around outside." He smiled. "I'm quite content staying here with my wife and daughter."

"But all you do is drink."

"That's not true. I only drink to relax. Then my happiness is complete."

There he was trying to look natural. But she saw him with her heart not her eyes; and her heart felt as though it were a pile of ashes being blown about in the wind.

"What's troubling you so, my dear?"

"Problems at work, maybe. But I'm not going to let them ruin our nice evening together."

Questions and answers, back and forth; and always the same result. Silent torture was all she had left. Searching for some reason for its existence was entirely futile. She noticed him looking at Lulu. He had a peculiar look in his eyes, but it disappeared while she watched him, became a glance of tender affection, a hugging, kissing, tear-jerking glance. Why was she then shuddering in fear?!

"Wouldn't it be a good idea to get to bed at the usual time?"

"Why should we go to sleep?"

She laughed feebly and gave him a worried look. "You're making fun of me," she said.

"Heaven forbid."

"You're really torturing me."

"God forbid that I should do any such thing ... "

"Is everything okay?" she asked, stroking his cheek gently.

"Yes."

"Nothing's bothering you?"

"Absolutely nothing." After a pause he went on in a pleading tone, "Don't worry. I promise you there's nothing in our life together to worry about. Here I am sitting happily with my little family. Sometimes I have a drink, other times I read. What's so alarming about that?!"

Reading had never been one of his pastimes. He would cast a cursory glance over the newspaper. She herself would just look at a page and then put it aside. Lulu would grab it, and before you could turn round the paper would be in shreds. But now he was trading books! What kind of books? *At the Very End of the World, The Sixth Sense, The World of the Spiritual.*

"What do you know about such things?"

"My faith has given me what I need to know ... "

"Yes, of course."

"So why are *you* reading all this stuff?"

"Just curiosity and amusement."

She made a mighty effort to convince herself that everything was quite normal and that it was her own fancies that were abnormal. It did not work. She felt like someone who consistently ignores the warning signs of a hidden ulcer.

"Tell me. How do you feel?"

"I'm fine."

"What about work? Don't keep anything from me, my dear. I'm your life-partner, remember!"

"Things couldn't be better."

"How will I ever find out what's wrong?"

He patted her on the cheek and kissed her, just as he used to do on the happy nights of the past. How different things were now! He was playing a part and could not conceal the fact.

"Has something come up?"

"I feel a little tired. That's all."

"Why don't we go away, just for a week?"

"That's a great idea, but not right now ... "

She glanced in the mirror and noticed that at last he seemed on the point of admitting that something *was* wrong. With all her heart she willed him to speak out. She prayed God to let him speak. But he flopped back into the chair again and started reading.

"You've turned into a bachelor again!"

"Me?!"

"It's as though you don't have a wife at all. All right, live by yourself, and I'll grieve till death us do part!"

"Can't a man feel tired once in a while?"

"What about a man who drinks wine and reads books about spirits?!"

"Wine is a spiritual drink. That's what they call it!"

"I'm sorry, my supply of laughter is all used up!"

"You'll be laughing at yourself when you finally realize that all your fancies are wrong. There's nothing to worry about."

"My heart never deceives me!"

She was right enough about that, he thought to himself. She always talked sincerely, more's the pity. Her heart was filled with a genuine sense of fear and she showed the signs, the premonitions of sorrow and a sense of its impending loneliness. He was enduring double torture, for himself and for her. But at the same time his thoughts were hovering crazily around the idea of the dissolution of matter, the refraction of light, the spread of ashes, and the diffusion of air. It might have been kinder, he thought, if he had found some refuge far removed from his own house, some bar where he could drink at a distance from the happy atmosphere in which his own body was transformed into three warm beloved bodies. But his emotions, his longing, and his profound despair all prevented him from running away and kept him tied to his beloved home. In fact, he sometimes felt like locking up the store and spending all his time with his wife and child, with Ismat and Lulu. He felt like kissing them both till his mouth was sore, clutching them both to his chest till his arms were tired.

He would have liked to play his role skillfully enough to deceive his wife. Unfortunately, this was beyond him. And so there he sat, reading, drinking, and sneaking glances in her direction. And as he held back his own tears and clung doggedly to his control, he had to endure the anguished looks she gave him. But he persisted, feeling that everything about him was disappearing: fatherhood, love, married life. Everything he regarded as an ideal seemed to be slipping away into oblivion and ruin. He felt that he was a nothing crying about nothing; even his tears were not real, no more real than the books he was reading, the liquor he was drinking, and the songs on the radio lamenting life. Why didn't he pull Ismat toward him and tell her his secret? But then, what was the point of that? That would only make everything even more complicated; things would just get more muddled, cruel, and gloomy. Why should he turn their evenings together into wakes, the singing into dirges? That would not change things at all but would instead destroy the family completely.

It was true that his loneliness was becoming more desperate, but he would tell himself not to give in to cowardice and selfishness. At least Ismat had not given up hope yet; and there was Lulu playing, singing, butting, and scratching. She seemed to be the only one worthy of being alive; for her, life was simple and she lived it without any particular meaning or thought. She was also the only one who knew nothing of death or depair; to her honey-colored eyes everything looked cheerful, possible, immortal. Even when the smooth surface of her life was ruffled by some minor disturbance, it only lasted a few moments. She might go yelling and screaming to her room, but she would emerge smiling a few minutes later. Even before her tears were dried, Lulu's expression made it clear that she had some new mischief in mind.

Ismat sits there each evening with him till it is time for bed. She knows nothing about what he goes through during the night. When she thinks he has settled down to sleep, she closes her eyes on all her sorrows. But he never closes his eyes. He *lies* there staring into the dark void. His brain churns at fever pitch, but no one knows about his dialogues in the dark, his fears, and his thoughts about the bottomless abyss beneath him. In the dark everything except death loses its shape. Death alone *can* see in the dark, and like the dark nothing *can* hold death back from its appointed time of arrival. With death, everything else loses value, reality, meaning.

What should he do, he asked himself, as he lay there aware of the breathing of his wife beside him? What did he want out of life in the time that was left to him? Back comes an answer: "Everything," and then another: "Nothing." In this context everything equals nothing. And yet his soul refuses to give in. Fear of the void makes him hang on to dreams. He sees now that he *is* no longer either husband or father. He is instead free to cross the distant horizon, to take a plane that hovers in the sky, or a ship that ploughs its way through the oceans; he can ride countless other vehicles. From forest to lake, from mountain to plain, he can speed across fields, deserts, cities; he can traverse regions so hot that steel itself would melt and frozen wastes so cold as to freeze fire. He could see people of all shapes and colors. But even this could not dispel the shadow of death or postpone its arrival, although it could transform the days that remained into a spectacular journey that would distract him a little. Sometimes he sees himself following whims, tossed about on the waves of fierce passions, relishing anything good, intoxicated by all that amazes, gratifying his instincts with adventure, excitement, and revelry, or with even stronger emotional states: brutal aggression. However, with him, such fantasies remained dreams, for even the prospect of death could not really let him forget that he *is* both a husband and father and therefore a human being. And so all these visions vanish into thin air. What remains is insomnia, the compulsion to continue working in the store and to come home each night, looking forward to a pleasant evening with his beloved family.

However, he had to have a drink occasionally and read spiritual books; there was no avoiding that. He was desperate for some peace of mind, however illusory, and for peace, however groundless. Even his deep-rooted faith gave way in the face of death. Not even poetry could be as intense and weighty as death. He can almost see death and feel it; the experience was so frightful that it forced him to bury the secret deep down inside himself and to keep it hidden from his poor wife. Let her worry all she wants, he thought; worry is easier to bear than despair. And let Lulu frolic all she wants in an atmosphere devoid of the terror of reality.

One day he went out to the Matatya Café, something that was quite unusual for him. It was late afternoon on a Sunday in autumn. He took a seat under the arcade at the beginning of the street but kept looking about him as though waiting for someone. Eventually he noticed a man walking toward him; the man wore a turban and a black cloak; he was obviously from the provinces. The two men resembled each other to an amazing degree. They embraced and sat down together at the table.

"How are you, Jum'a?" the new arrival asked. "What's the matter? Why in heaven's name did you fix a rendezvous in the café of all places?"

"You're worn out," Jum'a replied with a reticent smile. "I'm very sorry . . . "

"It's not such a bad trip from the Barrage.[1] But what's the point of meeting here in the café?"

Jum'a considered what he should say. His companion was staring at him anxiously.

"I know!" he said before Jum'a could speak. "There's been a family quarrel. I bet that's what it is. How are things with your wife, by the way?"

"'Ismat's fine, thank you," Jum'a replied. "There's been no quarrel."

"Strange! Then why didn't you invite me to your house?"

"I wanted to be alone with you."

"Away from your own home?!"

"Away from everything!"

---

1. These are the famous aqueducts built in the nineteenth century by Muhammad Ali Pasha, Egypt's ruler. People still go on festive occasions to picnic there.

Jum'a's brother looked at him carefully again. "Thing's aren't going well for you, are they, Jum'a?" he asked.

Jum'a made no comment.

"Tell me what's the matter," his brother said in alarm.

Jum'a gave him a slow look. "My dear brother," he said, "I need your help badly. I'll tell you everything. You have to believe me. I'm going to die in a few months!"

The sheikh's features froze, and his expression registered all the various stages of shock. "What did you say?" he asked. "Are you ill? How do you know you're going to die? Have you been to a doctor?"

Jum'a felt considerably more relaxed now he had got his confession off his chest. "I decided to take out some life insurance," he said relatively calmly.

"So?"

"I was turned down. I went to see a whole series of doctors. Now I'm sure that it's really serious."

The sheikh laughed sarcastically. "God's the only one who can be sure about such things," he said.

"Of course," Jum'a responded. "He's above everything. But I'm sure about the state of my health."

"What nonsense! I can tell you thousands of stories that show that doctors talk sheer rubbish!"

"And I can produce thousands of others," Jum'a retorted, "to show exactly the opposite!"

A heavy silence. A shoeshine boy came up beating on the side of his box, but he was soon sent away. A cool breeze was blowing under the arcade, and the busy Ataba Square[2] near the café looked like a nonstop merry-go-round of people and vehicles, a merry-go-round that never stopped.

"You must put these melancholy thoughts right out of your head," the sheikh said in a deep voice. "That's your only illness. If it's peace of mind you're after, then come back to the Barrage with me. You can visit a wonderful sheikh there. Even doctors go to see him when they're in bad straits!"

"Yes," Jum'a replied like an automaton.

"I see you don't believe me!"

"Let's put that aside for a while," Jum'a replied as he shifted in his chair. "I asked you to come because I wanted to talk to you about some urgent matters."

"But I don't like seeing you living with such destructive ideas."

"Let's not talk about that. For the time being please accept what I have to say on my own terms. Just listen."

"Very well," the sheikh muttered.

---

2. This square in the middle of Cairo is one of the busiest and most crowded spots of the capital.

"It's Ismat and Lulu," Jum'a said in a tone of voice that indicated both pity and concern.

"I knew it! I was sure you'd talk about them! I . . . " He was about to raise further objections, but Jum'a gestured to him to stop.

"I've a partner in the store who's a decent man just like you," Jum'a went on. "Even so, he will need some careful watching. I have to think about my family's security in the future. I'm sorry to burden you with more responsibilities than you already have, but I've no choice. I do have some cash in the bank, so I won't be leaving them . . . "

"Leaving them?"

"Please do what I ask and accept what I say on my terms. My family will not be in need of money, but they'll always need your protection."

The sheikh let out a laugh that was meant to express his ridicule at Jum'a's suggestion or at least to pretend to do so. He was about to reply, but at that moment the pulley of a passing trolley-car came off the electric wire overhead. With the brilliant electric spark came a loud crackling sound. For a moment the *shaikh* sat as though stunned. After a moment he said, "You asked me to go along with you, Jum'a, and I've done so. But do you really think I need to know the contents of your will? What a child you are! You know better than anyone how dear you are to me. Trust me completely. And now that I've been frank with you, I want you to give me some assurance. You must take a break and come home with me, if only for a week."

"Yes," said Jum'a. "I'll gladly do that. In a week or so I'll come to you, God willing. Now let's go back to my house."

But the sheikh found he was feeling some inner turmoil. He refused Jum'a's invitation and insisted on heading straight back home. Jum'a offered to take him to the train station, but the sheikh said no, he would take advantage of his visit to Cairo to make some important calls on the way to the station before heading home to the Barrage. So they said goodbye to each other in front of the café. The sheikh went off across the busy Ataba Square, and Jum'a headed straight to the bus station and boarded a waiting bus. The bus made its way round the square but had to stop by the Ezbekiyya Gardens[3] because the road was blocked by a large crowd. Jum'a looked out of the window of the bus and noticed that the crowd gathering around a car seemed to be getting larger and larger. He realized that there must have been an accident. For a while he looked at the crowd, then turned away. Before long the bus edged its way through the crowd and continued toward Opera Square.

Among the people gathered in the road was a shoeshine boy. He stared in shock at the corpse spread-eagled on the street in front of the car.

"I saw this sheikh just half an hour ago," he said loudly to the people around him. "He was sitting with another gentleman in the Matatya Café."

—*Translated by Roger Allen and Elizabeth Fernea*

---

3. The Al-Ezbekiyya quarter in the middle of Cairo was one of the most fashionable quarters of the capital at the beginning of the twentieth century.

Under a Starlit Sky

On the appointed morning the team gathered in a state of perfect readiness. Winter was on the retreat, and the weather breathed vitality into the soul. We all had woolen trousers and gray jumpers on. Our heads were covered with white cotton caps and our feet with rubber shoes. A medium-sized van arrived and was loaded with dry food and water bottles. A very tall man with clear-cut features and an awesome appearance came toward us. He was dressed like us except for a silver whistle that hung on his broad chest.

"I'm your guide," he said in a loud voice. "Have you read the rules?" We answered in the affirmative.

"Follow me!" he said as he gave us the signal to start.

Thus our journey through the desert began, the van following us slowly. It was an annual event organized by the Sports Club Association. The team would walk behind the guide, and each one would try to guess the destination oasis relying on his knowledge of the desert. The coveted prize went to those who guessed correctly. It could not be shared: all winners got the full prize, no matter how many they were. We set off at sunrise, keeping quiet and trying to remind ourselves of the rules for fear of being disqualified from the race on account of an oversight. We applied our full powers of observation and made use of all our knowledge, driven by our hope to win. The landscape extended infinitely and monotonously before us. Our feet plowed endlessly in the sand, and we began to feel the strain. Time grew heavy, and we wondered was there no place for rest? We felt the need to talk but that was forbidden. As for addressing our guide, that was considered a sin. It was an enjoyable and promising journey, but it was also arduous. More arduous indeed than we had imagined, and only those who experienced it could tell what it was like. It so chanced that two members of the group exchanged a couple of words for some reason. The guide halted immediately and turned on them. It was as if he had seen them with a third eye.

"To the van," he said firmly.

"I only asked him for a match to light a cigarette," said one of them.

"Smoking is forbidden too," he said decisively. "Go!"

You could read an expression of protest in the two men's eyes, but they had no choice but to obey. They walked to the van, trailing their disappointment behind them.

"My duty," he said categorically, "allows no leeway to the lax, the lazy, or the dishonest."

By noon we were overcome with exhaustion. Our alertness waned, and we came to realize fully what a difficult undertaking that journey was and what a cruel test for our sense of dignity even though it was regarded as a sports event and many saw it as nothing more than an entertaining game. We could feel the weight of the time growing heavier, and our souls yearned for a whiff of repose. It was then that the guide blew his whistle to draw our attention.

"Copy me!" he shouted at us.

He started to run. We had hoped he would invite us to take a break not to redouble our effort. We were obliged to imitate him, our hearts resentful and our faces gloomy. The sun ascended to mid-course above us, making its heat felt in spite of the fresh breeze. A young man stumbled, emitting a cry of pain, and stopped unable to continue the run.

"To the van," screamed the guide.

Thus the unfortunate fellow was out of the race, his expulsion serving to strengthen our wills. In the distance loomed a mighty rock that resembled the head of the Sphinx from behind. The guide ran in its direction, and we followed. When we reached it, he blew the whistle again. We stopped, breathless and near collapse.

"We will sit here to rest and have lunch," he said.

We sat on the sand. His assistants handed each of us a packed lunch and a small water bottle. Silently we started to unpack our lunch. It consisted of a roll of bread, some chips, a piece of tomato, a slice of cold meat, and an orange. We ate with great appetite and quenched our thirst, and then we lay on our backs to relax or perhaps to doze off.

"May I smoke a cigarette here?" asked one of us innocently.

"Go to the van!" replied the guide calmly.

The youth was struck dumb, but the man sitting next to him let out a sarcastic laugh.

"And you too, at once," the guide continued, addressing the one who laughed.

The guide stared at them defiantly until they succumbed to his will. We had hardly had enough rest, when he got to his feet, blew his whistle, gave the signal to start, and continued the march. We followed him, disaffected and silent. Was this man an idealist or a sadist? The truth dawned on me of a saying I once heard: "Power brings out both the best and the worst in those who have it." I remembered friends who advised me against taking part in the race, but I also was aware that to win was to have something to be proud of for the rest of one's life, and I was determined to put all my heart in achieving my objective. And oh, the demands the race put on participants! Alertness, a will of steel, unfailing memory, and supreme intelligence, not to mention patience, endurance, courage, self-discipline, and courtesy toward our tyrannical guide.

Before long we were overwhelmed by exhaustion again, and such were our misgivings about the guide that we came to expect from him another surprise even more violent than we had already seen. As the sun began its descent toward the skyline, the temperature came down and the air carried a tolerable coolness. Meanwhile, our guide increased his pace and trouble loomed in the air. Two young men suffered a disintegration of the will and gave up the race of their own accord. As they made their way to the van in a state of utter dejection, I asked myself, "Is this man immune to the tiredness we feel? Why does he seem as if he belongs to a superhuman race?"

Then what we had feared came to pass and the man suddenly accelerated the rhythm of the march into a rapid run. We started to run as night descended upon us. We waded through the darkness under the faint glimmer of the stars, terrified all the time that we might bump into something, step into a pit, or fall off a precipice. We were no longer able to think clearly or sustain our alertness to the extent that we came to believe that it was through good fortune alone that the race was ever won in previous years.

At long last and only after we had verged on despair, the whistle blew and the guide's voice was heard giving the order to stop. Our fatigue was such that we no longer aspired to the prize and only longed for a safe return.

"Dinner and then sleep," he said. "At midnight we continue the march and two hours later your cards will be collected with the answers written down. We reach our destination at sunrise."

A pole with a lamp hanging from it was stuck in the ground and we saw that we were not very far from a big hill. Dinner (which was no different from lunch) was distributed among us, as well as sleeping bags.

The guide approached one of us as we were eating our food.

"You've got a hip flask and you've had two sips from it," he said gruffly. "Go to the van!"

"There's got to be a despicable spy among us," the youth yelled angrily.

"Give me the flask and go to the van!" screamed the guide.

"I have no flask," came the defiant answer.

"I will have you searched."

"No one can lay a finger on me."

"No?" said the guide as he put out his arm as if to start searching him. The young man pushed the arm away in an amazing act of daring, at which point the guide slapped him so forcefully on the face that he was thrown to the ground. Suddenly our pent-up fury exploded collectively. We no longer cared for the race or the rules. The air all round us reverberated with our booming cries.

"This is an insult. We will not be insulted. You've got to know your limits."

The guide scanned our faces with charged calm.

"This is an all-out rebellion," he said. "I announce the journey canceled, and I will see to it that you are brought to account before the Association's Board of Directors. I'm withdrawing immediately."

He walked straight to the van followed by his assistants who carried away the lamp. Within a minute we could hear the engine revving up and saw the van drive off into the darkness leaving us without a guide. We stood together in a circle in a state of shock, then there was a flurry of reactions from every direction. "How dare he leave us in the desert without guidance?"

"We will raise the matter before the Supreme Committee."

"But we must think about the situation we're facing now."

"Perhaps we should stay where we are until the morning."

"Of course not. We must start moving straightaway. Every minute counts."

"Which way shall we go?"

"Let's put forward suggestions and then take a vote."

The conflict of opinion was so wild that almost no two people agreed on the same proposition. After a violent debate five schools of thought emerged. As we prepared to set out we gave in momentarily to our misgivings.

"We might get lost and die of thirst and hunger."

"Or be attacked by wild beasts or bandits."

"We must take the risk."

"Hadn't we better stay where we are until they find us?"

"Don't lull yourself with a wish that may or may not come true! There's nothing left for us but to depend on ourselves."

Eventually each group set out in the direction of their choice, firmly believing in the soundness of their opinion and driven forth by their hope of safe arrival. Before them stretched a path fraught with all kinds of probabilities in the dark night. It was as if they had an appointment with the rise of the sun.

—*Translated by Rasheed El-Enany*

Muhammad Makhzanji (b. 1950)

Egyptian short-story writer Muhammad Makhzanji is one of the most original talents to have appeared on the Egyptian fictional scene in the 1970s and 1980s. He reflects the new artistic sensibility that has been demonstrated by several others of his generation in Egypt, creating a fiction of life in crisis, usually in siege, where there is hardly any escape but where the will to live always tries to assert itself even against great odds. Makhzanji began his career by experimenting in the vein of such major fiction writers as Yusuf Idris, but reasserted his own particular terse, economical, and highly effective style and interest in his second collection, *People in Cages*, where he portrays a complete experience in very short stories. His other collections are *That Which is Coming* (1983), *Death Laughs* (1988), and *The Garden* (1992). Makhzanji works as a doctor in the city of Mansoura, Egypt.

BLUE FLY

I hate flies, and I have a particular loathing of the buzzing sounds they make. I'm an emergency room resident, who sits at night in an emptiness of waiting, surrounded by white walls.

This particular fly was making a noise like a hundred flies all together, and I rose in irritation, took off my white coat, and hit it. As it fell, I moved to stamp on it; then I noticed it was a huge and colorful fly. I decided to let it recover and fly away.

I brought across a crystal glass and tried to shove it off with my coat. It fell. I placed the glass upside down over it, then looked at it inside, huge now, with eyes like two half balls of glued crystal, and refracting a multitude of colors through the glass as it moved. I could see squares standing out in relief on its body, like the squares of a chessboard, and, beneath its cellophane wings, waves of color that glittered with a blue metallic sheen.

In its attempts to escape, the imprisoned fly kept hitting the glass walls at every movement; then it would try in another direction, and still another direction, ceaselessly. I soon grew tired of the repeated movements.

Bringing over the vial of local anesthetic, I lifted the glass slightly, sprayed a thick cloud inside, and let the glass down again. I saw the fly search desperately for a way out; then it stopped moving and looked as if it was beginning to die.

Suddenly it began to move in a circle with its lower end moving sideways, laying, with each tilt of its body, a small white egg the size of a pinhead, smooth and cream-colored. It laid one, two, three, four, five, six eggs. Then it grew quiet.

—*Translated by Mona N. Mikhail and Christopher Tingley*

THE GIRLS' WARD

The sign read: "Section 3—Tuberculosis—Girls' Ward," and I moved in the direction of the arrow. I was met by the nurse as she came out of one of the doors into the corridor, carrying a basket on her head with a pile of clothing protruding from it. I returned her greeting, then asked her what exactly she was carrying; she lowered her basket and told me it was the laundry from the girls' ward. I unfolded the bed sheets and pillow-cases and saw that the white sheets were almost completely covered with embroidery—hundreds of embroidered words reading "In Memory," followed by the names of the girls, decorated with flowers and boats sailing over waves and rising suns and birds in flight.

"Section 3—Tuberculosis." I read the instructions on the door and entered. At first I could see no one in the darkness, only the lines of bare beds stripped of their linen. Then I noticed her, alone at the far end of the ward, sitting on the edge of the bed beneath an orphan ray of sun that had strayed into the room from the only open window in the place. She sat hunched up, apparently preoccupied with something in her lap. Seeing me move toward her, she dropped the hem of her dress in confusion and stood up, so very thin, so embarrassed and pale and sensitive.

I told her I was the newly assigned doctor, and this reassured her. Then I went on to ask about the other young women, mentioning a few of the names I'd glimpsed on the sheets. She became clearly perturbed and simply said they'd all gone away; then, when she realized I hadn't quite understood, she quickly added, "May you live longer." She saw me looking at the hem of her dress, gave me an embarrassed smile, and said, "They've taken all the linen away, and this was all I could find to embroider."

On the hem I read the words "In Memory," stitched in sky blue and framed by two green flowers. The needle was dangling hesitantly with a pink thread still in its eye, sticking out from what, I later learned, was to be the first letter of her name.

—Translated by Mona N. Mikhail and Christopher Tingley

'Ali al-Makk (1937–1992)

Born in Um Durman in greater Khartoum, 'Ali al-Makk studied first at the University of Khartoum, then obtained an M.A. in public administration from the University of Southern California in 1966. He lectured at the University of Khartoum and was director of the Language Translation Unit. He spent 1988 as a visiting scholar at the University of New Mexico. His short stories revolve around Sudanese life in its various aspects, and several of his stories have been translated and published in English. He published at least five short-story collections, as well as many critical studies. An anthology of Sudanese literature edited by al-Makk was published in 1974.

THE CASE

The court convenes at nine o'clock in the morning . . . on paper, at least. No hearing has ever really started at nine, because the judge is not overly bothered by either appointments or time. He is not by any means lazy, since he turns up at his chambers at eight o'clock, but prefers to spend an hour or more reading . . . anything he can find on law and on tennis. On the other hand he is extremely careful to apply the full letter of the law. That is why everybody is afraid of him, especially those who live in the vicinity of his court and have become its clients. If they steal, they do not exaggerate . . . if they quarrel, they do so in whispers.

The docket on that particular Saturday morning, comprised only one case . . . although the "pack-up" was crowded with a large number of young Nubians, who had got drunk the previous night, then danced the Kempla in the public thoroughfare, which had resulted in a disturbance to the very precarious peace. They had been arrested and conveyed to the police station with the blessings of old-time Corporal 'Abdel Kerim, without putting up any resistance.

The defendant in the case was called Zeinab, a resident of the Sixth Alley in the town of Mahdiya. Her hobby was amassing money and traveling to the Hijaz every year. Forty-five years old, her obesity had destroyed her beauty.

The Hajja Zeinab, and her husband, Mahmoud, boarded a taxi, the driver of which immediately began adjusting his rearview mirror without appearing to pay them any attention. He wanted to be in a position where he could gaze on Hajja Zeinab. She realized what he was doing. "What they say about taxi drivers must be true. They have neither manners nor decency," she thought to herself. His gaze recorded her features. A few short seconds and then the decision, "She is not very interesting!" Most of the womenfolk of Al Mahdiya knew Hajja Zeinab, because she sold them their clothes, nylon wear, and skirts. She bought golden sovereigns and coins from the Hijaz and sold them to the womenfolk at a profit.

To himself Mahmoud reflected, "You were none too careful this time, Hajja, your end is near. In spite of the golden watch, the customs officer is now a person of some authority." In the past Hajja's suitcases had never been opened at Khartoum Airport. 'Abdel Fattah Effendi was the father of children who could not be fed on truth or clothed by honesty. The salary was small, snarled and snapped over by the creditors at the beginning of every month. 'Abdel Fattah Effendi used to know the exact date of Hajja Zeinab's return. He would chalk her cases through, and next day call on her at home, as though wishing her a happy return home and get his price. For five years, however, red tape had been unwinding its course. Promotion came as a blow to 'Abdel Fattah Effendi, because although it increased his salary by three pounds, it deprived him of Hajja Zeinab's bounty, as well as that of others. He was transferred to another station. "What an insufferable life! Hajja has been only three weeks in the Hijaz. A very short time but long enough to get you transferred from the airport customs." She was completely taken aback when she proceeded into the customs hall and 'Abdel Fattah Effendi was not there. The slim young man examining passengers' luggage was diligently and enthusiastically at work. When her turn came, he turned to her: "Are all these cases yours, madam?" Her searching eyes roved the length and breadth of the Airport Hall. "'Abdel Fattah Effendi isn't here?" The slim young man's voice answered, "All these seven cases are your luggage?" "Yes," she answered firmly.

Their eyes met. She could sense no comprehension or understanding between them. There was a pause, which came to an end when the slim young man opened the first suitcase. The contents, as though longing to escape their long and arduous confinement, poured out. Nylons, carpet-work, perfumes. "For your own personal use, Madam?" Hajja made no reply. The young man frowned and pulled out everything from the suitcase. The suitcase sighed with relief. He opened the second and the third. "Impossible! It's extraordinary! Do you intend to use all these things? Impossible, impossible!" Hajja suddenly realized that she had fallen prey to the system.

The young man's voice was sharp: "There is enough stuff here to open a shop in the European market." Then came the words that she had been dreading all her life: "Smuggling . . . contrabanding . . . all these things will be impounded." She found herself thinking, "Oh, if only he would be patient until he could come round the next morning . . . she could give him a pound and a Juvial watch, but that young man wouldn't be satisfied even with Big Ben. What, all these goods confiscated? Why? Was it the government that had bought them? Was it the government that had tired itself looking out for them or had performed the Holy Pilgrimage, hurled the rocks in the stoning rites, paraded round the house, or joined the processions between al- Safa and al-Marwa? Had the government gone aboard the aircraft and crossed the briny seas, suffering the horrors of takeoff and landing? Three hundred pounds lost to her. A sum collected with her sweat, tears, and patience." She was inspired with the words that came tumbling out of her mouth: "God have mercy on you, my son . . . your Aunt is a poor, miserable woman . . . " The young man laughed "Ha . . . ha . . . ha . . . " He went on "Poor? Miserable? You! It is really I who am miserable, Hajja!" After that Hajja wasn't sure exactly what happened, or of any of the events that followed, except that everything had run its course and she was now to come before the court.

The husband, Mahmoud, was hale and hearty. He was about forty years old and had no kind of employment to keep him busy. He was quite handsome, tall, broadly built, neatly dressed. Hajja looked after him from her income. She married him, although he had made no particular efforts in this direction. He had a gargantuan task to perform nightly for his food and drink. He rebelled inwardly but nightly enfolded to his bosom the gross bag of beans, disproportionately named Zeinab. On the eves of Monday and Friday he was expected to perform twice. The thoughts milled around his head: "Your evil actions have caught up with you, Hajja. You fool, Mahmoud; your name is on every tongue. What will you come to?" She knew exactly what was running through his mind. "Without my money, you would have starved to death on the sidewalk like a mangy pariah . . . but . . . " The taxi rolled along making its way to the courthouse. Both passengers were silent, their thoughts engaged in angry dialogue and severe accounting.

"Courts are for female bootleggers . . . tarts . . . and . . . and me? Your daughter, Abu Ahmad? *I* stand before a judge?" Her silence lengthened, her thoughts milled as they stood at the door of the waiting room.

The judge, who wanted nobody to know his name, save that of "Your Honour" had closed the door on himself and was busy with his own thoughts. He murmured to himself: "Phew . . . it's hot. Terrible, this concrete. If the loan comes through, I'll build my house of mud-brick . . . it's more moist. The roof will be of palm fronds." He looked around. The walls of his chambers were clean, so was the floor. The carpet was tattered and worn and of no particular color. The desk at which he was sitting was the worst thing in the room.

"Oh Lord, look on and marvel. A judge, who has the power to execute, jail, or set people free is sitting at a desk with one drawer? The chair is archaic! Not bad . . . not bad! Really, if I had my choice I would paint the walls gray. But the public works engineer says that only ministers' offices are entitled to gray. For the rest? White? Why? Am I a barber?"

When the judge heard the knock on his door, he realized that it could only be Corporal 'Abdel Kerim. Nobody else would dare to knock. He called out loudly, dryly, "Come in, Corporal 'Abdel Kerim." The door opened and the corporal looked in. He marched in bringing with him a blast of hot air and a babble of voices. The judge gathered that the courtroom was full to the brim. The floor of his chambers was nigh on splitting open with Corporal 'Abdel Kerim's martial stamp. Tramp . . . Tramp . . . Tramp.

He came to a brisk attention, his heels firmly together. His legs, however, were like two brackets that no system, however mighty, could ever bring together. Stomach well out; "Everything is ready, Your Honor; the contraband case." Tramp . . . Tramp. One step to the rear, a vigorous salute . . . he waited stiffly at attention. "Very good, Corporal 'Abdel Kerim. Thank you."

The greatest source of delight to Corporal Abdel Kerim was to see a well-filled courtroom, so that everybody could admire his diligence, energy, and dedication, something that filled his heart with pride and self-admiration. "Seventeen years in khaki. I consider myself very happy, because I went to school for one single day, then out at first break and have never been back again."

The courtroom was not spacious. There was quite a large number of windows through which the breeze circulated freely. At the western end was a high dais, with a desk for the judge, no larger than the one in his chambers. Yet it was clean and had a special majesty about it, maybe because it stood in such a high place.

The corporal himself was supervising entrance into the courtroom. "Calmly . . . quietly please. Let's have some quiet, you sheep. This is a courtroom, not a marketplace."

People crowded round the door, trying to get in, pushing away at each other. 'Abdel Kerim's voice, the voice of the corporal, rising again: "Don't you have any work to do instead of goggling at the tribulations of Allah's worshippers?" He said it without any particular ulterior motive. Order established itself . . . an ominous hush. The spectators seated themselves on the wooden benches . . . painted in brown but looking extremely uncomfortable. They did not have even a backrest.

When the judge appeared, everyone stood up. Hajja Zeinab had taken her place in the dock, flanked by an armed policeman, stiff as a helpless statue. Mahmoud sat not far off, where he could see her and where she, pouring with sweat, could see him. Her gown, wound round her body, revealed her obviously expensive, multicolored clothes. The gown was blue, the shoes gray. The long-sleeved dress was worked in heavy embroidery. She thought to herself, "Did what you do deserve all this suffering?" Mahmoud too was reflecting, "What if she is found guilty and jailed. What lies ahead . . . for me?" The judge surmounted the heavy silence: "Name?" His question was addressed to Hajja Zeinab. Despite the raw sea of silence, she did not hear him. A second and third time the judge called out, but still she made no answer. Irritated, Mahmoud replied, "Hajja Zeinab Ayoub." The judge flared up in anger and shouted, "Who gave you permission to speak? You are not in the street. Remove him from court. Contempt of court. One pound fine or ten lashes of the 'cat'." Mahmoud thought to himself fearlessly and with a trace of anger, "An insulting penalty." He sighed perplexedly as he followed Corporal 'Abdel Kerim out of the court with nothing more in his pocket than a one-pound note. It was as if the judge had intended to divest him of everything he owned. He began to contemplate rapidly whether he could bear the ten strokes of the cat, foolish as that line of thought might be. The lash however biting or fearsome could not deprive him of his pound note.

An atmosphere of dread and awe prevailed in the courtroom. It helped to revive Hajja Zeinab from her reveries. She was deeply concerned lest Mahmoud come to some harm. If he were flogged, that might be the lesser of the two evils, since it might curb some of his vanity. As for the pound, well, ultimately it was she who would be paying it. "How miserable this day is."

The hearing lasted about half an hour, after which the judge ruled that the goods be confiscated and Hajja Zeinab fined fifty pounds. The crowds slipped out of the courtroom as rapidly as they had flowed in, while the judge hurried back into his chambers. Nobody paid any attention to Mahmoud returning to the courtroom when it was cleared; or to Hajja, who crouched low in the dock, all fear now forgotten. "Three hundred pounds those articles cost me, to be effortlessly grabbed by the government? Did the government tour round the Ka'aba . . . stand on 'Arafat . . . or visit the mausoleum of al-Mustafa? Did it even cross the briny seas? But why the fine? Isn't it enough that they have looted me of everything I own?"

When Mahmoud came back into the courtroom, it was obvious by his expression that he was very deeply grieved. Silence reigned. In the courtroom stood only the harsh brown benches supervised by the judge's desk. The windows were empty; eyes staring sightlessly at the northern and southern horizons, the breeze hurried in and then out again with no desire to remain in this place.

"The thing that really enrages me is that this relationship has become so humiliating. I am not Mahmoud. I am Hajja's husband. The people in our quarter know me as such. They are right . . . very right. People are known by what they do, what they are. If anyone asked me what my job was, I wouldn't know how to answer. I have none. Unemployed, although I am healthy and strong. When asked, I say I'm a broker. Sometimes I say I run an agricultural project on the banks of the White Nile. That kind of reply makes the one who asks drool with curiosity. The question is prompt: 'Cotton cultivation, of course. Allah . . . your prosperity is assured.'" His reflections continued: "By Allah the Mightiest, I know no place in this widespread land save Omdurman. I do not even know where Kosti or Marwi are. Why? If I were to happen to come across the White Nile in my way, I wouldn't know it from any other of God's creations."

His eyes met those of Hajja. An open confrontation was obviously imminent. He felt her gaze piercing through him, inspecting him, wresting away any mask his spirit had donned. She asked, "Did you pay the pound?" and then waited silently, her gaze clinging to him. She went on, "We're finished. The government has taken all I have. Who knows, they are probably sharing it out among each other at this very moment." Mahmoud said nothing. His glances darted far beyond the walls of the courtroom but rested on nothing. He felt that a surge of rage was about to swallow him up, without him being able to protect himself from it.

She said, "It is Allah's will. It is far easier to pay the fine than to go to jail." He could imagine Hajja in jail. She would have to wear the long-sleeved prison uniform and feel no different from the other inmates. "Visitors would see you on Friday, Hajja, and you could sell tobacco leaf and maybe other articles to the prisoners. Ah ... but the nights would be so lonely." The thoughts ran on in his mind as he continued to stare at nothing, his longing for his freedom growing. Reflectively he thought, "A modest living ... a young wife to whom he could dedicate his energies. Not bad if he could find a homestead on a far off hill. Yes, those kinds of dreams need work and energy, neither of which he knew anything about." His thoughts swept on as though he were speaking to himself. "It is true I am strong, but you are a coward at forty, Mahmoud. A little effort exerted could perhaps wash the humiliation out of your soul. You could work as a navvy, for thirty piastres a day, road building. Your hands are not creative, cannot initiate things ... roads ... under the searing sun ... roads."

Hajja's voice broke into his train of thought: "We'll walk, shall we?" He made no reply. He felt something solid swell up inside him. He looked her straight in the face without fear or temerity. Slowly he pulled the pound note out of his pocket and returned it to her. Her eyes opened wide in astonishment. "You were flogged?" She said it pityingly, but he did not answer. He turned toward the door and started walking away with a light step. He felt her gaze on his back. He made his way into the street that drew his steps forward into the blinding sunlight, walking ... walking, alone under the glare of the sun.

—*Translated by Alec Magalli*

'Alya Mamdouh (b. 1944)

Born in Baghdad, 'Alya Mamdouh studied psychology at the al-Mustansi-riyya University in Baghdad, graduated in 1972, and began writing short stories soon afterward. Her first collection, *An Overture for Laughter*, was published in 1973 and was followed by *Notes of Mrs B.* in 1978. Her first novel, *Laila and the Wolf* (1981), brought her immediate recognition, and her second novel, *Mothballs*, was published in 1986. 'Alya Mamdouh writes with a freedom rarely achieved by male fiction writers, expressing the free and single-mindedly feminist attitude of a woman living at the turn of the twenty-first century. Her delineation of scenes from Baghdad and other cities of the world where she has lived and worked is both sensitive and daring. Apart from her creative writing, she works as a journalist and writes for Arab literary journals. She lives between Paris and Casablanca.

CROSSING OVER

I was, I felt, rather conservative but still capable of finding a more modern outlook. Each morning, before I went out into the street, I'd reflect how I had to protect myself ever more carefully; then, each evening, I could go out on the town and feel free. I learned to take long journeys through the narrow streets of Beirut, but still, you can never have enough protection in that city.

There were Europeans from all parts of the continent, of every color, permanent features of the shops and cafés. As for us, we were seemingly only to be there for a while, and yet we were making our unique contribution. I'd draw a veil over my pride and go out into the street.

Buicks and Fords and Mercedeses, churned out by the technological machine, passed by, but what did they have to do with me? As for the people in al-Hamra Street, their faces told you, more or less, that they'd never left the place since the day they were born.

There were a young woman and a young man, smiling fondly at one another. They were leaning against a car in a side street, supposing they were unobserved, but I saw them and caught my breath. As I came closer, I saw the young girl's face was different from any I'd known before, while the young man's face bore the promise of a long life to come. As I passed, I felt my respect for such people grow.

A car stopped suddenly close to me, and out from it came a young woman like a houri, positively dancing. She moved away from me without so much as saying good evening, then, a moment later, went into a fashion shop. I followed her in and came up so close behind her I was almost touching her. She was, I noted, speaking French. Nothing she saw seemed to appeal to her; she just kept turning away, smiling bleakly. Her skin was as clear as crystal, her face faultlessly made up, her eyes like wild flowers—though they seemed incapable of focusing on anything for long.

It was women like that, perhaps, that led to famine and fire. To look at her you'd say she was worth twenty other women, and when she left without buying anything she gave the shopkeeper a ten-lira tip.

A lady crossing the street nearby had a strange, artificial way of walking and moving: tack, tack, tack. As she reached the other pavement, the heel of her shoe flew off. She didn't turn back but limped on, before throwing off the other heel too. Then, evidently feeling the way she was walking was bad for her back, she took both shoes off, flung them in the nearest garbage can, and strolled barefoot into a café. What drew me to her was her smile and this small assault she'd made on life.

Suddenly I realized I was under siege from a man wearing dark glasses, tall and elegant, his hair neither short or long—I'd seen him before, I recalled, in more than one corner. He had a distinctly worried look on his face and gave the impression of someone who kept his thoughts to himself.

If it were only possible to make friends instantly, he was the one I would have chosen. Some faces are friendly and some are hostile, and some are between the two, but this face wasn't like any I'd known before. It was totally open, exposed. The thought kept haunting me: if only I could see his eyes! If I were in the police I'd stop people wearing dark glasses; but I'm just an ordinary woman wandering the streets, moving on from one shop to the next without buying anything, with a handbag inclined to poverty, though happy enough to carry slips of paper and telephone numbers (the police, perhaps, or the fire brigade, the emergency number, an empty cigarette packet, or the school bills for my only son). All I had on my shoulder was the handbag strapped around it; no sort of official insignia. Yet the man kept looking toward me, then away from me again, in all directions, without once venturing to take off his glasses. It wasn't just a matter, any more, of a man and a woman. The problem was how to rise above the curse of sexuality that raises barriers between one human being and another. The situation was becoming unbearable. I took off my own glasses and held them in my hand. It's the people around people who are my real enemies. Who was it that said, "I love humanity, but I hate people"?

Suddenly I felt full of joy, with a sense that the sun belonged to everyone. I stopped piling up the contradictions and imagined the man would take off his glasses as well. I went up to him where he was leaning back against a pillar, resolved, apparently, to say nothing. Yet, as I dropped my matchbox and bent to pick it up, he gave the impression of wanting something even so. As I stood right alongside him, I heard his voice for the first time, sorrowful and almost crushed.

"Madam," the voice said, "would you be kind enough to help me over to the other sidewalk?"

"You're like me, sir," I said, as I took his two hands. "You want to cross to the other side!"

—Translated by Salwa Jabsheh and Christopher Tingley

Samira al-Mana' (b. 1935)

Samira al-Mana' was born in Basra, Iraq, and holds a B.A. from the University of Baghdad and a Postgraduate Diploma in Librarianship from Ealing Technical College, London. After some years teaching Arabic language and literature in Baghdad, she became, from 1976 to 1980, chief librarian at the Iraqi Cultural Center in London, and from 1981 to 1985 worked in London as a freelance consultant librarian. Since 1985 she has been assistant editor of the literary magazine *Alightirab al-Adabi*. Her first novel, *The Forerunners and the Newcomers*, was published in 1972 and was followed by *A London Sequel* (1979), *The Umbilical Cord* (1990), and *Look At Me, Look At Me*, presently being serialized in *Alightrab al-Adabi*. She has also written a collection of short stories, *The Song* (1976), and a play, *Only a Half* (1984). Some of her short stories have been translated into Dutch and English and published in various periodicals. She is married to the poet Salah Niyazi and lives in self-imposed exile in Britain.

THE BILLY GOAT AND THE MENFOLK

She didn't die without a hard struggle. Her labor pains that evening had been excruciating, and everyone in the house had come rushing out on hearing her anguished bleating and the rumble of her heavy breathing. Mahmoud had come from his room in confusion, with just one of his slippers on, and Zakiyya's clogs could be heard clattering as she hurried closer.

The father was already there, by the goat's head, but there was little he could do. None of them could help this goat, which had been so generous before with offspring but was feverish and weak now and, it seemed, about to die—their coffee-colored goat with the wide eyes. They stood helplessly around her with their arms crossed, watching the half-born kid, as death worked its way through the mother's trembling frame. In a single heavy draught the goat drew in air from around her and, as her newborn dropped, turned her mouth away from it, her eyelids motionless with pain and fatigue. The newborn kid was just a lump of soggy, sticky flesh, with watery eyes and flabby limbs. Earth and fine bits of straw clung to it the moment it touched the ground and started wriggling closer to its mother, a dirty, viscous lump.

Soon the house was ablaze with anger and sorrow. The goat had died. Their house goat was dead! The neighbor, hearing the news, came running to the house with a troop of her children. She was an expert on difficult births, and she examined the dead beast, feeling all over the body for some throb of life. But, with the born obstinacy of sheep and goats, it wouldn't revive.

Meanwhile, it emerged the newborn kid was a male, a mere billy goat, whereas the dead mother had been fecund and given plenty of milk. The kid had killed their goat. It was because of him she'd died; even if he had some value himself, nothing could alter that. And what was the use of a billy goat without a mother, a billy goat that would have to live on bought milk? When he was full-grown, he wouldn't pay back the money laid out to foster him. In fact he wouldn't pay for a single drink of milk. How, after all, could a milkless creature pay?

The wretched kid had killed his mother. He lay prostrate by her side now, like an innocent child fearing punishment. The smell of the blood was still fresh on his soft body, recalling the mischance that had left this small creature untended and uncared for.

The family bade farewell to the goat with all due form and honor. She was placed on top of the dustbin and covered with a tattered mat to keep the flies away. The father went grieving back to the house, while Mahmoud trudged back to his room. As for Zakiyya, she stayed behind to clean up the spot where the goat had given birth to the last of her offspring—the last of her generous gifts to the family.

The eyes of the tiny kid were dark and sad. His little belly twitched like the belly of a coward seized with fear, his legs were folded beneath him, and his body was spread out limp and soft. Zakiyya took care not to get him wet and thought of fetching him a cover or laying him down by the fire in her room. She'd have to clean up all the mess he'd left, and she'd have to wipe him clean too, getting off all the things that had stuck to him. She fetched a rag and started drying him, till his skin was velvety and shiny and the little ears shapely and comely. He looked very small, but all babies grew, and this kid of their goat's would grow up one day too. He'd drink milk, which Zakiyya would feed him from a spoon till he could drink from a bowl himself. Perhaps he was hungry now. Why shouldn't she feed him? She started feeling a little happier, for the first time since the goat had died. The goat had been very dear to her, and she'd cried when its body was carried out, just as her mother had been taken from the house three years before.

Zakiyya had wailed and cried both times, but neither her father nor her brother had seemed to pay much attention to her grief. She'd grown used, after her mother's death, to milking the goat every morning and evening. She'd been ten then, and soon, as she and the goat came to be left alone in the house, a deep bond had developed between them. Her father would go off to work each morning, to the auctions at the market, while her brother, Mahmoud, who was a private in the army, was often away at his barracks. He had a day's leave each week, but he'd spend this with friends at the café, playing backgammon and sipping tea.

The goat had been very tame, very docile and gentle. She'd never bleated except when her feed of clover was late, and she knew the times of her meals well enough. Young though she was, without any experience of looking after animals, Zakiyya had had no problems tending her. The goat's part of the court-yard was still alive with her presence, with its own special homeliness, just as the barley and clover still scattered about was a reminder of her. Zakiyya's poor mother had left nothing but her clothes, which had been distributed among the poor, and her two children, Zakiyya and Mahmoud. If only she'd lived on, to give Zakiyya and her brother more brothers and sisters! She would have given them new names, Zakiyya thought, modern names. She wished she herself had been called something like Hana or Wafa, not given an old-fashioned name like Zakiyya, which made her hate herself sometimes. At least she'd give the kid a suitable name. She'd call him Shawqi. She even looked inquiringly at the kid, as if to see what he thought of his name. Then, imagining the kid's lips had actually moved to murmur something, she stifled a laugh.

If only she had a small sister. She'd sew all kinds of embroidered clothes for her and take her with her when she visited some of her friends. And she wouldn't let anyone cut her sister's hair. She'd let it stay long, so she could tie it in plaits to hang behind the ears. She liked little girls, but there was no reason, after all, why this tiny kid shouldn't be a male. She'd tie a green ribbon around his neck, and maybe a bell too, or anklets around his legs. And when he got bigger, he'd start drinking milk by himself, maybe come to the kitchen, whinnying in his own way, to say he was hungry. He could eat clover. It was plentiful and cheap in their district, and she'd ask her father to bring a bunch or two every day. She'd ask him to bring barley as well, and crushed date stones. There was plenty of animal feed, of all sorts, in the Abu 'l-Khasib district.

When she woke next morning, she found the kid huddled under the cover, just as she'd left him, peering about in an attempt to find someone he knew. She got busy preparing breakfast. Her father had his tea without any milk, resentful of how they'd been short of milk since the goat died—and all, he said, because of this kid not worth a quarter of a dinar. Zakiyya kept quiet. The kid would get bigger, she knew and, with a little patience, be worth a lot more than that. And why should he be sold anyway?

Before her father went out he told her to buy some milk and feed the kid, so that he wouldn't starve to death. She'd had exactly the same idea herself. How clever of her father, she reflected, to think of that. But her father just glanced quickly at the kid, with a calculating air.

"We'll slaughter him in two or three weeks," he said. "We'll slaughter him if he lives that long, God willing."

She felt her lips turn stiff and dry.

"But why?" she said. "He was only born yesterday."

"Why? Because it's no use keeping him, that's why. He's a male kid. What good will he be?"

Zakiyya plucked up her courage, then said entreatingly, "I want to keep him." Her father gave a sarcastic laugh.

"Keep him? How long are you going to keep carrying on like a woman?"

Zakiyya said nothing. She didn't tell him the kid's name was Shawqi, that this was the name she'd chosen for him herself. That would only have led to scenes, and her father would have made it a talking point at the market and with his friends, going on about her girlish ways. He would have made endless fun of her at home too. He hurried out, slamming the door after him and leaving her alone with the kid.

So, she'd tend him for just two or three weeks; that was her father's decision. She'd live with him till he died. There wasn't much to look forward to, beyond that short time, and there was nothing more to wish for him now. She couldn't hang a bell around his neck. And she couldn't give him a name—what was the point? She bought the milk, but he wouldn't take it from the spoon; he kept his mouth tight shut and the milk spilt. Nothing would persuade him to drink.

Still she tried, with dogged patience, to feed him. He should have had his feed the night before, but still he refused food, turning his head away, as if disgusted, to right and left. Could it be he knew what was in store for him? He'd been there, after all, when her father made those threats. That really would be sad. Still, he must eat something.

"Here," she said. "Have a taste at least. Just a spoonful, just one spoonful. Please!"

For two days the kid wouldn't take a drop. Then, on the third day, her father brought a rubber teat and handed it to her.

"Give him the milk in this," he told her. "That'll encourage him to drink it."

Zakiyya was jubilant at this. Perhaps her father had changed his mind and wouldn't slaughter the kid. He'd bought him something to get him used to feeding.

The kid sucked the milk with utter contentment now, closing his eyes and relishing it to the last drop. There was no difference, for him, between the cold rubber teat and the warmth of his mother's teats he'd never had the chance to enjoy. He had a full feed, and this was followed by others. He seemed certain to grow and thrive now. Zakiyya, delighted, had visions of him grazing in the neighboring field, along with the other sheep and goats.

After a few days he got confidently to his feet and started looking curiously around for herbage to graze. Zakiyya never left him alone for long; she was around him constantly, holding and fondling him. She was sure now he'd be good for something, and wasn't about to be slaughtered.

Early one morning, in the third week, her father put his cup of tea to his lips, not forgetting to remark on the poor quality of the milk, so different from the milk of their old, generous goat; and he remembered, too, her kid that he was going to slaughter that day, before inviting some friends of his to a sumptuous meal. Shaikh Dari was to be one of the guests, along with his son Ghazwan, and Taqi and Rahim might be coming. The kid should, he thought, be big enough for five or six people now. He gave his daughter precise instructions on how it should be stuffed with rice and the necessary condiments, then roasted in their earthenware oven. His mouth watered as he explained it all.

"Take care over the condiments, Zakiyya," he said. "Get them all just right. They're the secret of good cooking, the way your mother and our neighbor Um Jabbar used to cook."

Zakiyya said nothing. Then she asked, "Do you want another cup of tea?"

"No, no, I've had enough. I just wanted to be sure you won't let me down in front of my guests tomorrow."

Zakiyya remembered all the chickens her father had killed when they'd had guests; how he'd held them by the neck after first fixing their wings firmly under his feet, so they wouldn't flutter about and spatter everything with their blood. Sometimes, too, he'd go shooting in the Shatt al-'Arab district and come back laden with all kinds of birds, proud of being such a good shot and knowing where the best coveys and hides were. He'd take hold of the kid today, in the same easy, unconcerned way, and slaughter him neatly and efficiently.

But she knew this kid. She'd seen his two small sad eyes when he was born. They'd tended him, and she'd known his mother long before that. What harm would there have been in sparing the kid, in memory of past days? She was afraid, though, of revealing any of these thoughts to her father. He might be annoyed or else take the chance to make fun of her. She wished Mahmoud would say something to dissuade him, but he was quietly eating his breakfast. He finished it and went off with a muttered good-bye.

Her father spoke more sharply.

"Zakiyya," he said, "fetch me the rope and the knife—the sharp knife, not that useless kitchen one."

She gave him the knife and the rope but didn't tell him she was going over to their neighbors' house.

—Translated by Farida Abu Haidar and Christopher Tingley

Hassouna Misbahi (b. 1950)

Tunisian short-story writer, novelist, and journalist Hassouna Misbahi was born in a small village in mid-Tunisia, then studied in the capital, obtaining a degree in French from the University of Tunis. After working as a teacher, he was dismissed and lived a vagrant life for four years. At the beginning of the 1980s he began working as correspondent for various Arab periodicals outside Tunisia before settling in Munich where he worked as editorial secretary for the German review *Fikr wa Fann*. He is now the formal correspondent to the London-based Saudi newspaper, *Al-Sharq al-Awsat*. A great lover of freedom and a rebellious spirit, Misbahi challenges in his work outmoded taboos and restrictions. He has published several books of fiction, characterized by originality and zest. These include the short-story collections, *The Tale of My Cousin Haniyya's Madness* (1985); *The Turtle* (1996), which has been translated into German; and *Night of the Strangers* (1998); and three novels, *The Hallucinations of Tarshish* (Tarshish being a pre-Islamic name for Tunis), which was translated into German and recently won the Tukan Prize for the best book; *The Others* (1998); and *Good-Bye Rosalie* (2001), also translated into German.

THE AUTUMN OF '81

On the floor of the room were cigarette ends and some sad, desperate-looking papers.

On the iron bed were faded covers worn out by years of use.

There was a frightening confusion; everything was mixed up with everything else, everything dead, broken, and defeated. There was an unbearable smell too, the stench of a kitchen neglected for a week, and a toilet no longer working, and dirty clothes. Between the door and the only window was a picture of Pablo Neruda getting drunk in one of the taverns—in Santiago probably, or Madrid or Paris, gazing upward with a wide forehead like a bare autumn plain. Around the cunning eyes were clouds that warned of a storm, and between the wrinkles there was a poem, fluttering like a bird about to take its first flight. He remembered he had to finish *War and Peace* and then hang the picture of Tolstoy. "I like princes when they rebel," he said under his breath. He imagined him standing in his large garden among the grasses and trees, his wide robe billowing out in the wind and his beard trembling like a bush not of this world. Then he saw Rimbaud afflicted with skin disease, and the Africans carrying him beneath the rains of Ethiopia. Why did Rimbaud go there, he wondered. He recalled how, when he read his poems for the first time, he felt a terror he'd never experienced before, so that he couldn't sleep by himself any more. It was as if he'd been struck down by fever or by a permanent curse.

Since then he'd feared the dark, and people, and the old winding streets, and sunset over the empty barren plains, and winter coming down inscrutably from the gloomy northern heights. "Tomorrow," he said to himself, "I'll write my mother a letter and tell her I'm feeling sad. I'm sure she won't cry the way she used to." The last time he visited her, she told him her heart had grown cold. It was, she said, as if he, her son, hadn't really come from her womb, for now she was sure he was a failure and that fate had afflicted her with him; the books he read had crazed him, made him wander far and wide, away from the straight road. He imagined her walking in the streets absorbed in her thoughts, cursing the malice of fate, and the treacherous world, and the books that had spoiled her son and made him a vagabond in the streets of a heartless, remote city.

The man in the next flat was shouting.

"You've ruined my life, you bitch—you whore—"

The woman didn't say anything, or if she did, he didn't hear it.

He wished he could sink into a deep, blissful sleep, like the sleep he'd known when he was a boy. In those days he'd go to bed straight after evening prayer and enjoy the smell of the black cows and the sounds of the night. And before sleep finally closed his eyelids, he'd dream of a wide empty plain, with a red hut built there, for the birds to go and rest when they were tired.

The man was shouting again.

"What do you do in the streets every night! Tell me! What do you do in the streets from morning till night? Tell me, you bitch, you—"

The woman didn't say anything, or if she did, he didn't hear it.

Sleepless nights had become an endless wasteland. Everything now had taken on the harshness of barren open spaces filled with stones and thorns and silence.

"I'll tear you apart!" the man was shouting. "I'll show you who's master, you bitch, you—"

The woman didn't say anything, or if she did, he didn't hear it.

"You spend all your time in front of the mirror, and you put on a new dress every other hour. Are you trying to turn my house into a brothel?"

The woman didn't say anything, or if she did, he didn't hear it.

"When I can sleep again," he thought, "I'll go to that tavern in the street that suddenly turns and makes for the sea, as if it wants to get rid of the dust and the heat. I'll sit there on my own, in a corner, and drink one, two, five, ten, twenty—then I'll go out and walk toward the shore, quietly, and sit on the sand with my feet in the water. Then I'll listen to the night and the waves and the din of remote cities."

"You've ruined my life!" the man was shouting. "You've played around with my pride and manhood. Everyone's laughing at me!"

The woman didn't say anything, or if she did, he didn't hear it.

"I'm going to kill you, even if they hang me for it! I don't care about anything any more!"

"I'll write my mother a letter tomorrow," he thought, "and tell her I'm feeling sad."

Her nephew would read it to her, and when he'd finished, she'd tell him, "He's a worthless boy. He's been totally useless to me, and he's ruined his own future. All the other boys from the village have got on, all except him. He's an idle, degenerate boy. I should have thrown him down the well when he was first born." Then she'd go home, with her stick thrust out in front of her and her thick shoes thumping down on the ground.

"I'll show you who's master, you whore—you—"

The woman didn't say anything, or if she did, he didn't hear it.

The heat grew and he began wiping the sweat that was now pouring from him. He looked up at the ceiling, feeling very tired and wishing his childhood could return, and the smell of the black cows, and the moon that used to peep so shyly and serenely from among the cactus plants.

By the eastern gate on the outskirts of the city, where the desolate plains and the dust began, there was an old café where he liked to sit. He'd go there tomorrow with a book. He'd try and write something—though he knew already he wouldn't be able to. There was something standing between him and writing, something that lodged itself in the sinews of his hand or mind, heavy, viscous, as hateful as a spider or a beetle. When would the day come, the day when he'd explode with creativity, alone and with total finality?

"You're in the streets from morning till night! I can't look other men in the face any more!"

The woman didn't say anything, or if she did, he didn't hear it.

At that moment he remembered her. She descended upon him like a thread the color of the dawn, and his body was aflame. Did she still, he wondered, have that fiery desire in her eyes? God, where did she go? She used to come to him and leave him like a storm. And when the moon was full, the whole universe would melt, taking on the various colors of the rainbow.

He'd read *Lady Chatterley's Lover* with her and translated al-Sayyab's[1] poems for her. When she wrote to tell him she wouldn't be coming any more, he grew

---

1. Badr Shakir al-Sayyab was one of the major poets of the post-1950 modernist period of Arabic poetry and heralded many important changes in the Arabic poem.

his beard and wretchedly tramped the streets, read the lives of those who'd killed themselves for love, then decided that women were stupid and that he'd drown his past and return to the village. He'd line them up in a single row, then fire a hail of bullets at them and throw their corpses to the vultures on the mountains! Her name was Chantal. Where was she now?

A woman of light, or fire, with the smell of wild grasses! Where was she now? Her name was Chantal. She was born in Beirut, but all she could remember of Beirut was the corniche.

"Damn your father and damn your mother, you whore—"

The woman didn't say anything, or if she did, he didn't hear it.

"I'll break every bone in your body!"

Something crashed down with an enormous noise. The voice of a crying baby was heard.

"Shut up, you little brat, before I kill you!" shouted the man.

The child choked back its tears and began to sob aloud.

It hurt him to imagine the child's breast heaving, its lips working in convulsive fear.

A window opened in the building opposite and a man shouted, "Do you think you're the only man in the building?"

"Go to hell!" shouted the first man. Then he closed one window and a second and a third.

"Curse this city!" shouted the man in the building opposite. "And curse this life!"

From somewhere else another man shouted, "Aren't there any laws or police around here?"

Once he'd written to her, "The tree opposite my window has turned yellow, and in a few days it will be completely bare. The ugly old city shivers with the cold of the northern winds, and I sit reading the letters of Rilke to Salomi, and weep when I remember your eyes."

Her name was Chantal. She was born in Beirut, but all she could remember of Beirut was the corniche. The man was talking in an emotional voice, as if he was weeping, "I work like a dog to make you happy, and what do I get for it? You're in the streets from morning till night. I saw you smiling at that swine yesterday!"

He wondered why Rimbaud went to Ethiopia after he'd finished his "Chapter in Hell." He wished he could go away too, go where things still had no names. He remembered he had to finish *War and Peace* and hang Tolstoy's picture next to the picture of Pablo Neruda. Her name was Chantal. Would she remember one day and return like a beautiful storm? He'd take her to that gloomy southern village as usual and wake her at dawn so she could contemplate the sunrise in the oasis. She used to say, "The sky of your country at sunset is the color of honey." She used to dream of the return of the prophets, and all she could remember of Beirut was the corniche. Her name was Chantal. Why didn't she come back? She was like the birds, emigrating now to the countries of the sun and now back to the countries of ice. She used to embrace him and say, "I'm cold, like a polar bear." Her name was Chantal. She was born in Beirut, and all she could remember of Beirut was the corniche.

The man was almost whispering now.

"You know I only want you to be happy. I want you to be a queen all the time."

"I'll write tomorrow," he thought.

He heard a dress being torn, and he imagined the face of the sky was wounded and bleeding.

"I'll write tomorrow."

The bed in the next apartment began to make monotonous groaning noises, like a hearse moving toward the graveyard. Loud panting sounds were heard and moans, till he imagined the whole room was dancing and the books were embracing each other. He punched his pillow violently.

"I'll write tomorrow," he thought.

The sound of the moving bed grew more hectic, then a violet rope stretched between the sky and the earth. The bare field stretched out in his imagination, with a red hut standing in the middle of it. The cranes passed, flying southward with mournful cries; then silence spread like a shroud over a corpse.

The night struck him with gloom and terror, and he felt a thousand knives directed at his heart. He wept as he remembered her. Oh, if only she could come out to him from the cracks of the door, or from between the books, or through the window. Her name was Chantal.

"Tomorrow," he thought, "I'll write my mother a letter and tell her I'm feeling sad, and that autumn this year is full of lies and dust and flies."

—*Translated by Lena Jayyusi and Christopher Tingley*

Muhammad al-Murr (b. 1954)

Short-story writer from the United Arab Emirates Muhammad al-Murr was born in Dubai and studied at Syracuse University in the United States. He now works as a journalist in his own country, a profession that has given him great scope for expressing his ideas on culture and on general social issues. One of the generation of modern writers in the Gulf, he reflects in his short stories a particular involvement with the issues of poverty and human suffering. However, his great asset as a story writer is his capacity to entertain, excite, and interest the reader in the text and the outcome of the story—a quality many writers, eager to provide novelty and new orientations at the price of these first prerequisites of fiction, are finding difficult to achieve. In the last few years al-Murr has become interested in Arab calligraphy, becoming an expert on the great variety of script used for artistic reasons, and has been able to acquire a large collection, in part bought and in part commissioned, of these highly artistic objects. He has published many collections of short stories to date, among which are *Friendship* (1984),

A Little Tenderness (1985), and *The Surprise* (1985). Two collections of his works have appeared in English: *Dubai Tales*, translated by Peter Clark (1991) and *The Wink of the Mona Lisa* (1995), translated by J. Bricks.

SMILING AS LARGE AS LIFE

[1]

Saqr returned home, his body worn out by fatigue and exertion. He went into the courtyard of the house and called out to his wife, "Give me the rifle."

"Why?" his wife asked in an anxious voice.

"I'm going to kill this wretched monkey," he shouted.

"What's she done this time?" his wife wondered.

He sat down and began wiping the sweat from his brow. The monkey started to mimic him, and he slapped her on the hand with a bitter laugh.

"You wretched creature, do you want them to put me in prison?"

The monkey withdrew into a corner and pretended to be angry. "I tied her to the leg of the big chair outside the shop as usual," Saqr continued. "When I went out and didn't find her, I thought she was wandering in the back lanes and she'd come back to the shop before nine o'clock when I lock up. I waited till ten o'clock, and when I'd nearly given up hope, the telephone rang. A friend of mine, a police officer, summoned me to the police station to collect this stupid monkey."

"What did Um Kamil do?" his wife asked.

"This isn't Um Kamil," he said angrily. "This is Um Mujrim, Um Harami, Um Majnun.[1] When she slipped out of the chain tying her to the chair, she slunk off through the lanes and alleys and streets, and went into the Hyatt Regency Hotel, to the great banqueting hall that was crowded with a big wedding party. Can you imagine the uproar at the party because of this wretched Um Kamil honoring it with her presence?"

Saqr's wife sympathised with him, but she couldn't help smiling.

"Yes, laugh!" her husband said. "Suppose it had been the wedding of one of your sisters or daughters? The first thing she headed for was the big cake, which she overturned and started trampling on. The bridegroom ran away, with his cloak left behind and his headcloth and headband fallen off. The bride was frozen to the spot with fear. Then Um Kamil headed for the bridegroom's chair, sat down on it, and took the veil off the bride's head and put it on her own. The women and children screamed their heads off, the waiters and orchestra and relatives of the bridegroom and bride tried to catch her, and she turned the hall into a circus. She started dodging and weaving away from them, over the tables and under the tables, grabbing hold of the dresses of the women and throwing

---

1. Literally, "Mother of a Criminal, Mother of a Thief, Mother of a Lunatic."

plates of food and glasses full of drink at them. It took a big squad of policemen to catch her, after endless effort. By the grace of God the officer in charge of the police station was one of my best friends. If it had been an officer I didn't know, he would have handed me over to the court and there would have been a big case over it.

"But Um Kamil's very funny," his wife said with a laugh.

[2]

Saqr and his wife were fond of animals. They had a goat, a duck, a tortoise, a parrot, dogs, and cats. The year before Saqr had been wandering with his wife and small son around shops that sold animals, birds, and fish. In one of them he saw a female chimpanzee cracking peanuts. The owner of the shop had put a blue and white sailor's hat on her head and tied a red ribbon round her neck. She shook hands with Saqr's son, who liked her and insisted on his father buying her. His father asked how much she cost, and the owner of the shop replied that the price was five thousand dirhams. The father changed his mind when he heard how high the price was, but his son's screaming and crying and his wife's pleas and entreaties persuaded him to buy the monkey, which his wife called Um Kamil.

With Um Kamil's arrival at the house, the problems began. On her second day in Saqr's house she climbed onto the roof of the neighbors' house, opened the water tank, and went into it for a refreshing soak in the summer noon. Saqr had to pay a high price for the bath the pampered monkey had enjoyed. He bought his neighbors a new water tank and paid for it to be installed in place of the tank that Um Kamil had polluted.

Um Kamil became a constant terror to the grocer next to their house. When she escaped from her wooden cage or the chain they used to fasten her to the large almond tree, she'd head straight for the grocer, and the moment she entered his shop, the customers would flee and he'd be glued to the spot. She'd open the refrigerator, throw the bottles and cans of drinks on the ground, and eat some pieces of cheese. She'd climb onto the shelves of the shop, throw cans of foodstuffs, children's toys, and soap onto the ground, and select a particular kind of biscuit to take to Saqr's son, of whom she was very fond. Then she'd leave, followed by the whispered curses of the shopkeeper, who'd rush to add up his losses after Um Kamil's treacherous attack. He'd write these losses down on Saqr's bill, and Saqr would pay extra each month to satisfy Um Kamil's whims.

[3]

A month after the famous hotel episode, Saqr came in one evening, dragging Um Kamil behind him and hitting her on the head. "We've got to get rid of this monkey," he said angrily to his wife. "We'll sell her, we'll give her to one of our relatives on the other side of the creek, we'll put poison in her food. We must get rid of her somehow!"

Saqr's wife rescued the monkey from him and released her in the courtyard.

"She dared to go into God's house," her husband said in exasperation. "She got away from her chain, climbed the wall of the mosque near my shop, and surprised the congregation when they were performing the evening prayers. They were alarmed and stopped praying, and some of them ran out of the doors and the rest jumped out of the windows. When the imam noticed the noise and turned to look behind him, he saw Um Kamil heading toward him. He ran up the pulpit to get away from her, and she climbed up after him, so he jumped off the top and broke his right leg. I got enough curses from the congregation and the imam today to keep me in hell forever. Do you think that sort of thing's right?"

"But she's a dumb animal," his wife said, trying to make excuses for Um Kamil, "and your son loves her, and she amuses us. Today I've cooked meat broth with okra for you, and I've grilled the shrimps you bought this morning."

The mention of food calmed Saqr down. "When they told me she was in the mosque," he said smiling, "I rushed there and found people all over the place and the imam limping outside. Inside it was quiet. Um Kamil was standing on the pulpit. She'd put on the imam's cloak and started chewing the wires of the microphone."

Saqr and his wife considered Um Kamil's tricks and escapades over the year she'd spent with them. They laughed and concluded in the end that it would be better to keep her than get rid of her. So Saqr reiterated to his wife the need to build a strong iron cage for her inside the house; and when she was taken outside, she'd have to be fastened with an iron chain specially made for her, so she couldn't slip out of it whenever she felt like it.

When they went into the family room, Um Kamil was sitting with their son asleep in her lap. The Ceylonese maid was looking at them and smiling.

[4]

When Um Kamil had her first menstruation, Saqr was surprised and took her to the vet, who explained the matter to him. He went back to his wife, and they joked and chatted about the need to find Um Kamil a husband.

Two months after that Um Kamil disappeared. Saqr thought she was with one of the neighbors and that she'd come back the next day, but when two days passed and she didn't return, they became worried about her and they informed the police, who circulated it to all the police stations; but no trace of her was found. Their son cried at losing her and had a slight fever. They published an advertisement in one of the daily newspapers about the loss of their monkey, accompanying it with a photograph of her that Saqr had taken six months before, when she was putting spectacles on her eyes and smoking cigarettes. They promised a reward of five thousand dirhams to the person who found her.

One person brought them a sick monkey, totally unlike a chimpanzee, and when they showed him her photograph said irritably, "All monkeys look the same."

They went to a clairvoyant in the Satwa quarter, who was known for finding stolen objects, searching for people who were lost, and casting spells for sick people and lovers. After taking two hundred dirhams from them, he told them, "A toothless old woman, who lives between the water and the dry land, has taken her."

They searched everywhere. They even went to the zoo, thinking that instinct might have led her there in search of a male monkey. The employee in charge told them they weren't the only ones who came to the zoo looking for their lost animals. The fact was that animals escaped from the zoo, they didn't come to it.

All their efforts to find Um Kamil failed, and after a year all that remained of her was stories of her devilry and anecdotes about the devastation she'd caused.

[5]

When Saqr went at the end of the year to pay the annual rent for his shop to the owner, the owner told him he'd sold it to Ahmad Abdallah and that he should go to him to reach an agreement about it. When Saqr heard the name of the new owner, his memory took him back more than twenty years, to the time when they were both smuggling gold for a big merchant. They often used to go to the Indian city of Bombay and contact Indian smugglers. Those years they spent together had been full of danger and adventure, but even so they used to have late nights getting drunk and quarrelling over pretty girls and women of pleasure. After they stopped smuggling, they lost contact with each other, but Saqr heard that his accomplice had become rich through contracting, government tenders, and the construction of working-class housing. He asked for his address and was shown a large building overlooking the creek. In the headquarters of the company, which occupied three floors of the building, he saw Indian accountants, Pakistani engineers, and Arab secretaries, and he told Ahmad 'Abdallah's secretary that he wanted to see him. He felt confused and unsure of what would happen. Would his old friend know him? How would he receive him? Would he want a high rent for the shop? The secretary went in, and soon afterwards Ahmad 'Abdallah came out, embraced Saqr, and kissed him.

"My Bombay friend!" he said, with real or pretended joy, Saqr wasn't sure which. "God damn the world! How many years has it been since the smuggling days? Twenty, thirty years? Don't remind me; we've got old, our hair's gone gray. God, what a world!"

They went into the office, sat down on luxurious black leather chairs, and raked over a few old memories of Bombay and their smuggling days. The secretary came with glasses of tea and cups of coffee. Ahmad asked his friend Saqr how things were going with him, and Saqr replied by extolling his comfortable situation. His crony laughed.

"All your life you've been easily pleased about money," he said. "All the other people who worked in smuggling have become owners of big companies, and you're still in a small shop."

Saqr was surprised at his friend's comment. He'd thought of himself as a successful merchant, moderately prosperous, with a Mercedes car, a fine villa in the Humriyya quarter, and a little over a million dirhams in his bank account. But when his gaze wandered over his friend's luxurious office, and he saw the pictures of the buildings and projects his company had created hanging on the walls, he realized what an enormous difference there was between his modest achievement and his friend's great success. Saqr turned the conversation to the rent of the shop.

"The rent can stay the same as before," Ahmad said in a friendly way. "And if you'd like me to reduce it for you, I'll do it gladly. This evening you'll have dinner with me. We'll go to my house in half an hour."

Saqr wanted to excuse himself from accepting his friend's invitation, on the grounds that he had to close the shop and take his Indian employee home. Also, he hadn't told his wife he'd be dining out. But Ahmad wouldn't accept any of these excuses.

"We'll send one of my employees to close the shop and take your Indian employee home. There are four telephones here. Use any one you like to contact your wife and tell her you're having dinner with us."

Half an hour later Saqr and his friend Ahmad were getting into a vintage car. Saqr was surprised at its appearance and age, but Ahmad laughed.

"This car's worth 300,000 dirhams," he said. "It's an old, rare model that was made in America in the 1940s. There are only six of them left in the whole world, and this is one of them."

On the way to the house Ahmad complained about his poor health! "Life's full of problems," he said. "If you have money, you don't have health. Don't be deceived by my fat cheeks and plump stomach. I've got all the illnesses there are. I've got mild diabetes, mild gout, slightly high blood pressure, mild arthritis, mild allergy, and slight problems in my stomach and intestines."

He moved his headcloth slightly back from his temples and added, smiling, "Don't be deceived by this black hair either. Most of it's as white as candy floss; the credit belongs to modern dyes. Would you believe I use the same hair dye as my wife does?"

They arrived at a large villa in the middle of the Rashidiyya quarter. Ahmad pressed a small gadget in his hand, and the door of a garage large enough for four cars opened. They stepped out of the car, and Ahmad led his guest to the large hall for visitors, which was built beside the main villa. Saqr's feet sank into the carpet. He was dazzled by the chairs, the sofas, the curtains, and the many works of art in the hall. He sat on one of the chairs, catching his breath. Everything was shining: the chandeliers, the crystal, the tables, and the cabinets.

"I don't like a lot of furniture," Ahmad said, "but what can I do? It's what my wife wants, she's the one who's collected all these strange, shiny things that don't go together."

Saqr looked to the right-hand side of the room, and saw a complete set of iron armor of the sort European soldiers used to wear in the middle ages and that covered a soldier with iron from the top of his head to the soles of his feet. Ahmad pressed a bell, and an Indian servant came in, dressed in a uniform like a hotel porter or waiter's, with a cap on his head and brass buttons on his jacket. Saqr looked at the servant's clothes in astonishment.

"This is one of my gracious wife's wishes too. When I moved to this house, she insisted the servants should have a single uniform like the staff of restaurants and hotels. Her father was a fishmonger and mine was a sailor, and she wants to make aristrocrats out of us!"

Saqr looked to the left-hand side of the room, and found himself staring at an amazing, unbelievable sight. Um Kamil was standing behind the chair! His mouth opened wide in astonishment, and Ahmad turned to where Saqr was gaping, realized what had attracted his friend's attention, and laughed.

"That's Sabaho," he said. "Some workers in one of the buildings the company's putting up saw her and brought her to me. My wife was delighted with her, the children liked her, and my wife arranged for a servant to look after her. She was a clever, amusing monkey, but she was very lazy. By the time she'd been with us for a year, she'd become so lazy she didn't move from where she was, and then she stopped eating. We called a vet, but he couldn't cure her. The house was one big funeral parlour when she died. My wife insisted she wanted to keep the darling monkey forever as a precious memory. So we sent her to Bombay with some Indian engineers and had her stuffed there. There she is in front of you now, smiling as large as life!"

—Translated by Faris Glubb and Christopher Tingley

Video

Hamdan bin Khalfan was a cautious fellow who did not like being hasty or rushing into things. He left his intermediate school only after failing the intermediate certificate three times. When he took a job in one of the departments of local government, he stayed on working there after many of his colleagues had moved on to join federal ministries and earn better salaries. When he finally decided to leave, he realized that there were no longer any vacancies in the federal ministries, least of all for people who held lower-level school certificates. So he had to work in another local government department on only a slightly higher salary.

Hamdan did not get married until he was thirty years old when most of the pretty girls of his quarter were already married. He had to marry a girl who was nearly as old as himself and who came from another Emirate. On his wedding night he was taken aback when he saw that two of her teeth were made of gold. He did not agree to starting a family until he had been married for three years and then only when his wife threatened to ask for a divorce if they did not have a family. He continued to live in the same quarter after everyone else had left and the houses were occupied by people from the Indian subcontinent. He finally moved out as a result of pressure from his wife, who warned that if he did not take her away to a new quarter, she would take the little girls and go back to her own family. One of his wife's endless complaints really annoyed him.

"Everybody else has a video machine. The driver Ulwa has got one in his house. My family has got one. Why can't you relax with one, the same as everybody else?"

His argument that video films were the same as television programs fell on deaf ears. He put up resistance for two whole years but then gave in to his wife's pressure and bought a video machine. Without him knowing, his wife took out a subscription at one of the video rental shops. When he heard about it, he was no longer able to offer any objection, especially as he was becoming an addict of video films, especially for old Arab films and cartoons.

At the office where he worked, his colleagues knew he had bought a video machine. One colleague, Khalifa, offered to lend him a porno film. Hamdan, as usual, was against it.

"I don't think it's a very good idea," he said. "These films are immoral."

His colleagues laughed at him. Khalifa talked at great length about the porno films he had seen. Hamad, the best educated of the group, justified it all, saying, "This is sexual education. We learn everything at school except the subject that's important in the life of every person."

Hamdan continued to disapprove.

"This is poison from the West. They want to undermine our morals."

Khalifa took no notice of Hamdan's feeble disapproval. He described what had happened in the last porno film he had seen. The film had been clear and the colors were sharp and well defined. This was not the case with most of the porno films you could find in the souk. These were of poor quality because of the many times they had been used for copying. When he started to describe in detail what had happened in the film, Hamdan buried his head in the pile of invoices that were in front of him. He busied himself going through them, but his attention was distracted by what Khalifa was saying. Over the next few days his colleagues, and above all Khalifa, went on talking about porno films. At the end of a month Hamdan's curiosity was roused.

One day, as they were leaving the office, he said rather coyly to Khalifa, "Can you lend me one of those films of yours?"

"Certainly, certainly," Khalifa smiled. "As many as we've got."

That afternoon Khalifa called at Hamdan's house and handed over a tape wrapped up.

"Make yourself comfortable," he said with a laugh. "This tape lasts three hours. It's got Swedish, German, and American films. Three hours of pure artistic enjoyment."

Hamdan gingerly took the cassette and stammered his thanks. He went into the house and locked himself in the bedroom. He felt awkward. He closed the windows and drew the curtains, even the two little windows at the top of the wall. He checked that every window was fastened and then felt a little more relaxed. He put the cassette into the machine and sat down and watched. He was not aware of the fact that his little five-year-old daughter, Hamda, was asleep in her cot in the room, wrapped up in her blankets. After an hour and a half he switched the video off. He felt dizzy after these strange, arousing films that he had been watching for the first time in his life. He took out the cassette and carefully concealed it under the wardrobe opposite Hamda's bed, a dusty corner that even the maid never got round to cleaning.

He went outside to get a breath of fresh air. He felt that he had been tarnished by these films and their subject matter. He saw three of his daughters in the yard, Khulud aged nine, Amal aged eight, and Hana aged six. They were playing boisterously. He asked the maid about his wife. She told him that she had gone to the wedding party of a friend of hers. He recalled that she had told him about this the previous evening and that she would not take the girls, not even the older ones, Khulud and Amal, because the hosts had stipulated on the invitation that there would not be any children present. He remembered when he was young. Weddings were minor celebrations for the children, who would play and have fun. Curse this modern life! Children no longer had the right to listen in to wedding parties as their predecessors had done. He changed and went out. He went to the sports club of which he was a member. He did not think much of the conversation that was all about the English football season. He had not seen any of the games. He went back home early. He wanted to finish watching the cassette after he had had dinner. He was back home at eight o'clock and asked the Indian maid to prepare some food. He asked how the children were. She told him that they had been playing for an hour in the bedroom and had not gone out. He went to the bedroom. The door was ajar. He pushed it and went in. The girls were sitting quietly watching the cassette he had borrowed from Khalifa. It was almost finished now.

—Translated by Peter Clark

Sabri Musa (b. 1932)

Egyptian novelist, short-story writer, and screenwriter Sabri Musa obtained a degree in visual arts and, in 1956, joined the editorial board of the weekly *Sabah al-Khair*, of which he is now deputy editor-in-chief. He has traveled widely in the Arab world, as well as in Eastern and Western Europe, and has visited America twice. His collections of short stories include *The Shirt* (1956), *No One Knows* (1962), *Tales* (1963), and *A Design to Kill a Neighbor* (1970). He has written several novels, including *The Half Meter Tale* (1962), and has been awarded several prizes for his screenplays as well as for his fictional works, receiving the Pegasus Price for his original novel, *Seeds of Corruption* (1973), which was translated into English in 1980 by Mona N. Mikhail with the help of a grant from Mobil Corporation. This novel demonstrates an elevated style based on classical Arabic historical texts and opposes the ancient values of bedouin valor and pride and of mystical Islamic attitudes to modern-day materialism, lust, greed, and corruption. His other fictional works, however, have a much simpler language and style and employ a less serious tone, reflecting an ironic streak sometimes verging on the comic. His latest novel is *The Man from the Spinach Field* (1987).

Departure and Return

Shadwan's body was asleep, but his mind was awake . . .

His body had succumbed to the burdens of the long day, which had begun before the sun tossed the first strands of its glowing hair across the dark, dew-damp fields, and across the trees, the streams, and the southern canal. The muscles of his arms swollen, the veins of his thighs throbbing with the movement of his blood, his body had sunk down. The salt, onions, and cornbread had done their work. Shadwan had stretched out and become numb . . .

But his mind remained awake.

The walls of straw and mud could not keep out the groaning.

That heap of girls, his daughters, lying huddled under a cotton blanket on the dusty mat, could not keep out the screaming . . .

His wife as well, with her rancid warmth, the onion smell that emanated from her over their bed of palm leaves, could not keep out the groaning . . .

Of course, the groans were not noisy. In fact, they did not even sound like groans.

His aged father knew what was and what was not proper. He knew well how to keep things walled up inside and how to not let them out to others.

Besides, the pain was not new to him. Sixty years had been more than enough for a man to learn to accept and conceal pain when there was no point in bothering others with it.

From time to time a whimper here, a moan there, these were acceptable . . .

Only now the moans were like needles, and the whimpers were like awls . . . They tore through Shadwan's numbness and jabbed their sharp, pointed tips up along his nerves to pierce his ears. This was why his mind remained awake.

As he listened intently to his father's groans, Shadwan split in two.

"The old man would like to have a doctor see him, but is too shy to speak out," he said to himself. These were the words of Shadwan the Son—for whenever a blow strikes the root, the branch trembled.

However, Shadwan the Hamstrung, lamed by life, began to think: "What good is medicine when you're sixty?"

A few days earlier the old man had gone, with his chronic pain, to the general clinic. He had stood in line until his turn came, but there had not been enough time for him to spread his pain out in full across the impatient doctor's table—they had given him some all-purpose medicinal mixture.

The old man had returned from the clinic, his pains seemingly behind him, no longer groaning. Shadwan had been sure that the pain was still there, for the old man endured patiently; and yesterday his suspicion had been confirmed. The pain had reemerged, broken through the mantle of concealment, and spread throughout the house. And so once again the old man had gone to the general clinic, and again had returned with the same all-purpose medicinal mixture . . .

"The old man has to have a private doctor!" said Shadwan the Son.

But Shadwan the Hamstrung replied: "In the Name of the Prophet, be quiet! Where do we have the money for a private doctor?"

Shadwan wanted to fling off his anger, and he moved his stiff legs from under the blanket. But one of his legs did not respond because it had lost all feeling, so he began massaging to revive it.

Lying on the bench by the oven, the old man, thinking that everyone was asleep, let loose with his pain. Needles and awls swarmed in the darkness; they scraped across the walls of mud and straw, bounced off the sleeping children, and made their way to the bed of palm leaves, where they penetrated the ears of Shadwan the Son . . .

"Where can we get the money for a private doctor?" insisted Shadwan the Hamstrung.

"There's always a way," said Shadwan the Son. "I have two pounds. We need them of course—but my father's need is urgent!"

"And would a private doctor get up at this hour?" asked Shadwan the Hamstrumg.

"He will have gotten up by the time we arrive!" said the Son.

So Shadwan the Son and Shadwan the Hamstrung got up. In one body they stepped over the heap of daughters toward the storeroom in the back. Together they groped around in the dark for the donkey and woke it.

The donkey rose angrily and began to bray. Shadwan, one person now, scolded it and led it out of the storeroom. He carried his old father outside the hut, wrapped him up, and set him firmly on the donkeys' back. Meanwhile, from deep within himself, The Hamstrung, hobbled to the wheel of life, watched mockingly . . .

Nevertheless, Shadwan prodded the donkey with his stick, and it moved forward lazily. They turned their backs to the village and set out slowly along the dew-drenched road. They went through fields. They broke the silence over the paved highway.

Although Shadwan had thought that the trip would arouse in the old man a flood of hope that would numb his pain, the way was long and the night cold. The old man did not stop emitting his awls and needles.

At dawn they could see Giza. By the time the donkey, the man on its back, and the van behind it entered, the daylight was full and Shadwan himself had begun to ache as well . . .

The doctor examined the old man after Shadvan had paid him a pound.

"This old man needs an operation," the doctor said and started to scold Shadwan for having waited so long.

"We didn't know!" Shadwan said.

"You know now," said the doctor. "So what do you intend to do?"

"Operate immediately . . . I have another pound!"

The doctor laughed a dignified laugh as he announced that the fee for the operation was twenty pounds.

Shadwan the Son was stupefied. His heart began to pound.

Up spoke Shadwan the Hamstrung: "In the Prophet's name, pick up your father and let's take him back!"

"I appreciate your situation," the doctor war saying. "I will make it fifteen pounds. But make up your mind, for the old man doesn't have much time . . ."

"By God, man!" cried Shadwan the Hamstrung. "We haven't got a thing!"

"It won't be my responsibility," the doctor said. "His death will be on your head."

Shadwan the Son said: "I'll sell the donkey!"

"Are you crazy? It's all we have!" said Shadwan the Hamstrung.

"What!?" cried the Son. "Are you saying that the donkey is as important as my father?"

"The old man's useless," said the Hamstrung.

"But he's still my father! And anyway, the donkey is his . . ."

The doctor seized the opportunity and gave the order to prepare the operating room.

"I'll be right back with the money," said Shadwan the Son.

Shadwan rode his donkey to the market and returned, panting, with the money in his hand.

The doctor smiled with dignity as he stuffed the money, which had just been a donkey, into his pocket. And he said with pride, "The operation was successful . . . But the old man has died."

Carrying the body on his shoulders, Shadwan left Giza and returned home along the same road he had taken earlier.

The Hamstrung emerged and began his disparagements.

"That old man!" he said. "I knew him well—he just didn't want to leave without taking his donkey with him!"

—Translated by Lena Jayyusi and Thomas G. Ezzy

'Abd al-'Aziz al-Mushri (1954–2000)

Born in the village of Mahdara in southern Saudi Arabia, 'Abd al-'Aziz
al-Mushri failed to complete his education for reasons of ill health. He
worked as a journalist for more than ten years and then dedicated himself largely to creative writing, though he continued to produce articles
and commentary in Saudi and other Arab periodicals. He also painted,
showing his oil paintings, produced either in oil or Chinese ink, at various exhibitions, as well as in one exhibition in 1991 that was completely
devoted to his work. His journalistic range encompassed both literary and
social issues and, in the field of fiction, he wrote both novels and short
stories. From the early 1970s, al-Mushri was one of the major short-story
writers of Saudi Arabia. His first collection of short stories, *Death on Water*
appeared in 1979 and was followed by *The Confession of Wheatstalks* (1987),
Flowers Look for a Vase (1987); and *The State of the Country* (1987). He has
also published at least four novels, including *Al-Wasmiyya* (1985) and *The
Towers* (1992). He was highly sensitive to the small things of life around
him, as well as to the various factors controlling people's behavior and
interaction with each other, and was fond (as the two short pieces here
demonstrate) of drawing brief sketches whose tone ranges from pathos
to humor.

THE DOG

Abu Salim had a dog that he dearly loved. He would feed it from his own food
and make a warm bed for it on winter nights, protecting it from all harm.

There are set rules for treating a dog and about where it should sit and how
much it should be allowed to howl. The dog had learned to follow its master's
orders from the time it was a puppy and would have deserved to be shut away
had it not obeyed. And yet a creature's true nature rises, in any case, above what
it may happen to learn.

The dog, given the task of guarding the sheep and the yard, showed the faith-
fulness of a true guardian, one never to be surprised by any sudden attack. And
so Abu Salim loved the dog. The days flowed by as the sap flows in the trees, and
the flock multiplied before the very eyes of Abu Salim, who repaid his faithful
dog by loving it more and more.

Then one day the dog fell sick; and though Abu Salim offered it the best food
and drink, it failed to recover and died in the twinkling of an eye. Grief swept
through Abu Salim's heart, and he felt the dog's good deeds merited some reward. Taking his adze and choosing a spot on the hillside near the house, he dug

a grave for the dog then brought the animal there, wrapped in an old turban, and recited the prayer for the dead over it.

$$\Longrightarrow$$

A rancorous man, seeking revenge against Abu Salim, saw how he had prayed over the dog.[1] How, he thought, could anyone, from now on, accept the testimony of a man who had prayed over a dog?

When the village shaikh heard of it, he grew furiously angry and madly excited. Foam shot out around his mouth and he began to bellow. He recited prayers and incantations, and he cursed the devil, and the impurity of dogs' tails, and the length of their noses. Then he proclaimed that such an evildoer as Abu Salim could expect only death as his punishment.

Fear, added to his grief over the dog, made Abu Salim's heart beat faster. His beard shook with terror. Then he thought hard and said to the shaikh, "Sir, it's true I did this thing. But the dog, as it breathed its last, instructed me to present you with ten sheep."

The shaikh's pious rage abated. He looked to the right and to the left and saw many more people waiting there, seeking his judgments. He called Abu Salim to him.

"What was that you said?" he whispered. "How many sheep did the dog, bless its soul, instruct you to give me?"

—*Translated by Salwa Jabsheh and Christopher Tingley*

Sent with the Bearer

Life on the sidewalk is a bustling one. There's never any question of silence along those gray slabs.

There was nothing special about this evening—so many like it had found him here on the sidewalk. Life here had become still busier now, the feet slowing to something like a quiet crawl. He sat in his usual place, close to where the streetlight stretched out its two arms, and began dictating to his companion, who had his head bent over the paper spread on his right knee. He watched the movement of the pen between the other man's unsteady fingers.

He dictated in the Yemeni dialect, with a good deal of high-flown verbiage.

"And give my greetings to my loving mother, and to my brother Murshid and his wife, and to Aunt Rif'a and her children. My greetings also to my sister

---

1. A dog is regarded as impure by Muslims. Saying a Muslim prayer over it is, therefore, equivalent to blasphemy.

Hujja, and to my dear brother Hamid, and tell them that, God willing, I shall be with you all for next year's feast of Ramadan.

"And with the bearer of this letter, I am sending six hundred Saudi riyals, and I beg your forgiveness, father, for work is scarce nowadays, and foreign workers have become so much more numerous in this place, while we—we do not know English. But, Father, say some of your pious prayers for me.

"I shall give you the six hundred riyals when we go to our dwelling place, and, by God, place them in my father's hand, and embrace him from me, and kiss him on the cheeks and on the forehead and on the tip of his nose."

I had to be cautious, so very cautious, to be able to listen to them there. I had to use all my acuteness and instinct to pick up their conversation without letting them feel my presence.

And I was filled with compassion and longing, to the point of tears. I sent my gaze toward the broad expanse glittering with streetlights, and the lights of cars, and lights flashing and streaming with such warmth now.

—*Translated by Salwa Jabsheh and Christopher Tingley*

Mai Muzaffar (b. 1940)

Iraqi writer Mai Muzaffar was born in Baghdad and obtained a B.A. in English literature from the University of Baghdad, She has published several books of fiction and prose poetry, and has also published critical articles and studies in various periodicals on art. She was an editor at the English-language daily *Baghdad Observer,* and, from 1976 to 1986 an editor at the bimonthly magazine *Iraq.* She has participated in a number of conferences in Iraq and other Arab countries. Muzaffar lived in Amman, Jordan, with her artist husband, where she worked as researcher at the Royal Academy for Islamic Civilization Research, before going with her husband to live in Bahrain. Her published creative works include two short-story collections, *The Pelican* (1979) and *Texts in a Precious Stone* (1993), and two collections of poetry, *Fire Bird* (1983) and *Night Songs* (1994). She has also translated from English such books as *The Science Art of Visual Illusion* by Nicholas Wade, *Poetry in the Making* by Ted Hughes, and *Painting and the Novel* by Geoffrey Meyers.

MATCHES TO DRY WOOD

Wrapping himself in his thick woolen cloak, he breathed the early spring air and gazed up at the clear sky with its glittering stars. He longed, deeply, for a woman—a woman soft to the touch and smelling of perfume, whose free-flowing hair would make you sense the sweetness of woman, her tenderness and femininity.

The dampness of the garden seeped through his slippers, and he felt a touch of chill. He saw Samar's face, the laughter hovering between her eyes and dimples, sensed her softness and the grace of her movements, the voice that aroused such a mixture of nameless feelings in him. He stretched out a tentative hand, as if reaching for something in the dark, a woman's hair perhaps. A contented smile flickered on his face. He lit a cigarette and drew in a deep, restful breath.

"Sa'id!"

The voice came from the kitchen, a voice like a butcher's knife newly sharpened for slaughter.

"Sa'id, come inside! It's cold out there. You'll catch bronchitis."

The dream was shattered. He could feel the voice tearing into him like a handful of iron spikes, piercing his flesh.

He turned away to stifle a scream. His face filled with disgust, and he felt sick. A few words, curses perhaps, silently passed his lips. "Oh, God!" he muttered, gazing up at the sky. "Isn't there any way out?"

Two days before he'd been leafing through a calendar to mark the deadline for a paper he was writing on "The Concept of Freedom in Law," for a conference in a few months' time, and his eyes had been swept toward a particular date, which filled him with unease as he stared at it. In a few months he'd be sixty. And yet he was an old man already—had been marked, for many years now, by a deep, persistent sense of being old. Thirty years of his life he'd spent with what the world called a good woman—one with nothing womanly about her except the name.

It had happened soon after he returned from abroad, after she'd finished her own studies in pharmacy: he'd met her at the house of some relatives and seen in her the kind of woman he sought, enlightened and independent. Married life, though, had revealed two very different temperaments. He was open to life, hungry to acquire ever more knowledge, while she remained closed in her own world, content with what she'd achieved. Where he was peaceable, she was belligerent and domineering. He was attractive to other people; she was moody, a private, reserved person, satisfied with her realm of husband and two children. She'd established a strict way of life, to be observed in every detail, with no exceptions allowed: an utterly rigid regime, centered on a daily routine, based on a theory of economics she'd formulated and established through firm household principles. Clothes were strictly for practical use. Food was there to satisfy hunger and the inflexible needs of nutrition. There were various prohibitions: sitting in the living room wasn't allowed; windows couldn't be opened between certain hours; this and this and this couldn't be done in the house; that and that might be permitted on certain conditions.

She was tired all the time, from cleaning the house, or washing clothes, or preparing food; and if someone in the family was sick, she'd push herself to the limit to assure their comfort, too worried to sleep herself. Everything, though, was instantly turned into drama or lectures on morals and what was and wasn't done, and she was the perennial victim, her endless, exhausting efforts never properly appreciated. Her relations with her mother and brothers and sisters had their rules too—they couldn't just come and visit when they felt like it—and things were even stricter with his own family. And yet she was generous with his mother in matters of health, making instantly sure she had any medicines she needed. This in fact was a service she provided for both sides of the family, and she was never backward, either, in tendering what advice she could. She had little time for doctors, seeing them as leeches for the most part, making an exception only for two or three doctors she'd known as colleagues during her student days.

Thirty years together! The two children had grown up, married, and moved away, and his daughter had a baby boy, a few months old. And now he just couldn't take it any more. He'd made his own bed, it was true, and he'd tried to come to terms with his life over the years, but now the rope had started tightening, inexorably, around his neck. The days wrapped him round now, like a shroud around a corpse. It wasn't a proper woman he'd married—he'd realized that long since—and time had only dried her up more. And so he'd devoted himself to his books, to his reading, which had widened the gap between them still further, till now they had nothing in common but the house, a mere resting place filled with sanctions and prohibitions.

An unassuming man, he'd been all too ready to let her take control of things. His academic status, too, had brought some compensation, had even led him to accept things as they were. Besides, he was used to her now, used to the endless whirl of washing and ironing, used to the smell of onions and garlic and that ritual that took place every evening. Meanwhile the living room remained closed and without guests, the bedroom gloomy and dark. There was only one place, summer and winter, that had any life, the place of assembly for the family and guests and anyone visiting, and that was the kitchen, where chairs were set and a corner, which included a television, was arranged for everyday social life.

He had, though, been able to secure one small kingdom—a little study that was also his refuge and his paradise, arranged as he wanted it; a space he'd snatched and where he'd put everything he possessed. She hated this room, sensing in it a rival against whom she was powerless.

"How I'd love to put all these papers in a boat," she'd say, "and sink them in the river!"

The first time she saw the study, she'd been stunned.

"I've never seen so many books!" she exclaimed. "Have you really read them all?"

A library, he'd told her, contained different kinds of book: some that were read and finished with, some that were read many times, some that were used for reference, and so on.

"I don't believe in a lot of reading," she said, "or in a lot of thought and argument. It just gives you a headache."

In fact, intelligent conversation was one of the things not allowed.

Everyone in the house obeyed her. They obeyed her because she was well meaning and good-hearted and made so many sacrifices. She'd had her first shock, though, when her children insisted on choosing their own careers. When the daughter said she wanted to study literature, her mother had been up in arms straight away.

"Literature?" she said. "What is it? Just empty talk out of books. It's not a proper profession. Study one of the sciences, medicine, or pharmacy, or engineering. Something respectable."

But the daughter, secretly spurred on by her father, had opted for literature even so. As for the son, he chose aviation engineering, which saddened her too—she would have preferred a different kind of engineering. Aviation meant he might fly a plane one day, fly out of her hands, and she might lose him.

She dominated everything and she owned everything too, talking of "my house," and "my son." and "my garden." In the face of her children's insistence, she felt a threat to everything she possessed.

The family revolt was crowned by her children's choice of marriage partners—when she learned her daughter had been seeing her young man for over two years, coming to an understanding behind her back, the shock had almost killed her. She didn't like the girl her son chose, and she didn't like the young man her daughter chose either, regarding him as below her and generally unsuitable. She was astonished when both children were so insistent. Where, she wondered, had they got this stubborn streak from? As for her son, not content with marrying the girl, he cost her a lot of money buying furniture and a trousseau for the bride, and there was all the expense of the wedding, which she attended despondently and reluctantly, as if she was at a wake. She lamented her misfortune, looking on thunderstruck as the savings of years were squandered.

Watching this surprising revolt of his offspring, the father, for the first time, felt a spark of rebellion too. He found the spirit now to make the odd sarcastic comment about the meager food, or the rhythm that never varied a jot from year to year, or the constraints on their social life. In the past he'd kept quiet about things like that—had pretended, indeed, to be happy, out of respect for the work she took on herself.

But now rebellion had snaked its way into his blood. He'd started looking at what went on around him, had seemed to become aware, for the first time, of the beauty of other women he met, at the university or elsewhere, finding in some of them the fresh softness of an early morning breeze. He realized now how deprivation had pierced to his very bones, had gnawed through his spirit. Still, though, he kept the caution in which he'd trained himself so rigidly till it had become a screen over his eyes and passions. Not that he was so much affected by women's venturesome looks or by their passing comments or cunning questions. They tickled his vanity, true, and stirred him for a moment, but his spirits would droop the moment he walked back into the house, to face the gloom and the endless kitchen smells.

But Samar was unlike any other woman he'd known. There was a magic behind her honey-colored complexion, and her smiling black eyes, and her hair bound at the back of her head, an extraordinary elegance about her, and these things brought home to him what he'd missed for so long. She aroused something indefinable in him, prompting him to hold on to that subtle charm. She was not so much beautiful as gentle and soft, in a way that swept to a man's heart. Her laughter was mysterious, her conversation frank and attractive, her glances meaningful but without final commitment. Magic like hers, he'd think, somehow reflected the tragedy of all humanity.

He felt the power of poetry now, bursting out deep inside him. She'd once thanked him delightfully when returning a book she'd borrowed, and this had spurred him on to express the emotions filling his heart. He'd written down the verses that had come to him, then suppressed them out of shyness and a sense of what was proper. For the first time he felt a burning conflict deep down, forcing recognition of the iron bands penning his soul.

Once more he gazed up into the clear sky, reflected on all the untrammeled movements within that matchless starry system, all those small creatures reveling in their independence. Wasn't man a kind of star over the earth? He felt his deep loss, a longing to return life to his life. But how? His eyes filled with tears. He was bound, forever, by an iron law.

"Sa'id, do you want to catch your death of cold? Come in here!"

The hellish, shrieking voice brought him back to reality. He rose, feeling the cold without and within, the fresh, open air destroyed by something strong and choking. He saw his wife as if under a microscope: a heap of flesh and a sullen face, behind a large bowl into which she was peeling great quantities of bitter oranges, ready to make marmalade.

He looked at her stubby legs and plastic sandals, gazed at her toes that were like dry faded pebbles. It was Friday, the day of rest, and night had fallen, and yet there she still was, in the kitchen. She hadn't taken a bath, very likely wouldn't take one, because she had a touch of bronchitis. He gazed at her thick cotton dress, bought heaven knows how long ago, the only one he'd seen her wearing there for years. It was too tight for her now and clung around her breasts, emphasizing the flabby contours. He gazed at the face that had once had some semblance of beauty, buried now beneath the heap of flesh topped by that matted hair tumbling haphazardly over her brow.

Tomorrow, he thought, she'd put on her striped dress, pick up her big bag, and go off to her job at the hospital pharmacy. She'd learned nothing new since her university studies. When patients come to buy their medicines, she'd dole out her advice—telling them the doctors had overprescribed, that they should, for instance, take one pill rather than two. The patients thought a lot of her, and she was greatly liked all through the hospital, because she treated the sick with the care that came so naturally to her.

As he looked at her, he felt the silent protest deep inside him: "I don't want you, you no-woman! I want a woman! A woman!"

His palms felt dry, his lips chafed, his heart like a desert unwatered for a hundred years.

"If you want some supper," she said, "there's yogurt in the fridge. And there's some—"

He didn't answer.

He left the kitchen, went off to his study, and closed the door behind him. Then he lay back in his seat, deep in thought. Would he ever, he wondered, be able to break the collar laid on his neck over so many years? He, who had tirelessly fostered the cause of freedom, found himself a prisoner at last, pent in a small room that contained the only freedom he knew, powerless to defeat one solitary woman.

What exactly did he want? It was a disquieting question, to which he had no answer. There was a thirst in his heart and a strange sense of death.

He stretched out his legs and laid his head back on the rest, facing the bookcase with all those books set out on the shelves. But he wasn't even seeing what was in front of him. His thoughts were elsewhere. What exactly did he want?

Samar, a woman like other women. A vague new shape, no more. Yet she was ablaze like matches set to kindle dry wood. But then maybe, in a few years, she'd become a mere heap of flesh too!

He wanted to stifle his anxiety in some way, put off facing the issue. He focused his gaze on the shelves of books, his eyes flickering over all the different titles. At last he put out his hand and took one. Then he sat down once more, to read what Erich Fromm had written about *Escape from Freedom*.

—*Translated by May Jayyusi and Christopher Tingley*

Emily Nasrallah (b. 1931)

Lebanese novelist and short-story writer Emily Nasrallah was born in Kfeir in South Lebanon, studied at the American University of Beirut, and has worked as a journalist and teacher. She won instantaneous recognition for her first novel, *September Birds,* a sensitive portrayal of the tragedy of emigration from Lebanese villages, named as the best novel for 1962 and winning the Friends of the Book prize and other awards. This novel was followed by *The Oleander Tree* (1968), *The Bondaged* (1974), and her latest novel, *Sailing Against Time* (1981), a sequel to *September Birds.* She has also published several collections of short stories, among which are *Island of Illusion* (1973) and *The Fountain* (1978). Emily Nasrallah has also been active in feminist issues in Lebanon.

THE MIRACLE

She feels she is moving on a cloud with her three squabs fluttering around her: Samar, Laila, and Nadim. The earth is her domain, and space surrounds her head like a hat that she proudly wears. The golden sun of June permeates the waves of her hair.

All around the trees lean on one another, branches bending their heads in sorrow and confusion. Strange—why do the trees look sad while the trilling cries of joy fill the air?

Wondering where those cries of joy and life were coming from, she thought the jinn might be celebrating one of their legendary weddings in a nearby district of the city. She thought the city was opening its arms to embrace her; its streets were welcoming her to walk them.

The city looks different from what she remembers. It seems like an abstract painting, a flat, gray surface from which rise buildings with closed windows and doors, capped by sunrays. The morning sun descends from its high position lazily, like an exhausted person.

The youngest child, Nadim, might make a painting like this. She presses Nadim's palm with her tender fingers, and he presses his face against her dress, seeking protection.

Laila asks, "Where did the people go, Mother? The people we used to meet on the street?"

Her mother answers detachedly, "They might have gone to the wedding."

"Whose wedding?"

"The wedding of the jinn." Her eyes are fixed on an object that crosses the sky before them, lightning-fast. Laila keeps quiet but doesn't understand. Or maybe she understands more than she should. Samer interrupts, pointing, to explain to her, "It is a rocket."

Their mother smiles and says, "This is one of the jinn's birds—haven't I told you his story?"

Nadim is delighted by what he hears. Insistently, with all the innocence of his five years, he begs his mother to tell him where this bird came from. The mother presses his hand a second time, then bends to kiss his forehead reassuringly. She murmurs, "I will tell you later."

The mother and her children continue on their way, fascinated by what they hear and see, and by what they do not see. The city reverberates with echoes from the wedding celebrated by the jinn in the secret corners of the city.

An hour ago Su'ad knocked at her own door, the door of the house she lived in four years ago. Then she shared the life of the man who still lives there, a contented life, ripe with love and happiness. All this happened before the shock that made her unconscious. When she recovered, the doctor discovered that she had become mentally unbalanced. She underwent a long period of treatment, which didn't help. Her body was healthy but her mind remained ill. Occasional periods of clarity caused the people closest to her to forget that anything was wrong, but a sudden relapse would occur and her anguish escalate into hysterical bouts of destruction. She even tried to destroy herself.

Her husband tried to adapt to all this, he tried very hard to help her, but the situation was beyond his control and almost destroyed the family. The eldest of the three children was barely four when the doctor issued his decision concerning the family's future; he declared Su'ad must be hospitalized. Time and a miracle from heaven would decide her fate, but the miracle did not happen.

Now that Su'ad had been living at the hospital for four years, her condition seemed to remain stable as long as she stayed in familiar surroundings—her room, the garden, and the doctor's clinic. But if she left that secure domain, no one knew what would happen. Only a year ago the doctor had allowed her to begin visiting her home on weekends, hoping this step would gradually restore her to a normal life.

Her husband tried his best to make their hours together both relaxed and natural and to benefit both Su'ad and her children, who were now cared for by a very capable nanny.

A whole year passed without any incident. Everyone was getting used to this life. The children considered themselves to have two mothers, one who was bringing them up, feeding them, attending their needs, and another who visited them on weekends and other festive occasions.

When Laila explained this perspective to their father, he liked the idea, despite the pain it caused him. He thought, "Blessed are the children." He wished he had their innocence and could accept the situation as easily.

Today was not a holiday, yet Su'ad had come to visit her children. She did not inquire about her husband, who had been away traveling for a few weeks. The children had stayed home with their second mother, who was taking good care of them. It was Samer, the eldest, who opened the door. His mother kissed his forehead and embraced him, squeezing his soft body very hard. She wanted to make up for the days of her absence. Then Laila appeared, jumping on one foot, and singing, "Mama! Mama! Mama! Mama! Mama came!"

Nadim followed her, and the three gathered within her warm embrace. The nanny stood at the door watching the scene, finding it hard to believe the courage the woman had to be out on a day like this one, a day when even the chirping of birds had stopped and life come to a standstill. To convince herself it was all really happening, she asked, "How did you get here, Sit Su'ad?"

The woman answered with an eerie smile, the same way she did when the nurse objected to her going out and insisted she stay in the hospital. She would wordlessly smile and imagine the faces of her children shining like mirrors, bright as the stars surrounding a faraway planet. Their eyes flickered and darted like butterflies around her, calling her name.

The nanny repeated the question. "Could you get through on the road? Was it passable?"

Once more the woman's mysterious smile crossed her neutral face. She did not remember the road, nor could she understand the language of the nanny. What did the word "passable" mean? What was the meaning of this danger everyone referred to, were they only trying to alarm her?

She answered the nanny, "I am here now: I am among you now. I was missing the children."

They led her to their little room, singing. The windows were closed and the curtains lowered, which Samer described as the nanny's orders. They had not left the house since their father went out of the country to settle some business matters, and troubles had begun two days after he left. Samer told his mother the neighborhood had suddenly flared up and the sky rained bullets and black smoke that killed the roses.

She listened to him as if she were hearing a distant voice, centuries old. Then she went to the window and drew back the curtain, saying, "Let the sun come in. The sun is a good friend that brings us blessings."

The children were quiet, unsure what to do. The nanny's orders had been very clear: "We are not to open the doors or windows. We are not to stand on the balcony or look out the window into the street. When we hear shooting, we must hurry to the inner hallway. We must stay inside the house. If the explosions are very violent, we must go to the shelter with the neighbors."

They memorized her recommendations. She had been repeating them every morning for ten days.

Since their father was not able to come back, he kept calling them, and his calls made them feel secure. His voice was the hope of days to come. When he called in the evenings, the burdens of the day would be lifted.

Now their mother was here, breaking the rules and disturbing the order of things. Samer spoke up, objecting, "Mother Ratiba does not allow that." But his other mother persisted. "What do you say to a walk outside?"

Laila opened her mouth to object, but Samer covered it with his hand. His mother's enthusiasm was compelling. "Alright, fine idea . . . but we'd better not tell Mother Ratiba!"

He whispered his words while holding his mother's hand. The next moment they were stealing away together across the hallway. Laila and Nadim followed them. The little rascal remembered to leave the radio on, playing loud riffs of jazz that covered their escape operation.

Later when the nanny went to check on the children, she instinctively sensed that their human warmth had abandoned the house. What she was hearing were mere radio voices, mechanical vibrations. She opened the door into their room and stiffened. The curtain was drawn, but the outside door was open, letting sun and light pour in—and where were the children?

An enormous fear overwhelmed her and a black thought crossed her mind: Has Su'ad experienced one of her fits? Did she jump with the children from the balcony?

She stared down into the street, but no one was there. Bullets whistled past, echoing in her ears and unnerving her past any clear thought or action. Then she ran to the outside gate calling out, "Samer! Laila! Nadim!" No one answered. All she could hear was the broken rhythm of bullets being fired. Deeply disoriented, she did not know what to do: all she could think of was to knock on the neighbors' doors. Everyone greeted her with the same response, "Who dares go out under a shower of fire?"

Back at the house, she sat crying. All she could do now was shed tears of sorrowful regret. She spent a long time wrapped in silence, grieving and trembling fearfully, wondering what the coming hours would bring. What would she tell their father if he called to inquire about his children as usual or asked to speak with them? What could she say, how would she handle the situation?

The questions punctuated her mind like a hail of bullets. All her cells felt painfully alert and her heart pounded with each explosion outside. She wished her heart would stop; she wanted to rest, to escape her torture, but she could not. Around her stood the silent walls and stupid emptiness. She summoned her dormant power of faith, trying to recite her special prayer for the difficult moments. But she felt that her tongue was tied and her memory a huge barren desert, without water or vegetation. Her memory had become a room without windows or doors.

Finally she closed her eyes and slept on a chair at the entrance to the house. She slept like a person who did not ever wish to wake up, and her dreams were strange. Children running, the fire following them. Babies on their mothers' chests, mothers' faces ravaged with terror. Helpless men and women jumbled together, crying and shouting, while the world gaped open like the jawbones of a vast canyon. No one answered the calls for help, no one.

She tried to hold out a hand to the desperate people, she tried to rescue the children, pull them away from the mouths of fire, she tried to rise and run to their aid, but she could not. The chair she was sitting on had turned into a magnetic field that held her nailed to her place. It clung to her even when that terrible explosion resounded and a red gap opened in the ceiling above, pouring in raw tongues of fire.

When she awoke, hours later, she gazed around her and realized that all the colors had turned into one color, the origin of all colors, white.

She opened her mouth to ask where she was, but a young woman dressed in white, standing at the bedside, stopped her. She softly whispered in her ear, "Thank God for your safety; it is a miracle you have not been hurt."

—*Translated by Aida A. Bamia and Naomi Shihab Nye*

'Abdallah al-Nasser (1953)

Saudi Arabian short-story writer and essayist 'Abdallah al-Nasser was born in the Dir'iyyah near Riyadh and studied literature at King Saud University. Despite a demanding job as head of the Saudi Arabian Cultural Mission in London, he is very active in writing not just fiction but also comments on and analysis of contemporary Arab social, political, and cultural life, including an occasional comparison with Western culture, since he has lived for more than ten years in the West. He is the editor-in-chief of the London-based *Cultural Review*. His nonfictional writings reflect a deep preoccupation with the many problems that beleaguer the Arab world, and his approach to culture demonstrates a genuine love for the rich Arabic heritage and a passionate zeal to uphold and promote it. His fictional writings are varied in subject matter and approach but are always entertaining and illuminating about one or more aspects of Arab life. Two collections of his short stories have appeared to date: *Phantoms of Mirage* (1998) and *The Siege of Snow* (2002). A third collection, *Muzna*, is in press. PROTA's translation of a selection of his short stories, titled *The Tree and Other Stories*, appeared in 2004, published by Interlink Books.

THE WOLF

There he sat, in front of the big black camel-hair tent, watching and waiting for the moon to disappear. He began counting on his fingers. "I've killed six wolves in my time," he thought, "but not this cursed wolf. It's eaten twenty of my sheep in a bare six months, and still I can't catch it or kill it."

His father had retired to bed, where he lay with a heap of sand as a pillow for his head. "You should think of leaving this place, Shafi," he'd said, as they sat around the fire drinking coffee after the sunset prayer. "A wolf's a wolf. It's ravaged your sheep and you've found no way of stopping it. If you don't move off, by God all you'll have left will be sheepskins! A wolf can only be conquered by a wolf as strong as itself."

"Your son's a wolf all right, Abu Shafi," Shafi's wife had retorted as she handed him a cup of coffee, "but that other one isn't. It's a genie!"

Abu Shafi coughed from the smoke of the wood fire, which had covered his whole face and beard and seeped into his mouth. Then he laughed sarcastically and made a mark in the sand with his bare foot. "A genie?" he said. "By God, daughter-in-law," he went on with a wave of his hand, "if my eyes were good and my feet could still carry me, I'd kill this wolf myself and hang it up at the entrance to your tent."

The children laughed at their grandfather's remarks, exchanging meaningful winks as they crouched around the fire, till their mother silenced them.

Shafi, lying back on his pillow and stirring the fire with a stick, didn't answer. He was used to his father's sarcasm. In any case he wouldn't, from respect and reverence, have made any rejoinders to his father or argued with him, whatever the rights and wrongs of the case.

He tossed and turned on his bed, waiting for the moon to disappear; for the wolf attacked the sheep only in pitch darkness. Those words of his father, as they'd drunk their coffee after supper, pricked him like thorns, and he sighed and muttered to himself. This treacherous wolf had tired him out. So often he'd tried to ambush it, followed its traces in the valleys and among the hills, lain in wait for it along the tracks and pathways, set traps for it, put down dates poisoned with arsenic. All to no avail!

Misfir the shepherd, as he took down the bundle of clothes from his small donkey after settling the sheep in their fold, had talked of seeing the wolf at sunset. It had followed him from afar, he said, had appeared, then disappeared behind the neighboring hill. "That means he'll be coming tonight," Shafi thought. "When a wolf's hungry it's bound to attack. My father's going to see him tomorrow morning, hanging at the entrance to my tent."

Having cleaned his rifle, he raised the breechblock, pushed it forward, returned it to its place, and pressed the trigger, clicking it into the empty night. Then he filled the breech with five lethal bullets. The rifle was ready now. He aimed up at the sky to be sure his aim was sound. Finally, with everything checked, he put the rifle by his bed and waited for the moon to disappear. It was a long wait, for the moon seemed very slow that night.

He seized the small transistor radio his brother had sent him from the city and amused himself with it to pass the time. He moved from one station to another, hearing on one of them how a freedom fighter had killed twenty-five occupying soldiers. He felt elated at the news. How often he'd wished to become a freedom fighter, to liberate the occupied homeland from those treacherous human wolves that had devoured it along with all human dignity. Those wolves, he thought, are eating my people just as this wolf eats my sheep. If I could, I'd kill them all.

The desert breeze was blowing, cool and caressing. It was softly soothing, redolent with the fragrance of shrubs and wild herbs. It touched his soul, stirring within him tenderness and longing, a yearning too inscrutable and ambiguous for him to define. It was as though the breeze had swept a layer of dust from within his spirit. In the hidden depths of his soul many things shone, with a secret, enchanting luster he couldn't understand. He almost surrendered to a trance that was soft and sweet and lovely—then forced himself to rise for fear that shimmering, flooding longing would lead him to forget his watch.

He stole a look at his children scattered here and there, at his wife huddled in her black robe, at his father crouched in a heap inside his dark cloak.

The moon began to plunge into the sandy mountains. Only a third of it remained now. He breathed to the very bottom of his lungs, then moved his gaze to the sky where the stars were becoming more luminous.

The moon disappeared and darkness increased. He groped to touch his rifle, then got up, put it on his shoulder and walked slowly off. He entered the sheepfold, set himself in the midst of the animals, not knowing from which direction the wolf would come.

There he waited, watching the nearby valleys, raising his head, then lowering it again. Sometimes he'd just stare down at the ground, sometimes he'd gaze out to the horizon, seeking the figure of the approaching wolf on the skyline. He sensed a movement and prepared his rifle, placing his fingers on the trigger. He watched intently, scarcely daring to breathe. But his father kept coughing and his limbs were growing cold.

"If the wolf's around," he thought, "it must have fled by now." He shivered slightly. But still he waited and waited. The sheep were quite silent, as though they somehow felt all the safer for his presence there with them. Some were ruminating as they slept, their little ones sleeping on their mothers in a delicious slumber. The stars sank down. Soon morning would pierce the sky, and still the wolf didn't come. Could it have smelt his scent? Wolves can smell a human from a long way off. A question sprang suddenly to his mind. Had Misfir the shepherd been telling the truth? He might have been lying, inventing things that had never happened so as to stir people's curiosity. Or perhaps so that people would say: Misfir saw this or Misfir said that.

Shafi almost gave up and left; but finally he stayed, waiting there in his place. The sheep had all surrendered to a tranquil sleep, their heads on one another's backs. Twenty of them this cursed wolf had eaten. Pain and sorrow surged deep inside him, and he recalled his father's words: "Only a wolf can hunt down a wolf." A slight sound reached his ears, the sound of creeping . . . He felt exhilaration and caution wake together. He started looking about him with his sharp eyes, covering the ground on all sides. He gazed intently, narrowing his eyelids tight, staring into every part of the darkness.

The sound was closer now. He sensed, with his ears rather than his eyes, where it was coming from. For the moment, though, nothing appeared. The wolf was cautious and crafty. Perhaps it had smelt him, was hanging back—it would only attack when it knew it had eluded every watching eye. The sound was from another direction now. Perhaps it was circling the place. Nearer and nearer it came, with Shafi ever more ready and alert. At last—there it was! A heady joy took hold of him, triumph woke in his heart, but triumph mixed with caution. Nearer it drew, oh so slowly. It approached, then halted, and Shafi held his breath, his heart almost stopping, terrified it might elude him even now. If his father coughed, the wolf would shoot off, after he'd seen it with his own eyes. He actually wanted it to come nearer now. The nearer it came, the surer he'd be of a triumphant hit. What would his father say if he missed? He forced himself to be patient, to hold himself back. Little by little the figure approached, and a joyful elation swept through Shafi. He could make it out now.

He pointed the rifle straight at the wolf's body. His heart beat faster. He held his breath and pressed the trigger.

The explosion echoed to the horizon. The darkness was all afire, mixed with the smell of gunpowder. The sheep, suddenly woken, panicked, blundering into one another, almost breaking down the sides of the fold.

From distant tents the howling of wolves could be heard. He saw this wolf topple down, heard its voice thick with the warmth of death. The children ran out, followed by their mother, and there behind him ran his father, shouting, "God bless you, Shafi! Only a wolf can hunt down a wolf!"

Misfir the shepherd came, calling incoherently. Everyone ran toward the wolf, which had fallen soaked in its blood. His youngest son arrived first; then there they all were alongside the body. His little son burst out laughing.

"Father," he shouted. "You've shot the shepherd's donkey!"

—*Translated by May Jayyusi and Christopher Tingley*

'Abd al-Malik Nouri (b. 1921)

Iraqi short-story writer 'Abd al-Malik Nouri was one of Iraq's foremost story writers in the 1940s and 1950s. He published his first collection, *Messengers of Humanity,* in 1946 and his second, *Song of the Land,* in 1954, after which he stopped writing. This was a great loss for the Iraqi short story, as Nouri is one of the writers who established new fictional techniques by benefiting from the technical achievements of the short story in the West. His greatest interest has been in the psychological behavior of his characters, delineating the social and political reality of his society through the reactions and experience of his protagonists. He is also concerned with the various phenomena of life among poor and downtrodden people, portraying his observations in vivid and precise language.

THE WAITRESS, THE NEWSPAPER BOY, AND THE SPRING

She yawned lazily. Outside, the evening could be seen behind a veil of light fog. The street was packed with cars, and the last of the sunlight shone on the rooftops. Waves of people were moving along the pavement, and a strip of blue sky could be seen behind the front of the café.

There, in a small, dark corner of herself, she could feel something dying.

What a long day it had been, she thought, and it had all been spent waiting—long minutes of tedious waiting, moving wearily and so very slowly from one to the next.

She sat back in her chair and stretched her legs out under the small table. She'd tried this many times during her periods of work, closing her eyes, withdrawing right into herself, drifting far away—and coming back with nothing. She lay still, just as she usually did first thing in the morning, when she'd be stretched out beneath her quilt with her hands crossed over her chest and her feet warmly pressed together. Then ... she didn't know how it had happened, but she knew she'd never forget it for the rest of her life. Today, though, she'd tried as hard as she could and come back with nothing.

She gave a long look at the little clock. Soon her work in the café would be over for the day and she'd be able to go home. This immediately reminded her of the alley with its mud-filled potholes and the open gutter in the middle and the house with the decrepit staircase that she had lived in—a heap of sand with a few crumbling bricks and the marks of scrabbling bare feet in the mud. There was mud everywhere: in the yard, in all the rooms, on the faces and bare limbs of her young brothers and sisters, in the alley, in every corner of the lives of the people who lived there. They breathed it in, they ate it with their food, they slept and lived on it. The whole world seemed to her to be one great heap of thick, black mud.

Oh, God!

She heard a sound like snoring—it came from a gray-haired man who was sitting by himself, drinking tea. She slowly turned round. There weren't many people in the café. A young couple in the far corner were whispering to one another, and around the adjoining table the *ustadh* was reading an evening newspaper, while his companion sat in silent reflection, smoking a cigarette. Khalil, in his chair by the telephone, had his eyes fixed on the door, eagerly waiting for customers to come in and ready to leap towards them the moment they'd sat down. With his flat nose and swollen cheeks he always reminded her of one of those English dogs. Once she'd seen a dog race in a film, and it had reminded her of Khalil—she'd imagined the poor man running and barking with the dogs, just as if he'd been one of them. She took a grip on herself, trying not to burst out into sudden laughter in the silence of the café.

She squeezed the colored handkerchief tightly in her hands and, swaying her hips, walked to the glass door and called out to the newspaper boy.

"Boy, bring me *al-Kawakeb!*"

Once on the pavement she let out a long, quiet laugh. Then she trembled like the frond of a palm tree, overcome by embarrassment. Had anyone heard her? She shouldn't have laughed like that. She hid her mouth behind her handkerchief and quickly returned to her place in the café. The *ustadh* was looking at her—he always seemed to look through her these days, as if he wasn't really seeing her. He shifted the newspaper a little to one side, gave a quick glance—through her again—then went on with his reading. How embarrassed his glances had made her when she'd first come to work at the café! He'd always sit at the table next to hers, fixing her quietly with that direct, penetrating stare, looking only at her breasts, as though that was the only part of her he could see. Once she'd overheard him talking to his friend, and what he'd said had hurt her deeply. He'd looked at her, then opened his jacket and pointed at his chest.

"Look!" he'd said. "Mine are bigger than hers, aren't they?"

"She's still young," his friend had replied.

"What do you mean, young? She's at least seventeen. It's just the way she's made."

"If she'd only let us ... "

They'd regaled one another with dirty remarks that she preferred not to remember, and the *ustadh* had used a vulgar expression that had wounded her deeply for a long time. She was surprised that gentlemen like that could say such things—her father, for all his coarseness, had never spoken to her in that way. It was as if something inside her had been ripped apart, leaving a deep wound. She hadn't slept at all that night, had spent the whole night sobbing beneath her quilt. In the morning she'd worked out a way to turn those direct, penetrating looks away from her—she'd gone to the toilet and slipped some pieces of cloth over her breasts. After that she'd felt a little better.

In spite of what had happened, she didn't hate the *ustadh* at all and hadn't nursed any grudges against him. He'd still sit there every evening, at the next table, reading his newspaper and every now and then saying something to his friend. She'd been looking at him for so long that she could close her eyes now and picture his calm, handsome features.

She yawned again, then fixed her gaze on the glass counter full of pastries. Behind her were the street and the buildings opposite and the evening. A long line of cars stretched back at the traffic lights, the big bottles on the CocaCcola advert pointed toward the setting sun, and a forest of colorful fruit, stacked on the shelves of the still open grocer's shop, glittered, delicious and inviting, in the last rays of sunlight. If only she could have bought some fruit for her young brothers and sisters! But there wasn't enough money in her small black bag for that, and Khalil wouldn't lend her anything—she'd asked him often enough without success.

Shambling footsteps moved toward the door. The gray-haired man was leaving the café, and the long, weary day was coming to an end. She wanted to try for the last time. She couldn't do it in the house, within the four walls of the room that the whole family shared. Her little brothers and sisters would be playing on the bed they all slept in together, close to her own. In his bed her paralyzed father would be moaning and muttering to himself till late into the night, and her stepmother would be endlessly searching for something in this corner or that, with her disheveled hair falling over her lined face and her blind eye bulging out, looking like a white pebble in the darkness. She sometimes felt the very air in the crammed room was too heavy for her to breathe.

She sat back on the chair, closed her eyes, and tried for the last time. No, it wasn't possible here either. Khalil was rearranging the chairs—something he always did with a strange intensity and a lot of unnecessary noise, before going back to his place near the telephone. How she wished she could spit in his ugly, swollen, English dog's face! She turned her eyes away from him and looked outside in frustrated anger. The gray-haired man had left the door open when he went out, and through it a delightful spring breeze flowed into the café. Suddenly she felt deeply comforted and forgot Khalil. A gentle, loving hand was playing with her flowing hair, caressing her long neck, tossing against her face. She surrendered herself completely to the cool, delicious current and started to dream.

That morning, after crossing the gutter that stretched the length of the alley turning into the main street, she'd imagined she was entering paradise itself. Red flowers hung over the garden fences, branches like green wheat stalks surrounded her on every side, massed bunches of bright roses and huge eucalyptus trees covered the whole length of the pavement, white blossom shimmered like stars on the orderly lines of orange trees. And behind this brightly colored spring were the towering, splendid villas gleaming in the sunlight.

She breathed deeply in, filling her lungs with the spring. She wanted to live the same life as all the flowers, to grow and blossom in the sunlight as they did, to feel intoxicated with the spring air. She took a red flower and, with all her strength, breathed in the soft and gentle life it contained; then she felt pity at having picked it, not wanting it to wither and die in her hand. She walked on, swaying her hips, suddenly overpowered by the ecstasy of the new life flowing in her with the spring. And she thought about the dream with which she'd woken early that morning.

She'd been walking among the gardens of the rich, splendid villas. She wasn't alone, because her soul was filled with the spring and everything was full of beauty and wonder. She'd just come out from one of the villas, no, from a much grander one even. She was breathtakingly lovely with full breasts—a bewitching princess with her great coach waiting at the door. Everything full of beauty and wonder, everything the essence of spring . . .

"Hey! What's the matter with you?"

The voice jerked her out of her reverie, and she looked round in annoyance. The newspaper boy—all three feet of him—was standing in front of the table, smiling at her with his small black eyes and white, shining teeth. Everything about him reminded her of the cheerful-looking mouse she'd liked so much in the film of Cinderella she'd seen a few days before.

She laughed.

"What do you want, boy?" She said.

"You asked for *al-Kawakeb,* didn't you?"

He put the magazine in front of her. On the cover there was the picture of a dancer writhing like a snake. The boy went back to his work with the cheerful, naive smile still shimmering in his eyes. His feet were bare and the *dashdasha* he was wearing was split open to the stomach.

How cold this poor lad must get in winter! He'd sit huddled on a small stool next to the café with only a worn padded jacket over his *dashdasha* and a tattered kerchief to put on his head, and sometimes the kerchief would slip down onto his neck and make him look very odd and funny. He helped his brother sell newspapers and books and lottery tickets and would often come into the café and spend a long time getting warmed up, standing in front of her table, rubbing his icy cold feet together, and telling her a never-ending stream of childish stories. He was always cheerful: his walk was almost a dance and he never stopped laughing—everything made him laugh, and he never complained. What did the poor lad have in his life, except cold and hunger and weariness? She'd only seen him cry once, and she'd never forget the day it happened; she'd felt as if a flame was burning her from top to bottom. His brother was hitting him, hard, on his face and his backside and every part of his small body, and the poor lad just kept on screaming. She hadn't been able to get it out of her mind all day: his brother had picked him up and thrown him onto the ground, then started to kick him and trample all over him with his heavy boots. She sat crying in her place, almost out of her mind. All his bones, she thought, must be broken, and she couldn't take it any more. She started shouting and screaming at his brother, and cursing him, then she ran to the door of the café and thrust him back.

"Why are you doing that? Why?"

The brother had just smiled at her as if nothing had happened and had gone calmly back to his work. After a while the little newspaper boy had stopped crying, and he'd come up to her cheerfully with his usual dancing walk and started telling her about the lottery tickets. He'd only sold five tickets that day and he'd somehow lost 20 *fils*. He hadn't bought anything with it, he swore he hadn't, but his brother hadn't believed him and that was why he'd given him such a beating.

"I'll teach their fathers a lesson," the boy had said, showing his small white teeth in a cheerful little laugh, "and their fathers' fathers too!" He didn't seem to be hurt, but it had really upset her to see an innocent young life being squandered in the streets like that. She'd thought of her young brothers and sisters, too, with their bare feet and dirty faces, and felt something being torn apart inside her, leaving behind it a deep wound that would not stop bleeding. She'd leant her head against the counter and started crying silently, wiping the tears from her cheeks every now and then. No one had taken any notice of her—no one except the newspaper boy, who'd come up to her when he'd finished going round the café and stood in front of her with a deep, helpless pain in his small eyes, not knowing what to do, as if he was ashamed of something without knowing what it was.

"What's the matter," he'd murmured finally, from between his shining teeth, "why are you crying?"

God, how she'd wanted to hold him close to her and kiss him again and again, showering on him all the affection that was flowing inside her! He's the only one in the world, she'd thought, the only one who feels sympathy for me and shares my feelings and pain. Brushing away her tears, she'd gently tapped his dirty cheeks and smiled at him, almost hugging him with her smile. Very soon his small heart was comforted, and he'd looked happy, with his delicate white teeth showing again. He'd gone dancing off in his usual way and had come back with a pile of magazines and detective stories that he'd placed in front of her. When she'd left the café that evening she'd given him a big piece of cake that she'd paid for herself—30 *fils*' worth. A strange emotion had sprung up within her, happiness mixed with the kind of absolute joy that is free from any misery or despair. She'd seen the paperboy dancing on the pavement, eating the cake, and gesturing in a comical way to make his elder brother jealous. Going home that day she'd felt like a feather flying lightly and happily in the wind.

She glanced at the clock. In a few minutes she'd be leaving the café. The light outside seemed like molten wax now, running onto the passing cars and the pedestrians' faces and the windows of the shops opposite. In the grocer's shop the forest of fruit seemed dark and crammed among the bunches of bananas hanging from the ceiling, and the Coca-Cola bottles no longer pointed anywhere, for the sun had set now behind the tall buildings and all that remained was the fading color on the distant horizon. Everything was slowing down, coming to a stop.

Oh, God!

The evening paper crackled in the hands of the *ustadh*. The paper boy came in quickly, picked up his money with a smile, and rushed back toward the door.

"Oh, boy!" She said it louder than usual, and immediately felt embarrassed.

"Eh? What's the matter?"

"How many times have I told you? When you're answering people who call you, say 'yes', not 'eh'!" She looked timidly at the *ustadh*.

"O.K., yes, yes, yes! What's the matter?"

Smiling, she tapped his round face gently with her long fingers and handed back the magazine.

"I haven't got time to read it now. I'll read it tomorrow."

"O.K, tomorrow. Yes, yes, yes!"

He danced and laughed his way back to his small stool on the pavement and sat down on it triumphantly.

The *ustadh* got up and left the café with his companion. Khalil rearranged the chairs round the next table in his usual noisy way.

She felt a deep sense of loneliness, as though she'd left her country for some distant land. All day long she'd tried but to no avail. Now it was time to go home, to the mud and the shared room where everything got choked—she and her dreams and her young life that was blossoming in the spring.

She looked at her breasts and adjusted the pieces of cloth. Then she combed her flowing hair in front of the glass counter, took her bag, and slowly left the café.

Above her head the neon lights shone among the silvery evening shadows. The street was crammed with cars, and the great crowd of people walking irritated her. She stepped down into the street, then up onto the pavement again, no longer swaying her hips. The crowd pushed forward, and the big, hot buses panted from stop to stop, shrieking savagely sometimes as they came to a halt.

Escape! She wanted to escape as soon as she could from this street that was like a river flowing with hot metal and sweaty bodies and noise. Squeezing her bag and handkerchief hard in her fist, she walked on, following her own thin thread among all the many other intertwined threads. In the overwhelming din a brief scene from a film she'd watched came back to her—thousands of small silver fish heaving in the nets, then being emptied onto a small boat that stood alone on the wide sea, with the blue, foamy waves lashing at its sides.

She blended herself mysteriously into the scene, identifying herself with the things she saw; unconsciously she became the lonely ship in the midst of the waves of people and shops and cars and lights. The twisting and weaving and the hubbub of the street tired her. She began to push people aside with her soft fist, moving forward one small step at a time.

When she'd reached the roundabout she took a deep breath and looked up towards the dark blue horizon. Again and again she breathed in the scent of spring that drifted toward her from the flowerbeds planted there. Gradually, as her being filled with the tender, beautiful life of the roses, standing on their short stems amid a carpet of grass, she began to recover from the fatigue of the crowded street. When she left the roundabout, there was, within her, some of the fertility and keen scent of the earth after a rainstorm.

Comforted now, she turned into another, less crowded street and moved quickly past the lampposts and cafés scattered along the pavement and the Kebab sellers huddled behind their braziers. In a small area among the cafés there was a big bustle round a fire, where a number of bare-legged men were sitting broiling *masgouf*.[1] She remembered that scene for a long time, linking it with a trip she'd made one summer to an island a long way off. There'd been a strip of water there, shimmering in the moonlight, with a few boats moored to the shore, and scattered fires where, just as here, men sat down with bare legs preparing *masgouf*. A *gawriyya*[2] it was, and her uncle Yusuf had taken her there when she was very young, when her mother was still alive and her father hadn't yet been paralyzed by his illness. It had all been a long time ago and seemed like a distant dream now. Her uncle Yusuf had emigrated to India, and the family had had no news of him since; no one knew whether he was dead or alive.

The memory stayed with her as she passed into the main street. A sense of depression was beginning to weigh her down, a feeling of weariness, of something desperately nagging at her. Soon she'd disappear into the darkness of the muddy alley, walk alongside the gutter, and settle, like a piece of wet, sticky mud, in one of the corners of the crammed room. She remembered the piece of pastrami hanging beside the worn photograph of her grandfather, the little primus stove by the door, the smell of kerosene that filled the room in the morning, the endless curses of her father against her dead mother, the smell of rot and shoes and sweat and the musty clothes in the night. There was no window, just a small opening in the roof that gave a little light during the night hours. The air in the room was heavy and dark, suffocating almost.

Oh, God! Why, why?

She dragged herself along the main road, struck by the silence of the trees huddled together in the darkness and of the distant neon lights and the white walls of the villas. She walked on, empty of all thought, empty of anything. There were only a few people in the street. From time to time the lights of passing cars would flash in her eyes, and the huge trees watched her in silence, a deep, hollow silence that sucked her whole being from her. Ghostly figures

---

1. A famous and delicious Iraqi dish of *shabbut* (a large fish, similar to carp, found in the Tigris and Euphrates rivers), stuffed with spices and other ingredients and broiled over an open fire.
2. One of a number of small sandy islands in the Tigris River to the south of Baghdad. Most of them are submerged in winter, but reappear in summer, when they are used as popular holiday resorts with temporary accommodations erected.

hurried beneath the trees, the sound of their footsteps fading as they passed along the pavement, and a gentle breeze moved the branches that overhung the garden fences. Everything within her came to a halt, calmly, with a kind of sad peace; then silence stole into her, deeper and deeper, spreading inside her. She was lost in a long, empty dream.

She didn't know how she woke. Her reverie had lasted only a very short time, and she hadn't yet gone halfway along the street. A car stopped in front of one of the villas and several men got out. Another few steps, and she passed a knot of servants and chauffeurs. Neon lights shone on the green garden of the villa. Perhaps there was a dinner party going on inside. She'd often thought about the people who lived behind those handsome walls, conjuring up pictures of castles and towers like those she'd seen in historical films, of well-groomed men and women, eating and drinking continually, clothed in silk and with silk all around them. Over the years strange, exciting stories would unfold in those castles, like the stories from *A Thousand and One Nights.* She remembered the film *Thief of Baghdad* . . . Rashid Street crammed with cars . . . Khalil's swollen face. She'd expected the *ustadh* to turn and look at her when he left the café, but he hadn't; he'd just kept walking, upright, along the pavement, as he did every day . . . and the smile she'd prepared so expectantly faded from her lips. When she'd left the café, the poor boy had been sitting on his little stool. He'd put one leg over the other like a full-grown respectable man, and he was whistling a tune. She'd been instantly reminded, once again, of the cheerful mouse she'd seen and loved so much in the story of Cinderella.

She'd so enjoyed the film when she'd seen it with Mary a few days before. She'd wept for Cinderella and been happy for her—happy that it was Cinderella and not one of her ugly half-sisters who was married to the prince. She'd lain awake for a long time that night, reliving every scene in the film, and Cinderella had stayed in her mind ever since.

How she would have loved to see it again! But the week had gone by and now there was another film being shown. In any case she wouldn't be able to get to the cinema this week, because she'd have to pay for Mary next time. It wouldn't be right otherwise, because Mary had already paid for her twice and she didn't have much money. She was a simple working girl like herself, an assistant at one of the stores, who lived in the same building.

She stopped, listening amid the deep silence. A feeling like the one she'd experienced that morning was flowing peacefully through her. It's coming, she thought, it's coming now! She became perfectly happy. The neon lights were shining from afar, the blossoms on the orange trees were glowing like stars in the dark forest of branches, the lofty villas on the two sides of the street seemed majestic and still. It was coming now! A gentle breeze rustling the leaves on the trees, the scent of jasmine blossom filling the air, the dreamworlds of silver light in the green gardens. She put her hand over her heart . . . closed her eyes . . . stood motionless. Splendid music stole in from another world, bright, loving birds hovered and sang round her ceaselessly. "Wake up, Cinderella," they sang, "wake up

Cinderella . . . Cinderella!" She woke and knew he was there, waiting for her at the entrance to the palace, the handsome prince, his suit bright with gilded medals and silk ribbons. The coach was there too, the magnificent coach conjured up by the fairy with her magic wand. She didn't want to wake up!

That morning, too, she hadn't wanted to wake up. She'd lain stretched out beneath her quilt, without moving, her arms crossed over her chest, her feet warmly pressed together. She didn't want to move. He was there outside, waiting for her, looking up sometimes at her high window, weary with expectation. She appeared to him at the window, blew him a kiss through the air, and went to put on her glass shoes. Deep joy suffused her being. The lovely birds were flying in the room, filling the world with their joyful song, and she was still there, beneath the quilt. She didn't want to get up from her bed.

"The lazy girl hasn't woken up yet!" She hadn't heard the words at first—though she'd remembered them well enough during the day, at the café. After a while her father had started screaming at her: "Bahija! Wake up! Wake up, you've got to go to work!" Her stepmother, with her disheveled hair and her eye bulging out like a pebble, had been standing by her bed and shaking her violently by the shoulders. The dream had faded, the birds had vanished, the prince had gone away, and so had the coach and everything else.

In vain she tried to bring back her dream. But it didn't return.

Her stepmother with the one, red eye, her father with his insults, the café and Khalil, the dark, narrow room. That was all there was, that was her whole life. Soon she'd be walking back along the gutter of the narrow alley and she'd reach the broken stone staircase—sand and crumbling bricks and the scrabbling footmarks and mud. Everywhere thick, sticky mud.

Oh, God! Why were things like this? Why?

She leaned over the fence of one of the villas. She began to weep violently. "Why, why? Oh, God, why?"

A ripple of spring air was blowing through the long hair that came down over her shoulders. The main road was quiet, and on both sides the strange towers and castles wove their own legends in the darkness. Beneath the trees, moving further and further away along the pavement, the footsteps of the hurrying ghosts faded.

—*Translated by Salwa Jabsheh and Christopher Tingley*

Ghalia Qabbani (1953)

Syrian short-story writer Ghalia Qabbani was born in Aleppo. She went to live in Damascus, in order to escape the family strictures on women. Later on she went with her husband to London, where both of them work as journalists. Her rebellion against outmoded constrictions and habits lies behind her first collection of short stories, *Our Plight and the Plight of This Slave* (1990).

NEWS ON THE RADIO

His voice swept over the car, and silence fell. All at once the car seemed to be moving along without driver and passengers. The voice pierced every barrier, hovering like a stern teacher entering a rowdy classroom. It broke up the quiet talk going on till then and spoke of horrifying secrets.

"This is the voice of—"

As the summarized news item caught their attention, the five strangers in the taxi dropped all pretense of indifference, awaiting the detailed report with bated breath.

Ten minutes before fear came to grip its passengers, the car had stopped in a busy shopping area for two girls who entered and flopped down on the back seat. Before the car moved off again, a fourth passenger stopped it and asked, "Where are you heading?"

The driver looked at the two girls. "Do you mind?" he asked.

"Three different fares?" one of the girls answered, looking at the front passenger. "Is this a taxi or a bus?"

"I've been waiting for an hour," the young man pleaded. "This is the first cab I've found."

The two girls relented.

"All right then," they said. "Get in."

Opening the door, he squeezed his body into the seat with the two girls and their shopping bags. The car moved off, and the passengers started up a conversation about the taxi crisis in the town.

After that, talk wandered off in various directions. The driver and the front-seat passenger, with the young man joining in occasionally, talked about car problems: mechanical faults and the high cost of repairs. Meanwhile the two girls whispered busily to one another. One of them, it seemed, had a personal problem. None of the voices was raised too high in a way to annoy the others. The radio was playing a song of Um Kulthoum, whose voice formed a barrier, or perhaps a suitable background rather, for the quiet chitchat.

All this was before the news item on the important happenings in the country: "Large-scale detentions . . . Amnesty International has registered a protest at the detention of a number of people without trial . . . Also, . . . "

The silence that fell might seem unreasonable. Why, after all, should a cab driver and his passengers fall silent when a news announcer in another country spoke of events in this one? Well, then, let's try and find a convincing reason why they should have done it. The driver hesitated over whether or not to change the radio station, because he'd long ago lost all ability to weigh things up. Should he have changed the station and declared that the news was all lies and fabrication? But he knew very well the announcer was speaking the unspeakable truth. So, should he let the announcer carry on and perhaps have one of his passengers betray him, accusing him of collaborating in the spread of provocative rumors about the country? The four passengers turned their faces to the window, wishing they could be somewhere else—anywhere rather than the sticky situation they were in now. They tried not to look into the driver's mirror or into one another's eyes, fearing any reaction would be noted. Even the two girls stopped talking. Each turned her eyes from the other; they knew their eyes would give them away.

The young man in the back seat remembered his brother, who'd been missing for years now, put his hands in his pockets, and pressed hard, as if to squeeze out the tension.

Do you find this situation unacceptable? To be together in a taxi and start exchanging sudden silent accusations of treason and writing secret reports, all based on mere fear? Because the voice of an announcer on some radio station had crept into their souls, bringing their daily routine to a halt and releasing their fear?

Does the event furnish support for political condemnation of a particular regime? Is it typical of the kind of thing that happens in our country? Four passengers and a driver in a taxi had dropped all pretense of indifference, taking refuge in a remote corner of their hearts, hiding from the bright spotlight focused on them by the voice of a radio announcer from some faraway country. The voice had been distorted by loud drumbeats from that same corner of the heart.

—*Translated by Raya Barazanji and Christopher Tingley*

Muntasir al-Qaffash (b. 1964)

Egyptian short-story writer and novelist Muntasir al-Qaffash obtained his B.A. in Arabic literature from the University of Cairo and is now the managing director of the First Book Series at the Supreme Council of Culture in Cairo. He is one of the upcoming generation of Egyptian experimentalists and has so far published four collections of short stories: *The Innermost Secrets* (1993), *Permission for Absence* (1996), *An Unintended Person* (1999), and *To See Now* (2002).

THE SOUND OF FOOTSTEPS

I felt relaxed walking along this road. I liked its calm and the rustling of the leaves on the trees to each side. There were, I saw, many windows open, with rays of light seeping out, trying to penetrate to the far distance. Yet I had no sense of any life inside. It was as though only light dwelt there.

When I go home by the usual road, I feel I've lost the joy of walking. My footsteps only find what they seek on remote roads. I've thought sometimes that time might conquer this desire of mine, only to find my love my only companion—love for a road I can walk along without end.

What separates all these other roads from the road that leads to Uncle? Do they connect in some way, to form undefined maps? Do they make junctions, allowing my footsteps to find their way toward my end road?

Still I see the start of the roads stretching out in front of me, reminding me of his presence, but I don't feel any urge to walk there now. The road stretches on, and I can see Uncle carrying his charted maps, on their faded paper, where the columns of the ruined temple still stand firm, with stones strewn among them as though they'd just now fallen there. I never took any interest in this temple. Instead I'd contemplate my uncle's maps, walk with him along his roads, follow the movement of his fingers over the lines of the maps, and the way the fingers stopped to show where lines had faded.

He didn't get them out so often now from their leather bag. It was easier for him just to draw them, showing how the lines stretched out, or bent, or crossed, never adding or missing a single line.

I thought at first I was Uncle's only chosen companion along these roads. Then I realized many others had walked there with him too. He never named these people; he'd just keep saying that, when they returned, they all felt as though they'd never walked on those roads before. It was only with him that I lived these roads. When I walked on them alone, I found them, always, commonplace and silent.

He never talked much as we walked; but he'd be sure to stop, staring intently in front of him, be sure to look at the roads he'd crossed and point out with his hands the way we were going. It was as if all the houses and streets and farms and palm trees had emerged, summoned by those beckoning hands of his, to take their place in silence, with all the many different ages they represented.

I noticed, one day, that he didn't always stick to one map. He might stop to take a new road, then come back and take another. He'd move all over the maps, and I'd see none of the junctions between them—just see the roads opening up, as they recognized his footsteps, and knew, too, that he wanted them all. When he glimpsed a question in my eye, he'd take the maps and open one of them in front of me, then fold a part of another map, joining the rest of it with the first, then place a third map on another side, then fold a fourth, carefully revealing a single, continuous line among all the intertwining ones. Then he'd look at me, trying, all the while, to keep the pattern he'd made in place; and I'd watch his fingers intently, seeing how they held all these worlds together.

I don't remember him talking about the temple, which was the inner core almost from which all his roads spread out. When we'd reached the end of our walk, though, he'd raise his hands, inviting me to look, and I'd find the temple facing us a long way off. When I was with him, the roads would let me glimpse the life they concealed. I'd try and anticipate the moment he was going to stop.

Yet the moment always caught me unawares, and I'd be surprised, too, to see the temple appear suddenly, when I'd thought the roads were hiding it and taking us far away.

Did the temple reveal all its secrets to the roads? Or did they, rather, stretch out, completing the things concealed among its walls and columns and carvings?

In the great distances separating the temple from the place where our walk ended, I'd see my uncle's entwined hands, which I'd tried so often to read. Then Uncle's call to me would fade, and I'd listen to steps walking over roads that I'd traverse without knowing where they ended. I preferred him not to call to me then. I wanted that moment to be silent, offering me the vastness of space.

Was it time for me to draw those maps now? Or had Uncle simply closed the door on them, leaving me to go my way? He'd sit at the window, looking out continually, asking anyone who was by what was happening outside; and even before the answer came, his fingers would be marking lines on the wooden window frame. He told me, often, how much he wanted to go out again and walk, and he'd strike his legs, cursing the pain. He'd see the road once more, he said, when he started walking again. He told me which directions he'd take, and he pointed to the place where he'd stop, claiming he'd see the house and the window from there, through the columns.

He knew I didn't walk along his roads any more but let my feet stray far off. I thought he'd ask me what I'd seen, but all he did was produce his maps and ask me to write on the back of each one how I'd seen him when he walked there.

I found my words forming themselves into sentences, as if they alone knew where they were going and where they'd end. I didn't feel the pen in my hand. I just wrote down all I'd seen and known with him along his roads and wrote, too, of what had been revealed to me along my own remote roads. Junctions between the two seemed to take another direction among the columns, to settle in the hearts of people who had walked there, who were eager to pass over them till the day they died. But my words didn't stop where Uncle was—in fact the sound of his footsteps scattered them. I'd start calling to him once more, but my call would go off in all directions; I'd try to bring him back but find only his knowing, ever quizzical gaze.

His fingers stretched out, to stop me writing; then the tips of the fingers started moving cautiously among the lines, showing the maps my words had formed, where I could see my remote roads. I thought he'd speak, but he just produced quantities of papers where I read the words of those who'd walked with him and saw the lines by which he defined their maps. Our maps weren't too similar, but, for all the differences, you could make out junctions here and there.

There was a long silence. Then he went back to the window and started telling me of the whole land, about roads not found on maps at all, and about footsteps coming to us from far off, and eyes that will make known what was unknown before.

—*Translated by May Jayyusi and Christopher Tingely*

Yusuf al-Qa'id (b. 1944)

Egyptian novelist and short-story writer Yusuf al-Qa'id was born in the village of Al-Dahriya in Bujeira and received all his education in Egypt, graduating from the Teacher Training College. After teaching for three years, he
was inducted into the armed forces and experienced the 1967 defeat, which
had a great impact on his later writing. He remained in the armed forces
until after the October 1973 war. He has worked as a literary editor for the
magazine *Al-Suwak* and others. Al-Qa'id is one of the most sophisticated
writers of fiction in the contemporary Arab world, with a great control
over his art and a subtle and rare capacity to merge the tragic with the
comic as he emphasizes the more failed aspects of life. He is very concerned
with socialist thought and rural conditions in contemporary Egypt. He
has published many works of fiction and was very active at the end of the
twentieth century, publishing such collections of short stories as *The Trial of
the Bird in the Cage* (1991), *The Peasants Rise to the Sky* (1996), and *Impossible
Tears* (2000), as well as such novels as *The Bird's Milk* (1994), *The Vicissitudes
of the day* (1997), *Twenty-four Hours Only* (1999), and *The Train from Lower
Egypt* (2001). However, his best-known works are his novels *Today in Egypt*
(1977), and *War in the Land of Egypt* (1978), a superb novel that has been
translated into English for PROTA by Olive and Lorne Kenny and Christopher Tingley (London: Saqi Books, 1986 and New Hampshire: Interlink
Books, 1998).

RABAB GIVES UP DRAWING

Rabab was a little girl who when she went to school became well known in
al-Bandar[1] and the villages round about and, indeed, through the whole district
and the whole province. Her father was inspector of irrigation for the region,
though not a native of it, her mother was from a distant land, and Rabab herself
was a really beautiful little thing. There might have been no more to the story
than that—the uncommon name, the father's position, the beautiful face, the
sweet and innocent childhood—had it not been for the day when, for the first
time, a drawing teacher came to the school at al-Bandar. He asked the children
to take a pencil and a piece of paper and draw whatever came into their minds,
without thinking about it at all. There was a long period of silence, during
which the children drew; then the art teacher, who'd been an artist in his youth,
walked round the class to inspect the pictures. He questioned the pupils about

---

1. The capital of a rural district.

what the lines they'd drawn on the paper meant to them and talked a lot—in a way the children didn't understand—about the springs of virginity and innocence still unsullied and about hearts not yet trampled beneath heavy feet. Then he came to the bench where Rabab was sitting.

He stood there for a long time, examining the drawing from every angle, then looked at the girl and briefly asked her to bring her guardian with her next day. Baffled by this (and worried that the teacher might be angry with her for some reason), she told her father, but it was several days before the inspector of irrigation found time to go to the school, and during this time he became more and more puzzled as to why the art teacher could possibly want to see him, especially as drawing was such an unimportant subject—it didn't have to be passed before a pupil could move up to a higher class and it didn't have any importance for the child's future.

When the two men did meet, the drawing teacher lit his pipe, thrust his right hand in his right pocket and his left hand in his left pocket, and began to talk excitedly about talent that sweeps all before it like a flood, about creativity and originality. With the proper conditions for it, he said, Rabab's talent would flower and she'd become a unique artist, with no equal anywhere. It was easy enough to produce doctors and train engineers and to find officials, but (the drawing teacher said this with an enthusiasm that alarmed the inspector of irrigation) a true artist is only found once every century. The inspector of irrigation looked at him with a blank expression, devoid of all emotion or wonder.

"What exactly do you want from me?" he asked.

The drawing teacher talked about conducive atmosphere and suitable climate, about viewing paintings and reading the history of art, and, finally, about discovering oneself through the quest for a distinctive creative method.

"But where does it all lead to?" the inspector of irrigation asked, interrupting the flow.

He went off, partly convinced and partly rejecting the things he'd been told. "I don't understand this man at all," the drawing teacher said to himself. "Tomorrow I'll give Rabab a last piece of advice, and she can do as she likes with it." Next day he asked only one thing of her: that she should look deeply and carefully into her soul, do the same with the world around her, then take her pencil and draw, faithfully and with total abandon, whatever came into her mind, obeying only the truth that rose from the depths of her own young heart.

When the inspector of irrigation arrived home, he called for Rabab, sat down facing her, and asked her to draw him there and then, as he was. But Rabab said she'd draw him as she'd seen him at his office the one time he'd taken her there.

The drawing was made, and there he was sitting at his desk with importance, gravity, prestige, and resolution all clearly marked on his face. He was holding an enormous pen, and the office looked far more beautiful than it really was.

Rabab's father looked at the drawing.

"Why haven't you given me a secretary?" he asked.

So Rabab drew the secretary: pretty, graceful, with hair the color of ripe wheat and eyes like the pure blue of a summer sky. She wasn't more than twenty, and, as she leaned over him to hand him some papers, her full breasts hung pendulously down in front of the face of the Inspector, who seemed to be breathing in the scent of her skin. The first signs of satisfaction appeared on Rabab's father's face. Then he said, "Are you leaving your father without a messenger?"

He'd like her, he said, to draw an exhausted, unshaven creature in shabby clothes, with a jacket soaked with the sweat of a lifetime, worn-out shoes, and a body like a pyramid seen upside down.

"Why do you see Uncle Sirhan like that?" she asked. (Uncle Sirhan was her father's messenger.) "He's a good man, completely content with his life, and his *gilbab* is always spotless and as white as milk."

Uncle Sirhan, her father told her, was exceptional, a man from a good family who'd fallen on hard times. Most messengers, he said, were just the way he'd described them. She took issue with him on this, and they were still deep in discussion on the point when her mother came in and saw the drawing. She took one look at the secretary's full breasts and the flared nostrils of her husband, then the discussion was replaced by a battle between Rabab's father—who'd now become a mere husband—and the wife who'd caught him in the act of thinking about another woman.

"You took me like a piece of succulent meat," screamed Rabab's mother, "and now you're throwing me away like a bone!"

He explained the situation: it was Rabab, he said, who'd drawn the picture. So she pounced on Rabab and the picture together. Rabab was given a spanking and the picture was torn into small pieces, the largest of them no bigger than Rabab's little palm. Rabab swore she'd never draw again because of the troubles it had brought on her head.

Next day Rabab found herself drawing the owner of the estate near al-Bandar, who'd once invited them there for a whole day not because he liked her father but because her father had the power to make things easy for him in matters of irrigation. She drew the estate owner as a traditional feudal landlord unchanged since time immemorial: the huge belly, the hanging layers of flesh on the face, the veins sticking out. When she'd completed the drawing of him, his likeness seemed to come to life, and it was as if she heard him shouting at her, telling her that it was unheard of for a landowner of ancient family, still in possession of his lands, not to have peasants and laborers and soldiers, together with watchmen at night and servants during the day. Rabab thought about this and decided he had a right to what he'd asked for. She drew a person from each group: a peasant, a laborer, a watchman, and a servant, one at each corner of the picture, so that the landowner should utterly dominate them with his huge body and the space he occupied. When she'd completed their features, they came to demand things that they needed: houses to live in, food to eat, clothes to cover their nakedness, and money to spend. But the landowner shouted at them that they shouldn't present demands before they'd done their work: it was out of the question to pay them their wages in advance. But they answered that hungry people couldn't work; they needed the wages to buy food, then they could put all their energy into their jobs. The landowner insisted they should work first, then get their wages, and they insisted on food before work. Finally they came to blows, and the fight became so violent that the picture was torn and all Rabab's efforts were wasted. But this time she felt a new kind of curiosity: she wanted to know how the affair had ended and who'd been in the right and who'd been in the wrong. She'd carry on drawing, she told herself, whatever happened. She'd draw things that were far away from al-Bandar, far away from her home and the people she knew; that way she'd avoid the problems that cropped up after every picture.

She decided to draw the ruler of the country. And when she'd finished, he shouted at her, "Who am I going to govern?" A ruler, he went on, who doesn't have anyone to rule over is out of a job; if he goes on like that he'll be suspended as ruler. No one's ever satisfied, thought Rabab. She drew a person to be under his authority, who'd ask his permission to eat and sleep and go to the bathroom, and be altogether a docile subject. The ruler looked at her and said that this was a boring game: the person was too passive, he wanted him to have some life, sometimes saying yes and sometimes saying no, especially on secondary matters of no real importance. "I can decide," he said, "when he ought to say yes and when he can say no. That way the game will acquire new dimensions and won't be boring any more, and we can go on playing it for a long time." So she drew a querulous subject for him. It was quite simple: when she'd finished drawing the external features, she drew a brain inside the head, which the subject could use as necessary. The ruler decided on the matters where the subject should say yes and the ones where he should say no; the ones where he could use his mind and the ones where he wasn't allowed to. And together they decided on the punishments to be meted out to the subject if he made a mistake or went back on the agreement. On the first day the subject made a mistake and the ruler enforced the agreement. The subject found himself in prison and, from the walls of his narrow cell, said to Rabab, "Why have you made me suffer in prison like this?"

His part in this strange game, he asserted, was simply the result of a plot on her part, and he wanted the game to be stopped immediately. She tried to reconcile the two figures but realized that it was impossible. The uproar grew, with the subject demanding to be let out of prison and the ruler demanding a new subject, because he'd got bored again after putting the old one in prison; he wanted one now who'd toe the line properly and work within the general set of rules he'd made, only differing in his views, if at all, with the ruler's permissions. Irritated by the clamor of the imprisoned subject and the wrath of the ruler, Rabab tore up the picture and threw the pieces on the floor.

She didn't draw for many days after that, and she'd almost forgotten all about it when her brother, who dreamed of being an officer one day, came to her and told her the news was all over town that his sister was an important artist; a boundless future awaited her, it seemed, and her pictures would be as immortal as the pyramids and as rich as the waters of the Nile or the honeyed tones of the Egyptian dialect. He asked her to draw him a soldier, the soldier that he'd lead into battle one day, when he was a great officer, to liberate the occupied lands and throw the enemy back from the frontiers of the homeland.[2] So she drew a soldier for him, huge and dark and strong, and when she'd put in his bushy, twirled moustache and his huge government-issue boots and the eagle on the front of his beret, her brother said, "Where's his gun?"

Rabab started drawing a gun in the soldier's hand, but the soldier objected, pointing to the television behind her. On the screen was a dancer who'd danced for a quarter of a century before finally discovering a beautiful voice and a gift for singing, so adding a new talent to the one she already had. It was the first time in the country's history, apparently, that an artist had combined the two.

"The war's over, o–o–o," the dancer was singing, "the war's finished, o–o–o!"

"But the lands are still occupied," said Rabab's brother.

"The orders from my superiors," answered the soldier, "are that there'll be no more fighting after today."

"Isn't the enemy still lying in wait for us?" asked her brother.

"There are countless enemies," the soldier answered. "They're at the borders, and inside them, and in front and behind. But orders are orders, and my orders state quite clearly that there'll be no more fighting after today."

"The gun won't be any use then," Rabab said.

"They'll still be able to use it for parades and processions," her brother said, "and to keep peace inside the country."

To this the soldier replied that, with the war over, the presence of the gun was a danger; he couldn't answer for what would happen if he had it.

Rabab hesitated, but her brother insisted. A soldier without a gun, he said, cuts a pretty poor figure. The soldier said that a gun without a target to aim at was dangerous for them.

Rabab finally settled the argument by drawing the gun in the soldier's hand. She placed his eye close to the base of the barrel and pushed the butt firmly into the hollow of his right shoulder. "Since I have a gun," the soldier thought, "I'll have to use it. And since I'm forbidden to use it against the enemies in front of me, I'll have to use it against the enemies at my rear, until such time as I can decide for myself who to use it against." In a flash he'd turned, aimed the gun at Rabab's brother, and fired seven bullets into his body.

A charge was brought against Rabab in the court, to the effect that she'd drawn the soldier who'd ignored the instructions about the war being over, who'd disobeyed orders by firing the gun and killing the little boy. It was

---

2. The boy is referring here to occupied Palestine and the frontiers of his own homeland, Egypt.

mentioned, in extenuation, that the little boy had dreamed of becoming an officer, in an age that didn't want masses of officers who'd talk about occupied lands and liberating homelands and purging the country's frontiers of enemy columns.

The judge was pleased when Rabab stood up in court and declared, of her own free will, that she'd renounce drawing, that she'd never draw again, whatever happened, from that day on. She'd broken the pencils, she said, poured away the paint, and torn the paper, and she'd instructed her mind to shut her imagination up in a bottle, which would be put in a chest, which would, in its turn, be hidden in the seventh layer of the earth under the sea.

The judge instructed the court clerk to take a written declaration from Rabab, in her own handwriting, clearly stating that she renounced drawing of her own free will from that time on. The clerk produced pen and paper and went up to Rabab so that she could make the declaration. Only then did he discover that she had no hands; and when he enquired about this, she answered that they'd only been made for drawing and had no other use—when she'd decided to give up drawing, her hands had simply vanished. When, she said, she decided to start drawing again, and to draw a soldier able to choose his own destiny rather than having it decided by others, then she'd get back the full use of her hands. But now she was stating loud and clear, for everyone to hear, that she was renouncing drawing. That, she said, should be good enough for the declaration demanded.

—Translated by May Jayyusi and Christopher Tingley

'Abd al-Hakeem Qasim (1935–1990)

Egyptian short-story writer and novelist 'Abd al-Hakeem Qasim graduated from the University of Alexandria. In 1967 he was imprisoned for five years by a military court in Egypt because of his political activity, after which he went to East Berlin, where he continued his studies. *The Seven Days of Man* (1969), which depicts the gradual changes that happen to a boy away from traditional Islamic culture and modes of thinking and was published after Qasim's release from prison, is one of the most impressive novels in modern Arabic. It was translated into English by Joseph Bell and published there in 1989. Qasim has a particular skill in portraying haunting pictures of life and in reflecting a deep empathy with the human predicament and struggle. His novel *An Attempt to Escape* appeared in 1980, and in 1982 he published *The Destiny of the Depressing Rooms,* a description of the rooms occupied by the protagonist as he moves from his village all the way to Germany. *Al-Mahdi* appeared in 1987 and was translated into English by Peter Theroux in 1995, under the title *Rites of Assent.* His short-story collections include *Desires and Sorrow* and *Migrating to the Unfamiliar.* His death after a chronic illness was a grave loss for modern Arabic literature.

A WINTER NIGHT

The old barren acacia tree moaned humbly in response to the wind. In the sky there wasn't a single star transmitting sufficient light to distinguish its contours in the pitch darkness.

The decrepit windows were shut on the warmth and the faint light spread by lamps; but the wind's insistent whistle found its way through the cracks in the windows and walls. Fear pierced men's hearts as a thread goes through the beads of a necklace.

By the light of ovens—in oppressive rooms—old women wrapped black headscarves round their raisinlike faces. They were telling the story of the winds' moaning to the children. The children's eyes showed no traces of sleepiness. Their hearts were full of awe and wonder as they listened to the tales. Around the faces of the fatigued women one could discern locks of hair, disheveled and damp with their sweat, and these stuck to their brows and temples. As for the wise men sitting in the men's reception parlour, lit with lanterns, they were pensive. Their eyes took in the waves of pale light. Ah, there's no power save God's and in God.

In Sadiqa's barn, a ewe was in labor. She wasn't conscious of the source of her pain, but she felt iron fingers penetrating her body and pressing mercilessly on her abdomen. She sprang to her feet among other sleeping ewes, and her standing up caused a displacement of warmth on the barn floor. The other ewes trembled and jostled each other until the break was closed and the suffering ewe expelled from their huddle. She stood alone and entirely immersed in darkness. The cold air worked through her wool and smacked at her ears and the region under her tail. Pain pulsated in every vein of her body. The bleating came from the depths of her like the agony of a person being torn apart.

Sadiqa came running when she heard the agonized bleating. She carried a lamp in her hand, and its light inscribed a circle on the darkness in the barn. She stood in the light: a tall, broad-shouldered woman, with a flat chest and flimsy hair. She was bareheaded and wore a coarse black *gilbab*. The disheveled locks of hair showed up in the lamp's yellow flare.

At the back of the oven, embers of cottonwood could be seen blazing, tricking their red reflections over the room. The white mat was growing warm from those seated on top of the oven in the closed room. The old woman resembled a heap of black cloth from which a face like a dried fig peeped out. Whenever the wailing was carried on the wind, the black heap trembled and the folds of her wrinkled belly contracted.

"Do you hear?" she said. "It isn't the wind that's whistling like this. It's Abu Jubba!"

The little boy was busy embracing his thin legs, and resting his chin on his knees. As he listened to his grandmother's words, his heart trembled.

"She killed him on a night like this, thirty years ago. She bit his windpipe with her teeth and kept on until her teeth met through the skin and blood sprayed the canal bridge. Since then, from year to year, always at the same time, Abu Jubba's heard wailing at night."

The yellow wick in the funnel of the lamp slanted to one side. Its light increased in height. Darkness came from all corners to overtake it, and the smell of burning gasoline scorched the nostrils. Then the wick returned to its upright position, leaving a black print on the glass wall, like a lie.

The winter night outside was crowding the horizon with darkness. Its baying was like an encircling pack of black wolves. The lantern in the men's reception room grew increasingly frailer. The silence weighed. The suspended lantern tilted over feebly. Dark headless shadows thronged on the walls. Out of fear the little boy clung to his father's side. His voice came out, brokenly, "She bit his windpipe with her teeth until they met."

The father patted the frightened child and silently bowed his sorrowful face. His gaze swam over the waves of pale light:

"Thirty years, son, for thirty long years," he said, "the old women have sat on the oven tops, while the wind howls in the open spaces and the winter nights seem interminable!"

Angry looks met the speaker from all sides, "So it's just old women's tales?"

"But don't you see God's vengeance on her face?"

"She hasn't begun to suffer yet."

"Hair will grow on her face, and her teeth will grow into fangs. She'll be like a hyena!"

"God's vengeance! Since she escaped punishment by the government."

But the man remained silent and pensive, his eyes hung to the pale light.

"She was sitting there, son, under the acacia tree, a small tree whose branches were laden with yellow flowers that shone in the sunlight. I greeted her, 'Salaam, Sadiqa.' She was a shy little girl and pretty as a rose. She drew her veil over her face out of modesty and returned my greeting. That was on the day previous to the incident. Now that tree has grown old and twisted, standing alone on the top side of the field, bending in accordance with the wind's capricious direction."

The flames continued to glow red and dark in the oven's interior. The fatigued woman with the drained face parted her hanging feet and let the heat of the oven spread over her belly and thighs. She drifted out on her thoughts as she listened to the unabating wind, then turned and spoke to her sister about Sadiqa, "If only she'd married . . . Marriage might have helped soften her disposition!

"But who'd marry the woman who murdered Abu Jubba, the murderer who managed to elude all the men of the area!"

"God! She's become like a man . . . Every day she grows uglier."

"That's her fate; it's written and foreordained." The ewe was bleating with pain. Tears stood out in her glassy eyes. Sadiqua crouched near it, holding the ewe's pendulous belly. The lamp showed up Sadiqua's rocky face with the tanned skin full of scars. Her thick eyebrows were knitted together like two small moustaches that had never been trimmed.

Sadiqua's old mother was also woken by the ewe's bleating. The room was tight with layers of darkness, and she instinctively felt the bed only to discover that her daughter was not there next to her under the woolen blanket. She waded out through the darkness to the barn. There she saw her daughter's manly shoulders etched on the pale light. Her heart suffered for her daughter.

"Ah, my daughter," she thought, "the apple of your poor mother's eyes. May God punish them. They've killed you ... and they're still cutting your body to pieces by the ovens in these winter nights."

She continued to stare at the lamp until tears gathered in her eyes:

"The axe has no mercy ... It's squared your shoulders ... and furrowed the dead skin on your palms. Palms that have never been softened by kneading butter-drenched dough, or the churning of buttermilk in earthenware jugs. Oh, the gales of the fields and the gossip of people!"

Thirty years ago Sadiqa and her mother weren't alone. Muhammad was with them. Theirs was a happy home. Sadiqa was a lovely bride whom Ahmad loved, and he was in the process of preparing his house for their wedding. But Abu Jubba had decided to impose a penalizing tax on this happy household with the whitewashed walls. Muhammad retaliated by saying, "I made my fortune with my own hands, with an axe under the incandescent noon-day sun. I owe nothing to anybody."

Abu Jubba came to Muhammad carrying the murderous axe. "Muhammad!"

Muhammad got up.

"Yes, Abu Jubba!"

"You have to pay a tariff of wheat."

"No!"

It was a shame for one man to be afraid of another and for Abu Jubba to have the power to eliminate lives. But the axe sank into Muhammad's forehead, between his eyebrows. He collapsed on to the canal bridge under the small acacia tree. The little yellow buds of the tree floated in the stream of blood flowing from his head. At the time the ewes were huddled together in the middle of the bridge, with Sadiqa shepherding them, and carrying a thick stick in her hand.

She couldn't remember how it happened, but she had Abu Jubba lying dead next to her brother. At first she was imprisoned in the district jail. The judiciaries asked her questions, to which she replied honestly, omitting nothing of her story. They told her to go home.

The household was never heard to laugh again, and the only noise was that of the bleating of ewes, the cackling of chickens. The white paint flaked off the walls and no one noticed. Ahmad went and picked another flower. Who would marry a murderess?

The ewe was parting her legs and raising her tail upwards while simultaneously lowering her bottom. When she held her breath, her belly muscles would contract, and she would emit a stream of urine mixed with blood. After each labour pain had subsided, she would bleat pitilessly. Sadiqa sighed:

"Courage, my friend."

And she stroked the ewe's belly tenderly.

The embers turned to ash in the ovens. The lamps grew close to extinction. People huddled over their warm mats. Rain opened up, beating on the wooden shacks with a low, hesitant rhythm. The elements were rectifying their balance after the preceding fury.

The labor pains returned. The ewe's body stiffened and perspiration matted her coat. Blood poured out suddenly. The barn was full of the viscid smell of the bloody effluvia. Sadiqa's breath quickened and grew to an agitated sound. Then the baby ewe slipped out, all white, its wool tinged with blood.

A ray of light began to articulate the form of the acacia tree. It looked old, humble, and wet. Tears trembled on Sadiqa's eyelashes as she embraced the new-born lamb and rubbed her face in its soft moist wool.

"My child, my love!"

A numbing softness crept into her barren breast. The tears scorched her scarred face. The dawn broke in the east. The mother ewe uttered a sound in which joy was mixed with fatigue.

—*Translated by May Javyusi and Jeremy Reed*

Fakhri Qa'war (1945)

Born in Ajfour, Jordan, Fakhri Qa'war obtained a B.A. in Arabic and worked in aviation and tourism before becoming a teacher in both Amman and Zarqa'. He has worked for twelve years as editorial secretary of Jordan's prestigious *Al-Ra'iy* daily, where he was also a columnist. He is a member of the administrative committee of the Union of Jordanian Writers, where he has been very influential in courageously fighting hybrid misconceptions of Arabic culture. He has participated in many conferences and literary festivals, both in Jordan and in the Arab world, and has won, in conjunction with the writer Khalil al-Sawahiri, the *Sayf al-Irani* Prize for the short story. What is particularly interesting in his work is his talent for humor, and in an age that is dominated by loud denials of exterior and interior aggressions, as well as by grim depictions of life and experience, Qa'war's humorous episodes seem like a fresh breeze. His fictional works include *Why Did Suzy Cry So Much?* (1973), *Chess Playing Is Prohibited* (1976), *I am the Patriarch* (1981), *The Barrel and Other Stories* (1982), *The Palestinian Job* (1989), and *The Dream of a Night Watchman* (1993). He has also written fiction for children and has published books and essays on Arabic fiction.

LORD OF MY TIMES

Yesterday I had to commute by service taxi[1] in Amman and stood by the side of the road trying to stop a driver. I signaled once with my right hand, and once with my left hand, and once with my head, but no one would stop for me. My way

---

1. In many Arab countries a taxicab, often a Mercedes, will work a fixed route, picking up and dropping passengers at any point along it. The fare is a fraction of that for a normal taxi.

of signaling must, I decided, be all wrong. I wasn't getting my message across and would just have to find some new way of attracting attention. So I started smiling at my driver brothers, while simultaneously waggling the tip of my forefinger. That did the trick; one of them stopped, and I opened the rear door and got in.

The back seat was empty; there was just a plump woman in the front alongside the driver. This driver wore a short-sleeved shirt that showed off the gleaming muscles of his arms, and he had thick, twirled mustaches and piercing eyes like a hawk's. Near his right knee was a radio whose amplifier was blaring out a song called "Lord of My Times," sung by someone or other I didn't know. I tried my best to enjoy it, but frankly feared my eardrums might be punctured. Could I, I wondered hesitantly, ask my driver brother to lower the sound? I was afraid my meek request might open the door for a quarrel, and, once a door like that's opened, it doesn't close so easily and the consequences could be serious. I tried to tell myself these fears were just fantasies, that I was worrying myself for nothing. The driver's muscles, I reflected, were nothing to get anxious about, even if he did rub them with olive oil, and just because a fellow twirled his mustaches, that didn't make him some sort of wild man. I leaned forward, preparing myself, very gently, to tap his broad shoulders and say, "Excuse me. Could I ask you, very kindly, to turn down the radio?"

But before I could utter a word, he flicked his cigarette out of the window and the ash flew back at me, some of it going in my eyes. I retreated, leaning back in my seat once more. We didn't have that far to go, I thought. It was hardly worth making an issue over songs. Meanwhile, our singer brother was still banging out his refrain: "Lord of My Times!"

Suddenly the driver stopped the car to pick up a huge man with a vast belly, bestial looks, and thick arms ending in fingers like pliers. As the man got in and sat down next to me, the seat tilted straight over to his side. The car drove on.

"Turn that radio down!" the huge man told the driver, in a hectoring tone. "You're deafening us in here."

The driver twirled his mustaches and squinted sideways at my neighbor.

"That's Muhammad Adawiyya!" he said.

"I don't care if it's Muhammad 'Abd al-Wahhab in person,"[2] the huge man answered. "You've no right to inflict a row like that on us!"

At that point I remembered how the department of transport had banned the use of radios in public cars. What I really should do now, I told myself, was to write in about having amplifiers removed from the back too. That would finish the job properly.

The radio stopped of its own accord.

"I'm sure we all enjoyed that performance of 'Lord of My Times'," the announcer said. "And now," he went on, "let's hear Georgette Sayigh singing 'What Can You Do About Love?'"

---

2. 'Abd al-Wahhab is generally regarded as the greatest twentieth-century singer of the Arab world.

The driver was going to turn the radio down, but the huge man next to me got suddenly worked up.

"No!" he yelled. "Let's hear it!"

He laid his hand on the back of the seat behind me, taking up the room of two passengers with his vast bulk (he really was 'Lord of His Times,' I thought!), then started humming along with the singer.

The journey was only five kilometers, but it was starting to seem all too long for me. This, I felt, was the longest service car trip in the history of the world!

Suddenly the driver stopped the car, making my neighbor's belly jerk so violently my neck vibrated like a tuning fork. The driver glanced back at us.

"Sorry!" he said.

Another service taxi had braked abruptly just in front of him, forcing our driver brother to brake too. On the back of the other taxi was a sign reading: "Don't drive so fast, Daddy. We'll wait for you!" Its driver roared off again with the other cars and was lost to view.

It was a short trip but an exhausting one. Georgette Sayigh's song came to an end at the same moment that we reached my final destination, and I opened the left-hand door behind the driver. The driver wheeled round on me.

"What the hell do you think you're doing?" he shrieked.

I look around, trying my hardest to see what I'd done wrong but was none the wiser. I asked my driver brother what he was so excited about.

"You're not allowed to open this door," he said.

I glanced at his muscles, smiled in the most pleasant possible way, as if to say I hadn't realized, then flitted out of the other door behind my fat companion, thanking God for my safe arrival.

—*Translated by May Jayyusi and Christopher Tingley*

You Might Get Rich Today

I don't know why I've always had this odd idea—that one day I'll get rich with no effort at all, without so much as lifting a finger, just by buying a lottery ticket or whatever.

Long before the Union of Charitable Committees invented that expression "the less fortunate citizen," I'd felt less fortunate—fortunes being, I suppose, seized in this life from magic windows opening up on the roofs of houses, or from the veils of the unknown, or the folds of the sky or the layers of space. Yet I always felt—and do to this day—that misfortune isn't just a fate written on a person's brow, with no hope of release. Fortune might come, after all, from a lottery ticket bought by a friend or a relative, then slipped into my pocket unasked.

Fortune might come, too, from the death of a relative who'd emigrated to Argentina or Nicaragua or San Francisco. He would have tried, desperately but to no avail, to father progeny on a wife who'd died when he was in the prime of old age; then he would have died himself, and they'd find I was the sole natural heir! Or fortune might come from under a tile in the rented house where I live—there *is* a loose tile by the kitchen door. Suppose it got that way from all the gold bars or Turkish gold pounds stuffed underneath it? All the other tiles seem perfectly firm and in place.

As time passed, though, I came to sense, deep down, that the "less fortunate citizen" would never get rich, even if he put his hand in the hand of Onassis, God bless him! I started seeing my state as I knew it really was, stopped imagining wealth showering down on me from above or soaring up to me from below. What made me readier to accept my poor prospects was that hateful saying, "What's written on the brow the eye must witness." That was what made me raise the white flag—to proclaim my surrender to what was written on my brow. When people in responsible positions, who understand the nature and business of life, keep saying some citizens are more fortunate and some less, then I and others like me, who run small cars, and get meager salaries, and live in rented homes, find these endlessly repeated words seeping into their subconscious. There are many different sorts of people, we realize, and we'll never leave our skins. An ant doesn't turn into an elephant or a mouse into a fat cat.

Then, a few days ago, I met a young man who reopened my wounds, bringing back all my old lost hopes of getting wealth from some unknown source.

It was a credible story he told me, and a most original and interesting one. It opened with him standing by the door of his house, gazing at the people passing by, at the children playing and the cars driving past. There he stood, wondering how he could find the dowry to ask for the hand of the woman he loved. He smoked more than three cigarettes in the process. Then he saw a child dragging an old iron belt and called out to him to bring the belt over. The child gave it to him, and inside he found a setting of precious metals. The belt must, he thought, be an antique, and it might have some value. But he only had half of it there, so he asked the child about the other half, and the child promised to look for it. As for the first half, he bought it from the child for one dinar, promising him five when he brought the other part.

That evening his brother rang from Washington D.C., and our friend asked him if the Americans were interested in antiques and, on hearing that they were, described the belt and the precious metals inside. His brother told him to come to Washington at once, and when he'd arrived, he gave him the addresses of two businesses that bought antiques.

Going to the first address, he handed the part of the belt he had to an employee, who went off for a while, then came back and said, "Okay, we'll buy it."

He asked what they were prepared to pay.

"We can't give you more than thirty-five thousand dollars," the young lady said.

Suppressing his excitement, he assumed the firm look of a mountain of granite, then went straight off to the other address. They couldn't give him more than forty thousand dollars, they told him!

Much more fortunate now, our young man put the whole matter in his brother's hands, to follow it up and try and get a higher price. And a week ago, he told me, a third business, in another American state, had offered fifty thousand dollars for the belt, but his brother had held off in the hope of a better price still. Obviously, then, the unfortunate man may not stay that way for ever—he might come across a belt, and all his problems, all the financial trials and personal worries, would be solved. My young friend had, it was clear, asked for the hand of his beloved now, promising her a life of velvet and a gold cage, or maybe a platinum one, like no other one anywhere.

And now, this more fortunate friend dinned into me, I must examine every old metal item I came across, pore over every piece of pottery, anything that might bring in some money; and I've been looking for some sort of antique ever since. But all I've found is a wooden ladle in our attic, which goes back, apparently, to one of my gracious grandmothers. I'll spring this on my friend, today or tomorrow, and then he can spring it on his brother in Washington, who can either sell it straight off for ten thousand dollars or break it over his knee. I suspect he'll do the second, but still, less fortunate people never quite lose hope of being rich one day.

It's true, though, isn't it, that old saying people keep repeating? "The unfortunate will just find bones in the sheep's stomach!"

—*Translated by May Jayyusi and Christopher Tingley*

Mubarak Rabi' (b. 1935)

Moroccan novelist and short-story writer Mubarak Rabi' was born in Maachou in the region of Casablanca and obtained a degree in psychology from King Muhammad V University in Rabat, where he now lectures. His short-story collections include *Our Master, Fate* (1969), *Blood and Smoke* (1975), and *Journey of Love and Harvest* (1983). His first novel, *The Good-Hearted,* was published in 1972, followed by *Comrades in Arms* (1976), a political novel set on the Golan Heights in Syria confiscated by Israel as a result of the June War of 1967. His other novels include *The Winter Wind* (1977); *The Moon of His Times* (1983), which won instant acclaim; and his latest novel, *The Sultan's Road* (1999). He is one of Morocco's foremost writers of fiction. His work has shown a steady development toward greater sophistication and complexity.

ZINAH

By God Almighty, it would be much better to kill oneself. By God Almighty it would be; but he fears Zinah's commentary, referring to him as "Poor empty-headed Haddan, the deformed," and besides, he would never then be able to marry her.

It is not his fault he is deformed, God alone is perfect. (He is deformed in the upper part a little and in the lower part too.) Despite his condition, he fell in love with her; his love inspired him to call her Zinah[1] while the rest of God's creatures in the village use her real name, 'Arabiyya, daughter of the *Faqih*,[2] Si Nasir.

He went to her father in Masida, not to ask him for her hand—he certainly was no fool although they claim he is—but to ask for a charm to attract his beloved. He offered as fee a little basket of warm eggs, which he removed from under his old mother's only hen.

(*You understand, Mother, that your son is impatient for Zinah, so why be so angry with him?*)

The *faqih* asked for her name, but Haddan the deformed stuttered, refusing to divulge it. He was no fool, no matter what people said. Could he have uttered, "Faqih Si Nasir, write me words which will make your beloved daughter fall in love with me?" He could only give the *faqih* the first initial of her name.

"Oh, the first letter, the first letter, Sir, blessed be the letter, Si Nasir."

"Say it, say the name, Haddan, may God bless you."

"It is 'A—the first letter of her name, master Faqih."

The *faqih* wrote the first letter and stopped, staring at the paper as if he had discovered something strange . . . Had he figured it out? God have mercy! How could he recognize his daughter from just the first letter of her name? The *faqih* stared at Haddan's morose, frightened face and anguished posture, leaning to the left as if ready to run away. Now the *faqih* seemed to be trembling himself, almost strongly. Oh miserable, distorted Haddan, you'd better run away, he certainly recognized the name! The *faqih* gradually gathered his composure, with conscious effort. He spat around him, then invoked God's help and blessing and recited the Kursi verse and other such prescribed verses from the Quran. Then he grasped the anxious Haddan and, trying to persuade him to sit down, said, "Sit down, my son, sit down."

Again the *faqih* recited the Kursi verse and his features relaxed. Haddan too felt more at ease. Rejoice Haddan, the *faqih* knows and accepts!

The *faqih* whispered, "Oh my God, the infidel has conquered your soul, Haddan."

What could Haddan do if the *faqih*, rightly or wrongly, had guessed the wrong obsession when he stammered as he was about to mention her simple initial? It would not be the *faqih*'s fault, either, if he pursued a natural logic, realizing Haddan's passion by simple deduction: since Haddan the distorted was unable to pronounce her name, her initial was 'A, and he looked so pathetic, all this could lead to only one person, the nonbeliever, she whose name should never be mentioned[3] . . . in the Name of God, the Merciful, the Compassion-

---

1. Beautiful.

2. A Quran reciter, or a man learned in Islamic studies. The word can also point to some powers of divination attached to him.

3. The faqih is speaking here of an evil spirit that he thinks has entered Haddan's soul.

ate. Haddan's neck swayed, bent by the amulet attached to it by a black woolen thread. He leapt to her side as she was returning from the water wheel.

"Good morning to you, Zinah!"

She stiffened in surprise. "I won't bid you good morning, distorted and unlucky man."

His long stature quivered, losing its tentative balance, but he did not fall to the ground. He said, "You ought to be ashamed of yourself, Zinah, you ought to." Was he guilty because he had fallen in love with you? Because he was deformed and you were well built? Because he was Fatna's son, still living with her in the same hut? Was he at fault because all they possessed was a single cow tied to the large cactus tree? But she was expected to calve in two months time, and then they would have an abundance of butter and milk. It is for *your* sake, Zinah, daughter of the Faqih Si Nasir, that I deprived a chicken of its hatch and left it angry, its feathers ruffled! While *your* house is full of blessings. But poor Haddan's intention is to be your husband—that is, with the help of your father's amulet.

Haddan swayed like a drunkard at her side. Smiling, he thought, "The amulet is around my neck, my heart is filled with love for her, and patience solves most problems." He called out his secret name for her, "Zinah!"

"May you be deprived of all good, you twisted owl-owner." (By God Almighty it would be better for me to die, kill myself and get it over with. Is it my fault if my hut has been surrounded by thorny cactus trees since the days of my great-grandfather? I can't help it if the ill-omened owl[4] happens to like our place and stays, appearing there mornings and evenings, facing the hut. By God I will deal with this owl, one of us has to go.) With his eyes he followed a dark spot flying far off in the sky. As it shrank, he slapped one hand against the other, like a person washing his hands after a difficult job. Before entering his hut to rest, and feeling much more cheerful, he gazed at a gap in the dense growth of cactus trees. It looked as if a gun had shot through a strong citadel.

(He was musing . . . "You know, Mother, you who have understanding and knowledge, how hard it is to hear my Zinah calling me, 'The Owl Man'! "The cactus tree will spread until it fills in the breach. What is important is that the ill-omened bird has now lost its favored place and will look for another resting stop. One would be ready to cut off anything, even one's head, in order to escape the owl's gaze.")

"Good morning to you, Zinah!"

He was quivering and jumping at her side on the road she walked daily.

"Is it you again?"

(But the amulet was hanging on his neck, love was in his heart, and patience eventually pays well.)

"Yes, it is me again."

"How is your mother, Fatna, the poor woman?

---

4. In Arab society, the owl is regarded as an ill-omened bird.

(Joy, Haddan! Haven't you just begun to see results?!)

"We are all fine, Zinah. The owl has left the place. I jumped at it and surprised it."

She walked with swinging gait, laughing as if delighted by this achievement. (He mused, "Do you see, Haddan? Do you see, Mother, you are the one who understands.")

"Zinah, let me carry the jug." (He was musing, "Where do you find this sudden glibness and good manners? May none of your bones burn, hand of Si Nasir!")

It was not his fault that he swayed as usual and lost his balance. Some of the water in the jug splashed onto him and onto Zinah. But she reclaimed the jug, laughingly saying, "Let's leave it on my head, Haddan."

(Do you see how kind she is, Haddan? Didn't you just hear the most beautiful voice and enjoy the most soothing fragrance. By God Almighty, even if Zinah asked him to die, he would do it, happily.)

Was it his fault if, upon his jubilant return home, he found the owl quietly standing on top of his hut? It was on the very top of the top, over the *shashiya*.[5] Haddan froze at the sight of it.

He mused . . . . "Now what? My frightened mother told me to leave the creature in peace; its own God had given it the right to be here. But how could your son bear to hear Zinah say to him, 'Ha, the owl is nesting over the *shashiya* of your hut!'"

Hardly knowing if what he was doing was right or wrong, Haddan crawled around the hut searching for a long strand of dwarf palm. He gripped it, looped it over the hut, and twisted it around the *shashiya,* forming a trap. When the bird returned and alighted, Haddan pulled the strands and knotted them tightly in his hand. He went out to see the owl struggling blindly on the ground. Haddan reached the finest point of his plan when he poured petrol on the struggling bird. He lit the fuel while still gripping the ends of the palm. The owl was burning before his own eyes. Now Zinah would have nothing to say, except that he was deformed, a characteristic he admitted.

By God, it would be better to kill oneself.

Well then, Mother, you are lamenting and angry. But it is not my fault if the palm burnt first and I lost hold over it, and the bird was still able to fly, burning, to land on the roof of the hut, still in flames. All this was happening while your poor son Haddan was slapping his cheeks and calling for help, "My fire! My fire! Oh Mother, see this hut, I burnt it with my own hands!" It would be better for me to to kill myself than hear Zinah tell me tomorrow, "Go on your way, ill-fated man, deformed owner of a burnt hut."

Well, was it his fault if he did not own any reeds or straw or any animal to slaughter so he could gather people to help him build a new hut? Was it his fault

---

5. Textile that covers the roof of the hut.

if he needed to use his brain more than he ever had before? All that he wanted was to meet Zinah, or 'Arabiyya, one morning, and walk beside her, tall and proud, and say, blushing: "Good morning to you, Zinah."

She would swing her hips and reply, "Good morning to you, mightiest of men . . . how lovely you are, owner of a new hut!"

—Translated by: Aida A. Bamia and Naomi Shihab Nye

Hani al-Rahib (1939–2000)

Syrian novelist and short-story writer Hani al-Rahib is one of Syria's foremost writers of fiction. He was a professor of English at the Syrian University in Damascus, at the University of Sanaa in Yemen, and at the University of Kuwait, and his first novel, *The Defeated* (1961), won the *Adab* magazine literary prize. His early collections of short stories, *The Virtuous City* (1969) and *The Crimes of Don Qixote* (1978), won him recognition as a short-story writer, but his greater skill is evident in his novels such as *A Crack in a Long History* (1970); *One Thousand and Two Nights* (1977); and *The Epidemic* (1982), which deservedly won the prize of the Union of Arab Writers for the best fictional work. Although much of his work is based in Syria's cities and villages, it applies to most Arab countries and often has a strong element of symbolism that links it with the wider spectrum of present-day Arab experience. He has a deep sense of both country and city mentalities and likes to describe the pervasive aspirations of country folks to city life and to the attainment of middle-class comforts. His style developed with the years, arriving, in *The Epidemic,* at a vibrant beauty and sensitivity.

NOT ONLY THE HYENA

When evening came, an unexpressed feeling of the hyena's presence weighed heavily on the peasants' hearts. Lately, the growing whispers about the Devil's Mound had been charged with a disquieting expectation of evil. The village seemed to be surrounded by an army of hyenas. In the past, various man-eating animals had attacked the village and struck fear in the inhabitants for a time, before they were destroyed and made into food for memory. That was why, when all this began, the *mukhtar* simply announced that a detachment of police would follow the treacherous beast to its lair and slit its throat from ear to ear. One day the hyena seized three children playing at the Devil's Mound and left their naked bones behind. Thus it happened that evening and moonlight became two sources of fear, and young boys and girls no longer strolled down the village's white path.

The peasants had long believed that this accursed mound of rising rocks, where the roads from the three villages joined, was inhabited by Satan and would be so forever. To repel its evil, those who passed by would throw a stone at it, cursing the devil thrice and beseeching God's help against him. When the hyena devoured the three children, the people's sense of security was some-what shaken, and they feared an alliance between the hyena and the devil. They warned their children not to go near the Devil's Mound after dark, and they finished their work in the fields in time to be home before dusk. Little by little, their sense of well-being returned.

The *mukhtar* said that the hour of salvation was near; it was undoubtedly coming, he said. He doubled the number of police on duty. Strict orders were is-sued for people not to go at night to the mound where the vicious beast roamed with its cubs; not because the peasants were cowardly and dare not confront it but because the hypnotizing power in the hyena's eyes, sustained by the power of Satan, would rob them of their will and make them easy prey to its ferocious fangs. In fact, said the *mukhtar,* it was a cowardly animal; otherwise it would have appeared in broad daylight and fought with the farmers face-to-face. But it appeared only at night, when its eyes flashed with that mesmerizing light, full of treachery and deception.

The peasants remained in their homes and let loose their fantasies about the hyena. They pictured it, and fear seized them. Fear seized them, and made the picture still more fearful. What would happen if its hateful eyes pierced their own? In his imagination, Nimr al-Olaqy saw himself mesmerized, drained of strength . . . the hyena turning and walking slowly to its lair, confident that he would follow . . . looking back from time to time to see that he was still under the spell. There was general agreement that everyone should remain at home, since the hour of salvation was undoubtedly near. Of course the peasants did not forget the Devil's Mound; they would deliberately pass by it during the day to cast a rock or a stone. They heartily cursed the devil and implored God to cast him under a huge rock and to fill their bellies with food. After a time the mound became a hill, and, just before the moon set, it would cast a frightening, dark shadow. The stones and the curses piled up. Then there was yet another disturbing occurrence: the hyena seized a policeman on patrol in the area.

The striking thing about the whole affair was that nothing in the actual life of the village changed, except that there were no more evening walks to the hills or to the Devil's Mound. The peasants were a cheerful set of people who loved life, entertainment, and small talk and avoided troubles and worries. The schoolmaster saw in this an expression of true peasanthood: an ability to endure, despite oppression and injustice, which foretold the easy destruction of the hyena.

The peasants put their hopes in the growing number of police guards; one day they said, these guards would surround the hyena and shower it with bullets, tearing it to pieces. They began confidently to concern themselves with prepar-ing food and going out to visit one another. One of them, in fact, opened a restaurant, another a coffee shop. Both places typified the spirit of the age—with decoration, elegant tables, and polite manners. The village schoolmaster would

sit in a special corner of the coffee shop whenever the *mukhtar* asked him to prepare a speech to be delivered to the people. He would sit there poring over his
papers, covering them with his copious beard. The farmers were quite prepared
to pay an extra tax to cover police expenses, especially as shooting incidents
were on the increase, indeed, had become a familiar nightly event. Even funerals
became gala occasions, especially when the martyr was a policeman or a child.
For then, under the auspices of the *mukhtar*, speeches abounded extolling the
virtues of the deceased or his wonderful innocence; then he would be declared
a martyr, and his name would be added to the Roll of Honor (which would, no
doubt, have surprised him!), amid the respectful silence of all present.

But the hyena did not simply ravage police patrols. One day, with its cubs,
it raided the village, leaving blood, terror, and numbness behind. The villagers
stood before the ruins and the bodies in a dumb stupor, unable to understand
why all this had to happen. They felt bitterly the painful presence of an unintelligible fate that had descended on them, had taken them unaware; a fate they
had formerly believed to be no more than a bad practical joke. The sense of this
fate was no less painful than the sight of the bodies themselves. Village pride was
hurt, and the villagers were forced to take the hyena seriously—they felt bitter
because they were unable to capture it. The schoolmaster came forth with a
splendid epic poem, describing himself as defeated and dishonored and pointing
accusing fingers at the *mukhtar* and the police. But next day he sat in his familiar
corner in the coffee shop, bent over his papers.

The *mukhtar*'s official statement was important for one reason at least: it gave
farmers a good opportunity for sarcasm, they being born with a love of humor.
All of a sudden they found themselves accused of slackness, of being reluctant
to stone the evil spirit! They discovered that history was directly responsible for
the neighborhood's destruction, though they did not understand how! A writer
declared that he would renounce writing till his slackness had been overcome.
The cobbler's wife scolded her husband for talking to his customers in eloquent
language.

But now a new determination was born. First the number of police was
doubled again, and in a few days the village was filled with patrols roaming the
dirt roads day and night on noble, well-groomed steeds. As the villagers stared at
the horses, whose saddles shone brighter than the sweat of their own brows, they
pressed their hands to their stomachs, for they knew that more of their harvest
would be taken from them. Ali Abu 'Abdallah said that if the policemen's horses
had not stirred up so much dust, he could have groaned and sighed more easily
when handing out money and crops, and he began to eat half-cooked burghul
wheat soaked in water, which would swell in his stomach and satisfy him longer.
Subhi al-Naddaf, however, took to walking past newly opened restaurants and
licking his lips at all the different food there, which made his stomach contract
so painfully. He kept up this practice day after day, till the police finally arrested
him on charges of general indecency and breaking night curfew without a permit. These restaurants had been opened in response to a real need; patrol duty,

being a sacred thing, a thing that cannot be neglected, the responsible authorities came to realize that valuable time was being wasted by the police going home for their meals or to their headquarters. Enlightened villagers responded instinctively to this need and converted many of their houses—especially the new ones built of stone—into restaurants and coffee shops. This initiative characterized the more enlightened class of villager, which understood its duties and responsibilities toward the police in their war with the hyena.

It became the order of the day that there was no voice stronger than that of the police, especially after the beggars, parasites, and generally suspicious characters had become so numerous that the *mukhtarate*[1] had to imprison them in the fort.

Everyone's actions were governed by one paramount, frightening question: are our thoughts and deeds in harmony with the *mukhtarate*'s plans to destroy the hyena? If anyone ever felt the answer to be no, he was seized with the fear of being bewitched by the hyena and was overcome by a great feeling of guilt. One writer said that he could not distinguish between being possessed by the hyena and not being possessed; that the only real way of knowing this was to see whether a smile was bestowed on him by a policeman or *mukhtarate* official sitting at a table with a bottle of beer. Such a smile was difficult to come by in those fearful times.

Despite all this, enlightened villagers kept their humor and happy way of life. Their women wore the smartest clothes and set their hair in Farah Deeba[2] style, and their unexpected pregnancies became more frequent. As for the peasants, they preferred to sleep hungry or live on dry figs rather than admit their hunger publicly. They knew that revealing it was tantamount to complaining about the police, and they were not at all annoyed with the police!

One day, the farmer Abu Esteef thought that the truth was quite different. He looked cautiously around him and said to his wife, "The hidden cannot be explained by what is apparent. I have many feelings that arise suddenly, and I suppress them and believe them to be submerged, but they come to the surface again." Umm Esteef agreed with her husband saying, "True. But why are you philosophizing on the hidden and the apparent, and speaking in riddles?" "Oh Umm Esteef. Am I a writer who deals in symbols for fear of the police? I say what is in my heart, simply, if the police are not there. If they throw me in the fort, your needles can only knit a funeral shroud for me. Then how will you come by your daily bread, Umm Esteef?"

Another day, Fahmi the porter stared for a long time at the hearth, and his family demanded to know what he was thinking. He hemmed and hawed, then said, "The Devil's Mound, my people."

"What about it?"

---

1. The house where the *mukhtar,* the village mayor, conducted the village business.
2. Farah Deeba was the elegant wife of the Shah of Iran. She wore her hair high during one period of her life, and it became fashionable.

"The Devil's Mound doesn't make sense to me any more."

"It's not supposed to make sense. Is that why you're staring?"

Fahmi the porter stared at the hearth again, and the protests rose again.

"The Devil's Mound . . . I wonder . . . is there anything but earth and dirt inside it or underneath it? Sometimes I think that I, who have been a porter all my life, could carry the stones here and build a room for Samih and the rest of the children to sleep in." Umm Samith gasped, terrified and quickly sprinkled incense on the fire to keep away the evil spirits.

One moonless evening Miss Sumayya left her school as usual, and encountered the police patrol. One of them said, "Miss, you are exposing yourself to danger being here so late! The school, as you know, is right on the edge of the village." The young lady threw them a distrustful and determined look and continued her nightly walk without a word. For years she had been teaching her pupils that the hyena is a predatory animal, of the cat family, bigger and stronger than a dog, with a large head and powerful jaws. How it became a legend and came to permeate every detail of daily life was like a dream that is certain to end soon. Miss Sumayya sighed and murmured, "Yet it does not end . . . "

A mysterious event took place. The mangled bodies of four scoundrels were discovered, with the help of a flashlight, on the eastern outskirts of the village. No one knew exactly how they had gone there, why, and who had killed them. The dignitary Izzat Effendi Simlakh said that they were perverts and thieves; young men bored with village life, seeking to destroy its democratic institutions . . . they had got what they deserved! The owner of the Nidal Restaurant said that they had consigned themselves to perdition when they went to the Devil's Mound and that they had got what they deserved. But the more enlightened villagers wondered. Why did these men go to the Mound, when the devil had exhausted even the police? Everyone, though, was struck dumb with confusion and perplexity when Fahmi the porter returned and told of what he had seen: "The Devil's Mound is no longer a mound, and the stones have disappeared!"

This fired the peasants' imaginations. Ali Abu 'Abdallah forgot his chronic hunger. He yelled, patting his empty stomach, "The Devil's Mound is gone, my people." Another said, "When the hyena perishes, we will have our fill of bread and figs and olives; perhaps even eggs and milk." In a pleasant, bright dream, Umm Esteef saw herself entering the Cavaliers Restaurant and eating a whole slice of red watermelon. Old Kahla dreamt of a hundred white hens in her coop laying a hundred eggs—and the owner of the Princes Chicken Farm passed by, cast a distrustful look at the hens, and departed empty-handed. The waiter Hamdan pictured himself relaxing in a comfortable chair in the portico of the coffee shop, while the owner groomed his lovely mare, saying, "At your command, sire!" Those whom hunger had slimmed indulged themselves in nervous, humorless fantasies, such as seizing the storehouses of wheat and electing a new *mukhtar*.

A policeman stuck in the western outpost for days thought, "I get a strange feeling every time I walk down the village streets; the mysterious looks of the villagers, and the strange way that they behave, make me feel like one of the hyena's cubs—the very cubs that it's my duty to protect them against." His hand instinctively went to his rifle, and he stared into the obscure unfathomable darkness. A young police officer thought, "They envy us a morsel of food dipped in blood. They remember the morsel but they forget the blood." Stretching long and hard, he muttered, "Those rascals are really going to come to a bad end if they ever think of challenging our honor." Then he fell on a leg of roast chicken with an enthusiasm devoid of pleasure, cruelly, lazily, irritably.

But daydreams were not enough to satisfy the thirst of hoodlums and beggars. "Where is this hyena? Why doesn't anyone attack it?" they asked—not expecting an answer: "What's happened to our village?" And they answered, "Its life has lost color and taste and savor. Its sad heart is wounded. Darkness has covered its lovely open horizons."

In the darkness of the night they stole in groups down the village paths, searching for the hyena. Some went to the crossroads and walked back and forth where the mound was; they were not possessed by the evil spirit but returned and told of their experience. Some went to Cliff's Peak where the hyena's lair was and returned and told of their adventure. Some were arrested by the police and told no one anything. Some fought with the hyena and its cubs.

It was a bitter battle, for the cubs had grown into hyenas, and hyenas have always been accustomed to striking fear into humans. Some men shone their flashlights in the hyenas' eyes, and others showered them with bullets. They returned to the village with two bodies—one hyena, one human—and told their story.

The next day the hyena and its cubs attacked the girls' school, tore Miss Sumayya and three of her pupils to pieces, and lapped their blood. Immediately the *mukhtarate*'s statement was issued: "There will be no peace with the hyena. We will not recognize the Devil. There will be one common goal among us: that of driving the hyena out." Harsh measures were straightaway imposed to put a stop to the irresponsible behavior of those perverts who had set loose the hyena's evil and violence and released a river of blood.

Feverish anticipation descended on the village, and when evening came, an unexpressed feeling of the hyenas' presence weighed heavily and oppressively on the peasants' hearts. They pictured the hyena and their flesh crept; and as their flesh crept, the picture became still more fearful. Night time was pitch blackness and an eternity and distant stars; a dark crystal glass whose visions stunned their imaginations. Fear and laughter at fear. Hunger and evasion of hunger. Defeat and the anger of defeat. The mysterious link between dream and reality. Hope based on despair and bitter jokes. All this was brought on by the night.

Evening also brought sounds of shooting. Group after group stole down the village paths to kill the hyena. The sounds reverberated and bullets flashed brilliantly. Police officers said, "They want to provoke the hyena to kill peaceful villagers," and they became more determined than ever to protect the village. "They might escape us going, but they will never escape us coming back."

Bodies were scattered on the outskirts of the village mutilated as though by design. One evening there was a sudden bright flash, a bullet whined, and Esteef fell, a lifeless corpse.

There was no funeral party. He was not declared a martyr, and his name was not added to the Roll of Honor. Hoodlums, and beggars buried him and read over him the following short prayer:

> Not only are Byzantines all around you,
> Behind your back are Byzantines as well.
> So which direction will you take?[3]

—*Translated by Fateh Azzam and Christopher Tingley*

Hasan Rasheed (b. 1949)

Born in Doha, Qatar, Hasan Rasheed obtained a doctorate in the Philosophy of Art and Theater from the Academy of Art in Cairo and works as a special expert on communication at the General Administration of Radio and Television in Qatar. He is a member of the Jisra Administrative Council for Culture and Society and heads its cultural committee. He has so far published two collections of short stories, *The Dead Do not Visit the Graves* (1984) and *The Cold Fortress* (2001). He has also written on the short story and on drama in Qatar, and has written two experimental plays, *The Bleeding of the Rock* and *The Hostage*.

THE FINAL MESSAGE

Four decades of time—perhaps a little less, perhaps a little more. And yet nothing ever disturbed the flow of life. The nights and days were the same. There was a sense of sameness and surrender to fate, and yet a looking forward to the future too; a deep acceptance of what God had decreed.

A few years before Maryam had, every so often, examined the traces of time the mirror showed on her face. But finally she'd got bored with gazing, bored with her mirror and with herself, conceding defeat as she saw the lines and colors time had drawn.

The other sister, Sharifa, kept up her hopes, year after year, as the train of life still failed to stop at her station. But in the end she too surrendered. She'd tremble

---

3. A verse by the famous poet of classical times, al-Mutanabbi (915—965). He is addressing here Sayf al-Dawla, the ruler of Aleppo and his benefactor at one point. Sayf al-Dawla fought both the Byzantines on the west and the Persians on the east. Al-Mutanabbi here refers to the siegelike situation of the prince and his city as enemies surround it on all sides.

when she heard a girl in the neighborhood had sailed off into a new life of fertility and growth and giving, remembering, at those times, how her mother would end each pious wish with the words, "May God send you a good man"—then creep back into her corner, with a regretful sigh that showed her worry. Sharifa would look at her mother then, wanting to say something, then fall silent. "Where from, Mother?" she wanted to say. "When the train never stops? Why aren't we fit for fertility and giving? Are we destined to be wiped from the world's memory?"

Their mother too surrendered to fate, accepted that her dream would never be fulfilled. Maryam and Sharifa lost all links with it too—as days passed, the dream melted away. The image of the noble gallant lost all hint of form and feature. Everything vanished. He didn't ride on a winged horse, as he did in the myths and folk tales, didn't fly far off into the sky.

This figure wasn't important any more. It didn't matter now whether he rode a white horse or came on foot, whether he was handsome or plain. The important thing was that he should come. But when? And how was he to come? Maryam's world became one of nursing her father. Wasn't this her destiny? From first thing in the morning this father would sit apart in his corner, sipping endless cups of coffee, fiddling with his rosary, never leaving the house. Where would he have gone? Who would he have visited? Most of his childhood friends had died, and those that were left were crippled by sickness or old age. He himself had become a prisoner in his home, too sick to move elsewhere.

Sharifa was different. She had her own morning world, to which she could escape, live her own life, and find her place in society. As she sometimes angrily told her sister Maryam, she was educating the generations to come. Yet the link between the sisters came to have a very special flavor. In the evenings, when their father had fallen asleep, the two would sit whispering and chatting, dreaming and rejecting. They were closer than other sisters were, with a special bond, each playing her strictly defined role within this home of theirs. Maryam's focus was more on the house and the father, while Sharifa, for her part, strove to provide an honorable income. The father, though, felt ever more defeated as the nights dragged on. Sharifa could read it there in his eyes: failure and defeat. She could read the question etched on his face. What will you two do after my death? He was afraid to ask the question outright, but Sharifa knew well enough what was hidden in his mind. Which of the two sisters should ask the question? Or could their father ask it after all? One morning he finally summoned up courage and asked, with a father's tenderness overflowing, "Maryam, what will you do after I die?"

Maryam didn't answer. What could she say? Two tears flowed down her cheeks. There was still some sap of life in her! She said nothing—and that silence was like a knife plunged into him. Gazing at her, he stretched out a gnarled hand to pat her and said: "Maryoum,[1] why don't you answer?" But what could she say, and what tone could she take? She remembered well enough the number

---

1. An affectionate form of Maryam.

of young men who'd knocked at their door, hoping for her hand—only to be rejected as her father repeated that same, everlasting sentence, "He's not our equal." A meaningless, incomprehensible sentence. "Equal," Father? How do you mean, "equal?" But now, after all this time had passed, what could she say? She was silent for a long time. Finally she got up.

Again he tried to speak, in the same tender tone. "Maryoum," he said—then the words died away. What could he say either? She felt his suffering and went over to him, embraced the human wreck he'd become, then, laughing, planted a kiss on his forehead. He smiled back. What could she say? That she'd been turned into a nurse? Whose nurse?

Once more her eyes filled with tears. He gazed at her for a long time, till his own eyes became misty. "Why are you crying?" he said, fighting to overcome his emotions. He'd just discovered that Maryam, or Maryoum as he liked to call her, actually could cry. He must, surely, realize the reason for her tears. How could he not? Suddenly Maryam wanted to scream out loud, wanted to say, "You've wasted my life for me, Father, and wasted Sharifa's!"

But how could she possibly do that? How could she rebel, hemmed in as she was on all sides, with no means of escape? Sharifa at least had a job, could escape into a special world where she moved and met other people. And even when she came back home, to her sister's narrow world, she stayed in touch with that other world, through preparation and correcting homework. Heavy and monotonous her evenings might be, but still her lot was better than her sister's, whose world was limited to the father over there in his corner, gazing at his magical television. Maryam would float for a while in her own world, putting herself in the place of those people in the dramas on the screen, only to come back down to earth as she heard her father's order: "Maryam, I need some water." She'd wake then from her beautiful dream and hurry to get her father his drink.

When he fell asleep, though, the two sisters would carry on their own magical conversation, about a strange world, a dream that never came.

"Have you heard?" Sharifa would say. "Umm 'Abdallah's daughter Awoosh has got engaged."

The ghost of a smile would form on Maryam's face.

"The man must be blind," she'd answer. "She's not beautiful, not attractive at all."

"It's the luck of the draw," Sharifa would retort.

The names would keep piling up, only to meet the same amazement and protest, as if Maryam wanted to cry out, "Why? Why everyone except us? When will we ever enter this magic world?"

But life went on, humdrum and monotonous. Each of the sisters knew her allotted role, from early morning till nightfall. They were two symbols of the same bitter reality. As the days passed, they became like two soldiers who'd surrendered to defeat. There was no use striving or resisting. Even the roots of hope had died.

Suddenly, as if in a dream, the miracle happened: a strange visit from a distant relative. The visitor was Fatima or, as she liked to be called, "Umm 'Abd al-Rahman." A strange visit indeed. She sat with their father, whispering softly to him, and Maryam caught his murmured remarks—or were they rejections? Every so often he'd repeat the same sentence, "No, it's not possible." And then Umm 'Abd al-Rahman would pursue her errand unabashed. Finally Maryam heard the single word "*mabrouk*"[2] from Fatima's lips as she left the house. Why *mabrouk*?

That evening their father sat there talking and talking. What he talked about was strange: mostly about a girl's life, and how she was born full of tenderness and the ability to give, and how her chief role was to bring up the new generations. Now this man was saying a girl's destiny was her husband's home—now, after all these long years! Maryam wanted to shout, wanted to say, "Is it really you talking like this?" And yet for the first time she felt a strange ecstasy. Maryam and Sharifa both looked into their father's face, while he gazed far into the distance. What was he trying to avoid? Neither of them knew. Then he dropped his bombshell.

"Sharifa," he said, "my precious Sharifa, come here."

Sharifa went up, and he embraced her. For the first time she felt the warmth of those gnarled hands and the breast with its jutting ribs. For the first time she felt how beautiful, how wonderful this aged father was. She felt peace and security in his embrace. Did helpless old age have greater strength sometimes than real strength? Her father kissed her on the forehead, and she trembled through her whole body as she felt the flowing warmth and tenderness of a parent. Very gently she took his stiffened hand and placed a warm kiss on it. She didn't know how long she spent like this, but she woke from her reverie to hear her father whispering to his other daughter, Maryam, his voice choked with tears.

"Maryam," he said. "Come here"

He'd become like a bird now, folding his chicks beneath his wing. How was it that blood was moving now, in those stiffened limbs? He fell silent for a while, then once more looked into the far distance. (What was he looking at? What was he thinking?)

"This is how life is," he said, as the girls fixed their eyes on him. "Closeness and attachment. Remoteness and nearness. Staying and traveling."

Sharifa stared at him. What was this father of theirs saying? And why? Where had he learned to speak like that? Maryam felt an engulfing love of life, wished she could press this father to her breast; for the first time she knew the feelings of motherhood, without ever having borne a child. This pampered father *was* her child, and why not? Didn't she practice her lost motherhood on him, her motherhood she'd never known? Didn't she feed him, give him his drink, change his clothes? As for Sharifa, her feelings were indistinct. She sensed there

---

2. "May God bless" or "may God's grace enfold." It is said on numerous occasions: for new clothes, a new house, a new child, a betrothal, a wedding, etc.

was something behind those words but didn't know what. Was this aged father thinking of leaving the house, believing he'd become a daily burden? Did he mean to go into an old people's home? Was he thinking of selling the house?

Suddenly the father's eyes filled with tears. There was something unclear. Like an Arab mare, Sharifa started. She gazed at the pale face and the ravages of time etched on it, gazed at what was left of a human being. She went deep into the wilderness of words, wanting to know the secret of those strange things he'd said, and of his tears.

"Sharifa, my daughter—" Her father said the words with all the tenderness in the world. The unfinished sentence, the sudden flow of emotion, made Sharifa cling to him all the more. He embraced her again, then went on, with his faraway look.

"Daughter," he said, "destiny has brought you a husband."

He fell silent again. Sharifa couldn't say a word. He looked at her once more.

"I've given my consent. In a few days, you'll be in your own home. You'll have your own life. I want to live to see my grandchildren."

Maryam was silent, and all her suffering was in the silence. She couldn't speak any more. She wanted to embrace her sister, to tell her *mabrouk*. She so much wanted— Her father looked at her. She got up, feeling, suddenly, as if she wanted to scream. Why must we part, she thought? Why couldn't we be a fertile soil together, for growth and giving? She wanted to scream, to say: "Is it destiny I should live like this? Should I be turned into a nurse?"

Sharifa said nothing, helpless between curiosity to know more of her future, so long deferred, and her feelings for this man with his stiffened limbs. She looked at her sister, seeking refuge there. She felt the smallness of everything; for Maryam was her beautiful world. Tired from the strain of a day's work, she'd put her head on Maryam's breast, feeling safety and love there.

In her sister's eyes she saw two frozen tears. Sharifa was silent, sensing the screams locked up in her sister's breast. Maryam, she knew, was paying the price.

Maryam didn't sleep that night, and neither did Sharifa. Their father, though, never woke from his sleep. Had he delivered his message at last?

—*Translated by Salwa Jabsheh and Christopher Tingley*

Mu'nis al-Razzaz (1951–2002)

Born in Jordan to a Palestinian mother and a Syrian father who was also a well-known political activist, Mu'nis al-Razzaz grew up in a home dominated by a patriotic energy devoted to the dissemination of the seeds of rejection of present-day Arab political life and to bringing in enlightenment and the will to change. This immediate inheritance, however, did not instill in him the optimism his family embraced, and when he began writing, it was clear that there had seeped into his anguished soul a great amount of despair and pessimism. The atmosphere that reigns over his well-written novels is that of a disgruntled, irreconcilable critic of present-day Arab life. He worked mainly as a journalist, occupying prestigious positions in the Jordanian media, and as a columnist at Amman's two leading papers, *Al-Ra'y* and *Al-Dustur*. Since 1993 and up to his sudden death, he worked as counselor to the Minster of Culture. In 1992 he founded the Arab Democratic Party with some of his friends and was elected its president. His fiction includes the short-story collections *The Sea Behind You* (1977) and *Al-Namrud* (1980); and the novels *Alive in the Dead Sea* (1982), *The Confessions of a Muffler* (1986), *The Bewilderment of the Arab Bedouin Among the Skyscrapers* (1986), *Jum'a al-Qaffazi: The Diary of a Nobody* (1990), *The Annihilated Memory: Two Hats and One Head* (1991), *Memoirs of a Dinosaur* (1994), and *When Dreams Awaken* (1997).

ABU RICHARD

Abu Rashad and 'Atiyya al-Sakran sat on the pavement of a totally deserted alleyway. 'Atiyya pulled a cigarette from behind his ear, tapped it against the pavement, then lit up and made himself comfortable with his legs crossed.

Abu Rashad laid his walking stick beside him and leant back against the wall. His gaze lifted toward the horizon with the look of an eager visionary, a look betraying a hint of madness. He spoke musingly, as if out of a dream. "Rashad is coming back soon from Washington to cure my leg."

'Atiyya al-Sakran blew out the smoke from his roll-up cigarette and said, without looking at his friend, "You're always dreaming about Rashad. Aren't you overdoing it?"

A cloud of gloom and unhappiness settled on Abu Rashad's face. "I tell you: before the year's out he'll be back, a qualified doctor—and a damn good one, at that."

'Atiyya broke into mocking laughter, throwing himself flat on the pavement.

Disconcerted, Abu Rashad went on, "All right, laugh at my expense . . . but I can just see Rashad—may God make His face shine upon him—as he's leaving the library of George Washington University and . . . "

"George who?" cut in 'Atiyya as he repositioned himself.

"Washington."

"But Washington's a city."

"Yes, of course, and that's where George Washington University is. How many times do I have to tell you about the university?"

Abu Rashad began to trace the outlines of a map with his finger on the pavement, explaining to 'Atiyya:

"Look! Here's the White House, and this here is George Washington University. These are the university buildings. I can see Rashad at this very moment crossing the street between the university library and his faculty."

'Atiyya gaped at him in astonishment and mumbled lamely, "And just how do you know that?"

Abu Rashad twirled his moustache with a superior air and, with a condescending look, replied, "I bought a detailed map of Washington so I would know exactly where Rashad lives, where he studies, where he eats, where he spends his free time. When he comes home a great doctor, people in our quarter will applaud him, they will stand up before him to show their respect for his achievement."

'Atiyya al-Sakran gave a raucous laugh, "You're talking rubbish, you silly fellow! Who gets that kind of respect these days? Only the big construction contractors and the army bigwigs. Besides, I don't reckon Rashad's coming home at all. He left nine years ago, and he's never once been back or even written home. If he ever did come, he'd likely be bringing an American woman and a bunch of kids, not any kind of doctor's qualification."

Abu Rashad's face turned red as he shouted in a sudden fit of rage, "I'm telling you: right at this very moment he is in an autopsy practical. They are just wheeling in a corpse for dissection."

'Atiyya frowned, threw a skeptical glance at Abu Rashad, and muttered, "What do you mean 'for dissection'? They ought to have respect for the dead."

"You are an utter illiterate fool," spat out Abu Rashad with angry contempt.

'Atiyya crushed his cigarette-end with his foot and replied, "And you are nothing but a day-dreamer. You don't live your own life; you're living Rashad's. You get on my nerves. You never stop telling me about Rashad's life, as if you were his shadow: studying, eating, sleeping, you tag along with him like a ghost. You're driving me crazy."

Ignoring 'Atiyya's comments as if he had not heard them, Abu Rashad went on, "What time is it now?"

'Atiyya raised his head, which was round like a big football, and, looking up at the sun, said, "Maybe about four in the afternoon."

Abu Rashad's smile broadened to a laugh of pure joy, his mouth opening to reveal toothless gums. Then he mumbled, "Let's see now! That means the time now in Washington is . . . Oh, they're seven hours behind us . . . so the time over there is now . . . Are you any good at subtraction?"

'Atiyya shook his head in denial.

Abu Rashad went on musing absent-mindedly, "Rashad is sitting in the front row. He is paying attention to the professor's lecture. He could be talking about a new treatment recently discovered for curing paralysis of the leg."

Abu Rashad glanced angrily first at his stick then at his paralyzed leg, then added, "I can just see him writing down everything the professor is saying. Rashad's English is fluent. You can hear the professor taunting the American students, telling them that Rashad can read and write English better than they can. Rashad's professor, the one with the beard, says . . ."

'Atiyya interrupted with disapproval.

"What on earth makes you think Rashad's professor's got a beard?"

Abu Rashad's face took on an air of wisdom and dignity; to 'Atiyya it looked like the face of a second-rate comedian. Abu Rashad said, "He's got to have a beard. All professors there have beards."

'Atiyya restrained himself from jumping to his feet, and said instead in a bantering tone, "Pro . . . fess . . . or, is it? D'you really know what that means? Or have you just made up the word?"

Abu Rashad's self-important smile faded and he said in stern reproof, "You are a fool . . . a complete and utter fool . . . Of course I know what it means . . . it means 'teacher'."

'Atiyya asked stupidly, "So the teacher at the local primary school is a pro . . . fess . . . or, is he?"

Abu Rashad came to the rescue: "Professor . . . No! The primary school teacher is not a professor."

"Why not?"

"Because he doesn't have a beard."

An uneasy silence descended on the two men as they sat smoking their cigarettes and blowing puffs of smoke in the air. Abu Rashad's mind strayed again toward Washington, hovering around George Washington University. He said suddenly, "There he is now, going back to the library again."

Taken aback, 'Atiyya asked, "Who?"

"Rashad, of course," said Abu Rashad with a fixed stare.

His eyes burned with a blaze of terrifying, fanatical rage.

"He is preparing for his final exams."

'Atiyya clapped his hands together and shouted, "May God heal your crazy head, Abu Rashad! Stop your nonsense . . . How about trying to live in the present—with me, here? Hey, look at that woman crossing the road. Will you look at that! What a great head of long black hair, eh?" Abu Rashad cut in, "Rashad is going to marry his cousin. She is a very fine young woman."

'Atiyya paid no attention to Abu Rashad's abstractedness and went on, "Look . . . that good-looking young bloke—he's after her, he's pestering her."

Abu Rashad spoke, with a blazing glint in his eye:

"Rashad doesn't go after women. He is after doing his studies and getting his qualifications. There he is now, saying to the teacher, the professor, that he'd like to shorten his period of study by taking courses during the vacation, so he can get home sooner to treat my leg."

'Atiyya's heart beat faster as he spoke, his eyes riveted on the scene, "Look . . . that young bloke is holding the girl's hand."

Abu Rashad's dazed eyes rolled in their sockets, flashing with fury and impatience.

He spoke in a faint, faltering voice, "Look . . . there's Rashad holding a female patient's hand to take her pulse."

Now 'Atiyya al-Sakran leapt to his feet in agitation; he was shaking violently. Peering into the distance, toward the screen of cypress trees over the other side of the street across from the alley, he said, "Look . . . there, behind the cypresses . . . The bloke is just about to take the girl's clothes off."

Abu Rashad raised his head; his face had a strange glow and his eyes flashed and smoldered with madness. He said, "Yes, of course . . . Rashad is studying medicine, he has every right to undress young women. How else do you expect him to carry out a proper examination? No . . . 'Atiyya. It's wicked of you to slander Rashad like this."

'Atiyya looked round utterly nonplussed and said, "What?"

"Abu Rashad went on, "Now Rashad is placing the stethoscope in his ear to listen to her heartbeat."

'Atiyya struck his forehead in frustration and rounded on Abu Rashad furiously: "See here! For heaven's sake, will you stop living in Washington with your precious Rashad, stop living his life and come back to life here and now."

Abu Rashad's face beamed with joy, as if he had just seen a vision of hope. "I live in the future. I loathe and detest the present."

'Atiyya al-Sakran stifled a laugh that threatened to explode from his chest.

The hippy girl took Rashad's head between her hands and said reproachfully, "Look, Richard, you are far too heavily into drugs, and you go on far too much about what a hero your father used to be, way back."

Rashad took a long, deep drag from his joint, held it in, then exhaled a feeble thread of smoke through his nostrils. He passed the joint to his hippy girlfriend, feeling a sweet numbness that made time stand still and engulfed him in the euphoria of eternity where time and space are no more. His eyes roamed around the small, dingy room. His glance fell on the bed, and he said to the hippy girl, "My father lay on a bed just like this after he'd been shot in the leg."

The blonde hippy girl put her arms around him and said in disapproval, "Don't you ever stop going on about your father? You are living his life. You are always living in the past."

Rashad's legs went limp. He turned toward the blonde girl and saw her face through a distant blur. In a wooden voice he said, "He was wounded in the battle of Bab al-Wad . . . Did you ever hear of the 1948 Palestine War? Pass me the wine bottle! He was a soldier in the Jordanian army, on the Arab side."

The hippy blonde hid the wine bottle behind her back and said impatiently: "No, Richard! Not hooch and hash both at the same time! Just the hash should do us fine. And for chris'sake, stop living in the past. You are reliving your father's past for him."

Rashad's eyes opened wide. He stared at the dank, grim wall and said, "D'you see that heap of skulls peering out of the wall?"

The blonde hippy girl took a drag from the joint and replied, "No . . . I'm seeing skyscrapers going round and round like crazy."

Rashad took the joint from her, took a deep drag and kept the smoke in his lungs, then exhaled a thin plume through his nostrils. He spoke in a vaunting tone, "My father swooped down on them like a hawk. He went on fighting until he got hit in the leg. All our friends and relatives admit his legendary courage."

The blonde's face flushed and her eyes blazed with fury as she spoke in a voice at once appealing and full of reproof, "Why can't you talk about yourself? Why does it always have to be about your father?" Rashad said inconsequentially,

"He killed seven of them before he was wounded. There he is now, leaping out of the wall, attacking an enemy post. Can't you see the blood spurting out from all around?"

The blonde shouted in despair, "You are living in the past, Richard! It wouldn't be so bad if it were your own past. But it's your father's past."

Rashad took another deep drag and said, "And what's wrong with my father? Don't you like him? He is one of the heroes of the 1948 Palestine War. Look, there he is breaking through enemy lines." The blonde stood up, trembling. She rushed for the door, beside herself with fury and exasperation. But Rashad, left alone now with the ghost of his father, never even heard the door slam.

He was shouting, "Look out! On your right! You've been hit. You are staggering. You are screaming at the top of your lungs. Your leg . . . "

Rashad was yelling insanely. He gripped his leg with both hands and grit his teeth in anguish.

—*Translated by Yasir Suleiman with Sandor Hervey*

Yasin Rifa'iyya (b. 1934)

Syrian novelist and short-story writer Yasin Rifa'iyya was born in Damascus. Largely self-taught, he has distinguished himself as a literary journalist, working at some of the finest literary journals in the Arab world. His fiction reflects a very sensitive observation of human experience, with a great amount of empathy and understanding of life's conflicting situations. He endows his literary work with great gentleness and his characters, from whatever social stratum, with sympathy and affection. Among his short-story collections are *Sorrow Everywhere* (1960), *The Birds* (1974), *Dangerous Men* (1976), and *A River of Tenderness* (1983). His novels include his two fine novels *The Hallway* (1978), on the atrocious civil war in Beirut, and *The Slaying of Almaz* (1981), on the meeting and fight to the death of two traditional Syrian men, famed for their old-fashioned concept of manliness and honor. Both of these works have been translated by PROTA. Later works include *The Secrets of Narcissus* (1999) and *The Lightening Flash* (2003).

THE CHILD

The child was a star at night.

His eyes were a sky.

His face was the earth where men lived.

With his fingers he fondled the fair hair of the gentle woman. She held him to her breast and embraced him with all her longing. The child touched her lips with the tips of his fingers, and she felt as if spring had lowered its blossoming branches over her. The child's lips searched the tender flesh of her breasts, and an overwhelming joy engulfed her. She felt as if all the birds of the sky had started flocking to her home. She uncovered her breast, and the child suckled greedily. At that moment a warm sun shone, embracing all the snowy mountains of the world. A beautiful voice sang, and the valleys and plains resonated with echoes. The woman's joy was a voice speaking to a man still staring into the dark, "Look . . . he does resemble you. All your features are his. His eyes are your eyes. His hair is your hair. His forehead is your forehead. Even this dimple on his cheek is like the one on yours."

The man stayed silent for some time. Then he felt very tired. He slipped under the cover and looked at the woman who was already immersed in deep sleep. He touched her hair, which lay in a cascade next to his face, a burst of silken threads. His large palm continued lightly traveling on to her cheek, which was almost touching the wall. Its warmth made him realize his hand was very cold. Fear seized him. Was she sick? The room, despite its closed windows, was cold. The rain outside was pouring heavily. No, she could not be sick. An hour earlier she had told him, "I am going to sleep now," and he had said, "Good-night." She was in the best of health and complained of nothing. That day she had been particularly energetic: her mother had visited, then her neighbor. She had prepared a good meal for him in the evening and asked him to accompany her the next morning to the snowy mountain. He had promised to do so if the weather was good, and she slept like an innocent child. He always saw her as an innocent child, and she saw him in the same pure light. He remembered her words, "Oh, if only God could grant me a child! I would love it very much if he resembled you." He too wished she could beget a child, for their life had become like a mountain of ice over which the sun never shone. Ten years and no plant grew in their house.

Sleep overwhelmed the man at last.

The child was a star in the night.

His eyes were a sky.

His face was the earth where men lived.

The man played with the child. He threw snowballs at him. He made a snowman for him and placed a pipe in its mouth. He carried him over his shoulder and ran with him in the snow. And the child was a gazelle, a white bird. He was a misty cloud, a tree, a city of toys. The man became a bear carrying the child on his back. He was a sled crossing distances with him. The man became a wind and the child a flying sail.

And every morning the child was a sun.

The gentle woman awakened but did not find the child lying near to her.

The man woke up and did not find the child, or the snow.

The woman said, "Good morning."

The man said, "Good morning."

The woman made a cup of coffee for her husband. He drank the coffee and smoked a cigarette.

The woman said, "See? The Sunday sun is shining!"

"Yes, it is shining."

"Are we going up to the mountain?"

"Let's go up to the mountain."

They had their breakfast. The house was a graveyard. The house was a desert. The house was walls upon walls.

The woman dressed up and the man dressed up.

They left the house.

The man opened the car door and the woman climbed in beside him. The moment they found themselves on the road, they breathed freely. Today each would have a respite from teaching.

The car moved toward the mountain.

The woman remembered her dream. The man remembered his dream. She stretched her hand toward her husband's neck and drew nearer to him. She laid her head on his shoulder. The noise of the car covered their silence.

In a little while the snow crossed in shining white beams before their car. The road was busy and traffic was slow. The asphalt was slick and slushy. Their car kept on climbing behind the other cars. Near the top, traffic was even slower, and a loud din arose over which rang the excited sounds of hundreds of children.

They parked next to the snowy square. Children of all ages were playing on the snow, pitching snowballs at one another. The man watched another man building a snowman, with his children around him and his wife at his side. He kept staring at the snowman as it took shape under the other man's hands. The other man removed his hat and placed it on the snowman's head. Then he poked in two eyes for him, a nose, and a mouth, took the pipe out from his own pocket, and stuck it in the snowman's mouth. The children laughed long and loudly. Then they arranged themselves around the snowman, their mother standing behind them. The father stepped back to take a snapshot. Then the children began runnning about, throwing snowballs at the snowman. They each wore black or brown leather gloves.

Nearby a man was carrying a child on his shoulders. Only the child's dark eyes showed, for he was all wrapped up in woolen clothes. A beautiful woman walked beside them, her arm encircling the man's waist. They were walking slowly over the snow, while the child sang and giggled. An aura of joy surrounded them.

The man felt a stark chill enveloping his bones.

He looked over at his wife; she was kicking the snow with her toes. He hugged her, and they walked toward a quieter place.

As he stroked her hair, she turned her face to him and he glimpsed a bitterness in her eyes that he had never seen there before. He pulled her toward him till she felt his tenderness stir like a child in her womb.

The man took a few steps away from the woman. He gathered a snowball and threw it at her. The woman became a gazelle that hopped and leapt. The man laughed as he saw his child run and the snow flying up around her feet, like petals billowing out from the trees of spring.

The child ran exuberantly and the man ran, following.

The child disappeared behind a rock. While the man searched, the woman was seeing him as her own child. He himself. The same hair, the same eyes, the same mouth, the same dimple on the cheek.

The woman came out from behind the rock and ran toward the child.

The man ran towards the child that had emerged from behind the rock. Each of them was lost in the hug of the other.

A warm sun opened in their chests. They ran together tirelessly over the snow. They climbed one summit and slid down. They threw their bodies across the snow and rolled together down a slope. They threw snowballs at each other, built a snowman, and threw snowballs at it too.

The child inside the woman was tired.

The child inside the man was tired.

They locked hands and lay down across a flat rock engulfed by a joy mixed with deep sorrow.

—Translated by May Jayyusi and Naomi Shihab Nye

THE DOG

Ali always used to leave his home in the old quarter and go strolling in the new streets nearby, which were fringed with palaces on both sides. There he would breathe a different air and see people who were completely unlike the people in his own part of town. They were scrubbed perfectly clean and wore elegant clothes. In front of their palaces waited shining cars of various colors and shapes.

One day Ali paused in front of a large iron gate and stared at the palace inside. It rose from the middle of a fabulous flowering garden. Ponds studded the lawn—their waters gushing lavishly from brass fountains. Under a large striped umbrella sat the members of the family: a middle-aged man scanning a newspaper, a woman knitting, a young girl reading a book. In another corner of the garden a boy near Ali's age stood, surrounded by several jumping dogs.

Ali's eyes examined this fabulous place until the other boy noticed him. He slowly left his dogs and walked to the gate until he stood facing Ali. Ali stared at him quietly and noticed how clean he was, with well-groomed fair hair. He was about to walk on, when the boy asked him, "Do you like our garden?"

"It is a very beautiful garden."

"Do you have a garden?"

"No we don't."

"Do you have dogs?"

"We have no dogs."

"Do you have a car?"

"We have no car."

Ali sensed the other boy's pride as he continued, "Well, this is our place." He swept his arm. Pointing to the dogs, he said, "And those are our dogs." He pointed next to the luxurious car parked there and said, "That's our car."

Ali said, "Your life is beautiful."

He would have liked to leave just then, but the other boy invited him in. "Come on and look at the dogs."

Ali was tempted. The boy had already partially opened the gate. He took Ali's hand and pulled him in. He asked, "What's your name?"

"Ali . . . and yours?"

"Ziyad."

Ziyad whispered, "We must avoid my father and sneak behind those walls so he won't see us."

"Why?"

"Because he doesn't like dirty boys."

Ali was nervous and tried to turn around, but Ziyad had hold of his hand and kept pulling him forward.

They reached the place where the dogs were tied. Each of the four dogs was completely different. Far off stood a large well-built hut, which Ziyad pointed at, saying, "That is their home."

Ali tried to pat one of the dogs on the head, but it jumped back and barked ferociously. He pulled his hand away and retreated a few steps, but Ziyad laughed. Addressing the dog, he told it, "Shhhh! This is my friend!" The dog sat back tensely on its hind legs and gazed fiercely at Ali.

As Ali contemplated the dogs, an elderly man approached. He had a white napkin tucked under his belt. He untied the dogs' leather leashes from the ring in the ground. Ziyad asked him, "Where are you taking them, Uncle Abu Jamil?"

"It is time for their lunch."

Ziyad told Ali, "Come on, let's watch them eat!"

Ali trailed behind the dogs and Ziyad followed him.

The man entered a side room. The dogs followed him, growling. White froth gathered at their lips.

On the ground he placed three brass bowls—one was empty, one held milk, and the third held water. Then he produced a tray on which lay chunks of meat. He tossed one piece onto the brass bowl. The dogs rushed toward it and tried to snatch it.

Ali asked, "What are they eating?

Ziyad answered, "Lamb"

Suddenly Ali felt something strange happening to him. He felt he had acquired four legs. When he tried to speak, his voice turned into barking. Hungrily he leapt at the bowl trying to find a place for himself among the dogs. But they sensed that an alien dog had sneaked in among them and pounced on him all at once. The alien dog ran away, ran out of the room, but the other dogs kept chasing him till they expelled him from the garden.

Ali was trembling with fear. He left that place and roamed in the streets for a long time. He tried to find his way home, but he had forgotten all the roads.

—*Translated by May Jayyusi and Naomi Shihab Nye*

GOD AND THE FISH

Three children from neighboring huts called to each other to go on a holiday jaunt.

One boy's mother said, "Beware of cars."

The second boy's mother warned, "Do not go too near to the sea."

The third boy's mother said, "Don't stay too long."

The boys hiked swiftly away from their district of Karantina in east Beirut. Walid asked, "Should we walk to the mountain?"

Ahmad answered, "The mountain is too far away."

Antoine added, "To go to the mountain, we'd need a car, and we have no money."

Walid said, "Then we should go to the sea."

And Ahmad said, "The sea is closer. The sea is more beautiful."

The boys hurried toward the sea. Their little feet began to sink into the sands. The coast was littered. The boys chose a sandy spot, which was almost clean, and felt happy because it was free of people. They rested a little, then kicked off their sandals, unpacked their sandwiches, and placed them near their shoes. They approached the shore and waded in its salty waters. Walid wanted to build a house of sand. They worked actively until it was built, then sat next to it, feeling exhilarated. As they contemplated it proudly, a wave surprised them and devoured it. The house became a heap of sand that disappeared quickly in the folds of swelling waves.

Walid said, "The sea is strong."

Antoine said, "The sea is huge."

Ahmad said, "It is frightening, this sea!"

Then they had this conversation:

"Who created the sea?"

"God created the sea."

The boys raised their eyes to the sky. It was blue and clear.

"Who created the sky?"

"God created the sky."

The boys gazed off at the mountains. Their slopes were lush with trees.

"Who created the mountains and trees?"

"God created the mountains and trees."

Now Walid asked, "Why did God make us poor?"

Antoine laughed and said, "Because God loves the poor."

They returned to their belongings. They brought out the sandwiches and began eating. When they finished, they were still hungry.

Again they returned to the sea's foaming edge and plunged their feet into it. Walid shouted, "Don't go out too far! The waves might sweep you away."

Antoine shouted back, "Come on and play with us!"

But Walid was nervous. "No! Come out of the water right now! Hasn't your mother told you to beware of approaching the sea?"

The boys came out of the water. They sat soberly on the sand and Ahmad said, "I wish we had a boat."

"And could go fishing."

"How I wish I could eat some fish!"

Suddenly the children remembered God.

One of them raised his head to the sky and implored, "Oh God, please send us a fish!"

The second boy said, "God, send us a fish, *please*!"

And the third boy added "Oh God, Do please send us a fish!"

Then they began staring at the sea.

In a moment a huge wave rose up, rolling toward them. They jumped back. No sooner had it struck the sand than it delivered a huge fish at their feet. The fish convulsed rapidly, then gradually stopped moving. It lay there completely quiet.

The children could not believe their eyes. Walid drew back cautiously, then touched the glistening scales. He exclaimed joyfully, "It is really a fish!"

"And a huge fish too."

"God has answered our prayers."

The three boys raised their eyes skyward and gazed intently, hoping to see God so they could thank Him, but they saw nothing but the great, clear heavens. Their eyes blurred and they went back to contemplating the fish. Antoine said, "I tell you God loves the poor?"

Walid said happily, "How shall we divide it?"

And Ahmad said, "Why divide it? We'll carry it to our folks, and they will grill it, and we will all eat from it."

Antoine said, "My sister will rejoice when she tastes fish!"

The three began thinking of the best way to carry the fish. But they were suddenly surprised to see two huge men standing over them. They raised their heads in astonishment. One of the men said, "Get away from the fish!"

When the children refused to leave it, one of the men pulled a sharp knife from his waist, "Get away, or I will kill you."

The children drew back in fear.

The men picked up the huge fish and held it awkwardly. Before taking it off with them, they warned the boys, "If any of you leaves this spot, we will come back and kill you."

The children remained silent.

The men left with the fish. They walked on down the beach until they disappeared.

No sooner did the eyes of the boys meet than they all burst out crying. After a few minutes Walid said, "Do not tell anyone about the fish."

Antoine said, "Because no one will believe that God sent us a fish."

Ahmad said, "Do not tell anyone that the thieves took the fish away from us."

Walid said, "Because then they will make fun of us."

Antoine said, "Come on, let's beg God for another fish!"

Walid said, "If God should send us another fish, the thieves will return."

Ahmad said, "Come on, let's go home. Next week we'll bring our own knives, and we'll beg God for another fish."

The children hiked sadly to their huts. The sun was hiding its face behind the sea.

—Translated by May Jayyusi and Naomi Shihab Nye

Alifa Rif'at (1930–1995)

Marriage interrupted the higher studies and writing career of Egyptian novelist and short-story writer Alifa Rif'at until 1973, when she resumed writing and published her short stories in various Arab and Egyptian periodicals. She is one of a number of creative Arab writers in modern times (for instance, the Iraqi poet Zuhur Dixon, the Syrian poet, Muhammad al-Maghut) who seem to have absorbed a modern outlook and approach without having had a formal artistic background: her approach to fiction is amazingly modern and sophisticated and cannot be accounted for by what we know of her educational or social background. This spontaneous transcendence is a phenomenon worthy of further study by literary historians. Her short-story collections are *Who Can Be That Man?* (1981?) and *Distant View of a Minaret and Other Stories,* which appeared in Denys Johnson-Davies's English translation in 1984. Her novels include *The Pharaoh's Jewel* (1991?), for which she received two grants from the Egyptian Ministry of Culture.

An Incident in the Ghobashi Household

Zeinat woke to the strident call of the red cockerel from the rooftop above where she was sleeping. The Ghobashi house stood on the outskirts of the village, and in front of it the fields stretched out to the river and the railway track.

The call of the red cockerel released answering calls from neighboring roof-tops. Then they were silenced by the voice of the *muezzin* from the lofty minaret among the mulberry trees calling, "Prayer is better than sleep."

She stretched out her arm to the pile of children sleeping alongside her and tucked the end of the old rag-woven *kilim* round their bodies, then shook her eldest daughter's shoulder.

"It's morning, another of the Lord's mornings. Get up, Ni'ma—today's market day."

Ni'ma rolled onto her back and lazily stretched herself. Like someone alerted by the sudden slap of a gust of wind, Zeinat stared down at the body spread out before her. Ni'ma sat up and pulled her *gallabiyya* over her thighs, rubbing at her sleep-heavy eyes in the rounded face with the prominent cheekbones.

"Are you going to be able to carry the grain to the market, daughter, or will it be too heavy for you?"

"Of course, mother. After all, who else is there to go?"

Zeinat rose to her feet and went out with sluggish steps to the courtyard, where she made her ablutions. Having finished the ritual prayers, she remained in the seated position as she counted off on her fingers her glorifications of Allah. Sensing that Ni'ma was standing behind her, she turned round to her:

"What are you standing there for? Why don't you go off and get the tea ready?"

Zeinat walked toward the corner where Ghobashi had stored the maize crop in sacks; he had left them as a provision for them after he had taken his air ticket from the office that had found him work in Libya and would be bringing him back in a year's time.

"May the Lord keep you safe while you're away, Ghobashi," she muttered.

Squatting in front of a sack, the grain measure between her thighs, she scooped up the grain with both hands until the measure was full, then poured it into a basket. Coughing, she waved away the dust that rose up into her face, then returned to her work.

The girl went to the large clay jar, removed the wooden covering and dipped the mug into it and sprinkled water on her face; she wetted the tips of her fingers and parted her braids, then tied her handkerchief over her head. She turned to her mother and said, "Isn't that enough, Mother? What do we want the money for?"

Zeinat struck her knees with the palms of her hands and tossed her head back.

"Don't we have to pay off Hamdan's wage—or was he cultivating the beans for us for nothing, just for the fun of hard work?"

Ni'ma turned away and brought the stove from the window shelf, arranging the dried corncobs in a pyramid and lighting them. She put it alongside her mother, then filled the teapot with water from the jar and thrust it into the embers. She squatted down and the two sat in silence. Suddenly Zeinat said, "Since when has the buffalo been with young?"

"From after my father went away."

"That's to say, right after the Great Feast,[1] daughter?"

Ni'ma nodded her head in assent, then lowered it and began drawing lines in the dust.

"Why don't you go off and see how many eggs have been laid while the tea's getting ready."

Zeinat gazed into the glow of the embers. She had a sense of peace as she stared into the dancing flames. Ghobashi had gone and left the whole load on her shoulders: the children, the two *qirats* of land and the buffalo. "Take care of Ni'ma," he had said the night before he left. "The girl's body has ripened." He had then spread out his palms and said, "O Lord, for the sake of the Prophet's honor, let me bring back with me a marriage dress for her of pure silk." She had said to him, "May your words go straight from your lips to Heaven's gate, Ghobashi." He wouldn't be returning before the following Great Feast. What would happen when he returned and found out the state of affairs? She put her head between the palms of her hands and leaned over the fire, blowing away the ashes. "How strange," she thought, "are the girls of today! The cunning little thing was hanging out her towels at the time of her period every month just as though nothing had happened, and here she is in her fourth month and there's nothing showing."

Ni'ma returned and untied the cloth from round the eggs, put two of them in the fire and the rest in a dish. She then brought two glasses and the tin of sugar and sat down next to her mother, who was still immersed in her thoughts.

"Didn't you try to find some way out?"

Ni'ma hunched her shoulders in a gesture of helplessness.

"Your father's been gone four months. Isn't there still time?"

"What's the use? If only the Lord were to spare you the trouble for me. Wouldn't it be for the best, Mother, if my foot were to slip as I was filling the water jar from the canal and we'd be done with it?"

Zeinat struck herself on the breast and drew her daughter to her.

"Don't say such a wicked thing. Don't listen to such promptings of the devil. Calm down and let's find some solution before your father returns."

Zeinat poured out the tea. In silence she took quick sips of it, then put the glass in front of her, shelled the egg, and bit into it. Ni'ma sat watching her, her fingers held round the hot glass. From outside came the raised voices of women discussing the prospects at the day's market, while men exchanged greetings as they made their way to the fields. Amidst the voices could be heard Hamdan's laughter as he led the buffalo to the two *qirats* of land surrounding the house.

"His account is with Allah," muttered Zeinat. "He's fine and doesn't have a worry in the world."

---

1. The Great Feast: is the Feast of Sacrifice that follows the *hajj* or Muslim pilgrimage to Mecca. It is the bigger of the two major Muslim feasts, the other being the "Small Feast," which is celebrated at the end of Ramadan, the month of fasting.

Ni'ma got up and began winding round the end of her headcloth so as to form a pad on her head. Zeinat turned round and saw her preparing herself to go off to the market. She pulled her by her *gallabiyya*, and the young girl sat down again. At this moment they heard a knocking at the door and the voice of their nieghbor, Umm al-Khair, calling, "Good health to you, folk. Isn't Ni'ma coming with me to the market as usual, Aunti Zeinat? Or isn't she up yet?"

"Sister, she's just going off to stay with our relatives."

"May Allah bring her back safely."

Ni'ma looked at her mother inquiringly, while Zeinat placed her finger to her mouth. When the sound of Umm al-Khair's footsteps died away, Ni'ma whispered, "What are you intending to do, Mother? What relatives are you talking about?"

Zeinat got up and rummaged in her clothes' box and took out a handkerchief tied round some money, and some old clothes. She placed the handkerchief in Ni'ma's palm and closed her fingers over it. "Take it—they're my life savings." Ni'ma remained silent as her mother went on, "Get together your clothes and go straight away to the station and take a ticket to Cairo. Cairo's a big place, daughter, where you'll find protection and a way to make a living till Allah brings you safely to your time. Then bring it back with you at dead of night without anyone seeing you or hearing you.'

Zeinat raised the end of her *gallabiyya* and put it between her teeth. Taking hold of the old clothes, she began winding them round her waist. Then she let fall the *gallabiyya*. Ni'ma regarded her in astonishment:

"And what will we say to my father?"

"It's no time for talking. Before you go off to the station, help me up with the basket so that I can go to the market for people to see me like this. Isn't it better, when he returns, for your father to find himself with a legitimate son than an illegitimate grandson?"

—Translated by Denys Johnson-Davies

Mahmoud al-Rimawi (b. 1948)

Mahmoud al-Rimawi spent his childhood in Jericho, which he left in 1967 to follow a journalistic career, moving from Beirut to Cairo and then to Kuwait, where he remained for ten years before being deported in 1987. He now lives in Amman, Jordan. An original writer, his stories reflect the suffering and rootlessness he has known during his lifetime as an exiled Palestinian. Though these stories reveal a rather pessimistic outlook on life, this is combined with a faith in the ultimate success of the struggle. His greatest concerns as a writer are democracy; freedom from terror; and the situation of his people, the Palestinians, who are, he believes, capable of participating fully in the civilization of the age but who are denied the means of expression because of their political plight—deprived as they are of a homeland. His short-story collections include *Nakedness in a Night Desert* (1972), *Northern Wound* (1980), *Planet of Apple and Salt* (1987), *A Silent Garden* (1990), *Slow Beat on a Small Drum* (1991), *The Strangers* (1993), *Lonely Brethren* (1995), *The Train* (1996), and *All There Is* (2000).

THE TRAIN

It wasn't just filled with passengers and luggage but with feelings too. It was an old train, like the ones you see transporting soldiers in war films.

"It's been carrying us ever since they built it," said my neighbor, a doctor in his fifties. "Ever since it started rolling."

I didn't doubt it for a moment. I could hardly remember a thing beyond the moment I first got on board. I woke to its din, and I was nurtured on its vague promises; and, for all its high speed, time seemed to pass very slowly. Though we'd exchanged glances when we were shaken so violently about, I never had more than the odd conversation with this neighbor and companion of mine in the leather seat—the noise and tumult all around us cut off any desire for talk. More than once I'd tried to speak, but the light had gone out before I could utter a single word. I could have spoken in the dark, of course, raising my voice so as to let him hear me better, but talking without light just isn't the same. The sudden darkness would scatter my thoughts—to say nothing of arousing natural fears. What was to stop some quick crime being committed while the lights were out?

As for the two passengers opposite me—one short and fat, the other tall and bald—they were oblivious to everything going on around them, talking on, loudly and endlessly, about winning and losing, and financial conditions, and chances that shouldn't be missed, and what was proper and what wasn't. They talked breathlessly, with perfect understanding of each other. Nothing seemed to stop them; not the sudden darkness, or the almighty din and turmoil all around.

From time to time, though, I felt I just had to venture on a conversation with my neighbor, who was the kind of fair-minded man able to talk and listen equally.

"It's these tunnels," he whispered. "The lights go off in the tunnels."

How many of them there were, I thought! And how long they were!

"You've picked the wrong moment to start talking!" I said.

"You think so?"

"It's not a matter of thinking so. It's just the way things are."

Whenever we approached a tunnel, I seemed to feel the need to start talking—not realizing we were just going to plunge in. And though everyone realized it was the tunnels that made the lights go out, the passengers could never reconcile themselves to this. The air would be filled first with murmurings, then with exclamations, then with protests—all of which spurred me on to start up a conversation. It was a huge train, big enough to contain the people of a whole city, so long you couldn't see it all at once, longer than village nights in winter; and it had countless carriages, each roomy enough for a whole ordinary train, filled with people who all knew one another—even those who hadn't been acquainted before, like the doctor and myself, would get to know one another during the trip. And a long and dangerous trip it was, one that dragged on more than we could ever have dreamed, with the time of arrival uncertain. All we knew was that the train was on its way and must bring us to our destination eventually.

It was an odd situation—not like the case with ordinary train timetables, where the details are precise, the times of arrival and departure fixed and properly kept. In fact that's what I started saying to my neighbor, after several days when I hadn't spoken. He didn't seem surprised at my wonder, nor did he lose any of his cool poise; he gave the impression he'd heard all this before and that he'd answered the point scores of times.

"This train of ours," he said, with an assurance that didn't entirely mask a sense of irritation, "isn't like other trains."

He didn't look at me as he said it. You might have thought he was the driver of the train or that he was talking to someone else or to no one at all. But why, I queried? Why was our train different from other trains? And why couldn't we be like other passengers?

He lost his reflective air and spoke in a tone betraying his emotion.

"I'm not the one to answer that," he said. "I'm just a passenger, like you."

He wasn't, though, really like me. He spent his whole time reading, poring over old books and manuscripts and maps, and jotting down notes. Sometimes he'd go off for hours and only come back at nightfall.

How long was it, I wondered out loud, since we'd got on this train? But I knew the answer.

The man laughed, then repeated my question.

"How long?" he said. "Since the day they made the train and it started rolling. It's been moving along with us."

I hadn't spoken of this before, and didn't again. Nor did I hear anyone around me talk about it. It would only have made us miserable, got us all worked up and ready, as they say, to drown in the past. People older than us were constantly sighing, shaking their heads or else lowering them with an air of anger or sarcasm. We of the younger generation, though, would exclaim, vigorously and resolutely, "It doesn't matter how much time's gone by. What's important is how much there is left."

I said it myself now, folding up my sorrow like someone placing a document in the depths of his briefcase. Then, suddenly, a great din sounded, and there were women scurrying all around me and curtains being drawn. A woman, it transpired, was in labor; then she gave birth. And when the fifty-year old doctor sat down again next to me, I discovered it was he who'd assisted at the delivery.

"It seems we're getting new passengers," I remarked.

"Of course," he said. "Didn't you know that? It was a girl. There's a little girl with us now."

"A girl? What name have they given her?"

"Palestine."

"They really called her that?"

"Yes, they did. If the child had been a boy, as the father hoped it would be, they would have given him the same name. It's a name I dearly love."

"But what a name to give a child!" I said. I knew, I added, that everyone longed to call their daughter that, but few people actually went so far as to do it. "I can imagine her as a woman of forty," I added, "but not as a young baby. People are born, then they grow up and they die. Suppose she were to . . . God forbid!"

My neighbor listened to what I was saying, pleased, evidently, that I was expressing myself so clearly and fluently. When I'd finished, he took up the conversation himself.

"There are no preconditions at all for names," he said, speaking with a warm serenity. "A name may have a particular meaning, or it may have a certain effect, or it may simply be inherited. Every age has its particular names. Actually the Arabs don't usually name children after their country, but our situation's rather different. Otherwise—well, we wouldn't be here on this train."

I'd always call this man "doctor," from a sense that the title was more important than his own name, while he'd sometimes call me brother, sometimes *ustadh*.[1] No doubt we avoided names to prevent ourselves drowning in the past.

"They're lucky," he said. "They can cherish her and call her, always, by the name they hold so dear."

"Well," I said, "that's only right and proper after all."

Then I found myself adding, rather sarcastically, "They won't be able to tell her off or insult her. That's something they'll have to manage without."

But in spite of our talk, this matter of the baby on the train still intrigued me. What, finally, was her place of birth? When they asked her that, in time to come, what would she answer? Well, I thought to myself, that's no great problem. If only all our problems were as simple as that! Evidently, though, some of the passengers round about, both men and women, took it all as quite normal—amid all the noise, I heard one woman say how women gave birth up above the clouds sometimes, on plane trips of a mere four or five hours, or even less. So what was so strange about it happening during a journey on the ground? My neighbor heard it too, but I got my remark in first.

"Exactly," I said warmly, in an effort to convince myself. "What's so strange about this happening during a journey on the ground, in a train where people start off as passengers and end up as full-time residents?"

---

1. Title of respect given to an educated man, often a professor or teacher.

My neighbor tried to put things in perspective. He'd lost count, he said, of the number of times he'd helped women give birth on this train.

"I hadn't noticed," I said.

"Just because you didn't see something," he rejoined, "doesn't mean it hasn't happened."

"No," I agreed gloomily. "It doesn't."

The smile returned to his wrinkled face, and there was pity again, too, in his narrowed eyes as he leaned over me.

"Quite a few women have got pregnant over the trip," he whispered.

"You mean," I said, looking round me, "that sort of thing happens here?"

"Why shouldn't it?"

It was on the tip of my tongue to say I hadn't noticed. Instead I stifled my laughter.

"Do you expect life to stop," he went on, "just because the train doesn't?"

Clearly, though, he understood my surprise. He was older than I was, and I'd got on the train after him. Seeing this understanding, I made an effort to defend myself, as though against some accusation of stupidity and lack of shame.

"So in actual fact," I said, "we just live and die on this train."

His answer was assured and decisive, as if to rebuke me and put a final end to my naive ideas.

"When we stop at stations," he said, "it's not all in vain."

The train only stopped at remote stations, where you could see dim lights flickering in the four corners, along with a few scattered houses and single trees standing here and there like ghosts, so that those who saw them couldn't tell whether they were fixed or moving, drawing nearer or moving off. These stations were usually quite deserted, with no sign of any remnants of food or even a stray dog or cat. We'd stop nearby in the dead of night, finding them still more desolate and forbidding than the train itself. We'd get out and stretch our legs, gazing up into the high, dismal vault of the sky and stamping with our feet on the strange, dumb land, longing only for the train to start up again. If we looked at one another, it was merely to see how different each person looked outside the train, knowing full well we'd soon be meeting once more back on board. We didn't notice it when some people sneaked away, leaving their families on the train. It wasn't even clear, indeed, whether those left behind realized their relatives had gone. They'd just sneak off, finding a path through the darkness. As the whistle sounded, loud and piercing, for the train to depart, we'd hear, somewhere outside the station we were leaving, the sound of bullets. Then, even as we tried to work out where this was coming from, the train would dash off with a stifled squeal, along with its heavy load.

Then each of us would go back to his own compartment, forbidden to move to any other, except through the weary shift of tricking the guards or bribing them with money we could ill afford. My neighbor told me, calmly, that his wife and three children were in a different compartment. He hadn't seen them, he said, since the journey started.

"But didn't you get on the train together?" I asked.

Yes, he said, they had, but in all the confusion, and in all the fear of the train suddenly rushing off without them, they'd been separated.

"And what about you?" he enquired tentatively. "What about your family?"

"I don't have any family," I answered, going on to explain, with a show of stoical courage, that my mother was dead and my father had never got on the train at all. Turning my face toward the high, closed window, I saw the outside world in all its blind desolation. When my mother died, my father had chosen to remain there by her side, sending me on in his stead so that he could stay. And now here was this train, eating up great stretches of track, along with my own fortieth year. I turned back again, and my neighbor said:

"I was afraid it would be something like that."

"How did you guess?" I asked.

"There was no great problem. You just act like someone who's alone in the world."

His candor wounded me. I hadn't realized I was so obviously alone amid the throng. Now that we were on such frank, straightforward terms, I asked him if he really thought the train was going, after all this time, to reach its final destination. He was utterly sure of it, he replied at once, only he didn't know when.

I couldn't see this answer was so very new, or very useful either. He tried to make things clearer.

"The train might not arrive with us," he said. "But we'll arrive anyway."

"How's that," I asked. "What do you mean?"

He made no answer to my eager questions. Instead he gazed at me intensely, in a way I finally found bewildering.

"What's the matter?" I said. "Why are you looking at me in that odd way?"

He just searched through his coat pockets and produced a cigarette. A doctor, I thought, and he smokes? I'd never seen him smoking before. He didn't, though, light it, simply holding it in his fingers and gazing at me once more, as if wanting to see into my very depths.

"Strange, isn't it?" he said.

"What is?" I asked.

"That you haven't thought about the stations where we stop."

I felt my pulse beating faster. We were on a long-distance train, which just stopped briefly at stations, then moved quickly off again. We'd find our hearts sinking deep in such places; we'd feel them sinking, then we'd raise them up again and put them back in place. I never found anyone to welcome me there, or see me off, or even give me a letter for anyone. The only good thing was being able to breathe in some fresh air.

"The stations?" I said lightly. "Oh, I think about them all right."

I felt my pulse quicken once more. He came straight back at me.

"Are you quite sure of that?"

"Certainly," I said. "Do you have some reason to doubt it?"

His face relaxed, but he didn't abandon his usual air of sceptical reserve. He came closer.

"When we reach the next station," he whispered, in a brotherly tone, "you can take the things you need with you and just leave the rest here."

I nodded. He started off once again.

"It's no use," he whispered. "We'll never go back. We'll never be going back there."

'What a dream this is,' I thought distractedly. 'The train journey's been a dream, and now leaving the train, putting the train behind me, has become a new dream.' When they put us on the train, we told ourselves it was better than slogging along on foot. But all we'd known was travel sickness and dizziness from the movement. Whenever we felt at the end of our tether, one of us would just say, as a joke, that nobody had a right to grumble on the Orient Express!

"What a dream this is!" I exclaimed to myself. "And what a train!" As for my doctor neighbor, he was slumped over addressing his own heart. "Who knows?" he was saying. "Maybe they've gone. How can you be sure young men will have the will to stay on with the other passengers?" He was twisting his hands, speaking of the members of his own family.

As darkness fell outside, we got ready for the train to stop at the next station. Maybe, I thought, all this had happened to others before us. The expectation seemed longer than all the waiting we'd endured. We hadn't made up our minds to do anything—just to take what was left of our destiny into our own hands. We could hear, behind us and around us, lovely chants, about yearning and love, loyalty and promises, arrival and reunion. I could hear my mother's voice, full of feeling, above all the din, could hear her silence louder than my father's voice.

I found myself whispering to my companion.

"We won't just rush out in the thick of night." I said, with the rapture of one who'd agreed a meeting with the dawn. "We'll wait for the first rays of light, to help us on our way."

He nodded, but whether in agreement or as a warning to take care, I couldn't tell. I hadn't even thought of saying those words till I needed to answer his question—it was then the idea came gleaming into my mind, like a gold coin in the brain of a pauper. I started fidgeting in my place, then got up and walked around, seeing faces I knew and didn't know. I interrupted the reflections of some and the din of others, heard people talking of the Crusades, and the Ottoman Empire, and the British who'd brought in the Jews, and things about coughing and problems with breathing and convalescence, about whether a boy was better than a girl, or a girl than her sister, or whether an old system was better than a new one, or about what we could do if the train didn't stop and what we'd do if it did.

I heard them, but all they got from me was greetings and smiles. Some of them, though, invited me to sit down with them. When I finally got back, I found my neighbor listening to the conversation between the two passengers opposite, the short fat one and the tall bald one. They were talking of profit and loss, and about what would and wouldn't work. I knew from my neighbor that, when one of them left his seat, it was to wrap up a deal or make an appointment;

after which he'd come back and resume an earnest, heated conversation, with the regular use of phrases like "when we arrive" and "the moment we arrive".

Then suddenly, after all the earlier delay, things started happening quickly, quicker than the beatings of the heart, too quick for us to think or start sorting things out.

It was as though the driver of destiny—remote, unspeaking, screening us off and screened himself—had realized, along with his assistants and guards, just what we were thinking of; for there came, over the loudspeaker, the announcement that the doors would stay locked when we reached the next station. A new, global system was in force. No passenger at all was to leave the train.

The passengers, hearing this, started murmuring and looking at one another. Then, as amazement grew, they were seized by anxiety. Then they burst out into screams of anger. They got up and started hurling abuse.

"We're not prisoners of war," they shouted. "We're not hostages or some load being transported. And you're not our fathers or our masters."

With that they started smashing up everything they could trample or lay hold of, while our voices joined with those of the wise, crying, "No, not this way!" But still the protesting voices resounded, coming from every compartment, in a human roar tearing through the silence, sending echoes through the emptiness around us. The train seemed to shake and sway under all the pressure, and the only answer to our protests was the extinguishing of the lights, even though we hadn't entered any tunnel.

Darkness reigned. Then the engine fell silent. The train stopped and simply stood there, motionless, on the tracks.

On we rushed, smashing the windows. The doors opened, and the people poured straight out, the station yard filling in no time at all with huge angry throngs, though some of us, and not just the older people either, lingered, preferring to remain inside the train. And when we finally got off, the train, with its faded earth color, looked older than it really was. It was as though it had been stuck there, on that spot, for many decades.

—Translated by May Jayyusi and Christopher Tingley

'Abd al-Rahman Majid al-Rubai'i (b. 1939)

Iraqi novelist and short-story writer 'Abd al-Rahman Majid al-Rubai'i was born in al-Nasiriyya in southern Iraq. He took a degree in art in 1959 and taught painting till 1964, when he went to Baghdad to work as a journalist while continuing his education in painting at that city's Academy of Fine Arts. He worked at the Ministry of Information in Baghdad, occupying a responsible position, then moved on to Tunisia. He abandoned painting to concentrate completely on writing, is very active in literary circles wherever he goes, and has attended numerous literary conferences. Al-Rubai'i's short-story collections include *Other Seasons* (1970), *Eyes in a Dream* (1972),

The City's Memory (1974); *The Secret of Water* (1983), and *Fire for the Heart's Winter* (1985). His novels include *The Tattoo* (1972), *The Horses* (1975), *The Moon and the Walls* (1976), and *Lines of Latitudes and Longitudes* (1983).

THE KINGDOM OF BULLS

Sa'di yawned openly, then patted his chest and shook his numb arms. The customers flashed meaningful winks at him; he pretended indifference and let out a long sigh, after which he went back to yawning again.

Lips and ears exchanged secret cutting whispers about him, mercilessly exposing him to the world. He had long ago become accustomed to such mumbles, just as he had grown used to the occasional slaps dealt him by some of his more violent customers.

Someone said, "Look at him, sitting there like a sultan, the son of a bitch!"

Another said, "He's as haughty as Khosrow's Iwan!"[1]

"Don't you see his horns?"[2] asked a third.

"What? No!"

"Then you're blind!"

"So what if he has horns or ears, who cares? The important thing is he makes it possible for us to lie with that delicious whore, Salwa."

Sa'di, with his rosary beads and glass of whiskey, was sitting in front of his house. Customers would pass by and pay him in advance. As soon as the street emptied, he would send out the men who had finished, then return to his seat to direct the rituals of night and pleasure. He spoke like a conductor. "You came first, you came late. Don't be in a hurry, your turn will come. The night is long ... it's only five dinars. Haven't you ever taken a close look at her? She's beautiful and rebellious as a racehorse. She's worth fifty dinars, but we are not greedy people."

After two A.M., the door would close behind the last customer and Sa'di would concentrate on counting his takings. Salwa would stretch out on a sofa next to him, her loud breathing filling the place.

"Today's takings have been fifty dinars."

He wiped his thin cheeks with his hands, then poured another whiskey for himself. She did not answer but rose sluggishly and went to the bathroom.

She could never stand under the shower. She would place a chair under the spigot and sit on it, while the water poured over her body, massaging and refreshing it like a dozen hands of love. Later she would open her eyes, feeling more alert, put on her bathrobe, and go to her room.

---

1. The Iwan of Khosrow, King of the Persians, is a courtroom built with a raised floor; it is a famous, grand example of ancient Persian pomp and luxury.

2. This is an allusion to the fact that, as a husband, he was allowing other men to be intimate with his wife.

I expected you, Salwa, to be in a different situation. I expected to see blisters on your body, dirt filling your eyes, your clothes in rags, and you running in tatters from shade to shade, your hand outstretched for alms. Yes, this is what I expected! I tell you the truth without any exaggeration. But how could that ever have happened when you were so bewitching and so alone? One glance of yours would bring back the dead to life! Suddenly you stopped visiting me and I had no one I could ask to inquire about you. Then when I was released after a year and a half, everything had drastically changed. How did you manage this, Salwa?

He filled his glass again and called out, "Salwa, are you asleep?"

"No. Come and massage my back. My bones are aching, that fat dog tired me out."

I entered prison on another charge, only to emerge as a regal bull with two firm strong horns to protect his kingdom. Ha! I was completely immobilized in front of you, a hostage to the charm with which you encircled me. You sucked my blood until you were satisfied, then tossed me out like chaff. Whenever you opened your cloak to me, the dog inside me would begin to pant. Then I ran away with you. We executed the plan we had concocted in my shop. It was prayer time and our neighborhood was empty and quiet when we stealthily left for the train station. When I lay over you for the first time, I felt I was lying on top of the world, I had become the master of the seas and continents. I was singing praises at the top of my voice like a bedouin chanting to his camel in the moonlit desert night! I almost devoured you! Took you in with my body, nerves, and soul. I inhaled the smell of sandalwood and ebony, incense and forests. And you ran in front of me, neighing like a mare ... I chased you, falling and tripping over and over again ... then I would get up and continue. But where did I anchor at the end?

One of the customers whispered in my ear, "That damned woman! Where did you ever find her?"

"In this big wide world."

"I assure you that whoever sleeps with her once will remember her forever. That damned woman! I don't know what she does to you! She transforms a man's whole body into a sensual organ, and extracts all your sap."

Then he rose and went to her room, for his turn had come.

Sa'di poured down the rest of the whiskey and turned on the television to watch the evening's film program. What a monotonous life, Sa'di! The customers, the whiskey bottle, then the evening film program. And sometimes, but only rarely, he would listen to a news bulletin from a far-off station. The world was dead around him. People were dead. The time of black days and painful nights had arrived.

"Cheers to you!"

"To your health!"

"No, let's drink to Salwa's health."

"Ha ha ha ... "

Night laughter. Charm and bewilderment. A bad reputation. Lusts and desires.

"Open the door!"

"Who are you?"

"Jabbar, the builder. Don't you recognize me? Where's Salwa?"

"She's not here."

"I'll pay any amount you want. I've won 500 dinars in the races today. Al-Mughira has won the race. Get rid of everybody—I want Salwa all for myself tonight! Open the door! I'll get rid of them myself! Won't you open the door, you pimp?"

Ha ... let's plunge deeper and deeper into the sea of vice. Ah, the myth of honor, the destruction, the hallucinations, the flames, the repression, the hounding by family and tribe. The trip on a train of joy and sorrow. What's to come next, night? What's to come next, sky?

"I won't open the door."

Jabbar kicked the door.

"I want Salwa!"

He stood in the street, roaring, "I want Salwa!! If you don't let me have her, I'll kill you!"

Sa'di hurried to open the door, and motioned wildly to Jabbar to be quiet.

"Come in then, do not disgrace us! Lower your voice! Do you want to expose us to the neighbors?"

Sa'di closed the door after him.

"The neighbors think we are an ordinary couple. Do you think you are in al-Maidan?"[3]

"So why didn't you open the door then?"

"There were three men before you and it is now one o'clock."

"I told you that I have won five hundred dinars and I shall stay with her until morning. I shall pay you one hundred dinars, is that enough?"

"First sit down here, next to me. Let me fix you a glass of whiskey."

"I've had enough. I've drunk half a bottle already, and eaten a whole broiled chicken, and am quite ready for the ride—I've got to be careful or your mare will buck me off and trample on me.

When I was released from prison, everything had drastically changed. No sooner had I rung the bell than she appeared. God! It was Salwa herself, but how had she become like this? Coolly she whispered, "Is that you?"

Then she puffed her cigarette smoke into my face.

"Is this how you welcome your husband?"

She laughed bawdily before she said, "Now you wake up!"

"Shut up, you ... "

"Why don't you say it?"

"Why are you speaking like this to me?"

"Come in first. Come on."

I did. Good heavens! Where were our worn-out cushions that I had bought in the auction? Where was my own picture that used to hang in the middle of the wall?

---

3. A red-light district in Baghdad.

"I'll kill you!"

She let out another lewd laugh. "What are you waiting for then? You will only be biding time for me, nothing more. Since I ran away away with you, everyone has been looking for me. If you don't kill me, someone else will . . . "

"You've soiled my honor!"

Ha . . . O city of calamities and wonders!

"I have a gun, do you want it?"

"I shall hand you back over to your family."

"Then they'll kill us together. Have you forgotten?"

After a while in which bewilderment overtook me completely, I said, "I'm leaving."

"Where to?"

"I don't know."

"They'll run into you and ask about me. They will kill you, don't you realize this?" Then she threw herself upon me, embracing me affectionately. She mewed like a kitten and my legs trembled; my whole body rose up in hunger. I hugged her close to me with the repressed desire of a year and a half of deprivation. Oh, that terrible prison cell! Those long horrible nights, empty guffaws, and quarrels of thieves and drug addicts! And here was the warm body I had missed so much! The body I cried for, for a year and a half, since they arrested me in that loud demonstration I had joined out of sheer boredom. I kissed her lips and neck, her belly and legs. I devoured her.

She had asked Sa'di for his decision.

"I still don't know."

"Stay here, Sa'di, hide with me behind this door that protects us. This is the only solution. Let's prolong our lives until they find us. What do you say?"

"But what will happen to us after this, Salwa?"

"There's no future. The wall around us is quite complete. There's no use looking for an escape."

"I must think about it."

"It can be a safe life, Sa'di, before the end finally comes. It's true, it will not be completely free of annoyances, but you are strong enough and can protect me from those who might try to harm me. Isn't that right?"

And when he nodded his head, he felt it heavy as a big block of marble. He raised his hands to touch it, and they collided with two small horns.

—Translated by May Jayyusi and Naomi Shihab Nye

'Abdallah Rukaibi (b. 1932)

Algerian short-story writer and scholar 'Abdallah Rukaibi was born in Jamura near Biskra in the south of Algeria. After studying in his own country, he attended the al-Zaituna Institution in Tunisia and then obtained a Ph.D. from Cairo University. However, during the revolution he interrupted his studies to join the fighting and has now written his memoirs of those days. He taught at the University of Algiers and then served as Algerian Ambassador to Syria for several years, before returning to his teaching post in Algiers. His creative work reflects his continuing concern with the Algerian Revolution and its aftermath, when the national government took over from the French, two aspects well reflected in the short story presented here. His collection of short stories, *Rebellious Souls,* appeared in 1962, and he has since published in various periodicals. Rukaibi has also published several books of criticism, including his important work, *The Short Story in Contemporary Algerian Literature* (1969).

THE FIRE WITHIN

When his hand touched the doorknob, he felt a cold current run through his body. He heard the rain falling heavily against the door. His wife was saying good-bye, and how sorry she felt for him going out in such stormy weather, but he rushed outside without hearing her.

The rain lashed his face, and the wind made walking difficult. To be at the Hydra bus stop before seven, he would have to hurry . . .

The steady rain seeped through to his back. He walked briskly, almost running, but his shoes were of no help to him. At one point he tried to run, but he slipped and almost wrenched his leg. He cursed his rubber soles. Instinctively, he turned up his coat collar and pressed his hand to his neck, to protect it from the rain that was soaking through to his chest. He did not want to catch a cold. He had been plagued by nagging colds whenever the weather changed in the capital; and, in the capital, the weather changed constantly, several times in the course of one day.

He threw back his shoulders and raised them. This gave his thin figure the appearance of added height. His shoulder bones stuck out beneath his overcoat, which had become drab and faded. He had not been able to buy a new one for years. Thinking of this brought to mind his four children, and his wife, who had not bought a new dress in two years. His face was gloomy as he remembered these things; it went pale beneath the tan he had acquired years before. His nose stuck out, sharp and thin, bending a little to the left. It looked like the beak of an eagle about to attack its prey. With a determined air, the man clenched his teeth and walked faster.

At the bus stop, he saw that people were under the kiosk to get out of the rain. It struck him as strange that there were some who had umbrellas but were still seeking refuge under a roof. He ran, hoping to find shelter, but there was no room for him. He stood under one of the small trees planted nearby, but the water that trickled from it seemed heavier than the rain itself. He looked around for a familiar face but in vain.

He felt depressed. "No use, no use . . ." he murmured to himself.

The bus arrived, and people rushed up to it in a violent wave, breaking the order of the line. Those who had been keeping it shouted to protest the confusion. Women jostled each other.

"Show some respect for women!" shouted one of them.

"Get in and keep quiet, woman!" answered a voice, irritably.

"People today have no respect! No courtesy!"

There was a flash of lightning. Clouds rushed up against each other, thunder roared, and the rain intensified, as though mocking the man who was standing apart from the scene.

He could not bring himself to push into the crowd. The bus pulled away with its back door still open. With his eyes, he followed the hands and legs of the passengers who clung to it, until finally they were no longer visible.

He remained there, looking down the road, waiting for the next bus. Getting to the office after eight would require an excuse. He hated making excuses as much as he hated crowds, which filled him with revulsion, even on buses. He resigned himself but did not stop thinking. He recalled the image of his boss, and the hostility he saw everyday in his look, hidden behind an artificial smile.

"Why does he resent me so much?" he asked himself. "I've never done him any harm . . ."

The rain began to let up. There were fewer people waiting, since the first bus had taken most of them. The auxiliary bus arrived. He noticed the conductor. He had arrived late today. His delay, he thought, must have been caused by the rain; this was probably why people were so disgruntled.

He kept hearing the clicking of the ticket punch. Looking at the conductor, he wished he could change places with him. He could not bear his own monotonous job: writing lifeless words on a typewriter, carrying files to the supervisor, entering papers in the register, inscribing them with a brief remark that was almost always the same: "Accepted." "Rejected," "Accepted."

He thought of his supervisor, who was the cause of his depression, of his revulsion for his work, and wondered, "Why does he hate me?" But the noise of the bus interrupted his thinking. Passengers were moving about more quietly now. He sat up front, right near the driver. He felt safe in this place.

He looked toward the door, hoping to see a familiar face. Everyone who came on board showed signs of insufficient sleep: their faces were sullen; there were dark circles under their eyes; their breath smelled of tobacco. Their steps were unsteady, and their hands clutched the seats with obvious nervousness.

The bus moved sluggishly. Jammed up against each other, people swayed. More passengers got in; others got out.

"Watch where you're going!" shouted one of them.

"Excuse me."

"What a strange situation!" said a third person, grudgingly. "When will it end? We've become like overstuffed bags."

Al-Akhdar pondered all this, looking around at the passengers and feeling sympathy for them. Why was he looking at their shoes? He looked at his own shoes, too. He was struck by the variety: not one pair was like another. Why were people as different in the shoes they wore as in their faces and their thoughts? Was it coincidence? He could not explain . . .

At the People's Palace stop, the bus became more crowded. Two women tried to get on, but they were blocked by the people standing in the doorway.

"Let her pass," said the old one. "She's pregnant."

"Then she should stay home!" shouted the conductor at her. "If she is pregnant, why isn't she at home resting?"

"Who would support her children?"

He made no reply but glared at her with repressed anger. Frowning, aggressive, he was ready for a quarrel at the slightest pretext. The old woman gave him a five-dinar bill for tickets for herself and the pregnant woman.

"I don't have any change."

"This is all the money I have."

"Get off and find some change."

"How?"

"It's no concern of mine."

"I will not get off!"

The bell rang, and the driver stopped the bus. Voices rose in a jumble of protests. A girl standing beside two young men and speaking in French laughed.

"I'm going to be late!" said one person, waving his hand.

"This is scandalous!"

The features of the conductor were rigid as he ignored the protesting voices. Al-Akhdar remembered that he, too, would be arriving late; he remembered the Supervisor, his murderous look and malicious smile . . . Somebody paid for the two tickets, and the bus moved on.

Despite the narrow, curving streets, cars passed the bus at breakneck speeds. Al-Akhdar felt safer in the bus than he would have in a taxi, which he had taken only once, the time he took his youngest child to the hospital.

The bus halted at a stop on Didouche-Mourad Street. The other passengers scattered in different directions. Al-Akhdar was about to hurry off, like them, but he remembered that it was after eight.

"What's the use?" he thought. "What would I gain from it?"

He stopped in front of a bar near the bus stop and read its sign: "Bar Didouche-Mourad." He smiled to himself.

"Well, Hero," he wondered, "how do you like this? . . ."

When he pushed open the door of the building, which had the French letters *SNL* inscribed on it, he heard footsteps approaching. He turned to see the supervisor, who ignored his greeting and gave him a glowering look. Al-Akhdar felt as though something like a bullet was tearing through his body. The flush that the cold air had brought to his face disappeared . . .

Later, he tried without success to find an answer to the constantly recurring question of the supervisor's dislike for him:

"Why is it that he has always taken this attitude toward me? I have never done any harm to anyone ever since I was assigned to this position. Is it . . . is it because I don't hold a higher degree, like he does? It's true I don't have a long experience in administrative work, as he and some of my colleagues do. But I spent years out under the trees, fighting for the revolution.[1] I lost my health on the rocks. I slept on the ground and under the open sky. I lived with the birds, I savored the smell of gunpowder, singing for the valleys and the hills and dreaming of a better day . . ."

These were his thoughts as he looked out the window. His dreamy gaze did not notice the raindrops sliding along the pane of the window that faced him. He went back to the old days, to his comrades in the struggle. Despite all the hardships he had endured then, those had been better times than his present life. "Either times have changed," he said aloud to himself, "or I myself have changed. Or perhaps that's just the way life is . . ." He sank into his thoughts, which leapt about in disarray. He was unable to find the logic to hold them in any order. He felt that there were times when logic did not apply to life, which was characterized more by contradiction and confusion; and that anyone who tried to impose some order on it might get lost in its midst . . .

Absent-mindedly, he turned back to his desk and tried to arrange his papers in preparation for his usual work. As he felt those sheets, he saw them as living souls who spoke to him. He felt sorry for them; they were like his own thoughts, they needed affection . . .

While he was preoccupied in this way, he heard the voice of the supervisor's secretary calling him. Something inside him stirred. The moment that he had been anticipating, in torment, for a whole year had arrived. He had been expecting it every day, he had been smoldering, but no one had suspected it. Now, flames were erupting and were consuming even the objects in front of him; he could almost see the smoke rising. A strong feeling now took him unaware, and he was amazed by it: a feeling of fear, a feeling of impending change . . .

"I wasn't like this in the past," he said to himself. "Back then I wasn't even afraid of sudden thunderbolts. But today I am afraid of this boss!"

He walked steadily, while the eyes of his colleagues followed him dispassionately. Looks that meant nothing: empty, indifferent looks, neither sympathetic nor hating . . . What did it matter to them? Everyone took care of himself. They did not hate him, as the supervisor did, but neither did they feel any friendly sympathy for him.

He opened the door. He did not feel the same cold he had experienced when he touched the doorknob of his house. He felt a warmth radiating from

---

1. The Algerian Revolution began in 1954, against the French colonization of Algeria. It lasted for seven years, ending in victory and complete independence in 1962. The Algerian veterans are very proud of their victory, which was a great achievement in the face of the French's more advanced technological knowledge of warfare.

all sides of the supervisor's desk. He was met by that sluggish, black smile that hung, as usual, at his half-opened lips, suggesting some hidden meaning. The lips moved.

"You were late today."

"The rain . . ."

"Neither the rain nor anything else is any concern of mine."

He remembered the argument that the conductor had had with the old lady. Because of the bizarre coincidence, he almost smiled.

"What could I do?" he replied calmly. "I don't own a private car."

"Do you mean to imply? . . . "

"I don't mean anything."

"I know what you mean!"

"I'm not a malicious person, as far as I know."

"Are you boasting?"

"I've never boasted in my life."

"Your life? Your life is a failure!"

The blood boiled in his veins. He became agitated. He tried to control himself, perhaps so as to delay the end. He had worked hard in the past; didn't he deserve the right to a breath of fresh air, even a passing one? He controlled himself, trying to make the best of a thorny situation.

"I am not ambitious for success," he said.

"Without ambition or success, what can a man be worth?"

He avoided responding to this tone of sarcasm. What use was it to discuss success here?

As though the man before him had read his mind, he took his last bite; he breathed his poison: "I've been keeping an eye on you for some time, and I'm not pleased with you. I could destroy you. I could put a match to your whole life."

He could not remain silent. He had to put an end to this pretentiousness.

"I can put a match to you, too!" he shouted. "And to your house! I burned out your masters while you were one of their stooges in this country!"[2]

The black smile contracted, spewing its deadly tar. The round, pudgy face went pale. The eyes rolled in their deep sockets. In the sullen face, the years of rottenness were revealed. The huge frame quivered in the luxurious chair, and the feet pressed into the velvety carpet beneath them. One hand moved to keep the gold-rimmed eyeglasses from falling, while the other pointed toward the door.

"Get out of here! Get out!"

"I am not in your house!" said al-Akhdar, with such force that the other was taken completely aback.

---

2. Some Algerians were collaborators with the French. The Algerian National Front was very severe with many of these after victory.

The supervisor could not keep from shouting, "We'll see, which of us will make the other burn!"

"We're all burning, you and I. But let's see which of us will win at the end!"

Having said what he wanted to say, al-Akhdar turned. Nervously, but firmly, he walked out, slamming the door violently. He paid no attention to his colleagues, who had been listening to the exchange. Only now were they taking account of his presence: they were looking at him with sympathy, commiserating; maybe now that he was leaving them, they felt sorry for their previous attitude.

He went out into the street and breathed the fresh, pleasant air. The weight that had been pressing down on him for a whole year was gone. He strolled along the streets and decided to return home on foot. He lifted his head and saw rays of sunlight filtering through the clouds.

—Translated by Aida A. Bamia and Thomas G. Ezzy

Noura al-Sa'd (1964)

Born in Doha, Qatar, Noura al-Sa'd obtained an M.A. in literature from the University of Jordan in 1991 and has worked since as a researcher in the communications department at the Qatari Ministry of Foreign Affairs. She writes a special column in the paper *Al-Sharq*. She is married and has so far published one collection of short stories, *The Newspaper Vendor* (1989).

THE PIT

It was another tedious day. She rubbed her eyes hard, till they were red and began to feel loosened. She had an odd feeling that today would be different from the others.

At the college life began to seep slowly into her. She crossed the yard, then, standing in her space by the usual desk, began folding her *aba* and humming an automatic tune. The clammy morning greetings, dutiful and born of long habit, sounded around her.

Nawal languidly spread out her books, then, picking up one that had dropped to the floor, opened it and flipped over a few pages. Then she got up and went straight off to the lecture hall. It was still very early and the hall was empty. She smiled a meaningless smile, enjoying the echo of her footsteps. She really was there. It seemed quite natural for her to sit down in the end seat and take a light-colored pen from her satchel.

She decided to make some doodles on her desk. But there were, she saw, so many lines and circles already, faintly colored in all over the desk, that there was no space left at all—not even for a single line. There was no room here for a stranger. When the pen slipped from between her fingers, she didn't pick it up.

Time was cheap after all. Her comrades started coming in now, with their usual laughter sounding out in front of them. As they sat down beside her, she drew nearer and nearer to them, while, outside, the atmosphere grew colder. Her eyes drifted over them, looking for something different. "You're quiet today, Nawal," one of them said.

But she wasn't expecting an answer. The girls went on chattering, now criticizing the way one of them walked. She didn't remember any more what they'd been talking about. She wanted to tell them about the dream she'd had the night before: how she'd seemed to be sitting in a car going backward at great speed, and how the black trees appeared, through the window, to be racing forward, and how she hadn't dared put her hand out of the window.

But she decided not to tell them about the dream—they'd only laugh at her. After the lecture one of them suggested going to the cafeteria. They pulled each other along, then, after they'd gone, one of them came back again, remembering they'd forgotten to pull her along with them. She heard how they were talking about her with meaningful winks, how they were saying, "She's quiet today." She really loved them. They were decent and good-hearted, and they loved her too, even though she sometimes liked to suppose otherwise.

The ground seemed to crumble under Mouna's quick steps as she hurried to gather the girls around her. She waved her hand in that high-strung, endearing way of hers, then started talking all at once. "How are you?" she said. Turning to one of the girls, she said: "I thought you'd phone me yesterday." Then to another: "Where in Heaven's name are you going?" Back came the answers, quick and short and repetitive. With a sudden apology she went off to the lecture. "Nawal," she shouted from the distance, "why are you so quiet today?"

Nawal opened her mouth to speak. But what could she say? She didn't know the answer, and in any case, whatever it was she wouldn't have shouted it out to that girl fast disappearing among the crowd of other girl students. As for her, something quite different was engulfing her, something choking and congested. At the door of the cafeteria she felt, for some reason, very tense. She wouldn't go in, she thought. She felt no desire to sit down in her usual place, swallowing the usual food and scanning the faces around her without knowing what she was searching for. She wasn't going in to chatter about exams and the television serial, or play cards, then surrender, half asleep, to another lecture. No, she wasn't going in. Today was different. She called out loud, "No!" But no one heard her.

They were decent and good-hearted, she thought, but she wanted to be alone with herself. And yet she'd be alone even if she was with them, and when she was apart from them they'd still always be with her. She saw Mouna approaching at her usual quick pace. How graceful her walk was, and what a strong presence she had. Nawal gazed at her with admiration and a touch of envy. Mouna came up, took Nawal's hand in her own warm hands, pulled her off to a nearby spot, and started speaking with great animation on a large number of things. A few moments of silence followed, and then came the question that had been going around all morning. "Why are you so quiet?"

"Something's different maybe," Nawal said with a laugh.

Mouna got up, then started talking all over again, about the bad headache she was suffering from, how she needed so much sleep, ten hours at least. For a few seconds she spoke of the void, of emptiness, then made her excuses and walked toward the outer gate of the college.

Nawal wished she could stop her and ask, "Hasn't today been different?"

But she didn't. Everything seemed clouded to her and unfinished. In the cafeteria the girls sat chewing over their food and their talk. "We haven't read anything from you lately," Shaikha told Nawal. Nawal didn't feel like talking. "I'm thinking," she murmured.

"Shall we help you?" Shaikha asked.

"Drop the nonsense," Moza broke in. "We're eating."

After a few moments, Shaikha raised serious eyes and said to Nawal, "I've had an idea about a play set on Mars."

There was laughter, along with loud comments.

"Have we got so tired of earth," Sara said, "that we can't find anything down here to talk about?"

"Maybe you can dream up there," Moza said coldly.

Shaikha went on, as if in a dream, "We'd criticize everything that's bad, freely and objectively. We'd see the absurd things that happen here on earth, through a mythical telescope."

"Very exciting," Sara said with a light smile. "Maybe we could reform all these absurd things too."

"Could you pass that dish please?" Moza interrupted. Then, before she could stop herself, she added, "I reckon it would be more exciting if we abandoned earth altogether and floated about in space."

Nobody answered. Nawal felt conflicting emotions inside her. Her thoughts went back to those tense moments when she was sitting there in front of Nadia, finding in Nadia's confident eyes a refuge from her dreadful agitation. She remembered how Nadia had asked, in a calm and gentle tone, "What would you like to drink?"

"Nothing, thanks."

Hot drinks, Nawal thought, would make her more tense, and cold drinks would kill the feelings she was enjoying. But Nadia had got up anyway and brought a cup of coffee, setting it firmly down in front of her.

She'd watched the hot vapor rising from it, then began examining the room, feeling things sticking to her eyelids like dust. After a quick sip Nadia had said, "I read your last play. It was full of symbolism. Your symbols, Nawal, are different from the ones readers are used to. They seem like masks, like fortresses. It's as if you're mystifying the issues even as you try to express yourself; as if you're hiding them, afraid of them."

"What are you?" Mouna had asked her on another day. "Everything at once? We all complete one another. Doesn't this imply contradictory, conflictive stances? There can't be completeness as long as there's conflict. We're individuals after all.

"When I write, my individuality's lost, or takes a different shape perhaps. I become a girl of many selves, besieged by contradictory forces of destiny, and I find I don't know who I am.

"We all of us look away from our knowledge of ourselves, and we compromise with existing trends. We stop for a while when faced with a crisis of conscience, reflect for a few moments, then continue on our way. Don't you see," she added, finally exhausted, "that we're covering life up? There's so little time. Let's live spontaneously."

She smiled, eyeing Nawal in a meaningful way.

"But you can't do that, can you?" she said. She told her too, "Nawal, there's a time for words, there's a time for the sword. And there's something called being malleable, serene."

Nawal allowed a faint memory to return. "You're asking me about your play," Nadia had said a year before. "Yes, I did read it, but only once. And I'll tell you frankly, I hated it. It's just so tragic to see the heroine's problem finally plunged deep into the void like that, and then her suicide. It's futile, where what's expected is revolutionary force. It was all a mere crude expression of anxiety and anger and misery."

For eight months or so now she hadn't written a single word. All her attempts at writing seemed shallow and trivial. She'd hid all her earlier attempts too, couldn't even look at them.

"Oh, it's so cold," Shaikha said.

How wretched everything was here!

Nawal was perspiring all over, her burning body felt like a sun imprisoned in its place. Everything was turning, changing around her, but she remained mesmerized on her illusory throne. Umm Kulthoum's voice flowed from the radio, singing "The Days Rolled By."

"Time never stops," Sara said. "It seems to be our bitterest enemy."

Shaikha grumbled at the taste of the food, then launched into an endless torrent of epithets.

"You're never happy," Moza retorted, getting up.

"It helps pass the time," Shaikha answered.

When the last lecture was over, it was already late. Nawal watched them collect their things and walk toward the outer gate, after saying, "See you tomorrow." She collected her own things, with a sense of doing something strange and repugnant, then left. It hadn't been a different day after all.

—*Translated by Salwa Jabsheh and Christopher Tingley*

Nawal al-Sa'dawi (b. 1931)

Egyptian novelist Nawal al-Sa'dawi writes on society and social and psychological behavior, especially on issues dealing with women's lives and rights. A physcian and a psychologist, she is one of the major feminist writers in the Arab world and has paved the way toward more direct, honest, and scientific discussion of the Arab woman's life, sexuality, and happiness. She is renowned for her many enlightened and open discussions of a subject that had been, up to the 1960s, almost a taboo for the modern Arab writer. In her novels and short stories she continues the fight for feminine liberation. Among her novels are *Woman From Point Zero* (1974), *Two Women in One* (1975), and *The Death of the Only Man on Earth* (1976); and among her collections of short stories are *A Moment of Truth* (1962), *The Thread and the Root* (1967), and *The Demise of His Excellency the Minister* (1980). Her studies on modern sexuality include *Woman and Sex* (1972), *Man and Sex* (1973), and *The Female Is the Foundation* (1974). Because of her candid and scientifically open attitudes, she was dismissed from her government job in 1972 and suffered imprisonment and persecution in 1981, only to become world famous for her courage and persistence.

The Demise of His Excellency the Minister

Mother, place your hand on my head, stroke me gently on the hair and neck and chest as you did when I was a little boy. You're the only one left for me, your face is the only face I wish to see in these last moments of life. How I wanted you to reproach me for my absence during the last five years! I was not only too busy to see you, but too busy for the whole world, even for myself, my wife, home, and friends. You know how I loved playing golf, but I didn't play once during those five years! I never even had time to look at my own face. Hurrying out, I would cast a quick glance at the mirror to adjust my necktie or make sure my suit did not clash with its color. Even had I looked at my own face, I would not have seen it, and if I had focused on people's faces in the office or in the streets, I would not have seen them either. If they had spoken to me, even in loud voices, I would not have heard them. The truth is that the loudest shriek of a car horn would not have been audible to me. I stopped walking in the streets because cars almost hit me as I walked.

Mother, I was like one who could neither see nor hear, one who was not living in this world at all. Then where was I living? I was not dead, I had not read my obituary in the newspapers. A man in my position cannot die silently, without his obituary flashing in prominent headlines and a big funeral where people, including the head of state, walk in line. I used to find the deaths of dignitaries most impressive, so much so that I often wished I were the dead man in the coffin. But since I had never been inside a coffin before, I must still have been living in your world. But I was enormously preoccupied with more important matters.

Sometimes I was so exhausted I was unable to move my muscles, but my mind kept on working. Other times my weary mind would stop thinking, but my body would keep functioning, going to the office, attending meetings, presiding over conferences, receiving official guests at airports, attending celebrations, sometimes traveling abroad on official business. When I saw my body moving alone so often without the cooperation of my mind, I would feel quite surprised, Mother, even afraid, especially if I were sitting at an important meeting that required concentration. Still, the only really important meeting in *my* opinion was one presided over by someone superior in position to me. Ever since I'd become a government official, I hated having anyone in an office above me! But I had trained myself to disguise my hatred of bosses in front of them and only to vent my feelings in the office with my inferiors, or at home with my wife, as I used to see my father do with you. I never revealed my hatred in front of a boss even if he were an ordinary official such as a section head or department chairman. So can you imagine my repression of my true feelings when my boss was the head of state himself? I would sit before him with my mind extremely vigilant and awake, fearing he might ask me a question I could not answer, or if I gave the correct answer, I feared it would not be the required answer.

Yes, Mother, this is the *ABC* of politics we learn right from the beginning. The correct answer is not always the required answer, but the required answer is always the correct answer. A clever man is always ready to distinguish the right truth from the wrong truth, and it is a difficult job, Mother, harder than any other job in life. I had to sit at meetings with my mind and body completely alert, my left hand calmly resting in my lap, my right hand holding a pen ready to record the slightest sign, even a tiny movement of the head of the boss, or his hand, or finger, or lower lip as he puffed it a little to the front, or a small tautness of his facial muscles. I had to differentiate between the movements of his left and right eyes, to notice each change as it took place or immediately before it did, so I could interpret it. My mind, eyes, and ears were constantly anticipating.

Yes, Mother, in those meetings my mind and body became masses of sensitive nerves, like exposed radar wires wound around themselves. My stomach muscles trembled as if they were connected to an electrical current, especially when I stood next to him. The fingers of my right hand would tremble, though I held them with my left hand across my breast or stomach, and my legs were stiffly together. When cameras rolled, their lights would be directed at my face, panning my whole body to present me to the public. Sometimes I tried to disentangle my left hand from my right, but I would always find my hands heavy, as if paralyzed. Yes, Mother my love, this was the picture of myself I saw in the newspapers, and I would feel ashamed of myself. I would try to hide the papers from my family, especially my little daughter who would point out my face among the others with her slender finger and tell her mother, "This is not Papa, Mama!" However, her mother would always retort proudly, "Of course it is Papa! Just look what a great man he is, standing there with the head of state!" My wife's voice would ring in my ears and I would realize it was not her true voice, that under that voice there was another that she had suppressed since the day we were married. I knew she had hidden her true self and my true self within her in a deep fathomless labyrinth, and sometimes I could feel it like a tumor that had calcified and would never be exposed.

What do you say, Mother? I felt ashamed in the light of my little daughter's pure eyes, which were able to expose me and reveal the truth which no one else, even myself, could ever reveal. Do you remember when you used to tell me that all screens disappear in front of a child? I never believed you then, but later on I remembered it. My little daughter would gaze at me with her wide, steady eyes, and I would feel afraid of them, as if her stare were not the gaze of a child at all. No normal girl or boy should have a look as direct and fixed and impertinent as hers was, especially when they are looking at an older person who has authority over them. I was the father, lord, and pillar of the family, who had the right to respect and obedience from every family member!

Yes, these were the words that I often heard from you when I was a child. They stayed in my memory and I often repeated them to my wife and daughter, and to all employees under my authority. I even used to feel great self-admiration as I said them and saw admiration reflected in the eyes of those around me. My faith in the truth of what I was saying became stronger till I believed it was the eternal truth and anyone who advocated the contrary was blasphemous.

In all my experience, since I first was a petty official until I became a minister, I had not come across a single employee who contradicted me. This was why I absolutely could not bear that one female employee who enraged me till I lost my dignity. She drove me completely out of my senses, not by saying anything of great importance but simply by contradicting what I usually said, and I could not bear that. My wrath did not stem simply from the fact that she contradicted my ideas, or was a minor employee who differed with the minister, or a woman who stuck proudly to her opinion in front of a man, or because she called me "Sir" when everyone else called me "Your Highness, the Minister." It was because, when she talked to me, she raised her eyes to mine in a way no one else did. It was her strong fixed gaze that infuriated me. And I was not only angry because she did it but also because I could not fathom how she did it, how she ever dared to do it!

Mother, I wanted to find out how that woman could do that. My passion to discover her secret took such hold of me that it drove me to great lengths of anger. One day I sent orders for her to come to my office and left her standing there in front of me while I continued to sit, letting her feel invisible. I left her standing while I talked on the phone, laughing with the person on the other end. The strange thing is that she remained standing there, not appearing to listen to my voice or notice me but staring at a picture on my wall. After I finished my conversation, I thought she would turn to me, but she continued looking at the picture as if I were not there. Then she turned, fixing her strong steady eyes on mine. I trembled, feeling as if all my clothes had slid off me at once. I felt the same shame that I felt from my own daughter's eyes, but that shame changed quickly to rage and a burning desire to shame her back. I found myself shouting at her, "How dare you? Who do you think you are? Don't you know that you are nothing more than a small employee and I am the minister, and no matter how much you rise in your station in life, you will never be more than a woman whose place is in bed under a man?"

What would you say, Mother? Any woman who hears such words from a man might fall unconscious from sheer embarrassment, but what if the man were not only her boss but the minister? Besides, we were not in a private room: my office was full of men, high-ranking officials in the ministry. But the strange thing is that nothing seemed to defeat this woman. She did not look at all embarrassed, nor did she lower her eyes, or blink. Never before had I experienced such insubordination—and in the face of so many onlookers!

When I thought of the high regard others owed me because of my position, I became even angrier. How could a woman do this to me? How could she make me feel as if I was not the minister? How could she jeopardize my sense of authority, manhood, and pride? You may be able to understand how I hated that woman so much that my temperature rose one day to 105 degrees and I had to stay home, my boiling head swathed in ice pads. My temperature did not go down until I had issued all the orders I could to deal her a decisive blow.

But can you imagine, Mother, I was unable to finish her off, and she stayed on! People often mentioned by chance to me that she was still there. In truth I was spying on her, trying to find out about her secretly, hoping all the time I would hear some bad news about her, maybe that she had died in an accident. Yet she lived on in this world. Once I ran into her by chance and found her as she had always been, nothing had changed in her at all—still the forthright look of her unblinking eyes. What made me maddest was that my authority was unable to destroy her. She remained calm, while I was utterly unsettled. Her presence seemed to threaten mine.

I could not imagine how I had arrived at this state. How could an insignificant female employee still in the fifth or sixth level of employment threaten a minister's existence? She dared to do what I had never dared in my life: I had never raised my eyes into the eyes of any of my superiors, even if they had little jurisdiction over me. I never saw you raise your eyes into the eyes of anyone else. Had I seen you do that even once, Mother, I might have been able to endure this woman. Had I seen you raise your eyes to the eyes of my father, I might also have been able to raise mine to him and then to the eyes of other men in positions of authority. But I never saw you do that. I used to do things just as you did them. You were my example and I imitated well. So why did you never raise your eyes to those of my father? Had you done that even once, his awe in my heart might have diminished slightly, as would the awe I felt later towards every superior.

Now I want you to pat me with your tender compassionate hand as you used to do when I was little. You're the only person to whom I can open my heart and speak of my real tragedy—it is not simply that I lost my position as a minister but how I lost it! It would have been more tolerable if I lost it because of a serious reason or even a logical one. But the tragedy was more illogical than any one could believe. One morning I opened the paper and did not find my name among the new cabinet. I felt suddenly as if I had lost my identity, as if my name had fallen off my person and I had none now. Every day as I perused the papers looking for my name and not finding it, the feeling that I had become nameless was confirmed. And the telephone, Mother, which used to ring every single minute, asking for me became mute, as if it too had dropped me. I was falling, bitterly falling, tasting the bitterness as I fell, and realizing only now the real flavor of all I had lost. And I sat next to the silent telephone waiting, fearing that someone in my family would see me waiting. Then I would pretend I was not waiting at all, though I would have leapt at any ring from any man or woman, near or far, young or old, man or beast, any voice at all, even a donkey braying. Suddenly I discovered that this machine that I had so often announced that I hated was not hateful to me at all. In fact, it was lovable, and its constant ringing sent pleasure into my body, a pleasure greater than sex, or love, or food could offer. It was a peculiar pleasure, able to overwhelm fatigue and keep my mind working even in my dreams. It could make me stand on my feet in an airport under the scorching sun, a smile on my face, welcoming an official guest, or make me sit stiffly at any meeting or celebration, ready at any moment to take on that official attitude with my two legs tightly held together and my hands clenched over my breast or belly.

Ah Mother! All this pleasure is lost because of a trivial thing. And everything else is trivial compared to it. The loss is like death. One day I was sitting normally in my chair, alert and full of anticipation. I was sitting as usual, but suddenly my concentration began wandering uncontrollably as if my mind had started to operate independently of me. This would have been a catastrophe had it happened anywhere else, but it was happening at an important meeting presided over by the head of state. I was not thinking of the annual report I was about to submit or the new budget I was going to ask for. This would have consoled me a little.

But no, I was thinking of that insignificant female employee. I was cursing the first day I ever saw her, for since then I'd been obsessed with her. I would have been consoled, perhaps, if what preoccupied me about her was her womanliness, for after all, I am a man, and any man, no matter how great, can sometimes be preoccupied with a woman. But she was not a real female in my eyes. She was the lowest employee allowed to enter to office of the minister. And since she had first done this, I was no more myself, the person sitting in the chair was not me but another unrecognizable person. That was the issue that dominated my mind and senses during that fateful meeting; I was trying to resist and banish it from my head. I was so distracted that my left hand was making brushing motions as if to expel it from my mind, while my right hand held the pen as usual; anyone who saw my hand moving might have thought I was trying to brush off an obstinate fly. Since the meeting room was the cleanest room in the whole city and utterly without flies, my hand drew attention. I hated, Mother, to draw attention to myself at such important meetings and had always preferred to remain seated rather invisibly in my chair, so I would not have to face any questions.

I was not afraid of questions because I did not know their answers. The rightful answers were always obvious to me, as clear as $1 + 1 = 2$. What I feared was not to suppress the true answer but to say the true answer.

This was the great catastrophe that befell me that day. My hand must have caught his glance, so our leader's eyes focused on me, reminding me of my father's eyes when I was a child. I remembered how I used to move backward or forward in my chair, hoping the teacher's eyes would fall on the one sitting in front of or behind me. This time I don't think I noticed his eyes looking at me quickly enough, so I was unable to move. Or maybe I was not in my complete mind at the time, or perhaps I had a fever again. His eyes fell right on me with all their heaviness, just as death falls. And when he asked me his question, my mouth opened like the mouth of someone else, someone rash and unthinking. And the simplest answer came to my tongue, the most instinctive answer.

This was not the answer I should have given. The true answer was not the required answer. This is the *ABC* of politics, the first lesson I ever learned. At that moment, however, I had forgotten it. Later my grief was so great at having forgotten it that I felt numb, felt a kind of peace verging on joy. I felt that a huge load had fallen off my chest, heavier than my well-knit hands could contain, heavier than my body sitting mesmerized in my chair, heavier even than the seat itself and the earth over which I sat.

Yes, Mother, I felt rested. Even now in my last minutes I feel peace as I leave this world with all it contains. But the tragedy, Mother, is that despite the peace I feel and although I am departing this world, I still have the telephone next to my head, waiting, hoping it will ring just once more, so I may hear a voice, any voice, saying, "Your Excellency!" How I would like to hear this, Mother, once again, just once, before I die.

—Translated by May Jayyusi and Naomi Shihab Nye

Hadia Sa'id (b. 1947)

Lebanese novelist, short-story writer, and journalist Hadia Sa'id was born in Beirut. She studied for her B.A. at the Beirut Higher Institute, then worked in journalism, radio, and television in Beirut and Baghdad before going to London in 1992 to work at the Arabic review *Al-Sharq al-Awsat*. She is a prolific journalist and has written extensively for radio and television. Her short-story collections are *The Swing of the Seaport* (1981), *Oh Night* (1987), and *Exodus* (1989); in 1989 she also published *Women Outsiders: Stories of Love*, a collection of women's true stories. Her first novel, *Black Orchard* (1995), won her the prize of the prestigious London review *Al-Katiba*. A new novel, *Red Orchards*, appeared in 2002.

SHE AND I

Was I a relative of hers, the doctor asked? I nodded. What else could I say? "Well," I said, "we're distantly related. And anyway, she's like a sister to me now. Don't forget, doctor, we're both strangers here."

But he wasn't interested in what I was saying. He just wanted to tell me something, something he seemed to be carrying on his shoulders, as if he wanted to lay down his burden and rest. Well, I told myself, as I looked at his swollen eyelids, that was his right. We were standing on the stairs leading to his office, and patients and visitors were passing up and down them, with their bags and sheets and smells, noisily jostling one another.

"Poor woman," he said.

What was the matter with her, I asked?

"Cancer, God help her," he answered, in a firm tone. I heard his words, but when I spoke in return he couldn't hear me; it was as if we were two owls pointlessly shrieking. He couldn't tell her, he said. He'd had some fearful experiences telling patients what was wrong with them. And no, he wasn't worried about her feelings and fears, and all the turmoil the news might arouse in her. He wasn't worried whether she could take it or not. His only concern was to pass on the news to someone taking responsibility for her.

But where did I come in to all this? If only he knew what a jolt his news had given me! Who exactly had he supposed I was? A relative? A friend? Her sister? I wasn't any of these. We knew one another and yet we didn't. I'd ask after her health, and sometimes she'd send me flowers or a card. Sometimes, too, we'd walk together in the broad gardens of Casablanca chatting together. We'd talk and talk, knowing we'd turn eventually to the one inevitable subject.

Why was I the person he'd picked out to tell about her condition? "You're the only one who's come to ask about her," he said. "She's been here in the hospital more than a month. She thinks she's got a liver complaint or had some inflammation of the colon. But the tests show it's cancer."

"What kind of cancer, doctor?" I asked. "Breast, or womb, or intestine? Where is it?"

Just cancer. He couldn't be bothered to tell me what kind. He simply said it was well advanced, then started walking indifferently up the stairs toward his office. In a few minutes I'd have to put on a bright smile, take her the bunch of flowers, and tell her everything was all right, that she'd be leaving hospital soon. "Don't tell her, please," he said. "I've lost count of the number of patients who've learned they had cancer, then started on the wake early, wailing and crying and beating their heads against the wall, driving all the other patients to despair. They're better off with their illusions. Tell her anything except that."

But surely, I said, cancer's not such a frightening disease any more. He smiled at my ignorance, wiping his glasses and playing with a key that stuck out from a split seam on his white coat. His look proclaimed just how little I knew, and the smile was sarcastic, with no sympathy in it.

Why wasn't he prepared to discuss it with me? My own doctor says ignorance is bliss; the real misery comes from half-knowing. I remembered her words and started telling this doctor what I knew and what I'd heard about cancer. He became impatient. "Don't tell her the real facts," he said. "Just get that into your head. Everything's in God's hand."

He didn't say that with the pious conviction of our old neighbor, Haj Darwish! Our neighbor's eyes had real goodness in them, and his words had a solid weight of compassion and pity. If I tried to repeat those words to calm her down, I'd only get tongue-tied, convinced of the futility of the whole thing. You can't borrow faith. As for compassion, it's a gift, an endowment. Sometimes I did manage to feel like Haj Darwish, with a sense of great tenderness toward my mother, or my niece, or one or two other people, but that was before I grew up and went abroad. The years since then have worn me down. First I worked as a teacher, then as a secretary, till finally I married my boss and became his companion, secretary, and confidante all in one. My husband became a businessman, his fortunes thriving and dwindling according to circumstances, and the state of the country, and the people we associated with. As my life abroad with him developed—through the burning of the port of Beirut and the failure of his own factory in Damascus, through the ruin of his trading between Kuwait and Amman, then the flourishing of his projects between Casablanca and the Emirates—I became free and the mistress of my time. I was content to be married and bear children, to be always calm and quiet, while my husband turned into a successful businessman. He'd work and travel and bring in a lot of money, and I'd spend whatever we had at the time. I lived in villas and big houses but sometimes, too, in small apartments and dark rooms. I'd go out with my husband to the casinos or on other night outings, or I'd wait for him in homes that were like cellars or tombs. So often I'd laugh from the bottom of my heart, and so often I'd weep. All I could do was follow him and wait for him.

It was when I'd spent several years abroad, some time before I was expecting my second child, that I first met her. She'd always, she said, wanted to make friends with me. I remembered her then: she'd been in Beirut when we were there, when it was still Beirut. She was beautiful and graceful and elegant, but he'd left her to marry me, because I was more beautiful still and I'd captured his heart. Instead of telling her this, I gave a sly smile, and each time I met her, I'd smile a little more, asking about her and talking about my husband, playing happily on the chord of her jealousy. She'd turn pale as a ghost, dying of envy, then shed a tear that was black with kohl, trying to convince me she had a cold, though I knew she was really weeping. Well, let her weep and feel what jealousy and defeat were like! One day we were sitting in the garden of a small villa we had, before my husband had to sell it after an unprofitable deal. She hadn't been able to get him out of her mind, she told me. She was quite shameless about it! She spoke about him as though I didn't even know him, and, try as I might to change the subject, we'd soon be talking about him again, as though someone was pulling a rope with a drowning man hanging on to the other end. I was glad she'd come when he was away on a short trip. She'd never thought of marrying him, she said, because he wasn't right for the marriage she'd dreamed of: he was too traditional, too reserved, preferring a woman who was weak. I hid my fury behind a careless laugh, then went off to the kitchen to make coffee and curse her. I put some sugar in hers, even though she liked it bitter, and while she was sipping it, I told her I'd been careful only to put in a little. Then I sat watching her as she talked, like a silly child, of how she'd been entranced by him as he entered the cafés of Ras Beirut with that calm, handsome air of his, in those splendid days. Then I'd tell her, from my great store of wisdom, how enchantment and haste were some of the worst things of all. As soon as I saw her eyes shining, and noted how very elegant she was, I'd start up about how I concerned myself with the mind, with the power of the intellect, rather than empty appearances. One day she laughed, the way dancers laugh in films, as she told me of his clumsy attempt to kiss her. He was so shy, she said. Then she started talking all over again about how boring she found him and of her great love for that famous surgeon she'd married. He, I knew, had run off after a couple of days; but she'd never admit to anyone that her marriage had been a failure. They hadn't separated, she kept assuring me; it was just that his time was taken up with operations and conferences, while she looked after his property in various countries. At every visit, at every meeting, she'd try and talk about my husband and reminisce about him with me. All she knew was his smile and his quiet, reserved manner, and she always maintained he was uninteresting and limited. He, though, told me that all she knew of him was the surface of the lake, whereas I'd plunged into the depths, penetrating into his feelings. Whenever he and I were together and I mentioned her, he'd smile and make some sarcastic comment, then correct himself and tell me magnanimously I shouldn't take it too seriously. And then he'd laugh, and hug and kiss me, whispering things that made her seem far away. Once, though, I felt that he kept thoughts of her hidden in his heart; one night, when he was caressing my neck, it seemed as though it were the locks of her long hair he was seeking. I said nothing, clenching my jaw hard. I got angry then and started asking endless questions. He answered briefly: yes, he had known her, and had admired her till he discovered what she was really like. He'd realized she wasn't right for him and had never dreamed of marrying her. She was the one who'd wanted that, and hinted at it, before seeing how things stood and going off.

As for her, at the end of a long, hard day I finally got her to tell me what I wanted to hear. "Yes," she said, "I met him and admired him. I thought I loved him, but the feeling didn't last more than a few seconds. I found him boring. He couldn't see into the depths of me, so I left him."

I said nothing, and she was silent too, trying to think up another lie. I knew the way she was. She wanted to raise a whip and strike me with it. What made her want to act like that? She'd never known anything from me but gentleness and kindness. She'd drink my coffee, and sit in my garden, and peel an apple, speaking very softly whenever she found him and me together. The first whip she flicked in my face was when she said, "He married you as though he were marrying part of me." Then came the second flick. "There's something about you," she said, "that reminds him of me. I don't know what it is exactly. A look, maybe, or a tone of voice." Then she delivered a final kick. "I don't think it's your knees," she said, "or those bony wrists of yours."

A liar, wallowing in lies! How could I ever look like her, with my face and my hair and my figure? With my purity like the purity of children, or chestnuts, or ivory, and my rounded buttocks? How could such loveliness as mine be like that shriveled gypsy with her giraffe neck and her figure all out of proportion? I was more beautiful than she was! Every time we met, I'd try and see what on earth it was she had, then, the moment she left, seek out my mirror, feeling reassured and not reassured at the same time.

A month ago, when my husband had returned from a trip, she came to visit us, and I watched them. She was drinking coffee and he was asking after her surgeon husband. She stumbled at that and changed the subject, and she didn't ask him anything. I ordered coffee without sugar for her and, for my husband, prepared the juice cocktail he liked; I went off constantly to the kitchen, sending the servant off early. I watched her white hand as it moved like a butterfly between her cheek and her lap, and I gazed at her rounded knees and splendidly delicate wrists. She was getting on for forty, but still well preserved. I'd look at her lovely breasts, then count the taps of his restless foot till the rhythm resounded inside my head, and I'd hear the faltering in his voice and see how he swallowed and how his ears turned red. I tugged at his belt when she wasn't watching, signaling to him with my eyes to leave us. She was telling him about her husband's fame and success, as if to try and annoy him, while he was telling her of some new project he had on hand. When she let off her rocket, I got back with a bigger one, to make her understand my husband was a successful businessman, someone whose projects and trips were always reported in the papers—I didn't tell her my nephew's friend was a journalist, who was regularly fed these details. She didn't know the juice cocktail I'd prepared and the flood of tender care I was showing came not from love but because she was there. I hadn't missed him while he was away, and I wasn't really interested in his latest profitable deals or his meetings with well-known people. What I wanted was to get under her skin, to make her feel small so that she'd just melt away. I wanted her to make some mistake, so I could correct her with haughty sarcasm. I wished she'd let out some word to show how she admired him, or whisper to him behind my back, so I could give her a slap and throw her out. I wished he'd show stronger feelings toward her, so I could call him away to the phone, on the pretext of a call, then scold him and threaten him in the kitchen.

But she came and went, and my husband hung up his traveling jacket and put an end to those feelings of mine. He opened his cases and spread out the presents he'd brought, asking about the baby I was expecting as though this one were the first. Then he kissed me passionately. Next day he brought her to mind, saying that we ought to ask after her. The poor woman was having a lot of tests, he said, and her husband was away. I said there was nothing wrong with her, then added my own "poor woman," as if I was afraid of the comfort I was getting from her preoccupation with illness.

The truth is, I'm in a pitiful state too. It's as though she were some kind of duty I had to fulfill. But what exactly? What did I need from her? She wasn't a relative or a friend; I simply knew her the way I knew a lot of other people. It was a straightforward coincidence, the sort that happens a million times here on earth: a man was going to marry one woman, then he married another one instead. What was that to me all these years on? I wished I'd never let her name pass my lips that crazy night when I tried to dig down under his skin to bring out words, and addresses, and colors of clothes, and kinds of perfume, seeking out old laughter behind his smile, searching through his hair for the corner of a café or a casual meeting with a woman.

He was helpful, taking my hand and showing me how to dig further. His admission led me on to paths only this talk of ours had revealed to me. To please me, he told me everything, and I was pleased but so tired too. He was quite frank, talking of times that were dead and gone, but the emotions he aroused in me were exhausting. Something needed to happen to stop this deluge that had been unleashed, which was sweeping away first her, then him, then me too.

She'd come between us. I carried her inside me as I was carrying the baby growing in my belly; I'd let her into my house and into my life. I set her in the glass of my mirror and among the folds of my clothes. I became pregnant with her story, then aborted its contents nightly. Her life was there between us, as a rod against which to measure my own beauty and intelligence and powers of speech. I'm young, I'd think, but she's——. I'm from a good family, but she's——. My breasts, my figure—but hers——. Still she was there between us, between me and myself, between him and me, between her and herself. Something had to give, so all this could stop. She ought to go off to another country, or we ought to leave, or we should quarrel, or I should unearth some betrayal or treachery, or everything should end, in death. But who ought to die? She or I? I couldn't face the thought of death. I was afraid for my children, for my unborn baby, for my husband, who had nothing but me and his projects. My wishes for her death filled me with fear, and my mother's teachings returned to reproach me; but I fought down my fear, wishing she would vanish, vanish just like that, in some odd accident. I wanted to wake up one day, ask after her, and be told, "We don't know." "Where is she?" I'd ask. "We don't know," would be the answer. "Has she been kidnapped?" "We don't know."

I wished she'd vanish, so I could concern myself with the matter for a couple of days, say a few words about her to my husband, then forget about her and have some peace at last. But I never wanted her to have cancer! The thought of her death flared up for a moment, then I grew afraid and buried the thought as alarm bells sounded in my brain. I calmed down, as my husband had wanted me to, and started meeting her again. We went together to visit her, we heard her speaking to her husband over the phone and her peals of laughter. I heard one of my husband's friends, too, say what an important person she was, and how attractive and elegant, and it didn't worry me at all.

I simply had to find a way of calming down, and I found it after I'd spent a night with my husband on a farm belonging to one of his colleagues. What with the orchards, and the moonlight, we were split into a million lovers and wandered through the continents on wings, and I was able to lay her to rest in a remote corner. By dawn I'd reduced my secret feelings about her to dust, as a child crushes an insect to feel his strength. I grew calm and began asking after her. Only now did I realize a whole month had passed since I'd opened my battle with her, with the guns and the rockets, and the alarm bells my mother had set in my head. When her servant told me she was in hospital, I thought she'd gone there for a rest and to attract attention. But now the doctor's told me the news: "It's cancer. There's no possible doubt about it. It's at an advanced stage." She'll suffer, then she'll waste away and die.

I want her to get well. I want her to get well!

—*Translated by May Jayyusi and Christopher Tingley*

Amin Salih (b. 1950)

Born in Manama, Bahraini novelist and short-story writer Amin Salih studied as far as secondary school but augmented his knowledge of literary forms and techniques by his wide readings. One of the most modernist of the Arabian Peninsula writers of fiction, his experimental work imparts aesthetic pleasure as well as a message of real human significance. He has published several short-story collections to date, among which are *Butterflies* (1972), *Royal Hunt* (1982), and *The Fugitives* (1983). His first novel, *First Song of A. S.,* was published in 1982.

THE BARRICADE

The square is very big, stretching away like a desert. The sun revolves around itself. Time revolves. Shimmering colors revolve like eddies, penetrating temporal space. But there are no distances. The past has become the present and the future seems strange. Al-Hajjaj[1] is on horseback, brandishing his two-edged

---

1. Al-Hajjaj ibn Yusuf al-Thaqafi, the viceroy of Basra during the years 75/694—95/713, who is renowned for having taken oppressive measures to quench all rebellions for the benefit of the Umayyad ruler in Damascus. Al-Hajjaj has become an archetypal figure in present-day Arabic literature, particularly in poetry, as a symbol of oppression and iron-fisted cruelty, a symbol that has been very poignant for contemporary readers as it alludes to present-day oppressive men in power in the Arab world.

sword, then plunging it into the necks of the worshippers. "Men! The ruler has a sword. The man who spills his words before he thinks will have his blood spilt before his body knows it." The name of God affixed to the wall of the silent mosque falls down.

He was sprawled on the ground of the square. Sighs came with difficulty out of his lungs. The particles of sand near his mouth moved slowly as he breathed. A small trickle of blood oozed from the hole plowed into his forehead. It undulated, then was absorbed by the earth, going straight to the veins of thirsty seeds. He raised his head a little, trying to see ... to see anything. But he could see nothing despite his attempt to widen his eyes. He felt he was lost in a world of nightmares, with no doors or windows ... deep and convoluted labyrinths. Screams of terror. The earth itself was shouting. Huge men were trampling children's toys beneath their great feet.

He leaned on his elbows trying to get up, but again he failed. Was he going to stay like that, under the burning disk of the sun? He felt annoyed. He was very surprised when he tried to weep but could not. That day he failed to do many things ... to see, to move, to weep ... even to forget. The fountain of his memories was now actively at work, as if there were no relationship between his mind and the rest of his body. Past events began to float on the surface of the fountain, then flowed away like a little child's quiet dream.

The village slept in the heart of this calm and quietness. The waves of the sea were dancing to the tunes of an approaching dawn. The palm fronds were swaying with the touches of the violet sunrise, birds were chirping and the cocks were accompanying the village's *muezzin* in welcoming a new day.

Within this universal symphony played by nature, a woman of over thirty wakes up. Her face is worn with fatigue and weariness. She enters a small, humble room and stands opposite an old, worn-out bed; the yellow cotton stuffing shows through the many tears in the mattress. She picks up a book lying near the pillow. Before she whispers even one word, he has opened his eyes. *(He rested his head on the ground. He felt a sharp pain biting at his neck. It was a blow from a thick cane. He stretched out his lips and, with difficulty, he kissed the earth that had mingled with his blood. He whispered in a low, hoarse voice, "Mother!")* Her dark face shone in his eyes. A smile was dancing on her loving lips. She stretched out her thin hand and played with the hair that had fallen over his forehead. He had half an hour before the bus that would take him to his secondary school in the city.

He sat behind his desk, watching the smoke from the teacher's cigarette; it drifted out in the shape of empty, rounded words.

And so it appears clear to us on reading the oratory of al-Hajjaj ibn Yusuf in Basra that he had a strong personality, great willpower, and determination. "If I should order one of you to leave the mosque through one particular gate and he left through another, I should strike off his neck." This is the true and genuine relationship that should—and we must underline *should* here—exist between a ruler and his subjects.

He wished he could get up and hang those rounded words.

At noon, as he was returning home, his eyes were fixed on an invisible thread stretching to the driver's head. His father had worked as a tenant farmer for a long time in the orchards near his village, all surrounded by high stone walls. He dug the earth with his mattock and ploughed it with his fingernails. And when the fruit was ripe, the owner's spoiled sons climbed the tall palm trees and scattered it. They played with it. His was a laborious task with a pittance as wages, and there were many school expenses. Because of this his father had left the land and worked for the oil company. And now the teacher was talking about the genuine relationship between the peasant who rolled in the mud, where worms and snakes bit at his bones, and the owner of thousands of acres with their palm trees and birds and stones and herds and people. Authenticity is lost, driver, and the white hairs of your head are a witness to that. He felt tired, so he turned his eyes toward the sun that shone through the bus window. He saw that it was sad, or this is what he imagined. The palm trees were sad, too, and the cow seemed to him crucified and sad. He pushed the door and found his father squatting on the mat chewing hard at his food; his mother was standing there trying to check the flow of tears that was gushing from her sad eyes. *(You pained my heart, Father!)* It was not customary for his father to eat lunch at home; he worked at the company until evening. That was where he had lunch.

"Father, what's happened?"

His father poured some water into his parched mouth.

"The company doesn't want us."

"Why?"

"I don't know.

He remembered another scene. When he was a little boy, he climbed the wall of the adjoining orchard and was terrified when he saw the owner pointing a gun at a white dove that was pecking at some seeds near the fountain. The owner killed it with a shot that tore at his ears. Ah, Father! *(The particles of earth mixed with blood stuck to the side of his face. He crawled a little under the sun's rays, but could go no further. He sighed, then rested his face against the ground . . .)*

"Our hopes depend on you, my son."

So his father told him, sitting him down next to him. They talked about the future. His father would work on the neighboring land as a laborer, until the son finished his education and got a suitable job. They agreed on that. Sorrow was their witness.

The company fired thirty workers.

Silence became a crime.

"Every minute of silence adds another number to the list."

"Thirty-one, thirty-two."

"My father will have to wait a very long time before he finds work."

"I am afraid that the infant will die when the mother's milk dries up, and the cow will find nothing to eat but dung."

"What are we to do, Ustadh?"

The teacher adjusted his glasses with his forefinger.

"They have this world and you have the other."

"Has the one who is standing the right to kill the one who is sitting if the latter is unable to stand up?"

The teacher shook his head foolishly without understanding anything.

"And if the one who is sitting can stand up but never had the opportunity to do so?"

The wall of silence had cracked. The teacher fell to the floor, his strength exhausted. The crowd went out. In the square the dust and anger rose high. Bodies clung together and voices merged. Feet dug holes in the earth. The long-suppressed sparkle burst forth. Rejecting voices came to a climax of protest against their long silence. The crowds coalesced and began calling out, screaming, rejecting, drowning in a sea of anger. In the sky a black cloud appeared and began to turn and turn until it occupied the whole of the heavens. And suddenly a red arrow split these clouds. It plunged violently into the breast of a fledgling trying to make its first flight.

The veins in the men's necks were twitching. Anger and fury were drawn on their cracked foreheads. Women began running with the men. Weeping and screaming almost rent the women's cloaks just as they had rent their chests. Two words, "My son!" were all that came from their anguished lips.

People poured forth like logs of wood driven by a torrent, necks craned forward to see what was going on in the square, but the high barricade blocked their view. Their glances were lowered and stinging tears oozed from their eyelids. (*He felt great thirst. All the springs were dry and his throat was parched. He burrowed in the earth with his nails and dug a little hole. His body trembled as he imagined the hole growing to become a grave.*)

In the great square horses, helmets, and thick canes were ignorantly and foolishly demonstrating their power. Screams of terror clashed with the neighing of horses. Al-Hajjaj was shouting at the top of his voice, "Do not let anyone go out of the other gate!" He fell—he—after receiving violent blows on his neck and forehead and knee. Dust filled his eyes and nose and mouth.

No one can get up. He began to crawl toward the barricade. His fingers climbed the wall. He could not stand; he remained kneeling, his eyes closed. After a little while he felt cruel hands lift him from the ground and carry him. Two hard hands carrying his powerless legs. He opened his eyes after a great deal of effort. A steel helmet was in front of his eyes and stopped any question in them. There were two men wearing khaki uniforms carrying him away. He let his head fall against his shoulder. He was now outside the square. Men and women were gazing at him distractedly. They were unaware of anything that was happening around them, in front of them, or above them. A woman carrying a child was hiding it under her cloak and whispering in a trembling voice, "The young man . . . My God! . . . They've killed him!"

His body shook violently, then clashed against a metal surface. He sighed as he felt the blood flowing from his wound on to the iron surface. He heard the sound of a car engine. The car was off on its rugged way, leaving behind it silent prayers that climbed the mountains and the clouds, to arrive at a particular spot . . . in the sky.

—*Translated by May Jayyusi and Dick Davies*

Salima Salih (1942)

Iraqi essayist, fiction writer, and painter Salima Salih was born in Musol, studied law at the University of Baghdad, and between 1967 and 1970 concentrated on art, studying music and painting at the Institute of Fine Arts in Baghdad. She emigrated with her husband, poet Salih al-'Azzawi, to Germany where she studied journalism at Leipzig University before obtaining a Ph.D. in journalism. The couple has been living in Berlin since 1983. Other than creative writing, she has worked as the editor of several journals and newspapers and has also translated works from German into Arabic. Her first collection of short stories, *In the Wake of Life* (1961), was followed by *Because You are a Human Being* (1963), *Metamorphosis* (1975), and *The Tree of Forgiveness* (1996). Her novel, *The Revival,* appeared in 1974.

THE BARRIER

"It doesn't look as if the weather's going to pick up today," I said.

"No," he said. "This low pressure will be here for a couple of days yet. Then it'll move east. It'll probably go on raining tomorrow, then the weather will gradually clear. But we won't see any proper sun before Wednesday."

I was surprised he could talk about the weather in such detail. We'd been friends for twenty years almost, and we'd never talked about the weather—I'd only commented on it now because I couldn't find anything else to say. We'd found plenty of things to talk about in the past, but never that. I would have expected him to talk about anything else. To begin, for instance, with some statement such as, "I'm back. You can stop worrying." To which I'd reply, "Yes, right." Then he'd start, without any prompting from me, to tell me about all the things that had happened over the past three weeks he'd spent in one of the secret prisons. But he didn't. He just talked to me about the weather, the way a meteorologist would. It surprised me more than his visit, which, after all, I'd been expecting.

He'd opened the door and come in, and I'd got up from my desk and taken a few steps forward to welcome him. We'd embraced, then I'd gone back to my desk while he sat down in a chair alongside. It wasn't ten o'clock yet. I'd been surprised to see him come and interrupt the flow of my work, even though I should have known he might turn up at any moment.

"They're going to release him tomorrow," someone had whispered to me in a café, two days before. "They broke his glasses during the interrogation. He must have told them what they wanted to know. They never release anyone as quickly as that unless he's shown he's ready to cooperate. When they broke his glasses, they broke his resistance too. I know him. He could have taken a beating or any sort of torture, but without his glasses he was lost."

I hadn't asked the man where he got his information from. You never asked questions like that. You could believe what you were told or not, but you didn't ask where it came from. Even if you did, all you'd be told was, "Why should you care where it came from? I'm telling you. Don't you believe me?" Friends in the café would exchange information like that and rarely doubt it.

What had surprised me was to see Tawfiq come into my office alone. I might have expected a friend to come in first, to announce his arrival—tell me, say, that he was there in the next room, so I could get straight up and go and see him. Or else some friend might have come in and said, "Guess who's here," then stepped aside to let Tawfiq come in. None of this had happened. Tawfiq had opened the door exactly as he might have done three weeks before, without a word of the time he'd spent in prison.

Everyone knew how it had started. He'd been in the café with his friends when two secret police came and took him away. No one asked what he might have done or what he was accused of. There was never any point, because imprisonment could happen for no reason at all or for reasons the person himself wasn't aware of. These things came like fate. No one knew when they'd happen or who the victim would be.

"How are you feeling?" I asked Tawfiq.

"Fine," he said. "And you?"

"I'm fine too."

I called the caretaker, asking Tawfiq if he'd like tea or coffee.

"Tea, of course."

I smiled.

"Of course."

My pointless question had landed me in an embarrassing fix. I knew, after all, that Tawfiq never drank coffee. We met every day in the café and took our regular walks together through the city streets and around the bookstores. We'd eat our meals at a cheap restaurant, talking on till midnight about politics and literature. Toward the end of the month we'd share our money and search for someone to lend us some more. And here I was asking him whether he'd prefer tea or coffee, the way you'd ask a stranger.

I tried to end the silence that was becoming more stubborn by the minute.

"Tell me," I said.

"Tell you what?"

"Anything."

I looked at his face, then focused on his glasses. They didn't seem new. It was the same old pair he'd always had. Of course they might just have broken the glass parts. Tawfiq saw my questioning gaze but didn't know what was going on inside my head. He smiled, and I smiled back, searching for some new thing to say. But I couldn't banish the question from my mind: "Is he working for them now?"

—Translated by May Jayyusi and Christopher Tingley

Tayyib Salih (b. 1929)

Sudanese novelist and short-story writer Tayyib Salih studied at the universities of Khartoum and Exeter, England, and worked for many years as head of the Arab Drama Section at the British Broadcasting Corporation. In the 1970s he went to work as Director-General of Information in Qatar, then accepted a post at UNESCO. He now lives in London. Although by no means a prolific writer, he has won a formidable pan-Arab reputation for the technical brilliance of his work, especially for his novel *Season of Migration to the North*, which describes a rather violent encounter of East and West and was translated with great success into English by Denys Johnson-Davies (1969). Throughout his work, the fictional village of Wud Hamid appears as the recurrent setting for his themes, and he is deeply involved in exploring traditional Sudanese values in the face of modern progress and change. His novella, *Wedding of Zein* (1967), translated into English by Johnson-Davies and the author, has been made into a film. His third novel, *Bandarashah*, was published in 1967. His first collection of short stories, *The Doom Palm of Wud Hamid*, was published in 1960.

THE CYPRIOT MAN

Nicosia in July was as though Khartoum had been transplanted to Damascus. The streets, as laid out by the British, were broad, the desert was that of Khartoum, but there was that struggle between the east and west winds that I remember in Damascus.

It was British from head to toe, despite all that blood that had been spilt. I was surprised for I had expected a town of Greek character. The man, though, did not give me time to pursue my thought to its conclusion but came and sat himself beside me at the edge of the swimming pool. He made a slight gesture with his head, and they brought him a cup of coffee.

"Tourist?" he said.

"Yes."

He made a noise the import of which I did not follow—it was as though he were saying that the likes of me didn't deserve to be a tourist in Nicosia or that Nicosia didn't deserve to have the likes of me being a tourist in it.

I turned my attention from him so as to examine a woman with a face like that of one of Raphael's angels and a body like that of Gauguin's women. Was she the wife or the other woman? Again he cut through the thread of my thoughts, "Where are you from?"

"The Sudan."

"What do you do?"

"I'm in government service."

I laughed, for in fact I didn't work for the government; anyway, governments have broad shoulders.

"I don't work," he said. "I own a factory."

"Really?"

"For making women's clothes."

"How lovely."

"I've made a lot of money. I worked like a black. I made a fortune. I don't work any longer—I spend all my time in bed."

"Sleeping?"

"You must be joking. What does a man do in bed?"

"Don't you get tired?"

"You're joking. Look at me—what age do you think I am?"

Sometimes fifty, sometimes seventy, but I didn't want to encourage him.

"Seventy," I said to him.

This did not upset him as I had presumed. He gave a resounding laugh and said, "Seventy-five in actual fact, but no one takes me for more than fifty. Go on, be truthful."

"All right, fifty."

"Why do you think it is?"

"Because you take exercise."

"Yes, in bed, I bash away—white and black, red and yellow: all colors. Europeans, Blacks, Indians, Arabs, Jewesses, Moslems, Christians, Buddhists: all religions."

"You're a liberal-minded man."

"Yes, in bed."

"And outside."

"I hate Jews."

"Why do you hate Jews?"

"Just so. Also they play with skill."

"What?"

"The game of death. They've been at it for centuries."

"Why does that make you angry?"

"Because I . . . because I . . . it's of no consequence."

"Are they not defeated?"

"They all give up in the end."

"And their women?"

"There's no one better than them in bed. The greater your hatred for them, the greater your enjoyment with their women. They are my chosen people."

"And the Blacks of America?"

"My relationship with them has not reached the stage of hatred. I must pay them more attention."

"And the Arabs?"

"They provoke laughter or pity. They give up easily, these days anyway. Playing with them is not enjoyable because it's one-sided."

I thought: "If only they had accepted Cyprus; if only Balfour had promised them it."

The Cypriot man gave his resounding laugh and said, "Women prolong one's life. A man must appear to be at least twenty years younger than he is. That's what being smart is."

"Do you fool death?"

"What is death? Someone you meet by chance, who sits with you as we are sitting now, who talks freely with you, perhaps about the weather or women or shares on the stock market. Then he politely sees you to the door. He opens the door and signs for you to go out. After that you don't know."

A gray cloud stayed overhead for a while, but at that moment I did not know that the divining arrows had been cast and that the Cypriot man was playing a hazardous game with me.

The wave of laughter broadened out and enfolded me. They were a sweet family that I had come to like since sitting down: the father with his good-natured face and the mother with her English voice that was like an Elizabethan air played on the strings of an ancient lyre, and four daughters, the eldest of whom was not more than twelve, who would go in and out of the pool, laughing and teasing their parents. They would smile at me and broaden the compass of their happiness till it included me. There came a moment when I saw on the father's face that he was about to invite me to join them; it was at that moment that the Cypriot man descended upon me. The eldest girl got up and stepped gracefully toward the pool. With the girl having suddenly come to a stop as though some mysterious power had halted her, the Cypriot man said, "This one I'd pay a hundred pounds sterling for."

"What for?" I said to him in alarm.

The Cypriot man made an obscene gesture with his arm.

At that moment the girl fell face down on to the stone and blood poured from her forehead. The good-natured family started up, like frightened birds, and surrounded the girl. I immediately got up from beside the man, feeling for him an overwhelming hatred, and seated myself at a table far away from him. I remembered my own daughters and their mother in Beirut and was angry. I saw the members of the delightful family making their departure sadly, the daughters clinging to their mother, the mother reproaching the father, and I became more angry. Then I quietened down and the things around me quietened down. The clamor died away and there came to me my friend Taher Wad Rawwasi and sat beside me on the bench in front of Sa'id's shop. His face was beaming, full of health and energy.

"Really," I said to him, "why is it that you haven't grown old and weak though you're older than all of them?"

"From when I first became aware of the world," he said, "I've been on the move. I don't remember ever not moving. I work like a horse, and if there's no work to be done I create something to busy myself with. I go to sleep at any old time, early or late, and wake up directly, the *muezzin* says, 'God is great, God is great' for the dawn prayer."

"But you don't pray?"

"I say the *shahada*[1] and ask God's forgiveness after the *muezzin* has finished giving the call to prayers, and my heart finds assurance that the world is going along as it always has. I take a nap for half an hour or so. The odd thing is that a nap after the call to prayers is for me equal to a whole night's sleep. After that I wake up as though I've been woken by an alarm clock. I make the tea and wake Fatima up. She performs the dawn prayer. We drink tea. I go down to meet the sun on the Nile's surface and say to God's morning Hello and Welcome. However long I'm away I come back to find the breakfast ready. We sit down to it, Fatima and I and any of God's servants that destiny brings to us. For more than fifty years it's been like this."

One day I'll ask Taher Wad Rawwasi about the story of his marriage to Fatima bint Jabr ad-Dar, one of Mahjoub's four sisters. His loyalty was not to himself but to Mahjoub, and he used to make fun both of himself and of the world. Would he become a hero? It was clear that if it really came to it, he would sacrifice himself for Mahjoub. Should I ask him now? However, off his own bat, he uttered a short phrase compounded of the fabric of his whole life, "Fatima bint Jabr ad-Dar—what a girl!"

"And Mahjoub?"

Taher Wad Rawwasi gave a laugh that had the flavor of those bygone days; it indicated the extent of his love for Mahjoub. Even mentioning his name would fill him with happiness, as though the presence of Mahjoub on the face of the earth made it less hostile, better, in Taher Wad Rawwasi's view. He laughed and said, laughing:

"Mahjoub's something else; Mahjoub's made of a different clay."

Then he fell silent, and it was clear to me that he didn't, at that time, wish to say any more on that particular subject. After a time I asked him, "Abdul Hafeez said you'd never in your whole life entered a mosque. Is that so?"

"Just once I entered a mosque."

"Why? What for?"

"Only the once. It was one winter, in Touba or Amsheer,[2] God knows best."

"It was in Amsheer," I said to him, "after you'd buried Maryam at night."

"That's right. How did you know?"

---

1. The doctrinal formula in Islam: "There is no God but God and Muhammad is the Messenger of God."

2. Winter months in the Coptic calendar.

"I was there with you."

"Where? I didn't see you that morning, though the whole village had collected on that day in the mosque."

"I was by the window, appearing and disappearing till you said 'And not those who are astray. Amen.'"[3]

"And then?"

"God be praised. Poor Meheimeed was calling out 'Where's the man who was here gone to?'"

"And then?"

Suddenly the dream bird flew away. Wad Rawwasi disappeared, as did Wad Hamid[4] with all its probabilities. Where he had been sitting, I saw the Cypriot man, I heard his voice and my heart contracted. I heard his shouting and the hubbub, the slapping of the water against the sides of the swimming pool, with specters shaped in the form of naked women and naked men and children leaping about and shrieking. The voice was saying, "For this one I'd only pay fifty pounds sterling."

I pressed down on my eyes so as to be more awake. I looked at the goods on offer in the market. It was that woman. She was drinking orange juice at the moment at which the Cypriot man had said what he did. She sputtered and choked; a man leapt to his feet to help her, then a woman; servants and waiters came along, people gathered, and they carried her off unconscious. It was as if a magician had waved his wand and, so it seemed to me, the people instantly vanished; and the darkness too, as though close at hand, awaiting a signal from someone, came down all at once. The Cypriot man and I on our own with the light playing around on the surface of the water. Between the light and the darkness he said to me, "Two American girls arrived this morning from New York. They're very beautiful, very rich. One is eighteen and she's mine; the other's twenty-five and she's for you. They're sisters; they own a villa in Kyrenia. I've got a car. The adventure won't cost you a thing. Come along. They'll be really taken by your color."

The darkness and the light were wrestling around the swimming pool, while it was as if the voice of the Cypriot man were supplying the armies of darkness with weapons. Thus I wanted to say to him all right, I'll come, but another sound issued from my throat involuntarily, and I said to him, as I followed the war taking place on the water's surface, "No, thank you. I didn't come to Nicosia in search of that. I came to have a quiet talk with my friend Taher Wad Rawwasi because he refused to visit me in London and I failed to meet him in Beirut."

Then I turned to him—and what a ghastly sight met my eyes. Was I imagining things, or dreaming, or mad? I ran, ran to take refuge with the crowd in the hotel bar. I asked for something to drink; I drank it, without recollecting the taste of it or what it was. I calmed down a little. But the Cypriot man came and

---

3. The final words of *al-Fatiha*, the equivalent in Islam of the Lord's Prayer.
4. The village in which most of the author's novels and short stories are placed.

sat down with me. He had bounded along on crutches. He asked for whisky, a double. He said that he had lost his right leg in the war. What war? One of the wars, what did it matter which one? His wooden leg had been smashed this morning. He had climbed up a mountain. He was waiting for a new leg from London. Sometimes his voice was English, sometimes it had a German accent; at others it seemed French to me; he used American words.

"Are you . . . ?"

"No, I'm not. Some people think I'm Italian, some that I'm Russian; others German . . . Spanish. Once an American tourist asked me whether I was from Basutoland. Just imagine. What's it matter where I'm from? And Your Excellency?"

"Why do you say to me 'Your Excellency'?"

"Because you're a very fine person."

"And what's my importance?"

"You exist today and you won't exist tomorrow—and you won't recur."

"That happens to every person—what's important about that?"

"Not every person is aware of it. You, Excellency, are aware of your position in time and place."

"I don't believe so."

He put down his drink in one gulp and stood up, on two sound legs, unless I was imagining things, or was dreaming or mad, and it was as though he were the Cypriot man. He bowed with very affected politeness, and it was as though his face as I had seen it at the edge of the pool made you sense that life had no value.

"I won't say good-bye," he said, "but au revoir, Excellency."

It was ten o'clock when I went to bed. I did everything possible to bring sleep about, being tired and having swum all day. I tried talking to Taher Wad Rawwasi. I asked him about the story of his marriage to Fatima bint Jabr ad-Dahr. I asked him about his attendance at dawn prayers on that memorable day. I asked him about that singing which was linking the two banks with silken threads, while poor Meheimeed was floundering about in the waves in pursuit of Maryam's phantom, but he did not reply. Music was of no help to me, neither was reading. I could have gone out, gone to a nightclub or for a walk, or I could have sat in the hotel bar. There was nothing I could do. Then the pain began: a slight numbness at the tips of the toes, which gradually began to advance upward until it was as though terrible claws were tearing at my stomach, chest, back, and head: the fires of hell had all at once broken out.

I would lose consciousness then enter into a terrible vortex of pains and fires; the frightful face would show itself to me between unconsciousness and a state of semi-wakefulness, leaping from chair to chair, disappearing and reappearing all over the room. Voices I did not understand came to me from the unknown, faces I did not know, dark and scowling. There was nothing I could do. Though in some manner in a state of consciousness, I was incapable of lifting up the receiver and calling a doctor, or going down to reception in the hotel, or crying out for help. There was a savage and silent war taking place between me and unknown fates. I certainly gained some sort of a victory, for I came to to the sound of four o'clock in the morning striking, with the hotel and the town silent. The pains had gone except for a sensation of exhaustion and overwhelming despair, as though the world, the good and the evil of it, were not worth a gnat's wing. After that I slept. At nine o'clock in the morning the plane taking me to Beirut circled above Nicosia; it looked to me like an ancient cemetery.

On the evening of the following day in Beirut the doorbell rang. It was a woman clad in black carrying a child. She was crying and the first sentence she said was, "I'm Palestinian—my daughter has died."

I stood for a while looking at her, not knowing what to say; however, she entered, sat down and said, "Will you let me rest and feed my child?"

While she was telling me her story, the doorbell rang. I took a telegram and opened it, with the Palestinian woman telling me her formidable misfortune, while I was engrossed in my own.

I crossed seas and deserts, wanting to know before all else when and how he had died. They informed me that he had as usual worked in the garden in his field in the mornings and had done those things he usually did during his day. He had not complained of anything. He had entered his relations' homes, sat with his friends here and there. He'd brought some half-ripe dates and drunk coffee with them. My name had cropped up in his conversation several times. He had been awaiting my arrival impatiently, for I had written to him that I was coming. He supped lightly as usual, performed the evening prayer, then about ten o'clock the harbingers of death had come to him; before the dawn prayer he had departed this world, and when the aeroplane was bearing me from Nicosia to Beirut they had just finished burying him.

At forenoon I stood by his grave, with the Cypriot man sitting at the side of the grave, in his formal guise, listening to me as I gave prayers and supplications. He said to me in a voice that seemed to issue from the earth and the sky, encompassing me from all sides, "You won't see me again in this guise other than at the last moment when I shall open the door to you, bow quietly, and say to you 'After you, Your Excellency.' You will see me in other and various guises. You may encounter me in the form of a beautiful girl, who will come to you and tell you she admires your views and opinions and that she'd like to do an interview with you for some paper or magazine; or in the shape of a president or a ruler who offers you some post that makes your heart lose a beat; or in the form of one of life's pranks that gives you a lot of money without your expending any effort; perhaps in the form of a vast multitude that applauds you for some reason you don't know; or perhaps you'll see me in the form of a girl twenty years younger than you, whom you desire and who'll say to you: 'Let's go to an isolated hut way up in the mountains.' Beware. Your father will not be there on the next occasion to give his life for you. Beware. The term of life is designated, but we take into consideration the skill shown in playing the game. Beware, for you are now ascending toward the mountain peak."

—*Translated by Denys Johnson-Davies*

George Salim (b. 1933)

Syrian novelist and short-story writer George Salim was born in Aleppo and obtained his higher degrees in Arabic literature (1955) and education (1956) from the University of Damascus. He taught Arabic language and literature for many years in Aleppo's high schools before working at the Arab Cultural Center in Aleppo from 1959 to 1963 and then at the Aleppo branch of the Union of Arab Writers. His greatest interest has always been centered on writing, and he has participated faithfully in the literary activity of his country and attended many pan-Arab literary conferences. Salim is regarded as one of the avant-garde writers of the 1960s and 1970s in Syria. His work reflects a probing into the less ordinary aspects of the human condition, as well as an interest in the psychological, existential, and philosophic aspects of experience. His first publication was his novel, *In Exile* (1962), followed by several collections of short stories, among which are *The Destitute* (1965), *The Departure* (1970), *Dialogue of the Deaf* (1973), and *A Solo Playing on the Violin* (1976). He has also published several translated works of fiction and drama and several books of literary criticism, in one of which, *The Adventure of the Novel* (1973), he treats the beginning of the Arabic novel's rise to importance as a literary genre, thus providing a needed background for the study of the novel in Arabic.

REACTIONS

At last I could see it, the bend in the road that I wanted to reach; it was clearly visible now, and in a few steps I'd be there. A feeling of exhilaration overtook me as I started walking toward it. For some reason the road seemed to extend indefinitely, full of zigzags and holes. But all the same I felt sure that my direction would take me to that bend where the roads converge and lead to the forest. All the roads here, in this beautiful summer resort, end at the forest and then lose themselves forever among its ancient, densely canopied trees, which remain untouched by human hand. I saw no one on the road. Everyone was indoors at this hour of the afternoon, windows and doors shut to keep out the sun, despite the coolness of this resort, buffeted by strong winds from every quarter. No, I met no one on this road. It was as if the earth was uninhabited. If I did chance on people, they were doubtless invisible. As I looked into the far distance, I felt a sense of childlike joy, for I knew she'd come down from the top of the slope where she lived and continue walking until we met at this bend of the road; then we'd go into the forest, which seems to stretch out endlessly to the skyline.

For a moment I wondered if she'd change her mind and break our appoint-ment. But I quickly dispensed with this fear, angry that I should have entertained it. I tried to push doubt from my mind, but the nagging fear of being let down continued to disturb me. I recalled how she'd whispered in my ear, "We'll meet tomorrow at the bend," and pointed to it with her finger. I'd been too preoccu-pied with looking at her fingers to look in the direction she indicated, and then my interest had moved to the crystalline lakes of her eyes.

I asked myself "How do you survive throwing yourself into a deep lake if you can't swim?" It's true that I'm unable to swim, but her eyes asserted a predomi-nance that I was powerless to resist.

"If you really love me, then leave everything and follow me," she'd said.

That night I took an axe and tore down the guy-ropes and sockets that kept my tent bound to the ground. I did this in a mood of tranquillity, watching my past catch fire like a burning hayrick as I walked away from it.

When I first became involved with her, loneliness had made her mind bit-ter and twisted. She'd come here to convalesce, and my old sense of alienation gave rise to a sympathy with this innocent, sensitive girl who nurtured a grain of rebellion. I listened to her as I'd never listened to anyone before. It seemed to me that I'd always known her, and I knew she felt the same about me. And when we met in the streets of the resort, time seemed to disappear. Our meet-ings created that sense of calm and reassurance that is given to lovers. A few days before, when she'd laid her head on my shoulder with her hair brushing my arm whenever she made the slightest move, I'd felt as though we were one. We didn't need to speak, we could communicate by an enriching silence. For the first time in my life, I experienced a happiness that is indescribable.

I quickened my pace, for we'd decided to devote the day to exploring the forest and enjoying the savage beauty of nature. We'd walked over the resort together, and in every spot we shared a memory, and at every bend we whis-pered together. How beautiful the world had seemed and still does to my newly awakened eyes. I felt I loved it in its entirety and lived in it like a pip in a fruit. And this girl of mine was the heart of the universe, its throbbing center.

Then I caught sight of her in the distance, walking confidently toward me, and I heard the sound of her footsteps, soft and serene, with the high mountains sending them echoing into the distance. I looked toward the place where she was walking and saw white clouds filling the sky behind her, as if to embrace her and push her gently on.

I was startled suddenly by a car horn. Its abrasive screech seemed out of place in the surrounding quiet. I looked for the source of the sound but couldn't lo-cate it. There was no trace of a car anywhere. It seemed impossible, anyhow, that a car could attempt to penetrate the primordial wilderness.

After a few moments the horn sounded again, persistent and monotonously fierce. The sound disturbed me deeply; it seemed to din into my ears. I looked in all directions but couldn't see the offending car, and in doing so was diverted from watching the girl as she came down the slope, now appearing, now disappearing behind a bend in the road. I tried to follow the contour of the road, but I was again menaced by a horn and looked over my shoulder to see a small car standing just behind me. I quickly moved to let it pass, although the road was in fact wide and I presented no obstacle.

Without warning big black clouds massed in and covered the entire sky. I was still looking at the girl's tall figure as she walked toward me, her face radiating light.

I turned round again, but the car hadn't moved. I shrugged my shoulders, indifferent to its presence, secure in the knowledge that as soon as my girl arrived I'd take her arm and together we'd enter the forest as one being. But to my surprise another car appeared, this time in front of me, and I grew alarmed. I started to run away, but now cars of all different colors and make began to come at me from every direction. Gradually they formed an impenetrable shield, boxing me in and preventing any escape.

At the driver's seat of each of these cars was a man wearing a black mask. I let out a resounding scream, an inhuman shriek like the cry of a wounded, hunted animal. I rushed forward, blinded by fear, unable to find a way out of the trap. The least step I took, I found myself bumping up against hard, sharp iron.

I could see the girl about to reach the bend, and the involuntary movement of my hands was that of someone trying to defend happiness won at great cost and a love that gave life a meaning. But the circle of cars and the surrounding void left me impotent to attract attention. I screamed from the depth of my being, "Get away from me! Let me out!"

The scream became lost in the air, as if it had never been uttered. The darkness had intensified, so that I could see nothing of my immediate surroundings. I screamed again and again, trying to follow the girl's footsteps as she reached the bend in the road. Every second seemed an eternity gaping to swallow me. She was certain to be surprised that I was late, and she'd be hurt by my neglect. I'd promised I'd never cause her pain. I attempted to move my arm to signal to her, but my strength failed me. I fell to the ground with the reek of petrol in my nostrils, tried to get up, but found myself unable to move.

An almost imperceptible spark caught my attention. It grew from a seed to a raging flare, and I saw the red and yellow tongues of a fire catching around me, fanning themselves into a steady roar. "I'm trapped," I shouted, as the fire shook itself into the circular waves of a magic ritual, "I'm trapped!"

All at once there was a concerted blaring of horns that tore at the sky and broke through my frantic shouts.

Before I finally blacked out, I looked up and saw the girl standing there, her head bent, staring at me across the divide of flames. The last thing I saw before I expired was the tears streaming down her face and the sound of her own desperate cries.

—*Translated by May Jayyusi And Jeremy Reed*

Ibrahim Samu'il (1951)

Born in Damascus, Syrian short-story writer Ibrahim Samu'il studied philosophy and sociology at its university then worked as a social expert at the Institute of Delinquent Children in Damascus. His first collection, *Smell of Heavy Footsteps* (1988), drew immediate attention among young avant-garde writers for its unusual freshness and originality. He has also published other collections, among which is *Spaces on Paper* (1999), and has participated in the critical field of the short story in his book *Horizon of Change in the Short Story: Testimonials and Texts* (1990).

THE MEETING

The news jolted her, and she was about to dismiss it as untrue.

"It's just as I told you," he insisted. "The comrades have agreed for you to meet him, and they've asked me to arrange the details with you."

"All right then," she said, "when, and how?"

She was eager for the answer, her paleness gone in the flush of her excitement.

"Tomorrow or the day after, whichever works out better."

"Make it tomorrow," she broke in impatiently.

"Don't get worked up, Salma," he said, in a soothing tone. "He's been away from you for two years. What's the hurry now?"

She smiled mischievously.

"I've been in a hurry for the past two years. I'm always in a hurry. That's the way I am."

"Well, my dear, you can hurry any time you like, except when it comes to arrangements like this. If we're too hasty, it could cost both of you dear."

She gave a deep sigh of annoyance.

"Now you've started lecturing me! Look, tell me, when can I see him, and how?"

He smiled gently and got out a pencil and paper.

"Listen," he said, "if the meeting's tomorrow, it'll be in the evening." He looked at his watch. "About this time."

She nodded in agreement. He drew a circle on the paper.

"Do you know the Mujtahed hospital?" he went on, putting a cross inside the circle. "Directly opposite there's a small alley leading to a square in this side street." He drew a straight line crossing the circle.

"I know it," she whispered anxiously. "Is this the place?"

"No, wait a moment. In this street there are two turnings on the left" (he drew two parallel lines crossing the first line). "Go past the first turning, and right at the entrance of the second you'll see a narrow space with no houses and a big quinine tree toward the back of it (he drew two short straight lines close to one another, and at the end of them he put something that looked like a tree, together with a clearly marked cross). "You'll see him here, just under the tree."

She beamed and rubbed her hands together.

"That's marvelous," she said. "What time?"

He pressed his thumb and first finger together.

"Nine o'clock in the evening. Don't be even a minute late, but don't be early either. Exactly nine o'clock."

She pulled back her long black hair, and her eyelids quivered.

"Right, I'll do that."

He put the pen and paper to one side and twined his fingers together.

"Now listen carefully . . . "

She interrupted him, annoyed and astonished.

"Another lecture!"

"As many lectures as I have to give," he said, surprised in his turn. "Or would you rather get him arrested?"

Her fears had been swept aside by the radiant prospect of meeting him, but now they reappeared for a moment.

"What I meant," she retorted, "was that I understand the dangers from what you said last time." She began to mimic his voice and gestures: "Don't be late. Don't tell anyone. Don't show any nervousness. Keep a close watch on everyone round you. Try to . . ."

He interrupted her.

"That's what I want to stress this time. On the way, pay attention to who's round you. Your house might still be watched after the last search. That's why you should make sure no one's following you or watching you. We've agreed with Abu 'Omar that you should use your handbag to show everything's all right. And talking of 'Omar," he added, "don't take him with you. But take a picture of him, his father's asked for it. The important thing is that if your handbag's on your right shoulder and he has his prayer beads in his right hand, then it's safe for you to meet. If there's any doubt or suspicion, put your handbag on your left shoulder and don't approach him. He'll take the same precautions. O.K.?"

"O.K." she answered. She'd lost her flush now, and her face was becoming pale and slightly worried.

"I'm going now," he said. "Is there anything you need?"

"No, Abu Majed. Thank you."

He took a couple of steps, then turned back.

"Be careful, Salma. They don't know what he looks like at the moment. You're their only lead."

"Don't worry. Give my greetings to the comrades."

As she walked back she slid, suddenly dazed, into a bottomless pit of anxiety.

By the time she arrived home, drowsiness was overtaking her and, after taking a quick look at 'Omar, she threw herself into her bed.

She couldn't sleep, but this didn't, finally, displease her, for pleasant memories and visions of bygone days came alive in her mind. She dwelt on these old events as she lay there on her back—the day they met, the day they'd stood beneath a tree and promised always to stay together, the days when he angrily waited for her and she arrived anxiously.

She turned onto her face to try and sleep, and more memories of past days came back one by one. Their sudden marriage; the shock felt by their families; the day they'd had their first disagreement, and she'd cried and cried, vowing not to stay with him for another minute—and how, as she reached the door and they looked at one another, their surging emotion had flowed over and they'd come together, melting into one another, then quivered and grown finally calm, as love does in a heart wearied by sorrow.

Then she threw off the sheet and lay on her back again, as the memory of that dreadful day leaped before her eyes as though it had happened yesterday—the day they raided the house, looking for him! They'd turned his things upside down. They'd even looked under the mattress, and she remembered how, amid the darkness of fear, a sudden smile had stolen to her lips. Did they really think Majeed might be hiding between the mattress and the springs!

Her eyes were heavy, yet she couldn't close them. She buried her face in the pillow, trying to sleep.

The quinine tree spread its branches from the window of her imagination, and she clung to it and alighted. She saw Majeed coming from the trunk as though newborn, and she held him and sank her head into his breast and wept. He held her tight and she melted into his arms, flowing gently into him, breathing in the smell of pine that came from him; and now there opened up wide blue seas embroidered with loving beads of sunlight. She took him with her in the light of a sun setting behind the distant horizon—a horizon that had at first been bright but was now, little by little, being swallowed up in darkness.

As she shut the door behind her, fearful misgivings engulfed her at the thought of the meeting. She tidied her sky-blue dress and put the strap of her handbag over her right shoulder. She checked the time: it was a quarter to nine.

Stealing cautious looks around her, she crossed into Ibn 'Asaker Street, then turned right and walked straight on. There were plenty of cars but very few pedestrians. She felt as though all eyes were on her. This is how a thief must feel, she thought to herself, he thinks that everyone's watching him. She ignored the pedestrians and headed toward Bab Musalla Square.

Will I really see him, she thought, and will he agree to come back home with me? The walls of the house are longing for him, and so is 'Omar. Oh God, if only they'd let me take the boy with me! She opened her bag, checked that she had the picture of 'Omar, and shut it again. Fifteen minutes! She should have told them fifteen minutes wasn't enough, nowhere near enough! Last time it had been like a dream, then ... Only two meetings in two years!

"Hallo, my sweet!"

She was startled to see a young man standing in front of her, and she stepped aside in fear. Go away, you swine, she thought. She hurried round the square, then looked at her watch: it was seven minutes to nine. She crossed al-Mujtahed Street, onto the pavement opposite the hospital. I'm going to ask him how much longer he'll have to stay in hiding, she thought, and when this nightmare's going to end. They only raided the house and questioned me about him twice, and they never came back. How much longer do we have to go on like this? He and the other men must be exaggerating the danger. Who's going to spend all his time watching him or me?

Yet it seemed to her that she was being watched, for just as she was about to turn into the alley opposite the hospital she looked back and was shocked to find someone walking just behind her. Alarmed, she began to revise her earlier ideas. Could it be she wondered, as she resumed walking. In her mind she tried to go back over her journey. It seemed to her, vaguely, that his shadow had been pursuing her ever since she left the house. She looked back again, and again she saw him, but she was unable to make out his face. Could it be one of them, she thought. An alarmed expression came into her eyes, and she slowed down to see who it was. Or perhaps it's one of those men who follow women and make passes at them.

She slowed down again. He didn't overtake her, but he was keeping just behind her—she knew that from his heavy footsteps, which sounded like the blow of a hammer against her heart. She passed the old shop, her breast heaving, then, before turning into the narrow space, looked back again. He was still there! A helpless shudder tore through her whole body, and she pulled her handbag off her right shoulder and put it over the left. Then she walked to the space where the quinine tree was, dragging her feet along as though they were sinking in deep, sticky mud. I can't stand this silence, she thought. I wish he'd say something, just one word, to show that he's trying to make a pass at me! She saw the tree and was consumed with fear, her body soaked with perspiration, as if in a sudden fever. She felt as though impaled between the footsteps of the silent man behind her and the tree in front of her.

Majeed appeared from behind the tree, holding his prayer beads in his right hand. Her hand suddenly froze over the bag hanging from her left shoulder, and her feet moved slowly, so slowly, as if in a desperate nightmare. She came closer and saw his puzzled face, now framed by a beard, fearfully and silently questioning. Her eyes leapt to embrace him, then, as she passed him, she closed them. Her heart groaned within her, and she felt as though the heavy footsteps behind her were trampling out her life. She hurried on a little way, then moved toward the High Street and crossed it to reach the hospital. She spoke briefly to the receptionist, went in, walked around it twice and came out again. She looked behind her and around her, but couldn't see the man she feared. She rushed across the street to the road opposite and was almost run over by a speeding car, which stopped with a scream of brakes. She ran on, pursued by the driver's curses. "You slut!" he shouted. "Your customer won't run away!"

With her bag in her right hand, she flew back toward the narrow space and ran into it. The whole place was enveloped in darkness. She trembled with fear and, looking round, found only a ghostly silence. She looked round again and heard nothing but hollow emptiness.

She strained her eyes to look toward the back of the space and saw the great quinine tree standing there totally dumb, waiting for no one and with no one coming from behind it, its thick, intertwined branches disappearing into the darkness.

She came closer to the tree, then still closer. Then she put her arms round it, holding it next to her pounding heart, and began to circle it. Only the sound of her hands rubbing against the tree disturbed the emptiness of the place and broke its deathly silence.

She stopped as she felt her strength deserting her. She leaned her back against the trunk of the tree and gradually, in a daze, began to sink beneath the handbag that still hung from her right shoulder.

—*Translated by Salwa Jabsheh and Christopher Tingley*

Mahdi 'Issa Saqr (b. 1927)

Iraqi short-story writer Mahdi 'Issa Saqr was born in Basra. His work portrays an intimate knowledge of the southern Iraqi countryside and all the problems that face ordinary people as they struggle for subsistence and even sometimes survival in the face of the odds of Iraqi life before and after the revolution of 1958 that abolished the monarchy and established a republic. Saqr rose to fame in the 1950s as one of Iraq's most active writers of fiction. He has great talent for the description of minute details of experience and often resorts to the spoken Iraqi dialect to give greater reality to his work, writing in a powerful style with fluidity and punch. His short-story collections include *Good-Hearted Criminals* (1954), *The City's Anger* (1960), and *A Winter Without Rain* (2000); and his novels include *The Tombstone and the Negro* (1988), *The Other Shore* (1998), and *Eastern Winds . . . Western Winds* (1998).

FRESH BLOOD

Women's bodies were crushed in that weltering sea of people, and one could hear small children screaming, panting for air among those rough, strident feet, while thousands of voices were enthusiastically caught up in the chanting of elegies. Voices merged with each other and with the discordant noises coming from the far end of the city, with the ringing of bells attached to banners that fluttered above the throngs, the sound of palms falling harshly on the bare, bloodied chests of men,[1] the screaming of women and children; and from everywhere came the foul odor of sweat emanating from bodies that in turn commingled with the smoke drifting from large torches that fronted the procession. All of these contributing factors combined to come together on that big day, in *Karbala'*,[2] and separate it from other cities, other regions, indeed the whole world.

Qanbar 'Ali was a mere drop in that tumultuous sea. Whenever he tried to stand upright, he'd find himself walking despite himself, his feet not even moving as the current sustained him but pushed forward by the volume of people behind him, and upheld by those in front of him. He was crying emotionally, even without understanding what the crowd was chanting,[3] his tearful eyes fixed on his feet and the thousands of others, entangled together, tripping, hurrying. It was as if he were searching for something: something dear to him that had been lost five years before amongst this same remorseless march of feet. Every time Qanbar 'Ali visited the holy city, he would feel the old pain reassert itself. Nothing had changed: there were the same packed crowds, the forest of bare arms that rose and fell, the usual suffocating air that enveloped the city, that wailing that hadn't altered with the centuries, the same torches, bloodied chests, turbans, banners, women, children, and feet, millions of feet. Nothing had changed!

It was because of this that Quanbar 'Ali was anxious to attend the big day. Hidden within him was the desire to rediscover the sensation of violent pain, that same excruciating pain he had felt at the moment of the accident. Subsequent to this, he would return restored and tranquil to his native village in the north of Iran, there to pursue his uneventful life, until the recurrence of the festival. It was then that a new blood would fire his veins, tempered by a delicious feeling of melancholy, as he anticipated the jet of emotion that would suffuse every cell in his body as he became immersed in the dusty whirlpool of the crowd. In order to attend the occasion, Qanbar 'Ali, like millions of other Muslims living throughout the world, would find ways of financing the journey

---

1. Shi'a men, mourning the martyrdom of al-Husain ibn Ali (see note 2), beat their bare chests and backs until they are bloodied.

2. The holy city of Karbala', situated to the west and slightly south of Baghdad, was the site of one of the most momentous battles in Islam. The army of Yazid ibn Mu'awiya wreaked havoc on the much smaller fighting group of al-Hussein who claimed the Caliphate; then, taken by the Umayyads. Al-Hussein, his brother Abbas and his son Ali were all killed, together with the rest of the steadfast companions of al-Hussein. The battle of Karbala' took place on the tenth of Muharran, the first month of the Islamic calendar, known now as the day of "'Ashura." Al-Hussein's head was carried by the victorious army to Damascus, the capital of the Umayyads, and shown to Yazid I. It is believed by the Shi'as that it was brought back to Karbala' forty days later and buried with al-Hussein's body. This incident is believed to have taken place on the twentieth of Safar (the second month of the Islamic calendar), which is known to the Shi'as as the "Big Day." On this day each year, Shi'as from all parts of southern Iraq, as well as from other Shi'a locations, would come to Karbala' to walk in the mourning processions described in detail in the story. These processions are no longer carried out in present-day Iraq.

3. He is a simple Iranian, and the crowds are chanting in Arabic. More learned Iranians would understand and perhaps participate in the chanting.

by selling some of the contents of his home, or borrowing money, and would first travel south among the crowds of visitors to the holy city, then proceed with caution to cross Shatt al-'Arab,[4] a river likely to become a raging torrent if stirred up by the wind. He would surrender to the tyranny of the smugglers,[5] who in turn would save him from the unscrupulous border guards. He would take his place on board the small boat, together with the other pilgrims, and subject himself to the caprices of wind and water. The passengers would shiver with cold and fear, and their terror would increase if they looked for solace or comfort to the merciless smugglers. A wind would strike up, and the waves would billow into a roaring concourse. They'd feel the ice in their joints and would huddle together, seeking warmth in their camaraderie. They'd pray and entreat the waves to be appeased, even sacrificing valuables to no avail. Then one of the smugglers would shout at them, enjoining silence. They would then quieten down and, paralyzed by despair, fix their eyes on the dark shore in the distance. After what appeared to be a century of suffering, fear, and cold they'd arrive at the other shore, and rough hands would thrust them out of the boat. They'd walk, limping, wading through rivulets, feet deep in mud, cross ominous little bridges, trample through thorns, while all the time the wind whistled desolately through the palm fronds, and dogs would bark furiously, and weed-crawling insects would be crushed beneath their feet. At each step they'd expect to hear a voice calling on them to stop, or to hear a bullet whizz over their heads, or worse, to find the border guards emerging from a dark set of palm trees.

It was there, ten years ago, that one of the smugglers had tried to rape Qanbar's attractive wife. And how he had pleaded with him, cried and begged that animal to relent and leave the poor woman alone! He pleaded with him in the name of religion, invoking the Quran that descended upon the prophet Muhammad, and in the name of the Imam[6] whom they were visiting. His wife also pleaded and, overcome by fear, fainted. The smuggler was delighted when he saw she had lost the power of resistance, and he slapped Qanbar on the face. His friend used this as an opportunity to charge the frightened husband, tie his hands behind his back, and force him to the ground, to facilitate the other's intention of rape, after which he himself would do the same. It was at that critical moment the frontier guards appeared with their rifles from behind the palm trees. Quanbar experienced joy and not fear at their intrusion and surrendered himself to them. Both he and his wife were led off to prison, before being returned to Iran, and denied their visit to the holy city that year.

---

4. The place where the Euphrates and the Tigris rivers meet near the town of al-Qurna, just north of Basra.

5. These are the men who smuggle pious Iranians intent on visiting the holy Shi'a shrines on the "Big Day" to participate in the ceremonies.

6. An *imam* (in lower case) is the *shaikh* who heads the prayers and usually delivers the Friday sermon; every mosque has its *imam*. *Imam* (in upper case) is one of the Shi'a holy leaders, here, al-Husain.

After that terrifying incident, Cawhar refused to accompany her husband on his future visits to the holy city. And when, five years ago, he had suggested taking their son, Jamshid, with him, she protested strongly and would not allow the little boy to accompany his father. But Qanbar insisted on taking the boy with him to visit the holy tombs of the martyrs[7] and to witness the vast crowds lacerating their bare chests until the blood ran from them, in the panoply of banners streaming above the throng, and to see the torches as their bearers swayed with the force of the processions. Jamshid held fast to his father's hand, while the crowd jostled them toward the crossroads. There the violence of the opposing stream buffeted them, so that they were forced to retreat a little but met with an increased pressure. Jamshid began to cry. Qanbar 'Ali looked to the other street and saw a headstrong procession clearly attempting to race the other to the Imam's tomb. A man fell in a confused uproar. Then everything became chaotic. The crowds converged on each other like the wind-driven waves of the Shatt al-'Arab, each man beating the other without any premeditated enmity. The torches were dragged down and fire spread. The earth was stained with blood and the trampling of feet on everything: women, old people, and children. In the resulting panic Jamshid broke free from his father's hand in the middle of the stampede. Then, when the pointless anger of the crowds subsided, the bodies of the dead and wounded were removed from the street, and the unstoppable voices went back to chanting the elegy on the martyred Imam.

And Qanbar carried his child, who had been torn by the feet, and buried him somewhere in the holy city.

From then on Qanbar never failed to attend the big day. For, in that atmosphere which knew no change, he could renew the violent emotions surrounding his son's death. Qanbar 'Ali looked at the closed shops around him and realized that he had strayed a long way from the place where he had been standing without moving his feet, pushed forward by the flood of people pressing toward the golden minarets. And now, as he felt an opposing current gathering its momentum, and saw a huge procession rush on from the other street in the attempt to arrive at the Imam's tomb first, and sensed in the charged atmosphere how hands reached for their weapons, he realized that fresh blood was about to flow!

—*Translated by May Jayyusi and Jeremy Reed*

Salma Matar Sayf [Maryam Abu Shibab] (b. 1961)

Short-story writer from the United Arab Emirates Salma Matar Sayf [Maryam Abu Shibab] was born in 'Ajman. She studied chemistry and geology, but her greatest interest remained in reading literature and in writing. She

---

7. These are the tombs of all the martyrs who fell at Karbala', includeing al-Husain, his brother al-Abbas, his son Ali, and all his men who fought gallantly at his side and fell in action.

has also worked as a journalist. She is one of the most gifted women writers in the Gulf area, reflecting a sophisticated and liberated outlook on women, on their destiny and their tribulations. Her style is vivid and she has a future as a writer with both depth and vigor.

THE HYMN

"If I ever see you with that damned woman again, I'll slaughter you like an animal in the cattle pen," my grandfather said, bearing down on my neck joint heavily with his big thick foot. The more emphatic he became, the harder his foot pressed. Then he stepped away, leaving my body throbbing as if it were one large heart. Lying there, I felt as if I were withering, a desert plant sizzling under the heat of the sun.

Approaching my mother when I had recovered, I looked up into her eyes and asked, "Is he forbidding me because she is a black woman?"

"Your grandfather cannot bear anyone crossing him. He has the heart of a skipper of one of those pearl-diving ships;[1] he coldheartedly buries his dead sailors by tossing them overboard. Ah, I doubt he is capable of feeling any reaction to the pain you suffer under his foot—just don't stir up his hatred for the woman."

I wondered about the reason for his hatred. Ever since Dahma had moved next door to us, I had noticed how distraught he was. He had no appetite and he rarely left the house. I became accustomed to seeing him lying prostrate on his side, with gloom clouding his harsh face. I would always get up several times during the night and hear his cough and smell the smoke from his pipe. It seemed something was bothering Grandfather so much it was making him deathly sick, and this change had definitely come over him with the arrival of our new neighbor. When he discovered I had visited Dahma, he flew into a rage, exploding in front of my mother and throwing me to the floor with such cruelty I couldn't believe I was his own flesh and blood.

I went back to visit Dahma again, urged on by Grandfather's hatred of her. I was completely perplexed about his feelings, as I didn't see anything about her to fear. One might only be afraid of staring too long at her—she was so beautiful. Youthful and firm, with a body formidably built like one of the mythical goddesses invented by Babylonians and Sumerians, she was fascinating in the way that bustling refined cities are fascinating to the repressed. Her palms were incredibly wide and her rocklike head as round as a dove's.

---

1. In the literature of the Gulf area, there are numerous stories about the pearl-diving days, before oil was discovered. Pearl fishing had its own rules and customs, and although most stories and poems express a deep nostalgia for the pre-oil days, there are also quite a few that describe the hardships and greed and tyranny of the ships' skippers.

When I looked closely, I noticed that her brown neck was brutally scarred—it looked as if she'd been severely beaten by someone with no human mercy. During our strange visits she never broke her silence except to communicate with that broad smile she flashed from time to time when she met my wild and fascinated gaze. I was desperate for her to speak. Being in her presence made me feel insatiably thirsty.

"Mother, what *is* Dahma's story?"

When I asked about Dahma, my mother too would start as if I had burned her.

"Mother, I'm going over to Dahma's, and Grandfather can do as he likes with me!"

Taking my hand, she sat me down beside her. She was shivering like someone with a fever.

"This woman has a bad reputation, and . . . "

I went over to Dahma's. Her eyes were haunted by dark shadows like clouds that hang heavily in the sky but shed no rain. I examined her up and down, every aspect of her. Her body did not look like one likely to throw itself down for whoring. I saw it somehow mythically, standing tall like a tree, recreating itself while standing, growing, and being. Oh, I really felt my mother's eyes were missing the truth.

"Mother, what *is* the woman's story?"

Her face turned strangely pale. Swallowing hard, she begged, "Your grandfather will show you no mercy! Give the woman up!"

"Mother, I'll ask Grandfather about her . . . "

Looking at the floor, Mother roared, "The woman that fascinates you so is nothing but a carousing drunkard! Just look at her eyes!"

The next dawn I visited Dahma and stared straight into her eyes. I saw the traces of what my mother had mentioned. Her eyes were bloodshot, but they were not the red lines of alcoholics; to me they looked like the signature etched by fire, or the result of insomnia, or tortuous memory.

"Grandfather, *why* do you forbid me to go to Dahma? Is it because she is black? She is beautiful . . . I have come to love her."

Grandfather gripped my hair, pulling it hard from the scalp. This was how he communicated with me. "You are disobedient and unruly, damn you! I'll pound this head of yours to a pulp! Are you asking about this whore? Ask about her ten bastard sons!"

I waited until it was time for Grandfather to leave for his frequent rendezvous with the men in the village market square, then I rushed next door. I didn't understand what intrigued me so about our neighbor; Grandfather said she had ten bloody bastards, but to me she seemed like a lone woman living in silence. Still, the mystery about her caused him to beat me severely. What astounded me most was how Grandfather grew weak at the mention of her name.

When I entered, I found she was not alone. Sitting beside her was an elderly poet whom I knew well. I often saw him in the streets and alleys and heard his voice at dawn singing with frightening passion as if, out of madness, he were rejecting the world and everything in it, dedicating himself to one thing only— possibly a woman or some obsessive belief. Now, beside her, he was relaxed and peaceful. I thought perhaps this madman explained her secret and I could ask him. But when she drew me near to her, I caught a whiff of a smell emanating from her. She smelled like a palm tree. When I observed her closely, I perceived this was not the right time to talk to her and that asking the poet what he knew about her would not give me any more satisfaction.

She patted me gently without uttering a word.

Back home, I tearfully asked my mother about Dahma again. Mother pulled away from me to seek out Grandfather, but he wasn't home.

"She is a mentally deranged woman who has no sense of things. Her mother was a lunatic who would go out into the streets and into houses naked, refusing to cover herself with even a stitch of clothing . . . people here stoned and beat her." Staring hard at me she added, "Then she was found murdered in one of the ruins."

I noticed my mother's brow furrowed in fear. Turning to me like a wounded animal, she went on, "People here were dying from starvation. The sea brought them nothing but tragedy. Therefore they fell back upon their black slaves.[2] Everyone did that, the poor and the powerful . . . They began selling them for very low prices. Dahma's mother heard that her owner was going to sell her, so she shut herself up in a tent where she remained a long time. Then her anxiety made her go mad."

"But why does Grandfather hate Dahma?"

Mother did not answer. I began to understand the different ways people react when searching for a way to save their own skins by trafficking in other people's bodies and souls. Perhaps Dahma was eternally silent because of her mother: perhaps she was hemmed in by the immorality of the world. Whatever the reason, I felt a hatred toward my grandfather. I became more and more sleepless, twisting and turning the whole night facing a wall that opened wide to reveal the face of the woman clothed in silence, wearing her uneasy smile.

One morning at dawn when Dahma drew me close to greet me, I sniffed the scent of dust wet with dew.

"Don't pester your poor mother," she murmured. " Your grandfather is merciless."

Later, staring at my grandfather, I realized his features could only be described as the features of a cruel skipper who grew powerful by sucking the blood of his sailors. But why was Dahma silent while my grandfather openly declared his hatred for her? Had he realized that I was so attracted to her, he might have stifled the life out of me.

---

2. It was only recently that the slave class in the Gulf area was finally freed. Historically, women slaves were regarded as being the lawful sexual property of their masters. Numerous children of these slaves were born and now live in the Gulf states and Saudi Arabia as free and equal citizens.

Simply, I enjoyed the woman's mysterious presence—she filled me with new ideas with which to view my frightening future. Yet her presence in our alley was causing Grandfather to waste away.

One night there was a full moon. The mad poet tapped on my window with a stick and took me with him next door. Dahma had lit a fire in the middle of her house that she was keeping blazing with sticks of firewood. Her limpid eyes seemed more brilliant than stars over the desert at night, and her movements as she fed the flame were graceful and strong, filled with the peace that follows suffering. They were like a dance in which joy and pain, words and ideas, silence and speaking, are all united. The poet and I sat at a distance. Under the full moon I was overcome with emotion. I had never seen anyone more beautiful, yet my mood was alternately jubilant and depressed.

"Who *is* this woman? Why does my grandfather hate her? Is she a whore?"

"Her mother went mad, and the villagers killed her because she went around naked," replied the poet, patting my leg. "Dahma stayed with her master as an adolescent. Her beauty, as you can see, was enough to topple an upright man, let alone a shameless one. Under cover of darkness he would take himself to her bed, empowered by the fact that he was her legal master and she his slave. The first night, spreading her legs apart, he tied each leg to a bedpost. He repeated the same thing night after night, sobbing with savage delight, until the girl's belly began to swell and his wife realized what was going on. Filled with cruel resentment against Dahma, she ordered the girl to jump down from a height so the fetus would abort; she also beat her on the neck and stomach. But the fetus stayed curled in its place like a letter protected inside its envelope. She finally threw her out."

I looked at Dahma, who was still gracefully bending over and straightening up to feed the fire. I noticed she had a drum in her hand.

"She lived alone in a shelter made of stripped palm fronds. I used to bring her food and in due time she gave birth. Intoxicated with joy, Dahma sang heart-rending hymns as she nursed her son. The day came when she refused to let me bring her food and went out in search of work. One day she returned home from work to find her son's throat slit."

Dahma had begun beating her drum lightly, but now the beat intensified and the fire flared up like red birds vanishing into space.

"After her son's murder I took her under my wing. She was changed: she no longer spoke. Her silence was a terrible silence. One morning she moved her tent into the heart of the village. I didn't realize what was going on until the men of the village, losing their self-control, swarmed around her tent like flies around honey."

Dahma, her face lit by moonbeams and night shadows, was hugging the drum close to the cleavage of her full breasts as she beat upon it. Her head was thrown back like an animal when its jugular vein is being severed.

"Even the wealthy, beside themselves with rapture, lost their reason."

"Does she have ten bloody bas . . .?"

"She would choose the men. If one of them took her to himself, she would cleave to him for days on end till she felt her belly swelling. Then she would shut herself up in her tent avoiding all the men. But the chosen man would still hover around the tent like a dog. When the child was born, the echo of her hymn singing could be heard permeating the houses and alleyways and creeping into the hearts of everyone in the village. The song would continue until she weaned her baby, at which time she would carry him to his father's house. The father would cover the baby's face to hide its resemblance to him, but all the children had skin the color of Dahma's. Then the man would become worse than a rag soaked in water."

Dahma began to sing. Her voice rose in its hymnal cadences like the voice of a woman having labor pains.

"She did this with ten men."

"She has ten sons."

"She has hundreds of songs. She never stops singing while the village silently screams. I heard one of the men tell quite openly the truth of what happened to him with Dahma. He was crying like a child. Dahma was the earth that turned the seed into a tree."

"Why does my grandfather hate her?"

"Your grandfather was one of the men."

Rising to her feet, Dahma sang, and the mad poet sang with her. I approached Dahma with a spinning, swelling sensation throbbing inside me. I clung to her and echoed her hymns.

Later my grandfather beat me, his cruel skipper's heart pounding, and he screamed at the top of his voice, "This child is demented, touched! I'll flog her till I drive this strange spirit out of her! She's touched!"

—Translated by Olive E. Kenny and Naomi Shihab Nye

Mahmoud Shaheen (b. 1947)

Palestinian novelist and short-story writer Mahmoud Shaheen had an unhappy childhood and was taken out of school in the eighth grade by his father and forced to become a shepherd. He had, therefore, no formal education. Three years later he ran away from home and spent the next few years working at various strenuous jobs to earn a living. After 1968 he joined the ranks of the Palestinian resistance and worked for the Palestinian Information Office. He is deeply involved in the traditional and folk music of Palestine and is an accomplished flute player. Shaheen became a painter of original creations in rather strong colors, which turned out to be popular with the foreign visitors of Damascus who look for original artistic material. While his artistic gift was maturing, he also began writing in a surrealistic fashion that involved metaphysical notions—a move away from his early more realistic approach to fiction, which, although highly

creative at times, was still part and parcel of the daily life of the Palestinian community. In addition to his work in fiction and journalism, he has
written a fifteen-hour documentary series on Palestinian life under Israeli
occupation. His two collections of short stories are *The Visitors* (1979) and
Ordeal by Fire (1979). His first novel, *Forbidden Land* was published in 1983
and was followed by *Migration to Hell* (1984), *Crossing Over to the Homeland*
(1985), and *Usurped Land* (1989).

ORDEAL BY FIRE

*According to village law, the village judges resort sometimes to the ordeal by fire when the
accused denies the accusation. They heat the coffee roaster, and he has to lick it. In some
"previously agreed upon" cases, they put a live coal on the tongue of the accused. If it burns
his tongue, then he will be convicted of the crime: if not, his innocence will be declared.*

Hajjeh Safiyyeh raised her hand holding the thread of wool and spun the
spindle on her bare leg. The thread twined and, twisting it round the knob of
the spindle, she said, "Neighbors! Have you heard that they want to put 'Ali al-
Khatib through the ordeal by fire?"

Aisha Musallam was lying on her stomach, with her back bare up to the
shoulders for cupping. She said, "May they burn in hell. By God, I swear by my
orphaned children that 'Ali al-Khatib is as innocent of assaulting Maliha Abu
al-Jadayil's honor as the wolf was of Joseph's blood."

The Tarmuzian woman set fire to a piece of paper, put it in a cupping glass,
and quickly slammed it down on 'Aisha Musallam's back. Holding her collar
band and shaking it,[1] she said, "But then, what was he doing at her place after
midnight as naked as the day he was born?"

'Aisha al-'Allan put the beater through the threads of the loom and, holding
it from both ends, she pressed it several times to distance the threads, then said,
"May God forgive you, woman! Did *you* see him?"

"Maliha said so, and, anyway, people saw him running away carrying the axe
Maliha described, his face all muffled up."

"What would he need an axe for? To cut her up?"

"No, to frighten her so she'll keep quiet."

"The story doesn't make sense to me. A man, after midnight, breaks the
window into a woman's room, as naked as the day he was born, his face masked
and, as if that isn't enough, he's also carrying an axe in his hands. Yet people
don't hear the woman scream except when her husband arrives late from his
job and knocks at the door. Only then does she scream! When her husband
asks, 'What is it, Maliha?' she answers: 'Ali al-Khatib has assaulted me!' 'And

---

1. A gesture used in popular culture in Palestine, which means she is proclaiming her innocence of originating the rumor.

how could you tell when he's masked?' 'I tore the mask off his face.' God! This *is* too much! A man who has to support seven people, who has spent his life harvesting for the Abu Jadayil family, and whose reputation with them has been clean—then comes a day when he assaults their son's wife! I swear by the soul of my father—may you live long—that this whole story is a pack of lies, and if I am wronging Maliha, may the blood freeze in my veins!"

Hajjeh Safiyyeh cast the ball of wool off her arm and dumped the spindle to her side. Her gaze ranged over the women's faces: "I have made the pilgrimage to God's house ... those who have seen Maliha after she has heard that they want to put 'Ali al-Khatib to the ordeal by fire say that her face is black with fear. God has no stones to throw at people, neighbors, and Maliha *is* afraid, afraid that the fire won't burn 'Ali al-Khatib's tongue. She will be in disgrace then, and so will the Abu al-Jadayil family. And 'Ali al-Khatib will return to his children with his head held high."

The Tarmuzian woman placed more cupping glasses on the back of Aisha Musallam. They filled up with smoke and emptied of air, so that the skin was sucked up into them. 'Aisha Musallam was in pain. Without lifting her head but looking from the corners of her eyes, she said, "May God have mercy on us. My arm is stuck under my breast, and the cupping glasses are on my back. I cannot spit in my bosom and shake my collar band, but I say that Maliha is a woman who plays around and God will make her pay for it. He will make the fire as cold as a lump of ice on 'Ali al-Khatib's tongue."

'Aisha al-Allan stopped weaving for a while and said, "May God listen to you, Aisha."

The Tarmuzian woman began pulling the cupping glasses off 'Aisha Musallam's back—*pop, pop, pop* ... Only the fourth glass didn't pop ... 'Aisha Musallam got up, adjusted her clothes, and shook the dust off her gown. The Tarmuzian woman asked, "And suppose the fire remains fire and doesn't become like a lump of ice?"

Aisha al-Allan answered, "Then you may feast. You can buy a load of henna and tint your ... "

Hajjeh Saifiyyeh said, "Have patience with each other, women! Tomorrow, when they light the fire in the shrine of the Prophet Moses, all that is unknown will be revealed."

Aisha Musallam said, "I heard that they don't intend to take him either to the shrine of Moses or to that of the Prophet Shu'aib.[2] They are going to do it in the Square in front of the *mukhtar's* house."

The sun was setting now, and the shepherds were returning to the village. Hajjeh Safiyyeh put away her spinning kit in its canvas bag and said, "Goodbye, neighbors. In the morning everything will be clear. I must go now and get some

---

2. Palestine is full of shrines of old prophets, which are visited by people for guidance and blessings. The shrine of Prophet Shu'aib (identified sometimes with Jethro, the father-in-law of the Prophet Moses) is in the village of Hittin in Galilee.

barley for the goats." 'Aisha al-Allan stretched her warp threads tight and attached them to the beams of the loom, then took the shuttle and started weaving. As the shuttle was thrown between the warp and the weft, a monotonous sound began—*tuck, tuck, tuck, tuck*—accompanied by her secret prayer: "Please God, protect 'Ali al-Khatib and his children."

[2]

O Lord! Give us of your bounty, let us be content with Your will, and satisfied with what satisfies You . . . Keep away from us all evil, by the blessings of all Your saints, of the Ka'aba and of the Holy Books. God, *You* know the truth: Maliha, wife of Khalid Abu al-Jadayil, wants to avenge herself on me . . . O Lord, I ask your forgiveness and turn to You in penitence . . . I told Maliha, "Have pity, Maliha. What do you want of me? I am a man with children who need bread to fill their mouths. I appeal to God against you—keep your evil away from me, woman. One day you expose your breasts to me. Another day you take off your—Forgive me, Lord, forgive me!" "By God Almighty, I shall revenge myself on you, 'Ali al-Khatib . . . " Her words still ring in my ears, ever since that day. "Don't you have any pity, woman? What have I done to you?" "You've done it all, 'Ali!" Well, Lord, You know the truth better. I was scared of her, scared that she'd ruin me one day. I told her brother-in-law, Rizq, I told him, "Rizq, your brother's filly is out of harness." He understood. By God he did, and told his father, but I don't know what came of it. What a man you are, Rizq! The best of friends. He never passed by while I was harvesting his father's crop without saying, "God grant you health, 'Ali, rest you awhile, man; what are you in such a hurry for? The world is here today, and gone tomorrow. Are you anxious that my father's crop will not be harvested? It will be, man. You will die as Hussein Arshud died, while you're harvesting his crop! Take it easy, man, take it easy!" He came to see me last night. I told him, " Rizq, brother, do you believe me?" He said, "I believe you." I said to him, "By God, if I were to enter my own sister's house with bad intentions, I would enter that of your brother's wife." He answered, "You speak truly, 'Ali. You don't have to swear. I believe you, and I feel with you and am worried about you. What are you going to do?" I told him, "I will submit to the ordeal by fire." Rizq began swearing at the ritual and at 'Ayid, the *mukhtar,* who has become a judge of late, arbitrating among people: "The wretch could have made you simply take an oath and have two or three, or even five, vouch for your integrity, and the problem would have been solved. But my father is behind him . . . My father knows something, 'Ali, which he is concealing. Since this has started, he's been acting like someone with a snake in his bosom; he can't sleep at night or during the day." I told him, "Don't worry, Rizq, my faith in God is great, and my confidence is even greater. I shall not be frightened even if they put all the fire in the world on my tongue . . . It is only an instant. It will pass, and the truth will be revealed." He said, "Be sensible, 'Ali, fire is fire, and fire never uncovered the truth. Disappear, 'Ali, disappear, then perhaps my father will accept that you take an oath at the shrine of Moses, an oath that you have never entered the house of my brother's wife, and the problem will end there." I answered, "What, Rizq, disappear and have the accusation stick to me? Do you doubt me, Rizq?" He answered, "Of course not, but to have the accusation confirmed with your tongue intact is better than having it confirmed with your tongue burnt . . . And then where will you get the money to pay the fine and the costs of reconciliation and settlement?" I laid my hand on his knee and said, "Come, Rizq, you suspect that I assaulted your brother's wife, otherwise you wouldn't talk like this." He was silent for a moment. Then he looked at me, and I saw the tears springing to his eyes. He held my arm with both hands and said, "'Ai . . . " I said, "Yes?" He said, "I told you that I believe you, and this means *I believe you*—but fire is still fire, it burns everything that gets in its way. God has nothing to do with it. Do you understand?" Saying this, he went away.

"Fatima!"

"What is it, 'Ali?"

"Are you asleep?"

"No . . . "

"Our prophet, Abraham,[3] when they put him in the fire, God said to the fire: 'O Fire, be cold and peaceful to Abraham.' Didn't this come to pass and nothing happened to our Prophet Abraham?"

"True, 'Ali, but still, I'm afraid."

"Why, Fatima?"

"That was our Prophet Abraham!"

"Why, woman, God forgive you, does He discriminate among His worshippers?" "I don't know, 'Ali. May God punish the evil-doers." She stretched out her hand and fondled the children's heads, and her eyes brimmed with tears.

[3]

Ah, my cousins, my kinsfolk! I said to myself, 'Ali al-Khatib is a stallion with no equal, Maliha! Year follows year, and his wife bears a child . . . *I* have a husband, oh my misfortune! He's good for nothing . . . Ever since he became a sergeant with the State Cavalry, I see him only once every three months. He comes home to me, dragging himself and dangling his balls, his helmet tilted over his eyebrows . . . and he sleeps at my side like a dead man . . . He stays one or two days on his way to the East Bank. All he's good for is to brag about the bedouin woman he mounted in front of him on the saddle of his mare . . ."

---

3. The Muslims believe in most of the Jewish prophets. Abraham is the father of Ismail, who is regarded as the father of the northern Arabs.

I said to myself, there's no one for me but 'Ali al-Khatib . . . One afternoon
he was harvesting alone in the fields . . . I went to him . . . I carried a pot of
tea . . . I saw him harvesting, flinging himself on the crops and singing a harvest song—"My scythe falls swinging through the crops—my strong scythe, I
brought it from Gaza . . . " "God grant you health, 'Ali!" I told him. "And you
too, Maliha! How is it that you come our way today?" "You came to my mind,
'Ali, my soul. I said to myself, 'Ali is reaping alone in the fields, ever since morning; I'll take him some tea to quench his thirst." "Bless your hands for the tea,
Maliha." "And yours, my soul." I looked around me, at the hills, at the valleys, not
a sign of a person around. I wandered among the crops, plucked an ear of barley
and stuck it under my breasts . . . I looked at him. He was lost in thought. I put
my hand on my breast and shouted, "'Ai, help!" "What is it, girl?" "Something
is stinging my breast, 'Ali." "Where?" "Here—ooh, 'Ali!" "Wait, don't move, let
me see, where?" "Here, 'Ali, here." I loosened my collar, and unbuttoned my
shirt, my breasts showed. "I don't see anything, girl." "Under my breasts, 'Ali, my
love." "An ear of barley, an ear of barley, don't be afraid; there it is, just an ear
of barley!" "Only an ear of barley, my soul, my love? I almost froze with fear.
I said, God knows what is in my bosom!" I let myself go, and sprawled among
the crops, my breasts coming out of my shirt, ready to swell . . . 'Ali came and
pulled the ear of barley out and went back to drinking his tea. I returned home
with my sorrow and torment.

I said, try your luck again, girl! After a few days, he was moving the crop
from the fields to the threshing floor. I saw him coming up the road . . . I went
to the threshing floor . . . Even the lobes of my ears were dripping with sweat
from the heat. This time, I placed the ear of barley in my cunt . . . When I put the
ear in the hair down there, my kinsfolk, I felt it swell . . . But I held on. I took
the rake and began raking the hay, feeling the ear of barley swimming around
down there. The pain almost drove me mad. 'Ali al-Khatib arrived: "God grant
you health, Maliha, what are you doing?" "And grant you more health . . . Well,
I found myself with nothing to do and said, I'll go rake up the hay, let the sun
reach it so it won't rot." He took down the bundle from the mule's back and
separated it. I put my hand over the lower part of my belly and screamed, "Help,
'Ali!" "What is it, woman?" I threw myself down on the hay: "Come to me,
my soul, there's something in my clothes." "Where, girl?" "Under my clothes,
my love, under my clothes!" "God is my help! Don't be afraid, it might be an
ear of barley." "No, my precious, it is something that swims. Hurry, save me, for
God's sake!" He lifted my gown a little. I said to him, "Up, 'Ali." He lifted a bit
more. My underclothes showed. I took my hand off my garments and placed
it on the ear of barley over my underclothes. "Here it is—here!" I pulled and
raised the ear of barley: "Here it is in my hand, my precious, it is so big. It could
be a scorpion . . .! Pull them down, 'Ali!" "I beg You for forgiveness, Lord, and
turn to You in penitence." He pulled, while I held the ear of barley in my hand.
"Open your hands. Let me see what it is," he said. I loosened my fingers a bit.
"'Ali, my precious, take care it doesn't jump . . . take hold of it, here, see what it

is!" I opened my fingers while he held my hand in both his own. "It is an ear of barley, didn't I tell you it was an ear of barley?" "Oh, my soul, my love, these ears of barley, they swim, they swim like snakes. This is the second time they have frightened me to death. Oh, my precious!"

He blushed, the sweat dripping off the tip of his nose. He looked at me, and looked. I realized that he was going to bridle the wild stallion stirring in his heart, and bridle it he did, oh, my cousins, my kinsfolk! By God, he did and stood up. The likes of such a man I have never seen! I told him, "I beg you, 'Ali! Don't leave me dying here on the hay . . . I am thirsty, 'Ali, I am thirsty. Slake my thirst, 'Ali, revive my spirit." He told me, "I have children . . . " He said many things that day. He insulted me, and he humiliated me. And I said, "By God, I shall revenge myself on you, 'Ali al-Khatib!"

I went to Hajjeh Safiyyeh. I said, "Hajjeh, here is a restive filly. Have you anything to mount her?" She understood. She said, "Saqr Abu al-Jadayil, your cousin and your husband's cousin. A big thing he has, longer than your stretched palm." "Is it so?" "That's your good fortune." I went home, swift as a bird. Oh, my God, I spat in my bosom and shook my collar band. What! Has she measured it? I remembered then that the *hajjeh* used to set out for Jerusalem when the cock crowed, carrying the bundle of mallow on her back and walking alone . . . According to the women who sell mallow, and chamomile, and thyme, and snails, they used to hear, as they passed by the mound of Um al-'Asafeer at dawn, a lot of cooing and purring from the hollow behind the mound. I couldn't forget, my kinsfolk; the *hajjeh's* words kept ringing in my ears. When my mother-in-law died—may her children live long—and her daughter fainted over her body, I rent my dress to the waist and my breasts were pouting like two young pigeons. I left the funeral room. I pretended I was looking for Rizq to tell him that his sister had fainted. Rizq, bastard that he is, guessed when he saw me. He said to me in formal Arabic, "You wretch, go and sew your dress, or else I shall dispatch you after my mother!" I overheard him murmuring, "Fie on you and your husband who does not satisfy your lust." On my way back I looked among the graves. The place was packed with people . . . Then I saw Saqr. "How are you, cousin?" he asked. "God preserve your youth, why don't you visit us, apple of your cousin's eyes?" "Tonight, God willing." "I'll be waiting." Then I went into the funeral room with the women.

That night when the cock crowed, I heard tapping on the window. I jumped up. "Who is it? Saqr? Oh, my cousin, my soul, come in." He entered. He wrapped me in his arms, and I wrapped him. A ram, my kinsfolk, a ram—a peg like those still dug in the ground since the days the British staked out the land. I said in my heart, "How happy you must have been, Hajjeh Safiyyeh!" He jumped on me and said, "Ride, wife of my cousin!" I rode. "Gallop!" I galloped. "Charge!" I charged, to the right, to the left, forward and backward. "Ah, wife of my cousin!" "Soul of your cousin's wife, my cousin and my husband's cousin!" "Lower your voice!" "Oh, cousin, my throat is parched, glut me, glut me." Ah, my cousins and my kinsfolk, I wish you all good health!

After a few days, before the cock crowed, I heard knocking at the door. I thought, Saqr usually raps on the window, who is this knocking in the night?

I opened. "Who? Father-in-law?" "Yes, follow me!" "Where to, Uncle?" "I'll be waiting for you in the valley, next to our plantations." Woe to you, Maliha! He must have seen Saqr coming to me, or else he must have heard of what I have done with 'Ali al-Khatib! Or he wants me himself . . . I seemed to have glimpsed a rope and a stick in his hand. God, what did he want with the rope, now, after midnight? And what did he want with me? Follow him . . . this is an ominous moment, Maliha.

I followed him, Oh my kinsfolk! It was a dark night—so dark that if I were to put my finger in front of my eyes, I would not see it. Then I got used to the dark . . . I was able to see the road and the figure of my uncle in front of me. I followed him down the valley. Without uttering a single word, he threw me on the sweet clover growing to the side of the crop. The smell of sweet clover assailed my nostrils. I sighed. He lifted my gown. I remained silent. He pulled down my underclothes. I remained silent. He stripped me bare as the day my mother gave birth to me. I remained silent. He folded my legs until my knees touched my shoulders, then tied my hands behind my legs with the rope. My patience ran out. I said, "Oh, my uncle, father of my husband, I beseech you! Have mercy on me! You are the father of men and the very soul of your son's wife and your brother's daughter." He remained silent. He trussed me up like a chicken ready for the grill and grabbed his stick. I knew at that moment that my uncle wanted to torture me. I said to myself, "I would not be Maliha, daughter of your brother, 'Ayyash Abu al-Jadayil, if I did not make you, Uncle Ahmad Abu al-Jadayil, unleash your stallion tonight and let it drink from my pool." He swung his stick, he did . . . I parted my lips in anticipation. "What did you do with 'Ali al-Khatib?" "By the life of my uncle, I did nothing!" He brought down the stick along my thigh. I gasped. "Say what you did!" "I am thirsty, Uncle, I am dying of thirst. I told 'Ali, 'for God's sake, 'Ali, slake my thirst.' But he left me thirsting and went away, Oh soul of your son's wife." "So that's how it was?" He brandished his stick, he did, and held it high. Then he brought it down on me and it began rising and falling. I felt the pain bursting out of the bottom of my skull. I withstood it. I cooed, I sighed. He said, "Your voice, you bitch! Do not expose me!" I said, "I'll expose the whole family rather than expose you, my Uncle, my love." I howled like a fox. I bayed like a wolf. I purred like a cat in February. His head spun, my kinsfolk. His eyelids drooped, and his lips loosened, and he began hovering around my thighs. Then he flung his stick away and lifted his garment.

Such a thing I have never seen, my kinsfolk! An axe's haft, my cousins . . . He made love to me once, twice, three times. He cut his bridle and gulped his fill from my pool.

[4]

The bitch! I got up and left her tied up, howling like a wolf . . . I went back just before the dawn and found her shivering with cold. I said to her, "Have you learned now that God is right?" She begged, "Untie me, Uncle, for pity's sake!" "Do you repent?" "I repent." "From now on, I don't want to hear anything about you." "I promise, Uncle." It took her an hour to be able to stand up. I said to her, "Hurry up, you bitch, before the dawn breaks. Don't ever let me hear anything about you any more." She went home ... For a whole month I didn't see her leave her house. Then suddenly we heard her cries in the middle of the night. We hurried to see what the matter was and, God save us from the Devil, we saw a man as big as a giant fleeing naked, masked, and holding an axe high in his hand. He disappeared in the dark. I went into the house. I found her husband, the ox, just back from his job. "What's up, Maliha?" "'Ali al-Khatib has assaulted me." The story didn't make sense to me. But many people came that night, and it became a scandal. The next day, the family came to consult with me. "It is our honor that's at stake, Uncle Abu 'Ali, what are we going to do?" I said, "Don't speak with any member of the 'Ubaidat family." "But these are not our customs, Uncle, we will not be assuaged except by 'Ali al-Khatib's blood." I said, "Don't do anything, *I* will act." The notables of the Shuqairat family came to buy a truce for the Ubaidat. I accepted the sum of fifty pounds for one month of truce, with no other conditions. We agreed to meet the Ubaidat family in the house of Shaikh Daud, chief of the Uweisat, and to appoint Shaikh 'Ayid, chief of the Za'atra family, to be the judge.

My son—the ox—came to me. He said, "Father, I'm going back to my job. Take care of Maliha." I looked at him and saw him for what he was—an ox with two long horns. I said to myself, "By God, you are not of my stock!" Then aloud to him, "Go, Khalid, my son, go. All the toil and sacrifice and expense I incurred in bringing you up have been in vain. You ask me to take care of Maliha? Why don't you ask *her* to take care of *me*? Be gone, now, be gone."

I went to her at night. I said, "Walk in front of me, you bitch!" I took her to a well in the open country and stripped her of her clothes. I tied a rope round her waist and said, "Now tell me the truth. Who was with you when you screamed?" "By God, it was 'Ali al-Khatib, Uncle." I dangled her in the well, she clung to the rope and started screaming before reaching the water. "Will you tell me?" "By God, it was 'Ali, Uncle, I swear to you by the life of my father and my husband." I lowered her even more. She reached the water. I submerged her in it to the neck, or so I thought when I let down the rope. She started to scream, the echoes resounding in the well. I could not understand what she was saying. I plunged her in and out, in and out. Then I hauled her up a little so I could hear what she was saying. She almost killed me, damn her, she was so heavy. "I beg you, Uncle, pull me out!" I pulled her out. Her teeth were chattering. I let her be for a while. "So, who was it?" "My cousin Saqr." "Saqr Abu al-Jadayil, my nephew? Your cousin and your husband's cousin? Curse you! Oh, you hapless 'Ali al-Khatib! You still haven't forgotten him! Do you realise what you have done? Families and clans are about to slaughter each other because of you—or don't you know?"

I thrashed her with the rope until her skin was striped all over. I made her dress and walked her in front of me, all the time slashing her with the rope until we were near the village.

What am I to do? What *can* I do? If only people hadn't seen the bastard fleeing like an unreined horse, we would have made 'Ali al-Khatib swear an oath, with five of his relatives vouching for him, that he hadn't set foot in the house of my son's wife, and the story would have been forgotten. But what am I to do when people have seen a naked man actually fleeing from my son's house? Is it *possible* for me now merely to accept an oath from 'Ali al-Khatib—even if vouched for by all his relatives—and even in the holy Kaaba itself, and suffer for ever after the taunts of people about the naked man we couldn't identify . . . ?

I sent four lambs to Mukhtar 'Ayid and told him, "Shaikh 'Ayid, all I want from you is to judge fairly and squarely between us and the 'Ubaidat." He caught my meaning in a flash, and said, "By God, man, you'll get justice all right. You want me to put 'Ali al-Khatib to the ordeal by fire so that the truth may be revealed?" I said, "You are a seasoned judge, Mukhtar, I want you to let the embers consume his tongue so that he'll know that other folk's women are not easy prey. After that, Mukhtar, we will not disagree. The hundred pound fine for his entering from the window goes to you, and the hundred pound fine for his exit comes to me." "Come, come, Abu 'Ali, there's no need to mention this. May God forgive you, brother, may God forgive you!"

[5]

In the Square opposite Mukhtar 'Ayid's house, rugs were spread out. Notables of different families began flocking in. The notables of the Shuqairat family arrived, led by Shaikh Ibrahim; they were seated next to Mukhtar 'Ayid in one corner. They were followed by the notables of the Uweisat family, led by Shaikh Daud, and they were seated by him in the opposite corner. Then the greater part of the Sahaiqa family, headed by their eldest, Shaikh Ahmad Abu al-Jadayil, arrived and took their place in the third corner. And lastly, the 'Ubaidat family, led by their chief Muhanna and other elders, with their nail-studded canes and their glittering daggers, arrived to the last man. 'Ali al-Khatib himself walked in the rear with some of his intimates. Mukhtar 'Ayid seated them at the fourth corner of the square. He seated some elders from his own family—it being the host family—among the other clans, and seated himself next to the 'Uweisat family, since it was neutral. As soon as the coffee was served, Mukhtar 'Ayid ordered the coals and the brazier to be brought in. The fire was kindled, and the smoke rose high so that everyone in the village knew that 'Ali al-Khatib's hour had come . . . As she stood by the loom and watched the clouds of smoke rise, 'Aisha al-'Allan said, "God, stand by the side of 'Ali al-Khatib!" 'Aisha Musallam said, "Lord, have mercy on his wife and children. Let the fire be as cold as a lump of ice on his tongue." The Tarmuzian woman said, "Lord, don't punish us with the sins of sinners." As for Hajjeh Safiyyeh, she said, "O Lord! You are beautiful and you cherish love and beauty—protect lovers, O Lord!"

'Ali al-Khatib's wife sat in front of their shack with the children playing around her: "O God, exact your vengeance on the unjust!" Ahmad Abu al-Jadayil's shepherd hugged the white goat, which he used to leave unmilked in the morning so that 'Ali al-Khatib could have its milk with his breakfast while working in the fields, and spoke to it while gazing at the smoke from the opposite mountain: "I swear to God that, should 'Ali come through the fire unscathed, I shall dye your udders with henna, hang bells around your neck, and feed you two pounds of barley a day."

The cake vendor tied his donkey's halter and announced to the children that he would not be selling cakes now. Saqr Abu al-Jadayil had disappeared from the village since morning . . .

The fire blazed. Bit by bit the smoke drifted away, and the lumps of coal started to smolder. 'Ali al-Khatib sat composed: "O Lord, I have entrusted myself to you. You know the truth, O God. Your wisdom is supreme." Maliha locked herself in her room. She threw herself on the floor and began trembling from head to toe, her face drained of color. Ahmad Abu al-Jadayil could not keep still. With every passing minute he would adjust his position, forcibly holding himself in check so as not to reveal the trembling of his hands. Mukhtar 'Ayid, laboring to keep his expression calm, said, "Bear up, Abu 'Ali, the truth will be revealed and everyone will get his due!"

The children, in their tattered rags, hovered around the guests. Women stood at front doors and on rooftops. Rizq clasped his head between his hands, staring at the horizon. Hassan Hamdan, the idiot, sat on a rock and began banging one stone on another.

The smoke finally disappeared. The embers glowed. Mukhtar 'Ayid stood up. He approached the brazier. With tongs in hand, he began turning over the embers. He signaled the elders to bring 'Ali al-Khatib to him.

Composed, head held high, 'Ali stood up, a towering figure. His eyelids did not flicker even once. Shaikh Daud took hold of his right arm, and Shaikh Ibrahim took hold of his left arm, and together they advanced toward the fire. Hamdan Abu Ratta said to himself, "I stake a hundred sheep that you, 'Ali al-Khatib, are innocent." And Yusuf al-Dakhil, also to himself, said, "I stake two hundred acres." Mukhtar 'Ayid raked the embers and with his long tongs chose one as big as a cake. A woman who had come from a distance peered over the children's heads and said, as she saw the ember glowing between the *mukhtar's* tongs, "O you who have no fear of God!" The *mukhtar* banged the tongs against the side of the brazier to shake off the particles of ash clinging to the ember. Then he stood up to face 'Ali al-Khatib. "Put out your tongue!" 'Ali al-Khatib stretched out his tongue as far as he could. A heavy silence fell on the crowd. People's mouths dried up. Mukhtar 'Ayid's hand shook, and Abu al-Jadayil trembled like a feather in the wind. Maliha began screaming in her room. The cake vendor pulled at his donkey's halter, and Hassan Hamdan, the idiot, stopped banging the stones against each other. Mukhtar 'Ayid's wife emerged from her house, remnants of dough sticking between her fingers.

The crowd listened intently, fixing their gaze on the scene and swallowing hard. The mad woman refugee suddenly appeared, sweeping through the village, her hair disheveled, beating her breast with two stones and singing in her mournful voice, "Oh, my sorrow, they packed and departed, leaving me alone." Mukhtar 'Ayid brought down the ember on 'Ali al-Khatib's tongue. The flesh sizzled, eaten away by the fire. 'Ali al-Khatib jumped up in the air, letting out a monstrous scream. He fell to the ground writhing and kicking, clutching his head with his hands.

Ahmad Abu al-Jadayil regained his composure, and Maliha breathed a sigh of relief. Saqr Abu al-Jadayil was seen emerging from a cave in one of the valleys. Shaikh Muhanna declared that his family disowned 'Ali al-Khatib, and pledged in front of the whole crowd that the Sahaiqa family would receive all the monies due to them. He tore off his headband and brought it down on 'Ali al-Khatib's head for having besmirched the honor of the family.

The voice of the singer, Abdu Musa, boomed out from a radio nearby:

"Jordan's sun is shining
High up in the sky."

—*Translated by May Jayyusi and Anthony Thwaite*

Hanan al-Shaykh (b. 1945)

Lebanese novelist and short-story writer from Nabatiya in South Lebanon Hanan al-Shaykh grew up in a traditional Shi'ite environment, which has influenced her work deeply. After studying in Cairo and Beirut, she worked in journalism for a few years, writing mostly on women's issues. Since the Lebanese civil war, she has been living outside Lebanon and has now settled with her family in London. Her first novel, *Suicide of a Dead Man* (1968), was followed by *The Guards of the Devil* (1975) and her acclaimed novel, *The Story of Zahra* (1980), about the life and tribulations of a Shi'ite girl from Southern Lebanon, which appeared in English in 1986. Her novel, *Women of Sand and Myrrh* (1983), reflecting the universal experiences of women anywhere but with the particular characteristics of local Arabs in the Gulf, and depicting the meeting of an expatriate community with native dwellers, was chosen, in its English translation (1983), as one of the fifty best books by *Publishers Weekly*. She has also published two collections of short stories, *The Rose of the Desert* (1983) and *I Sweep the Sun off Rooftops* (1995). Her latest novel to date, *Only in London*, which recreates Arab expatriate life in London and demonstrates the irreconcilable modes of behavior and thinking among this now extensive community, appeared in Arabic in 2001 and in English in 2002. The novel reflects her great sensitivity not only to human nature in its universal phenomena but also in the cultural imprints of society. A delicate line of comparison is drawn here between East and West and between Arab and Arab. Her two experimental plays, *That Afternoon Tea* (1992) and *Paper Husband* (1994), have been performed on the British stage.

THE WOMEN'S SWIMMING POOL

I am in the tent for threading the tobacco, amidst the mounds of tobacco plants and the skewers. Cross-legged, I breathe in the green odor, threading one leaf after another. I find myself dreaming and growing thirsty and dreaming. I open the magazine: I devour the words and surreptitiously gaze at the pictures. I am exasperated at being in the tent, then my exasperation turns to sadness.

Thirsty, I rise to my feet. I hear Abu Ghalib say, "Where are you off to, little lady?" I make my way to my grandmother, saying, "I'm thirsty." I go out. I make my way to the cistern, stumbling in the sandy ground. I see the greenish-blue water. I stretch out my hand to its still surface, hot from the harsh sun. I stretch out my hand and wipe it across my brow and face and neck, across my chest. Before being able to savor its relative coldness, I hear my name and see my grandmother standing in her black dress at the doorway of the tent. Aloud I express the wish that someone else had called to me. We have become like an orange and its navel: my grandmother has welded me so close to her that the village girls no longer dare to make friends with me, perhaps for fear of rupturing this close union.

I returned to the tent, growing thirsty and dreaming, with the sea ever in my mind. What were its waters like? What color would they be now? If only this week would pass in a flash, for I had at last persuaded my grandmother to go down to Beirut and the sea, after my friend Sumayya had sworn that the swimming pool she'd been at had been for women only.

My grandmother sat on the edge of a jagged slab of stone, leaning on my arm. Her hand was hot and rough. She sighed as she chased away a fly.

What is my grandmother gazing at? There was nothing in front of us but the asphalt road, which, despite the sun's rays, gave off no light, and the white marble tombs that stretched along the high mountainside, while the houses of upper Nabatieh looked like deserted Crusader castles, their alleyways empty, their windows of iron. Our house likewise seemed to be groaning in its solitude, shaded by the fig tree. The washing line stirs with the wind above the tomb of my grandfather, the celebrated religious scholar, in the courtyard of the house. What is my grandmother staring at? Or does someone who is waiting not stare?

Turning her face toward me, she said, "Child, what will we do if the bus doesn't come?" Her face, engraved in my mind, seemed overcast, also her half-closed eyes and the blue tattoo mark on her chin. I didn't answer her for fear I'd cry if I talked. This time I averted my gaze from the white tombs; moving my foot away from my grandmother's leg clothed in thick black stockings, I began to walk about, my gaze directed to the other side where lay the extensive fields of green tobacco, towering and gently swaying, their leaves glinting under the sun, leaves that were imprinted on my brain, their marks still showing on my hands.

My gaze reached out behind the thousands of plants, then beyond them, moving away till it arrived at the tent where the tobacco was threaded. I came up close to my grandmother, who was still sitting in her place, still gazing in front of her. As I drew close to her, I heard her give a sigh. A sprinkling of sweat lay on the pouches under her eyes. "Child, what do you want with the sea? Don't you know that the sea puts a spell on people?" I didn't answer her: I was worried that the morning would pass, that noonday would pass, and that I wouldn't see the green bus come to a stop by the stone my grandmother sat on, to take us to the sea, to Beirut. Again I heard my grandmother mumbling. "That devil Sumayya . . ." I pleaded with her to stop, and my thoughts rose up and left the stone upon which my grandmother sat, the rough road, left everything. I went back to my dreams, to the sea.

The sea had always been my obsession, ever since I had seen it for the first time inside a colored ball; with its blue color it was like a magic lantern, wide open, the surface of its water unrippled unless you tilted the piece of glass, with its small shells and white specks like snow. When I first became aware of things, this ball, which I had found in the parlor, was the sole thing that animated and amused me. The more I gazed at it, the cooler I felt its waters to be, and the more they invited me to bathe in them; they knew that I had been born amidst dust and mud and the stench of tobacco.

If only the green bus would come along—and I shifted my bag from one hand to the other. I heard my grandmother wail, "Child, bring up a stone and sit down. Put down the bag and don't worry." My distress increased, and I was no longer able to stop it turning into tears that flowed freely down my face, veiling it from the road. I stretched up to wipe them with my sleeve; in this heat I still had to wear that dress with long sleeves, that head covering over my braids, despite the hot wind that set the tobacco plants and the sparse poplars swaying. Thank God I had resisted her and refused to wear my stockings. I gave a deep sigh as I heard the bus's horn from afar. Fearful and anxious, I shouted at my grandmother as I helped her to her feet, turning round to make sure that my bag was still in my hand and my grandmother's hand in the other. The bus came to a stop and the conductor helped my grandmother on. When I saw myself alongside her and the stone on its own, I tightened my grip on my bag in which lay Sumayya's bathing costume, a sleeveless dress, and my money.

I noticed as the bus slowly made its way along the road that my anxiety was still there, that is was in fact increasing: Why didn't the bus pass by all these trees and fallow land like lightning? Why was it crawling along? My anxiety was still there and increased till it predominated over my other sensations, my nausea and curiosity.

How would we find our way to the sea? Would we see it as soon as we arrived in Beirut? Was it at the other end of it? Would the bus stop in the district of

Zeytouna,[1] at the door of the women's swimming pool? Why, I wondered, was it called Zeytouna?—were there olive trees there? I leaned toward my grandmother and her silent face and long nose that almost met up with her mouth. Thinking that I wanted a piece of cane sugar, she put her hand to her bosom to take out a small twist of cloth. Impatiently I asked her if she was sure that Maryam at-Taweela knew Zeytouna, to which she answered, her mouth sucking at the cane sugar and making a noise with her tongue, "God will look after everything." Then she broke the silence by saying, "All this trouble is that devil Sumayya's fault—it was she who told you she'd seen with her own eyes the swimming pool just for women and not for men." "Yes, Grandma," I answered her. She said, "Swear by your mother's grave." I thought to myself absently: "Why only my mother's grave? What about my father? Or did she only acknowledge her daughter's death . . .?" "By my mother's grave, it's for women." She inclined her head and still munching the cane sugar and making a noise with her tongue, she said, "If any man were to see you, you'd be done for, and so would your mother and father and your grandfather, the religious scholar—and I'd be done for more than anyone because it's I who agreed to this and helped you."

I would have liked to say to her. "They've all gone, they've all died, so what do we have to be afraid of?" But I knew what she meant: that she was frightened they wouldn't go to heaven.

I began to sweat, and my heart again contracted as Beirut came into view with its lofty buildings, car horns, the bared arms of the women, the girls' hair, the tight trousers they were wearing. People were sitting on chairs in the middle of the pavement, eating and drinking; the trams; the roasting chickens revolving on spits. Ah, these dresses for sale in the windows, would anyone be found actually to wear them? I see a Japanese man, the first-ever member of the yellow races outside of books; the Martyrs' monument; Riad Solh Square. I was wringing wet with sweat and my heart pounded—it was as though I regretted having come to Beirut, perhaps because I was accompanied by my grandmother. It was soon all too evident that we were outsiders to the capital. We began walking after my grandmother had asked the bus driver the whereabouts of the district of Khandaq al-Ghamiq[2] where Maryam at-Taweela lived. Once again my body absorbed all the sweat and allowed my heart to flee its cage. I find myself treading on a pavement on which for long years I have dreamed of walking; I hear sounds that have been engraved on my imagination; and everything I see I have seen in daydreams at school or in the tobacco-threading tent. Perhaps I shouldn't say that I was regretting it, for after this I would never forget Beirut. We begin walking and losing our way in a Beirut that never ends, that leads nowhere. We begin asking and walking and losing our way, and my going to the

---

1. An elegant district in West Beirut where there are many embassies, nightclubs, and hotels. *Zeytouna* means an olive.

2. An area in the center of West Beirut where many businesses, including publishing houses, are situated.

sea seems an impossibility; the sea is fleeing from me. My grandmother comes to a stop and leans against a lamppost, or against the litter bin attached to it, and against my shoulders, and puffs and blows. I have the feeling that we shall never find Maryam at al-Taweela's house. A man we had stopped to ask the way walks with us. When we knock at the door and no one opens to us, I become convinced that my bathing in the sea is no longer possible. The sweat pours off me, my throat contracts. A woman's voice brings me back to my senses as I drown in a lake of anxiety, sadness, and fear; then it drowns me once again. It was not Maryam at-Taweela but her neighbor who is asking us to wait at her place. We go down the steps to the neighbor's outdoor stone bench, and my grandmother sits down by the door but gets to her feet again when the woman entreats her to sit in the cane chair. Then she asks to be excused while she finishes washing down the steps. While she is cursing the heat of Beirut in the summer, I notice the tin containers lined up side by side containing red and green peppers. We have a long wait, and I begin to weep inwardly as I stare at the containers.

I wouldn't be seeing the sea today, perhaps not for years, but the thought of its waters would not leave me, would not be erased from my dreams. I must persuade my grandmother to come to Beirut with Sumayya. Perhaps I should not have mentioned the swimming pool in front of her. I wouldn't be seeing the sea today—and once again I sank back into a lake of doubt and fear and sadness. A woman's voice again brought me back to my senses: it was Maryam at-Taweela, who had stretched out her long neck and had kissed me, while she asked my grandmother: 'She's the child of your late daughter, isn't she?'—and she swore by the Imam[3] that we must have lunch with her, doing so before we had protested, feeling perhaps that I would do so. When she stood up and took the primus stove from under her bed and brought out potatoes and tomatoes and bits of meat, I had feelings of nausea, then of frustration. I nudged my grandmother, who leant over and whispered. "What is it, dear?" at which Maryam al-Taweela turned and asked. "What does your granddaughter want—to go to the bathroom?" My mouth went quite dry and my tears were all stored up waiting for a signal from my heartbeats to fall. My grandmother said with embarrassment, "She wants to go to the sea, to the women's swimming pool—that devil Sumayya put it into her head." To my amazement Maryam at-Taweela said loudly. "And why not? Right now Ali Mousa, our neighbor, will be coming and he'll take you, he's got a car"—and Maryam at-Taweela began peeling the potatoes at a low table in the middle of the room and my grandmother asked, "Where's Ali Musa from? Where does he live?"

I can't wait, I shan't eat, I shan't drink. I want to go now, now. I remained seated, crying inwardly because I was born in the South, because there's no escape for me from the South, and I go on rubbing my fingers and gnawing at my

---

3. This is the Imam 'Ali, head of the Shi'a sect. The heroine is, like the author, a Shi'ite Muslim.

nails. Again I begin to sweat: I shan't eat, I shan't drink, I shan't reply to Maryam at-Taweela. It was as though I was taking vengeance on my grandmother for some wrong she did not know about. My patience vanished. I stood up and said to my grandmother before I should burst out sobbing, "Come along, Grandma, get up, and let's go." I helped her to her feet, and Maryam at-Taweela asked in bewilderment what had suddenly come over me. I went on dragging my grandmother out to the street so that I might stop the first taxi.

Only moments passed before the driver shut off his engine and said, "Zeytouna." I looked about me but saw no sea. As I gave him a lira I asked him, "Where's the women's swimming pool?" He shrugged his shoulders. We got out of the car with difficulty, as was always the case with my grandmother. To my astonishment the driver returned, stretching out his head in concern at us. "Jump in," he said, and we got in. He took us round and round, stopping once at a petrol station and then by a newspaper seller, asking about the women's swimming pool and nobody knowing where it was. Once again he dropped us in the middle of Zeytouna Street.

Then, behind the hotels and the beautiful buildings and the date palms, I saw the sea. It was like a blue line of quicksilver: it was as though pieces of silver paper were resting on it. The sea that was in front of me was more beautiful than it had been in the glass ball. I didn't know how to get close to it, how to touch it. Cement lay between us. We began inquiring about the whereabouts of the swimming pool, but no one knew. The sea remains without waves, a blue line. I feel frustrated. Perhaps this swimming pool is some secret known only to the girls of the South. I began asking every person I saw. I tried to choke back my tears; I let go of my grandmother's hand as though wishing to reproach her, to punish her for having insisted on accompanying me instead of Sumayya. Poor me. Poor Grandma. Poor Beirut. Had my dreams come to an end in the middle of the street? I clasp my bag and my grandmother's hand, with the sea in front of me, separating her from me. My stubbornness and vexation impel me to ask and go on asking. I approached a man leaning against a bus, and to my surprise he pointed to an opening between two shops. I hurried back to my grandmother, who was supporting herself against a lamppost, to tell her I'd found it. When I saw with what difficulty she attempted to walk, I asked her to wait for me while I made sure. I went through the opening but didn't see the sea. All I saw was a fat woman with bare shoulders sitting behind a table. Hesitating, I stood and looked at her, not daring to step forward. My enthusiasm had vanished, taking with it my courage. "Yes," said the woman. I came forward and asked her, "Is the women's swimming pool here?" She nodded her head and said, "The entrance fee is a lira." I asked her if it was possible for my grandmother to wait for me here and she stared at me and said, "Of course." There was contempt in the way she looked at me: Was it my southern accent or my long-sleeved dress? I had disregarded my grandmother and had taken off my head shawl and hidden it in my bag. I handed her a lira and could hear the sounds of women and children—and still I did not see the sea. At the end of the portico were steps, which I was certain led to the roofed-in sea. The important thing was that I'd arrived, that I would be tasting the salty spray of its waters. I wouldn't be seeing the waves; never mind, I'd be bathing in its waters.

I found myself saying to the woman, or rather to myself because no sound issued from my throat, "I'll bring my grandmother." Going out through the opening and still clasping my bag to my chest, I saw my grandmother standing and looking up at the sky. I called to her, but she was reciting to herself under her breath as she continued to look upward: she was praying, right there in the street, praying on the pavement at the door of the swimming pool. She had spread out a paper bag and had stretched out her hands to the sky. I walked off in another direction and stopped looking at her. I would have liked to persuade myself that she had nothing to do with me, that I didn't know her. How, though? She's my grandmother whom I've dragged with my entreaties from the tobacco-threading tent, from the jagged slab of stone, from the winds of the South; I have crammed her into the bus and been lost with her in the streets as we searched for Maryam at-Taweela's house. And now here were the two of us standing at the door of the swimming pool, and she, having heard the call to prayers, had prostrated herself in prayer. She was destroying what lay in my bag, blocking the road between me and the sea. I felt sorry for her, for her knees that knelt on the cruelly hard pavement, for her tattooed hands that lay on the dirt. I looked at her again and saw the passers-by staring at her. For the first time her black dress looked shabby to me. I felt how far removed we were from these passers-by, from this street, this city, this sea. I approached her, and she again put her weight on my hand.

—*Translated by Denys Johnson-Davies*

Muhammad al-Sharikh (b. 1937)

A Kuwaiti short-story writer and businessman, Muhammad al-Sharikh has exploited his abundant creativity with ingenious business acumen, creating a vast computer programming enterprise in the service of culture and knowledge. Whenever time permits, however, he writes, often creatively, about social and political experience, and his stories apply not only to Kuwaiti life but also to contemporary Arab life in general. He lives and works in Kuwait.

THE INTERROGATION

He hated the sound of the telephone when it started ringing. He let it ring, then heard the sound of his wife's slippers hurrying towards it. He gave a cold, hard stare at the door.

"Yes," his wife was saying, "he's in. Who is it, please? Just a moment." He heard her slippers coming down the corridor to his study. "Hatem." she said. "Who's Hatem?" He would have liked to say, "I don't want to answer the phone" or, "Why did you say I was in?" But her face and eyes were saying, "What's the matter with you? Why don't you get up and answer the phone?" He got to his feet and dragged himself along, tightening the belt of the dressing gown he was wearing and shaking his head to get rid of the sweat sticking to his shirt.

He picked up the receiver.

"Hello."

"Dr. Ahmad Mansour?"

"Yes, Ahmad Mansour speaking."

"Good morning."

"Good morning."

"I'm sorry to disturb you on a Friday morning, but I've read a copy of your latest lecture at the university, and I'd like to meet you."

"Thank you. They're just the ordinary lectures we give our students. Do you work at the university or have a son or daughter studying with me?"

"Neither, Doctor. I work at the Ministry of the Interior. Your lecture, or rather your last two lectures, reached me last week, and I thought I'd like to meet you if you wouldn't mind."

"By all means. Would you like to drop in at the university? I'll be in the economics faculty at eleven tomorrow."

"In the morning?"

"Yes."

"I'm sorry, I'm busy then. When does your lecture end?"

"Around one."

"Excellent. Would you like to have a cup of tea with me? The police station where I work isn't far from your house. I know that, you realize, because I know your car. It's the blue Chevrolet, isn't it, number 11429L, which nearly collided with the sanitation truck last week? You were coming from Dr. Abdallah's house, weren't you, wearing a yellow shirt?"

"You mean the station in al-Zuhur Street?"

"Yes."

"But it's lunchtime at one o'clock. How about if we met on Sunday?"

"All right then. I'll be at the station at one o'clock on Sunday."

"But that's lunchtime, and my wife ... "

"Doctor, I've been wanting to meet you since last week, I assure you, and I've already postponed our meeting by a day. In any case we won't be keeping you long."

"You mean I have to come and see you?"

"If you would."

"The day after tomorrow?"

"Yes."

"As you wish."

"You haven't asked me my name, Doctor. I'm Lieutenant Hatem, and I'm on the second floor."

"All right."

"We'll meet on Sunday then."

"All right. Good-bye."

The telephone clicked shut, and he replaced the receiver, leaving his hand lying on it heavily, his eyes fixed on the black machine with its white numbers.

"So who is Hatem?" he heard his wife ask.

"He's from the Ministry of the Interior."

She tiptoed up to him, unable to believe her ears.

"The Ministry of the Interior?"

He looked at her and nodded.

"Yes."

She took him by the hand, and they walked silently to the study, where he sat down on the rocking chair and wrapped the dressing gown round his waist. Then he shook his head slightly as he felt the sweat breaking out on his body.

"What do they want?" his wife asked, sitting down opposite him.

He shrugged his shoulders and pursed his lips.

"I don't know, but he talked about my lecture."

She threw him a compassionate look.

"Didn't I tell you?" she said.

He sank his eyes into the elaborate, brightly colored Afghan rug and started thinking about the wording of his lecture and how he was going to answer Hatem on Sunday. There was nothing particularly significant in the lecture— and yet it was all there. How could he explain the theory of distribution without examples? And was he to use examples from America or Belgium or the Comoro Islands? How could the students be expected to understand economic theory unless the examples were taken from their own country? It had also distressed him that he was producing government clerks rather than economists, and now here he was bringing trouble on himself, with his own hand. Could he really have worked as an expert in one of the ministries or departments or banks, turning out reports that, for all their elegance and different colors and graphs and columns on Japan and the Argentine, would have been mere ink on paper? What was the point of studying in that case?

Fear was running through him now: fear of humiliation and the need to answer pointless questions. They wouldn't of course do anything to him—he'd done nothing wrong, after all—but he'd be humiliated; yet if he was going to be afraid of humiliation, why had he, finally, given illustrations of an ideal distribution of wealth within the country? Wouldn't it have been cleverer of him to keep out of trouble? It chilled him, even now, to think of Adnan al-Qassar, who'd killed himself the year before in the entrance hall of the economics faculty. He was twenty-one, and he'd been one of the brightest students, although Dr. Yahya never stopped attacking him, rightly or wrongly, for his article on the relationship between production and distribution on the faculty's wall sheet.

Suddenly his mind was flooded with the image of Adnan, lying sprawled out on the ground with a gun in his hand and teachers and students all round him, in the faculty's entrance hall. It was one o'clock in the afternoon, lunchtime, and students were going home or moving toward the cafeteria. Adnan stopped. "There's no hope for me," he told his fellow-students, "as long as Dr. Yahya's head of the faculty." Then he took a gun out of his briefcase and said, "I'm going to kill myself before he turns me into a clerk." He fired a shot, and the students jumped like startled birds rising together. Adnan smiled, his left leg bent forward. "For all your education," he said, "you'll die as hirelings." Then he fired a second shot into his head and fell straight to the ground with blood pouring from him. May, who loved him, ran forward and sat on the floor, supporting herself on her arms pushed out behind her and cradling his head in her lap. She looked, stunned, at the people standing round her; her breast was proudly high and her ebony black hair disheveled. Without a word or a tear she rocked his head in her lap and looked at us in despair. When the ambulance men arrived and lifted Adnan up, May took hold of Dr. Yahya, whose eyes held a horrified gleam behind his thick glasses, and brought her face close to his, while he strove desperately to avert her gaze. She shook him. "He kissed me yesterday," she said. Then she shook him again, with greater force, her eyes flashing. "He kissed me yesterday!" Adnan had left a note for May: "I was afraid my love for you would stop me killing myself. I'll take yesterday's kiss with me."

Dr. Yahya shook himself free and looked round at the crowd, his hair flying. "Where are the police?" he screamed, panic-stricken. "Has the ambulance gone?"

In the staffroom Dr. Yahya declared that Adnan was demented and that he'd been expecting something to happen to him, because he was a discontented, troublesome, complicated student. He should have been happy, said Dr. Yahya, because he was from the desert and he'd left the dust and the scorching sun and the misery behind him. Here the university had given him lodging and food and clothing, and there'd be a job for him when he graduated. What more could he have wanted?

He learned later that Adnan had been a chaste and cheerful sort of person and had played football, on the left wing. He'd loved poetry and food, and he'd often said that the beef from the cattle of the city of Kobe in Japan, which were specially fattened for their tender meat, was the best.

Ghassan had told him about Adnan. Adnan, he said, would streak down the left wing like a Red Indian arrow and pierce any defense. He'd stand with the ball as steady as a rock, then turn and pass it; he never lost a ball and every pass went to the feet or head of the striker. When the stadium filled with the shout of "Adnan! Adnan!" he'd immediately start singing proudly with the crowd, rather like the Harlem Globetrotters who prance around between passes.

Ghassan was a member of the Wild Cattle, a club founded by Adnan and May, which had a large and surprisingly various membership among students of law, arts, economics and literature. It was a literary club producing wall sheets and posters, and the club's own sticker, designed by the famous artist Nabil Salim, was of a cow's head surrounded, in a high Ottoman script, by the motto "No pride except for those who refuse to suffer injustice." This motif spread like wildfire and could be seen on the notebooks and cases of most of the students. The administration hated the club because of all the things it represented. "Wild cattle?" they said. "Wouldn't 'cattle' have been enough? And cattle don't suffer injustice anyway. What is this crazy fashion? Who's Adnan's father?"

When Adnan published his poem "Wild Cattle," the administration decided to act. Some of the students were to sing it in the law faculty cafeteria, and Ghassan hung it up in his home, written in gold-embossed Kufic script.

It ran as follows:

Oh wretched cattle of Kobe, share my joy; for I am one of the wild
    cattle.
I run like the gazelle. Everywhere I find the scent of flowers.
What beauty lies in my wide, honey-brown eyes! Why are your eyes
    drowned in sadness?
I gaze above me and before me. Why is your head bowed to the floor of
    the stall?
Oh wretched cattle of Kobe! Do you move in a cramped, narrow stall?
My color is light red speckled with white. Why is your color dark and
    gray?
Oh wretched cattle of Kobe, I will not pray for you."

He felt hemmed in, and the folds of his flesh and the smooth roundness of his neck disturbed him. The image of his fat white body, naked in front of the mirror, flashed before him. He felt he'd lost his manhood, despising the fear that he felt. "Why did I bother to study?" he thought.

His wife was watching him, silently and anxiously; she was plump and white-skinned, with a long neck and full lips. He looked at her. He'd loved her the moment he met her, and he'd loved her throughout their thirty years of marriage, in which she'd borne him Imad, Ghassan, and Khaula. She enjoyed philosophy and politics, and they'd graduated in America in the same year. They'd married and gone to live there, and on the way they'd stopped at Rome, where they'd visited all the tourist attractions: the Coliseum, the Tivoli Gardens, the gardens of the Villa d'Este, the Spanish Stairs, the Egyptian Obelisk, the Vatican. They'd listened to Duke Ellington and his jazz band; it all came back to him now, the sound of the trumpet, the man's sense of rhythm and puffed-out cheeks; the whole thing resounded in his ears and surged in his heart like the waves of the sea. They'd watched Aida at the Caracalla and seen the Harlem Globetrotters playing basketball like magicians. Her father had been the Imam at the mosque where he went to pray with his own father. Looks had been exchanged, then came smiles, and finally the tryst, the pledge, and the eventual marriage. When they came back from America, they lived in a furnished apartment provided by the university, and she'd taught in the arts faculty while he'd taught in the faculty of economics. He'd been made a professor seven years before, and all his books had been published. Imad was married with two sons, and Khaula too was married, to the head of a news agency. Ghassan was studying civil engineering, but he also loved the arts and was a friend of Adnan and May and all the other young men and women who dreamed of changing the world after they'd graduated.

His wife was looking at him anxiously.

"Are you afraid?" she whispered.

He turned down his lips.

"What of?"

She felt his fear and brought him a bowl of cold water, so that he could soak his feet in it, as he liked to do. As he sank his feet into it, he went over his lecture word by word in his mind: the first page, the fourth, the eighth, the last paragraph . . . His wife, he noticed, was watching him without saying a word—as she continued to do all that day and the next, directly or covertly, listening for every sound.

All his life he'd avoided both professional prostitution and political disputation. He'd decided to teach economics in a realistic way, which meant that teaching students about national income involved not simply a general theoretical analysis but also a pragmatic analysis of the sources of the country's income, together with the reasons for its growth or underdevelopment. Teaching about market mechanisms laid emphasis on the country's lack of pragmatism in this area in the face of constant government interference. Econometrics was useless, given the lack of relevant data. The study of production led to the theory of the distribution of surplus revenue.

These young people had to learn how short life was. Surely this was their opportunity. Why should they suffer as he had, studying at the best universities, only to be crushed by the brute need to make a living? Were they all to spend their lives trying to find a place to live, a problem that, for no good reason whatever, had now reached crisis proportions? Why wasn't the price of land reduced so that all young people could buy their homes in installments from their salaries? "You're an economist," the Minister of Finance had said to him one day, "why don't you write about the housing problem?" "That's not a matter of economic policy," he'd replied, "it's a political issue." From that day on he'd never been invited for consultation by any of the different ministries or government agencies. His wife's turn had followed. She'd been at a dinner party at a neighbor's house when a pleasant police officer jokingly said, "Didn't Adnan kill himself because of all the things you debate on Tuesdays at your home?" It had never occurred to him that he might have caused someone's death.

After the invasion of Beirut, Adnan and many other young people had come on Tuesdays to discuss some momentous questions, the most important of which was whether the backward state of Arab political philosophy had encouraged the invasion. His wife took a strong scholarly interest in the various opinions on this and in the strange phenomenon of 150 million Arabs keeping silent during the attack. Ghassan plunged himself into the issue body and soul and felt he must demonstrate or write about a matter on which he felt a burning conviction and deep agitation. Young people of Ghassan and Khaula's age would attend the meetings, and afterward his wife would always discuss their views with him. No one was trying to curry favor; one of the young people said to her, "What are you achieving at the university?" Imad and his wife would have liked to found a new theatre, though they realized well enough that this was impossible. Then there was a young Palestinian who kept repeating, "I don't understand." One evening, as they were watching a television film of Israeli soldiers surrounding the camps so as to hand them over to the mercenaries—exactly like those films where heavily armed gangs and vainglorious murderers surround an isolated Mexican village to burn and loot and kill—the Palestinian leaped up from his chair with wild, appalled eyes, then rushed to the wall and began to beat against it with such force that the pictures hanging there fell.

After that the meetings had ceased, in order to avoid repercussions. He'd always avoided political or administrative work, and he'd preferred not to be involved in drawing attention to government corruption or any other glaring issue. He'd been careful to keep both body and soul untroubled.

That Sunday morning, he went to his room, put on his blue jacket, placed his blue dotted handkerchief in his pocket, and knotted his tie. He looked at his reflection in the mirror, noting, as he did every day, how elegant and neat his moustache was.

He got into his car and drove to the university. Here were the same buildings, the same roads and road signs, the same people: newspaper sellers, vegetable sellers, fast drivers, religious men marked out by their beards and dress. He had the impression that there was a car following him; and when he parked in his usual space at the university, he felt he saw this other car park nearby. He walked through the university gates, past the guard standing there with his automatic rifle, and proceeded slowly to the College of Commerce. Students who knew him stopped their conversations as he went by and made way for him respectfully. He went up to the faculty of economics on the second floor (observed, he felt, by a person wearing a blue suit, like the person in that other car), then leaned over the balustrade and looked into the college courtyard, across which students and teachers were sauntering with their books and files. He didn't want to see them. He turned to go to the lecture theatre, then, after two steps, he returned, leaned on the railings again, and closed his eyes. No, he didn't want to see them! He wished he could blow the last trumpet, he wished he could play an Indian magician's flute, he wished he had a long whip in his hand, he wished he had Moses' staff to expose the lies they were concocting. He gritted his teeth hard and knit his brow.

Hatem was waiting at the door of the police station and greeted him with extreme politeness, looking at his watch. "One o'clock exactly," he said. "I was afraid you'd be late." He conducted him to the stairs leading to the second floor, talking very pleasantly all the while. "I'm sorry to bother you, Doctor, I know it's lunchtime. Hisham tells me it's your birthday today. Is that true?" Slowly they walked to Hatem's small, clean office. It had a wide window and a glass-topped desk on which there was a photograph of his children and three telephones, and the wall behind it was adorned with a large colored picture in a gilt frame. "Please come in," Hatem said. Would you like tea or coffee?"

He sat down on a chair by the side of the desk, while Hatem sat down behind it, rang a bell, and ordered coffee. He called in Hisham, who greeted the Doctor rather shyly and with profuse respect, and instructed him to sit down and record the proceedings.

"Let's begin, shall we, Doctor?" said Hatem. "Your name?"

"Ahmad Mansour."

"Your full name, please."

"Ahmad 'Abdul-Latif Mansour 'Abdallah.'"

"Your age?"

"Fifty-two."

"Where was your father born?"

"At al-Ruhaybiyyeh."

"And where were you yourself born?"

"At Syrs."

"Why?"

"What do you mean, why?"

"I mean, was your father working in Syrs or visiting it?"

"He was working there."

"What was your mother's name?"

"My mother?"

"Yes, your mother."

"Khadija."

"Her full name, please."

"Khadija 'Abdallah.'"

"Her grandfather's name?"

"Her grandfather's name!"

"Yes, his name."

"I'm not sure I know it. I think it was Fouad."

"When was your father born?"

"I can't remember."

"You can't remember?"

"No, I can't remember, but I could bring you the date later. I have a record of it."

"And your mother, where and when was she born?"

"I'm sorry, but I wasn't expecting you to ask for all these details. But I can bring them later."

"I'd like you to bring them tomorrow. You may not regard them as important, but in fact they're essential information. But we all want our lunch as soon as possible, so let's get to the point. Where did your father work?"

"He was a tax commissioner, posted to various cities. When he died, twenty years ago, he was working here in Syrs."

"And your mother. What work did she do?"

"My mother?"

"Yes, your mother."

"My mother didn't work. She was a housewife."

"Did your father have any special hobbies?"

"Special hobbies?"

"Yes, hobbies."

"I can't remember any. He used to sit with his friends in the evening, in the big Beradi Cafe in Ibn al-Ahnaf Street."

"Was that his only hobby?"

"It was a habit rather than a hobby. He didn't have any hobbies."

"None at all?"

"I don't know."

"Weren't you living with him?"

"Yes, of course I was. But I don't know of any hobbies."

"And your mother?"

"What do you mean?"

"Didn't she have any hobbies?"

"Did your mother have any hobbies, Mr. Hatem? What are all these questions for?"

"Please keep to the point."

"What point, Mr. Hatem? My parents' hobbies?"

"Please let us do our job, Doctor."

"I'm not stopping you, Hatem. But what is all this about hobbies?"

"You mean they're not important?"

"Of course they're not important. I don't understand what you're looking for. You wanted me to come and discuss my lectures, and now you're asking me about my father's birthday!"

"Don't get worked up, Doctor. I don't understand economics. Do you think you understand about interrogations?"

"I didn't say I understood anything about interrogations. What I said was ... "

"Don't let's go into what you said or what I said. If you don't want to cooperate with me, I'm quite willing to pass your file on to another officer. I wanted to help you. Let us try and help you, Doctor."

The professor stood up, buttoned up his jacket, and pulled out a handkerchief with which he proceeded to wipe the sweat from his brow. Then he looked closely at Hatem.

"I think that's a good idea," he said. "Let's pass the file on to another officer."

"There's no need for that, Doctor. What I mean is, don't be hasty. I want to help you. Hisham and I both want to help you. Please don't be hasty."

"I'm sorry, Mr. Hatem, but I have to leave now. I can't go on with this now. I'm sorry."

"You're tired, Doctor. But it's better if we finish the interrogation. It's a pure formality. I hope you won't make an issue of it."

"An issue! I can't stay now."

Hatem stood up.

"Tomorrow then."

"Yes, all right."

"I'm sorry, Doctor, I didn't mean to insult you."

"Please don't talk like that, Hatem. I didn't say you insulted me. Please, all I said was that you didn't ask me about the lecture. I thought you told me on the phone that you wanted to discuss the lecture."

"I'm sorry you're so irritable. Yes, I did say I wanted to discuss the lecture, but that isn't important. Let's finish the interrogation. Please let's finish it."

"All right, we'll finish it. But please, Hatem, I can't do it now."

Hatem saw him to the door, shook hands with him, and agreed to meet the following day. Hisham, who'd recorded the interrogation, was alongside him, dressed in a blue suit. The professor pretended not to see him, but when he reached his car Hisham stepped forward.

"We could have finished it today, Doctor."

The professor turned towards him and looked at him closely.

"You're a friend of Ghassan's, aren't you?"

"Yes, of course. You remember me?"

"You were a student of mine last year."

"Yes, of course. I studied the theory of production with you."

"And you work here?"

"Yes, of course. I work and study at the same time."

He looked carefully at Hisham, took out his sunglasses, and, still scrutinising him, placed them over his eyes. Then he slapped him hard in the face, pushed him to one side, and climbed into his car. He drove the car forward, then reversed, while uproar broke out among the police and passers-by.

He drove toward the station, where there was a *shawarma* shop that his wife liked. Every weekend they left from here to go to Imad's house, just as, at one time, he'd driven off every weekend with his wife for the fresh mountain air and forests and lakes all round Chicago, where they'd studied. He used to drive her to Niagara sometimes, because she loved waterfalls. He stopped for a second at the *shawarma* stand, then got back into his car and made for home. In all the time he'd known her, she'd never done anything to annoy him. She'd only buy a dress after he'd seen her in it and liked it on her. How lovely she looked in that yellow dress with black roses, with her thick eyelashes and her long neck! And the white dress with the open circles at the waist, which he'd bought for her after losing a wager in Rome during the first week of their marriage! How tenderly she'd look at him, and the way she winked her eye at him whenever he was in the wrong!

When he got home, she was at the door waiting for him.

"How did everything go?" she asked, looking at him closely.

He shook his head angrily.

"Worse than you can imagine."

She closed the door.

"Dr. Yahya called me a few minutes ago," she said, "and told me that you came to blows with the investigator. He said you slapped him and then ran away. Is it true?"

He sat down on a chair opposite her.

"No, it isn't true. It was Hisham I slapped—a friend of Ghassan's. Do you remember him? I expect he came to your meetings last year—a tall boy with blue eyes."

"Was he there?" she asked.

"Yes, he works for the police."

"What!"

"That's right."

"I can't believe it!"

"Shall I tell you about the interrogation?" he said.

As he told her, she leaned back in the chair, staring at him with angry eyes.

"So that's the way it is!" she said.

"That's it."

"They did the same thing with the painter, Nabil Salim," she said. "He was without a job for two years and had to report there every day; they'd ask him questions about trivial things, and every time the investigation would be deferred with a demand for documents they hadn't asked for before."

"The same as with me," he said.

She clapped her hand to her mouth.

"I can't believe it!"

"That's how it is," he said, nodding and feeling his moustache.

Her eyes clouded with thick, unshed tears, and she asked him, in an attempt to make things easier for him, "Would you like some cold water for your feet before lunch?"

As he went to his room, he saw all the dishes laid out in the dining room, probably his favorite dishes, cooked by Khaula, or maybe by Imad's wife. They were all coming in the evening, with their children, to celebrate his birthday. He took off his jacket and tie and went to the bathroom, where he washed his face and neck with cold water, then carefully scrutinized his neck.

He opened the drawer where he kept his gun and, still standing in front of the mirror, he loaded it and released the safety catch. Then he raised the gun to his neck, pulling up the skin as he did during his daily shave and feeling for the spot he'd pinpointed at the time of Adnan's suicide. Then he pulled the trigger.

—*Translated by May Jayyusi and Christopher Tingley*

Yusuf Sharouni (b. 1924)

Egyptian short-story writer and critic Yusuf Sharouni was born in the Egyptian Delta, studied philosophy at Cairo University, and taught for many years in both Egypt and the Sudan. In 1956 he was appointed to the Higher Council for the Arts, Literature and Social Sciences in Cairo, where he came to hold the position of under secretary. One of the finest short-story writers in the Arab world, Sharouni has been instrumental in establishing the short story as a major genre in Arabic. He has published several collections to date, among which are *The Crush of Life* (1969), *Midnight Chase* (1973), *The Last of the Bunch* (1974), *The Mother and the Beast* (1982), and *Musical Chairs* (1990). He has also published studies on Arabic literature and has received several prizes both for his creative writings and for his criticism. A full collection of his short stories, titled *Blood Feud*, has appeared in English, edited and translated by Denys Johnson-Davie (1984).

BRIEFLY

I was about to turn off the light, the nearby clock having struck midnight, when I heard my roommate say, "I can hear you yawning; I'd better make my story brief."

There was only one hotel in the town, and I occupied its last vacant bed. I'd entered on tiptoe so as not to disturb my roommate, but found that he was still awake. It was clear that he wasn't expecting my arrival at this late hour and had sat up with a bottle and glass. The smell of liquor and cigarette smoke permeated the room. A man of about thirty, he was sitting in white pajamas in the middle of the room.

We exchanged formal greetings. As I began quietly to take off my suit, I was searching in my mind for a clue to diminish our evident distance from each other and to ensure our nocturnal companionship would be harmonious. The first thing I noticed was that my roommate had failed to hang up his suit in the wardrobe, having preferred to discard it carelessly on the back of the chair next to his bed. I also noticed that the necktie draped over his suit was black. The young man was mutually occupied in observing me, for he quickly offered me a drink, at the same time saying, "Or don't you enjoy what God has prohibited?"[1] I thanked him for his invitation and declined on account of my stomach, which can't tolerate liquor. "Then I don't suppose you intend to sit up with me?" he said. "I'll have a last glass and then we can put out the light. I really mustn't disturb you."

I had the impression that he wished to unburden his mind of something that was bothering him. "I noticed you looking at this black necktie," he said, "I wear it because my sister died forty days ago, and I've just returned from attending her

---

1. This is a reference to the Islamic prohibition of liquor.

forty-day memoriam.[2] I came to this hotel, because as you probably know, the train doesn't pass by the town of *N* where the service was performed.

"God rest her soul," I answered, as I slipped off my shoes.

We continued in silence for a few minutes, before I asked out of politeness, "Was this sister of yours a little girl or a grown-up?"

The young man poured another glass before answering.

"She was a mother and leaves a boy and girl behind. But that's hardly an explanation. The story's a long one, and we're getting ready to go to bed. I really shouldn't disturb you with my talk."

"Death has no logic," I said, condolingly. "It comes at any time, with or without a reason."

While undressing, I heard the nearby clock chime midnight. At that precise moment my roommate confronted me with the question, "What would you prefer: to live on the margin of life for a hundred years or to live intensely at the center for thirty or forty years?"

Before giving me the chance to consider, I heard him say, "My sister answered this question. She preferred to live life to the full and die at thirty, rather than face seventy or eighty years of mediocrity. That's what I mean by 'living in the heart of life.' I suppose the story begins in part with her heart problem, although, of necessity, I shall be brief. If you don't drink, would you join me in having a cigarette? You don't smoke either? I don't smoke as a rule either, but I take refuge sometimes from sorrow, anxiety and insomnia in smoking and drinking. But I clean forgot to introduce myself. I'm Khalil Asfour, an employee in the Property Register, although the job's not much use to me. It's funny, but I've never bought an acre of land, or secured my own home, or been party to an inheritance."

Mr. Asfour laughed and as abruptly stopped, without any apparent reason. As it was my custom to read for a short time before going to sleep, I had no objection to substituting an oral for a written narrative. The man continued:

"Briefly speaking, the doctors advised her not to marry and have children if she hoped to live to a reasonable age. But she preferred to disregard their advice and sought to live intensely, even if it meant risking death. When they told me that a member of my family had died, I immediately assumed it was my grandmother. She's eighty, shriveled to the bone, incessantly quarrelsome, and weak of memory. But it wasn't she who'd died; it was my sister who hadn't yet reached thirty. Her funeral was wonderfully majestic. The whole town walked behind her coffin, headed by the police superintendent representing the president of the republic. Perhaps you can imagine what it was like to see her face

---

2. The dead are formally remembered after three days, one week, and forty days. Usually an open house is maintained where people come for condolences and remembrance. In certain Arab countries, the passage of one week and forty days after the birth of a child is also significant.

in death, hardly altered from its complexion in life, apart from an additional paleness. Moreover, her corpse showed no deterioration, although it had been a day awaiting our arrival. She died at five o'clock in the evening and was buried around four the next afternoon ... Have you ever heard of the dead awakening in their graves a few hours after burial? My sister nursed this morbid fear. She'd read an article somewhere that described how certain people requested that their jugular veins be opened subsequent to death, and my sister asked that the same should be performed on her, so that there was no possibility of her waking up frightened in the grave. However, we had no need to enact her wish, for her corpse had lain dormant for twenty-four hours. No greenfly, attracted by the smell of putrescence, had settled on her to impregnate the skin with its eggs as usually happens, so that later on, when the corpse is buried, the eggs hatch into the worms that are responsible for the body's dissolution. In this instance, no fly appeared to approach her."

Mr. Asfour extinguished his cigarette and finished the contents of his glass. I thought that he'd concluded his story and proceeded to turn off the light as the clock was announcing midnight. I moved slowly, so as to allow him time to cap his bottle and put it away. Then he said, "It's better without the light, only the air inside this room is stifling. As it's not cold outside, and the moon's silver will light up our room indirectly, I'm sure you won't mind if I open the window. In big cities like Cairo, we seldom enjoy moonlight, as the tall buildings and artificial lights screen it away from us. I feel rested when I'm engulfed by moonlight. What do you think? Do you believe in dreams? I've already dreamt twice of my sister since she died. The first time I woke up frightened and tearful, but the dream was too complex to analyze, although its disturbing effect weighed heavily on my chest for two days. The second time I saw her ... but I know you're tired, as I hear you yawning, and I'll try to be brief. Will you forgive me if I ask whether you're married? Do you have children? And if so, do they ever get tonsillitis? And if the answer is yes, then they should have a tonsillectomy immediately. My father used to fear his children being operated on, a suspicion that I've retained, although I succumb to the need when it arises. Can you imagine that my mother had her appendix removed without letting my father know? She pretended that she was traveling to see her mother but went to the hospital instead. We're not poor, we were, but that no longer applies. Sometimes I get confused in my own mind as to whether my father's fear of operations for members of his family originates from an overprotectiveness about their lives or a dread of the expense that an operation entails, he being used to economize since the days of poverty. In brief, my father refused to have an operation performed on my sister, Safa. I still can't get used to saying "bless her soul" when I talk about her, for I can't accustom myself to her death, even though we'd been expecting it for so long. She was two years younger than me. I remember how my parents left us alone one evening, when we were still young children, and went to visit a relative. My sister and I availed ourselves of this opportunity to devise a game whereby each would attempt to frighten the other into submis-

sion. I began by contorting my face, distorting my ten fingers, standing, doubling, approaching, and retreating, and all the while making frightening noises
that appeared to come from somewhere else. My sister tried to follow likewise.
I ended up as the winner, something I attributed to her being younger than me,
and the bleak evening atmosphere. She soon forgot I was her brother and took
me for a devil or demon of the jinn and began periodically to scream with terror and take refuge by embracing me. She was hysterical, unable to control her
nerves. Her own terror communicated itself to me, and I too started screaming
and held her tightly, crying all the time. Had it not been for our parents entering
at that moment, we would have lost our senses.

"Safa suffered regularly from tonsillitis, but my father remained adamant that
she shouldn't undergo an operation. And then, at the age of thirteen or fourteen
she was hit by rheumatic fever, which in turn affected her heart, putting her
health in jeopardy. She had to remain motionless in bed for eight months, while
Dr. Tawhida, who was looking after her, became the friend of the family, even
refusing to ask for her legitimate fees.

"When Safa was better, Dr. Tawhida advised us that her tonsils should be
removed. They were, and optimism led us to believe that my sister's troubles and
our own were at an end; but the illness recurred, in a milder form, some three
or four years later, and she was confined to bed for six months."

It would seem that the combination of drink and darkness encouraged my
roommate to continue his narrative, for I saw him light another cigarette before
continuing, "As far as I know, Safa was sixteen when she first fell in love. I think
my father apprehended a letter that the young man had sent her; but no, I'm
getting the sequence of events confused. I remember now. She was alone in
the house when my father returned home and found the young man with her.
He feared that something had happened between them. The young man went
out shaken, while my father would have thrashed my sister, were it not that my
mother prevented him, on the grounds of Safa's fragile health. But I swear to
you that nothing ever occurred between them; their love was honorable and
innocent. Since I was of the same age as that young man and could more readily
understand his motives, I went to see him and asked him to return my sister's
letters. He apologized for what had happened and rationalized the incident by
saying that he'd come to the house to ask me for the loan of a book—I forgot
to mention that he was a neighbor of ours—and he additionally assured me that
he was officially going to request my sister's hand in marriage. The young man
enjoyed a good financial situation and, more important, he and my sister had a
perfect understanding. You, of course, can appreciate this, although you neither
drink nor smoke, for you're still a young man. Of course, you might think differently if ever you should become a father . . . What? You're yawning again? . . .
Still, I know you're listening to me.

"Anyhow, formal proceedings for the completion of the marriage agreement
were instigated. Safa was wild with joy when she learnt that our father had raised
no objections to the proposed marriage, for she'd anticipated his opposition in

view of what had happened. But it was I who'd been successful as an intermediary between them. In a way I've been responsible both for my sister's way of life and her death. Sometimes I reproach myself for having been too enthusiastic a supporter of her views, or at least for not supporting the chorus of those who advised her to be more of an observer than a participator in life. But what meaning can such a life have? Then one evening we had a surprise visit from Dr. Tawhida, who was in a very agitated state of mind; she'd heard that my sister was getting married and viewed the consequences with extreme gravity. She advised my sister, and all of us who loved her, to abandon the idea completely, as it would entail certain death. As a doctor she knew that my sister's heart couldn't withstand the stresses of marriage or the consequences of pregnancy and childbirth.

"The marriage never did take place, because the bridegroom stopped visiting us and seeing my sister. To avoid embarrassment, he moved with his family to another quarter. Later on we heard that, when her efforts with us failed, Dr. Tawhida had visited the young man's family and explained the potential risks of such a marriage. After this they pursued the project no further. Poor Safa suffered such an emotional setback that it almost reactivated her illness. The incident caused her great anxiety. She lost her faith in people and would spend whole nights unable to sleep; or, if she slept, she'd wake up startled by a terrible dream, her heart pounding, and we were powerless to know whether her heart problem induced these dreams or if nightmares were the cause of her heart condition. She used to take yeast, or sleeping pills to try and prevent herself from waking in the night with the feeling that someone was approaching her to strangle her or that they'd buried her alive and she'd woken up in the grave screaming, trying to disentangle her arms and legs from the shrouds they were bound in.

"Safa nursed a profound resentment against Dr. Tawhida and felt that the doctor had no right to interfere with her personal life. She saw the doctor as representing an obstacle to her future. At that early age the critical issue of her life was not fully realized by Safa: that of choosing a long life of complacency or enjoying the natural aspirations of a woman by getting married and having children. She may even have thought in the enthusiasm of her youth that Dr. Tawhida had exaggerated her report on her health. She even went so far as to construe the doctor's motives as those of jealousy; the latter being over thirty and still unmarried. Dr. Tawhida was neither pretty nor plain but had decided that marriage would distract her from her career. Dr. Tawhida insisted that my sister's treatment should not end with the abatement of the symptoms . . . What do you make of this so far? I have the feeling that you're cold. I'll close the window. Now, where was I up to? Oh yes, yes, I remember now. As it turned out, no one asked for my sister's hand for the next three or four years. She had to watch her girlfriends get married one after the other, while she feared that her destiny was to remain a lonely spinster. As her insomnia persisted, I arranged for her to see a psychiatrist, but she never took advantage of his possible help.

The clock announced one in the morning. It seemed that Mr. Asfour was afraid of getting drunk, so he closed the bottle and put it away, and lit another cigarette. I was trying hard to overcome my drowsiness, and his protracted sentences reached me from a great distance and lacked all unifying cohesion. But I fought off the recurring drowsiness, and heard him resume, "Briefly, marriage seemed the only way to calm her nerves, and after an interval of time a young man came to ask for her hand. He seemed eminently suitable, and since Safa's illness hadn't manifested itself for a number of years, we all of us believed her to be cured. In the meantime we'd severed our relationship with Dr. Tawhida on account of her quarreling with my sister, and as a consequence the former had no opportunity to acquaint the new bridegroom with my sister's medical history. For our part, we had no wish to unearth the past, and so the marriage took place. And by way of an aside, as you mentioned that you were single, let me advise you when the time comes to marry either a relative or a neighbor you know well. We ourselves have a poor neighbor who married a young man last year. Neither she nor her family had the opportunity to know him well, and the marriage took place only fourteen days after the engagement. And what happened after that? It soon became clear that the young man had tuberculosis and that his family had devised the marriage in order to afford him some degree of pleasure before he died."

Then in a voice that was hardly audible, Mr. Asfour whispered, "They say that those who have tuberculosis develop a keen sexual desire. It was undoubtedly this impulse that drove him to get married. The poor girl became pregnant within two months of being married and then discovered her husband's illness. He was admitted to hospital shortly afterward, where he soon died. I'm of the opinion that there should be government offices for the compulsory examination of all who plan to marry. Of course, in Safa's case, the situation was far from clear, and we viewed her marriage as a hopeful end to the anxiety and constant agitation from which she suffered. Almost every girl feels happy in the initial stages of marriage, unless it's a union without her consent. And I believe that Safa's was deliriously happy. Her husband was only an employee, rather as we are, but he was young, and she was happy and proud to have her own home, just like any other girl, and fortified by the trust that she wouldn't have to live alone and dry up like a tree in autumn. This was clear to us whenever she came with her husband to visit the family or when friends and relatives visited her in her new home. On such occasions she'd take a delight in showing them around the rooms of the house and in pointing out the furniture and the sheets and cushions that she'd embroidered with her own hands. Later on we watched her elation as she revealed the cute embroidered clothes she'd made herself for the baby she was expecting.

"Four months after her marriage, Safa felt the first movements of an embryo living within her. Our repeated warnings were to no effect, for she'd answer that she'd prefer to die rather than deprive her husband and herself of at least one child. 'I'll see to it that this is my only pregnancy,' she'd say. But the old illness reappeared, this time in the form of a hacking cough. We called the doctor, who decided that the cough was the result of the baby's pressure on a weak heart.

When he heard from us that she'd already suffered from heart disease, he was, predictably, of the opinion that she should have avoided marriage and pregnancy. When her feet started to swell and her temperature rose in accordance with the cough, we all felt that she was about to die imminently. Despite the risk it entailed, the doctor indicated that an abortion would be less dangerous for my sister than continuing her pregnancy.

"And what do you think she did?" said Mr. Asfour, banging on the table in front of him to rouse me from partial sleep.

"She never set foot again in that doctor's surgery and consulted another practitioner called Dr. Ra'fat, who was sympathetic to her wishes and her determination to continue with her pregnancy. Consequently he attempted the impossible in the effort to save the lives of mother and child. My sister fought heroically, and her morale was high despite the danger of her condition. I used to wonder at her resolution to keep the child in view of the certain death that threatened her. The first thing Safa did after giving birth to a son was to call him Ra'fat. That's why I still remember the doctor's name.

"In brief, my sister regained her health and the baby was a healthy one. It might have been possible, despite the disadvantages of her condition, to live a normal life, had she not become pregnant again. The second pregnancy resulted in a relapse, and she didn't recover after giving birth to a daughter. She used to say that she wanted to have another child as a companion to her son, and she hoped it would be a girl. However, she never really intended to have a second child but conceived in spite of the contraceptive precautions she and her husband took.

I must have fallen asleep at some point, and I didn't hear the rest of the story, although I vaguely recall hearing him cry out at something. I've no idea when I fell asleep; I only know that I woke up in the morning to the sound of footsteps near me. At first I thought I was in my own home, before I opened my eyes to an unfamiliar room. I remembered all the events of the previous night and saw my roommate standing with his suitcase in his hand. I hardly recognized him at first, except for his black necktie, for the sad, intoxicated, chattering nocturnal phantom in pajamas, with bare feet and an unshaven face, had disappeared. In his place I saw a well-groomed, cleanly shaven person whose shoes mirrored the light. It was as though he'd been purged and reborn from that nocturnal confession. Even his voice was different, for he no sooner saw me move in my bed and open my eyes, than he said slowly and serenely, "I'm sorry for bothering you as I did last night. I realised you were asleep when I heard you snoring."

Before he took his leave, he turned to me and said, "By the way, I forgot to tell you that Dr. Tawhida died two weeks before Safa did, although she never did marry or have children. She hadn't been ill either. She died suddenly, just like that, with no apparent cause . . . just as you said."

—Translated by May Jayyusi and Jeremy Reed

Sulaiman al-Shatti (b. 1943)

Born in Kuwait, short story-writer, critic, and scholar Sulaiman al-Shatti studied for his B.A. and M.A. at Kuwait University, then obtained a Ph.D. in Arabic literature from Cairo University. He teaches literary criticism at the University of Kuwait and has served as head of the Kuwaiti Union of Writers, whose literary review, *Al-Bayan*, he has edited. He is also a member of the prestigious National Council for Culture, Arts, and Literature in Kuwait and a very active member of the Kuwaiti literary scene, representing his country in many pan-Arab conferences and writing on its literature. He has published three collections of short stories, *Low Voices* (1970); *Men From the Upper Echelon* (1983), and *I . . . Am the Other* (1994). In his fiction al-Shatti is preoccupied with the tremendous change that has taken place in Kuwait since the discovery of oil; he speaks in a nostalgic tone about the past, which represents to him a period of calm, security, and stable human relations. His critical work includes *Symbol and Symbolism in Najib Mahfouz* (1976); *Introduction to the Short Story in Kuwait* (1993), and *Three Readings in Arab Classical Criticism* (2000).

OBSESSION

The cold of early morning and that sparkle that distinguishes the beginning of each day; leaves that drift without aim or direction, blown about by the wind and the gusts of air escaping from the paths of speeding cars.

The day's journey began.

His hands began to gather his clothes around his neck, while his eyes froze into a dim and lifeless stare fixed on the ground . . . it was not like the usual hostile glance that he bestowed daily upon his huge residence, cursing the times that had brought him to live in one of these imported houses . . . But we will not hear the bewildered question that he reiterates in anxious, angry tones with the dawn of each day.

"How . . . I say how is it that people import their houses and lose all links with their environment. And yet—believe it or not—they can laugh feel happy, having lost all feeling. No feeling . . . no emotion . . . woe betide a person when he cannot feel . . . when no nerve throbs in him . . . never throbs . . . never ever."

We will not hear these words from Abu Madi, for something has changed. Things are not what they used to be. This is a journey different from former ones. He will cross the same road, ride in the same cart, and arrive at the same place . . . but is it really the same place? That's the problem . . . his emotions began to take charge . . . is he still as he was in the past? Which past?! The distant past or the day before yesterday?

There were many things that Abu Madi wished for. Dreams had not left him since the day he left his home to live in that cramped and alienating house, as he called it. He thought of the years he had spent trying to establish a footing in his old home, of the quarter he had built with his own two hands during the long years of his life. He had resisted the move to the last, tried to remain in his old place, but how could he when the government invoked its right to demolish the house, and his wife, with whom he had lived all his life, did her best to make him imitate the others . . . woe unto women, they form no bonds with anything at all but, rather, always seek to abolish the past, because for them the past is past. She had finally convinced him that he had an obligation to move out . . . it was a necessity. The deadly portents of that necessity began to appear, to gnaw at the houses, which collapsed in front of that hateful procession of machines, and the enormous room that had represented his final work began to disappear. Every day a section of it would fall down, until only the northern face that overlooked the road remained. The pickax continued to descend. They chose the sites one by one, they meant to humiliate and torment him slowly. They chose the houses whose construction he had been responsible for, starting with the most recent and proceeding with deadly slowness toward the remainder, as though they were cutting his limbs off, slowly torturing him. Everything had compelled him to leave his home in order to live in that cramped and alienating house, yet he could not keep away from the objects of his love, the things he had spent his whole life preserving with his magic hands that renovated everything they touched.

It had become a familiar sight to see Abu Madi going off each morning to the old neighborhood to wander among the old houses that awaited their fate and watched their own approaching end, made manifest every morning by the frightful noise of machinery. But Abu Madi continued to wander around, gently stroking the walls of the houses, sitting in different corners, drinking tea that he was careful to have daily at an appointed time, the self-same hour at which he used to take his rest in days gone by. People who were familiar with that neighborhood would not feel surprised when they saw Abu Madi repairing one of the houses; how could they when this had been a constant sight for all of thirty years? If anything was different, it was the cessation of all movement within those houses. Some, no doubt, would feel sorry for this purposeless labor or comment meanly that Abu Madi was repairing the mistakes of the past, having so few days left before he met his Maker . . . All the same he went on repairing these houses: each day a house or a corner of a house.

Today . . . the dread that had stirred in him ever since he got out of bed was different. He had spent all yesterday in a very old house that now stood solitary. He had left it in the evening, lonely in the darkness of a great open square that had unexpectedly come into existence. It would not be able to hold out. If only this day were not to be its last. He was beset by the feeling that all would be ended today, that all sense of existence would perish within him.

He began to walk faster. Cars passed him, blasting him with gusts of cold air, wheels screeching loudly on the asphalt, crunching the ground.

There was the sound of brakes and a multicolored car skidded to a halt in front of him. The driver bent to peer through the window and called out, "Haj . . . the market—?"

He turned his head away to show that he wanted nothing to do with such people and stared into the distance, waiting for Musa'id's cart and its gray horse, while the driver spluttered incoherently.

Minutes passed, one by one. The cold almost froze Abu Madi's bones, but his gaze remained fixed, awaiting Musa'id's cart. The distant shape of the cart came into view, followed by the sound of the gray horse's hooves as they clattered discordantly upon the asphalt . . . they had lost their harmony. Slowly the sound faded, and was replaced by that of the cart's wood protesting in its old age.

"God bless you, and good morning to you, Abu Madi . . ." The words of the greeting were lost as he clambered aboard the cart, whose discordant noise broke out again.

That feeling of dread whose nature he did not understand persisted. The road he traversed each day had greatly changed with the years. He turned his gaze to examine the silent Musa'id, the only person who was not visibly changed. If they conversed together, perhaps he could get rid of whatever lay so heavy on his breast. Once again he took to scrutinizing the road and those hateful houses on each side of it, painted in pathetic colors, each clashing, each house different.

"Look . . . Musa'id . . . look at these houses."

"Well?!"

"Their colors."

"Well!"

"Running wild."

"Well!"

"Do you know what that means?"

"Well!"

"Not well . . . far from well . . . don't you see that that disparity of the houses means discord and alienation. Don't you know that these people are missing something irreplaceable?"

A short silence ensued.

"Do you know what it is?"

"Well."

"Far from well, Musa'id . . . nothing is well . . . they have lost everything, neighbors, friends, everything . . . it is not well at all . . . and never will be."

This was the first heated conversation between them. Silence had been their bond ever since this new situation had arisen. Work was what had united them before, but now there was this silence hovering over them as they went along the road, coming and going.

Everything was as before; no sound but the cart creaking and shaking, the gray horse struggling to pull its load.

A triptych . . . Abu Madi, his head bent in thought, Musa'id with eyes fixed on the distance, the horse plodding on its four hooves . . .

A thought occurred to Musa'id. For some time now he had wanted to ask Abu Madi a question, but silence had separated them. Today, however, part of that wall of silence had fallen. He felt a compulsive desire to ask his question; he was sure of the form that answer would take, but the wish to ask was insistent. He turned to his only passenger.

"Abu Madi . . . I have a question."

Abu Madi took his hand from his forehead, and turned to look at him, surprise written over his face at this unexpected announcement.

"Go ahead."

"What stops you from going back to what you were?!"

"How?"

"Returning to work in construction."

Things became confused immediately . . . The cart shook while Abu Madi shivered with anger. His faded smile was replaced by rage. Musa'id's hands tightened around the reins, jerking up the horse's head. Abu Madi let out a hoarse gasp.

"What?!"

It was a cry filled with pain; it frightened both Musa'id and the horse. They realized that something had just gone terribly wrong, but it was too late to do anything to avert it. This was true enough. A wound had been reopened, and Abu Madi burst out, "What did you say? I am to work at these filthy jobs? Don't you understand, Musa'id, that these buildings are the biggest of frauds?"

Abu Madi ran out of breath. He got up to his feet to cool his rage, then sat down. His voice faltered, as if tears had run down into his throat.

"Beneath those brilliant names, behind which those all-crushing machines have disappeared, have you observed people's eyes? Our eyes can no more express any meaning. They are bewildered, robbed of dignity and life. Bondage alone looks out of these eyes, and the sweat of our labor that flows like a river, this sweat only serves some people's pleasure. And then you tell me, 'Fake with the fakers!' Why didn't you sink into this hell? Do you know why? Because you have never really lived, so that in the end all things have the same value for you. Do you really know what you are saying? I to work with these people?! I'd have them sentenced to death instead! They don't deserve to live! Do you know how those shoddy houses have been built? You don't know at all! As for me, I'd have them all destroyed!"

Musa'id muttered, as if talking to himself:

"But you are the one who's victimized—"

He choked and stopped speaking. Abu Madi gave a hacking cough. Silence was resumed. But it was a silence broken by sporadic mutterings, choked with anger and rage. Little by little they died down, till they ceased altogether.

The cart continued to make its way calmly along the road, the two figures swaying with its movement. The remains of a wall began to loom in the distance. Abu Madi became more and more aware of it as his eyes focused upon the old gate that had been placed in the middle of the big green roundabout . . . The wall was as nothing beside these loathsome buildings. Abu Madi's throat began to feel tight as his glance fell on these remains. He bent forward, his hands cupping his face; a shriveled, furrowed face. The hair of his head was white, his eyebrows, once black, were whitening. He was approaching sixty, but a close observer would think him much older. He was a man who had experienced much, known much, and suffered much, his life a series of troubles and anxieties. But he was now experiencing the cruelest moments of his life. He wanted to say something, wanted to speak to these ruins, that some life might return to them. Musa'id said, "Abu Madi . . . forgive me . . . I did not mean to vex you."

Both were feeling hurt. However, Abu Madi's hand slid from his head and despite the black looks he had given at first, his features began to relax little by little till a kind of glow returned to them. A gentle atmosphere dominated now and separated them from the noise around. The cart began to descend eastward toward the shore. As they exchanged glances, their lips began to twitch with laughter. They smiled at the same instant, as though a mutual thought had passed between them at that moment, then they began to laugh. They were not laughing at anything in particular, but there was nothing to stop their laughter, either. Each was laughing for the other's sake, yet a different kind of feeling began to seep into them, for despite the new atmosphere they felt that the horse was changing its gait and was slowing down, its steps getting heavier one minute and brisker the next. Musa'id gave it a tug at the reins. Still, they continued to laugh . . . and to laugh without joy, except for the feeling that each was making the other happy. They forgot the horse. For the first time their third companion slipped from their attention.

The sound of Abu Madi slapping his thigh rang out. His hand stretched to point, fingers rigid: "Look!"

"What?"

"Do you see that house . . . the yellow house?"

"I don't see anything."

"All your life you don't see anything. Look well. Its Haj Salih's house . . . see, there are its ruins."

"Aah, Haj Salih's house."

"Don't you remember anything? A story?"

"Nothing."

"These ruins . . . there, thirty years ago was our first meeting, when we began to repair it."

"I remember. Yes, I remember, I remember everything now."

"For the first time you remember something. We met here, our hands sank into the mud together. That summer was a scorcher . . ."

"Yes . . . yes, I remember; our meeting was at summer's end. Yes, at summer's end."

"And yet, we worked the whole day long. Young men, we were brimming with youth then. But now, look . . . us and our work together, both finished. God have mercy on you, my old teacher, do you remember Khalifa?"

"God have mercy on him."

"He used to say that everyone's work decays and perishes, except for the builder's. His work has more permanence, so he should be worthy of it. But nothing has remained of my work save ruins."

And he felt a shiver go through him; it was that morning's premonition again. He was not going to be able to forget it. The depression returned to his spirits because of the dread that would not abate.

"We have arrived, Abu Madi."

Musa'id always said it, and then fell silent. Wish we had not arrived, the fate that I do not want, huh.

He repeated, "We have arrived." And there was nothing to arrive at. Abu Madi alighted. A vague urge prompted him to watch the gray horse as it retreated; its gait was changed, much changed.

The high-rise buildings that stood there concealed the ruins of the old neighborhood, those few that had remained. The morning's premonition became more intense. Abu Madi was lost between the two soaring buildings, behind which the barren land, once teeming with people, movement, and abundance, lay empty and desolate now. He began to walk faster; only a few more yards and the actuality of the old neighborhood would be revealed.

He certainly knew that all the houses had disappeared; even their ruins had been flattened to the ground and become dust. Only the last house, the oldest of all, still stood alone, open to the winds. He pushed the door and entered. Severed from the outside world, he was once more in the house he had left the day before. He had been working on it recently, restoring what had fallen, having noticed some time before that water was seeping in through the ceiling, which needed repair. He gathered all the tools that he had brought from Hai Fahd's house two days before its demolition. Everything was ready. He began to repair the ceiling. Three consecutive days he had worked and found the place where the water had collected, and he was able to repair it. After that he spread the ceiling with a layer of cement. Everything was finished. The day before he had to test the ceiling and the water's flow across it. He poured water over it in the morning and went down to see if there was any problem; this was what he used to do in the old days. His eyes fixed themselves again on the ceiling, studying its different nooks and crannies; everything was as it should be. And suddenly, those terrifying shrieks arose, followed by loud sounds that filled the yard. He rushed to the door and looked out.

He wished he had not looked; the front of an enormous bulldozer was evident; it rose above the ruins, with the wall mashed to a pulp beneath it. They met face to face. Some of the small stones began to scatter, while the dust rose high, blotting out almost everything then slowly dispersing. The ruins were mashed to pulp beneath this great monster. For the first time they meet face to face. The enormous bulldozer towered above him.

The noise grew louder as he scrutinized the bulldozer. It was like a beast spreading out its arms to clutch its victim. As he stood contemplating this thing standing in front of him in the receding dust, the sporadic noises it made gave him the feeling that this huge machine was fatigued. But the noise continued to grow louder. He felt a hand grasp hold of him and shake him angrily, "What are you doing here, man. Do you want to kill yourself?!"

And another man at his side was also talking agitatedly, apologizing to the circle that had formed around Abu Madi, "I had examined all the rooms—by God—before giving the go-ahead, but I did not see this man. I am certain that nobody was in the house. As for him, God only knows where he sprang from."

Abu Madi began to examine the staring faces. One of them yelled, "He's a madman. Look how he stares at us."

Another cried, "He really is a madman. I see him every day round here. I've known him for some time. I went into one of the houses once, before its demolition, to relieve myself, and I was looking for a suitable spot when I heard movement in one of the rooms. It took me by surprise, so I stood still. After that I heard talk, which became clearer, but I was not able to make anything out, so I pricked up my ears to listen and edged closer and closer, until I saw . . . do you know what I saw? This man, with his head leaning against the wall, muttering strange words that I could not understand. He is definitely mad."

It was as if the talk was about another person whom he did not know and with whom he had no connection. But it stopped when he felt one of them take hold of his hand and lead him outside the house. The man began to pat him on the shoulders, his eyes full of pity, while his lips enunciated meaningless words. He came to as the man removed his hand from his shoulder, saying, "Go now to your own house. Do you know it?"

He went, leaving all that noise behind him. But the men's laughter reached him more clearly. He crossed the road, his mind still ruminating on what had happened. The thing whose image he could not banish was the bulldozer that crouched over the mashed wall; an image he would never forget. The road was empty of life, stretching before him without end. These then were his last minutes, after which there would be nothing left but detachment, awaiting the end of the end, whose portent had loomed ahead already. From a distance, a shadow appeared, walking slowly. There was nothing to indicate that they knew each other. It was Musa'id coming toward him, without his constant companion. It was difficult for either of them to make the other out.

They approached each other . . . their eyes met, and Abu Madi got out a question.

"The gray horse?"

A tremor shook Musa'id's voice.

"He is dead."

—Translated by Lena Jayyusi and David Wright

Muhammad 'Ali Taha (b. 1941)

Palestinian short-story writer Muhammad 'Ali Taha was born in the village of Mi'ar in the Galilee. Taha's family became refugees in 1948 and lived in the Palestinian village of Kabul. He did his secondary studies in Kufr Yasif and obtained a degree from the University of Haifa. At the end of the 1970s he joined the Israeli Communist Party. He has chosen a teaching career, but is also involved in a wide range of literary and political activities and attends many world conferences. Much of his fiction reflects the oppressive conditions of Palestinians under Israeli rule, and he has shown particular interest in the life of Palestinians in refugee camps, depicting it in terms that are as realistic as they are gripping. His collections of short stories include his first, *For the Sun to Rise* (1964), and at least three others: *A Bridge on the Sad River* (1977), *'A'id al-Mi'ari Sells Sesame Cakes in Tal al-Zaatar* (1978), and *A Rose for Hafiza* (1983).

THE EVENING WALK

He was walking slowly along the sidewalk as he always did, taking one step, then a second, then a third, then stopping to watch the pedestrians. He'd look at their clothes, and their bodies, and their ample bellies, then gaze into the shop windows, contemplating the goods so smartly and temptingly laid out there. He'd note the prices of the various items, nodding or shaking his head and moving his lips, sometimes thrusting them out as if to say "Ridiculous!" or "What sort of price is that?"

Then he'd go on with his daily walk.

This walk was linked to the sun. Every afternoon he'd shave, then put on his best clothes and some perfume, peering several times into the mirror to make sure the little hair he had left was neatly arranged, that his mustache was properly trimmed, that his clothes looked smart and his shoes were polished. Then he'd glance at the wall clock to check it was an hour before sunset. Then, finally, he'd leave the house.

This was the daily ritual he'd planned with such care three years before, when he'd taken early retirement. It changed with the seasons, for in winter he'd leave the house at four o'clock, in summer around seven. Between these times, summer and winter, and winter and summer, he'd take care over the right time. The important thing was to leave the house at least an hour before sunset and return home an hour after sunset. Perhaps this kind of schedule sprang from his village past, when time had been defined by the rising of the sun, and its daily journey across the sky, and its setting.

People, especially curious ones and the ones with nothing to do, knew the times of his daily walk from his house to the main street. If, one day, they happened not to see him, they'd suppose he was sick or else that—God forbid—some accident or mishap had befallen him, and some of them would feel concerned. As for the owners of the shops and kiosks in the main street, they'd long since got used to seeing him walk along, stopping from time to time, used to his clothes and his appearance. He'd become, it seemed to them, a very part of the street—of its people and its goods, its customers and its life.

He'd stand at the top of the street, gazing at himself in the shop window, checking once more on his appearance and his clothes, his hair and his necktie, then read over the prices handsomely inscribed on the goods. He'd watch the people on the two sidewalks, laugh at a driver who'd lost his head in the traffic. He'd stop by the entrance to the cinema, contemplating the pictures for the film being shown. He'd walk on a few more steps till he reached the fountain, at which he'd gaze in wonder, plunged in thought. Then on he'd walk once more. He'd rarely fail to stare at the legs of the young women in the short skirts they were wearing—though the very word "wearing" struck him as ridiculous. He'd swallow, then repeat a favorite saying of his: "You wretched girls, we're gasping already, and still your skirts get shorter." And then he'd tilt up his head and thrust out his chest, to reassure himself about his health and that he was still a young man, even if he was well into his sixties now.

An hour and a half he'd spend, looking and discovering, studying the faces of people, and how they looked at him, and the way they moved. Then back he'd go to his house in 'Abbas Street, feeling fit and contented, quite reassured all was well with the world and with him too. He'd sit down in his favorite chair and gaze at the sea, at the port, and the ships.

Then, one particular evening, something unexpected happened, to shake him out of his daily routine.

He walked a few yards down the main street, stopping two or three times as he always did; and as he did so, he spotted, on the other sidewalk, a beautiful girl looking at him—unmistakably at him. It was usual enough, of course, to see young women. There were plenty of them in this street every day, because most of the shops and big stores had women's clothes, women's shoes, cosmetics, and similar things. But to have a girl, and such a beautiful one too, gazing at him. That was unusual!

He glanced at her a few times, then turned to peer into the window of a bookstore and started reading the authors' names. A lot of the space was taken up with cookbooks. Was culture, he wondered, becoming just culinary culture in this world of theirs? And anyway, did properly accomplished women, daughters of good families, really need a cookbook?

He smiled at the thought of buying a book like that for his partner of a lifetime. What would she learn from it? He almost laughed out loud at the idea. Then, turning suddenly toward the sidewalk opposite, he found the beautiful girl was still looking at him.

A sudden anxiety swept through him. What did this young woman want? He felt powerless against those looks of hers; or maybe he feared the unknown, which he couldn't explain. He examined his clothes, his small belly, his shoes, then turned back to gaze at the books. He walked on a yard, seeing authors he knew from other books, and books by people he'd never heard of: Albert Camus, Sagan, Isma'il Cadreh, Kundera. He smiled as he saw the title *Lolita*. He'd read that thirty years or more ago, he recalled, then hidden it to make sure his sister didn't read it!

He took a few paces more, watching as the twilight sun eased its way between two high buildings, its golden rays flirting with the garden trees. There
were different sorts. Some were tall trees affected now by the fall, their leaves
growing pale and some of them dropping; then there were trees of medium
height, green and fresh and some small trees hugging the earth, stretching to
find the blue sky.

He made an attempt to recall the names of the trees and plants in the garden.
He started listing them: cypresses, palms, olives, walnuts, willows, oleanders—he
just couldn't name them all.

On he walked. One step, then a second, then a look over at the other sidewalk. To his surprise that same girl was still gazing at him.

He looked back at her, inspecting her closely. She had a graceful figure, the
way girls had today. Her hair was short, the way girls' hair was today. Her complexion was fair.

Fair? Was she Russian maybe? The streets were full of Russian girls these days,
and so were the cafés and hotels and all kinds of other places. The newspapers
never stopped talking about them.

No, no, the girl couldn't be Russian. Russian girls were on the plump side,
and their faces were rounder and the white of their complexions was mixed
with red. No, no. He pushed all his instinctive skills to try and work out where
the girl came from, what her origins were, but he didn't succeed.

As he eyed her, from head to foot, he saw she was smiling at him—a smile
that lit up her face and made him feel as if something had stung his own. He
turned, walked on another pace, then a second, gazing at a jeweler's window,
with its earrings, bracelets, rings, small watches, and brooches of various sorts.

The jewels were beautiful, and one particular brooch was wonderfully elegant.
I bought a lovely gold brooch once, he thought. Salwa's still got it. Time simply
flew by. Twenty-seven years! Curse this life, as short as the skirts of the girls here in
the street! If only you could live your life all over again, Suhail, he thought!

He felt the girl's gaze boring into the back of his neck. Just what did she
want with him?

He turned away, his body beginning to waken, while the girl walked a few
yards alongside, on the sidewalk, then stopped by a florist's, then leaned her
graceful body against the iron railing separating the street from the sidewalk, her
proud breasts defying the passers-by and his sixty years. Her smile had grown
wider, her looks more frank and provocative.

He took a lingering look at her, shaking his head, as if to ask, "Can she really
be following me? Is she really attracted to me?" Then he saw to his surprise that
she was shaking her head too, smiling even more broadly than before.

He looked around, left, right and behind him, checking there was no one
there who knew him, who had seen what was happening. Then he went back
to gazing at her figure, her hair, her face, her breasts, the black blouse she was
wearing, her blue jeans.

If it does work out, Suhail, he thought, where are you going to fly off to with her? You don't have a car, of course, but there are plenty of taxis. All you've got to do is hail one and your problems are over. You can just tell the driver, "Panorama Hotel, please." We can walk together there. It's a romantic spot, with those trees and flowers and the quietness. We'll sit together on a wooden seat, watching the sea, and the ships and the harbor. And yet!

Why did the girl have to be wearing jeans? Was it fitting for him to walk with a girl in jeans? If only she'd been wearing a short skirt, that would have been better—and easier!

No, no. People mustn't see him walking in the street with a girl in jeans, a twenty-year-old girl walking with a man in his sixties, wearing a formal suit and a necktie!

But what if this girl was just a coquette, who wanted to trap him in her meshes, make him a laughing stock for decent and worthless people alike to gloat over, turn him into a standing joke?

He felt afraid. Walking on a few more yards, he reached the entrance to the cinema, stared at the placards and the faces of the actors and actresses. It looked an exciting film, French, about a young man in his twenties and a seventy-year-old woman. He kept staring at the pictures. No, it should be the other way round—a girl in her twenties and a man in his sixties!

Love! That's something you haven't thought about for years, Suhail, he reflected.

He remembered the innocent experiences of love before he met his wife. How he'd come out of them in one piece but with scars on his heart and in his memory.

Love! Was it possible a girl in her twenties could be attracted to a man like him? Retired and washed up?

Well, why not?

He'd read, in novels and other books, plenty of stories about adolescent girls and older men. There was a particular type of girl who preferred relationships with old or middle-aged men rather than young ones. And anyway, he reflected, I'm not that old and decrepit. I still have my graceful figure, and there aren't any wrinkles on my face, and I walk like a young man!

Turning toward the other sidewalk, he saw the girl had advanced a few paces and was approaching the pedestrian area near the fountain.

Suhail gazed at the fountain and the white arcs of water and saw a wondrous rainbow there, from the reflected rays of the sun as it slanted toward its setting. Joy surged through him as he counted the different hues and saw the girl walking on, her body passing through the rainbow, its colors breaking over her breasts and belly and legs.

She walked on to the edge of the pavement, then stopped and gazed at him. He stopped in his turn and gazed back.

Should he open the conversation? Should he ask her out to dinner?

He calculated how much money he had in his pocket. There was the two-way taxi fare, the price of a meal for two at the Panorama, and the cost of a room—a room for two hours, or just for one . . .

He saw words form on her lovely lips, like snapdragon flowers on a dewy morning. He read the expressions in her honey-colored eyes, and her smile lured him on, one step, then a second step.

Delight filled him once more as he saw her approaching now, walking toward him—her graceful body, her jutting breasts, her long white neck, her alluring rosy lips, her fair-skinned face, her honey-colored eyes. Honey. Honey.

He felt youth creep back into him, his age shrink away little by little, as if he were still in his fifties. No, in his forties—no, in the very prime of youth! The blood surged in his veins.

A smile formed on his well-shaven brown face. He took two further steps toward her.

"Good evening," he heard her say.

"Good evening," he replied, "full of roses and lilies and jasmines."

She blushed. He stretched out his big hand to clutch her small palm in greeting.

"Hello," he said. "Welcome! Welcome!"

"I'm Amal," the girl whispered.

"I'm honored. Welcome! Welcome!"

The smile on his face grew broader, the blood poured into the cells of his body, awakening such youth as still remained there.

"Aren't you Mr. Suhail?" she said.

"Yes. Yes, I'm Suhail."

At this peak of his ecstasy, it hardly occurred to him to think how strange the question was, to wonder how it could be she knew him.

Anyway, why shouldn't she know him? Hadn't he been an important official once? Wasn't he known among all the different ladies in society?

"Please," the girl said, "give my best wishes to Maha. She was my classmate at secondary school. We shared the same desk. I saw you once, when the principal called you in, after the two of us put a pin on the Hebrew teacher's chair!"

The girl was speaking fluently now, the smile widening on her small face. As for the man, he stared at her in embarrassment, stunned and quite at a loss.

The girl walked on along the pavement, her body disappearing among the other walkers. Then she was lost among all those great bellies.

He stood there, motionless. The sun and the rainbow vanished from the fountain. A cold fall breeze sprang up, and the yellowing leaves were plucked from the trees in the garden.

Suhail heard a group of youngsters laughing their heads off as they crossed the pedestrian area. One of them said, "Make way for us, sir!"

Then they burst out laughing again, while he gazed at them, stunned, utterly thunderstruck.

—Translated by Sharif Elmusa and Christopher Tingley

Baha' Tahir (1935)

Egyptian short-story writer and novelist Baha' Tahir was born in Giza near Cairo. After studying history at Cairo University, he worked as a cultural programmer for Radio Cairo, later becoming its deputy director. In his capacity as program director he produced a range of drama from Classical European to Western modernism, as well as writing drama criticism. In 1977 he moved to Switzerland to work as translator in the Arabic section of the United Nations in Geneva. Though he is not prolific, he is unanimously acknowledged as a skilful writer of the short story. Tahir's life in the West has inspired his comparisons between life in the West and in the Arab East. This theme was successfully taken up by the Egyptian writer Tawfiq al-Hakim in his *Bird from the East*, and subsequently by writers such as al-Tayeb Salih of the Sudan, who brought the subject to great artistic and cultural heights in his novel *Season of Migration to the North*, and, many years later, by the Lebanese writer, Hanan al-Shaykh, who treated Tahir's theme with a new sophistication in her novel *Only in London*. His collections of stories include *The Engagement* (1972); *Yesterday I Dreamt of You* (1980), and *I Am the King, I've Arrived* (1985).

THE ENGAGEMENT

I'd taken care of everything. A trusty friend took me to a well-known barber who cut and arranged my hair, massaged my chin, and was paid a pound, and after that we bought an expensive red tie and silver shirt buttons. In the end, when I stood in front of the mirror, I was like a stranger—not more attractive but different, with shining hair lying flat as if plastered onto my head, a chin that was also shining and reddish in color, and a stiff, neat shirt-collar. For the first time in my life I fastened a tiepin in my tie; I felt all the time that it was going to slide off and fall, but it stayed in place until the end.

The doorman was surprised at my appearance and asked me, with a laugh, if I was going to get engaged. I told him I had an important appointment at the bank, and for no reason gave him five piastres. He looked at me in astonishment. I told him to pray for me, as I was expecting a promotion, so he thanked me and raised his hands to heaven, murmuring. I felt confused and hurried out of the door. The wind stung my face, and I realized that my temperature was high. In the taxi my heart began beating hard; I was sure all the words I'd prepared had gone and I wouldn't be able to say anything to her father except "Good evening." I started to sweat.

As I pressed the doorbell, I told myself that everything would depend on the father, and that I could confine myself to answering questions. A girl of eleven, dark-skinned and demure, half-opened the door for me, then stood behind it and faced me with lowered eyes. When I asked for the father, she nodded her head, opened the door, and led me without a word to the sitting room.

I remained alone for a while, smelling the usual smell of sitting rooms: wood preserved by little ventilation and rare use. The Venetian blind was closed, shutting out the ashen glint of the sunset, but by the brilliant light of the chandelier I saw the pictures: an oil painting of two sailors standing at the two ends of a gondola, each of them holding a long oar inserted in the water, their faces covered by broad hats. As a background to the brown gondola and the blue sea there was European countryside with its bright green and red hues. To the right of the painting hung a photograph of a man placing his hand on the shoulder of a woman in a wedding dress. Then there were pictures of children at various ages, and my gaze was drawn to the picture of a girl spreading her short dress to one side with her hand, and raising her other hand in the style of Pharaonic dancers. I didn't know whether or not it was Laila.

I stood up as the door suddenly opened. He came in, in shirt and trousers, spectacles and slippers, and stretched out his hand to me, smiling slightly. His hand was cold. He sat down opposite me and asked me whether he should open the blind or not; I looked at the blind for a long time but couldn't make up my mind. He said the spring in Egypt is changeable but mainly cold, and I agreed with this. He said the real spring in Egypt is the autumn, because it isn't humid; on the other hand, in the spring there are the *khamsin* winds. I added that the *khamsins* bring a lot of dust, which hurts the eyes. He leant back in his chair.

"Welcome," he said.

Silence followed. He crossed one leg over the other, and shook his slipper on his foot, so that his heel protruded from it, smooth, clean, and extremely white, like a large egg.

It couldn't be put off any longer, so I began talking without looking at his face. I told him that I was a colleague of Miss Laila at the bank and that I was asking his permission to marry her, and I told him about my degree, my salary, and my father. When I raised my head at the end, I found he was leaning his head forward on his chest, as if he hadn't heard a word I'd said. But at last he raised his head and asked, "What town in Upper Egypt did you say you were from, Sir?"

I told him for the second time about my hometown.

"From the Arabs of Upper Egypt?" he asked.

"Yes."

"Do you know 'Abdul Sattar Bey?"

I didn't know him, and he told me he was the director of the Educational District there. Everybody knew him, he said. I explained to him that I'd been educated in Cairo and taken a job there after graduating, and that this might be why I didn't know 'Abdul Sattar Bey. He shook his head, apparently unconvinced by this, then turned toward the door where the dark-skinned girl was advancing, cautiously carrying a glass of lemonade on a tray. She put the glass in front of me and left. "Please," he said to me. "Please, go ahead," I told him. He told me he didn't drink anything because of his colon and turned his face the other way. It seemed to me that he was angry with me about this, but while I was drinking the lemonade he told me he was honored that I'd asked him for his daughter's hand, and he thought I was a sensible and very deserving person. He added that there weren't many sensible young men about these days. Then he told me a joke: "A young Beatle went to the barber, and he sprayed him with DDT." He started laughing at this, and I also laughed gently. Then I thanked him and said I hoped he had a good opinion of me.

"As a matter of fact, young man," he said quietly, "parents give their daughters their freedom these days. It wasn't like that in our day. The father used to arrange everything, and the daughter only had to get married. Now the father educates his daughter and doesn't take a *millim* from her after she gets a job, and she rejects anyone her father advises her to marry. In the end she chooses whoever she wants, and the father has to put up with everything whether he likes it or not. But on the whole we're a conservative family."

"Of course."

"Of course, Laila isn't like other girls. She wouldn't ever disobey me. I brought her up and I know her. When she wanted to work, I asked her if she lacked anything, and she said she didn't. Why work then? I asked her. I've educated you, so your degree can be a weapon in your hand if, God forbid, anything happens. She said, 'Father, all my friends work. Please, father, please!' Finally I agreed. Because she insisted so much, not for any other reason."

"Of course, that . . . " I stopped.

"Yes?" he said.

"That's the reason," I answered.

"Of course, 'Abdul Sattar Bey was my colleague at the Higher Teachers' College. But never mind about that. You say you don't know him. But I tell you, and I beg you to listen to me carefully, I can't agree to anything that isn't in Laila's interest."

"I wish you'd be so kind as to explain to me . . . "

"Yes, in fact Laila's spoken to me about you more than once. And I asked about you, and I know a lot of things . . . a lot of things."

He started searching carefully in the pockets of his trousers as if he was going to take out certain documents, but in the end he took out a handkerchief and started wiping his face and hands. "Shall I open the blind?" he asked me again.

"If you like."

He looked at the blind, then said slowly, "When you were at university, you lived with your maternal uncle, didn't you?"

"Yes."

"And now you're living alone."

"Yes."

"Why?"

"I don't understand."

"Why did you leave your uncle's house to go and live by yourself?"

"I graduated, and it wasn't right for me to remain a burden on him."

"Really? It wasn't because your uncle was angry with you?"

"Certainly not."

"I'm glad to hear it. By the way, this is a somewhat delicate question, and I hope you'll forgive me, but consider me as your father. The lands in your home town, are they in your father's name or your mother's name?"

"I explained to you, sir, that we're not rich. It's a small piece of land that my father cultivates, and I think it's in his name."

"No, I think it's in your mother's name."

"Maybe, but I don't understand the meaning of this. I haven't lived in the town, and I haven't worked in agriculture."

"Nor have I, but I understand a lot of things. One plus one equals two. Why didn't you live with one of your paternal uncles in Cairo?"

I was silent and began turning the empty glass around on the tray. Then I suddenly realized what I was doing and left the glass where it was.

"Do you think Sir," I asked in a low voice, "that that's an important question?"

"More important than you think."

"Then the fact is that there's a disagreement between my father and my paternal uncles."

"Maybe more than a disagreement. Maybe a complete estrangement. Do you know the reason?"

"There was a disagreement over inheritance, I think."

He laughed. "Inheritance?" he said. "Never mind about that. I don't think you know much about the matter. This . . . disagreement, as you call it, has been there since before you were born, and certainly your father didn't tell you about it. But now I beg you to be honest with me. Everything between us will remain secret. You're asking to be the husband of my daughter, so it's my right to know everything."

"I haven't told you any lies."

"No, I know you haven't. But now tell me, why did your maternal uncle divorce his wife?"

"Do you think too . . . "

"I beg you, tell me the truth."

"Believe me, I swear I don't know the reason. My uncle was secretive about it. I think the reason was that she didn't give him any children."

"But he stayed with her for ten years without having children."

"Yes."

"And he didn't marry again after he'd divorced her, did he?"

"No."

"So?"

"Perhaps that wasn't the reason."

He suddenly leaned towards me and grasped my hand, which I'd put on the small table between us. I trembled as he began whispering, his face almost touching mine.

"You mean you don't know that . . . that . . . It was said that your maternal uncle's wife was having an affair with you?"

"That's a lie," I shouted.

"Please," he said, "keep your voice down. I didn't say it was the truth, I said that was what was said."

"Who said it? It's a lie, a contemptible lie! Whoever said it is a liar and contemptible."

"The people who said it are your paternal uncles."

"They said it to you?"

"Of course not, but I knew. No, don't ask me how I knew. But why did they say that?"

"I didn't know they did say it."

"Do you visit your maternal uncle?"

"Sometimes."

"And does he visit you? No, I don't need to ask that. Has your maternal uncle been to your hometown even once since his divorce?"

"I don't remember."

"But that's an easy question. He used to visit the town once a year, during his holiday, and stay as a guest at your house, with his sister."

"Yes."

"When was the last time?"

"Not since . . . Three years ago. Not since the year I graduated."

"Yes, just before his divorce. He hasn't gone once since then."

"Why?" I asked.

He laughed loudly, showing clean, shiny teeth with no gaps between them. "I . . . it's me that's asking you that," he said, still laughing.

I didn't answer, gazing instead at the picture of the gondola hanging above his head. It seemed a little gloomy. When I touched my forehead, my hand became wet from the copious sweat on my face and round my eyelids. I raised my hand to the collar of my shirt and tried to open it, but my fingers fumbled with the firmly fastened button. I contented myself with loosening my tie a little. Her father's face became serious.

"I'll open the blind," he said, moving to stand up.

I stretched out my hand toward him quickly. "There's no need for that, please. What concerns me now is to know . . . what . . . what do you mean exactly?"

"Surely that's clear by now?"

"You want to refuse to allow my engagement to Laila, Sir, and so you're telling me about . . . about these rumors?"

"What rumors?" he asked, his face hard.

"This strange story about my maternal uncle's wife."

He leaned towards me again. "I don't understand," he whispered. "The matter must be as clear as daylight. You're from Upper Egypt, from the Arabs of Upper Egypt. And you understand these traditions better than I do."

"What traditions? Could I please ask you to be clear. There's no need to beat around the bush."

"God forgive you. From what I've heard, your maternal uncle, who's also the son of your father's paternal uncle, was the only one of the family who remained on good terms with your father, isn't that so?"

"Yes."

"Because of the relationship by marriage, of course. The whole family ostracized your father because he squandered his inheritance on ... let's say on pleasure. All of them except your maternal uncle. The man was prepared to put up with threats of death."

I threw back my head and laughed. My eye fell on the oars of the gondola, aimed like bayonets, as his voice rose a little.

"I don't know whether you chose to ignore it or simply didn't know about it," he said. "But at that time they all went to him, to your maternal uncle, and said they'd put up with everything your father did, but they couldn't bear this 'disgrace,' as they called it ... that is, his wife having an affair with you. They said either he should divorce her, or they'd kill her and kill you at the same time."

"Nonsense. Some contemptible person wanted to defame my reputation, and invented this ridiculous story."

"Perhaps. But how can you prove it's a lie?"

"There are a thousand proofs. I tell you, it's a lie. I'm not so low as to think, even to think, of my maternal uncle's wife. She was ... she was like my mother ...just like my mother."

"I'm not discussing that now. I respect your word. I don't believe there was anything. But what's your proof that the rumor didn't lead to these results?"

"I've never heard of them."

"That's not a proof. You say you've never heard of them. What's the proof you've never heard of them?"

"I swear it."

"All right. Nevertheless, you yourself said your maternal uncle was secretive about the matter. Right?"

"Yes."

"You wouldn't expect him to talk to you about it himself, when you disassociate yourself from your paternal uncles and their children. In fact you don't even know them, do you?"

"No."

"So you're not likely to hear from them, either."

"Would they have been satisfied with killing then?"

"I don't know. That's something I don't understand. You don't think, of course, that I made this story up merely in order to tell you that I don't want you as a husband for my daughter? I could simply have refused with an apology."

"So?"

"So the story is true. I don't say the story of the relationship, that's none of my business, but the story of the threat and the divorce. Unless you have any proof to refute it."

"Yes, I have, of course I have. If it were . . . If it were true, it would have spread everywhere and I would have known about it. If it were true, my paternal uncles would have exploited it to slander me and my father."

"And so bring shame on themselves? No, they wanted to contain the matter, not spread it."

"So how did you come to know about it? From 'Abdul Sattar Bey?"

He laughed slightly. "Would a man in his position concern himself with things like that?" he said. "No, no."

"So how did you know?"

"That's my business. But I assure you it will remain secret between us."

"Why should it remain secret? Spread it. Spread this rumor everywhere."

"I'm not malicious. And please, keep your voice down."

"Why should I keep my voice down? Isn't that what you want? Don't you want Laila to hear this despicable story? Isn't this your plan to keep her from me? Why should I do this for you? I'll tell her about it myself. Ha, ha! My maternal uncle's wife . . . Why wasn't it my maternal aunt herself . . . or . . . or my grandmother for example? Ha . . . ha . . . ha."

Having failed to keep me quiet, he stood up, shook me by the shoulder, and said quite loudly, "Be a man. If I'd known you were going to act like this, I wouldn't have spoken to you in the first place. Are you a child? You're a guest in my house."

"Do you want me to leave?"

"No, I want you to be a man and hear me out. Shall I get you a glass of water?"

"No, thank you."

"I'm sorry if I upset you. But believe me, I didn't realize you were unaware of all this."

"I was happy to be unaware of it."

He went back and sat in his place opposite me, clasped his hands together and looked at me silently.

"I apologize for what I said," I told him.

"I understand your feelings," he said, gesturing with his hand.

"Thank you," I said, standing up. "Will you excuse me if I leave?"

He stood up again and placed his hand on my shoulder till I sat down. "No," he replied, "we haven't finished talking yet."

"If I've understood you correctly, you think I'm a person with a bad reputation and you don't want me as a husband for your daughter. And I can't deny the bad reputation, since I've no proof that it's untrue."

"I didn't say you have a bad reputation. Let's say you're a victim of rumors."

"There's no difference."

"And I didn't say I refuse you as a husband for my daughter."

"So what's the meaning of all this?"

"Please understand me. I'm concerned for Laila."

"Why don't you say it right out?"

"You want me to be frank? All right, I will. You know that in the bank, in a job like yours, a person's reputation is the most important thing?"

"Are you starting your insinuations again?"

"No, but . . . "

"I simply won't agree to this kind of insinuation. Tell people what you know. Tell them everything you know. I don't mind what you say!"

"Please!"

"What about my work? There's nothing to harm my reputation in my work. If you're referring to the accusation of embezzlement, I was cleared of it. The Administrative Prosecutor's office itself cleared me and shelved the case. It confined itself to drawing my attention to the matter."

"I swear I wasn't referring to that. I don't even know about it."

"No? That doesn't work with me any more. Since you insinuate that, I want you to know it was a frame-up. They took advantage of my good intentions and planted some papers on me that I didn't know anything about. The Administrative Prosecutor's office discovered that itself. If it had been embezzlement I would have been put in prison. Do you hear? That's clear. But the prosecutor's office drew my attention because they said my good intentions were regarded as a kind of negligence. Do you hear?"

"Yes, Yes, I hear."

"I'm not a thief."

"I wasn't accusing you of that. Are you crying?"

"No. Why should I cry? This is sweat. Sweat. Look."

"So why don't you want me to open the blind?" he asked, getting up from his seat. I couldn't see him clearly, and all I could see of the painting was a red and yellow blur.

"I never said I didn't want you to open it. I said it didn't matter to me. I don't care whether you open it or don't open it. I only want to know what you want."

He put his hand in his trouser pocket and hesitantly handed me a handkerchief. "Thank you," I said. "I have a handkerchief."

I began carefully wiping the sweat off my face, from my forehead and around my eyes. When I'd finished I saw he was no longer there in front of me. In fact he wasn't in the room at all. Only the canvas confronted me with its two sailors with their faces blotted out. Then I found him standing in front of me, handing me a glass of water. I drank a gulp of water and, when he sat down again in front of me, noticed that there were fine beads of sweat appearing on his wrinkled white forehead. His face was pale and we remained silent.

"The gondola ought to be in Venice," I said after a while, surprised that my voice should come out so loud.

"Yes?" he said. "What did you say, Sir?"

"This picture. The gondola should be in Venice. I mean, in a city. But this picture shows it in the countryside. It's wrong."

He turned his body as he sat, and began gazing at the picture hanging behind his back as if he were seeing it for the first time. Then he turned to me and said: "Yes, you're right. Do you know about art?"

"No, but we studied that in history. At school."

"I studied it too. But I never noticed."

Then he said with sudden vehemence: "Listen to me. Laila loves you."

"And I've . . . come to become engaged to her."

"Put yourself in my place. If you were her father, would you agree?"

"You could have said that at the start. I'm sorry, and I won't trouble you or Laila again. I'll say you've refused."

He turned towards me. "No. No. No," he whispered hurriedly. "I don't want you to put it like that."

"Please, what do you want exactly?"

"Let's talk frankly as you suggested. There are certain stories or rumors about you that it's important to you nobody should know."

"Yes."

"Even Laila herself might be influenced by them, might believe them."

"So?"

"For my part, I won't say a thing, I promise you that, but I urge you to cooperate."

"Co-operate in what? If you would be so kind . . . if . . . "

"I beg you not to laugh. I really need your help. If you told Laila I'd refused you, she'd only cling to you more, I know that. She'd hate me, and I might find myself forced to tell her everything."

"I understand. So am I to tell her I'm the one who refuses her?"

"No. Not that either. Tell her I've agreed, and I've made another appointment with you in a week or two, so we can come to an understanding."

"What?"

"There are ways. You understand these things much better than I do . . . There are girls inside the bank, and girls outside the bank (he laughed and put his hand over his mouth), and I believe you know how to deal with girls."

"You want me to . . . "

"You undertand quite well what I want," he interrupted, gesturing with his hand. "You can convince Laila in a thousand ways that you've changed your mind about marriage. But enough of that. Do you know Mr. 'Abdul Fattah, the head of the cancelled debts section in the bank?"

"Yes. What's he got to do with it?"

"He's got nothing to do with it. He's an old friend of mine. In fact, between you and me, he's the one who gave Laila a job in the bank. He's a good man, and very helpful. I heard him say they want to open a branch of the bank in Heliopolis, and they want a manager for the branch . . . What's your grade? I mean, how many years have you been with the bank?"

"One moment, please. Are you offering me a bribe? Is that it, that I should leave Laila in exchange for a promotion?"

His face hardened again. "Why should I want to bribe you?" he asked. "What could you do to hurt me? I'm offering you a service in return for a service. It's in my interest that you should go away from the place where Laila works, and it's in your interest to work in the new branch."

"Why?"

"You yourself said a moment ago that your work record isn't completely clean. This is a chance to regain your good name."

"Listen, please. Don't try to . . . "

"I'm not trying anything. You're trying to break your promise. You're more dangerous than I thought."

"What promise? Listen. I won't surrender to threats. I love Laila and she loves me. I'll tell her everything and she'll understand. Do you hear me? That's what I'll do."

He closed his eyes and turned in his seat. Fine beads of sweat had collected in the folds of his lined forehead, close together and crystallizing, until they looked like the surface of an iced glass. He laughed softly, shaking his head with his eyes closed.

"Yes," he said. "Yes. I know this kind of courage. I've known a lot of people who reject the voice of common sense. They're ten a penny now. But believe me, this isn't really courage. Courage is knowing what comes after this and accepting it."

"I know it, and I accept it."

"No, you don't know anything."

"Oh, I do. You can dirty my reputation at work, maybe you can get me transferred to another town, and you can fill Laila's head with suspicions of me . . . "

"I can do more than that, believe me. I can spread the rumor that your paternal uncles have been so careful to cover up. If I do spread it, no one knows what your paternal uncles or your father or your maternal uncle might do."

"But that's impossible."

"What's impossible?"

"You can't do that."

"Why not?"

"You can do what you want to me, have me transferred, kill me, but what have my relatives to do with this?"

"But you want to destroy my daughter, my own daughter. Why should I be concerned about people I don't know? Think about it carefully. Do you think I'd hesitate? Look at me. By the way, do you know your maternal uncle tried to commit suicide once?"

"Please be quiet!"

"It was just after the divorce. Nobody from the family knew."

"What do you want from me exactly?"

"They took him to the hospital in a bad state, but . . . "

"Please be quiet. I'll do everything you want. But please, don't say anymore."

He sat back in his chair. "I felt right from the start," he said, "that you were a sensible sort of person. No, don't get up now. Dry your sweat before you go out. You might catch cold outside."

I did dry my sweat before I went out. But as I was going down the stairs, I stumbled and fell flat on my face. I got up quickly, brushed the dust off my clothes and body, and leaned a little on the knob of the large outside door until I'd calmed down. The doorknob was a large brass-plated flower.

Outside night was falling, and the cars, with their red rear lights, were moving slowly along, one behind the other. I stood waiting. It wasn't cold. When the cars at last gave me a chance, I crossed to the pavement opposite, where there was a barber's shop crammed with mirrors. I saw myself, and saw dust on my sleeve and a large, swollen scratch above my eyebrow, which I felt with my hand: the skin was torn, but there was no blood. The barber stood leaning against the door, with his hand in the pocket of his white jacket. I noticed he was looking at me with interest. When I caught his eye, he invited me to come in and take a piece of cotton wool. Then he started laughing to himself and turned his face away from me. I didn't reply; instead I quickly lowered my hand from my forehead and crossed the pavement again. I dusted my sleeve thoroughly in front of the door and noted my reflection in the shining brass flower. Then I began to climb the stairs again.

—*Translated by Faris Glubb and Christopher Tingley*

Fu'ad al-Takarli (b. 1927)

Iraqi novelist and short-story writer Fu'ad al-Takarli studied law at Baghdad University and worked as judge in Baghdad for many years. Considered one of the leading writers of fiction in Iraq, much of his work springs from his experience as a judge and delineates problems of sexual morality, particularly incest. His collection of short stories, *The Other Face,* has appeared in two editions, the first in 1960. His first novel, *The Remote Echo,* was published in 1980 and has been translated into French. Two other novels have been published, *The Seal of Sand* (1995) and *Joys and Heartache* (1998). In 1999 al-Takarli won the prestigious 'Uweiss prize for fiction.

THE TRUTH

Yes, Your Honor, that's correct. I did not tell the truth the first time. I kept quiet for a month or maybe longer. But then, I was in jail all that time. And you know that honor is dear and one often does not know when to tell the truth.

I am innocent, Your Honor. I killed Farha, the wife of my brother 'Abd al-Hamza, because she had committed adultery. I surprised her in the act and was overcome by my Arab pride. Yes, I did lose my head, for honor is precious to us, and our custom is to avenge the loss of the family honor with blood. I loaded my hunting rifle, the one you see there in front of you; I fired at her once, while she was in the act of adultery. As for the lover, permit me, Sirs, to tell you all about him.

It is true I did not see him with her. That day, at dawn, Farha came out of her room to prepare breakfast for the family. She was wearing a red dress, with white dots. I saw her out in the courtyard heating up the oven to bake the bread. She told me she had sinned, that she had committed adultery; she said she wanted to kill herself. She lit the oven and then started preparing some lead shot to throw into the oven and kill herself. Your Honor, at that the blood boiled in my veins. I pointed the rifle at her and fired. She dropped dead.

Sirs, honor is precious to us, for we are genuine Arabs. We cannot allow shame to soil our family honor. It has always been our custom to kill the adulteress; this is our way, not to allow her to stay among us. Such a woman is like dirt that has to be wiped away.

Farha herself told me, Your Honor, that she had betrayed her husband in their marriage bed; she took advantage of his detention by the police to make a rendezvous with her lover, to tell him to come to her after dark. I did nothing except defend the honor of the family. Her husband is my brother, and she is my cousin. She used her youth and beauty to lure her lover to come for that illicit rendezvous. Yes, Sirs, she was nineteen, a beautiful face and eyes like honey.

As for my half sister, Halima, no, she saw nothing. I swear that to you on the Holy Book. True, she was with me, but she did not participate in the action at all, because she was not there at the time. She was in another part of the house. Let me explain to the respected court how we live. We are a poor family, and have one mud brick house with several rooms. On the east side is the room of my brother, 'Abd al-Hamza the husband of Farha, the adulteress. Next to it is my mother's room, then my own family's room.

Yes, Your Honor, I am a married man, I have been married for ten years and have four children. I served in the army and was promoted to the rank of corporal; I have never before been accused of or tried for any crime. The oven is in the middle of the courtyard near the room of my half sister, Halima. Halima has a small room to herself. I had completely forgotten to tell the court all this.

The morning the incident took place, my sister, Halima, woke me. In fact, I was already awake; maybe it was my aunt, Nuriyya, who called me. Nuriyya had spent the night with Farha, my slain sister-in-law. Maybe she was the one who called us, asking about the sound of shooting. I came out into the courtyard and saw Farha. She was lying on the ground next to the oven and the bullets were exploding inside it. That was where the noise was coming from. Yes, this is the testimony I gave before, Your Honor, in front of the magistrate, but it is not the truth. I forgot myself and repeated it to you just now; I beg your indulgence for my forgetfulness. The tragedy came upon me suddenly and I had to say whatever seemed best at the time. But the truth cannot be hidden; it will not go away, unfortunately.

The real truth is as follows, Your Honor. I was asleep that night when my sister, Halima, came to me about four or five o'clock in the morning; she woke me, whispering that she had seen someone running across the courtyard. I got up and went to my own family's room. They were asleep. Then I went to the room of Farha, the deceased, and found her by herself. My sister, Halima, is a young girl of seventeen, with a sharp temper; she has already testified before you, I believe, that she saw Farha, the deceased, sleeping with a stranger, committing with him the act of adultery, and that is why she had come to wake me up. Well, Sirs, I put on my clothes and came out to investigate. There was Farha, preparing the oven for breakfast. Yes, Your Honor, this is how things happened. The sky was white and the oven was burning furiously, with red-hot flames leaping up. Farha, without turning, said something to me about adultery and honor and suicide. I was embarrassed as I listened to her, but then my blood boiled up in my veins and I took the rifle from Halima, pointed it at Farha, and pressed the trigger. I fired one shot at her, only one shot from that hunting rifle that was found next to the body. I was acting for the good of my family, defending the family honor.

I beg of you, Sirs, to appreciate my position and to take into consideration the situation of my large family and the fact that I am a self-made man from a poor background who has taught himself to read and write and who is a former corporal. I killed that shameful woman, Your Honor, because she had committed adultery, she confessed her sin to me, face to face. She stood there next to the flaming oven in her red dress and announced that she had sinned, that she had stained the family honor.

What? The testimony of the other witness, Nuriyya? You mean the testimony that she, Nuriyya, was in the same room with Farha all night long? That testimony has no value, Your Honor. The woman is crazy. Why, the deceased herself confessed to me that she had committed adultery. Also, my sister, Halima, herself saw Farha in a shameful situation that neither honor nor law should condone. What can one say about a young woman who takes advantage of her husband's detention in jail to make a rendezvous with her lover, a young woman who asks that lover to come to her marriage bed after sunset to commit the evil crime of adultery. Yes, honorable Sirs, while the rest of the family was worrying about her husband 'Abd al-Hamza's arrest, what was the wife doing? She was busy arranging a meeting with that criminal, her lover.

I am not an educated man, Sirs. Some might call me simple, but I know my position in society, Sirs, even though I am not yet thirty. I explained to the deceased very clearly that the crime of adultery could not take place in our house. We are an honorable family, a conservative tribal family; we cannot allow our honor to be defiled by such a crime. I tried to convince Farha to abandon her fantasies and not to accuse anyone of immoral acts, but like a demented person, she persisted in doing so. So then I left her to go to her own room in the hope she would come to her senses. I told Halima what had happened and then went to take a bath. I had not finished bathing when the shot rang out. I ran into the courtyard. It was flooded with a misty white light, Your Honor. The red flames were leaping out of the oven, and Aunt Nuriyya confronted me to ask who had fired the shots. I pushed her aside and ran to the room of my brother 'Abd al-Hamza where I found Farha and her lover together. She was already dead; perhaps she had killed herself. I took the gun and returned with Halima to her room.

But now I am straying from the truth again. This is a habit to which you are not accustomed, honored Sirs, a habit that probably doesn't appeal to you. We poor bedouin tribesmen cannot concentrate on one subject for any length of time. In other words, our minds are disorganized. We think about one idea but before finishing that thought, we move to another idea that seems more attractive or at least nearer to our heart's desire.

We may be simple people, but we are honorable people, we want to live and eat our bread in peace. All the rumors circulated about us are lies. As for me, I personally am a totally innocent person, as I have said before. You know that honor must be defended. Honor is always the same; it does not change. In honor, all men are equal. We are doomed to be honorable and to defend our honor with blood. I did no more than any many would do, a married man like me who is responsible for the future of a large family. Perhaps the situation seems complicated but in fact it is not.

Yes, Your Honor, I will try to put the true facts in front of you once more, for the last time. We were one family living together in a single house. My brother, 'Abd al-Hamza and his wife, the slain Farha, lived in one part of the house; next to them my mother and father, then I and my family. I have a wife and four children, Your Honor. Next to us my half sister, Halima, has her own room near the well. The oven is near the middle of the courtyard. Now, on the day of the incident we are discussing my brother was arrested. In spite of my advice he had broken the agricultural reform laws; the police took him away. Aunt Nuriyya came to spend the night with Farha, his wife. Simple, uncomplicated facts. Then the lover of the deceased sneaked into the house, we don't know when. And at midnight or maybe a little after, the honor of the family was defiled, again and again. All was quiet until dawn, when breakfast is usually prepared and the bread baked. It was then that the shameful acts were uncovered all at once.

This is how it happened, Your Honor. The deceased, Farha, this woman who had been indulging in adultery all night long, gets up! Yes, instead of being tired and going to sleep, she gets up before sunrise as if she had done nothing and comes to pry on others! Sin did not lie quiet in her soul, honorable Sirs. No, no, she woke us up. Her eyes flaring, her hair disheveled, she announces that it is better for her to commit suicide than to see adultery in our house! As if she had not already done enough, with her hideous crime, her adultery! At that, Halima responded she had seen Farha sleeping naked with her lover, yes, committing adultery all through the night. Farha was shocked and unable to speak, she was so taken aback by the truth spoken so openly. She covered her mouth with her hand and rushed out of the room.

What to do then? I had no choice but to wipe away the stain of that woman's shame with her own blood. Remember, honorable Sirs, this is how shame and dishonor are removed in our society, they are washed away with the blood of women. I put on my clothes, took my hunting rifle, and went out to her. As I told you, she was standing by the oven. The early morning sky was white, and the flames leaped out of the oven. We were alone. She told me she was going to commit suicide because she could not bear to see the sin of adultery go unpunished. I had no alternative but to fire at her with my hunting rifle. After that Halima unintentionally threw a handful of cartridges into the burning oven. The explosions woke everybody in the house.

This is the truth, Honorable Sirs, the whole truth. Anything else is mere fabrication.

Nuriyya is lying when she says she was with the deceased, Farha, all night long. She is lying when she says she saw no man enter and commit adultery with Farha. If you believe this woman, Nuriyya, ask her how it is she never saw Farha wake at dawn and come prying into the affairs of honorable people? And who asked Farha to light the oven for breakfast in the first place? And, if her motives in making breakfast were good, why did she come to Halima's room? And since when has Halima ever helped prepare the breakfast?

Yes, I have heard that false testimony. Nuriyya claims to have seen the deceased, Farha, pointing at us . . . at me and trying to say something before the rattle of death silenced her. This is not true, Your Honor! For it was I, and no one else, who dragged Farha from the side of the oven where she had killed herself, took her to her room, then dragged her back to the side of the oven again. I alone know where Farha fell and where she died.

The coroner's report is also untrue. The report claims the deceased was fatally wounded by a shot from a revolver. After all, I pulled the trigger myself, I should know what kind of weapon I had in my hand.

Whatever has been said in this court about Halima's role in the whole incident is lies, lies. In the name of God, Your Honor, I beg you to leave this innocent girl out of it. She knows nothing of the matter. I am the culprit—if you want to call it that—who defended his honor and silenced that hypocritical Farha once and for all.

I am innocent, honorable Sirs. If I have committed the crime of murder, it was for a noble cause—to uphold the honor of my family. Thus I ask you to be honorable yourselves, Sirs, and to be merciful in passing judgment on me. Believe me, there is someone who will grieve for me. Yes, there is.

And this is the truth, Your Honor, the whole truth.

—*Translated by May Jayyusi and Elizabeth Fernea*

Zakaria Tamir (b. 1929)

Syrian short-story writer Zakaria Tamir is a largely self-educated man, who rose to become editor of the prestigious literary magazine *Al-Ma'rifa* in Damascus. Now retired and living in the United Kingdom, he is still writing his highly allegorical, well knit, and terse experimental fiction. Tamir was one of the earliest Arab writers of fiction to use material from Arab history,

connecting the past with the present and using historical events and personages to allude to present-day political and social experience. His angry,
critical, and symbolic work is one of the major experiments that inspired
other short-story writers in the Arab world. Tamir's first collection of short
stories, *The Neighing of the White Horse* (1960), which won him instant recognition in avant-garde literary circles, was followed by *Spring Ashes* (1963);
The Thunder (1970); *Damascus of Burning Fires* (1973), and *Tigers on the Tenth
Day* (1978). He has also written fiction for children.

THE BEARDS

The birds fled from our sky, the children stopped playing in the alleys, the singing of the caged birds turned into soft trembling sobs, and sterilized cotton wool
began to disappear from the pharmacies, for there, gentlemen, were the armies
of Tamerlane[1] encircling our city. Fortunately, terror did not strike the sun, and
it continued to rise every morning.

We were the men of the city. Our faces did not go pale. Rather we smiled
and praised God who had created us as men with beards and did not create us
as women without beards. We held a consultative meeting to discover how we
could avoid defeat by Tamerlane. The first speaker was a rash youth who worked
as a salesman of women's clothes, and he shouted enthusiastically, "Let's fight."
Instantly he was greeted with contempt so that he became not only silent but
embarrassed. At that point the owner of the biggest beard in our city rose up
and spoke with composure, "No one needs war except he who does not exist,
and we—praise be to God—are bearded, and, therefore, we exist." Immediately
voices were lifted in encouragement and support, and it was decided after a short
argument to form a delegation to negotiate with Tamerlane. The delegation was
headed by an old man who had a beard that hit his knees when he walked.

There were seven gates to our city, and the delegation exited from one of
them preceded by a white banner and went forward among soldiers more numerous than the stars or locusts. The soldiers were preoccupied with hunting
for lice in their underclothes, and they left their swords for the sun to dry what
blood or mud had stuck to them.

With slow dignified steps the delegation entered Tamerlane's tent, and they
saw that Tamerlane was a youth who had the eyes of a child and the smile of
an old man.

The head of the delegation said, "We seek peace, and our city is yours without war, but our city is small and poor; it owns neither gold nor fuel; our women
are like goats, and we would be happy to be rid of them."

---

1. *Tamerlane* or Timur was the Mongol conqueror who invaded Persia, India, and many countries of the Levant, including the Arab world, in the fourteenth century. He was notorious for
acts of atrocity and may have butchered more than eighty thousand people.

Tamerlane answered, "I hate shedding blood, and I do not want gold or beautiful women. But I have learnt that the barbers in your city are hungry because you have let your beards grow. This is an injustice that I decry, especially as my life is dedicated to championing the oppressed and spreading justice in the far corners of the earth, for men must not go hungry."

Astonishment took hold of the members of the delegation, and they exchanged bewildered looks.

Tamerlane said, "My armies will not depart your city until after you have shaved your beards and the business of the barbers prospers."

The head of the delegation responded, "What you ask is a weighty matter, and it is necessary for us to return to the city before giving a final answer."

Tamerlane said, "Either you shave your beards or you perish. Choose."

Silence and terror spread through the delegation, and life at that moment seemed to them to be as beautiful as a deep blue sky or crimson roses or *mawwals* recited by a tormented lover, or as the first cries of babies or the trembling mouth of a woman. But then the members of the delegation soon imagined themselves standing in front of the mirrors staring at their smooth-shaven faces, and horror and indignation overwhelmed them, and death at that moment turned into a red fish glistening under a sun of gold.

And the head of the delegation spoke, feeling that all the men of our city were listening with reverence, and he said in a cold voice, "Tomorrow our city will choose its future."

And the delegation returned to the city and repeated to us what Tamerlane had said. We were angry and shouted, "What is the use of living if we must lose our beards?"

And on the next day the armies of Tamerlane attacked our city, leveled the walls, destroyed the gates, and slew all the men.

Thus was the opportunity given to Tamerlane to stare with satisfaction at a mountain of men's heads, and the faces were yellow and blood-stained, but they were smiling, proud of their beards. They did not frown—as has been said, nor did their happiness and pride recede except at the moment that Tamerlane ordered the barbers to cut off their beards.

That is how, gentlemen, we were defeated without being avenged, and a shame that cannot be erased by any blood crowned us.

—*Translated by Lena Jayussi and Samuel Hazo*

WHAT TOOK PLACE IN THE CITY THAT WAS ASLEEP

No—

In the courtyard of his house the old man was sitting on a low wooden chair. He rested his back against a white wall. His eyes were closed and he was bathed in the light of a warm sun, imagining that he had become a king before whom heads were bowed and that the earth would tremble when he was angry. And he was also imagining a cat coughing and saying, "I will die because I smoke cigarettes," and he imagined a child on fire calling to its mother for help but the mother would not heed him and continued grooming herself as she stood in front of a big mirror.

The old man opened his eyes when he heard the door of the house open and saw his seven sons enter carrying wood, a saw, and hammers. So he said to them questioningly, "What are you carrying?"

But none of them answered. They put down what they were carrying on the floor of the courtyard and began their work silently.

The old man asked them, "What are you doing?"

When they did not answer, he said mockingly, "You must be making a chest." "What do you want to do with a chest? Will you put your tattered clothes in it?"

The sons did not reply and continued working quickly. The old man said, "I know what you are making. You are making a cupboard to keep food in. What use is such a cupboard since mice have stopped coming to our house for years because they found nothing to eat?"

The seven sons remained silent, working with grim faces. So the old man said to them in an angry voice, "God's curse on you! What is this behavior? Your father addresses you and you do not answer? Sons have to respect their fathers. What a waste of my efforts on your upbringing!"

And the old man closed his eyes again and imagined drunk men dying on the pavements, wailing and saying, "How ugly is both our life and its end! We did not pray. We did not fast. We did not perform the pilgrimage. We did not give alms."

And a rough hoarse voice said to them, "You lived like dogs, so die like dogs."

A sudden silence filled the courtyard of the house. The old man opened his eyes and saw that his sons had finished their work. So he cried in astonishment: "What have you made? You have made a coffin? Which of you intends to die?"

One of the sons said, "The coffin is for you."

The old man said: "What a silly son you are! You always speak the words of madmen. A coffin is for the dead. As for me, I am still alive and able to marry a girl of fifteen."

The seven sons approached the old man with slow steps and scowling faces, so he said in panic, "What is the matter with you? Have you gone mad? What do you want to do?"

He tried to resist when his sons lifted him and placed him in the coffin, but their strong arms pinned him to its bottom. The old man wept, and his tears wet his long white beard and furrowed face, and he said, "You are mad".

One of the sons said in a calm voice, "It is time for you to die."

The old man shouted, "Do you know what you are doing? You are killing your father? What have I done to be treated this way?"

The first son said, "You taught us how to bow our heads."

The second son said, "And you taught us to kiss the hand that slaps us."

The third son said, "A woman's dress frightens us."

The fourth son said, "We become limp as socks at the sight of a woman's knee."

The fifth son said, "You taught us to sleep on the days of the storm."

The sixth son said, "We have no past, no present and no future."

The seventh son said, "We do not dare look up at the sky."

So the old man shouted, "But I have not died yet."

But the sons did not heed his cry, and they hammered nails into the lid of the coffin, then burnt all the cloth in the house that could be made into a white banner, and they carried the coffin into the cemetery.

—*Translated by Lena Jayyusi and Samel Hazo*

LOVE

The warning sirens let out their sharp, drawn-out cry, so the city turned out its lights and tried to choke back a gasp of terror.

Eagerly a man and a woman embraced as they lay on a narrow bed.

The man said, "Are you afraid?"

"I won't be afraid."

The man said in a low voice, "Here we are after such a long absence."

And he touched her hair with a trembling hand and said, "Every night the pillow would ask me about you."

The woman laughed. Her laughter had the wings of a small bird.

She said: "And what would you say to it?"

"I would say to it: I am a jealous man. Why do you ask?"

"And what would it say to you?"

"It would say: 'I long for her black hair.'"

"But it is silent now."

"Happiness has robbed it of speech."

And he felt her close to him, a live naked body like green moss or a river of stars, and as the stars went seeping into his veins, he pressed his mouth to her mouth.

And at that moment the enemy planes approached, circled in the sky of the room and dropped their bombs.

—*Translated by Lena Jayyusi and Samuel Hazo*

TIGERS ON THE TENTH DAY

The jungle moved farther away from the caged tiger, but he could not forget. He stared angrily at men hovering around his cage while their eyes contemplated him with fearless curiosity. One of them spoke in a calm but authoritative voice,

"If you really want to learn my profession, the profession of animal taming, you must never forget that the stomach of your adversary is your first target, and then you will find that this is a profession that is both easy and difficult at the same time. Look at this tiger. He is ferocious and wild, very proud of his freedom, his strength, and his power, but he will change. He will become meek and gentle and as obedient as a small child. Just watch what will happen when I control his food and he doesn't. Watch and learn!"

The men hastened to say that they would be loyal students, so the tamer smiled and mockingly questioned the tiger, "How is our dear guest?"

The tiger said, "Get me something to eat. It's time for my dinner."

The tamer feigned surprise, "Do you give me orders when you're my prisoner? What a ridiculous tiger! You have to realize that I am the only one here who is entitled to give orders."

The tiger said, "No one commands tigers."

The tamer said, "But you are not a tiger now. You are a tiger only in the jungle, but now you are in a cage. You have become a slave, and you must do whatever I tell you to do."

The tiger said impatiently, "I will not be a slave to anyone."

The tamer said, "You will have to obey me because I control your food now."

The tiger said, "I don't want your food."

The tamer said, "Then stay hungry if you want to. I won't force you to do what you don't want to do." And he added, addressing his students, "You will see how he will change. Pride and stubbornness won't fill a hungry stomach."

And the tiger became hungrier and hungrier and remembered the days when, unchained, he would race along like the wind chasing his victims.

On the second day, the tamer and his students surrounded the tiger's cage and the tamer said, "Aren't you hungry? Certainly you must be having hunger pains by now. Say that you are hungry, and you will have what you want."

The tiger remained silent, so the tamer said, "Do what I say and don't be foolish. Say that you are hungry and you will have all you want to eat."

The tiger said, "I'm hungry."

So the tamer laughed and told his students, "There he has fallen into my trap, and there is no escape." And he issued orders for the tiger to be given a good supply of meat.

On the third day, the tamer said to the tiger, "If you want to get food today, do what I say."

The tiger said, "I won't obey you."

The tamer said, "Wait a minute, my request is very simple. You are just roaming around your cage; when I tell you to stop, I want you to stop."

The tiger said to himself, "It's really a trivial request. Why should I be stubborn and go hungry?"

Then the tamer shouted, "Stop."

So the tiger froze immediately, and the tamer said in a pleased voice, "Well done."

So the tiger was happy and ate ravenously while the tamer was saying to his students, "He will become a paper tiger after a few days."

On the fourth day, the tiger said to the tamer "I'm hungry, so ask me to stop again."

The tamer said to his students, "He has started to like what I order him to do."

Then he turned and said to the tiger, "You will not eat today unless you imitate the miaowing of cats."

So the tiger suppressed his anger and said to himself, "I will amuse myself and do what he wants."

And he imitated the cat's miaow, but the tamer frowned and said disapprovingly, "Is that the best you can do? Do you consider growling to be miaowing?"

So the tiger once again tried to imitate the cat's miaow, but the tamer remained grim and said contemptuously, "Be silent, be silent. Your mimicry is still a failure. I will leave you today to practice the cat's miaow, and tomorrow I will test you. If you succeed, you will eat, but if you do not succeed, you will not eat."

And the tamer walked away from the tiger's cage with deliberately slow steps, his students following him whispering and laughing among themselves. And the tiger longed to be back in the jungle, but it was very far away.

On the fifth day the tamer said to the tiger,: "Come on, if you sound like a cat today, you will get a big piece of fresh meat."

The tiger mimicked the cat's miaow, and the tamer clapped his hands and said happily, "You're great. You miaow like a cat in February."

And he threw him a big piece of meat.

On the sixth day, no sooner had the tamer approached the tiger, then the tiger began miaowing like a cat. But the tamer remained silent and frowned until the tiger said "But I'm miaowing like a cat."

The tamer said, "I want you to bray like a donkey."

The tiger said with annoyance: "I am a tiger, feared by the animals of the jungle and you want me to bray like a donkey. I will die rather than execute your request."

So the tamer departed from the tiger's cage without uttering a word.

On the seventh day the tamer came to the tiger's cage and smiled and said to the tiger, "Do you not want to eat?"

The tiger said, "I want to eat."

The tamer said, "The meat that you will eat has a price. Bray like a donkey, and you will get it."

The tiger tried to remember the jungle and he failed, so he burst forth braying with eyes closed. The tamer said, "Your braying is not successful, but I shall give you a piece of meat because I pity you."

And on the eighth day the tamer said to the tiger, "I shall recite the opening of a speech. When I finish, I want you to clap."

The tiger said: "I will clap."

So the tamer began reciting his speech, "Citizens . . . we have previously on many occasions made our positions clear regarding all matters of destiny, and this frank and steadfast position will not change however much the enemy forces conspire, and with faith we shall be victorious."

The tiger said, "I don't understand what you said."

The tamer said, "You have to admire everything I say, and clap with admiration."

The tiger said, "Forgive me, I am ignorant and illiterate, your speech is marvelous, and I shall clap as you wish." And the tiger clapped, so the tamer said, "I do not like hypocrisy or hypocrites. Today you will be deprived of food as punishment."

On the ninth day the tamer came carrying a bundle of grass, threw it to the tiger, and said, "Eat."

The tiger said, "What is this? I am a meat-eater."

The tamer said, "As of today you shall not eat anything but grass."

When the tiger's hunger grew, he tried to eat the grass, but its taste shocked him. He drew back from it in revulsion, but he returned to it again; little by little he began to relish its taste.

On the tenth day, the tamer disappeared, as did his students as well as the tiger and the cage. The tiger became a citizen, and the cage became a city.

—*Translated by Lena Jayyusi and Samuel Hazo*

Sahar Tawfiq (b. 1951)

Egyptian short-story writer Sahar Tawfiq was born in Cairo. She studied Arabic language and literature at Al-Azhar University College and has published her short stories in a number of Egyptian and Arabic periodicals. She is one of the avant-garde younger generation of writers of fiction in Egypt, and her work tends to be symbolic and sometimes allegorical, where the direct approach is only a mask for the involved psychological and emotional life of the protagonists. Her latest collection is *Taste of Olives* (2000)

IN SEARCH OF A WILDERNESS

That evening, as was customary, the thin pale man with the pronounced bony fingers came and sat on the same stone seat, his eyes fixed in one dimension, their gray pupils constricted to a narrow space and contemplating one point in his visual field. He sat alone and distracted.

The first time she saw him they exchanged a few words about music. After that he never paid her any attention, made no sign of their having met, and remained silent.

Sa'id came.

She got up and left the place with him. They walked for a short distance before turning toward the bridge. There was nothing there except the river. After a little while, he began to talk. He talked of many things, of his friends, of his mother and father, of work and fatigue, loneliness and the state of the world. He also spoke of love and said that he loved her. After talking of primordial and fundamental things, he looked at her questioningly, and when he saw that she did not answer, he said, "Why don't you say something?"

The river reinforced the solitude.

When she spoke it was to tell him that his talk of love appeared absurd and was meaningless now.

Then she spoke to him of herself, and how her first relationship with a man had gone wrong. She had known right from the very start that there was no future in it, yet she did not resist it until things grew to a final irreconcilable head and put an end to the affair.

"I loved a man once," she said," and he loved me. Everything appeared beautiful. Nothing could come between us."

"So what happened?" he asked.

"Nothing," she said.

"Why did you leave him?" he asked.

"I didn't leave him," she replied.

"Did he leave you?" he questioned.

"No, he didn't," came her reply.

"Then what was it that happened?"

"I don't know," was her answer.

She was suddenly depressed. Her pace slowed, and she withdrew her hand. They walked on in silence. Eventually she said that she wanted to go back.

She was sitting with her girlfriends, and they were talking about the mermaid that had appeared in Yemen. One of them was describing its legs, its protruding knees, and its body and head, which resembled those of a fish. Then they spoke of the spirits and jinn of their new stories and of what had happened to them recently.

One of the girls said, "It's a sign of the imminent end."

She walked through streets that were dark, wondering why she could not believe those tales.

Death is unreal, she thought, but it happens. She wasn't sure of the meaning of truth, but she felt threatened by the darkness.

The early morning saw her sitting by the Nile, a book in her hands. She thought back to her first days of love. She had been a small, fragile, naïve girl, but she had experienced something intangible then, a sense of surety and simplicity. It was like getting to know the streets. At first, she used to lose her way a great deal when she walked the main streets of Cairo and would go round and round, and finally by a series of detours she would come out at a familiar place. Later on, she realized that by familiarizing herself with one street, she would come to know the names of those other streets that intersected with it. Thereafter it was easy, she had got to know all of the streets, and today, there wasn't a side street or a main one that wasn't known to her. But still, she often wished she could lose herself, for there was a challenge in finding oneself fallible. Her thoughts returned to the perplexing subject of the mermaid. The old man came. He sat in his own world, and she had the impression that it was a long time since she had seen him last. His small eyes were of an indeterminate light color, and whenever she thought of him, she couldn't recall the color. She had decided, deep down inside, that one day she would follow him in order to know where he lived. He was carrying papers and busied himself with leafing through them. She tried to make out the print but could decipher nothing. She continued to watch him, the boats, the tower, al-Andulas Gardens, and the cars passing over the bridge.

Sa'id came, and they sat in silence. After a while the old man got up, and she stood up too. "Where shall we go?" Sa'd asked; and she, growing tense, replied, "Let's walk a little."

As they went along, she said, "I brought you some sweets."

A natural exuberance overtook her, and she quickened her pace, laughed, ran, and doubled back. She was watching the people, the river, and the trees.

They sat down in a quiet place. "What's the matter?" he asked her.

"Nothing," she said.

After a short interval, she said, "I don't know. I feel some change is imminent, and then everything will be defined."

They walked on, both feeling tense. He took her home, and she straightway went to bed and fell asleep. That night she dreamt that she went out in secret to meet him, but someone saw her, she couldn't say whether it was a man or a woman, and she didn't know what to do. She struck the person on the back with the flat of her hand and he fell down dead. After that she felt fear, panic, remorse. She hid in a hole so that no one would discover her, but they found her and took her away in a closed car. The car accelerated to a rapid speed, and she couldn't make out why she had done it, there was no apparent reason, and now it was inevitable that she would either be imprisoned or hanged, and she could accept neither. She felt greatly oppressed and genuinely innocent.

She woke up at last. Her head was burning. She went out in the street, not knowing what to do. She imagined that if she were to see Sa'id now she would throw herself into his arms and go on crying as he comforted her. He would know everything without her having to say a word.

She went to Tahrir Square. She climbed the steps to the bridge and walked up and down it several times. She grew tired and thought only of sitting on the stone stairs. She came down and walked to the Corniche. The old man was sitting there, reading a small book. She wished she could sit next to him and that they could read the text together. Or she wished that he would read out loud to her, quietly, and she would listen and look at the water and remain silent. After a time he got up, and she followed him. He crossed Abdin Square and entered an area that she hadn't seen before. It was full of small quarters and narrow crowded alleys. At last he arrived at an old pale-yellow house. He entered through a door and went down some steps. The entrance was dark. She continued to stare at it for a long while. When she turned to go back, she discovered that she was lost. She continued to walk in a state of confusion round the alleys and quarters until she arrived at the square.

She took a deep breath, and looked at the expanse of sky above her, and at the noonday light flooding the square. She walked briskly smiling at everyone and everything. It was time for Sa'id's arrival, but this was no longer important. She stood in a crowded place, shielding her eyes from the sun. A clock was chiming. She made a great effort to recall the old man's features, but to no avail.

—Translated by May Jayyusi and Jeremy Reed

Maguid Tobia (b. 1938)

Egyptian short-story writer, novelist, and screenwriter Maguid (also written as Mageed) Tobia was educated in Cairo. After teaching math for eight years, he studied script writing and film direction, graduating in 1971. Widely published, he was awarded first prize for a cinematic story and wrote a number of film and television scripts. In 1979 he was awarded the State Encouragement Prize for the best novel. He was also awarded the First Class Medal for Literature and the Arts. He has published five novels, including three published in the 1990s: *The Story of Beautiful Reem* (1991); *The Emigration of the Banu Hathut to the Countries of the South* (1992), and *The Moon is Born on Earth* (1995); and two novels for older children, as well as five collections of short stories, among which are *Five Unread Newspapers* (1970) and *The Next Days* (1972).

THE JOKER

THE FATHER

My father was strong as a stallion and randy as a billy goat. Women were his greatest pleasure.

At least that's what my mother used to say.

One evening when he came home, she was angry.

"You choose!" she said to him. "Make do with me alone or I'll leave you and go home to my family."

"Why?" he asked. "Have I ever denied you anything?"

"No."

"Have I ever failed to satisfy you?"

"No. You've taken me beyond my wildest dreams! But you won't leave other women alone, and I can't stand it!"

My mother said that my father frowned.

"You're incredible, woman," he said. "I've got enough juice in this body to keep you happy and many others too. Why should I lock myself in?"

Then he grabbed her, pulled her down on the bed, and only left her when the cock crowed next morning.

He dressed and went out to the fields.

My mother rested for a bit and got up feeling happy and full of energy. She made a delicious lunch and decided to take food out to my father in the fields.

But though she looked and looked, she did not find him.

And he never came back again!

In due course my mother gave birth to my brother and myself.

When we were first born, my mother said she didn't quite know what to do. But then she thought to herself, "I was created with two breasts. Fair enough, each can have one." She would rock the two of us together; the left breast was mine to suck and my brother got the right.

"Whichever of you finished first," she told us with a giggle, "used to kick the other one with his feet."

After we learned to walk, she dressed us in identical clothes and put identical skullcaps on our heads. My brother would get behind me in the street and copy the way I was standing. When the village men saw the two of us together, they would shout, "Look at those kids, it's incredible. Must be like looking at yourself in the mirror."

My brother thought up some great games to take advantage of our likeness. He would make the boys stand in the fields of sugar cane, while the two of us hid together among the tall stalks. After a bit, either my brother or I would come out, and the boys would try to guess which one of us it was!

THE TATTOO

My mother had a tattoo, three vertical lines on her chin. In the village and in the fields, she always walked confidently, her full breasts almost pushing out of her dress. She never looked behind her, sure that we would follow her. And I did, imitating every move she made. But my brother would take off at any turn in the road, cut through the fields, and sit down to wait for us. Sometimes he would circle round her, capering and cavorting and yelling his head off. She never seemed to pay any attention to him, and yet she had a happy smile on her face when she looked at him.

He would climb the Pharaonic ruins in the fields and clamber over the broken statues. He would even jump on the factory train and ride till the watchman discovered him, whereupon he would run off, making a noise like a steam engine.

One day while my mother was watering the sugar cane, she stopped suddenly. I saw her clench her lips tightly together and grasp her right breast. But it was only a moment. She shook her head and called us to her.

"Look, boys, see these?" She had grasped some of the canes heavy with seeds. "The seeds will be put in the ground and they will send up other new stalks. But the new ones will never be as strong as the original ones . . . "

I looked and listened in amazement, but my brother was off again, like a kid after a brief snooze. He came up behind me, jerked my *gallabiyya* and pushed me, running, ahead of him. His hand circled round, I could see, like the pistons of a steam engine. We ran this way across the cane fields, through the old temple, gathering boys and girls from the village as we ran.

We crossed the train tracks, pushed through a herd of goats and made our way toward the village. The play-train grew longer and the high-pitched whistling sounds of the children's voices filled the air, shrill as the shrieks of virgins. The row frightened a small mule that ran away in panic from its mother's side.

On the way we passed the gypsy fortune-teller, a basket on her head, red spangles glittering on her head scarf, a long bead necklace jangling against her chest.

"Secrets revealed!" she called, the gold ring in her nose trembling violently as she raised her voice. "Fortunes! Tell your fortunes!"

My brother dropped out of line and drew closer to the gypsy; in a second he pulled at her thin over-dress, revealing the red silk dress beneath. The train's procession faltered and began to break up while we waited to see what my brother would do next.

"Secrets revealed!" cried the gypsy, and my brother crept up behind her, grabbed the edge of her dress and pulled it as high as he could. We could all see her anklets, legs, and part of her thighs. One of the boys sniggered, and a group of women passing by gaped at us. But before that gypsy woman could even turn round, my brother had fled. The gypsy's basket had fallen to the ground, and we ran home.

In a moment, the gypsy woman stood there in the doorway of our house. The gold ring in her nose shook as she demanded that the rude child be punished. My mother probably guessed who had done it, but she chose to resort to her usual ruse.

"Well, there they are, the two of them," she said, pointing at us. "Tell me which one it is, and I'll beat him for you."

The gypsy woman stared at us. "Good Lord, lady, that's not easy. They're just like two peas in a pod."

"But only one pulled up your dress, right?"

"Right."

"So the other one's innocent."

"Beat them both," said the gypsy, "and the guilty one will be sure to get it."

"How about forgiving them both," my mother said, "Then I'll have been fair to the innocent one."

The gypsy woman growled out something and turned to leave, but my mother called her back.

"Watch what she does," she whispered in our ears, "And be careful. Gypsies will steal the kohl off your eyelids if you give them half a chance!"

The gypsy woman sat down her basket in our courtyard. She got some water from my mother and mixed it up with the paste for tattoos. Holding onto my mother's right breast with one hand and rubbing that breast with the other hand, she muttered prayers and phrases I could not understand. She began on the tattoo by first piercing the skin and making a design, then rubbing the paste mixture into the skin. At the end she gave my mother a green scarab and told her to put it under her bed at night.

"God willing the cure will work," she said.

Before she left, she looked at my brother again and at me. For some reason, I do not know why, I could not meet her stare. But when she looked at my brother, he stared boldly back.

"Aha!" she cried, pointing at me, "That's the one who lifted my dress up!"

My mother chuckled and looked at my brother. For a moment he stood there and then rushed out of the door, laughing loudly, a laugh that rang in my ears long after he had left the courtyard.

Next day, we could see the tattoo the gypsy woman had made, a crescent moon on our mother's right breast. We still did not understand what was happening. I felt jealous my brother's breast was getting all this attention. Mother still clasped that breast from time to time and clenched her lips together in a straight line.

THE *Zar*[1]

We crouched on the bed against the wall, totally absorbed in the scene before us. A fire flared in the middle of the room. When the flames died down to coals, my mother drew on some incense and a few black seeds with red eyes.[2] Musk-scented smoke drifted up to the ceiling. The red-eyed seeds in the coals seemed to wink at us.

A big woman stood up and raised a tambourine. Our eyes focused on the palm of her hand as it measured out a steady beat. My mother began to circle around the fire rhythmically, turning behind two other women.

We were fascinated by the dance. My mother moved faster to keep up with the quickening beat of the tambourine. The women swayed back and forth. Through the smoke we could see the dancing figures shimmering in the vague light, their bodies rippling and moving beneath their loose clothes.

Suddenly my brother jumped up and joined them, shaking his head and his body. But the women pushed him away, and he came back to sit beside me.

"Look," he said, pointing to the woman with the tambourine.

---

1. A ceremony of African origin for exorcising demons that are believed to cause illness, disease, or psychological problems. The medium is usually a black woman.
2. Called in Arabic "'Ain al-'Afreet," they are burned as a kind of incense in the *zar* ceremony.

The buttons of her dress were undone, and her breasts were clearly visible, swaying and jiggling together, whiter than her face and neck. My brother could not seem to take his eyes from that white expanse of bosom.

After what seemed a long while my mother, utterly exhausted, threw herself down on the bed. I noticed she had pinned an amulet over her right breast. Why, I asked myself, does she take that extra care of the breast my brother sucked and not mine? I was jealous.

I stared at the fire; the coals were turning to ash, and the demons' red eyes were fading away. "That tambourine woman's got breasts like milk pudding." my brother whispered in my ear. "Or like two large pomegranates."

From time to time the coals dropped and snapped, and the sharp crackling sounds mingled with the outside noises, the barking of dogs, the croaking of the frogs, and the rustling of the wind in the fields of sugar cane. Before I fell asleep, the train whistled as it passed through our village, wailing, shrieking like a virgin.

Next morning in the fields we saw Azhar, one of the village girls, driving her sheep toward us.

"Hey," cried my brother. "That girl's grown up before her time!"

And he pushed through the sheep, went right up to Azhar, and pinched her breasts in a brazen way. She screamed and cursed him, beating the sheep with her stick to move them along quickly so she could get away from my brother.

"You saw what he did, didn't you?" she hollered at me.

For a moment my brother paled. I gave him a scolding look, but soon I saw his whole body shaking with laughter. That loud laughter must have been heard all across the cane fields. Even the birds seemed to me to stop singing to listen to my brother laughing.

"You won't tell on me, though, will you?" he asked.

Well, Azhar came to our house, and she talked to my mother, but she never complained about what my brother had done to her or even asked me to back up her story. All she did was to turn her face away from him in anger.

THE LEAF AND THE GRASS

I asked my mother if anything was hurting her. She said no, but she had covered herself and was feeling her right breast again.

"Go out," she told me, "and find me a leaf from the Barbary fig."

"Why? Where?"

"Past the statues," she said, and her face crumpled suddenly in pain. "Go on to the edge of the valley and you'll see the tree. Take a good leaf. Go on now, and don't ask any more questions."

I took a short cut to avoid the winding alleys and came out onto the fields. From the swaying stalks of cane, Khamriyah, the waterwheel maker's slender wife, emerged. She came toward me, a strange look in her eyes, a mixture of modesty and boldness. When I looked suprized, she hesitated, but when I smiled, she smiled back and came closer, looking into my face. I smiled once more, but when I spoke and she heard the sound of my voice, she suddenly drew back, frightened. Her face turned pale, her eyes lost their brazen expression, and all that was left was embarrassment. She turned and ran away.

I kept on walking toward the valley, my heart full of bitterness against my brother. *For a few days he had disappeared and left me all alone to work in the fields. The work was exhausting. On the way back in the evening, men stopped me. "We can't make you out!" they said. "Just a few minutes ago you were laughing and telling jokes, and now you just look grim and tired. What's the matter with you?"*

I crossed the railway tracks. Near the temple, I heard voices somewhere among the statues, and there was a glimpse of a slim woman's fine back; she was running to hide and I could not see her face. I tried to follow her, but my brother suddenly appeared and stood in my way, smiling broadly. I moved to the right; so did he. I tried the left, he did the same. I bared my teeth; he imitated me. I growled angrily and he echoed me. And then he laughed, that loud laugh that rang across the fields.

I kept walking, but he caught up with me.

"Don't be angry with Khamriya. She's your blood relative."

I frowned and plodded on.

"I mean it. Her daughter's birth is registered with the government, with the waterwheel maker as her father. But actually, you're her uncle by blood."

"Get away from me!" I yelled.

"You're her real father's twin, that's what I mean." And he let out another of his laughs.

I kept on walking toward the edge of the valley.

"See the gypsy tents over there?" he asked, running beside me. "I've got a girlfriend there too."

"You lecher!" I screamed.

I remembered the first time he had left the field and followed the gypsy girl; he came back in a few minutes. The next time he caught up with her, but soon came back, and this time he was furious. "Those gypsies sure know how to play hard to get." he said. The third time he left me working on my own and ran after her, saying, "Third time lucky!" He was gone for some time and came back grinning from ear to ear. He hummed to himself as he set about working. The girl passed by us on her way back to the gypsy tents but never looked up. "The tall canes are wonderful cover, you know," he said, laughing.

I was very jealous of him.

Here was the Barbary fig. I pulled out my knife, and my brother started and moved back, frightened. I felt very pleased that he was frightened. I took hold of a large green leaf and cut it off.

"What's that for?" he asked.

I ignored him, and turned back home.

My mother took the thorns out of the leaf, then chopped it to a green paste, which she pounded in the mortar. She rubbed her right breast with the viscous leaf paste, wrapped it in an old cloth and put the breast back inside her dress again.

"Tell me what's hurting you," I asked.

"I'm getting old," she replied.

She lay down on the bed. "From now on," she sighed, "I'm going to stay home. You two will have to look after the field. I've taken care of it ever since your father left. All these years I refused to let any of the men help me in case I took a fancy to one of them." Her eyes glistened. "I was afraid I might find some strange man attractive, not, believe me for your deserter of a father's sake but because of you and your brother."

"Don't tell your brother what I have been doing with his breast," she said. "He might get angry."

For a long time she just stayed in the house, sitting and sleeping. Then one morning she got up and made her way to the Nile. There she carefully picked out some green leaves growing on the embankment and brought them back to the house. She put them in a pot with some water and placed it over the fire. Green-colored smoke began to rise from the pot. She squeezed her right breast till the nipple stood out, and then put the nipple into the smoke.

At that moment my brother came in, He stood in silence, without moving. She did not notice him. The smoke was turning the brown nipple deep red. My brother gasped. She looked up and pushed the breast quickly back inside her gown.

For a long time there was silence. The water boiled and bubbled on the fire.

"We must call a woman doctor," he said.

"Never," she said.

"You should have told us from the start," he said and went out.

She groaned. "The sparrow is grieving," she said to me, "because its nest has been destroyed."

She buried her face in her hands and her whole body shook. "Go and stop him!" she yelled at me.

"The medicine the doctor can give you is much better than the leaves and wild grass," I said, "and it'll hurt less than the tattoo woman's needle."

THE DOCTOR

The woman doctor held my mother's breast in her hand. The nipple was encircled by a dark halo like that around the moon on the night before it wanes. The doctor was looking at her nipple with a magnifying glass. I leaned over to see. So that was where the milk had come from, the milk that had poured into my brother's mouth so his baby appetite could be satisfied. Did his breast, I wonder, give more milk than mine? Was it even the same kind of milk?

The teapot rested on top of the coals. All around the fire the men were sitting and chatting. They always treated us the same in the beginning. They made a space for us. But my brother would begin to talk and make them laugh. His own laugh burst out, the blood rushed to his face, he looked handsome, even fascinating. Everyone's attention was focused on him. I got up and left, but no one even noticed . . .

And there were veins on *"his"* breast, thin blue veins that at times seemed to disappear under the green tattoo the gypsy woman had made. The skin of my mother's breast was lighter than her face. All around the nipple were tiny pimples that vanished when the doctor took the magnifying glass away.

The snake coiled its way out of its hole in the Nile embankment, pushed out by the flood, drunk with so much moisture. I aimed the gun and took off its head with a single shot. My brother gave me a stunned look.

"Can you shoot that accurately and that fast?" I asked, defiantly.

"I can stare at any woman in the village, whisper a few sweet nothings in her ear and make her blush. Can you do that?"

I was furious. I picked up the dead snake and shoved it near his face, but he turned his back.

"Watch out," he said gesturing threateningly with his finger. "Every snake has a companion. He'll come looking for her."

And away he went laughing. I was jealous. Perhaps I envied him . . .

The doctor let go of my mother's breast. It did not droop, but stayed upright, jutting forward.

"I still have to do some tests," said the doctor, "and take some X-rays."

A few days later the doctor announced the verdict. "The picture is completely clear now," she said stiffly.

My brother gave my mother one of his smiles and she looked back at him, her eyes bright.

"It's a cancer," said the doctor after a pause.

I was frightened.

"Never!" my brother muttered.

"The breast will have to be removed," the doctor continued.

"Never!" said my mother this time.

"It's malignant and it'll have to be removed," the doctor repeated.

"Never!" my mother said looking at my brother.

"That's the only way you'll be comfortable," the doctor said.

My mother did not take her eyes off my brother.

"Can't it be treated with drugs?" I heard myself ask the doctor.

"No. Surgery is the only treatment there is."

My mother hugged my brother. "How can I allow it to be removed," she asked, "when this son of mine suckled on it?"

The doctor collected her equipment.

"I can still feel his tiny nails touching it," my mother went on.

The doctor moved toward the door.

"And I can still feel his sweet little bite on the nipple."

All the color drained out of my brother's face and he stared off into space.

"Your breasts have dried up," the doctor said from the door. "Your child is grown; he's a young man now. He doesn't suckle any more."

"It's wonderful to have you back home again," I heard myself telling my mother.

"You won't be in pain any more," my brother intoned hoarsely, "that's what matters."

Her black headcloth covered her chest. When she took it off, he stole a look. Just one breast. On the right side the dress hung down straight from the shoulder ... *When we were small, she used to take money from inside there so we could buy sweets ...*

There was something about my brother's look that I had not seen before. For the first time ever, he looked defeated; his eyelids were quivering.

My mother patted the mattress of the bed and then sat down on it crosslegged. "It's time for you both to go to the field," she said without looking at us.

On the way we met some men of the village. They stared, for my brother looked as grave and worn as I did.

"Give us a break, talk, laugh, *do something,*" one of them exclaimed. "Which of you is the funny one?"

"My mother's the only one who can tell us apart," my brother told me. "She may be squatting in a corner, but she knows who it is just by the way we come in. She'll call out our name without even looking around. Or she can tell by the way we walk, like a cow who knows her calves by their scent."

"And when we grew up," I said, "she knew us by the time we came back home. I always came back in the afternoon exhausted from work, while you cam back late at night, and usually tottering."

The villagers, on the other hand, are just waiting for his laughs and jokes to start again, I told myself, so they'll gather round him. And once more I'll find myself outside the circle!

"I used to love resting my head against that breast," he told me when we reached the field.

I started on the weeds that were choking the cane.

"It was soft and warm. I used to feel her breathing when I put my head on it," he continued.

"Get to work and stop thinking about it," I said.

"I could even hear her heart beating, although it is the right breast." His voice was trembling. All his life he's been the joker, I told myself; he'll get over this sad business before long. When we came across the waterwheel maker's daughter playing, I tried to distract him by pointing her out. He looked at her tenderly. The girl stared back and even gave him a wink! He did not laugh.

"You remember, of course," I said jokingly, "that I'm her uncle by blood, being her father's twin ... "

But he still did not laugh. The little girl ran toward us, imitating his languid walk and sad expression. He managed a smile. She laughed; it was a shrill little girl's laugh but it had that ringing quality. He replied with one of his own ringing laughs, and together they laughed and echoed each other.

But when he came home again and saw my mother's one breast, he looked glum and went out to walk in the open air. The factory whistle hooted.

"My mother's not a whole woman any more," he sighed.

The Train

I tried everything I could think of to get him laughing again. I told myself it was better to have him back as the joker, even that joker of whom I was jealous, rather than see him sorrowful and preoccupied.

I took him to the provincial capital. We looked in the shops and stared at the city women, but his mood did not change. We finished the day drinking tea at the gypsy camp, watching a girl with a gold tooth shaking her body. Her eyes were heavily darkened with kohl, and she had drawn a beauty spot on her cheek. Although plump, she had a lot of energy and shook her body vigorously. The dress she wore revealed most of her ample breasts. They jiggled with every vigorous movement she made. She leaned forward a long way, displaying her bosom to the audience, which cheered with excitement. She smiled at them. Even though she was getting old, she was still beautiful.

On the way home my brother was silent. I tried to get him to talk but failed. His only reply was to nod his head. In the dark I could see his expression. When we came to the sugar factory, light fell on us from the high windows and we could hear the sound of the machine inside.

"Do you remember the game we used to play on the factory train?" I asked. He nodded.

"And the line of children who used to make up a train?"

Again a nod.

"And do you remember the miller's wife?"

In the light of the window I could just detect a glimpse of a smile. I could hear the bubble of the machines . . . *The factory whistle hooted. Work was finished for the day, and the seasonal laborers came out of the building to change their work shifts for their regular clothes. The daily inspection was over. For a moment they stood there in the yard, naked. And then we both saw her—the miller's wife, hiding in one of the empty box cars—hiding to stare at the naked men!!*

"*She's looking at the men's private parts, is she!" said my brother.*

She was concentrating so hard she did not notice him until he surprised her from behind. She started and tried to get away, but he took her round the waist just as a tomcat grabs the neck of a female cat. She stared at him.

"*What do you want with me?" she asked, pushing his chest as she resisted him. "Let me be! Let me be."*

He laughed and pulled her to the floor of the wagon and she went down with him without a word. A few months later her husband the miller was walking down the village streets shaking bits of flour off his gallabiyya, announcing that his wife was pregnant. At last, said the village folk. She had almost given up hope. Everything in its own good time . . .

In the light of the next window I could see him smiling I laughed out loud and so did he, but his had a different ring to it:

"I had forgotten," he said, "that you were with me that day. Believe me, she was excited. Her body was warm. We kept rolling over, and all we could see was the top of the tall palm trees and the smoke from the factory, the sky above and then the floor of the wagon below."

THE SON

In the days that followed he went out alone at night and came back at dawn. It was always at dawn; he would come home exhausted to find my mother still awake. He would kiss her three times, one on each of the tattoo marks on her chin, and then she would smile at him and forgive him everything. But it was never like that with me. I used to kiss her in my heart, with my eyes, but I could never bring myself to show my feelings in such an open manner.

We harvested the sugar cane, carted it to the factory, and made our way home at sundown. My mother fed us both. I went to bed immediately, but my brother washed his face and went out again.

Next morning I woke to find my mother pale, her eyes red from weeping.

"He hasn't come home yet," she whispered.

I went to the provincial capital to look for him and then to the gypsy camp. But the gypsies had moved on; no one knew where. And I remembered that night we watched the gypsy woman dance, the one with the gold tooth. *He had not taken his eyes off her breasts. He had not bothered with her round hips, her half-parted lips, or even her heavily kohled eyes. He had stared only at her breasts as they moved beneath the thin fabric of her low-cut dress.*

I went back to my mother feeling thwarted. She looked even paler than before and just sat silently, refusing to eat.

One day she drank some water and said, "That cursed damned father of his." But her voice was full of love.

The village men believed the gypsy woman had seduced my brother and the two had run away together. He was now working as a drummer with the gypsies, they said, and was wearing a gold tooth in his mouth. The waterwheel maker's wife wept, and the pregnant wife of the miller started to come by our house and sit with my mother. A number of other women came to visit too.

In summer one of the village men went to Cairo and came back saying he had seen my brother hanging around the railway station at Bab al-Hadeed;[3] he said he was sitting by the fountain in front of the great statue of Ramses, laughing as usual!! Someone else said no, that was wrong, he had heard that my brother was working at the Cataract Hotel in Aswan!

Then one day another of the village men came to say that he had seen my brother sleeping beside the Sayyida Zaynab Mosque in Cairo; he had a beard and was wearing ragged clothes; he had become a dervish, laughing with other dervishes who were possessed by God in different ways.

---

3. The main railway station in Cairo.

My mother believed none of this. She stayed inside the house, but she looked always at the door, which was kept wide open during the day and slightly ajar at night. After a time I could not tell whether she was waiting for her son or for her husband.

Once in a while she would rub the place where her lost breast had been. I would then walk through the dark village night missing the ringing sound of my brother's laughter. Nothing was the same again.

The village men look at me differently these days. Their silent and insistent stares seem to be saying, 'The joker's gone and now we're stuck with you?!'

The fields of sugar cane are green again and the tall palm tree is sending its branches up into the sky like a gigantic rose. I think about the three-line tattoo on my mother's chin, and the way my brother used to kiss her; I see my mother's tears running down her cheeks.

And I feel guilty because I used to be so jealous and envied my brother so much.

I wonder if the joker will ever come back!

—*Translated by Roger Allen and Elizabeth Fernea*

'Abd al-Salam al-'Ujaili (b. 1918)

Syrian novelist and short-story writer and one of Syria's earlier writers of fiction, 'Abd al-Salam al-'Ujaili is a practicing physician and a passionate traveler; he is also a prolific writer and has at least thirty books in print. He has served in several ministerial positions in the Syrian Government, including the post of Minister of Culture. His fiction deals with a wide variety of subjects that stem from his observation of human nature and his knowledge of his own culture and provide a comparative outlook on the cultures of foreign countries he has visited. He has also written on his travels both in his fiction and in travelogues. His fiction contains the first prerequisite of fiction in any language: the capacity to entertain and, at the same time, enhance the reader's awareness of the human condition. Among his short-story collections are *Seville's Lanterns* (1956), *The Horseman of Qantara City* (1971), and *Horses and Women* (1979); his novels include *Hearts on the Wires* (1974) and *Men Obscure* (1979).

THE DEATH OF MUHAMMAD BEN AHMAD HINTI

Muhammad ben[1] Ahmad Hinti opened his eyes and saw glittering spots on a dark blue background. His first thought was that they were the stars and that the background was nothing but the dark sky. But why were the stars not above

---

1. "Ben" is the form used by the writer and people in this part of Syria for the more normal "ibn," meaning "son."

his head but in front of him, and how could they appear so close? Moreover, he thought, if those glittering spots were really stars, why then were they running away from him as though driven by a whip?

Certainly Muhammad ben Ahmad Hinti was perplexed when he opened his eyes and saw those glittering spots. However, he might not have expressed, even in his own inner thoughts, his perplexity in the language we have just used. Hinti was a man of simple background and intellect. Before the events of this story began, he had been no more than a caretaker of some grain warehouses in the Bab al-Nairab quarter of Aleppo. He was later forced by circumstances we shall see in the course of this story, to become a peddler in the Zaidi desert north of the Euphrates in Northern Syria. It is clear, then, that Hinti was incapable of analyzing the reasons for his bewilderment when he saw glittering spots resembling stars running away from him or of tracing it back to its origins. This is why we have taken it upon ourselves to do so for him, and to relate the story of some of his experiences in life. We have analyzed these events and arranged them so that his story can be understood, accepted, and enjoyed.

Muhammad ben Ahmad Hinti thought at the beginning that he had been attacked by a spell of dizziness. But he knew that stars, when one is dizzy, revolve around one's head, while the earth under them and the sky above them clash together, one rising, the other falling. But here the sky was not falling or the earth rising. All that he saw was that the sky and the stars were quickly receding. He therefore tried to turn his head in order to make sure that this phenomenon was really happening. He also tried to move his body so as to fix his own position under the sky. He could do neither. His neck did not obey him when he tried to turn his head. As for his body, when he tried to move his foot he felt a sharp pain, as if a blade was being plunged in his bowels, one that moved whenever he tried to move his foot and even when he simply thought of moving his foot. So he abandoned his attempt and surrendered to the feeling of perplexity, his gaze following the clusters of stars running away from him. He saw that whenever a cluster of stars disappeared, another took its place. However, his lack of movement did not spare him from the pain, for, as soon as he became conscious of his condition, the sharp penetrating pains began to awaken again in his body. The sharp pain in his bowels was becoming stronger and more real. Gently he tried to feel the source of the pain in his abdomen, but he could not move his hands. They felt heavy, as though chained. His breathing was heavy too, as if someone was squatting on his chest. He now realized that he was not standing but lying down. Yet what was this thing, he wondered, that was moving under him, rising and falling with him, and what was that din that filled his ears, and that cloud that rose on his right and left, hovering over and submerging him, filling his chest with dust?

Suddenly, the darkness lifted from Muhammad ben Ahmad Hinti's mind, and he knew now the reason why he saw all those stars running away as though driven by a whip. He was lying on a rough hard bed of sacks filled with wheat or barley in the back of a large truck that was crossing the dusty desert in the darkness of the night ... And here Hinti tried to smile, to laugh at himself as he thought he must have been plunged in deep sleep and had therefore been unable to comprehend why the stars were fleeing in front of his eyes. He tried to smile, but his lips would not obey him, for the pain, that of the sharp blade, suddenly stabbed again in his bowels as the vehicle lurched into a depression in the desert road. This cut short his attempt at a smile and stirred a new question in his mind: How had he come to be lying on sacks in a vehicle instead of being behind his two donkeys, one laden with grain and the other with goods to be sold to the bedouins in the Zaidi desert? Moreover, what was this pain that spread all over his body and was stirred up again whenever he moved or the vehicle moved him? He remembered that at sunset he was behind his donkeys at the foot of the ancient ruins, hoping to reach the well and the house beside it, where he could rest and sell the remainder of his goods. He also remembered that bedouin coming down to him from the direction of the ruins, with a cigarette between his fingers, asking for a light. The bedouin was veiled; it was strange that someone wanting to light a cigarette should be veiled. However, despite it, Hinti was able to see the bedouin's features and remember them. When he drew near him . . .

At this moment, the truck shook as it crashed over another bump in the road, and Hinti's bowels were torn with unbearable pain, cutting off all connection between his feelings and his consciousness. His memory could no longer follow the course of events . . .

When Muhammad ben Ahmad Hinti regained consciousness and opened his eyes, he remembered the spots of light that he had seen running away from him as a result of the movement of the truck. This time, however, he found the situation different. The spots of light were not receding from his vision; they were above his head, much nearer than the others that he had thought were stars. It may be that they had not been stars at all. He had no more confidence in himself. He was dizzy and his mind was clouded . . . But the important thing was that these spots of light were different. They were brighter, nearer, and multicolored, some white, some red, some green. They—and this he found to be quite amazing—went on and off all the time. When they came on, they dazzled him, preventing him from distinguishing anything around, seeing nothing but their brightness. When they went off, he was immediately drowned in deep darkness and felt just as though he had been blinded. This constant change from dazzling light to pitch darkness made him feel as though his eyes were afflicted with the same piercing pain that was afflicting his bowels, a pain that increased whenever he closed his eyes.

It was necessary that Muhammad ben Ahmad Hinti should try to think, try to resolve this new mystery to which his eyes were exposed, but, as we have said, he was a man of simple upbringing and intellect and had little interest in following a problem to its roots. He therefore stopped trying to find the causes of his confusion and surrendered body and soul to what was going on around him. If it had been possible he would have liked to have been able to stop both seeing and hearing. This, however, was difficult. It was more difficult to stop hearing than seeing, for he could close his eyes so as not to see, but he could not close his ears to avoid hearing the voices that had now started to rise and the din that surrounded him.

The din around Hinti began to rise now by degrees; or maybe it had been loud right from the beginning, and it was his sensibility that had started to sharpen. Little by little, he realized the presence of this din more clearly. The first thing that Hinti distinguished from all the noise around him was a question he heard as if coming from below him:

"What, Doctor? Have you arrived safely?"

A voice that seemed to Hinti to be near him answered, after a sigh of relief, "Yes, thank God. Be reassured."

Had Muhammad ben Ahmad Hinti been in full possession of his strength and clear in his mind, he would have realized the heavy sarcasm in the voice of this man now thanking God beside him. But Hinti was not in control of his senses, which were transmitting the various stimuli to him, without, however, arousing in him any thoughts or rational reaction. Noises assailed his ears with this conversation, and shadows now assailed his eyes as a dark mass came between him and the flashing lights that had been dazzling them. This was the shadow of the man who had been speaking beside him. He heard him shout, "Tell the servant to fix this light, so I can see what kind of patient I have on my hands. How can I distinguish anything in this flashing light?"

A voice that arose from below the place where Hinti was lying answered, "This flashing light is the 'Jalaa' Hotel; Innkeeper's Pride,' Doctor. He brought a technician all the way from Aleppo especially to make it go on and off in this wonderful way. How can you expect a stupid servant to do anything with this miracle?"

The man who was standing near Hinti shouted angrily, "I think I am the first doctor in this town who has had to examine a patient lying on a pile of sacks ten meters above ground in a light that goes on and off ten times in a single minute. Where is your wound, lad?"

It was clear that the last sentence was directed to Hinti, who heard it without realizing what it really meant. However, the vibrations of the word "wound" began to drum themselves into his consciousness until they aroused some thoughts in his mind: wound . . . wound . . . wound . . . At the same time, the man at Hinti's side, whom we now know to have been a doctor, was talking to another as if not expecting a reply. "You say that he came from the Zaidi desert? This means he has come a hundred and fifty kilometers on the back of this luxurious vehicle, supplied with all the necessary medical equipment . . . a hundred and fifty kilometers in the dust of the desert and the chill of night, on a bed of wheat sacks in a truck like this. A wounded patient with a bullet in his bowels! This is exactly what the surgeons of the University Hospital would want for their intensive-care patients . . . What can I do with this man here?"

The doctor's hand had been fumbling under the shabby fur coat that covered the body of Muhammad ben Ahmad Hinti, feeling his rigid abdomen. As for

Hinti, he was in a different world, for the echoes of the word "wound" took him back to the scene he had witnessed at sunset when the veiled man came down toward him . . .

Muhammad ben Ahmad Hinti's surprise at seeing a man asking for a light while keeping his face veiled was normal and logical. In fact, as soon as the man faced Hinti, he stretched his right hand to his left side, and before Hinti realized the meaning of what he was hearing and seeing, the veiled man had pointed the muzzle of his gun at him; a dark muzzle, with a dull metal rim. Hinti heard him say in a voice that was audible above the loud noise of the shot, "Die—may God never have mercy on you!"

It was now very late at night. The doctor climbed over the wheat sacks heaped on the truck; everything was covered by a thick layer of red dust that left its marks on his dark suit and, in the flashing light of the Jalaa' Inn sign, he examined Hinti's wound. When he gave his opinion, he was merely guessing, for it was impossible for him, in such bad conditions, to make an accurate diagnosis. However, he was of the opinion that the body sprawled in the cold of the night on top of those wheat sacks was in danger of losing its life before another day passed. The only hope for the patient, if any, was to attempt to treat him in a fully equipped hospital. This meant that he had to be moved to Aleppo, some two hundred kilometers away. The doctor gave his opinion decisively, relieving himself of further responsibility and giving himself the opportunity to go back to blissful sleep in his comfortable bed with an easy conscience.

The doctor's suggestion to send Hinti to Aleppo was a sound one, particularly because the patient's family lived there. However, some impediments prevented the immediate execution of the doctor's recommendations. One of these was that the officials at the control point for agricultural products stationed at the entrance to the Bridge refused to let the driver of the truck continue his trip to Aleppo because they did not believe that the weight of the cargo was no more than nine tons and three hundred and twenty kilograms: they estimated the weight to be two hundred and eighty kilograms more than the driver claimed. Therefore they would not allow the truck to continue on its way before the cargo was brought down and weighed, sack by sack. There was indeed another method by which the driver could have convinced those officials, but he preferred not to resort to it, as he had not been authorized to bribe them by the owner of the wheat. Moreover, he himself was not the owner of the truck but merely a hired driver who cared little if it spent the night at the guard post or continued its journey.

It would have been possible, of course, as the doctor recommended, to send Hinti to Aleppo in another vehicle, a smaller, more comfortable, and quicker car. But another impediment intervened: who would look after the wounded man during the trip and, more important, who would guarantee payment of the fare? It was inevitable, therefore, that Hinti should remain where he was. The fact that Hinti himself fell into a deep coma without moving or making any sound made this solution even more acceptable. At this, the people concerned—the driver of the truck, the desert guards who had accompanied the wounded man under the supervision of their corporal, and the officials of the control point for agricultural products—were able to forget about him and go to sleep leaving things for the morning.

The morning arrived. *The morning* here does not mean the coming of dawn and the rising of the sun on the eastern horizon; it means *work,* it means that the judge, the court clerk, the doctor, and the chief of police have started work. It is not simply related to the position of the sun in the sky but to earning a living and the psychology of all these people. The morning of this day, therefore, began at almost ten o'clock. It found Muhammad ben Ahmad Hinti stretched on the floor of the government clinic in his shabby fur coat and dirty 'abaya. He was in a coma. The doctor took his pulse, looked at his watch, and then told the judge that the pulse was weak, one hundred and twenty. The doctor dictated to the court clerk the particulars of the wound and direction of the bullet as it penetrated the right side of the abdomen from the top left. He also estimated the number of holes made in the intestines to be between sixteen and twenty, remembering that bullet holes are always double. This was not prepared as a report to be registered in the minutes taken by the court clerk but was said by the doctor to explain to those present how little hope there was for Hinti to survive.

At the door of the government clinic, the corporal of the desert guards who had brought in the victim and the assailant was standing telling his story to a group of traders, originally from Aleppo, who had gathered there when they heard of the plight of that peddler, a man from Aleppo like themselves, intending to help him and move him to the hospital in Aleppo. Since each of these traders had already paid his share for the hire of the car—which was not yet hired— each felt it his right to hear the whole story, with all its details, from the corporal. He in turn saw it as his duty, a very palatable one, to relate the information he knew to these good men, repeating at intervals as he plucked the seam of his military uniform, "I implore God to forgive me!" thus relieving himself of the responsibility of accusing a possibly innocent person, a heavy responsibility in bedouin custom, particularly when the accusation is that of murder—as was that against Mu'aishir ben Dhabban—or of assaulting the honor of a woman—as was that directed against Muhammad ben Ahmad Hinti.

And here it is proper for us to go back to Hinti himself, for he had just begun to regain consciousness. However, this was not apparent to the eyes of the judge, the doctor, the chief of police, and the rest, because those gentlemen saw his limbs motionless, his eyes closed, and his lips still half open and stiff. They thought, therefore, that he was still in a coma and could neither hear nor see. This allowed them to continue their conversation in loud voices in front of Hinti without considering that he would hear them. It was now the turn of the corporal of the desert guards to speak, and he began to relate to the judge in detail all the efforts he had made since he had learned of the incident. The corporal was modest and mentioned that circumstances were on his side, for he

had been touring near the ruins and was therefore able to arrest the culprit easily. However, the way he related this made it clear that no other corporal of the
guards had been able to take advantage of the circumstances as he had. When
the judge asked him how he could be sure that it was Mu'aishir who was the
culprit, he began recounting the excellent reasons that had prompted him to
arrest that bedouin. In the first place, he said, Mu'aishir was found near the site
of the incident, and second, he was carrying a gun that smelled of newly fired
gunpowder. Third, and this was the most important reason, he was the brother
of a girl called Sabha who was rumored to have been raped the spring before
by a peddler—"And may God forgive me!"

What the corporal had said was not trivial, and its effect was quickly apparent on the faces of all those present. The chief of police ordered that the people
who were coming nearer, curious to hear, should be kept back even though they
had paid the fare of the car that was to take Muhammad ben Ahmad Hinti to
Aleppo. The court clerk settled himself more comfortably on his chair in order
to register this part of the minutes clearly and legibly. Even Hinti, despite his
apparent coma, made a faint movement as though about to participate in the
conversation, but his strength failed him and his attempt remained unnoticed.

The judge, a young bachelor newly appointed to the office and inexperienced in hearing scandal, began asking the corporal what he knew about the
assault on the girl called Sabha, but with a curiosity he could not mask with the
pretence of carrying out his professional duties. The corporal recounted all he
had heard from the lips of people in his distant desert area, asking God's forgiveness all the time. He said that Sabha's stepmother forgot to buy a comb of black
bone from the peddler touring their district and asked Sabha to catch up with
him before he went too far from their camp and exchange a pack of wheat for
the comb. Imploring God's forgiveness all the time, the corporal described how
the girl caught up with the peddler as he was driving his two donkeys along
the bed of a green valley, how the time was twilight, and how the bed of the
valley was shady and covered with green grass dotted with spring flowers. And
notwithstanding the wagging tongues, who can know how the action took
place then in the quiet solitude, as the eighteen-year-old bedouin girl leaned
toward the young stranger full of youthful strength and seething with desire
. . . This had happened many months earlier, but every secret in the desert, and
even outside the desert, always gets known. And this, may God bear witness, is
the result of that . . .

Having detailed all his information, theories and comments to the judge,
the corporal fell silent. One thing remained now: to bring the young bedouin,
Mu'aishir, whom he had arrested the evening before near the ruins carrying a
gun smelling of gunpowder, as an easy mouthful for the judge. Everyone who
had heard the account of the corporal, an officer supposed to speak dispassionately, was able to imagine the rape in the green valley on an evening in spring,
which fires the blood in the veins of young men and women. However, Muhammad ben Ahmad Hinti, the peddler now lying in his shabby fur coat and

tattered *'abaya* on the tiled floor of the government clinic, remembered a story of rape (and let us accommodate the corporal and call it "rape" too) but differently from the way those present—the judge, the doctor, the chief of police, and others—imagined. Was it the same story that the corporal had related, or was it another?

Despite the fact that Muhammad ben Ahmad Hinti had now regained consciousness from the coma brought on by excruciating pain, hemorrhage, and inflammation of the peritoneum, as well as journey of a hundred and fifty kilometers in the dust of the desert and the cold of the night, he could not differentiate between the narrative of the corporal of the guards and the rape that he himself recollected. There was some confusion in the narration of events, some similarities, and some differences that Hinti, in his weakness and exhaustion, the lack of blood flowing to the convolutions of his brain and that blood's heat as it raced through his veins, could not discern. It was impossible for him to recognize the relationship of the two narratives and the share of truth in each of them. Hinti would have liked to get up, after the corporal finished his narrative, and tell him, "Stop and listen to my story." He would then have narrated the story more clearly, with a greater inner knowledge and richer details. But Hinti was unable to do or say anything. The most he could do was to tell the story to himself, in the depths of his consciousness, or maybe it was the story that told itself to him; and we will follow it.

Yes, it was spring, and it was almost sunset. However, it was not in the desert but a narrow alley in the quarter of Bab al-Nairab or on the fringes of that quarter in the city of Aleppo. At that time, in such an alley, the place would be dark and quiet, and the pedestrians few. Hinti was on his way home from the grain warehouse where he worked as a guard. He was well groomed; he had twirled his moustache, he had tilted his tarbush forward on his forehead, and he had wound perfectly his wide belt from which the shining chain of his cheap watch was dangling. He walked slowly on his way through the alley, his eyes fixed on a narrow round window at the top of the wall to his right. From this window, from behind a chain of heavy barriers, the high thick wall with its smooth stones built so close to each other they seemed to suffocate the little window, and the dark curtain that covered the opening as if it were the hand of a criminal suffocating a little child, the wide eyes of Raqqush would watch him. And when Raqqush drew back this curtain with her plump fingers tinted with henna, another dark screen, that of her black veil, would cover her beautiful face below the wide eyes.

Despite this chain of barriers, Muhammad ben Ahmad Hinti was at the height of happiness every evening when he saw the light shining from the black eyes of Raqqush penetrating the dusk, the darkness of the alley, the curtain, and the black veil. Every evening except this evening, for his eyes looked in vain for the rays of light in the closed window at the top of the wall. He felt sorrow fill his heart. But his sorrow did not last long, for another surprise was awaiting him at the door of Raqqush's house. No sooner had he arrived near the door than he saw it open, revealing a slim soft form wrapped in a black veil, and he saw the wide eyes shining in that part of Raqqush's face that was not covered by the veil, which fell from its knot on the forehead and was held by the young girl's hand as if to cover half her face. That was, as we said, something that Hinti never dreamed would happen, and it is not surprising that he felt his heart beating against the wall of his chest as though it wanted to fly out of his ribs. His feet would not obey him. In a husky voice that almost choked his dry throat, he stammered, "You?"

He did not receive an audible answer but saw the hand that was holding the end of the black veil drop to reveal a round face, rosy cheeks, and a lovely mouth with parted lips. He felt the open door calling him in and suddenly found himself behind that door, looking at the inner part of the house and close to a young, plump body whose warmth he felt penetrating his clothes and hers, feeling the blood racing in her veins as it was in his.

This is what happened to Muhammad ben Ahmad Hinti that evening. It had never happened before in this part of the city, or maybe it had, possibly many times, but people had not heard of it and spoken about it. Hinti was therefore experiencing a mixture of uncertainty, joy, ecstasy and anxiety, and could not think straight about his situation. All that he understood from the few words that Raqqush mumbled was that the women of her family, as well as the children, were in the public baths, and that she had been with them but had returned earlier to be with her crippled grandmother, and that it was not the hour when the men returned, and that she was afraid, for he should not have come in . . .

But Hinti had already come in, and if there was no one in the house except a blind and deaf old woman, and if the men were not returning now, when then should she be afraid? At this point, the girl's body drew nearer to him, and blood gushed hotly through the veins of his head. At the beginning, when he was only holding her by the shoulders, he experienced a strange kind of pleasure as his fingers dug into her plump flesh, but when he felt her rounded breasts pressing against his chest and his nostrils were filled with the warm fragrant smell of Aleppo powder evoking in his mind the image of a woman's naked body sprawled on the tiled floor of the bath, the feelings of simple pleasure changed into passionate desire. All that he said and did after this was dictated not by his own free will but by that overwhelming passion that he felt like a fire seething in his veins and surging with every beat of his heart. His eyes were fixed on Raqqush's face, its rosy color had changed into deep red tinged with blue as she held her breath in her efforts to free herself from the encirclement of his arms and legs. The veins of her throat were blue and swollen as she held her breath in her resistance, and whenever she relaxed and breathed for a moment, she would entreat him in a hoarse voice, repeating, "Don't want to, don't, I don't want to."

This girl's features, the strangled sound in her throat, her tense limbs, all indicated that she really did not want to. But Muhammad ben Ahmad Hinti was now a body dripping with lust, ready to do anything to possess that other body in his arms. It was a battle that Hinti thought would never end . . . but suddenly, at the moment when he thought the girl's body was at the height of its resistance, he felt it go limp. Only her head, from which the black veil had fallen to reveal her soft chestnut hair, continued to move, expressing a lingering resistance in a soul whose fire of rebellion had really subsided, while her body yielded to his.

All that remained in the memory of Muhammad ben Ahmad Hinti of that battle was his great astonishment at the surrender of that body to him after its stormy rebellion. Did he experience sexual pleasure then? It was possible he did; but now, as he lay on the tiled floor of the government clinic, he could only repeat over and over again, in his delirium, his astonishment at the surrender of Raqqush to his desire. Why did she demonstrate all that resistance at the beginning, when she had all that passion too? And they call that *rape*!

When Hinti arrived at this point, he opened his eyes. The very fact that he could arrive in his thinking at this level of complexity was a proof that he was regaining part of his consciousness. The doctor now expressed his opinion that the wounded man would be able to answer the judge's questions provided they were brief. The first thing the judge wanted to know was whether Muhammad ben Ahmad Hinti had actually seen his assailant when he was shot. By moving his head Hinti indicated that he had, and the judge asked him, "Would you be able to recognize the man if you saw him again?"

A weak "yes" escaped from Hinti's lips, but it indicated that he had enough strength to understand and discriminate. The judge signaled to the corporal of the desert guards to bring in Mu'aishir, while Hinti closed his eyes as if that short moment had weakened him further and put him back into a coma.

However, the truth was that Hinti did not relapse into a coma but went back to the train of his thoughts. Yes, of course he knew Sattouf, Raqqush's brother. He knew him quite well—he used to see him every day either coming out of the low gate in the high wall of their house or in his carpenter's shop. He was a young man of medium size, his back a little bent from leaning so long over the carpenter's bench or crouching over the wooden boxes he made for the shepherds. He used to wear a striped vest and red slippers and always carried a penknife in his breast. Hinti wondered how Sattouf had reached him and shot him in the Zaidi desert, when he could have torn his breast with a single stab of his knife either in the Bab al-Nasr Road in Aleppo or when coming out of one of the taverns in Bab al-Faraj. As for himself, Hinti, the only reason he had left his town and his job and started a new business, that of a peddler in the Zaidi desert, had been in order to avoid meeting Sattouf in town. So how could Sattouf have followed him here? This was a new mystery for Hinti, like the mystery of Raqqush's sudden surrender to the violence of his passion that evening . . .

However, the gentlemen around him would not leave Hinti to his puzzling mysteries and conflicting thoughts, for he heard one of them shout to him, "Muhammad!"

Muhammad ben Ahmad Hinti opened his eyes. The judge now pointed to Mu'aishir and asked him, "Do you know this man?"

Hinti was silent for a long time, his eyes fixed unflinchingly on the face of the young bedouin with its thin nose, its light beard, and the locks of black hair flowing around it. Hoping to help Hinti, the judge asked the bedouin, "Are you Mu'aishir ben Dhabban?"

"Yes."

"Do you have a sister called Sabha?"

The look in the eyes of the bedouin froze, and he did not answer. The judge repeated his question, "Speak, Mu'aishir. Did you have a sister called Sabha? And where is she now?"

At this point, Hinti closed his eyes, saying to himself, "What have I to do with Sabha? And this is not Sattouf. This bedouin may resemble the other bedouin who came down to me from the ruins, but I do not know him, and he does not know me. He may have mistaken me for another peddler ... As for me, I am sure that he is not Raqqush's brother."

The pulse of Muhammad ben Ahmad Hinti had reached one hundred and sixty beats a minute now, as the traders carried him to the small car that was going to take him to the hospital in Aleppo. The doctor told the judge that the testimony of a man in that condition of exhaustion, fever, and peritonitis, his denial that he had ever seen Mu'aishir before, was certainly no proof of the bedouin's innocence. As for Hinti himself, he was now falling into a deep coma, dreaming that he was crossing the desert in an enormous truck, perched on top of a hill of wheat sacks, wrapped in the cold of the night. The stars were shining above him and dust was blowing around him. It was a red, sticky dust that gathered at his nostrils and covered his lips, suffocating him little by little. In vain did Muhammad ben Ahmad Hinti try to free himself from this stifling dust, for his hands were tied and Sattouf was squatting on his chest and arms as he used to do on the wooden boxes he made for the shepherds in that shop with the low ceiling in that narrow dark marketplace in that quarter of Aleppo ...

—*Translated by Elizabeth Hodgkin, with the help of the editor, and Anthony Thwaite*

Layla al-'Uthman (b. 1945)

Born in Kuwait, short-story writer and novelist Layla al-Uthman studied up to secondary level but has augmented her education through her wide readings in Arabic as well as Western literature in translation. She is one of the Peninsula's foremost women writers of fiction, whose short stories reflect skill, economy, and a diversified outlook, ranging from local issues to general Arab, particularly Palestinian experience. Although a profusion of women writers is currently appearing in the Gulf area, al-'Uthman remains the best-known fiction writer among them. She is completely dedicated to her writing, despite her many family responsibilities. Her collections of short stories include *A Woman in a Vessel* (1977); *Departure* (1979); and *Love Has Many Images* (1984). Several of her short stories have been translated into East European languages, including a complete collection into Yugoslavian. Her novels include *The Woman and the Cat* (1985) and *Wasmiyya Comes out of the Sea* (1986).

GOING ON A JOURNEY

The golden light of the sky played on the pillow where his head lay, and I looked at his body stretched out in front of me. I couldn't believe he was dead. But for my mother's screams and wails, I would have believed he was sunk in a long sleep and would wake up soon.

My brothers and sisters were moving around the bed, looking at his pale face. Was he really bidding them farewell forever?

I was the only one not to mourn this body lying in death. As I looked at it I was filled with resentment, and my glances were accompanied with sighs of frustration that I'd so often suppressed. I felt an overwhelming desire to scream and would have screamed if my mother's lamentations hadn't been drowning every other sound.

"Get your uncle!" she was wailing. "Get the neighbors! Call an ambulance! Do something!"

My brothers rushed to do as she asked. One of them crossed from the bed to the bedroom door as if in a trance. Another lifted the receiver and started dialing, but I couldn't follow the movement of his fingers—he must, though, have made a mistake, because I saw him press down and begin redialing. My mother was still wailing.

I stood apart from all this, gazing at his face, then letting my eyes wander over the whole luxurious room: the ivory bed, the rare painting on the main wall over his head, the two candlesticks (which, I was sure, were there just for decoration and had never been lit), and, near the bed, the gilded hanger from which his clothes dangled: a silk *dishdasha* with its sleeves sagging under the weight of the gold buttons and his white *ghutra* beneath its *igal*, swaying a little in the cold draughts of air from the air conditioner, as if they were mourning their owner. His crocodile shoes lay one on top of the other on the mohair carpet.

Going on a journey, that's what they say.[1] That was why my mother was careful never to let my father's shoes lie on top of one another like that, because she hated it when he went away and left her. But in fact he traveled all the time. Once she'd tried to keep him at home for a month, on the grounds that she wanted them to celebrate the New Year together for once, and he'd looked at her with utter distaste and said, "Why should I stay here with you? Are you short of anything?"

---

1. It is popularly believed in several parts of the Arab world that if shoes fall one on top of the other when taken off, their owner will be going on a journey.

"I just want you here with me," Mother had said.

"The children will all be with you," he'd answered soothingly, patting her on the shoulder.

Then, before leaving, he'd looked back at her and said, as if to reassure her, "I'm leaving you ten thousand dinars. I may be away for some time."

I couldn't keep my eyes off my father's shoes, laid there one over the other. He'd gone on one of his trips, but this time he'd be away forever.

I approached, intending to separate the two shoes, then drew back, afraid he might wake up and decide to stay with us—which was the last thing I wanted. I left the shoes and began once more to gaze at the body, resting with such dignity on a bed equipped with all the amenities of modern life: buttons and more buttons, serving various functions: this one for my mother, another for his secretary, Mun'im, who'd come in with all the papers needing his signature and all the checks made out for such fantastic sums of money, a third button for the houseboy Sallum, who'd come in carrying the pot of Arabic coffee from which he'd pour and pour, and that my father could apparently never have enough of. Sallum would wait impatiently for my father to shake the cup in his hand, as a sign that he'd had enough.[2] I'd often watched Sallum's disgruntled face as he waited for this sign, and several times I'd caught him drinking the rest of the coffee in the corridor that separated my father's bedroom from the large hall where he received his male guests. Sallum was huddled at the end of the bed now, like an animal awaiting its master's orders; his two elbows were resting on his knees, and he was leaning forward on his arms with his head hung low between them. There was a tear on his dark face, and I felt real compassion for him.

But why was he crying? Was he wondering what his future would be, now that his benefactor wasn't there any more? Or was he really mourning my father, whose face he'd never see again and who he'd never again pour coffee for? Sallum had really liked my father, despite the beatings he got from him for the slightest reason. Now he sat there, like a faithful dog, weeping for his master.

The telephone rang shrilly. My brother lifted the receiver and shouted into it, "Yes, he's dead, Uncle. Come quickly!"

He was talking to my maternal uncle. My mother stretched out her hand and seized the receiver before he could put it down.

"Brother, he's dead! Buhamad's[3] dead. The father of my children, dead!"

I wondered why on earth she was wailing like that. Despite my father's generous gifts to her, she'd never been happy with him.

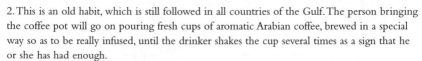

2. This is an old habit, which is still followed in all countries of the Gulf. The person bringing the coffee pot will go on pouring fresh cups of aromatic Arabian coffee, brewed in a special way so as to be really infused, until the drinker shakes the cup several times as a sign that he or she has had enough.

3. This means Abu Hamad, i.e., the father of Hamad.

We'd hear them quarreling all the time. My mother's sobs and the sound of her weeping pierced the wall of the room and unleashed a torrent of resentment in us against my father. He didn't hesitate to hit her in front of us with his *igal* or shoe, and then she'd look sad and ashamed and cover her tear-stained face so that we shouldn't see it. Then, after a day or two, we'd see her smiling at my father as he presented her with a piece of gold or diamond jewelry. She'd accept it, then choose her moment to say, "I'll invite some of my friends to tea tomorrow."

Then my father would smile cunningly, realizing she was taking the opportunity to show off her new present to her friends. She always managed to find a convincing reason to stress my father's generosity and love, but she knew, in her heart, that the present was a compensation for the slap she'd received.

Once she cried for two nights out of humiliation and sorrow.

Now she was wailing. Why in heaven's name was she sad? Why wasn't she singing? Why didn't she face my father with joy and take her revenge for all the past days and years?

And Sallum was crying too! Why was he huddled up like that near the bed? I went up to him.

"Get up and make some coffee," I said. "My uncle's coming."

He got up quickly, which surprised me. It was as if he'd been hoping I'd ask him to do that, so that he'd no longer have to be polite and show sorrow—or perhaps he wanted to be alone and cry to his heart's content. Who knows? But did Sallum really feel sad?

I alone gazed at the body with resentment and hatred, with questions burning in my brain. What if he came back now? Perhaps I'd scream in his face:

"I don't want all this. I don't want it!"

Then, in a louder voice, I'd say:

"Just say 'No' once, Father, just slap me once, the way you slap my mother, and ask me why my grades were low, even though I had private teachers as well! Spit in my face, just once, when I come to you after I've smashed my new car or broken my gold watch! But you never did that. You just looked indifferent, then, next day, you'd come up to me and say, 'Hamad, here's a new watch in place of the one you broke. It cost me a thousand dinars. How do you like it?'"

I'd shake my head and never show any admiration. I only wished I had the courage to throw the watch back in your face or wished it could get stolen next morning. I'd even try and arrange this myself, taking it off and putting it on the table of the club where I used to squander my days. But the caretaker of the club would always follow me with it.

"Mr Hamad," he'd say. "Your watch! You left it on the table. God has preserved it for you!"

Then I'd take the watch, feeling it was as heavy as the time around me, and keep it till I finally managed to lose it, certain that another one would soon imprison my wrist again.

The hands of the clock on the bedside table were dancing now. Time was passing, and I watched his pale face, hoping it would never return. Tomorrow, perhaps, I'd be able to get back some of what I'd lost, do something I really liked: get on a bus or a small truck or a motorcycle and race and bump against all the luxury cars! I wanted my life to begin again and never again to hear his voice rebuking me, "Why do you mix with poor people's children and study with them?"

I never again wanted to hear his words smothering my ambitions whenever I had bad grades, "Not to worry, Hamad. Education won't be any use to you. You're blessed, thank God, with a wealth a lot of people are jealous of. I've opened a big store for you. I've put a lot of big buildings in your name and they'll show a good profit. I've put a lot of money in your bank account—you can spend three thousand dinars a day if you want to and go on like that for years."

"But Father," I'd protest, "I want to get a degree!"

He'd silence me. "Commerce and money are the best degree," he'd say. "Just look at me! Do I have a degree? Yet I've done everything I wanted to do, for myself and for all of you." Then he'd smile in the sarcastic way I hated so much. "Leave degrees for poor people's children," he'd continue. "Here, take these . . . "

And he'd offer me the keys to his car.

"Go and have a ride in the Rolls Royce. When you drive it along the corniche, you'll have a thousand girls chasing after you."

My mother was crying. Did he, for heaven's sake, deserve a single tear from her? Scores of other women would feel sad when they heard about his death, because it meant he wouldn't shower money on them any more, but mother's rights were safe. I touched her tenderly on the shoulder.

"Try to stop crying, Mother!"

Her eulogy of my father poured out: "He was so good, he was so generous, he was—"

Oh, Mother, don't tell such lies. He hardly ever looked at your modest face. He used to scold you, shout in your face, even hit you. Have you forgotten? You used to find lipstick on his clothes and smell the perfume of other women in the folds of his body. And when, once, you asked him for an explanation, he didn't even look at your questioning face, but just retorted, "It's none of your business!"

Then, when you persisted and humbly asked him if he had another woman, he laughed sarcastically, and said, "One woman? Ten women! I'm a man, I'm free!"

But you were never free, Mother. You were the prisoner of your fear for your jewelry and luxurious clothes, which were the envy of women as humiliated as you, while the phantoms of other women haunted you even in your sleep, in my father's very breath. He was an enormously rich man. And that wealth's yours now, Mother. Yours!

I shook her gently. "Try not to cry any more, Mother. Father's dead. Nothing will bring him back now."

I alone rejoiced, as I felt the gates of life opening wide for me, beckoning me to throw myself into the arms of freedom. From this time on I'd change everything, I'd trample on everything my father imagined happiness to be. He'd done all he could to shatter my ambitions and aspirations, but now I'd be able to hope, to aspire. He'd tried to sweep away all my dreams, but now I would dream. I'd plunge into the sea of life, whereas he'd tried to plunge me in a sea of luxury and high living, a sea in which I was forced to swim against my will, while my poorer friends, whom he despised, became doctors and lawyers and pharmacists, each with a profession that gave him a living from the sweat of his brow. Now, after all the long dreaming and running and struggling and toiling, they reposed on a carpet spun from their own efforts. They'd achieved their goals.

Again I looked at his face, scrutinizing his features that were now covered over with the pallor of death. His eyes were closed in peace. Suddenly, as my feelings woke, I trembled and fought to hold back the large tear that filled my eye. A strange emotion throbbed in my heart. My father was dead, gone forever. Had I been waiting for him to leave life, so that I could enter life? My eyes slid down to where his shoes lay, still one on top of the other. He was going on a journey! Slowly I went over, bent down, and arranged the shoes on the carpet. It was then that the large tear fell.

—Translated by Salwa Jabsheh and Christopher Tingley

THE DAMNED INSINUATION

One day someone whispered in my ear that my wife was being unfaithful to me. I trembled and my face froze. A violent storm raged in my breast, but I bided my time till work was over for the day.

I stayed behind at the office, pondering the matter, turning it over and over, probing all the various aspects, in the hope of finding a single hint to prove the truth of the damned insinuation that had pierced the walls of silence in my ears.

My eyes began wandering around the office, over the walls, the shelves, the desks and chairs, the papers scattered over the tables. Nearby lay coffee cups, the dried-up coffee in them tracing crazy patterns. Everything wagged its malevolent tongue—the damned insinuation was knocking, hammering at the door of my mind! Then the door opened, and it entered, darting here and there inside my brain, establishing itself, then, at last, focusing on a particular point.

Come on, you sluggish brain, get moving! Make an effort, just for a few minutes! Think, would my wife really be unfaithful to me?

The walls lengthened before my eyes, grew higher too. My wife just loved cleaning walls.

"What is it with you and walls, darling?" I'd ask.

"The flyspecks collect on them."

"So, who has time to look at them?"

"I want the house to be clean. That's my job."

I moved my feet, hitting the waste paper basket. Then, gazing under the table, I saw the scattered remnants of sandwiches, along with the pickles my colleagues brought, to nibble on and pass the time at work.

"How often, darling," I'd ask, "do you stir up the dust out there in that cursed street?"

"Do you expect me to let the garbage collect for a whole day before I throw it out?"

"It's a waste of time."

"It's my job. I want the house to be clean."

My agitated gaze moved to the desks with their disarray.

"Please, don't mess up my papers, darling," I'd say.

"They get on my nerves. They have to be tidied up. I can't stand things being untidy."

"It's just a waste of time."

"I want my house to be neat and tidy."

"But, darling—"

I felt hungry. What, I wondered, had she cooked today?

"Ugh," I'd say. "You always smell of onions and garlic and cauliflower."

"You like eating what I cook. It doesn't matter what I smell like, does it? The important thing is for you to eat and be filled up."

My eyes grew heavier, and I nearly fell asleep. The delightful state between waking and sleep began to take over.

"Come in and snuggle up next to me," I'd say. "I want you with me."

"Oh, go to sleep, can't you? There are clothes waiting to be washed and there's ironing to do—and the baby needs changing—and—"

"All right, all right! I don't want you anyway. Just get on and finish those boring chores of yours."

Poor woman. How all the chores pile up on her. How many worries she has weighing on her heart.

The damned insinuation stirred. *That heart of hers is unfaithful to me. How, and when? And why? What time does this woman ever have for any love except mine? What sort of man is it she's giving her affection to, after a whole, exhausting day in the kitchen and the rest of the house? She never has a single moment to herself. When could she be unfaithful?*

So, she's lying to me! She must be lying to me. Yes, that's it, she makes me think she's always busy so I'll leave her alone. Maybe it's while I'm asleep, during the midday heat. Or perhaps it's at night, when she gets out of bed because, she says, the baby's crying in the next room. Or maybe it's at dawn, when she gets up because, she claims, she's got to get breakfast, or prepare the meat, or whatever.

You damned insinuation! You've stirred up a whole nest of troubles. What a fool I've been! What am I to do?

I stretched out on a chair. *Right, I'll take the time away from her—and the lie. I'll do everything myself. Then there won't be any room for deception. She'll see.*

For months now I've been splitting my energy between home and work. The work's never once stopped, I'm just dashing about without end, all my free time swallowed up. I've started feeling pains in my back and thighs, and my fingers are chapped from all the soap and cleaning agents. My body's started falling apart, and there are new lines on my face. I've wrinkles around my eyes, from a whole series of worries and cares. I've grown old before my time.

In the midst of all this endless exertion I strove to fix a timetable for my periods at work, so as to work out how much time my wife was able to steal from her work and throw herself into that other man's arms.

What an incredible woman! How did she find enough time? It's heavy enough even to weigh down the shoulders of a man like me. How could she bear it all by herself, for the three years she's spent with me, inside the walls of our house where she couldn't stand the sight of a flyspeck even? What a cursed woman! Where did she find the time, in the middle of all this constant pressure, to fly off to the arms of that other man?

The confusion of the office was mirrored in the house now. There was no difference between the office and my place of rest. My baby was always crying, always dirty-faced and wet. I started going off to the restaurants across the road, eating, day after day, the same food they'd decided on—meat, meat, meat, till I hated the sight of meat.

The flyspecks collected on the walls, became etched on the fans. I never got to bed before late now, only for my exhausted body to be thrust from it at dawn, then, next night, back in with the bed untouched, with no one having made it or changed it, the linen covered with filth. There were cigarette butts crushed on the tiled floor, on the table, in the ashtrays, filling the whole house with their stale smell.

And my wife—how alluring she was! She wore the loveliest clothes now, and every shade of makeup appeared on her eyes, on her cheeks, on her lips. Her hair, which I hadn't seen hanging down behind her since our wedding night, I now saw rippling gaily over her shoulders, the smooth skin of her back revealed by the dresses she'd worn when we were engaged, which she'd had to give up just a month into our marriage, because her body had begun to fill out and swell.

Only my wife disposed of time and beauty, during the seven months the damned insinuation had settled itself peacefully in my head. I wasn't concerned any more about investigating the time she stole from all her pressing duties. Today I saw a blurry figure moving about in the nursery next door.

"What does my wife do," I wondered, "with all the free time she has?"

And how I envied her!

—Translated by Olive F. Kenny and Christopher Tingley

Faruq Wadi (b. 1949)

Palestinian novelist, short-story writer and critic, Faruq Wadi was born in Bireh, near Jerusalem, then went to study in Jordan, obtaining a B.A. in Psychology from the University of Jordan. He is active in the literary life of Jordan remaining in touch with men and women of letters in the Arab world. He has worked as a journalist, as a chief researcher at the Center for Palestinian Research in Beirut, and now edits the Palestinian review *Financial Samid*. He has participated in many literary conferences and film festivals. His first collection of short stories, *Exile, My Love!*, appeared in 1976; his second novel, *Road to the Sea* (1980), won instant recognition for its deeply penetrating depiction of the human spirit slowly discovering itself, and its reflection of feelings hitherto rarely addressed with such candor in Arabic. His novels *The Smell of Summer* (1993) and *Places of the Heart: The Book of Ramallah* (1997) each combine a maturity of both style and subject matter with an intimate and disturbing treatment of his Palestinian subject that distinguishes itself from the loud tones and bravado of political literature. In 1981 he published a book of criticism, *Three Moments in the Palestinian Novel*.

The Secret

Only he knew. Even though a river, and the enemy, separated him from them.

When the rounding of Maryam's belly betrayed her secret, the news lay on people's tongues, to start with, like a timid bird that seeks to reveal itself and proclaim its existence but consents, after all, to be pent within closed walls, echoing in the merest whispers. Then, as the belly swelled still further, the walls broke down to show the secret behind, and the windows and doors opened—kindling talk beneath the summer trees and reaching the faraway school near al-Suwwana.

And so the secret was a secret no longer. The bird was out, now, from those secret walls.

"Maryam's pregnant!" Every tongue in Saffa repeated the words, and still, as the belly grew bigger by the day, the news was confirmed, more solid than the rocks of the surrounding mountains the village feet knew so well. "Maryam's pregnant!"

And behind this secret that was a secret no longer lay no answer at all—that was the secret now. Who could the father be, with her husband, Yusuf, so far away? Should they ask her perhaps? But who'd venture to approach her?

The men all drew back. "If I'm seen talking to her," they said, "people will claim I'm the one responsible. It would be fatal." And the women couldn't talk to someone like Maryam, who was, they said, a disgrace to them all. As for the children, they kept their eyes and their ears open, watching and listening.

The men were sitting and talking in the café near the village square.

"We did tell him," they said. "Listen Yusuf, we said, keep your voice down. Walls have ears. Don't let your tongue land you in a cold prison cell or force you to run off. Look, Yusuf, the flushed face reveals the secret; it speaks and gives a man away completely. Come and bury your head among the other heads. Be like everyone else."

But Yusuf's voice had grown ever louder, till at last it knocked against the walls of the sky. His face had grown ever redder, more flushed. Finally, he'd had to flee.

He'd fled through the rugged mountains while the village slept, pursued by the constant barking of dogs on his track and the feet of the occupying soldiers; fled toward the East Bank of the River Jordan, leaving behind a parched land and a woman, joined together beneath the burning sun. "Maryam was thirsty," people said. "She opened her legs to some passing man who came and hammered on the door of her house, while her husband, Yusuf, was away."

That night was a calm one, its quietness welcoming the footsteps cleaving the wilderness, while the parched land slept. Maryam's eyes had been half-closed, but now they opened wider as the sounding footsteps approached her house; opened wider still as she heard the light, cautious knocks on the door. She got up, spurred on by familiar sounds able to drive off all sense of fear and desolation.

Opening, she saw the figure of a tall man rising above the low door frame, standing there silently, a smile lighting up his face. The light in his eyes pierced through her to the very heart. She gasped, and the man, whose figure was so familiar, put out his hand to cover her lips. Then she melted into his arms.

She remembered, later, how they'd said so many things to one another. Her sharpest memory, though, was of how, at the end, all barriers between them fell, and they became one, pulsing with warmth and desire.

Come, man, and cover the parched body. Send your springs gushing into the fields, make the water flow through all the furrows. Infuse every part of the body that pulses with longing and thirst. Let the land quiver, in ecstasy, for the springs of water.

He too remembered how they'd said so many things; but his memory plunged itself, above all, into the moment their two bodies melted in the joy of their union.

The tragic thirst is quenched. Tremble now as you embrace my body and wring it with your love. Draw it to you more firmly, for the spring is there in the depths. Promise me, Maryam. Promise you'll keep the secret of this night etched deep inside you, no matter what; and I'll promise, too, only to reveal the secret when the proper moment comes; till then I'll burn it into a fiery rock of al-Suwwana. Tremble with love now, and quench the tragic thirst within our two bodies. Let the night witness the coming together of a man and a woman who trembled in love's ecstasy, then hid the secret in their depths.

Only he knew. When he'd left that night, stooping to emerge through the low opening of the cave, the village was plunged in sleep, and his footsteps had opened no eyes. But the village that slept that night was woken, later, by the swelling of Maryam's belly.

Who, they wondered, could it have been? A passing man, some said, who knocked on her door one night. Others said a regiment of soldiers had occupied her body. While others still . . . But, whatever they might say, he knew. Only his eyes, awake in the dark village, had pierced the blackness. Only Yusuf recalled the events of that night.

There were just the three of us.

My buttocks were numb, I told the others, from sitting so long; but neither of them answered. I put my gun down at my side and stretched out to relieve my stiffness, feeling the damp of the cave seeping into my limbs. Then I put my hand to an old wound on my chest, feeling no pain as I pressed it. As I started peeling off the scab, little by little, Maryam's face returned to me, sharply and insistently; and, as it still persisted, I surrendered to it, losing all power to resist. The distance between us shrank, and I threw caution to the winds.

"The joy of joining with a woman's body," I said, "is the most wonderful thing in the world."

"Don't be a fool, Yusuf," Abu 'Abbas said, as he caught my drift. "There are people hunting us the whole time."

"I only wish, Yusuf," Haytham added, "I could do something about that sex drive of yours. That's what gives you all those nightmares!"

"But look," I protested, laughing. "Saffa's not so far away. Just a few yards really."

It was too dark for me to see the expression on Abu 'Abbas's face.

"Actually," he shouted furiously, "it's a few *miles*."

I managed to laugh. Then I started telling them, all over again, how it was actually no distance at all, that I could take the mountain track. When I stopped, I could feel the silence pressing down on the cave; and, in the desolate stillness, I surrendered to the fiery longing that clung to me like Maryam's face.

I got up abruptly and stood at the entrance of the cave, carelessly breathing in the air. A voice told me to come back inside, but I didn't answer.

"I'm off," I heard myself saying. "I'll see you in the morning."

Then I added lightly, "I'll leave my gun with you. I'll be up before dawn and I'll race the sun back here."

A voice from inside was still trying to hold me back.

"Come on, Yusuf. Come back in here!"

Still the voice pursued me. Then, finally, it gave up.

I started walking through the darkness, feeling quite sure of myself. It was as though the mountain track was smoothly paved under my feet, the small stones breaking as I strode on through the night.

I don't remember too much about that walk. But what I do recall is the moment I knocked at the door of our old house and my eyes fell on the face suffused with sorrow, along, now, with a shock that refused to leave it.

I remember how we said so many things. I remember everything.

He remembers everything. So where has all your sorrow come from, Maryam?

As you pass by, all the palm trees of the earth withhold their shade and hide their delicious fruits.[1] Eyes strip you naked, wandering over your body. People say, in their ignorance, that a stranger planted his seed in you, in the furrows of a land parched through your husband's absence.

Where will you find a palm tree, Maryam, and shade when weariness takes you? What can you say to the questioning eyes? That no man ever touched you at all? Did the swelling come through God's spirit or through the warmth and ecstasy overflowing from those two bodies?

Bury the scream in your heart, Maryam; keep the burning pain locked tight in your ample breast. Remember your promise and keep the secret hidden.[2]

He remembers everything and keeps the secret safe in his heart. And as he knew the way from the river to al-Suwwana, and from al-Suwwana to the sea shimmering so brightly before his eyes, so he knew all the other things, even though a river, and the enemy, separated him from them.

—*Translated by May Jayyusi and Christopher Tingley*

---

1. The reference here is to the chapter of the Quran in which Maryam (the Virgin Mary), when in labor, is told by God to shake the trunk of the palm tree so that dates will fall for her to eat.

2. Divulging her hunted husband's return would expose her to danger from the occupying Israelis. She could not even let the other villagers know.

Al-Taher Wattar (b. 1936)

Algerian novelist and short-story writer Al-Taher Wattar was born in a rural area of Eastern Algeria and received his first education in the "free" schools (conducted by the Association of Algerian Muslim *Ulama,* which taught Arabic during French rule). He later studied language and religion in Constantine and at the Zaytuna Mosque in Tunisia. Despite the crucial and often somber subject matter of his fictional work, he never abandons the first prerequisite of a storyteller: to sustain the elements of excitement and fascination for the reader. One of North Africa's major novelists, Wattar became known broadly in the Arab world with the publication of his first novel, *Al-Laz* (1974), about the Algerian revolution; his other well-known novels are *The Earthquake* (1976), translated into English by William Granara (2000), and *The Wedding of a Mule* (1978). Other novels include *The Fisherman and the Palace* (1980); *Experiment in Love* (1989), and *The Candle and the Corridors* (1995). His short stories have been collected in *Smoke from my Heart* (n.d.) and *The Stabs* (1969). He has also written two plays. A leftist, much of his nonfiction work deals with the crises and problems of postrevolutionary Algeria.

THE MARTYRS ARE RETURNING THIS WEEK

As he handed him the letter the post office employee told him, "It came for you from abroad, Uncle al-'Abed, from a very distant land."

He made his way toward the shade of a tree to sit on a rock, asking himself, "Addressed to me?" In all his sixty years al-'Abed ben Mas'oud al-Shawi had never had any connection whatever with the outside world. He opened the letter, bent over it, and immersed himself in its contents.

For four hours he stayed there, never once moving, as the sun fixed itself above him and then went into its decline, casting shadows from the wall. At last he folded the letter and put it into a small bag hanging around his neck. Then he rose heavily and began to make his way along the road that sloped down from the edge of the village.

Old al-Mas'i was passing by and greeted him. Al-'Abed stood for a moment and beckoned him to come closer. When he did, al-'Abed took his hand and stared deeply into his eyes.

"Al-Mas'i, have you ever thought that your martyred son might return some day?"

"I swear by the Almighty God that the image of my son has never left my eyes in seven years. Whenever lunch or supper is laid I look to the right and to the left, waiting for him to join me ... "

"I'm speaking seriously, al-Mas'i."

"And do you think I'm joking? Anything having to do with the martyrs is extremely serious."

"Imagine that a telegram arrived this minute, informing you that he would arrive tomorrow."

"Well . . . as a matter of fact, a late return like that could give rise to many problems, difficult problems. During the first two years of Independence, it would have been possible; but now . . . "

"It has reached me that they are all going to return. Farewell."

Al-Mas'i stood watching him walk away and mused, "His mind has gone soft, he is on his way to madness. People have moved forward, but he is still tied to the past, grieving for his son. If his son had returned, al-'Abed would have been treated no better than anyone else—they might have given him a tavern to run, or a taxi license, or probably would have neglected him completely. But as fathers of martyrs, every three months since Independence we have been receiving sums we had never dreamed of. If aid is to be distributed, or loans given to the peasants, we are first in line. If we were to appear in court, our sons would attend the case and enable us to win. Thanks be to God for what is left, and God have mercy on all the martyrs . . .

"Good evening, Si Qaddour."

"Welcome, welcome, Uncle al-'Abed. What fate brought you here this evening? Would you like a bottle of soda? As you can see, at the end of our life we have taken to selling liquor, so we can earn something to support the army of children and relatives dependent on us."

"God's will, my son. This is how it was written that you should take their place. I have come to ask you to repeat to me the story of my son Mustafa's martyrdom as it happened."

"We were coming down from the Oras[1] mountains on our way to the border, carrying the *wilaya*'s mail. It was a moonlit night, and he was walking ahead of me. About an hour and a half's walk from the electrified fence, I saw him stop suddenly and freeze. 'Allahu Akbar!'[2] he cried out. 'There is a mine under my foot! Stay where you are!'

"'But I must help you!'

"'You cannot. Lie flat so that the shrapnel will not fly out at you!'

"No sooner had I dropped down when one, then a second explosion took place. Mustafa threw himself into a hole in the ground, and the mine he was standing on exploded. His bad luck—the hole was also mined. I rushed to him,

---

1. The Oras Mountains, or Aures as they are known in English, are part of the massive Saharan Atlas. They were the center of the Algerian Revolution against the French colonization of Algeria, which ended in victory for the Revolution in 1962.
2. "God is great." Muslims pronounce this often but especially in moments of emergency, stress, or wonder.

to find him dead. His chest, God have mercy on him, was ripped open. I buried him there, Uncle al-'Abed, and continued on my way."

"You say you buried him?"

"Yes, indeed. With these two hands. How I wept! He was more to me than a brother, Uncle al-'Abed."

"Listen, Qaddour, my son: your tale is true and there is no room for doubting it?"

Qaddour started, and glanced at him sidelong, "Of course."

"But my dreams are also true. Mustafa stood this morning, after prayer, at my head, and told me very precisely, 'I have not died. I escaped the mine through a miracle. I will return to you within ten days at most.'"

"Did he tell you anything else?"

"This is what he said."

"God have mercy on the martyrs, Uncle al-'Abed! Your son is now enjoying eternal paradise! Have a drink, Uncle al-'Abed, think of yourself . . . "

"May God increase your bounty."

With that he made for the door, leaving Qaddour astounded, the blood returning slowly to his face.

"How are you this evening, Uncle al-'Abed" It was young 'Abd al-Hameed.

"I am well. I want to ask you a question, in your capacity as head of the village council and principal of its school."

"Please do."

"What would it mean to you, as head of the village council, if all the village martyrs were to return—or at least some of them?"

Inwardly 'Abd al-Hameed said to himself, "If your son Mustafa were to return I would avenge my father! I would eat his flesh with my teeth!" But he smiled at al-'Abed and asked, "Why this question?"

Al-'Abed, thinking, "I will not tell him about Mustafa for it was he who assassinated his traitor of a father," answered, "Just a question that came to my mind. And I beg you to answer it with complete frankness."

"The matter to me is simple. They are down in the register of deaths, and they would have to prove their lives anew. That would not be possible for them, at least until my period of office was over."

"But these are martyrs—real fighters, I mean!"

"So what? They would not be here a week before they became fake, before they reverted to what the others have reverted to."

"And what if they came back with all their weapons?"

"Then it would be out of my hands, and a matter for the state. It's all very simple, according to the law."

'Abd-Hameed proceeded on his way, certain that poor Shaikh al-'Abed was on his speedy way to madness. He did not look well, he thought, his eyelids were droopy, the muscles of his face were rigid, and his hands trembled.

Al-'Abed continued down the road, his back stooped, his head hanging low. "The law! The fighters, according to the head of the village council, whether they are martyrs or not, are dead and must struggle to prove they are alive! Son of a traitor! The people of the village all know that, but they elected him unanimously. I myself voted for him. Son of a traitor! Our naive supposition that as the son of a former head of council he would be more successful than someone else . . . the absolute surrender to the wave of general amnesty for the past, that is what caused us to elect him . . ."

"How are you, Uncle al-'Abed?"

"Is that you, Si al-Mani? I want to speak to you."

"But I am busy. I have a meeting, Uncle al-'Abed."

"One minute—no more."

"Go ahead."

"Do you believe that all the martyrs are really dead?"

"No, Uncle al-'Abed. They are alive and prospering near their Lord."

"I do not mean that. I mean, are they alive in this world, eating bread and walking in the marketplace?"

"God knows!"

"It is more than that. The village martyrs are all going to return."

"What? Are you well, Uncle al-'Abed? I do have a meeting . . . "

"No, this is serious. My son, Mustafa, whose headquarters were in your house before you left the desert for the village, will return this week."

The face of the District Organizer went pale, and he felt a desire to sit down. "I don't know how he heard that I informed on him to the enemy," he thought, "And that an ambush was set up for him in my house. The soldiers remained hidden there for a month, but he did not come. At the end of it I was forced to move to the village. He sent me a letter saying I was a traitor to my country, and that I would be killed sooner or later. It was my good luck that he died a month later . . . "

"From where did you hear that, Uncle al-'Abed!" he asked confusedly.

"After the morning prayer he stood at my head and said to me: 'I was not killed, and I will return to you within a few days.'"

"Isn't this a dream?"

"I have not had a false dream in all my life, Si al-Mani'. My son will return within ten days. He mentioned to me some matters and some names. I do not remember them, unfortunately."

"Did my name pass his lips?"

"I do not think so. But please, answer me. What would your position be, as district organiser, if all the village martyrs were to return?"

"Ah. I would take them to see all the achievements that Independence has brought about. Then I would present them with the folders of party membership, with the Declaration of Commitment to the Revolutionary Authorities. Then, once they had met all the conditions and standards, and proven their obedience, loyalty, and self-sacrifice, they would be promoted to the militants' cells."

"That's all?"

"And what more do you want? All people are equal under the law."

"Even the sacred ones? The precious in whom we take most pride?"

"We will finish our talk another time, Uncle al-'Abed. Farewell."

Sheikh al-'Abed trudged on, his mind preoccupied: "What do they think during the moments of silence when they stand in remembrance of the martyrs' souls? Do they say, 'May God in His wide-ranging mercy bless your souls, you heroes who chose death over life in order to make your country and your brothers happy'? Or do they say, 'Lord, Thou art kind to thy worshippers, for hadst Thou not relieved us of them, we would not have been able to enjoy the things we are enjoying now in this life'?

"Ah! Depression fills my heart and suffocates my soul . . ."

"Good evening, Uncle al-'Abed."

Al-'Abed went straight to him, grasped him by the arm to stop him.

"You have descended from the heavens . . . remove my bewilderment, son, for no one but you can do that!"

"What's up?"

"You are the only one in whom I have confidence in this village. Your past is purer than milk—a fighter in arms from start to finish! And you have not been willing to sell your conscience for a tavern, or to ask for a loan at the expense of your brothers, or to give false testimony so a traitor can obtain the fighters' ID, despite great temptations. You are the angel of our village, my son!"

"You exaggerate, Uncle al-'Abed."

"By my son's head, no! This is the truth!"

"But you said you were bewildered, Uncle al-'Abed . . . "

"Do you know what the head of the village council said to me?"

"No."

"That the martyrs, if they were resurrected, would have to struggle all their lives to remove their names from the registry of deaths."

"Son of a traitor! What else did you expect him to say?"

"And do you know what the district organizer said?"

"No, by God!"

"That he would hand them the applications for enrollment, and after studying them would accept them as members."

"Listen, Uncle al-'Abed. My heart is full to the point of overflowing; do not add to its unhappiness. The proverb says: 'Whatever direction the living shall desire, the head of the dead shall be turned to.' The living are the law; they are the ones who watch over its application. And the dead, they are dead. Everything today has to come by the ID, Uncle al-'Abed. A revolutionary past has to have an ID to testify to it. Struggle has to have an ID to prove it. Good conduct has to have an ID. Treason alone has not been given an ID. We all know the traitor but we cannot confront him, because the ID is the only means of proving the truth. There is something called bureaucracy, Uncle al-'Abed. It is what wins in the end."

"But my son, do we have anything more to be proud of, more sacred, than a million and a half martyrs? What is left for us if we lose our reverence for them?"

"Why do you say these things, Uncle al-'Abed?"

"Ah, I forgot to tell you. My son, Mustafa, you know him?"

"And how not? God have mercy on all the Martyrs, although their absence in these circumstances is a mercy to them . . ."

"He will return this week."

The organizer of the veterans' division bent his head, thinking, "Is Sheikh al-'Abed sick? No. He is as well as can be. What is he saying? He is a trustworthy man, who weighs his words before letting them out . . . This matter of the burial, I'd never really thought about it before today . . . Near the electric barbed wire, enemy posts all around them, two mines explode, and Qaddour has sufficient time to bury Mustafa? Would he have had the necessary courage even to wait for him had he merely been wounded? Is Mustafa really returning, or has longing for his son so shaken Sheikh al-'Abed that he wants to know all the details of his death? He is following a dangerous method in his investigation if that is his intention . . ."

"The meaning of your words is great, Uncle al-'Abed."

"Great, my son. Very great."

"And from where did you get this news?"

"I have come to know it of a certainty, my son."

"The important thing, Uncle al-'Abed, is that the matter of their return be on the agenda. And the saw has taken precautions against the matter. I do not know whether it is better that they return singly or as a group."

"That depends on what is fated for this nation, my son."

"This nation's fate is in the saw. Prince 'Abd al-Qader, for example, was a martyr for seventeen years and remained alive for a century and a half after. The only thing that affected the destiny of the generations is what they did with themselves. With their own hands. I am standing in front of you. Am I not a living martyr?"

"I am about to fall! My head is spinning! My knees do not have the strength to carry me! Do not talk any more to me . . ."

And before he left, the organizer of the veterans' division told him in a soft voice, "If you are able to get in touch with him, advise him not to return to the village. God's land stretches wide. Tell him to practice life in another place first."

Sheikh al-'Abed's head felt heavy, as though filled with bullets. No one welcomes their return. Neither the loyal nor the opportunist, neither the militant nor the traitor. Those people, what is the matter with them? What ogre has stultified their feelings? It is as though they have all gotten into a railroad coach that does not move, it has become separated from the rest of the train and remains in a tunnel, but they do not realize this. They will not realize it until another train approaches, collides with their coach, and pushes it forward . . .

"Sheikh al-'Abed! In God's name! Has some ill befallen you?"

The head of the militia unit was passing by, carrying a black leather briefcase in his hand.

"Wait, my son, I want to ask you something."

"Go ahead, even though I am in a hurry. The wives of the martyrs, they have been causing us a lot of anxiety! There is a fight in the house of one of them now, with sticks and daggers; she turned her house into a tavern and a whorehouse, and this is the result. We warned her more than once, but she paid no heed."

"This is the matter I wanted to touch on with you."

"What, Sheikh al-'Abed? Do you have new information to add?"

"They are going to return."

"Who are they?"

"The martyrs."

"They do well to," said the Head of the Militia Unit, and then bowed his head, musing, "If anyone who knew me returned, that would be quite a problem! No one knows of my capture the day of the battle in which all the members of our unit were killed. No sooner had the first shots rung out than I put up my hands and ran toward the enemy, abandoning my post as guard of the unit's machine gun. Because no one else was able to reach and man it on time, they all fell . . . "

"At last," said Sheikh al-'Abed to himself, "someone who welcomes their return. He was a genuine fighter, no doubt about that!" Then he raised his voice:

"Are you serious in what you say, my son?"

"Allow me to ask in turn, Sheikh al-'Abed, would you accept that your son, Mustafa, God have mercy on his soul, should return and remove from you the honor of a martyr's father and cause you to lose all the rights that follow from it? Truly, you yourself were a militant, imprisoned and tortured during the Revolution; but what militant or fighter enjoys the honor that a martyr's father enjoys? Think well, they should have joined us on the first Independence Day, for now it is too late. The procession has passed."

"But what if they really did come back—all, or at least some of them?"

"The answer is very simple, Sheikh al-'Abed. We would arm their women and leave the matter to them."

Al-'Abed's head grew heavier, and he felt a lump and a bitterness in his throat, and a burning in his eyes, so he pushed forward along the sloping road. "The railroad coach is totally detached," he thought, "and no one is aware of it. Are we not like one who lives beside a cemetery and allows his cow to graze over the graves? So much does he tread it and pass through it that he forgets it is a cemetery, holding the remains of people who were once alive like him, among whom there were individuals who were dear to his heart. When you raise the matter of their return, it does not occur to anyone that they alone are the legitimate bearers of a right, for were it not for their martyrdom things would have remained as they had been. If we had indeed wanted to change things as they did, we would not be alive now: we would have plunged ourselves forcefully into the battle, and not have continued to trick death in one way or another.

"Lord . . . if the returnees were to realize this truth, would they not regret their sacrifice? If the coming generations were to realize this truth, would they be ready to sacrifice in their turn?

"Oh! My head, my heart, my knees, my stomach! They are all aching!"

"God be your aid, Uncle al-'Abed."

He started and made in the direction of the voice, his hand outstretched to grasp the caller.

"Good evening, my son. Wait. Wait. There is a question I wish to raise with you."

"Go ahead."

"If they should return, what would the stance of the treasury be?"

"Who should return?"

"The martyrs. For whose death the treasury pays their fathers a grant."

"But this is impossible, Uncle al-'Abed."

"It has reached me from an informed source that the village martyrs—or at least some of them—are going to return. Do not argue with me over this. Answer me only in your capacity as head of the treasury who pays the grants."

"This is something that has not occurred to anyone at all, Uncle al-'Abed. But pending the returnees' proof of life in the courts—and this is a matter that requires long proceedings, which take many years—we would stop the grant immediately."

"And what about the grants already paid?"

"Ah. Here you find me perplexed. But from the legal point of view the matter appears clear. Monies have left the treasury needlessly, so the treasury would demand, of the person concerned or his heirs, no less than that they be returned."

"But at any rate they would retain their rights, as veterans if not as martyrs?"

"They would have to obtain many forms in order to make up the application folder, which would not be easy for them unless they obtained a certificate of life first. From a purely legal point of view, they might not obtain this certificate at all. Imagine: society, and at its forefront their own kinfolk, would deny them or ignore them, or even take legal proceedings against them on the grounds that they were imposters . . . No, the best they could do is submit to the status quo and remain marginal. The honorable among them would commit suicide, no doubt."

"But they are all honorable, my son, they are the most sacred thing in which we take pride!"

"There is no one who returns from the grave and brings good luck, Uncle al-'Abed."

Perturbed, Shaikh al-'Abed continued his descent down the street that approached the center of the village.

"Has some problem befallen you, Father al-'Abed?"

"Ah. Is that you, Communist?"

"That time has passed, Father. Now I am in charge of the local Union of Railroad Workers. Do you remember what the officer used to say when he tortured us together?"

"I remember. They tortured you more than us. They wanted to kill you."

"The warden in charge decided to remove me from the party and the union, Father al-'Abed. I can still hear his words to this day: 'The dangerous germ in this movement' . . . "

"Yes . . . but I want to ask you a question. If the martyrs should return . . . "

"Do you mean all the martyrs?

"Yes."

"The population would increase and social problems would accumulate."

"I am not talking about this angle. Would you accept them or not?"

"A way would be found to accept them. They would be summoned immediately to the training centers, where they would remain for many years without arms and without any contact with the outside. Then their release would proceed: one by one the noble officers would be given important loans or appointed managers of firms, which would have increased by that time; the simple soldiers would be dispersed round the self-management farms that would be allocated to them in all fairness, as they merited and deserved."

"You are more honorable than to say these things!"

"But you did not ask me my personal position. You asked whether we would accept them or not."

"And what is your own position?"

"I cannot declare it without first and foremost contacting them. It depends on the ideas they come back with. I am a trade unionist, Father al-'Abed, and things are intertwined, so that it is difficult to take an off-the-cuff position like this."

Shaikh al-'Abed thanked the head of the local union and continued his way down the road, more perplexed than ever: "A loyal revolutionary," he thought, "I can testify to his steadfastness in prison in the face of extreme torture. Yet he was not enthusiastic about the news of their return. Does he doubt that they would support him as he expects them to? God is great, God is great! What ideas could they return with other than those with which they went, other than those for which they died? . . . If we, the living, have fallen into the snares of traitors and opportunists, have drowned in the material things of life, and have not noticed that the coach we are riding in has been separated from the train, those dear sacred ones, in addition to having been the most sincere among us because they sacrificed more than we did, have not yet been tainted by life's problems . . . They are the train that will enter the tunnel and push the disconnected coach ahead of it.

"Perhaps the train will come from the other direction to push the coach backwards.

"God is great!"

"Father, what is the matter with you?"

His son addressed him, taking hold of his arm, at the crossroads in the center of the village.

"Is that you? Where did you come from?"

"From home. I was looking for you, you have been absent since morning. Where have you been?"

"Why do you ask about me? Listen, if your brother Mustafa were to return, what would you do?"

"My brother Mustafa return?"

"Yes, return! Return! He is returning this week!"

"And what would *you* say, Father?"

"Get out of my sight! The fault is not yours! It is mine! Our fault! All of us! Go, tell your mother and your wife and your children!"

He withdrew his arm from his son's grasp, muttering, "I have to talk to the Imam of the Mosque. He is the most knowledgeable of us all!"

He made his way directly to the Mosque, waited until the Imam had finished with the afternoon prayer, and gestured to him.

"Were you not praying with us?"

"I have not made my ablutions. I want you to give me your professional judgment regarding a certain matter. You know that my son Mustafa did not return from the war."

"He died a martyr."

"Let us say that his wife, with whom he parted after four months of marriage, waited in my house until we were certain of his martyrdom."

"And after that?"

"I married her off to his youngest brother, and he has had four children by her."

"You did that? It is a sin! Heresy! Adultery!"

"What are you saying?"

"How dare you give in marriage a woman who is not divorced!"

"But her husband was dead, and we have his death certificate, and we signed the marriage contract at the judge's . . . "

"This is heresy, Sheikh al-'Abed, heresy against God and His Prophet and His Book. Your son is a martyr, and the martyr is not dead, he is alive and prospering near his Lord. Haven't you read the Quranic verse that is hung in all the village squares? The death certificate here is a legalistic trick to formalize things that have no meaning, from the point of view of the *shari'a*.[3] When the case is related to a martyr's wife, there is no recourse but divorce. This is adultery, God save us! Even the accusation of absence and desertion does not apply to them, for we know their location."

"What is to be done, Sir?"

"The religious law will be applied to the two adulterers."

---

3. The Muslim canonical law.

"Just like that, Sir?"

"And the choice remains for the first husband either to divorce or his wife back to his house. With regard to you, the matter goes beyond adultery. It is heretical to the Holy Quran and its explicit verses. Do you not know that the living status of martyrs is something upon which all religions concur? To this day the Christians await the return of Christ, for he is a martyr . . . You all have to declare your Islam anew, and to atone and repent."

"The problem of the divorce is easier than the problem of this heresy, Sir."

"And how is that?"

"The first husband, my son Mustafa, is going to return this week."

"You are still being heretical, man!"

"But . . . "

"Do you take your son to be Christ or al-Mahdi?[4] God forgive us! Yours is a cardinal sin; according to the Ibadi[5] creed, you shall roast in eternal fire! The repentance of those who commit cardinal sins is not acceptable! Leave the mosque, you heretic! Renew your Islam according to one of the other sects and repent!"

Humiliated and broken-spirited, Sheikh al-'Abed left the mosque and made his way to that part of the village through which the railroad passed.

The district organizer opened the session: "We are meeting here to confront a great agitation being planned in our village, and perhaps in other villages as well; and I am certain that it has connections with the outside. One of the elements of this movement, who has already been discovered, is in contact with persons abroad, and has received a letter from there only today. This massively restive movement rests on the claim that the innocent martyrs, God have mercy on them, shall soon return from the hereafter, and that the reason for their return is to reform matters that they claim we have failed to reform, or have caused to deteriorate.

"Just imagine what this means . . . an armed mutiny in which a million and a half of the best sons of this nation will participate, with the purpose of turning the situation upside-down.

"Of course the return of the martyrs is impossible, but who knows, perhaps there are dissidents who have taken to the mountains, or a big army might come from abroad to occupy our country again.

"As a militant committed to the Revolution since 1954, and as one who is in a position of authority, I saw it to be my duty and a sign of vigilance to

---

4. Literally "the one who is rightly guided," but al-Mahdi refers to a divinely guided religious leader designated by God to bring His true believers, the Muslims, back to the right path when they go astray. The Mahdi is expected to appear at times of stress, especially at times when Muslims are oppressed by foreign domination. There is a popular belief in some Islamic sects that a Mahdi will return, just as Christians look forward to Christ's second coming.
5. The 'Ibadites are a subdivision of the puritanical Kharijites, the earliest religiopolitical sect in Islam.

meet with you so we could put an end to this movement while it is still in its cradle.

"We must arrest Sheikh al-'Abed, and interrogate him, and inform the higher authorities immediately!"

"I agree!" said the head of the village council. "Shaikh al-'Abed contacted me this evening and said some perplexing things. I imagined at first that he was mad, but it becomes clear to me that the man is a deliberate agitator."

"If you knew what is being said inside the homes!" piped out the head of the women's union. "All the women are in a great quandary! They are saying that the martyrs are going to return this week armed with swords and cannons, grenades and machine guns, each armed with a long list of persons to kill. And that they will not be killed by bullets or stab wounds or even fire, and that after they have accomplished their mission God will take them to Him again."

"Did I not tell you the matter was serious?" asserted the district organizer.

The head of the youth organization said, "I can no longer control the youth. You know that they already hold ideas imported from abroad, and they criticize the authorities strongly. They have declared themselves on the side of the martyrs—or rather, the insurrection. You have done well in inviting us to this meeting, Brother Al-Mani'!"

"We, the scouts, have not been affected by this nonsense. We have decided to form units of vigilantes to inform the authorities of every stranger that enters our village and of every suspicious movement."

"We have faith in the scouts!" said the district organizer. Then he turned to the head of the veterans and the head of the local union, waiting to learn their stance.

"There is confusion indeed, but poor Sheikh al-'Abed is innocent. The memory of his son and his poor health are all that move him to imagine that his son will return this week," said the head of the veterans.

But the head of the village council interrupted him: "He says *all* the martyrs will! And what about the letter he received today from abroad?"

"We might say," put in the district organizer, "that the veterans, or at least their organizer, is an accomplice in the movement of agitation."

"What are you saying?"

"Be quiet! I did not give you the floor. And what is the position of the union?"

"You know that the workers are not interested in such matters. Sheikh al-'Abed may be ill, or he may have received a letter from his son. Perhaps his son was sent abroad for treatment and was afflicted with amnesia after the shock of his accident, then recovered his memory. This is not an impossible event."

"You too are an accomplice of the foreigners! Commander of the militia, in view of the open agitation, it is necessary to arrest Sheikh al-'Abed, the head of the veterans, and the head of the local union.

"This seems to be an exaggeration. The matter has not reached the degree of seriousness you imagine. Sheikh al-'Abed is sick, there is no doubt about that . . . "

"And what about the confusion, the panic of the women?" asked the women's organizer fervently.

"The only thing," answered the commander of the militia unit, smiling, "that will lessen the problems in the village, as you know, Aunt 'Aisha, is such propaganda from time to time. Only this evening three women have been killed—a martyr's wife and two girls, one sixteen and the other seventeen years of age . . . "

"Those three must be arrested!" the District Organizer said, and the head of the village council added:

"The matter is serious, and I shall immediately alert the district commander, and perhaps the *wali* himself."

"All I can do is summon Sheikh al-'Abed and ask him for the letter," said the militia commander.

"That should take place this very evening. Now, if possible. We will wait for you here at headquarters. The session is closed."

When the commander of the militia unit went outside, he was met by an unusual commotion. People—men, children, and old folks—were all running together, down towards the railroad tracks.

"Sheikh al-'Abed! Sheikh al-'Abed!"

He ran down as well, and at the tracks found other members of the militia standing near Sheikh al-'Abed's body, moving people away.

"He threw himself in front of the train," the driver said. "Some of them saw him waving this letter," a militia man said.

The commander of the unit took the letter from him and muttered, "It really is true . . . Glory be to God the High and Mighty!"

—*Translated by Lena Jayyusi and slightly abridged by Thomas G. Ezzy*

Muhammad al-Yahya'i (b. 1964)

Omani short-story writer and journalist Muhammad al-Yahya'i was born in Al-Haradi and obtained an M.S. in globalization and communications studies at the University of Leicester in 2002. He now works as a journalist in Oman. He has published two short-story collections, *The Magic Bead* (1995) *and The Day Khazina Shed Off the Dust* (1998). His *Democratization and the Arab World: The Role of Globalization and New Media is now in press.*

THE DEATH OF THE GOOD CITIZEN

He rested peacefully for an hour, then slept and died. When morning came, and news of his death broke, they washed and embalmed him, then walked behind his coffin and buried him. Then they all went back to their different homes. When night came, the man rose up out of his tomb, shook off the traces of death, rid himself of his shroud, then went back to his home, as naked as on the day he was born, as if starting life afresh.

The morning after his death he drew two buckets of cold water. Then he put on his clothes: the white robe, together with the green belt, adorned with its dagger whose red threads matched those of the turban over his forehead. Then he walked his usual morning route to the street overlooking the village, to wait for the ministry bus. The bus arrived at its usual time, and he climbed in to join the other employees, who were finishing off their broken morning sleep.

He sat down by the window, and very soon he too was asleep.

When the bus stopped in front of the ministry, and the employees got out, the driver noticed one lazy employee still hunched there on his seat. He went to wake him. Then, as he shook him, he found the man was dead.

The other employees gathered around, carried him inside and laid him out in the lobby of the ministry. Then they washed him, embalmed him, put him in a shroud, prayed over him, then walked behind his coffin and buried him. Then each one returned to his duties.

The man had learned wisdom, lying there in his first grave. His death, he felt, had been a grievous mistake, for a good citizen should only die on the job.

—*Translated by May Jayyusi and Christopher Tingley*

Hussa Yusuf (1948)

Poet, short-story writer, and writer of children's literature, Hussa Yusuf (al-'Awadi) obtained a B.A. in communications from the University of Cairo, with a special emphasis on radio and television, and has subsequently led a very active cultural life in Qatar. Much of her activity has been dedicated to children's education: she has occupied important posts in various media channels devoted to child education and culture and has written some twenty books dedicated to the enlightenment and enjoyable entertainment of children. Because of her own creative work and her serious dedication to the betterment of Qatari cultural life, Hussa has been awarded several prizes, three for poetry (1971, 1975, 1977), one for the short story (1980), one for the ideal woman (1996), and two for the best children's book (1997 and 1998). Her three poetry collections are *Words for the First Time*; *Birth,* and *Waiting* (in press); and she has published two short-story collections, *Starting Anew*, and *Faces Behind the Sails of Time*.

THE TURNING POINT

She lifted the receiver and answered calmly as usual. An urgent voce came back, "Hello, Maryam—I—I need to talk to you. Please, I must see you."

He was stammering and sounded confused, as though he was completely churned up inside. He wasn't usually like that.

She didn't want to refuse—even if she was engulfed by a stifling depression from which she could find no way out. She followed carefully as the strange words tumbled out one by one, but she still couldn't find the reason for all this wild turmoil.

She arranged a time to see him, then calmly replaced the receiver. He was in a dreadful state. Something very serious must have happened. She knew Ahmad well, knew he wasn't the sort to fly into a rage and start recklessly hitting out at things around him. He was the only person she felt comfortable with—the ideal person, she thought, for any girl who dreamed of a life of calm and contentment. But Laila, for all her twenty years, was still a child in everything she did. A child in her way of behaving, aware only of what she wanted, knowing only the childish whims that so often worried Ahmad and tired him out—as they did Maryam.

She was Maryam's pampered friend, her big pampered baby.

In fact she was Maryam's very special friend. Maryam was the first girl Laila had met as a child, on their very first day at school together, and she leaned on Maryam as a compensation for having no brothers and sisters of her own, coming to view her as sister, mother, and friend. They'd played together, studied together, grown up together day by day. But Maryam had grown up ten years for Laila's one.

While Laila grew up with all her childhood joys, life engulfed Maryam in a thick cloud of sorrow, depriving her of her childhood, closing the doors of her heart. She knew no way to joy. Merriment had fled her life, as the soul leaves the body at death.

In the evenings she worked to help her crippled father and support her young brothers and sisters. Maryam never came to know happiness; it left her when her mother left the tumult of this world, in childbirth. Her mother's breath had grown short, her voice had rattled in her throat, then it was silent forever. But out of death a new life was born. Maryam found herself mother to a newborn baby girl, to six children in all. She was just fourteen.

Only the day before she'd played alongside them, a child as they were; now, suddenly, she was their new mother. For all her young years she was firm, strong despite her innocence; and when her father became bedridden after the accident, her strength and resolution grew to be like steel.

No one could know what was going through that small head of hers. She spoke like a grown woman now, running the house like a calm housewife, rearing her brothers and sisters with a mother's tender heart, foreseeing every possible problem. She felt, too, as though she were Laila's second mother, even if Laila did get her fair share of pampering—much more than her fair share. Laila couldn't do without her little mother, Maryam. If she cried, it was Maryam's hand that wiped away her tears, and if she laughed, it was Maryam's heart that received her joy. Two small friends—a mother and her child!

But this phone call from Ahmad boded badly. What could it mean? Had things started going wrong between him and Laila?

It was just a few months since Ahmad and Laila became engaged, but many times already Laila, with her childish tantrums, had almost lost Ahmad, the young man who loved her in the hope her nature would change—who'd chosen her in the face of parents who wanted him to marry a young relative. Laila's behavior was almost driving him mad now. Was it his parents' wrath that lay behind this, or was it God's? And what had Laila done to lose the fiancé she loved?

The questions swarmed in Maryam's mind. She must, she felt, save this bond from snapping, save her friend from a suffering brought on her by her own conduct.

As she waited for Ahmad to come, at four that afternoon, Maryam lay on her bed and found herself gazing at a picture hanging on the wall—Laila and Ahmad on the evening of their engagement. Maryam had been abroad with her father, returning just in time to attend the evening. There were drums and music, and no sooner did Laila, the little bride, see Maryam enter the house than she leapt up, forgetting what her mother had told her—that her place was there next to her fiancé—and rushed to take Maryam in her arms. The people at the party were shocked by the young bride's behavior, and Maryam herself tried to make her see what she was doing, but Laila didn't care. She pulled Maryam by the hand and took her over to Ahmad.

"Look, Ahmad," she said anxiously. "This is Maryam. Isn't she marvelous?"

Ahmad was ready to gaze deep into Maryam's shining eyes, but she averted her own gaze, turning to his bride who was ready now to receive the congratulations of Maryam and the others. For all the sorrow and care that had swallowed Maryam's life, she was radiant that evening, with a lovely, enchanting glow, for all to see, Ahmad included.

It was the first time Maryam had met Ahmad, but it wasn't to be the last. Laila and Ahmad visited her constantly at her home, taking her out with them sometimes too, to give her some diversion.

While no one knew of Maryam's sorrow, Laila sensed it nevertheless and tried every so often to release her into Laila's own private world, full of joy and merriment and flowing with hope and life, a world glowing with beautiful dreams—a perennial, burgeoning spring in which she and her fiancé, Ahmad, would one day live, in their little house with its green fence, with little ones, their little ones, playing in the garden. The life of Laila and Ahmad was going to be wonderful!

Maryam believed it would be. Laila, for all her immaturity, loved children, and she loved Ahmad. She'd surely put in every effort to make him happy. As for Ahmad, while Laila's behavior didn't always please him, while he was often silent, he loved her in the teeth of his parents' objections. He'd chosen her for love and would surely devote his life to her happiness and their little home. No doubt this strange problem, on which Ahmad was apparently seeking her advice, was a passing disagreement of the kind that had cropped up so many times before, the sort of thing that happens between couples, a mere fleeting summer cloud.

With this in mind she waited for Ahmad. And there he was now, standing in front of her with his usual silent, calm manner. But before he spoke, before she could speak, he grasped her hand, tried to draw her to his breast, while she strove desperately to break loose, silently protesting, the tears streaming from her eyes, till she dropped down almost. At last she let out a cry, but stifled it, feeling her heart fluttering.

"Oh, God!" she murmured. "What is this happening? This terrible thing?"

It had all been a nightmare, terrible and terrifying. It wasn't Ahmad she'd seen but a dream.

Thank God. It was just a dream.

She gasped with relief. It hadn't been Ahmad but his resemblance. She looked at the picture again: there was Ahmad, surrounded by the drums and singers. The doorbell rang.

She looked at the clock. It was four. Heavens, she'd slept a long time. This must be Ahmad.

It was. But he wasn't his usual calm self. He was trembling as he looked into Maryam's face. His hand touched hers in greeting, then he quickly pulled it away. His lips were moving with difficulty and his eyes never left her face for a minute.

"What's the matter, Ahmad?" she cried. "You're frightening me!"

She really was frightened. It was the first time she'd seen Ahmad lose his poise. He seemed so agitated Maryam herself was shaken and disturbed.

"What's the matter, Ahmad?" she asked again. They were still standing there in the doorway.

"Can I come in?" he said.

She made way for him. When they were inside, she thought, he'd tell her what had happened between Laila and him. She was used to Ahmad coming to her in cases like that; she, after all, knew Laila better than anyone—and knew Ahmad better than anyone too, really understood him. She was the final recourse for both, the sole person who could persuade Laila of right and wrong. She was her little mother, her second mother.

One thing, though, she'd never managed to implant in Laila, try as she might. That was that she should live Ahmad's thoughts and ambitions as a woman ought to, a woman of proper maturity and wisdom. Would she ever be able to do it?

The winds outside the house were light, and there were just a few clouds in the sky. Maryam commented on this as she closed the window, trying to hide her agitation, ready to listen to what Ahmad had come to say. His voice was choked now. He made to say something, tried to begin, then broke off again.

As the teacup trembled in his hand, the thoughts sped through her mind. Why didn't he speak? Why was he so tense and upset? Why was he gazing into her eyes like that? What could he want? That glint in his eyes reminded her of the evening of the engagement. Whatever had happened?

His eyes swept her thoughts away, and a silent dialogue began between them. For the first time Maryam was speaking through her eyes alone. It was a long dialogue, very long, and Maryam woke from it at last quite terrified.

"No!" she said. "No! No!"

She gave a loud cry, then began to weep.

He stood beside her trying to calm her, to stop her weeping. His eyes held a thousand meanings, but his hands were empty of everything; even the engagement ring wasn't there. At last she knew what he wanted. She knew everything, read all the secrets in his eyes.

"Maryam," he said. "I—"

She broke in, her voice choked with tears.

"Don't say anything more. Just leave now."

He looked at her, trying to win her round, to make her change her mind. Then, suddenly, she fell on her knees, her face in her hands.

"Ahmad, please, I beg you. Have pity on me—" She began to weep once more.

Ahmad smiled. He had his answer at last.

—Translated by Salwa Jabsheh and Christopher Tingley

Muhammad Zafzaf (1945–2001)

Moroccan novelist and short-story writer Muhammad Zafzaf was born at Qunaitra, did his higher education at Muhammad V University in Rabat, then taught Arabic in Casablanca. He published many collections of short stories and novels and is regarded as one of Morocco's foremost creative writers. His short-story collections include *A Dialogue Late at Night* (1970); *The Stronger* (1978); *The Sacred Tree* (1980); *King of the Jinn* (1988), and *Vendor of Roses* (1998); and his novels include *The Woman and the Rose* (1972); *Walls and Pavements* (1974); *Graves in the Water* (1978); *An Attempt at Life* (1985); *The Back Quarter* (1988), and *The Fox that Appears and Disappears* (1989). He also wrote plays and criticism.

MEN AND MULES

That day they collected all the mules of the village.

"Why the mules, particularly?" we asked ourselves. But then they came back and rounded up all the donkeys as well. And no one was able to know why they had gathered all the mules and donkeys, for they, and they alone, had the answer.

Late that night our mules and donkeys returned to us. As they arrived, a trumpet blared, and we awoke in panic. We discovered that behind our own donkeys and mules was a line of other donkeys and mules, and that behind them was a line of barefoot men—people like us, who had come from other villages in the plain.

And behind them came armed soldiers. Of these there were only a handful, which could be counted on the tips of one's fingers. They singled out the young men among us.

"Put your hands above your heads!" they said. "And don't try to make any noise by scraping your shoes on the ground!"

This was a rather silly thing for them to say, since not one of us had any shoes to wear, not even slippers, in fact.

Yet one of the foreigners struck me with the butt of his rifle and insisted: "Got that? No shoe-scraping!"

Feeling still heavy with sleep, I bent my head to see if I might actually have come into a pair of shoes. He hit me again. I straightened out and woke up. He passed on behind me and harangued the others, perhaps with the same warning.

The ground was cold. Because it had been raining there were small puddles beneath our feet. As the mules and donkeys filed falteringly by, we could hear the squishing of their hooves, and every so often water would spatter under our *jilbabs* and up to our thighs. This felt chilly, for at the time we owned no trousers—neither of the European nor of the baggy Moroccan types. Our bodies winced, but we stayed shivering where we stood. We could not even budge because the slightest stir might provoke a rifle shot.

For a while we remained standing among the puddles. Then they pushed all the women and children and old people into the huts. To the rest of us they said, in an Arabic that was hard to understand, "Each of you is to take charge of a mule. Do you see those mountains? We will split up into smaller groups and rendezvous there.

"If any one of you makes one false move—or gives us any kind of trouble—then, one single bullet will take care of him!"

I was certain that none of us would make the slightest move, so the warning did not seemed called for. Or, perhaps it was: one of us might make a wrong move unawares. And, as a result, one single bullet would take care of him . . .

Though we did not know it at the time, the mules were loaded with arms—each was carrying two cannons, in fact, and it had been decided that we would all have to climb those rugged hills. No one could ride his mule except for the foreigners, who were to march behind and guard us in case someone tried to escape and hide among the thick trees that grew in various places. I was sure that none of us would dare such a thing, especially since the weather was chilly and rain was threatening to fall any minute. And besides, what could any of us hope to do against these foreigners, with their rifles and pistols?

We walked in a single column, each behind a mule. The mules were not close together but spaced, with intervals between them. The foreigners had taken part of the mules on another road. I did not know whether friends of mine from our village had gone with that group because we were not allowed to turn our heads either to the left or to the right. What we had to do was look straight ahead of us and keep walking behind our mules toward those mountains. As to what the mules were carrying, it was none of our business to know: it was only later that we found out about the cannons, the big iron chains, and the rest of it.

And as to where we were going, and why, that also we found out later on . . . Some of the tribes had risen in revolt against the authorities, and these weapons were to be used to put down their uprising. This had not been as easy as one might think: so far, the foreigners had not been able to make their way across any of the valleys without being ambushed from behind the rocks. One night, after a battle in the mountains in which the tribes had beaten the foreigners, these latter, in the belief that we too had been there shooting at them from above and behind, had descended on our village, bent on avenging their honor. They had killed a good number among us, slashing open the bellies of pregnant women to remove the embryos, and then they had completely withdrawn and not come back again.

Until today. Now here they were, pointing their rifles at our backs and chests. There were both whites and blacks among them. The blacks, it was said, were Muslims like us, who prayed and fasted and gave alms. We did not find this too surprising, since it was a well-known fact that there were Muslims in the foreigners' army . . .

As we walked, we kept expecting that the sun would rise soon. When it didn't, we began to suspect that the time was not close to daybreak, as we'd thought, but closer to midnight instead. The cold was biting and the wind was strong, and the wolflike howls of animals came to us from the valleys. There was no light, and the dark was intense; we could not see the mountains, but we could visualize them. We had to bear the cold and keep pace with all the others. Occasionally a cursed mule or donkey would stop, and one of us would get the blame. I would hear the grunting of a mule and then hear the sound of a hard blow, I would imagine the blow falling on a man's back; but whenever a man did not cry out, it was safe to assume a mule had got it that time.

We had heard that those tribes had rebelled again, but we had not been certain of anything, since we lived in the plain. There had been rumors that some of our men, despite tight security, had actually gone to join the tribes in the mountains and were there now fighting beside them. I wondered why they should have accepted any of us even though we had never in our lives had any experience in the use of arms . . .

"Walk, Bourkabi!" said a foreigner behind me. His Arabic was so clear that I suspected he was not a foreigner at all (later we learned that some of the officers were Algerian, though their fair and ruddy complexions made them look like foreigners).

For fear he would strike me, I hurried to catch up with my mule, which had started running despite the weight of his load. Other mules were not doing this, and I had no idea what had got into mine. Nevertheless, I took hold of his tail and let him pull me along with him.

We could hear the growls of distant dogs, which grew louder until their echoes reverberated everywhere. The darkness deepened, so that I could not make out the outlines of the other mules. I felt very tired and envied the foreigners their privilege of following us on muleback. I thought of running away, but how could I? They could have flushed me out of anywhere, even my mother's womb . . .

At last the mules began to work their way up the slopes, and deep fatigue came over all of us. I held on tighter to my mule's tail and felt he was dragging me along. I realized that if it hadn't been for this, I would not have been able to make the climb, especially after such a long walk . . .

It seemed clear that the foreigners intended to surprise the tribespeople in their sleep and then do to them what they had done to us before: slaughter and dismember them, skin them and tan their hides. I did not believe that they would succeed, however, because the tribespeople were armed, while we had not been . . .

As the mules kept climbing, I could feel an intense cold rise up from the ground, seep under my *jilbab,* and spread into my belly, my chest, and the whole of my body. To top it off, rain began to fall—slowly at first, then hard and strong. Mules began to lose each other beneath the sheets of rain. They stumbled and almost fell beneath the weight of their loads.

The order came for us to stop. At first we thought it was because they had taken pity on us, for most of us were wearing clothes that could not protect us from the cold and rain. I was one of the lucky ones because I was wearing a *jilbab,* and I thought of those who had on only shirt-dresses. How could they bear this damnable weather?

Mules and men, we huddled beneath a great overhanging rock. Up and down the column, other teams were doing the same thing. We could not see them, but we learned of it later on. The rains poured down so heavily that the mules began to whimper. One of the foreigners chose a well-protected spot, lit a cigarette, and began to smoke it. Someone approached him and began to speak to him. We ourselves had no right to speak, and we heard that person tell us, "The Shoulouh want to kill every last one of you. But we will not give them the chance to!"

The man was a Moroccan, then, who spoke the foreigners' language fluently. I wondered where he had learned it. For all I knew, he might even have been one of the Sholouh, but the foreigners had been able to turn him into another kind of person—into a foreigner like them . . .

I thought of sitting down, but I was afraid of the foreigner. They had forbidden us to sit. Two mules began to move and stamp the ground with their hooves. My mother, God rest her soul, had once told me that if a mule cut a groove in the ground with its heel, this meant that one of your relatives was dead. I became afraid that death had snatched one of my family . . .

My *jilbab* was now clinging to my body, and still the foreigner took no pity on us. I pressed close to the mule, but it moved away from me. The Moroccan returned to the foreigner and spoke to him in his own language. The foreigner leapt to his feet.

"Get ready, all of you," the soldier told us, "We have not been able to take them by surprise the way we wanted to."

How could we prepare ourselves to kill our brothers in Faith, I wondered; moreover, we had no training in the use of arms ...

The soldier walked hurriedly into the darkness until we could no longer see him. At the same time the foreigner in charge of us began to wheel around and jabber at us in his own language. I wondered if he had gone mad. He shouted in my face, gave me a hard shove, and gestured toward the mule. I saw my neighbor shivering with cold. He was someone I knew. There were six men in our group, aside from the foreigner.

When I showed no sign of understanding what he said, the foreigner came back and said, "*Cochon!*" (I found out later this means "pig,") He gave me a sharp slap and a kick in the belly. I felt pain but kept silent. The rain was still pouring savagely. At last he ordered us to continue our ascent, one mule after another and a man behind each.

In the dark we came upon a small hut with no light showing and its door open. With his rifle at the ready, the foreigner approached it and told one of us to enter and bring out whoever was inside. When the man came out and reported that the hut was empty of any trace of humans, the foreigner did not believe him, so he pointed a flashlight inside the hut. All of us could see there was no one inside. Then he ordered us to continue climbing.

Exhausted, we walked on. Then suddenly we heard rifle shots. The mules became recalcitrant. They grunted, brayed, then stopped in their tracks.

The tribespeople were on the alert then. The foreigner ordered us to beat the mules so we could get going, but none of us had a stick. We began to hit them with our hands, but they did not budge. The shots stopped, then rang out again. The reports resonated from the valleys and mountains, came to us mixed with the wind and the rain. From out of the dark two other soldiers joined us and began beating the mules with their rifle butts. With reluctance, the mules began to move. Their task accomplished, the soldiers headed back to where they'd come from. It seemed to me I heard one of them stumble and fall to the ground. The shooting intensified, and I became afraid for myself.

The foreigner told us to walk close to the rocks for cover. No sooner had he spoken than a volley of bullets whizzed over our heads. I saw something gushing out of my mule's body. It was blood. He had been hit, whether by one or many bullets I could not tell. I used him as a shield and could hear the foreigner moaning. The other mules scattered in the dark and pressed up against boulders.

There was no sign of the rest of the men. I was certain they had all got away. Nearby, the foreigner was stretched out beneath a small jutting rock. He was wounded. He fired a few shots, until pain overwhelmed him. I drew back a few steps from him, but he ordered me to stop where I was. I did not understand his Arabic at first, but I stood as he aimed his rifle at my chest. Then he let it fall. I reached out into the mule's saddlebag, which was close to me. When my hand touched a piece of light metal, I pulled it out and hid it behind my back.

In his pain, the foreigner was screaming into the downpour, "Get back here, *Cochon!* Where are your friends? Come closer!"

There was no sign of my companions, who had escaped with their lives. Even the mules—except for mine and another one further up—had disappeared under the hail of bullets and rain. I started to draw near him in the dark. I felt an anger that had no limits. The blood boiled in my head. The piece of metal trembled in my hand; I wanted to pounce on him with it, but I hesitated. Slowly, I began to move backward. The mule had moved lower down the slope.

Once again the foreigner ordered me to stop and come closer. This time he did not point his rifle at me right from the start. Then as he did, I heard him give a loud scream. Obviously, another bullet had struck him. I began to quake with fear that perhaps a stray bullet might hit me. I threw the piece of metal down. Ignoring his orders, I found myself running downhill. Then I stumbled into a mule stretched out in the road. I fell to the ground. Bullets were still whizzing through the air, coming from somewhere or other. In my panic I stood up and ran, with no idea of where I was going.

"Halt!" called a voice, this time in the Sholouh tongue. When I kept going, a shot was fired at me. I stopped. A man wearing a short *jilbab* and a *barnous* sprang on me. Another man joined him.

"Are you with them, traitor?" asked the first man.

"No, by God! I'm not a foreigner! They took us by force! I don't even know how to use a gun!"

"Be quiet!"

"They slaughtered us! Then they took our mules . . ."

"Let him go," the second man said. "He's not one of them."

But the first man paid no attention. He grabbed me, led me to a small tree, and tied me to its trunk. I offered no resistance.

"Stay here until we come back!" he said.

But they did not come back. Who knows, perhaps they were killed?

By the time the sun came up, I could no longer hear the whine of bullets. I tried to figure out where I was but could not. The whole place was enfolded in silence; the rain had stopped falling and the ground was wet. With great difficulty I untied my knots and made off, exhausted, looking for a path that would lead me back to my village.

In that battle, the tribes had captured the cannons, the arms—everything, even the mules. And despite the fact that they are Moroccans, like us, and Muslims, they have still not, to this day, returned our mules to us.

—*Translated by Lena Jayyusi and Thomas G. Ezzy*

Latifa al-Zayyat (1923–1996)

Born in Egypt, Latifa al-Zayyat obtained a Ph.D. in literature at the Egyptian University and has taught English literature at the Women's College of 'Ain Shams University. One of Egypt's most highly respected women in the public sphere, she was, before her death, head of the Department for the Defense of National Culture, and her seventieth birthday was the subject of a major celebration. Her work is particularly interesting for its treatment of subjects rarely touched on hitherto by women in modern Arab culture. A poignant example of this is her long short story, "Growing Old" (included in her collection), which is a heartwarming description of the process of growing old, as the fears, the aches, and the traditional dependence on the younger generation eventually gives way to a realization that, in the modern world, a woman's antidote to the loneliness of old age is the utilization of her own potential. Her literary work ranges from criticism, *The Image of Women in Some Arabic Novels and Short Stories* (1986) and *Naguib Mahfouz: The Image and the Ideal* (1986), to creative work in the various genres. Her first novel, *The Open Door*, was published in 1960. In 1986 she published a collection of short stories, *Growing Old, and Other Stories*, followed in 1991 by a short novel entitled *The Man Who Knew His Accusation*. Her play, *Selling and Buying*, was published in 1993. In 1994 she anthologized a collection of short stories by thirteen women, entitled *All Those Beautiful Voices*. She has also published an autobiographical account of her life and experiences, *A Search Raid: Personal Files* (1992), which may be regarded, for its candor, sincerity of approach, and fluent style, as one of the most attractive personal accounts available in Arabic.

The Narrow Path

The mother stood at the window in the early afternoon, eager to see her daughters, Siham and Muna, coming home from school. She leaned out of the window in the hope she might glimpse them in the distance, then quickly stopped herself. Would she never learn from experience? You couldn't see any distance, because there was an old gray house two houses down that blocked off most of the street, leaving nothing visible but a narrow path. Siham and Muna would only appear after they'd crossed that narrow path, and then you'd see Siham walking with her head tilted back and her lips set in determined lines, while Muna ran behind with longer, more persevering strides, trying to catch her up. She'd run, then hold on to Siham's arm as if she was afraid of getting lost.

The mother moved back, wiping the drops of perspiration that ran down her brow and onto her eyelids. Something had happened to Siham over this last year, something to make the heart ache. The girl had started walking as though there were a battle waiting for her at the next step, in which she'd have to defend herself, a battle she rose miraculously above with every step she took.

The sun was a little lower now, but it was still fiercely hot. The very slabs of the street seemed to have it stored up in the gaps between them, sending it back like a hot wind laden with the smell of fried onions, and old urine, and the rotting garbage lying in heaps on the street corners. There was a cat that always seemed to be searching in the garbage along with Um Muhammad's children, and now it emerged from a heap in the shadow of one of the houses and stretched out, peaceful and content, darting its tongue backward to lick itself.

The train's whistle sounded once again, disturbing the quiet noontime street. The cat crouched fearfully low, while the madman who lived on the roof of the house opposite emerged as usual, driving his imaginary train. He'd send out a whistle for the start of the journey, then breathe loudly in and out the way trains do, using his arms and legs for the wheels. The "train" gradually speeded up, then accelerated into a mad thrust, as if there were no wall there to hold it back. The madman had fled from reality into illusion, as he always did. In his world there was no narrow path and nothing was impossible; everything was possible in the madman's world. He duly crashed into the wall, let out a new whistle and started all over again, only to end, once more, where he'd started, bleeding heavily.

The madman's blood flowed onto the wall day after day, and yet he never stopped beating his head against it. 'Amm Jum'a, the greengrocer transformed into boutique owner, would invoke God's mercy on him as he heard the whistling start up, while Suad Husni's latest song would sound out, for the thousandth time, from the cassette recorder of Sayyid, the mechanic's boy, who now owned a kiosk for imported tobacco and also sold sweets, and children's toys, and pills and sex.

Sayyid the pimp was stealing glances at the house opposite, along with two men, strangers to the neighborhood, who were there with him. And soon the two strangers would disappear across the narrow path as one of the doors opened to reveal a woman. Those houses had belonged to decent families once. Who was the woman appearing there now? Whose daughter was she?

The path of virtue, the mother knew, had become a pretty difficult one. Things were moving faster and faster, and you could believe anything now. But the realization never ceased to hurt her, and fear would stab at her as she saw the door open to reveal this or that familiar neighbor, or that young girl she'd carried as a baby. Suad Husni was still singing, and the flies covered Um Muhammad's bare breast as she sat nursing her baby, while her other children, boys and girls together, the oldest no more than eight, would bring up the chosen items of garbage little by little—rags, and glass, and tin cans, and remnants of food that might satisfy their hunger just a little, while the madman's blood flowed daily on the wall. It was just surprising the sane ones didn't go mad.

In the kitchen she peeled some eggplants to fry. The rice wasn't properly cooked yet; she'd got home late because of the traffic, and Muna would start complaining loudly when she found lunch wasn't ready, while Siham—but with Siham it was more complicated. At eleven, she'd grown up before her time.

When she was Siham's age, she'd been like a kitten with its eyes still closed, knowing nothing of the world. She'd hang her festival dress over the board of her mother's brass bed and turn happily around it, gazing joyfully at it the whole day, then go to sleep dreaming of the moment she'd put it on next morning. She never knew what the latest fashion was, or what kind of cut or material was in vogue, and neither did any of the other children, in the street or at school. The festival dress was always a new one, and that was enough to make it beautiful in her eyes and in the other children's. If she ever fell sick during a festival, the dress would stay hanging for three days over that board of her mother's bed, where she slept too, and she'd gaze at it through her fever, imagining herself running, wearing it, out into a street bustling with colors and children and laughter and screams; with friendships that sprang up suddenly and quarrels that melted away as though they'd never been; with a sense of belonging, and games in which all the children took on a role they gravely acted out, whether policemen or thieves, in an enchanted childhood world to which adults had no entry—a world with its special language and expressions and values, where everyone was regarded as equal and no difference was made between one child and another.

She cut her finger slightly on the edge of the knife. Facing her daughter Siham had, she suddenly realized, become something frightening. She washed her finger, seeing the water grow reddish, then clear. Then she finished off what she'd started, the wound smarting as she dipped the slices of eggplant in salt water. The world had changed, she decided. There was no childhood any more and no more children. Divisions between wealth and poverty, light and dark, were mirrored all the time now, even in schools, even in the playground of the street.

The barrier that had once separated the adult world from the world of children had crumbled, and sometimes, as if by magic, the light was darkened by life's harshness—for life might grant darkness the glitter of savage, murderous gold, and power. Everyone saw it and knew it and grew old knowing it!

She put the pan full of oil on the fire, thanking God Siham liked to keep herself to herself, that she'd excuse herself from making visits or going to birthday parties. Did Siham really dislike mixing, she wondered, as she waited for the smoke from the oil to turn dark gray, or did she just hate appearing in front of her schoolmates in clothes Muna would eventually inherit, then wear till the hem just couldn't be let down any more?

Two days ago Siham had asked a question that stunned her. If a Mercedes, she asked, cost eighty thousand pounds, how much did a Rolls Royce cost? She was bewildered, unable to believe her ears, and asked Siham to repeat the question; and the girl repeated it. What, the mother answered sharply, did any of that have to do with Siham!

She realized now that she'd made a deliberate show of losing her temper, to give her time to digest such a strange question and work out why the girl had asked it. She guessed a Rolls Royce was more expensive than a Mercedes, though it hadn't really registered with her till that moment—even now, in fact, she wasn't really sure of the difference between the two. It was amazing a car costing eighty thousand pounds should exist in the world (how could it?) and that the school where the two girls studied should have children from families who could buy cars like that. It disturbed her that Siham should take an interest in matters outside, so unimaginably outside, her own family and background. When she saw what the question meant, she became still more agitated, telling the girl to know her place and just concentrate on her lessons.

Would it be possible, Siham wondered, if she kept doing really well, and saved every penny of her pocket money, and from her work after she'd passed her exams, to buy a car when she was grown up, even if it was only a Nasr?[1] The question embarrassed her, and she took refuge in the old proverb, "We can all get on if we work hard." Yet, even as she parroted it, she knew she didn't really believe this saying, which might have fitted the old life but not the one they had now. Still, you had to hold on to it, the way a drowning person holds on to the life-saving rope. It helped keep you from going astray or else going mad.

She moved back as the eggplant slices sank into the boiling oil and the oil began to spit. She remembered how, on her way to work, Siham had looked at her clothes and said, "That's an old-fashioned style. No one wears things like that now. It might be better if you took up the hem." She'd inspected her mother with a strange expression on her face, as though she were a pupil and not her mother at all. That look of Siham's still hurt, for the girl's sake rather than her own. How terrible, she thought, to see sometimes with the eyes of a stranger and for those we love to see us with strangers' eyes. We stand there naked, and we both feel strangers.

As she turned the eggplant slices in the boiling oil, guilt flooded her again, as if she'd committed some crime. Siham would see how, for the sixth day in a row, there was no meat on the table at lunch, and if she was in good spirits she'd say, "Did the cat eat the meat, Mummy?"

She might swallow Siham's sarcasm or just smile back, and the family might get happily through to the end of the meal, in an atmosphere of light-hearted banter, without any bitterness in it. There was nothing hurtful in banter and joking about things. Anything was easier than Siham's silence, her holding back from saying anything. She no longer had any idea how to treat her daughter, and that made her responsibility as a mother harder than ever.

The hot eggplants sizzled as they settled in a glass dish of garlic and vinegar. How often, she wondered, had she been on the point of telling Siham, bluntly, about the state of the family's finances? With the crazy cost of living today, the father's salary from his main job, plus his extra job, along with her teacher's salary and her income from private lessons, only just covered the girls' school expenses and the bare minimum of clothes and food. The ordinary necessities of life were becoming extras now. And meat, for two years, had been down the list of extras, except for one or two days a week, with fruit regarded as a luxury too, and even vegetables finding their place on the list now. She could no longer provide the family with a bowl of fresh salad every day, even if it was important for the girls to have their daily vitamins. If the rent for the apartment hadn't been an old one, even bread would have been out of the question.

So often she'd wanted to let Siham share the responsibility, but out of pity she couldn't bring herself to do it. So many times that sullen, knowing face would

---

1. A small car, assembled in Egypt and much cheaper than other cars.

upset her, and she'd try to explain, to make the expression go away, retreating in the face of stab after stab, knowing, all over again, that the knowing face was just that of a child who'd grown up before her time, because of a poverty no one had ever predicted, inflicted on two well-educated parents who each worked more than twelve hours a day in the most respectable government jobs—while that boy Sayyid, the pimp, now owned a building, and a greengrocer's store had turned into a boutique, and a car costing eighty thousand pounds was run by an employee who shouldn't be earning any more than the fathers of other girls at the school.

No, she wasn't going to collaborate with time, to wage a war against Siham. What she'd learned, so young, was enough, and the passing of the days would teach her enough and more.

Muna appeared now and, unusually, without Siham. She was hurrying, rolling her plump little body along, while the quarter settled into the afternoon and the madman kept on hitting the wall. Muna stopped under the window, then started making strange signals with her arms, which her mother could make nothing of. She put her school satchel on the ground, then began jumping in the air, higher with every leap.

Her mother almost screamed in terror as a car, driven by a mere boy, just missed hitting Muna, but she managed to hold the scream back. At that moment Siham arrived, picked up the satchel, and pulled Muna unwillingly into the house.

The mother left the door of the apartment open for the girls and, wondering why Muna had acted like that, went into the kitchen to heat a pot of vegetables left from the week's allowance of food. As she bent to pour hot water over the vegetables, which had frozen in the fridge, she heard Muna's rushing steps in the hall.

She almost stumbled into the flame and the pot, as Muna, with a mad thrust, came and hugged her legs from behind. She patted Muna's shoulders to make her let go, then turned to look at her. Muna's eyes, raised up to her, were gleaming with a thousand lights. The mother quickly drew her away from the fire, into the middle of the kitchen.

"What is it, Muna?" she asked. "What is it, darling?"

Siham, standing at the kitchen door with her arms folded, answered contemptuously, "She's going to act in the school play, Mother. She's nearly going mad about it."

"I'm playing the silk merchant," Muna said, with a kind of pride she'd never shown before. "In the story of Harun al-Rashid."

She let out a laugh like the sound of a rooster crowing, then started whirling round and round, her ringing laughter mingling with the madman's whistle. Then, out of breath, she raced into the hall.

The mother's eyes met Siham's as she gave her the plate of bread to put on the table. She felt, once more, the sense of embarrassment she always felt when she tried to communicate with her older daughter. The words stumbled on her lips and, when they did come out, the tone was midway between the one she used for adults and the one she kept for children. "And what part are you playing, darling? The queen?"

Siham's hand stopped on its way to the table. Then her eyelids went hooded, and she scanned her mother with that knowing look, as if to say, "Who are you making fun of, Mother? Me or yourself? I know my place in life, and there's no illusion could make me forget it."

Her mother stretched out a trembling hand, to pat the hand that was holding the bread plate. Siham blushed, then pulled her hand away in a violent gesture that almost upset the bread. Then, at the kitchen door, either as an apology or to escape a moment pregnant with emotion, she said, "I'm hungry, Mummy. I want to eat."

Her mother took the hint.

"Straight away, darling," she said, escaping the moment in her turn. "Do calm Muna down somehow, before she starts shrieking."

But Muna wasn't going to let anyone calm her down. She went out of her way during the meal to show she was independent and didn't need anyone, to the irritation of Siham, who was used to having Muna follow her like a shadow. Their father wasn't there to see the change in relations between the two girls, but even if he had been he wouldn't have noticed anything. He was just too busy with the problems of getting a living for himself and them.

Muna barely touched her food. She kept banging at the plate with her fork and spoon, her hand moving slowly and gracefully from one side of the dish to the other, her ear noting the accelerating rhythm, which she corrected whenever it started losing its tempo. Siham tried several times to quieten her down, but Muna insisted she knew how to play, and finally paid no more heed to Siham's rebukes. Her rhythm mingled, now, with the sound of the madman's starting whistle.

At the end of the meal Siham tried to restore the old relations between her sister and herself. Rather than help, as she usually did, with clearing the table and washing the dishes, she left the table with a lot of noise, then slowed down, meaning Muna to race after her like a shadow. But Muna didn't leave the table and didn't even notice Siham leaving it. Siham slammed the door violently to attract her attention, but Muna watched the door close with indifference, still banging the same rhythms on her plate.

The rehearsals for the school play went on for two weeks, during which Muna would leave with Siham in the morning but come back alone at five in the afternoon. Siham, for her part, boycotted the rehearsals, because she felt they were mere acting, something rather childish. Despite her mother's repeated insistence, she refused point blank to wait for her sister till the rehearsal was over.

The first time Muna came back alone, she said she knew the way perfectly well, declaring, with newfound pride, that she wasn't a little girl any more. In just three months, she said, she'd be nine.

Thereafter she'd mostly sit all by herself and say nothing, and Siham, whenever she saw Muna huddled alone in a dark corner, would say her sister was fast going mad. The house didn't resound with Muna's crowing laughter anymore, or with Siham's sarcastic comments that made other people laugh.

Throughout the first week of this, the mother tried, without success, to draw Muna out of her reserve and to persuade Siham that it wasn't madness but just physical exhaustion from the rehearsals. She was too busy with housework and correcting her pupils' homework to note the symptoms that Muna was showing now, but Siham saw them. It disturbed her to see her sister choosing to free herself from her power, and she watched, day by day, as the symptoms continued to appear, though she held back from any comment for fear of making things worse.

When the performance was a few days off, the mother busied herself making a new dress for Siham, with material she'd chosen herself and using a pattern taken from one of her friends at school. As she sat there doing the final stitching of the hem, Siham came out of the two sisters' bedroom on tiptoe and signaled to her mother to follow her.

In the girls' room Muna was sitting on her bed, staring into vacancy, and every now and then the pupils of her eyes would narrow and shine with a brilliant glitter, as if she was seeing something immensely beautiful.

"She's going mad!" Siham exclaimed. "I told you she would."

Muna woke as if from a dream and looked first at Siham, then at her mother. She wiped the drops of perspiration that had gathered over her brow, then gazed around the room, till her eyes focused on the bare floor, and on a cushion with the stuffing coming out of it, and on a crevice in the opposite wall that was deepening day by day. She had the look of a mouse in a trap. Then she made a sign with her hand as if telling her mother and sister to leave the room, then she lay back on her bed and pretended to go to sleep.

The mother, certain her daughter was feverish, went to fetch the thermometer, but she'd completely forgotten where she'd put it, while Siham distracted her by insisting Muna had stopped eating. She searched the shelves of the cupboard one by one. She'd resolved so many times to tidy things up, but there was never a moment, in the maelstrom you lived in these days, to put things in order and catch your breath.

"Look!" Siham went on triumphantly. "She's even forgotten to give the other children her sandwiches, the way she always does now."

The mother was still desperately searching for the thermometer, while Siham kept saying how Muna never slept at all, but spent the whole night lying on her back with her eyes open. Yet, she continued, Muna was cunning, because she'd no sooner see the light than she'd close her eyes and pretend to be asleep. The mother, finding the thermometer at last, stood up straight again and said, "Muna's sick, Siham."

Again and again she put the thermometer in Muna's mouth, but it never went above 37, and Muna kept protesting, "I'm not sick!"

Next the mother took all Muna's clothes off and turned her this way and that, feeling every part of her body, sure there must be something physically wrong to make Muna behave so strangely. But Muna's body would grow tense and hard beneath her hands, reminding her of the futility of her attempts, rejecting and banishing her.

With a sense of defeat the mother turned off the light, while Muna pulled the coverlet right over her body, to the top of her head.

The school hall was lit up and the curtain raised so the people in the audience could see their children on the stage. The children exchanged smiles and greetings with their families in the body of the hall and up on the balconies, and the place resounded with repeated clapping interspersed with cries of "Bravo!"

Again and again the mother tried to attract Muna's attention, but she didn't succeed. Muna stood on the stage, there yet not there, and, though she looked happy during the play, she looked miserable when it was over. Right through the performance she seemed contented, absorbed in her part in the lovely, imaginary world of which she seemed an indivisible part, moving with sure steps and speaking with a strange new eloquence. Muna embraced to the full the world of singing and dancing and joy, of warm silk colors and diamond jewelry and gold crowns, and it embraced her in its turn. Not for a moment did she leave her imaginary world; she was conscious of nothing else. Because of that she'd mastered her part better than any of the other boys and girls taking part in the play. Why, then, was she so downcast when the play was over? Why that look of the mouse in a trap, as she stood there among radiant children receiving the audience's applause?

The mother had a long wait for Muna, in the lobby outside the hall. Indeed, if she hadn't let Siham go home with the neighbor and her family, she would have sent her in to hurry her sister up. She watched the families, one group after another, leave with their children, able to note, in the process, who didn't own a car and who owned a car driven by the father or older brother, and who owned a chauffeur-driven car, with the driver wearing the sort of chauffeur's uniform you saw in the television plays.

The families who were on foot walked down the side of the hall, disappearing into the dark even before they'd reached the bottom of the stairs. As for the ones who owned cars with the father or brother driving, the owners would produce the car keys with an unnecessary, ostentatious flourish, perhaps because the sight of the shining luxury cars stopping to block the entrance assailed them as it assailed her—as the owners of those cars dallied in front of their splendid vehicles, exchanging conversation, while the drivers in their smart outfits opened the doors one by one, and ladies climbed in, their evening clothes embroidered with beads and sequins. Some were wearing Muslim dress. But what dress! How many pearls were there embroidered like a crown on the headdress, or coiled around the soft neck like a bracelet!

Her eyes met those of another mother waiting for her child, and they exchanged smiles, relieving their sense of alienation in this hostile, intimidating atmosphere. They recognized one another as teacher or employee, each wearing the somber, classic suit they kept for special occasions, which did duty year after year, with just a scarf added here or a new blouse or artificial flower there. She grew increasingly anxious as her colleague waved goodbye, then vanished into the dark.

The last group was leaving now, and still Muna didn't appear. The place looked almost empty, and the stage lights were gradually being turned off. Why, oh why, was Muna so late coming? Calling her constantly by name, she went into the hall and, seeing a door to the side, climbed the stairs to it and walked down a long corridor dimly lit by light emerging from a closed door. Then, pushing at this door, she entered to find herself in a room, long like the corridor, with the clothes from the play heaped up in confusion where the children had torn them off. She kept calling out to Muna, to no avail. Then she found her, at the far end of the room, huddled in one of the corners and still wearing her stage clothes. She went up to her and shook her.

"What's the matter, Muna?" she said. "Don't you want to come home, darling?"

Muna lowered her head and puckered her lips. Then, her face darkening, she allowed her mother to take off her stage clothes, but she insisted on putting on her own clothes herself, before following after her mother with a defeated air.

At the door of the dressing room, Muna turned to take a last look at this place reeking with the odors of smelly silk clothes, and remnants of food, and bottles of fizzy water, and the remains of gold and silver paper crowns thrown down on the floor, and artificial flowers trodden by so many feet hurrying out, and the golden brooch of Harun al-Rashid around an unlit paper lantern. Muna looked ready to cry. Then she slowly went out with her mother.

Muna was weeping soundlessly as she crossed the narrow path on the way home, and she took her hand away from her mother's the moment she saw the children gathered there to chase the madman, as they did every night. Then she ran the section from the path to the house, trying to avoid the flying stones.

She began to weep out loud as the children scattered, pursued by the madman's curses, only to gather again and pursue him with their stones and laughter. The song was being heard for the thousandth time.

Siham opened the door of the apartment, stood there for a moment watching her sister's tears, then drew back to make way for her. Muna stood there in the hallway, wiping away her tears with the back of her hand, while her mother embraced her from behind, patting her shoulders and kissing her hair. But Muna broke loose from her mother's embrace and, ignoring Siham's outstretched hand, trudged to the bedroom, her head tilted back and her lips pressed closed.

Muna, her mother realized, had grown up in her turn. The giddy speed of life made her feel suddenly dizzy, and she clutched at the edge of the table so as not to sink under the pressure of it all. Siham had grown up some time after ten, now Muna had grown up before she was nine.

Tears flooded her eyes as she stood up, remembering how her father had cried when she had her first period, at twelve years old. Even then, when morality was the rule rather than the exception throughout society, he'd cried because he feared for her. She felt the weight of her new responsibility as a mother. And she longed for times past.

Then, taking off the clothes she reserved for special occasions, she begged God to help the two girls go safely across the narrow path.

—*Translated by Salwa Jabsheh and Christopher Tingley*

3

SELECTIONS FROM NOVELS

Radwa 'Ashour (1946)

Egyptian novelist, short-story writer, and scholar Radwa 'Ashour was born in Cairo. She obtained a B.A. in English literature and an M.A. in comparative literature at the University of Cairo and, in 1975, a Ph.D. in African-American studies at the University of Massachusetts at Amherst. She is now professor of English literature and chair of the department of English at Cairo's 'Ain Shams University. She is also an active member of the Egyptian Higher Council for Culture, the Arab Organization of Human Rights, and other distinguished cultural organizations. Her works of literary criticism include *Gibran and Blake: A Comparative Study* (1978) (in English), *The Novel in West Africa* (1980), and *Critical Essays* (2001). 'Ashour has published two short-story collections, *I Saw the Palm Trees* (1989) and *The Reports of Mrs. R* (2001), as well as several novels, including *Warm Stone* (1985); *Khadija and Sawsan* (1989); and her acclaimed trilogy on the state of Muslims in Spain after the fall of Muslim Granada in 1492 to the Spaniards, *Granada, Mariama,* and *Exodus,* which was awarded first prize of the First Arab Women Writers' Book Fair in 1995. Her latest novel is *A Slice of Europe* (2003).

GRANADA

The fall of Granada, the last bastion of Muslim Spain, to the Spaniards in 1492 marked the end of roughly eight hundred years of Islamic civilization in Spain. This civilization illuminated the Middle Ages up to the end of the fifteenth century with its splendor, love of learning, and a multireligious and pluralistic culture that ensured that Muslims would live in peace and harmony with the Christians and Jews of Spain. With the conquest of Muslim cities by the Spaniards, this liberal and humane concept of a multicultural life was suddenly revoked with vengeance. 'Ashour's trilogy is an account of what happened to the Moriscos, the Muslims who continued to live in Spain after Granada's fall, and the fanatical humiliation, forced conversions, torture, and even the extermination to which they were subjected until their final expulsion in 1609. The following account is a description of one episode mirroring the suffering of Salima, one of the early Moriscos, under the notorious Spanish inquisition (the trilogy as a whole continues the history of Salima's family over three generations, until their final expulsion). 'Ashour wrote her trilogy over several years, after intensive research in Arabic, English, French, and Spanish historical sources. Reading her today, one cannot help thinking that history repeats itself, and that the modern world is still not free of the roots of terror and rationalized fanaticism that were in evidence during the times of which she writes.

[1]

Salima was led backward into the hall. To walk, contrary to all God's creatures in reverse was passing strange; it was one more of those weird things that she had encountered since she was brought here two days before.

She turned and saw them. The four men were staring at her with inquisitive eyes. Three of them, right across the shining black table, were seated next to each other; the fourth, in the corner, with inkpot and papers, was holding a plume.

The residing judge, an old man with a wrinkled face, cleared his throat, moved his head back, and held his hands together. Salima noticed the brown freckles on the back of the ivory hands. He cleared his throat a second time, and the scribe dipped his plume in the inkpot and started to write down what the old man dictated.

"In the name of our Lord, Amen.

"In the year of our Lord, 1527, being the fifteenth day of the month of May, in the presence of Inquisition Judge Antonio Agapida and his assessors, Alonso Madera and Miguel Aguilar, we started investigating the truth of the reports that had come to our ears that Gloria Alvarez, whose original name is Salima bin Ja'far, is suspected of witchcraft, the possession of harmful seeds, herbs, potions, and . . ."

Salima was listening with great attention lest any of the meanings of the Castilian words should escape her. However, she could hear the scratching of the scribe's plume on paper.

". . . her deeds constituted a threat to the Catholic Church and state security."

Straining his eyes, which almost disappeared under his swollen eyelids, the judge pointed at her with his index finger to approach. He asked her to swear by touching the Bible to say the whole truth concerning both herself and others. She did.

He resumed his dictation and the scribe went on scribbling: "After the accused was sworn in by touching the four gospels of God, we questioned her as follows:"

"Your name?"

"After baptism, Gloria Alvarez; before baptism, Salima bint Ja'far."

"Place of residence?"

"Albayacin."

"Your parents' name and are they alive or dead?"

"My father, Ja'far ibn Abu Ja'far the bookbinder, died before the Christians entered Granada. My mother, Umm Hasan, who was baptized Maria Blanca, is living."

"Have you or any of your relatives been accused of witchcraft?"

"No."

"Are you married?"

"Yes."

"Your husband's name?"

"Carlos Manuel; Sa'd the Malagan before he was baptized."

"Where is your husband?"

The three inquisitors exchanged looks that Salima failed to understand. She was sure that she had given them the wrong answer; her throat constricted, her breath fluttered in her breast before it was slowly expelled.

"When did your husband leave home?"

"Years ago."

"How many years?"

"Almost six years."

"Do you have children?"

"Yes."

"How many?"

"One, a girl."

"What's her name and how old is she?"

"Her name is Esperanza, she is three years old."

"You have just said that your husband left six years ago, haven't you?"

"He came back once. After we made it up he went away."

Again they looked at each other. The eyes of the young inquisitor seated to the right of the judge were glittering and the smile of the scribe showed his front teeth.

"Do you practice witchcraft?"

"No I don't."

"How do you account for the things we found in hour place?"

"They are seeds, herbs and potions which I use to treat my patients."

"Where did you learn to treat patients?"

"I learned on my own."

"On your own or from books?"

She paused, then said, "I have no access to books. I do not read Castilian. And Arabic books are forbidden by the law."

"What about the books we found in your possession?"

"They are not mine. They do not belong to anybody in the family. We do not have any books; we have never possessed any."

"Then you confess that you practice witchcraft and that the devil taught you those things you call medicine?"

"I didn't say that!"

"Don't you believe in witchcraft and that witches can raise tempests, cause cattle to die, and harm people by planting diseases in their bodies and destroying them?"

"I think that all those things—I mean tempests, the death of cattle or human beings—have natural causes that we might ignore because we lack the necessary knowledge, personally or in general. No sir, I do not think that there are witches."

"Why do people hate you?"

"Do people hate me?"

"Why do they hate you, fear you, and avoid your gaze? Once you told a person: 'Don't talk to me like that!' You looked him full in the face and afflicted him with terrible pains that kept him awake all night. You touched the belly of a pregnant woman; two days later the woman was dead. Another woman asked for your help because her son was sick; you went with her and caused the boy to bleed and die."

"The first incident is probable. Somebody must have hurt me with his words or action and I answered back, 'Don't talk to me like that!' But I don't recall when or to whom I said those words. What the person experienced on that night was simply a matter of coincidence.

"The second incident you mentioned is correct. I met that woman on the street, she's a new Christian, an Arab like myself. She was wondering why the baby inside her was so still. I put my hand on her belly and thought the baby was dead. The woman died because the baby inside her had poisoned her body. The third incident is also true. A Castilian woman came to my place, she was crying; her son was very sick and she wanted me to see him. My brother thought that I should not go out to strangers, but I went with her. The boy was bleeding, his face was extremely pale and his fingernails blue; he was dying and I could do nothing to save him."

"You confess that you have been practicing witchcraft?"

"I said that I don't believe in witchcraft."

"Don't you believe in the devil?"

"I don't know!"

"Do you believe in the existence of the devil? Answer yes or no."

They were staring at her; the judge from behind his heavy eyelids; the skinny young man on his right whose eyes were glittering, she could not understand why; and the third on his left, with a wax face and stony look. The scribe had lifted his eyes from his papers; he seemed to be entertained by the scene.

"I don't think that there is a devil!"

She answered in a low voice and realized right away that she must withdraw what she said; the inquisitor's eyes were shining with malicious victory.

"Yes, I believe the devil exists."

"And you worship him?"

She was bewildered.

"Worship him, how?"

"You worship him instead of the Lord."

"Of course not!"

"How do you explain this?"

Triumphantly, the judge held up a small piece of paper as if it were the unshakable evidence of her crime. His two assistants, well pleased, nodded in agreement and smiled.

"What is this? Come near, look at this paper, look well."

Salima contemplated the sketch. It looked like a sheep or a gazelle. When she looked at it again she could remember.

"I am not good at drawing."

"You confess that the drawing is yours?"

"I had a gazelle that I was very fond of. I tried to make a picture of her."

The judge laughed loudly; his two assistants and the scribe followed him.

"It is a goat not a gazelle!"

"Mr. Judge, I said that I am not skillful at drawing."

"It is the goat with which you copulate and to which you travel by night!"

"The goat with which I copulate?"

"Yes, the goat that seduced you and caused your husband to leave you. It is the devil in whose service you work!"

Neck thrust forward, head frenzied, and face inflamed, the judge was pointing his index finger at her, shouting at the top of his voice.

Was it a nightmare that involved her in an absurd game run by idiots? The judge accused her of sleeping with a goat, using for evidence a senseless piece of paper. Those who arrested her had been even more ridiculouss; when she tried to stop one of them from fidgeting with her books, he jumped back terrified and yelled: "Don't touch me!" as if she were a snake or a scorpion whose sting would make an end of him. They arrested her, tied her like an angry bull, and put her in a basket! No, bulls are not carried out in baskets, a little lamb maybe, a hen or a rabbit. And she, Salima bint Ja'far, was carried out tied in a basket! She conjures it all and laughs, her laughter comes out like weeping, then she laughs no more,

Before she was led to the presence of the inquisitors, a huge woman with a hard face shaved her hair, stripped her naked, and searched her armpits, between her thighs, her nose, mouth, ears, and the inner part of her body. What was she looking for? Absurdity, or sheer madness? And the judge sticks his index finger in her face as if he means to pierce her eyes, and says, "The goat with which you copulate!"

Alone in her prison cell, Salima was scared because she could not understand. At the beginning she thought that it was Sa'd they wanted, but now, after the interrogation, it became clear that it was she they were after. But why? She thought they would accuse her of not going to Sunday mass, but the judge did to make any reference to that. She needed to collect herself, to ponder and reflect and understand, but how could she, with all that humiliation? And that woman throwing a woolen rag to her, leading her into the presence of the judges, unlike all God's creatures, backward? "Turn!" the woman said: she turned to face the three inquisitors: wax faces, sharp noses, and searching eyes piercing her soul. What do they want from me? Disturbed, frightened and bitter, Salima felt like throwing herself on them, breaking their heads and tearing them to pieces. This, at least, would appease her fury, but the humiliation, what would she do to appease her humiliation? Nothing. What happened to her happened . . . "The goat with which you copulate!" What can she do, laugh or cry or knock her head against the wall and break it instead of breaking theirs? . . . "The goat with which you copulate!"

All through the interrogation it never occurred to Salima that her judge was a good man of great knowledge and integrity. He held the scales in all fairness and checked his assistants' tendency to go to unnecessary extremes. They discussed the matter as befits scholars versed in the learning of the ancients and schooled in the minutest details of the canon.

Alonso Madera, the youngest, was fervently eager to protect and defend the sanctity of the creed. He spoke as he usually did, with zeal; his eyes flashed with enthusiasm, his voice rang loudly, the pointed nose and thin lips that made him look stern mellowed, and the face softened.

"We have to arrest the child. She carries the seeds of the devil. Her confessions leave us in no doubt. Her husband left six years ago, the child was born three years after. The child is the fruit of an intercourse between the accused and the devil who assumed the form of a goat."

Judge Apagida smiled; he was patient and kind with his assistants, aware that the fervor that drove them to extremes was due to their faith and their earnest desire to serve the Church.

"Dear Alonso, the devil is a spirit and not a living body. He is unable to produce a single seed of life."

"But, Father, the devil, it has been proved, wanders from one end of the earth to the other collecting seeds, including men's seeds, to produce the fruits he wants. Saint Augustine, in part three of his book on the Holy Trinity, referred to the devils that collect human semen and preserve them in other men's bodies. Also, the great scholar Wellfrid Strabo in his commentary on Exodus 7 wrote that devils go about the earth collecting all kinds of seed and using their power to produce extraordinary creatures. The same commentary, which has a reference to the sons of God who tempted the daughters of men, points out that giants are the offspring of lustful devils who shamelessly copulated with women."

Miguel Aguilar had the long experience and erudition that gave him self-confidence. He was calm and sober as he talked.

"The devil, as Father Antonio said, is a spirit; to produce a child is one of the properties of living body. However powerful devils are, however extraordinary their abilities, they are unable to give life to the bodies they assume or to cause those bodies to produce life. Devils can fill the earth with diseases, stir up hurricanes, make men impotent, carry hell with them wherever they go, possess the bodies that do not resist them, and harm people and destroy them. Devils can do all those things, but they cannot produce one single seed of life that will grow into a human being."

"That child then is not the devil's?" Alonso said miserably.

Father Agapida answered, "No, it is not the devil's, it is the child of another man whose semen the devil took either directly from him or from another devil because devils differ in degree. In this case the devil carries out the necessary act for generation to take place but the pregnancy is not due to the power of the devil, not to the body that he has possessed but to the life power of some man somewhere, a man unknown to us and to the accused."

"She won't be burned?" Alonso said, disappointed.

"She will not be burned!" said Agapida with a stern finality.

A short silence followed, interrupted by Agapida's words, "It is not this question that has been preoccupying me. The writings of pervious scholars, ancient and modern, provide us with clear answers. But the question that must be discussed is whether this woman should be exposed to torture to make sure she has confessed everything."

Miguel Aguilar answered, "Today, the accused made three confessions. The first is a direct one: she did the drawing of that goat. The second she made and then withdrew: she said that her husband went away six years ago and that her daughter was three years old. The third is clear evidence of heresy: she said she did not know whether the devil exists."

Alonso Madera said, "This confession alone is enough evidence of her heresy. Today that she does not know whether there is a devil is a denial of one of the principles of the Catholic creed. However, I think that exposing her to torture is necessary to make sure that she does not have more to say."

Turning to Father Agapida, he went on, "Father, didn't you tell me that first time I accompanied you to an interrogation that witches who are deeply involved in their dealings with the devil are unusually calm, talk quietly, do not weep, and do not cry because they find powerful support from the devil, who assists them and makes them think that he can save them from torture without any damage?"

"It is true, and it was obvious today. The accused did not weep, did not beg, did not lose her calm. This is sure evidence of her powerful bond with the devil . . . what do you suggest, torture or a second interrogation?

Miguel Aguilar coughed and said, "Another interrogation could be useful. We shall repeat the same questions to see whether she will return the same answers, and we shall ask her new questions too. In this light we should be able to decide if torture is necessary."

They seemed satisfied with their resolution. They ended their meeting and went out to have supper and rest their minds and bodies from a long working day.

[2]

Alone in her cell, Salima was trying to take it easy. She could not sleep because with her eyes open and wide-awake she could drive the rats away and avoid the nightmare that possessed her sleep and made her scream, terrified. How could she cast off that oppressive burden, take it easy, and restore her peace of mind? The giant woman who brings her food said that it had been proven that she was a witch and that the inquisition, as in hundreds of other cases, would consign her to the flames. She visualizes the execution. They will lead her, tied, to the square crowded with staring faces waiting for her to be burned . . . like the books . . .

How could her grandfather endure it? How could he see the fire spreading from one book to another, devouring the sheets one by one, each sheet coiling as if to protect itself from the flames that went on spreading, eating, drying, and scorching. Then nothing, nothing but light ash. What about the things written there? Where do the writings go? And man, isn't man an inscribed sheet, a string of words each of which has a meaning that, put together, connotes the whole that man signifies? She, Salima bint Ja'far, aspired to vanquish death, then stepped back and brought herself to accept a less impossible career. She read books and treated patients and intentionally set aside the injustice of Castilians. Like other women, she walked in the markets; but, unlike them, she was not obsessed with markets because uppermost in her thoughts was the face of a woman who did not respond to her treatment. She racked her brains thinking of the symptoms and contemplating why that woman did not respond and what medication would help her. "Salima bint Ja'far, why do people hate you?" the inquisitors asked her. They lied because they never asked the people of Albayacin. Would they bear to look at her the moment of burning? Would they bear what her grandfather could and she couldn't the day they burned the books? And 'Aisha? She shakes off the image and the thought and evades that which defeats body and soul and brings madness to the mind. She runs to her grandfather who inscribed the first word in the book. It was neither her father nor her mother who did. It was her grandfather who said that she would go to school like her brother. He whispered to his wife that Salima would be like the women scholars of Cordoba. Her grandmother giggled and repeated her husband's words. Salima heard them and they became the first inscribed in the book ... why was she cruel to Sa'd? She loved him and still does. "I made things difficult for you, Sa'd, would you forgive?" she repeats to herself, aware that she does not even know if he is alive or already there. This "there." Is it reality or illusion? Would she meet them "there," her grandfather, Sa'd, her departed baby, and her father? How would she recognize her father and how would he recognize her? He wouldn't, because the little girl he left behind is now a middle-aged woman who will soon be forty. She might recognize him when she sees a person who looks like her brother Hassan. Poor Hassan! He wanted to protect his folk, and trouble came to him where he least expected it. But Hassan is not alone; Mariama warms his home, looks after his children, and takes care of 'Aisha too. She choked with tears; her body trembled as she tried hard to suppress her sobbing.

When Salima went through the ordeal by red-hot iron and walked the stipulated paces, the inquisitors did not deduce, as was expected after such a trial, that she was innocent. They decided that she had strong support from a very powerful devil that helped her endure pain.

On the previous day they had questioned her, She did not have any confessions. However, she raised suspicions when the judge asked her if she traveled for long distances by night, riding a winged beast. She answered that she never heard that anybody ever did except for Mohammed, the prophet of the Muslims. They asked her to explain what she said and make herself clear. She told them about a winged beast that carried Mohammed from a mosque in Mecca to another mosque in Jerusalem. When the judge wanted to know if she believed that such a thing did happen, she evaded the question and said, "I was baptized. I became a Christian."

These new details drew the inquisitors' attention to a new fact in the case, which might have escaped them; namely, that the accusation of heresy might be limited to the accused's dealing with the devil but might extend to her very faith. In spite of baptism, she had not relinquished her Mohammedan faith. If that were the case, her dealings with the devil would have been intended to harm the Catholic Church.

The inquisitors tried to make her confess it; when they failed, the judge told her that she could choose. He warned her, "Don't think it easy. You will have to carry a hot iron rod." She said she was ready. The three inquisitors watched her walking with the rod, which she carried with both hands. How? The question made them shiver, even the notary whose desk was put in the yard so that he could follow everything and write it down.

When they left the yard, the judge congratulated himself and his two assistants on having taken the necessary precautions to protect themselves from such a powerful witch. Each of them had, under his black priest's robe, a parchment where the last seven words uttered by Jesus on the Cross were inscribed.

"No alternative to torture!" Father Agapida said.

His assistants agreed with a nod of the head. Alonso Madera seemed elated with the rightful punishment of a heretic woman. Miguel Aguilar, whose face was calm, seemed resigned to the usual measures taken to extract the truth from proud and obstinate sinners whose vice turned Satan from a noble angel of the Lord to a devil.

Before the pronouncement of the sentence, they took Salima to Bab al-Ramla square. The guards cleared a path for her among the crowds that had gathered to watch the execution.

It was an agony to walk, but Salima tried hard. Her feet were inflamed and swollen from torture. She tried to avoid contact between her hands, tied at the wrists, and her clothes. They were still hurting from holding hot iron. Plunged in her thoughts, she did not look around her. They will condemn her to death. Her stomach does not convulse with fear. She does not scream in terror or fury. Why? Is it because she has wished for death and asked God for it so much that it now seems a deliverance from an agony unbearable to the soul and the body? Or is it that she has accepted her fate like those deeply pious persons whose hearts are filled with serenity and acceptance even when the ways of God are inscrutable and unacceptable? Or is it that she has decided without previous thought or consideration that she will not humiliate herself by screaming or begging or looking scared like a trapped mouse? She will not add to her humiliation. Reason makes man beautiful and pride makes him sublime. Now she can say, "Yes, I am Salima bint Ja'far, brought up by a dignified man, a bookbinder whose heart was burnt the day he saw the burning of the books and departed in noble silence. My grandfather, I screamed when they tortured me, I did, my mind and body lost their balance, for moments, only for moments, grandfather. But I said nothing of which you would be ashamed. I read books, exactly as you taught me, I treated the sick and suffering and dreamed, my grandfather, that one day I would write a book and dedicate it to you. In it there would be a record of all the knowledge I acquired through reading and touching the bodies of people. That was my dream, grandfather, which I could have realized had it not been for the fetters of the times."

Salima looked around her. A strange silence had enveloped the crowd. The three inquisitors were seated on a high pedestal nearby. The judge was reading in a loud voice reverberated in the square.

". . . We were keen to make absolutely sure whether the accusations were true or false and whether you were walking in the light or the dark. We summoned you, interrogated you on oath, asked witnesses, and observed all the regulations assigned to us by the canon. And because we wanted to achieve the utmost degree of justice, we consulted distinguished scholars whose authority in theology was unquestionable. We carefully discussed all sides of the case and the interrogation minutes and reached the conclusion that you who are now named Gloria Alvarez, and whose name before baptism was Salima bint Ja'far, are guilty of heresy because you have been a tool of the devil, working at his service, keeping the seeds that he collects, and preparing devilish potions that harmed beasts and humans.

"In spite of your denial, it was proven by the evidence of the witnesses that you caused the death of a baby inside his mother's womb and destroyed a sick child.

"Your relapse has also been proven by the evidence you have rejected the Church that embraced you and wanted salvation for your soul. It became clear to us that in spite of baptism you retained your Mohammedan faith and remained loyal to the prophet of the Muslims.

"However, we wanted and we still want you back in the fold and to abjure, renounce, and evoke your heresy and your loyalty to the devil and to return to the bosom of the holy Church and to the Catholic faith to save your soul in this world and the next. We tried hard and long; we postponed the sentence hoping that you would avow your repentance, but your pride, obstinacy, and sinful disposition tempted you to persist in error. Therefore we declare with the greatest sorrow and pity that we have failed to make you repent your sin.

"For the benefit of every lucid mind and healthy nature wishing to be delivered from heresy, and for all to know that infidels will not go unpunished, we, Judge Antonio Agapida, pronounce on behalf of the Church, while here in front of us lie the four gospels of God, our sentence, taking nothing into consideration but the Lord and the honor and glory of the creed:

"We sentence you as you stand before us in Bab al-Ramla square to the stake for your heresy."

The clamor of voices and the uproar of the crowd mingle like big hammers in Salima's head with her heartbeats and the pulse in her stomach. She refrains from looking, she does not want to look at the eyes, the eyes of Castilians smiling ready for the excitement of the scene and the Arab eyes whose tender or frightened look cause the heart to overflow. She does not look. They take away part of her fetters and drive her in the direction of the stake.

—*Translated by Radwa 'Ashour*

Layla al-Atrash (b. 1945)

Palestinian novelist Layla al-Atrash was born in Beit Sahour, near Jerusalem, where she received her high school education. She completed her university education at the Arab University of Beirut, Lebanon, where she specialized in Arabic literature. She also holds a degree in law. She started her career as a journalist and press reporter, then entered the broadcasting field, first in radio programs then as a TV news anchor and program producer, covering a range of cultural and social themes. During the same time she was also gradually establishing her novelistic career. As for many Arab women novelists, the issue of women's independence and rise into the public sphere is a major preoccupation for al- Atrash, one that she addresses skillfully. Side by side with her probing into the depths of the Arab woman's anxiety and courageous push into the world, she also very poignantly depicts some of the major weaknesses she believes are inherent in Arab men. Having lived long in the Gulf where she held an important television position in Qatari television, she has also brought out in the open both the methods used by heartland Arabs to attract help from Gulf countries for their causes and the way the indigenous people of the Gulf countries behaved: their intent on status, their premodern understanding of money and generosity, and their ever changeable moods. Her work, especially in *A Woman of Five Seasons,* is not only entertaining and refreshing to read; it is also a social document of great interest to present and future students of culture and cultural change. She has so far published *The Sun Rises from the West* (1988); the acclaimed *A Woman of Five Seasons* (1990), which has been translated into English by PROTA (2001); *A Day Like Any Other* (1991); *Two Nights and the Shadow of a Woman* (1997), and *The Neighing of Distances* (1999).

A WOMAN OF FIVE SEASONS

While describing, the relations that develop between indigenous high officials in the oil-rich countries and the heartland Arabs who go to work there in search of affluence, this novel also explores male-female relationships in the Arab world. The novel cogently delineates the way men, whether businessmen living in the commercial world or revolutionaries

working for a higher cause, have preserved their old high-handed, exploitative, and preda-
tory outlook toward women and poignantly depicts the coming of age of the Arab woman
and her successful quest for independence and self-fulfillment.

Nadia didn't raise her eyes from her book as Ihsan came laughing into the room.
She simply went on reading. How beautiful she still was, for all the thickening
of a waistline no longer in harmony with her shoulders, onto which her hair fell
black and shining, accentuating their broadness. She still insisted on wearing those
narrow skirts, ignoring Ihsan's comments about the way they revealed the faults in
her figure. She'd combat his comments with silence, then go on wearing them.

Now, though, he resisted his urge to criticize her, as she raised her baby face
toward him and he saw that radiance once more—saw the face he loved as if
enchanted by a talisman. He always saw her looks as a good omen. She folded
the corner of the page she was reading and set the book down next to her. He
picked it up and leafed through it, noting the small print and long chapters,
then tossed it aside.

"You'll hurt your eyes," he said.

How, he wondered, could she show such patience? She and Jalal? Jalal was
forever reading. Crazy the pair of them, by God! They wasted their time on the
pages of books when life, after all, was the best school and culture. What was the
point of it? There was Jalal, he thought, endlessly memorizing books, endlessly
discussing things, theorizing about things. But you, Ihsan, you're the clever one,
just reading what's written on the back cover, then dipping in here and there. In
the end you know much the same as he does, and you don't just benefit from
the bits you read, you learn from his comments too.

"Where are the magazines, Nadia?" he asked. "What artists have divorced or
married this week?"

The joke had grown stale now. She looked away, saying nothing, then leaned
back in her chair. Why, she thought, must he always belittle everything? This
book in my hand annoys him. From the first day of our marriage he'd insist on
pulling it out of my hands, till I started setting it to one side when he came in
the room. I wanted to be his wife! I spring, don't I, from that bedouin woman
of long ago, whose advice to her daughter's been passed down through generations of women? "Don't disobey any of his orders. Don't reveal any of his secrets.
Let him meet only the purest fragrance from you." I wanted to be that skillful
woman who wraps her husband around with love and tenderness. He actually
took that good book out of my hands, and he put stupid magazines in their
place, and I read them! He asked me what was in them, and I told him. When
we came to Barquis, he planted me with his friends' families, with people who
thought of nothing but money and getting money. The emptiness started hemming me in. I felt it when I was with him, and when I was with other people,
till it started choking me.

"Nadia," Ihsan said, "you haven't asked me what's happened today. My plans
are working out, and quicker than you think too."

He rubbed his hands happily. She said nothing.

"What do you say," Ihsan went on, "to visiting his wife and daughters? You need to get on good terms with them. The man's the height of good taste and kindness. All my dreams are bound up with him."

To his surprise she sat up irritably.

"For heaven's sake, Ihsan," she said impatiently, "do what you want. Plan and scheme to your heart's content. Just don't involve me in your games. I can't take any more of this."

"Of course you can! You're beautiful and intelligent. You really must get rid of this silly shyness."

He raised her face toward him. She was wearing the expression that had perplexed him for so long now—that same mixture of surrender and rejection. And now, for the first time, the rejection had been expressed in words.

"You've had three children," Ihsan went on, "and you're still as shy as a new bride! You'll have to change, my lovely kitten, because our life's going to change, believe me."

She jerked his hand from her chin.

"For heaven's sake, Ihsan," she said, "will you please stop calling me by that wretched name! Do what you like. Just don't involve me in your schemes."

Did he ever think, she wondered, of what happens to me now? Has he any idea of the way a great snake bites at me when he sees me just as his "woman"? A rebellious snake, but helpless too. It coils around, deep inside me. There's another person inside me, sexless, a person who feels and thinks and suffers and makes me suffer. A person who doesn't know what female and male mean, who rises above anything Ihsan ever thinks about. It burns me with its whip whenever Ihsan pleases himself by arousing the female in me. But it's an inner suffering too, weak and suppressed, powerless to rise to resistance and refusal when Ihsan treats me as his toy, then goes happily off to sleep. I lean on the edge of the bed, overwhelmed by a feeling that's inscrutable, something like a vision. And there, at the edge of the bed, a pit opens up, profound and bottomless. I'm cloaked in a light dizziness, and I slip, and I rush, helplessly, into the thick darkness—toward the pit, not knowing how far it goes, how far it stretches, and I've no power to stop.

I tremble, then I take hold of myself. How many times has this happened? So many! Is it a vision? Or is it a feeling or a fantasy? It's been with me a long time now. It grew stronger after my third child was born.

We surrender again, my defeated person and I, when next Ihsan approaches and enfolds me, looking for the woman in me. Winter wraps my rebellion around, blocks my vision. I long for a spring, from which my entrails burst out, revealing the human being I want to be and possess, one who rebels and mutinies and rejects. I know now, since we've been married, how he's been rushing around, matching his strength with competitors and phantoms, with the phantom of Faris stronger than the rest. When Faris came to Barquis, the city became a different world. How often I've wished Ihsan was like Jalal! If I'd married Jalal, surely he would have understood me better. Jalal's cultured, different altogether. He would have felt what I was going through, without any need for me to explain. He wanted me—there was no mistaking his looks as he followed me. He did that so many times, through the alleys of Damascus, then stopped as suddenly as he'd begun. He wouldn't even look at me. I used to try, deliberately, to let him see me, but he'd lower his eyes and disappear. If he'd loved me, would he have let his younger brother marry me? "You're full of fancies," they used to tell me. "You build castles in the air." A romantic, building a castle from a single tender word. Perhaps I am. His face did change, even so, whenever he saw me, revealing something he couldn't control. Ihsan used to fondle and embrace me more in front of Jalal, in a different way. Or am I just imagining things?

"So, what do you say, Nadia? Will you go?"

"Please! Just leave me out of it. Be successful, the way you want to be. You can do that without me. I've tried already, but I don't like that atmosphere. Do you know how things are there? Every one of those women wears a set of different masks, changing from one to another the moment you turn away from her. They're schizophrenic—they're blinded by boredom. I've been there several times now, for your sake, but I won't go any more. Do you know what it means, to have to be someone else? What's the point of it? Do what you want and let me be."

"The things in those books have taken a grip on you," Ihsan said. "All these impetuous, cultured people and their rebellious ways. You must stand by me. You must stand by me, just this once. Then I won't ask you again."

"I'm not going, Ihsan."

"Of course you are. You're a sensible woman, aren't you, who stands by her husband and supports him?"

He ruffled my hair, then went off to his room.

The person inside me moved. I felt it wake as Ihsan pushed me toward the slope. I hate to be what I'm not, to smile when I'm not happy, to repeat words I don't believe, to kill time in empty sitting-room talk where there's only hypocrisy and falsehood. I waited to hear the person inside me scream, refuse to go, stand firm in the face of Ihsan. But then I felt it go limp as Ihsan disappeared behind his door. I cried out, silently, for it to come to my aid, to describe the feeling of nausea that rises because everything around me's false and unreal.

Tell Ihsan how much we've suffered, you and I. I remember when you first started beating against the walls of my soul, the day that political activist, Najwa Thabit, stood up at the head of the table. If the table had a top, that is—it just stretched on and on! There were seven grilled lambs shining with fat, set on beds of rice fragrant with saffron, with countless broiled chickens arranged around them, decked with parsley and covered in boiled eggs and raisins and pine seeds and nuts, and all the other dishes there, full of food of every kind and color. "There's enough here to feed a whole refugee camp," I thought, and the idea shocked me. Did Najwa Thabit think the way I did? She didn't so much as stretch her hand out, didn't taste anything.

When the hostess called her to the table, the smell of food mingled with the smell of incense and women's perfume. The air conditioners were roaring away on all sides. The servant came in with a box covered in blue velvet, which the hostess took, then handed to Najwa Thabit.

"This is my father's sword," she said, "which was handed down to him by his father. When my mother died, he gave it to me. There's nothing more precious than your revolution, to offer this sword to."

Najwa Thabit opened the box, and the gold blazed out, the diamonds and rubies glittered in the brilliance from the great chandeliers on the ceiling. Najwa Thabit's face remained calm, though her eyes shone with dazzled wonderment. After a few moments she took hold of herself. Had she ever seen anything remotely like it before?

A doctor's wife began to ululate, then cried out, "A generous woman, the daughter of a generous man! May God bless the womb that bore you! All your life you've been one of us!"

Then everyone present burst into applause, to the hostess's exuberant joy. She stood there proudly with her short frame, her plump figure showing clearly through the long robe. Najwa Thabit had no choice but to respond.

Was it her slow, deliberate manner that didn't fit? Didn't fit the anxious look in the eyes of the hostess, or the impatient air of the women who'd lifted their full plates once more, or the curiosity of those gazing at the glitter of the sword and the vast size of the diamonds and rubies set in its handle? Najwa Thabit closed the blue velvet box and set it down by the side of the table. Then, moving her eyes over the faces of the people there, she launched, unexpectedly, into a forceful speech.

"In the name of the revolution," she said, "I should like to thank Her Highness and her people here for having always been with us. Here in Barquis you eat lambs, while our people live in refugee camps that are often demolished over their heads. They suffer poverty and deprivation. If each of you would stop for a moment and reflect on her people's plight there, many families would be able to live and scores of young people could have an education. We need support, financial support. And those who strive with their money are equal to those who strive with their lives. All we need is for you to pay for amenities."

"There's no strife," Her Highness broke in, "like the strife of the spirit."

"To hell with her," one of the other women murmured. "How about the five per cent taken off our salaries each month? What do these people think we are? Do they think we own a bank?"

"She won't be satisfied till she has all our salaries," whispered another, "so the revolution can buy Persian carpets!"

Did Najwa Thabit hear the whispers? She ended her speech abruptly, and the women sighed with relief. The place was filled with the sounds of knives and forks and the chink of plates.

And I, Nadia al-Faqih, felt this person inside me rebelling, kicking, revolting against all this falsehood. Here our homeland was a song, a dress, a hanger. It had vanished as a reality. When I arrived here, I thought the homeland was planted deep in people's hearts. I'd heard them sing about it so many times. But where was it when our help was needed?

Like her I didn't touch the food. For all the roaring air conditioners, I began to feel the sweat trickle down my body, felt the heat about to stifle me, till I was ready to die from distress!

Ihsan was there, holding on to the door.

"We're agreed then, are we, Nadia?" he said. "You'll go."

"All right. But this is the last time!"

"My darling!" he cried joyfully.

He blew a kiss toward her, then disappeared behind the door with a beaming smile as happy as it was sarcastic.

Every time I threaten this will be the last. And yet every time he knows I can't refuse him. I used to stand out against going to these gatherings of women, all devoured by boredom, with nothing to talk about but money and clothes and perfumes and husbands. Men have their world, and women have their own limited world too. There they'll sit, waiting for the husbands to come home from their work or their pleasures. Then the man arrives heavy with fatigue, his waiting wife eaten up with longing. He's a man, who vents an urge, while she's a woman looking for talk and tender affection, which she finds only with women like herself. The years pass, and he's still a man and she's still a woman.

I'm no different from the others. I left everything I loved, when the man came for me and I became his wife. Marriage filled my mind, pushing me to the corridors of the unknown, gripped by wonder. I was consumed with desire to discover, learn all about that secret unknown. It was a dark maze hemmed in with danger, an indistinct happiness I couldn't imagine; something we were forbidden to discover. We'd etched its image on our imaginations, from what we'd heard, as small girls, whispered by women in our mothers' sitting rooms. A comment or a gesture would escape from one of them, and then they'd exchange winks, and even the most straitlaced would laugh. And we'd hover around them, driven by a devouring curiosity to know. But all we'd have was a reprimand, and one of them would laugh gaily and cry out, "Careful! There are girls here!"

—*Translated by May Jayyusi and Christopher Tingley*

Liana Badr

See Liana Badr's biography in the short-story section.

THE STARS OVER JERICHO (1993)

This is the story of Jericho over the span of three wars—from the 1948 Palestinian catastrophe, when the city became the center for three of the largest Palestinian refugee camps, housing numerous Palestinians who had been ousted from their homes in the part of Palestine occupied by the Jews in 1948, to the June War of 1967, which caused the deportation and migration of large numbers of its citizens; to the Gulf War (1991), which dispersed and made destitute anew most of those who had remained. All this horrific history lives in the collective oral memories of Palestinians, preserved through tales recounted by women. The novel unifies the personal with the communal and depicts the stories of family, neighbors, and place over three decades to revive the image of place despite the exile that had forced the author, herself one of the city's original inhabitants, to live away from Jericho for almost three decades. The stars, symbolizing the stars that led the three shepherds to Christ, are the same stars that lead the Palestinians, the author among them, back to Jericho, where memory imposes a new birth out of annihilation and confirms the presence of a people, the Palestinians, that was made absent by occupation and annihilation and the confiscation of identity.

The Battle of the Shorts actually started on the farm of the headmistress, Sitt Fakhria, where we spent most weekends. The hours flew by as we plunged through soil that was red, brown, ocher, or crimson, and I expected my shoes to turn, any minute, into a scarlet anemone. Sitt Fakhria's son Sari made fun of me for the thousandth time. "Who do you think you are," he said, "Little Red Riding Hood?" And for the thousandth time my saucy tongue was tied—I was too embarrassed to tell him my mother had bought me the red shoes because of all the times I'd wept over Red Riding Hood ending up in the wolf's belly, before the hunter came with his axe to rescue her. All she'd done was choose the longer path because she loved flowers and wanted to pick some! If she'd gone the shorter way, she wouldn't have been able to gather that bouquet for her sick grandmother.

Sari was much the same age as me, and we made a point of traipsing through the vegetation so as to get free from his younger sister, who would have trailed along and spoiled our excursions. Every time he asked me the same question, and he was always delighted by my failure to respond. He didn't like little girls making comments, he said, though actually he wasn't much older than I was. But he'd stare at me out of those orange eyes, the same color as the vitamin I had to drink every morning, and say, "I'm much bigger than you. A lot bigger!"

When we got back from our outing, the gardener's wife was getting ready to bake *shrak* bread, or *shrah* as the people of the Jordan Valley called it. She turned over the round iron griddle and lit a small fire of dry grass and twigs beneath it, then she cut the dough into little balls, which she rolled out with the help of a big wooden sieve until they were as thin as handkerchiefs. She stretched each smooth circle of dough between her fingers, patting it lightly, and flipped it onto the heated griddle. Bubbles of air ballooned up in the dough, leaving the finished loaves pocked with little brown circles.

We pounced eagerly on the warm bread, ignoring the grown-ups' entreaties not to spoil our appetites before dinner. It took a while, the time between hunger and satiety, before a small stack of loaves built up untouched by our teeth.

Between biting off one mouthful and swallowing the next, I heard my mother and Sitt Fakhria discussing what to do with the new cloth the school had received from the UNRWA warehouse. There was a lot of it, and it didn't match the colors of the school uniform.

"We'll make shorts for phys ed," my mother said. "It's hard for the girls to move their legs in the standard uniforms. I'll ask the seamstress to take the measurements, then start right away."

And what a unique piece of outfitting it was. Once word of the new phys ed uniforms had leaked out, the forbidding school walls were powerless to repel the entire male population of the camp, which descended on the school en masse. Groups of boys and youths kept a continuous vigil on top of the walls (even though they had to be climbed with ladders), and when the first class of sixty girls, still not twelve years old, came down to the playground, catcalls and curses echoed round the place. Chaos reigned, and all 'Amm Abu Rish's broomsticks weren't enough to quiet the storm of hands and tongues and mouths and feet. The class had to retreat into the hallways, which, luckily, were no longer mere fabric tents housing a hodgepodge of ages and levels. Next day my mother, refusing to surrender to the provocations of the day before, insisted on trying again with another class, but the procession of boys dangling over the wall was thicker and rowdier than ever, and once more the class was forced to retreat within minutes of beginning the lesson. Still my mother wouldn't give in, telling the headmistress she'd be carrying on with her struggle against the backwardness plaguing her people, assisted by Abu Rish, who by now had earned the displeasure of the neighborhood. But she couldn't win the tiniest victory, as the swarms of boys occupying the walls contrived a whole array of indecent noises, from braying and howling to hissing and jeering. In the face of all this, the long-suffering troops of schoolgirls managed to go on exercising for ten minutes or so before retreating. After a few days a group of camp notables formed a committee, along with members of various political forces opposed to the Communist party to which my mother belonged. They planned to start by attacking the camp manager and end by having the stubborn teacher transferred to some distant post.

"Exile?" Abu Rashid asked, his lank figure wrapped in a traditional Arab cloak. "This teacher's from the town I grew up in and supports the party I belong to myself, whether you like it or not. All the devotion she's shown to teaching and public service, and you want to exile her to God knows where? And for what? A couple of pairs of shorts! No, by God, if any of you decide to fight her, I'll be the first to get my townspeople together to defend her! And if you've any problem with that, there's the door!"

Fierce tribal instinct, though, produced a consensus to banish the stranger. "What's all the fuss about?" the women asked, when they heard about it. "We're used to it, and anyway, our school's the most orderly in the district now. So the girls are taking phys ed lessons, inside the school walls! What are all these men and boys going crazy about? Uncouth Peeping Toms, that's all they are. Let our daughters exercise in shorts—it'll do them good."

My father's aunts in Hebron felt differently. "That daughter-in-law can't leave well alone," they complained. "How does she keep her house so clean when she's gadding about from sunrise to sunset? They say she has the whole school exercising in shorts now."

Abu Rish, ta'ish, ta'ish. Long live Abu Rish.

A few years later I came back to ask you for the story of Fuad Hill. You were embarrassed and combed your bushy mustache with broad fingers. "No," you said. "Look, why don't you go and see Professor Abu Samir instead?" Ah, you don't let me sit alongside you any more, in the front seat, and watch you maneuver the speeding car around the bends with one hand. Finally I was admitted into another school, as an observer. I don't know how I got through first grade, because I was never given a notebook to do my homework in. Then, when the heavens shone down on me and I was duly enrolled in second grade, they gave me a tattered copy of the reading primer. I cried for hours because all the new books had been passed out and my turn hadn't come till there were only ragged copies left. "Don't cry, sweetheart," Sitt Fakhria said, when my mother explained my attachment to schoolbooks. "Soon you'll grow up and be as sick of books as we are. School's nothing but nasty inspectors and stupid employees. Maybe you don't understand that now, but it isn't worth crying over! I'll give you a dozen books, honey, don't cry."

What she gave me was ten young pigeons to add to the birdcage hanging over Ras al-Wadi.

I'd get depressed because of the reprimands that kept, endlessly, beating in on me. *Don't jump on the bed. Don't wander about with sticks in your hand. Be careful. Don't play horse like a boy.* I didn't know where it came from, this danger they were so worried about, though I sensed it intuitively and was amazed adults were naïve enough to regard little girls' legs as so vitally important. *Don't repeat the things you hear at home when you're outside.* What cowards! Why did they say things if they were afraid of people finding out? *Don't accept sweets in other people's houses unless they offer them several times. Always be polite and don't act as if you're hungry.* Why? What if I want what they're offering me? *Kiss great-uncle's hand.* I don't want to. I don't like him. *Don't raise your voice in front of people.* Why not? *Don't throw yourself into the arms of your father's friends when they come to visit.* But they spoil me, and I reckon they're my friends too, so what's the problem? *Don't tug at the elastic band holding your hair under the kerchief.* But it hurts. I'm going to pull it off even if the teacher scolds me. No, no, no.

All this turned into yes, yes, yes in the magical forest that was the home of Abu Samir, who taught calligraphy at the Nuwayima School for Boys. He lived near the camp of 'Ain al-Sultan, the Sultan's Spring, and near the springs of life as well. At the front door I was surrounded by the fragrance of honeysuckle blossoms, that tantalizing aroma that seemed to fluctuate between the scents of carnations and ginger, gardenias and nutmeg, allspice and sweet honey. All those elements together made up the smell of honeysuckle, *'abhar*, whose letters could also spell brilliance, dazzlement, spiciness. Its curly-edged, bell-shaped flowers hung in white, yellow, and sometimes pink clusters, around an entryway shaded by grapevine trellises. From the doorstep I could see the orange-red fruit on the Seville orange tree, from which Umm Samir made the fragrant, refreshing drink she stored in glass jars sealed with wax and covered with cheesecloth. The moment I entered the house, my mouth would water in anticipation. The entryway led through an open courtyard, where the blue sky prepared one for the pleasant touch of darkness in the inner room prepared for guests. There the dimness was like cool water, rinsing the body from the excessive light outdoors, where sunshine reflected off loofah vines with yellow blossoms, white lilies with their dizzying aroma, curling tendrils and purple petals.

Abu Samir and his wife had got to know my parents after the famous Shorts incident, in which a number of plots against the girls, the school, and the head-mistress, and against my mother in particular, had been foiled. When certain political forces tried to use the incident to show the immorality of the Left, the patriotic Abu Samir took my mother's side. That was how our families got acquainted and I found paradise spread out before me: an enormous garden bor-dering on the springs of 'Ain al-Sultan, with little streams and rivulets flowing into it, a vast green expanse, thrusting with every kind of fruit tree imaginable. Grasses, bushes, and vegetable plants carpeted the ground, beneath sycamore, mulberry, mimosa, and *sesban* trees. An ocean of perfumes wafted across the air. Butterflies flitted about like tiny suns and giant weeping willows trailed their hair in the brooks. Most important of all, there were children, among them a girl of my own age called Marmara. No one followed us to see what we were doing or how far we went. No one cared if we spent the whole day barefoot in the murmuring silvery streams or stayed up in the trees for hours on end. "There's nothing to worry about," Umm Samir said to my mother, who was amazed to see how happy her daughter was. "The girl's cooped up at your place. Let her run around here and have some fun." Umm Samir was forever in a housecoat that buttoned up in the front—she dressed up only on the rare occasions she left the house to attend a wedding or pay condolences. Wherever she went she was accompanied by an aura of happiness as rounded and undefined as her own body, and the magical dishes she prepared filled the air around her with tantaliz-ing aromas: fragrant gum Arabic in rice pudding, sweet golden puffs of *zalabia* dough, the warm thirsty smell of roasted watermelon seeds, soft lupin seeds in brine, dripping pickles, custards scented with orange-blossom water. There were so many delicious nourishing treats, always available, and we didn't have to wait for mealtimes or sit down at table with everyone else. We could have what we wanted, whenever we wanted it, without being scolded.

The one matter that plagued the boys and their sister, and tormented me as well, was the tiny room next to the garden, where Abu Samir would disappear for hours on end without saying a word to anyone. This was his workshop, where he crafted the plaques he later sold to shop owners—proverbs and say-ings that people hung in their shops for good luck: phrases urging patience, sincerity, fairness, and so on. But something else went on in that room, some-thing none of us had ever laid eyes on. There was a canvas, propped on an easel and draped with muslin, and this had never been so much as glimpsed by the children, who were not allowed into the room alone. Years passed, and still the painting sat there in the same position, and the family found out nothing about it, though they knew Abu Samir worked on it when the door was shut tight. With his round spectacles perched on his nose, his bushy mustache protruding over his upper lip, and the dark vest he wore day in and day out, Abu Samir had all the forbidding aura of a traditional father figure. He was lenient within certain limits that his children could never exceed. They could demand their own rights but could never earn the right to meddle in their father's affairs, and woe betide them if they dared cross the line between the two. And so we had all of us, from the eldest to the youngest, to work together in a joint campaign, stealing glances whenever the door was ajar. We'd overcome greater obstacles in the past, breaking rules in a way that could have got us severely punished, as on the day Marmara and I watched through an open window as a neighbor gave birth. Yet, for all the momentous nature of what we'd seen, the fluids gushing from between her legs before the baby's head appeared, it was Abu Samir's authority that we felt to be our Great Wall of China, which we'd never manage to beat. Who would dare sneak into that room in secret, and lift the cloth to reveal what we were all burning to see? We knew well enough about the teacher's cane he kept among his things, and we knew he wouldn't hesitate to use it on us in a moment of anger. We could roam the house at will, at any time of the day or night, we could stay out in the garden till dawn, and never hear a word of warning or reproach—but that room was another story. Umm Samir refused to intercede or pay any attention when her children begged her to join their ranks. They'd throw comments her way like a stray camel pushed into the enemy camp, but since Umm Samir, with her unruly mop of hair, would very likely have told her husband about the children's curiosity, earning them instant punishment, they never dared suggest she help them open the door or provide them with a copy of the key; instead they simply offered to help with the cleaning. That, though, was something she'd never agree to, and Abu Samir never gave her the key anyway, not even to clean the place. When curiosity, time after time, prompted them to bring the subject up, she'd silence them with the two dark arches of her eyebrows, which usually looked more like question marks that had wandered onto her forehead by mistake and stayed there. In the evenings, beneath a canopy of blossoming lemon trees, what was on Abu Samir's mysterious easel would be the main topic of conversation. Quranic verses he was scripting as a mark of devotion? He was a believer but not overly religious, content to follow the basic teachings of the Holy Book. Besides, why should he preach to himself, when he believed he was the only one who was right and the rest of the world was wrong? Perhaps it was a portrait of a nude woman. But no, that couldn't be it, when he was so concerned about traditional clothes and folkloric costumes. He was always, after all, scolding Umm Samir for wearing housecoats instead of traditional embroidered dresses; and Umm Samir would point to her plump midriff and varicose veins and say, "You want me to wear a long, tight dress? How am I supposed to do the cooking and hop around the plants in the garden? I'd be tripping on the ends of it the whole time. Is this how you want me to walk?" And then she'd launch into her comic ballerina imitation.

Yet he was deadly serious as he explained the beauties of folkloric garb to his many offspring. When people were seen in their "birthday suits," he explained, their foolishness was exposed, whereas folkloric clothing concealed this foolishness. At that his oldest son would wink at us.

"Is everyone stupid without clothes, father?" he'd ask innocently. "Men, and women too?"

At that the unsuspecting Abu Samir would reaffirm his beliefs passionately. And was this the kind of man to paint a nude woman in secret? Impossible!

"My father dreams of the alphabet at night," Samir would say. "He goes on and on about the letters of the alphabet, as if they were famous people."

It wasn't hard for me to get in on some of the calligraphy lessons Abu Samir "practiced" (as Umm Samir would say) on his children.

One holiday Abu Samir took us all to the Palace of Hisham Bin 'Abd al-Malik at the border of Nuwayima. We crossed a dry wadi, which looked nothing like the one near our home, except for its rounded yellow boulders, and we passed vast farms and orchards said to belong to a single family; then, finally, we reached the eight-point stone star, raised on two pillars. What had it been? A gateway or a decoration on an interior wall? We listened and nodded, enthralled, as Abu Samir explained. After pointing out the Kufic script etched on the walls, he showed us the most beautiful mosaic in the history of Islam: an orange tree laden with ripe fruit, with a gazelle on one side and, on the other, a second, hapless gazelle being attacked by a wild beast. We gasped in delight at this magical assemblage of tiny stones, so unlike the pictures we were used to in books and magazines, while Abu Samir watched us with a mixture of satisfaction and disapproval. He was about to discover the transforming effect of art on people he'd considered dull and apathetic: for a whole week after this splendid experience we followed all his instructions and advice to the letter.

"Look carefully at the expressions on the gazelles' faces," he said, pointing. "On this side a pair of gazelles are grazing safely. On the other side a terrified gazelle is being devoured by a lion. Caliph Hisham wanted to show the boundaries of safety and danger. He was supposed to be seated on a dais behind these mosaics, though actually he never was. Maybe he wanted whoever crossed that mosaic to think carefully before approaching his throne. That was how he planned things; and yet, after four years of building, he never got to live in his palace. There was an earthquake. Maybe it destroyed part of the palace, or maybe some learned man warned him. Do you know why the Golden Gate in Jerusalem was sealed off? During the reign of Sultan Salim a learned sheikh had a vision of a swarm of rats and mice trying to enter the gate. The people of the city interpreted this as foretelling another crusade and had the door sealed off.

"No," he added, coming back to the mosaic. "It's not an orange tree. It's a type of citrus similar to a Seville orange. Looks like an orange, but it isn't."

He used to immerse us in lessons and lectures, but he did it behind Umm Samir's back; when she was there she wouldn't let him clutter our minds and spoil our appetites with his "tragedies," as she called them. He did his best to convince her they were no such thing, that knowledge was much more important than the fancy dishes she spent so much time on. Umm Samir, though, didn't care what he said and fought back fiercely—that's why it was better for us all to deal with things like that out of her earshot. And so we went over script and calligraphy, then moved on through pottery (which Umm Samir despised, considering it a step below glass) to Tal 'Ain Sultan and the history of Jericho. Originally, he told us, it had been named after the moon goddess, and when Umm Samir wasn't looking he sketched, with quick strokes, the ancient urns that had been excavated. Neither did Umm Samir hear him talk about Miss Kenyon, head of the Department of Antiquities I think, who'd been a pioneer in her field, proving that Jericho had had no wall during the time of Joshua, son of Nun. This was one historical figure whose name we quickly learned, because in Arabic it was spelled just like Jesus, with three extra dots, and because the second name, Nun, reminded us of the Arabic letter *noon*. For years before his time, and for thousands of years after him, there were walls and temples, which few cities in the region had then. Why had they built the original wall—the only one of its era—then changed their minds till thousands of years later? Maybe, he suggested sadly, they'd been under attack, like us.

Our escapades were cut short the evening Munir was stung by a scorpion. Despite the gardener's insistence that he diligently uprooted weeds and burned thistles, somewhere under the poplar trees, among the willow roots by the big canal, a scorpion had managed to hide, and Munir's foot, shod in plastic thongs, found it. His skin turned blue, and almost the whole family rushed him to a nearby clinic, with just Marmara and I left at home in case my parents should arrive and find the house empty. We waited, not knowing whether there was any hope of saving this boy in the prime of his life, while the rest of the family tasted gray fear during the time it took for the nurse to find the proper vaccines and the doctor to administer them. We weren't there to hear the one phrase Munir kept repeating despite his sickness and terror. "Yaba," he said, his whole body shuddering. "Father, you have to show us the painting. The one on the easel covered with the navy drape."

"Is that all?" Abu Samir cried, the tears dropping from his thick glasses onto his bushy mustache. "Whatever you want! Just get better, and I'll give you the easel and everything on it."

"My God!" The distraught Umm Samir wrung her hands. "All this comes from the old wives' tales and superstitions you've filled their heads with. You just couldn't leave them to their studies. The boy was sane before, and now look at him trembling, and us trembling over him, all because of the nonsense you've put in his brain. Come on, son, get up. God and His Prophet bless you! Your face looks much better, and there's nothing to worry about now you've had your injection. We caught it early, thank God!"

And so Abu Samir ushered us into his little room. "As you know," he said, "my father was from Acre. We didn't move to Jerusalem, where my mother was born, till after the '48 war."

"Yes, Yaba, yes," replied a chorus of voices, broken only by my discordant "yes, Uncle, yes."

He glanced round at the tribe of children encircling him. "To tell you the truth," he said, "I don't like to show anyone my painting because I regard myself as a top-notch calligrapher and don't want to be considered an inferior painter. But what can I do? It was what Munir wanted, and God brought him back to health, so for his sake you're going to see the painting I've never shown anyone before."

It was a seashore scene, with fishermen casting their nets.

"This is the eastern gate of Acre," he explained. "The fishermen are dragging out their nets and singing, as they do every morning at sunrise. And look, here's the wall overlooking the sea. Now don't think the sea looks the same wherever you go in Acre. No, in some places the sand's red, and in other places it's pure white, white as poplin. In some places the beach is sandy, and in others it's rocky. And of course there are different kinds of fish, depending on where you go. Every night, before I go to sleep, I imagine this scene. I wonder why Ahmad al-Jazzar built it. He was a man with good points and bad points. Every day he had execution parties for the rebels and people he just didn't like. Look, over here you can see the *halvah* factory. We used to be able to smell it from miles away. East of the port is the girls' school, run by the nuns. We used to wait for the girls after school. Acre's a city like no other. God never created anything like it."

The older boys sighed in obvious disappointment. The secret had been revealed; there could be no more covert plots to lift the little drape and find out what lay beneath.

"You asked to see it," Abu Samir said. "Personally, I didn't want to show it to anyone. That way I could see it clearly and imagine it better and better. Ah, that *halvah* factory. You could smell that warm, sweet smell from so far away!"

None of us stayed to take in what Abu Samir was feeling. We were too young to appreciate the places and people a paintbrush can render. Besides, Abu Samir had deliberately made us feel (or had he just anticipated our reaction?) that the painting was a second-rate effort, not to be compared with the fine talent he bestowed on his calligraphy and so not worth looking at for too long. It would take us years to realize that this painting was the most beautiful of all his works, telling as it did of what went on upon that shore. Little did we imagine that the fishermen still battled the waves every morning, with rhythmic motions, a physical movement Abu Samir could no longer follow now because of the occupation of Palestine. Had Abu Samir meant us to be disappointed with his painting? Had he meant to persuade us to go back to our games and leave his dreams alone? Every day he had to oversee dozens of little boys at school. Did he resent our intrusion into that calm, magical world where, each evening, he returned to Acre?

Things change. Puberty brought aches and pains as our bodies adjusted to their mysterious cycles. Breasts began to appear, fuzz on upper lips, plans for the future. My old friend Aida and I had been separated; we caused too many distractions in the classroom, and the teacher had moved her to a different section. She'd formed a clique with some other girls, who all planned to go to the same college, live in the same dormitory, and major in the same subject. But although I was in a different section, I was in on all their plans and meant to join them. Marmara was one of them too. Grown now, nearly my height, she was no longer a plain child but a strangely beautiful young lady. Her clear complexion was free of the pimples that constantly plagued the rest of us. Her long, slender legs seemed as graceful as a gazelle's, and she glided around with an angelic ease we could scarcely aspire to. While we droned on and on, like so many bees, about the way our parents misunderstood us, she enjoyed a blissfully serene relationship with hers. Her chestnut ponytail gleaming in the sun, she'd rattle off the household tasks she completed before and after she did her homework. She got up early to mop the house and sweep the courtyard, while the rest of us were always being scolded for laziness, or oversleeping, or bad behavior. Like some kind of guardian angel she seemed to wrap us around with sympathy and guidance, without ever overstepping the unspoken boundaries that exist between adolescents. Maybe it was the white lilies from her garden, reflected in her eyes, that made her pupils so bright.

I didn't often visit Marmara now. Coming back to the city after several years away, our family hadn't managed to find a house in the same area, and besides, schoolwork and household chores didn't leave much time for visiting. Abu Samir's home no longer had the same meaning for me. Marmara and I weren't allowed to run around with the younger boys, as we once had, or wade barefoot through the silvery canals. We were supposed to be ladylike now, to act our age. No one believed that, even though our feet were bigger and our breasts were starting to show, we were still the same inside, just as childlike, or mischievous, or silly, call it what you will. We were forced to sit there quietly in a corner of the sitting room or kitchen, without making a noise or giggling, with nothing to do but make tea or coffee when called on. What with all these new constraints, and the distance between the two homes, I rarely visited, as I said. Yet we all loved Marmara because she had something we lacked: the ability to adapt to reality. We all of us, except for her, got mad at our parents and blamed them for our unhappiness. We all of us, except for her, resented our strict upbringing and the restraints imposed on us. Perhaps it was because she was the only one to have grown up in a spacious garden, with banana trees that renewed themselves every year, a garden that had been her magic kingdom since childhood. Whatever the reason, I seized every opportunity I could to spend recess with her. Standing in the schoolyard munching falafil doused with hot sauce, we'd discuss trivial matters as though they were the most important things in the world. She gave me that same faith in the beauty of nature as I'd found in her garden as a child, as well as the pleasure of true friendship untainted by envy or doubt. I tried to learn contentment from her as well, laying before her endless complaints about my differences with my parents. Marmara would laugh. "Relax," she'd say. "Little things like that aren't worth so much worry and gloom. Try and go along with them a bit. It'll make them happy, and things will get better."

1967. Sirens going off, screaming explosions. Civil defense patrols enforcing the blackout. Why can't they leave us alone? We sit in our homes, waiting anxiously. All morning the newscasts have been tallying the number of downed enemy planes. All afternoon we've been dissolving bluing agent to darken the windows. Who has time for all this? Our arms and legs move, our mouths speak, but our hearts and eyes are paralyzed. We repeat the figures we've heard, and doubt sinks down into our souls, settling there like mud. The voice on the radio trumpets claims of victory; the figures become more and more astronomical. And yet we discern something bitter in that tone, a worm eating its way out of the apple. No one wonders aloud; voicing a doubt might break the spell and bring vengeance crashing on our heads. Better to listen to the broadcasts and say nothing. Was this really possible, we asked ourselves, secretly, as though even our innermost thoughts could bring us to ruin. Could this really be happening? Was it possible to wipe out an enemy state in the blinking of an eye, as though the whole thing were some musical on a stage?

The days passed—two, three, four. Wave upon wave of refugees fled, toward the bridge and the east bank of the Jordan. We couldn't believe any of it, neither the victories claimed on the Arab airwaves nor the multitudes migrating before our eyes.

To me, and to Marmara and Aida and the rest of our schoolmates, it was all more like a game. Everyone was playing hide-and-seek; they couldn't see us, but still, they might find us any moment. Who would have thought this could happen, in such a tender land of mint and oranges, its soil emblazoned with white jasmine blossoms? Where we lived was more than two hundred meters below sea level. Perhaps that was why God had forgotten us. Or maybe He simply closed His eyes as the three big refugee camps around us were gradually deserted.

Then—the infection reached us. Our very neighborhood, our own building, the heart of our home.

We opened our eyes each morning to the sound of shelling pelting down from fighter planes. We all fell victim to a campaign of terror. White leaflets filled the sky like a flock of dead birds fluttering down on us, threatening death unless we raised white sheets from our windows and rooftops in surrender. The inhabitants, who'd had no weapons in the first place, finally tired of raising white flags and decided to make a break for the safety of the east bank, just sixty kilometers away.

That was why—I just couldn't. I couldn't bear the news that Marmara hadn't made it across with us.

She'd been in her grandparents' car. They'd decided to escape the inferno for a few days and visit one of their sons, who worked for the UNRWA in Amman, and Umm Samir, concerned for her beloved daughter, had suggested Marmara go with them till the situation calmed down. Abu Samir, who loved his daughter more than life itself, had been insistent she go, even though she said they needed her help with the housework.

"We're in the middle of a war," he scolded, "and you're worried about cooking and cleaning? Don't worry, I won't let your mother do anything till you get back."

And so they finally persuaded Marmara, the apple of their eye, to leave, out of concern for her. Who could have guessed the old man's hand would be too slow to stop the car and flee, before the bomber above them emptied a whole tank of napalm? Maybe he trusted the pilot wouldn't bother with a wreck like his old Ford. Maybe—The only certainty was that there was no more Marmara, not even a body for Umm Samir to bathe in tears or for Abu Samir to commemorate with a headstone engraved with verses of solace and comfort.

There was no more Marmara.

This was in the nineteen hundred and sixty-seventh year of Jericho's time.

From that time on our souls were to follow the script of misery. We were to be like the wind, with wings only God could number, hovering placeless, as in the Book of Genesis.

We stopped in front of a modest apartment building on one of Amman's hills. I couldn't believe this was Abu Samir's home: a three-story building surrounded by dumpsters heaped with stinking garbage and with mangy, colorless cats with sick eyes slinking around them. We climbed a narrow staircase to the first floor, and I rubbed my eyes, remembering the fragrant, flowering vines that had surrounded the entrance to their old home in Jericho. When Abu Samir appeared at the door, I saw time had turned him ashen, and his hair, once coal-black, had turned a dull plaster gray to match his face. It was he, but he was no longer himself. A strange silence hung over the dim apartment, fenced in by wooden planks that blocked the light. I couldn't believe it. Where was Marmara? Dry, leafless stems stuck up from the flowerbeds.

—Translated by Sima Atallah and Christopher Tingley

Halim Barakat (1936)

Syrian novelist, sociologist, and researcher Halim Barakat was born in the village of Kafrun, Syria, and raised in Beirut where he received his B.A. and M.A. in sociology at the American University of Beirut in 1955 and 1960 respectively. Later on he obtained his Ph.D. in social psychology from the University of Michigan. He was a research fellow at Harvard in 1972–1973, taught sociology at the University of Texas from 1975–1976, and in 1978 joined the faculty at Georgetown University where he still teaches. Halim Barakat has written two books on psychology and has authored one collection of short stories and a number of novels. Barakat faithfully depicts a world at war, in the grip of political intrigue and failed struggle, and in most of his creative work has been one of the most vigilant novelists regarding the political situation in the Middle East,

particularly in Palestine. His novels include *Six Days* (1961), in which he anticipates the war of 1967; *The Return of the Bird to the Sea* (1969), which unfolds the
existential drama of the June War of 1967; *The Crane* (1988); and his latest novel,
Inana and the River (1995). His work has been translated into English, French,
German, and Japanese.

THE CRANE (1988)

*The Crane intelligently summons the past of the author, connecting it firmly with the
present and portraying his experience of a continual exile, an experience shared by numerous Arab intellectuals living in self-imposed banishment. The novel employs various
novelistic devices: memories, flashbacks, dreams, fantasies, and realistic depictions. Resorting
to the collective consciousness, it transcends the personal into the universal, delineating a
world of alienation and uprootedness but, at the same time, reflecting an honest revelation
of the author's personal experience and innermost thoughts. The "crane" here is a symbol
of the alienated Arab intellectual, flying all over the globe in search for a salvation for self
and nation and trying to find answers to the crucial questions that have filled the world
around him. A touching and vivid account of experience, this novel is a departure from
Barakat's political involvements into the realm of personal narrative, reads more like an
autobiography, and is probably Halim Barakat's best creative work.*

Suddenly, with a mighty clamor, a flock of cranes appeared in the skies of al-
Kafroun. They boomed in their pride, proclaiming the coming of autumn after
the hot summer and the end of the seasons of grape, fig, and pomegranate.

We raced barefoot, watching them intently, fascinated by the patterns of their
flight and by their huge wings and long necks. They drew closer, in stately flocks,
their figures tracing lines of black between the clear blue of the sky and the
shadows cast in the river by the trees.

First came a group shaped like a *V*, with an enormous crane at its head. Then
other flocks approached from various directions, from Nab' Karkar, Nab' Shaikh
Hassan, and Nab' al-Shir. Then the *V* shapes changed to circles, hovering over
the river and over the two mountains of al-Sayyida and al-Sa'ih that slant one
toward the other as though they'd been quarreling and were pondering reconciliation, two mountains towering over a valley deep as an ancient wound.

The cranes stretched their great black wings right out, revealing their white
breasts. They glided through the air like clouds, fell like thunderbolts, rose like
gods, then stayed motionless in one spot, fierce as the sun. Still they climbed and
rose, fell and soared.

We marveled at them, seeing how they held sway over a vast sky, seamless
but for wisps of white cloud like the pieces of fine scarves. They roamed freely
through all that expanse, as if spellbound by its bare transparency, like a young
woman viewing her breasts in the water's mirror. They sported as though oblivi-

ous to hunger and thirst, paying no heed to the hunters who'd gone onto their rooftops, or up into the hills, with their rusty rifles.

Through all the years, stretching back like anxious threads, the shots echo in my mind. One after the other they came, like irregular heartbeats, still blazing out in every direction, as though war had broken out after a long period of peace.

The picture changed. Suddenly the pattern of flight broke up, the circles dispersing as if from a vast explosion within them. The wings, mirroring their hearts, fluttered rapidly, and the very sky changed, the calm, clear expanse of blue stained by spots of gray cloud where the shots had been fired.

The startled cranes scattered in their terror, with sharp screams, some of them falling helplessly to their death, into valleys deep as the heart's worries, their feathers swaying and fluttering down through the air.

I still recall, so sharply, their cries of grief, yet I can find no words to describe them to myself. Their cries mingled with the feathers, black and white, floating down as though intent on play amid the danger.

The crane fell in front of me beneath the kite's nest at the crumbling al-Dahr rock, like a thunderbolt bounding over the earth, its sharp, confused screams expressing fury, pain, protest, terror, all together. I leapt toward it, thinking to pick it up, then fear held me back, fear both for myself and for the bird. I drew slowly closer, so as not to startle it; then, as its screams and struggles grew fiercer, I retreated again. Once more I approached, cautiously, stretching my hand gently toward it. How could I make it understand I wasn't a hunter? It had no reason to trust me. Conquering my fear, I approached and leaned over it, then, as it grew a little calmer, gently rubbed its long neck with the palm of my hand. It didn't trust me, nor did I trust its hard red beak. Yet I knew I must find the courage.

I saw that its right wing was broken, with blood flowing from it, staining the white and black feathers a deep crimson red. It was helpless, and I knew no way to heal its wounds. Afraid I might cause it pain, I couldn't stop trembling.

At that critical moment Ra'if came racing up, like a hungry tiger scenting the blood of prey, and before I knew what was happening he snatched the wounded crane from me and shot down toward the river, displaying it proudly to everyone he met. Then, as curious people gathered round, he ran off for fear they'd snatch the crane from him just as he'd snatched it from me.

I learned later that Ra'if had slaughtered and skinned the crane, then roasted and eaten it. Only long afterward did he confess the meat had been tough and bitter-tasting. Still, he didn't regret it, because he'd sold the long legs to a man who used them to make cigarette holders for wealthy smokers.

From my imaginary voyages I returned to reality, saying to myself, "I congratulate you on your illusory victories, Don Quixote." My wife was collecting leaf samples, and I asked her whether she'd marry me again if we were divorced. She didn't hesitate. She'd often repeated mistakes in the past, she told me, but that was one mistake she wouldn't repeat. "I wouldn't agree to a divorce anyway," I told her, "because I'd only ask for your hand all over again."

I kissed her, then released her, and we wandered aimlessly, side by side, down narrow back roads, returning by the main road. A chipmunk jumped from in front of us, into the trunk of a dead tree, and we read a small sign referring to the tree and its relationship with life and death: "The dead tree is actually very much alive. When a tree dies it no longer fights the invasion of beetles and bacteria and fungi. As the wood grows soft, ants and centipedes, grubs, and worms, move in. . . . A rotten tree is much like an apartment house, providing homes for many living creatures. . . . Its nutrients return to the soil, so nourishing a new generation of trees."

These words pierced below my consciousness and multiplied there. I reflected on the forests of the future, born from the roots of forests themselves murdered. If nothing lasts, nothing ends either, and death is no departure to a further world. Is that how you see it, Elias al-Akhras?

A cloud of sorrow covered my face, its shadow reflecting in the eyes of my beloved, as the lakes mirror the sky and the trees. I said to the crane, "My death and rebirth are like yours."

All this was in the days of harvest, as spring ended and the summer began. The golden stalks of wheat swayed here and there, in harmony, on the rolling hills, meeting and touching like the dancers of *Swan Lake* or *The Nutcracker*.

As the hot day turned to rainy night, trees, roads, and houses were cleansed of their dust and bathed in cool air. My father washed off the weariness of his day and climbed into the hammock he'd set up to sleep in during the summer, between two trees in front of our house. But Najib and Mighal came and entered on a long discussion about a dispute they'd had that day, over who should be the first to irrigate his land.

I fell asleep before they'd finished, and when I got up next morning my father wasn't there. He'd gone off to Marmarita with the dentist, my mother told me; he'd spend a day or two there, and would also go to Hab Namra where he'd order a new saddle for his mule.

Two days later he returned, sick and bent double with pain. That night he grew worse and couldn't sleep. My mother called my grandfather Salim and my uncles Jamil and Yousef, and the neighbors, hearing of it too, came there to spend the night with my father. Then, before dawn, they sent my uncle Jamil to al-Mashta to fetch Dr Tu'ma. I don't remember where I was; I must, I think, have been asleep. According to my father, my uncle returned an hour later and told them the doctor had refused to come without three lira paid in advance, upon which my mother gave him the money and he went back to al-Mashta. Then, suddenly, my father began to feel better. He got up, washed his face, and talked about various things with my grandfather and my uncle Yousef.

When the doctor came, he examined my father and joked with him. Concluding that he had pneumonia, he gave him an injection, gave my mother instructions for his care, then left to pay a visit to one of our distinguished neighbors. The visitors left too, and my father returned to his bed, while my mother went to prepare the compress the doctor had ordered and I remained alone with him. I remember nothing more than that, but my mother has told me he lost consciousness as soon as the doctor gave him that cursed injection, and ever after she'd count up the doctor's other victims in our village and the districts round about.

My father, I remember, motioned to me to go and sit next to him, and I approached him fearfully, as I had the injured crane. I saw his face, bronzed, the color of honey, grow ever more pale. Outside the clouds returned to encircle the earth and smother its breath, their dark shadows entering the house, reaching up to where I sat alongside my father. The air was still, and hunched on his breast was thick cloud without rain. I sat by him, alone, while my mother lit the fire outside, to prepare his compress. He said nothing to me, nor did I know what to say to him. I didn't know how to bandage his broken wing.

He stretched out his hand to take mine, and I found it was hot and trembling. He made an attempt to smile, but the smile, cold, pale, and wasted, was no longer the same. Drowning in that deep silence, I was afraid, having no idea what to say, while the dark shadows from the clouds lay in wait on the walls, making the corners almost invisible. I remembered the silk seasons of the year before, when the house had been dark like this. My mother had rented Mr Qterah's mulberry trees to raise half a dozen silkworms, borrowing money she hoped to pay back at the end of the season and selling her sewing machine, too, to fund the project. But the weather had been very bad that year. 'Aboud al-Haddad immortalized what happened in popular songs containing verses about my mother:

Mariam raised silkworms
All died but one
With it she bought a whistle to quiet little Halim.

Village people are quite extraordinary at times like this, making fun of people's misfortunes, then acting as if nothing had happened. Yet in spite of this heritage, which is a part of me too, I remain capable of feeling, and I'm deeply sorry for you, 'Aboud al-Haddad. You hoped to die with honor, and instead you lived long and suffered, going to stay with your children in Beirut so the village shouldn't see your last days. In your days of glory the village was your stage: no one could equal you at the *dabka*, or at singing, and you entranced the young women when you danced at weddings and festivals.

You may care to know that Mariam, who rented the mulberry trees from Mr Qterah and failed in that, her first project, had a hard struggle after my father's death. She gathered the harvest in the eastern plains, baked for the people of the village, worked as a maid in Beirut, washed clothes, swept and mopped floors, ironed and cooked—all so as to send us to the best schools and preserve our dignity. She devoted herself to the task, working tirelessly, and when she was alone, I'd hear her reciting popular verses to herself:

Misery and hardship must be
But ease will come, these anxious days pass
The long branch of the tree will bend
The short branch will grow longer
Lovers must part
Even if bound by the strongest twine.

No doubt you too have recited the traditional verses of patience and hope. Do you remember that popular verse, "Be patient, oh heart, and make the burden lighter"? We should learn to struggle proudly, and this was a problem for me as a poor child among the rich pupils at the school. Because of my mother's job I never felt at ease with them, felt, always, that my relations with them were those of helpless humiliation and pity. I hate the word "pity" as much as I love the word "justice," and it was during this period of childhood that my religious beliefs began to form. My relations with the rich worsened, especially when I excelled them at school and they retaliated with wounding taunts like "poor people are poor because they're lazy." One of the ladies my mother worked for advised her to take me away from school so I could work and help keep the family, but my mother didn't take her advice. And she was too modest to say, "Who'd teach your children if my son left school?"

I remember what I wanted to tell you. My mother's old now and no longer the person you or I knew. I'll tell you a secret I never told anyone before, which I haven't even dared admit to myself. Everyone knows how much my mother did for us, and I worked so as to pay her back for those things, to provide her with a life of dignity and happiness in her later years. But there were problems even before she had her fall. For some time her life had been full of illusions and doubts; then, when she'd turned eighty-seven years old, she withdrew right into herself, feeling quite isolated, with no thought for anything but her problems. What frightened her most was that she might not be able to look after herself any more. "Oh God," she'd say, over and over again, "please take me into my grave." Then came that bad fall, but the grave didn't claim her—she's buried above ground, not beneath. And even before the fall she wasn't sure of how people felt toward her. She'd pray constantly to God, begging Him to take pity on her, to help her bear her pain, to soften people's hearts toward her and protect her from her enemies. To overcome the fears and the desolation and the tedium, she transformed her life into a set of rituals centering on her problems and illusions. She became very forgetful—of names, faces, facts, what she'd said or heard. Then, after the fall, sheer oblivion took over. It's a bitter thing to see your mother decline so completely.

She wouldn't let me help her, having, as she did, the conviction that children should listen to their parents and not the other way round. When she ignored my advice, I'd lose my temper with her; I tried to be patient, knowing I ought to show understanding for the mistakes she made, but a man can't always keep his self-control. I'd get angry, shout, curse, and threaten, but all in vain. She didn't realize she was wrong; or else, on the very rare occasions she did realize it and admit it, she'd make me feel ashamed by saying, "Let God take me now. I've gone senile. Please be patient with me, son, and forgive me." Sometimes she'd try and make me feel guilty (she was very good at this) by reminding me of all the sacrifices she'd made, and that made me more furious than ever. With time I began to counter these tactics with sarcasm. "My father didn't die," I'd tell her. "He ran off." This provoked her, though she learned to swallow it in time. The most important lesson I learned from all this was that a man must know when he's going to die, and I hope I shall know when to loose my hold on life. There's nothing more wretched than to be preoccupied with oneself, and I feel the utmost pity for those busy with themselves rather than trying to make a contribution to society. Perhaps this is a key to the wretchedness of the Americans and of their loneliness as deep as the depths of the desert.

This is how my mother became even before her fall; after it her problems multiplied and deepened, took on new forms. Talking to her became an ordeal, because she no longer understood what I was saying. Perhaps I didn't understand myself. What a mercy death would have been had it come earlier. And yet how difficult death is in the flower of youth. That reminds me of Ilias al-Akhras. He married late and had a son who brought him such joy. Then, when this son grew up, he went hunting, like Adonis, and never returned. Later they found his body. Had the wild boar gored him as it had gored Adonis? But his blood didn't flow in the river, and, after that day, the spring never flowed from the life of Ilias al-Akhras. Oh Uncle Ilias, death in youth is as hard as granite. Now you are dead too and at rest.

My father's hand reaches out to take mine. He puts it to his lips and kisses it. He draws me toward him and lays his face against mine, laughing as he feels me try to wriggle my own face away. "Am I scratching you?" he asks me. "I haven't shaved today."

Suddenly his hands rise toward the ceiling, then slowly come down again. He gnashes his teeth and I gaze at him in terror. His eyes are totally changed; he must have seen death face to face. Unable to move, I call my mother in a strangled voice. He's still gnashing his teeth.

I woke suddenly from a nightmare. Beneath a great tree in the Shenandoah Mountains, I felt my beloved's hand on my shoulders, as though a bird had come to settle on my branches. A golden leaf trembled, then fell into a brook in al-Kafroun. It was swept, quickly, toward the waterfall.

"Do you remember," I asked my beloved, "the waterfalls of al-Makhada in al-Kafroun?"

"Do you call those waterfalls?" she answered. "You can't compare them with the smallest falls on the Potomac. What made you think of them now?"

"The crane."

"The crane?"

"Yes. The crane made me think of them."

"That reminds me," I went on, "of the child who asked his mother where he came from. 'The stork brought you,' she told him. Then he asked her, 'Where did our neighbor's children come from?' 'Samir came out of a cabbage head,' she said, 'Fadi came out of a lettuce head, Fadya came out of a rose, and Salim came out of an apple.' 'Then I suppose,' the child said, 'men and women don't sleep together in this town.'"

My beloved didn't laugh, even out of politeness. We'd both heard the joke so many times it wasn't funny any more. "You didn't tell me," she repeated, "why the crane made you think of the waterfalls at al-Makhada."

"It carried them in that hard, long beak, under its great wings."

"Don't be silly!"

She was quite serious, looking at me despondently, waiting for me to give a serious answer.

"When you put your hand on my shoulder," I said quietly, "I was daydreaming, imagining a bird lighting on a sycamore branch by the river bank in al-Kafroun. When the bird hopped onto another branch, a leaf fell into the river and the current carried it off to a small waterfall."

The current of death swept my father off to another world, and his face faded like a golden autumn leaf. Death came down on al-Kafroun with its green valleys below, searching out his exhausted soul. He'd suffered long in vineyards that bore no fruit. Now death swooped down like an eagle, caught him up, and flew far off.

Tears were shed, by the broken-hearted wife and the son. The lonely, desolate daughter wept and wept. The handsome small one, who'd inherited his father's features, didn't understand what was happening yet felt a tragedy had entered his world. They all saw death approach, like an eagle swooping to earth at astonishing speed, seizing my father from his homeland with no chance to whisper a farewell. The little one, sadly, knew nothing of that other homeland. My mother appealed for help, and the neighbors and relatives quickly came. The bells of sorrow tolled in the church.

The young girl, Fahida, asked, "Who's died?" "It's your brother!" they told her. She took the bundle of corn from her head, took off her wooden clogs, and ran off barefoot. Next moment the face of Marianne, so compassionate, so beautiful and loving and cheerful, was transformed by fear, and she too ran off barefoot, weeping, to the house of her favorite cousin. All the other village people arrived, then more people came from the villages round about and summoned the doctor, who was still on his visit with the chief village notable. He sipped the rest of his coffee, then came hesitantly over; and when the visitors cleared a way to the bed, he looked at my father, briefly checked his pulse, and pronounced him dead. (May God add the years he did not live to your own life.) He consoled my mother with a pat on the shoulder, leaned down to kiss me, then darted out.

I was lost in the crowd of mourners weeping and wailing. I'd heard of death before, seen it face to face even, but never before this moment had I felt it with such bitterness. I wept and wept and took myself apart, but people pulled at me, so that my cries mingled with theirs. When I heard them weeping, I sighed, and when they heard me sighing, they filled the skies with their weeping. I can still see my mother beating her face and breast with her hands; and when I beat my own face, she held me to her breast and wept more softly. Our neighbor whispered to Ghassan to take me to his house, and he came up with Jamal and Nasri and Salim, and they wrenched me away. They washed my face in cold water and brought *mankala*, and persuaded me to play with them, so as to cheer me up. When I heard myself agree to play, it felt strange.

"Just imagine, I played *mankala* straight after my father died."

I said that now, to my beloved, and another deep-held secret was out. I'd never dared tell anyone about it before, had tried to bury it in my own mind by busying myself with other things.

"Why are you thinking about all these things now?" my beloved protested. "How strange you are! Why not enjoy this lovely world? Is there anything better than that?"

"I do enjoy it, believe me. I'm not sad. It seems to me there's a thin, invisible thread joining desolation and deep joy. Sometimes I think death was a matter of joy for the children in our village, made it into one of our most unusual games. We made our own toys because we couldn't buy them like the city children. They just get bored with one toy, then get over that by buying another one, and their toys and lives pile up in forgotten corners. When a man died in the village, we children would drop everything and go off to the cemetery. We'd watch all the expressions on people's faces, and listen to the hymns, and climb the trees, or else peer through the legs at the casket being lowered into the grave and showered with earth and rocks. Then, after the mourners had gone, we'd pick the acorns and galls from the great oak trees. The acorns were our chestnuts, and we'd play or make bets with the galls."

"We get very emotional when we meet death," she answered, "the complete opposite of Western people. They exaggerate their solemnity and we exaggerate our weeping. It never occurred to me that death could be a game."

I remembered how my beloved's weeping turned to breathless sobs, how she fainted almost in my arms, when she saw the bodies of her father, and her brother and his wife, and her aunt, in a funeral home in Detroit. (They had died all together in an automobile accident.) I shouted to her to control herself, but her uncle, the physician, thrust me to one side and told people to give her room to breathe.

Remembering the accident, I changed the subject. "Fall," I said, leaping up to reach a low bough full of colorful blooms, "can be so beautiful. It's like spring. These colors make up a kind of enchanted symphony, their harmony's like glorious music." I'll never forget the evening we heard Beethoven's Ninth Symphony in the Hill Auditorium at Michigan University. Surely that work's the greatest symphony ever produced by the human spirit. I remember how the chorus were all around us, how their voices seemed to move us back and forth, like small boats tossed by the waves. How sublime it is to ascend to the heights of the universe, how sublime to descend to the depths of the earth! We gazed down on the Himalayan peaks, we sank to the bottom of Dante's inferno. Oh waves, oh storms, oh thunderbolts, oh lightning, shake the foundations of this world, then build it again! That's just how I feel, too, when I see the waterfalls in front of me. Was it this, I wonder, that made me climb down the great rock and cross the log bridge to reach a rock in the midst of the gushing river?

I gazed at my beloved. "My world's changed," I told her, "since I met you."

"So has mine," she said.

"I fell into your waterfalls and your clouds raised me as high as they were."

"You're good with words. That's all you give me."

"They're free, a gift."

"I'll pay you for them if you like."

"They aren't for sale."

We stopped by another plaque describing the history of a crumbled rock with plants growing from its crevices. I remembered the great rock that had given birth to a fig tree in al-Kafroun and recalled with sadness how they'd destroyed it to make a wide, straight road. I cursed those whose work is that kind of "development." Development's their name for destruction. How dare you accuse me, Munif, of wanting the village to remain backward, only because I spoke out against a project that would send sewage into the river!

According to that small plaque in the Shenandoah Mountains, the tree would eventually be destroyed. Thousands of years ago the forces of nature succeeded in making cracks in the rock, as rain penetrated the surface, then turned to ice, causing the fissures to expand. Then, after that, earth went down into the cracks causing plants to grow, one of these becoming a tree and splitting the rock. So it went on. More rain and more earth. More plants and more roots. More holes and cracks and crumbling. Now the rock was in the process of falling apart.

"Death's a matter of transformation."

"That's true enough."

"The trees and rocks show that."

While we were playing *mankala*, the mothers of Munif and Salim passed on their way to go and console my own mother, and as my eyes met those of Munif's mother, she sent me a strange look. "Is this the dead man's son?" she said to Salim's mother. "The poor little boy's playing. He doesn't know what death means."

"He's only a child," Salim's mother answered. "Poor thing."

I bowed my head in shame and embarrassment, then ran back toward our house, to get lost all over again in the crowd of mourners. They'd laid my father

in a wooden casket and made the arrangements to take him to the cemetery—
they'd decided to bury him there and then, just a few hours after his death. Out
of pity for my mother and us children, his friends bore him to the cemetery
where he'd lie, forever, beneath the great oak trees.

This speedy burial didn't, though, shorten my mother's grief. Her sorrow
grew deeper, staying with her till the end of her long life. The day he died, she
cried out, while the other women kept hold of her, "They took you away from
me, my beloved. They took you away. Give him back to me. His body's still
warm. You buried him while his body was still warm." Then she sang to him,
quietly, "You vanished beneath the earth like a grain of wheat. Who will give
me rivers of tears to weep with?"

The day after my father was buried people told how a man from the neighboring village of al-Mahairey had passed through the cemetery the evening
before and had heard moans from within my father's grave and fled in terror.
When one of the neighbors told my mother of the rumor, she fainted, and
ever afterward, applying such scientific principles as I had in my grasp, I tried
to convince her the rumor couldn't possibly be true. But I tried in vain. Still
she believes my father died from the doctor's injection and that the people who
buried him just a few hours afterwards were brutes.

A few days before her fall I was talking to her about many things from the
past. She was still angry and bitter. "Above all things in this life," she said, "I pity
your father. May God take Dr Tu'ma's life. But for that injection he gave him,
your father would never have died. He'd got up from his bed, washed his face,
and talked to us as if there was nothing wrong with him. He talked with his
father and his cousin Yousuf about his trip to al-Mashta and Marmarita and Hab
Namra. Then, when the doctor gave him that injection, he lost consciousness.
That doctor's killed scores of patients, may God make his way hard! The people
in our village are monsters, son. They buried him while his body was still warm.
Why did his father and brothers and cousins let them do it? They wrenched
him away from me. He died at noon, and they made his casket, dug his grave,
and buried him in the afternoon. Why couldn't they leave the burial till next
day? That man from al-Mahairey heard him moaning and instead of calling the
village people, he just ran away. How can I ever go back to that village? I can't.
I can't. May God blight the lives of those savages!"

My mother came to hate the village as much as I loved it, and I tried in
vain to change her view. Once an idea stuck in her mind, there was no way of
changing it. And for all her deep faith, she never forgot how the doctor and the
priest took the eight lira my father had left. "Doctors and priests," she'd say, "take
the money of orphans and widows." I must admit these words of my mother's,
which I heard right through my life, influenced my view of the clergy and the
rich.

When I was a student at university, I met a beautiful young woman who was,
it turned out, related in some way to the infamous doctor who'd treated my
father. We became good friends, almost, indeed, developed a relationship, till I

made the mistake one day of telling her about the doctor's injection that had, we believed, killed my father. She took fright and vanished from my life.

As for the priest who buried my father, I gather he later became insane. In his last days he'd tear his clothes off and run into streams, and at night he'd roam through the vineyards, so that his family had to go out searching for him. It was said, too, that he'd go off to the cemetery and collect the skulls of the dead, then preach sermons at them, threatening them with the fires of hell. He'd arrange the skulls in a long line, then climb an oak tree and look down to make sure the line was straight. I felt pity for him.

I learned to rise above petty things and fight only battles that were worth-while. I leapt into the world, to be exposed to its various currents; and the more I was exposed, the greater my appetite for life grew. I crossed oceans and came to understand that my own departure from the world would be a death from certain suffocation, like a fish taken from the water.

Yes, I'm full of anger longing to surface, and what angers me most is op-pression. The history of humanity is a history of oppression and war, and I feel guilty that I haven't devoted my life to a struggle against such things. There's so much killing in the world, so many masks, so much fear. We should fight against oppression as Makhul did. What am I doing in Washington and the Shenandoah Mountains? Why wasn't I there in Beirut, when the siege was on? Why didn't I resist the Israeli tanks crushing the wild flowers of Southern Lebanon? Resis-tance is the salt of the earth.

I reject you, you errant civilization, as a paltry thing, and I declare your leaders too to be paltry and abject. They call freedom fighters terrorists. I say they are the terrorists. They divide the world into civilized and barbarous. I call them barbarians; it's a word I hate, but they're capable, perhaps, of understand-ing their own language. Their elegance is a mask. Their beautiful clothes are a mask. There's a connection, I believe, between fat people's preoccupation with losing weight and the hunger of Africa. Their rotten capitalism is a polite form of rape. A rich man reads an advertisement: a Rolls Royce, it tells him, is for "those unique individuals who possess an inner motivation to achieve the high-est of life's aspirations." Straightaway he decides to buy his wife a Rolls Royce for her birthday, at a cost of a hundred and fifty-six thousand dollars, more than many poor third-world families have to live on through their whole lives. It's his money, they'll say, and he can do what he likes with it. I say he must be a thief. You jewel thieves of hungry Africa, where will you run to? You women, who wear the fur of rare seals clubbed to death in their infancy, where will you flee? You who smoke cigarettes in holders made from the legs of cranes, how long will your power last? When will the limits of exploitation and injustice be reached? When will oppression end? When will there be an end of luxury built on others' deprivation? You've reached the point now of employing im-poverished women to bear your children. You put your sperm in their womb, then, when the woman gives birth, you take the child from her lap. And when the woman becomes attached to the child, when it's become the flower of her heart, as my mother always said, and refuses to give the child up, you take her to court, using your money and influence against her. You strip motherhood of its humanity. Where are the limits of greed and luxury? And why do I use words only as a weapon?

Why, I wonder, am I so full of anger? Why do I busy myself with such issues and concerns here in this enchanted setting? How can I free myself, for just one moment, from my convictions and my anxieties? I should so like, for one moment, to be without worries and concerns.

How do I dare to be angry in the midst of this vast joy and enchanting beauty, this utter peace? Why am I haunted by such issues, so gripped by them, devoting my energies to them even in this glorious place? Why do I take pleasure in wakening the oppressed from their quiet state? I believe life is joy, beauty, peace, only when it's shared with others. I try in vain to free myself from my concerns. Self, be filled with concerns. I'm like you, crane, in my constant death and rebirth. Why, I wonder, should the death of a tree in the Shenandoah Mountains make me think of my father's death in al-Kafroun, the murder of the wild flowers, the fall of cranes, the suicide of my homeland, the slow death of my mother? Why this flight into childhood? Where is the line between death and confrontation?

Since as a child I left al-Kafroun, I've plunged into the world, joining its battles on all fronts. Without something to fight for, I'm like a fish out of water. During a battle I'm like the salmon Hani told me about. They swim up rivers and streams, against the current, ascending to the place where they were born. Then, when they've arrived there after bitter struggle, they lay their eggs and die.

Like you, crane, I've crossed continents, flown over mountaintops, passed over seas and rivers. I've faced death and, each time, been reborn. I've pierced clouds both translucent and dense and touched the naked sky. I've stood in the rain, fought the storm, conquered new horizons. I've left the flock and rejoined it, I've wandered the four points of the compass and taken root in the earth. And I've known desolation and deep joy.

—*Translated by Bassam Frangieh and Christopher Tingley*

Huda Barakat (b. 1952)

Lebanese novelist Huda Barakat was born in Beirut, obtained a B.A. in French literature from the Lebanese University in Beirut, and worked subsequently as a teacher, journalist, and translator. In 1989 she left Beirut to live in Paris with her two children, working as a journalist at the news media desk of Radio Orient. Her novels combine a powerful, passionate and vivid style with a deep insight into life in all its joyful and tragic aspects. She maintains a marked control over her work, instinctively avoiding redundancy, and her description of outside events blends magically with the characters' inner experience and feelings. She promises to be a strong feminine voice in the art of the novel among Arab women writers and, while not necessarily targeting feminist issues as a main theme, seems certain to exemplify the major role of women in the Arabic literature of the twenty-first century. Her books include *Women Visitors*, a collection of texts dealing with the lives of women in war-torn Beirut and with famous women in history. She rose to sudden recognition with the publication of her first novel, *Stone of Laughter* (1990), revolving around the violent civil war in Lebanon, which was awarded a prize by *Al-Naqid* magazine and has been translated into English, French, and Dutch. Her novel *People of Passion* (1993) is being translated into Italian, French, and English, and her latest novel is *Plower of Waters* (1998).

People of Passion (1993)

Against a background of war and sectarian hatreds, two lovers, a woman from the western sector of Lebanon, probably a Muslim, and a Christian man from the eastern sector, are involved in a relationship of extraordinary passion. Sudden fierce shelling forces her to escape with him, and he takes her to his house, occupied only by him and his unmarried sister, Asma'. There she remains with him for months, initially happy, then anxious and unsettled. When she tries, on one occasion, to escape to her home, he brings her back forcibly, then goes on living with her in constant fear she will leave him again. She does so, but returns to him next day, whereupon he kills her. Wandering half mad in the hills, he is captured by two fighters from the western sector, who kidnap him and, seeing blood on his shirt, torture him to discover whom he has killed. He is returned to the eastern sector in an exchange of prisoners, and is committed to a lunatic asylum. His story is related during his moments of clarity and sobriety, which alternate with long spells of oblivion. However, the story is not really about the war, but about passion and what it does to people, attacking them like a fierce torrent, leaving them no protection against its anguish, fears, and possessive madness. It is a passion devoid of true tenderness or affection, and of all mercy or tolerance, sweeping everything before it, so that nothing remains for the characters except the long nights of love so vividly described by Huda Barakat.

After I'd killed her, I sat on a tall rock.

I closed my eyes for a long time, till my breath grew calm and regular, till my joints relaxed and my limbs flowed into one another, reconnecting like waters that flow after sweeping into other waters. My skin was cooling down in the soft breezes, and I felt I'd found it again now. Now that I'd reassumed my strong protective covering, all gaps and openings closed. New.

I lay down on the rock and found it was smooth and soft, like a luxurious bed; it followed the curves of my body and contained them. I opened my eyes onto a great low moon. The sky was dark blue, swollen with many raw stars that shone brightly, as if they'd just burst out in the sky. The sky was fresh and near—as it had been when I was a child—I could touch it, I knew, if I stretched out my hand. I was so sure of its nearness I didn't trouble my hand by stretching it. There was nothing between the sky and me but air, that soft, weak barrier, the air that flew into my open lungs, making them part of its vast regular motion.

At that hour I'd entered the world. I was breathing it vigorously in, growing full. Now, I knew, I'd begun to possess what I'd searched for all my life. I'd begun to possess my self, which entered this space now and became part of it. It was as though I was being born. I gave myself to the winds and the forest, to the valleys and the sky, and they gave themselves to me.

I knew, when I killed her and saw that I'd killed her, that I drank her soul, drank her spirit, and it came inside me. The sky, the space, opened for me, and my body opened. I knew I was a saint, that my body had begun its slow but sure ascension, that one day they'd open my grave and not find me—find nothing but my loosened bandages and empty shroud—and there'd be women pouring perfume on the earth and running with the propitious news of my disappearance.

Those who haven't killed can't know.

Those who haven't killed remain the victims of their suffering, of their wearisome search for some wonderful redemption. Their lives will be spent like the lives of flies on the dunghill, forever revolving in the same place, replete to nausea with their empty questions, then dying and sending no noise into the air.

The one who hasn't known passion, and a love complete like the sun, complete, like a huge nuclear mushroom, with just one everlasting explosion, doesn't know. He doesn't know how the seed of death descends in the apt dampness of the dark. When we realize, from the first touch, that it is it, the very skin, with its perfect temperature, fitting so totally with the heat of our own skin. The seed of murder.

But this passionate desire can never be complete in little souls, the little souls that grow sick, devote their time to weeping and listening to songs, and to the sad contemplation of old photographs. Those stunted souls, forbidden to grow complete.

Now I overflow over the suckling world, like blessed milk. Overflow but am never diminished. There's no way of diminishing me. I've been granted pardon—bliss. The bliss of the seed fertilizing in the warm dampness of my soul, growing and flowering and burgeoning. Then to pluck the fruit and eat it. Eat the fruit and enter paradise, deserving entry to it.

I rose from the rock and walked. I walked lightly, flying even. I opened my arms like St. John and sang. A pile of gold came from my mouth. I sang in the name of the God I knew, the God I'd touched and embraced. I walked, and sang loudly, not looking behind me where I'd left her near the heap of stones. This was because I knew she wasn't there any more—that she was inside me, or had ascended to heaven.

The dawn was about to rise. I saw the roofs of the small villages on the mountains opposite, still drowned in the violet haze of the sleepy dawn—I started singing aloud to the sun that was about to rise for me, and engulf me in its mighty heat.

They believed I was sick in my mind, and they pitied my condition. What had happened to me had come, they agreed, from my long captivity and the torture by my captors.

The young doctor, and my sister Asma', and the nuns, along with the male nurses, all put it down to my kidnapping and torture, my vanishing for so long in the western sector of the capital[1]—so long they'd believed I was dead. After discharging me from Arzat Lubnan hospital—I don't know how long I was there—they'd brought me to Dayr al-Saleeb. My sister Asma', supposing I was completely oblivious to things around me, told me all that as if it had happened to another man, someone I didn't know.

When Asma' repeated what had happened to me, which she did many times, she'd change a lot in the telling. I used to wonder if she did that deliberately, to probe my consciousness and powers of concentration and see if I'd realize she was mixing things up, or whether she had her own reasons for changing the story, adding things or omitting them, or whether she wanted to forget too, or because she was overanxious about me and wanted to make me understand she loved me and wanted me to go back to her, to the region she knew was mine. And so I'd listen to Asma' with the wonder of someone hearing the story for the first time, and that made her still surer I was oblivious to all that had happened to me and would go on being oblivious—so she'd repeat the story over and over again.

I knew I was in the hospital—when I was in Arzat Lubnan, I mean—but I'd forget sometimes, especially when they kept plying me with their questions—and when they'd be there around me talking, ignorant of the true reason for my illness, which they attributed, insistently and with great resentment, to the fact that I'd been kidnapped and tortured in the basements of the western sector.

For, as I was coming down that dawn, singing on the slopes of the mountain, with the sun about to rise, some young men also crossing the mountain stopped me. I didn't see them till they were almost on me, because their clothes had markings that camouflaged them among the rocks and grass.

Seeing the traces of blood on my shirt, they surrounded me on all sides, before slowly approaching, their guns pointed at my chest. Then they took off my clothes and forced me to kneel on the ground with my hands placed together above my head. I was somewhat upset at this but decided they were nothing to do with me, that I wouldn't speak to them. They spent some time searching through my clothes and, when they didn't find any identity papers, began talking among themselves as if I didn't exist. That, I told myself, was all right. They were silent for a moment, then they came up and started beating me and

---

1. The western sector (al-Gharbiyya) was inhabited mainly by the Muslim factions, the eastern (al-Sharqiyya) by the Christian Maronite factions. During the Lebanese Civil War, which lasted about twenty years, the two sides would frequently kidnap one another's young men.

asking questions—I reflected, in despair, on the misery of that coincidence, that I'd had to meet these people at the very moment of my supreme happiness, the moment in which I'd clutched at my fresh, complete, pure soul, born that very moment, when I'd thrown off all relationship with this whole world, the moment in which I was swimming over it, seeing it run and flow under my feet, in which I was singing. Oh God, I said as they beat me, oh God.

They went on hitting me for a long time, but, in one single moment, I learned something surprising, which made me realize I hadn't lost my happiness at all. In one second, just like that, I knew, as I watched the blood spurt from my mouth onto my whole naked body, that my pain was no pain at all. Not like the pain I'd known in the past, which would make me, for all my strength, roar with fury if my knee so much as hit a sharp corner. I began to feel pain as if in a dream. It was I and it was not I. It was my body and it was not my body. It was as if I were a spectator, as if I had two bodies, not like those other two bodies that would torment me when they separated and when they united. Two bodies, but two other bodies, different.

They were hitting me, and I was watching and not believing. They'd hit me, and I'd fall and see the small stones so close to my eyes and hear the sound of my breathing in the flying earth that stuck to the blood on my nose, as though I were just watching, following every small detail with something like interest. My body would shake with every blow, but the pain would stay in the place where the blow fell and wouldn't reach my head or my heart. When I saw that, I started laughing. Then they tied my hands and feet and carried me off to some remote place.

When I woke, I found they'd bound my waist, very tightly, with a strong thin thread. I was lying alone on the floor, in a dark place. My body, I realized, was swelling, swelling quickly. Every so often they'd come up and sit down beside me, trying, kindly and calmly, to make me speak, so I could be saved from the situation I was in. Sometimes they'd eye me with surprise, and I'd hear one of them say I really was mad, not just pretending to be. Then the other would answer that I was dangerous and a liar, that I'd killed someone and they must know what had happened. At other times they'd decide they ought to kill me and get rid of the smell of me, but soon they'd go back to hitting me and asking me questions. "Talk, talk!" And there I was with my head empty, nothing inside it but the desire to go on singing the song whose melodies filled me, as I climbed down the mountain slope, in that lovely dawn.

"Talk!"

"What should I say? What should I say, brothers?"

They'd get furious then, furious or else afraid of me, and start hitting me really hard, and I'd look at the places where their blows fell and see very little in the dark.

Because of my many lapses into oblivion, I don't remember how and when they moved me to a dark room where I found myself with other people. I was better there as far as physical pain went, but I'd get diarrhea. I'd sleep a lot, and wake up, sometimes, to find my companions had changed, that the faces I saw weren't the same faces I'd had beside me before I went to sleep.

One day they came carrying navy blue sports outfits, beautiful ones with white stripes. I was overjoyed when I saw, along with them, the young man who liked me and would always joke with me. He'd pamper me, bringing me tasty chocolate bars, and give me antidiarrhea pills and talk to me. I knew he laughed at me sometimes, making fun of my appearance to his friends, but I felt he liked me, and I'd tell myself he was just doing it because of them. I'd feel contented when he was there and miss him if he went a long time without coming.

That day they washed me without any grumbling or screaming or blows. Then they put the navy blue sports outfit on me, saying they were returning us to our families in an exchange of prisoners. They ordered us to be ready. A man next to me started weeping with joy and loudly thanking God. I spent a long time scouring my brains, wondering what it meant, that they were returning us to our families. Then I found Asma' there and realized they were returning me to Asma'.

We were all happy, except for one. Watching him closely, I remembered he'd been with me for a long time. He was, I recalled, a university professor—he'd gone on repeating he was a university professor and had nothing to do with any of this, till finally he'd decided to keep quiet, just like me, or almost like me. But he was fearful and tense. And when they asked him why, he said, "You fools, they're going to kill us. They're going to take us out of here and kill us." "Why should you say that?" said the man who was thanking God and weeping. "Do you think they've put us in sports outfits to kill us?"

A long time passed as we waited in our outfits. For myself, I plunged into oblivion.

Now, as I close my eyes and slowly breathe in the smell of her neck, I know that what happened was inevitable; now, after it's some time since she was with me and my great wonder's subsided. My wonder at her presence in front of me, and my wonder at how swiftly things happened.

It happened in late morning, one Sunday. A young neighbor passed by and we drank some coffee. He wasn't sure what to do; he had to go down to the capital, but his car didn't have enough gas. There was none for sale anywhere, but he'd heard there was a gas station at the entrance to our village that might get a tankful that morning, and he asked me to go with him in his car and wait in front of the station. As we waited, I saw her passing in her car, going toward her village. Come on, I said to my friend, let's go to the village near here, there's sure to be some gas in the stations. He, though, didn't dare. It was out of the question, he said. We might be kidnapped, or, at best, insulted. We weren't women, and they'd soon see we weren't one of their own people. Then we heard the sound of shelling and saw the smoke from shells falling in the valley near where we were. My friend tried to start the car engine, so we could get away, but it died before we could move off.

We got out of the car and took cover behind the walls of the gas station, though we knew well enough it was likely to explode the moment a shell hit it. At that moment I saw her coming back in her car, toward our village. I followed her, shouting, and she stopped. I climbed in next to her, and we began to see the shells falling on the road, before our eyes. We got out of the car and started climbing up into the forest to the right of the road, to take shelter behind its high rocks. She was very frightened, and I was dragging her by the hand. I didn't know where I was taking her. She kept repeating, "What's happened?"

We were still sheltering behind a tall rock when night fell. We could see the red shells flashing in the sky before falling on the two villages and the land around them. Then I found myself holding her tight, her head on my breast, and guessed this hadn't just come from fear.

By dawn the shelling had completely died down. I thought she was asleep but didn't want to move her to find out. I could feel her regular breathing all over my body, and I wasn't really aware what state I was in.

She stood up and looked first at the sky and then at me. I thought she'd go to the road where her car was and return home. But she came back and sat next to me. I thought of taking her back to my home but didn't do it. Then we heard the sound of trucks and military vehicles, along with screams and bullets. I knew we wouldn't be able to pass the barricades they'd set up on the road; they wouldn't let us at a frantic time like this. They wouldn't let us pass, in either of the two directions. I looked at her, dizzy and fearful, my eyes flickering, yet joyful too, with a strange, deep joy. "Come with me," I told her.

We walked a long way before finally reaching a narrow, abandoned road. The sounds of shelling made it impossible to decide exactly where we were. I asked her if she was hungry, but she didn't answer. She didn't speak because she was looking at me the whole time. I saw she wasn't afraid, even though she stayed close to me all the time, touching me. At that moment I had no doubt whatever she'd decided to stay with me. Up to then I hadn't dared ask her if she wanted to come back. But now I no longer had any fears.

There would, I told her, certainly be a car passing by. "Come on," I said. "Let's wait under the trees, where there's some shade." We sat under the trees. "Do you have any tobacco left?" I asked her. She stretched her legs and put her head on my stomach. My chest felt ready to burst as I tried not to move at all. Then I found I couldn't move anything in me. I was gazing at her face, not believing what I saw. I could see my own soul in front of me. Then she opened her eyes to look at me, and I could see nothing but her lips.

When I kissed her I felt as though I were leaping into the void. My knees were knocking, and the earth sank very low, far away from me. Her lips were warm and soft, and filled with juice. I'd pull her to me so hard that I felt my breath stop, then I'd go back to her lips and my breath would stop again.

Her smell was in my nostrils, and in my mouth, like hot water. Hot mercury that would fall apart, then reassemble itself to fall apart again, and I'd start collecting it from the whole of her. How easy it was. To coil then open along with my movement, as if, for the very first time, I was leaving the weight of my large body, as if I were at once many men and the shadow of a single man, heavy yet flying, empty yet full, warm and malleable, as if I had no bones.

For the first time I didn't see the body of the woman I was making love to. I didn't see her body. It was as though it were liquid to drink, as though her warmth seeping into me were stronger than any form my eyes could discern, as though I were blind so that my other senses could fulfill all their potential, their utmost strength. I saw nothing, not her skin, or her belly, or her thighs.

In the same way, I didn't see my desire. I didn't know what had taken me over. As if all this had happened in a moment; in a moment I'd pulled her hard, kissed her, entered her, and screamed. As if what I did to her, with her, had nothing to do with sex or with making love to a woman.

Now, when I remember, I see other things. Other things coming back to me after I'd stretched out close to her, looking in her face with fear and awe. Because when I came out from her, I knew I'd never come out from her, never. I was frightened, because many days of screaming, crying, and dancing wouldn't satisfy my joy, my regret, my belief in my victory and the loss of myself. My fathomless regret, because such pleasure would never come again, because, in trying to regain it, I had to be with someone else, someone other than myself. Because it wasn't possible for me to endure the tie to anyone outside myself. It wasn't possible to endure the submission to another body that would grow old, grow sick and die and leave me. No one could do it. People had attributed pure love to God alone, because they knew they'd never see Him. They didn't create a body for Him, or a death. He doesn't leave, because He's in all the places that are empty of Him.

I was lying alongside her. Her body had separated, gone back to its motion to which I'd be magnetized till I found my calm and removed myself from my place. I was sad. I knew I was sad now, as I gazed at the little moles scattered over her face and neck, and saw a few short hairs growing between the two eyebrows, and some small black spots over the nose and at the edge of her upper lip, and a tooth with a small broken edge.

I understand, now, the meaning of my wonder and my emptiness, of my inner knowledge of victory and the loss of my self.

In the truck that picked us up in the narrow side road, I continued to gaze at her. At her hands. I could see the edge of the dead skin of her nails, the nails glittering under her transparent, rose-colored manicure. I saw the nail of her index finger, with some earth sticking under it. I started cleaning it with my teeth.

The truck was full of people fleeing from the shelling. There was one woman who wouldn't stop screaming, while the rest were torn between pity for her and annoyance, in case her screams guided the shells to us. "Just thank God," they were telling her, "that the others are safe."

I didn't hear anything. I remember now, the woman was screaming because her baby had fallen from her as she climbed into the truck, and the truck didn't wait, but left it there.

As for me, her fingers were in my mouth.

~

We didn't stay long in the school building where we were given shelter. I said she was my wife, and no one asked to see her papers. They gave us a bed and two blankets in the corner of a room, where there was already a family: a couple, a grandmother, and four young children. We set up a green sheet around our bed. The family didn't like us because we didn't talk to anyone, didn't tell them about ourselves, didn't go with them to ask for water and complain because the food they distributed to us was off. Also, because we managed to get some water and took a bath twice.

I'd put up the green sheet, then embrace her, put my head on her neck, and breathe . . .

At night we'd climb onto the roof of the school, where many other people went too, to enjoy the coolness of the night. I'd wrap her in the blanket and massage her feet until they warmed up. She felt the cold a good deal, her feet were always cold, like two fish. This, I'd tell her, was because she ate so little. I used to wonder what I could talk to her about. Only the occasional idea came to me. I'd talk about the fall and how it rained a lot. I'd tell her how soft the air was and point to the stars and tell her their names. Then I'd go to the shop they'd opened in the administration room, buy her a box of biscuits or a chocolate bar, then come back and insist she eat. She'd laugh, then she'd eat— We'd stay on the roof until it was empty, sometimes only just before dawn, so I could kiss her repeatedly, strip off her clothes, and sit there gazing at her, seeing how she looked anxious. She'd look around and draw the edges of the blanket over her. I'd sit gazing at her, each time as if it were the first time, and I'd see something else, new things, quite different, I'd tell myself, each time. Here she is, I'd think, in front of you, with you, waiting for you, her master, whenever you desire and want. And she wanted too.

Sometimes I'd go up and cover her, spreading the blanket over her as her nakedness became too much for me. The light of her breasts and the moon of her black nipples. I'd spread the blanket and stretch out next to her, stroking her hair, braiding it, untying and kissing it, with that desire to cry slowly aloud to restore my breath as I looked at the sky. Stronger than me and too much for me, stronger than all my potency, stronger than the space of my skin. I was bound to her, and I was lost, with no strength at all. Exhausted even before I took her to me. Frustrated and weary, while my palm drank from the warmth of her naked shoulder. I'd breathe her in drop by drop, from the tip of my toes, from the moment my mother gave birth to me, but I couldn't be filled, was never filled. Then she'd open the blanket and take me to her.

Sometimes she'd fall asleep. I'd feel happy she was forgetting me now, leaving me alone. I'd breathe over her mouth to draw in the air coming from her lips, the air that had passed within her body and purified her blood. I'd lean on my arm and watch, for a long time, the vein throbbing on her neck. I'd envy the blood that flowed in her. And I'd stay without moving, so she could stay asleep close to me, calm and quiet, as I remained alone. I'd count the pulse of the visible vein, then slowly put my hand on her, trying to penetrate it to the red liquid that flowed within her, under her skin, and through all her organs.

One day, I told myself, she'd leave. Not that I supposed she'd go back to her husband or family or that she'd grown bored with me. I didn't imagine she'd become bored with me. I simply knew, for a certainty, that she'd leave, just because she was separate from me physically, had a body she could give orders to at her own will. She'd get up and walk in a direction I didn't know and couldn't imagine. That's all. She'd order her feet to walk away from me to a place where I wouldn't be. Not in my direction but in an endless number of directions, none of them coming toward me but where I'd never be. She'd stand up like that and walk, and I'd stay in the spot where I was. She might die too, like all those many people who were dying.

Oh, Mother! Sometimes, as I looked at her sleeping by me on the roof of the school, I'd feel like screaming and waking her up, putting her clothes on her, and asking he,: "Where will you go? What direction will you take, and not return?"

I'd remember she was a woman and wonder a good deal. Wonder how she had a body that wasn't mine. It was enough, I'd say, for her to stay a long time with me, so I could learn to endure her. To stay along with me, till time had wrought its subtle work.

Time will pass over the things of this world like a sword, cleaving it in two and saving me. It will disinfect the first part the way those disinfectants do that are so strong and evaporate with such speed. It will separate them from their organic origins, and they'll dry up and become light and sterilized but sink down too and move no more. As for the second half, its remnants will fly away on the first wind, then sink and gather in distant places we know nothing of. Our bodies remain in their sterile state, while our thoughts and memories fly off and settle far away. Our bodies, which time sterilizes as it passes over them, dry off from their sex. And so things become neutral as to their origins. Man and woman become one form, one body; their organs settle into one sex. A woman grows small mustaches and a little beard, and a man's mustaches and beard grow to the same size. Two small breasts grow on a man, limp like the fate of the woman's dry breasts. Even their sexes become twins: fragile, small, limp, with protruding veins.

This is how mummies become cleansed over the ages. This is how they celebrate the loss of their sex, in perfect sterilization. No eggs, no hormones, these have been so long forgotten. And so no parasites ever enter, no parasites enter unless the mummies are brought out from their time and drawn into a time that intrudes on them. A different air.

Time will pass over us, I and my woman, then we'll become alike. We'll have one body, one sex, not two. I shall reclaim her sex, endure it, and equalize it, and become free.

But time passes over us, also, as a woman who destroys our capacities, keeps us at her side, sterilizes us before ages pass. A woman depriving us of the bliss of parasites, and their mercy.

She had to come back.

She had to come back, and I had to kill her so that madmen, saints, and all those about to die will continue on their road, etched in the void of chaos.

Because our stopped lives are always like this, with no justice to expect on this earth, not when our souls will come out from their two nostrils, leaving behind them traces that, let us agree, have nothing to do with the nature of the soul. I had to kill her because one woman wasn't enough, because the exception to the rule is the ultimate torment of the rule. Because every woman we love is the exception to the rule and its greatest possible torment.

Because the rule is for those who grow old slowly and are then extinguished, or for those who are snapped off in wars knowing nothing of it beforehand, suddenly, like the rain whose sound we suddenly hear outside the window, when it's long been streaming down. We hear it only when we stop our conversation and prepare to say goodbye to the evening visitors.

Because the rule isn't for those who die of passion, who die from their suffering and their desire for lightness and light and the phantom of the beloved. Because the rule is for those laid out on stretchers, in the emergency corridors of government hospitals, those who tripped, confounded, as they walked, by their days and their ill-starred awakening among the buses.

For those on the lines of stretchers, stunned, sinking deep, not just into comas but into wonder at the destruction of their physical machinery. In the coma, they see their bodies like complex machinery, strange and remote. Pointing to this machinery, they ask not where they were, but what that was.

And so it is that the look their families knew vanishes, and those looks they had at the very start return, stunned, searching for their physical beginnings. As if the empty gaze they send us were something fulfilled, and returning inside them.

The rule is for these, for God's normal creatures, for the masses crowded together, moving parallel to one another and stifling one another, for those who lie on clean beds and hospital stretchers. The torment of the rule is for us: for the heavy laden, the madmen, the saints of phosphorus, the rabid dogs, the lovers, the failed murderers; and for her.

CONCLUSION

I know a long time has passed since I came here.

I know I'm tired, and sick in my mind. That's why, when I return from all those spells of oblivion, I think I didn't kill her. I think I didn't kill anyone, that my sick mind was disjointed, leaping inside my head, erring where it willed.

Perhaps that woman never was, the one I'd see in a circle of sunlight, sitting motionless in the garden beneath my window. I might even have composed her from the many women I've known, so as to fulfill my desire. The doctor keeps hinting I harbor many unjustified fears.

One day I told the doctor I might get well, that I see the signs of health when I'm able to walk blindfold, in the hospital or the garden, without knocking into any thing or person, when I can see, not just the things but the outline of things, not just the people but the movement of people, and so avoid them.

Perhaps I never killed her. I doubt very much whether I held her head, then smashed it against the rocks till it gaped with wounds and she died. I doubt if my body had the strength to do this, and the idea repels me. She wasn't there when I wandered blindly over that rugged mountain, and the two young men found me and took me as a captive to the western side. She wasn't there, not because she'd ascended to heaven but because I never killed her.

Perhaps she's back with her husband and never came back to me on the night of shelling, as my sister Asma' tried to persuade me she'd return that next day. Perhaps she's with him now, near him, in the peace of the country that has settled now into a purity, full and final, in their distant home I could never imagine having a form at all; while I, here, am still huddled in the night of shelling where she left me, contemplating my final disposal of her, just before dawn, like all people of passion.

—*Translated by May Jayyusi and Christopher Tingley*

Najwa Barakat (1961)

Lebanese novelist Najwa Barakat was born in Beirut and now lives in Paris. She read theater studies at the Fine Art Institute in Beirut, graduating with a D.E.S. in 1982. She later obtained a diploma in Cinema Studies from the C.L.C.F. in Paris. She has worked as a press and radio journalist, and was a film writer and director from 1984–2001, when she participated in at least two documentaries and two feature films. In 1997 she won the Prize for Best Literary Creation of 1996, in Paris; and in 1999 she won first prize at the Amateur Theater Festival in Amiens, France. Although Najwa Barakat can reflect a grim outlook on the world and on human negative streaks, her novels have the authentic quality of the storyteller and entertain as well as horrify, thus escaping much of the unrelenting heaviness of some contemporary Arabic fiction. Her capacity for details is rare, and her insight into human nature reflects both an instinctive and an intelligent approach. She has published four novels to date: *The Transformer* (1986); *Hamid's Passion* (1995); *The People's Bus* (1996), and *Ya Salaam* (1998).

THE PEOPLE'S BUS (1996)

The People's Bus *explores the lives of a number of people who are on a bus journey from Beirut to one of the southern villages of Lebanon. The journey is made much longer and more difficult by three incidents: a storm that forces the driver to make a halt; the intrusion of a pregnant woman who gets on the bus when it stops, then goes into labor and is helped to give birth by the other women passengers; and an encounter with a random patrol. As the journey progresses, we become acquainted with the lives, mentalities and past experiences of the passengers, whom Barakat chooses from various walks of life, mainly from the humbler sectors of Lebanese society. The following passage deals with the different sides of Khaddouja, a widow taking her daughter, Maryam, to be married to a man in the south. Here, the bus is being made ready for the journey.*

Meanwhile Khaddouja was busy urging the porters to take proper care of other people's property. "Just remember, you people," she said, "that's a bride's furniture there. Make sure it doesn't get scratched!"

The bride modestly bowed her head as her bedroom furniture was loaded up onto the roof of the bus: bed, cupboard, mattress, and mirror, along with cushions, an eiderdown, sheets, and a bedspread, all packed in bags for protection. There were baskets, bundles, and further luggage belonging to the other passengers too. Everything had ropes tied around it to fix it firmly in place . . .

The passengers sank back in their seats dreaming of what was waiting for them at the journey's end. Maryam, Khaddouja's daughter, was deepest in reverie. She closed her eyes to escape her mother's scrutiny; then her desires, shot through with silken threads, began weaving their way toward the place where the bridegroom's ardor awaited her. As she leaned her head out of the window to cool herself down, the winds untied the knot on her scarf and flung it off, setting the long locks of hair free to dance in the air like flapping fish newly brought from the water. Khaddouja sprang to her feet like a woman possessed and retrieved the scarf from the passenger next to her, striving, with her other hand, to hide what had been revealed. "Cover it," she cried, "may God preserve your honor!"[1]

Then she turned to her neighbor, Malik al-Radiyy.

"Excuse me, brother," she said, with an apologetic smile. "I think I heard you say you were a notary public."

"That's right," he said. "In the courts."

"And you deal with matters of inheritance and marriage?"

"Yes, we do."

Khaddouja sat down again and turned toward him to continue the conversation.

---

1. Muslim women are supposed to cover their hair in the presence of male strangers.

"God sent you to me," she went on, "so I could ask your advice. I come from a family whose men have been fated by God to die young."

Her neck already stiff from turning round, she got up and asked Yusuf, the hydraulic engineer, to change seats with her for a while. Then she settled down next to the notary public.

"Where was I?" she asked.

"You were saying you come from a family whose men are fated by God to die young."

"God's will be done! The menfolk die, the women are left as widows or orphans, and the estate's squandered because there's no heir."

Hearing one particular word, which seemed to scream in his ears like a siren, Yusuf fidgeted in his seat,[2] while Khaddouja turned to her daughter, who was sitting stiff as a board next to him, to check all was well with her.

"My daughter here," she went on, "may God preserve her, is getting married soon. I've fitted her out with a whole bedroom suite—I'm just praying it'll arrive safe, without getting scratched. Did you see the mirror? It was the finest one in the market and the most expensive. I'm going with her myself, you can be sure of that, to her bridegroom's house, to be sure everything's in order. Then I'll be coming back. Are you married?"

"No."

"God's will be done! My fear is her husband might turn out to be a scoundrel. I'm afraid he'll grab what's left of her father's estate, then throw her out in the street. Shouldn't I be taking precautions? Is there some way of protecting her?"

Malik al-Radiyy's eyes took on a moist glitter, and he hastened to swallow the spittle flooding under his tongue.

"It's easy enough," he said. "Just let her keep her independence within the marriage."

"Independence?"

"Yes. Only let her marry on that condition. If it's not too late, that is."[3]

"What would that mean exactly?"

"It would give her the power to decide whether the marriage continued or whether it was revoked"

"So she could divorce him whenever she wanted?"

"Exactly."

"Hey! You mean it's really possible to fix things like that?"

---

2. It emerges later in the story that Yusuf was an orphan as a child.

3. Muslims often sign the marriage contract before the actual wedding. If this had happened here, there would be no way of revoking the standing law whereby the husband has the sole right of decision. However, the law allows for a condition inserted into the marriage contract allowing the would-be wife to divorce her husband, which would give her independence and volition within the marriage.

The bus is forced to halt because of the storm, and the driver's assistant starts selling tea, soft drinks, and snacks. There is not, though, enough sugar for the tea, and this leads to protests from the passengers. Remembering that one passenger, Mu'awiya al-Matmati, was carrying a large bag of sugar when he got on, the assistant asks him to provide some in return for some free food.

Mu'awiya al-Matmati gave him a long look, then answered loudly for everyone to hear.

"You see this bag of sugar?" he said. "My wife sent me out to buy it over thirty-five years ago. And now I've bought it, you want me to give it to you?"

The assistant raised his eyebrows, utterly bewildered, while some of the passengers laughed, taking the answer to be a joke or some kind of play on words.

There is considerable confusion among the passengers.

Mu'awiya, filled with a sense of unexpected importance, turned to the nearest passengers, at which Khaddouja looked at him, nodded, and said, "It seems you have a story to tell." Everyone got ready to listen to the story, which might make them forget the storm and help pass the time, little by little, as they drank their mint tea.

Mu'awiya cleared his throat.

"I was at home," he said, "receiving some unexpected guests, and, as we were talking and laughing together, my wife broke in to say there wasn't enough sugar for the tea. So I left my guests and went off to the shop close by, promising to come straight back. When I got there, though, I found to my amazement that the shop was shut, even though it was still early.

"I asked why this was and was told the shopkeeper had closed up and rushed off to the fountain in the square. And when I went there looking for him, I found a crowd of people gathered around a man who was speaking most eloquently, like an imam addressing his congregation.

"'You Arabs,' he was crying, 'Palestine's lost, and we must take it back through holy war!'

"His words riveted the people, and they felt their consciences burning within them.

"'By God,' I cried, flinging away my house key, 'I shall never return home till what's been lost is free again!' And with that I followed him."

A silence descended on the passengers, and the sound of the wind whistling through the cracks of the windows increased their sense of awe. Mu'awiya took a brief sip of tea and continued. "Off we marched behind the speaker," he said, "a small group of us from our village, till we reached the appointed place for fighters to travel on to the gates of Palestine. Our numbers grew on the way, just as a river swells from all the tributaries that feed its flow and the might of its waters. I won't describe all the setbacks we met crossing the desert or tell you how many people had to be left behind because their legs wouldn't keep them going over a long march like that. Jamil al-Baghdadi—God bless his soul!—was one of us, and whenever I think what happened to him, I break down and weep. We'd run out of food and water and were so parched with thirst our skins were chafed and our lips felt as if they were made of mud. Some people fainted under a sun that turned your brain, but three of us, of whom I was one, volunteered to go and look for water, and God, in His mercy, led us to a well. I said I'd go down inside, but Jamil al-Baghdadi strode forward, swearing by the life of his children that he and no other would go down; and since the rope was worn and he was the smallest and lightest, we felt bound to agree. We tied him around the waist and started lowering him, but the rope snapped and the poor man plunged on, down and down, till we heard his bones smash against the sides of the well."

Mu'awiya fell silent, then made a sign to the assistant to bring him some more tea to moisten his mouth. He took a quick sip, then continued, "Still we marched on, through thirst and hunger and suffering. Every night, before going to sleep, we'd sit in a circle around a small radio one of the fighters had, to find out the results of the latest battles. As we heard the good news, of Arab armies marching in every direction, we'd breathe sighs of relief, our spirits buoyed right up, and next day we'd march on with all the speed we could muster, so as not to miss our part in defeating the enemy and ending victorious.

"Then, when we'd almost arrived, great crowds of people from that country met us on the roads: women and tottering old people and children, who'd abandoned their homes and were wandering along the roads to escape the bullets and the enemy. There was wailing and moaning, and wounded people filled the plains. And when we asked them how the battles were going, about enemy losses and the heroism of our comrades, they'd stare at us astonished, as if we'd come from some remote planet. The radio played martial songs that made the blood boil in our veins, repeating, over and over again, that victory, victory was so near, the enemy crushed and about to be flung into the sea; and still the refugees poured on, in unbelievable numbers, to be met at the neighboring borders with blankets, clothes, and food.

"We understood at last that the battles we'd come to join had never taken place on real ground, only on the radio. I picked up my rifle, and I swore: 'By God! By God! I shall never lay this rifle down till we've gained back what was lost.' The cause of Palestine became my own, and I followed it from place to place, heedless of any sacrifice, however great. If we abandoned it, after all, everything would be lost, and what would history say about us then? What would we tell our children? How could we explain away the loss, and the way we'd done nothing about it?"

⸎

Early next morning, when the storm dies down, the driver moves on very slowly through the forest, constantly crushing storm-felled branches beneath his wheels. Then he stops, fearful of the unknown terrain. When daylight comes, he finds they are on the verge of a precipitous slope down to the seashore and wakes his assistant, telling him to go and find out where they are. On the shore the assistant makes out a group of highly agitated women, all moaning and weeping.

⸎

The assistant froze with fear, unsure just where he was and what he ought to do. Shouldn't he go back, he wondered, or try and find someone to ask the way? He heard himself murmuring, "In the name of the Merciful, the Benevolent"; then, turning back, he bumped into someone standing there just behind him. He shuddered with fear, the blood streaming to his head. Then, seeing a woman gazing at him with expressionless eyes, he grew confused and tried to stammer out an apology. She, though, reassured him somewhat by asking, "What are you looking for, stranger?"

The assistant told his story, briefly but with a good deal of dramatic emphasis on all the worry and surprise and confusion they'd suffered. Then he ventured to ask her, in turn, about the things he'd seen and heard on the beach, at which she moved off, making a sign for him to follow. It seemed the women of the village had come to wait for their menfolk—fathers, husbands, brothers, or sons—who'd put out to sea the previous afternoon, then been caught in the sudden storm, and failed to return. She was waiting there for her own husband, she said, though she was sure it was fruitless, that the sea had taken him.

"Listen, stranger," she said, "I'll show you the way, on condition you take me with you to my family, so I can have my child there. My time's right on me. If you'll just put me down not too far from where they live, I'll go the rest of the way on foot."

Seeing her bulging belly, which made walking a big effort, the assistant felt sorry for her and hoped the driver would agree to take her along for part of the way. They entered the olive grove, and he started walking toward the bus. She, though, stopped him, took him by the hand, and drew him toward a large sack of olives she'd hidden there.

"If I sell this in my village," she said, "I'll have some money for clothes for myself and my baby."

The assistant followed on behind her. How on earth could she be so sure, he wondered, that her husband wouldn't return? Was it the famous female intuition everyone talked about? He was prevented, though, from asking further questions by the sheer size and weight of the sack. He panted on behind her, his knees bent and his shoulders almost crushed under the burden.

When they arrived, they found the passengers had got out of the bus and were walking among the trees, talking about the storm and, above all, of that gaping abyss just below them. The assistant, ignoring the questions they were hurling at him, went straight over to the driver, and the two of them stood apart, talking together under a tree.

Then the driver climbed into his seat, while the assistant went up onto the roof of the bus and called to someone to help him lift the olive sack. Finding his hands sticky from the contents, this other man asked the assistant what was in it. The pregnant woman stuck her head out from the window of the bus.

"Just olives," she cried. "Black olives!"

~

One of the main characters in the novel, 'Abd Al-Fattah Ben Salha, is a man who delves into all kinds of witchcraft. His antecedents are dubious, his father being unknown. His mother was a cook, famous for her wonderful dishes and regularly hired by families for weddings, festive occasions, and funerals. His childhood was spent following her from house to house, helping her in different people's kitchens by sorting the vegetables, washing, peeling, and chopping them, and so on. The women of the house would come and joke with him and play with his hair, so that he became completely used to female company.

~

The kitchen! The enchanted world to which his eyes were opened, the world of women par excellence. The sensuality of their movements, their comings and goings and their clamor. The way they dealt with all the matters of cooking. The hands that boiled, plucked, minced, crushed, ground, cut, stuffed, hashed, chopped, sprinkled, mixed, kneaded, mashed, sifted, sorted, beat, and took to taste; the co-quettish hands shining with oil, with butter, with water; the hands that clapped, snapped with their fingers, took on suggestive shapes as jokes and comic stories were told; the hands with rings and bracelets and patterns of red henna.

The kitchen! The world of flavors and secrets. The world of bellies and legs and breasts. The smell of burned sugar, of henna, of sweat and perfume; the smell of firm young bodies and old, flabby ones; the smell from between the breasts, from hair, and from under the arms; strong, pungent smells and light, coquettish, playful smells; the smell of laughter and forbidden talk, of greasy talk; the smell of spices and kerosene.

The kitchen! The female world, the kitchen paradise!

~

Such was the world in which 'Abd al-Fattah grew up. Now, as he sits in the bus, we find him reminiscing about the experience that shaped his future life. He was at a bakery owned and run by a widow.

"I've run out of change here, 'Abd al-Fattah," she said. "Come over to the house with me."

The boy followed her down the dark, narrow corridor, then stood by the door as she went into the bedroom. The light in the room was pink like the curtains, which were drawn even though it was daylight. Opening the cupboard, she thrust her floury hand between the sheets and tablecloths, while 'Abd al-Fattah looked stealthily around him, marveling at the beautiful dressing table on which stood a round mirror reflecting perfume bottles, makeup, and small vessels with various thick colors for her long red nails. She beckoned to him. "Come on, lad," she said. "Don't be shy. Give me that box over there." . . . Then she squeezed him between the cupboard and her body.

This marked the beginning of his precocious sexual experiences. When, though, the baker's relationship with 'Abd al-Fattah began to attract attention, she carried it on by imprisoning the boy (with his consent, apparently) in a room in the house, after he himself had told the people of the quarter he was going away to study. Meanwhile the baker quenched his thirst for knowledge by giving him her late husband's books on the spirit world, witchcraft, and every kind of fortune-telling and talisman. The novel provides a skillful description of the relationship and, in particular, of the way the boy is lured and initiated into a life of adult lechery and sexual abandon.

After two years 'Abd al-Fattah, pallid but master of a new profession, emerges to launch himself on a career devoted largely to women and their needs and demands.

And so 'Abd al-Fattah ben Salha returned after his long time away, his face pale, his hands wise and skilled in healing. He returned with a large yellow rosary and bearing great quantities of drugs, and potions, and ointments, and prescriptions. When the news spread through the quarter, the local people showered him with plaudits and gave hair-raising accounts of the miracles he'd performed.

The women would come and throw themselves at his feet. "Cure me, you blessed saint!" they'd cry. Or else, "Get me back my husband, or lover, or fiancé, so-and-so, the son of so-and-so." Or else, "Unite me with my lover." Or, "Unbind me from this charm!" Or, "Save me from dying unmarried!"

The women grew sick with love, wilting like tender plants, and 'Abd al-Fattah felt sorry for these wondrous creatures in the thrall of the kings of the jinn. His heart melted to see their condition, their bodies drooping, parched for the juices of his manhood through which they could ripen and blossom and feel life returning. They tumbled into the vessels of his lust like ripe fruit, gave him, to taste, the harvest of seasons made sweeter and more delectable by their arousal, and Abd al-Fattah grazed blissfully in their pastures, like a stallion. Slowly he wove his nets, then scaled the walls of their ripe womanhood or springtime youth.

'Abd al-Fattah never, though, assuaged their desire for long. Like a hunter, or a murderer, he exercised his arts once only, never a second time, avoiding lasting relations, avoiding complications—and avoiding, too, the fury of brothers and husbands and fathers. He'd tear himself away to alight in new pastures, where there were new gazelles and deer. He loved them, helplessly, in their tens and hundreds and thousands. On he rushed—there was no time to waste. What he left behind was nothing to speak of; what lay ahead held the promise of sweetest fruits.

And now here he was, today, finished with the regions and villages of the north and traveling south. Husniyya was a stop along his way . . .

Husniyya is traveling on the bus with her husband, who is a butcher. She is a tall, stately woman of voluptuous charms, a remarkable contrast to the small, wizened husband she clearly rules. 'Abd al-Fattah has no problem awakening her and arousing her lust. The description of their secret meeting in the woods (during the night, when the bus has stopped because of the pregnant woman's labor) is charged with sexuality and vivid evocations of desire, without, though, descending into pornography—Najwa Barakat's touch is at its deftest here.

The pregnant woman's difficult labor ends with Khaddouja's help, and she and her baby boy are sent on to the woman's village by cart, in the care of a peasant. Soon, though, the bus suffers yet another serious mishap. It is stopped by a random patrol, which makes a rough search of the top of the bus, not only breaking Khaddouja's expensive mirror but also toppling the olive sack, which spills open to reveal a severed head. Now almost everyone is a murder suspect.

Mu'awiya al-Matmati sinks into silent reflection:

Will they believe me, he wondered, when they find out the truth? Tomorrow they'll look up my stunning record, and then I'll be the prime suspect. You fool, Mu'awiya! What possessed you to start spouting lies the moment you came out of prison? But how was I to guess, he thought, that I'd end up accused of a crime committed by that black owl of a woman? It's incredible! We weave a white lie, then smother in the heart of it. We're squeezed from all sides, like some prey in the grip of an octopus!

I kept on telling those fools, warning them! If they hadn't let her on the bus, we'd all be safe now. Haven't I paid enough over all these years? If they'd only dropped her off when she started complaining about her labor pains, she would have remembered that cursed sack of hers all right. We could have dumped them both together, there on the road. What hypocrites they are! They pretend to do good, but they're like scorpions. The moment you start trusting them, they turn around and sting you.

Women! They ought to be trodden underfoot like insects. That whore, saying she wanted to go back to her village because her husband had been lost at sea! You can bet your life she got rid of him so she could sleep with every other man in the world. Poor devil! Hacked to bits like a dog, or a calf at the slaughterhouse. He must have been a weak-kneed creature though—a real man would have made sure she went first. Damn her and damn all women! You can't trust any of them. To hell with the lot of them! If only I hadn't got on this bus. If only I'd come along late and missed it.

Mu'awiya al-Matmati was blazing with fury, grinding his teeth in his passion. If someone came along now and stabbed him, he thought, there wouldn't be a drop of blood coming out of him—that's how hard he was holding himself in, ready to burst with curses and abuse! He felt a numbness in his feet and tried to move them, but only met the feet of the driver sitting opposite and had to pull them back again. In the end he crossed them and leaned forward with his elbows on his knees.

Suppose, he thought, they started questioning him again next day. Do you really think, he'd say then, that I'd spend all those years in prison, then come out and commit another crime a few hours later? That made sense, surely. Anyway, he wasn't some sort of random killer, was he, who wandered about knocking people off just for the fun of it? What did he have to do with all these strangers? The crime he'd committed had brought him a life sentence, reduced to thirty-five years for good conduct—or, at least, that's what they said. Actually the real reason, so some of his comrades had told him, was that the prison was overcrowded and couldn't hold the hundreds of new prisoners who were being arrested now. So they'd let him out.

He'd been twenty-four when he went in, and now he was nearly sixty. Surely they'd believe him! His original crime, as he'd point out, had been against the person closest to him—there'd been a proper reason and impulse to kill. But as for that severed head, what earthly connection could he have with it? Yes, they'd believe him all right, they must. Where was he supposed to have met the head's owner? In his prison cell?

God! After he'd taken that last step, walked those last few inches that separated prison from life, he'd stood there and gazed up at the sky. "Pray God, Mu'awiya," he'd whispered to himself, "you can spend what's left of your life in peace and happiness now, there in your village in the south!" Then he'd flung away the bag with all those things that reminded him of the dark years past and walked toward the square, hoping to find a bus to take him home. And when, late though it was, he'd heard the driver's assistant calling out for passengers, he'd taken it as a good omen, hoping his luck was about to turn at last.

Before that, though, he'd passed a shop and couldn't resist going in and buying something, to assure himself things hadn't really changed during all that time away. He was seized by the desire to perform some action, to convince himself he could go around and do things like anyone else now. And so he'd asked for a quantity of sugar—not just for the pleasure of it, though it was a pleasure all right, but to put an end to something he'd left, as he recalled, unfinished. He picked up that sugar like someone who'd finally found the end of a rope, one that made him feel his life had never been interrupted—as if he'd just gone out to buy something, not thirty-five years before but a few minutes back. He was running a quick errand, then going back home.

It had been his first experience of love and marriage, and she'd been so beautiful—a lovely young woman, with a smile that squeezed the heart tight, then made it open again. A pretty, plump, white-skinned bride, like sugar. He'd forbidden her to go out. After all, if he couldn't even bear men looking at her when he was with her, how could he have stood it when they were apart? He'd sealed her up behind doors and windows and walls—that way he could feel safe when he went off to work. And still she smiled.

Like the sun that smile of hers burned him; and like the sun it blinded him. He couldn't understand where this sun rose from or how he could make it sink. In the end he couldn't take any more. He laid siege to her, he kept her apart, made a recluse of her, orphaned her, severed her roots and nipped her leaves and blotted her out. He wrung her dry and crushed her. And still she smiled—not outwardly, it was true, but he could feel the smile there inside her, behind the lips and eyes, down in the depths of her; drifting slowly out and nestling in the corners, spreading like some subtle organism, shimmering in a fleeting gleam he could never capture.

Why was she still smiling, after all that? He stripped her of her possessions, all her ornaments and finery, cut her off from her clothes and sold her jewelry. Then he seized hold of her hair and hacked it all off, so that the locks tumbled on the floor like severed snakes and the skin could be seen beneath.

And what next? She got up, fetched a pail and a broom, and wiped the floor clean, her smile creeping over her shaven head, cascading down her back. Why hadn't she shrieked out? Why hadn't she wept and wailed and beat her head, against the wall or whatever? What kept her going in the face of what he was doing to her? Where did she find the strength, the endurance? She'd end up killing him, he knew, if she went on like this. She'd finish him off.

And what next? He abandoned her, flung her out of his bedroom, made her sleep on the floor. And the smile, the smile he couldn't see, pursued him still, haunted his dreams in the shape of demons, like suns, like fire, like jinn, till, exhausted, he was robbed of his very soul.

One day she made him some tea as he'd told her to, but it was bitter. He'd flared up and cursed her, then gone to fetch some sugar but found they'd run out. He'd go out and buy some, he said, but he might be a while coming back, as he was going to drop in on some friends. Then he went out, leaving the door unlocked and, his trap laid, hid some way off to watch.

For several minutes the door stayed closed and there was no sign of her. He started feeling happier; then his fears sprang up all over again, and he waited on. Then the door opened. He smiled in anticipation. Out she came, into his trap. For a while she stood there under the walnut tree in the inner courtyard, frozen to the spot. He couldn't see her eyes or where she was looking. What made her stand there, just stand there like that? Had she come out for some fresh air? Well, what if she had? What was wrong with that? He started walking away, then stopped as a further thought struck him. Had she maybe come out to see someone or be seen by someone? And if so, who was it? He turned and ran back to his home.

And what next? He found her sitting in front of the mirror, holding the shell of a green walnut, rubbing it over her lips till her mouth was the color of old wine. She hadn't betrayed him at all. She was making herself beautiful for him. She was alone after all, with no fear in her eyes, not a flicker of alarm or surprise. He drew near and kissed her. She started and drew away. He came up and bit her, but she stood there frozen in his arms, as cold as ice. He breathed his burning breath on her, but she didn't smile. "Who is it?" he asked. "Who are you making yourself up for?" She didn't say she was doing it for him, that he was her husband, the man she longed for and loved. Instead she burst into tears. He slapped her, then hit her, and she stopped crying. But he felt he had no power over her, that she was defying him. "Who's it for, you whore," he yelled, "if it's not for me?" He started hitting her again, hoping she'd utter at least one word in response, that she'd moan, scream her innocence, cry out to reproach him, even with a curse, with something at least. He went on hitting her and hitting her, till her whole body was scarlet like red wine, like the ruby lips colored with the walnut shell.

And what next? It was all over. She lay there in a red pool, her mouth and ears gushing blood, then finally stopped moving. That had been her destiny, written and laid down, to die by his hand. If she'd been innocent, he wouldn't have gone on in that blind rage, would he, kept beating her as if she were a mere object between his hands? He would have found, once and for all, the reason for her smile.

And now, next day, they were sure to try and pin that severed head on him. He'd already murdered once, hadn't he? What's more, they'd say, a man who kills his wife because she puts on some makeup might just as easily kill a man because he didn't like his face. Well, he'd answer, if you'd been in my place, back then, you'd have done the same. I'm not sorry for what I did. It was the hand of fate, and I was the chosen instrument. No, I'm not sorry for it. There's no shame in going to prison. Prison's for men.

Well, he thought, they released me in the end, and they kept in that imbecile who'd pounded my eardrums with his talk of the struggle. If he knew I'd taken over his identity, he'd be delighted—he'd feel as though he'd been set free himself, from being a prisoner of war. He was the bane of my life with those stories about that friend of his, Jamil al-Baghdadi. I ended up knowing them all by heart, and I told them to those cunning people on the bus as if they were etched there on the palm of my hand, as if my memory was a book open in front of me. What difference does it make anyway? What I said wasn't a lie, even if I was a liar myself. And even suppose the stories themselves had been lies, that every man had invented his own epic about the struggle, would it be my fault if I'd believed them?

I lied and those people believed me! They respected me! They left me to myself! If I'd admitted the truth, would they have treated me as an equal? No, by God they wouldn't! People are like scorpions. The moment you start trusting them, they turn around and sting you.

And what next?

Further events unfold as the book develops. We learn that Khaddouja is not Maryam's true mother; of Malik al-Radiyy's homosexuality; of Yusuf's memories of an orphaned childhood, and so on. The passengers spend the night in police custody, awaiting questioning about the severed head, but are saved when the formerly pregnant woman dies, having first confessed to her husband's murder.

—Translated by May Jayyusi and Christopher Tingley

Saleem Barakat (b. 1951)

Syrian poet and novelist of Kurdish origin, Saleem Barakat lived in Beirut for many years working as a journalist and is now associate editor of the prestigious quarterly *Al-Karmel*, the literary review of the Palestinian Union of Writers. Both as poet and as novelist, he is one of the most original and compelling authors writing in Arabic today and has enriched modern Arabic literature with his courageous use of words and expressions that are rare and unfamiliar but semantically apt and aesthetically exciting. He has published several volumes of poetry, the first five of which have been collected in one volume titled *The Five Collections* (1981). A later poetry collection, *With the Nets Themselves, With the Foxes that Lead the Wind*, was published in 1987. His several novels include *Sages of Darkness* (1985), which won him immediate acknowledgment; and *Geometric Souls* (1987); *Feathers* (1990); *Camps of Eternity* (1993), and *Astronomers in the Tuesday of Death* (1997).

SAGES OF DARKNESS (1985)

Set against the backdrop of the crude agricultural struggle and brutal life of tobacco smugglers, Sages of Darkness *is the story of two magical and snowy winters in a small Kurdish Syrian village on the Turkish-Syrian border. An aberrant child, Bikras, is born to Mulla Binav on a freezing, snowy morning and reaches the age of marriage by the waning of that winter day. From this day on, the village and the lives of its inhabitants become fantastical. Bikas joins the violent, shadowy smugglers of the night and the sages of darkness, who are planning to take over the village through wizardry. Through the bewildered eyes of the mulla's younger son, ten-year-old Kurzu, Saleem Barakat portrays the uncanny events in the life of the beleaguered village: a grandfather confines himself to an old cupboard, while the cut fingers of a communist teacher grow in the garden, a eucalyptus tree turns into amber, scarecrows devour the cornfields, the village mosque slides away to the south, and some villagers develop gills under the ears. Then Bikas bears a child, and the time of the sages of darkness has come.*

The following are excerpts from the first and third chapters.

A few starlings alighted on the electric wire hanging across the courtyard of Mulla Binav's home. From above, their eyes lazily searched for hidden food under the quiet snow. It was the morning following the night of Bikas's wedding.

The rooms in the courtyard were still calm. Only the boy Kurzu was out, creeping alongside the wall like a ghost, so as not to frighten the birds away. He set two traps, concealed them, then returned as cautiously as he had set out. He opened the door and entered, and a little while later the curtain was partly pulled back to reveal his eyes darting a cautious look at the movements of his intended black prey on the high wire.

The boy's face vanished, and the mulla's face appeared in turn behind the curtain. Unlike his son, the mulla was not looking at the birds but at the room of Bikas and his bride, Sinam. Above it, there was some light smoke quivering at the opening of the tin chimney of their stove. The mulla smiled, supposing that the couple in the room were awake. It never crossed his mind that Sinam might have forgotten to turn off the stove by closing the little round fuel tank that provided oil to keep the fire burning.

The mulla's face disappeared, and Kurzu returned to his observation post. One starling came down from the wire and alighted on the snow to explore; hopping a little, it approached the two traps, then stopped. Other starlings followed, equally quiet, then they too stopped. Two yellow pieces of bread attracted the attention of the birds' round, fast-moving eyes, and the boy began to breathe heavily, so that the glass was almost covered with a thin vapor, which he rubbed off with his palm. Then, suddenly, there were loud knocks on the outer gate of the courtyard. The starlings were startled; they spread out their wings and returned to their high place. The boy cursed aloud and, obviously angry, hurried to open the gate. Khati, the mulla's sister, entered, and Kurzu's hands moved in quick, jerky gestures.

"They flew away," he shouted. "You frightened them."

"What's the matter with you? What flew away?" Khati shouted back.

"The starlings. They almost fell in the trap. If only ... "

"Curse your starlings! How long have you been awake, you puppy?"

"And you, you cow, don't you sleep?" retorted Kurzu.

At that point, the mulla's voice reached them from inside: "What's happening out there, dung cocks?"

This put an end to the shouting of the boy and the woman, which was about to turn into a quarrel. The boy threatened his aunt in a thick, choked voice, then ran to his two traps and kicked them savagely, mixing mud and snow together. Then he leant back against the wall, ready to sob with rage.

Khati opened the door without waiting for permission and entered. As was usual on winter mornings, the family was sitting round a bowl of warm crushed lentils. The mulla's sister made room for herself between two boys and took a loud sip, using the spoon of one of them. When the boy asked for his spoon back, she told him to get another one for himself, and he got up resentfully.

"How's the bridegroom?" she asked, addressing nobody in particular, the spoon moving quickly up and down between the bowl and her mouth.

The mulla's wife answered Khati by asking, as she looked at the father, "Shouldn't they have breakfast?"

"Give them a bit more time, woman," the father mumbled, from beneath a moustache now wet at the edges with lentil soup.

Then he looked at one of his children and added, "Look out of the window, Ziwan. Perhaps they're up."

The boy got up, went to the window, and lingered there.

"Hey, Ziwan?" muttered the father, as the boy failed to give him the signal he expected.

The boy burst out laughing. "Kurzu's sprinkling oven ash on the snow, all over the courtyard," he said.

"I told you to look at Bikas's room, not at Kurzu," his father reminded him furiously.

"I can't see anyone," said the now crestfallen Ziwan.

The family finished breakfast in silence, and the empty bowl was taken away and a large black kettle brought and put on the stove. It was teatime, and streams of tobacco smoke mingled with the steam of the dark liquid in the cups. The mulla's silver tobacco box passed from his hand to his sister's, then to his wife's. The smoke from the thick cigarettes summed up the inquisitiveness of those sitting there, about what Bikas and Sinam were doing. Suddenly, the father said to his sister with evident impatience, "Please, go and see whether they're all right."

Khati got up quickly, as if anticipating such a command. "I'll see, I'll see," she said, closing one eye to protect it from the smoke of the cigarette, which never dislodged itself from her sternly tightened lips.

In the courtyard she saw Kurzu, who seemed to have accomplished his task of angrily sprinkling black ash everywhere. Even the lonely little olive tree was not spared and had its leaves all covered with ash, while black vengeance was exercised on the submissive white snow!

Khati tried to understand the wisdom behind this mischievous act but could finally see none; it simply seemed the prank of an angry boy, and nothing more. She pressed her lips together and headed for the door of Bikas's room. Gray snow stuck to the edges of her shoes, and the tracks she left behind her had a ludicrous appearance. She knocked fiercely on the door, then placed her hands beneath her armpits to protect them from the cold.

There was a clatter inside, then Sinam opened the door, thrust out her bare head with its two thin braids, and said, "Ha! Ha!"

Khati contemptuously ignored the dull-witted head and called out, "Bikas, aren't you hungry?"

"Ha! Ha!" repeated the silly creature standing at the door.

"Bikas!" cried the mulla's sister, ignoring her and looking nowhere in particular. "Are you still asleep?"

Sinam chuckled stupidly again, and Khati raised her hand toward the silly creature's face but did not touch it. "That stupid chuckle comes from the devil," she said. "May the chickens eat your tongue! Where is Bikas?"

She pushed her aside and entered. The room was empty, but Khati did not appear to be too upset.

"Is he in the toilet, then?" she asked in an ordinary tone of voice.

Then, as though correcting herself and realizing that Sinam would never answer her question, she said, "I'll wait for him. Close the door, jackal."

Sinam obeyed, closed the door, and returned to sit near the stove, where the mulla's sister had preceded her.

The two women looked at one another in very different ways. Khati was wondering what such a silly creature could possibly give a man, and Sinam was absorbed by the face opposite her. The silly creature's expression held no question about anything and no wonder. She was attracted only by movement, which tickled the depths of her soul.

"Ha! Ha! Bikas is a cock," she remarked.

Khati opened her mouth, about to insult her, but instead she said, in a sarcastic, mocking tone, "And what are you, Sinam?"

"Me? Ha! Ha!" the silly creature answered, "My mother called me pantie elastic."

"Pantie elastic," muttered Khati. "That's a good name for you. Are you wearing underpants?" she asked scornfully.

"Yes . . . Ha! Ha!" Sinam answered, about to pull up her dress.

The mulla's sister stopped her with an exasperated motion of her hand: "It must be the first time you have. Your mother finally taught you how to wear them, did she?"

Khati's face took on a sly look. "And what did you do last night, Sinam?" she asked.

"A man has two testicles," Sinam answered without hesitation, "just like a cock. My mother said we'd kill the cock for our guest, Hishmat's son."

Khati stopped her, "I don't want to hear any of your stories," she said.

Sinam continued to tell her story nonetheless, heedless of the commanding tone of the mulla's sister. "I was the one who got hold of the cock. Ha! Ha!"

"May God get hold of you!" Khati commented.

"My mother's going to feed the chickens today," the silly creature continued. "Isn't my mother coming here?"

"Your mother, your grandmother, and your cow as well," Khati answered.

She looked around for any trace of the man who had been in the room, but she could see nothing.

"Where is Bikas," Khati whispered. "Will you please tell me?"

"He went out in the night," the silly creature muttered, giving a chuckle at every word. "He'll be cold. I'll never go out in the night."

Khati frowned. "He went out in the night, did he," she said, "and he hasn't come back?"

"His beard's got long," Sinam answered. "I haven't seen his eyes. Why haven't I seen his eyes?"

"When are you going to say something I can make sense of?" asked the mulla's sister, exasperated. "Where is Bikas?"

The mulla got up and made for the window, where he raised the rough curtain with its pattern of yellow flowers and blew cigarette smoke through his nose as he looked out. "The little swine, I'll put him in the oven!" he threatened, as he saw the ash sprinkled on the snow in the courtyard.

Then he looked toward the door of Bikas's room, "Has Khati died?" he asked angrily.

A few seconds passed and questions welled up from deep inside him. He returned to the stove, removed the hot cover by holding it with the edge of his head kerchief, and threw his cigarette in the fire.

His wife raised her head from the pillow. "Khati still hasn't come," she said. "Can't someone tell us what's happening?"

"I wish we could forget yesterday and what happened yesterday," the mulla answered. "I wish we hadn't woken up today."

"Kurzu-u-u!" he shouted furiously.

Kurzu hurried at first on his way to the house of his grandfather Avdi Sari (Avdi was not really his grandfather, but he called him grandfather out of respect for his father's wife). Then, after he had crossed half the white open space on the north side of the western quarter, his pace slackened. He had to walk in a curved line to enter the alleys, in which the houses stood in neighboring rows next to the open space. Further to the north there were gaps between the houses, which were scattered and surrounded by the fields of the men from Aleppo, all the way up to the barbed wire of the Syrian-Turkish border.

After covering half the distance, he did not seem to hurry as his father had told him to. Dispersed in groups of two in that white velvety space, the starlings occupied part of his thoughts and made him dream of traps. The other part was occupied by his father's words that Bikas had died. When did Bikas die? He had heard the conversation between his aunt, his father, and the silly creature in its entirety. No one mentioned the words "He died"; rather, they said "He went out in the night."

"Why is my father lying?" he wondered to himself.

The only explanation he could find was that his father hated Bikas.

"But what did Bikas do to be hated by his father?" he wondered again.

He dismissed from his mind the sorry destiny of a person whose strange fleeting existence on earth had been beyond belief. He tried to remember his brother's features in the open space of his thought as it related to the snowy open space around him, but he was unsuccessful. Only his strange brother's movements near the stove continued to appear before his eyes: his quietness, his lowered eyes, his rosy hands stretched out to his brothers, his fondling of his little brother and the little brother's fright, his account of catching birds.

He had the feeling of being tickled by a tender strangeness, which seemed to him like the odd desire that induced the starlings sometimes to fall victim to his uncamouflaged traps. He looked at the snow around him, from which he had been distracted for a short while, and he saw the lazy black birds spread out on the ground in larger flocks.

The boy was about to strike his chest, regretting bitterly that he had left his traps behind. Ah! What if he had traps as big as all this open space, some in the snow and others in the air? He would besiege all the wings; the clapping of the metal closing on the birds' necks or legs or beaks would be heard all over; and the birds would fall from above, fluttering in fear, their wings unable to obey them in their attempt to rise again.

A winged fever took hold of the boy. He opened his arms and ran toward the birds, now to the left and now to the right. The woolen scarf with which he protected his head and face slid off and fell on the snow, and the edges of his long, capacious lined coat fluttered like a flag over his robe. His thick plastic shoes shortened his steps in this earthly flight of his. He was coming to the starlings with his whole body as a trap, with his depths in which there were traces of birds' legs and remnants of abandoned birds' nests.

He was struck by wonder whenever a flock flew off as he approached it with his open arms.

"No," he said, his utterance mingling with the vapor of his warm breath, "don't fly away!"

He wanted only to be a companion, not a hunter. All the time he caught birds he tried to tell them that. But they were always afraid of him. He caught them in order to establish a dialogue with them at short range, but their necks became limp in his hands and they died. How much longer would his tender dialogue be so difficult for them? How much longer would they continue to be afraid of him and oblige him to set traps for them?

"I'm Kurzu-u-u-u!" he shouted, prolonging his shout in an attempt to make them calm.

But they continued to fly away.

An hour after that unavailing running, Kurzu fell to his knees from exhaustion. He looked at the sky and saw the slow starlings crossing the field of his total despair.

"Kurzu!" a voice called from some hiding place. "Kurzu!"

The boy listened intently in order to determine the source of the voice. He thought what he heard was the echo of his shout in the cold, white kingdom stretching before his eyes. But the voice repeated his name, at a distance of a few steps only. He was startled and jumped to his feet.

There was a hump of snow being peeled off, slowly, and a creature of some kind rose from it, yet remaining in a kneeling position, as though it had been performing a prostration beneath the snow. The boy took a couple of backward steps so as better to determine the features of the form he was seeing, while fear covered his eyes with a transparent film of gray steam.

Only the eyes and nose of the creature appeared at first, but the mask of snow broke up gradually with the movements of his jaws and lips, as he muttered again, "Kurzu, come here."

The boy approached, staring, then uttered a stifled cry, "Bikas, Bikas!" and knelt down next to his brother.

Bikas raised his flabby hands to his face and brushed off the snow from it. His face was flabby too and blue in the midst of a colorless beard. He smiled, or so the boy imagined.

Kurzu pulled himself together. "What are you doing here?" he whispered.

"Where am I supposed to be?" Bikas answered in a faint voice.

"At home," the boy replied.

"And why should I be at home?" his brother asked.

Kurzu looked in confusion at the white stretch of snow around him and came up with a simple answer: "Aren't you cold?"

Kurzu was cold. His teeth were rattling and he placed his hands beneath his armpits to warm them up. With languishing eyes, Bikas stared fixedly at his brother's face, as though he expected to hear a story the boy was hiding and simply could not put together.

Suddenly Kurzu remembered why he was there. "I was going to Avdi Sari's house," he said, "to tell him you were dead."

Then he smiled like someone who has found the solution to a puzzle. "We'll go back home," he said. "You're not dead."

After a short silence, an urgent question forced its way out: "Why is my father lying, Bikas?"

Bikas patted his brother's knee. "My father isn't lying, Kurzu, and in a little while you'll tell my grandfather Avdi Sari that. Don't forget."

The boy pursed his blue lips. "What shall I tell Avdi?" he asked.

"He's dead," Bikas replied. "Tell him Bikas is dead."

"So you're lying like my father," Kurzu said, his voice slightly angry.

Bikas bent his head, then raised it again. He stared at his brother, smiled, then whispered, "Look."

He opened his wool-lined cloak. It was his father's, which he had worn on his own wedding night. Simultaneously, the boy raised his hands to his face to protect it.

From under Bikas's cloak, stormy flocks of starlings rushed out and bumped against the boy, who coiled himself up in surprise. When the noisy fluttering of wings had died, Kurzu slowly opened his eyes. Bikas was no longer there, and all he could see was a black flock of starlings, flying high in the sky, heading north.

—Translated by Issa Boullata and Christopher Tingley

Muhammad Barrada

See Muhammad Barrada's biography in the short-story section.

Game of Forgetfulness (1993)

This autobiographical novel is written in honor of the author's childhood and of both his benevolent and gracious uncle, Si Tayib, who brought him up, and Tayib's charming first wife who left indelible memories in the child's mind and heart. It is also the story of the city of Fez, its deeply rooted traditions and political struggle under French colonialism. The author depicts actual conversations, which gives the novel its air of realism. Despite this use of the colloquial, which might pose considerable difficulty for the non-Moroccan reader, the novel never loses its endearing touch and its attractive and exciting narrative.

He'd get up early every day, putting on a light *jilaba* in summer and two woolen ones in winter, and he'd move about carefully, so as not to wake the other people in the big house. Then he'd pass by the Moulai Driss Mosque to perform the dawn prayer and recite as much as he could of the Quran, before heading off to his weaving. He was a tailor like his father before him, and his work didn't conform to the common standard—his character spurred him on to tailor as many meters as he could, of his usual high quality. He felt a natural bond with the loom and shuttle, with the *sabra* threads and their colors of red, blue, green, and yellow—intricately woven into the bright-colored cloth that would shimmer over the heads of L'Arabi women, and around their waists; strong tones, imbued with the colors of the trees and flowers that grow on the fertile banks of the Fez valley.

There in the weaving workshop the hands and feet never stopped moving, and the tongues never stopped their melodious hum of chatter and comment and laughter; this was a cell of master-craftsmen and apprentices, caught in a natural race against the hands of the clock. Respected and loved, Tayib (or Si Tayib as they called him) was at the heart of all this. With his tall stature and strong build, he led the workshop in its daily struggle against the other shops. You only built a reputation among the buyers with work that was well done and contained a good variety of designs and shades.

When the call to noon prayer sounded, they'd stop work, and one of the apprentices would be sent to fetch the lunch. Then, after the prayer, they'd gather to eat their meal and carry on with their talk.

The events of the war formed their main topic. They'd discuss its various angles and repercussions, from the common use of dates to sweeten tea, in place of sugar, to their admiration for Hitler and the Germans, and the swastikas the children drew on the alley walls. "The Germans are strong," they'd say. "They'll rid us of the French and their tyranny. They'll give us back our freedom, and we'll be independent at last."

The favorite topic, though, for these men of the weaving workshop, was the spring celebrations and the outings to Anzaha, on the outskirts of the city. There they'd listen to singing and stories from the *Thousand and One Nights,* and eat various tasty treats. It was a cherished tradition, for which preparations started long before the event, with friends invited—a chance to leave the dim workshop with its cramped spaces and rickety walls. The gardens lining the walls and gates of Fez would receive them, and they'd plunge themselves in the greenery, delighting in the songs of the various birds, in the strumming of the lutes, and the moans of the *mawal* singers. There was laughter there, for a soul refreshed after all the weary toil. Tayib was filled with joy when spring came, throwing off all his burdens as he listened to the reader of the *Thousand and One Nights.*

"I'm speechless," he'd say. "God bless Lalla's life . . . How she loved! . . . It's a wonderful thing when women love you like that . . . Lalla Zubaida, my dear friends . . . I'm lost before her beauty . . . "

But, balancing this craving for life and pleasure in Tayib's heart was a love for the songs praising the Prophet and his descendants, whose company he himself sought out. Tayib attended many of the nights when these songs were performed, joining in the chanting, and he never tired of the whirling and ecstatic dance. Stories of the Prophet's life enraptured him, and his deep voice and bald head gave him a striking aura. On the night of his first wedding (to a woman from an Ashraf family[1]), the strains of Andalusian music alternated with the soaring voices of the singers of eulogies. Dressed in a fine white *jilaba,* Tayib was rosy with excitement, drawn irresistibly to the circle of these singers and, against all tradition, raised his voice along with them, singing, "My love for you is eternal." Did he know who he was marrying that night?

She was beautiful; with her milky white skin and coal black hair, and her fleeting smile. She was exquisite softness, an elegant symmetry that seemed from another world. He was happy for the seven days of his wedding, and in the years that followed; then her life was extinguished in a flash.

Tayib's deep voice, along with his strong body and full, trimmed beard, trembled as he wept; man though he was, he wept at the funeral without shame, and no one could comfort him with counsels of patience and consolation. Nor would he ever talk to anyone of the love he had known with his departed wife.

---

1. A family descended from the Prophet.

He wondered, at first, if he or she was the barren one. Then, a year into their marriage, he embraced his nephew and joined him to his family. Hadi became their pampered child; and when Lalla Ghalia went off to Rabat to live with her daughter, Tayib kept Hadi with him. He lived a life of perfect contentment, with his wife (who loved the nephew too), his weaving work, and his evenings at the mosque or with the singers of religious chants.

The war was in its third year now, the angelic wife was gone, and years of misery and anguish seemed to lie ahead. But Tayib, like a tree rooted deep in the soil of this old city, didn't crack, never allowed the wind to tear up the roots that linked him to the world and penetrated to the depths of his being. But then his mother, the grandmother, whispered to him one evening that he should marry again.

And so, once more, a wedding filled the house with lights, though the joy this time was muted. The second wife was from a different kind of family, a modest one: the eyes were blue and bold, the hair light, the skin fair and freckled, the character excitable and impulsive, lacking all softness. But things would still have taken on their old, familiar flavor, had the child, Hadi, not declared war on this new woman come to take the first wife's place and to supplant him. Tayib was torn between this strong new wife of his and Hadi, who answered his need for children and evoked the fragrance of the vanished phantom. His wife would tell him of the hurtful gibes she endured from Hadi's tongue, and how he challenged her orders and mocked her in front of the other women of the house; yet even then Tayib couldn't bring himself to beat him. He'd calm her down and promise to punish Hadi; then, when they were alone together, he'd appease the boy, giving him coins and gifts in exchange for peace with the new wife—a game that ended only when Hadi was sent to Rabat to live with his mother.

Next, Tayib's eldest nephew, who'd been well into his studies at Qarawiyin University, used the war conditions to take up trading, starting off by smuggling linen and other cloth from Casablanca to Fez. His aim was to regain with all speed the funds his father had lost in the Senegal trade. This nephew asked Si Tayib, along with Hadi, to travel with him and carry pieces of linen strapped to their bodies, and other children from the family joined in as well. The nephew would wrap the linen and other cloth around the children, then lay them down to sleep on the suitcases in the fourth-class compartments. Everyone was doing the same on those night trips, and the passengers conspired to stop the inspector finding the smuggled items. The trips were profitable and enjoyable too, and they helped the eldest nephew to launch himself in due course into the world of commerce and money. Soon he was to leave the old city for suburbs gleaming with new-won wealth, while the others in the house sighed with longing pride. "God granted him success," they'd say, "and he built a villa on the Imouazar road."

As for Tayib, when the war was over, he stayed on in his weaving workshop, in the old house, in the city's dim dusty alleys that stretched like veins secretly and constantly renewed. Slowly time ate away at his frame, but still he worked, and went to the mosque and out to play cards, and looked forward to visits from Hadi, who'd made a busy new life for himself in Rabat and abroad.

His sharp edges were rubbed away, and in his depths a boundless kindness settled, a dignity flowing in his very blood, as though he'd never been assailed by whims or tempted by desires. He became like a very part of the house, the focal point for all who lived there. He knew now he was barren, yet his love for his second wife, through intimacy and habit, grew strong enough to weather any storm.

In that house he was like a place of shade, living joys and woes with a heart wide open, clinging to the transcendent and everlasting, spurning the earthly and ephemeral.

ILLUMINATION

We loved him first because of his voice, whose resonance echoed in our souls. Si Tayib always spoke loudly; we'd hear him in our rooms, his laughter coming to us along with his humorous comments. The days passed, and as our bonds with him and his sister Lalla Ghalia strengthened, we began to think of him as an older brother. He'd sit with us sometimes, teasing us but always showing us respect. A model of honorable courtesy, he'd ask how things were with us and about our families; he'd advise and guide. Our husbands loved him too, and he'd invite them and receive them generously. He, along with Lalla Ghalia before she left, became the center of that house. We shared the happiness of his first marriage and suffered with him at the loss of his tender, kind-hearted wife. He was always there, attentive and friendly to everyone in the house.

After his second marriage he mixed a little less with the others; but the people of the house soon involved his new wife in their daily rituals and chores. Kindness smoothed every wrinkle away.

When Lalla Ghalia went off to Rabat, she took her eldest son, Taya'a, leaving Hadi there with Si Tayib. We'd never seen any love like the one he bore that slight boy who moved and talked with such violent energy. The first wife spoiled and worshipped him too, and after her death Hadi declared war on his uncle's new wife.

Almost daily there'd be the same scene. At eleven Hadi would come home from school, and his uncle's new wife would give him a glass of milk and a piece of *ghraiba*. Then, when he rudely asked for more, she'd refuse to give it him unless he kissed her, and he'd race toward the door.

"Don't touch me, cat eyes!" he'd shout.

"Curse you!" she'd answer. "Just you wait! By God, I'll tear you apart if I catch you! Don't you dare come near me!"

"You've got cat's eyes!" he'd yell. "Like foreigners have!"

Then the poor woman would turn to us, and say, "You saw how this little devil behaved. When his uncle comes home, tell him about the foul way his nephew talks to me. He'll say I've ill-treated him otherwise!"

Nothing could make Tayib angry except things to do with Hadi. He loved the boy, and loved his sister too on his account, and couldn't bear to live without him. We were the ones who persuaded Lalla Ghalia to take back her son, to stop Tayib's life becoming utter hell. This, though, was one more addition to Tayib's anguish from the time of his first wife's death.

Our husbands loved him, and they respected his character and the way he treated his neighbors. They also—though they only mentioned this in secret—admired his adventurous outlook and love of life. This came, they'd say sometimes, from his trips to Casablanca during the war and the money he made to help his sister 'Aisha's son, and from his change of profession when, for a while, he became a cloth merchant in a store his nephew built for him in the New Fez neighborhood. He lived merrily then, regaling himself with drinks and enjoying nights filled with folk and Andalusian songs. He was a stallion of a man who talked in the most pleasing way, but, though we were attracted to him, he never showed us more than brotherly feelings. We didn't get upset, or hold it against him, when he stole the odd moment of pleasure away from his thin, fair wife who spoke with the tongue of a scorpion. They say he fell in love with a broad-hipped Jewish woman with golden brown eyes and skin, one of his customers at the store. He started spending his profits on her, then dipped into his capital.

After he'd passed fifty, he started spending more time in the house. He went back to his old job and started going to the mosque and attending the circles of religious study and eulogies, and he'd invite friends, too, to play cards with him. He hated being beaten at *tris*, and he'd bellow with fury if his partner made a mistake. He was happiest when Lalla Ghalia and her son Hadi visited from Rabat; every visit would be a cause for celebration, one that involved everyone in the house. Si Tayib's old gaiety and love of talk would return as he quizzed the visitors about every kind of thing, teasing Hadi with questions about the far-off country where he was studying.

"Have you chosen a wife yet?" he'd ask. "When are we going to celebrate your wedding?"

At these times Si Tayib seemed like a central column holding up that house— and we felt this when, once a year, he went away. He and his wife would go and visit his sister and other relatives in Rabat, and we'd keep telling each other, loudly, how we longed to have them back:

"By God," we'd say, "Si Tayib and his wife have left an emptiness in our hearts. How we miss them! They've stayed away too long."

He fell ill at times, but his strong build helped him recover quickly enough. He wasn't a greedy eater, yet he had a strange affection for certain dishes he insisted on for his dinner. He was always ready to spend money on food, and he disliked eating alone, constantly inviting someone to join him and his wife. When anyone fell ill in the big house, he treated them kindly, spoiling them even. He became the salt of our daily life. We never felt our poverty or deprivation when he was there.

When television came in, he was quick to buy a set and invited us to watch films and other programs. We were happy to be around Si Tayib, with our husbands, and laugh with him. We found amusement, even as life chugged along under the heavy weight it bore. And he stood erect and firm, even after he'd passed seventy.

Are you trying to remind us he's dead? We can't speak of his death. We can still hear his voice resounding, "You upstairs, come on down. The evening programs are just starting."

We grew used to Si Tayib's generosity, which was never failing.

A DIMNESS

Shall I start by describing your death? Or was that your true beginning?

I'd always found you a beautiful source of strength, and I'd yearned for you within the overwhelming, terrifying whirl of life. When I saw you, images of the past surged up in my mind. The weddings, and our joys at outings, and the celebrations of the community in the big house, and the generous delight you took in giving to others.

I arrived late that day. They'd just finished washing your body and placed you in a white shroud. Around you were four *faqih*s reciting the Quran:

> He created death and life to determine who among you are the gooddoers and He is most Exalted, most Forgiving. He created seven heavens successively, and you shall not see discrepancies in the creation of the Merciful One. Turn your gaze to God's creation, do you see any faults? Turn your gaze again, and your sight will return disgraced and weary.

I wouldn't see again, not even one last time, the smile that was your special language to me. And I wouldn't see your full, round face, glowing with such energy and strength. The body had failed, but the face remained raised and proud. They began sprinkling perfume on your shroud, knotting the ends where they met at your feet. My lips began to move with those of the reciters.

I could barely hear the sobs of the mourners in the spacious courtyard. They all loved you. You knew that, and it was confirmed when you were bed-ridden. I tried in vain to fathom what it meant, as I saw you stretched out before me in your coffin, quite dead and soon to leave us. Five years ago you were safe beside me, even as your sobs convulsed you like a snake-bitten child at the sight of Lalla Ghalia's body. Should I stretch out my hand and unveil your radiant face from under the thick white linen? Who knows, your eyes might have opened and your lips quivered in a smile.

They wouldn't let me do it, I knew that. But it would have been in keeping with the reckless spirit that filled me, as I saw you dim and lifeless, hidden within that white shroud. Voices were rising now. There was the rattle of empty buckets someone had stumbled over, the washing board set against a wall, the voice of the washer telling everyone to leave; and we stumbled awkwardly out, with tears in our eyes. There were condolences exchanged, and children tugging at the adults' legs, gazing desolately at it all. There were many visitors, all saying repeatedly, "Our grief is one." Your funeral was like a wedding. The chanters and singers of eulogies, who thought of you as one of themselves, came to sing a funeral song full of eloquence and poetry, addressed especially to you. We stood there around your shrouded body, in the middle of the house beside the fountain that was silenced now. They recited from the Quran, then chanted eulogies, the singer straining with his lovely voice, as though pleading with you. A rapture filled my heart, shattering those reckless feelings I'd harbored. I imagined you, too, enraptured in your shroud; you loved those words and the lofty worlds they wove in your imagination. We listened and focused on the sounds, forgetting you were departed forever.

Rain fell gently on the heads of the men gathering round to bear you. And rain fell gently on the coffin that held you. Gracious and kind-hearted Tayib, did you hear us? Did you hear the voices whose anguish and weeping were forgotten now?

When we bent to lift your coffin to take you to the mosque, then on to the cemetery, the women's wailing rose to a sharp and painful pitch; but the voices of your friends rose, too, in joyous farewell:

Praised be the Lord of Dominion, Lord of the Realm
  Praised be the Lord of Glory, Lord of Omnipotence
  Praised be the Living Who never dies
  Extolled and All-Holy, Lord of angels and souls

The voices echoed within the walls of the cramped alleys, and passers-by left the way clear. The happy procession, as those who knew you proclaimed, was leading you to heaven like a bridegroom.

It was thirty years now since I'd left you and the big house; and I'd been chock-full of boldness and daring and love of adventure. You never slapped down my childish desires, no matter how rash they were. With that great love, I felt I could do anything. Then a new, daunting world confronted me, cutting the cord that bound me to the world of childhood and dreams. Yet, when I returned to you, those thirty years of distance would melt away; the visions and fantasies would vanish, and I'd become a child once more, crouching on the earth of childish folly. My spirit rose as memories of that rich past welled up in it. The door was always open, the faces of the women and children beaming with contentment and good cheer, and there you were in the middle of the room, with your long *jilaba* and fez, gazing at the courtyard or chatting with your wife or one of the neighbors. You'd embrace me and the knots balled up in my chest would untie. My doubts would vanish, along with my sense of fear. As you talked on, with the simple eloquence and humor that came from your lips, I'd feel no need for long speeches. How can language be separated from its speaker? How could I resist the magic springing from the depths of memory, from those walls and faces?

"Oh yes," you'd said, "I still see them. They came and had dinner with us a couple of days back. Lalla Mena isn't too well. She's worried about her daughters too, and that doesn't help. Oh yes, and 'Abdelaziz has that little shop of his. Times are difficult now. Everything's dear and no one's happy. They even put the price of sugar up and told us point blank it wouldn't be coming back down. And this is the blessed independence we waited and waited for! You've studied. You understand these things. Tell me, what has this independence brought us?"

You turned toward me, crinkling your eyes and trying not to laugh, taking a huge delight in teasing me. My voice dried up and my words lost their meaning. I preferred to listen to you, to defer, still, to the authority in your words.

"Si Sallam was asking about you. Do you remember him? He's so poor now he doesn't have two coins to rub together. The poor fellow always asks me: 'How's the *ustaz*?' We should go and visit him. Even he can't make a go of anything. Everyone's having it hard. Nothing's the way it should be any more—people just cheat openly. The milk's half water, and you can walk till your throat's parched and you won't find any fresh butter. As for the people who write in the newspapers and preach in the mosques, they must have lost hope of anyone ever listening. Oh David, who would you sing your psalms to now?"

With the eyes of a mesmerized child, I see you knock on the outer gate, calling us to unlock quickly. Inside the house everyone was crammed on the ground floor, for fear of stray bullets from the roof, where the Senegalese soldiers were stationed to watch the rebellious city. The war was coming to a close, and the nationalists' hot fervor was spilling out in the alleys and streets, flowing in people's veins. You were just back from the Qarawiyin Mosque, where you and the others had been under siege since the morning, chanting the *Latif* supplication as a protest against the despotic measures and detentions. We'd been fearful and worried about you, and the families above had come down when a bullet ricocheted over their heads, piercing one of the doors. The house echoed with cries of alarm, tempered only by women and men chanting the *Latif*. You rushed in and shut the door behind you, your face pale. The people in the house thronged around you.

"Well," you cried, "they've killed the stool pigeon. They've killed that police informer, Ismail. They cut his throat from ear to ear, the swine! It was shameless the way he sneaked in here, to spy things out for his French masters!"

We stared at you as the words streamed from your mouth. We followed what you were saying, trying to imagine the dreadful scene. I wished you'd taken me with you, so I could tell the exciting news to the other children. You'd often remind me of this, which you yourself called "the Nationalists' cry of forty-four." You formed the words with such unforced eloquence that the events became secondary. And now I won't hear you telling your stories any more, giving color to people and things. You'd speak; and with your words you'd create a magical, surging ocean that flowed inside my very skin. And as I journeyed further from you and saw new people and new worlds, those marvelous words of yours stayed lodged in my memory: words eclipsing the things they described.

—*Translated by Khalid Mutawa' and Christopher Tingley*

Mohamed Choukri [Muhammad Shukri] (b. 1935)

Muhammad Shukri was born in the al-Rif area of Morocco but has lived in Tangiers for many years as an integral part of this cosmopolitan city's literary façade where he also met and befriended some of the European and other Western writers who sought peace and calm in the city's creative atmosphere. Born to a poor family, he has never acquired wealth, but he enjoys the admiration and affection of many writers and readers around the world. His three most famous writings are the novelistic autobiographical accounts of his life, *For Bread Alone* (1973); *A Time for Errors* (1992; published in Beirut under the title *Scoundrels;* translated into English by Ed Emery and published in 1996 under the title *Streetwise);* and *Faces* (2000). The dissemination of the first two of these creative books made Shukri famous in many literary circles of the world. The trilogy is characterized by candor, sometimes an extreme candor that can arrive at a crude depiction of experience. However, by holding on to an instinctive thread of sympathy and affection, Shukri escapes the edge of the ribald and pornographic, which explains his popularity.

A TIME FOR ERRORS (1992)

Like its predecessor, For Bread Alone, *this novel operates within a semi-fictionalized world inhabited by a cast of characters living on the fringes of society, struggling to eke out the barest of existences. A modern picaresque novel, it revolves around the episodic adventures of the writer/narrator as he takes his first tenuous steps into maturity, literacy, independence, and self-esteem. Choukri's honest and spontaneous narrative produces a rich mixture of fantasy and reality, death and life, past and present, despair and hope. Where the voice in* Bread *is young, impressionable, innocent, and victimized, that of* Errors *is mature, tested, wary, and wiser. In the first of the following chapters, Mohamed returns to his family home during a summer vacation and is haunted by the memories of a battered childhood. Caught in the middle of a vicious father and a nurturing but helpless mother, Mohamed struggles to make sense of his world, narrating in alternating stark and poetic images the rapid changes of his physical environment and his evolving intellect and consciousness. In the second, he writes of his first forays into the artistic and literary world as he grapples with the continuous harsh realities of his and his family's existence.*

When I gained admission to the Teachers' College, I felt reborn. I really believed I'd built an impregnable wall between myself and society's contempt, ignorance, and misery. And how foolish I was! As it turned out joy was soon overtaken by misfortune: my father only gauged my success from what I'd give him out of my monthly check, and actually started charging me for my food, and taking rent for living in that rat-infested shack, even before I got my hands on the first installment of my training grant.

My father worshipped money more than he worshipped Almighty God, but he never lifted a finger to earn it, expecting other people to earn it for him instead. All my old hidden hatred of him seemed to resurface then, and all the animosities between us came back—though why he was so keen to settle scores with me I have no idea. He watched all my comings and goings. I always fancied his face was like a criminal's, the face of someone who'd just been released from prison after a sentence with hard labor and corporal punishment. How long, I wondered, did I have to endure the hatred I felt for him?

The 1960 summer vacation had arrived, and it was quite some time now since I'd spent any time with old friends from Tetouan. In fact some of them had become just names, and I wondered whether we'd recognize one another when we met. The only one left was Tafarsiti, whose business was booming—he had a near monopoly of ice stands and ice carts, with three stores besides, and I usually had to search him out if I wanted to meet him. And to think we were fed at the breast of the same mother of misery! Perhaps he wanted to cut himself off from his old self. Sunk in his depraved lifestyle, he mingled with the other merchants and hobnobbed with influential friends bragging about their newly acquired positions.

We were still celebrating independence, and once he took me to the Villa Rosa brothel on the road to Martel. I could never have imagined such scenes of decadent extravagance. There were bottles of champagne flowing at the feet of Spanish whores, mixed with screams of ecstasy and chants of "Long live your mother, Mohamed!" That night I drank alone, at his expense, till daybreak, not even noticing that he'd disappeared. Then I walked back to town. Not wanting to spoil what was left of the previous night's high, I told myself it wasn't his fault or mine, but the fault of the drink.

I was still drunk. Fishing for a cigarette in my pocket, I found some crumpled notes, several hundred pesetas. He must have thrust them in my pocket when I wasn't looking, or maybe he gave them to me and I forgot. There was just a black hole in my memory.

I sat down in one of the cafés in Fedan to smoke some *keif* with the other customers. I didn't have to pay. Then I played cards for a while, but not for money. My mother usually gave me money for tea and cigarettes, but I didn't always have to spend it. Sometimes I was treated by a customer who liked my conversation.

Often I'd go to the British Library and read till closing time, and once I offered my services as a tourist guide to a middle-aged British couple. I knew just enough English to give them a tour, and they were delighted with my company.

I now have a map of the old city quarter firmly embedded in my memory. They took pictures of me with each of them and gave me a hundred pesetas, which kept me going for several days.

≈

"He doesn't know any more than I do. He's just a loafer. How did he get into college? They must have made a mistake admitting him."

That was how my father talked about me to the neighbors, to his comrades who'd been wounded on the Fedan Plains in the Spanish Civil War and to unemployed people all over the place. There's no end to his vindictive malice toward me; it's going to follow me wherever I go, even years after he's finally dead. If my mother dared protest, he'd strike her and curse her, the way he'd always done to all of us.

Some of the people he spoke to were inclined to accept what he said. They had sons of their own who wallowed in depravity, and why shouldn't I be down in the mud like the rest of them, the way we all are? But of course there were exceptions. One day an elderly man stopped me on the street.

"Aren't you Haddu Alal Choukri's son?" he said.

"That's right," I said.

"Is it true you're studying to be a teacher?"

"Yes."

"God bless you! Lots of people wish they had a son like you. And yet your father says you're an idiot and makes fun of you. He's the one who's a fool."

"I know he is. He was born to hate everyone. He doesn't even love himself."

"God protect us!"

≈

I still look fondly back on my childhood games in the alleys and quarters and suburbs. Those were days of mischief and scrapping: one neighborhood gang attacking another; stealing fruit from people's gardens; stripping naked by the river bank and having masturbation contests, to see who'd come first, who'd come second, and so on. I visited the 'Ayn Khabbaz quarter. Our old house was near the plant at Benyenas. We used to pelt one another with sticks and stones. We'd celebrate the spring rains, and the sun coming out, and the sparrows. We'd dance and shout. An invisible rooster crowed nearby. There was a rainbow in the sky. We'd mount donkeys and leap onto the backs of moving trucks. What was left of a burnt fence was still partly standing, partly falling down, on what remained of its wooden stakes. A fig tree, still in green leaf, stood tall, but climbing weeds had gathered around it and robbed it of some of its beauty. Beauty recalled is always more beautiful. Wonder doesn't grow any less down the generations.

I wrote several chapters of this autobiography in 1990. Last summer I was visited in Tangier by a Japanese friend, Notahara, together with his wife, Shuko. He's a Middle Eastern scholar, and he was translating my novel, *For Bread Alone*, into Japanese. After doing thirty pages he stopped.

"It occurred to me," he said, "that if I could actually see some of the places where the events in the book took place, it would make things clearer and more accurate."

We started off in Tetouan, meaning to end the trip back in Tangier. The first place we visited was the reservoir, which he photographed many times from different angles. When he'd finished, he smiled.

"In your book," he said, "you described the reservoir and the things around it as being really beautiful. And it isn't true at all. What is there here that's so beautiful?"

I replied with equal politeness.

"That's what art's all about," I said. "Even the uglier sides of life we embellish. This reservoir seemed beautiful to me, through my child's eyes, so it's natural I should look back in the same way, even though it turns out to be just a muddy pool. I've been away for a long time, you know."

The noonday sun beat down, and I stood there by the edge of the reservoir thinking of the house where we'd lived in the early forties—that splendid house of misery and daily battles with my parents. It glistened in the sunlight now, with its white paint and shining new door. When we moved into it, the paint was peeling, the color was faded, and it was barely standing. In fact it had to be patched up several times and reinforced with assorted boards that were older than the house. An elderly woman came out, her breasts huge and sagging, but with a beaming smile on her countrywoman's face. Behind her appeared a young woman with two small barefoot children around her.

"We used to live here," I said.

"Whose son are you?" she asked.

"Maymouna's."

"We moved in after you. I know your mother. I haven't seen her in ages. Where do you live now?"

"In Sidi Talha. Barrio San Antonio."

"How is the poor dear?"

"She's fine."

"I'll go and see her soon, God willing. Give her my greetings."

"I'll do that."

I had nothing in my pocket to give the two small children or the woman. Making my excuses, I thanked her and left, then walked along the palm-lined road, calling back memories, sad and happy, of that particular neighborhood. The Pilar Institute was still there. I'd never known what to do with my spare time, when school was over. In Tangier I would never have known that kind of bore-dom; I could squeeze some pleasure from the most depressing, impoverished days. Being alone there meant a kind of freedom, like the taste of wild berries. Here, though, solitude was something forced on me, and it had the bitter taste of colocynth. I walked round the district that had the Pergola Cabaret, the Tango, Carlos Gardel, Consha Bakir, the Flamenco, Las Cublos (which were folk songs), and the gipsy dancing.

I used to stand in front of an Italian girl's house, rummaging through the garbage to find lipstick-stained cigarette butts, which I'd get an erotic thrill from smoking. One day she took me by surprise while I was picking them out and never threw them there again.

I passed by Lovers' Park, and couldn't even buy myself a glass of tea at the Café Magara. Al-Hadi Jouaini was singing "Evening Under the Jasmine Tree." My mother's business slackened off toward the middle of the month and some-times she had nothing to give me. A scented breeze lulled the mind as the novice lovers paraded proudly through the lush greenery. There were only a few colored fish left in the pond; the drunks who came round at night fished most of them out, so it was said, then fried them and ate them. All the ducks had disappeared from the park too. There was a monkey in a cage that the chil-dren used to tease, and a photographer who went gaily around offering to take snapshots of the lovers.

Moroccan passion, dazzled by its own bold freedom, had begun to emerge from its hiding places, from behind the windows out onto the streets, into the movie houses, under the trees, decked out in European fashions and neckties. There were clashing colors. Women stumbled on their high heels. There was naïve coquettishness and flirtation. The age of passion had still to mature. I'd gone regularly, more than once a day, to Trancats, and Upper Souk, and Guersa El Kebira, and Mellah, the Jewish Quarter. All that bustle, the craftsmanship and the noise of vendors and artisans, soothed away the tension my idleness and boredom gave rise to. The thought of going back there one day, to work in one of those trades, filled me with terror. It was enough that I had to work there as a young apprentice.

My brothers and sisters and I slept in one room and my parents in another. We didn't talk, and I'd stay out till the middle of the night to avoid meeting my father. If he did happen to hear me coming in, he'd launch into a volley of curses mostly directed at me. My mother was usually asleep. I never heard any conversation between them, but he'd talk at her as though she was listening. She may have been awake, of course. Who knows? Whenever he was tired, he'd make insulting remarks about her and the pigs she'd borne him, then fall asleep mut-tering. We were set, the two of us, on our separate tracks: he didn't accept me as his son, I didn't accept him as my father. He cursed us every day. He wished, he said, we'd never come into the world, and he was forever going on about the misfortune we'd brought him and how pleasant life would be without us. He never showed affection for man or beast unless there was something in it for him.

September came, and I was longing for the wretched summer to end, to fall into the bosom of autumn, then into winter, where there's warmth in the abyss of dreams of beauty recalled. At the end of days like this I hardly ever went back, hungry and exhausted, to that hut of curses and daily misfortune. My brother 'Abdelaziz sold nuts and candy to the neighborhood children, from a crate he took to be some kind of grocer's shop. He was born with a merchant's mentality, and he'd make a point of counting his few coins in front of us, over and over again, beaming with delight over what he'd made and challenging our two sisters and me to do as well as he had. When he got the chance, he'd even challenge our unemployed father.

I found Habiba, a quiet, thoughtful sort of person, talking to my mother and my sister Arhimu, while my mother held my little sister Malika asleep on her lap and stroked her hair. Their warm relations sprang naturally from my mother's friendship with Habiba's mother who, like mine, had suffered torments from a violent and lewd husband. She, though, had dared to stand up to him, and he'd retaliated by marrying Habiba, their only daughter, to a middle-aged sheep merchant who happened to be a friend of his—she was barely seventeen at the time. He'd divorced her after a year and a few months, because she hadn't borne him a child, and thereafter, with no one to protect her, her father and aunt had treated her shamefully.

She'd finally been taken to a mental hospital because she kept smashing things in the house and because she'd rip her clothes and anyone else's she could lay her hands on. At the hospital she'd dance around in a screaming frenzy till she fainted or was given sedation. Then, after a few months, she was released, apparently cured and able to live a normal life.

One summer she made friends with a young man who was holidaying with his family at Martil Beach, and soon afterward he married her in Tetouan and took her to live with him in Rabat, where he worked in a car repair shop. They were blessed with four children, but he began to treat her very severely, to the point of beating her till she bled, whereupon she fled, abandoning both him and the children. Then, when he divorced her, she went off to Ceuta, and madness took hold of her once more.

There, in Ceuta, she began her frenzied dancing all over again, walking drunk through the popular quarters and behaving immorally, flirting shamelessly with the men and taunting the women. People called her the beautiful idiot. Having nowhere to live, she'd spend the night wherever a beggar was able to lodge her in one of the abandoned shacks in the Bernissi.

Sometimes Habiba would make garlands of flowers and set them on her head and drag four tin cans behind her tied to a rope, with a loud, rattling noise. She'd tell people the cans were the four children she'd left behind with her violent husband. In her few quiet moments, when she seemed at peace, she'd accept clothes and food from people who knew her and even from strangers.

In the end her madness reached such a pitch of violence that they took her once more to a mental hospital in Tetouan, to try and stop the frenzied dancing through medication. Again she was released after treatment, to resume a normal life, this time so sedated she seemed oblivious to everything. She put her life in order, then bought some bright new clothes, which she'd show off like a child through the streets of the city.

Habiba's father owned several shops and apartment buildings, and in one of these she took the ground floor, immediately below an aunt who was widowed and had no children. Her father allocated her so much money per month, just barely enough to live on, waiting to see what would happen to these two unfortunate women.

After years spent on the street, Habiba married for the third time but died of cholera in the seventh month of the marriage, while her husband was waiting for the birth of their first child.

—

I enjoyed her company when she came to see my mother and talk of her worries about her husband and children in Rabat, and it was during one of these visits, while my sister Arhimu was out visiting her hunchback friend, Fatima, a neighbor of ours, and my mother was in the kitchen in the courtyard, and my sister Malika was asleep, that Habiba invited me to come and have dinner with her.

She lived in the Malaga district. Pressing a thousand-franc note into my hand, she said, "Take this and buy something to drink. I'll be leaving soon. Wait for me in front of the movie house."

My mother was busy cooking, and in any case she never bothered whether I was at home or not. Sometimes I slept at home and sometimes I didn't—it didn't matter either way. That's the way things were between us.

"I'm going out," I said. She was putting something in the oven.

She nodded but didn't say anything. She didn't usually gaze at people. She had a look in her eye that was vague and sad at the same time. She always treated me with consideration, more than she did my brothers and sisters, perhaps because I was her oldest, or perhaps because I'd managed by some miracle to avoid being hungry, or because I'd been born in the village and could talk to her in the village language. Or maybe it was because I lived a long way away. My brothers and sisters were all born in Tangier or Tetouan and couldn't speak the village dialect, though they could understand it to some extent. Actually, they weren't interested in learning it, answering anything she said in *derja*, the colloquial language of the city. They do their best to hide their village roots, because they think country areas are all backward. I've met a lot of people, young and old, who think like that.

Even now I've no idea how many of us children there were. I may have had a brother or sister who was born and died while I was away in Tangier, so that I never knew about it. I never asked her, right up to her death on June 8, 1984.

I drank two glasses of white wine in a Spanish wine bar in the Barrio de Malaga, then bought a bottle of the stuff and left. Habiba had described her building to me, and inside the apartment was simple and clean, reminding me of Fatima's home in Larache. It was a woman's studio, used as a bedroom and living room combined. Her things were neatly arranged and the furniture was nicely polished, seeming somehow part of her.

Hanging on the wall was a picture of her as a little girl with her father in Bab El Tout, and another of her in a traditional wedding dress, and another, fairly large-framed one of her mother. Above the armoire rested two dolls, and there was a ticking clock plus a cuckoo clock on the wall. She had a small night table with a lamp on it, and another table, marble-topped, with a mirror and a vial of makeup. There was also a nicely carved vase with red roses surrounded by white blossoms.

We drank wine and had a meal of fish stew. Then, after dinner, we smoked and talked over our worries, agreeing, after prolonged discussion, that people only truly come to know themselves and other people when disaster's struck.

When she visited our house, she always wore her hair in braids, but now she let it down, and this made her more beautiful. Her movements were subtle and refined, her voice soft and gentle. She spoke slowly and happily and glanced in a drowsy, sometimes distrait way. I told her of my studies in Larache and about my life in Tangier, and I was delighted when she asked me to spend the night there, because it meant I wouldn't have to listen to the pointless curses my father hurled at me every night in that wretched shack.

She insisted I should take the bed while she slept on the sofa, but I wouldn't hear of it. I must sleep on the sofa, I insisted, and I lay there fully dressed. It was silent and pitch dark. I thought over all my past wishes and desires. This evening might not have been the best I'd ever spent, but it was certainly one of them. I tossed and turned continually, a sure sign of my usual insomnia. Desire was beginning to possess me—it was more than two months since I'd touched a thigh or a breast, since my head had spun with any real, gratifying pleasure. But masturbation does have its own kind of pleasure, and its advantages too. There's more freedom, and it doesn't bring the lingering anguish of long-term relationships, to say nothing of the fear of social diseases. Actions are judged by their intentions. Each to his own.

Had she invited me just out of charity, or for the company our common misery seeks, or in the prospect of some relationship, now or in the future? Perhaps the invitation had sprung from some genuine desire. I'd no idea what lurked behind her strange madness, and I didn't want to be the spark that made her frenzied dancing flare up all over again. But the desire to release a part of myself into her aroused me and drove me to her.

How often in Tangier I'd wake up in a hotel, or in some friend's house, with no idea who it was lying next to me, or with no memory how someone had left, unseen, in the middle of the night, while I slept on only to recall next day that I'd been having sex with someone. It was drinking, maybe, and a chance night meeting that would have brought us together.

But Habiba wasn't a one-night stand, and we weren't drunk. I was resolved, if she resisted, to manipulate her kindly feelings toward me. Why couldn't I have been content with a night of warm companionship and serene silence? Just as reckless passion destroys every beautiful thing, so I rose, crept to her bed fully clothed and crawled next to her. She was curled up asleep, her hair hanging over her face. Her body went limp, then stretched and became taut. Then she curled up again and pleaded, in a drowsy, dreamlike whisper, "Let me sleep."

"I love you."

"Don't try and take me in with your night lies."

How stupid I was. She was right, of course. I was just acting out a comedy of my own. I went on kissing her and touching her body, testing her resolve, but she resisted firmly without doing anything dramatic. She was simply sure of herself. Suddenly my foot slipped and I felt her body quiver, then stiffen. A warm trickle wet my pants. Was she pissing, while awake? Did she have a pissing madness the way she had a dancing madness? Once, in a brothel in Tangier, I slept with a woman who worked in a public toilet, and she'd never pissed on me. But Habiba did!

I slipped away before I stirred up some other kind of madness in her, then took my pants off and lay face down on the bed. Habiba was crying. Maybe she'd wet herself because of my insulting behavior, or maybe she was just crying to console herself and calm herself down.

I wasn't prepared to act a part in her play. Some women are only calm and amenable when they're crying, but I didn't have the patience for a scene of that kind. What had made her wet herself? Was it fear or some overwhelming nervous compulsion? Whatever the reason, Habiba wasn't either jelly or mildew. Nor was she like some overripe melon tossed out in the burning sun, as my misogynist friend Yusuf would say, to rot in a mental hospital.

I'd always believed human fruit must be plucked in time, or it would rot. But I was wrong. The time of harvest hadn't come yet. . . .

When classes began at the Teachers' College, my mother bought me a jacket, two shirts, and a pair of pants. When I told her I'd stayed with Habiba, she merely replied that I knew what was best for myself.

The demon of literature began to possess me, and I grew more interested in literary works than I was in books on pedagogy and the psychology of education.

I was particularly taken by texts in Arabic, in which my professor was expert. He'd analyze the passages, then parse them all out on the board.

My professor of literature was immoral and a true believer at one and the same time; he had this world in his left hand and the hereafter in his right. Every Friday he'd lead the prayers and deliver the sermon at a small mosque, while at night he'd be raising hell in El Rincon or Ceuta. I often traveled with him in his old car, in which he had a trap set beneath the back seat—he'd got it firmly into his head that there was a mouse living in his car, so smart it could eat the bait without getting caught in the trap. Or so he said anyway!

My professor of education and psychology caught me reading *Les Misérables* and ordered me out of the class. This was a classroom, he yelled, not a library. I started hanging out at the Café Continental, which was quite comfortable with a mostly very chic clientele who looked as if they'd all been born with silver spoons in their mouths. The forty-nine thousand francs I received as a grant was a lot of money in 1960. I gave part of it to my mother and kept the rest.

I divided my time between reading Arabic and Spanish and carousing in bars—the Ribertito Bar, with its bulls' heads adorning the walls, being the most cheerful spot. I enjoyed, too, the songs on the gramophone at the Continental, and there were three songs I never tired of hearing: the "Subhiyat" of Nat King Cole, the "Tempo" of Lucho Gatica, and "Besame Mucho" by Antonio Machin. There was one well-dressed young man there surrounded by a flock of admirers, and I asked the fellow sitting next to me who he was.

"Don't you know him?" he answered. "That's the writer Mohamed Sabbagh."

"What does he write?" I asked.

"Prose poetry."

I bought his books: *Wounded Agony*, *Cataract of Lions*, *The Tree of Fire*, *The Moon and I*. The last two have been translated into Spanish. They're short books, and I read them right through in two days. Did people show such respect to people who wrote books like that? Surely, I thought, I could do as well, if not better. Being a writer, it seemed, was a mark of distinction. It had never occurred to me that writers might appear in public places and talk to people, as Mohamed Sabbagh was doing in that café. I thought writers kept out of sight when they weren't actually dead.

I wrote something, over three pages, entitling these spontaneous scribblings *The Garden of Shame*. I started following Sabbagh everywhere. Then, one day, I saw him sitting alone, drinking his expresso coffee, and I nervously approached him.

"Mr Mohamed Sabbagh?"

"That's right."

"I'm a great admirer of your books. I'd like to be a writer myself. I'd be very grateful if you could cast an eye over these few pages and tell me what you think. They're the first I've ever written."

He took the sheets graciously and put them in his pocket, then I said my good-byes and quickly left the café to save us both any embarrassment. The café's nearly empty at noon, and he usually had his coffee there before going back to work at the public library. Next day he gave me back what I'd written.

"Your language isn't bad," he told me. "Keep on writing and read a lot too."

We drank black coffee together, and I told him bits and pieces about my life in Tangier, and my studies at Larache, and my training at the Teachers' College. He aroused my interest in Arabic and Spanish poetry: Gustavo Adolfo Becquer, Antonio and Manuel Machado, Alexandrey Vicentes (with whom he corresponded), Pablo Neruda, Cesar Vallejo, Gabriela Mistral, Rafael Alberti, and others.

In the course of my reading I discovered for myself the pleasure of the romantic poetry written by women: Rosalita de Castro (translated into Spanish from Galician), Emily Dickinson (in Spanish translation), Juana Ivarburro, and Alfonsina Sattorni. But I barely scratched the surface of this group. Some of them had written more than one book, while I was still trying to write my first decent sentence. The first Moroccan literature I read was 'Abdelsalam Baqqali's *Stories from Morocco.*

The newspaper *Al-Alam* published a short piece I'd written entitled *The Stream of my Love*, along with a picture of me in a bow tie. I was delirious with joy and got dead drunk to celebrate my newly discovered literary talents. I bought loads of copies of the paper too, passing them out to my fellow students at the college, to make them feel how important I was. Here am I, I thought, sprung from a shack, from human filth, writing literature and getting it published! I emphasized my new importance by buying a fancy suit of clothes, some bow ties, and a gold-plated bracelet.

Pride and arrogance took me totally in their grip. I no longer went to the lowly cafés of Fedan or Trancats or the Barrio Malaga. I started being seen, instead, in the lobby of the Hotel Nacional and the Marvel Night Club. To me, now, the Café Continental seemed second rate, the La Parra Bar third rate. I shaved once, even twice a day, and became obsessed with the idea of smelling nice, even carrying a small bottle of cologne in my pocket. The camel driver's son living among vermin had become elegant, civilized, developed, jumping out of a coarse skin and into a soft one. Inspiration? You have to have some source of inspiration. The son of the mud seeks inspiration.

One day I started following a young girl with an olive complexion. I found out where she lived and where she was from, and every time I caught sight of her, I'd stalk her and keep vigil outside her house or her aunt's house. She was a friend of the daughter of a Moroccan big shot—I'd laid myself open to a cracked head with that attachment! Then there was Halima. She was illiterate, but she was beautiful, able, perhaps, to rouse me to write a gipsy ballad, though her calm disposition held less appeal for me. I'd grown used to fiery natures.

Habiba had given me a key to her house, so that I could come and go as I pleased. Sometimes she didn't come home at night, but that's another story. More than once I saw her in a car or walking with someone or other. I didn't know who she was seeing in the streets of al-Nuzha, or what side paths she herself was wandering down. That was her business anyway. Once she stayed out, then came back a couple of days later, with traces of black or blue around her left eye from some brutal blow. Someone had a powerful hold over her.

My sister Arhimu went down with tuberculosis, and my father and my brother 'Abdelaziz were coughing incessantly too. There's a history of disease in my family; only my sister Malika and I have stayed healthy. My mother was cured of the disease, but she's still under constant medical care. My father insisted on treating himself.

Finally, when Habiba hadn't come back for two days, I moved out and went to stay at the Black Jewel, a small family hotel run by two Spanish brothers, Rosario and Carillon, where a room and three daily meals cost me twenty thousand francs a month. Habiba, I had no doubt, was plunged in some tawdry amorous adventure.

I went to visit Arhimu and 'Abdelaziz in hospital, and they burst into tears when they saw me. A woman in Arhimu's ward had just died, and she herself still wasn't convinced you could be sick and not die. It was a miracle our mother survived.

I went with Mohamed Sabbagh to his home. His was the room of someone totally given over to his art. There were grapes, apples, and pears on a tray. A pale light made the poetic silence more intense. There was Chopin, *Evenings in Majorca*, and readings of Mikha'il Nuaimy's *Letters*. As I left, I longed, some day, to have a self-contained home like that. He criticized my writing with chiseled words and sharp perception. He, though, had been molded from one kind of clay and I from another. He hadn't been brought up, torn and bleeding, on the garbage the privileged threw away; he'd never been plagued by lice or suffered from cracked, bleeding heels. I don't know how to write about "sparrow's milk," or the embracing touch of angelic beauty, or the pearls of morning dew, or "cataracts of lions," or the melodies of nightingales. Nor do I know how to write with a crystal broom inside my head. For me a broom isn't an ornament but a weapon of defiance.

I went to see Habiba, to give her back her key. She had a gaunt look and seemed distracted and depressed. She spoke in a coarse, choking voice.

"Why did you go? Did something upset you?" She looked as though she'd been crying.

"I didn't want to be a bother to you."

"You were no bother at all."

On the coffee table were two empty beer bottles and a pack of cigarettes. A new worry seemed to be gnawing at her. She'd gone to pieces. Even her aunt wouldn't see her any more, regarding her as a whore. That's the aunt who was screwing away with the guard at the local repair shop! Habiba had no friends at all. When I suggested going to get us something to drink, she beamed with delight, and I hoped her new mood would last. Her depression had reminded me of Fatima in Larache when her daughter Salwa fell ill—Salwa, of the one cold, rainy day in a deserted park, Salwa, who I might never see again, who I never let put her hand into her little purse. A faint smile flickered on Habiba's face, then opened out into full bloom. She looked more beautiful and suddenly younger.

We arranged to have dinner together: lamb casserole with artichokes and peas. A cool, refreshing breeze slapped my face, along with a slight drizzle. I bought a glass of sherry at the Spanish grocery, where two elderly Spaniards were engrossed in talk about bullfighting. Business was slack. They were fondly remembering José Bardenas, Marcel Lacanda (The Heroic Chicolo), Francisco Piralta, Joselito El Gayo, Manuel Benfinida Mejjias, Juan Luiz de la Rosa (a fascist killed in Barcelona at the start of the Spanish Civil War), and The Great Manulitti. As the discussion turned heated and they began arguing, the Spanish grocer stepped in to patch things up, politely calming them down.

I had a second glass of sherry, then bought a bottle of white wine. As I returned, I was thinking about Habiba. It would be better for her not to fall into the clutches of love again; otherwise she might end up dancing back in the mental hospital or in some street in Ceuta. Perhaps she found a sort of ecstasy sometimes, some distraction to soothe her worries over her frenzied, anchorless life. Her last divorce had taken away much of her purity, yet she was barely twenty-five. She'd borne her four children like a rabbit, twins first, then two more one right after the other. She used to tie their legs to the bedposts, or to the different legs of the sofa or table, to stop them scratching one another and snatching one another's biscuits. There hadn't been anything pleasurable about her life, only the odd moment of stolen happiness. She'd been plagued by misfortune from early on.

A delicious smell of cooking seeped out from the kitchen, filling the whole room, and there was a joyful energy surging inside her. As she spoke, the dust of depression began to be wiped away from her face. We drank one another's health and exchanged smiles, then, suddenly, she was radiant, as though she was a guest at some grand banquet. I praised her cooking skills. Lamb casserole with artichokes and peas was the best thing she did, I called her "Prime Minister." Her features softened. She said, "I've never met anyone who understands me the way you do."

"We shouldn't put too much trust in happiness," I said. "It comes and goes. And when we try and take hold of it, it slips away from us. It's like a beautiful bird sitting on our balcony rail and flying off the moment we get too close. Do you expect a bird to sit on your shoulder and sing to the pair of us the way we'd like it to?"

"I understand."

"Well, that's happiness. It doesn't rest chirping on our shoulders. It stays on the balcony rail."

Again she assented, her mind whirling, at last, to a point of rest.

"You're right," she said.

I was consoling myself too. After all, my life was no better than hers.

—*Translated by William Granara and Christopher Tingley*

Ghazi A. Algosaibi (b. 1940)

Ghazi A. Algosaibi was born in Al Ihasa', Kingdom of Saudi Arabia, and educated at universities in Cairo, Southern California, and London. He first taught at the King Saud University, then began a career in the government. He was Minister of Industry and Electricity from 1975 to 1982 and was appointed Minister of Health in 1982. He became Saudi Ambassador to Bahrain in 1984 and Ambassador to the United Kingdom and Ireland in 1992. His published works of poetry include *Poems from the Pearl Islands* (1960), *Drops of Thirst* (1965), *Yes Riyadh* (1977); *Fever* (1982); *Obituary of a Former Knight* (1990). His prose works include: *Face to Face with Development* (1981). His second novel in Arabic is *Al-'Asfuriyyah* (1996).

AN APARTMENT CALLED FREEDOM

This novel caused a sensation when first published. With extraordinary frankness, it relates the experiences of four young men studying at university in Cairo in the late 1950s before returning to their home countries in the Gulf. They have left the protection of family and community for the first time and face many totally unexpected challenges. Released from the restraints of strict religious conservatism, they find themselves plunged into the easy-going ways of Cairo. The free mingling of the sexes is the most bewildering change they must adapt to. They also find themselves challenged by new political ideas—Arab nationalism, Baathist ideology, Communism, secularism, and Nasserism. The protagonists symbolize the process of development of a generation of young men who, before the great oil boom, were sent abroad from their highly traditional home countries to face the new world of revolutionary Egypt.

The novel begins with the attempt to destroy Nasserism—when Britain, France, and Israel collude in late 1956 to invade Egypt in reprisal for the nationalization of the Suez Canal Company. The young men react in a variety of ways to this sudden eruption of violence into Egypt. Throughout the novel the author gives a powerful account of the dramatic political events of the late 1950s in the Arab world. He describes wars, plots,

*coups, revolutions, declarations of unity, secessions, and the arrival of sudden unimaginable
oil wealth. The impact of all this is bewildering to the young men in the midst of their
often comic attempts to come to terms with the challenges of adolescence in the form of the
World, the Flesh, the Devil . . . and Cairo.*

*The narrator, Fuad, a young Bahraini, the son of a merchant, is arriving in Cairo
on his first ever trip away from his home. The time is at the end of summer 1956. He
reflects as his flight approaches Cairo on what his new life holds. He is to be a pre-uni-
versity student and will live in the capital of Arab aspirations to unity and resistance to
the colonialists.*

He thought of how well he knew Cairo before he had even seen it. He had seen
the city in films and newspapers, and people had told him about it. His Egyptian
teachers in the primary and secondary schools had loved talking about Cairo.
He had acquired a mass of information. The Andalucia Gardens were the most
beautiful in the Middle East. The zoo was the second biggest in the world after
London's. There was an astonishing clock made of flowers in Cairo, a clock that
talked. In Helwan there was a Japanese garden the like of which did not exist
even in Japan. And as for the capital of Bahrain, you could put it in any one of
Cairo's streets. You could hide it in the middle of the Shubra quarter and not
be able to find it.

And what about the girls? All as beautiful as film stars, like his favourite,
Iman. And they were emancipated like all girls in films and in the stories of
Ihsan 'Abdul-Quddus. In Bahrain a girl from a well-known family had refused
to wear the *'abaya* and this had caused a great uproar. No girls went unveiled
in Bahrain except a few Christians and Jews from Iraq. In Cairo they were
all unveiled except girls from the country districts and old women. And who
wanted *them* to be unveiled? He concentrated on this delicious theme. Would
he have his own girlfriend? Would they go together to the Metro Cinema? To
the Andalucia Gardens? To the zoo? How would he find her? The university was
coed so there should be no problem. But he had a year ahead of him in college
before the university, and the college was not coed. But he might get to know a
girl in the residential block or nearby. He had heard that a number of friendships
had grown from a smile that had been carried, like a butterfly, across the street,
from one balcony to another.

But there was one thing he would never do and that was to go with prostitutes, no matter how attractive. Some of them were young, nice girls and you
could hardly tell them from ordinary girls. But he knew that he could never love
a body that could be bought for just a few dirhams. He recalled Grandol—the
red-light district in Bahrain, one of the most hateful gifts left behind by colonialism—and the panic that had seized him a few months ago when one of
his friends had suggested they visit one of the houses there. He would have a
girlfriend in Cairo but he would never make a friend of a whore.

But he had to address again the problem of the visa. He had none, but he
hoped he could get an emergency one at the airport and later get his residence

permit. Why worry? Mr Shareef would organize "everything" he had assured his father a number of times. Fuad had known Mr Shareef for three years. He had been headmaster of the secondary school. Everyone said he had been the most energetic headmaster the school had ever known. During his short time in Bahrain he had quickly established solid ties with many people and he had got to know Fuad's father and they had become friends and he had persuaded his father to send Fuad to school in Cairo. But Mr Shareef was very strict. Would he be able to enjoy his stay in Cairo with a supervisor such as he?

Fuad's thoughts were interrupted by the steward asking him if he had filled in his form. He had as he scribbled down "ten thousand gallons." Would he be the winner? And what would be his prize? He decided that he would make the competition the omen for the journey: if he won or was close, this would be a sign that all would turn out well; but if he did not win . . . then there would be a big hassle with the visa, customs, and where to stay.

"May God open it before your face, my son!" He recalled how his mother had called to God for him as she embraced him in tears before he set out. She repeated her prayer and embraced him again. And for the tenth time she asked him if he had written down that verse from the Holy Quran. "Dearest son, have you written down the *ayya*?"

His mother would never let anyone travel unless they had written on the wall the verse from the Noble Quran: "He who gave you the Holy Quran will return you to your abode." His mother had an unshakeable faith that anyone who wrote this verse must return home safely from any journey, God willing. This time she had been more insistent than usual and would not be calmed until he had written it three times.

Fuad was astonished that he had been able to part from her: what would his life be like without her smile in the morning and her care throughout the day, the stories she would tell in the evening? The way she doted on him was bantered about at home even by his father who seldom went in for jokes. It seemed to Fuad that his mother's tendency to spoil him increased as he grew older: the favored, stifled, youngest child. Sometimes he thought that his mother believed he was no more than five years old and never would be, that his height of six feet was no more than a disguise, behind which hid her young child, Fuado, as she would call him.

This journey had created tension between his parents. "Abu Nasser, how can you let Fuad live by himself in Egypt?"

"Fuad has become a man."

"A man? He is still a child of thirteen."

"Woman, is your son getting younger or older? He'll soon be seventeen, or he may already be seventeen. Have you forgotten that I married you when I was younger than he is now?"

"But Abu Nasser . . ."

"That's an end of it, he will travel by himself."

Fuad is now established in an apartment with other students, Adnan, Majeed, and Qasim, all expatriates like himself, but with different approaches to the questions of the hour, such as the Anglo-French-Israeli attack on Egypt, now going on. Fuad is also facing the reality of the huge difference between comparatively wealthy Gulf students such as himself and his new Egyptian friend, 'Abdul-Ra'ouf.

Qasim kept trying to spoil Fuad's dream of nationalist fervour with bits of information that he would bring in each day but that Fuad knew came from the son of the Pasha. Qasim insisted that the British and French aircraft had destroyed every one of the Egyptian aircraft and that news broadcast by Egyptian radio that they had only destroyed wooden decoys was rubbish. Qasim said that the British and French forces occupied Port Said within hours and that all the talk about heroic popular resistance was pure lies manufactured by the German experts employed by the radio station, The Voice of the Arabs, who had been trained by Goebbels. Every day Qasim would come along with more malicious rumors: an imminent military coup; the return of Nahas Pasha; the suicide of Gamal 'Abdul Nasser. When the cease-fire was announced, Qasim said that Nasser was about to escape from Cairo and he had only been saved from death by President Eisenhower.

Fuad spent many long hours debating the fighting and its consequences with his flatmates, 'Adnan and Majeed, who held identical views. They all agreed that the confrontation had ended in a historic victory and that the aims of the attack had been to bring down Nasser and regain possession of the canal. The Tripartite Aggression had failed in both aims since Nasser had not fallen and the criminals had not regained the canal. Quite the opposite: Gamal 'Abdul Nasser had emerged stronger than ever and the Egyptian character of the canal had been reasserted. But when Yacoub joined in the discussion, a new element entered the debate.

"With the announcement of the Soviet warning there was an end to U.S. domination of the world. When Khruschev threatened Britain and France with nuclear warheads, the threat was really directed at America." But when Qasim tried to talk about Eisenhower's role in bringing the fighting to an end, his colleagues had nothing but contempt: his reactionary views were not worth discussing.

Fuad did not know when the friendship between himself and 'Abdul-Ra'ouf began. Both of them were usually very shy, and neither formed new friendships easily. He had met 'Abdul-Ra'ouf on his first day at the Saeediyya School, and at first their love of literature was the only thing linking them. Fuad had already published his first short story while 'Abdul-Ra'ouf was hoping to do the same.

They soon realized that, between them, they had read more books than the rest of the class put together, and then gradually they became aware of other things they had in common: a wish to analyze everything, or "philosophize," as 'Abdul-Ra'ouf called it; an unwillingness to take life just as it was, as others did; the ability to see the funny side of every situation, as well as the tragic side, since they both recognized that comedy was hardly different from tragedy. They shared a tendency to be oversensitive to other people's reactions, criticisms, or praise . . . and women. During the break the two of them would go off together to talk school, the world, and people, and always the talk would come round to women.

"What do you think of Aqqad's position on the subject of women?"

"Isn't it just the same as Hakim's?"

"Has either of them come up with anything new?"

"How can a bachelor possibly understand women?"

"Do women's feelings differ from men's?"

"Which one is the hunter and which one the hunted?"

"Which of them is the more predatory?"

"Which of the sexes is the more faithful?"

They had many more questions about women than they had answers.

As his friendship with 'Abdul-Ra'ouf became stronger, Fuad came to understand something of a problem he had never seriously thought about before: poverty. In Bahrain all his companions had been middle-class, like himself, and there had been few differences between them. Usually in class there would be two or three sons of wealthy "merchants" and two or three from poor families, but the rest were all on one level. The question of wealth and class did not occupy much of his thinking. He assumed that life in his home was not very different from that in any other home in Bahrain, with all the children sleeping in one room, going to school on cycles, used to buying new clothes only at Eid, and being unfamiliar with both hunger or luxury.

Before he got to know 'Abdul-Ra'ouf, Fuad was never aware that he moved in a world that was separate from the majority of people. He had never felt privileged before. His father had bought a car some years before but seldom used it, and it had made almost no difference to Fuad's life. But now he began to realize that he was, whether he liked it or not, one of the rich. Poor people did not own cars or have jewelry shops or eat meat regularly and did not send their sons to study abroad with five suits and a monthly allowance of twenty-five pounds.

The friends sharing an apartment, now with the addition of 'Abdul-Karim, have decided to take the ultimate step to discover the facts of life. They invite a number of prostitutes to the apartment and fortify themselves with alcohol.

But it was generally agreed in school that manhood began only with beer and cigarettes: you were half way there, and only the other half remained: women. Yacoub was the only one who had carnal knowledge, which he had acquired at Grandol, the red-light district in Bahrain, and various secret locations in Cairo. Fuad had never had any wish to touch beer either in Bahrain or in Cairo in spite of the mockery of his companions. Even 'Abdul-Karim had drunk it with the rest. God alone knows what would have happened if his father the sheikh had discovered that his son, who claimed to be going to "private lessons," was actually heading off to bars. Fuad decided that the ceremony of inaugurating Apartment Freedom deserved a glass of beer. What surprised him was how bitter it tasted since he had imagined that it was sweet like Pepsi or had a neutral taste like water. He had to spit out the sip he had taken and splashed his clothes to the amusement of his friends. They explained that beer was drunk not for its taste but for its effect.

The ashtrays filled and the bottles of Stella disappeared with astonishing speed. Laughter rose into the air, and Fuad found himself launching forth in a way that he had never before experienced. He swore for the first time and told questionable jokes. Yacoub was singing in his lovely voice one of 'Abdul-Halim Hafez's songs that he could imitate beautifully:

Greet him, you lovely one, to go with the longing that is in his eyes . . .

The girls sang along and then came the dinner, so the party was going swimmingly. Qasim whispered that it was getting near 9 P.M. and that it would be better not to waste any time.

Zeezee was with Qasim in his room, the smartest room in the apartment, with diverse pictures on the walls. His father's portrait, his mother's, and his uncle's. There was a colored picture of Elvis Presley, one of Brigitte Bardot, and one of President Eisenhower taken from the cover of *Time*. Zeezee contemplated them and stood bewildered in front of Eisenhower. Qasim could not hold back his laughter.

"Wot's up with you, wotcha laughing at? Who is he, I mean?"

"Eisenhower."

"But wotcha put his picture in your room for?"

"I am an admirer of his."

"Admiring an ugly old guy like him?"

"It's not his face I like, Zeezee, it's his politics."

"Hey, wot's politics got to do with us?"

"All right, then, we'll forget about politics."

"Yeah, much better, no headaches. Er . . . is there anything wrong with us?"

"No. Why?"

"Everything's OK but aren'tcha going to strip off?"

In a rapid movement that did not seem to Qasim to last more than a second Zeezee had got rid of all her clothes and had sat down on the bed. Qasim blushed and could not speak.

"Aren'tcha going to strip off?"

Qasim felt a chill strike him, reaching his limbs and paralyzing him.

"Wot's up? Aren'tcha going to strip off and get into bed? Now, wot is it? Don'tcha like me?"

"No, no, it's not that, it's just that I'm . . ."

"You're wot?"

Qasim had imagined that the room would be darkened and that things would get started with delicate whispers and soft kisses. But for things to start in the glare of lights with a woman who expected him to undress like her in a second and then pounce on her like an animal—well, this was a real dirty trick. He tried to save the situation. "May I put the light out?"

"Oh, yer can't get it up. Why didn't yer say so? Anything but that. But why make out you were a man?"

Qasim felt an overpowering rage. Why should he put up with these insults? Hadn't she come just for the money? And hadn't she been paid already? With a show of resolution he told her, "I've changed my mind. I don't want to tonight. Get up and get dressed. I'll wait outside."

⌒

The time is now February 1961. Fuad has become more involved with political issues, in addition to mastering his subject, law, and coping with the emotional demands of Cairo. He meets a member of the Baath party who is to have a future role in Arab politics.

⌒

"We feel that the union is in danger. The entire move toward unity is in danger. We fear that popular enthusiasm is feeble now. Can you believe it: the Ba'athists have become the enemies of the enemies of union and the enemies of the enemies of Gamal 'Abdul Nasser? There's an urgent need for new blood. The movement needs you, Fuad."

"Me?"

"Yes. I've had a long talk about this with Dr Ahmad Khatib. He agrees with me that you will be an asset. We need mature young men."

"Mature young men! Me?"

"Fuad, drop the sarcasm. If you came in it would be based on conviction, and after all, you have been through some tough intellectual experiences. You could be a really effective member with your brains and your pen."

"My pen? Are you going to ask me to write stories about revenge?"

"We won't ask you to do anything you don't want to do. What do you say?"

"Listen, Majid. How about a compromise? Accept me as a sympathizer and I'll cooperate. But as for joining the movement, let's leave that for the moment."

"Okay. A short transitional period and then you join the Movement officially. This is your first assignment: there is a Ba'athist refugee from Iraq, called Saddam Takriti, one of the bunch who tried to assassinate 'Abdul-Karim Qasim. Although he's still young, some of the brethren in the movement think that he'll soon be a star in the party. We have to know about opinions and inclinations. You are well placed to find out because Saddam is a close friend of Suad."

"I offered to be a helper, not a spy."

"In the nationalist movement gathering information on the enemy is a noble assignment, not spying."

"The Ba'ath Party is the enemy?"

"Yes, regrettably."

Suad was alone in a corner of the faculty cafeteria when Fuad came up to her. "I won't disturb you long but there's a favor I'd like to ask."

"Go ahead!"

"I'd like to meet Saddam Takriti."

"Haven't you met him yet? He often comes here."

"Maybe I've seen him but I haven't been introduced."

"Why do you want to meet him? Planning to come back to the party?"

"I've heard a lot about him and his attempt to assassinate 'Abdul-Karim Qasim and his escape. I'd like to see him."

"We could meet here Thursday morning. He's generally here then."

"Comrade Saddam. Meet Comrade Fuad Tarif from Bahrain."

The tall, swarthy, handsome young man with piercing eyes rose and shook hands warmly with Fuad. "All strength to Bahrain. Its population is half Ba'athist."

"And the other half is on the way," said Fuad, laughing.

"With the help of God."

The three of them sat down. Saddam chain-smoked. Fuad noticed a bluish tattoo on his hands. He asked about the assassination attempt, which pleased Saddam, and he launched into details. Fuad then asked him about his escape from jail. This pleased Saddam even more, and he told the full story. He even rolled up his trousers to show Fuad the bullet mark from when he was hit in his escape.

Carefully Fuad asked, "And what of the future, Comrade Saddam?"

"In three years' time the party will be in power in Iraq and will remain there. The Arab Nation is bound up with the future of Iraq and that is bound up with the future of the party. The center of gravity will shift from Cairo to Baghdad. Regrettably, Nasser has shown that he is just a politician subject to the calculations of personal gain and the reports of his intelligence people. He has abandoned the revolution and leadership of the nation and is content to be the president of the UAR [United Arab Republic]."

Fuad was astonished to hear this criticism coming from a man who was here as a guest of Nasser. Saddam seemed to read his thoughts. "Look, this is a state of intelligence bodies, a police state. I'm sure that a whole platoon has been assigned to keeping me under surveillance. If you were to look around now, you'd see three or four detectives. Gamal 'Abdul Nasser is no longer a leader of the masses. The only hope now is the party."

"Well," Fuad asked cautiously, "What about the Arab Nationalist Movement? Isn't cooperation possible with them?"

"They're just puppets of the secret police. We tried to reach an understanding with them, but it was a waste of time. The only hope is the party."

"That's true. But as an interim measure till the party comes to power can't we make use of Gamal 'Abdul Nasser's leadership?"

"I used to think that was possible," said Saddam, "and so did the comrades in Iraq. But then we had one shock after another. The day we fired on Abdul-Karim Qasim, Nasser was supposed to act, and we had an agreement that he would send in aircraft. If he had sent just one plane, Abdul-Karim Qasim would have fallen. But Nasser didn't budge. And then there was the uprising by Al-Shawwaf, and Nasser encouraged it, but then he simply stood by as a spectator while it was wiped out. If ten planes had flown in from Syria, the attempt would have succeeded."

"How do you explain his attitude?"

"He's got used to being a president and has forgotten the struggle."

September-October 1961. The UAR (Egypt plus Syria) has collapsed as Fuad pays farewell calls in Cairo, having graduated and decided to study further in the United States.

Some day the time would come for writing, but right now was the time for farewell. This city, which clutched me to its bosom. The city that gave me a degree in law with a grade of "Very Good"—and I would have had a place of honor if it had not been for that teacher of French who would lead anyone astray! The city that gave me my first collection of short stories or, rather, half a collection! The city that led me to my first night of love. Cairo, choking with its millions of people. This young man who left some part of his life on the number six bus and in Tahrir Square in the revered Mugamma' and in Sa'eediyya. And a great deal in Apartment Freedom. This young man is saying farewell now. He opened his spirit and stored there as much as he can of Cairo: the faces, the smells, the cafés, the delicious Kushari, and the bread rusks and the boiled eggs . . . The moon is on the gate . . . It is you alone who are my beloved . . . The Ezbekiyya wall. The Island of Tea. Recite the *Fatiha* to the Sultan. Shoeshine, Your Excellency? "Rose El-Yusuf"; "Sabah Al-Khair"; *Al-Ahram*. The pickpockets. Will you remember this young man who will be taking all these things with him to New York? And when the skyscrapers crowd in upon him and the cowboys assault him, he will stand up, challenging, chewing seeds and spitting them out, and yelling at the Yanks, "Hey, you lot! What an evil lot! That's the truth!"

My Cairo! Cairo of the capitalists and socialists and sometimes of the Marxists. Cairo of the oppressors and the oppressed. The deprivers and the deprived. The rulers and the ruled. O Mother of the World. Will I ever see you again? And what if I should see you? Would we meet as strangers? . . . I know the answer. I've become a stranger in fact, myself, after an absence of only four months. Written on my forehead at the airport in invisible ink was the word "Tourist." The word has remained. Welcome to His Excellency the Tourist! Mr Fuad Bey Tarif, the lawyer. I'm just Fuad. Your old friend. The student. Students are students and tourists are tourists. But I'm not a tourist. I did not come to shout for Gamal 'Abdul Nasser by day and spend the night with the girls, as so many of our Nasserite brethren do. I only came to say good-bye. To cast a long glance over my life here. To see Cairo, to see Apartment Freedom. May God have mercy on Freedom! Unity! Revenge! And Socialism too.

Qasim shook him. "Fuad. Have you been asleep?"

Fuad looked out of the window at Cairo, which was sinking below the horizon. Tears poured from his eyes.

"Fuad, why are you crying?"

Slowly Fuad pulled out from his pocket the piece of paper with the names of the ANM members in America and tore it up, putting the pieces in the ashtray.

"Fuad, what are you doing? Why are you crying?"

Fuad looked toward the city, which had now disappeared completely and made no response.

—Translated by Leslie McLoughlin

Emile Habiby

See Emile Habiby's biography in the short-story section.

THE SECRET LIFE OF SA'EED, THE ILL-FATED PESSOPTIMIST

Emile Habiby's novel is unique in contemporary Arabic literature. Sa'eed is an informer for the state of Israel, but he is a rather stupid, cowardly little man, whose uncanny behavior makes him the fool and victim rather than the villain. Yu'aad is his first love from whom he is separated during the upheaval of the 1948 War when thousands of Palestinians lost their homes and lands and were driven to neighboring Arab countries. Sa'eed marries Baqiya, who bears him his son, Walaa', destined to join the Palestine resistance and die, with his mother, at the hands of Israeli soldiers while asserting his just rights. Even this tragedy is not enough to cause Sa'eed's change of heart. This happens when, immediately after the June War of 1967, Sa'eed, being the fool that he is, makes an idiotic blunder. This arouses immediate suspicion toward him, and he is sent to the notorious Shatta prison where he is beaten heavily by the prison guards and put in a cell with Yu'aad's son, also named Sa'eed, a noble freedom fighter who mistakes Sa'eed for a comrade. This produces the final reversal in Sa'eed. However, although he rejects his former role as spy, he is still crippled by his natural cowardice and limited intellect and unable to become a hero. The dilemma in which he finds himself is symbolized by the impaling stake on which he sits at the end of the novel, to be saved only by the miracle of the man from outer space who picks him up and disappears with him into space. In this novel all the tribulations and aspirations, fears and hopes, self-betrayal and self-assertion of the Palestinians are depicted in a style that mixes the humorous with the tragic to produce one of the most original fictional works of contemporary Arabic literature.

A FLAG OF SURRENDER, FLYING ON A BROOMSTICK, BECOMES A BANNER OF REVOLT AGAINST THE STATE

I met Yu'aad where meetings in Israel often occur—in prison. Actually, I was on my way out of prison at the time. I got there in the first place when I overdid my loyalty bit, so that the authorities saw it as disloyalty.

It all came about on one of those devil-ridden nights of the June War. I was tuned in, to be on the safe side, to the Arabic-language broadcast of Radio Israel. I heard the announcer calling upon the "defeated Arabs" to raise white flags on the roofs of their homes so that the Israeli servicemen, flashing about arrow-quick all over the place, would leave them alone, sleeping safe and sound inside.

This order somewhat confused me: to which "defeated Arabs" was the announcer referring? Those defeated in this war or those defeated by the treaty of Rhodes? I thought it would be safe to regard myself as one of those "defeated" and convinced myself that if I was making a mistake, they would interpret it as an innocent one. So I made a white flag from a sheet, attached it to a broomstick, and raised it above the roof of my house in Jabal Street in Haifa, an extravagant symbol of my loyalty to the state.

But who, one might ask, was I trying to impress? As soon as my flag was flying for all to see, my master Jacob[1] honored me by bursting in on me, without so much as a "How are you?" So I did not greet him either.

He yelled, "Lower it, you mule!"

I lowered my head until it touched his very feet and asked, "Did they appoint you King of the West Bank, Your Majesty?"

Jacob seized me by the lapels of my pajamas and began pushing me up the stairs toward the roof, repeating, "The sheet, the sheet!" When we reached the

---

1. A Sephardic (Oriental) Jew who was Sa'eed's immediate boss and with whom he formed a lifelong friendship.

broomstick, he grabbed it, and I thought he wanted to beat me with it. So we fought over it, as if doing the stick dance together, until finally he collapsed at the edge of the roof.

He began to weep, saying, "You're finished, old friend of a lifetime; you're finished and so am I along with you."

I tried to explain: "But I raised the sheet on the broomstick in response to the Radio Israel announcer."

"Ass! Ass!" he responded.

"How is it my fault if he's an ass?" I asked. "And why do you only employ asses as announcers?"

He then made it clear that I was the ass to whom he had referred. He also pointed out that all Radio Israel's announcers are Arabs; they must have worded the request badly, he commented, but I must still be a fool to have misunderstood it.

In defense of my own people, the Arabs who worked at the radio station, I said, "The duty of a messenger is to deliver the message. They say only what is dictated to them. If raising a white flag on a broomstick is an insult to the dignity of surrender, it's only because broomsticks are the only weapons you permit us.

"However," I continued, "if, since the outbreak of this war, they too have become some kind of deadly white weapon we are not permitted to carry without a permit, like the shotguns only village chiefs and old men who've spent all their lives serving the state are permitted to carry, then I'm with you as always, all the way. You know full well, old friend of a lifetime, of my extravagant loyalty to the state, to its security and its laws, whether promulgated or still to be so."

My friend Jacob, standing there with his mouth open and listening to my gabbling, was unable to stop either the tears pouring down his cheeks or my raving.

Finally he regained his composure and explained how my "misunderstanding" had been considered something quite different by the Big Man,[2] nothing less than a case of rebellion against the state.

"But it's only a broomstick," I objected.

"That announcer," he emphasized, "was telling the West Bank Arabs to raise white flags in surrender to the Israeli occupation. What did you think you were up to, doing that in the very heart of the state of Israel, in Haifa, which no one regards as a city under occupation?"

"But you can't have too much of a good thing," I pointed out.

"No," he insisted, "it's an indication that you do regard Haifa as an occupied city and are therefore advocating its separation from the state."

"That interpretation never so much as crossed my mind."

"We don't punish you for what crosses your minds but for what crosses the Big Man's mind. He considers the white flag you raised over your house in

---

2. An arrogant Ashkenazi (European) Jew who was Jacob's boss and who oppressed him and mistreated Sa'eed.

Haifa to be proof that you are engaged in combat against the state and that you do not recognize it."

"But," I objected, "you know full well that I serve the security of the state to my utmost and would never do anything to harm it."

"The Big Man has come to believe that the extravagance of your loyalty is only a way of concealing your disloyalty. He recalls your parentage and character and regards them as proof that you only pretend to be a fool. If you are innocent, why was it 'Yu'aad' you loved, 'Baqiyya' you married, and 'Walaa' you had as a son? All these names are highly suspect to the state."[3]

"Has the big man ever stopped to ask why I was born only an Arab and could have only this as my country?"

"Come along and ask him yourself."

But instead they took me to the Bisan Depression and imprisoned me in the awesome Shatta jail.

How Sa'eed Finds Himself in the Midst of an Arabian-Shakespearean Poetry Circle

We got out of the van in front of the iron gates of the jail. The soldiers also alighted from the dogcart; three of them approached and put me under close guard. The Big Man himself headed the procession. He knocked just once. A dog barked inside, and the gate opened.

There was the prison warden himself, mind you, in the flesh—and he had lots of it—preceded by his pet bulldog, coming forward to meet us. The master smiled welcomingly while the dog growled. The Big Man and the fat warden played with the dog awhile, patted him, then climbed a flight of stairs, while I remained standing in the inner courtyard surrounded by the soldiers.

Eventually one of the soldiers ordered me to go with him, and we climbed some stairs to a corridor, then to another and then another. At last we reached the warden's office, where we found the two men sipping coffee with audible pleasure.

The warden smiled at me and said, "On the recommendation of my dear friend, the Big Man, I shall give you special treatment. I have learned from him that your past is as white as snow, without so much as one black mark except that of the white flag. He has told me, moreover, that you're an educated lad and quote from Shakespeare."

This made me feel most relaxed, and I settled comfortably into a chair.

He promptly offered me coffee and conversation on Shakespeare. He began quoting from Anthony's speech over the body of Caesar, with me filling in the lines he had forgotten, while he exclaimed, "Oh, bravo! Bravo!"

---

3. Yu'aad means "to return," Baqiya "who has remained," and Walaa' "loyalty."

Then he stood up and began acting the role of Othello giving Desdemona the fatal kiss. I stretched out on the ground like her, but he said, "Get up! It's not time for that yet!" I did get up, but I was beginning to feel a little uneasy.

"However," he explained, "in the presence of the other prisoners we shall treat you as we do them. You understand, naturally."

"Yes, I understand, sir!" I glanced over at the Big Man reassuringly, and he returned my look in even greater measure.

The warden pressed a button and a guard entered. I shook hands with the warden, then with the Big Man. I asked him to look after Jacob for me. I kept on thanking this one and praising that one until the guard pushed me out of the office. As we penetrated the length of the second corridor, I said to myself, this guard is my friend, my brother; we have walked together along two corridors in the same prison. It is like sharing bread and salt. I commented, "What a highly cultured warden."

"What were you speaking about?" he asked.

"Oh, about Shakespeare and Othello and Desdemona."

"You know them then?"

"I quote from the first and lie down like the third."

"Good for you."

Then he led me into a dark room with no windows or furniture. When he switched on an overhead electric, light, I found myself standing in the middle of a circle of jailers, all tall and broad-shouldered. Each one had sleepy eyes, arms at the ready with sleeves rolled up, thick, strong legs, and a mouth wearing a smile worse than a frown. They all seemed to have been formed in the same mold.

I tried my best to carve on my own mouth that same smile, but the left side of my face kept collapsing, and when I corrected it, the right would promptly collapse. Having corrected that, I would feel my lower lip give way, and when I would repair that, my teeth would chatter.

While I was engrossed in this labial exercise, I heard the guard who had led me to this nightmarish room tell the thick-thighed jailers, "And he quotes from Shakespeare, too!"

This was the signal for the beginning of a literary competition the likes of which the entire history of the literature of the Arabs since pre-Islamic times has never recorded.

One of them began with the comment, "Quote some Shakespeare for us, you son of a bitch!" Then he gave me a tremendous punch.

Another jailer caught me and said, "Here, take this, Caesar!"

I tottered toward first one jailer and then another until they got bored with punching me and began kicking me. Then I rolled around at their feet as they booted me again and again. At times I was quicker than them, but then I would feel several feet trampling on me all together. I screamed but could hear nothing, just stifled noises coming from the beating, kicking, and punching. Then I could no longer feel the blows but could only sense them faintly, as if they came from somewhere far away. They had stopped repeating verses from Shakespeare and were concentrating on the poetry of sighs and moans, with them sighing at this display of their strength and me moaning in exhaustion. I kept up this moaning as they did their sighing until I felt their boots cutting off my breath, and I sank down unconscious, completely defeated.

The last thing I heard them say was, "Welcome a thousand times, our very own Shakespeare!" This nickname stuck to me for as long as I was in jail—and after I graduated from it as well.

SA'EED AT THE COURT OF A KING

The day was coming to an end when a hand shaking my own woke me up. I found myself lying on a straw mattress in a dark, low-ceilinged room. The chamber was illuminated faintly by a little daylight forcing its way, wounded, through the netted and barred opening at the top of one wall.

The hand to my left was shaking mine and pressing it reassuringly. I found I was unable to move my fingers, so I turned my head to the left and saw a very long form lying there on a straw mattress like my own. He was naked, and at first sight his body seemed to have been painted with a deep red pigment.

Had it not been for his eyes smiling silently to me in encouragement, and for his hand pressing mine and telling me to be brave, I would have thought the body lying to my left was a corpse.

I said "Hello," but it came out "Ah!"

Then I heard the man clad in the crimson cloak of kingship whisper, "What's your story, brother?"

"Is this the cell?" I asked.

"There is a room without windows—"

"And there is a hope without walls—"

"What about you?" I asked him.

"I'm a *fedaiy*, a guerrilla and a refugee. And you?"

I did not know what to reveal about my identity before the majestic figure laid out there who, when he spoke, did not groan and in fact spoke in order not to groan. Should I tell him I was a mere "sheep," one who had stayed on in the country, or should I confess that it was through crawling that I entered his court?

I disguised my shame by emitting a lengthy groan.

He forced himself to stand up. And I saw him bend his head down so that it would not hit the ceiling; or perhaps he was bending his tall figure down to look at me.

"Stop it, man!" he shouted suddenly.

Well, I told myself, I've become a man now that I've been thoroughly booted by jailers!

He seemed to be very young, his cloak of crimson only emphasizing his youth.

"Where do you hurt, brother?"

Had we met outside, would he have called me brother?

There was something about his eyes that took me back twenty years to the playground of my youth and the slopes of Jabal Street. In his voice, as he asked me where I hurt, I heard the screams of Yu'aad when, so many ages ago, the soldiers hurled her into the car for deportation: "This is my country, this is my home, and this is my husband?"

I burst into tears, like a child.

"Patience, father."

I did not stop crying, but now it was from pride and gratitude; my tears were those of a soldier whose leader is awarding him a medal for courage.

"Be brave, father."

Trample all you like, you huge boots, on my chest! Suffocate me! And you, black room, crumble over my helpless body! Were it not for all of you, we would not have been reunited! Those brutish guards, if only they knew, were merely guards of honor at the court of this king. That dark and narrow room was the outer hall that led to this, the throne room!

I have become his brother! I have become his father! Laugh at that, if you can, my jailers!

A feeling of enormous pride spread over me, a pride I had never felt since the day that Yu'aad had shouted, "This is my husband!"

I am your father, O King! I do have a son like you, but his cloak is of sea coral.

I did not want to tell him I was from Haifa and go into lengthy explanations, so I told him instead I was from Nazareth.

"We have every right to be proud of our brave people there," he said.

Then he asked, "A Communist, of course?"

"No, a friend of theirs."

"Fine, glad to meet you indeed."

He healed my wounds by talking about his own. He kept widening that single tiny window in the wall until it became a broad horizon that I had never seen before. Its netted bars became bridges to the moon, and between his bed and mine were hanging gardens. I told him of myself, what I had always aspired to for myself. I did not want to lie, but I did not want to soil the majesty of the moment by speaking of personal details: these the jailers had stripped from me when they stripped off my clothes. Here we were, one naked man facing another. Would Adam ever have left Paradise of his own free will?

The guards, however, did not leave me there. They removed me from Paradise and transferred me to a large hall in the prison where the inmates lay huddled together, each lying on a straw mattress on an iron bed. For many days I disobeyed the rules so that they would return me to the cell where I would meet again that young man who had called me father. But they did not.

I learned from the prisoners that he was a Palestinian *fedaiy* who had crossed over from Lebanon and had been taken prisoner when wounded.

They also told me that his name was Sa'eed. "Just like me," I commented.

"But he was never nicknamed Shakespeare!" they pointed out and smiled consolingly.

I occupied myself binding my wounds and looking out for this second Sa'eed until finally I met his sister, the second Yu'aad, as I was leaving prison for the third time.

—*Translated by Salma Khadra Jayyusi and Trevor LeGassick*

Ben Salim Himmish (1949)

Ben Salim Himmish was born in Meknès, Morocco, and studied philosophy and history in Paris, obtaining a *doctorat de troisième cycle* and a *doctorat d'état* from the Sorbonne. He now teaches the philosophy of history and the philosophy of Islamic thought at the Mohamed V University in Rabat, Morocco. He has written a number of books in his field, including *Critique on the Need for Marx* (1983), *Ideological Formations in Islam* (1988), *On the Readers of Ibn Khaldoun* (1990), and *Orientalism* (1991). He has published four collections of poetry, and his novels include *Marriage Brokers* (1987); *The Learned Man* (1987); *Power Crazy* (1990), for which he was awarded the Al-Naqid Prize; *The Tribulations of Young Zein Shama* (1993); and *Brokers of Mirage* (1996). Himmish's novels, which take a historical approach, are characterized by marked originality of subject matter and strong structural balance, and he has the capacity, when writing about history, to manipulate language in order to bring forth the flavor and mode of the old Arabic style, in itself a remarkable achievement.

POWER CRAZY (1990)

Himmish's is a fine historical novel, one of the experimental attempts of contemporary Arab novelists to merge the past with the present and to allude to the present by vividly depicting the acts, attitudes, and concepts that have pervaded the past in Arab history and demonstrating the constant recurrence of patterns of public and personal behavior that determine the destiny of people. A great attitudinal difference can be immediately detected between this novel and the colossal work of Jurji Zaydan (discussed in the introduction to this volume), who is rightly regarded as the father of the Arabic historical novel in modern times. Zaydan, who wrote at the turn of the twentieth century, saw it as his mission to present a civilization to the Arab reader, highlighting the great points of triumph and tragedy in this long and rich history. The facts of this history obliged him to acknowledge the points of failure and chaos, but his great emphasis was on the more illuminating moments, on the glory that described the Islamic Arab Empire at the height of its power in medieval times. Himmish, on the other hand, belongs to a different generation, one that has acquired sophistication in novelistic techniques and that has already suffered the numerous setbacks of modern Arabic history. Quite a few contemporary novelists refer to events in the past as compulsively recurring in the present—a kind of mythological time syndrome connecting disparate times to produce a pattern only too well known and suffered. In Power Crazy, *Himmish depicts the strange, oppressive, and utterly inhumane behavior of the Fatimid ruler who ruled Egypt between 996–1021, wreaking havoc there, and there is no denying the unvoiced comparison with some present-day autocrats in the Arab world. After many years of unbelievable persecution and tyranny (including the cloistering of women in their homes,) this mad ruler disappeared, presumably killed probably with the blessing of his beautiful and worthy sister, Sitt al-Mulk, who ruled for a few years after his mysterious disappearance. Himmish has consulted historical sources for the details of this work, and in certain parts of the novel has tried to duplicate the old style of historical narration. However, the whole novel, which makes unusually charming reading, is written in a style that clearly belongs to a different age of prose narrative in Arabic. Linguistic specialists, who study style and the development of language, might find much to ponder about these experiments, which seem to be deliberate, deviating from the normal development of style. In this Himmish joins some other writers who are consciously trying to benefit from the immense riches of old Arabic narrative literature, which has been long neglected in favor of poetry, the Arabs' more beloved art form. The novel, translated by Roger Allen, is now in press.*

Four years after the death of al-Hakim, Sitt al-Mulk took charge of the affairs of state. She restored the kingship to its former prosperity, replenished its coffers, and appointed trustworthy men to positions of power. Then she fell gravely ill and died of dehydration. She was knowledgeable, competent, and highly intelligent.

—*Ibn al-Sabi', Kitab al-Tarikh, being a supplement to the History of Thabit Ibn Sinan*

Sitt al-Mulk arranged for her brother al-Hakim to be assassinated during an excursion in one of his secret hideouts. He was struck down and the matter kept secret until the Feast of the Sacrifice [10 Dhu al-Hijja] in the year 411 A.H. Extremists within the Fatimid faith claimed that he was secretly absent, and that he would return unexpectedly to regain his power and glory.

—*Ibn al-Qalanisi, Appendix to the History of Damascus*

Sitt al-Mulk, the daughter of the caliph al-Aziz bi-Llah, held a special place of affection in her father's heart. As long as he was alive she was the apple of his eye and the object of his adoration after God. She was his consolation and his coat of armor against any troubles or anxieties afflicting him. When her father passed away, her brother, Abu 'Ali Mansur al-Hakim bi 'Amrillah, succeeded him on the throne.

Even during the turbulent period of her half-brother's rule Sitt al-Mulk continued to radiate beauty, intelligence and grace. She was a shining star not only to the cloistered and subjugated women of Egypt but to all classes of people, who loved her and referred to her as Lady of the Realm, Our Princess and Mistress of All.

Ah, her beauty!

About her beauty poets composed verses that became famous throughout the realm and would be sung again and again by the minstrels and bards. Neither they, nor anyone enamored of Sitt al-Mulk, would ever dare to utter her name for fear of swift and deadly punishment from her threatening tyrannical brother. Instead, they would refer to her by one of her many epithets, such as The Magnificent Treasure, The Rising Sun, or The Incomparable Beauty.

People would vie, indeed, in their descriptions of her, extolling her braided hair, her ample stature, her slender waist, sturdy shoulders, and straight back. They likened her eyes to those of a gazelle, her neck to a long-necked silver urn, her legs to a slender palm tree, and her hair to wild flowing silk or else to clusters of ripened grapes. The rival poets were joined by composers of prose and rhymed prose, one of whom wrote, "Tender, slender, wispy as a feather, strong and sturdy all set together." They would describe her in prophetic terms, saying:, "Her leg can be seen from behind the flesh of beauty."

One of her more ardent admirers wrote, "Some nonbelievers looked into the face of Sitt al-Mulk and saw proof of the existence of God. And so they put their faith in God and pledged allegiance to the Islamic faith and the rule of the Fatimid dynasty . . .

"For should anyone fail to bring forth some eloquent description, and buy no share from the most celebrated poets, he need only stop at any part of her blessed body and say: God, how great thou art!"

As witnessed by any who had the honor of attending her sessions, or being close to her when she passed by or came out to speak, Sitt al-Mulk exuded natural scents of perfumes and musk. All agreed that they were fragrances from heaven, that the odor of these fragrances came not from man-made perfumes but from the remarkable scent of her body, which permeated her small palace. Anyone coming close to her was overwhelmed and humbled by her essence. People would flock to be near her and bow in deference and adulation.

Ah, her intelligence and poise!

Sitt al-Mulk was never obsessed by her beauty, nor did she exploit it in her relations with people or in any attempt to influence them. She deemed the intelligence and poise bestowed on her to be greater by far than her beauty and more useful and lasting. These, she considered, were the qualities and principles on which the Fatimid dynasty was founded, and she was fiercely proud that these sprang from Holy Fatima, the daughter of the Prophet, may God bless her memory! From Fatima it was that she inherited her justice, enlightenment, and faith in the One and Only God.

It was a clear sign of her intelligence that she was among the very first to pay homage to her brother, al-Hakim bi Amrillah, in spite of his tender age. She became the first to care for him, to nurture him with affection, to provide him with caresses and good advice, and to shower him with the most marvelous and costly gifts. This was her way of celebrating his ascent to the throne and of extending her protection to the glorious Fatimid dynasty.

According to some historians, Sitt al-Mulk presented her brother, when he was named caliph, with thirty saddled horses, one of the saddles being studded with gems, another with crystal, and the rest with gold. She also gave him twenty harnessed mules, fifty servants, ten of whom were Slavs, and a crown and a fez, both encrusted with precious stones. She gave him baskets of aromatic perfumes and a garden fenced in silver and seeded with many kinds of trees.

Sitt al-Mulk showed no disapproval or aversion toward her brother (and even then such bitter feelings never affected her intelligence and poise) till she had grown aware of his fearful fits of misrule and his bloodthirsty instincts. It racked her with grief and distress to see how he slaughtered innocent people, so making a mockery of the sacred Fatimid heritage, destroying it with his devious designs and heinous crimes, and exposing the state itself to destruction and extinction.

The beauty of Sitt al-Mulk, how wondrous it was!

The many cares of Sitt al-Mulk only added grace and dignity to her beauty. The few white hairs that shone on her head did not lessen the number of her admirers, nor did the few wrinkles that crept into her face blot out the twinkle of joy in her eyes and her smile.

Her intelligence, God be blessed! It only grew more refined through her experience of the world, stronger in the face of her brother's swelling violence and of deepening disasters. Awaiting some sign of hope following despair, Sitt al-Mulk spent many a sleepless night in prayer and supplication, cut off from the rest of the world, in deep reflection and awe.

From all of this sprang a vigorous resolve to seek some salvation, some release from this fearful dilemma, a resolve fed by visions that came to her in her sleep. She dreamed Holy Fatima appeared to her, giving her sound counsel on how the Fatimid government might be saved. So she would do till dawn drew its golden curtains; and then she would vanish into the horizon glistening with the first light of day, spreading her sacred sash across its fold.

Sitt al-Mulk passed night after night in such sleepless confusion, able to find sleep only with Fatima's appearance and advice. Fatima began, indeed, to appear to her even in visions by day, enveloped always in the same halos of sanctity and splendor, accompanied now by a rainbow, now by a galaxy of lucky stars and good omens. In one of her last visits Fatima added a new piece of advice, urging Sitt al-Mulk to go to her tyrannical brother and counsel him against his atrocities and wild behavior.

Having reflected on this counsel with due care, and deemed it apposite and judicious, Sitt al-Mulk resolved to take on the task. It was the morning of a momentous day when she appeared, unannounced and unexpected, forced a way into her brother's chambers in his palace and entered on perilous discourse with him. Holding nothing back, she revealed all to him.

Al-Hakim responded, his blood boiling with rage:

"How painful it is to suffer the disobedience of a rebellious sister. You have not probed my depths, nor have I plucked out your secret. You come to me uninvited, pent up and ready to burst, like poison biding its time. You it is who are the scourge of my kingdom and the thorn in my side. So, daughter of an infidel Christian woman, reveal your black secrets and burst before my wrath devours you!"

Striving hard to remain calm and level-headed, Sitt al-Mulk responded:

"'Silence in the kingdom of tyrants is an act of faith'; so says our master, Imam Ja'far al-Sadiq. But how can I remain silent when I myself, dear brother, am from the founding dynasty of this kingdom? How can I find rest in peace of mind and absence of suspicion, when I spend every waking hour, as you try my patience, hoping for a thing that will never happen? My fear, dear brother, is not of death or of your clear intention to destroy me, but rather of the destruction of our dynasty at your hands, and the destruction of our lives and our religion by enemies."

Al-Hakim cut her off, screaming, with sparks of hatred and rage spewing from his mouth:

"Do not talk to me of this dynasty, which I raised up on foundations of iron and steel. Leave well alone what you know nothing of, and tell me rather of your own house, which you have turned into a brothel. You bring in men and lovers to work on you around the clock, to have open access to your degraded womb and cursed body. I heard of that degenerate poet on whom you lavish gifts and visits by night, and who has written a poem on you, boasting: 'How often I sighed for her bosom, that appears, proudly swaying, in its glittering crown!' That and other such scandalous things! I should have kept you under lock and key from the moment you left childhood, when your lewd breasts grew hard and lust consumed your body, and the young, obedient, innocent virgin in you died."

Sitt al-Mulk could not hold back the tears swelling in her eyes.

"Shame on you, brother! You have every excuse in the world to kill me, but to defame my honor you have no right!"

Al-Hakim answered, his face and voice still quivering with anger:

"All those tears you are shedding are wasted on me. I no longer feel any affection for you, so spare me your efforts to sway me. Tomorrow, I swear by our pure and honorable Fatima, I shall send midwives to you to test your virginity and search your well-plowed womb for adulterous bastard seed. And if I find truth in what my spies and old women have said of you, I shall slay you with my own hands, without hesitation or mercy. Now, leave my sight, lest my anger thrust me to my sword, and my sword to your neck!"

Sitt al-Mulk left her brother's palace and made for her own, convinced more than ever that her brother was beyond redemption, that there was no hope he would end his atrocities or undo his brutish, tyrannical deeds. And that night the voice of Holy Fatima returned to her, confirming all this and urging her to find some way out from this impending doom.

By the following dawn, Sitt al-Mulk had devised a sound plan to be rid of her brother. To put it into effect she chose the person of Sayf al-Dawla Hussein Ibn Dawwas, leader of the Kutama tribe, which had suffered grave loss and mistreatment under the rule of her brother, al-Hakim bi Amrillah. That night she set out disguised and alone. On finding him at home, she removed her veil, and Ibn Dawwas, seeing who his unexpected visitor was, knelt before her and repeatedly kissed the earth between her feet. She seized his shoulders and ordered him to rise. He obeyed, then began to speak, his heart pounding with astonishment and joy, "To what do I owe such an honor? For a long time to come, memory of this blessed visit will afford me sleep in comfort and peace. Neither the sword nor the venom of al-Hakim will disturb me. My nightmare is past. My lungs will now, for the first time in many years, breathe air that is fresh, an air both fragrant and calm. And all on your account!"

"God bless you, Sayf al-Dawla," replied Sitt al-Mulk. "You are master of the tribe whose valor and courage helped fix this Fatimid dynasty in North Africa, and in Egypt and the lands of Syria. You it is who embody the pride and glory of your people. I see in you, who have sought out the oceans and ridden the crests of waves, a high-flying sail for our flagging ship, to fend off our enemies and those given over to wickedness. Oh, Husayn, you are our only hope! The swamps of the butcher al-Hakim have sucked the oars from your grip, so that you now seek only safety and deliverance. How long will you stand by, a panic-stricken witness to unjust letting of blood and severing of heads? How long will your swords lie idle, turning to rust in their sheaths?"

"Your words, My Lady," said Ibn Dawwas, "are like perfumed water and carvings and fragrance of amber, weaving for me a cloak of warmth and potency, a cloak of resolve for our country. Through them I feel myself like the rains of deliverance soon to fall from the sky, from which my lips drink drops of mercy and healing."

"Your words and feelings do not deceive you, Hussein," continued Sitt al-Mulk. "There are indeed rains soon to fall, rains that will water the arid meadows of our land and wash away these desperate cares from our souls. The waters of our Nile will be clear and shimmering once more. We cannot change what is decreed."

Ibn Dawwas fell to the ground and kissed her feet, clutching at the hem of her garment. Understanding the tenor of her words, he begged her to release him from the awesome task in prospect. In a trembling voice he spoke: "The disaster through which we live, My Lady, is great. But greater still is the fear of my own impotence and failure. Now he has abused and tortured so many, there is none alive who would dare raise a fist against al-Hakim, nor any who would strike him from a distance with bow and arrow, or a slingshot."

As she mounted her carriage, draping his head in the hem of her garment, Sitt al-Mulk said, "Shame on you, Sayf al-Dawla! Do you think I have taken no account of your fears? I do not wish your hands to be stained with the blood of al-Hakim, nor even that you should be present at the scene of his demise. You will choose two of your servants who do not know al-Hakim's face and in whose staunch loyalty, courage, and fierceness you have full confidence. Then you must deceive them into thinking a rebel means to harm their master, the caliph, and will wait for him tomorrow night at the trail of the Muqattam Mountain, mounted on a gray donkey and disguised in clothing like the caliph's. You must promise them a reward of money and land, and high office in the government, if they return with the rebel's head and entrails in a bag, having buried, deep in the bowels of the earth, his corpse and the corpse of his donkey, along with those of any companions who may have been with him. The moment their mission is accomplished, you must destroy them, so this secret will remain between the two of us. So long as you harbor this secret in your heart, you shall see yourself blessed with all and every favor. You will administer the affairs of state for al-Hakim's successor, whom I will appoint in due time. As for myself, I shall remain as I am, a woman behind a veil."

Sitt al-Mulk did not leave Sayf al-Dawla filled with fear or apprehension; rather, she left him full of praise for her blessed cleverness and her flawless and righteous plan. When she was quite certain he understood her orders to the letter, she bent to kiss him gently on his ear as an expression of her approval. Then she took out from the sleeve of her garment two sharp knives. Placing them in his hands, she said: "These were forged in Morocco. Do not doubt they have strength enough to do the job!"

With that she stood up and began to take her leave. Ibn Dawwas followed her to the gate, repeating words that showed full understanding of what he had to do. He promised to bring her the bag the following night, just before the break of the new dawn.

On the evening Sitt al-Mulk devised her plot and set Sayf al-Dawla to carry it out, al-Hakim rode out to the reservoir northeast of Cairo. He inquired about the last caravan of pilgrims, whom he had bidden farewell months before but who had not yet returned. He was told they had sought asylum at the Ka'ba[1]

---

1. The central and most holy place of Islam. It is a large cubic stone structure, covered with a black cloth, which stands in the center of the Grand Mosque in Mecca.

in Mecca and were still seeking refuge there. Then he asked about the gifts and the pilgrimage bequest he had sent along with them and was told Qarmatian bandits[2] had attacked the pilgrims on the road and stolen the holy *kiswa*,[3] along with wheat, flour, oil, candles, and perfumes. Striking the side of his leg, he said angrily, "In the past I forbade Egyptians to make the pilgrimage, then I rescinded my order. I now restore that order strictly and formally."

At that point al-Hakim felt a stab of anxiety and abruptly dismissed his servants and bodyguards; then he turned his mount toward the Lu'lu' Palace to take some exercise. No sooner had he arrived than anxiety assailed him anew. He imagined the trees were soldiers compassing him around and that the trunks of trees were swords drawn against him, ready to strike and rend him apart. He turned back and headed home, toward the Tarma stables, where, having ordered that all other animals be cleared out, he insisted on spending the night with his donkey, Qamar. And there he remained, in the pitch black of night, lying on the ground by the snoring donkey, amidst the whiffs of dung and hay. Suddenly he began to speak, as though in a trance. What could be heard sounded like jumbled, riddled words, shrouded in obscurity and doubtful meaning.

At daybreak, when al-Hakim was still lying on the ground in the stables, his guard entered and asked him if he wished to be taken to his bed. He acceded and gave the order, then, once in his bed, began once more to babble in riddles, shuddering violently all the while, till a deep, restless sleep took hold of him. When he awoke, his last evening had begun. He rose and called for astrologers to be brought to him but was reminded he had banished most of them from the kingdom and killed off the best. Only one astrologer, they told him, remained, and he was blind and totally crazed, his dwelling unknown.

Al-Hakim raised his head and looked out at the stars, crying, "I see you, unlucky star!"

After gazing some time at the sky, lost in thought, al-Hakim left his quarters and paid a visit to his mother, Queen 'Aziza. He kissed her forehead, then her hands, and told her of his unlucky star. The mother cried out in anguish and begged her son not to go out that night, as he usually did, to the reservoir at the Muqattam Mountain. He answered her, submissive and quivering, "I must act firmly tonight, before daybreak. It is as though, Mother, you have been destroyed by the hand of my sister. I fear no one, on your account, as I do her. Take this key to my safe. Inside are chests holding three hundred thousand dinars. Bring them here to your castle and use them as your provision for defense. I see you kissing the ground, imploring me not to ride out tonight. Yet my spirit is quite cast down. Either I ride out tonight and gaze at the world, or I shall die. Farewell then! We are all God's creatures and to Him we must all return."

---

2. A group of rebellious Muslims who espoused radical egalitarianism.

3. A black brocaded carpet covering the walls of the Kaaba, until recently made annually in Egypt and transported with the pilgrimage to Mecca.

When only a few hours of the night remained, al-Hakim left his palace and, as though drawn by some invisible force, he mounted his donkey; then, ordering his guards not to accompany him, he set out for the Muqattam Mountain. His sole companion was a young scribe bearing an inkwell, some pens, and paper. Sitt al-Mulk, meanwhile, was watching his every action and movement from the windows of her palace. When he reached the top of the hills and went down into the canyon, he cried, again and again, "You will soon be rid of me!"

He rode up once more, now shrieking in a high voice, now speaking in a low murmur, "This night is like no other. It is the endless abyss, drawing me to its overflowing beauty; as I gaze at the night sky with its stars, I long, with passion, for the essence of my existence and the indivisible whole. This night is the eye that does not sleep but, rather, entices and allures me to the treasures of immortality and the blessings of the hereafter.

"How little I care for the extinction of my body, for the total destruction of each shred of my flesh on this night, unpolluted by concern and efforts!

"How paltry I consider this wide earth, beside this dark void studded with glimmering pearls.

"Were my spirit to fly away, to depart this world of iniquity and return to the elements, then my death would be easy and sweet.

"But what disturbs and offends me is that I perish betrayed, split in two, my limbs severed by the weapons of base men.

"My unlucky star shows my death will be at the hands of a woman of closest kin to me. The plot will be carried out with a Moroccan dagger, by order of this woman, who will then slay my slayer and those knowing the secret of my murder. Woe to the leader of the Kutama tribe, and woe to all those who have conspired against me!"

The murder of al-Hakim bi Amrillah took place on the twenty-seventh day of Shawwal in the year 411 (1020 A.D.). He was thirty-six years and seven months old, and his reign had endured twenty years and one month. Had the assassins not forgotten to bury the donkey's hacked carcass, Sitt al-Mulk's plan would have found total success, with no questions or rumors passing between the noblemen and through the towns and villages. Yet, despite this palpable error, Sitt al-Mulk found ways, calmly and clearly, of facing out the rising tide of questions and insinuations.

"Al-Hakim," she explained, "told me he would be absent for a time, and we should not trouble ourselves in the least on that account. As for his donkey, Qamar, either he died from bearing too heavy a load or else from simple exhaustion. Or maybe al-Hakim killed the beast himself, as he often threatened to do."

Throughout the first weeks of al-Hakim's disappearance, Sitt al-Mulk waged a fierce battle against time. To her this period of waiting, along with the empty seat of government, seemed like a two-edged sword: either she must strike first, or be struck. Her gamble would, she knew, pay off only if she seized the moment. She gained the allegiance of the Maghribi and Turkish forces in the army, distributing money and gifts among them and granting their officers fiefs of land. Also, to broaden her scope for action, she deemed it necessary to tell the prime minister, Khatir al-Mulk, of al-Hakim's secret murder, drawing from him a sacred oath of loyalty and silence.

Next Sitt al-Mulk ordered the prime minister to recall the crown prince, 'Abd al-Rahman Ibn Ilias, from Syria and commanded him to arrange for the young man's "suicide"; on no condition would she agree to a cousin of al-Hakim succeeding to the caliphate. When the due time arrived, Khatir al-Mulk carried out his orders to the letter. One account of what happened was provided by a scribe of the prime minister: "We brought poisoned figs, almonds, and pomegranates to the crown prince in his prison cell, and said to him: 'Here is your portion of this season's fruit, which is a gift to you from the Empress. Eat your fill and take pleasure in it!' The prince seized a knife and plunged it into his stomach, till faintness overtook him. Then he devoured the fruit. He managed, in his death throes, to say, 'Curse al-Hakim and his throne! I am going to my Lord, taking with me anxious questions that never end.'"

All this time the tongues of the common folk continued to wag in gossip and speculation. Even among the ranks of judges and magistrates strange stories and rumors about Sitt al-Mulk abounded. She swiftly summoned a delegation of them and addressed them harshly: "Shame on you all! Are you the trusted agents of state or the dregs of society? Are you minded to abandon the sacred Shi'ite principles, of the hidden, secret, esoteric reading of holy scripture? Do you desire to bring down the pillars of the Fatimid mission? Shall I count you among the degenerate, the negligent, and the superficial[4] about whom the jurists and *imam*s have warned, 'There is no eternal reward for them. When they die their souls will not separate from their bodies, and they will remain forever punished, eternally afflicted with suffering'? Therefore, renounce your transgressions and spare me your suspicions. Cleanse yourselves with the waters of morality and preserve your honor. Should you fail in this, then await the condemnation of God and the retribution of a woman behind a veil."

Faced with Sitt al-Mulk's display of indignation and feigned innocence, the magistrates and judges conferred among themselves and proclaimed her innocence, humbling themselves before her. They begged her forgiveness and besought their own safety; and she pardoned them and assuaged their fears.

When this one, solitary storm had blown over, Sitt al-Mulk began to feel sure of taking control once more. Using the occasion of the Feast of the Sacrifice, she installed her candidate on the throne, she herself placing the crown on his head. He was the young son of al-Hakim, Abu al-Hasan 'Ali, and was given the

---

4. The term *al-Zahir* (outer, external) is clearly used with reference to Sunni Muslims, in contrast to *al-Batin* (inner, esoteric), which refers to a basic precept of Shi'ite Islam.

honorific title of al-Zahir li-I'zaz Dinallah. After the ceremony she summoned Ibn Dawwas to come to her forthwith and spoke to him with unusual directness: "I am just as you have known me, and as I promised you I should be. So, be just as I have known you, and as you promised me you would be. The souls of free men are the sanctuaries of secrets. Never forget this! I am placing this young man's education in your hands. You must take him by the hand and teach him how to steer the helm of government and hold the reins of power, how to fortify our state and see that it endures!"

On hearing these words Ibn Dawwas bowed his head and kissed the ground, declaring his unswerving loyalty. She dismissed him and summoned Khatir al-Mulk, speaking to him as she had to Ibn Dawwas. Then she added, in an imperious tone, "You will assemble a procession, luxurious and ornate, for the new caliph, and parade him among all the subjects with an escort of slaves, announcing, 'Your mistress presents to you your new lord and protector. Pledge your loyalty and obedience to him.'"

Sitt al-Mulk now had what she wanted. Khatir al-Mulk carried out her orders with skillful cunning. Apart from one young servant, who was killed because he refused to pledge fealty to the new caliph and spoke too of the imminent return of al-Hakim, all the palace servants spent their days kissing the ground and rubbing their cheeks against the pavement, vying fiercely in their shows of obedience and compliance. People came in droves, from every alley and every walk of life, to profess their loyalty and proclaim their joy.

Soon after the coronation of al-Zahir li-I'zaz Dinallah, and the ensuing celebrations, Sitt al-Mulk declared a three-day period of mourning for the disappearance of al-Hakim; and when this time had passed all seemed to be well. The affairs of state returned to normal, the waters ran their courses, swords were returned to their sheaths, and tongues were silenced. But before long a new wave of malicious gossip and dangerous stories rose in the main palace, concerning Sitt al-Mulk's complicity in the murder of al-Hakim. Fanning the fires of these rumors was the discovery made by a team of skilled searchers and diggers three days after al-Hakim had disappeared. Scouring the Muqattam Mountain from top to bottom, they found, close to the pond east of Halwan and Dayr al-Baghl, al-Hakim's clothes, seven buttoned robes all stained with blood. At first the searchers withheld their findings from public knowledge, from fear of Sitt al-Mulk and a desire to remain in the good graces of the new caliph. But soon word got out and spread like wildfire.

Sitt al-Mulk shut herself in her chambers for a full day, desperately seeking some means to keep control and find a solution. Just before sunset there burst out within her sudden, resistless flashes of satisfaction. The meaning and significance of these was as follows: that just one soul should harbor so many secrets, and that making them into one secret and burying it within her soul alone meant all other secrets must be destroyed. To return the secret of al-Hakim's murder to the grave of her soul, and thereby put an end to all rumors, she must, she concluded, kill it by killing those who harbored the secret or had any knowledge of it.

It struck her, too, that this action would not simply acquit her and cleanse her hands of al-Hakim's blood but also accomplish several other goals for the better security of the government. First, it would free her from the rivalry between Ibn Dawwas and Khatir al-Mulk, for influence and autocratic power, which existed because both were guardians of the secret. Second, it would quell the rumors, spread by missionaries among the simple common folk, and among enemies of the state awaiting their chance to attack, that al-Hakim had disappeared only for a time. Last, it would put a stop to all the stories of the madmen who claimed to be al-Hakim's killer, or who disguised themselves as al-Hakim, displaying themselves in the hope of claiming his throne and his power.

At once Sitt al-Mulk summoned Nasim the Sicilian, the head of the palace guard. She ordered him to refrain from continual kissing of the ground in her presence, then said, "Rise, Nasim, and tell me. What is a secret?"

"A secret," he responded humbly, "according to my knowledge and profession, is like a buried link or a veiled knot, something my eyes may see but my tongue does not utter. A secret is what is beyond my comprehension and about which I dare not ask. A secret, My Lady, is a precious kernel, a special nugget, which, once exposed, is lost; if the soul of one harboring it is tormented by it, then the soul of one not harboring it is still more tormented. A secret, in politics, is the key to authority, and, in war, a secret leads to surprise and victory. A secret, My Lady, in its highest and noblest form, is what man carries in his soul to his grave. Yet this is the merest fraction of what scholars and learned men have said about secrecy and a secret."

Pleased with this response, Sitt al-Mulk said, "You know, I am sure, how well I think of you, just as my brother did. Indeed, I hold you in still higher esteem. You have no doubt heard much talk about al-Hakim's death. I wish, here and now, to put an end to all of that by revealing what my own inquiries and investigations have uncovered, concerning certain members of the nobility who always hoped to destroy my brother.

"Go out and, in the very presence of Ibn Dawwas, tell the servants this: 'My mistress has clear evidence that this Sayf al-Dawla is he who slew al-Hakim. Therefore slay him!' Then go and do the same with the prime minister, Khatir al-Mulk. Demand his neck and the necks of all those who conspired with him in the matter. Then, when you have carried out these orders, return to me and report what you have accomplished."

Nasim and his squad of palace guards set out in search of Ibn Dawwas but did not find him at his residence. Then they headed toward the Kutama Quarter, where they found him making the rounds of his tribesmen, urging them to attend to one another's needs. The head of the guard then told him Her Highness requested his presence, forthwith, on an urgent matter. Then, when he was led far enough away from the quarter, Nasim spoke as Sitt al-Mulk had instructed him to do; and, as expected, the palace guards drew their swords on Ibn Dawwas. Striving to defend himself with his own weapons, he called out in vain to his fellow tribesmen; and after a few brief moments, having slain two guards, Ibn

Dawwas sank beneath the many gashes. As he sank into death, he was heard to murmur, "I escaped the hell of al-Hakim, only to fall victim to that treacherous serpent his sister. Curse this government of secrets and calamities!"

While this was taking place, Khatir al-Mulk was at his home, telling his wife of a nightmare that returned again and again to haunt him. In it al-Hakim appeared to him, now as a fearsome ghost, telling him he must reveal the secret of his murder or fall victim to some evil revenge, now in the form of a woman of giant size, clutching his neck with her many hands and taking pleasure in choking him. His wife could think of no way to assuage his anxieties and fears, except to serve him cup after cup of wine, of which she herself partook liberally too.

When they were both quite intoxicated, she removed all his clothing, then, standing before him, herself disrobed slowly and seductively. In her eyes and in her movements there was every sign of suppleness and enticement. Then she descended on him as he received her on his mighty body, responding twofold to her every kiss and hug and embrace. They appeared as though they were one body, one entity, not to be separated or told apart. Then, in the midst of this rapture and ecstasy, at the very moment of ultimate pleasure, Nasim and his henchmen burst in upon them and thrust them with deep, piercing stabs, like flashes of lightning, tearing their flesh apart.

In the early part of that bloody day, Nasim returned panting to Sitt al-Mulk, together with his burly slaves, bearing great bulging sacks dripping with blood. Bowing before her, he said, "Your will is done, My Lady. These seven sacks contain the corpses of Ibn Dawwas and Khatir al-Mulk, along with five of their treasonous cohorts. The others will come later. Shall we place the heads in a single bag and throw the trunks to the wild beasts?"

Sitt al-Mulk shrieked, the tears rolling from her eyes, "No! Nothing shall remain. Bury all these sacks in a single ditch outside the city. Keep your hands from their necks, and let the blood flow in their veins, not on the tips of your swords."

Sitt al-Mulk spent the following days breathing sighs of relief. Her palace attendants bathed and massaged her body and embellished her with cosmetics and perfumes. By now this was her only pleasure, and she demanded ever more of it, each lady vying to please every part of her blessed body.

Indeed, Sitt al-Mulk knew a kind of rebirth in these days, freed from the bloodshed and turmoil of the past weeks. She took comfort at reaching, as she felt, safe shores. She even began once more to oversee the affairs of state, while the young caliph al-Zahir was learning, in her shadow, the ropes of responsibility and decision, and how to undo the repressive policies of his father.

Then, a little time after, Sitt al-Mulk reorganized the various branches of government, making them more secure and durable. She launched a wide-ranging purge of the treasury, which had collapsed beneath al-Hakim's excessive patronage and corruption, and the criminally swollen salaries he had doled out. At the same time she reinstated income and customs taxes on a fair and equitable basis.

The first signs of health returned to the treasury, along with indications of a sound balanced budget. In addition to these much needed fiscal reforms, Sitt al-Mulk encouraged al-Zahir to cancel and abolish all al-Hakim's edicts crushing and curtailing individual rights, along with those sanctioning the mistreatment of citizens of other religion. When these new proclamations reached the ears of the people of Egypt, a sense of tranquility warmed their hearts and a spirit of tolerance and comradeship prevailed among peoples of every race, color, and creed.

Once convinced normal life had returned to their neighborhoods, the people began to exercise their rights and enjoy their new freedom. They came out of their homes, into the alleys and streets and squares, men and women alike, of all classes and ages, rejoicing and praising God, chanting wishes of victory and glory to the caliph and his aunt, and cursing their enemies to defeat and damnation. They formed processions, throwing rose petals and spices at one another, exchanging pleasantries, all to express their surpassing joy at receiving the ultimate blessing, second only to Heaven itself.

—*Translated by William Granara and Christopher Tingley*

Moussa Wuld Ibno (b. 1956)

Born in Mauritania, Moussa Wuld Ibno obtained a doctorate in philosophy from the Sorbonne. He also obtained a degree in journalism from the Higher Institute of Journalism in Paris and now teaches philosophy at the University of Nouakchott in Mauritania. He has published two novels in French: *L'Amour Impossible* (1990) and *Barzakh* (1993). *City of Winds* (1996) is his first novel in Arabic. He is the major writer of fiction in the Arab world to have addressed the question of technology and its negative effects on human life, a crucial subject hardly touched upon as yet in modern Arabic literature. Wuld Ibno treats his potentially gloomy and depressing subject matter philosophically and with great sophistication, and his style, symbolization, and deft treatment of his narrative produce a very good read.

CITY OF WINDS (1996)

City of Winds, excerpted here partly in translation, partly in retelling, is a novel about the human condition in its more negative aspects. The novel straddles centuries of recurring abuse of power and of the spiritual and physical enslavement of the weak by the strong. This continuing and repetitive drama, in three cycles of time and space, takes place in a desert both actual and symbolic and demonstrates both the capacity of indigenous peoples

to enslave their fellows (here the Africans) and also the West's unrelenting attempt at hegemony and its ravenous intentions toward peoples of the Third World. The main character,
Vara, finds himself dying in one cycle only to find himself thrust into a further cycle of
misery, suffering yet another drama of incarceration. There is always a Western figure, or
figures, attempting to exploit a still innocent and virgin world, a point fully highlighted in
the third and final episode, with the introduction of advanced technology as a weapon of
evil and a means of human subjugation. In the author's philosophy, humanity is unable to
free itself from an inborn egocentric cruelty and a relentless will to acquire hegemony, riches,
and power at the expense of the weaker majority. Even the introduction of the fantastic, in
the figure of a beautiful jinn who strives to save the hero, provides no permanent solution
and, in the end, cannot save the novel's protagonist.

The first episode below begins with the main character experiencing his final death
in the third round of life on earth, having lived through various but essentially similar
experiences in all of them.

THE TOWER OF THE BLACK

I am in a new world, assailed by strange and trivial memories of the life now
leaving me. The pangs of death have brought a clear truth, and I am no longer
oblivious to anything. My eyesight is sharp. The pangs of death have lit, have
magnified many thousands of times, the folds of my life, while the dark corners
are as though thousands of angry desert suns were directly blazing on them. All
barriers between external and internal, apparent and hidden, known and unknown, have crumbled down. All distinguishing qualities have melted now into
one single quality at the center of light! The bottomless lake of my consciousness has split off in all directions, as if it had crashed into a planet fallen from
a height of millions of light years. Consciousness now is working outside the
realm of consciousness. I am in the region of the afterlife, on the borders before
death; I am winding in the reel of my life, hearing it, seeing it, realizing it in
all its detail, with nothing before or after—I, who have spent my days striving,
vainly, to connect my life with my dreams, my feelings with my subfeelings, my
consciousness with the consciousness of others, so as to pronounce judgment on
others, on myself, on time, only to have all my attempts bounce back, defeated
and despairing. But at this moment—at the hour of my death—I witness what,
through all my life, I could never see spontaneously realized. And now, having
left the field, I see the outcome of that decisive battle, between my life and my
dreams, take form before me in boundless truth, each detail in its proper place.

In an initial episode, Vara is taken as a slave by salt merchants, and we are
given a detailed description of his miserable life of bondage in a caravan of wild
and primitive men, on their way first to Ghana, then to the city of Odavest.
There, in Odavest, he is put up for sale.

The salt caravan's souk attracted many of the people of Odavest: those merely curious; smiths looking for leathers or precious metals needed in their trade;

people searching for rare goods; slave merchants; hunters after the latest news, after anecdotes, rarities, and quaint narratives. There were great bands of poets and musicians, all eloquent of tongue, seeking recompense. There too were the wizards, the snake charmers, the sellers of amulets; there were the tricksters of all kinds, offering protection against the jinn, or the evil eye, or iron weapons, claiming to bring about success in love and happiness in marriage, or else prosperity in business. Then there were the various Sufi sheikhs, and those who said they could make connection with the other world, and the professional prostitutes. A motley throng met there, of every breed and color: veiled Muslim women, bareheaded Tuareg women, and pagan black women with their heads shaven.

He is put on display among other slaves and, after some weeks, is bought for a cheap price by a man called Izbaghra, whom he accompanies five times daily to the mosque, carrying the man's ablution jug and prayer mat. Although his life is fraught with difficulties, it is here that he comes to know love.

During this time of hardship, I came to know Fala, a bewitching Berber slave girl who'd come to fetch water from the mosque's wells. She was of middling size, with eyes clear as a rain-washed sky. Each night we'd meet, in an abandoned house in the artisans' quarter, set on a lonely street reached only by faint echoes of the city. Sometimes, during the late hours of the night, when the moaning winds blew and stones would break from the cold, we'd light a small fire in the old hearth. Then the strange, dancing shadows would begin to rise up the walls, and the house would fill with the spirits of its old inhabitants. The wind's intermittent gusts would bear to our ears fragments of voices, their fullness lost before they reached us: a disjointed fragment of music, a single "Allah Akbar," a remnant of a prayer call.

Eventually Fala tells Vara she is pregnant with their child. She takes him to her grandmother, who reads his fortune, then tells him, in frightening tones, that he will live a very long life but be killed by his own son. In the following episode, as in the others, there is a certain Matall, a leader among men. Fala takes Vara to a slave meeting led by Matall, who urges his hearers to a slave revolt that Vara joins. However, the plot is discovered and all those taking part are severely punished. The only person who speaks to him during his days of imprisonment is Abu 'l-Hama, a wise slave who is also a dwarf. One day Abu 'l-Hama tells Vara an old tale.

"In olden times virtue reigned supreme on earth. But after a while it grew bored and began to wonder what its opposite could be—and from that time on the kingdom of evil grew ever wider, the kingdom of good ever smaller."

"But what of human beings?" I broke in.

"They're the latest inventions of evil, its most dangerous device. Take, for instance, the one who betrayed you."

"You mean someone betrayed me?"

"One of the slaves, whose side didn't win the vote over what to do."

"I don't care any more what happened. All I want now is to escape from this slavery, to live in another time, where people are better."

"One day, perhaps, your dream will come true. If you reject fate, then flee humans, take refuge in the desert, and await God's will."

I lowered my face from the sky and gazed hard at this mighty dwarf who was speaking with me.

How strange it is, I thought, to see such hideous ugliness yet know, from his tone and his expressions, what depths of beauty lie behind that ungainly mask.

Eventually Vara is sold on to a caravan traveling to Sijilmasa. There follows a long and fantastic description of the hardship and harshness of the desert.

As we traveled steadily on, the sands would appear in all their forms: waves, mountains, hills, valleys of silky soft sands, boundless expanses of dry black or white pebbles, long seas of sands, flat seas, seas surging or calm, sands heaped up or scattered, sands in great heaps surmounted by streams of moving sands, their shape constantly changing.

The noon call to prayer sounds, and men perform their ablutions and face the *qibla*. He stands to pray with them, and reflects.

Why this equality in prayer and oppression in life? Why should people's share of religion lie in its outer forms, while the pure essence stays neglected and people are left to live beneath the tyranny and injustice of others?

During this journey, having suffered the immense hardships of the caravan, he manages to escape.

In my endless wanderings through this ocean of sands I lost all sense of identity, no longer able to remember who I was. Was I that young pagan boy who'd lived so happily in the land of gold, or this Muslim slave crossing the great wilderness, not knowing where I was bound? Or that earthbound being in whom dwelt strange, universal elements, which led me on to wander in other worlds? Might I be not just one of these but all of them together?

THE TOWER OF THE WHITE

The fugitive remains for forty days and nights on the top of a hill; starving, parched and feverish, assailed by wild birds and exposed to unbearable heat by day and bitter cold by night. Constantly he hears Abu 'l-Hama's words, "Flee humans, take refuge in the desert and await God's will."

Once more the fantastic intervenes, this time in the person of the Muslim saint al-Khadir, who tells him as follows:

"I am the sign you have been waiting for. You rebelled against the ordinary ways of humans, but you will never be rid of your humanity."

It is clear he is speaking to Vara in a period later than the one in which Vara had been living. Odavest is now an industrial city on the verge of causing an environmental disaster. He grants Vara a new chance of life, a crossing to another time, in which he can stay if he wishes. If, though, he chooses to leave, the next station will be his last.

He is rescued by four black men, who carry him down the hill to a caravan presided over by the eternal white man, the archeologist Vostpaster, with whom there is once more a Fala. He is taken along with the caravan.

I fell into a deep sleep. My consciousness of the other time returned, and I knew who I was. I wondered about the time in which I now found myself. Perhaps I wasn't in another period at all. The sun, the winds, the sands in the great wilderness—these were still just as they had been. The men, the caravans, the masters and slaves were the same. Could it be the king of time had deceived me? This caravan, though, was strange, not like the ones I'd known. It couldn't be from the time of Sijilmasa . . . and Fala! How she'd changed—I struck fear in her now. How had she come to find herself in the caravan with Vostpaster? Was she someone else, alongside the same me? Strange how alike they were! When she woke, I thought, I'd talk to her, remind her of our long nights in Odavest, in that abandoned house in the artisans' quarter. I'd ask her too for the latest news of the slave revolt.

As he recovers, he realizes Fala is a great favorite with the European archeologist, who is searching for ancient remains that will tell him of the life of people in bygone times, and is trying to discover the site of the old city of Odavest, the city of lost caravans.

Filled with questions, he finds himself able to remember the old Odavest in his sleep, and he speaks out loud, describing it in detail. Vostpaster is called to hear the sleeper talk about the goal of his search. On waking him, though, he finds Vara has forgotten all he said while asleep.

After a furious desert storm lasting for some days, Vostpaster vainly tries to gain more information from him through hypnosis. In his dream Vara remembers everything.

I was, I realized, outside time, and I found many of the answers to Vostpaster's questions. I was on the point of telling him my father's name when I woke. Afaramoul! How could I have forgotten my father's name? If Vostpaster wanted to delve into the depths of my hopelessness, I'd give him every scope till he was satisfied. I was filled with hopelessness, till it gushed out from me. The source of my very being had brought the greatest shock of my life. My life itself was a great and unforgivable error. My father, who'd abandoned me to the shackles of the salt caravan—the thought of killing my father keeps returning to me, obsessively—the failure of the Odavest rebellion—and the eternal caravan with its masters and slaves in the great wilderness. Imagine! For nine centuries I've fled it, only to find myself hurrying back to it. The king of time has saved me from one hell, only to fling me into another. Where's the good in moving on from one time to the next, if human beings are evil in every time? They become worse, even, as each period passes. But I don't want to leave Vostpaster's caravan. I must lead him to the remains of the city he's searching for. Would it be best, perhaps, to flee into the desert, die on some hilltop, and so put an end to this whole charade? And yet I've always told myself to wait, to see what was to come. I've no choice at any rate, either here or there, whether asleep, awake, or dead. It will happen as it will, and I've no control over events. When I wake, I no longer know who I am. I become cut off from my past and future, and I can remember nothing. No matter how much I decide, while I'm dreaming, to remember a thing when I wake—I never do. My conscious action has no will to guide it. My will's a counterfeit, for behind it there's another will.

It is Fala who eventually succeeds in hypnotizing him. When he wakes, he finds an excited Vostpaster writing furiously and boasting how he will be the first archeological explorer to find the remains of the lost city of Odavest; all the missing links have now been supplied by this being from outside time. He kisses Fala passionately and happily. His plans have changed now. They will, he tells the guide, go to Tijafja to collect all the oral history they can about Odavest and Ghana, then make their way toward the place where Vara said Odavest existed before. When they reach Tijafja, however, they find the place "a museum of horrors": there are burned corpses of people hanged by their necks from palm branches with short ropes and swinging in the tongues of fire beneath them. The rebels have, it emerges, killed Capolani, who was among the few interested in Vostpaster's research. They are met by Lieutenant Efrirjan, who has assumed control following the European's murder. There are a number of old men in chains, their beards sunk in the sand and their arms tied behind them. These are the dignitaries of the city, taken hostage till they reveal the names of the fleeing rebels. They seem proud that the rebels have thwarted the colonial dream. Vara's spirits are raised by the rebellion.

When I was left to myself in sleep, that first night in Tijafja, the disaster seemed to me too vast to conceive. Man traverses nine centuries, and the whole of the great wilderness, looking for virtue, only to end as a guest in the pit of oppression! I feel revolted and sickened. Khadir! What time have you sent me to now? In that first time we were free in our land, whether masters or slaves. But now, see this shame! Here's Fala, sleeping with an invading nonbeliever. I've lost all desire to know Odavest's shifting fortunes. I must flee, just as soon as I can, this demon that pursues mere phantoms. Didn't al-Khadir tell me? If you have no wish to stay in your next station, then do as you have done now. Flee humans, take refuge in the desert, and await God's will. But, if I do that, I'll lose my chance of traveling through time. Well, what if I do? Could any station to come be worse than the one I'm in? Better, perhaps, to stay here and help the resistance. But the Europeans might arrest me, treat me as they've treated the people of Tijafja. They might torture me, hang me from the branch of a palm tree, and light a fire under me. Then I'd lose my last chance to travel far and forward, where humankind might be better.

Vostpaster, having placed Vara under constant surveillance, finishes collecting oral memories of Odavest and wishes to leave, but the lieutenant will not permit him. The resistance, having learned of the murder of Capolani, is now active. It is led by the Prince of Adrar, who becomes Vara's idol. The colonists are awaiting a military aid caravan with fresh ammunition and provisions. When it arrives, Vostpaster's caravan begins its journey, with Vara in it.

After three days the rebels attack the caravan and Vara finds himself hiding among the dead and wounded. At nightfall he manages to creep out and climb the heights of Izhar, where he settles in a seclusion he hopes will be everlasting.

THE TABBANA TOWER

He remains for a long time on the heights, trying to ward off the attack of eagles seeking prey. He spends much time in prayer, making the following pledge to God.

"I swear by God the Creator never to return to the rotten human race; to live a life of even serenity, far from the oppressors, till the day I die."

The radical change within him does nothing to change the law of the universe. But nor is his will shaken by the fierce heat of the day or by the bitter cold of the night, or by hunger or thirst. Whenever he feels his resistance fray, he hears Abu 'l-Hama's voice saying, "Flee humans, take refuge in the desert and await God's will."

Stiffness of limbs, high fever, and a feeling of total degeneration follow, leading to incipient coma. He is visited once more by al-Khadir with his green aura: "So, for a third time you've chosen to change the century you're living in?"

"Everything's quite dreadful there. It's been a time of terror, filled with injustice wrought by evil people. The children of Europe are there in their hundreds now, at the head of armies invading from all directions, aiming to subjugate the whole region. Even the masters have become their slaves, slaves to the European. I detest this nation, I can't endure it. I want to live among another nation, or else die."

"Very well. Surge on. Follow your inclinations. Change your people for the last time. But this last station you'll be unable to leave, and you'll perish in it."

Waking in a new century, Vara descends and finds himself, soon, in the world of advanced technology. We have a description of technicians carrying out their duties, of vast walls stretching endlessly, of tongues of fire of various colors, and of ubiquitous propaganda posters. He falls into a faint and, when he awakes, finds himself tightly bound on a chair, alone in a closed room. Two men, speaking a language he does not understand, enter and begin to beat him violently, then force him to swallow two pills. We are given a chilling description of this place: a center for storing toxic waste and dangerous chemicals, which has become an important source of hard currency. Workers are subjected to a constant barrage of propaganda. Video episodes are repeated continually, over and over again, with no respite, accompanied by the same explanatory voice describing the Imdel Center, one of many such centers in the great wilderness for the storage of dangerous and poisonous substances. There are notices everywhere, all written in English, prohibiting smoking and pointing out other urgent precautions. The whole place is an advanced image of hard-core technology, with a frightening absence of any human concern. Men are regarded as mere robots, who must yield to the harshest discipline in a perilous place including, among other things, live nuclear material buried in deep wells. The wells give way under the extreme heat of their contents, so that fissures appear on the top, but these are closed daily. This station forms part of the Democratic Republic of the Isthmus Heights, presided over by Tanvall ben Matall, a ruler much glorified in the reels of incessant audiovisual propaganda and praised for having built these centers for storing the profitable waste and other substances. We are given a detailed description of the protective measures taken by the authorities to prevent the release of dangerous materials, measures that render humans subject to automization and a life without volition. He speaks with another new comrade, who tells him as follows:

"I'm from the Namadi tribe, the old deer hunters they talk about in the video. We were masters of the great wilderness, living in freedom in those harsh, magical expanses. We refused technology and its world so as to protect our land; but when Tanvall came to power, he signed an agreement with the United Nations to store poisonous waste, and the great wilderness was chosen as an international region for storing it, along with other dangerous substances. They pushed us all out toward the coastal regions—our land's been a storage site for a long time now. I myself was born in the City of Winds, some time after my people were exiled. This place is assigned now, by the world order, as a storage place for the refuse of all the tropics. The only ones living here are the rejects and weaklings of the tropical world, the ones who've been contaminated and exposed to radiation. The first chance they had, they sent us for forced labor in these centers. No one here lives more than two years at the most."

That night Vara sees al-Khadir again and speaks with him.

"Oh Khadir, what disaster have you found for me? You know well enough I'm a traveler from no time, searching for a better human race, and this is the worst of all! Don't, I beg you, abandon me."

The features were as inscrutable as ever behind the green aura.

"Have you forgotten our covenant, Vara?" he asked.

"No, I've forgotten nothing."

"You must remember how I permitted you to travel into the future, to change your people."

"Yes, I remember. But I thought the future would be better than the past."

"And so you chose to explore the future. Two earlier periods I permitted you to discover. First you wanted to escape the Odavest time. Then, nine centuries on, you could choose to settle in the second time or travel on toward another. But you fled the Capolani time and found yourself in the Tanvall time. And now you press me to grant you yet another chance! I remind you once more of the covenant. Your travels through time are over. You must stay in this time till you die."

"Have pity on me! I must leave this accursed people! Could any evil be clearer to see than here?"

"There is refuge for you no longer. What human before you had the chance to live with three peoples, in times so far apart? You're meeting your just deserts, because of your ignorance. You can't run away from fate forever! There's no way out for you now. You're bound to live in your new nation. In any case, what you're witnessing now is the last face of the earth. Were you to travel further into the future, you'd find it had turned to a heap of ashes, the sun blotted out."

With that he vanished behind his green aura.

"No, wait," I cried. "Wait! Khadir! Khadir!"

After decontamination at the end of the day's work, the inmates are fed, then taken to the man directing the place, a bulky European who tells him that, having been caught in the act of trying to sabotage the center, he is to remain incarcerated there and put to hard forced labor. His revolt has led him nowhere. After his first paycheck he had been allowed, for the first time, to go to the club, and there he had met a beautiful woman called Solima who was, it turned out, a jinn looking for a good soul. She was wearing a bracelet with a stud, which was, she explained, a compass leading her to such souls. Vara, though, was the first good person she had found.

"For thousands of years now I've traveled in a black void, from one place to the next in the Tower of Tabban, but good souls are hard to find. Many deserts I've crossed searching for you. I'm not permitted to drink twice from the same fountain, and so I had to travel on—looking for new blood, for new water, for another good soul. If you're not happy here, I can help you escape. I'll give you one of my suits of clothes, which, if you once put it on, will make you invisible. Then you can leave whenever you wish."

He tells the Namadi he intends to run away. Though incredulous, the man gives him the address of a woman called Fala, at Itweel, the second site after theirs. He succeeds in fleeing the center, wearing the magical garments, and finds Fala, who is, it emerges, a rebel against the present state of things. She tells him, "There are disasters all around us, and yet we make no proper effort to ward them off. I'm afraid the temperature will rise so high, the earth will be turned to an inferno."

The novel ends with his joining Fala and her group in trying to sabotage a convoy, which is guarded by dogs trained to attack and kill. He is captured and sentenced to death. While awaiting execution, he wonders what had happened to the beautiful Fala, who was also captured, supposing that she will be executed too. Just before his death he learns, from a newspaper that comes to hand, how she has actually become engaged to the ruler she had been attempting to overthrow. The date of the wedding has been fixed, and she has received many gifts from her fiancé. The human bent toward evil, which Vara so loathed throughout his three existences, has finally triumphed.

—Translated by Salma Khadra Jayyusi and Christopher Tingley

Sun'allah Ibrahim (b. 1937)

Egyptian novelist Sun'allah Ibrahim studied law before eventually taking up journalism. From 1959 to 1964 he was imprisoned for his political activities, an experience recounted in harrowing detail in his acclaimed short novel,

That Smell, originally published in 1966 and subsequently banned. This novel bears eloquent testimony to the power of censorship in the contemporary Arab world, for, until quite recently, the complete version was available only through its translation by Denys Johnson-Davies, entitled *The Smell of It* (1971). After his release Ibrahim spent time in Moscow and East Berlin, working on a graduate project never finally completed. His work, which demonstrates great sensitivity of language and viewpoint in conjunction with a concerned outlook on life and society, has won him considerable fame and popularity. His better-known works include the novel *Augustus Star* (1974), an account of Egyptian society during the Nasser presidency set against the building of the Aswan High Dam; *The Committee* (1981), an exploration of the dynamics of bureaucratic tyranny; *Beirut, Beirut* (1984), in which a writer is commissioned to write his comments during the Lebanese civil war; and *Dhat* (1992). He also writes children's fiction.

THE COMMITTEE (1981)

The "Committee" is a faceless authority that can decide your fate and channel your destiny. The protagonist is summoned to appear before this committee and suffers the humiliating array of questions that impinge on his life, his thoughts, his conduct, and his individuality. Ibrahim's novel, with its strong reminders of Kafka, can be described as a revelation of how a person is forced to bend to the standard acceptable to society and the authority that rules it, as well as of the ways in which any genuine individuality is rejected and fought. A mindless bureaucracy dominates everything, creating a paranoid atmosphere that crushes a human being and imposes the harshest sentence on him. Ibrahim's handling of this novel reflects a mastery of style and narrative dexterity.

I reached the building where the Committee met at half past eight in the morning, a full half hour before my appointment was due, and had no difficulty finding the room, in the quiet, dimly lit side corridor set apart for its meetings. An aged guard in a clean yellow coat was sitting in front of the door, wearing the serene expression of those who, finding they've reached the end of the road, hoist the flag of surrender and withdraw from the hurly-burly of life with all its ephemeral struggles.

The members of the Committee didn't, he told me, usually arrive before ten. This didn't surprise me in the least, though I felt a bit put out even so, especially as I'd turned up for the appointment in good time, sacrificing several hours of sleep to get up so early.

The guard's seat was the only one around. I stood there beside him and, putting down my Samsonite briefcase, offered him a cigarette and lit one for myself. Try as I might to keep a grip on my nerves, I found my heart pounding constantly, and I had to keep telling myself that any sign of anxiety would lose me the chance I'd been offered. I wouldn't be able to concentrate, as I needed to so badly during the coming interview.

After a while I got tired of just standing there and, picking up my briefcase, I walked down to the end of the corridor then back again, keeping my eye on the door all the while in case the Committee should arrive and call me in. But still there was just the guard sitting there, staring meekly in front of him, his toothless gums moving constantly as though chewing on some imaginary morsel of food.

Once more I started pacing the corridor, looking at my watch from time to time. It was almost ten-thirty when I saw the guard finally get to his feet, put his cigarette on the floor under his chair, turn the handle of the door, and cautiously open it. Then he disappeared inside.

I hastily took up position alongside his chair, my heart pounding more fiercely than ever. When the guard emerged, I was expecting him to tell me to go in, but he merely picked up his cigarette, sat back down, and went on quietly smoking.

After a while I plucked up the courage to ask him, politely, whether the Committee had arrived yet.

"Just one of them," he replied.

"I didn't see anyone going in," I said.

"They come in by another door," he explained.

For yet another half hour I stood there by his chair. Meanwhile various members of the Committee arrived, and several times the guard went to the buffet to fetch coffee for them. Each time he did it, I tried to sneak a glance into the room, but, whenever he opened the door, he was careful only to open it a tiny crack, just enough for him to get in but not enough for me to see anything. Once he emerged from the room with a pair of leather shoes, called over the shoe-shine boy who was standing at the end of the corridor, and gave them to him. The boy proceeded to sit down by the door, but the guard shouted at him and told him to go and do it where he'd been standing before.

So I started walking around all over again, shifting my briefcase wearily from one hand to the other. I hadn't slept well the night before, even though I'd taken a sleeping pill, and I could feel a slight ache in the back of my head. I hadn't reckoned on something like this, even though I'd spent the whole of the past year preparing for anything that might happen today. Still, I didn't dare go off in search of an aspirin in case the Committee suddenly called me in. Wandering up and down, I finally came to the place where the shoe-shine boy was sitting on the floor, energetically cleaning the Committee's shoes (so I called them instinctively, laughing to myself as I thought about it). I saw, to my astonishment, that he was polishing the soles as well.

I made my way back to where the guard was sitting, put my briefcase down alongside him, offered him a cigarette, and lit one for myself. Then I stood there by him, smoking. After a while the shoe-shine boy finished cleaning the shoes and brought them back to the guard, who took them carefully and carried them back into the room, closing the door, carefully again, behind him. A little later he reemerged with a tray full of empty coffee cups, which he took back to the buffet. Then he came and sat down again.

As it was almost eleven-thirty now, and no one else had joined me by the door, it was clear I was the only person the Committee was going to interview today. Probably, I thought, they were discussing my case at this very moment—a most disturbing thought if true, because it meant they'd arrive at a provisional decision, and, if that was unfavorable (as it most probably would be for a number of reasons), anything I might do during the interview would have far less impact. They had plenty of reports on me, I knew, but even so my whole future was going to depend on the coming interview. Not, of course, that I'd actively sought the meeting. I'd simply been told an interview with the Committee was mandatory, and so I'd come.

At noon precisely the guard went into the room, came straight back out again, and asked me what my name was. Then he gestured to me to go in.

I picked up my briefcase in my right hand, using the other to check my tie was properly adjusted. Then, assuming a confident smile, I reached out for the porcelain door handle I'd gazed at so many times over the past three hours, turned it, pushed the door, and made my way into the room.

I made two mistakes right at the start.

First, in the panic I was vainly trying to hide, I forgot to close the door. I heard the soft tones of a woman's voice near to me.

"Close the door, please."

The blood rushed to my face and I turned toward the door. I grasped the handle in my left hand and pushed—but it wouldn't shut. The door panel was old, and it needed a lot of pressure to close it; as I was still using my right hand to hold on to the briefcase, I had to use my knee to push the door. The sweat was pouring down my forehead.

"Put your briefcase down," said the soft female voice, "and use both hands."

I realized I'd lost the first round.

The Committee would, I knew, be asking various questions, not designed merely to find out how much I knew but to probe my character as well, and assess my intellectual capacities. The content of the answer wasn't everything, though that certainly carried weight. What really counted was the ability to face up to questions.

As I explained earlier, I'd spent the whole of the past year getting ready, in different ways, for this particular day. I'd made a detailed study of the language used at the Committee's meetings, and reviewed my knowledge of a whole variety of subjects. I'd read about philosophy, art, chemistry, and economics. I'd set myself dozens of different questions, then spent whole days and nights finding the answers to them. I'd watched the quizzes and general knowledge programs on television and read through the letter columns of newspapers and magazines. I'd had one stroke of luck: my brother, who's twenty years older than I am, had kept a complete series of "True or False," dating from its very first issue thirty years ago, wrapped in a rubber band.

That wasn't all though. I'd made strenuous efforts to get a clear idea of how the Committee worked, seeking out people who'd been interviewed themselves—only to find that the few people I unearthed couldn't remember what had taken place in any detail, and that what they could remember seemed contradictory. Other information I gathered from a variety of sources was no more helpful. The only thing I gleaned from it all was that the Committee seemed to have no specific set of rules for doing things.

I tried to find something out about the members of the Committee, so as to have some idea how to answer their questions, or some notion about their attitudes, but a veil of rigid secrecy covered their names and professions. Everyone I asked just looked at me sympathetically. The one thing everyone agreed on was that the Committee always set a number of cunning traps for the people it interviewed. In view of this, that business about closing the door had clearly not come about by chance; and my confusion had shown them, even before the interview got under way, that I was inclined to panic and lacked initiative.

You can imagine how I felt after a fiasco like that: I just stood there in front of them, with the sweat pouring off me. Yet I felt too, deep down inside, an odd sense of delight at what had happened, as though a part of me was actually afraid of being successful—a feeling that was somehow stronger than either my anxiety or my overwhelming desire to please the Committee.

It was a really big committee, with members sitting in a line behind a long table that stretched right across the room. I couldn't concentrate enough to count just how many there were. Some of them were whispering among themselves, while others were thumbing through the papers in front of them. Most were wearing dark glasses, but even so I managed to recognize some of them from photographs in newspapers and magazines. In fact, as I now realized, I knew the woman with the soft voice, an unmarried woman I'd met a number of times before, and I blamed myself for not having paid any attention to her then. She was smiling at me, though, in a friendly looking way. I wasn't surprised to see a couple of soldiers among their number, with red tabs on the collars of their uniforms, embossed with gold, which were evidence of their high rank.

Right in the middle sat a decrepit old man with thick glasses, who was trying to read a document held so close to them the two were almost touching. The document had, no doubt, been taken from my file. When the old man had finished reading, he put the paper down and turned first to the left, then to the right, to indicate to his colleagues that the session had started and they should stop talking. Everyone looked toward me.

I fixed my gaze on the lips of the old man, whose sallow complexion made him look as remote from life as anyone could possibly be.

"Before we begin," he said, speaking to me directly, "I should like to express my appreciation, and that of all my colleagues here with me, for your decision to come here. That doesn't mean, of course, that we shall be showing you any partiality; our attitude toward you will depend on a number of factors, and we're here today to reach a decision in that regard. However, I wish to emphasize that appearing before this committee of ours is, as everyone knows, not compulsory. Everyone, in this day and age, enjoys complete freedom of choice. Your decision to come here reflects considerable perspicacity and good sense on your part, and we shall certainly be taking it into account as we consider your situation. But now we should like to hear what you have to say about all this."

According to those who'd appeared before the Committee before (and other sources too had confirmed this), there was one standard question addressed to everyone who came for interview, namely the reasons and factors that had prompted them to come. As such I'd prepared my answer in advance, but, realizing the Committee would be expecting me to do just that, I'd thought long and hard before deciding on the proper way of responding. I didn't want to give them some hackneyed answer they'd heard countless times before, obviously designed to flatter them. It should, I decided, be something unusual, something that would seem simple and spontaneous, as though the question had taken me by surprise. In this way I'd demonstrate my honesty and reliability. I'd give an accurate picture of myself, without going into specific detail about, for example, the real reasons behind certain things I'd done; I'd simply refer to these in a way that would absolve me from responsibility for anything that might put me in a bad light—which would, on the contrary, lead them to form a favorable view of me. Given the special means and wide powers they had to find out everything they wanted to know about me, this was actually a very difficult thing to do.

I swallowed several times, then started to speak—so quietly that the old man leaned forward with his hand to his right ear. "Excuse me," he said, "I'm rather deaf in one ear. Would you mind speaking up?"

I did as he asked, launching into the response I'd prepared in advance. Of course, being so anxious, and concentrating so hard on not making any grammatical errors in their language, meant that I forgot a large part of what I'd intended to say. Still, I managed to give them a general picture of my upbringing and the course my career had taken, in circumstances over which I'd had little control. Yet, I told them, I was spurred on by lofty ambitions, and was eager to foster and utilize such talents as I possessed to the best possible advantage. I made a special point of citing the ethical principles and ideals from which I took my guidance.

I went on to discuss the ordeal I'd been through, and how it had left me vulnerable to sickness, attributing this in the main to the wide gulf between my aspirations and what I was able to do in reality. This, I said, had led me to be dissatisfied with everything. The only solution, so far as I could see, was to change my way of life completely.

I supported my speech with various theatrical gestures I'd rehearsed in advance. Then, picking up my briefcase and opening it, I produced a set of testimonials from various sources, praising my abilities and confirming all the information I'd sent them about myself. Since most of these were in Arabic, I talked about them in the Committee's language. They listened carefully, looking over the documents in front of them as I did so. I noticed, though, that a member with blond hair and blue eyes, sitting on the old man's left, paid no attention to the testimonials, leafing busily through a file that no doubt contained secret reports about me.

A short, ugly-looking member, seated to the old man's right between him and one of the army officers, raised his head in my direction. "I find that hard to understand," he said aggressively. "You seem to have had plenty of experience, and yet here you are, at your age, wanting to make a new start. Don't you think it's a bit late for that?"

"A lot of people start a new life after they're forty," I replied nervously. "And in any case it isn't really a new start, more the culmination of the original beginning—a complete exploitation of all my different kinds of potential. I look at it, from numerous points of view, as a natural development of my personality."

My diminutive questioner started muttering angrily to himself, and I wondered just why he felt so hostile toward me. I got the impression, somehow, that the way I'd set out my talents and presented testimonials from respected and influential quarters had annoyed him. It occurred to me, considering the matter further, that he might perhaps have been in my position himself in his younger days. Perhaps the Committee had approved him, then he'd failed in what he'd set out to do, ending, eventually, as a mere member of the Committee itself; for, important and influential as the Committee was, some people, myself included, regarded membership of it as a sign of inferior talent, or even complete failure.

The next to speak was a dignified old lady sitting on the far left, next to a fat man in a white jacket who'd crossed his legs and was staring at the ceiling as though he wasn't with us at all.

"Do you know how to dance?" she asked.

"Yes, of course," I replied.

The short, bad-tempered man broke in.

"Show us then," he said.

"What kind of dance would you like?" I asked. The moment I'd said it, I realized my mistake. What kind of dance indeed! As if there was any other kind!

I hoped the speed and dexterity I showed now would count in my favor. Not finding anything to tie around my waist, I simply took off my tie and knotted it just above my pelvis, where the body's particularly supple, taking care that the knot was on one side the way professional belly-dancers have it. This, as I soon found out, had definite advantages, because it almost separates the top and bottom halves of the body, giving each half the maximum scope for independent movement.

I started shaking my hips and dancing with my heels raised slightly from the floor, keeping my eyes fixed on the ground and my arms raised above my head. For a while I gyrated energetically, even trying to click my fingers together like castanets. I was too absorbed in what I was doing to notice what effect it was having on the members of the Committee. Finally the chairman of the Committee, the one who couldn't hear or see properly, made a gesture with his hand. "That's enough," he said.

One of the army officers, his face almost completely hidden behind dark glasses, now leaned forward. "From the papers we have available," he told me, "we know pretty well everything there is to know about you. There's one thing, though, we haven't been able to find out. What were you doing in that particular year? Could you tell us?"

I set about taking my tie from my waist and retying it around my neck, trying, all the while, to work out what year it was he meant. For all my limited knowledge of the Committee's language, I realized the demonstrative adjective he'd used wasn't referring to the present year we were in. If he hadn't mentioned a specific year, then the omission was deliberate, and the whole thing was an obvious trap he was setting for me—especially as they did, after all, have comprehensive reports on me.

I couldn't ask him to specify the year he had in mind, or I'd fall into the trap. Clearly I was supposed to work things out for myself, just as quickly as I could.

It was all thoroughly difficult. The only solution, I decided, was to rule out some of the likely years (1948, for instance, or 1952) on the grounds that I'd been too young then and that they'd be outside the scope of the inquiry. That left 1956, 1958, 1961 and 1967. Just as I was despairing completely of finding the appropriate response, I had a sudden flash of inspiration: there was a brief reply, which wasn't too far from the truth but wasn't absolutely specific either. "I was in prison," I said.

For all its brevity, my answer seemed to leave them nonplussed. No one asked any further questions on the subject, and some of the hostile atmosphere I'd sensed at the start began to clear, or so it seemed to me—though I found it difficult to interpret the expression on the face of the man with the blond hair and blue eyes. It seemed somehow sarcastic.

I saw him write something in red ink on the report in front of him. Then he leaned over to the old chairman and whispered in his good ear, handing the report to the short man as he did so.

"You've told us at some length," the chairman said deliberately, "about your talents and abilities. But we have a secret report here that says you weren't able to have sex with a certain woman. The report seems quite reliable—indeed, it was the woman in question who submitted it. What's your explanation for this?"

The question took me by surprise, and I was at a total loss how to answer it. Actually it hadn't happened just with one woman, but with a number of them, for a variety of different reasons. Since the Committee was so precise in its work, my answer would have to be specific too. And how could it be when I didn't even know which woman they meant?

It was the short man, spurred on no doubt by his rancor and unable to restrain himself, who saved me the bother of replying. "Maybe he was impotent," he yelled.

But the blond-haired man had different ideas. He leaned over and whispered in the chairman's good ear: "It's usually a case of—" I couldn't hear the rest, but it wasn't difficult to guess.

The blond-haired man beckoned to me to come and stand in front of him, then told me to take off my trousers, which I did, standing there in front of them all in my underwear, shoes and socks. I put my trousers over an empty chair and took hold of my underpants. "Shall I take these off, too?" I asked.

The blond-haired man nodded, and I took them off and placed them on top of the trousers. The eyes of the Committee were riveted on my private parts. The blond-haired man told me to turn around, then, when I'd done it, told me to bend down and I felt his hand on my naked buttocks. Then, when he asked me to cough, I felt his finger inside my body. He took his finger out and I stood up straight again, facing them. I saw the blond-haired man look at the chairman.

"Didn't I tell you?" he said.

For the first time the decrepit old man smiled. Then all the members of the Committee started talking at once; there was total bedlam, and I couldn't make out a thing they were saying. Eventually the chairman banged on the table with his fist and the talking stopped.

"The century in which we're living," the chairman said, when the din had finally died down, "is beyond all doubt the greatest in history, whether one considers the number and momentous nature of the events it has witnessed, or of the horizons opening up for the future. For which events—wars, revolutions, inventions, and so on—do you think this century of ours will be remembered?"

I was delighted to be asked this question, even though it was such an obviously difficult one, because now I could show them how much I knew about my favorite subjects. "That's a vitally important question," I replied. "I could cite a large number of significant things."

"We only want one," broke in the blond-haired man. "And it should be something of worldwide significance either in itself or through the influence it's had. And it should be something, too, that embodies the loftier, timeless ideals of our culture."

"That's an extremely difficult question, sir," I replied, smiling. "We could cite Marilyn Monroe, who, as an American beauty, was a feature of world culture in every sense of the word; and yet it was an ephemeral feature, which has now completely disappeared. In the hands of gifted people like Dior and Cardin the yardstick of beauty changes day by day. Human existence itself is doomed to extinction. And by that criterion we must also exclude Arab oil, which will very soon be exhausted. We might, too, mention the conquest of space, were it not that it still has to produce anything of benefit for mankind. By the same measure most revolutions must be discarded. We might perhaps pause to consider Vietnam, but that wouldn't, I think, be wise, because it would drag us into pointless ideological irrelevancies.

"I'm saying all this because you asked me to give you something for which our century will be remembered in the future. But wouldn't it be preferable if the thing itself continued to exist in the future, serving as a permanent memorial in its own right? All this leads us to search in another direction, and we'll have no trouble finding the right road. Unfortunately, though, it's a long and congested road, like the one to the airport. All along it there are signs bearing names like Phillips, Toshiba, Gillette, Michelin, Shell, Kodak, Westinghouse, and Marlboro. I think you'll all agree, ladies and gentlemen, when I say the whole world uses the items these companies manufacture, just as the companies, for their part, make use of the world. They turn workers into machines, consumers into numbers and countries into markets; which is precisely why they're such a vital product of the scientific and technological achievements of our century. What's more, they're not subject to obsolescence or depletion. They're made to last."

"So which one should we take?"

I allowed myself a calculated pause at this point, and looked around at them all. "Not any one of them!" I went on with a theatrical gesture.

There was a murmuring among the members of the Committee. I raised my hand.

"One moment please, ladies and gentlemen," I continued. "I didn't mean to suggest I can't answer the question put to me by this august committee; only that I wouldn't give one of the names I mentioned earlier. My choice, ladies and gentlemen, is a word made up of two parts: Coca-Cola."

I was expecting some kind of comment at this point, so I could gauge the impact my reply had made, but there was total silence.

"None of the things I've mentioned, ladies and gentlemen," I went on, "so embodies this century's culture, products or indeed horizons like this small, slender bottle with its top thin enough to fit in any man's backside."

I smiled at them, hoping they'd join in my attempted joke, but they just went on looking at me with stony faces.

"It's found almost everywhere," I went on, "from Finland and Alaska in the North to Australia and South Africa in the South. When it got back into China after a gap of thirty years, it was the kind of shattering event that will be the very stuff of this century's history. There's no threat to its ingredients, and people's taste for it won't change, because it's able to form a habit bordering on addiction.

"As for its significance, I'd refer you, ladies and gentlemen, to the article published in *Le Monde Diplomatique* in November 1976, where it's stated that it was the president of the Coca-Cola company, along with several other presidents of giant American companies, who selected Jimmy Carter as candidate for the presidency of the United States, long before he actually became any such thing. This article, which you've all read, I'm sure, notes that the presidents of the aforementioned companies have created a committee of ten politicians—including the president himself and the vice-president, Walter Mondale—to represent the American branch of what is known as the Tripartite Committee, which was established by David Rockefeller in 1973 and administered up till recently by Professor Zbigniew Brezinski, the national security adviser to the American president. The term 'tripartite,' applied to the committee, refers to its bringing together of North America, Western Europe, and Japan with one specific purpose, namely to confront the Third World and the forces of the Left in Western Europe.

"This shows how far-reaching Coca-Cola's influence is in the greatest and richest country in the world. And in that case you can imagine the stature it has vis-à-vis the Third World, and our own poor, tiny country in particular.

"The fact is that we should believe what people say about this innocent-looking bottle. It plays a decisive role in the way we choose our life, our tastes, the kings and presidents of our countries, and even the wars we join in and the treaties we sign."

By now there seemed to be a pall of silence hanging over the Committee, and I wondered if I hadn't perhaps spoken longer than necessary. Then, after a little while, I came to the vague realization that I'd "put my foot in it" (this being a colloquial expression in the Committee's language, implying that someone has unwittingly said or done something wrong).

I was still standing there before the Committee without my trousers and underpants, which made me feel completely naked, not only in the literal sense of the word but figuratively as well. I felt I was completely at their mercy. Yet the strangest thing of all was that, in the last few minutes, I'd somehow come to feel I could hit back at them, strike out at them in some way, if I only wanted to.

The short man, with whom my relations had been so rancorous, cleared his throat, then turned to the chairman and asked if he might put a question to me.

"This comprehensive answer you've given us," he said in a contrived tone of voice, "shows your command of contemporary events. Now we'd like to check you have the same degree of learning with respect to historical questions—"

I couldn't resist smiling at this point.

The blue eyes of the blond-haired man gleamed. "If you'll permit me," he said to his short colleague. Then he turned toward me. "Let's examine that now," he said. "And let's make the great pyramid our topic. No doubt you'd like to sit on top of it. However, I'll leave it entirely up to you what perspective you wish to take in talking about it."

For the first time in the interview I felt really delighted. Because I'm an Egyptian, this was a subject I knew a lot about and I could go on talking about it till the next morning if necessary. Yet I knew instinctively that a huge trap had been laid, and I prayed to God to send me the inspiration to avoid it and wipe out the bad impression I'd made with my previous speech. And soon God answered my prayers and sent me illumination. I started talking calmly and confidently: "The collection of structures comprising the three pyramids and the Sphinx, built some five thousand years ago, remains a riddle to challenge human ingenuity and a witness to the genius of mankind. All of us, I'm sure, have been following the recent attempt by American scientists to investigate the matter using advanced electronic technology, but in fact nothing new has been revealed.

"Scholars are still divided on the purpose of the pyramids and the precise means by which they were constructed. Some think they were built to provide places to record what had happened in the past and predict what would happen in the future. Davidson notes that the exterior surfaces of the great pyramid were designed to reflect light, the pyramid thus serving as a sundial to determine the times for sowing and harvesting. As further evidence he points out that the horizontal projections to the Northeast and Northwest, from the East and West sides of the pyramid, correspond exactly to the boundaries of the agricultural area within the Delta on the day the Egyptian farming year traditionally begins, namely November the first, and also that the pyramid is placed at the apex of the Delta triangle.

"There is, of course, another, more likely possibility, namely that the purpose of the pyramids was to preserve the names of the kings of Egypt and protect their corpses; they were intended, in other words, to provide eternal burial places. But while Khufu may have succeeded in making his name survive longer than that of any other king who ever lived, the primary purpose of building the pyramid, that of preserving his corpse, was not achieved. Despite a labyrinth of internal passageways and chambers deliberately incorporated when the pyramid was created, the body has long since disappeared.

"A further, unusual theory is that of Adams. This makes use of the *Book of the Dead*, which speaks of an unusual structure made up of passageways and chambers. Adams claims that the pyramids and the *Book of the Dead* are both leading us back to the same basic structure, one doing it in words and the other through stone.

"The internal and external functions of the building are in fact linked, and the upper passageway was designed in such a way as to demonstrate this link permanently. The building specifications reflect a great deal of accurate calculation and a wide knowledge of architectural design, which makes it clear that the whole thing was built to perpetuate not only the king's name, or his corpse, but something else as well.

"We learn from Herodotus that the stones used to build the great pyramid were transported along the River Nile, and also by way of a road built by a hundred thousand workers over a period of ten years. Then, once at the site, the stones were raised from one level to another using hoists made from short branches. Yet scholars are still baffled as to how exactly this staggering structure was erected. There is no evidence the Egyptians made use, at any period of their history, of any mechanical devices other than hoists, pulleys, and inclines; and for that reason many scholars are disposed to believe that the size and precision of the structure point to the use of unknown mechanical devices whose secret has been lost for ever. This may serve as a starting-point for the argument that now arises over the role of the Israelites in building the pyramids. Some maintain that Khufu was himself one of the kings of Israel, but kept the fact hidden—in accordance with the traditions of that people, who, since the very dawn of history, have been forced by continual persecution to shroud all matters in the utmost secrecy for their own defense. Others say that Khufu was an Egyptian pharaoh who made use of Jewish genius to solve the complex problems involved in erecting this architectural wonder.

"As I said earlier, the building specifications of the great pyramid show a wide knowledge of architectural design and an incredible ability to innovate and improvise, two things which the Egyptians do not of course possess. That is why they most probably made use of foreign Israelite expertise. Some people maintain that the Israelites were slaves of Khufu, forced to work on building the pyramid by the tyrannical king. This, however, is a controversial point; for, while it would be difficult to deny that the Egyptian pharaohs were despotic over the years, it's equally hard to imagine a building of such size and precision being the product of a slave regime. What seems more likely is that it arose from a profound religious belief that set the pharaoh at the very pinnacle of human existence.

"This leads us, then, to give preference to the theory that Khufu was one of the secret kings of the Israelites, particularly since we know that the architect supervising the building of the pyramid, whose name was Ham-iyunu, was the nephew of the pharaoh himself.

"In any case, this incredible structure, made up of one million three hundred thousand blocks of stone, is a monument to the genius of the Israelites. There is evidence to show that copper saws, each nine feet long, were used to cut up the huge blocks of stone. If all these blocks were to be cut into smaller sections, each a foot long and placed side by side in a straight line, they would cover two-thirds of the earth's circumference. It is also established that cylindrical drills were used in the unloading process, and that modern boreholes actually show none of the precision or finesse of the ones the Israelites drilled five thousand years ago. They are a marvel indeed."

I felt the tension in the room relax, and the hostility in the air seemed to lessen palpably. The members of the Committee had all been listening to me very carefully—even the fat man sitting to one side withdrew his gaze from the ceiling for the first time and looked at me. When I'd finished, the second army officer gave me an approving look which made me feel very happy. Then the members began to show signs of movement again and embarked on a series of whispered conversations. At that point I realized the lower part of my body was still naked. I tentatively picked up my underpants, then, as no one stopped me, quickly put them back on and put my trousers on over them.

They appeared, finally, to have reached a decision, and the blond-haired man was delegated to convey it to the chairman via his good ear. The old man pointed to the papers I'd submitted.

"You can take those now," he said. "We have no more questions. We'll let you know when we've reached a decision on your case."

I started gathering up my papers, making every effort to appear confident about the decision they'd eventually come to. Even so, I was still on edge, and had no idea of what I was doing. I stuffed the papers in my briefcase in no particular order, closed the case, and (remembering what had happened at the start of the interview) took it in my left hand. Without a word I bowed to the members of the Committee, then made for the door and turned the handle with my right hand. To my delight it responded easily, and the door opened. I left the room, not forgetting to close the door behind me, put down my briefcase, and lit a cigarette, which I smoked with relish.

I knew, though, that I wouldn't be able to sleep, or to rest, until the Committee had come to its final decision about me.

—*Translated by Roger Allen and Christopher Tingley*

Jabra Ibrahim Jabra (1920–1994)

Palestinian novelist, short-story writer, poet, and critic, Jabra Ibrahim Jabra was born in Bethlehem and studied in Jerusalem and Cambridge, England, where he obtained an M.A. in English literature. After the 1948 debacle in Palestine, he sought employment in Iraq and settled eventually in Baghdad, where he took Iraqi citizenship. His several volumes of literary criticism, which include *Freedom and the Deluge* (1960); *Closed Orbit* (1964), *The Eighth Voyage* (1967); *The Fire and the Essence* (1975) and *Sources of Vision* (1979), contain some of the more cogent and valuable criticism of poetry and fiction in contemporary Arabic. He published two collections of prose poetry, one collection of short stories, *Araq and Other Stories* (1956), and at least six novels, one of which, *Hunters in a Narrow Street* (1955), was written in English. His most important novels are *The Ship* (1970) and *Search for Walid Mas'ud* (1978), both of which have been translated into English by Roger Allen and Adnan Haydar, appearing in 1998 and 2000 respectively. Jabra has himself translated widely, and among the most useful of his translations was part of James Frazer's *The Golden Bough* (1957), a book that in Arab literary circles in the 1950s helped to shed light on ancient mythology and its possible use in poetry. At the end of his life Jabra published two accounts of his own life and experience: *The First Well* (1987) is an autobiography of his impoverished childhood in Palestine, and *Princesses' Street* (1994) is an account of his youthful life and experiences in Baghdad after he was forced to leave Palestine during the Diaspora.

SEARCH FOR WALID MAS'UD (1978)

As in his other novels, Jabra deals here with the life, ideas, and experiences of Arab intellectuals. He depicts them facing the issues of a contemporary Arab world hampered by internal and external obstacles while demonstrating strong and genuine promptings toward freedom and liberation from both internal sexual and political repression and external (represented by the State of Israel) aggression and coercion. Written in a style as vivid and picturesque as it is lucid and erudite, it is the story of the life and mysterious disappearance of a Palestinian intellectual, Walid Mas'ud, who has been able to acquire wealth through a thriving business in Iraq and the Gulf countries. Mas'ud the Palestinian works toward the deliverance of his country from Israeli occupation, and the novel thus hints that this is the major dream and effort of all Palestinians everywhere. The loss of his son, who had become a fida'i, in a raid inside Palestine, only enhances Mas'ud's own purpose and determination. His final disappearance in mysterious circumstances leaves the question open as to the fate of the Palestinian: was it the Israelis who kidnapped him; were his kidnappers emissaries of the Arab establishment that is suspicious of his endeavor to liberate the world around him; or was his disappearance the result of some personal grievance on someone else's part? The question rightly remains open.

Walid Mas'ud Passes Through Rain That Keeps Recurring

Rain. How sweet it is, how bitter. Love, fear, anticipation; all these things I feel for the rain. I watch for it, I want it to continue and to stop at the same time. The sound of rain drumming, sputtering, pounding, excites me. It makes me want to sing and to love. It makes me want to fade away and die. The rain used to come down so hard it filled the valleys and roads and made a mockery of our flimsy houses. It leaked through the thin roofs exposing the innermost secrets of the houses. Do the poor have secrets, I wonder? Children and mothers, can they have any secrets if the rain pours down on them at night? As it comes down in torrents it looks so wonderful battering the windowpanes, pounding the leaves on the trees and covering the world with a cloak of silvery beads. Suddenly a rainbow appears over the hills and valleys, and then the rain begins to fall again, murmuring, knocking, and pounding as it dispatches the waters of the flood over the farthest regions of the earth.

How lovely it is, at nightfall, to walk along the city pavements in the rain. The water is streaming into gutters and people are hurrying along trying to keep dry with raincoats and newspapers. And how pleasant it is to stumble through the puddles that reflect the gleam of the city lights. Hair gets more and more tangled on top of heads and around faces, and tiny rivulets of water cascade down cheeks, nose, and chin. Rain, rain. Showers pound the stonework of the great black walls of the city, walls that for countless centuries have stood there in the broad expanse of darkness. The walls have stood in a darkness pierced by tiny distant lights, from time to time cracked by thunder and lightning, and punctured over time by whistles and howls, by the sighing of the wind.

Near the entrance to al-Khalil Gate[1] burns a fire made of old boxwood; dampness, exhaustion, and cold. A woolen scarf around the neck, a heavy black raincoat, and wet feet that refuse to warm up. The flames leap up, twist and smoke, and in the dancing light our faces change from one mask to another. A silent question seems to emerge as if from the depths of a bottomless well: who am I? Who are you? What am I doing here? And who are these people who are laughing, laughing in the face of death while the city is being devoured limb

---

1. The Jaffa Gate on the southwest section of old Jerusalem and its famous wall.

by limb, hour by hour, by that savage beast, the enemy? And all the while the rain pours down in torrents, roaring in storm. All this sadness around us, what dire catastrophe does it foretell? Everything seems black, old, or decrepit. Still the rain comes down. Rain, rain, rain, rain, rain . . . With the rain life can burst forth, black changes into green, the old begin to dance, and the dead bloom once more . . . Rain, rain, rain . . . Let me die! I wanted to die that night.

Bashir, Tahbub, and I took the British soldier to a room near the neighboring police station and stripped him of his khaki uniform so that I could use it as a disguise. He did not put up a fight. A few hours later the whole operation was completed, and I could hear the shattering, screaming, reverberating sound of explosions in the distance. I could picture the whole thing in my mind. Let me die now, if my death will allow you to live on, my city. Saint Augustine of Carthage, what would you have to say if you knew about it? Here are my defenseless people; they are being killed, uprooted, decimated, scattered like torn limbs across the valleys and mountains of the earth.

Rain, rain, rain, rain. Very well, let me kill and afterward let me die. The walls collapsed, and a cry went up. The rain kept on falling; the waterskins of the heavens were spewing their entire contents over the poor wounded city, the beloved city, abused by the rain at night and constantly violated, in the morning and at noon, in fair weather and in cloud, in storm and calm. I wept silently, while my face was buffeted by the wind and rain. I mourned my dead brother, my murdered people, my friends, and my nation; I even mourned those who had been killed at that moment and those who would be killed in the future. The rain kept pounding on the doors and windows, trying to penetrate houses to uncover the depths of human secrets, to flow into hidden nooks and crannies, presaging death, and saving from death those whom I love and whom I will father. Still the rain proclaimed life to glow, to rage and to love, to reproduce life . . .

O rain, O black dawn that never brightens, O hours laden down with debris and destruction, O morning choking with streams of blood that pour forth today, tomorrow, the day after, next year, on and on without ceasing through fifty years of oppressive, tear-laden hours of struggle, of wounds.

After something less than twenty years, they came to my house in Bethlehem and knocked violently on the door. The rain beating down provided accompaniment as they pounded on the door. Three of them came in, shaking the rain off their coats.

"Walid Mas'ud al-Farhan?," they asked.

"Yes," I replied.

"Come with us."

"In this rain?"

"We're sorry to bother you. Do you live here all the time?"

"So what's that supposed to mean? This is my country, isn't it, my city, my land?"

"Okay, okay, okay. Come along with us."

"Will you allow me to put my coat on?"

"Yes. Who lives here with you?"

"No one."

"We'll search the house."

So they searched all the rooms, turned the chairs over, opened all the cupboards. They put handcuffs on me and pushed me toward the door. We went down the steps. A military jeep stood some twenty meters from the front door of the house; we all got soaking wet in the pouring rain. They put me in the back between two of them, while the third sat in front with the driver. The roads were deserted. The whole town was covered with the rain as a bereaved woman wears heavy mourning.

I had seen this town, in times past, gleaming like a jewel; I'd seen its skies full of swallows. I'd seen it with almond and apricot blossoms clinging to its houses and heard joyful ululations from its windows. I had seen the city when the roads and roofs were covered with snow as white as a bridal gown. I saw it on the seventh of June when Israeli guns pounded its houses and killed its people; and I saw it later that same afternoon when the Israelis entered as conquerors and occupiers. After the olive harvest, during the first rain of autumn the whole atmosphere of the town seemed to be saturated with tears. And now, getting in the back of the jeep with handcuffs on my wrists, I looked out on the wounded city, silently gazing at the valley and the distant hills through the mists. My city, if you can live through my torture and my death, then let them torture me and let me die. Who are these faceless invaders? I know them and I don't know them. I have seen them in the annals of history. They come, they destroy, they kill, and then they fall down and collapse.

The jeep rattled and groaned its way downhill towards al-Mawrida and then started uphill on the twisting road that goes past the monastery of Saint Elias. Every rock and every tree I knew was still in its place. But where were the children's swings, the peddlers, the people squabbling and laughing round the well; where were the sellers of kebab, the smell of grilling meat wafting among the olive trees? Where were the bottles of arak, the beautiful girls, and the ballad singers? My poor hills, you are silent; are you weeping? Should I jump out of the jeep into your orchards, bury myself in your mud and become part of your soil, your flowers, and your thorns?

We kept climbing, up to al-Khalil Gate. The huge stone walls were there still, like wild beasts, waiting, under the onslaught of the rain and the pounding of the invaders' army boots, waiting. Not smiling and not weeping. Waiting, We climbed up parallel to this wall and went into the Moskobiyya, the old Russian church. But then they took me in another direction and put me in a cell. Later they took me into a room full of men whom I knew instantly without having seen them before, tired, pale, stubborn, beautiful men. I heard cries, screams, the noise of bodies being dragged along the floor. I faced my interrogators as they launched into that vulgar, endless process that has become standard practice all over the face of the globe.

Your name, age, address; your father's name, your mother's. A slap across the face that blinds you for a couple of moments. (Sabri hit me on the face with a rock once because I had won five colored eggs from him on Easter Day, but he hit me and then ran away.) In this place they do not run away. They hit you and stand right over you because your hands are tied behind your back just as your whole nation is tied. What's your relationship with Fatah, they ask. You emigrated to Baghdad. You lived in the Gulf. You lived in Beirut. What are you doing in Bethlehem? Whom did you see in Hebron? In Bait Sahur? In Nablus? In Ramallah? In al-Bira?[2] The only person I saw was my wife. Your wife's a pretty feeble excuse. Never.

The cell was damp, and I was too tall to stand up in it. They locked the door. It was completely dark; there were no cracks in the walls, not even a keyhole. Only a latrine can. Oh, if only I could sleep and lose consciousness.

Hours later I could hear screams and moans from my cell. Walid, remember your childhood. Think of your days at the monastery, the war days in Milan and Rome, days in Jerusalem. Remember the shattered remains of Elias buried under the debris and that wonderful, terrifying night with the rain pouring down when you drove that "sequestered" jeep loaded with dynamite across area C, then area A, then area B. You were wearing the British soldier's uniform, and alongside you was the other "English soldier" who was also in search of revenge. Winter 1948, and it seems like yesterday! Twenty years, man, do you realize that? And they ask you whom you've seen, and what you're doing here. The crucial thing is not to break down. It's enough that Rima has had a breakdown and is living the life of the dead in a sanatorium. They pulled me by my arms and my hair, kicked me in the backside, pushed me into the other room full of comrades whom I don't know, and yet I know so well. "Beware of Shimon," they say. We whisper our names to each other: Tahir, 'Umar, Yasir, Zuhdi ... and the interrogation starts again.

A stick came crashing down on my shoulders and sent an electric charge right through my body. They threw me to the ground on my back, grabbed hold of my mouth viciously, and used their fingernails to thrust a hose into my mouth. They filled me up with water like some waterskin. I'm going to die, I told myself, but I must not break down. Then they turned me over on my face on the filthy floor, and the water came pouring out along with vomit.

The interrogation started once again. They gave me a cigarette and offered me hot tea. This time, they were laughing with me.

"We know all about your books," they said, "your movements too, and your membership in Fatah. We want to help you. Who are you, exactly? Whom have you seen? Who, who, who?"

Back to the cell and the black darkness, then back once more to the horrible, brilliantly lit room for more questioning. And then came a foul attack that caught me by surprise. They tied my arms behind my back and pulled my

---

2. Bait Sahur, Ramallah and al-Bira are small towns around Jerusalem. Nablus is the famous city of resistance in the south of Palestine, about an hour's drive by car from Jerusalem.

trousers down. Suddenly Shimon grabbed hold of my testicles and started burning the skin of my scrotum with his thick cigar now here, now there, and then stubbed it out slowly on my penis. I screamed. It was the scream of a forty-six year old man who feels in his heart he is a proud young man of twenty-six. My crying helped ease the pain.

"Where's Tahbub?" they asked me suddenly.

"Who is Tahbub?"

"Weren't you with him on that demolition operation in Ben Somekh Street in 1948?"

"I don't know what you're talking about."

So they know about that wonderful, terrifying, rainy night twenty years ago; they mention Tahbub. It's as though they can read my mind. Even so, I realized from their questions they were not sure of anything. If they were, then why all this torture and madness? The crucial thing was not to break down. Endure and remain silent till death. But where was death? Death would seem so easy if it came. Pain is far more terrifying than death. Has the rain stopped? Has the sun come out and begun to warm the city once more? They dragged me off to the cell again. I no longer have any idea of time. They pull me from one room to another. My companions keep changing, and so do my torturers; or perhaps it is merely that I can no longer distinguish between their faces? The dampness, the walls, and the cold floor all remind me of things hidden in the recesses of the past. I will tell all this to Marwan when I see him; if I don't die, that is. I wonder what he's doing now in Brummana.[3] Is he studying or playing basketball? You're very good at basketball, Marwan; they made you captain of the team. Marwan, dear boy; remember your father; keep his name pure, even if they kill him here like a dog. The important thing is not to break down. People do break down. I'm not made of steel, but I will not break down.

Suddenly a scream fills the whole world, a hoarse scream followed by women shrieking. Major Shapir. How can one man harbor such a horrific amount of hatred in his heart?

"Hatred," he said. "There's no hatred here; we just want to help you, and put an end to your torture. Don't imagine you're Tarzan. You'll confess, sooner or later. Here's a piece of paper. Write on it ten lines of things we've asked you about, and it'll all be over. Have a cigarette. Oh, so you don't want to smoke? You refuse to write anything?

"Take him away."

Always the same, again and again, time after time.

"Take him away, make him understand, fix him, get him to talk."

At last through a tiny window at the top of the wall some magnificent light from a blue sky pours into the cell; the thick bars convert it into squares. Ten, twenty, how

---

3. The Brummana College for boys, a Quaker institution to which the sons of affluent families were sent, founded at the end of the nineteenth century in the small town of Brummana in the eastern Lebanese mountains.

many men are we, I wonder. We go to sleep on the floor close to one another. Time is divided into segments by the occasions when a tepid broth is thrown to us in tin cans, a dry substance they call bread and a cold liquid they term tea.

For several days they left me alone. But they kept shouting out names continually through loudspeakers; they would open the door suddenly, and then we all had to stand up. They forced us to our feet with sticks. By now I could only get to my feet with an enormous effort. Every muscle in my body groaned. Every bone felt as though it was cut off from the rest. Each time they would take one or two of us away. The one they took might never come back or might come back utterly shattered; his clothes would be torn, he would be splattered with blood and would lie spread-eagled on the floor, groaning.

One day they called my name and number and took me away. The interrogation room was full of them: Shimon, Shapir, and many others. Some were seated, others standing. They brought in Mahmoud Kamleh. He looked as though he had just come out of the grave. He began to walk round the room in a daze; his hands were tied behind him.

"Do you know this man?"

"No."

"Do you know him?"

"No."

"Do you know him?"

"No."

They made us face each other. Mahmoud was magnificent. His mouth was bloody, his face was ashen, his eyes gleamed in their deep sockets, but he did not bat an eyelid when he saw me.

Good God! I musn't break down! Mahmoud was my key contact in the region, as firm as a knife edge and not yet thirty years old.

Shimon gave a nod to one of his assistants who caught me unawares with two vicious punches to the stomach.

"Do you know him?"

"No."

From that moment reality became confused with dreams and nightmares. Consciousness, unconsciousness, and the sounds of groans and screams became mixed up. I was dragged backward and forward. Time passed, as heavy as lead, as black as the night of the dead.

I longed for Baghdad. I longed for my home, for music, for the valley of Bethlehem, for Abu Dhabi, Beirut, Shemlan, for Marwan! My mouth was full of blood. Mother, O mother, are you crying? Is my father weeping too? And the angels, are they weeping? And what of God Himself, is He weeping? Saint Augustine, is he beating his breast and weeping? Monica and the Virgin Mary, how about them? Are they also weeping? Days went by until the nightmares became commonplace, merely punctuation for the barbaric days.

They gave me some papers in Hebrew and told me it was an expulsion order. They pushed me into a jeep. The three soldiers and the driver said nothing. The rain was pouring from a sky gray as ashes. The soldiers' boots, belts, and rifles filled up the small space in the jeep, and I sat there in silence, squeezed between two of them, watching the rain. They were grumbling to each other about the rain and how long the trip was. "There won't be any rain like this," they kept saying, "in the Jordan Valley."

After two hours, one of them said in an Iraqi accent, "We're going to leave you. Will you go to Baghdad?"

I looked at his face; his eyes were sad, very sad.

I nodded my head.

At the destroyed bridge there were other formalities. I was so feeble I could hardly stand on my own two feet. There I was, my dusty raincoat billowing around me like a sheet since I had lost half my weight in two months. The Arab soldiers there at the bridge looked at me as though I were returning from the world of the dead, just like Mahmoud. But the sight of people returning from the world of the dead was no longer a shock to anyone. It is repeated a thousand times every single day. The important thing was that I had to stay on my feet, I could not break down; I had to reach Marwan.

I was lucky. Others suffered miserably and many still suffer. I was a wanted man because I had struck the enemy more than once and because I had participated in several organized attacks. I was lucky because I had managed to outwit the enemy once again; even though my body had been torn limb from limb, my mind had held together. Even so, if my body were to be exposed to the same kind of torture today, I wonder if my will could stand up to the horrors of it all and bring about the miracle of my steadfastness a second time.

I emerged from this experience with the feeling that I had won a whole new life again! How good it was to breathe the cool air, how delicious! I came back to life with the spirit of a child, though my body was crippled and I had to put together the pieces of my physical self. But intellectually and psychologically I felt I was running over the expanses of the earth like a panther, like a gazelle.

However I was still faced with some problems, and in order to deal with these problems, I had to learn certain things from the beginning, as a child learns the alphabet. And what an alphabet it was, more taxing to the mind than cuneiform or hieroglyphics. In these new lessons I saw my Arab homeland, for which I was prepared to bear the tortures of hell, itself apply the same tortures to its own people, those who fall into the hands of influential men. I heard screams in all the Arab nations from the north, south, east, west, from the Gulf to the Atlantic Ocean; I heard weeping and the sound of sticks on bone, the thud of plastic hoses on flesh. The secret police seemed to be everywhere, up in the highest mountain peaks and down in the lowest valleys. In capitals and other cities men in neat civilian suits walked back and forth and arrived in their cars like a thousand shuttles in a thousand looms, coming and going, taking to the centers of darkness tens, hundreds of people. In labyrinths of cells and dungeons people were lost, while the sound of questioning, denial, and confession could be heard night and day, along with the noise of rubber coming down on naked flesh and the screams, the cries. All of this went on among my own people so the accusations and calumnies could be recorded, filed, and piled up in dossiers and the people's mouths could be filled with blood. I do not know how I can ever learn the implications of this alphabet and come to accept it as a part of life.

Rain. Marwan, whenever rain falls, I think of you; I remember all those I love; I remember Tahbub, Bashir, and Mahmoud. Then my heart swells with pride. But whenever rain falls, I also record the plight of my Arab people, their errors and their pains, and then my heart is filled with wrenching grief.

—*Translated by Roger Allen and Elizabeth Fernea*

Ghassan Kanafani

See Ghassan Kanafani's biography in the short-story section.

ALL THAT'S LEFT TO YOU (1966)

See the introduction for a discussion of Kanafani's All That's Left to You.

He could now stare directly at the sun's molten disc and watch its crimson fire-ball hang on the rim of the horizon before disappearing into the sea. In a flash it was gone, and the last glowing rays that lit up the path of its descent were extinguished like embers against a gray wall that rose shimmering at first, then turned into a uniform coat of white paint.

Suddenly the desert was there.

For the first time in his life he saw it as a living creature, stretching away as far as the eye could see, mysterious, terrible, and familiar all at the same time. The light, retreating slowly as the black night sky descended, played over it and transformed it.

It was vast and inaccessible, and yet the feelings it aroused in him were stronger than love or hate. The desert wasn't entirely mute; it felt to him like an enormous body, audibly breathing. As he set off into it, he felt suddenly dizzy. The sky closed in on him noiselessly, and the city he had left behind dwindled to a black speck on the horizon.

In front of him, as far as the eye could see, the body of the desert was breathing, alive. He felt his own body rise and fall at its breast. In the depths of the black sky-wall that stood up erect before him, panels began to open one after another, revealing the hard, brilliant glitter of stars.

Only then did he realize he wouldn't return. Far behind him, Gaza with its ordinary night disappeared. His school was the first to vanish, then his house. The silvery beach was swallowed up in darkness. For a brief moment the street-lights, dim and faint, remained as suspended pinpricks; then they too were extinguished one by one. He continued on his way, hearing the stifled swish of his feet as they met the sand, and, as he did so, he recalled the feelings that always filled his breast whenever he threw himself into the waves: strong, immense, utterly solid, and yet at the same time possessed of a total and shattering impotence.

As he plunged into the night, it was as though he was anchored to his home in Gaza by a ball of thread. For sixteen years they'd enveloped him with these constricting strands, and now he was unraveling the ball, letting himself roll into the night. "Repeat after me: I give you my sister Maryam in marriage—I give you my sister Maryam in marriage—with a dowry worth—with a dowry worth—ten guineas . . . ten guineas . . . all deferred . . . all deferred." Eyes had bored into his back as he had sat in front of the sheikh. Everyone there knew very well that it wasn't that he was giving her away, but that she was pregnant, and that the bastard who was to be his brother-in-law was sitting next to him, audibly laughing inside.

All deferred, of course, with the child already pressing against the walls of her womb! Outside the room he took her by the arms. "I've decided to leave Gaza," he said. She smiled, and her mouth with its badly applied lipstick looked like a bloody wound that had suddenly opened up beneath her nose. "Where will you go?" she asked, her mouth still open, as though she wanted to tell him that he couldn't do that. "I'll go to Jordan over the desert." "So you're running away from me?" she said. He shook his head. "You were everything to me, but now you're dishonored, defiled, and I'm deceived . . . If only your mother was here."

Tomorrow he knew she'd say to the bastard she'd borne, "If only your grandmother was here." And he'd grow up in turn, get married, have children, and say to his son, "If only your great-grandmother was here." If only . . . if only . . . for sixteen years he'd been saying that to her, "If only your mother was here!" Something he would repeat whenever they quarreled, when they laughed, when she was in pain, when she didn't know how to cook, when they fired him from his job, when he got work, always the same phrase would occur: "If only your mother was here, if only your mother was here."

His mother had never been there, even though she was only a few hours walk away in Jordan, a distance no one in sixteen years had succeeded in crossing. Even while he was saying, "I give you my sister Maryam in marriage," he had resolved, unconsciously, to make the journey.

He was on fire, tasting a deep bitterness right down to the pit of his stomach, while she stepped back a little, still wearing that wounded smile. Behind her the swine growled, so she said to him, "Your brother-in-law Hamid wants to leave Gaza." But the other man never so much as looked at him, treating him as though he wasn't there. "Hamid says a lot of things, there's no need to take him seriously." At the same instant as he asked himself, 'I wonder where it happened?' he looked at the gentle curve of her belly beneath the dress.

One day, no doubt, he left school early; probably he got permission from the headmaster, saying he had a headache. That was always his way: to plead a headache and then sneak to the house in my absence, and she'd be waiting for him. There he undid the buttons of her blouse and she pretended to feel nothing. But when?

She turned round without a word and began talking absently to the guests: "May you enjoy the same." A word rang out—congratulations . . . congratulations. Cold hands reached out to shake his own, while his eyes were focused on her. Fired by his boiling rage, for two months he'd taken refuge in the fantasy of killing her. He'd imagine himself rushing to her bed, armed with a long knife, uncovering her face; then while she looked up at him with eyes like a madwoman's, he'd grab her by the hair and say something brief yet cuttingly final—or else he wouldn't speak at all, but just look at her so that she understood everything, and stab her straight through the heart. Then he'd rush outside to look for him, his brother-in-law. "I give you my sister Maryam in marriage for a dowry worth ten pounds, all deferred." His brother-in-law . . .

She'd allowed this man to tarnish her; her fifteen minutes of surrender had denied the bond between them. When the intruder had planted the child in her womb, he'd had him where he wanted him. "You're free to marry her off to me or not. I'm not the one who will suffer." "But why didn't you say you wanted her?" He had just shaken his head, smiling like an honest merchant. "It just happened this way." He'd felt like standing up and hitting him, but the man had gone on smiling. "You don't want to hit me, do you? They'll say that you hit the man who . . ."

Enough!

The man was slight and ugly as a monkey, and he was called Zakaria. Hamid could, if he'd wanted, have put his big hands round him and squeezed him to death, but he was powerless to act; his sister Maryam was listening behind the door, with the child growing all the while in her womb. When the last guests had left, his brother-in-law shut the door and came back in as though he owned the house. He flung off his shoes and stretched out in a chair, looking like an accidental blemish that didn't belong there. He took a deep breath, clasped his hands behind his head, and stared with malign contentment at the objects in the room. At last his eyes came to rest on her, and he began speaking, exaggerating the contours of his mouth. "So he wants to go, he intends to cross the desert . . . He hasn't congratulated me yet, even though I'm his brother-in-law—to say nothing of the fact that I'm older than him." Then he jumped up and began pacing around the room, eyes trained on the floor. "He's threatening us, Maryam, so why don't you tell him we don't care about him?" But she'd stood silently leaning against the wall, looking for all the world like an old woman who's just remarried. He stopped and looked at her again, striking the pose of an eloquent orator. "In one night the desert swallows up ten like him." He turned his back on him and faced her: "First he has to cross our borders, then theirs, and theirs again, before he finally arrives at the frontier with Jordan, and these are just small dangers compared with the endless deadly threats the desert holds in store . . . are you sure this isn't one of his stupid jokes?" She didn't answer, and the atmosphere in the room grew tense and oppressive.

A thread of sweat darkened Hamid's collar. He realized he was breathing heavily. If he spoke out he would, he knew, appear ridiculous, but he couldn't help himself. He got up from his chair, headed straight for the door, and then at the right moment swung round, "I'll leave tomorrow night."

As he went down the steps, he wanted to hear a sound, to hear his sister's voice calling out to him—"Hamid, come back." He wanted her to cry out, to say something. But the only sound he heard was the sound of his own footsteps clattering down the stairs. Even before he'd reached the street, he heard the door slam behind him. No solicitous word broke the silence.

The darkness was uniform now. A cold wind had sprung up and was whistling across the surface of the desert, its rhythm like the gasps of a dying beast. He no longer knew whether he was afraid or not. There was one heart beating in the reaches of the sky, in that universal body stretching to the rim of the horizon. He stood still for a while, staring at the perforated black tent of the sky, while the expanse of the desert stretched out dark as an abyss. He pulled up his coat collar and thrust his hands deep into his huge pockets. Suddenly, his fear melted away. He was alone with the creature that was with him, under him, and within him, breathing in an audible whistle as it floated sublimely out on a sea of studded darkness. When a roar reached him from the distance, he greeted it without surprise. Nothing in this vast expanse had the power to shock him; it was a world open to everything, and whatever sound came to him could only be small, clear, and familiar. At first the noise had seemed to come from all four quarters, then he was able to distinguish its source. A straight beam of light swept the rim of the horizon like a white stick describing a semicircle. In the next instant two shining eyes were narrowing in on him, bouncing as they came forward with a circular motion. Without fear and without hesitation, he flung himself to the ground and felt it like a virgin quiver beneath him. The strip of light brushed the sand dunes softly, silently. Instinctively, he flattened himself into the sand and felt its soft warmth rise to meet him. The roar was on him now as the car accelerated forward. He dug his fingers into the flesh of the earth, feeling its heat flowing into his body. It seemed to him that the earth was breathing directly into his face, its excited breath burning his cheek. He pressed his mouth and nose against it and the mysterious pounding mounted, while the car suddenly turned and sped by, its rear lights receding redly into the night. "I give you my sister Maryam in marriage." He laid his cheek on the sand again and felt a cold breeze wash over him. The red taillights had disappeared, as though a hand had wiped them out. If only my mother was here, he reflected. He turned and brushed his lips against the warm sand. "It's not in my power to hate you, but how can I love you? In one night you'd swallow up ten like me. I choose your love. I'm forced to choose your love. You're all that's left to me."

You're all that is left to me, and even though you share my bed, you are irretrievably distant. You leave me alone to count the cold metallic strokes beating against the wall. Beating, beating insistently, inside that wooden bier opposite the bed. He'd bought it one July. He'd carried it back from the market, and when he'd got to the door, he couldn't get the keys out of his pocket. It was heavy in his arms, as he told me, and he stood there, perplexed, wondering what to do. Then he forgot himself and remained standing there till I arrived. When he looked at me, sweat was pouring off his body, but he showed no anger. He just said to me, "Why are you late?"

"I'm not late . . . what's that?"

He looked at it. "It's a wall clock, but it's like a small bier, isn't it?" When we entered, he went straight to the room where we slept. There was a big nail fixed directly opposite his bed and he hung the clock on it, while I held the chair for him. He got down, stood back, and admired it. But it didn't work. As he contemplated the clock face, I said to him, "Perhaps it needs winding." He shook his head in disagreement. "I think it's because it's not hanging straight," he said. "Wall clocks with pendulums go wrong if they're tilted." He climbed on the chair again and altered its angle, as though he were preparing to take precise aim at a target. The next instant it began ringing. We both noticed that its metallic strokes were like the sound made by a solitary cane. When we put the chair back in its old place, I came out with the question he must have been anticipating. "How much did you pay for it?" His answer was unexpected. "I didn't buy it," he said. "I stole it." And ever since it's been hanging there with its cold metronomic beat. It goes on remorselessly, Zakaria, measuring time without any letup. And now all that's left to me is you and it. We let him desert us without so much as a word. When I heard his hesitant footsteps on the stairs, I thought he'd return, and I felt torn between him, who stands for the past now, and you who are all my hope for the future. And yet neither of us acted, and he didn't come back. Then you stepped forward and slammed the door, putting an end to everything, and went into the next room. When I followed you, you assured me that he'd come back; that he was too young to take on the desert alone. You said that in time he'd come to see how trivial all this is, however important he thinks it now.

If my mother had been here, he would have taken refuge with her, as I would have done too. There would have been a chance to discuss the problem with her. We wouldn't have erased him from our lives the moment the door closed behind him.

I received his first message from the baker's boy: "I'll be leaving today at sunset. I'll write to you from Jordan, if I ever get there." Appended to this was the small signature "Hamid." The note was as composed as the notes he always wrote if he had to leave the house for some reason—when he'd write "Back soon—Hamid" on the back of his cigarette packet and leave it propped up on the radio where he knew I'd go straightway. But we've deceived him, Zakaria. We've deceived him, let's admit it! He'll have been walking for a good three hours by now. I'm counting his steps, one by one, with the subdued metallic strokes on the wall in front of me. It's like a death march.

They are strokes charged with life, which he beats out endlessly against my breast. But my breast gives no echo back, it holds nothing but terror. As he

struggles on against the black wall that towers above him, he seems a paltry creature, resolved on an endless journey charged with fury, sorrow, suffocation, even
perhaps death, night's solitary song that parades my body. From the moment I
felt his approach, I knew he was a stranger; and when I saw him, my suspicions
were confirmed. He was totally alone, unarmed, and perhaps hopeless too.

Despite that, in that first moment of terror, he said that he asked for my love
because he was unable to hate me.

You won't find it in you to despise me, Zakaria, I know that. You're all that's
left to me. As for him, he's gone, all traces of him wiped out, except for the incessant monotony of metallic strokes beating on the wall like a cane that's lost its
direction. Counting those strokes is all I've left to do, while you're lost in sleep,
within my reach, but as distant as death.

You don't really know him, even though you worked with him for a short
while in the tent called the camp school. And neither did he know you. Only
I know you both. His opinion of you was always the same, expressed concisely;
no experience ever altered it. When we first met you together by chance in the
street, I learned that your name was Zakaria and that you were his colleague at
the camp school. When I asked if you were a friend, he said, "No, he's a swine."
Even when he found out, he uttered one thing, "He's a swine!" and left. That
was all. He never ever changed this term. "He's a swine."

—*Translated by May Jayyusi and Jeremy Reed*

Edward al-Kharrat (b. 1926)

Egyptian novelist and short-story writer Edward al-Kharrat was born in
Alexandria, studied law at its university, and has always been an avid reader
of literature and philosophy in Arabic, English, and French. He was the
deputy secretary-general of the Afro-Asian Peoples' Solidarity Organization
and of the Afro-Asian Writers' Association, but is now completely dedicated
to writing. Apart from his translations from English and French literature,
he has published two collections of short stories, *High Walls* (1958) and
Hours of Pride (1972). His novel *Rama and the Dragon* (1972), which reflects
a wide spectrum of experience transcending the boundaries of place and
time while never losing track of the immediacy of present-day experience
in his country, won acclaim in avant-garde literary circles and confirmed
the author's role as a major modernist influence on contemporary Arabic
fiction. His difficult, slow-flowing, and ambiguous style has not been a
deterrent for selective readers. His novels include *The Other Time* (1979);
and *City of Saffron* (1985), and *Girls of Alexandria* (1990), both translated into
English by Francis Lairdet (1989 and 1993, respectively). The last few years
saw a profusion of works: *The Certainty of Thirst* (1997), *Agonies of Realities
and Madness* (2001); *The Rocks of the Sky* (2001), and *The Path of the Eagle*
(2002). His latest collection of short stories, *Conflicting Passions*, was published in 2003.

RAMA AND THE DRAGON (1972)

This symbolic and lyrical epic novel contains fourteen sections, each of which can be read as an independent prose poem as well as a chapter in the narrative. Set in Egypt between 1970 and 1978, the political and the metaphysical, the realistic and the mythical merge in the intimate dialogue between the hero and himself, the hero and his world, and ultimately, the hero and the universe. Stylistically, the novel reveals itself on different levels and scattered internal references to an anagrammatic fable. The following excerpts are the outcome of unraveling the discrete story-within-the-story. The inner fable is both asserted and parodied, invoked and radicalized, thus giving the entire work an ironic status.

[1]

He began to tell her a children's story. He was enjoying the tale and yet mocking it, as he fumbled through it. His voice trembled with a passion he had never before found in himself: "Once upon a time, there was a little princess who went into the forest looking for something that was unknown, but that she knew was there. The princess traveled over God's whole wide world, moving from one country to another. In her search, she came across trees, clouds, monsters, and children . . . But she did not find what she was looking for. The sun rose and the sun set . . . Always, the darkness returned . . . and the search went on."

She interrupted him in a drowsy voice with a hint of sarcasm. "This is not the way to tell a story. You should give the name of the Princess and describe her to me."

Rama. Rama.

All of a sudden, he answered her with a shrill laugh, "You only have to listen to the story till you fall asleep."

But she replied in a submissive voice that touched his heart—a little girl searching for refuge and unwilling to be without it, "All right then. Please finish your story, my love."

And when he told her how the princess did find the knight she was looking for, he could not bring himself to believe in such a stale and foolish old tale. The few salty tears in his eyes remained unwept.

She said, "Don't leave me till I fall asleep."

He did not say to her, "What are you afraid of, my love? What is the secret of this barren void, of this infinite desert all around you?"

[2]

Your continuous presence. Your silence. Your closeness to me, and yet the remoteness of your life on those various paths that you guard so tightly with such sharp, alert intelligence. As if your life flowed into locked compartments, one barred from the other, each one separate, and you heroically protecting each dividing wall. Do you think, dear heart, that you—the real you—exists inside this maze of walls and ramparts? That you exist behind these barriers and fortresses that you put up in front of my face, in front of the world's face, and in front of your own face? Do you think that you, yourself, exist in the world of each of these spheres that touch and yet do not overlap, which go together but never join; in each one of these solitary worlds that exists in a strange remoteness from all the others?

He said to her, "Do you know, dear love, that Michael, the archangel, is my patron, my guardian angel, and that I was named after him? This is what they told me when I was small. I was also told that the Nile won't flow unless the archangel Michael comes down on holiday into the land of Egypt, and weeps.

"One drop of his tears and the waves, rich with fertility and the redness of the earth, will pour out; the thirsty plants sway with joy as they spring up; the cracks in the barren soil are filled with plenty; and prosperity reigns."

He said to her, "When I was little, they used to make *fatir* cakes on my birthday, the day of St. Michael, the archangel and the leader of God's soldiers, with his two-pointed sword. When I ate the oiled, shining cakes, decorated with the ancient Coptic script, I used to see him, my angel, my guardian, my brother, with his silvery armor and his long lance fighting all the lies and all the devils crowded all around us in the dark."

No. He did not say any of this to her.

He did not say to her, "Truth for me is the demolishing of ramparts and the overflowing and joining of life's waters in a sea with an infinite horizon, floating on its turbulent surface, two lovers in one tiny, frail wooden vessel."

He did not say to her, "What I want, what I want more than anything else, what I want for you and for both of us, is that you be free with me, free from the need to justify yourself. My little one who has met with phantoms in her long search in the night, you are justified because you are loved. Love is the only thing that needs no justification. It takes and gives without question. Dear heart, I think I know you; I know your mettle; I know you though I know of no explanation or justification for you. Love for me is knowledge, and candor is a burning desire. I don't want to say that I accept you. Why should I accept or not accept? I want to say that I love you, you, all that is you, unconditionally and without reserve.

"And when I say this I know I am breaking all the rules of the game. Yes, it is a game; life is a game and so is love. I am taking a risk. I am letting my heart, naked, trembling, throbbing, stubborn in its faith, suffer the agonies of confession, and with nothing to protect it. What happens when the barriers and the dams give way, and the imprisoned, anxious, pent-up waves gush out from the fenced-in areas and collide, carrying stones and rocks with them? Is it frightening? Yes, I know the warmth of hidden darkness and preserved secrets, but I also know of the bitterness and loneliness behind the ramparts. What happens when the self unveils its intimate disarray, its incomprehensible and unjustifiable long-ings, the force of its frenzy and its hidden demands?"

[3]

She said to him, "You shouldn't have come with me. We should have said good-bye to each other in the hotel. It doesn't make sense for you to insist on coming with me to the station, especially as you are leaving this afternoon. You will be coming to this station twice in one day. Do you know . . . you have slain the dragon."

Somewhat startled, he said, "What was that?"

She said, "You have slain the dragon. You know, in the old legends, in the tales of courtly—and uncourtly—love, the knight demonstrates his devotion by slaying the dragon. He goes out to the desolate woods, having given his beloved a handkerchief or a token. Then he goes off alone, conquers all difficulties, overcomes every challenge . . . and endures great hardship . . . until he slays the dragon; and you have slain the dragon . . ."

Then she quickly added, "And I do not mean to be satirical or funny . . . I mean what I say."

He did not say to her, "Do I still need to demonstrate my love? I do not want to demonstrate or refute anything. All of this is beyond demonstration and refu-tation. Do you, yourself, need proof and evidence to demonstrate or to refute? You never stop, at any time, speaking as if you were wondering, as if you were uncertain . . . Don't you feel that which is breaking loose, day and night, in my deepest being? Doesn't it show itself? Don't you feel that which can never be separated from my life?"

A hoarse roar bursts through his ribcage, an earthquake shudders his whole frame. Broken, solid stones, torn by nails and claws from the core of his heart, thunder down. The two hands with their tensed fingers gouge out ponds filled with blood in the harsh blank walls of his body. They scrape off the petrified heart, which goes on, stubbornly and regularly, beating.

He screams in the still silence: "Aaaaay me! Aaaaay me!" . . . He bellows but holds back his gaping mouth from the fullest cry. His scream, never held back, never uttered, fills all the breaches, all the holes, all the wounds, all the gaps in heaven and earth.

He said to himself, "I have not slain the dragon. I am living with him. His teeth are piercing my heart in an embrace-without-end until death."

[4]

The hooves of the horses slam down with a dreadful rhythm on the black basalt, sending repeated echoes along the street, now empty of traffic and all its familiar noises. In the swaying body of the city new, solid, stubborn knots are forming, which soon dissolve and melt in mists of tear gas. In front of the slim ranks carrying shields, clubs, and helmets, other small knots are gathering. They bulge slowly and are filled with cries like the explosions of an old painful disease, like the gushing of stagnant turbid water under the oppression and suffering of daily agonies that have no explanation or solution. The howling of the machine guns with their intermittent echoes seems unimportant, leaving in front of it small bodies that fall suddenly as if they were insignificant heaps of sorrow and rags. They are lifted up and carried over quickly to the sidewalk in the hope of finding a mercy that may or may not come. Slender plants bend under the blows and are broken down. These flowers that bloomed only for one day and then were smashed, will they leave behind them seeds from which they can grow again? The fire of these bitter flowers is soon extinguished.

As if Michael felt the wounds, the cracks, and the burns in his frail, finite body, in his other body stretched out buried between the desert waves and the belly of the soft soil. The dragon fidgeted from the stinging of the sharp cuts left by the stabbing spears. If he rose with his blazing eyes and wide-open, flame-throwing mouth with its thousand teeth ... If he raised his strong, firm back, balancing himself on that huge tail covered with scales and taut muscles, then the pillars of heaven would sway and rock the lower world on which the black earth is mounted.

[5]

He said to her "Of course you know that it is not at all important what you narrate, and what tale you tell. Maybe what is important is that you, yourself, are the narrator."

She said, "I don't know what you mean."

But there was a look of understanding and knowledge in her eyes.

He made no comment.

[6]

But he was silent.

Why silence?

He said, "Surely words impoverish, because they put fences around things that cannot be enclosed."

He said, "Because there are deeds. Only deeds can give silence its meaning."

He said, "Deeds may also contain ambiguity. In fact, they are mysterious in themselves. They are the thing and they are its opposite. They are finite too, and they set limits."

He said, "This is precisely their value."

He said, "Escape where? A deed is more than one thing and less than one thing."

He said, "Words too are deeds, and the deeds of words, their tone, warmth, allusion, spontaneity, reserve, inarticulateness, are all necessary, inevitable and vital."

She said, "You make my head whirl. Isn't all this absurd?"

[7]

The trumpets of alarm sound out in despairing lamentation. The stars fall and crumble between his fingers. The smile of pleasure on her beautiful face appears in a rusty brass mask that stretches out and is crushed by shields. The waves of all the oceans of the universe cannot wipe out the bitterness in his mouth or vanquish the pain bursting in his ribs. A tremendous earthquake hurled him about. He was tossed around by the walls of the confining room that contains heaven and earth, everything having become a vast ruin swept by the wind. The braids of her honey-colored hair are drooping from the sun, and the green-eyed moon drips blood. His eyes shed pebbles of tears. The seven seals are locked. They do not open in the clamor of the earthquake nor are they broken by his fingers, which go on fumbling with their locks. The black steed rips the ceiling, breaking free with a rapid beat of its thundering hooves. The guts of the dragon are open, throbbing and pouring out a bloody flood, gushing in the glow of fires in the dark, which is then swallowed by the wasteland. The two great olive trees have shed their fruits in the roar of the flooding waters. The six wings are not broken in a war that ends in neither victory nor defeat. Heaven's towers are collapsing, but the supple, feminine body in his tightening embraces is chaste. It has not been touched by the flood of water replete with corpses. The great sunflowers with their rounded tips and dark-colored centers rise up, thriving and swaying among the flames, and he has fallen.

He calls out voicelessly in the clamor of the earthquake, "O Michael! O Archangel! O Leader of the hundreds!"

[8]

And she said to him, "Michael, is this the first time that you break the chains and are free from repression?"

Later on, he reflected she had not said that his lovemaking was romantic, even chaste and purging, in a certain sense, nor had she said that it had in it a tenderness and a sensuous devotion verging on ritual worship, and that his hands, lips, and tightly tensed body were unravaged by use or vulgarity.

He said, "Yes, it is the first time."

She said, "That pleases me."

Without any quaver in her voice, she decides something that is important but arouses no excitement. As if the matter has not been, for him, a stunningly beautiful discovery, an earthquake shaking the walls of his life, breaking and piling the split, cracked but clean-cut, fine-edged rocks.

How impossible she can be to communicate with when she chooses—or when her taste or distaste chooses. She rebukes him with her sheer presence! Her presence alone denies him, negates him, silently, voicelessly, and without effort.

After six days, she told him, "You have slain the dragon."

And she said, "Thank God we are traveling today and moving on."

He said to her, obstinately, "Thank God if you like. But I cannot say, here and now, and despite everything: Thank God; had it not been that to Him alone one offers thanks."

She said to him, "Of course, you are free in what you say, and what you don't say."

He accompanied her to the station, nevertheless, and embraced her, believing that this was good-bye, though he knew in his innermost being that it was not.

From the dragon's teeth planted in my heart, thick dark-green reeds flourish and sway.

[9]

This dragon inside me is forsaking me, is slipping free from me. I feel him as an Other, as a stranger, close and clinging to my innermost being. How often I tried to deny him. Michael said to himself "When the cock crowed three times . . ." And he laughed. Who hung himself? Who is Peter? And who is Judas?

[10]

Michael said to himself, "Tell al-Zaatar and Abu Zaabal. The circles of the Colosseum, the graveyard of Caracalla, and the dungeons of the inquisition. The helmets of the Vikings, the hounds trained to savage the blacks in Zimbabwe, the power of the papal pardons, and the statement of politburos and central committees. Spartacus, Jesus, and Husayn ibn Mansur crucified with thieves, rebels, and fugitives. The cells of the Bastille, the swords of the crusaders and the chains of the Saracens. The prostitutes of Saigon, and the victims of black September, black June, and all the black months. The devil's islands no matter how their names differ: Sing-Sing, Tura, Robbens Island, and the islands in the Aegean. The floating corpses in the Nile in Uganda, the bodies stabbed by poisoned spears in Burundi and Rwanda, the crushed ones in Chile, and the squashed ones in Bangladesh. The snows of Argentina and the ovens of Dachau. Quartering of limbs, guillotine blades, and execution blows. The Khartoum of Kitchener, the Victorian factories of Manchester, the Commune of Paris, and the fields of sugarcane and cotton in Mississippi and Upper Egypt. The huts and putrid wounds covering the face of the earth, and the ghettos of Harlem, Odessa, and Warsaw. The barbed wire of Siberia and Saharan oases, and the electrodes on women's breasts and men's genitals in Algeria and Haiti. The caravans of the Karmathians and the fall of Baghdad under the strikes of Hulagu. The pyres of witches and white soldiers harvesting jungles and valleys with wide-mouthed cannon. The slave boats from Guinea and Zanzibar. Whiskey, syphilis, opium, and bullets for Red Indians, and the same for black and yellow Indians. From Beirut to Guernica, from Berlin to Leningrad, from Sinai to Deir Yassin, from Carthage to Constantinople, from Jerusalem to Shanghai, from Buchenwald to Munich, from Bombay to Dinshawai, from the Huns to the Mongols, from the Hyksos to the Mandarins to Vietnam, from the Mamluks to the tycoons. Isn't this the story of all our days? Of the first day and the last day? Isn't this the principle and the rule? Isn't this the story of this wise, inventive, dreaming, upright, articulate, intelligent, ravishing ape? The bruised living limbs that are stamped and torn, and the wounded spirit behind the stifled, hidden eyes; the mind in anguish, starved by oppression and paralyzed by degradation; all the cards and the values, all the gods and the systems; all the beasts and the victims; all the heroes and the sites, all the epochs and the masks; all the victims and the freaks; all the lists do not and cannot end. And the dragon is one, unslain, and the lance of St. Michael is blunted—but is still brandished among the stars.[1]

[11]

He said, "Revolutionaries, everywhere, are alike."

She said with a dreamy almost erotic look, "Ben Ammar was a revolutionary, of the pure type, able to let bygones be bygones and start from scratch each time, after each failure, without regrets, and especially without bitterness."

---

1. Every name on this long list refers to human atrocity and suffering through history. For example: Devil Island in the Caribbean was the site of a French penal colony. Dayr Yasin is a village in Palestine near Jerusalem where on April 9, 1948, the inhabitants found in the village, mostly children and women, were massacred by Zionist militia of the Irgun faction led by Menachem Begin. At least two hundred and fifty of them were murdered in cold blood. Warsaw refers to the Nazi occupation of the Polish capital from 1939—1944. The Nazis persecuted the inhabitants, and tens of thousands, mostly from the intelligentsia, were sent to death camps (mainly at Auschwitz), and thousands were tortured to death in prisons. The Jewish ghetto uprising in 1943 caused the Jewish population of the ghetto to be taken to extermination camps. When the Soviet armies were approaching the city in 1944, the Nazis methodically destroyed the city, burning palaces, churches, museums, libraries, and many buildings. Tel al-Zaatar was the Palestinian camp in East Beirut that was savagely overrun by the Lebanese Christian Phalangists in 1976. At least fifteen thousand people, mostly civilians, including women and children, were massacred there.

[12]

My intimate companion, never known to betray, Invited me to drink, as a host would invite a guest. As the cup went round, he called for the block and the axe. The fate of all drinkers of the dragon's midsummer wine.

Thus spoke Hussein ibn Mansur al-Hallaj[2]

—Translated by Ferial Ghazoul and Alan Brownjohn

Ilias Khouri (b. 1948)

Lebanese novelist, short-story writer, literary critic, and columnist Ilias Khouri studied history at the Lebanese University and read sociology in Paris. An enthusiast for the Palestine cause, he joined the editorial board of the Palestinian cultural magazine *Shu'un Filastiniyya* and was its deputy editor-in-chief between 1977 and 1979. In 1981 he won a fellowship from the Institute of Arab Studies, which operated in Belmont in the early 1980s, and spent that year in the United States. His short-story collections are *The Green Mountain* (1977), which was translated into English by Maia Tabet, and *Beginning and End* (1984). His novels include three that have been translated into English by Paula Haydar: *City Gates* (1993), a complex work written in a surrealistic style; *The Journey of Little Ghandi* (1989); and *Kingdom of Strangers* (1993). Other novels are *White Faces* (1981), a mystery, and his prestigious *Door of the Sun* (1998) on the Palestinian experience, which won him an award from the Palestinian Ministry of Culture. He is an experimental writer who has succeeded in writing each of these books in a distinctly different style. He has also written at least four books of criticism on contemporary fiction and poetry.

CITY GATES

This is a tale, told in repetitive parable fashion, of a man's endless quest: for an entry to a city, for the city's center, for his lost possessions, for women, for a reason, for himself. His wanderings take him round and round in circles, as in a maze, and the tales told of various lives he encounters on the way are simultaneously mysterious and alienated.

THE COFFIN AND THE KING

The man spoke to the man. He looked up and found no one beside him, but he spoke, saying, this is the king, and these things that look like flowers are his coffin.

---

2. Muslim mystic (857—922) who taught Sufism against orthodox beliefs. Standing firmly by his beliefs, he was finally arrested and crucified.

And the man was alone, the flowers were like his memory: piles of torn leaves and a smell; the smell of memory.

The stranger's head sags and his limbs drop onto the soft sand, questioning. The old man who seemed like an ancestor is absent, far away, and cannot answer. It was the woman, the one who kissed him seven times on the forehead, who told him. He cannot remember now what she said, but he remembers the odor of dead flowers lying by the wayside. He remembered then that there were no roads in the square, and that he was incapable of bending down to smell the flowers, but their smell rose into his nose and mouth until it spread throughout his chest. And he sat aside, alone on the ground, sending up a cloud of white dust; he tried to open his eyes but couldn't, as though he had been kneaded one with the dust. How could he see? He couldn't see. He tried. But the woman who was beside him rose lightly, he tried to rise, "I can't" he said, she whispered something, scattered sand over his head and body, his head lifted and he looked up . . .

Above, in white space, a black dot was spiraling up and up. It circled the tomb and the square and then drew nearer. It is getting close, the man said. I am afraid. Of the bird that soared above, he said this is a bird of prey who will feed upon our eyes. The bird flew closer, and dust went up in a column that linked the earth with the sky.

The man said this, and looked around. He saw voices in the shape of tiny birds circling his head. He was afraid and wanted to. The woman grasped his hand. He walked beside her. He wanted to ask her about the women, but she placed her finger on his mouth and kept walking. The man saw a deep pit, and sat down beside it.

"This is the king," she said.

As he looked at her, the woman receded further away, until she was a distant point. He wanted to follow her but couldn't rise. He looked down into the pit and saw a sarcophagus of stone and numerous rocks scattered about.

"I shall go down where the king is," he said, "I will look there, there find it, and maybe." He felt himself slide down, the dust come up through his nose, and he hoped. He went down slowly, as though falling piece by piece.

The man found himself alone, and he found the king. It was no king but a sarcophagus of white stone, covered with the engraving of a man gripping his beard with his right hand, left leg broken, the other hand flat against his body. He went closer to it, bent down, and knelt, feeling a need for water.

The man tried to remember the city gates but could not recall their color. He thought of the women but had forgotten the colors of their eyes. He thought of his briefcase, but he had forgotten why he was looking for it. He thought of the letters he had found but had already forgotten why he had found them. Memory is something like a flower, he told himself, and he sat down by the coffin's edge to wait, and he saw.

When he opened his eyes, the bird was flying close by his head. He had seen a dream, the man told himself. It was the king; the king had opened the lid of his coffin and risen, not much like the image laid down over the coffin but an old man who coughed, with bones that creaked.

The king had sat on a chair, surrounded by his ministers and attendants. When the king coughed, they fell silent and remained so.

"Why are you silent?" the king said.

They bowed to him and began to speak. He raised his hand and everybody left. Then the king called, in a voice full of wrinkles, and she made her entrance . . .

A woman white as buttermilk came in on the tips of her toes. Her hair reached down to her ankles. In her colorful dress, eyes flashing, she kissed the king's feet and sat down. She held an 'oud, on which she started to play. She sang. Her voice was sad, the tune emerged from her fingers to enfold the court, to wrap itself around a body. Enough! he said.

She stopped singing and playing. He called. Several men came and secured the doors. He coughed and drank from a pitcher by his side. She got up and began to dance and sway. He approached and stripped the dress off her, she shivered as she swayed, her long neck arched downward and her eyes swam around the court.

Panting louder, he went closer to her, his face—I saw his face—it was the face of someone who strains without wanting to. Her laughter resounded at the center of his face. His face resembled nothing. Kings' faces look like nothing, the man thought to himself. Her eyes grew wide, and his eyes filled with tears. She knelt down at his feet and kissed them, crying aloud. He kicked her in the face, closing in on her with both hands raised. She tried to run. Gates locked, with king and guards. He came closer. Don't kill me! she screamed, I am yours! With tears in his eyes he came closer . . .

"But this is you," the man said questioningly.

"Yes," she said.

"You were standing by one of the gates in the wall."

"Yes," she said.

"And I saw you weeping with the other women."

"Yes," she said.

"Why?" he said.

"Yes," she said.

On his knees the stranger fumbled around the tomb, as though looking for something. He heard a voice request that he kiss the king's hand. He kissed the one that gripped the beard, bending lower as he moved around, and then he saw horses, three horses, and three knights whose swords were flashing as they raced about, their faces broad and tattooed, and they ran, emitting strange sounds. The first knight dismounted; the other two followed—he bowed down, and they bowed down with him. Then he returned to his horse and mounted, still as stone. The stranger approached. He spoke to the knight, but the knight did not answer.

Wandering off, the man saw three women walking, who carried a large animal on their shoulders. It is a long way, the stranger thought, but the women don't look at anyone.

"Where are you going?"

"We are taking sacrifice to the king," one of them answered, in a voice the man thought he had heard before.

The woman fell silent and walked ahead with the others. The animal's body lunged forward on its way to death.

The man reeled around. He was carrying a spear with a little serpent at its tip. The serpent's jaws were open, and it was coiled around the spearhead. The bearer kept walking. He would ask him nothing, the man thought, because no one answered anyway. Suddenly the serpent dropped off the spear. The bearer bent down, and the women bent with him. The king remained stretched out on his wooden bed, seemingly unperturbed. One of the women picked up the serpent and put it back in place. The bearer bowed his head and continued his march forward.

The stranger felt exhaustion slither down his back. Am I afraid? Why should I be? A dead king and piles of stones ... He sensed that he had turned into a deep abyss. He trembled. The pit was gaping downward, but where could he scream ...? He heard a loud noise and saw the faraway bird approaching from a distance. Its wings were long and remote, its head was darting downward, its fluttering filled the tomb with the odor of dead flowers, the women wept louder.

Why doesn't he come and sit beside me? the stranger thought. I am perfectly willing. I shall weep for the king and die for his sake ...

But there was no answer. Only the distant bird, coming closer, a terrible wind, and sounds of rushing water. The man closed his eyes and leaned against the serpent; he heard a hissing noise grow louder. He tried to open his eyes but couldn't. Then he tried to lie beside the coffin. He tried ...

He heard a voice then and saw a man, an old man sitting at the edge of the coffin. The lid of the coffin had been pushed aside. He opened his mouth to speak.

This is the king, he thought, I must bow.

"You needn't bother," said the king. "Come and sit beside me."

"But I do want to—" said the man.

"Will has no place here. I'm too old for that sort of thing."

"But they're above us. Don't you hear?"

"That's above us. But you come and sit beside me."

The man said he wanted to go back with the woman. The king started to cry. But kings never cry, thought the stranger. The king spoke about other kings, about his back, which had grown crooked from so much bending. But kings never kneel, said the man. He spoke about the dead, whose corpses kept piling up. But kings ... About going back to the city. The stranger felt misgivings. He was wrong, he shouldn't be speaking to the king. The king was pointing to the bird: "Now, after an endless number of circles, it will come down to us. Then, when it is gone, I will return to my place and you will come with me."

"I want to go where the women are."

"You will stay with me," said the king.

"But I am afraid."

"How can you be afraid of a king?"

"I am afraid of the serpent and the women who carry the beast; of your eyes, sunken in white. I'm afraid of your men, who all circle around you without your knowing it."

"But I do know. Only, I want . . . Only, I can't . . . Only, I . . . "

The stranger raised his eyes and saw the bird come down. He felt sharp knives slicing through his clothes, his limbs being torn off.

"All I did was look for my briefcase!" he cried. "It contained some paper, nothing more!" And the bird kept descending, and the man was transfigured, grew smaller and smaller, white as sand. Naked as the forest whose trees are cut down, the square that has no beginning. He struggled to get his eyes open and to scream. He saw an endless staircase and attempted to climb. He rose, he saw a hand stretched out to him, he grasped it and started to climb. He started gasping for breath. He was up, then he stood still and fell to the ground.

The seventh woman said.

The first woman said.

Darkness was spreading the hands stretched out to him. The women took him in their arms, they carried him around. Then he opened his eyes and saw that all around him was sand and dust.

"Woman!" he cried. His voice fell in circles onto the grounds of the square. He grew attentive to distant sounds. He noticed a black dot getting larger, and he waited.

"The woman is calling me. I'll tell her it's not me."

"I know it's not you, but she keeps calling."

"She's calling, and I shall certainly go," said the man. He listened to the rustle of her dress and saw the dust rising from under her bare feet and pierce me through the head.

—Translated by Sargon Boulus and Thomas G. Ezzy

Naguib Mahfouz (b. 1911)

See Naguib Mahfouz's biography in the short-story section.

THE THIEF AND THE DOGS

The Thief and the Dogs is one of Mahfouz's greatest novels, combining his interest in the antihero, who is himself a victim, and his capacity to delineate, with subtlety and skill, psychological situations that ensue from poignant existential problems. Sa'id Mahran, a thief has just been released from a four-year term in prison, to face a double betrayal: the wife whom he had loved and cherished has betrayed him with another man, and the friend, Rauf Ilwan, who had been his moral support and political mentor, and taught him the principles of socialism, has dramatically changed, becoming an opportunist after the Egyptian Revolution of 1952 which took place when Mahran was in prison. The plot revolves around Mahran's reactions to this double betrayal. His attempt at avenging himself against the man who took his wife results in the killing of bystanders. His attempt to get even with Rauf Ilwan results in failure. Caught in the web of his own mistakes, as well as in the mechanism of the social order, the thief now turned fugitive revolves in vain around the pivots of love (his attachment to Nur, the good prostitute) and faith (his loyalty and attraction to the holy old man who was his father's spiritual teacher) as he tries to flee a world of treachery that proves that even a thief and a murderer can be a victim. At the story's end the prostitute who gives him love and the holy man who gives him pity become unattainable, and he is once again left alone, for police dogs to tear him apart.

CHAPTER 11

Not a day passes without the graveyard welcoming new guests. Why, it's as though there's nothing more left to do but crouch behind the shutters watching these endless progressions of death. It's the mourners who deserve one's sympathy, of course. They come in one weeping throng and then they go away drying their tears and talking, as if while they're here some force stronger than death itself has convinced them to stay alive.

That was how your own parents were buried: your father, 'Amm Mahran, the kindly concierge of the students' hostel, who died middle-aged after a hard but honest and satisfying life. You helped him in his work from your childhood on. For all the extreme simplicity, even poverty of their lives, the family enjoyed sitting together when the day's work was done in their ground-floor room at the entrance to the building, where 'Amm Mahran and his wife would chat together while their child played. His piety made him happy, and the students respected him well. The only entertainment he knew was making pilgrimage to the home of Sheikh 'Ali al-Junaydi, and it was through your father that you came to know the house. "Come along," he'd say, "and I'll show you how to have more fun than playing in the fields. You'll see how sweet life can be, what it's like in an atmosphere of godliness. It'll give you a sense of peace and contentment, the finest thing you can achieve in life."

The sheikh greeted you with that sweet and kindly look of his. And how enchanted you were by his fine white beard! "So this is your son you were telling me about," he said to your father. "There's a lot of intelligence in his eyes. His heart is as spotless as yours. You'll find he'll turn out, with God's will, a truly good man." Yes, you really adored Sheikh 'Ali al-Junaydi, attracted by the purity in his face and the love in his eyes. And those songs and chants of his had delighted you even before your heart was purified by love.

"Tell this boy what it's his duty to do," your father said to the sheikh one day.

The sheikh had gazed down at you and said, "We continue learning from the cradle to the grave, but at least start out, Sa'id, by keeping close account of yourself and making sure that from whatever action you initiate some good comes to someone."

Yes, you certainly followed his counsel, as best you could though you only brought it to complete fulfillment when you took up burglary!

The days passed like dreams. And then your good father disappeared, suddenly gone, in a way that a boy simply could not comprehend, and that seemed to baffle even Sheikh 'Ali himself. How shocked you were that morning, shaking your head and rubbing your eyes to clear away the sleep, awakened by your mother's screams and tears in the little room at the entrance to the students' hostel! You wept with fear and frustration at your helplessness. That evening however, Rauf 'Alwan, at that time a student in law school, had shown how very capable he was. Yes, he was impressive all right, no matter what the circumstances, and you loved him as you did Sheikh 'Ali, perhaps even more. It was he who later worked hard to have you—or you and your mother, to be more precise—take over Father's job as custodian for the building. Yes, you took on responsibilities at an early age.

And then your mother died. You almost died yourself during your mother's illness, as Rauf 'Alwan must surely remember, from that unforgettable day when she had hemorrhaged and you had rushed her to the nearest hospital, the Sabir hospital, standing like a castle amidst beautiful grounds, where you found yourself and your mother in a reception hall at an entrance more luxurious than anything you could ever have imagined possible. The entire place seemed forbidding, even hostile, but you were in the direst need of help, immediate help.

As the famous doctor was coming out of a room, they mentioned his name and you raced toward him in your gallabiya and sandals, shouting, "My mother! The blood!"

The man had fixed you in a glassy, disapproving stare and had glanced where your mother was lying, stretched out in her filthy dress on a soft couch, a foreign nurse standing nearby, observing the scene. Then the doctor had simply disappeared, saying nothing. The nurse jabbered something in a language you did not understand, though you sensed she was expressing sympathy for your tragedy. At that point, for all your youth, you flew into a real adult's rage, screaming and cursing in protest, smashing a chair to the floor with a crash, so the veneer wood on its back broke to pieces. A horde of servants had appeared, and you'd soon found yourself and your mother alone in the tree-lined road outside. A month later your mother had died in Kasr al-'Aini hospital.

All the time she lay close to death she never released your hand, refusing to take her eyes off you. It was during that long month of illness, however, that you stole for the first time—from the country boy resident in the hostel, who'd accused you without any investigation and was beating you vigorously when Rauf 'Alwan turned up and freed you, settling the matter without any further complications. You were a true human being then, Rauf, and you were my teacher too.

Alone with you, Rauf had said quietly, "Don't you worry. The fact is, I consider this theft perfectly justified. Only you'll find the police watching out for you, and the judge won't be lenient with you," he'd added ominously with bitter sarcasm, "however convincing your motives, because he, too, will be protecting himself. Isn't it justice" he'd shouted, "that what is taken by theft should be retrieved by theft? Here I am studying, away from home and family, suffering daily from hunger and deprivation!"

Where have all your principles gone now, Rauf? Dead, no doubt, like my father and my mother and like my wife's fidelity.

You had no alternative but to leave the students' hostel and seek a living somewhere else. So you waited under the lone palm tree at the end of the green plot until Nabawiyya came and you sprang toward her, saying, "Don't be afraid, I must speak to you. I'm leaving to get a better job. I love you. Don't ever forget me. I love you and always will. And I'll prove I can make you happy and give you a respectable home." Yes, those had been times when sorrows could be forgotten, wounds could be healed, and hope could bring forth fruit from adversity.

All your graves out there, immersed in the gloom, don't jeer at my memories!

He sat up on the sofa, still in the dark, addressing Rauf 'Alwan just as though he could see him standing in front of him. "You should have agreed to get me a job writing for your newspaper, you scoundrel. I'd have published our mutual reminiscences there, I'd have shut off your false light good and proper." Then he wondered aloud "How am I going to stand it here in the dark till Nur comes back near dawn?"

Suddenly he was attacked by an irresistible urge to leave the house and take a walk in the dark. In an instant his resistance crumbled, like a building ready to give way, collapsing; soon he was moving stealthily out of the house. He set off toward Masani Street and from there turned toward open wasteland.

Leaving his hideout made him all the more conscious of being hunted. He now knew how mice and foxes feel, slipping away on the run. Alone in the dark, he could see the city's lights glimmering in the distance, lying in wait for him. He quaffed his sense of being alone, until it intoxicated him, then walked on winding up at last in his old seat next to Tarzan in the coffeehouse. The only other person inside, apart from the waiter, was an arms smuggler, although outside, a little lower down, at the foot of the hill, there was considerable noise of people talking.

The waiter brought him some tea at once, and then Tarzan leaned over. "Don't spend more than one night in the same place," he whispered.

The smuggler added his advice, "Move way up the Nile."

"But I don't know anyone up there," Sa'id objected.

"You know," the smuggler went on, "I've heard many people express their admiration for you."

"And the police?" Tarzan said heatedly. "Do they admire him too?"

The smuggler laughed so hard that his whole body shook, as if he were mounted on a camel at the gallop. "Nothing impresses the police," he said at last, when he'd recovered his breath.

"Absolutely nothing," agreed Sa'id.

"But what harm is there in stealing from the rich anyway?" the waiter asked with feeling.

Sa'id beamed as if he were receiving a compliment at some public reception in his honor. "Yes," he said, "but the newspapers have tongues longer than a hangman's rope. And what good does being liked by the people do if the police loathe you?"

Suddenly Tarzan got up, moved to the window, stared outside, looking to left and right, then came back. "I thought I saw a face staring in at us," he reported, clearly worried.

Sa'id's eyes glinted as they darted back and forth between window and door, and the waiter went outside to investigate.

"You're always seeing things that aren't there," the smuggler said.

Enraged, Tarzan yelled at him. "Shut up! can't you? You seem to think a hangman's rope is some sort of joke!"

Sa'id left the coffeehouse. Clutching the revolver in his pocket, walking off into the open darkness, he looked cautiously around him, listening as he went. His consciousness of fear, of being alone and hunted, was even stronger now and he knew he must not underestimate his enemies, fearful themselves, but so eager to catch him that they would not rest till they saw him a corpse, laid out and still.

As he neared the house in Shari' Najm al-Din, he saw light in Nur's window. It gave him a sense of security for the first time since he'd left the coffeehouse. He found her lying down and wanted to caress her, but it was obvious from her face that she was terribly tired. Her eyes were so red it was obvious that something was amiss. He sat down at her feet.

"Please tell me what's wrong, Nur," he said.

"I'm worn out," she said weakly. "I've vomited so much I'm exhausted."

"Was it drink?"

"I've been drinking all my life," she said, her eyes brimming with tears.

This was the first time Sa'id had seen her cry, and he was deeply moved. "What was the reason, then?" he said.

"They beat me!"

"The police?"

"No, some young louts, probably students, when I asked them to pay the bill."

Sa'id was touched. "Why not wash your face," he said, "and drink some water?"

"A little later. I'm too tired now."

"The dogs!" Sa'id muttered, tenderly caressing her leg.

"The fabric for the uniform," Nur said, pointing to a parcel on the other sofa. He made a gesture with his hand affectionately and in gratitude.

"I can't look very attractive for you tonight," she said almost apologetically.

"It's not your fault. Just wash your face and get some sleep."

Up in the graveyard heights a dog barked and Nur let out a long, audible sigh. "And she said, 'you have such a rosy future!'" she murmured sadly.

"Who?"

"A fortune-teller. She said there'd be security, peace of mind." Sa'id stared out at the blackness of night, piled up outside the window, as she went on, "When will that ever be? It's been such a long wait, and all so useless. I have a girlfriend, a little older than me, who always says we'll become just bones or even worse than that, so that even dogs will loathe us." Her voice seemed to come from the very grave and so depressed Sa'id that he could find nothing to reply. "Some fortune teller!" she said. "When is she going to start telling the truth? Where is there any security? I just want to sleep safe and secure, wake up feeling good, and have a quiet, pleasant time. Is that so impossible—for him who raised the Seven Heavens?"

You too used to dream of a life like that, but it's all been spent climbing up drainpipes, jumping down from roofs, and being chased in the dark, with misaimed bullets killing innocent people.

"You need to get some sleep," he told her, thoroughly depressed.

"What I need is a promise," she said. "A promise from the fortune teller. And that day will come."

"Good."

"You're treating me like a child," she said angrily.

"Never."

"That day really will come!"

FROM CHAPTER 12

Sa'id shouted in anger to the darkened room: "Are you really the same one? The Rauf 'Alwan who owns a mansion? You're the fox behind the newspaper campaign. You too want to kill me, to murder your conscience and the past as well. But I won't die before I've killed you: you're the number one traitor. What nonsense life would turn out to be if I were myself killed tomorrow—in retribution for murdering a man I didn't even know! If there's going to be any meaning to life—and to death, too—I simply have to kill you. My last outburst of rage at the evil of the world. And all those things lying out there in the graveyard below the window will help me. As for the rest, I'll leave it to Sheikh 'Ali to solve the riddle."

Just when the call to the dawn prayers was announced, he heard the door open and Nur came carrying some grilled meat, drinks, and newspapers. She seemed quite happy, having apparently forgotten her two days of distress and depression; and her presence dispelled his own gloom and exhaustion, made him ready again to embrace what life had to offer: food, drink, and news. She kissed him and, for the first time, he responded spontaneously, with a sense of gratitude, knowing her now to be the person closest to him for as long as he might live. He wished she'd never leave.

He uncorked a bottle as usual, poured himself a glass, and drank it down in one gulp.

"Why didn't you get some sleep?" Nur said, peering close at his tired face.

Flipping through the newspapers, he made no reply.

"It must be torture to wait in the dark," she said, feeling sorry for him.

"How are things outside?" he asked, tossing the papers aside.

"Just like always." She undressed down to her slip, and Sa'id smelled powder moistened with sweat. "People are talking about you," she went on, "as if you were some storybook hero. But they don't have any idea what torture we go through."

"Most Egyptians neither fear nor dislike thieves," said Sa'id as he bit into a piece of meat. Several minutes passed in silence while they ate, then he added, "But they do have an instinctive dislike for dogs."

"Well," said Nur with a smile, licking her fingertips, "I like dogs."

"I don't mean that kind of dog."

"Yes, I always had one at home until I saw the last one die. That made me cry a lot so I decided not to have one again."

"That's right," said Sa'id. "If love's going to cause problems, just steer clear of it."

"You don't understand me. Or love me."

"Don't be like that," he said, pleading. "Can't you see the whole world is cruel enough and unjust enough as it is?"

Nur drank until she could hardly sit up. Her real name was Shalabiyya, she confessed. Then she told him tales of the old days in Balyana, of her childhood amid the quiet waters, of her youth and how she'd run away. "And my father was the *umda*," she said proudly, "the village headman."

"You mean the *umda*'s servant!"

She frowned, but he went on. "Well, that's what you told me first."

Nur laughed so heartily that Sa'id could see bits of parsley caught in her teeth. "Did I really say that?" she asked.

"Yes. And that's what turned Rauf 'Alwan into a traitor."

She stared at him uncomprehendingly. "And who's Rauf Ilwan?"

"Don't lie to me," Sa'id snarled. "A man who has to stay in the dark, waiting by himself, a man like that can't stand lies."

CHAPTER 17

Late in the afternoon and then again during the evening the landlady returned. "No, no, Madame Nur," she muttered as she finally left, "everything has to come to an end sometime, you know."

At midnight Sa'id slipped out. Although his confidence in everything had gone, he was careful to walk very naturally and slowly, as if merely taking a stroll. More than once, when the thought struck him that people passing by or standing around might well be informers, he braced himself for one last desperate battle. After the encounter on the previous day, he had no doubts that the police would be in occupation of the whole area near Tarzan's café, so he moved off toward Jabal Road.

Hunger was tearing at his stomach now. On the road it occurred to him that Sheikh 'Ali al-Junaydi's house might well provide a temporary place of refuge while he thought out his next moves. It was only as he slipped into the courtyard of the silent house that he became aware that he had left his uniform in the living room of Nur's flat. With the realization infuriating him, Sa'id went on into the old man's room, where the lamplight showed the sheikh sitting in the corner reserved for prayer, completely engrossed in a whispered monologue. Sa'id walked over to the wall where he'd left his books and sat down, exhausted.

The sheikh continued his quiet utterance until Sa'id addressed him: "Good evening then, Sheikh 'Ali."

The old man raised his hand to his head in response to the greeting, but did not break off his incantations.

"Sheikh, I'm really hungry," Sa'id said.

The old man seemed to interrupt his chant, gazed at him vacantly, then nodded with his chin to a side table nearby where Sa'id saw some bread and figs. He got up at once, went to the table, and consumed it all ravenously, then stood there looking at the Sheikh with unappeased eyes.

"Don't you have any money?" the Sheikh said quietly.

"Oh, yes."

"Why not go and buy yourself something to eat?"

Sa'id then made his way quietly back to his seat. The Sheikh sat contemplating him for a while, then said, "When are you going to settle down, do you think?"

"Not on the face of this earth."

"That's why you're hungry, even though you've got money."

"So be it, then."

"As for me," the Sheikh commented, "I was just reciting some verses about life's sorrows. I was reciting in a joyful frame of mind."

"Yes. Well, you're certainly a happy Sheikh," Sa'id said. "The scoundrels have got away," he went on angrily. "How can I settle down after that?"

"How many of them are there?"

"Three."

"What joy for the world if its scoundrels number only three."

"No, there are very many more, but my enemies are only three."

"Well then, no one has 'got away.'"

"I'm not responsible for the world, you know."

"Oh yes. You're responsible for both this world and the next!" While Sa'id puffed in exasperation, the Sheikh continued, "Patience is holy and through it things are blessed."

"But it's the guilty who succeed, while the innocent fail," Sa'id commented glumly.

The Sheikh sighed, "When shall we succeed in achieving peace of mind beneath the doings of authority?"

"When authority becomes fair," Sa'id replied.

"It is always fair."

Sa'id shook his head angrily. "Yes," he muttered. "They've got away now all right, damn it." The Sheikh merely smiled without speaking. Sa'id's voice changed its tone as he tried to alter the course of the conversation. "I'm going to sleep with my face toward the wall. I don't want any one who visits you to see me. I'm going to hide out here with you. Please protect me."

"Trusting God means entrusting one's lodging to God alone," the Sheikh said gently.

"Would you give me up?"

"Oh, no, God forbid."

"Would it be in your power, with all the grace with which you're endowed, to save me then?"

"You can save yourself, if you wish," came the Sheikh's reply.

"I will kill the others," Sa'id whispered to himself, and aloud said, "Are you capable of straightening the shadow of something crooked?"

"I do not concern myself with shadows," the Sheikh replied softly.

Silence followed and light from the moon streamed more strongly through the window onto the ceiling. In a whisper the sheikh began reciting a mystic chant: "All beauty in creation stems from You."

Yes, Sa'id told himself quietly, the Sheikh will always find something appropriate to say. *But this house of yours, dear sir, is not secure, though you yourself might be security personified. I've got to get away, no matter what the cost. And as for you, Nur, let's hope at least good luck will protect you, if you find neither justice nor mercy. But how did I forget that uniform? I wrapped it up deliberately, intending to take it with me. How could I have forgotten it at the last moment? I've lost my touch. From all this sleeplessness, loneliness, dark, and worry. They'll find that uniform. It might supply the first thread leading to you: they'll have dogs smelling it, fanning out in all directions to the very ends of the earth, sniffing and barking to complete a drama that will titillate newspaper readers.*

Suddenly the Sheikh spoke again in a melancholy tone of voice: "I asked you to raise up your face to the heavens, yet here you are announcing that you are going to turn it to the wall!"

"But don't you remember what I told you about the scoundrels?" Sa'id demanded, gazing at him sadly.

"'Remember the name of your Lord, if you forget'."

Sa'id lowered his gaze, feeling troubled, then wondered again how he could have forgotten the uniform as depression gripped him further.

"He was asked," the Sheikh said suddenly, as if addressing someone else, "'Do you know of any incantation we can recite or potion we can use that might perhaps nullify a decree of God?' And he answered: 'Such would be a decree of God!'"

"What do you mean?" Sa'id asked.

"Your father was never one to fail to understand my words," replied the old man, sighing sadly.

"Well," Sa'id said irritably, "it is regrettable that I didn't find sufficient food in your home, just as it is unfortunate that I forgot the uniform. Also my mind does fail to comprehend you, and I will turn my face to the wall. But I'm confident that I'm in the right."

Smiling sadly, the Sheikh said, "My Master stated: 'I gaze in the mirror many times each day fearing that my face might have turned black!'"

"You?!"

"No, my Master himself."

"How," Sa'id asked scornfully, "could the scoundrels keep checking in the mirror every hour?"

The Sheikh bowed his head, reciting, "All beauty in creation stems from You."

Sa'id closed his eyes, saying to himself, "I'm really tired, but I'll have no peace until I get that uniform back."

—*Translated by Trevor LeGassick and M.M. Badawi*

Hanna Mina (b.1924)

Prolific Syrian novelist and short-story writer Hanna Mina came from a very poor Christian background and began working very early in life, first as a laborer, then as a barber in Latakiya. He early adopted left-wing leanings, reflecting in his writings an affinity with those who are downtrodden in life but showing at the same time a passion for the values of courage, resistance, and chivalry. Having grown up in the Mediterranean towns of Northern Syria, he had a rare opportunity to learn about a marine culture, which he portrayed in his fiction, becoming Arabic literature's most prominent marine writer. He has published many novels, some of the most famous of which are *The Sail and the Storm* (1977); *The Blue Lanterns* (1954); and *Fragments of Memory* (1975), which was translated for PROTA in 1993 by Olive and Lorne Kenny. His novel *The Sun on a Cloudy Day* (1973) was translated by Bassam Franjieh and Clemmentine Brown in 1997. He published two short-story collections, *Who Remembers Those Days* (1974) and *White Ebony* (1976).

FRAGMENTS OF MEMORY (1975)

This autobiographical novel by one of Syria's foremost novelists is a recollection of his early childhood in northern Syria. It is a tale of the vicissitudes of a family caught in the vortex of the storm of adverse circumstances in Syria after the First World War. The irresponsibility of the drinking, carousing, womanizing father, whose harebrained enterprises in pursuit of "the imaginary loaf" always end in disaster, only adds to the family's wretched misery. This is counteracted by the fortitude and faith of the mother who would sacrifice herself to the limit for the love she bears her children and her sense of responsibility toward them.

The various side issues in the story afford the reader an understanding of the customs, traditions, folklore, religious beliefs, and superstitions of the author's society. However, this is all dealt with dramatically and artistically, arousing the deepest sympathy of the reader without ever verging on the sentimental. Although it deals with circumstances in a par-

ticular place at a particular time, the novel remains a vivid account of universal human experience often at the point of crisis.

The weather became hot in May, and all the silkworms finished spinning their cocoons. The bluffs were dotted with mulberry bushes upon which the blessed worms had woven themselves into silk. They no longer needed to be fed, and all we had to do was to harvest the raw silk, stuff it into bags, and take it to the village *mukhtar*. After weighing it, he would put aside for us one out of every four bags that we turned in. Out of that one bag we paid back our debts to him, and the rest was ours. If none were left, the *mukhtar* would start another debt page for us in the ledger for the new year.

That year the bushes on the bluffs looked like giant trees decorated with resplendent yellow silk cocoons rather than with snow or cotton. Father always liked to take a sprig from one of the bushes and bring it to us. The sprig, all covered with elongated silk cocoons that sprang out like little fingers, looked like a complete little tree itself with part of the stem visible. The cocoons were so intricately woven that any loose threads fluttering in the wind would wrap themselves around the cocoon to form a single mass of silk. Each individual cocoon, however, was totally independent of the rest. Each maintained its own shape and its own place on each beautiful sprig on each bush. It was all so well arranged, without a trace of neglect, without crowding and without enmity. It was as though each silkworm had carefully estimated the amount of space it needed, then settled to spin its cocoon, leaving just enough space for the other silkworms to weave their cocoons.

So many times, while holding one of those sprigs laden with golden yellow cocoons in his hand, father would proudly exclaim, "I'd win a prize if there were one! Perhaps I'd even get first place. I doubt whether any of the other sharecroppers have a better harvest this season. None of their bushes are as laden with silk as mine. If I weren't shy, I'd take one of my bushes and show it off in town."

One day, accompanied by his deputy, the *mukhtar* appeared for an inspection tour of the sharecroppers' homes. As usual, the visit was unannounced and was made to assess the harvest, so that none of the sharecroppers would be able to hide or smuggle out any of the crop. The *mukhtar* always overestimated the harvest and then accused sharecroppers of theft every time there were discrepancies at the scales. And discrepancies were thus inevitable, just as were the problems that followed.

The *mukhtar* circled our bluffs and then climbed them, examining every bush with his one good eye. His face remained as frozen as his other eye, which was made of glass. He never seemed to have a nice word for Father. We, the children, watched from a distance. We usually hid because we were so frightened of the *mukhtar*. Mother had told us so many bad stories about him that we had a frightening image of him in our minds. We prayed that he would leave quickly and not harm our parents.

But this day I noticed that my mother was smiling at the *mukhtar*. I thought maybe that was her way of deterring any evil that might emanate from him. She was pretending to forget all the harm she had received from him, about which Father knew nothing. Perhaps it was the good harvest that had wiped away all bad memories.

Father invited the *mukhtar* to sit with us on the stone bench. He refused. Instead, he walked away to inspect the mulberry grove and the summer vegetable garden.

"Enjoy, eat, and enjoy!" he said, in an envious, resentful tone. "The land is mine but it's you who enjoy the fruits."

"Oh, but the land, the fruits and everything is all yours, sir," replied Father. "Yet men are greedy: only a handful of dust will satisfy their eyes."

"Don't be insolent!" the chief said. "Is this the way a sharecropper talks to his landlord?"

Like farmers, silkworm growers used to compete. True, there were no prizes to win, but the best grower earned fame. Father had a good reputation among the growers, and that year he won a bottle of arack from the *mukhtar's* own vintage. And he came back home, ready to start picking the cocoons then stuffing them into bags.

So we began the harvest, picking the cocoons one by one, each member of the family working on his own bush. We would throw them onto a sheet that Mother had spread inside the room. The cocoons rustled down softly onto the sheet, and a strong scent of raw silk filled the house. The cocoons were like peanuts in their shells, only much bigger; the pile got higher and higher.

Father was full of praise to God while he scooped up the cocoons from over the sheet with both hands and put them into the bags that Mother held open for him. We all felt overcome with pride and success. We did not talk about our good feelings, but we experienced them. We sensed them deep in our hearts that year when we sat down to eat and drink. The entire house became as bright as though there were a different and more intense sunlight inside. Father and Mother spoke to each other in sweeter, more tender tones. There was no more fear, no more separations with Father. Father was with us, and we felt like we owned the world.

Ours was the joy of harvest. It is true that we were not farmers, but we sowed and reaped like them, and here we were filling the bags with our crops while Mother sang and we followed her. When Father took a drink, we sat around him and exchanged glances of joy, hope, and happiness.

"Persevere and win," said Father.

"We've persevered through many bad times, haven't we?" Mother said.

"Yes, yes," repeated Father. "Don't remind me, please. You don't know how much I suffered . . . A man doesn't tell his wife everything. But the important thing now is that our blessed worms have given us a good harvest this season. Life has become as pleasant as a summer breeze. We'll move away. I won't stay even if they fill my hands with gold. God's world is vast."

Mother closed her eyes tranquilly in a way that we had never seen in her since we had come to that village. She went off to work, praying and rejoicing over the prospect of paying back debts and regaining her daughter who worked as a servant for the *mukhtar*.

But the good summer breeze quickly changed. The delightful days of honey and hope were transformed into a time of gloomy depression. Despair replaced joy, for the news from town was bad. The silk dealers who usually flocked into town and lined up to buy the silk crop did not come. Only a handful showed up. Even those who had paid in advance for the raw silk were slow to claim their share; the landlords who owned the mulberry groves took their portion of the crop reluctantly and refused to buy from the sharecroppers. At the same time, they refused to allow the sharecroppers to sell as they pleased. This meant that no debts were paid and no new loans were available.

Early in the mornings the men would set out for town or go to see the landlords and the shop owners. They would remain in town for long periods of time but always came back empty-handed. Even the street peddlers were now few and far between. Those who were on the street refused to take raw silk in exchange for their pastries and other items, as was customary.

Father filled a small bag with cocoons and took it around to all the nearby shops. If he had been caught by the *mukhtar*'s deputy, he could have been thrown in jail on a charge of theft. He could even have gotten killed if he had tried to resist. In any case no one took his silk in exchange for the flour, oil, and kerosene that we needed. He was forced to take the lowest price so he would not have to carry his load back home.

"Oh, God," Mother lamented, with tears in her eyes. "What is happening to us? Why have You withdrawn Your mercy?"

"Because you've given Him a headache with all your pleas, that's why," Father shouted back. "Be quiet now! We're not alone. Whatever has happened to us has happened to other people."

"But we're not from here, we're strangers," she insisted. "We say we intend to move on, but how can we when our daughter is still in the *mukhtar*'s custody. I simply cannot leave her here as his hostage and servant."

The men gathered from all over the area. They came together because they shared the same plight and because they had nothing to do. They talked and cursed as they poked the ground with small, dry sticks. They squatted on the floor in a circle, muttering and brooding over their troubles. Whenever we heard them say something that we did not quite understand, we asked Mother to explain. We heard them carry on the same conversation over and over again.

"Indian silk has destroyed us!"

"You mean Chinese silk."

"No, it's Indian silk."

"The silk be damned anyway! We haven't seen it. They say it's lousy—an artificial silk. Yet it's sold everywhere abroad. What can we do? The dealers are only go-betweens. They buy to sell, and if customers from abroad turn them down, they'll turn *us* down."

"Don't you believe any of that nonsense! Ours is natural silk. It's strong. People can't do without it. This is just a nasty trick to lower prices. As soon as we sell, prices will go back to where they were before. We'll be the only ones who lose."

"So?"

"So—those who have some money can wait. But those who don't? What will they do? Eat dirt?"

"You can't eat dirt. The kids are hungry. If only the sons of bitches would buy, we'd sell at any price."

"Let's hold on a little longer. They'll buy. The prices will go up."

"We have to hand in the crop, and the one quarter that we get to keep won't even be enough to pay back our debts."

"Let's keep the whole crop," suggested Father. "Let's not turn in one single cocoon before the *mukhtar* actually buys our shares."

"What about the government authorities?"

"They can go to hell!"

"What are we going to eat?"

"We can sell a small amount for any price, but we could keep the rest until the prices go up."

"You're putting your life in danger; you don't know landlords and their cohorts!"

"Oh, yes, I do, I know them well. I've dealt with them. They can shoot me if they like. But the kids have to have food."

What could the men accomplish? Even if they defiantly refused to turn in the raw silk, what would happen? There, in the village, the summer begins in May, and at that time every year the raw silk cocoons are bagged up in burlap sacks and taken to the landlords and dealers. Then a process begins to choke the worms in their cocoons. Otherwise they burst the cocoons open and the little butterflies fly out. The raw silk would be spoiled and would lose its value completely.

In May, people used to say, the wheel of the year has turned full circle. They meant that the silk season had begun, that the cocoons were ready to be opened. After the cocoons are opened, the silk is ready to be spun. But not everyone had spinning wheels! Most were owned by landlords. Sharecroppers made their own small wheels, to spin some of their silk, which they then wove at home for their own clothing. The dealers, however, took their raw silk to the city, with the cocoons still unopened.

But the spinning and weaving activity came after the "choking" process, an elaborate, technical operation. First, the bags of silk cocoons are put into a pitlike room. A fire is lit in a corner, and when smoke fills the room, the worms choke and die inside their cocoons. But it has to be done quickly. This is why everyone rushes to turn in their crop and the landlords are also in a mad rush to either sell their harvest or begin this choking process. After that, the spinning wheels begin to turn, the air is filled with smoke, and the looms begin to roar.

The town bustles with activity in the main square and in the harbor. There, the purchased goods are loaded onto barges and shipped away. The sharecroppers, who have waited all year to receive one quarter of the crop, pay their debts and buy food and clothing, then return to their fields to plough and plant greens. They pick the figs and dry them for winter. They press the grapes and olives, either working for themselves or for others in return for small wages. In the fall they gather firewood and cattle droppings and save as much as they can for fuel. That is the season for celebrating weddings and other happy occasions. In the winter they hibernate in their mud houses that are scattered across the fields.

Mother knew all about it. She had experienced it all as a young girl and remembered stories her folks had told her when she was a child. Through her discussions with Father and with the neighbor-women, we could always tell what was going to happen in summer, fall, and winter.

However, that year the predictable work cycle was disrupted. Everything came to a full stop and was set backward. The silk season used to be like a river that carried in its flow the boats and barges of our little town. But suddenly it struck a satanic dam and everything was hurled backward in rage and murky agitation. Scared and threatened creatures were strewn in the middle, their barges near collapse and they themselves near drowning.

For the dealers never came to buy the crop that year, and the very few who did arrive waited until they could impose their own low prices. The greedy landlords hoped to acquire the sharecroppers' shares for an insignificant price. But some of the sharecroppers refused to sell. Father refused to turn in any of the crop. Everyone held onto their boats in the river flow. But just before the waters struck the satanic dam, everyone suddenly surrendered and unloaded their barges into the wild flood to escape from drowning.

On the last possible day, Father ran home to get one of the cocoon-filled bags to take to the *mukhtar*. The latter would not let him use one of his mules to transport the bags of raw silk. Father tried to rent a mule but could not find one. That day all the village folks were busy carrying their cocoons to their landlords or to the "choking" rooms, hoping to prevent the final catastrophe.

But the heat had been already intense that season, and the cocoons that had not yet been choked burst open and let out tiny butterflies. The butterflies filled the house and flew out to the fields and across to neighboring houses like a wave of invading locusts.

What a great catastrophe it was! What sorrow befell my mother as she cried over our bad luck that day! Father kept shouting for help at the top of his lungs. He wanted us to grab as much as we could and follow him to the *mukhtar's* house, where there were long lines of people waiting to use the "choking" rooms. He picked up a large double sack; Mother carried a single bag on her head and had a full basket in her hand. My two sisters carried a basket each, and I was the only one with empty hands.

The road was long and rugged. Even empty-handed I could hardly walk, so I was told to stay and guard the house until they got back. I wept and caught up with them, but Mother begged me to return and stay at home. She scolded and threatened me, then ran along behind my father, with both my sisters following her. I tried to run and catch up with them, but I fell and did not feel like getting up again. I was expecting Mother or my sister to come back and pick me up or stay with me, and for this I cried and rolled in the dirt. But they didn't. I cried until I was weak and fell asleep there, lying in the dirt under the hot sun.

On the way back they picked me up. Night had fallen, and it was dark inside our house. Mother and Father did not speak except for a few words. They simply sat there on the stone bench in front of the door and allowed silence and distress to envelop them.

Mother said that Father had gone to Antioch. He walked all the way because he did not have a mule or even enough money for the bus. Mother prepared some food for him at night from what the *mukhtar*'s wife had given her.

She told us he had promised not to be gone too long. He would not stay away, he said, and leave us hungry, cold, and an easy prey for the increasing number of brigands and highway robbers.

In the evening, Mother gathered us together to pray for Father's safe return. "Let him come," she prayed, "with a cart to carry us away from this wretched place where bad luck has landed us."

She continued to call on the *mukhtar*'s wife and get whatever she could spare. But because Mother never wanted to go empty-handed, she began to embroider long strips of white lace for the *mukhtar*'s wife, like that with which people used to trim the edges of sheets and pillow cases. Mother used to wind the thread around the tip of her left forefinger, and with her needle she'd gracefully pull the thread in and out. No sooner would she finish embroidering one lace flower when another would emerge next to it. Later, she very carefully wrapped a long strip of these flowers in white cloth.

Usually when Mother embroidered, she talked or sang, working away almost like a machine. She seemed to know exactly how many stitches she had to take. But during those days, when she looked so extremely thin, she embroidered silently, almost with sadness. I heard her confide to her neighbor that the embroidered lace was for the *mukhtar*'s wife, to decorate the hems of her trousers. I had only seen the trousers that Mother made for us out of printed calico, so I was surprised to hear that this beautiful lace with its white flowers was for the trousers of the *mukhtar*'s wife. I wanted to ask Mother what those marvelous trousers looked like, and why the *mukhtar*'s wife would need lace for them. I even hoped that Mother would take me along when she presented the *mukhtar*'s wife with the gift. I wanted to hear what she would say about it.

But now I don't even remember whether Mother ever finished that lace or if indeed it did eventually decorate the trousers of the *mukhtar*'s wife. So no one knows whether the *mukhtar* got to appreciate those ornate embroidered flowers at the bottom of his wife's trouser legs.

That year our distressed village with its unsold silk was struck by another misfortune. A disease broke out. Some said it was yellow fever, and others

thought it was the plague. Still others were certain that it was the result of famine, and indeed famine was spreading everywhere. Scabies also broke out, and
we caught it. An infectious rash appeared all over our bodies, and we itched.
Mother rubbed us with salt water.

One day, she went to the *mukhtar's* house and was turned away. The *mukhtar*
was obsessively frightened of catching disease, and his paranoia drove him mad.
He shut himself up completely in his room and allowed no one, including his
wife, to enter and see him. At mealtimes he would receive his food through the
window, which he would shut immediately after, and if people needed to talk to
him, they had to stand at a distance to say what they had to say. No one was allowed to cross the threshold of his house, which had become like a jail for those
trapped inside. Mother was unable to see my sister or the *mukhtar's* wife and she
came back empty-handed. In a fit of despair, she said she saw no solution to our
predicament. We were no doubt going to starve to death, she added.

It was on a cold autumn afternoon that Mother took us out in the fields
along the canals to pick some edible weeds. I refused to stay home, so she dressed
me in warm clothes, covered my head with a scarf, and carried me along. We got
to a nearby creek, baskets in hand. Mother and my two sisters cut the sour weeds
with a knife until they had gathered a fair amount. Then we returned home and
sat around while Mother washed and chopped the weeds. Our hungry eyes did
not look away from the little stove upon which she was cooking them. As soon
as they were boiled, she dished them out onto a large plate. We attacked the sour
weeds and ate and ate until our teeth gnashed together.

That desperate grassy meal was a terrible mistake, leaving us with an acidy
sensation in our teeth, nausea, and a lousy case of diarrhea, despite all the salt
that Mother had used.

Nevertheless, we had to eat that grass. Mother thought that if we drank some
hot water, we would get rid of the diarrhea. She said that she knew a place
where that grass grew profusely and she was going to take us there the next
morning to gather a large amount. But the next morning we felt so weak from
the vomiting and the diarrhea that we retired to one corner of the house. Our
faces were pale, and we were like wilted boughs that have been lopped off and
left under the July sun. Moreover, our faces and hands were swollen from the
scabies rash.

When children get sick, their weakened young bodies lose their vitality and
inspire fear and pity. About all they have left is their eyes, which move around
defeatedly. Children don't know what lies in store for them. They become helpless and as limp as a coil of silk. Their lips part to show their teeth. Their eyes
simply follow their mothers' with a beseeching look.

Well, we were exactly such children. We were emaciated from not eating
and now dehydrated because of the diarrhea. Like wet rags, we simply lay there
on a mattress in the corner, my two sisters huddling near me. Mother covered
us and lit the heater. She looked gaunt and emaciated. In the end she had to
comply with her exhausted body's demand for sleep. She threw herself onto a

bed and closed her eyes. What a relief it must have been to her to give in in that way! Snow, dirt, sand, all are convenient beds to a tired-out body. The end can come then whenever it wishes, whether arms are raised in surrender or not. The last breath may then escape from our chests and leave us in peace. The conflict between life and death weakens as the body weakens. Then it stops, and death creeps in under a mantle of black clouds.

On that morning itself there were black clouds. It was cold, and we were like small candle stumps about to burn out. It would have been enough for Mother to close the door and simply lie down next to us and let the cloud enshroud her and rest overcome her. We would then have remained buried in our mud house until someone realized we were dead and came to bury us.

Later, Mother would tell us the whole story. She'd remind us of every bit of detail. We would sense then a great fear that we had not felt even at the time it all took place, when our weakened bodies were lying there, wilted and as pale as sheets. We had been on a journey from which there was no escape. And halfway through it the pain had ceased, and so did our ability to feel pain. If it had been completed, the journey would have been like asphyxiation by gas, a journey of slumber and hunger.

That day, in her despair about the whole world, Mother was all prepared for the end. If it had not been for us, she would have died happily. It was her right to die. Perhaps she thought it over but was unable to see us die. She had tried the last and harshest remedy to keep us alive, which was to feed us those deadly weeds.

Our door was shut, and no one knocked on it or opened it. My sister cried and fell silent. Then Mother got up and left. She did not say where she was going nor did she really know.

The day before, she had been turned away from the *mukhtar*'s house. The houses in the nearby fields were empty. The mulberry trees were being chopped down for firewood, and the men had gone away. They had left by themselves or with their families. The roads were filled with migrant people on the move. Highway robbery and murder became commonplace.

Mother continued her story.

"You see, my son, famine had spread everywhere. The people who hadn't moved away were eating up what they had left, or just as we did, they were eating weeds, and cooking roots. I hadn't tried them before, and I couldn't tell the good weeds from the bad. When the three of you fell sick, I realized my mistake and feared it was going to be fatal for you. I pulled myself up and dragged my feet out for help.

"I was very cold," Mother went on. "The fields were bleak and the houses abandoned. Not a soul was in sight. The wind was so strong it slapped at me and blew me along. I lost my strength, I leaned against trees, I fell down. I thought I would never see you kids again. I wanted to come back just to say good-bye. I shouted, hoping someone would hear me from the road. I stood up, held onto a tree, looked in every direction, and waved my hand and handkerchief, but nobody saw me. My voice was lost in the wind.

"The rain poured down, and I was drenched. There was mud everywhere, and I was right in it. I raised my face to the sky and prayed to God, I begged Him for mercy from the bottom of my heart. I stood in supplication for long moments, sometimes without words because none came to my mind. Then I ended my prayers but never let go of the mulberry tree that I'd been leaning against for support. I closed my eyes, and shivered with cold, rain, and fatigue.

"But the good woman rescued me. The widow they said was a sinner, she rescued me. Don't you believe everything you hear, my son. Only God knows for sure. Only He can see and judge. God willing, that woman will go to heaven. I pray for that. Even if she is a sinner, she'll go to heaven. Even if she did have affairs with men, including your own father. God forgive sinners. He will forgive her and reward her well in both worlds. She was so kind to me. She had so much courage and strength. Later, I kissed her hands. 'I am a sinner, and I don't deserve this!' she said. 'Of course you do!' I replied. We immediately became friends and enjoyed each other's company and cried when we went our separate ways. When we parted, I took off my own head scarf and covered her head. This was a gesture to signify that I wished her safety from people's lashing tongues. I wanted God to protect her from scandal and make up to her for the loss of her dead husband."

Mother recalled several times how that widow rescued her. She talked about it a lot with quite a bit of exaggeration, praising the widow and praying for her. She would describe again and again the widow's courage and her beauty and would express the hope of seeing her again some day to pay her back for her generosity.

The widow, Mother would say, had gone to look for her cow in a nearby field. But for some reason known only to God, the cow had gotten out of the field and was lost. The widow went out looking for it. It was all she owned. She thought someone had stolen that cow. It seemed obvious that someone would indeed steal it, would slaughter it and eat its flesh raw in those days of starvation. The widow followed the cow's tracks and found it at the edge of our field, where she found Mother as well.

"Wouldn't you say the cow got lost just for me?" Mother would go on recalling. "And God guided the widow to come and save me? Praise be to His name! He makes miracles happen. He made one happen for me, I, His sinning subject. She saw me from a distance, called out, and I heard her. I thought that I was in the middle of a nightmare. But I heard my name called out several times, and I felt a strong hand slap my cheek. So I opened my eyes. I sighed and tears began running down my cheeks.

"'Poor woman, what on earth are you doing here?' the widow said, 'Where are you headed?'

"'The kids ... my kids are dying at home,' I muttered. You were the only thing on my mind, my only concern and my only hope. My fears for you made me so weak, more than hunger, more than the rain or the mud. I'd forgotten about everything except you kids. I'd forgotten about my own well-being and about my whole life. When I got so weak that I could not remember anything, I still had you in mind. When I regained consciousness, I uttered your names, and the widow anxiously asked me, 'What happened to them? Where are they?' I pointed toward our house and passed out.

"Later," Mother went on recalling, "the widow told me that she carried me on her back. She was strong enough to do it. She pulled off the belt of her dress, tied it once around the cow's neck and once around her waist, and pulled the cow behind her, me on her back. She walked barefoot in the mud, under the rain and against the wind. She took me to her house though it was farther away than ours. She knew she'd be able to care for me better there. She lit a fire, changed my clothes, and gave me a hot drink. She called out to the neighbors, but no one answered. Had they all deserted their homes and fields? I don't know. Many did leave, and those who remained took refuge each in his own corner, hungry or sick or frightened by the storm. Alone, the widow walked out in the rain and struggled through the mud and brought you to me. She fed us all and saved our lives. While we were still in her house, don't ask me how, she managed to get some sulfur ointment from Antioch, and she showed me how to use it for the rash you kids had. She said that some man in town had told her it was good for curing scabies.

"I was overwhelmed by her hospitality. I begged her to let me take you back home and care for you there, but she refused. One morning she lit the fire and heated some water. Bringing some soap and a clean cloth, she helped me wash and scrub you all. Then she dried you and rubbed the ointment into your skin. Then I also bathed and rubbed myself with some of that cream. It was strong and it hurt, and I was pained to see you cry. But the widow said to us, laughing, 'Pain for a brief moment is better than pain for a long time. After a while, the ointment won't hurt anymore, and tomorrow we'll be bathing and rubbing again.'

"After three of those treatments, you kids got better. And when we came back home, the widow gave me some flour and cracked wheat. 'Don't worry,' she said, 'things will get better. But do come back here if you find yourself in need. I'm a widow and you are a woman alone. My husband is dead and your husband has gone away!'"

I heard Mother say once that the widow resented my father for leaving us under such trying circumstances. She had loved him once. She had even been his mistress at some point. If she'd wanted him to abandon us for her, he'd have done so. He was very much a slave of his desires. But the widow refused to let him abandon us for her. And when he left us that way, she began to despise him. When Father came back, he abused the widow and said she was a whore. She did not challenge or reprimand him, and his accusations did not seem to bother her. She simply mocked and ridiculed him before our eyes. It was as though she was taking revenge for our mother, for herself, for women in general; or she did it simply because she was a generous and courageous woman who hated hypocrisy and lack of human feeling.

Father returned toward the end of the winter. In a burlap sack, he had brought back a few things for us. Of these, I only remember a meringuelike candy that we called "Khamirah." It was light and sweet and melted in the mouth. Father also had a little money in his pocket. He went to town and bought some flour and oil and told Mother that we were going to move to the city of Iskandaron.[1] He said he had made arrangements for the move and for a job. We regained some hope and tranquility.

—*Translated by Salah-Din Hammoud and Elizabeth Fernea*

'Abd al-Rahman Munif (1933–2003)

'Abd al-Rahman Munif is one of the foremost novelists of the Arab world. A naturalized Iraqi citizen, he was born in Amman, Jordan, to a Saudi Arabian father and an Iraqi mother. He studied at university in Cairo, then in Yugoslavia, obtaining a doctorate in oil economics in 1961. Between 1975 and 1981 he edited the Iraqi journal *Oil and Development*. In the latter part of his life, he lived in Damascus, completely devoted to writing. Munif's appearance on the literary scene in the 1970s with such novels as *Trees and the Murder of Marzouq* (1973), *East of the Mediterranean* (1975), and *When We Left the Bridge* (1976) took both readers and critics by surprise. The novels reflected versatility, maturity, and power of style; a commitment to the problems of freedom and liberty; and such important values as resistance, courage, perseverance, and reverence for one's ideals; they also reflected an intimacy with and a love for nature rarely found in contemporary Arabic fiction. He has published more than ten novels, among which are *Endings* (1978), translated by Roger Allen and published in English in 1988. His five-part novel, *Cities of Salt* (1984–1992), regarded as a most important novelistic event in modern Arabic fiction, opened a vista of major importance on contemporary Arab life, depicting the decisive role the oil countries have played in changing concepts, ethics, and attitudes in the rest of the Arab world and anticipating, with the author's deep foresight and unmatched power of observation, a colossal conclusion to an era of fabulous happenings and irreconcilable contradictions. The first three volumes of *Cities of Salt* have been translated by Peter Theroux (*Cities of Salt* [1987]; *The Trench* [1993], and *Variations of Night and Day* [1993]). Munif was one of the most outstanding novelists among the post-Naguib Mahfouz generation. His unmatchable work will gain in importance in the coming decades, not just for its fictional quality but also because it has, in fact, recorded the ethical, social, political, and, in part, economic history of the post-1950s era in the Arab world, particularly in the Gulf countries.

---

1. A Syrian Arab town appropriated by Turkey and now within the Turkish domain.

TREES AND THE MURDER OF MARZOUQ (1973)

This novel in two parts deals with divergent contemporary issues in the Arab world, the first revolving around the political predicament and social hypocrisy in urban Arab society, and the other around change in the rural landscape as a result of a new commercial spirit that has dominated village life and taken charge of the fate of many peasants. However, the novel also deals with individual uniqueness and fortitude, human persistence and single-minded defense of one's beliefs and ideals. The first part of the narrative takes place on a train journey during which Ilias, the dispossessed peasant, recounts his long tale of struggle and woe to Mansour, the urban official who has just succeeded in getting permission to leave his country after years of suffering. The second part of the narrative deals with Mansour's life before and after this journey, and ends with him becoming demented and taken to a lunatic asylum because of his incapacity to solve the many "unendurable" problems of contemporary Arab life, particularly the life of the Arab intellectual.

"Life is delightful and difficult ... yes, difficult." He said that nodding his head obscurely. Calmly he turned to look at me until his eyes came to be luminous, tearful, and perplexed, silently saying many things. I trembled inwardly. I wished that he would turn away those eyes, and look somewhere else instead, but he fixed them on mine, his gray head shaking like the pendulum of a clock.

He said, the muscles in his face tensing slightly, making him look morose, "I remember that after that I came to hate everything, I wanted to kill myself, but the people around me held me back. I have never found a solution since, except by becoming somewhat cruel in order to avenge myself.

"Do you realize, my friend, that this person sitting here had a really difficult life? Perhaps a pleasurable one? No, it was never pleasurable, in fact. It was a life of hardship, but no matter, it was a life for all that. Yes, it was a real life, especially after I took the rifle I had inherited from my father and went to the mountains. In the mountains I became a bandit, an outcast, an animal. I spent four years there. I don't regret it now. What is life? No one knows.

"Since that day, my life changed. It became, at once, serious and foolish."

Doubts began assailing me that he was either delirious or drunk. I asked him, "What are you talking about now?" Sarcastically, he answered, without changing his tone, "About the delightful and difficult life. Don't be astonished. I will tell you everything.

"I was twenty-four years old. I was hooked on gambling. The story began simply, in a small way, as many things in life begin. At the outset, a person does not realize that his life will change. In the beginning we gambled on walnuts, then on the chicken. A day came when I staked the three calves I had ... and at the end I gambled with the trees. Sometimes I would win and sometimes I would lose. I lost many times and many times I won. But I was lucky most of the time and therefore did not heed the losses I made.

"Then the day came when I began to hate the village. I saw it as a big cage. Especially when it had changed a great deal after the peasants began cutting down the almond, apricot, and walnut trees to plant cotton in their place!

"Farming was changing in our village, and with it life too was changing. At-Taybe, which once had been a huge orchard growing all the fruits and vegetables that one could desire, was transformed overnight into an arid, desolate land. Don't be upset if I tell you that peasants are stupid and bear a great resemblance to monkeys. All they know is how to imitate. For after the western parts of the village had been planted with cotton and had produced an abundant harvest, people's lives changed. They cut down all the trees of at-Taybe, they dug wells everywhere, and the village became, during the picking season, a white meadow that extended as far as the eye could see. Nothing could be seen in at-Taybe except cotton and the trees of my orchard. I did not want to cut down the trees, for it was I who had planted them with my father. I still remember everything. As we planted the trees, my father would say, 'Ilias, these trees are like children, more precious even than children; I can't imagine anyone in this world killing his children, so look after them when I die. I leave them in your charge. Should you cut down one tree before its time, my body will turn over in the grave.'

"I helped my father a great deal in planting the trees. I saw them grow day by day, and they bore fruit in my father's lifetime. They thrived better than all the other trees in the village.

"A mysterious bond grew between us, and I was sad when our neighbors cut down their trees. At first I cursed them in my heart, then I spoke harshly to them while looking into their narrow, mocking eyes. I told them that by cutting down their trees, they were destroying their own livelihood and transgressing against life, and that God would certainly punish them. They were enraged and plotted against me, boasting all the time about the money they were making.

"One day, a month before cotton planting was to begin, when the trees of my orchard had already blossomed and were turning green, the men came to me and said, 'The cotton harvests have made us rich men; you are the only one in the village who has land that doesn't yield him any profit. You are still poor, Ilyas!' They also said, 'The trees in your orchard have become our foes.' They fell silent for a while, then continued, 'Tonight we will play only for the trees. We will pay you money and you will pay us with trees.' I did not want to play. The trees of the orchard were in blossom, promising a full harvest, and I could not see anything in the whole world as beautiful as they were. They were lovelier than girls in their prime and more delicate than a spring of water.

"I sensed that the men were conspiring against me. I told them that we could bet on anything except the trees. 'Forget the trees, men. They no longer mean anything to you, but to me they are my only link with this life.' But they insisted, and we didn't play that night!

"Oh, if only the world had come to an end that night. Had we quarreled, had we come to blows, nothing of all this would have come to pass, and the trees would have remained. But the following night, even a wish for death seemed to erupt in me. I felt I was in the power of a forceful drive. I had taken no decisions on anything in particular, but a strong feeling began to stir and surge inside me. I felt that life didn't deserve that men cling to it tenaciously.

"That night after drinking and singing to celebrate the circumcision of the son of the eastern sector's chief, I saw the men testing me with their glances. Their provocative and inciting voices tempted me to play: I agreed to gamble with the trees. At first, I said I would play only on the almond trees, then I changed my mind and said I would play only on the trees of the western part of the orchard.

"The western part of the orchard was rectangular, its soil limy. The trees there were frail and not as fruitful as the trees in the eastern part. A latent hostility was growing in my heart toward this section in which I had labored more than in any other part, but, despite my labors, those trees had remained frail.

"At the beginning of the night I won a lot of money. I thought the money was sufficient for me to plant a new orchard two or three times bigger than mine. I could imagine the trees shooting up, rising high on the horizon until they had eclipsed all the cotton fields; I could imagine the village becoming green after those three years of aridity.

"And I went on playing. Before the night was out, I had become a nervous, irritable man as I saw the trees toppling down one after the other. At the outset we played on single trees, then on two, and by the end I was betting on ten trees at a time.

"Yes, I lost that night. Of the western section only seven trees and the big walnut tree remained. I forgot to tell you that the big walnut tree stood at the entrance of the orchard like a formidable guardian, feared by all, and was so old that my father could not remember when it had been planted.

"That same night, I dreamt of this walnut tree. I saw it in pain, weeping, and I saw my father also, his face full of scars. In fact, they were more than scars, they were bleeding wounds. This scared and pained me. I felt that I wanted to go to the men as soon as it was light and tell them, 'I will pay you whatever you want in exchange for the trees I lost!'

"But once again, the following night, we played. I regained many trees, but I also lost many. I suffered hell as I saw myself losing the trees I had planted with my own hands four years before; they were about to bear fruit that very year. The world darkened in my eyes, and a shudder shook my whole being. I saw the trees disappearing, sinking in the earth, turning into piles of firewood, while I was impotent to do anything to save them. I stopped thinking. I stopped winning, and started losing persistently. Not one tree was returned to me. They all disappeared, felled down, while I grew more insistent and fierce. I was shouting at the top of my voice: 'I have to regain them, luck cannot go against me to this extent . . . Everything must have an end.'

"But it ended by my losing all the trees. The western section as well as the eastern section. The walnut tree, which stood like a goddess at the gates of the orchard, I lost that too!

"Without thinking I said to the men, 'These trees are mine, mine alone, not one of you will take them.' They laughed. They scoffed at me. They said: 'We play every night, and we have lost a great deal; we cannot let you have the trees.' I told them, 'These are my trees; you have betrayed the trees and no longer know their worth. I am the only one who loves them, and it is I who will be their owner.'

"When I found that their determination was stronger than my desire, I said to Zaidan, my neighbor in the land, who had won the bulk of the trees, 'Hey Zaidan, I'll let you have the land but I want the trees to remain standing as they are now.' He said, 'We played only for the trees. We want you to be one of us, planting cotton, as we do.' I said, 'I have no wish to become rich. Any way the village needs fruits and vegetables. I will be the one to supply you with the crops of this year and the following years.' All the men said with one voice: 'No . . . we want only the trees.'

"Rage possessed me. Before the night was out I had killed a hundred sheep in Zaidan's pen. I descended upon them and with a big knife I struck again and again, until I had cut them all down. I struck them on their heads, their bellies, their backs. My father's rifle was slung over my shoulder and I had decided to kill any person who stood in my way. As soon as I left the pen, with the cries of the animals and the smell of their blood and urine saturating every cell in my body, I found Zaidan carrying a lantern and running toward the pen. I stood in his way and told him, 'If you take one more step, I'll kill you.' He froze on the spot, struck by fear and unable to do a thing. I drew near him and peered into his terrified eyes. I grabbed his neck and squeezed it. I wanted to kill him. However, at that moment a crazy idea took hold of me.

"I said to him: 'I will not kill you, Zaidan. I can kill you, but I will not.' He did not believe me. He was crying like a woman and looking at me imploringly. I said, 'I want only one thing from you now.' But he didn't answer. He went on weeping and wailing.

"I said, 'I want you now to strip off your clothes . . . nothing else.' He pleaded with me. He said that he did not want the trees and that he would not demand the price of the sheep. All he wanted was that I leave him alone. But I did not leave him alone. I said, 'Choose whichever you prefer, to die or to strip off your clothes.'

"His appeals vanished with the winds. All that possessed me was the desire . . . to see Zaidan naked. I don't know why!

"He stripped off his clothes. I took them and put them in a pile on the ground, and with a branch I broke off one of the trees, I began flailing his body. I wanted to carve into his body a memory that he would not forget until he died. He was screaming as the branch bit into his flesh; crying for help while I engraved my hatred on his back, his buttocks, his chest.

"I said to him, 'These marks will remain as long as you live, And remember that these are the marks from one tree only. Should you cut down the trees, then each tree will carve marks like these on your body. Think carefully of what

I'm saying . . . I shall go now, but you will see me again.' I spat on him, took his clothes, and headed for the mountains.

"Yes, I went to the mountains to live there. I lived alone. I ambushed people on the road several times, but mostly I relied on hunting to satisfy my need for food. In the mountains, I was lost in reflection and sadness, but the image of the trees did not leave me for a moment. I thought of them day and night. I saw them, standing high with an invincible loftiness amid barren, dust-filled plains. I saw them flirting with the wind and cuddling the birds. I saw them in spring, bursting with blossoms, and in summer with fruit. I could see them in winter, all chilled, thin, and bare, huddling close to the ground when the wind blows, seeking protection and warmth.

"The trees were the only thing I saw and thought about day and night."

My view of Ilias had changed, now, becoming a mixture of fear and admiration. I asked him, "How did things go after that?"

He said, "Won't you have a drink now?"

Eagerly I snatched the wineskin and offered it to him. I wanted him to resume his story without interrupting his train of thought.

"As I told you, my friend, I went to the mountains, and there I lived for four years. I lived in caves. I ate plants and birds and occasionally some animals. I drank from a small spring that flowed down the mountain toward the valley until it reached at-Taybe. During this period I went down only three times to the village. I wanted nothing from the village. I did not even desire cigarettes. The only thing that I valued had ceased to exist. I went down to the village in the fourth month; I had then become very lonely. I wanted to reach some agreement with the people. I was prepared to pay for the sheep and to pay Zaidan any price he wanted for his wounds and scars. I was prepared to plant cotton.

"Yet when I arrived at my orchard that night, I found it bare and disfigured. At first I could not recognize it. A cold shudder passed through me, seizing me from head to toe. The cotton plants had grown big, and without realizing it, I found myself like a madman, uprooting them, trampling on them, destroying them. Within an hour not one cotton plant had remained. And without stopping at any house in the village I found myself returning to the mountain.

"As soon as I reached the mountain this time, I felt contentment. I felt peace spreading throughout me. At-Taybe appeared to me as a small and narrow village, and life in it was unbearable. I wondered how I had managed to live there all those years.

"You know that when a person changes his place of residence, his habits and frame of mind change too. When this time I found myself alone in the mountains, I began reflecting on this life, so full of misery. I wondered why people hate each other, but I could not find the answer. I asked myself once, 'What did the people at at-Taybe gain by cutting down Ilyas's trees and making him miserable like this?' I thought of this and other matters and became confident that if those people were to live in the mountains as I did, they would become capable of making at-Taybe a better place a thousand times over.

"In the mountains a person is transformed into an amazing creature. His hearing becomes sharper than the hearing of the people at at-Taybe, and he sees better too. The wind, the stones, and the moon, everything appears far clearer to him. Stones lose their hardness and become closer to man. Whenever I reclined on a rock in the mountains, I felt comfort and pleasure. I would look at the moon and see its face, sad and almost on the verge of tears as it looked over at-Taybe. The cave I slept in was the strangest thing I've ever come across in my life. It was warm in winter, bursting with heat, but in summer it became a cool place, cooler than the water reaching at-Taybe from the mountain spring.

"Were you to ask me about the animals there, I would say that they had strange habits. At first they were frightened and would run away, but scarcely a few months had passed than I saw them coming closer to me. I gave some of them beautiful names, and we would talk from a distance. I understood them, and they understood me except for those occasions when a man is hungry and cannot find anything to eat. On such occasions I would be forced to kill some of them. I did not do that often. However, when I killed Rummana, the gray rabbit that lived near the cave, I felt a sorrow surpassing everything else, and I regretted it deeply. I understood the dreams and pain that afflicted me after that to have been the result of guilt feelings, for sin had touched me, making me a disfigured man.

"Although I meditated a great deal and saw everything there was to see in the mountains, I remained sad. I wanted other human beings to talk with. I wanted trees to water and look after every day. But the people of at-Taybe had deprived me of all that. I met only shepherds, and even they, like the animals, did not get used to me quickly. But once they felt reassured, they began giving me milk to drink, and every once in a while they would kill a young lamb for me.

"We would talk of the people of at-Taybe, of trees and sheep; but they always left quickly, before the sun reached halfway down the valley.

"One day I found myself, with my sharp short stick, digging and searching in the soil that surrounds the castle of Murad Agha. Suddenly, I found coins, which at first I took to be gold, but after putting salt on them and rubbing them strongly, they turned red, the color of copper. They had drawings and other marks that I did not understand.

"Despite that, I spent long hours contemplating the castle and searching its grounds. True, I did not find anything, except for the coins, but I came to love the stones and the shadow cast by the castle over a wide area. During the summer days I slept long in this shade.

"Had I been in at-Taybe at that time, I would have shown people those coins and we would all have gone to hunt for treasure. But when I returned to at-Taybe after all those years, I could not find in myself the desire to tell anyone. The only man who saw the coins said to me, 'Don't bother, Ilyas. They are not worth anything. No one in at-Taybe or anywhere else will give you even a piece of bread in exchange for them.'"

I asked him eagerly: "Where are those pieces now?"

"I still have some of them." And he pointed into the distance. "I put them in a chest my mother left me after her death. If Adma has not encouraged our children to open the chest, they must be still there."

"These pieces are worth a great deal . . . You can sell them."

"I offered them for sale once, when I worked in the hotel, but no one bought them, except for one that I sold to an old lady for one Turkish gold pound. She said she would make a pendant of it.

"I think they are worth a lot. You should take care of them."

"I did not choose to sell them. I said to myself, 'keep them, Ilias, in memory of your days in the mountains.'"

"Oh, if only you had them now!"

"What if I had them now?"

"I would see them."

"And tell me their value?"

"But I know nothing about old coins."

"You will see them one day . . . I will keep them until you do."

"And did you stay on in the mountains with the animals and shepherds? Did you not miss at-Taybe?"

"I stayed for two years without anyone seeing me. I saw the people of at-Taybe occasionally. I would stand near the road they frequented leaving or returning to at-Taybe, but I never let them see me, not once. I could have killed a great number of them. I could have waylaid them on the road, made them dance like monkeys, but I chose not to.

"They sent me a message with the shepherds saying: 'Return to the village. Your mother has reached an agreement with Zaidan; everything can be settled.' But I would not listen. I knew that all they wanted was to trap me, to take their revenge on me. I knew Zaidan, I know him only too well. We once had a disagreement over watering, and as a result he sent someone to pick the fruits of my trees before they ripened. He never confessed, and nothing was proven against him. However, I came to know this at a later date from one of those he had hired to pick the fruits.

"'And now,' I thought, 'What would Zaidan do should he see me? Would he leave me without trying to maim and mutilate me?' I did not fear him; only I saw him as a man who smiled as he betrayed. He would kill a man then walk in his funeral. I don't like this kind of man, and I was apprehensive that seeing him would turn me into a madman. I would not let him get away this time, especially since he'd cut down the trees. I had imagined that he would hesitate a great deal before cutting down the trees, but he had not.

"Once they sent me a message with a shepherd who'd worked for my father. He said to me, 'Ilias, your mother is ill and she wants you to return so she can see you before she dies; had she been up to it, she would have come herself.' At first I did not believe it. On the third day he came to me again and said, 'Your mother is dying . . . You might not arrive in time.' This time I could not stay away.

"Not long after, I secretly stole into the village. When I entered the house, my mother was sleeping as usual in her bed. True, she looked old, but she seemed to be still in good health. As soon as I looked at her, she woke up. She had sensed my presence. Mothers, my friend, possess a penetrating insight into things; they are like trees. They don't talk much, yet they have a beautiful way of expressing themselves.

"I said to her: 'Why did you lie to me, mother?' She answered. 'I would not have seen you had I not lied. I tried many times before, but you never came.'

"I said: 'So you lie?'

"She said: 'The lie of a mother who wants to see her child is a prayer.'

"I said: 'But you know Zaidan. If I should see him, I would kill him, and if he should see me, he would not give me a chance to get back to the mountains again.'

"She said: 'We will pay Zaidan what the *mukhtar* and other notables of the village will determine, and you will return.'

"I said: 'Is it for this that you asked me to come?' She wept, she implored me. I said to her, 'Mother, I can no longer bear the village. A village in which no trees grow cannot be inhabited by humans. At-Taybe, which once was as green as a sprig of mint, is today a graveyard, a dustbowl. I cannot bear to live in it even for one single day.'

"Before dawn had arrived, I had left the village. I heard my mother's voice pleading, calling me, but I did not heed it.

"Three days later, the same shepherd came. He knew the watering place that I frequented. He said, 'This time the old woman has died. The previous time, she did not want to die because she hoped you would return. But today she died because she despaired of everything.' He did not stop there but went on, 'The people of at-Taybe heard of your return. They swore a great deal and said Ilyas will remain cursed forever!' Is it for this they call you the prodigal son?'

"Partly because of this, and partly because I could not agree to anything when I finally returned to at-Taybe."

"When did you return?"

"I spent four years in the mountains, during which time Zaidan died and the village became more wretched after its waters had dwindled. The water was no longer sufficient for irrigating all the cotton they had planted. They had planted cotton everywhere: in the gardens of their houses, at the roadsides, in the plain, once full of trees. And in every square foot of ground they dug wells. Within two or three years the wells had dried up. They became rat holes, producing not water but mud and an ugly stench.

"You know that wells, like trees, don't give to you if you don't give to them. Once they had cut down the trees, what did they have to offer the wells? It was the trees that brought down the rains, gathering them up from the furthest reaches of the world, until black clouds settled over at-Taybe and would continue pouring down day and night. The rains would not stop. Sometimes they flooded the plains, and my father would say: 'God protect us from the flood.' But now the years pass and the rain comes only like the pissing of dogs: an instant, then it stops. It is trees that bring rain. Trees are like children, and in the same measure that the Lord keeps an eye on children, protecting them, He keeps an eye on the earth through its trees. When people cut down their trees, then the Lord forsakes them and grants the rain to others, to those who have trees.

"This was how at-Taybe lost everything; it lost the trees and it lost the cotton. And you, my friend, know that the loss of trees is like the loss of men, they are irreplaceable.

"People began pondering the matter. They appealed to God, they deepened the wells over and over again. But the wells didn't produce and the cotton shrank and dried up before it was fully grown. The harvests failed, and people began to emigrate.

"Until one day they said, 'It was Ilyas who has brought us this bad luck, and we have no choice but either to kill him or bring him back to at-Taybe.'

"I told them, through that same shepherd who'd acted before as a messenger between us, 'I will return to the village, but abundance will not return. If you want it, then you must look for it in the trees.' But they did not understand!

"The day came when I returned to at-Taybe. I said to myself, 'Go back Ilias, and what will be will be.' I saw sorrow filling the hearts of the men. They were tired, perplexed, not knowing whether they were alive or dead, not knowing whether to plant or not to plant.

"I said to them, 'Oh, people of at-Taybe, if you believe that Ilias brought you bad luck, then here I am back. Should you want to flourish again, then the trees are your only way to life. I will not stay in the village until I can plant my orchard once again. If you want this misfortune to cease, then give me a part of my land and help me to plant it. As for the rest, I will renounce it in favor of Zaidan's children as a price for the sheep.' I did not say a word about Zaidan's wounds. Zaidan deserved those wounds!

"I left them for a few days, then returned. I asked them whether they agreed.

"After some thinking, they agreed, then changed their minds. They agreed again, and again they changed their minds. So I took matters into my own hands, and said, 'I will stay, but I will keep away from the land. Plant what you want.'

"I opened a bakery in the village after I had sold the land. It was the first bakery in at-Taybe; people were amused. They mocked me, and said, 'Look, he's bringing dates to Mecca!'[1] Before a few months had passed, the money was spent and the bakery closed down.

"Had they wanted, I could have stayed in the village. They could have strangers and passers-by and some shepherds; as for them, they ate the bread they themselves baked, all the time mocking me.

---

1. This is the equivalent of the English saying, "carrying coals to Newcastle."

"One morning there was nothing else o do but go eastward. I took the carriage that journeyed to the distant city and said to myself: 'I will leave al-Taybe and its people and depart.'"

—*Translated by May Jayyusi and Anthony Thwaite*

Ibrahim Nasrallah (b. 1954)

Palestinian poet and novelist Ibrahim Nasrallah was born in the Wahdat refugee camp in Amman, Jordan. After studying at the Teacher Training College in the Jordanian capital, he worked as a teacher in Saudi Arabia, then returned to Jordan as a journalist, before being appointed as the cultural Director of the Shuman Art and Cultural Center, Darat al-Funun, in Amman. His experience in Saudi Arabia deeply affected his outlook on life and resulted in one of the most moving modernist fictional experiments in Arabic, his novel, *Prairies of Fever* (1984), which PROTA has brought out in English translation. His other novels include *Terrestrial Waves* (1989); *The Barking Dog* (1990); *Just Two Only* (1992), and *Guard of the Lost City*; and, under the general title *The Palestinian Comedy*, a series of three novels so far: *Birds of Caution* (1996); *The Erasure and the Child* (2000), and *Olive Trees on the Streets* (2002). Nasrallah has published several volumes of poetry, among which are *Horses at the Outskirts of the City* (1980) and *The Rains Inside* (1982); and his last, well-acclaimed collection, *The Youth River and the General* (1987). He has received three literary prizes for his poetry from the Union of Jordanian Writers, and in 1997 he received the prestigious al-'Uweiss Prize for poetry.

PRAIRIES OF FEVER (1984)

This is one of most important Arabic modernist novels to be written in the 1980s. A negation of chronology and sequence, a cohesive relationship between form and content, and a temporal parallelism of events, memories, and dreams give the novel a fresh and original flavor all its own. The main themes are the subjugation of human life to the harsh reality of place, the severe force of inherited mores many centuries old, and the blind, automatic machinery of state. The main character, a young teacher hired, like hundreds of other teachers from all over the Arab world, to teach in a remote and isolated place in the Arabian Peninsula, recounts a harrowing experience of alienation and loneliness as he is afflicted with hallucinations, fears, phobias, nightmares, and extreme deprivation from the basic requirements of normalcy. He lives in perfect victimization. There is often a complete fusion of actuality and dream, of fact and fantasy, and a strange unity between the animal and human worlds. There is also an eerie absence of woman, who becomes an unachievable dream, a source of torture and fantasy, an undefinable phantom surrounded by taboos and danger. The force of place—here the desert— is so strong that it obliterates time, which runs in every direction, unsystematically spanning the past to the future and regressing to the past, emphasizing the supreme sovereignty of place. This is a novel about the extreme anguish that has been the hallmark of the experience of thousands of young individuals since the discovery of oil in the Arabian Peninsula.

Exploding fists almost broke the door of the room into splintered fragments. They always come at the end of the night. They traverse obscure passageways, unlimited distances. I've given them everything, and now there's nothing left to take. The desert stretches to the sea's edge, and I own almost nothing of it, a narrow area the size of an airport, but all it can contain is thirty sacks of corn, two beds and a sandy table, and unlimited thousands of white ants, white to the point of madness.

What do they want now? Let them go away. Let them turn over every stone in the hope of finding him, or let them climb to the summits of mountains and search for him in the eyes of hawks and the wings of crows. They might find him there. Do they really want to plant in my head the belief that I am he?

It won't work!

Their fists exploded, and again the door was almost smashed to firewood.

"What do you want?

"We want you."

The cock woke up. The brown hen had grown tired of raising its head from beneath its wings, while the white hen gazed with closed eyes, framing an expression of indescribable stupidity.

In a light so pale one couldn't determine from which of last night's stars it fell, you recognized the face of one of the policemen, and said to yourself, "Thank God!"

The officer's lips opened, while his two colleagues whispered, "It's him . . . he's not changed much since noon."

You stared into the policeman's face, the same one who'd chased you all day, but saw nothing. You drew near to him. He was very thin. It hurt you that his night was disturbed by looking for Ustadh Muhammad. Secretly you whispered, "The world's still a good place."

An interval of silence ensued, broken finally by the howling of a wolf on the rocky slopes of the mountain. The officer resumed shaking his head, "Yes . . . it's him . . . he's the one."

A sudden storm got hold of you. Your leaves shook, your throat went dry, your eyes widened.

You wondered, have they caught him, or have they come to arrest me?

You were torn between conflicting probabilities. The storm racked you again, stars in the distance shiveringly dispersed, and the eyes of foxes converged in a single beam.

It had been a cruel day, but you'd learnt one thing that you wouldn't have been able to discuss with yourself.

Just imagine if I had been Ustadh Muhammad, try to conceive of him as me. That isn't especially difficult. And what would happen to me if I knew that no one ever asked about me but the police?

But the world's still a good place!

The wind returned. The cold stung you, you shook like a bird in the snow, you withdrew into yourself, feeling your warmth evaporate.

"We were going to arrest you, but Haj Sa'ud's insistence that we join him for dinner made us abandon the idea. We spoke a lot about you, about you and Ustadh Muhammad."

You asked yourself, "What did Haj Sa'ud say to change the mind of the police? He's a good man, and this action isn't unlike him. But what on earth did he say?"

You said, "That's OK, but the important thing is that you came. You know, someone must ask in the end, someone has to, even if it's a policeman."

But have you found him?

"We've come to ask you: 'Has he returned home?'"

"No . . ."

"Do you think he will?"

You didn't know how to answer. How can you say he'll return, or he won't? How? But you answered, "No . . . he won't return!"

"Then you're aware of his departure?"

"No . . . not at all."

"And why shouldn't he return?" asked one of the two policemen. You couldn't distinguish which of the two had spoken.

"He may return, but there again he may not," you said.

The officer shook his head and said: "It's not important any more."

"Then I assume you've found his corpse!" you replied.

You were about to burst into tears when the officer said: "No, he isn't dead."

"Then why is the matter no longer significant?" you asked.

"Because we know he's still in the district. He's really here."

"He's really here? Why keep me in suspense when this is the news I've been waiting to hear."

"The important thing is that you're well and comfortable. The rest is our concern."

"But," they continued, "Can you describe him to us accurately? This will help us considerably. And if you have a picture of him, then so much the better."

"He's fairly tall . . . almost like me," you said, "and has brown curly hair, resembling my own, and brown eyes, and wheat-colored skin, and a melancholy look."

"Almost like you?" they said.

"Yes."

"And has the same name?"

"Yes, that's another coincidence."

"Are there other similarities with which we're not acquainted?"

"No."

"Where did you meet the first time?"

"I don't remember. Sometimes I can believe that I've known him since child-hood, but I can't be sure of that since he does nothing to jolt my memory. His predominant mood is one of silence, and incommunicativeness characterizes our relationship. I'm sure he hoards an unfathomable secret in his heart. It could have been that we first met in Jeddah, no, in al-Qunfudha, when we came down from the jeep. We shook the dust from our clothes and faces. He looked pale with fatigue. In those days I could draw a clear picture of him, an image I was always trying to get to know . . ."

"And the picture? Do you have any likeness of him?"

"No. I told you he looks like me. Do you want me to give you my pho-tograph?"

"He resembles you and carries your name too?"

He began shaking his head again.

"I told you. It's just a coincidence!"

"We'll see you tomorrow night, then."

And you replied; "Why don't you come in and rest until the morning."

They said: "We'll carry on looking for him."

"I'll come with you."

"No, look for him around the house."

You said: "Try to be kind to him."

They said: "We assure you: no harm will come to him."

And before you could recompose your hand, which was in the action of wav-ing goodbye, they'd disappeared.

. . . .
. . . .

You stared at the sky. It was crowded with tired stars, and then your focus returned to the cock and the two hens. The white hen was still frozen in its uncomprehending inertia, while the brown hen had remained static. The cock momentarily modified the position of its legs.

Before commencing the search, you stepped back into the room. You crossed the threshold. More than one night was crowded into the interior. One night outside it, one night inside, and the endless multiplication of time and space.

Once again you tripped on the pot . . . you felt a sticky liquid on your feet. You said: "How many times have I told him to wash the pot!"

I felt the edge of the bed . . . the remains on the table . . . the table, the soft sand. Then I found it near the suitcase. It's the torch. I should have found it much earlier, but here it is, and from now on I shan't lose it, it won't go astray and delude me. It's the last of the night stars. It's the only star that lights up this room.

The circle of light began to move, a magic eye probing the dark.

As the cleaver blade pierced the ground, its wooden handle stood upright, as though an entanglement of roots deep in the sand had fixed it secure.

Suddenly, with the swiftness of an arrow penetrating the door, he'd crossed the threshold, trembling and foaming ... then came down with the cleaver on the ground.

It would have been possible for the blood to burst out of the particles of sand, but a kind of miracle had happened.

"You musn't stay here another minute, otherwise one of us will go to the grave."

You didn't understand anything of what had happened. Only that a face had drawn near you, its features lined from the ravagement of the wilderness, and fires blazing in its eyes; you don't know who it is or where it's come from.

You said, "And why should we go?"

He looked at his shack, the one that stood out like a clown's hat and said, "My woman's there: my honor's being trampled on today. How could Haj Sa'ud agree to sell me for a hundred *riyals*? How?"

At that moment things came clear.

You said, "We rented this room from Haj Sa'ud, so you can speak directly to him."

He said, "But you must go away now, before my blood boils." He bent to the ground and extracted the cleaver forcibly from its place, then his eyes searched your face anew:

"You must go now."

Ustadh Muhammad wasn't there. Most likely he wasn't around at all, otherwise your answer would have been more daring.

"I can't tell you anything except to go and speak to Haj Sa'ud. If he tells us to leave, then we'll leave."

It seemed that the man with the cleaver relented a little.

This was your second day at Thriban. Why didn't he come yesterday? And as if he was reading your thoughts, he said, "I didn't know there were strangers living in front of my family. Otherwise, no one would have slept in this room while I was alive.

"Everything that was happening pointed to a bloody struggle, to the omen of more than one unpropitious bird.

"I'll give you up to this evening. After that, no one will be able to prevent me from throwing you into the valley."

After saying this, he picked up his cleaver and left.

I stood there bewildered in the middle of the room. You must do something. You must talk to Haj Sa'ud.

The noon's incandescence was red with flames. Everything had gone into hiding, the hawks, the sand and stones shrunk from the glare, the trees, the shadows, the crows and sparrows .. But are there really sparrows here? Ah!

You called out, and Haj Sa'ud appeared from one of the shacks outside of the field of your vision.

Five shacks punctuated a small hill; there was a common threshing ground, there were some corn sacks, and two wives inside about whom you heard later on, but whom you never glimpsed.

"What's up, Ustadh?"

You answered in the manner of someone who wishes to make a request to a bedouin sheikh, "When we live in your house, aren't we under your protection?"

"I'd protect you with my life."

"Then get that madman off our trail."

"Who?"

I told him what had happened. He said, "So now we have Ghabshan to deal with. Leave him to me, Ustadh, I know how to deal with him."

Ghabshan made no further attempt to cross the threshold, with his emaciated face. He simply sat on a black rock in front of his shack, spanning the divide with his fiery looks. He then circled the building, drew near to the room, then stopped in a state of suspended threat, and returned. He repeated this approach several times, approaching, then stopping in the same spot, his suppressed anger checked by some invisible line stretching between our door and his shack that was taboo to cross. He couldn't cross that barrier.

Ghabshan . . . Who's Ghabshan?

You knew nothing about him. Worn through to the skeleton, dry as a piece of wood, stooped like a roof about to collapse, his sixty years contained in a shriveled body. And try as you will, you can't find an excuse for what's happening.

Yes, you caught sight of a woman yesterday, but only her shadow, wrapped in a cloak. You couldn't distinguish whether she was going or coming, then she disappeared inside the shack and never reappeared. Had anything happened to call for all this anger?

You said, "Ustadh Muhammad, there's a woman . . ." He said: "There's a cloak. It's not a human being. All you see is a black tent moving."

You said, "I see a cloak moving."

"And you can't be sure of what's inside it!"

Everything ended with this and began from this.

A cleaver embedded in the ground, its handle upright, smooth like a snake. And a man foaming in the middle of the room.

Night fell, and in succession red suns rose and were extinguished. A night and a day, a night and a day, and Ghabshan was still approaching and pulling up short at the secret line between the cleaver and blood, between the shack and the stone room.

You said, "Ustadh Muhammad, I think we should tell the police."

That was the first time you ever thought of the police.

He said, "No, . . . don't worry . . . he won't do anything. Have you spoken to Haj Sa'ud?"

"Yes."

"And did he promise you anything?"

"That no harm will come to us."

"Then relax. If Ghabshan was intent on doing something, he would have done it by now."

But you couldn't rid your mind of his image; a man approaching only to return. Even after you'd locked the door and gone to bed, your fear persisted.

You reassured yourself that Haj Sa'ud's word possessed irrefutable power. It was his influence that stood as a barrier between the cleaver blade and blood.

Two days later you discovered the presence of bats in the room. They occupied half of it, hidden by corn sacks, their heads pointing downward, while their claws held to the wood.

You'd heard of the notorious blood-sucking bats. True to their name of vampire bats they'd suck blood from a sleeper's outstretched foot, and retreat into dark corners, and he wouldn't so much as wake.

You wielded a long stick and rushed into the dark interior of the room. The bats fled. You drew back, you closed the windows and the door and went to bed.

As though to comfort you, Ustadh Muhammad said, "There aren't any vampire bats in this country." But you still took the precaution of seeing that your limbs were concealed by the cover.

When you got up the next day, and before you opened the door, the bats were zigzagging from one corner of the room to another. You were horrified as you pointed to them.

"Look! How did they get in? How?"

Ustadh Muhammad said "From there" and pointed to a small hole in the wall. You hurried and blocked it with a large stone, packing it into place with smaller ones.

Haj Sa'ud said, "Ustadh, Ghabshan is a good man, and remember this is the first time a school teacher has come to the village. You should make allowances for him. He's over sixty and has a beautiful woman. He's jealous to the point of possession."

You said: "But we won't eat her up!"

He said: "I've spoken to him and warned him. He won't be able to harm anyone."

But Ghabshan, whom you hadn't seen on your immediate arrival, was still circling round and round the shack, like an African dancing around a fire, tense, overstrained, foaming, the evil blazing in his eyes and communicating itself to the stones.

Ghabshan, after long thought, seemed suddenly to have found the solution.

A jeep drew up. A woman approaching sixty climbed down, evidently exhausted, her stooped back looking almost broken, her complexion blackened from age and exposure. She carried a stick in her hand.

She looked once toward you, then toward the room. She muttered some imprecation you couldn't hear. A few moments later, a cloaked woman came out of the shack. She climbed into the rear of the jeep, while Ghabshan sat next to the driver. The jeep took off in a cloud of dust.

You said, "What's happened, Haj Sa'ud?"

He said, "Ghabshan brought his old wife here, Aunt Jarada, and took his new wife to the village."

You said, "But can Aunt Jarada endure staying here all by herself?"

He said, "But Ghabshan comes here before dawn and goes to the corn field, then returns before sunrise to the village. He takes Aunt Jarada provisions, then goes away."

"So Ghabshan's run away with his young wife and brought the old one here to this wilderness?"

But the next night you were still unable to sleep with your limbs exposed. What an unbearable prospect was presented by the idea of bats sucking blood from your toes and then flying off without you feeling anything!

They say that they leave wounds that are hardly visible. They perform the act rapidly and disappear before the pain registers with you.

You bolted the door again.

Ustadh Muhammad said, "Why don't you try and relax? Ghabshan won't be able to harm us!"

"But I'm afraid of the bats. They can kill us in the night by sipping our blood."

You can't recall how long it took you to realize that those bats were of another species.

And when you adopted a rational means of interacting with them, Ustadh Muhammad began to interact with them in a different way!

In the shadow of the complete absence of surprise, the destitution of a world of joy, the glory of Sa'ad's daughter increased. Her only rival was Aunt Saliha's daughter.

In the permanently dark, stone-walled grocery with its narrow entrance door, Sa'ad's daughter exercised her beguiling charms on both stone and men.

There she'd hold sway, but her fruits were always expensive and untouched by human hand. Her voice would undulate like a waist burning with desire. She'd go deep into the recesses of the shop, as though the earth had swallowed her. Now near and now far, she appeared inaccessible, an illusion, or a nightmare that concentrates itself in an empty spot, a fathomless abyss, or she steps out of a cactus forest, soft . . . wounding, and no hand can touch her.

There she'd shelter, but her fruits would always be out of reach, fruits that no one had ever touched except Ustadh Waleed, if we're to believe the rumor. But who can stay here seven years for Sa'ad's daughter?

Ustadh Waleed went on a long journey this year, and they say she cried when someone secretly told her he wasn't returning in the coming year.

That was the only time Sa'ad's daughter lost control of herself and her father's shop. She ran. But Ustadh Waleed had discovered that seven years was enough. During that time he'd revolved around her, and when he caught hold of her at last, it wasn't before he'd begun to write letters to himself.

He used to go up to Baljarashi and project them down in the direction of Sabt Shamran. The letters would come winding down from the heights of

'Aseer, tumbling down with the floodwater and its cargo of rocks, then quickly accelerating.

Ustadh Waleed used to watch the floods and await his ship, await the world that he'd left a long time ago, seven whole years. He'd run in the direction of the mail, where water and desert meet. He'd open the letter and return looking happy and proud.

The thought of Sa'ad's daughter was no longer sufficient comfort. The desert didn't rise above the solitude of its sands. It remained there, lurking in the corners of desolation and oblivion.

But already rumors were abroad. People had got an inkling that Ustadh Waleed was in love with Sa'ad's daughter and that, driven to distraction by love, he went every week in the direction of Baljarashi.

"Where are you going, Ustadh Waleed?"

"To Baljarashi, I want to visit my brother and some friends."

But they all knew that those friends would run away in time. They'd collect their torn limbs and jostle each other, running through the dark nights in the direction of light, any light that appeared. Some of them would fall down, and the crows would prey on them, returning them north, wrapped in their wings, their voices a hoarse outcry. And some of them would struggle with death until life exploded in their veins. They'd then gather together their remains and disappear.

There, in that corner of the world called Sabt Shamran, Ustadh Waleed would huddle down, trying to savor his last good days with Sa'ad's daughter, but for a long time that had proved an inadequate compensation.

Sa'ad's daughter ran, but the desert was larger than her body. She ran, but Ustadh Waleed, who one evening on a dark night almost decided to remain forever, left his body and went away in the wilderness, and no one ever found him.

Sa'ad's daughter ran in the direction of every bird that soared that year, expecting to find his corpse. But the eagles and ragged crows would rush in her direction, beating their wings, and she would smell in them the odor of blood and would follow them. But a huge gulf of time had opened since that year.

Sa'ad's daughter withdrew. It was said that no one saw her after that fateful year and that she grew old and wrinkled, her stiffness emphasizing her decrepitude. But her voice remained youthful, for she was always calling for Ustadh Waleed, her lover.

Some said that Sa'ad's daughter was over a hundred years old and that even when Ustadh Waleed was here, she was an old woman, but when he saw her, he abandoned his body and was never seen again.

You trembled at the beginning. You were about to step toward the corner from where the voice issued, kindled, resonated, but you lacked courage to unravel this secret.

Ustadh Muhammad told you, "I heard that whoever touches her disappears. You must keep away from her." Then he laughed loudly. Ustadh Muhammad himself disappeared, and you know in truth that he'd never even entered Sa'ad's daughter's grocery and had never touched its darkness.

Sa'ad would enter the grocery and find her there, among the sacks of rice and sugar and the cans of processed food. She'd draw sufficiently close to touch Pluto's shoulder with her palm, he who'd come from Milan, or the hand of one of the school teachers, then retreat a little. And Sa'ad would smile and go into an adjoining room, as though he were one of the ancients.

You said, "Pluto, you teach me Italian, and I'll teach you Arabic."

He shook his head.

We'd already smashed the English language out of all recognition.

The paved road had almost reached Sabt Shamran. Someone pointed it out saying, "It'll go from here." It had seemed impossible at the beginning.

For two years the Italians had been paving the desert to arrive at al-Qunfudha. As for us, we used to reach it in a night and a half. Two whole years to arrive at al-Qunfudha in six hours!

However, no one wanted to contract time to arrive there that quickly.

"But the moment a proper road reaches us, our whole life here will change," said Shaikh Hajar.

"I see no good reason to open a road here," Ahmad Lutfi pronounced.

"We'll be a part of the new world," the teachers responded.

Fatima remained silent.

"Ustadh Muhammad," I said, " they say that the road works have now reached the village of Namira."

"But why should you be happy about that?" he asked. "There'll be a street, but the only time you'll use it is once when you enter that hell and once when you leave it."

The Italians searched unsuccessfully to find something in the landscape that corresponded to themselves. The desert was vast. At the beginning they confronted it with wonder: Oh! The desert!

At first they were fascinated by its gold face. When the sun rose, they'd rush toward it, throwing sand at each other, as though they were running on a beach. And in the evening, preoccupied with the shadows skirting the edge of the dunes, they'd run again.

They'd come very close this time, by going too far. And there, in that complete desolation, they'd hear the voice of Sa'ad's daughter, burning, with desire, and they'd rush toward her. Unable to define the source of that voice, they hurried toward each quarter. Some of them ran south to the borders of Yemen, while others continued eastward, stopped only by their collision with the 'Aseer mountains. Then the bloodied floods burst forth and the detonations of thunder rocked the center of the world.

Although their company attempted to provide them with everything from matches to whiskey, the alcohol-free beer they consumed took on a special flavor near Sa'ad's daughter.

She moved elusively through them like a magic bird, her hair brushed with perfume and crowned with basil leaves. But no one saw her face.

"Pluto," I said, "do you believe Sa'ad's daughter is a hundred years old? That's what they say." And I told him everything I'd heard.

"You're crazy," he said, "You're like the rest of your people—mad! Nothing fascinates you more then improbable superstition."

"But, Pluto," I said, "the age of legends is a thing of the past."

"That's what you think," he answered.

When we stood at the door of the grocery, her voice was unashamedly provocative.

Pluto looked at me and said, "You're mad. Such a voice can only belong to a complete woman, one full of femininity and voluptuous embraces."

But who was it who dared hold her hand. Antonio? Or Ustadh Fathi, who came looking for her from Namira?

Who was it who dared touch her hand?

Suddenly the world spun out of orbit.

The voice shrilled, and the wilderness was full of it. Everything took cover from the source of that scandal. Thunder slammed across the sky, and the floods followed. Sa'ad came, he bellowed and swore, although his voice remained inaudible.

Then the night grew serene.

It became calm, as though a radiance had entered the angry core from which its circles and black spears emanated. There was repose in the sky, it became a night like any other in the world, subdued, and offering assurance by its calm. It grew quiet until you could believe that you were dreaming in a room open to the world and looking out on to a narrow street, somnolent and innocent. A world like the one in which a person can actually smile.

Perhaps the cold had seeped to you through the sands of the room's floor. You'd forgotten even the white ants and were about to forget the storm.

That moment of peace enveloped you with multicolored birds and warm songs. You fidgeted and turned over again. You drew the blanket up to your head. You huddled into yourself, placing your head near your knees. Sa'ad's daughter seemed to you now like a nightmare without clearly defined features or form.

Why doesn't life retain this equipoise? Why do they all occur again—hawks and greenfinches and storms, and Sa'ad's daughter, and white ants?

You threw off the blanket, sat up, and found yourself on the floor. Your hand stretched out to touch the sands. You stood upright and took a decisive step. Now you were over the bed, you stretched out, looked up at the ceiling, but didn't see the bats. Your hand searched for the torch but couldn't locate it. You didn't know how long you stayed sleeping on the sands.

I used to tell Ustadh Muhammad that white ants could be prevented from climbing the bedposts, by placing the legs in empty bean cans. The ants couldn't perform the feat of climbing up the can, down its inner side, and then up the bed's legs.

Haj Sa'ud said, "If you put gasoline or oil inside the can, they can never reach you."

You had to summon the courage to place your feet on the ground, before reaching for the oil container or the gasoline tank. You found yourself jumping; a bat scuttered away. Your hand fumbled in the corner . . . here's the pot, here's the cooker.

The oil was here, and so was the gasoline, but both had disappeared. You tried to remember the last time that you and Ustadh Muhammad had filled the cooker with gasoline or the last time you used the oil. You tried, but . . .

A voice arrived out of nowhere, its tone not entirely unfamiliar. It was weak and frail to start with, and when you pricked up your ears, you felt them moving. You wanted to ascertain the precise location of that voice.

Not in the direction of Thriban . . . the motorcycles are coming from Sabt Shamran. Fear overtook you, you stood at the ready, took a step toward the door, then returned.

"If I go outside, they'll see me." You revolved around yourself, once, twice, you fell down, stood up, and again took a few steps toward the window. You shook the bars . . . You rattled them until blood oozed out of your palms.

You shouted, "I told them I didn't want to see them . . . I told them that . . . and they promised me."

You turned toward the ceiling. "You're witnesses to that, you're witnesses!" You were pointing to the bats.

The noise approached, came near to the house, but didn't climb the little hill. Instead it continued its forward thrust, accelerating away into the distance.

You said, "Perhaps they've missed the road."

And despite the fact that it was almost dawn, and that the light would assist them in finding you, you wished that the morning would arrive.

You shouted, "Dear morning, why are you so late?"

Pluto had said, "Do you think we'll be able to cross the threshold?"

There wasn't any distance between you and Sa'ad's daughter.

"Pluto," you said. "Where have you come from?"

"Milan," he replied.

"From Milan . . . to here?!" you questioned with astonishment.

But perhaps he didn't understand you, and maybe you didn't register your surprise in an interpretable language.

A human explosion had occurred. Everything turned to its opposite. At first they rushed, jostling each other, in the direction of Sa'ad's grocery, and Sa'ad took everything. As for them, they never arrived.

Pluto said, "Will you come with us today?"

"Where are we going?" you asked.

"It doesn't matter," he said, "Will you come?"

'I'll come," you answered. Every trip one took was like a hammer that broke the sharpness of time.

The Italians gathered in the wide square, in front of their camp. They looked into each other's faces, then ran toward the cars. You ran too, bewildered.

Scores of motors roared into collective action and dispersed in different directions. Something was going on in their heads; they were ablaze with energy.

The cars stopped, and the Italians stood in a circle. The cattle's instinct told them that something was wrong, that a plan was being hatched against them. As the men closed in on them, they tried to find a break in the approaching human circle. The men were trying not to alarm them, but terror showed in their big eyes, their necks . . .

The cows were preparing to stampede, and then no one would be able to catch them. They'd lived here a long time, unintruded on, so could only panic at the white alien faces that came toward them, eyes shining with latent madness.

The animals formed a protective herd, their heads raised high. The human circle narrowed, and the beasts knew that they were trapped.

When the white hands started brandishing ropes, the cows huddled together in one massed body. That was all they could do. It was their only means of self-defense.

Suddenly the ropes twitched in the air, aimed toward their cautious necks, but the strokes went wide of them. They lashed out again. This time the cows moved in fright and were about to disperse. But they regrouped in the middle of the contracting human circle. They reared, they bolted, but everything had closed in on them; space, the desert and the mountains crowded them and almost blocked the flow of the valley.

The Italians drove the cattle in the direction of the cars, and five or six of the herd huddled there, alone.

They were realizing that this was the end of the wilderness and the freedom of their lives.

The engines roared into action again.

And there . . . behind the wide square, bulldozers had prepared a gaping wide hole, something like a communal burial ground. The men and cattle alighted, and you stood there bewildered.

The Italian laborers rushed on . . .

Pluto shouted to you with joy, "Come on!"

There was a rapid exchange of laughter as they ran their hands over the cow's wombs.

But a wave of weeping overtook them.

And they broke.

The voice of Sa'ad's daughter could be heard again in the distance. They trembled, they ran with half-raised trousers, in the direction of the voice. They stormed on . . .

Some were running to the east, some to the west, and some to the north. And the voice was filling the desert with its secret flames.

—*Translated by May Jayyusi and Jeremy Reed*

Hani al-Rahib (1939–2000)

See Hani al-Rahib's biography in the short-story section.

THE EPIDEMIC (1981)

Hani al-Rahib's fourth novel reflects his steady artistic development. It covers one hundred years of modern Syrian history, from 1870 through the two twentieth-century world wars, spanning three generations and surveying the tragic history of a beleaguered people. An important element in the novel is that it brings to light the rise of the middle class in the Arab world—originally proponents of social justice but ultimately focusing on their own political gains, abandoning the masses, and surrounding themselves with reactionary movements in order to protect themselves and stay in power. The Epidemic includes historical characters from the author's village and society, presenting Syrian social, political, and economic problems through real families and political personalities. Unlike other Syrian and Arab novelists, who speak of a more remote past—such as that of the Ottoman or French presence in the Arab world—al-Rahib speaks directly about the present, addressing current political situations: the government and living characters and personalities, even, who have benefited from the political environment at the expense of the principles they once propounded. The Epidemic was read by political prisoners in Syrian jails with reverence and joy, and the author received a torn copy, sent to him after having been circulated in a prison. This copy had more than one hundred signatures and many positive comments on its pages.

The place is beautiful. Perhaps the most beautiful place in memory and certainly the loveliest in the village. Nobody can remember when the people made it a place for their dead. Radiant wild flowers spread around the hermitage and the graves. Some of the graves are stone shrines decorated with markers identifying the dead. Others are barely visible above the ground. Most of the graves are so old and decayed that the only sign of them is the flowers that have sprouted over them. A breeze blows through the cemetery, roams among the graves, then heads toward the village carrying fear and memory to the living. To the north of the hermitage is a huge oak tree bordered by an earthen arch that drops down to the edge of the surrounding forest. To the east a curved path reaches for Al Rameem Valley and the distant mountain range. To the south the landscape slopes down to a dense thicket bordering the big river. Westward stand groves of fig trees, the main road, and the eastern part of the village.

Ten years ago he indicated to me that he preferred to befriend the dead, so he went to the hermitage—there atop a cliff that jutted out of a smooth mountain peak. The villagers said this was where the secret and the evidence had been revealed. There he stayed, getting closer to God and distancing himself from the people. The villagers became more modest in their daily lives, obsessed with a renewed feeling of shame because of his ability to transcend life and befriend the dead in contrast to their inability to overcome their self-deception. They said that manna would inevitably come down to him from heaven to help his soul overcome his body and his body overcome his soul. Indeed, they said, it had already come.

He did not react when he heard that war had begun—war of a type that humankind had never experienced. The limited news reaching Al Sheer was outdated and unreliable. He knew that the war was everywhere, that it might consume everything and kill millions of people. One day it might even reach his hermitage. His daily routine did not change. He continued following the sun and synchronizing his movements with its movements: he rose with it, revolved with it, and turned westward toward the village when it set. After sundown he slept in the silent hermitage among the silent graves.

A day came while the sun was still hanging on the horizon that he left his usual place for the village. He had become entirely white—his hair, his clothes, his shoes and his rosary. Only his eyes were black.

In the beginning of the eighteenth century the land of the Al Sindyan family extended as far as the eye could see: from the top of the Al Sheer mountain to the sea. The head of the family used to wear a white turban and a loose, long-sleeved white garment. He strutted on the road leading his ten strong sons born of only two mothers. They wore sharp and terrifying daggers on their belts always. There were other landowners, but they all sought Shaikh Al Sindyan's protection. Not only because of his extensive property holdings and large family but also because of the religious status he inherited from his forefathers as guardian of the law and morality of the people.

In those slow times a strange group of people migrated to Al Sheer. No one knew anything about their history or origins. It was said that this group came from as far away as four days' journey by donkey. That was not unusual; it was part of the way of life for people to be nomadic. They also were strong men. Once they bought some land, the villagers grew afraid of them. One thing about them stood out: a brown goat accompanied them and lived in their house with them. It was said that they drank its milk, ate its cheese, sold its droppings, and braided its hair. Before long the villagers began to refer to them as the Goat family.

One day the Goat family held a banquet in honor of the Al Sindyan family. That evening the village was quiet except for the barking dogs. The ten sons came. They walked through the village three abreast, with the eldest in front. Their hosts welcomed them profusely outside the house, taking their guests' outerwear and belts and leading them to the room of death.

No one knew exactly how it happened. Except that ever after that night was called the Night of Blood. The Al Sindyan sons had suddenly found themselves held hostage, bound tightly with strong ropes. Then their hosts had sent for Shaikh Al Sindyan to come witness the death of his ten sons. It was said that they had seated the *shaikh* on the floor on something like a straw mat, after which they had slain the ten sons one after the other over his knees.

After the Night of Blood, the Goat family had invaded and taken up residence on the *shaikh's* property, which was close to the village. A few years passed before they could persuade any of the villagers to work their newly acquired land. By the time they were able to convince some of the peasants to work for them, the middle letter of their last name was dropped, leaving a surprising improvement in the meaning of the name. At first they were called Al-Anz, meaning Goat; once they were more established, they changed it to Al-'Izz implying glory.

Shaikh Al Sindyan was seventy years old. He did not cry. He did not speak. They let him go.

The day following the Night of Blood Shaikh Al Sindyan awoke as if nothing had happened. He went to the fields. He prayed under the old oak tree. He watched the sunrise. He drank from the spring. He listened to the songs of the birds. He contemplated the trees for a long time and touched the blossoms of the white flowers that dropped from their branches. When his men gathered around him, he was sitting under the oak tree. He told them he wanted to marry and asked their advice.

They were pleased to oblige. That evening he married a young lady, seventeen years old. Nine months later his wife gave him a son. Sixteen years later the son married for the first time. Forty years later the son killed ten strong men of the Goat family.

1916: World War I reached Syria.

During the retreat of the Turkish army, destruction prevailed in Greater Syria in a way unknown since the Turks' entrance into the country four hundred years before. The crops failed and surplus food was stolen. Livestock disappeared and money was taken. Men were hanged. People wandered around, trying to elude death. Tens of thousands. The more people, the more victims. They left their houses and roamed over the land. From the deserts and the coasts they poured into Jerusalem, from Beirut and Houran to Damascus, from the mountains to Hama and Lattakia, from the plains to Aleppo. In the streets the only audible word was "bread, bread." Along with their scant, cheap possessions, they carried deadly diseases. Among these, typhus held the strongest grip on them. Lice found fertile ground in their heads and under their arms. Typhus spread faster than people died. And they died faster than was expected.

Somehow the village of Al Sheer was protected from the disaster. Perhaps it was the only village so protected. Not because the Turks were too tired to penetrate the clouds to reach the flat crown of the mountain; no one believed that. The Turks were capable of moving the moon. No. Al Sheer was safeguarded because Sheikh Al Sindyan never left the village. Among the villages throughout the country, from the seacoast to the eastern forests, Al Sheer alone was graced by a man with God-given mercy, who received daily manna from heaven. He changed none of his habits. He continued following the movements of the sun. He was seventy-eight years old and walked without a cane. When at last he died, the village fell silent in sadness. In the days leading up to his death, they had suspected at first he was only secluding himself. But three days had passed during which he had apparently disappeared into his hermitage. On the sixth day, typhus drove 'Um Kahla to her death, even she whom they had thought immortal. They remained uncertain about Shaikh Al Sindyan, enduring a silence that cloaked them. Then just before morning prayer some of them heard a great cry and awoke. A few saw a burst of light shatter the sky and flood the universe. They had no clocks to tell how long it lasted, but it was enough for a few of them to see Shaikh Al Sindyan climbing the heavenly towers while the light explosion was transformed into songs glorifying God.

In the morning four others died, and for the first time the Turks were able to cross into Al Sheer. They killed eight people. The silence had been a warning. Suddenly an entire world collapsed. It was as if a thunderbolt had struck and left nothing but terror. The day the Russian Revolution broke out, the inhabitants of Al Sheer joined the human procession crawling from the villages toward the city: fleeing death; carrying their death to the city.

Shaikh 'Abdel Jawad Al Khayyat was one of them. He carried Ahmed Salim in his arms; he was sick. The mother carried Daoud; he was an infant. As for Salih, he walked between his parents. The wavy land around them seemed like a city without houses. A family here and a family there. All walking with those slow, wandering steps motivated only by fear of death.

Nobody greeted anyone, but in their proximity they became accustomed to sharing fear and despair. Some of them had come from distant villages and they began to scratch their heads violently before the others, searching for lice. Catching one bug and crushing it between two stones was a joy to be discussed and to make them believe in living long enough to take a few more steps. Another victim fell, a young woman. Her face had appeared swollen four or five days earlier. She reddened with fever but kept walking. The fever rose and walking became difficult, but she continued. On the seventh day she fell. Her relatives hesitated for a while and exchanged guilty looks. Their eyes filled with tears when they forced themselves to leave her behind.

Shaikh Abdel Jawad was standing in the courtyard of his house, thinking, He believed that he had been born in 1885, but five years earlier or later would not have made any difference. What mattered was that people were born, they lived, and they died. So what if they did not know their exact birthdays? Eventually mankind would cease to exist, anyway. Death itself did not mean anything to him. His earthly existence was not eternal, so a quick departure from it would be better than prolonging it. He went through a phase during which he loved the thought of death because it would bring him close to God. He even loved the misfortunes life entailed because he knew God was testing his faith. Therefore, after Daoud had died under the bridge and Salih had choked to death on some beans, he named his fourth son, Ayyoub (Job). But he hated sickness because it was a form of torture and a disruption of nature. He hated such things as blindness, deafness, and broken bones because they disfigured the absolute beauty of nature. He had been born and raised in the lowlands among people who knew humility. His spirit had been fortified by the pride and might of the clear winds whistling through the surrounding mountains. And because the calcified land always yielded less than the peasants wanted, he vacillated between generosity and stinginess. Because food was scarce, he was content with little. Because the journey was long, he became patient, yet remained as passionate as ever.

He moved between the village and the city at a time when such travel was a noteworthy event. He knew why his grandfather the *shaikh* had preferred the isolation of the hermitage. His grandfather had lived in the city during the war and the temporary independence, only to return to the village later to work as a serf. He had returned to the city once again to put his children in school. Nothing had changed in his mind about the image of the world. For him it continued to expand infinitely, every aspect of nature proclaiming divine revelations of one single divine origin.

That had been in the past—now Shaikh 'Abdel Jawad, his grandson, stood here in the village, where his grandfather had once stood. Like the old man before him, the younger man watched the seasons come and go, and he saw them as monotonous, beautiful and joyous. The colors changed in the face of eternal nature with the cycles of rain and drought, the wheat and the harvest, the wind and the calm, the bitter cold and the heat. He had seen the face of nature as immovable, timeless, unchanging. He did not see anything less than the absolute in life—not even in death—not even in the sunset. He stood, observing the little boys playing in front of the big house. A strange thought occurred to him.

Perhaps it was the thought of Shaikh Al Sindyan, his grandfather. The death of the shaikh has been like an earthquake. Suddenly he had disappeared, but his presence lingered, a symbol of the permanence of the stars and the movement of the sun around the earth.

With his death, his power to protect Al Sheer from death had failed. Death had invaded the mountains, valleys, vegetation, and people. Everyone had tried to escape instead of meeting it with sad resignation. The distinguished Al Sindyan family broke up into three families. Shaikh Ibrahim retained the original family name, while Shaikh Abdel Jawad took the name of Al Khayyat and Shaikh 'Abdel Hadi assumed the name Al Rihan. Others took different names. 'Abdel Jawad was the least fortunate of the three, the most ascetic and the most learned.

—*Translated by Bassam K. Frangieh and Clare Brandabur*

Mu'nis al-Razzaz

See Mu'nis al-Razzaz's biography in the short-story section.

ALIVE IN THE DEAD SEA

This novel is set in Beirut, the Arab city that can embrace a mélange of Arab racial, sectarian, and ideological variety. It is, in fact, a symbol of the Arab world, which the author regards as dead and ineffective. All its protagonists meet a tragic end: the representative of Aab nationalism, the dominating ideology in the novel, ends in a lunatic asylum, the Marxist rebel is killed, and his colleague, the Marxist thinker, ends up with heart disease.

This 'Enad fellow, I told myself, has to be tamed, or 'Abd al-Hamid's going to be angry. So I started hatching my plans and maneuvers. I was sure it would work—I'm not without initiative, after all, and I know just how to manage anything that might crop up.

The first stage of the plan worked perfectly. Bullets rained on 'Enad's car (my men were good enough shots to fire over him and underneath him without hitting him directly), and he was scared out of his wits—and agreed to having bodyguards to protect him. That's the way I am: I can go round and round a mine without setting it off and plant it where I like. Next, I ordered the arrest of his friend Mariam, and, just as I expected, along he came to plead for her release—or rather, he stormed into my office, his eyes blazing with fury. She wasn't a communist, he said, and my men were idiots. I kept my temper. With the cunning of an army engineer turned intelligence officer, I said I knew nothing of the matter and actually denounced the arrest in stronger terms than he did. I even summoned an officer and slapped his face in front of 'Enad.

"Release her at once," I shouted.

Then, while 'Enad was still in the office, another officer came in as arranged, with a big file that he threw down in front of me—and there were pictures of Mariam naked, making love with someone under a picture of Lenin, along with a photocopy of a letter in her handwriting, cursing the president, calling him a chauvinist and comparing 'Abd al-Hamid to Ivan the Terrible. There was even better to come, though: part of the letter was about 'Enad himself, saying he was a guileless fool who could easily be used for "our purposes." "He fell right into my trap," she added.

I rose from my chair, working to plant mines of doubt in his mind. My expression changed: I narrowed my lips, widened my nose and frowned, then looked at him in a way fit to melt a heart of stone.

"And we thought she was innocent," I shouted. "Take that whore back to jail!"

I was killing the boy in 'Enad. He collapsed onto the sofa, unable to believe what he'd seen, turning, before my eyes, into someone who looked very old; then he buried his face in his hands. He looked like a barricade torn apart by a bomb. I watched him fold, gazing at him as he stepped on the mine, as it exploded in his face, shredding him in a million pieces. He gave the impression of a soldier whose body had been torn by bullets and who was begging the doctor for just one more bullet to put him out of his misery. He'd already split in any case; we just came and plucked him up by the roots. Still, I didn't want a mere shell of a man, who was no use to anyone. I loved him just the way I loved my younger brother. He was like a wild horse, and I was breaking him in for his own good—before he fell into 'Abd al-Hamid's trap.

Had 'Abd al-Hamid seen this file, I asked the officer? No, he answered. I dismissed him and was once more alone with 'Enad. The bomb was getting ready to explode. I approached the debris of his body, but he didn't raise his head, or utter a single word. Then I took the file and burned it. He did raise his head at that, his eyes alight, and I could see he was bewildered. He staggered to his feet, white as a sheet, and stood there in front of me, the tears still lingering in his eyes. He stayed motionless for a time, saying nothing; then his head sank onto his chest and he retreated into his gloom.

"I'll have her released tomorrow," I said calmly.

He nodded and moved toward the door. Before opening it, he turned and shot me a grateful glance. Then he went out.

It makes me downright sick! The fever of socialism has every one of those scheming bourgeois swine in its grip. All they do is brag, all over the place, how their great-great-grandfather or great-great-cousin or father's father's step-mother was—a peasant.

Some of them even go so far as to claim the father of their grandfather or grandmother was a "worker"! Where were they ever "workers," for heaven's sake? At the steel mill in the Empty Quarter? Or the Fiat factory in the Sahara? Or maybe in one of those factories making military aircraft in the villages? It's all total rubbish! God curse times like these, when people have to dig right down in the roots of their family trees to find a peasant or worker to brag about! And if they couldn't find one, be sure they'd still drag some great-grandfather up from his grave. "He got his hands dirty working," they'd say. Or, "he was a peasant." And here I've been, searching all my life for some sort of rich relative, one I could take pride in when things weren't going right.

Even 'Enad al-Shahed claims his grandfather was a peasant; and if his father was rich, he says, it was because he was a self-made man. He actually apologizes for his father's wealth. God curse these times, I say! "Show me your grandfather,"

I told him. "Let me see he really is a peasant." Being part of the peasant class is a guarantee of good behavior now.

And just what are peasants? I'll tell you. We gave them loans, and they used them to pay their sons' bride prices and marry them off. And to put the lid on it, Marx himself, so the minister of culture told me, said the peasants weren't revolutionary at all. A couple of days back I'd finally had enough and went to the jail where that lousy red Mahjoub 'Abd al-Sattar was kept.

"You son of a bitch," I said, "didn't that Jewish son of a bitch, your leader, say peasants were backward and reactionary?"

I was gloating inwardly, proud of showing off my knowledge and intelligence. It must have come as a shock to him—they claim we're ignorant, after all. But this old man, sixty years old, just looked away and remarked condescendingly, "Actually, it was Lenin who said that."

"I don't care who it was," I yelled furiously. "You're all alike—just like the Chinese or the blacks. Lenin, Marx, what does it matter? Didn't one of your leaders say peasants were backward?"

I didn't wait for his answer—I was afraid he'd flush out some other mistake I'd made, and that wouldn't do for someone in my position, with the jailers there behind me. I just cursed the minister of culture to hell and back.

I tell you, "civilized" people—"cultured" ones, I mean—don't have any balls. They're all ditherers. Deep down they admire people like me—and it's because they secretly admire us that they feel so drawn to attack us and run us down. But, as I said earlier, if an officer's been an expert in mines and explosives, then turns his hand to dealing with revolutionaries, and reds, and backward people, and enemies of unity—well, you've found the perfect, ideal man for handling security matters.

How I hate that minister of culture! He sits there as if his chair were some kind of imperial throne. For me it's just a toilet seat, which he got through our machine guns, not through his education and university degree. And the imbecile deceived me—saying it was Marx who talked about the peasants like that. He shamed me in front of the jailers and guards. I left my office and went straight to his, only for his stupid secretary to tell me he was at the radio station. I gazed at the man contemptuously.

"You dirty little pen-pusher!" I said. "Collars as white as a baby's puke and university degrees just fit for the toilet!"

By the time I reached the radio station, I was boiling with rage.

"What the hell do you think you're doing," I yelled at the minister, "sending out these songs of 'Abd al-Halim and Farid, about how bright the day is and how dark the night is? This is a time of unity, isn't it, my fine friend? A time for rejoicing, not sobbing and weeping and mourning. What's wrong with Faida Kamil? And how about that patriotic singer I sent you last week?"

The minister just gaped at me, his mouth spread out wide like a hooker's legs. He went white and turned to the employees around him, but he didn't say a word. He wanted to say the patriotic singer was just a whore, but he didn't dare, because he knew she was a friend of mine. His cowardice worked me up even more, and I went right over the top.

"And how about that poem by 'Enad al-Shahed?" I screamed. "How dare you tell him it couldn't be published?"

I started heaping the vilest curses on him. Suddenly he started shaking. His voice trembled, and his face and whole body seemed ready to fold.

"Actually," he said, "it was an employee in the Department of Censorship who turned the poem down. For the same reasons you were against 'Abd al-Halim and Farid—that it was gloomy and bitter."

I stared at him with contempt, burning to vent my aggression in some way. Before I left I issued him with a warning.

"I'm giving an order to the captain," I told him, "the man in charge of the people guarding this station. He's to tick off anyone who tries to let those romantic songs of 'Abd al-Halim or Farid go out on the air. He'll make sure you broadcast patriotic songs."

I'm not a Leader yet, it's true. But I'm a major even so—and a man to be reckoned with! From the time I started growing up, I had this distinct feeling I was a great man. A sense of destiny took me over completely—and yet I had no scientific evidence to support it. That, in fact, was my mistake. A feeling like that is just a feeling—it isn't supported by rational argument or logical proof. It's more like the kind of spiritual call where the searcher only finds a solution through direct contact with the divine—through revelation, or intuition, or a call. But fate sends out her invisible signs to the one who's chosen, and only he can see them. Once, after I'd taken a bath, I walked naked to the mirror and gazed at my broad, handsome, hairy chest and strong, rippling muscles that have attracted so many girls. For the first time I noticed the moles on my chest were shaped like a crescent. I gazed at them for a while. "This is a sign," I said to myself. And all that came true when the time of unity was here, and I found myself a major.

A few years back, I admit, I was a fool like my friend 'Enad al-Shahed. To the outside world I seemed bold and decisive enough, but deep down I was confused and awkward, especially if I knew someone was important. I wasn't so important in those days, not someone to be reckoned with as I am now. Those feelings, which were hardly in keeping with my rank, sprang, I think, from a sense of resentment and inferiority in the face of intellectuals and powerful people. Once, before the time of unity came, a friend arranged a confidential meeting for me with someone close to the president—a man who was widely read, and knew all about the personal life of Chou En-lai, and had had personal contact with Krushchev, even going with him, sometimes, on his trips in his private yacht on the Nile or the Black Sea. On the way to this meeting (I still laugh when I think of it) I was sweating, even though it was pouring with rain. I was wearing a smart suit of my friend's and kept a constant watch on the shoes I'd spent so long polishing—they were glossier, I tell you, than Hollywood stars!

"Now don't chatter on," my friend kept warning me. "Just remember, he doesn't like being interrupted."

A great thinker, he added, talks in such a way that the listener's never quite sure if he's finished or not. It would be better, too, if I didn't smoke during the session, unless the teacher smoked, or he himself offered me a cigarette. It was impressed on me that I should rise whenever the teacher left the room for a call of nature—he was close to the president and a friend of Krushchev—and again when he came back. Also, I shouldn't cross my legs in the presence of this great thinker—the president's theoretician, as my friend referred to him.

All these instructions made me more anxious than ever about the meeting—I even thought quite seriously of canceling the whole thing. I remembered my father, who was so strict I couldn't smoke in front of him even after I was married—I used to go to the bathroom when I needed a cigarette. I felt as though I was going to sit for some difficult exam. As we rang the bell, my heart skipped a beat and my hands started trembling. I hoped the guard would tell us the thinker wasn't in—I had an impulse, even, to turn tail and run off as fast as I could, especially when I saw the mud smeared around the legs of my pants. Then I took a grip on myself. "Keep going," I thought. "The gates of history are opening for you, right now."

The theoretician's face emerged, glowing, it seemed to me, with the mystic light you only see on the faces of saints and holy men. My hand was trembling as I put it out to shake his; then, finding it was wet with sweat, I jerked it back (even though his own hand was already extended) and wiped it quickly and clumsily on my jacket. I nearly fell down with mortification, then, to everyone's surprise—including my own—I started giggling hysterically. I had no idea why I was laughing, what demon had suddenly possessed me.

The important thing, though, was this. While the meeting was a disaster in one way, it also showed me I was a genius chosen by destiny. As an officer in the engineering corps, I'd learned, crucially, to handle people the way I'd handle mines: carefully, deviously, and in a hostile spirit—in other words, with what the psychologists call "social intelligence." Now do you see what a well-read intellectual I am? How I'd love to explore this matter of social intelligence further. You'd see just how cultured I am! One of my worst flaws, though, is a temptation to elaborate and digress. It takes a great man, needless to say, to admit his faults, and everyone tells me how totally honest I always am with myself.

Now, where were we? Oh yes. We went into the reception room and just stood there, while the thinker, for his part, was evidently waiting for us to sit down. Then he put out his hand, as a sign for us to sit, and, in my confusion, I automatically put my hand out to shake his again. He shook out of politeness, then, clearly irritated, he gave up, smiled, and sat down, whereupon we did the same. It seemed to me the thinker must be amazed how stupid I was. Maybe he was thinking to himself: "God help me through this evening!" I blushed, and things started swimming before my eyes. I sat down and folded my arms like an obedient schoolboy.

"Welcome!" the thinker said.

"Thank you, Teacher," my friend answered respectfully.

I furtively watched the thinker as he started asking my friend about our country. His face and eyes were quite ordinary, no different from ours, and so was what he was saying, except, of course, for the dialect. He spoke slowly, only glancing at us between one sentence and the next. Actually I wasn't listening to him, because I was busy watching the movements of his face and the gestures he was making with his hands. His muscles were alternately tightening and relaxing. I even took note of his tone of voice. I was enormously surprised. I'd been expecting someone arrogant and haughty; and what I found, instead, was a humble, modest man. I'd been expecting him to talk in a lofty way, barely deigning to glance at us with eyes that were hard and fixed and proud; but to my surprise his look was one of shyness and simplicity.

And that wasn't all. Every now and then, as he talked on, he'd crack jokes, then laugh uproariously just like a little kid. I was taken aback. Where was the dignity I'd been expecting from him? The dignity and solemn authority you'd expect in a leader? He wasn't a real top leader, of course, but still, he was a first-rank leader within the hierarchy. The president himself, it's true, has a pleasant, humorous face, but I felt this man here risked being taken advantage of by fools and people on the make. In any case, the president's the exception not the rule; and I've noticed, besides, from the newspaper and magazine pictures, that his expression's firm, imposing his authority on anyone that's by. I've tried endlessly, in front of the mirror, to imitate that look of his, but I've never succeeded.

I compared the thinker, too, with the marshal, whom I'd met a little while back. The marshal, I noticed, talked without looking at his listeners, and I realized later that this endowed him with an aura of solemn authority, one that put the listener on the defensive—especially when the marshal did surprise his hearers with a sudden piercing look that caught them as their attention was drifting, making them feel confused and small. And I noticed too that he'd lower his voice sometimes—deliberately, so that the person next to him couldn't make out what he was saying. The poor man would strain to hear, even nodding in agreement and smiling respectfully. Then, after mumbling inaudibly for a while, the marshal would clap the listener thunderously on the shoulder, and say: "What do you think of that, eh?"

I did find it daunting, it's true, when this teacher, this thinker, harked right back to the Middle Ages to support his theories. He'd quote Bismarck, maybe, then move on to a story about Garibaldi, or Charlemagne, or Haroun al-Rashid, followed by a long list of names and incidents I'd never heard of. But what really amazed me was the way he answered most of my friend's questions.

"Actually," he'd say, "I don't really know. I've no idea. I haven't read that. I've no information on the subject. It's all rather unclear—I can't figure it out."

What was this? How could he let himself "not know"? How could he admit he didn't know, in front of someone like my friend, who wasn't one of us? That changed things completely. I stopped watching his every move, had no wish to memorize and imitate the way he behaved, as I usually do with important people I meet. I must say I started feeling superior. The coffee cup stopped shaking in my hands. I wasn't afraid of this leader any more. It occurred to me, suddenly, that this thinker looked like my father, or as if he ought to be a hermit in a refuge, not a leader close to the president and the marshal. I'd been dying for a pee all the while. Now I asked him where the bathroom was, and, when I came back, I crossed my legs and lit a cigarette. But what really made my respect for him plummet was when he said hesitantly, "We heard about the part you played with 'Abd al-Hamid in the rebellion. I'm full of admiration for the courage you showed. If we'd had just a hundred soldiers like you in the Arab world, we'd have been united long ago."

I said nothing. I felt proud, filled with a sense of self-satisfaction—and of disdain for the thinker. He admired me, did he! If he'd said he admired 'Abd al-Nasser, or Mao Tse Tung, then fair enough. But once he'd said he admired me, that made me the one who was admired and him the admirer—and there's a wide gulf between the two. I noticed, too, how he agreed with every stupid thing I said. "Right," he'd say. "Exactly. Precisely."

When he got up to leave the room, excusing himself politely, my friend got straight to his feet, but I didn't stand. When he came back, my friend got up again, but I stayed planted on my backside.

After we'd said goodbye and left, my friend asked me curiously, "Well, what did you think of him. What was your impression?"

I felt a sense of irritation.

"These wordy intellectuals," I answered, looking straight in front of me, "were just born to chatter in cafés like women—not to lead the nation. It's people like us, firm, decisive people, who make history. They don't make history. They just write it."

Yes, they write history. There's a world of difference between those who make history, like the president, and fellows like that who just write it. Now unity's here and I'm in a responsible post, I'm surer of that than ever.

Just look at 'Enad al-Shahed. For all his negative criticism and idealism, he's jealous of me because I'm firm and decisive. But as for me, why should I be jealous of his intellect? Aren't I the leader of all those baying for the blood of intellectuals? Anyway, these bourgeois types with their eyeglasses buy all their dozens of books for decoration, to show off, not to read. If 'Enad al-Shahed read all the books he decorates his library with, he'd be more important than Mao Tse Tung or that American philosopher, Hemingway. Intellect belongs to real men. He just philosophizes because he doesn't want to work.

Take Farajallah, now. He said a few clever things and everyone admired him. Then I put a simple question to him. "What decides the fate of nations?" I asked him. "My cannons or your theories?" He couldn't give me an answer. These cultured people are full of problems. They chatter day and night about socialism, and what is socialism anyway? Just a handful of measures for nationalization. That's all it is. We achieved unity without any theories or rubbish like that. Power was there, and we took it.

But 'Enad al-Shahed—It's true I love the bastard because he looks like my little brother, God rest his soul, but he couldn't ever lead. You have to be decisive to lead. Before I met the thinker, I thought leadership was something pretty difficult, but afterward I realized I had more ability than any of them. I asked 'Enad al-Shahed one simple question, and he couldn't get the answer right.

"Suppose you were president," I said, "and you found I was plotting against you. Would you have me executed?"

"Of course not," he answered, in his stupid, childish way. "You're my friend. And we've been through so many things together. And—"

"Then clear off!" I broke in. "You're not fit to be a statesman."

And yet I love this son of a bitch who looks like my brother and reminds me of my youth. I've warned him, more than once, to keep his mouth shut about all those high officials and security people. But he's so stubborn and stupid. He just won't listen. I even told him we had a huge file on him, as thick as a telephone book. But it was no use. My criticism was constructive, he said. He was trying to be creative, he said. He said—well, anyway, he's an idiot.

Yesterday, though, I hatched a plan to make him a bit more positive. I'm going to give him a taste of authority—let him wallow in it. Of course he's already part of the system—and anyone who's a part of that has power. He's one of us, yes. But he's never known real authority. He's still just active in the popular organizations. Some day I'll put him in a post he never dreamed of. He'll have security guards, a chauffeur-driven limousine. I'll take him out of that apartment, which isn't even fit for students, and put him in a classy villa. Maybe, one day, he'll write a novel and put me in it. Or compose a dramatic poem about me. At any rate, I'll be free of his criticism constantly nagging away at me.

I chuckled, happy with this idea of mine. An engineering officer, I thought triumphantly, a specialist in dangerous mines, had more cunning than 'Amr ibn al-'As himself [1]—especially if he combined all that with the experience of a police officer.

—*Translated by Eliane Abdel-Malek and Christopher Tingley*

Yasin Rifa'iyya

See Yasin Rifa'iyya's biography in the short-story section.

The Hallway

In war-torn Beirut a young Christian woman is attempting to visit her sister in hospital. Suddenly a fierce bombardment forces her to take refuge in the hallway of a building, where a young Muslim man has stayed to try and ride out a crisis that has already forced

---

1. The seventh-century general who conquered Egypt and established Islam there.

others in the building to flee. Trapped together as the fighting becomes constant outside, the two help and comfort one another as best they can, forging a strong bond in the process. Eventually, after a first escape attempt has failed, the pair break out from the building once more; the woman just manages to escape, but the man is killed. The book demonstrates, in chilling fashion, the evil and pointlessness behind a violence in which ordinary, decent individuals, whatever their religious background, become mere playthings of chance.

It was evening now. Rana, exhausted, was leaning against the wall, while the man moved back and forth between the doors of the kitchen and living room. But the bullets, greedy as ever, hadn't grown tired. One shot followed the next as though alive and pursued by hordes of wild beasts, streaking left and right without pausing for breath, swifter than the wind, faster than sound, screaming in waves from the steel muzzles, under the relentless pressure of fingers on triggers.

How could such a city, so clean, so well ordered, be transformed to one filled with all this hatred and filth and blazing destruction? These people all worked together in the same factories or stores or offices, lived in the same buildings, went to the same restaurants and beaches, ate the same bread, and drank the same water. They met morning and evening, and paid the same taxes, and watched the same television programs. They all loved Fairuz, Wadie al-Saafi, 'Abd al-Wahhab, and Um Kulthoum.[1] They spoke the same dialect of the same language, tried to outshine one another with their cars, attended the same soccer matches. They all observed Sunday as a holiday, spent their summers in the mountains, sunned themselves at the seaside, and bathed in the same waters. Their children played together. They read the same newspapers, elected the same leaders, were homesick when they traveled, were hospitable to travelers themselves. Their joys and sorrows were one. They all bore the name of citizen, proud of the lovely homeland of which they were part. So how could everything go to pieces at once, to be replaced by hatred, shooting, and killing, as though they'd always been enemies, at war with one another since time immemorial?

Who was it thinking these things? Herself or Mahmoud? Rana was thinking and questioning; and there was this man pacing back and forth in front of her, in a space of just two meters—was he reflecting on these things too? Was he, like her, wondering just who gained anything from all this destruction?

Rana observed him closely, a tall, brown-skinned man, on the thin side. What would she do if this siege went on? And what would he do?

"You're thinking about your fiancée, aren't you?" she said.

"And you're thinking about your husband and daughter!"

They fell silent. Was it really true, Rana wondered? Was he thinking about his fiancée or about how to escape? She'd almost forgotten her past. She just wanted to escape herself. But how, with all this fierce shooting and these explosions, with the smell of burning and gunpowder filling the whole dark hallway?

"Would you like some coffee?" he asked.

---

1. The four leading popular singers in the Arab world.

"Yes, I would, please," Rana answered.

The man went into the kitchen.

How long are we going to stay here in these few square meters, she wondered, unable to move, tormented by fear of the unknown? But was it so unknown? Wasn't death there, at the door, at the windows, in the street, on the sidewalk—just a meter or two away? The building itself might come down on their heads from one moment to the next. How could you talk about the unknown when everything was so clear? The weakest of threads separated life from death at every moment. Death strode forward from one conquest to the next, slaying dozens in a flash, extinguishing the light of the eye, freezing all motion. Death was racing in all directions, gleaning each trembling heart, each moving hand and fluttering eyelid, bringing everything to a stop at a blow. Frail life had taken flight, hiding behind walls, in hallways, shivering with fear. Chaos had crept its way in, morning and evening, sleeping and waking; because death had declared war on life, so that you could no more distinguish morning from evening, sleeping from waking.

Rana was surprised to find herself reflecting like this. Hadn't she once wanted to be a movie star, or a writer, a poet or journalist? She'd devoured books both in French and Arabic and gone to the cinema several times a week, pondering over these things, discussing and probing, wishing she could commit her thoughts to writing. She was the one her women friends came to with their troubles, and she'd advise them, as though she'd been through trials enough to turn her hair white. And yet, in the springtime of life as she was, she'd never thought of death; she was blooming, after all, and death was a long way off.

She'd been right too, this beautiful woman whose eyes reflected the varied colors of the olive grove, whose skin was like the brown of coffee fields. Those who praised her beauty marveled at the changing expressions in those clear eyes of hers. She was spirited too, meek though she looked. Whenever she looked at her face and body in the mirror, she knew her beauty was greater than that of any of her friends. She was afraid now, feeling the skin on her face with one hand and, with the other, caressing the cross around her neck. What, she wondered, if the water was cut off and she lost some of her beauty? Hadn't this stranger, this man sharing the narrow hallway with her, praised her beauty, in the midst of all the terror? She wanted to seem beautiful in his eyes as well as her own.

At the moment he came in, with the coffeepot in his hand, she was smoothing her silky hair with her two hands. For all the darkness, there was a glimmer of light filtering from the kitchen, falling on one side of her face. He gave her a fleeting glance, she thought, before turning to put the tray on the stool at the far end of the hallway. He poured a cup, which he gave her, then another for himself; then, after offering her a cigarette, which she declined, he lit one for himself. As he struck the match, she saw his eyes focus directly on her own eyes and face, with the ghost of a smile playing on his dry, dark brown lips.

"I'm getting used to the sound of shooting," she remarked.

"You'll get even more used to it with time," he answered. "Little by little you'll lose your fear."

"I hope to God we'll stay safe."

"So do I!"

"Were there armed men in this building last time too?"

"No. In fact half the occupants were still here then. This time, though, it looks as if there's no one but us, along with those armed men at the entrance and up on the roof—and maybe in other places too."

"So it's really more dangerous this time."

"Yes, it is. Still, no one's going to bother with us. They get their pleasure from firing at one another. Try not to think about it."

The darkness had deepened, and the explosions were getting more frequent.

"Have you noticed," she whispered, "how the fighting seems to get fiercer at night? How can they see each other?"

"Who says they can? Each side's safe behind its barricade, shooting toward the other. Nobody dies except innocent people who've nothing to do with what's going on and don't take care. There are more bullets and explosions at night to stop the other side advancing and give the impression they're there in force."

"So really it's a war no one can win."

"Exactly. There's no victory in a battle where the fighters just stick behind their barricades. They're destroying the city—quite simply. And it's the innocent they kill, sniping at wretched people who have to move around to find a piece of bread. It's the most miserable, futile sort of war there is. Nobody wins, and nobody loses either—except for people like us. We're trapped here under siege, not knowing what to do, because we don't belong to either side."

Rana lay down and tried to sleep, while the man did the same on the other side of the hallway. It was around twelve o'clock maybe—should she ask him the time? She'd forgotten to wind her own watch, and it had stopped. Perhaps he was asleep. But he wouldn't have kept his hands under his head like that if he had been. No, he was staring up at the ceiling. What was he thinking about? About his sweetheart perhaps? And what was Michel, her husband, doing? He must have lost all hope of finding her. Was he asleep? No, he wouldn't be able to sleep. He loved her. How would he be able to sleep when she was so far away, knowing nothing of her fate? What would he be saying to Hilda—to sweet, wonderful little Hilda? And how would Hilda be asking for her? Would she be saying, "Where's Mummy? Why's Mummy been away so long?" She'd be crying, wanting her Mummy.

Emotion welled up in her. She tried to resist, then, for the first time, suddenly started sobbing, trying not to let the man hear her, but finding her voice rising even so. She wanted to apologize to her companion, who'd pushed the stool aside and drawn near, placing his fingers on her lips. His hand was cold. Or was it her lips that were warm?

"Don't apologize," he said. "I know what's going on inside you. You're thinking about your daughter and your husband."

She gave way to her emotions now and started to weep. Taking a handkerchief from his back pocket, he tried to dry her tears, and she took the handkerchief and covered her face, wishing she could block out the sound of the explosions and screaming bullets outside—though when there was a pause in the dreadful din, she would shiver and shake, lonelier and more fearful than ever. In a hoarse voice she cried out to him through her tears.

"We have to get out of here somehow. We have to get out!"

He tried to calm her. If she'd just pull herself together, he told her, they'd talk about it. But she couldn't get the image of the sleeping Hilda out of her mind. She was afraid, too, that Michel might be forgetting her. He might be mourning her, supposing her among the dead, but be thinking too, at this very moment, of finding some other woman to live with in her place. The idea made her sob harder still. Might Hilda grow up under the care of another, strange woman and come to call the woman "Mummy"? Would she forget her?

The man came still closer, cradling her head and trying to comfort her.

"Why are you so afraid?" he said. "Don't worry, you'll get home again, to your daughter and husband. No one's going to attack this house, believe me. The fighting's going to end eventually, just the way it did last time, and you can go back."

His cool hand was pressed against her feverish forehead, then it moved back to her hair as he pressed her closer to his breast. Feeling calm returning, she stopped sobbing, though the tears continued to flow. Unconsciously she snuggled up close to him, like a child seeking shelter from an ogre about to devour her, while he placed his other hand on her back and gently stroked it.

"Don't be afraid," he said. "I'll stay with you. We're in this together, and your fate's mine too. Tomorrow morning I'll try and think of some way we can leave. Maybe we can sneak out through the back. Then you go back home safe."

Rana was silent, clinging to him so hard her body seemed to be blended with his. She felt, for a few brief moments, that this man embracing her saw her as a daughter or a sister, and the thought upset her; she started weeping again, her thoughts straying in every direction, without focus or control. Her daughter—death—her husband—death—home—her sister at the hospital—death—her mother—her father—her family—her friends here and there—people—childhood—death—cities going back thousands of years, without walls now—death—and this calm, sad man holding her to his breast, to whom she was clinging as if to life itself.

She came back to the present, for the first time, it seemed to her, since she'd left her home. She felt tranquility winning out over the firing and explosion outside and inside her head. Still, though, she sobbed, to make him believe she was afraid, so he'd hold her more tightly. Then, without knowing quite how it had happened, she put her own arm around him, pressing him to her. They clung to one another more tightly still, as though one interlocked body beat with two hearts, twined around with four arms, as though each part sought to escape but was prevented.

For a long time Rana hovered between sleep and waking, a multitude of thoughts coursing through her as she wavered between fear and hope. She slept maybe one or two hours. Then, it seemed to her, a bullet grazed her forehead or her chest.

She had a vision of herself lying on the sidewalk, a bullet piercing her body, with blood, dark and red, gushing out. But she knew she wasn't dead, because she could see countless eyes, mad and tireless behind their rifles, their only target her warm, trembling body. As all the guns aimed, at her head, at her eyes, she felt the bullets piercing her face, yet still saw the men clearly, their eyes hateful and vengeful and stony behind their masks, laughing out loud as they fired. Then one of them hurled a grenade at her, and the rest eagerly did the same. And yet, for all the explosions in front of her, and in her breast, she didn't die.

Then the whole building against which she was leaning tumbled down on top of her, covering her with dirt. There were dozens of wounded alongside her—children and women and old men, groaning and stretching out their hands, unable to reach her. She tried to help them but was glued to the ground, her sticky blood holding her fast to the sidewalk. She tried to get up, but they had her surrounded completely, aiming their bullets at her earrings. Though they tore her to pieces, Rana found, to her amazement, that she still hadn't died.

Looking around her, she saw great numbers of corpses scattered about the street, motionless and gnawed by mice and rats, polluting the air with their putrid smell. And now she saw the bullets flying slowly like snowflakes, then exploding in the air, alongside her ears, against her breast. She tried to cry out, but no sound came.

She saw the city she loved in flames, and all the memories of her youth returned: the corniche, the green mountains, the snows of Farayya, Hamra Street. This city, adorned with a million flawless stars like a bride, was now, here in front of her, like a heap of paper or dry wood going up in flames. She went to stretch her hand to heaven to beg God's help, but a bullet pierced her palm and flung it to one side. She felt no physical pain, but she saw the funerals of thousands passing before her, among them funerals for her loved ones, while she lay paralyzed on the sidewalk. There was her husband's coffin, followed by his friends who briefly glanced at her as they passed. Then she almost burst into tearful screams as a small coffin passed by on its hearse, with a cross shining on the black-draped wood. A small head broke out through the wood, its silky fair hair fluttering in the breeze, Hilda's head. "Mummy," she cried out desperately, "Mummy." Rana strove desperately to go to her aid, but the coffin slowly receded, with Hilda gesturing to her, while still her sticky blood glued her to the sidewalk. She tried to brush away her tears but found the very palm of her hand covered with blood. She wanted to die, to throw herself on her daughter's coffin, but she was still alive, watching those funeral processions. There was her mother, her sorrowful, shrouded, white-haired mother, gazing at her silently, followed by headless bodies, by phantoms and ghosts. The whole city, it seemed to Rana, was moving to the graveyard before her eyes, with its crosses, and minarets, and *muezzins*, and church bells.

Only the bullets were grinning from ear to ear, dancing their mad dance. No sooner had the processions passed than the masked men returned with their guns in their hands, hemming her in on every side, staring at her with boorish arrogance. And now, before her eyes, these men, from their different factions, formed into ranks, and the first rank fired at her. She felt the blood spurting from the holes in her body but was conscious of all that was happening. When the first line moved aside, the second advanced and opened fire, tearing her body more. The third followed suit, and the fourth and fifth and sixth, and still the blood spurted, from fresh holes, to form a river flooding the street, sweeping away the corpses, along with the masked men and shattered buildings and burned-out cars. The bloody river flooded every part of the city, and the heavens were a mass of yellow flames. She wondered how she, alone, was staying alive to witness all this.

In her desperation she grasped the cross around her neck and kissed it. She didn't know why, at that moment, she thought of Mahmoud, the noble knight who was all that remained to her. She hadn't seen his funeral procession, nor had she glimpsed his eyes among the hard eyes of those firing at her—she would have recognized them among a million others. She called out to him, but no one answered. Still the river of blood swelled, spreading to become a sea without ship or sailing boat, a stagnant red sea, without wave or shore. She didn't know how she was witnessing this, or from where. She noticed, once more, that the blood was all springing from her own body and tried in vain to stop up the holes with her hands. Then, her hand on the cross, she begged God to deliver her from this carnage, to spare her the fearful spectacle. It seemed then that some powerful force bore her aloft then threw her down on the earth, and she woke with the smell of dust in her nostrils.

She was aware of Mahmoud trying to rouse her; and the moment she got up, he pulled her into the kitchen and clasped her to him. Aware of her pounding heart, she drew back and stared at him. As the light of day began to creep in, she noticed his face was pale and his lips dry and trembling.

"We were almost killed by an explosion," he said. "There was a direct hit on the building, maybe on this very front wall."

The explosions redoubled, drowning out the sound of the small arms fire. Rana suddenly caught sight of his left hand, wounded and covered in blood, his wrist watch shattered.

"Your hand!" she exclaimed fearfully.

The man looked at it, then at his watch. "I don't know how it happened," he stammered. "It was probably when that huge explosion shook the place. Maybe

I jumped up suddenly and hit my hand on the wall, or on some glass. I just don't know."

Rana approached and took the hand in both of hers.

"It isn't serious anyway," he said.

She gazed at him once more, seeing how his face had changed, showing signs of utter exhaustion, and how a beard had started to grow. Then she thought of herself, touching her face—no doubt she looked the same to him as he did to her, worn out and pale as a sputtering candle.

"What are we going to do?" she asked.

He didn't answer straight away. He turned on the faucet, but not a drop of water came out; and when he went over to the jerrican, there was only a little left there. As she approached, he told her to hold out her hands, then poured some water into them so she could wash her face. He did the same, washing the back of his injured hand too, then took a bottle of eau de cologne from the shelf and poured some over the wound, the aroma spreading through the air. She opened her hand to take some also, rubbing it on her neck and behind her ears, then went to the bathroom for a few moments. Looking in the mirror, in the faint light, she was taken aback by her appearance. She went to find her handbag and returned with a small comb with which she tidied her hair. She looked a little better now, like a brown filly preparing to canter over the boundless fields.

When she returned, she found Mahmoud leaning against the kitchen door, gazing out through the window at the dark clouds of smoke. Realizing she was there, he turned toward her.

"We'll try and get away," he said. "We'll leave this place. What do you say?"

"Are you sure we can?"

"We'll go out through the inner courtyard and make for the other buildings to the back. There's a narrow alleyway behind the building next to ours, and if we can get out through that we'll reach the street at the back. If we make it that far, I think we'll be safe."

Rana thought about this.

"You know the district and I don't," she said. "If you've really worked it out and think it's the best thing to do, I'm with you."

She saw the hesitation on his face.

"If you were on your own," she said, "what would you do?"

"I don't know. I really can't think what I'd do. Anyway, I have to think of how things actually are. You're here with me, and I have to protect you."

She took his hand in both of hers.

"I think, " she said, "that you're a—a noble-minded man."

"And you're a brave woman," he rejoined, "a wonderful woman." She felt delighted at the compliment.

"It seems to me," he added, "there isn't quite so much noise and fighting now."

"Maybe they're tired."

"Or maybe they've run out of ammunition. Now's our chance."

"Whatever you think best."

The man hurried inside, then returned with his jacket.

"Will the sandals bother you?" he asked. "Can you move fast in them?"

"They're OK. Better than women's shoes anyway."

"Keep your eyes open. Now—are you ready?"

Rana thought for some moments, then she said:

"Yes, OK."

"Come along then."

Hand in hand they went to the window, and when he jumped out she followed suit. They rushed to the wall on the other side of the building, and the man leapt up on it, then took Rana's hand and pulled her up too. Then they flung themselves down into the courtyard of the neighboring building. As the firing grew fierce again, they took refuge within the angle of the building, panting for breath, watching the surrounding buildings, most of which had their windows closed, with no sign of movement. Then Rana trembled as she caught sight of a man appearing suddenly on the rooftop opposite, then disappearing again, to be replaced by the muzzle of a rifle aimed straight at them.

"A sniper!" she yelled.

Mahmoud retreated with her, his hand in hers. Was she the one who was shaking, or was it him?

"I got a glimpse of him," she said. "He was looking at us, I'm sure of it. I was afraid he'd shoot us."

"God protected us," he whispered, trying to force a smile. "Now, let's go."

They ran together toward another building. "It's better if we stay behind these buildings," he said.

"There doesn't seem to be anyone in them."

"Maybe not. Or maybe they're hiding, like us."

They reached the wall. "The alleyway's on the other side," he said. "From there we can get out to the street beyond."

He leapt up and took her hand, at which she jumped up too, and they leapt down together onto the other side. Rana opened her mouth in terror and dismay.

"My God!" she cried. "Those bodies. Two children!"

Some meters further off she saw a man's bloated corpse too, then a wrecked car, broken glass and a blown-up shop. She was seized by trembling fear and tried to go back, but Mahmoud stepped toward her to shield her body.

"We're right in the middle of the shooting," he shouted. "Let's go back."

Rana, though, was jabbering senselessly, making the sign of the cross first on her face, then on her breast. Mahmoud advanced cautiously toward the middle of the alleyway, only to be met by a hail of bullets.

"There's a barricade there at the end of the alley," he said, "and a bunch of men behind with machine guns. They're firing at us."

"Let's go back. Please!"

Her knees, she found, were knocking violently together, and she saw Mahmoud fearful and hesitant too, pulling at his lips and pressing them between his fingers, saying not a word. He went back to the wall, jumped onto it, then took Rana's hand and hauled her up. The instant they flung themselves behind it, bullets rained over her head, even, she realized, touching her hair. She knew it when she brushed her hair back and a lock came away, singed at the end.

"They almost killed me!" she cried.

Mahmoud looked at her dejectedly.

"What are we going to do?" he said. "I wish now we'd stayed where we were."

"This time we won't get past the snipers on the other side."

"Whatever happens to us will be what God decrees. Be brave, please."

"We will be brave. We must go on living."

"We *will* go on living."

He pulled her by the hand, and they ran to the side of the other building. Then he took a hasty look around at the windows and rooftops.

"I'm not sure where we are," he whispered.

He glanced nervously around once more, then cried, "No, no! There's the building. There it is, just behind this one. Come on, jump up!"

He went first, and she jumped up behind him. Then they ran as hard as they could toward the last wall separating the courtyards of the two buildings.

"We're nearly there," he cried, fighting for breath.

She was panting too. "Oh God, save us!" she cried, repeating the entreaty as she grasped his hand. She glimpsed a number of heads moving from one rooftop to another, then the bullets started raining down on them. Certain the end had come, Rana started silently praying, but Mahmoud was edging nearer the wall, silent and self-possessed now, keeping an eye on the rooftops. Suddenly he lifted Rana in his arms, threw her onto the top of the wall and shoved her over, then leapt over behind her. Then he raised her to her feet, took her hand, and ran with her toward his own kitchen window. Yet again he lifted her up, pushed her through, and jumped in after. It had all taken just a few seconds, and Rana didn't even realize they were there in the kitchen. When she came to her senses and saw she was safely back, she threw herself on Mahmoud's breast and burst into tears.

—*Translated by Lorne Kenny and Christopher Tingley*

Ghada Samman (b. 1942)

Syrian novelist, short-story writer, and columnist Ghada Samman studied in the Arab world and read English literature in Britain. She lived for some time in Paris and settled eventually in Lebanon, alternating her time between Beirut and Paris. A leading and outspoken feminist, she uses the vehicle of fiction and journalism to raise major feminist issues. Writing in a vivid and often fiery style and practicing what she preaches, she has done more than any other writer, with the exception of the Egyptian Nawal al-Saadawi, to drive the ideas of women's emotional, sexual, and social liberation into people's consciousness. Her short-story collections include *Your*

Eyes Are My Fate (1962), *No Sea in Beirut* (1963), *Night of the Strangers* (1966), *Departure of Old Harbors* (1973), and *The Time of Another Love* (1979); and her splendid stories of marvels, *The Square Moon* (1994), translated into English by Issa Boullata in 1998. Her many novels include *Beirut 75* (1975), translated into English by Nancy N. Roberts (1995); her superb novel on the horrific Lebanese civil war, *Nightmares of Beirut* (1976), translated by Nancy N. Roberts (1997); and *Billion Night* (1985), *The Impossible Tale: A Damascene Mosaic* (1997), and *A Costume Ball for the Dead* (2002).

Nightmares of Beirut (1976)

This novel provides a detailed description of the horrors of the civil war in Beirut in 1975. There are over two hundred nightmares, some of which are realistic descriptions of the situation. Some, interwoven with factual descriptions, are hallucinations and nightmarish dreams. The strong element of fantasy in the novel, the occasional humor, the ponderings on human nature, sometimes mischievously thought out but often exhibiting pathos and confessional candor, help to mitigate the level of horror and at the same time bring out, through more than one literary mode, its grotesque contours.

For eight months the battle had raged. Only the narrator on the third floor and the landowner, his spineless son, and their Sudanese servant have remained in the building. It was an old, vulnerable Beirut house, situated right in the middle of the two warring factions. Gunmen had occupied the towering Holiday Inn opposite. "The hotel overlooked our little house like a cement and iron mountain overshadowing the hut of some peaceful farmer in the bottom of a valley."

The narrator had already lost to the war the man she loved, murdered in front of her, a victim to religious prejudice and tyranny, for he was of a different religion. Her own brother had managed to escape from the beleaguered area, only to be arrested and thrown in jail.

Caught in the midst of the battle of the hotels in Ras Beirut and exposed on all sides, any approach to the house was impossible. "We were like the inhabitants of the valley of lepers: no one dared approach us, not even thieves. Only bullets and missiles knocked at our doors and walls."

The novel relates the history of those terrifying days until rescue arrived.

Nightmare 14

I saw the man emerge out of the heart of darkness. I saw the man place a black mask over his face. I saw the man knock at the great door. I saw the man meet the "big" man. I saw the deal being struck, I saw the man coming out carrying with him the "manic power." I saw the man receive the price. I saw the man climb the mountain. I saw the man throw the powder into the spring from which Beirut drinks. I saw the "manic powder" touch the spring, and fire kindle in the water, and burning bubbles break to the surface . . . I saw the man bend over the spring and drink, his ten fingers turn into animal claws, his hair grow long, his clothes fall off him like a dry skin, and his body emerge transformed into the body of an angry gorilla. The ape stretches out his hand, breaks off a green branch, and carries it, running excitedly towards the city. Flames ignite from his footsteps, and inside him erupts an irresistible savage volcano, and a thirst for blood . . . for blood . . .

The "manic waters" gush forth to give drink to the people of the city.

NIGHTMARE 22

I saw them lead a young man toward the pavement. His only sin was that he had passed along a road on which a few minutes previously a car holding armed men had stopped. The brother of one of the armed men had been killed, and he was looking for a scapegoat. Who he was was not important, only his religion. He had to be of a different creed.

They dragged him to the pavement. He asked them, "What am I guilty of?" The dead man's brother replied with angry curses. The armed men began to squabble. Do they kill him here or take him with them? Who should kill him? How? One asked, "How would you like to die?" He answered, "I do not want to die!" Another suggested a quick shot in the head and moving off instantly before any others passed by. He replied, "I do not want to die." The bereaved brother insisted that it was his right to kill the young man. The young man said, "I do not want to die."

They asked him, "To what party do you belong?" He replied, "To the party of life." (He was a philosophy student.) They asked him, "What's your name?" He said, "Lebanon." "Your family name?" "Arabi." They said, "This is no time for jokes, who are you?" He answered, "My name is Lebanon the Arabi, and I do not want to die."

An argument started among the armed men whether to kill him at once or later. They pointed their weapons at each other. The young man seized his chance. He exercised the only means of fighting that he knew: he ran . . .

He started running like a madman on the pavement. He ran for what seemed forever, but he heard the sound of steps running after him . . . he stumbled and fell. The running footsteps stopped, and he saw the face of the armed man who wanted to kill him . . . he saw him with astonishing clearness . . . like him, he was weeping . . . "My brother was a fireman. He went to put out a fire and they killed him and brought him back to us a corpse." The young man thought that he was unburdening his sorrow to him, and his heart began to soften. He was about to ask him for more details, when the brother's face was suddenly transformed to the face of an executioner as he said, "And you shall die in return for that . . . they are of your religion . . ."

The young man was still lying where he had fallen in the street. Exerting a great effort to extricate himself from the grip of his executioner and stand up, he found himself clutching a marble molding on a wall ... his senses were at their acutest, and in the pale light of the street he read an inscription on the marble: "A Public Fountain for the Glory of God. Donated by Salim al-Fakhouri, 1955." The fountain was dry. Not one drop of water. The armed man pressed his victim's neck against the marble edge of the fountain, and his knife soon found the main artery ... The young man gasped and it was all over for him ... the armed man went on slashing his neck even after the body had slumped, while blood gushed from the dry fountain. It flowed ... and flowed ... and flowed ... it washed the street ... rose higher ... and higher covering the roads ... reaching the windows of the houses. It was like a legendary spring that would not stop flowing ... inside the houses ... inside the rooms ... up to my knee ... my waist ... my breast ... my neck ... I gasp and scream as I suffocate with blood ... And I wake up.

NIGHTMARE 64

A sniper sits on the roof of a building that faces the sea. He has one huge solitary eye in the center of his face. For months he has not changed his position, performing a task he cannot remember how or why he took on. All that he knows is that he has to kill as many people as he can.

To start with, he had imagined his task would be more difficult, that he would have to do a lot of running round the edges of the roof to hunt people down ... Hunting humans, he supposed, would be more difficult than hunting birds. But what amazed him was that people came willingly to him ... When he began shooting from the building, he thought that people would avoid it and that he would have to move to another. The incredible thing was that people came in flocks to stand willingly in his range of fire. Day after day they came, one family after another, complete with all its members, old and young, and he would fire at them. When the bullet hit them, they would wave gratefully, walk a few steps toward the sea, and fall ... A minute or two later a wave would come and sweep them away, making room for the next family to follow ... and so on ...

He feels the people of Beirut were practicing a voluntary collective suicide while they came willingly like this ... They have deprived him of the pleasure of the chase, transformed him from a temperamental sniper into an executioner burdened with work ... He craved the pleasure of hunting a man, frightening him, firing first in front of his feet, then wounding him in the hand so he could go on running, then shooting him in the belly that he might die a slow and painful death ... but the people of Beirut bewilder him with their appetite for death, their strange collective suicide..

He sees a man coming from the end of the alley, walking cautiously, as frightened as a hunted animal. He could well be the last man in the city, thinks the sniper: it would be better to spare him so as not to be left alone. But his blood begins to burn . . . he forgets his fears . . . the old blood lust revives . . . his energy and hunting instinct mount in him; he aims and shoots. The bullet hits the ground in front of the man, exactly as he intends . . . he wants to frighten him first. The next bullet hits the man's hand; it begins to bleed. The sniper feels happy and does not register that his own hand has begun to bleed as well, in exactly the same place. A third bullet hits the man's thigh; he falls, and his thigh starts bleeding. The sniper does not notice that blood is flowing from his own thigh as well. A fourth bullet hits the man in the stomach. He can no longer crawl but surrenders to a slow death. The sniper does not see that blood is also flowing from his own belly, from the very same spot. He feels extremely tired and decides to give his victim a coup de grace to finish him off. But first he feels a great desire to see his face. He runs to him, turns him over, and finds that the man's face is his own. It is as if he were gazing into a mirror. It was then that he felt the terrible pain in his belly, and he knew he was going to die a slow and painful death. The rifle was too long for him to put a bullet into his own head to end his suffering.

NIGHTMARE 65

The shelling stopped and again a tense quiet reigned . . . that hush of battle, so different from any other . . . you can listen to it. And if you listened hard to the noise of silence, you could hear many other things . . . I heard the rustling of the animals in the pet shop nearby. So they have not yet escaped! I wondered if the rest of the people of the neighborhood had got away.

All the windows were shut like mine. On one of the balconies a child's clothes were still hanging on a rope. The child's mother had not dared to collect them . . . or had they perhaps left the house? Presently, the door of the balcony slowly opened a crack. A frightened head popped out and disappeared. A hand emerged from inside to feel the washing. Then a pregnant woman, her belly preceding her, crept quietly out to collect it. She seemed afraid. Her hand trembled and her laundry pegs fell to the ground. She continued to gather the child's clothes as if she were stealing them. Suddenly a bullet rang out. Was its target her belly, the heart of the fetus, or her own heart, I wondered? The woman fell to the floor of the balcony, and I could no longer see her. In his own way the sniper was saying "good morning" to the neighborhood. No one came out to the balcony. Doubtless her husband did not even dare to drag her inside. I heard the voice of a child bitterly crying . . . perhaps it was her child, whose clothes she will never wash again!

NIGHTMARE 84

Uncle Fu'ad and his son got tired of gathering their silverware and storing it in special cases and came to sit with me to rest. I said teasingly, "The thieves will thank you for your work, when they find everything of value neatly packed into expensive leather cases that only need picking up and walking away with."

My joke apparently did not please them, for Amin frowned and said, "Are you trying to say we may be burgled?"

He got up and vanished into one of the side rooms for a moment, then returned carrying a number of dusty black velvet boxes . . . I soon realized that they were not boxes but albums containing the family photographs. Amin's family was rich and had passed its wealth from father to son through several generations.

Amin began turning the pages of the albums where I could see pictures of the daughters of one of Lebanon's most prominent personages. I glimpsed some of their wedding snapshots: they had all married Arab princes. The late wife of Uncle Fu'ad was standing next to the newlyweds, for there had been an age-old friendship between the two families. I did not look at the faces of the brides or the other women—all society ladies whose pictures regularly appeared in the society pages of magazines. What I gazed at were the jewels that dangled at their necks like corpses of birds. A large diamond hung from the neck of the bride, reminding me of the albatross in Coleridge's "Ancient Mariner." Ah! Those ill-spent riches! All those velvet cushions, all that spectacular wealth announcing itself even in the gilded glasses they carry in their hands! Looking at them, I felt an obscure despression, while Amin gazed at them with affection, as if they helped him to escape from the gloomy present. When he asked me to savor them with him, I refused. I felt that this ostentatious past was responsible for this exploding, bloody present.

NIGHTMARE 109

Shakir had a hardware store. He was neither rich nor poor, neither handsome nor ugly, neither a saint nor a criminal.

Shakir's shop was in one of the downtown markets of Beirut. He made a moderate profit. He cheated a little so he could make enough to help pay the school fees of his seven children. Every time the fees went up, Shakir cheated a little more, and every time prices soared, he felt he had to cheat just a little bit more, asking God to forgive him and cursing the bad times.

One morning Shakir was on his way to his shop when a security roadblock stopped him. The security guards told him that the market had burned down and all the shops as well. Shakir inquired where they had been when the market burned down and why they had not been there to prevent it, instead of now stopping its owners from going there. No one answered. He spent the day eaten up with worry and misgivings. Had his shop, his only source of livelihood, burned down? He bought all the newspapers and scrutinized the photographs of the burnt market, it seemed to him that his shop . . . but no . . . this burnt-out shop has two windows and his has only one . . . This was his shop . . . but no, his shop has an old embellished molding over the roof and this has none, no trace of molding.

He tried to sleep but anxiety hammered at his lids and kept him awake. He cursed his children and his wife and quarreled with them for no reason. They escaped from him to their beds, and he felt resentful because they were able to sleep and because he was responsible for feeding those mouths that were now emitting snores and a regular, relaxed breathing.

Next morning he went, resolved to see his shop even if it were to become his tomb ... Though prepared for any adventure, he was surprised to find the market teeming with shop owners, journalists, and cameramen. At first he could not find his shop. It was difficult to make out in a street whose features were now confused by rubble, soot, and ashes, and half-collapsed blackened walls ... when he finally found it, he could not believe his eyes.

When he left, carrying what remained from his shop, he could not believe his hands! He took away in his old car what worldly wreckage was left to him, and it was wreckage indeed!

NIGHTMARE 110

The first day Shakir went out with what he had left to sell, his children's hunger compelling him to do so. He took it in his car to al-Hamra Street. He spread his goods consisting of pots, spoons, plates, and other housewares over the roof of his little car, spread the remainder on the pavement, and stood waiting. The crowds were thick, but no one bought anything. The pavements seemed strange and hostile.

In the past he had taken pleasure in going out to the sidewalks of al-Hamra to steal looks at the slender legs of the girls, thinking with regret of the legs of his wife, the mother of his many children, resembling in size and veininess the two trunks of some ancient tree. He would also pass by this sidewalk on feast days, accompanying one of his many children to the cinema, looking at the festive decorations, at the passers-by, at the succession of colors, listening to the sounds and rhythm of fast, vigorous living. He would notice, from time to time, disabled beggars—most of them frauds—sitting on the pavements begging from passers-by.

There was one blind beggar who always insisted on singing in a high-pitched, funereal voice. Shakir would give him charity in the hope that he would be silent or lower his screeching a little ... Oh, the mockery of fate ... here he was now occupying his place, having spread his wares where the beggar used to sit. However, Shakir was silent, indeed unable to call out about his wares like other destitute salesmen on the sidewalk beside him.

Throughout the day he did not sell much. He heard a woman tell another that all the goods were stolen. A valuable container of his that a small child tripped on got broken, and the child's mother cursed him because he had caused her son to fall to the ground.

Despite everything he spent a long day nailed to the pavement of al-Hamra Street ... he would sell a little and often feel miserable, remembering with regret his account book and the comfortable chair in his shop. In the evening, as he was returning home in the dark, an armed man stopped him at the corner of the alleyway to his house and sternly demanded what money he had. He had made little profit, and this money was for his children's bread. Dazed, Shakir asked the thief, "Who are you?" The armed man said, "I am a hunter." The poor salesman answered, "At your service, hunter."

NIGHTMARE 111

The next day the police stopped Shakir from entering al-Hamra Street. So he went with his companions in misery to the Qintari neighborhood and spread out his wares again. Rain poured down and the wind blew. The customers fled except for one tired woman who argued with him for a whole hour just to buy a kitchen knife and some spoons. Then she bought the spoons and left the kitchen knife. On his way back home at night the same armed man, the "hunter." stopped him, demanding money.

He had made little profit, and his money was intended for his children's bread. Nevertheless, he gave it without hesitation. He was tired and afraid. As he handed it over he said, "At your service, hunter!"

On the third day Shakir carried his wares to al-Qintari, only to find it taken over by rain and bullets, wind and fighting. So he continued on his way to al-Rawsha[1] and set up his spread on one of the sidewalks . . . the sidewalk had become his shop front, the winds his customers, and the rain his executioner. He wept a lot and sold little. In the evening when he returned home, the same armed man stopped him at the entrance to the alleyway. Before the armed man could speak, Shakir handed him the proceeds of his day, saying, "At your service, hunter!"

On the fourth day Shakir did not go to work. He did not carry his spread, and he did not sell anything. He slept throughout the day, and when evening approached carried the kitchen knife that he had failed to sell and stood at the entrance of one of the alleyways, waiting for the sidewalk salesmen to return to their homes.

He had decided to become a predator.

NIGHTMARE 118

On my way back to the kitchen I glimpsed Uncle Fu'ad sitting in his chair in the parlor . . . surrounded by the piles of silverware that he had carefully

---

1. The seashore of western Beirut. Before the civil war it was the area of fashionable cafes and restaurants, elegant apartment buildings, and swimming clubs. However, with the intensification of the civil war in central Beirut, and the burning of the Sursuq and other shopping centers, many of the shops moved their goods to make-do stores on the Rawsha, overlooking the sea.

wrapped, the objets d'art and antique Sèvres vases, each of which cost, to my great amazement, more than an entire library! I was too tired to wish him a good morning, had I not ... had I not sensed that mysterious hidden presence ... the smell that the soul and not the senses inhales ... no ... it was not his posture, his head thrown against the chair, nor his stiff body. There was a dark light radiating from his presence, which I sensed through the pores of my skin rather than my eyes, through those hidden senses that science has not yet uncovered, which simple people, but few scientists, apprehend.

I went toward him like one entranced, and it was no surprise for me to find him dead ... I had known it while I was in the adjoining room, even before I had touched his blue frozen hand, even before I was frightened by the look of remote indifference in his eyes. I had guessed it ... I had picked up the vibrations from it ... had realized without knowing how ...

When I looked at him surrounded by his antiques, he seemed to me to be like a scarecrow guarding a field of ashes ...

He was wearing his ancient official Ottoman uniform and had covered his breast with his old medals as though expecting an important visitor ... and the visitor had kept his appointment.

NIGHTMARE 122

Amin's screams woke me up. For the first time in a long while I awaken to a human voice instead of the explosions of shells and bombs ... but his voice was not exactly human ... it was more like the cry of a frightened animal ... at first I leapt out of my bed, afraid that he had been hit by a bullet ... then I remembered Uncle Fu'ad, whom I had left dead in his chair. No doubt Amin had discovered his father's corpse.

Amin was crying, and the servant had joined him in his lamentations ... it seemed to me that their weeping had more fear than grief ... as Uncle Fu'ad's death was a telegram warning us all of an inescapable death, of a death that one had no option but to forget in order to go on with the game of living. Amin was lamenting him in a sorrowful, frightened voice, as though lamenting for himself, and crying, "They have killed him ... they have murdered him." Then to my surprise he started running about everywhere and searching the house, though it was sealed on us as tight as a tin of sardines. I said to him, "Don't you see it's clear he died of something internal, a heart attack or a stroke, not a bullet from outside?"

But Amin insisted that his father had been murdered.

Because murder was so rampant around us, it was no longer possible for anyone to believe that someone could die a natural death. I said to him, "There's no trace of a bullet or shrapnel in his body. Terror and fatigue could have wiped him out more effectively than any bomb, but, can't you see with that his body was not hit?" Amin said, "Perhaps he was strangled."

I said, "There are no marks on his neck, and the doors and windows are all closed as we left them last night . . . the man has died a natural death, as most do."

But Amin was not convinced. It seemed very strange to him that in these days someone should die an ordinary death, and it was obvious that the old servant shared his opinion. I left them searching the house for the traces of the alleged killer, while the sound of bullets chased them. I sat in a chair opposite Uncle Fu'ad and said to him, "The killer is hiding inside you . . . he emerged from within you and killed you . . . Love killed you . . . love for your endangered antiques."

And it seemed to me that I glimpsed in his eyes the gleam of conspiratorial agreement.

NIGHTMARE 123

Amin and the servant were still wandering round in fear, searching for the alleged killer. I left them to let physical activity loosen the tension of their initial shock. As for me, I was facing a difficult practical problem: I had been a prisoner under one roof with three men in a state of emotional collapse, and here I was with two men and a corpse. The problem now was the corpse . . . We were unable to bury it for fear of the sniper who could certainly kill us while we dug a grave in the garden. It would be like digging our own grave . . . No one was able to come near the house to help us escape or even to collect the corpses from the neighborhood!

So the corpse was going to remain with us . . . and it would rot. We were going to face a worse disaster than the loss of electricity and the shower of bullets . . . and hunger.

Nearly an hour later Amin came and collapsed in the seat next to me . . . and started wailing, "Oh, Father!"

I said, "He's no longer your father. He is now a corpse. And we have to do something so that its smell does not suffocate us when it rots. We have to think about putting it in some suitable place before it stiffens and becomes difficult to move . . ."

He seemed quite dazed. It was obvious that he still saw in the blue lifeless body in front of us a man he loved, who was his father. He had not yet taken note of the problem posed by the presence of a corpse in a situation such as ours.

NIGHTMARE 130

Amin, his servant, and I are staring at the corpse that had become quite rigid, its features beginning to swell and change . . . the jaws had parted a little and something akin to a very sarcastic smile had taken shape on the blue lips, now parted to reveal a set of dentures. It is the Mona Lisa! The Mona Lisa of the civil war! Mona Lisa of Beirut '75?

I burst out laughing. The servant burst out laughing. Amin too. We fell silent suddenly, and all that remained of the laughter were gasps that turned into sobs in Amin's throat.

Night was rapidly descending on an ominous winter evening. It was nearly four, and a chilly wind carrying toxic rain bore with it the grey motes of a bleak evening.

Today was Saturday or Sunday, a time when people used to think of familiar homely problems, such as where to spend the weekend and should they make the cheese sandwiches with radishes or tomatoes? But this Saturday or Sunday evening I was thinking of a different kind of problem: What do I do with the dead man's corpse in front of me? And what do I do about thirst, with the water cut off, and about hunger, with the food running out?

In countries where people are facing famine, the weekend becomes a desolation that they have to spend in burying the dead. How did the yachtsmen at the St. George Hotel and the skiers at the Mount Cedar and Farayya hotels fail to notice this simple truth, with the hungry refugee tents scattered along the roads that took them to their playgrounds? How was it they saw without seeing?

Amin was the first to speak. He said, "We will carry him to his bed." I said, "We shall need his bedroom. It is the safest room in the house, because the adjoining garden wall gives it a double protection."

"We shall carry him and lay him out on his bed," he insisted. I said, "His smell will spread to your room and mine, which are both next to his."

Again he insisted, "We will carry him to his bed, as is proper."

We carried him to his bed. We stretched him out. He was heavier than his thin shrunken body would indicate. I moved his pillow to place his head on it . . . There I found four loaves of bread that he had hidden. Under the other pillow I found two apples and a bag of roasted chickpeas. I was too hungry to be shocked or angry and began to devour one of the loaves without even thinking of washing my hands . . . after the first few bites I felt hungrier than ever . . . As though food enabled me to feel the extent of my hunger! Amin glanced angrily at me. How could I eat in the presence of his father's corpse? I went on eating, much as if I were a wolf devouring a rabbit, unaware that what it is doing is labeled savagery by those animal species that do not experience hunger.

Then in turn Amin took hold of a loaf . . . and bit into it.

NIGHTMARE 134

Amin woke me up. The wind still blew its storm of hale and rain. "What's up, Amin?" "We must move Father." "You mean his corpse," I said. He ignored my remark and repeated, "We must move Father." "Why?" "It's his smell." I replied, "But it has not yet spread."

"Frankly," he replied, "I'm afraid. Whenever I close my eyes, he calls me and asks me to accompany him. His room is next to mine. Let us move him to the drawing room."

We gathered round the corpse, Amin, the servant, and I. A dull, resigned look in the servant's eyes; a very sharp one in Uncle Fu'ad's. I went forward to lift him by the head and tried to close his eyes for him, but the lids resisted with unexpected firmness and his eyes went on staring. The smile had become stronger, and the face looked healthier—or was it swollen? . . . No doubt Uncle Fu'ad was enjoying this game of moving him from one bed to another . . .

Once again I glimpsed our shadow against the wall, huge and nonhuman, and it seems to me that our labored breathing was rising from it. I felt as if we were the ghouls of the legends and had emerged from the covers of a horror tale to live out our miserable lives, our nights spent running about with corpses under a hail of bullets and the stormy wind. At last we stretched him out on the large settee in a drawing room that was relatively distant from the bedrooms.

When I lifted my eyes to Amin. I saw that he was not quite satisfied. And I knew that he was going to go for me again. I said to him, "What do you think about moving him to another place?"

He said, "Such as?"

I said, "We'll put him in the big refrigerator . . . It is true that the electricity is cut off, but it is closed tight . . . that way you won't hear his voice however much he screams, and you won't smell him either."

The servant asked, "You mean we should cut him up into pieces?"

I said, "I mean that we take the shelves and drawers out of the refrigerator, and take off some of his clothes and medals, and stuff him into it whole. It won't be a comfortable position, of course, but he will sleep at any rate!"

No one laughed at the joke. Amin did not agree. Silently we went to bed. I saw that Amin was still not satisfied with the position of the corpse. And I knew that he was going to go for me again!

He did.

This time he was wailing, and I was shaking with anger . . . Looking for sleep in these circumstances and capturing it was more difficult than catching a griffin, and there he was waking me up the very moment I was about to close my hands on the fleeting butterfly of sleep . . . I knew what it was. He wanted to move his father again.

I shouted at him, "Out with it. What do you want to do with the corpse? It's a corpse and you have to face that. And we are three living beings and we have to face that. What exactly is it that's bothering you?"

(I heard my voice commanding. Cruel. Cold. As if it were not my voice, once so soft and tender.) He cried, "Frankly, I am afraid . . . I don't dare sleep under one roof with a dead man . . . with a cor . . . cor . . . cor . . . corpse." I said, "Great! Now we know where we are. Then you want him outside the house?"

He nodded in assent.

I said, "Digging a grave in the garden is impossible. They will think we are planting mines. These days snipers' rifles see well in the dark . . ."

He nodded his head in assent. I went on, "And we cannot throw the corpse into the street because the garden surrounds us on all sides . . ." Again he nodded his head.

I continued, "The only remaining possibility is to place him in front of the main door of the house, as is 'proper' . . . and in the morning look further into the matter—if we are still alive."

We woke the servant up. He looked as though he were still asleep as he helped carry the corpse. Uncle Fu'ad's smile had broadened . . . I wondered how long since anyone held him in her arms and rocked him? Since he was a child perhaps?

I did not know that I had so much strength in my slender body . . . or so much hardness and cruelty . . .

I directed the transportation of the corpse, while Amin was in a state of utter collapse. As for the servant, he seemed nervous. I understood the reason when I saw that some gold medals had disappeared from the breast of the dead man. Perhaps he had crept up to the corpse in the dark, trembling as he took them. I did not blame him. It was the logic of hunger and poverty.

At last, like a gaggle of lunatics amusing themselves with a corpse, we reached the door. We propped it up against the wall, where it looked like a tired beggar crouched under the door, its hand unable to reach the bell overhead. We returned silently, each to his bed . . . but there was in Amin's eye a secret look of dissatisfaction . . . I knew he was going to go for me again. So I stretched out on the bed and did not go to sleep.

This time when he came to wake me up, I was expecting him. He said, "I can't go to sleep . . . he won't stop ringing the bell . . ."

"It's impossible for him to ring the bell. Have you forgotten that the electricity has been cut off? And he is a corpse . . . He'll never ring a bell again."

"But I can hear him ring the bell—then he knocks at the door with both hands and cries out, asking to be let in, saying he is afraid and the cold is hurting . . ."

"All right. What do you want us to do with him?"

No use. He was in a hysterical state; joking and sarcasm were no good.

I began to consider the predicament. There was a corpse, which we had to get rid of. It could not stay in the house because that frightened Amin or outside the house because it would knock at the door and that frightened Amin as well. What was wanted was a place neither inside nor outside.

I said to Amin, "What can we do to reconcile your feelings about death and your feelings for propriety and tradition?"

Suddenly he said, "We will put him outside the garden door where there is no bell for him to ring."

"He will knock at the door with both his hands . . . I mean, you will hear him knock at the door . . ."

Finally, he said with resolution, "We will put him in the trash can in the garden near the back door, and close the lid tightly."

When we woke the servant up this time, he was mutinous. He said he was tired and did not wait for a reply but obstinately closed his eyes.

This time I let Amin carry the trunk of the corpse and pretended to carry the legs, but I was cheating, for I was extremely fatigued, I let him drag it along the floor till we got to the back kitchen door . . . We had barely opened it when the wind assailed us like a rebuke from some mysterious metaphysical power. But, I cried in my heart, he is a corpse, and we are alive and in the midst of circumstances that do not allow any compromise. His old official uniform and medals and decorations will not stop his body from putrefying. There is no escape from burying that portion of the past that rots, and his body is a putrefying past. That is what I was telling myself while we were putting the body into the trash can. It was a much more difficult task than I had expected. The corpse had ceased to be a body and had become a marble statue. Bending the limbs in order to get them into the can required an enormous effort indeed, and more than once I thought of using a hammer to help . . . Bullets were raining down, and the longer the task took, the more exposed to danger we were. It was loathsome to be weighted down with hunger, fear, cold, drowsiness, and a corpse! When we finished depositing him in his round metal coffin, I was surprised that Amin closed the lid tightly as though he was afraid that his father would run away.

I did not wash my hands before I went to bed . . . I kept the water for drinking.

—*Translated by Lena Jayyusi and David Wright*

Ahmad al-Tawfiq (b. 1943)

Moroccan novelist Ahmad al-Tawfiq headed the National Library in Rabat then became Minister of Religious Affairs. Most of his novels deal with the past in Morocco, evoking experiences that are still alive in Moroccan folklore but have been threatened with extinction by the concepts of modern life. Although his work occasionally deals with violent experiences and negative attitudes, mirroring the human condition in its less fortunate aspects, he has a strong penchant for that which is spiritual, virtuous, and beautiful, thus defying a trend in some modern Arabic fiction of depicting a world less attached to the strong traditional values and mores that infuse a more robust life. This kind of work, just to give a single example, is well exemplified in Naguib Mahfouz's novel, *Chattering on the Nile*, with its portrayal of the apathy and degeneration of its upper-middle-class protagonists. Another great quality in al-Tawfiq's work is its capacity to hold the reader spellbound. His novels include *A Henna Tree and a Moon* (1998), *The Deluge (1998)*, and *Abu Musa's Neighbors* (2000), the latter translated by Roger Allen (in press).

ABU MUSA'S NEIGHBORS (2000)

The narrative is set in the Moroccan port city of Sale (and to a lesser extent in the Ma-
rinid capital city of Fez). Abu Musa is a strange mystical figure whose influence pervades
the action of the novel, and yet the work's main protagonist is the beautiful Shamah, a
woman of Andalusian descent, whose culture, manners, and outstanding beauty make her
the cynosure of all eyes. She is initially married off to an elderly judge, counselor to the
sultan in Fez, but, after a disastrous naval expedition, the sultan is deposed by his son and
Shamah is given as a maid-servant to the deposed sultan's mother, Umm al-Hurr.

With just a few days remaining from Shamah's required waiting period Umm
al-Hurr was ordered by the sultan to perform the obligation of the pilgrimage
to Mecca. She was permitted to take with her whomever she wished from her
female retinue. She chose ten of them, one being Shamah. Two days later the
sultan gave his consent and issued instructions for the company to make ready; it
was to carry with it a gift to the ruler of Egypt. A senior member of the sultan's
own entourage was appointed to lead the company.

That night Umm al-Hurr stayed up later than usual. Shamah was at her side,
and they spoke about Al-Jawra'i. Umm al-Hurr noticed Shamah's sweetly innocent loyalty to her dead husband. She was still wary about the possible effect
on Shamah's sensitive spirit of what she had really wanted to say from the start,
but she decided to say it anyway. "My daughter," she announced tersely, "God
has released you!"

The sultan permitted his deposed father to travel from his exile in the western desert to meet his wife as she traveled along the desert route, but he fell
seriously ill and died a few days later.

Umm al-Hurr's company took three months to reach Egypt; most of the
Maghribi pilgrims that year followed behind. A message had been sent on ahead
announcing the imminent arrival of the former consort of the sultan of Morocco and the sultan's gift. Over the course of an entire week the company was
welcomed at the Egyptian ruler's palace with all due honor and respect. However, some of the Egyptian ruler's imbecile sons blackened their father's name
by suggesting to the leader of the Moroccan company that he could further
enhance the sultan's gift by including some of Umm al-Hurr's female entourage.
However, the Zanati judge who was in charge followed Umm al-Hurr's instructions and purchased some female Circassian slaves in the Egyptian market so that
her company could continue on its journey to Mecca.

While the company was waiting for a laissez-passer at the port of Aydab, it
was attacked by a group of masked horsemen who made off with Shamah and
one of Umm al-Hurr's maids. However, a Sufi ascetic who had been a disciple
of one of the Moroccan sheikhs had given orders to his followers to protect the
party while it passed through his zone of influence. As soon as he heard about
the attack, he dispatched his horsemen in every direction. Before sunset on the
very same day they brought back the two kidnapped women, having snatched

them from the clutches of a group of men who, along with the head of the Egyptian postal service, were taking them to Fustat.[1]

During the rituals of pilgrimage and penitence Shamah stood alongside her mistress, Umm al-Hurr; in the process she recovered all the spiritual traits that she had acquired in her youth at the side of her other mistress in Sale, Al-Tahirah, wife of Judge Ibn al-Hafid, who had been her companion in ritual washing and vigils. Left alone, Umm al-Hurr and Shamah spent half the night performing prayers, intercessions, and supplications; half the day was spent circumambulating the Ka'ba and running between Safa and Marwa. When the time arrived for the pilgrimage rites, the tears of devotion shed by the two women transformed them into two kindred spirits poised to shake hands with the angels.

The long trip concluded with a visit to the Prophet's tomb in Medina. There once again their two spirits blended in the celestial realm of penitence. One morning Umm al-Hurr asked all her female attendants to tell her about their dreams since they had arrived in the region of the holy places. With Shamah she waited till they were alone together. "After we returned from visiting the tomb of the beloved Prophet," she said, "I fell asleep before sunset and dreamed that you, my lady, were giving me a present, a white horse from Granada." "God willing," replied Umm al-Hurr with a smile, "that will happen!"

On the return journey to the Maghrib the company had reached Sijilmasah when Umm al-Hurr was afflicted with severe pain. An Egyptian doctor had already diagnosed the problem as a stomach ulcer while they were still in Kinanah territory. Throughout the trip Umm al-Hurr had been suffering because of changes in water and food that had been quite different from what she was used to in the palace. As they approached Jabal Fazaz, Umm al-Hurr spent a really bad night. Next morning she summoned the company leader and two jurists, asked them to convey her satisfaction to the sultan who had looked after her interests, and prayed for his continued happiness. She then gave instructions regarding her sons and daughters, as well as details about the place where she wished to be buried. She specifically asked that the sultan should respect her wishes regarding her married servant-women who were foreigners by returning them to their families if they so desired. Regarding Shamah in particular, she requested that she should be returned immediately to the care of Judge Ibn al-Hafid in Sale.

No one in the company knew for sure when Umm al-Hurr passed away; they were just about to enter Fez itself. The sultan came out in person to greet the company, which now included her corpse. Ibn al-Mubarak, the leader of the group, stood before the sultan; handing him Umm al-Hurr's will with its various requests, he mentioned all her virtuous acts during the journey and in the holy places.

The day of Umm al-Hurr's burial saw a big ceremony in Fez. The sultan used the occasion to pardon all of his deposed father's former retainers. After the Quran and third-day intercessions had been recited, the sultan ordered her will

---

1. Another name for Cairo

to be carried out to the letter. As part of that process the judge in Fez wrote to Judge Ibn al-Hafid in Sale consigning Shamah, by the sultan's command, to the care of his wife, Al-Tahirah. The task of taking Shamah and the letter back to Sale was entrusted to two servants and a maid from the Sultan's palace.

—*Translated by Roger Allen*

Jurji Zaydan (1861–1914)

Jurji Zaydan was one of the most distinguished Arab writers of modern times. He came from a humble Christian Lebanese family (Syrian in those early days before colonialism established a schism in greater Syria by creating the state of Lebanon). His father was a restaurateur, and his early simple education was interrupted for several years because he had to help in the family business. However, he early discovered his aptitude for learning, and he used every minute of his life to acquire knowledge in many fields. His love of literature was matched by his love of science, and he was able to enter medical school in Lebanon but, because of political dissent, had to leave for Cairo where his real erudition flowered. One of the most enlightened minds, he realized the vast dimensions acquired by Islamic civilization and dedicated most of his career to disseminating its virtues and greatness. His historical and cultural works pertaining to Arab/Islamic civilization include *The History of Arabic Literature*, in four volumes; the *History of Islamic Civilization*, in five volumes; *The Arabs Before Islam*; and *Famous Men of the Orient* in two volumes. Zaydan also wrote twenty-two novels delineating almost the full history of Islamic civilization, the first of which was the *Wandering Memluk* (1890). One of his greatest achievements, which benefited generations of readers through the twentieth century, was the founding of the prestigious *Al-Hilal* monthly, which published a mixture of science and literature. His general oeuvre, particularly as the father of the historical novel in Arabic, has been discussed at greater length in the introduction to this volume. He was a great pioneer, a visionary historian, a matchless intellect dominated by a benevolent passion to serve and create. The fact that he was a premodern novelist should not detract from the immense value of his work, which is entertaining, informative, inspiring, and an integral part of the history of modern Arabic fiction.

AL-AMIN AND AL-MA'MUN

Zaydan's novels on Islamic civilization have been a source of enlightenment to generations of young readers over the four or five decades after his death. They are, as the present novel illustrates, packed with information, particularly on the manners, lifestyle, beliefs and ethical concepts of the particular period treated, but they are also a delight to read. Al-Amin and Al-Ma'mun *depicts the critical last days of the reign of Harun al-Rashid, and the ensuing struggle for the throne between his two sons al-Amin and al-Ma'mun. It also portrays the character and lifestyle of the famous Zubeida, Al-Rashid's ravishingly beautiful Arab wife, who was the mother of Al-Amin and a proud descendant of the Abbasid dynasty, and details the Persian plot to ensure the ascendancy of Al-Ma'mun, Al-Rashid's son by a Persian slave woman and destined to become one of the most learned and sophisticated caliphs ever to rule the Arab empire—certainly a good deal fitter to reign than his pampered brother Al-Amin. Another principal character is Bahzad, a brave Persian fighting on the side of Al-Ma'mun and also, it emerges, the avenging grandson of the famous general, Abu Muslim al-Khurasani, who had helped establish the Abbasid caliphate but was subsequently killed by the Abbasids themselves to avert any Persian aspiration to the throne. A little later, another Persian empire-builder, Ja'far al-Barmaki, was also killed by Al-Rashid for the same reason; his mother, 'Abbada, and daughter Maymuna also play a major part in the novel. Maymuna and Bahzad are in love, but Maymuna is captured by Al-Amin's soldiers and kept as a prisoner in the palace, where Zubeida, having discovered the girl's lineage, urges Al-Amin to have her killed. Al-Amin, though, had promised to protect Maymuna after his own niece had befriended the captive girl. The crucial point here is that the astute Salman, one of Bahzad's men, contrives to be appointed chief soothsayer at Al-Amin's palace, where Maymuna is being kept. Feigning ignorance of the young girl, he is able, through apparently clairvoyant knowledge of her identity and the events surrounding her life, to save her through hints that she is innocent of any intrigue.*

FROM CHAPTER 61

Meanwhile Salman, in the guise of a soothsayer, was trying to persuade Al-Amin to block his brother's succession to the throne, through the offices of his chief minister, Al-Fadl ibn al-Rabi', and his general, Ibn Mahan; while Al-Fadl, serving his own interests, urged the same course, since he feared vengeance if Al-Ma'mun should ascend to the Caliphate. Al-Amin, though, hesitated, not through any fear of the consequences but from a wish to keep the covenant made on the matter, or perhaps mindful of the ties of brotherhood. He leaned toward Al-Fadl's advice, but thought it best to consult his mother, Zubeida, in whose sagacity he had complete confidence. She was then at her palace, Dar al-Qarar, and he wavered between riding there and inviting her to his own Al-Mansur palace.

After some thought he decided to divert himself by fishing in a large pond in the palace garden, where fish had been brought from other waters. Accordingly he took his rod and line and started fishing there, surrounded by groups of eunuchs dressed in women's clothes, some of whom baited the hook or drove the fish from other parts of the pond toward Al-Amin, while others carried nets, and still others prepared further rods and hooks. Al-Amin remained immersed in his sport, which included playfully hauling up one of his retinue, just to show how powerful his muscles were, then throwing him back into the water—upon which everyone would laugh and praise the matchless strength of the Commander of the Faithful. Al-Amin was in fact famous for his physical strength, and once, so it is said, actually wrestled with a lion and killed it.

While he was so engaged, some eunuchs came to tell him, "The procession of our Lady, mother of the Commander of the Faithful, is approaching."

He was pleased at this, remembering how he wished to consult her, and issued orders for the manner of her welcome. The palace superintendents, both male and female, began setting out the rows of slave boys and slave girls, including the group of lovely, slim slave girls presented to him by his mother, Zubeida, when she noted his preoccupation with slave boys rather than women. She had had them wear young men's clothes, along with turbans, and ear-rings, and jewelry above the brow and down the sides of the face, dressing them in tight trousers and vests to show off their figures and rounded buttocks; and he, after seeing them march before him, had found them pleasing and displayed them in public,[1] both to the upper classes and to the commoners, attracting numerous imitators. His mother, he knew, would be pleased if he received her surrounded by these women. He also ordered the appropriate official to line up the *ghilman*, or slave boys, under the slave Kawthar, with whom he was famously infatuated.[2] And so the lines of eunuchs and *jawari* (slave girls), along with other types of *ghilman* and bound women, some white, some Ethiopian, were duly assembled, each group wearing special clothes, in their own colors and fashions, from short to long, from red to blue to sky blue to pink to yellow, with some *ghilman* in the garb of women and some women in the garb of boys. There were lute-players among them too, and drummers and sprinklers of perfume.

The slaves stood in lines from the great court right to the outer gate of the palace, while *ghilman* stood between them, burning incense or bearing flowers or declaiming poetry, and Al-Amin walked between the two lines to receive his mother at the palace gate. She was seated on a large seat of sandalwood, carved with silver and ebony, on which embroidered curtains hung from fixtures of gold and silver. The seat was in a howdah borne by two mules wearing silver saddles and led by slave boys who, being in fact soldiers, had the state insignia on their clothes of embroidered silk. The fragrance of musk was all around her.

As the howdah halted at the palace gate, all those round about drew off except for the superintendent of the eunuchs, who helped the Lady Zubeida alight. Al-Amin approached and kissed her breast, then she kissed his head and proceeded on foot. She wore slippers studded with jewels,[3] and on her head was a veil woven with gold threads edged with precious stones, revealing her gem-encrusted headband and diamond necklaces and earrings behind. Covering her

---

1. This description is taken from volume 2 of *Muruj al-Dhahab* ("Fields of Gold"), by the medieval historian Al-Mas'udi.

2. Based on volume 6 of the *Kamil fi 'l-Tarikh* ("Complete History") of Ibn al-Athir.

3. From the *Kitab al-Aghani* ("Book of Songs") of Al-Isfahani.

shoulders and sides was a garment in gold-colored silk, open to reveal a robe of pink silk that covered her feet behind but not before, exposing her studded slippers—Zubeida was in fact the first woman in Islam to wear embroidered sandals. But anyone seeing Zubeida was taken not with her sumptuous, costly clothes but with her radiant beauty and the greatness this beauty conveyed, along with all the signs of splendor and dignity.

No sooner had she come to the gate than news of her arrival reached 'Abbada, mother of the slain Ja'far, who had ventured to join her granddaughter here under the guise of her old nurse and now trembled with fear at the exposure of her deception. Maymuna, though, was eager to see the procession of the caliph's mother, of whose sumptuous glory she had heard for so long, and gazed furtively out at it from a window of the palace, full of admiration for Zubeida's beauty but awed, too, by her air of grandeur....

FROM CHAPTER 62

Al-Amin and his mother walked, at her behest, to a private sitting room where she wished to talk to her son; and he was pleased at this, because he wished to consult her too. Before Zubeida seated herself, the dress servants came to help her off with those things too heavy for indoor wear, and male and female slaves stood by fanning her or busying themselves in preparing food and drink. But she said to Al-Amin, "I wish, Muhammad, to see you with no one else present. I have no desire for food."

Al-Amin thereupon made a sign for everyone to leave, and he remained alone with his mother. Then she seated herself on a sofa, gesturing to Muhammad to sit beside her, which he did.

"This is a happy hour indeed, Mother," he said. "It is as though the meeting were arranged, for only this morning I thought to come and see you, or invite you here, so as to consult with you on certain matters. And now here you are, of your own accord. It must surely be a good omen."

She smiled diplomatically, but there was anger in her eyes.

"In fact," she said, "I have come to you for a different reason, which is of moment for both of us."

Al-Amin showed his interest.

"And what should that be, Mother?" he asked.

"Is that wretched waif still here?" she asked in her turn.

"Who do you mean?" he said, puzzled.

"I mean the daughter of our enemy who planned to supplant you as crown prince. Who strove to persuade your father, Al-Rashid, to appoint the son of Marajil in your place."

Realizing now that she was speaking of Ja'far al-Barmaki's daughter, Maymuna, he said, "Yes, Madam, she is still here, among the palace *jawari.*"

"And why have you kept her here? Did you sense no danger?"

"She seemed a poor harmless orphan, and my niece, seeing I should never release the girl, urged me not to see her harmed. And so I kept her here under guard, to ward off any threat she might present."

"A poor orphan! A vicious traitress rather. And, strangest of all, you look favorably on your niece's intercession, when your brother is the greatest of all your enemies. Did he not seek out the Persians of Khurasan as allies against you? Do you think he would lose any chance to seize your throne? And who was it put this overweening ambition in him but Ja'far, the father of this girl? Your father, may God bless his soul, was wiser than you in the knowledge of men and had him put to a fearful death; had he not done so, in good time, you would not now be sitting on this throne. And she is a poor orphan, you say, and your niece sought your protection for her! Persian blood is stronger in your brother than Hashemite[4] blood; he has taken more from his mother, Marajil, than from his father, Al-Rashid. That is why you see him seeking the aid of her brothers against us."

As she spoke, her eyes blazed with mounting fury, and she grew pale, losing her red lips and rosy cheeks. All this fitted well with Al-Amin's own thoughts of debarring his brother from succession to the throne, and he hastened to seek her opinion on this.

"But did my father," he said, "not fix the Caliphate first on me and then on my brother, in the covenant he hung in the Ka'ba?"[5]

"The covenant was worthless," she broke in, barely able to stifle her rage. "It was written at the behest of that treacherous minister, from a wish to tear the Caliphate from the Hashemites and place it in your brother's hands. But are the sons of slave girls fit to assume the Caliphate while the sons of freeborn women are alive? Can the son of this slave girl, Marajil, be compared to the son of Zubeida, daughter of Ja'far al-Mansur?[6] Do you know who this Marajil is? How she contrived to snare your father and bear him 'Abd Allah?"[7]

"No," he replied. "I do not."

"Then let me tell you. This Marajil was one of my own slave girls, no different from Mariya, Farida or any other. When I found your father neglecting to visit me, going instead to a singer called Dananir, a slave of his minister, Yahya,[8] and passing most of his leisure with her, I complained to his uncles, who advised me to find other slave girls to divert him. I accordingly made him a gift of ten slave girls, among them this Persian, Marajil.[9] She bore him this son, 'Abd Allah, who, from childhood on, has been brought up by Ja'far to love the Persians. And

---

4. The descendants of Hashim, the Prophet's ancestor, from whose progeny the Abbasid Caliphate originated.

5. The chief Muslim shrine, in Mecca.

6. One of the earlier Abbasid caliphs, son of the dynasty's founder.

7. The first name of Al-Ma'mun.

8. The father of Ja'far al-Barmaki.

9. From the *Kitab al-Aghani*, volume 16.

you see how it has all turned out. How can he have the same status as you? As for this covenant in the Ka'ba, send to have it returned, then tear it up, for it was written in treachery."

"You think, then," Al-Amin said, calmer now, "that I should debar my brother from the succession?"

"You mean it is still not done? Debar him now! Before he seizes your throne."

"I wished to consult you first," he said, raising himself in his seat. "And I see now you are of the same opinion as my minister, Al-Fadl."

"Debar him and settle the succession on your son Musa, young as he is. In this way the Caliphate will be rooted more than ever in the Hashemites. You are the first caliph of the Abbasids born of Hashemite parents; and so your children are more firmly of the Hashemite family than any other of the line."

Al-Amin was much encouraged by this. Still, though, he preserved a heavy silence.

"Let us return to the traitress," Zubeida went on. "The best course is to have her killed and be rid of her."

"Kill her? What has she done to deserve that? What possible threat does she pose?"

"You have no notion, Muhammad, of the things happening around you. You remain plunged in your pleasures, ignorant of the designs of flatterers. I, though, watch over your interests. I know what goes on in your palace and in your bedrooms. I tell you, the presence of this girl, constantly here in your palace, is a still greater danger than your brother's right of succession. You must kill her."

Al-Amin was astounded at her insistence, for he had seen nothing in the girl to merit death.

"She can be killed easily enough," he said, "for I have hundreds like her, thousands even, in my palace. Only I promised my niece, Um Habiba, to keep her under my protection."

At this Zubeida rose furiously from her seat.

"You are too trusting," she shouted, "and too easily snared by trickery. If you had any astuteness, you would have seen how suspicious this intercession by 'Abd Allah's daughter is. Know that this Maymuna is betrothed to one of the fiercest enemies of the Abbasids. They have exchanged letters speaking of his aim to avenge the deaths of Abu Muslim al-Khurasani and Ja'far al-Barmaki. He views the Abbasids as treacherous. If you do not believe me, read this for yourself!"

With that, she took Bahzad's letter to Maymuna from her pocket and gave it to Al-Amin. He took it and, by the time he had finished reading, found his hands shaking and his very fingers trembling, such was the abuse poured out against the Abbasids and the rancor and threat expressed. Then he looked toward his mother, who was now once more reclining back on the cushions, consumed with rage.

"Such a poor orphan!" she said. "We, according to this betrothed of hers, won our way through treason and treachery, and he is to avenge her father's death, traveling to Khurasan to that end. How can you let her live here in your palace, among your very retinue, where she can learn everything of you and your aims? Does she really present no threat to your plans and secrets?"

Al-Amin was astonished by his mother's vigilance on his behalf.

"How did you come by this letter?" he asked. "Who brought it to you?"

"I was able to take it from the very heart of your palace, because I am vigilant, while you remain asleep. Oh, let us not stay talking here!"

Al-Amin was now greatly aroused.

"I shall order," he said, "that she be flung into the Tigris."

"And will you fling her into the Tigris," Zubeida asked, "without questioning her first?"

"Let me just be rid of her!"

"How innocent you are!" his mother rejoined. "Before killing someone like this, you must first find out from her how things stand with our enemies. She will certainly be privy to their secrets. Then, when you have gained what you want from her, you may kill her or drown her as you wish."

"I shall summon her here at once," he said, "and we can question her together."

"Do so," Zubeida said.

He clapped his hands, and, when one of his eunuchs entered, commanded him to bring Maymuna.

Maymuna was in the most remote room of the palace (for fear of being seen by Zubeida), eating with her grandmother, while 'Abbada, for her part, was praying to God that Zubeida should return without noticing her. When the eunuch came to summon Maymuna into the presence of the Commander of the Faithful, 'Abbada knew Zubeida had come to urge her son to do away with Maymuna. Maymuna, though, had no option but to obey the order, and followed the eunuch until they arrived at the caliph's sitting room. The eunuch then announced her, saying: "The slave girl is at the door, Sire."

"Let her enter," Al-Amin said.

Maymuna came in, her head bowed and her knees knocking from fear. Her eyes fell on Zubeida as she reclined on the cushions, her air of dignity and majesty made still more awesome by her anger, with Al-Amin sitting beside her like one of her slave boys. As Maymuna stood there and greeted them, Al-Amin said, "Approach, Maymuna."

She walked toward him, gazing at the floor and utterly terrified. Al-Amin stretched out a hand with the letter and said, "Do you know to whom this letter belongs?"

Recognizing the letter at once, she knew her secret was out. Panic fear seemed to take all strength from her hand; and when she at last forced herself to take the letter in trembling fingers, it dropped to the floor. She bent to pick it up from the carpet, then fell herself on the ground, utterly overwhelmed, trying vainly to rise as the tears coursed down her cheeks. She tried to appear innocent, to read through the letter, but was overcome by weeping once more. She threw herself at Al-Amin's feet, kissing them and weeping, unable to utter a word.

"You wretch!" Zubeida shouted. "Why are you weeping? Do you think tears will save you? Who is this Bahzad? Is he not your lover, who has borne the sword of rancor against the Abbasids?"

At this point, though, Zubeida decided to change her approach and trick the girl into revealing her secret.

"Do not be afraid," she said, speaking softly now. "Tell the truth and you will be spared. Tell us where your lover is now and what you know of the Khurasanis. If we find you truthful, we shall set you free and let you live. If not, you must die."

"Believe me, my Lady," Maymuna answered unsteadily, "I know nothing whatever beyond what is in this letter. If you read it, you will see—I knew nothing of this young man before—I swear by the head of the Commander of the Faithful that, since reading it, I have heard no more of him."

Zubeida laughed sarcastically.

"You swear this," she said, "by the head of the Commander of the Faithful?"

"So I do!" Maymuna said. "And I am true to my oath."

"Tell us the truth, girl," Al-Amin said then, "and you have nothing to fear. But if you will not do so, we shall bring the head soothsayer to unveil the secrets of your heart. And if we should discover something you have withheld from us, your punishment will be severe."

"It is for the Commander of the Faithful to decide," Maymuna said. "I have nothing further to say." . . .

From Chapter 63

The *Mandal*[10]

The caliph clapped his hands and ordered that the head soothsayer be summoned. Maymuna had remained humbly standing, but Al-Amin now told her to sit down. She was unaware the head soothsayer was Salman, believing him, after his long absence, to have fled or died.

Soon Al-Malfan Sa'dun[11] arrived in his large black turban, with a long cloak over his honey-colored robe. He wore a belt from which an inkwell hung, and had a long flowing beard flecked with white and joined to two thick sideburns, along with other aspects typical of Christians or Jews. He was, of course, quite different from the Salman that Maymuna knew. Only his eyes and nose could have told her this was he, had she ever suspected such a thing.

Sa'dun entered and greeted them, then stood there courteously, hugging his book and stealing glances at the people assembled, recognizing both Maymuna and Zubeida. Then his eyes fell on Bahzad's letter, there in Al-Amin's hands and,

---

10. Divination from various substances (in this case embers); an ancient practice found in certain countries.

11. The name taken by Salman in his guise of soothsayer.

since it was he who had borne the letter to Maymuna, knew at once why he had been summoned. But he showed no sign of all this.

Al-Amin then ordered him to be seated, with no barrier or curtain between them, and he squatted on his haunches, his eyes fixed on the floor.

"We have summoned you, Malfan Sa'dun," Al-Amin said, "to reveal the secrets of this girl. When we questioned her, she denied all knowledge of the matter in question; and so we have threatened to have her secrets uncovered at your hands. Let us know the truth."

Zubeida gazed silently at the soothsayer, waiting to see how skilled he was in his science. Though having scant faith in the abilities of soothsayers, she had agreed to have him summoned in the hope that Maymuna would take fright and confess from fear of punishment. As for Sa'dun, he produced his book and asked for a censer to be brought with embers of burned olive wood, claiming that only such a wood, which was easily found at a caliph's court, would permit successful divination. The fire was brought in a silver censer placed on a tray; and, since he seemed to be intent on his reading and muttering, with everyone else silent, the tray was placed beside him. He then took a piece of fragrant incense from his pocket and, throwing this into the embers, asked for a cup with water, which he took in his left hand, between thumb and forefinger. Having gazed at the water for a time, he asked the caliph to have Maymuna approach and place her hand on his book, which she did, trembling with fear. Sa'dun then took her other hand, read the lines there, raised the first hand from the book, and told her to be seated. He opened the book and read from it in a whisper, smiling triumphantly. Then he nodded his head, looked at Al-Amin and said, "This girl has a long history, and her story is an important one."

Zubeida gave a mocking laugh, as if to say there was nothing prophetic in this. Sa'dun, catching her drift, looked toward her, though he refrained, out of courtesy, from gazing at her direct.

"I do not say this," he told her, "from any wish to delude or impress. I mean simply that she is not of common stock but of high and honorable lineage, slave girl though she now is."

"If you are so sure of that," Zubeida broke in, "tell us all about her, without further ado."

"Shall I do so in her presence?"

"Yes."

He gazed once more into the cup and then into her face. Then he said, "She is the daughter of a great minister, who died a violent death."

When she heard this, Maymuna felt a chill pass through her whole body, and her face turned pale. As for Al-Amin, he looked triumphantly at his mother, seeing her no less astonished than he was. She, though, took no heed.

"It may be you are right," she said. Then, stretching out a hand holding Bahzad's letter, she continued, "Tell me what I am holding in my hand."

"A letter."

She laughed heartily.

"Such skill!" she said. "Why, even a child could tell that! But if you are a true head soothsayer, as they call you, tell me what the letter contains."

"Your lack of faith in my knowledge grieves me deeply, my Lady. It may be fitting, hereafter, to hold back what I know. What I will say is that you are holding a letter of fire; indeed, fire itself would be of less consequence to that gentle hand than what is written there. What you are holding is a letter, to this young girl, from a Persian man. The letter exalts the Persians and denigrates the status of the Abbasids, so that you and my Lord, the Commander of the Faithful, are angered. If this general description does not convince you, let me venture to give you the details. My science has never yet caused me to stumble, but perhaps it has failed, now, to lead me to the truth."

Zubeida was astonished at this, and filled with admiration in spite of herself.

"You have spoken truly, Malfan Sa'dun," she said. "But now, since you have uncovered the secret of this letter, tell us where its writer is."

"He is very far away, my Lady. He is in Khurasan."

"And what is his connection with this girl here?"

"The connection is quite new, and if she has claimed otherwise, then she is a liar. There is no point in questioning her about the threats of vengeance in this letter, for she was totally ignorant of these before the letter arrived and has heard nothing of its writer since."

Maymuna was still more surprised at this than the others, knowing the man had read her mind. She could have expressed none of this more clearly herself. Her face became radiant, and she seemed relieved of her fears, gazing silently at Al-Amin as if urging him to be merciful.

Zubeida, too, felt her anger cool toward Maymuna, though deep down she hated her still.

"You believe then," she said to Sa'dun, "that this girl is innocent?"

"So I read in my divination, and I know from experience that this science does not fail me. Ask the Commander of the Faithful, and he will confirm this from his own knowledge."

Zubeida made a sign to Maymuna to leave; and Maymuna departed, scarcely able to believe her escape.

—*Translated by Salma Khadra Jayyusi and Christopher Tingley*